BATTLE FOR NEW CANAAN

THE ORION WAR - BOOKS 1-3

(Including Set the Galaxy on Fire)

M. D. COOPER

Version 1.1.0

ISBN: 978-1-64365-045-6

Cover Art by Andrew Dobell
Edited by Brenda Tippin Deliantoni, Krissy Smith, Amy DuBoff, Jen McDonnell

THIS BOOK & THE AEON 14 UNIVERSE

This book picks up where The Intrepid Saga left off, with the Tanis Richards separated from the *Intrepid* after a strange cosmic event following the ship's departure from Kapteyn's Star.

Because The Intrepid Saga omnibus contains Destiny Lost (which is also within this omnibus) I have included Set the Galaxy on Fire, a collection of novellas and short stories that follow the events of Destiny Lost. With that collection in this omnibus, there is nearly a 30% savings over buying the books individually.

If you have already read Destiny Lost, then I recommend you jump to Set the Galaxy on Fire.

To learn more about the books of Aeon 14, and where this collection falls within the ever-expanding story, you can pick up the free Aeon 14 Reading Guide.

To get the latest news and access to free novellas and short stories, sign up on the Aeon 14 mailing list: www.aeon14.com/signup.

TABLE OF CONTENTS

DESTINY LOST

THE ORION WAR – BOOK 1

BY M. D. COOPER

ACKNOWLEDGEMENTS

This book is in your hands today in no small part because of you, the readers. Your emails and excitement for the series always inspires me to keep writing.

In addition, the author community, with whom I have found companionship, has helped me hone my craft, and shared stories of encouragement—as I have with them.

Beyond them are the hard-working folks in the aero-space industry, who are working day and night to bring our species to space in a meaningful way. Their dedication and advances are what gives me hope for our future.

Lastly, as I've mentioned before, this book stands on the shoulders of giants. Writers whose stories and imaginations have forged a shared vision of the future, and our destiny, that we call Science Fiction.

AN UNEXPECTED CARGO

STELLAR DATE: 06.30.8927 (Adjusted Years)
LOCATION: Coburn Station, Trio
REGION: Trio System, Silstrand Alliance Space

Sera slammed the shooter down with a triumphant grin and watched with reddened eyes as the man from Thoria reached for his next glass. Around them, the crowd chanted their names as money changed hands.

Her opponent downed his drink and tossed the glass onto the table where it rolled against the two-dozen empty shooters between them. With a wave of his hand and an unappealing grin, he indicated that the floor was hers.

She took a deep breath to steady herself, chanting an internal mantra of *just one more, just one more.* The act of raising her arm caused Sera to sway in her seat, the smell of bodies pressed close around not helping her deepening nausea.

The Thorian saw her hesitation and his grin grew wider.

"Ready to give up?" he slurred, his putrid breath washing over her.

Sera didn't reply, only fixed him with a steely glare—at least she hoped it was a steely glare—and grasped the glass in her fist, throwing it back without further hesitation.

The alcohol washed down her throat like fire, and her tongue felt swollen in its wake. If she didn't know better, she'd assume the bartender had poured a stiffer drink.

She set the glass down and took slow, deep breaths, using all her concentration to keep the fire in her stomach and veins under control.

The Thorian grunted and stared at the row of shots before him—likely deciding which one to pick up. Finally selecting his drink, he grabbed it with a swift flourish and raised it high to throw it back.

In his current state, the gesture failed miserably and the drink splashed across his face. His features crumpled in confusion and his arms rotated slowly as he slid sideways out of his chair to the floor. No one attempted to catch him and the man's head hit the deck-plate with a solid crack.

Cheers and grumbles erupted around her as Sera was declared the winner. The victors were paid out, and the losers turned to the bar for another drink. In the midst of the post-contest exchange, one voice rose above the others.

A short, but well-built man in a dirty shipsuit pushed to the front of the crowd.

"Cheater! She had to cheat; there's no way that waif could drink Greg under the table!" He slammed his hands on the table, bent over, his face inches from Sera's. "You used nano to clear the alcohol from your bloodstream."

Most people had some of the tiny nano-machines in their body, it was nearly impossible not to; they were almost as common as bacteria. A person's nano was controlled by their internal computer or AI—if you had the money or influence to hire one. Sera's nano could clear her bloodstream with ease—though that wasn't a fact she advertised. It took a lot of nano to filter that much booze over such a short period; a lot more than a simple freighter captain should possess.

Sera worked her mouth for a moment, making sure it would respond the way she wanted it to. "I did not. Have the bartender do a check." The words were slurred, but understandable.

Bartenders on Coburn Station were not allowed to let their patrons get too drunk—an ordinance they rarely enforced. They had scanners on hand that could do a blood-alcohol level check and determine, based on that person's size and metabolic rate, if they were too inebriated to have another round.

The bartender had already stepped into the crowd, eager to do whatever it took to avoid a fight on his shift. He pressed the scanner against Sera's wrist and took samples of her blood for the reading.

"She's pissed," he said as he straightened. "Consistent with the amount and time she's been slugging them back." Smirking, he turned back to the bar. "Those shooters are only a third of what she's had tonight too."

The winners cheered all the louder and the losers ceased their grumbling. Everyone knew that bartenders altered their scanners, so they could give people more liquor than they should. If it said she was drunk, then she should be totally pissed.

<*One of these days, the losers aren't going to care what the scan says and take their satisfaction out of your hide,*> Helen admonished in Sera's mind.

Sera sent her internal AI a mental shrug. Helen didn't like it when Sera drank; she claimed it upset the chemical balance of Sera's body in a way that made the AI feel weird. Sera wasn't sure how that was possible, not that it would change her behavior. She liked the feeling of chemical imbalance.

<*My hide's been through worse.*>

<*I know; I've been there each time. Doesn't mean I want a repeat. You know how disconcerting I find it when you get hurt that badly.*>

Helen could be annoying at times with her mothering, but Sera knew that her AI's concern was genuine. Pulling her thoughts from the familiar debate, Sera looked around the bar.

To smooth things over, the winners were buying the losers a round. Sera had put a hundred SIL credits down on herself and collected three hundred back. The odds had been stacked nicely against her.

Betting was illegal in Silstrand Alliance space, so money always changed hands in cash. The prohibition didn't seem to diminish the illegal activity; it just meant no one had to pay taxes on their winnings. Sera thought about that for a minute. Maybe that was why it was illegal; officials probably liked to gamble tax-free, too.

Stuffing the hard money into an inside pocket on her leather jacket, she rose slowly, nearly teetering over at the last moment. A steady hand appeared under her elbow and Sera turned to see the dark smiling face of Cargo.

"Good haul on that, Captain." He guided her out of the bar and into the bustling main corridor of the station's promenade. "I made a couple hundred credits on your drinking skill."

"It's good to be useful," Sera slurred as Cargo led her toward a small coffee shop which was renowned for its after-drunk-sober-up brew. Once inside, Sera ordered two of their strongest and let Cargo wait at the counter for the order. Her leather clothing squeaked noisily as she collapsed into a chair. Cursing the café's bright lights, she leaned back with a hand over her eyes, praying for a power outage.

<*You're not masking the squeak. What gives?*> Sera asked her AI.

<*It's what you get for drinking. I can't deal with two organic peculiarities at once. If you drink, I won't mask your clothing's noise. Take your pick.*> Helen was really on the warpath, determined to make Sera suffer. Thank god Cargo had shown up.

Her first mate knew she liked to get one last round in at a bar before they left a station—OK, maybe more than just *a* round. He often would find her and bring her back to the ship before she was too far gone.

Sera splayed her fingers and looked through them to see Cargo returning with an insufferable grin on his face. He had a coffee for himself and two of the sober-up drinks for her. He set them on the table and pushed them toward her, his smile widening.

"I bet those are going to taste horrible."

Sera stuck her tongue out as she leaned forward to pick one up. "Prolly."

"You should have let me know you were gonna get into another drinking contest," Cargo said and took a drink of his own beverage. "I would have had more cash on hand and made a larger wager."

"I'm sorry I didn't think to let you know so you could sate your gambling needs," Sera said while delivering another sour look.

"My gambling habit doesn't have the unpleasant side effects of your station drinking binges."

Sera eyed him blearily over the rim of her cup. "What side effects are those?"

"The first day of any trip. You're not exactly sunshine and roses the day after a binge."

"Am I ever?"

Cargo paused, appearing to ponder the statement with great cogitation.

Her mind echoed with the light watery sound of Helen laughing at Cargo's pause. Sera scowled and swatted at him. "Thanks!"

He gestured with a nonchalant wave toward the second cup, indicating she get to it. Sera had already used her nano to clear most of the alcohol from her bloodstream and contain it for the next time she visited the head. However, Cargo didn't know she could do that and she needed to keep up appearances.

Sera raised the cup to her lips and took a long pull of the vile liquid anyway. She didn't want to seem ungrateful. After downing it, she leaned back in her chair, feeling much steadier than when she first sat down.

"All things considered, it's not a bad bit of extra credit to finish the visit with," she said and patted her pocket.

Cargo grunted, "One day you'll run out of people who haven't seen you win a drinking contest and then what will you do for fun?"

"Dunno, I guess I'll have to find a new way to fleece the common man."

Cargo laughed heartily in response.

Several minutes later—with Sera moving under her own power—they made their way down the promenade and onto the commercial dock front. There was just as much traffic here, but of a different sort. Cargo transports trundled down the deck plate and service trucks were everywhere, delivering supplies or repair equipment.

Sabrina was in berth 724 Station South. Long before she could see the ship around the curve of the docks, Sera could hear Thompson's voice berating some poor cargo handlers. The echoing shouts eventually resolved into words, and Sera hid a smile behind her hand as they approached.

"You lazy dolts. Can't you even lift a crate? I've seen hundred-year-old bots do a better job than you oafs. If you drop one more container, I'll take it out of your scrawny, mal-nourished hides. Now get to it,=; I don't have all day."

Thompson was a large blond man who had been her supercargo for over six years. To avoid confusion with Cargo, they just called him the Super. He wasn't a very outgoing man, mostly taken to brooding and stumping about the ship, but his attention to detail made him a good crewmember. Combined with his size and skill with a pulse rifle, that made him the right sort of super for *Sabrina*.

"How's the last shipment?" Sera asked when she and Cargo reached the ship.

"Fine, if these morons can manage to hold onto an effing handle." Thompson tossed the two dockworkers a contemptuous glare. "Don't know why they insist on using humans for this. Either way, we'll be loaded up with plenty of time to spare; don't worry, Captain."

"Good to hear," Cargo said. "Send the final docs up to me on the bridge when you're done."

Thompson nodded and turned back to the handlers as another crate slipped from their grasp. "God's great black space! What is *wrong* with you two? Is this your first day on the job? I told you I was going to take it out of your hide and now I am. Which one of you wants to get your ear ripped off?"

"Somehow, I don't think that is helping them with their work," Cargo laughed.

"Yeah, but I bet it makes him feel a lot better," Sera grinned.

"I'll see you later, Captain; I've got to wash off the smell of that bar you were in before my shift starts."

Sera took a deep breath. "Dunno, I kind of like that malty musk on you."

"In that case, I'm gonna take an even longer shower," Cargo laughed and walked onto the ship. Sera stuck her tongue out at him and walked over to an inspection port to admire the sleek lines of her girl.

Sabrina was not a regular boxy freight hauler, having started her life as a pleasure yacht. Her previous owner had fallen on hard times and lost possession of the ship in an outer system. *Sabrina* had needed repairs, and the local shipyard, where she had been in storage for owed taxes, didn't have the funds to make them. So, she sat for ninety years before Sera found her. With a hundred years of service before being impounded, she was getting on, but that didn't diminish the impact Sera felt when she first laid eyes on the ship.

There was an influential man who owed Sera a favor or two, and she got him to give her the money to buy the ship and furnish it with the necessary repairs. The finer aspects of the yacht's interior had been stripped out long before Sera saw *Sabrina*, but it was the size of the vessel and the engines that mattered. This ship had the room to haul cargo and the power to do so quickly. There were some other modifications that had been made, but like her advanced nano, Sera didn't advertise those.

She noted with approval that the damage they had suffered on their last run had been repaired. They had been parked in a planetary ring, moving along with the flow of the rocks and ice, when a stray rock had damaged the port sensor array and left a long rent across a goodly portion of the ship. However, the profit from the questionable cargo, which had put them there in the first place, more than paid for the repairs.

Thompson let loose some final curses as the dockworkers finished loading the last crate. She turned to watch with a smile; the dockworkers were visibly trembling as they got on their cart and drove off.

Sera returned to viewing her ship. She enjoyed these final quiet moments alone before going on board and filling out departure docs; these last few minutes when it was just her, *Sabrina's* sleek hull, and the call of empty space. She could forget her past, previous failures. Here she was a good captain, *Sabrina* was prosperous, and she had a good crew.

Her reverie was interrupted by a stinging slap on her butt and Sera turned to see her pilot, Cheeky, standing behind her. She wore a coy smile and her hands were resting on tilted hips.

"One day I'll get you to give me some of that luvin' you lavish on *Sabrina*," Cheeky said.

"One day I'll get you neutered and save us all a lot of hassle." Sera rubbed her stinging butt; Cheeky could really deliver a good slap. She found herself becoming aroused as she looked at her pilot.

Cheeky was an attractive woman who wore as little clothing as local law or custom would allow. On Coburn, that meant she wore little more than three triangles of cloth, her shoes and a purse.

Sera shook her head to clear her mind. Cheeky also had altered glands that could put out much higher levels of pheromones than any human should be allowed to. "Make sure you shut that off and take a long shower. You know what happened last time your love smell filtered through the ship."

"We all had a good time." Cheeky wiggled her hips suggestively and blew her captain a kiss as she walked up the ramp. From behind, it was obvious why Cheeky had the name she did. Sera found herself wondering if it was a conscious effort to walk like that or if the woman had resorted to surgery.

Following her pilot onto the ship, Sera's internal AI flashed a notification that they had made a secure connection to the ship's private net. Sera checked the ship's general status and greeted its AI.

<Good evening sweetie, how are you holding together?> Sera asked Sabrina.

<Well enough, though I take offense to the question. How else would I be holding together?> The ship's mental tone conveyed annoyance.

Sabrina had been in a strange mood as of late. Sera chose to ignore the reply and smiled up at the nearest observation camera as Helen passed her authentication token to the bridge's net. Sera checked in, finding Cargo already working on departure paperwork; he must have decided to skip the shower.

<Station given us our departure time yet?>

<0900 ship time tomorrow.> His mental tone was relaxed. He enjoyed the little details of running the ship. Sera preferred to sit in her captain's chair and give orders.

<Everything delivered and stowed?>

She could imagine him flipping through the plas sheets, checking them against the records logged in their databases, before he answered. Cargo hated making mistakes.

<Just one package left.> There was a significant pause; Sera could feel his mental discomfort even over the net. *<It's from one of Kade's people here.>*

<Kade? Why didn't I know about this?> Sera asked Cargo and Helen.

<It came on the list when we were out,> Helen supplied.

Cargo muttered something rude and the bridge's net flashed with an image of Cargo's avatar doing something very unpleasant to a representation of Kade. *<At least we're delivering it at the regular drop point with the rest of his stuff; there's no extra trip.>*

The regular drop point was an out of the way FTL jump point that Kade's people used for trading with other ships—his people being a pirate organization known as The Mark. Most of their people and ships were somewhat less than welcome at the more reputable stations, such as Coburn.

<They never can schedule things ahead of time,> Sera sighed.

<They're not exactly an "ahead of time" sort of organization.>

Sera told Cargo she'd be making the rounds and passed the active monitoring of the bridge's net to Helen.

When *Sabrina* had been a private yacht, the main deck was where the owners presumably threw their parties and spent most of their time. Now it was the freight deck. The cargo hatch was on the port side, and from there Sera walked into the main corridor, which ran from the bow to the stern engine shielding. The various freight holds were located off this corridor. Some had normal air and gravity, some were refrigerated and some had low, or even no gravity.

Also along the corridor were the lifts and ladders to the other decks. Sera walked toward the bow of the ship and slid into one of the vertical ladder shafts, which ran through all the decks. From there, she opened an access hatch to a maintenance tube. Inside the hatch were some knee and shoulder pads that she slipped on; it wouldn't do to scuff her leather.

The tube ended in a sealed inspection port. Sera opened it and peered out at the newly-installed sensor equipment. The workmanship looked good. Everything was straight and attached firmly. The exterior indicators all showed green.

Beyond the array, Sera could see the space elevator that carried cargo and people between the surface and the station. Seeing it reminded her how far humanity had fallen from the glory it once held.

Millennia ago, when humanity had first set out to cross the stars, they had no faster than light technology. Interstellar travel was made possible only by utilizing massive fuel scoops. Ships had vast electrostatic funnels that spread for kilometers in front of them and allowed the gathering and compression of interstellar heavy hydrogen. The hydrogen, typically Deuterium and Tritium, was burned in nuclear fusion reactors to produce the thrust that pushed the ships between the stars.

Journeys between the stars took decades, or even centuries.

With the considerable effort and expense required to get to even the nearest stars, humanity strove to make the most of all available resources. Technology and engineering made impressive advances as societies demanded better use of raw materials.

The space elevator stretching from Coburn Station down to Trio was an example of the different sort of technology humans used to have. In present times, few worlds could afford to build elevators to their space stations. The materials were just too expensive and the process took too long. A ship's grav drive was more efficient in the short term. However, over centuries of use, the elevator would use much less power to achieve the same volume of transport. It was another example of the long-term approach that people used to take as opposed to the current mindset, which was decidedly shortsighted.

It was a shift created by the advent of FTL.

People had always suspected—at least once the significance of 299,792,458 meters per second was known—that some method of exceeding the speed of light was possible. Many theories of wormholes, space-time folding, alternate realities, and slipstreams were put forward and attempted. In the end, the workable form of faster than light travel encapsulated many of the ideas behind some of those theories, though it turned out to be much harder to harness than originally hoped.

Before FTL, each star system was isolated from the rest of humanity, but once a trip between two stars was reduced to a matter of weeks and not centuries, everything changed. Traveling to an uninhabited star to mine asteroids was something that could be easily achieved, and people's attitude toward conservation and efficiency disappeared within a century.

Helen injected a long yawn into Sera's thoughts. *<Enough already. We get it, you yearn for the good old days.>*

<I don't really miss the days…just wish people could appreciate the way things used to be.>

Helen didn't agree. *<You just miss your people. This isn't your world and you know it.>*

<It is now; it has to be.>

Helen didn't respond. It was an old conversation, one they performed out of habit more than a real expectation of change.

Sera walked through the freight deck's main corridor, poking her head into various holds, ensuring that everything was secure and ready for departure. The familiar smell of deck cleaner and oil wafted past and an unbidden memory of her first weeks on the ship came back.

She and Flaherty had spent many a day hauling equipment through these halls and shafts back when they were first refitting *Sabrina*. It had been long days and longer nights, but she was proud of what they had built.

Helen flashed the date of her memory over her vision and she was surprised to see that it had been just over ten years ago. Somewhere in the last few months, she had passed her ten-year anniversary with *Sabrina* without marking the occasion. No wonder the ship had been a bit snippy of late.

Sera chided Helen for not reminding her of the occasion, nor for cluing her in on the cause of Sabrina's poor temper.

<*I was unaware you were interested in marking anniversaries with AI.*> Helen was unrepentant.

<*What are you talking about?*> Sera replied. <*We always celebrate our anniversary.*>

Helen inserted the emotion of mild surprise, followed by a pout into Sera's mind. <*I thought that was just for me.*>

Sera laughed and her avatar stuck her tongue out at Helen. <*Don't give me that; I'm not some little girl that you can twist around your ephemeral finger anymore.*>

Helen didn't respond, and Sera let out a long sigh. For being one of the most advanced AI in the Inner Stars, Helen could certainly be childish.

<*Sometimes I think Sabrina is rubbing off on you,*> Sera said to her one-time mentor and guardian.

<*I resent that,*> Helen retorted. <*Just because the ship's AI can't deal with the fact that I am her superior in every way doesn't mean I have to dumb it down.*>

<*You're superior to most planet administration AI we run into, but you don't go out of your way to make them feel inferior,*> Sera responded, mildly surprised to be the one to advocate maturity in their relationship.

<*Maybe I could be more accommodating for our dear Sabrina,*> Helen eventually responded.

<*Glad to hear it. Now I have to figure out how to make it up to her,*> Sera said.

<*Make what up?*> Helen asked innocently and Sera let out an audible scream.

She completed her review of the freight deck and took the aft ladder shaft up to the crew deck.

When she first bought *Sabrina,* the ship had lifts for reaching each deck, but Sera had removed all but one of the conveniences. Shafts were faster and still worked when the ship was under fire and conserving energy.

<*Nothing to do with how you like to climb the ladders in front of the men on the ship?*> Helen suggested.

<*I do it to Cheeky, too.*> Sera smiled to herself as she stepped onto the crew deck.

<*Funny, I thought you preferred it when she did it to you.*>

The ladder was across from the galley and she stepped in to find Thompson and Flaherty eating their supper. She saw that it was nearing the end of second shift; most of the crew would be calling it a night soon.

"Evening, Captain," Thompson said around a mouthful of his sandwich. Flaherty looked at her, nodded, and went back to his meal.

"Hey guys," Sera smiled at them as she poured a cup of coffee and hunted for fresh cream.

Thompson and Flaherty made an effective and efficient team when it came to managing the ship's cargo. Neither of them talked much and managed to communicate just about everything with grunts and gestures. They didn't even use the Link to talk—Sera had checked the logs.

Sera doctored her coffee up just the way she liked and bid them goodnight before taking the corridor to the bow, then climbing the ladder that led to the top deck. This was the smallest deck on the ship, containing only the bridge forward and a small observation lounge aft. The lounge had a magnificent view of the light flare from the engines when they were under heavy thrust, and Sera had often sat back there, gazing out at it as the ship cruised through space.

Cargo was still on the bridge, readying the reports Sera had to sign before they could depart. Cheeky was also at her console, having added a tight halter top and tiny skirt to her ensemble. She yawned and stretched as she stood.

"You just had to make a final course alteration right before bed," she complained. "I had to plot it out and re-file with system traffic control."

"Sorry about that—I didn't think you'd already filed the report," Sera apologized.

"When else was I going to do it, when I was sleeping?"

Cargo laughed. "I thought you had gotten all of your 'sleeping' in on your shore leave."

Cheeky stuck her tongue out at the man. "Jealous."

Cargo couldn't help it as his eyes strayed down to the bold, black print across Cheeky's chest. It read 'Got Milk?' He sighed wistfully. "I might be."

"Really?" Cheeky asked.

"No, not really," Cargo grinned.

"You're such a tease," Cheeky said as she turned and left the bridge.

"I'm a tease?" He murmured softly as she left.

"You are, you know," Sera said.

"How so? I don't flirt, I just do my job."

"Exactly!" Sera smiled as she shuffled the plas she had to sign into order. "You're totally unflappable. It's the ultimate come-on."

"I'm going to start the pre-warm-up checklist so things'll be ready in the morning."

"See! Always back to business with you."

"Do you want to do it?" Cargo turned, half rising out of his chair.

"Heck no, I've been up for thirty hours already."

Cargo nodded and sat back down.

Coburn, like many stations, required a full warm-up and test of all ship systems before undocking. The warm-up had to take place four hours before departure and Cargo was taking the third watch to run the sequence at 0500 hours.

She turned to leave the bridge when Nance, the ship's bio, appeared in her mind.

<*I just wanted to let you know, take short showers for the next while—I know how you like to luxuriate for an hour or more.*>

Even though she was looking at Nance's mental avatar, the bio-engineer still wore a thick, tight hazsuit. Whereas Cheeky showed every inch of skin she could manage, Nance was the opposite, rarely showing any skin at all—even virtually.

<*What's up?*> Sera asked. <*I have the stink of a hundred drunks to wash off.*>

The bio scowled. <*Well, let's just say that you don't want to come down to environmental until I clean up. The regulator on tank nine malfunctioned, and a line blew. Contaminated all sorts of shit with…well…shit.*>

<*Was it that one you bought at Rattlescar?*> Sera asked.

<*Yeah, I knew I shouldn't have, but it was such a good deal,*> the bio replied.

<*Ripped off at Rattlescar again. You should know better.*>

Nance's avatar nodded sullenly and Sera laughed. <*Well, I'll let you get to it. Can I at least have ten minutes?*>

Nance nodded. <*Yes, but a second over and I'm switching it to full cold.*>

<*Is that any way to treat your captain?*>

<*Do* **you** *want to come down here and clean up?*> Nance retorted.

<*OK, OK, ten minutes, got it.*>

Nance disappeared from her vision as Sera slid down the ladder to the third deck. She walked quietly past the crew cabin doors to her quarters at the end of the corridor. She palmed the door open with a yawn and entered her outer office where she handled the ship's business.

It was the standard utilitarian sort expected of a captain; her various certifications hung on the wall and a large oak desk dominated the small space. She laid the departure plas sheets on its surface and pulled up holo of each one. This was the part about captaining a starship she liked least. She was near finishing up and getting ready to peel off her leather when Cargo called her over the Link.

<*Still up, Captain?*>

<*Barely.*>

<*Hate to bother you with this, but you're the only other one awake. Kade's boys are down at the hatch with that last shipment.*>

Despite his words, Cargo's tone didn't carry any apology.

Grumbling that she should have told Thompson to have himself or Flaherty wait up for it, she pulled her jacket back on and slid down the ladders to the freight deck. At the hold's opening to the station dock, two men were waiting with a large crate on a gravity pad. They were looking nervous and just a bit twitchy. Either they had some bad drugs in their systems or Kade was foisting something pretty damn dangerous on her.

One of the men spoke up as soon as he spotted her.

"Permission to come aboard?" he asked.

Sera granted it and the two men all but ran onto the ship and moved out of direct sight from dock traffic, the cargo container following them on its float.

"So, what does The Mark have for me today, boys?" Sera asked, none too pleased about the late hour or the obviously illegal contents of the crate. "What am I sticking my neck out for this time?"

Most cargo The Mark had her run was just semi-illegal. Either OK in the system where she was picking up or delivering to, just not both; or some stopping point along the way. There also had been the odd shipment that was illegal no matter where they were; this one had that feel.

The man who had asked permission to board grinned in what he probably thought was a winning fashion. It really wasn't. "S'nothing to worry about, just a little something that Kade wants."

"I don't care about that," Sera said as she reached over and snatched the bill of lading from him. "I care what *this* says it is." Scanning the pad, she found that the crate purported to contain a prize racing hound in a holo sim. The dog thought he was in a regular kennel with other dogs for companionship and humans feeding him. The reality was just a crate with a feeding system, but he wouldn't know the difference and would be better for it.

"That really what's in there?" Sera didn't bother to hide her skepticism.

"Yeah, the dog's not as special as who used to own it." The man grinned again and Sera held up her hand.

"Yeah, sure. I really don't want to know more." She signed off on the delivery. "Any need to open it and check it out?"

The men went rigid and hastily assured her that the dog would be fine and there was no need to check it out. That clinched it for Sera; she would definitely have to check this cargo out once she was underway. If it had any type of tamper seal, she'd make up some excuse for it later.

Once it was secured in the fore port hold, she informed Cargo that the delivery had been made and stowed. Then she closed the main cargo hatch and the auxiliary personnel port. Cargo confirmed the seal from the bridge and checked it off the pre-warm-up list.

<*Get some rest, Captain, gonna be a long day tomorrow,*> Cargo advised.

<*Cargo! Now you've gone and jinxed it!*>

JUST A ROUTINE DAY

STELLAR DATE: 07.01.8927 (Adjusted Years)
LOCATION: *Sabrina*, Coburn Station, Trio
REGION: Trio System, Silstrand Alliance Space

At 0600 hours, Sera sauntered onto the bridge and greeted Cargo, who was hunched over his console, finishing up departure plaswork. She handed him one of the two coffee cups she carried and he absently took it, thanked her, and cast her an appraising look.

"Forgoing the customary clothing-matches-your-mood policy?" he asked.

"I never break my clothing-mood policy. I'm feeling good, but mellow. Blue fits."

Cargo eyed her with suspicion. "This isn't like that one time you wore pink to fake us out, is it?"

"How many times do I have to tell you? That was a dare from Cheeky." Sera set her coffee down and eased into her chair. "Checks went OK?"

"*Sabrina* purred like a kitten, just like always," Cargo replied.

<*Of course I did. When have I not?*> Sabrina asked.

"Never, my dear," Sera replied with a smile.

Cargo shook his head and swallowed his coffee in two quick gulps. "Tug is scheduled for 0845. I'm getting sack." He stood and left the bridge without even his customary morning stretch.

"Is it something I'm wearing?" Sera called after him, laughing.

Sera ran a hand down the tight leather skin-suit covering her body. She spent a moment enjoying the tactile sensation before beginning her routine. The first order of business was finalizing the freight manifests and trade route they would take after the drop-off for Kade.

When Cheeky came on duty at 0700, she took in her captain with a long hungry look, unable to keep a hand from straying toward her captain's well-defined chest. Sera slapped it away.

"There'll be none of that."

"You are such a tease, Captain." Cheeky grinned as she sat at the pilot's console.

Sera laughed. Cheeky was one to talk; she was wearing her customary departure uniform, little more than the day before and a pair of 'sensible' heels. Sera used Cheeky's arrival and coverage of the bridge to make a quick visit to the galley, followed by a final visual inspection of the ship. She returned an hour later to go through final checklists with the station.

Departure tug charges were billed and their accounts were closed. Station umbilici retracted and station personnel confirmed inner seal on the dockside airlocks. At 0830, *Sabrina* broke hard connection with the station and floated in her berth, with only the station's security tethers still in place.

The tug showed up on time and made a solid grapple to their bow anchors, pulling them gently away from Coburn Station. Sera felt a mild flutter in her stomach as they left station gravity and their internal systems took over.

"Coburn Tug 19 confirming successful undock," the tug pilot's voice announced over the comm.

"Free and clear, Tug 19," Cheeky confirmed as the ship drifted away from the station.

The tug maneuvered *Sabrina* out into their designated departure lane. For a relative backwater, Trio was a busy system. They took plotted courses and space traffic lanes very seriously.

"Oh, sweet mother!" Cheeky exclaimed. "Is he ever going to turn on his grav drive? If he uses thrusters to pull us all the way out, you should register a complaint."

Sera had dozed off. She stretched and checked the holo on her console. "He's still on thrusters? We're a thousand klicks from the station; he could have turned on his grav drive at the five hundred mark."

"Trio System law states that all outbound ships must use thrusters only until fifteen hundred kilometers from stations," Sabrina provided via the bridge's audible systems. "It's a recent change they made after some accidents."

"I guess that explains the size of that tug bill; must take a pile of fuel to pull a ship that far on thrusters only."

At the prescribed distance, the tug's gravity engines unfolded from its main body and activated. Because the graviton waves would disrupt the ship behind it, the engines extended far to either side of *Sabrina* before activating.

"We could have been on a fusion burn by now," Cheeky complained, yawning with boredom over the long departure.

"You may be a good pilot, Cheeks, but I don't relish the thought of being on a station where half those moron captains can turn on their fusion engines near me. I like my skin actually attached to my body."

Cheeky made a dismissive sniff. "You can always get new skin, but lost time is gone forever."

Sera laughed. "I'm still wearing my original birthday suit, thank you very much."

"Like I'd know, you never let anyone see it. Always with the leather."

"I could say you have the opposite problem."

"You could, but would I care?" Cheeky sat up and looked at her console intently. "Damn tug's got the vector wrong. We want a parabolic around that inner planet, not a collision."

That was what Sera liked about Cheeky; fun to chat with, but able to switch to business in an instant, when it was called for.

"Tug 19, this is *Sabrina*. Come in," Cheeky called over the comm.

"Tug 19 here."

"Check your vector, 19, you're moving off course."

There was a moment of silence and then the tug pilot's response came over the comm. "Sorry about that, my primary nav was reading sensors wrong. I'm on backup now and correcting. Tug 19 out."

"Roger, *Sabrina* out," Cheeky said, switching off the open comm.

"I think that Tug's AI is senile," Sabrina said over the ship's speakers. "It told me that my humans and their advice are not welcome."

"Yay for tugs," Cheeky's voice dripped with sarcasm.

"I suddenly feel somewhat less than safe." Sera finished her cup of coffee and double-checked scan. "At least he corrected properly. How long till we can ditch this dude?"

"Seventeen minutes," Sabrina replied. "And it won't be a moment too soon."

Sera chuckled in response.

Sabrina was an unusual AI. Usually ships' AI were officious and only spoke when directly addressed—and then only over the Link. However, Sabrina had a habit of simply speaking her mind whenever she chose. On their first voyage, when it was just Sera and Flaherty, having Helen and the garrulous Sabrina was comforting—especially since the AI were much better at casual banter than Flaherty.

Finally, the tug reached its departure point and released its grapple.

"Tug 19 signing off. Have a good trip."

"You too," Cheeky said and closed the channel. "Dork."

"We're not on our proper course," Sabrina observed.

"I know," Cheeky sighed. "I just didn't feel like mentioning it again. I can fix us up in a minute."

Cheeky laid in her course corrections and activated *Sabrina's* gravity drive. They were accelerating toward the center of the system, the drive throwing negative gravitons in front of the ship, essentially sucking them forward.

Their flight path took them past the innermost planet, a rocky world spinning below them at over sixteen thousand kilometers per hour. Sera watched the world's surface as the daylight termination line raced across the craggy landscape, casting long, dancing shadows over the world.

"Hate to be working a mining rig on that thing," she said with a shake of her head.

"Can you say 'hourly earthquakes'?" Cheeky asked.

Sabrina skimmed close to the surface of the world in a parabolic arc, Cheeky applying a hard burn of the fusion engines at the periapsis of their passage. The ship's velocity picked up considerably during the maneuver, lining them up for a close pass-by of the local star.

"Gravity assist one completed at one hundred percent efficiency," Cheeky said with a grin. "Now to beard the star."

Gravity assists were one of the wonders of physics. The faster you flew, the more kinetic energy a burn gave. When a burn was made at the closest point of an arch around a heavenly body, the more relative velocity was imparted.

Cheeky referred to it as planet slalom.

"We at the scoop deployment point yet, Cheeks?" Sera asked, feeling too lethargic to use her Link. Maybe she *was* still feeling the after effects of yesterday's binge.

"Just about. When we hit 0.113*c* we'll have the right *v* to do it smoothly."

"You on it with Sabrina?"

Cheeky turned and looked at her captain. "I *have* done this before."

<*Me too,*> Sabrina added.

Sera laughed and raised her hands. "Sorry, I apologize for my backseat piloting."

Several minutes later, a slight vibration ran through the hull as the scoop deployed. It wasn't large, only a kilometer wide, but its electro-static field funneled the stellar wind through a system that stripped out the heavy hydrogen and helium, storing the gasses in the fuel tanks for later consumption.

<*Sabrina,*> Cheeky addressed the ship as they passed 0.15*c*, <*my board shows green for fusion burn. Confirm?*>

<*I am green, as well,*> Sabrina acknowledged. <*Good to initiate burn at plot point tango.*>

<*Roger,*> the pilot replied.

Despite the terms used, Cheeky wasn't sitting at a board with green lights, and Sabrina most certainly was not. Piloting a ship like *Sabrina* involved manipulating controls in a three dimensional holo projection. At any time, the pilot had to monitor dozens of visual indicators, as well as the data feed her Link to the nav computer provided.

"Initiating fusion burn," Cheeky said as she activated the fusion engine's super-lasers and started the flow of helium and heavy hydrogen into the engine.

Although she had just initiated an atomic fusion reaction only one hundred meters aft, there was no noticeable change on the ship. Powerful inertial dampeners in the form of gravity fields protected the rest of the vessel from the engines. Without them, the thrust from the fusion burners would cause *Sabrina* to do a large-scale impression of a crushed can.

"All dampeners and stabilizers read normal; radiation shielding is showing green, as well."

"You know, Cheeks," Sera said. "It's just me up here; you don't really need to do the whole status announcing thing."

Cheeky cast her captain a sour look. "I don't do it for you; I assume you're checking everything on the Link. You know I've always dreamed of being a military pilot, you know, flying one of those big cruisers. Well, I saw some Silstrand military holos recently where they announce everything. I'm trying it on for size."

"Don't let me stop you, then," Sera smiled.

"I wasn't going to. You may dress like a dominatrix, but you don't frighten me."

Sera sighed and sat back in her chair.

<*Well, you do,*> Helen said.

The course Cheeky followed took them over the star's north pole. *Sabrina* was on a course to pass within a hundred thousand kilometers of the star, putting them on the right outsystem vector while picking up at least thirty percent of the total velocity they would need before hitting their jump point.

Sera carefully examined the ship's scan readout to make sure there was no potential flare activity. System scan said the star's northern hemisphere was quiet, but she liked to check for herself.

She was comparing the two scans when she noticed several ships enter the system through a seldom-used jump point stellar south of Trio and Coburn Station. Scan showed them traveling at over seventy percent the speed of light, far too fast for a busy system like Trio. Sera imagined they could expect a hefty fine when they docked.

Sabrina lost its Link to the system's dataflow as the ship approached the star; radiation played havoc with any signal. The ship's shields showed nominal fluctuations—they were rated to hold against far worse, including having a fusion warhead detonate against them.

As the ship passed over the star, Cheeky applied full burn to the fusion engines, the effect multiplying their acceleration by a factor of five. At that rate, it took less than a minute to complete their arc around the star and they exited the gravity assist maneuver at just over a quarter the speed of light.

Sera examined the data from the passage over Trio Prime, impressed to see the precision with which Cheeky performed the maneuver. Even the switching of the grav drive from negative to positive was done at the optimal time—the gravitons it threw now pushing them off the star's mass.

Ship's Link reconnected to a nearby beacon and Sera turned her attention back to the ships she had spotted earlier. System scan showed the vessels remained on a direct course for the world of Trio, though they weren't slowing down much, if at all.

At *Sabrina's* current distance from Trio, scan lag was an issue. The beacon they were stripping data from was ten light minutes away from their current position; Trio was another seven lightminutes past that. Considering the speed those ships were traveling, they could already be at the station, or past it.

As Sera was pondering what those ships could be up to, Sabrina alerted them to a call on the local emergency band.

"This is a system-wide alert. Three ships of unknown origin have attacked a Trio defense emplacement and are on a vector for Coburn Station. Their intentions are unknown. All ships are advised to stay within the protective range of a system station or fleet patrol until further notice." The alert paused and then restarted the same message.

Sabrina muted the alert. <*I'll let you know if it changes,*> she said.

"Thanks, that's not terribly auspicious—Silstrand really needs to deal with these pirates; it's getting worse all the time," Sera said with a shake of her head.

"Uh, you realize that we smuggle for those pirates," Cheeky said with a smirk.

"Well," Sera smiled back, "I said they should; I didn't say I thought they actually would."

Cheeky chuckled and Sera reviewed their current vector. There were no planets or stations anywhere near their outsystem route. They would just have to keep pushing forward. Chances were slim those ships would even come within fifteen million kilometers of *Sabrina,* though Sera wasn't about to bet her ship on it.

"Crank our burners up all the way, Cheeky. I want to put more distance between us and that mess," Sera said, before calling the crew to their stations, updating them on what was happening on the other side of the star.

Cargo stepped onto the bridge a few minutes later with coffee for himself and the two women. He made a show of only looking them in their eyes as he passed out the brew, then sat at his console, looking over the scan and their course.

"That's a lot of velocity those buggers have on them," he commented.

"They're going to get a speeding ticket," Sera agreed.

"What about a blowing-up-a-defensive-emplacement ticket?" Cheeky asked. "I hear systems are sticklers about that sort of thing."

"Alert said three ships, right?" Cargo asked.

"Yeah."

"Scan just updated from a relay south of the star. It shows five jumped in. Where are the other two?"

"That's disconcerting," Sera said. "I don't see them anywhere on system scan."

"Why does that statement insert small circus animals into my stomach?" Cheeky asked.

Cargo leaned forward and looked at Cheeky's flat stomach. "I don't see how even a couple of dancing mice would fit in there."

"Maybe it's a flea circus," Sera commented.

"Ewwww!" Cheeky shivered convulsively. "There's a mental image I just didn't need."

Another relay a few million kilometers south of the star updated scan data and they got their answer on the missing ships.

The feed showed the two vessels veering off from the other three and plotting a course around the star's south pole. They were running fast, thrusting on antimatter pion engines, from the look of the gamma rays trailing behind their ships.

"Does Trio allow AP engines in their inner system?" Cheeky asked.

"They blew up an emplacement. I don' think they care about AP regulations," Cargo said.

<Trio special regulations state that no antimatter engines may be used within twenty million kilometers of the star, or within two million kilometers of any station or outer planet,> Sabrina supplied the ruling anyway.

<What's up with her? She's being so proper today,> Helen said privately to Sera.

Sera sent her AI a mental shrug, but didn't comment further.

"Cheeky, what's the chance those two bogies will get within a million klicks of us?" she asked, though it looked like Cheeky was already on it.

"Based on their current course, they're going to get closer than your tight leather outfit, Captain. I'm guessing they plan to pay us a visit."

As though on cue, a signal came in from one of the ships and Sabrina patched it through the bridge speakers. A harsh voice called for them to cease burn and divert to a position that Sera would bet local stellar scan couldn't monitor.

"Like hell we will," Sera muttered. "Sabrina, are we ready to do an AP burn?"

<*We're always ready to make an AP burn. It's my favorite pastime.*>

Sera chuckled, <*Don't I know it. Bring up the gamma shielding and extrude the AP nozzle.*>

<*Spooling.*>

Sera could hear the ship's secondary reactor spin up and she watched readings show power flowing to the gamma shields. The AP drive smashed Hydrogen and Anti-Hydrogen, annihilating them and producing pions that were focused out the AP engine's nozzle. The pions quickly broke down into gamma rays and accelerated out the nozzle at just under the speed of light. The longer the nozzle was extruded, the more thrust *Sabrina* would get from the burn. Sera saw that Cheeky and Sabrina were spinning it out all the way.

"Good thing we declared our antimatter and allowed the containment inspection before we docked," Cargo said. "Blood suckers at Trio would fine us if they caught us using undeclared antimatter, pirate attack or no."

"You're thinking pirate, too, then?" Sera asked.

"It's way too small a force to actually attack a Silstrand Alliance member. They're here for something that they think a small, fast force can snag."

Sera's thoughts immediately went to the small crate she had taken on the night before. She couldn't imagine anything in that crate being worth an outright attack on an Alliance member system, but it was the only thing she carried that could possibly have that kind of value.

The AP drive began to add to the ship's velocity and the holo display showed their kph relative to Trio Prime increasing so quickly that the lower digits were a blur.

<*Oh this feels good!*> Sabrina crowed. <*I wish we could run out the AP engine more often!*>

"Not concerned who we're running from?" Cargo asked the ship's AI.

<*Sera will take care of me. I'm not worried about any pirates,*> Sabrina replied confidently, causing Sera to suppress a smile.

"What are the chances that these guys are just checking all the outbound ships?" Cheeky asked.

"Then they'd split up. Both of them are on a vector to meet up with us well before we get to our jump point. I'd say we're the ones they're looking for."

Cheeky looked perplexed. "What could we have that pirates would want?"

Sera and Cargo shared a long look, his eyes showing mild recrimination. Sera sighed and told Cheeky they were carrying something extra special for The Mark.

"Figures," the pilot sulked. "I don't know why you do runs for them. From what I can see, we're pretty profitable even without all the extra risks."

Sera's expression was stony. "I have my reasons."

"Well, I hope they're worth dying for."

"We're not going to die here; we've got a few tricks up our sleeves," Sera said. In her mind, where only Helen could hear, she said, <*Yes, it's worth dying for.*>

Sera checked scan and saw that the two unidentified ships had fallen from their entry velocity of $0.73c$ to $0.45c$. Their vector around the star had not been clean and they lost velocity breaking out of its gravity well.

Cheeky was looking at the same data. "Damn, those ships must be all engine to only lose that much v during such a sloppy maneuver."

"Don't forget the guns," Cargo added. "All engines and guns."

Sera switched her display to show their outsystem course. Their destination was an FTL jump point several million kilometers beyond the last of the outer planets. The interior of Trio system was a good seven light hours across and they still had just over three hours to the jump point on full burn.

She widened her view and saw that the two ships behind were accelerating again. Both were back over half the speed of light, nearly at their previous velocity of $0.73c$. Sera looked down at *Sabrina's* indicators and saw that they were accelerating slower than expected and the ship was developing an odd vibration.

"Scoop!" Sera cried just as Sabrina reported that the scoop was still deployed and slowing them down. Cheeky cursed and quickly killed the electrostatic field that had been scooping hydrogen for fuel.

The pilot turned her slightly red face back to Sera. "Sorry, Captain. It sorta slipped my mind."

Sera's brow furrowed. "Mine too," then she nodded. "Now the ol' girl's picking up."

<*Who are you calling old?*>

<*Sorry, it's just an expression,*> Sera replied and only received a mental 'harrumph' from her ship. She really needed to think of something to make up for the forgotten anniversary.

Cargo looked over his shoulder. "Stellar medium is a bit lighter on our vector. We should be able to hit 0.60 c with all drives burning hot, but they'll," he jerked his head to the stern to indicate their pursuers, "get that advantage, too."

Helen had been examining their outbound vector and brought an issue to Sera's attention. Sera cursed silently. Things were always working against her.

"Ladies," Sera asked Cheeky and Sabrina, "if we do this burn for another forty minutes, what are the chances we can hold shields at max while we vector for the jump and keep all three drives online?"

"Planning to melt us?" Cheeky asked.

<*She's right,*> Sabrina said. <*Power plant could melt down if we tried to run all that—even with the auxiliary plant online.*>

"What about the SC batteries?" Sera asked.

"They're way low," Cheeky replied. "Pansies at Trio get all nervous with a hundred fusion reactors humming around their station. You said they charge too much for station power, so we ran on batts while docked."

"Huh," Sera grunted. "Well that was shortsighted of me."

When traveling at any appreciable speed, *Sabrina* always ran her forward shields. Even a speck of sand, traveling at even a tenth the speed of light, would punch right through the ship. It could destroy the reactor, and certainly any humans in its way.

However, with ships chasing them, they now had to deploy shield umbrellas over the entire vessel, and that was going to run them beyond their power generation limits.

Flying directly behind a ship running grav, fusion, and AP engines was a recipe for a bad day. If they were smart, their pursuers would fan out and flank *Sabrina.* From those positions, they would be able to hit nearly any part of the ship. The only advantage was that they couldn't shoot straight up the engines.

<*Helen, I'm betting these guys are going to use lasers, probably ten centimeter beams; they're going to take out some of ours so they can board us. Work up some tactics and prime our defenses,*> Sera said to her AI.

<*I'll load the routines. I think our best bet is to try to refract their beams with some precise grav waves. With the batteries low, we can't run refraction shield-wide,*> Helen replied.

<*You can do it girl, don't let those bastards put holes in Sabrina.*>

<*Her I'm not so concerned about. You, on the other hand, are a priority.*>

And so, the battle of the AIs continued.

"Do we have a solid intercept time, Cheeky?" Sera asked vocally.

"Not one hundred percent. They have a few course corrections to make that may slow them down a bit, but even if they have one-eyed apes flying those tubs, they'll catch us before we jump."

"Any chance we can jump early?" Cargo asked.

"Not unless you want to see how you look smeared across a clump of dark matter," Sera told her first mate, while looking over their course. "There's gotta be something…" There was always a way out of these situations; it just took some creative thinking. "Cheeky, you've got one more correction to make, right?"

"Yup, shortly before our transition we've got to angle down and get back into the main plane of the system," Cheeky said, highlighting the position in the plot on the ship's main holo.

"Would you be able to make it now, and have it be shorter? It may be enough to get us out of this mess."

Cheeky pulled up several holos and manipulated them, plotting positions where she could make the alteration, looking for the one with maximum efficiency, lowest drag, and best time-to-jump improvement. The incongruity of her nearly naked, oversexed pilot furiously processing advanced spatial calculations on a dozen holos was not lost on Sera; she hid a small smile behind her hand as she watched.

<*It's like you don't take this stuff seriously,*> Helen admonished.

<*I totally do, but look at her, she's wiggling all over.*>

Cheeky turned and Sera schooled her expression.

"There's a point coming up where we can do our burn that would work well, but I don't like traveling in the main plane at these speeds. You never know what uncharted rock is out there, waiting to end our little race."

"Trio's pretty busy; I'd imagine they have everything charted."

"Who? The people with senile tug AIs and faulty nav comps?"

"AI can go senile?" Cargo asked.

"We have evidence," Sabrina said, her voice dripping with implied meaning.

"I'll take the chance of a stray rock over the surety of their lasers. Plot it out," Sera replied.

She leaned back in her chair. Despite the humor she found in the small things around her, Helen was right; this was serious. But her crew was smart, and her ship was a pro. This would work; they'd make the jump before the pirates caught up with them.

Cheeky made her computations, rechecked them and then had Sabrina review them, as well. They passed muster and Cheeky announced stellar south course alteration in just under five minutes. The time came and the change occurred with no noticeable sensations in the ship.

Sera ran the computations again, *Sabrina's* nav systems telling her that they had insufficient data to provide an accurate model due to unknown deceleration capabilities of the pursuing ships.

In addition to catching up with *Sabrina,* the two pirate ships also had to show some care in matching speeds. At the velocities they were traveling, even miniscule speed differences would cause immense differences in position. If the pirates didn't match *Sabrina's* speed precisely, they would flash past faster than the human eye could even detect.

High relative *v* also made targeting with lasers tricky at best. Good gunners with powerful AI could do it, but even they missed a lot. Her real worry was that if *Sabrina* managed to avoid being boarded, the pirates would resort to relativistic missiles.

Apparently, Cargo had been thinking along the same lines.

"Do you think they have RMs?" he asked.

"Pirates can get their hands on those things?" Cheeky asked, her entire body getting a bit paler than it already was.

"Yeah, but even if they have them, I doubt they'd use one. Those things aren't cheap."

Cheeky was looking over her nav board again. "How fast can they accelerate?"

"It varies and it's not linear," Sera replied. "At the speeds we're traveling, I'd guess they could go from seventy percent to ninety-nine percent of the speed of light in a few minutes."

"Ninety-nine percent?" Cheeky choked.

"They don't have the word 'relativistic' in the name for nothing." Cargo's voice dripped with sarcasm, which earned him a scowl from the pilot.

"They can't burn too long, though," Sera said. "Only so much fuel in them."

"Probably because they usually kill things before they run out," Cheeky commented.

Scan showed their pursuers making course corrections to match the burn Cheeky had made. The calculations now showed that their pursuers' loss of *v* from the adjustment would be just barely enough; *Sabrina* would make it out of this.

Apparently, the two ships behind them had come to the same conclusion, as the comm board suddenly lit up with an incoming message.

Sabrina activated the connection and a very unhappy face appeared on the main holo. From the lack of uniform and a glimpse of the bridge, it was confirmed; they were definitely pirate ships.

"Ship designated *Sabrina,* you were ordered to cease acceleration and divert to the transmitted course. Why are you not complying?" The man was trying to sound officious.

"'Cause I like my skin on my body," Sera said with copious amounts of sarcasm. "Why don't you tell me why you have such a keen interest in my ship?"

"That's none of your concern," the man snarled. "Now comply with our directive."

Sera almost laughed. This was the saddest line she'd ever been fed. "Don't be ridiculous. I'm not diverting. I have a schedule to keep and I'm not going to interrupt it to have tea with you." With that, she killed the connection and looked to Cheeky. "Time to FTL?"

"Twenty-three minutes," came the pilot's reply. "Those looked like Padre's men, didn't they?"

"Yeah, I'm starting to get a suspicion about who Kade stole that 'racing hound' from."

Cargo turned from his station. "They're still trying to make contact. Let's hope that's as mean as they get." He glanced back at his board. "Never mind that, scan shows energy signatures on their bow. I'm guessing lasers."

"Any room to twitch?" Sera asked Cheeky.

"Not unless we want to do another burn to correct, but that would put them right on top of us when we make the jump."

Sera cursed their luck.

"Sabrina, do we have the power to extend the shielding back over the AP engine nozzle? It looks like they're warming up their heaters and I bet that's gonna be the first target," she asked.

<*It'll weaken our shields overall,*> the AI replied. <*But I see the logic. Doing it.*>

The shields that protected *Sabrina* were not a firm shell around the ship, but rather an anti-gravitational field that repelled any objects and particles. Complex systems allowed the shields to detect laser impact on the hull and diffuse the beam with targeted gravitational waves. It was a tricky system to operate and often worked better in stellar space where the leading edge of a laser beam could be detected by refraction from the particles it had to travel through. Out in gasless interstellar spaces, lasers were much harder to counter.

Unfortunately for *Sabrina,* that was just the type of space they were entering. They had cleared the Kuiper Belt, and the Trio System had a stretch of very empty space between their current location and the jump point.

The shield extension came just in time, as invisible beams lanced out striking at *Sabrina's* AP nozzle.

Sera turned to Cargo. "What tricks do we have up our sleeves?"

Cargo mulled it over for a minute. "Could pepper them with some beams right on their bow. It would cause them to throw some force off the front of their ships, but I don't know how much good it would do. Could also drop a mine or two; might be able to do it accurately enough to force them to twitch out of the way."

Sera looked at the numbers again on her screen; although they were on course to jump before interception, the nav systems still showed a much closer race than she'd like. "Do both."

Cargo called down to Thompson and Flaherty and told them to get two magnetic proximity mines loaded into the tubes and ready to drop on the bridge's mark. Sera watched him run a few simulations to see if it was possible to hide the mines' presence with a bit of a light show from the aft lasers.

"Think it will work?" she asked.

"Worth a shot. Gonna be shooting at them anyway."

Cargo initiated the laser sequence, and seconds later, dropped the proximity mines. The mines had their own small propulsion units, which allowed them to reach the desired position as the lasers flickered around them.

Right before the lead ship was about to hit its designated mine, the vessel twitched and avoided impact. The other ship wasn't so lucky. Under constant fire from *Sabrina's* lasers, they never saw the second mine.

"Score!" Cargo shouted.

The resulting explosion was too small to see at the ten thousand kilometer distance, but scan showed a direct impact. With its forward shields maxed out, the pirate ship didn't appear to take damage, but the shaped charge managed to shed enough of their velocity. They were out of the race.

Scan updated, showing the first pirate ship's maneuvers to avoid its mine had placed it over a hundred thousand kilometers further away, now far to port. It was out of the running, too.

"Great work, Cargo," Sera said to her first mate with heartfelt gratitude. She thanked everyone over the Link for their calm, steady response to the trouble. Before she could finish, Cargo interrupted her.

"Captain, I wouldn't get too excited yet, we've got an RM inbound."

"Shit!" Sera swore over the open comm. "Belay that happiness, missile on our tail."

Sabrina was five minutes from the jump point. The relativistic missile was four minutes from intercept.

Sera ran the math and couldn't see any way they could get to the point before the RM hit them. Even killing aft shielding and diverting more power to the engines wouldn't give them enough extra thrust to pull it off. She looked to her pilot.

"Two options, Cheeks; we twitch and jump on whatever vector we end up on, or we dump to FTL now and hope there's no dark matter between us and the point."

Cheeky bit her lip as she pulled charts of the local dark layer onto the main holo.

Dark matter occupied its own sub-layer of space-time, which is where ships transitioned when they made FTL jumps. However, dark matter orbited its host star erratically and charts never displayed it with perfect accuracy. Jump points were positions with outsystem vectors that were always clear of dark matter. Ships could enter FTL without fear of colliding with a solid mass.

Cheeky zoomed the holo in on their course and pointed to a rather large clump of dark matter. "Can't do the jump on our current vector, there's a big lump of the black stuff in our path. Let me see if there is a clear path outsystem parallel to our vector."

Though it took Cheeky less than thirty seconds to find a course they could twitch to, it seemed far longer with the main holo showing the RM closing on them. Sera was tempted to try a mine again but the nav computer showed that the RM could compensate even if it had to avoid the mine. The damn things were just too fast and maneuverable. Sera was ordering Thompson and Flaherty to load another proximity mine anyway when Cheeky let loose a triumphant cry.

"I've got it! There's a clear path to port, if these charts are right, that'll take us out of here. DM does orbit through, but it should be clear right now."

Moments rolled by as Cheeky double checked her work and then laid in the burn time and vector that would give them a spare twenty thousand kilometers from the RM. She called out the count as everyone held their breath.

"On five, four, three, two, one, burn for three, two, one, kill!" The eight seconds stretched into a lifetime and then the two more seconds dragged on while scan updated. The RM had overshot and was compensating to approach their position. It had dropped down to 0.8 *c* as it maneuvered, but was quickly up to 0.9 *c* back on a direct course for *Sabrina*.

"It's on us again, Cheeky. How long to jump?"

Cheeky spared a hand to wave behind her at her captain as she concentrated on her console and the numbers rolling across it. She made a few final alterations and then rechecked them.

"Kay! FTL transition in T minus fifteen."

She began counting down the seconds to the transition as Sera brought the RM's time to impact up on the main holo. It was only a half a second behind Cheeky's count. Through those long seconds, Sera's mind raced over the thousand things that could go wrong, praying that they would make the jump in time.

Then, with the customary gut-twisting wrench, they made the transition and were in the lightless void of the dark layer.

TANIS RICHARDS

STELLAR DATE: 07.01.8927 (Adjusted Gregorian)
LOCATION: *Sabrina*, Interstellar Dark Layer
REGION: Galactic South of Trio Prime, Silstrand Alliance Space

Sera took a deep breath as Cheeky leaned over the side of her chair and threw up. Without a word, Cargo rose and walked out to the corridor. He returned with cleaning supplies from the small head just outside the bridge.

Sera rose from her chair, shaking far more than expected. She moved to Cheeky's console and rested a hand on the pilot's shoulder. Cheeky was quaking, and Sera helped her stand, wrapping her in a tight embrace. She choked back tears of relief and Sera did her best not to join in.

"Girl, that was the best flying I've *ever* seen!" Sera gave her pilot a squeeze.

Cheeky offered a weak smile. "Thanks, Captain, I'd appreciate it if you guys didn't tell anyone about this little after effect, though." She looked down at the spattered deck-plate.

Cargo bent down to clean up the mess. "What after effect?"

Cheeky reached down and smacked his head. "I mean it…I can't have anyone thinking I'm less than ladylike."

Sera laughed, wondering who might think that Cheeky was ladylike to begin with.

The distraction had calmed Cheeky and she sat back down at her console, reviewing the ship's readouts.

"Everything looks bang on, Captain," she turned and said after a minute's examination. "Mind if I hit my cabin for a bit and clean up?"

"Whatever you need to do, Cheeks. Cargo and I can hold the ship together while you're gone."

<*I resent that,*> Sabrina huffed.

<*Sorry, love, I didn't mean you,*> Sera stroked a console affectionately.

Cheeky left the bridge with a slight wobble in her step as she navigated around the consoles in her heels. Sera sat back in her chair and gave the crew the good news over the ship-wide net.

<*Thanks to everyone's hard work, we just outran a couple of pirate gunships that were looking to turn us into a bright, fluffy cloud. I'm sure you all noticed that you're still alive,*> Sera added a smile to her comment.

<*I did notice a distinct not-dead feeling,*> Thompson replied dryly.

<*Yay for our side!*> Nance's hazsuited avatar did a jump and a kick in everyone's mind.

<*Our SC batteries are totally drained,*> Sabrina interjected. <*Going to keep the auxiliary plant running; we'll have to watch the heat, though.*>

<*You do that, Sabrina. Me, I'm going to have to re-hydrate—I must have pissed a gallon when I saw that RM right on our tail.*> Thompson somehow managed to convey both thirst and the urge to urinate in his message.

<*What on earth did they want anyway?*> Nance asked. <*What could we have worth using an RM on us? Those things must cost as much as a small mining platform.*>

<*I have a suspicion,*> Sera said. <*Give me ten minutes to square some things away, then Thompson and Nance, meet me in the fore port cargo hold.*>

<*Will do,*> Thompson said while Nance's avatar managed a stiff nod.

Sera laid their interstellar course over her vision as she brought up the nav computer on her console's holo.

<*How far off will we be when we exit FTL?*> she asked her AI as she worked through the calculations herself. Helen would have the answer before she was half done, but Sera liked to test herself. People who let their AI think for them didn't take long to degenerate into little more than automatons.

<*We entered the dark layer not too far from our original jump point, but our vector was slightly skewed by the twitch. Not to mention we made the transition at over twice the originally-plotted speed,*> Helen said, giving Sera a bit more time to finish the math on her own.

<*We must have shaved almost five days off the trip,*> Sera said idly as she flipped through a matrix of figures.

<*Five days, three hours and twenty-one minutes.*>

<*You just can't help it, can you?*>

Helen sighed. <*No, I can't. It's actually a bit annoying. You take for granted how easily you can think in abstracts.*>

<*I suppose I do,*> Sera admitted. <*Well, based on this, it's a good thing we shortened the trip by a few days; we're going to spend every one of those saved days braking from this ungodly speed if we don't want to use up the rest of our antimatter.*>

<*It will take three days of braking and then a final day to arrive at the drop point,*> Helen supplied.

Cheeky returned to the bridge several minutes later, for once wearing pants and a shirt. Sera didn't comment on it, and the pilot began working out the details of when they needed to drop out of the dark layer and back into normal space.

"Have I mentioned that I hate special relativity math?" she asked. "An RM up our ass I can forgive; making me adjust calculations for all this time dilation is something else."

Sera smiled. "You have fun; I'm going to see what's in that crate we got from Kade's boys at the eleventh hour."

"If it's something nasty, kick it for me," Cheeky said.

Thompson and Nance were already in the cargo bay when Sera arrived. The burly super was sliding a gravity lift under the crate, while Nance, wearing her hazsuit with the hood sealed tight, stood nearby.

"How are you doing?" Sera asked.

"Mm, good," Nance replied.

Sera saw that the lenses of her bio's mask were fogged up and the woman's limbs had a slight tremble.

"Nance, honey, take off the hood; let me see you."

<*Sure, why not try now,*> Helen chuckled.

Sera had never seen Nance out of her hazsuit, and had only seen her face a few times, when Nance had her suit's hood only half-off. There was a pool on the ship with a big pot for whoever finally got her to reveal her entire head.

Without speaking, the bio reached behind her head and unsealed the hood. Sera held her breath as Nance slowly slid it off her head.

"You have hair!" Sera exclaimed. "It's beautiful!"

Nance stepped back as Sera reached out to touch the dark brown locks, a frown creasing her brow.

"Of course I have hair; it's a normal thing to grow on a person's head."

"Damn it!" Thompson swore. "I can't believe you picked now to try that—and it worked!"

"You can't believe I won," Sera said with a grin. She turned back to Nance and reached for the bio's hand. "Seriously, though, are you OK? You seemed fine on the Link."

"I think you missed my sarcastic tone," Nance replied. "I was scared shitless."

"I guess the suit masks it," Sera replied.

Thompson got the lift under the mysterious crate and it rose into the air. He leaned against it and eyed Nance.

"That *is* a pretty amazing amount of hair."

"Says the blonde ape," Sera smiled.

"Hey, nine thousand years ago, this amount of body hair was perfectly normal."

"Yeah, and nine thousand years ago, people had just upgraded to pooping in public troughs," Nance grimaced.

"Don't try to distract me, Nance," Sera said. "I had never even imagined that you had hair. How do you keep it so soft while it's plastered to your head all day? Doesn't it get sweaty?"

Nance made a disgusted sound. "I don't sweat. I had all those oozing glands removed years ago."

"I enjoy a good sweat," Thompson said, with thinly-veiled innuendo.

Sera sniffed in his direction. "That's no secret."

Thompson ignored her. "Don't you get hot, Nance?"

"No, my suit has a cooling system."

"I'd think you'd still get itchy," Thompson frowned. "All that flaking skin with no sweat to lubricate it."

Nance shivered convulsively. "Ewww! I have a controlled shedding, which my nano activates when I'm in the shower. I don't have flaking skin."

Sera peered at her bio's face, hands held back so Nance wouldn't flinch away. "You do have really smooth-looking skin. And it looks so clean…"

"You'd be amazed what lives and accumulates in your pores. Thank god I don't have those anymore," Nance looked at the super. "Look at those crevices on your face. And Cheeky wonders why my suit has tinted lenses."

Thompson seemed to decide that there was no way this conversation would favor him, and back to the situation at hand. "So, what do you think is in here that they wanted so bad, Captain? I'm betting it's no dog."

"If it is, it's getting its shots," Nance said. "No way I'm letting some dirty mutt run around the ship and contaminate my environmental tanks."

Nance pulled a holo display into the air over the crate. Initial scan showed that some living creature was inside, but its vital signs were masked by cryostasis.

"I'm not getting a reading on anything hazardous," she said and looked over Sabrina's scan on the emissions and power levels in the crate. "No heavy metals, probably running on an SC Battery."

"Let's take it into the sealed chamber. I don't like little tiny surprises any more than you do, Nance."

It never hurt to pop a container that seemed harmless into the biohazard chamber and check it out by remote. Their lives were dangerous enough without extra unknowns adding risk. Not many ships had a hermetically-sealed chamber, but from time to time Sera found it necessary to determine the exact level of danger a cargo presented for herself and her ship. If it was more trouble than she'd been told, extra charges were applied to the transport.

Once the container was in the chamber, they stood back and watched as Sabrina used robotic arms to crack the seal and lift off the lid. Inside was the cryostasis pod Nance had detected.

"Either it's a kid, or an adult that's going to have some serious cramps," Thompson observed.

"You don't cramp in stasis," Sera said.

"Depends on how good the system is and how long it took the stasis to kick in," Thompson replied. "Once I had to hop in an evac pod on a gas platform; it took the stasis over an hour to fully set in. That's not an experience I'd wish on my worst enemy."

"Owww," Nance said, casting an appreciative look at the super.

"What do the readouts look like, Sabrina?" Sera asked.

<All outward controls show nominal,> the ship's AI responded. *<I'm making a filtered connection to its controls for a direct reading.>*

A robotic arm extended and fitted a physical data connector into the cryo pod. Sabrina had done this before and knew to exercise extreme caution. All the systems within the sealed chamber were isolated from the rest of the ship. Sabrina felt the same way about foreign computers as Nance did about germs.

<The system looks normal, and it is a person in there—a woman of indeterminate age,> Sabrina announced moments later. *<I can't say if she's totally safe without a blood sample, but if you wear hazsuits in the med lab you should be OK.>*

"Nance, it's finally a party you're already dressed for," Thompson said with a smile.

Sera caught a glint in his eye when he said it.

<*Is Thompson flirting with Nance?*> Sera asked Helen.

<*Beats me, if he is he sucks at it.*>

Sera gave her head a slight shake and addressed Thompson. "Take it into the med lab, Thompson. Nance and I will pop it open and see what we see."

Nance looked as though she was being asked to juggle flaming knives. She pinned her hair up and pulled her suit's hood back on. <*Let's get it over with.*>

Sabrina re-sealed the crate and Thompson entered the chamber and keyed the grav lift to float it down the hall and into the med lab.

Ten minutes later, the stasis pod sat on the floor of the med lab with Sera and Nance standing to either side. Thompson and Cargo were both outside peering through one of the observation windows.

<*You want to pop it open?*> Sera asked.

<*Hey, this was your idea. I give you first crack at whatever bio weapon is waiting in that person's bloodstream.*>

<*You really are a bit of a pessimist, you know that?*> Sera smiled through the clear faceplate of her hazsuit.

<*I'm a realist.*>

<*You're also the one-zillionth pessimist to say you're a realist. Your prize is an all-expense paid trip to the Disney World. You'll get to spend a full month with an entire planet full of people modded into animals and fairies,*> Sera chuckled while Nance made a soft gagging noise.

<*Just pop it open already so I can declare this person healthy, or dead, and get back to that blown regulator I'm dealing with.*>

Sera sighed and bent to look the console over. The controls were fairly standard and Sera entered the sequence to open the pod. Immediately, the pod's interface flashed a warning and prompted for additional access codes. She attempted to bypass it with some of her usual tricks, but the pod locked down entirely.

<*Giving you some trouble?*> Nance asked as she leaned against the examination table.

<*Nothing I can't handle, I'll have it open in a minute.*>

Shielding her actions with her body, Sera pressed the tip of her finger tight against the hazsuit's glove and spoke to Helen. <*Send some of the little guys through the suit and into this pod to crack its security. Just make sure they patch up whatever holes they make.*>

<*Want me to have them cover their tracks and reprogram the pod with something you could crack by hand in a minute?*>

<*Yeah, we need to keep up appearances.*>

<*OK, Fina, the nano are on their way in.*>

Sera ignored Helen's mothering tone and use of her childhood nickname. She acted as though she was working on the pod's interface while the nano completed their task and the interface altered to a simple security setup, set to the final stage of a basic hack. Sera manually entered the final sequence. The pod's outer cover hissed open, and she left her index finger on the edge of the console until Helen informed her that all the nano were back in her body.

<*Easy as pie,*> Sera said to Nance as she looked up at the bio.

<*Mustn't have been that hard,*> Cargo said with a grin from the other side of the observation window.

The pod flashed a short countdown as it pulled its occupant out of cryostasis, then the inner shell split open. Sera stood and peered in as Nance pulled one of the scan arms over from the examination table, her other hand double-checking the seal of her hazsuit's hood.

The occupant of the container was a woman. She had the same ageless look that most people acquired after their first rejuvenation treatment. She was also naked; whoever had placed her in stasis hadn't bothered to put her in a stasis suit, or even put a salve on her skin to deal with the quick freeze.

<*She's going to have a nasty rash when she wakes up,*> Sera observed.

Nance looked at the med scanner's readout as it hovered over the pod. <*Not any time soon, though. She's heavily drugged. Pod pulled her out of stasis smoothly, but she's going to sleep for a few more hours, even with a mild flush.*>

<*Works for me; gives us a chance to check her out before the yelling and screaming starts,*> Sera replied.

<*If you don't mind, I'll skip that part,*> Nance grimaced.

<*I'll stay with her. I imagine you can do any checks remotely.*>

Nance's avatar smiled at Sera. <*Happily.*>

They lifted the woman out of the pod and Thompson let a whistle loose as they set her naked form on the table, earning a cold look from Sera. Cargo grinned but was smart enough not to add more.

Nance pulled a blanket over the woman, then lifted her head, smoothed her hair, and placed a low pillow underneath. The action was very gentle for someone who eschewed tactile contact. Sera peered at the bio, but the opaque lenses of her hood hid any expression that may have been behind them.

<*This is odd,*> Nance said as she looked over the data from the medical scanner.

<*What?*> Sera asked.

<*See these slight discolorations all over her skin?*>

<*That's discoloration? I thought maybe it was the lighting in here,*> Sera peered closer and dialed her vision in to a higher level of magnification. <*Bruises, I can see the pattern from the broken vessels.*>

<*Scanner shows she got them within two hours of going into stasis.*>

<*That can't be right, those bruises are almost healed, and they were some serious shiners. Things like that don't heal during stasis, at least not in a pod like this.*>

Nance's expressionless face looked up at Sera. <*I'd agree with you except for what we're looking at.*>

<*Curiouser and curiouser.*>

Sera looked down at the woman. She appeared to be normal. Her body showed the tall frame of a person raised in lower gravity, but her muscle tone indicated time spent in full gravity, as well. The readout put her at one hundred and eighty-four centimeters; just shy of ninety-seven kilograms, though probably well under seventy without her internal tech—which was considerable.

Her features were classic Scandinavian, from the slight slope of her brow and high cheekbones to the perfectly straight, blonde hair. Of course, none of that meant she had a drop of Scandinavian blood. It could just indicate a good rebuild.

<*She certainly isn't hard to look at,*> Thompson commented.

Sera looked at the two men. <*Don't you two have something else to do?*>

They looked at one another and shrugged.

<*I guess I could use a meal,*> Cargo said, and the pair sauntered off.

<*Her skin may be all patched up, but she's got a fractured skull, three broken ribs, a bit of internal bleeding that looks to have stopped up, a broken ankle, and her left leg is broken in three places.*>

<*Someone wasn't too gentle with her,*> Sera said with a shake of her head.

<*That's the understatement of the year. I'm going to send some of the med nano in to start patching her up,*> Nance said as she pulled the IV line down from the array of devices above the examination table. It would be primed with the nano machines that would begin knitting the woman's bones back together.

The women turned to the med system's status display, watching the nano filtering through her body, moving toward the injuries.

<*Looking good,*> Sera commented.

<*Seems to b…what the? What!*> Nance exclaimed.

They both stared as the med unit lost contact with the nano in the woman's body and then reported that they had all been destroyed.

<*That can't be good,*> Sera shook her head. Med nano was hard to kill; the mystery surrounding this woman was growing.

Nance pulled up the detailed logs on the med nano's ill-fated venture and looked them over. <*They were destroyed…by her nano,*> Nance closed the log and then initiated a more detailed scan. <*Doesn't make sense; our med nano broadcasts the standard Red Cross signal. A person's nano should welcome them, not kill them.*>

<*I don't think her nano needs the help,*> Sera said, and pulled a high-res holo image of the woman over her body. <*It looks like it's doing the healing on its own.*>

Nance scowled at the images, then took a blood sample with a biohazard extractor.

<*I'm going to take this down to my lab; I've got better containment down there. Let me know if anything changes.*>

<*Good luck,*> Sera said as Nance stepped into the scrubber and then out into the corridor where she walked briskly toward the nearest ladder.

<*Does that look at all familiar, Helen?*> Sera asked her personal AI.

<*It looks as good, maybe better, than our nano. I don't know if your bots could repair bones that fast.*>

<*I was thinking that, as well. I wonder if we could send an investigatory probe in.*>

<*It's worth a shot. We could send it with the med signal, as well.*>

<*No point, it would just get squished like the others. Send it with the standard OFC signal. We'll see if her comp is running.*>

Sera pressed her index finger against the woman's arm and several of her nano passed through the hazsuit and into the flesh under it.

<*We've got communication,*> Helen said in an agitated tone as she patched the message through.

<*This is Angela. Please cease inserting your foreign nano into Tanis's body. I have her well in hand and will wake her in one day, five hours, three minutes and seventeen seconds. Thank you for the IV supply. No other assistance is needed.*> The signal cut out as Helen indicated their nano had been eliminated as well.

<*Snippy thing, isn't she?*>

<*You have no idea. That was the human version. The one she sent me was far less companionable. It includes things like silicate hussy and other such terms.*>

Sera laughed out loud. <*Sometimes I wonder why you AI grow personalities; they seem to cause you more trouble than they could be worth.*>

<*You have no idea the extent to which that debate rages,*> Helen said dryly.

*****

"So how's our visitor?" Thompson asked as Sera stepped into the galley. Everyone except for Nance was around the table tucking into a dinner of soup and sandwiches.

"Helen and I managed to get ahold of her AI. It told us quite simply that our assistance isn't welcome and it will wake her tomorrow."

"Is she OK?" Cheeky asked.

"Yes and no," Sera replied equably as she poured herself a cup of coffee and grabbed a sandwich.

"That is the opposite of clarifying," Thompson grunted.

"Her body has been put through the wringer. If she were stranded on some backwater, with no nano, she'd be in a hospital for months. If she were relying on our med nano, she'd be taking it easy for a week. With her personal nano, she'll be up and about tomorrow."

"Her personal nano is that good?" Cheeky asked.

Thompson and Flaherty didn't say a word as they chewed.

"Yeah, she's got some seriously impressive stuff, and a prickly AI running the show. It nuked our med nano and even my bots after it delivered its message of displeasure."

"Can't say I blame it," Thompson said. "I'd hope my AI would have my best interests in mind if I was beat up and somewhere strange."

"You don't have an AI…or even I," Cheeky said with a grin.

"Har, har, that's original," Thompson replied.

Flaherty gave an uncharacteristic snort of laughter, which earned him a sour look from Thompson.

"What does her DNA say?" Cheeky asked.

"Nance took blood samples; she should be up shortly with the results. Hopefully it may shed some light on the identity of our…stowaway?"

"I don't know how accurate that is. We stowed her ourselves," Thompson offered.

"I deem her our 'reluctant hitchhiker'," Cheeky said around a mouthful of her sandwich.

"Actually, her name is Tanis," Sera offered. "Her AI, Angela, gave us that much info before telling us to go screw."

"Her DNA said about the same thing," Nance stepped into the galley and slipped her hood up, exposing her face. "I couldn't find DNA anywhere similar to it in any of our records. It's not as though we have an extensive library, but we do have a sample from nearly every inhabited world."

"What, the rest of us don't get to see your hair?" Cargo asked.

Nance cocked her head at Sera, who lifted her hands defensively. "I've only been here for a few minutes. I didn't blab."

"What?" Thompson said. "You've got nice hair."

"Come on..." Cheeky said with a winning smile, "I want to see, too. How could you show Thompson your hair and not me?"

Nance sighed. "OK fine, only because you'll bug me for days if I don't." She reached up behind her head and slipped open the seal on the hood, pulling it off in a smooth motion and placing it on the table beside her.

"Wow!" Cheeky said. "It's so fluffy!"

"Poufy would be the word," Nance replied.

"And you have really nice almond eyes," the pilot smiled. "I command you to show them more often."

Nance laughed. "I'll reset my lenses to be transparent when you are around."

"So, nothing on the DNA at all?" Flaherty asked, appearing to be uninterested in the discussion of hair and eyes.

"Well, she actually *is* of Scandinavian descent, pretty pure blood, too. If I didn't know better, I'd say she was actually from Earth...'cept no one's from Earth," Nance said as she pulled a bar from her personal food cupboard.

"Some people are still from Earth," Cheeky offered.

<*There are no Scandinavians on Earth anymore,*> Sabrina said.

"Aren't you Scandinavian?" Sera asked Nance.

"Not really. One of my ancestors settled on New Sweden and the names infiltrated the family. I think my family is actually from the Madrid moon in Procyon."

"OK," Thompson said. "Time to lay odds on where she came from. I have a hundred Sil creds that say she's actually from Sol. Any takers?"

REVELATIONS

STELLAR DATE: 07.02.8927 (Adjusted Years)
LOCATION: *Sabrina*, Interstellar Dark Layer
REGION: Galactic South of Trio Prime, Silstrand Alliance Space

Sera sat on a chair in the med lab, waiting for their 'reluctant hitchhiker,' as Cheeky still called her, to wake.

At exactly the time prescribed by her AI, the woman began to stir, and then her movements became almost violent—as though she was having a nightmare. After almost a minute of thrashing, her body remembered what it was like to function with a conscious mind in control; her movements slowed and finally her eyelids fluttered open.

Sera waited for Tanis to acclimate to her surroundings. The lights in the med cabin were dim—she knew from experience how painful bright lights could be after coming out of a few days of unconsciousness.

She watched the woman's eyes struggle to focus, and then adjust to the dim light. A flicker of panic raced across her features when she tried to raise an arm, only to find it restrained. Almost as though by reflex, she closed her eyes and her breathing calmed. She retained that posture for several moments and then, in slow stages, she opened her eyes again; taking a second, more careful stock of her surroundings. Sera decided this was as good a time as any to make her introduction.

"Welcome aboard *Sabrina*, Tanis. I'm Captain Sera."

The woman's eyes flicked over to Sera. She opened her mouth to say something, but all that came out was a dry rasp.

"Ah, sorry about that," Sera's smile was friendly as she provided a bottle of water with a straw. The woman sucked on it eagerly and then pulled her mouth away to signal she was done.

"Thank you," she whispered as Sera set the bottle down.

"No problem," Sera smiled again. "I've done a few imitations of a dead person myself; it's thirsty work."

"Am I a prisoner?" the woman asked as she looked down at her wrists strapped to the table.

"Not at all." Sera leant over and undid the fastener on the wrist closest to her, allowing Tanis to free her other arm. "It's just hard to predict a person's state of mind when waking up unexpectedly in a strange place."

The woman nodded as she rubbed her wrists, her expression guarded. "Where is 'here', exactly?"

"Here is home," Sera said as she waved an arm about her in an expansive gesture. "This is my fair *Sabrina*, a starfreighter. We're currently in FTL transit outside of the Trio System."

A look of incomprehension followed by shock passed over the woman's face. "In...FTL?" she said with an edge of panic to her voice. Her eyes darted around the room as though she was looking for some indication that the ship was moving faster than light.

"Yup, on our way to Edasich, with a few stops along the way."

"E-Edasich…as in Iota Draconis?" the woman stammered. "How long will it take to get there?"

"Depends on how big a rush we're in. A few months depending on exactly where the trade takes us."

The blood all but drained out of the Tanis's face. It was the strangest reaction Sera had ever seen someone have to being told they were in FTL. She was wondering how stable the woman was after all.

"Let's start with the basics, though. As I mentioned before, I'm Captain Sera. Your AI introduced you as Tanis."

The woman frowned. "She told me someone tried to infiltrate my body with nano. Logs show it was med and then comm; sorry about her reaction, she's very protective. My full name's Tanis Richards."

"Two names? That's somewhat uncommon in this neighborhood. What star system still does that? Our med NSAI didn't recognize your DNA as coming from anywhere particular."

"I'm from Earth," Tanis said so matter-of-factly that Sera let out a chuckle before covering her mouth.

"Aren't we all?" Sera said and took a deep breath to stem her laughter. What was surprising was that Tanis appeared somewhat put out by her amusement. "It's OK." Sera smiled once more. "You don't have to tell right away. I'm betting that you didn't beat yourself up and hop in a stasis pod for kicks. I assure you that we mean you no harm, though we are curious. What happened to you anyway?"

Tanis didn't respond immediately and Sera suspected this woman would be a tough nut to crack.

* * * * *

They were getting closer. No matter how hard she ran they gained steadily on her; the sound of their boots hitting the deck echoed through the hall. Tanis was terrified. Nothing was as she expected it to be; the lights were wrong. Words were strange and no one made any sense. It was a horrible nightmare and she yearned to wake up.

As if her desire alone were enough, she found the nightmare slowly fading and wakefulness returning. There was light pressing against her eyelids and she knew it would be uncomfortably bright when she opened them. Steeling herself for it, Tanis opened her eyes and tried to focus. The light wasn't as bad as she expected, but she couldn't manage to see properly. Everything was grey and her limbs all seemed to be throbbing.

<Good morning, sleepy head,> Angela greeted her.

<Where am I, Angela?>

<*As best I can tell, we are on a ship of some sort. I haven't gotten much information, but I do know that we're in transit. You were near death when they put you in that stasis pod,*> Angela sounded concerned.

<*I remember that…I remember feeling almost dead. The nice men with the big meaty fists got a bit carried away, didn't they?*>

<*You're lucky I wasn't damaged. The pod didn't do true stasis…it was…. Anyway, while you were in there, I reconfigured your spare nano for med duty and pulled your body back from the brink.*>

<*I owe you my life, dear, again.*>

<*I wasn't entirely selfless. If you die, I stand a pretty good chance of joining you. That's a journey I'm not ready for yet.*>

<*Is the baby safe? Did its stasis get disrupted?*> Tanis felt worry crash into her at the thought of the unborn child within her, carefully held in stasis in her womb.

<*She is well, perfectly safe,*> Angela replied. <*She's just a few cells, still, not a lot can go wrong with her yet.*>

Tanis relaxed and tried to push that worry from her mind. Plenty of time to think it over later.

<*Are we safe here? Are these the same people that were beating me before?*>

<*No, we're on a different ship. No one has talked out loud in your presence, and I didn't open your eyes in case someone saw. They have a good nano suppression field and their Link is weird. I haven't tried to force access—not while you were out. I did hear the sounds of two women at first. Right now, there is just one, to your left somewhere. I think she's wearing leather; it squeaks whenever she moves.*>

<*I guess that rules out some sort of official or doctor,*> Tanis replied.

<*At least not the sort of doctor you'd want to see.*>

Letting out the slightest of sighs, she cracked her eyes open, but even the dim light of the room was more than she was prepared for. Instinctively she tried to raise her hand to shield her eyes. It didn't move. She was surprised to find her wrists restrained—though she supposed it was to be expected.

Unbidden, a thought of Joe flashed into her mind; where was he, and would she ever see him again. What of their child? Would she raise her alone?

Tanis took a deep breath, forcing herself to relax. Opening her eyes again, she looked around and identified her surroundings as a medical lab of some sort. A voice spoke, and while the words were soft, her ears throbbed from the sound.

"Welcome aboard the *Sabrina*. I'm Captain Sera," the woman's voice said

Tanis's eyes darted to her left where the woman sat. Even as she smiled, the woman's face looked hard, and her eyes appeared to have some great weight behind them, though her warm expression seemed genuine enough. Jet-black hair glinted in the light and framed a pale face with high cheekbones—definitely the complexion of a spacer.

Tanis could feel the faint vibrations of a reactor nearby and determined that either this ship had its med lab in a strange place or it wasn't that large. Maybe it was a small shuttle or transport heading to this woman's main ship. She opened her mouth to reply, but only a dry rasp came out.

The woman made an apology, and offered her a drink. Tanis thanked her; then asked if she was a prisoner. The woman smiled again and, though she seemed somewhat wary, the smile did reach her eyes.

"Not at all," came the reply. Tanis noted how the woman only unfastened the wrist closest to her—she didn't reach over Tanis's body to release the other. Usually, only people familiar with violence showed that sort of caution. The woman explained that the restraints were just a precaution against an unfavorable reaction to waking in strange surroundings.

It was a plausible explanation.

Tanis took the opportunity to ask where she was. The woman confirmed her suspicion that they were indeed on a ship, though it was a freighter. However, three letters the captain uttered caught in her mind: FTL. Tanis was familiar with the term. It meant *Faster Than Light*, though neither she, nor anyone else for that matter, had ever been on a ship that exceeded the speed of light.

She glanced around the med lab, unable to reconcile the fact that an aging freighter could achieve such speeds. Through all her furiously-racing thoughts, three words escaped her lips.

"We're in FTL?"

The captain responded that they were headed for Edasich. Tanis quickly dredged the reference up in her mind. Edasich was a star system just over a hundred light-years from Earth. If they were traveling at the speed of light, or even faster, it could still take decades to get there. If it was that star. She asked after it by another name, Iota Draconis, and the captain confirmed it was the same star.

Tanis re-examined what the captain had said; they would be making some stops along the way. Perhaps she could manage to get off the *Sabrina* at some point and return to the *Intrepid*—though she was dying to know how long such a trip would take. The number she was given was unbelievable; just a few months! This woman spoke of a trip of a hundred light-years as though it were a simple jaunt across the Sol System!

Tanis could feel alarm setting in and forced herself to breathe deeply. She didn't want this woman to think she was unstable and sedate her again. Even as she steadied herself, a part of her mind was screaming. This was wrong, it was all terribly wrong. Humanity didn't have FTL capability. No human had ever come within twenty light years of Edasich. She was trapped in a nightmare, one where the *Intrepid* could be on the other side of the galaxy for all she knew; one where she may never be able to get home to Joe and her ship.

<Relax, dear; I'm having a not dissimilar reaction. I'm sure it will all make sense soon.>

<It better, because if I'm not insane already I may try it out.>

The woman noticed her discomfort and started over by re-introducing herself as Captain Sera and asking her name. Her mind latched onto the question. This was within the realm of her understanding, and she answered calmly that it was Tanis Richards, biting back the desire to add her rank.

"Two names? That's uncommon in this neighborhood, what star system still does that? Our med system didn't recognize your DNA as coming from anywhere particular," the captain asked.

What an odd question. Why wouldn't they be able to determine her origin from her DNA. Though if they used spectrographic analysis on the isotopes in her body, that would likely confuse them, given her time on Victoria. Tanis replied that she was from Earth—a small lie—and Captain Sera seemed to suddenly stifle a laugh. This was all becoming too much.

<*Am I on some sort of hallucinogenic?*> she asked Angela.

<*If you are, it's affecting me, too. Something is not right with this.*>

"Aren't we all," the captain said with a hint of sarcasm.

<*Well yeah...*> Tanis thought. <*I'm really starting to dislike this Captain Sera.*>

<*I think she's trying to soften the blow…whatever that blow is.*>

<*I hate pussyfooting around things,*> Tanis sighed.

<*Really? I hadn't realized that about you.*>

"It's OK," the captain said and smiled; Tanis couldn't help but believe it was genuine, even though the woman was a bundle of contradictions. "You don't have to tell right away. I'm betting that you didn't beat yourself up and hop in a pod for kicks. I assure you that we mean you no harm, though we are curious. What happened to you anyway?"

Tanis thought about it. Honestly, she wasn't entirely certain what *had* happened to her. Moreover, she wasn't entirely certain that she wanted to relate the story just yet. The captain seemed to sense her indecision and apologized.

"I'm sorry; I forget how disorienting all this can be. There are some clothes on the stand beside you. Once you get dressed, I'll show you to your cabin where you can freshen up, before joining us in the galley for the second-shift meal."

Tanis looked over to the clothing on her right. Reaching out she put a hand on it. It was soft cotton; natural, too, by the feel of it. A captain wearing animal skins and now natural cotton. Perhaps she was on some colony world where such materials were more common than synthetics.

<*Could this be some sort of interrogation technique?*> she asked Angela.

<*If it is, it's the most unique I've ever been exposed to.*>

Sera seemed to take her reaction as disdain for cotton. "I hope they're alright. Everything I own is custom fitted to me. Those are Nance's. She doesn't really wear clothes anyway, so she won't miss them. I'll be right outside the door."

The captain stepped outside the med facility and Tanis could see her back as she waited in front of a window. She sat up, clutching the sheet as she pulled the clothes to her lap and examined them. They sure felt like cotton. If they weren't, it was the best synthetic she had ever seen. Looking under the sheet, she blushed to find herself totally naked. Well, better naked and alive than the alternative.

Tanis dressed quickly in what turned out to be simple shoes, cotton leggings and a loose, sleeveless shirt. Running a hand through her hair, she wondered if this ship of contradictions would have water showers or the good ol' sandblasting a freighter ought to have.

The captain flashed another one of those hard, yet genuine smiles as Tanis stepped out of the med facility. "Amazing how getting into at least a scrap of clothing can make you feel so much more human, isn't it?"

Tanis nodded in response and Sera turned, leading her down a long, well-lit corridor. She couldn't help but smile to herself at the incongruity of Sera's statement. The captain certainly seemed to believe in a lot more than just a scrap of clothing, what with her skin-tight outfit covering every inch of her body from the neck down.

They stopped at a ladder and the captain climbed up to the next level.

<OK...if we are being pranked, then they really suck at this,> Tanis laughed in her mind. *<Ladders on a ship with FTL?>*

The captain looked down and noticed her disbelieving expression.

"*Sabrina* does have lifts, but I find that on long trips you need all the extra exercise you can get. I put the ladders in after I bought her. Also much better than lifts if the AG fields ever have trouble." She turned and led Tanis down another corridor with a series of doors on the left.

There she went again, referring to a trip that was probably only a few months as 'long'.' While Tanis tried to wrap her mind around FTL again, she realized the captain had mentioned AG fields. Massive ships like the *Intrepid* could generate artificial gravity, but how could a small freighter—where the engines couldn't be more than fifty meters from the med lab—have AG? Sera *must* be playing with them now. FTL and AG in one day was far too much to swallow.

"Here we are," Captain Sera said. "We use this cabin for passengers we pick up from time to time. Consider it yours for the trip."

Tanis peered in; the surprises just kept on coming. How did a small freighter have cabins of this size? It was at least four meters across and had a bed, dresser, and desk. There appeared to be a closet, and it even had its own toilet and shower.

The captain looked pleased. "*Sabrina* used to be a pleasure yacht. I know I could probably shrink these cabins down, but it sure helps in hiring crew when you show them their own private bathroom."

"It's a water shower?" Tanis asked, hoping it was, because she wanted one, yet wishing it wasn't, so that something made sense.

"Of course, do we look like savages?" The captain laughed. "Second-shift meal is in about thirty minutes in the galley," she gestured aft, down the corridor. "We'll be expecting you."

With that, the captain slid the door shut and left Tanis to herself. She stood for several moments taking everything in, trying to make sense of what she was seeing. It occurred to her that this could be some sort of holo suite, or an elaborate ruse to fool her. But fool her for what reason? Sure, the *Intrepid* was very valuable, but no one trying to gain her trust would use such ridiculous methods.

<They wouldn't, would they?>

<I'm still stuck on the first batch of impossibilities. I know you flesh and blood types like to be clean—why don't you take a shower while I try to keep my cortex from fracturing.>

All was not lost; Angela still had her wry sense of humor.

Glancing over at the bulkhead, Tanis noticed a porthole. A porthole in FTL? Was that safe? She couldn't resist the urge to see what was out there. Peering through the window, she saw only blackness. There were no stars, not even streaks or smears of light as the ship blasted past photons in space. Tanis had always been certain that some light would be visible in FTL. Wouldn't the ship be intercepting light that was already there? Light toward the bow of the ship should surely be visible? The porthole showed none of this.

She caught herself pondering all the types of FTL she had heard postulated or seen in holos. Most utilized a space folding, or space compression/stretching technique to achieve a circumvention of relativity's limits. The amount of energy to achieve either of those effects was proven to be completely impractical. Earnest had created stable wormholes in previous research, but creating one over interstellar distances, stable enough to safely transfer matter, turned out to take as much energy as a star emitted over a billion years.

This had to be a farce. If Earnest couldn't determine how to achieve FTL, then there was no way that this yacht turned dingy freighter could exceed *c*. Yet, if they were traveling at the speeds she thought, it must be much faster than light speed—hundreds of times faster. It was mind-boggling. How did the ship even hold together?

Tanis suddenly felt very unsafe. Though, she rationalized, the ship must have been through an FTL trek more than once in its decades of service. It could last a few more weeks for her. Besides, after the torture and beatings from her previous hosts, a shower would feel amazing—even if it was a holo shower.

She spent as much time as she could under the flow of hot water before getting out in time for the meal Captain Sera had mentioned. Feeling greatly refreshed, she stepped into the corridor. At the end of the hall, the sounds of cutlery clinking on plates came from what must be the galley.

Tanis entered and saw Captain Sera and another man enjoying a meal at a large table. Tanis couldn't help but admire the quality of the wooden table and surrounding chairs. It reminded her of her cabin back on the *Intrepid,* which in turn made her think of Joe. She forced those thoughts down. She didn't want her first impressions to be all warbly-voiced and teary.

<*We'll find him, we'll get back,*> Angela said softly in Tanis's mind.

<*We will. We have to.*>

"Hey Tanis," Sera stood to greet her. "This is my first mate, Cargo."

The man stood and offered his hand, which swallowed hers to her wrist. His skin was dark, as though few of his ancestors had spent any time in space; his voice was soft, but very resonant, as he greeted her and offered a chair.

"You're in luck," Sera said, as she spooned some vegetables onto her own plate. "We're just out of station, so we have fresh food. A week from now, we'll be on to frozen stuff. Enjoy it while it lasts."

Tanis picked up a plate from the counter and sat across from Sera and Cargo. She scooped some salad onto her dish, and poured a creamy dressing over it.

"You were just at a station?" she asked as she mixed the salad up. *<I swear my mouth is watering after what the pirates fed me.>*

<I tested it with some nano; it's clear,> Angela supplied.

<Thanks, Mom.>

"Coburn, in the Trio System," Cargo filled in. "Picked up some cargo, including you."

Tanis set aside the part about herself being freight to be picked up, and asked about the location. "I don't know any places named Trio."

"No?" Sera cocked her head and gave Tanis a quizzical look. "It's a pretty well-known system. I forget what it used to be called, before it was colonized. It's about ninety-six light-years out from Sol. Lemme see if Sabrina knows."

She watched Sera's eyes blink a few times, as the captain chatted with the ship over the Link.

"Looks like it was cataloged as HD 111232 before it got settled and named."

Angela provided Tanis with an image of the system, relative to Earth and 82 Eridani. It wasn't possible; they were well over a hundred light-years from where she should be. On the far side of Sol from the *Intrepid*!

She forced herself to remain calm.

"You said you picked me up. Are you slave traders or something?"

The Captain looked genuinely appalled. "No! You were packed in a shipping container that was supposed to have a prize-racing dog in it. After we came under attack leaving Trio, I decided to see what we'd risked our necks for." Sera wore a smile that made Tanis want to cringe. "Someone wants you real bad."

"You came under attack because of me?" Tanis couldn't make any sense of this. Events just wouldn't line up for her, and her mind still felt sluggish from her prolonged incapacitation.

Sera related the story of how they came under fire while leaving the Trio System. Tanis felt numb as she took it all in. The acceleration and maneuvering the freighter captain described was unheard of. No ship could do that and not kill its inhabitants—unless they were in shoot-suits, or augmented like Joe. As she mused over the meaning of this information, the captain fixed her with a very level stare.

"I know you probably are still feeling out of sorts, but my crew and I would really like to know exactly why you're so sought after. You came this close," Sera held her thumb and index finger very close together, "to getting us all turned into fine stellar dust. We would like to know why."

<You know what has happened, right?> Angela asked in Tanis's mind.

<I really don't want to, but I think I do—but how far? Everything has changed! It's like we moved to another dimension.>

Tanis knew many people who wanted to kill her, but—if her suspicions were correct—none of those people were alive, or if they were, she couldn't imagine that old grievances were relevant anymore. She certainly had no idea why she was over a hundred light-years from where she should be—being chased by pirates, no less.

<We need to know when we are. I haven't been able to get into their Link without outright hacking it and that's not something I want to do while we're trapped on this ship.> Angela's tone had a level of anxiety Tanis was not used to hearing from her AI.

<Do you think all this tech exists without humanity having ever creating picotech?> Tanis asked.

<Maybe…if they worked out how to generate gravitons efficiently without pico…I could see a very different course for humanity.>

The pirates had to be after the *Intrepid.*

Tanis took another bite of her salad and looked at her two dinner companions. It was impossible to tell if they had been truthful or not. This still could all be a ruse to get the *Intrepid's* location.

She decided to play dumb.

"I…I really don't know. I don't understand what someone would want from me."

Sera pushed her chair back, a look of exasperation washing across her face. She looked to Cargo and waved a hand, indicating he should try.

"You seem like a smart lady, Tanis," he said softly. While there was no threat in his voice, she imagined it wouldn't take much for it to appear there. "Surely you can at least determine where the current course of events began and tell us the tale of how you came to be in that cargo container."

<I don't think they'll buy damsel in distress,> Angela chuckled inside Tanis's mind. *<Especially since you really suck at it.>*

Tanis weighed her options. Getting back to the *Intrepid* and Joe was really all that mattered. Perhaps honesty would be best—if these people double-crossed her, she could kill them and take their ship. Though there was something about the captain—she felt a kinship with Sera.

"I haven't been entirely honest with you," she began. Neither of them looked surprised. "My name is Tanis Richards, yes, but I'm also a major on a ship you would know as the *GSS Intrepid.*"

<So much for honesty, ***General*** *Richards,>* Angela said. *<But good call on the pretend demotion.>*

<Well, I was a major when we signed on.>

"Well that explains a lot," Sera slapped the table with a laugh. "Go on."

Tanis gave her a sidelong look. She wasn't certain if the reaction was good or bad for her. She decided to give them the paraphrased version.

"We had some ramscoop problems as we were passing by LHS 1565 on our way to our colony world. We managed to slingshot around the star, but an x-ray flare baked one of our engines. We lined up with Kapteyn's Star and drifted for a good seventy years."

Tanis considered telling them about the Victorians, but decided to leave that colony out of it. "Once there, we managed to mine a few small comets and asteroids to get the materials for repairs."

Sera was giving Cargo a strange look, and Tanis decided to keep going. "It took us some decades to get everything ship-shape, then exit the system and get back up to speed. It was only 8.9 light-years to 82 Eridani, which we were calling New Eden, so everyone went to stasis for what was expected to be about a sixty-year trip with the deceleration burns. Only something happened—we got trapped in some sort of gravity well and accelerated out of control. Our sensors were completely off the charts and we couldn't make heads or tails of what was going on. All we could tell was that we did not appear to be in regular space-time."

"Kapteyn's Streamer," Sera said with a nod. "You can get some amazing speed cutting across that thing, but if you hit it at the wrong angle it'll take you for a ride."

"Or crush you to powder," Cargo added.

"It has a name? What is it?" Tanis couldn't believe that this was a known phenomenon.

"It's a supermassive stream of dark matter streaked out beyond Kapteyn's. If you hit it just right, it will accelerate you and then dump you out the far side into a gravity tunnel that has a very unpleasant lensing effect. Significant time dilation occurs," Cargo said bluntly.

Tanis was dumbstruck. They had just described what had happened to the *Intrepid*. She noticed then that Sera was giving Cargo a scathing look.

"You sure know how to break things nicely," she sighed.

Cargo just shrugged.

"I already figured out we moved forward in time a fair bit," Tanis said. "How far? Hundreds of years, a thousand?"

Sera stood and pulled a bottle of whiskey from a cupboard. She grabbed three glasses and poured everyone two fingers. Cargo gave her a long stare, but said nothing.

The captain sat back at the table and tossed hers back before answering.

"I'm guessing you're from a colony ship that probably left Sol sometime in the late fourth or early fifth millennium. You were headed for 82 Eridani, which interestingly *is* now called New Eden. You hit the Kapteyn's Streamer and then found yourselves somewhere in the vicinity of 58 Eridani, about 28 light-years further out than expected; wondering how the hell you got there and what the heck the year is."

Tanis hadn't known where the *Intrepid* ended up, but 58 Eridani was along the ship's trajectory.

"Yours isn't the first gen ship to dump through there. The first one managed to settle 58 Eridani, named it Bollam's World, and is doing fine now—for a system full of greedy assholes, that is.

"Anyway, due to the vagaries of space-time, they probably left Sol after you. Unluckily for you, there isn't a single habitable planet within a hundred light-years of where you came out that's not already taken."

Tanis couldn't believe it. The *Intrepid* had spent hundreds of years of blood, sweat and tears to make it to a colony; a world she could call home. She slumped in her chair; it would take centuries to travel to a new world. If the FGT had any worlds available—if the FGT still existed.

"But how is that possible?" she all but whispered.

"It's all thanks to the greatest advance and the greatest tragedy of mankind: FTL. While all you gen ships were still chugging through interstellar space sucking up hydrogen in your ramscoops, some brainiac back on Procyon figured out the gravity drive," Sera said.

"I remember hearing something about graviton experiments at Procyon while we were at Kapteyn's. Our engineers were very excited about the possibilities," Tanis said with a furrowed brow.

Sera nodded. "I know it doesn't seem like the *biggest* discovery ever, but trust me it is. Once we could create gravity to react against other gravity, all the other pieces just lined up. Ships got AG fields to provide internal gravity, without rotation, thrust, or phantom mass. Inertial dampeners came out of fiction and into our ships, and we discovered a lot more about dark matter."

Tanis was glad she hadn't eaten too much. She was certain she was going to be sick.

"You know that scientists have always known about other dimensions, as well as sub and super-layers of space-time. But transitions to those other layers were prohibitively expensive, energy-wise, or it ended up being a one-way trip."

Tanis nodded slowly; this was basic physics.

Sera continued. "With the ability to manipulate gravity, they discovered how to drop into the same layer of space-time where dark matter resides. It was always postulated to be like this. Dark matter has all this mass, but isn't bending light like it should. To be honest, the exact nature of the dark layer, as it's called, still isn't perfectly understood. Some think it's utterly void and frictionless, while others think it's Einstein's universal frame of reference. I suppose someone knows, but they're not sharing the details."

"Either way, when you move into the DL your speed relative to the normal universe multiplies exponentially."

Tanis looked down at the whiskey and downed the glass in one shot. The captain gave her an appreciative look and continued.

"Gravity manipulation gave us other things, as well—namely methods for cheaper antimatter production. Once that was available, hitting speeds up to 0.70*c* with an antimatter pion drive became trivial. The end result? A trip from Sol to Alpha Centauri takes four days instead of four decades."

Tanis had always prided herself on being strong. Granted, the decades with Joe aboard the *Intrepid* had taught her about her softer side—but she still considered herself strong, a rock.

Until now.

She felt her foundation slipping away. She had understood her place in the galaxy so well. Known how to operate within all the parameters. Now, she knew nothing. She felt like all her value was lost.

<*Hold it together, girl,*> Angela didn't sound that together herself as she gave the advice. <*We've been through worse and come out the better for it.*>

"Have we?" Tanis whispered.

"Pardon?" Captain Sera asked.

Tanis felt like she was going to have a mental breakdown. She thought of the harrowing events on Toro, the Mars Outer Shipyards, and the Cho. Of her awakening on the *Intrepid* as it was falling into a star and the desperate battle against the Sirians above the fledgling colony world of Victoria.

She thought of the picobomb.

"It was all for nothing," she muttered.

"What? No! That is the furthest thing from the truth. At the very least, there's no more Sol Space Federation, so your colony mission doesn't owe anyone a cent. They fell apart millennia ago," Sera said and then clasped a hand over her mouth, realized her misstep. "Oh shit."

Tanis's head snapped up. "Millennia?"

Cargo laughed. "And you said I stepped in it."

"Ummm," Sera shifted uncomfortably. "Well I guess in a way it doesn't really matter much; you never expected to see anyone you knew again anyway. Like Cargo said, the Streamer has a pretty wicked time dilation effect if you pass between the gravitational arms like you did. You skipped a few thousand years of relative time on that transit. By your calendar, it's just about the year nine thousand…or so.

Tanis rose, her legs shaking slightly. "If you'll excuse me, I need some time to myself."

Not waiting for a response, she left the galley and dashed down the corridor to her cabin, where she quickly closed the door. Praying no one would hear her, she began to sob.

TIME TRAVELER

STELLAR DATE: 07.02.8927 (Adjusted Years)
LOCATION: *Sabrina*, Interstellar Dark Layer
REGION: Galactic South of Trio Prime, Silstrand Alliance Space

"That went well," Cargo commented as he reached for another baked potato.

Sera ran her hands through her hair. "I didn't even get to tell her the good news."

"What, that aside from the positions of galaxies, everything she knows is no longer valid?"

"No, that like all good classics, her gen ship is worth a hundred times what it took to make the stupid thing. If they're early fifth millennia, they've got amazing tech. I've heard biological android were even common then. Do you know what a bio-droid with an advanced AI neural net goes for on the market?"

"Haven't a clue," Cargo said around a mouthful of potato.

"More than my sweet *Sabrina* will make in the rest of her life, that's how much."

<*I thought you said I was priceless,*> Sabrina groused.

Cargo perked up at that. "You don't say."

"We're not hard up for cash, but the tech her ship carries is worth more than a dozen star systems. I wouldn't object to a bit of a reward."

Cargo chuckled. "Well, what are you waiting for? Go talk to our little flower."

"Not yet...with what she's been through—and I bet we still only know the half of it—she's gonna need a bit of time to settle down. I'll go check on her in an hour or so."

Sera killed the hour running through a few checklists and doing a circuit of the ship. She stopped in the galley at the end of her tour to see Tanis sitting at the table alone, another glass of whiskey in front of her.

"Mind if I join you?" Sera knocked on the wall.

The major looked up and nodded.

Sera sat and poured herself another drink.

"It's a lot to absorb," Tanis said, her voice devoid of emotion.

She nodded. "I can only imagine. But you left before I could tell you the good news—well, sorta good news."

"I already know it," Tanis replied. "The *Intrepid* is worth an immeasurable amount now."

Sera wondered exactly how Tanis knew that, but let it slide for the time being.

"I knew you were smart; that clueless act you tried to pull was pretty pathetic," Sera chuckled.

Tanis joined her in short laugh. "Yeah, it really was—not sure what I was thinking."

"Let's go up to the obs lounge. Its small, but it has a nice view of *Sabrina's* ass," Sera said as she stood and picked up the whiskey. If there was ever a good reason to break her 'no drinking onboard' rule, this was it.

They climbed up the ladder to the bridge deck and then followed a short corridor aft to a small room. There were several low couches and four windows facing out over the rear of the ship. Nothing beyond the ship was visible in the dark layer, but the inspection lights were on, casting the stern of the ship in a soft glow.

"Don't your engines emit light here?" Tanis asked, when she noticed there was no illumination coming from the back of the ship.

"We kill 'em in FTL; the hum you probably heard back in the med lab was our reactor. Our batteries are a bit low from the excitement in Trio, so we're charging them. There's nothing to thrust against here in the DL anyway. You can't maneuver or accelerate—except with grav drives against globs of dark matter. Once we come out of FTL, we'll need to do some serious braking since we entered it at well over half the speed of light. It took Cheeky some time to figure out when we'll need to drop back into normal space."

"Cheeky?" Tanis asked.

"Our pilot. You'll meet her soon enough."

"How big is your crew?"

"Six humans. Seven with you aboard."

"AI?" Tanis asked.

"There's Sabrina, the ship's AI, and Helen who is embedded with me. Nance, Cargo, and Cheeky have what you would probably call NSAI—sort of. Flaherty and Thompson don't have a lot of mods."

"Well, at least I won't have to remember many new names and faces, though I'm going to have a bit of work learning about the last five millennia."

"To be honest, things have been a mess," Sera responded. "FTL has been the bane of humankind."

"It has?" Tanis asked. "After more than a hundred years drifting through interstellar space, I sort of imagined it would be the opposite."

"What could never really happen in your time?" Sera asked by way of response.

Tanis knew the answer. "Interstellar war—though I wouldn't say 'never'."

Sera nodded. "Bingo. Let's just say there have been some setbacks. Humanity has only just recently begun to pull itself out of the toilet. For instance, there was even a period in the eighth millennia when the bulk of humanity completely lost knowledge of nanotechnology. It's been rediscovered since, but believe me, your nano is better than any you'll find across a thousand systems."

<*She's not being entirely honest,*> Angela said.

<*How so?*> Tanis schooled her expression, not wanting to show suspicion to Sera.

<*Her nano may have been more advanced than yours. It didn't put up a fight when I destroyed it, but it could have.*>

<*Will the mysteries ever cease?*> Tanis asked.

<*Could they please? I blame your "luck".*>

Tanis realized Sera had continued speaking while she and Angela talked.

"...I'm willing to bet you've got tech on your ship that the rest of mankind would kill for—probably has killed for. That's why we found you in a shipping container. I bet that Kade wants to have a nice long chat with you about where your ship is."

"Kade? Who's he?"

"Local scumbag. We have some dealings with his group, called The Mark, from time to time. Pays pretty well."

"I do hope you're not going to turn me over to him. I won't go quietly," Tanis's voice was level and dead calm.

Tanis watched Sera's face grow more serious as they stared into one another's eyes. She wondered how she appeared to this not-so-simple freighter captain: a problem and an enigma, but a possible payday as well. The moments dragged on, but Sera must have come to a conclusion about Tanis because she suddenly smiled and leaned back in her seat.

"No, I don't transport slaves, and I certainly wouldn't turn you over—threats notwithstanding."

"Good, that makes our relationship a lot more agreeable." Tanis took another drink from her glass and relaxed into the deep leather couch.

"However, Kade's going to expect to get you and I can't directly cross him or my ass is grass. How's about you tell me the rest of your tale so I can make sure whatever we work up jives. How did you end up at Coburn Station?"

<*She's lying,*> Angela said to Tanis.

<*I picked up some tells, too. Which part do you think is a lie?*>

<*Well, not really lying. From her body language and what I can read in her voice and smell, she's not afraid of Kade at all. He could make things difficult for her, but she is hiding something about her relationship with him.*>

Tanis held that conversation with Angela as she ran a hand through her long blonde hair. "I don't know how I got there, but I do know at least the start."

"We didn't exit gracefully from what you call Kapteyn's Streamer. In the split-second we transitioned out, something hit the ship at relativistic speeds. I was in the bow and managed to get to an escape pod. We ejected and then the *Intrepid* was gone. Angela and I were trying to find it when a small ship appeared out of nowhere—using FTL I now realize—and snatched the pod."

<*I've been meaning to tell you, now that I've reviewed the data I managed to get during that hack attempt we did back on the ship that captured us, there was an anomaly that might have been the* Intrepid. *I think they popped out a few AU further down than us,*> Angela informed Tanis.

<*Intact?*>

<*It didn't scan like debris, but it's hard to say. It was a long ways away.*>

While querying Angela, she continued her recitation to Sera.

"When they boarded the escape pod, I could tell right off that they weren't any sort of official representatives…of anywhere. Though, I must admit, they had some good nano suppression tech in their interrogation room. I almost got past it a few times, but I had a limited supply of bots and I decided to hold back to repair what they were doing to me."

"They beat me for a few days trying to get any detail they could from me. I was pretty messed up—Angela tells me I was on death's door. I guess they—what? Cryostasis?" Tanis sputtered as Angela fed her more details. "This *is* the dark ages!"

"Sorry, I should really give you Link access so you and your AI can chat with the rest of us," Sera apologized. "Sabrina, can you give the major and Angela our protocols?"

"Certainly, Captain," the ship said somewhat icily.

"No wonder everything aches," Tanis said while rolling her shoulders. "I can't believe it. How long was I under?"

Sera looked perplexed. "What's wrong with cryostasis? It's pretty common; keeps you alive and all that."

"No, *stasis* keeps you alive, *cryostasis* freezes you! As in it makes you very cold!"

<*I'm sorry, Tanis, I hadn't gotten around to sharing that with you sooner; I figured you had enough on your mind. You were iced for one hundred and nine days,*> Angela joined the conversation over the public net now that they were Linked.

Tanis's eyes widened and she flexed her fingers one-by-one as though she expected to find defects.

"Oh wait…you have true stasis on the *Intrepid,* don't you?" Sera sat up, eyes wide.

Tanis nodded. "Yes, when we left Sol, everyone had stasis; no one had used cryostasis in hundreds of years. I can't believe I was frozen!"

"There's some tech that'd be worth a pretty penny," Sera said with a smile. "True stasis tech was lost thousands of years ago. No one could figure out how the null field was created without ridiculous amounts of energy."

<*It's not complicated tech…how is it that things like that have been lost?*> Angela asked.

Sera sighed. "War, people hoarding tech and not sharing it, piracy, you name it."

"This is going to take some getting used to," Tanis said. "So what's our deal here? I'm guessing you're more than happy to take me back to the *Intrepid* if we provide you with something in trade to make it worth your while."

Sera leaned back again. "Look, I'll be honest. I won't hand you over to Kade, but I also won't traipse across human space on a courier run without payment—especially when everyone and their dog probably wants to find you and get a piece of your hide."

"I have one priority," Tanis said. "To get back to the *Intrepid* and ensure it remains safe. I can personally guarantee that you will be exceptionally well compensated."

Sera took a sip of her drink as she considered Tanis's words. She certainly believed what she was saying, but the shrewd businessperson in her wondered what ability Tanis had to deliver on her promises. What sort of deal could she make with a major that would be binding? There was a lot of risk here.

"I would love to help you, Tanis, but how do you know that your ship will still be there? They may have retreated to interstellar space, or been captured by some other force. This is a pretty big risk."

"I can promise you one thing," Tanis said. "The *Intrepid* is there, and it is still sovereign. There is no force in the galaxy that can stop that ship—especially given the state of things right now. They will reward you handsomely for returning me. If they're not there, then I will give you specs for enough advanced tech that you'll never have to work another day in your life."

"You have them on you?" Sera asked.

"Yes, I've taken to carrying a lot of data with me."

Sera nodded. "Very well, before we enter into this deal, I want to make sure I know how many factions are involved. Did you notice anything significant about the ship that attacked you?"

"Not much. It was obviously not a cargo hauler by primary trade. My scan of it showed some big lasers for such a small ship. When they tortured me, I noticed that they both had an odd tattoo over their right eyes."

Sera pulled a plas sheet from a pocket and marked a pattern on it. "Like this?"

Tanis nodded. "That's the symbol. What's it mean?"

"Padre. It's his sign; all his guys have it tat'd on."

"Padre, as in a priest?"

"Priest? No, he's a pirate. One of the distinctly less pleasant ones. It was his guys that chased us out of the Trio System." Sera took another sip of her drink. "I'm betting that somehow Kade got wind of what Padre had found and snatched you up. We're supposed to deliver your container to him in about seven days."

"What a mess," Tanis sighed.

"It's gonna take some fancy footwork to pull one over on ol' Kade. I'm probably going to have to fake logs and show that Padre's ships boarded us and toss your container out the hatch here in the DL so he won't find it if he comes aboard."

"What about finding me?" Tanis asked.

Sera winked. "You're much smaller. I'm sure we can tuck you away somewhere."

A STARSHIP NAMED SABRINA

STELLAR DATE: 07.02.8927 (Adjusted Years)
LOCATION: *Sabrina*, Interstellar Dark Layer
REGION: Galactic South of Trio Prime, Silstrand Alliance Space

It certainly was a motley crew, Tanis thought as Sera introduced her to each of them around the galley table. Cargo, the first mate, seemed to be the only normal one in the group, which was a disturbing thought.

The bio and life-support engineer, who apparently was just called the bio in the ninetieth century, seemed to live inside of her hazard suit. She didn't even pull off the hood as she ate, and only unhooked the mouth filter, which exposed a circle of pale skin around her lips. She seemed passionate about her job, though. At first, Tanis couldn't understand the need for a dedicated bio on a ship this size, but she was realizing that technology wasn't quite as foolproof as what she was used to.

Everyone taking a shower or two a day probably didn't help with the volume of waste management.

Angela had already gotten to know the other AI. Sabrina seemed a bit touchy, almost as though she was a little insecure in her place as the ship's AI. Angela was obviously superior in capability, but even without that, it seemed as though Sabrina had already felt threatened.

Angela expressed surprise to find that Helen was something of an equal, though evasive on her origins.

Sera was correct in that Cheeky didn't have truly sentient AI, but it wasn't an NSAI either. Cargo's and Nance's were similar; both clear violations of the Phobos accords.

<*I'm certain that Sabrina is a violation, too,*> Angela added. <*She was created—not born—for this ship, and she's never left it. They even left her active while the ship was impounded for decades!*>

Tanis was appalled at the thought and looked around at the ship's crew. They didn't seem like barbarians, but their treatment of AI would have landed them in prison back in Sol.

Thompson and Flaherty didn't have AI at all, just simple Link interfaces—most of their information access was through retinal overlay. It was crude enough that Tanis could even see it on the backs of their eyes when she dialed up her vision.

Though she suspected that Flaherty might have an additional interface, since his retinal overlay rarely showed any information. Initially, she thought him to be little more than a deck hand, or perhaps an enforcer of some sort, but something about that assessment didn't fit.

He had glanced at her when she entered, and then again when Sera introduced him. He nodded his greeting, not saying a word. His build wasn't heavy like Thompson's or Cargo's, yet that didn't diminish the growing impression Tanis had that he was the most dangerous person in the room. Every movement he made was both spare and precise.

She had no doubt that he had also observed her completely and had formed his own silent opinions.

An additional clue was Sera's introduction of Flaherty. It was obvious she had a personal connection with the man, and was very comfortable around him. Yet, his lack of internal AI and little more than a personal Link, combined with what was obviously the lowest position on the ship didn't make a shred of sense.

Even though the pilot was a self-modified nymphomaniac, Tanis found herself taking a liking to the woman. Cheeky had bounced into the wardroom on what had to be twelve-centimeter heels, wearing a miniskirt that barely covered her ass, and a tight top with a semi-lewd slogan dancing across her breasts.

She had gushed how happy she was to meet Tanis and how cool it was to meet someone over five thousand years old. Her smile and laughter was infectious and Tanis found herself reminded of Trist.

"Watch out for her," Sera said. "You are witnessing the mating ritual of the sexually aggressive Cheeky. In the wild, they are truly dangerous. She's tamer than usual since she gets a lot of it out of her system when we're docked."

Tanis laughed. Perhaps the woman was a bit more like Jessica.

Sera moved on to the next member of her crew, a large man named Thompson. She was amazed at the presence of body hair. Tanis had to restrain herself from touching the peach fuzz on his arm. It looked like pictures of men from the nineteenth and twentieth centuries. She had always thought it would be repulsive, but seeing the somewhat rough blonde man with his soft blond hair in person, she found it to be quite the opposite. Despite that, Tanis noticed how he shifted uncomfortably when he shook her hand and had shot Sera some significant looks.

"So, what's the biggest difference you've noticed so far between your time and the ninetieth century?" Cheeky asked after the introductions were done.

Tanis pondered the question for a moment while the crew stared at her, greatly interested in the answer.

"Aside from the obvious FTL and gravity drives, it's the attitude you're able to have about the galaxy and humanity's place in it. I grew up in the crush of Sol—people everywhere, a military with a million warships. Yet if you wanted to get away from it all, you could. You could go to a colony world and live a simpler life—knowing that the overpopulation of Sol would just be a memory—you would never encounter it again, because you were just too damn far away. Now it would be a week's trip and you'd be back in it."

"I wouldn't have thought of that," Cheeky said. "I can't imagine how different it must have been. You lived in the time of greatness, the planetary rings, space elevators everywhere—moving worlds, terraforming everything…near immortality, it must have been amazing."

"Is all of that lost?" Tanis asked.

"Not all," Sera replied. "Worlds are still terraformed; planets are moved, but not commonly—not like in your day when Sol had dozens of habitable worlds. There are few rings left; in Sol, only High Terra remains."

Tanis felt her breath catch. That meant the Mars1 ring was gone. Ceres, the Cho, all no more. She knew losing a ring was no small thing—it meant those worlds may have been destroyed, as well. She decided not to ask; she didn't want to know.

"We didn't have all those things," Tanis said. "No one was immortal."

"I guess not," Cheeky replied. "But they lived a long time—over five hundred years from what I've read. How old are you? If you don't mind my asking."

"Cheeky, really..." Nance sighed.

"I don't mind," Tanis held up her hand and smiled. "I'm still pretty young, only about two hundred and eleven years of real-time on my clock."

Thompson whistled. "You look pretty good for two-eleven. None of us are over fifty. Two hundred is about the best we can hope for—unless we strike it rich somewhere along the line."

"Or live in the AST," Nance added.

"AST?" Tanis asked, trying to guess at what that could be.

"If every time needs to have a dark, greedy empire, the AST is ours." Sera's expression was grim. "It is what has grown from the first interstellar government that started with Alpha Centauri, Sol System, and Tau Ceti. Hence, the A. S. T. At least, that's what everyone else calls them. Their real name is The Hegemony of Worlds."

Tanis nodded. It made sense that those systems were at the core of a large empire. Alpha Centauri and Tau Ceti were two of the most powerful colonies when she had left Earth. Alpha Centauri even had slow, but regular trade with Earth.

"Who knows what could happen?" Tanis shrugged. "If we really have a treasure-trove of tech, and it is stuff that's completely lost, we could trade it for a colony world. You guys could end up living as long as I plan to."

"Girl, you could trade that tech for a hundred colony worlds and still have money to burn. Heck, you could trade it for fully populated worlds," Cheeky exclaimed with arms flung wide.

"We have a few systems to hop through before we get to Bollam's World. You can shop around," Sera laughed.

"So it's Bollam's we're off to," Thompson said with a frown. "Are you sure that's wise?"

"I've struck a deal with Major Richards," Sera nodded at Tanis. "We'll be well compensated—enough that each of you can retire after this run."

Thompson looked about to say something else, but Sera shot him a dark look and he closed his mouth.

<So, did you pick up on the bit when you were talking about age and immortality?> Angela asked.

<I noticed Sera had a funny look on her face,> Tanis replied. *<Is that what you're referring to?>*

<Not just her, Flaherty too.>

<*The plot thickens—I noticed Sera also gave a little twitch when they referred to the AST as the big bad empire of the time. I wonder if she's originally from there.*>

<*I'll see what I can learn from the other AI,*> Angela said.

The rest of the meal progressed pleasantly, Tanis asking questions that would help her understand the present time as best she could, but she found herself coming back to the odd behavior that Sera displayed and Angela's earlier warnings that Sera was hiding something; something significant.

RENDEZVOUS

STELLAR DATE: 07.05.8927 (Adjusted Years)
LOCATION: *Sabrina*, Interstellar Space
REGION: Galactic South of Trio Prime, Silstrand Alliance Space

Sabrina exited FTL three light days away from her previously-anticipated exit, an unfortunate consequence of entering the dark layer at an irregular vector. Cheeky's calculations were as accurate as could be; it was just impossible to predict a ship's precise location in space, when you weren't even in space.

However, Cheeky had things well in hand as she rotated the ship a hundred and eighty degrees. Starting with a slow burn, she lit up the fusion engines and brought *Sabrina* down on the meeting location.

The rendezvous was deep in interstellar space. No stars shone nearby; there were no planets, or moons, or bodies of any sort. The only marker for this meeting place was a clump of dark matter resting alone in the void.

During the days of FTL transit, the crew had ditched the cargo container in which Tanis had been found, and faked the logs to show that instead of outrunning the Padre's ships, they had been stopped and boarded. Logs now showed the container being removed and then *Sabrina* being allowed to leave the Trio System.

Regarding Tanis, Sera decided that the best place to hide her was in plain view, as a new crewmember.

"Too bad we don't have access to any advanced modifications. Those cheekbones are pretty distinctive," Cheeky had commented.

"Amusing statement for someone named for their own cheeks," said Tanis.

"I'm not known for those cheeks." Cheeky pointed to her face, then placed her hands on her butt and swished it side-to-side. "These cheeks, though..."

"Believe me, I harbored no confusion on that fact," Tanis smiled. "Though, I can do something about my cheekbones, if you think it's necessary. Will he know anything about me?"

"He may. There are ways to send messages through FTL far faster than a ship can travel. If you can mask your appearance in some way that will stand up to inspection, do it," Sera said.

The major sucked in a deep breath as her face changed right in front of their eyes. Slowly, her jaw widened and her cheekbones became less prominent. Her lips filled out and the corners of her eyes turned up.

"Hot damn! I'd forgotten how much that *hurts*!" Tanis said in a somewhat huskier tone, as she touched her face gingerly.

"Wow! That's amazing!" Cheeky reached out to feel Tanis's face. "How in the stars did you do that?"

"I worked counterinsurgency in the TSF." Tanis's statement was met with blank stares and she laughed. "I may as well have said Praetorian Guard; it's probably better known."

"Praetorian? Is that what the Regulan military calls its Royal Guard?" Nance asked.

"Yeah," Sera said. "But they ripped it off from the Romans. The Praetorian Guard is the military unit that guarded Caesar."

"The salad?" Cheeky asked, visibly confused.

"The Roman Emperor."

Cheeky's mouth formed an O, but the expression on her face indicated she had no idea who the Roman Emperor was, when he lived, or on which planet he had ruled.

Tanis was dumbstruck. "I guess a lot changes in five thousand years."

"It has a lot to do with location, too," Sera said. "I'd bet people in the Sol System know all about the Romans. People on rim worlds don't care to know much about AST worlds."

<*What story did you settle on?*> Sabrina asked, clearly impatient to get to her task.

Tanis spread her arms with a flourish. "Rachel, at your service. After serving as a station comm and nav tech on Coburn Station for a few years, I grew weary of it. Now, I'm working on my pilot's license, and managing scan and comm here on *Sabrina* while Cheeky shows me the ropes and helps me get my practical experience hours in."

<*Nothing more?*> Sabrina asked.

"If Kade asks more than that he'll already be suspicious and we won't be able to fool him with anything further," Sera said.

"That's an encouraging thought," Cheeky said.

Both Tanis and Sera began to say that they'd gotten through worse and stopped, eyeing each other for a moment. Then Tanis smiled and Sera let out a laugh.

"I doubt it'll be the last time either."

THE MEET

DATE: 07.09.8927 (Adjusted Years)
LOCATION: *Sabrina*, Interstellar Space
REGION: The Mark's Interstellar Drop Point, Silstrand Alliance Space

Sabrina had finished deceleration and was drifting near the meeting point.

Sera wasn't sure if Kade himself would be at this transfer, but she hoped not; this whole 'hiding human cargo act' was making her stomach twist enough as it was. Her misgivings aside, Tanis was actually fitting in with the crew quite well. She had picked up the comm and nav systems with appreciable speed and had watched Cheeky's final maneuvering of the ship with great interest. The crew had helped her flesh out a few parts of her story in greater detail, but Sera was still of the opinion that if too many questions were asked it was an indication that they were already in trouble.

Flaherty and Thompson had moved cargo to be transferred into the few rooms off the bow corridor. They also placed a few containers in the corridor itself. It made for some tight maneuvering, but the sooner they could transfer the cargo and get on their way, the better.

Tanis had argued very strenuously that perhaps they shouldn't stick around for the meeting, but Sera said she needed the business with Kade right now and couldn't afford to run across the Orion arm just to avoid him.

The meeting time arrived and they expected The Mark ship to show up on scan at any moment, decelerating toward the meeting coordinates. Sera was certain they had a few passive probes floating quietly in the area, so they would know who was around and be able to drop back into FTL if something were amiss.

As much as Sera wanted to look for those scan probes and tap into them, the chances of The Mark picking up on it were just too high.

Even though there was plenty of room, the bridge felt crowded with four of them up there. Tanis was operating scan at the comm station and Sera wondered what it would be like to go from what had to be a very clean, crisp, and ordered society to working on *Sabrina*. Tanis's back was straight and her movements spare and efficient. If she was feeling any anxiety over this cargo transfer, she wasn't showing it.

She surveyed the rest of her bridge crew. Cheeky was wearing a bit more clothing than normal—she didn't much like being ogled by the types that made up Mark crews. Cargo was as inscrutable as ever as he checked over ship's systems and did whatever it was that always seemed to keep him busy at his station.

Sera accessed her Link again to see if scan showed anything, to be informed yet again that The Mark ship hadn't arrived.

<*Would you cut it out?*> Helen said. <*It'll go fine, they'll never suspect anything and we'll be able to carry on as usual.*>

<*Pardon me if I don't share your perennial confidence,*> Sera replied.

<Trust me, I worry, too. I just calm myself down faster than it takes to even mention it.>

Even as Sera was pondering the possibilities, Tanis spoke up. "There they are. Just came up on scan."

"They? There was only supposed to be one."

"Two ships, one an obvious freighter, the other looks a bit smaller, larger engine signature—you have it on record as the *Vertigo*. Both have turned and are firing AP engines to decelerate." Tanis plotted out where the two ships would come to a relative stop and sent the coordinates to Cheeky, who laid in a course.

"And we've got contact," Tanis announced. "They're still a good thirty light minutes out, so it's just a welcome." She sent the message to Sera's screen, who saw with dismay that Kade had made an appearance himself. The message was brief. It instructed them that Kade's ships would decelerate to 0.15c and maintain their current course. Sera was to bring *Sabrina* up to a matching speed and set a course to intercept. The maneuver would make for a faster overall rendezvous.

Sera piped the pertinent information to Cheeky, who put *Sabrina* on course to match up with Kade's ships. Once that was done, she sent a message over the ship's main net.

<Kade has dropped from the DL and we are accelerating to meet him at a 0.15 c *rendezvous. He's here himself in one of his pirate boats, with a freighter, to pick up the wares, I imagine. Our ETA on meet-up is about eight hours. I'll put it on the clocks.>*

It was easing into the third watch and Sera decided that things would be hectic soon enough. She slated everyone to get at least six hours of sleep before the rendezvous.

She opted for sleep first. If anything interesting happened, it would be later rather than sooner.

After her allotted six, she was awake and back on the bridge nursing the first cup from a fresh pot of coffee.

Humans may have done a lot in the previous ten millennia, but so far nothing had been invented that was better than a cup of coffee after waking up. Well almost nothing, but people didn't invent that.

By the time a soft seal was made against the *Vertigo,* Sera had quelled her anxiety over potential conflict with Kade. Her concern was more due to the wrench it would throw in her plans. Kade had made it clear he wanted to meet with her and look over the cargo, which was something he had never done before.

Sera was starting to wonder if they should have just thrown Tanis in a hazsuit and dropped her in one of the nastier enviro tanks, one that no one would go peeking in. Too bad she hadn't thought of that earlier. They could have kept the container she had been in and shrugged when it was found to be empty.

Sera cycled the bow airlock herself and let Kade and his two companions on board. She was tempted to wait for him on the bridge, but this was no time to antagonize the pirate with power plays.

He came through the lock first, just as she remembered him from the last time they'd met. His long, dark hair was somewhat greasy, and, although his clothes were crisp—and probably cost more than the value of all the cargo they were about to transfer—they somehow didn't transmit that wealth to him.

With him was a person that Sera had dealt with many times, and liked less on each encounter—Kade's right hand woman, Rebecca.

Rebecca was a beautiful woman who had no compunctions about using her looks to her advantage in every way possible. She also looked nothing like a pirate, more like the unlikely combination of a princess and a dominatrix.

Where Sera gleamed in her tight leather, Rebecca sparkled with necklaces and bracelets. All made of diamond, platinum, and whatever was currently the most expensive gem in vogue.

Beneath the jewelry, her body was sheathed from head to toe in a tight, black material that reflected every light in the corridor. The combined effect made her almost difficult to look at—though Sera certainly appreciated the appeal.

Kade probably hoped that some of Rebecca's style would make him look better than he did. Unfortunately for him, the opposite was true—having her nearby just made him look somewhat dumpy.

Rebecca's eyes raked over the corridor crowded with cargo and locked on Sera, the expression on her face filled with distaste for all aspects of *Sabrina*—including her captain.

<*I hate the way she looks at me,*> *Sabrina* said.

<*I know how you feel, dear,*> Sera replied.

The third person was a man Sera did not recognize. He looked cowed by the company he was keeping and Sera wondered why he was here.

"Welcome aboard *Sabrina,*" Sera said.

Sera knew that Kade harbored desire for her; as she offered her hand, she tilted her hips and smiled. She was fully prepared to do whatever it took to remain in the pirate's good graces.

Kade took it and smiled, his eyes traveling over today's leather outfit—dark green with yellow piping down her sides. It was more formal than usual, with the pants loose from the knees down, where they fell over low-heeled boots. The jacket was form fitting and fastened with a double row of brass buttons down her chest. She'd even topped it off with a captain's hat in matching green leather. Kade practically licked his lips.

"Sera. You know Rebecca, and this is Drind. He'll be going over your scan logs to learn what he can of Padre's ships that took my property."

Had she not known better, the emphasis he placed on 'my' would have caused Sera to believe it actually was his. It certainly seemed as if Kade's ethics did not take into account the fact that he had stolen it from Padre in the first place, or that the property he spoke of was a person.

"Of course," Sera said in the polished voice she used for speaking with the pirate leader, which drew a dark look from Rebecca. "You'll pardon the mess. The men have things ready for transfer to the *Starskipper* so that we don't cause any delay. This way to the bridge." She gestured down the corridor.

Kade smiled magnanimously. "Of course. I've instructed the *Starskipper* to dock while we are here and transfer the cargo while we talk." As though his words were prophetic, she heard the light clang as the *Vertigo* disengaged from the soft dock and maneuvered away, to allow the other ship room to link to *Sabrina*.

Sera hid her thoughts behind a mask of pleasantness. Kade must have felt either invincible or unthreatened by her, if he didn't feel the need to have any type of escape route during parts of their meeting. For her part, Rebecca looked more concerned with scuffing the shine on her outfit than finding out about the missing freight container.

Sera used the lifts to bring them up to bridge deck. They stepped into the command space, where Cheeky, Tanis, and Cargo were all at their stations coordinating with the *Starskipper* for its soft dock.

Kade noticed Tanis right away. "New crew? I didn't know you were looking, Sera; I could have furnished you with anyone you'd need."

<*If we wanted that, we could have just contacted Moles R Us,*> Helen said privately to Sera.

Sera introduced Tanis as Rachel and explained that she would be assisting with comm and scan. She didn't go into details as to why, after years with the same crew, she had decided to add another member. Offering it unasked would be too suspicious.

Whatever stars watched over *Sabrina* smiled and Rebecca asked the question first, and Sera explained it was to expedite dock duties. Currently, Cheeky, Cargo, or she had to remain on the bridge while docked to watch scan and comm. This way, they could all be out on station at once.

Kade and Rebecca seemed satisfied with this answer and didn't press the issue further.

"Perhaps our technician could look over your logs with your new comm tech while you and Cargo join us in your lounge to discuss some things?" Kade phrased it as a question, though it wasn't one.

Sera acquiesced and called down to the galley for Nance to bring up some refreshments. She spared a glance for Tanis as Drind sat with her to go over scan from the Trio departure. She was impressed; absolutely nothing about the major belied the tension Sera knew she had to be feeling.

The four sat in the observation lounge. A moment later, Nance, looking more than a little uncomfortable, entered with a selection of drinks she had previously prepared. The bio wasn't wearing her hood—Sera had asked her not to—in an attempt to show they had nothing to hide. She asked preferences, and quickly began to pour the drinks.

"Are you having some sort of environmental issue?" Rebecca asked Nance, frowning at her hazsuit.

"No, I just wear it all the time in case something happens," Nance said. "That way we don't lose precious time while I get suited up."

Rebecca didn't seem convinced, and started to question Nance further, but Kade stopped her.

"She always wears it, though I've never seen her face before," he said with a leer. "Has anyone ever told you how beautiful your hair is?"

Nance flushed, but managed to give a steady reply. "I've heard it once or twice before."

With that, the drinks were served and Nance quickly left the lounge.

A few minutes passed while mild pleasantries were exchanged before they got to the issue at hand. "I'd forgotten your curious aversion to alcohol onboard your ship," Kade mused, as he drank from his cup of dark roast. "Any other captain would have his or her best wine in front of me."

"My equivalent is my best coffee, which this is," Sera said with a smile she did not feel.

"It's damn good," he nodded. "However, I'm not nearly as pleased with you, Sera. I'd think that one of my captains would try to defend my property against Padre a bit better than you did." He sighed as though this was very vexing to him. "I'm not sure what to do with you."

Sera sipped from her cup and spoke calmly, as if they were discussing the weather. "I do make runs for you, but I'm not one of *your* captains. I'm under no greater obligation to protect your cargo than any other consigned to this ship. I'm certainly not going to risk *Sabrina* or my crew just for some racing hound." Kade seemed taken aback by her calm response, obviously expecting something else; perhaps fear.

To his left, Rebecca was giving Sera the blackest of looks.

Sera rolled the dice and pressed on.

"Since it was your cargo that Padre was after when his men chased us clear across Trio, I find myself thinking I should bill you for the antimatter we burned." Sera enjoyed the expression of consternation that flashed across Kade's face, and let an edge of anger slip into her voice. "Hell, they fired an RM at us! Who did you piss off enough for them to do that, and what type of racing hound is worth an RM?"

Cargo was making 'stop it' eyes at her, and Sera decided that she had pushed as far as she should.

Kade shook his head and made a soft clicking noise with his tongue. "I'm sorry you feel that way. That hound was very precious to me. I'm feeling very much like it is you who should compensate me."

Cargo seemed to decide he had better speak up before Sera said something they'd regret. "That's not the type of business this is and you know that, Kade. There's no insurance when things don't go according to plan," he gave Sera a pointed look. "We know that, too."

Kade seemed somewhat placated by Cargo's smooth, even tones.

Sera nodded and said nothing, which seemed to allow the tension to pass.

Kade sighed and finished his coffee before rising. "Very well, let's see if my tech found anything useful on your scan data." They filed out of the lounge and back to the bridge, where Drind was chatting amicably with Tanis.

"What do you have for me?" Kade asked brusquely.

Drind's attention instantly snapped to his employer and then back to the console, where he brought up several pieces of pertinent data.

"The ships were definitely Padre's. From what I see here, they really did attack Coburn Station, but broke off when it appeared their quarry wasn't there. Not sure how they got that message. Two ships that weren't in on the station attack circled south of the star to chase after the *Sabrina*. It was quite a ride, the crew here pulled out all the stops to get away; pushed this old bucket of bolts faster than I'd feel comfortable with."

<*Why do humans continually insist on referring to me disparagingly?*> Sabrina groused.

<*They don't appreciate your finer qualities,*> Sera said, sending a wave of calmness to her ship.

Drind continued, "Their pursuers actually launched an RM and that was when the *Sabrina* ceased acceleration and allowed the boarding. They wouldn't have escaped the missile."

<*And he keeps using the word 'the' when referring to me. That's just rude,*> Sabrina said with a pout.

"And they didn't take anything else? Just that one container?" Rebecca asked with a quirked eyebrow, while Kade appeared to be mollified by the explanation.

Drind responded affirmatively, "That's all the records show."

"Bastards," Kade said. "How did they know where we stashed it?"

Sera didn't miss that Rebecca touched Kade to stop him from saying more, just as Cargo had stopped her earlier.

"Very well," Rebecca said. "How far along is the cargo transfer?"

Tanis had been monitoring the progress and announced that it was complete and that the *Vertigo* was preparing to connect once more. Kade announced that they were finished and Rebecca asked that Sera accompany them to the airlock.

The request felt suspicious to Sera. She always walked Kade off her ship, but for Rebecca to request what was the norm told her something was off. She could see that Cargo felt the same way.

All in all, this was going far too easily.

Sera led the two visitors off the bridge to the lift. They stepped inside and Sera pushed the button for the freight deck. The lift shuddered a bit as it started its descent. Suddenly, between the crew and freight decks, it stopped. Sera smiled innocently at the three guests.

"Sorry about that. This lift doesn't get used much and sometimes seizes. It'll free up in a moment."

True to her word, the lift started down again half a minute later. Down on the freight deck, the corridor to the bow airlock was free of cargo except for one last crate. They stepped around it and Sera keyed the bulkhead controls to begin pressurizing the airlock while the *Vertigo* made soft dock on the other side.

Having entered in the codes, Sera turned, only to find herself staring directly down the muzzle of a gun.

Rebecca's angry scowl was at the other end of the weapon. "You didn't think we fell for that whole Padre chased you thing, did you? There was no way he could have known you had the container."

"Are you insane?" Sera asked. "Put that thing away, it'll hole the hull if you fire it."

Rebecca laughed. "I'm not stupid, Sera. An old tub this may be, but I know your shields will hold air even if I put a dozen holes in the hull."

Sera looked at Kade. The expression on his face told her everything. He wasn't in on this. Rebecca was acting on her own.

"She doesn't have it," Kade gave an exasperated sigh. "Sera wouldn't lie about something like this, and she couldn't fake scan well enough that Drind would be fooled."

The look that Rebecca shot at Kade was pure hatred. "How stupid are you? Have you become so complacent that you can't see how she plays you? She knows exactly where that container is and she's gonna tell us, or little Sera will have to see how hot her sexy little captain's outfit looks with a few holes in it."

Cargo's voice came smooth and steady from behind Kade and Rebecca. "I don't think that will happen."

Kade turned to look back, but Rebecca kept the gun trained on Sera. The Mark's leader cursed as he saw Cargo, Thompson, and Flaherty filling the corridor, pulse rifles leveled.

"I think you'll toss that blaster to the deck and then you'll get on your ship and we'll pretend this never happened," Sera said evenly.

"Do what she says, Rebecca. You're acting insane. I know you've always been jealous of Sera, but this is too much."

As Kade spoke, Sera wondered that she'd never realized how much of a complete coward he had become as his wealth increased.

The same thought must have been on Rebecca's mind, too. She swung her arm until the muzzle of the blaster pointed at Kade's head. "You are a complete and utter moron. It's like you get dumber by the day, and frankly I can't stand it anymore." Her voice dripped disdain and hatred, but somehow sounded toneless at the same time.

She paused for just a second, cocked her head, and pulled the trigger.

Everyone was stunned as Kade's brains sprayed across the bulkhead. All eyes followed Kade's toppling form as it hit the ground, spilling blood, tech, and grey matter onto the deck.

At that precise moment, the airlock finished cycling and behind Sera, four heavily armored soldiers stepped into the corridor. Their visors were down and their weapons leveled.

Rebecca's voice was surprisingly calm. "They just killed Kade. Take Sera alive and then secure this piece of crap."

The four soldiers raised their weapons to their shoulders in a single fluid movement. In the same instant, Cargo and Flaherty dove behind the remaining freight container while Thompson hit the deck and rolled through an open hatchway. Sera fell to her side and kicked at Rebecca's knees as the troopers unloaded their clips into the corridor. They weren't the ship-friendly pulse rifles that Sera's crew held. These were full power beam weapons. Sera cringed as she thought of the holes their shots must be tearing through her *Sabrina*. If it weren't for the heavy shielding around the engines, their beams would have punched clear through the ship.

Rebecca crashed to the ground, and Sera gained a pyrrhic sense of satisfaction that her bucket of bolts ship dirtied the other woman's shiny black skinsuit. Rebecca locked eyes with Sera and grinned. Sera looked up just in time to see one of the troopers smash the butt of his weapon into her face.

She fell back and watched the world slowly fade from view. The sounds of weapon fire tearing her ship to shreds took a bit longer to leave her hearing.

LOSS

STELLAR DATE: 07.09.8927 (Adjusted Years)
LOCATION: *Sabrina*, Interstellar Space
REGION: Galactic South of Trio Prime, Silstrand Alliance Space

Cargo ducked back behind the freight container as the beam fire continued to flash overhead. Sera and he had suspected the possibility of an altercation with Kade, and this container had been left in the corridor for precisely the purpose it was now serving.

It contained a small shield generator, providing a secure shelter. The wall Thompson was using for cover wasn't faring as well, but so far the burly super had managed to avoid being hit.

Cargo accessed his Link and told the other two men to narrow their rifles' band and match frequencies. They'd take these goons out one at a time. On a three count, they all broke cover enough to get a clear shot and fired at the helmet of the leftmost trooper. The harmonious frequencies from the pulse rifles amplified one another and the tight beam focused the pulse wave to achieve lethal intensity.

Cargo noted with satisfaction that the trooper's faceplate cracked as the shots struck true and he slumped to the ground. At the same time, another of the Mark soldiers cracked his rifle against Sera's head and he saw the captain slump to the decking, unconscious.

"Mother fuckers!" Thompson cried out as he was forced to duck back behind the bulkhead for cover. "They hit the capt'n."

This wasn't good. *Sabrina* couldn't take much more of this abuse. They had powerful exterior shields, but on the inside, other than around the engines, there was no sectional shielding. Before too long, those beams were going to tear through something that responded badly to tearing.

Cargo contacted Cheeky over the Link. "Cheeky. Dump to FTL *now!*"

<What the hell is going on down there? It sounds like a fucking war!> the pilot responded.

<Just do it, we're going to be swimming in Mark soldiers if you don't.>

<But we're still at 0.15 c. I don't know what we'll hit if we enter the DL right now.>

<We're never gonna hit the DL again if you don't do it now.> Cargo wasn't in the mood to discussion. *<Do it now!>*

<All right! It's gonna take a minute.>

<Take less.> Cargo cut the connection.

He counted with his fingers to indicate when to make another timed shot at the two other men. On three, they broke cover again to fire on the enemy furthest to the right. Ready to make the shot, it took him a moment to grasp what was happening.

The fallen soldier was still on the deck and two others had taken positions within the airlock for cover. Past them, Rebecca was back aboard the *Vertigo* with the fourth armored figure hauling Sera's unconscious form into the other ship's airlock.

Cargo pointed to the man on the left of the airlock, so that they wouldn't chance hitting the captain, and they fired in unison once more. The man attempted to duck to the side, but he was flung against the outer hull as the shot clipped his shoulder.

At the far side of the umbilical, Sera had been pulled into the *Vertigo*'s airlock and several more troopers were ready to step around her and join the assault on *Sabrina.*

Cargo called Cheeky over the link again. <*Any damn minute now!*>

<*Hold on, in less than a sec,*> came the pilot's frantic response.

Two of the reinforcements were in the umbilical, and the pair in *Sabrina's* airlock were leveling their weapons to fire as Cargo motioned for Flaherty and Thompson to get down. The wrenching feeling from the shift to FTL washed through them, and, before the sensation had passed, Flaherty broke cover and leapt over the freight container.

He rushed down the corridor, firing his rifle on its highest setting while the remaining enemies were still off balance from the shift. The one who had already been clipped in the shoulder slumped to the deck after taking two more hits.

Flaherty got three more shots off at the other trooper before crashing in to him and slamming him against the bulkhead.

At that moment, the transfer to FTL completed and the airlock yawned open to the total void of the dark layer. Their ears popped as air rushed out into the space between *Sabrina* and its shielding. Beyond the shield, two soldiers who had been in the umbilical could be seen floating away in the void.

Flaherty pulled a beam rifle off one of the unconscious enemy soldiers and took careful aim before firing a shot through each of the drifting men's heads.

"Why the hell did you do that? You should have let the dogs suffer," Thompson said, as he approached the airlock.

Flaherty didn't look away from the void. "No one deserves that."

Cargo stepped beside Flaherty, silent, his breathing ragged. Then, with a curse, he slammed his fist into the bulkhead. The trooper who Flaherty had crashed into made a noise and stirred from the sound. Flaherty reached down, tore his helmet off and slammed his head against the hull.

The other soldier was also moving, his breathing sounded strained through his helmet and he was moving his head erratically. Cargo reached down and pulled his helmet off. The man looked haggard, his face a massive bruise from the effects off the pulse rifle. His eyes were bloodshot and barely open. He still managed to scream as Cargo fired the pulse rifle point blank into his left eye.

The trooper's head crumpled, but the scream didn't stop. That was a first, Cargo thought, until he realized the sound was coming from behind him. He and Flaherty turned to see Thompson holding his gun to Drind's head. Completely forgotten, the tech had been curled up on the floor.

"Want me to ice this bastard, too?" Thompson asked.

Hearing that, followed by seeing the cold eyes of Cargo and Flaherty upon him, Drind seemed to shrink inward even further. "Please, please don't do that to me, too. I'll do anything you want, please just don't kill me." He was sobbing now, his shoulders heaving and hands over his head.

"No. We've done enough killing for one day," Flaherty said.

"Stick him somewhere out of the way," Cargo agreed, and Thompson nodded wordlessly as he gestured with his rifle for Drind to stand up. They were all feeling the loss of the captain; it was best not to do anything else rash just yet.

"What's that sound?" Thompson asked.

They all stopped, Flaherty turning his head as he listened.

"It's not out there," Cargo said. "It's in here." He tapped his head.

"It's Sabrina," Flaherty replied.

"I'll be on the bridge," Cargo said as he took off at a run.

Less than a minute later Cargo stepped on to the bridge, and confronted the concerned faces of Tanis, Nance, and Cheeky.

"Something's wrong with Sabrina," Cheeky said. "She won't respond and is making this strange noise on the net, almost like a whimper."

Cargo looked around at the bridge's observation cameras. "It's OK, Sabrina. We'll get her back."

"Get who back?" Cheeky asked, the color draining from her face.

"SHE'S GONE!" Sabrina screamed over both the Link, and the ship's audible systems. "I CAN'T HEAR HER ANYWHERE!"

"That's because we're in the dark layer and she's not with us," Cargo said with more compassion than he would have thought he could manage at the moment.

"She's what?" Cheeky screamed and Nance let out a gasp.

The wailing coming over the Link and audio was increasing in pitch; Cargo was starting to have trouble thinking with the sound slicing through him.

<*Sabrina.*> Flaherty's voice broadcasted onto the ship's net. <*Listen to me, Sabrina,*> he insisted, but the ship didn't stop her cry. <*Remember. Remember what Sera said to you back when we first met and saved you from that place?*>

The keening lessened and Sabrina spoke, <*I do remember. I do.*>

<*Good,*> Flaherty said. <*Remember that. Remember the things she told you and you'll be ok.*>

Sabrina made a noise that sounded uncannily like a sniffle. <*OK.*>

As the sound faded away, Cheeky fixed Cargo with a hard stare. "You told me to go to FTL. Why would you do that if they had the captain?"

"Because we'd be crawling with Rebecca's soldiers if we didn't get out of there."

"Rebecca?" Tanis asked. "What happened to Kade?"

"Rebecca killed him."

"She what?" Cheeky yelled and leapt back to her console. "Kade's one thing, but Rebecca *hates* Sera. She'll kill her! I'm pulling us out and getting back there right now!"

"You'll do no such thing; they'd waste us in a second," Cargo said, his trademark calm becoming ragged.

Cheeky couldn't speak; for a moment she just stared at her controls and then let loose a sob.

Tanis knelt down beside her and stroked her hair. "What do you propose?" she asked, her eyes hard as she looked up at Cargo.

"We need to drop out of the DL, alter course and then get back in, or they'll get higher v and then skip along waiting for us. They know how fast we're going and can predict our course with ease. Figure out a new course on a different vector and get us on it. We need to get safe and then figure out what to do." Cargo said.

Tanis turned to her console and began pulling up plots while Cheeky looked up at Cargo.

"I abandoned her."

"You did as you were ordered. I am the one who abandoned her, and I intend to get her back."

"How are we going to do that?"

"We've got that Drind guy. Since he was the big expert with the scan and nav, I'm betting he'll know where they'll go with her."

They all clung to that hope as Cheeky and Tanis worked out a new vector and effected the transition to regular space. Cheeky quickly altered course and dropped back into FTL. Scan didn't pick up any of Kade's ships when they were in regular space, though that didn't mean there weren't any sensor arrays nearby relaying information. They made two additional course alterations before they began to feel comfortable.

With Sabrina monitoring the bridge, everyone met in the galley to work out what they hoped would be their plan to rescue the captain.

"What is our damage report?" Cargo asked once the coffee had been poured. No one wanted to talk about their missing captain just yet.

"Not much," Thompson replied. "The meatheads hit a few power couplings, but secondaries re-routed. Lucky they didn't hit those, too, or we would have disintegrated when we tried to go into the DL. Most blasts hit engine shielding, which held without a problem."

"Hit a return flow pipe on an enviro system," Nance added. A return flow pipe was a nice way to say sewage. "It was clear at the time, but no one use the cargo deck's port-side head till I fix it or you get to clean up the mess."

"Repair time?" Cargo asked.

"Not long."

Cargo was silent a moment, but he couldn't withhold the details from the crew. They needed to know. "Kade had fallen for our little ruse. Rebecca hadn't. She pulled a blaster on the captain and then Thompson, Flaherty, and I showed up with the pulse rifles, and we told her to stand down. Kade was on our side and told her to back off, as well. So, Rebecca turned the gun on him and took the top of his head off."

Sabrina was an on-the-fringe sort of freighter, running a bit of this and that, things she probably shouldn't. They'd even gotten in a few dockside shootouts in some seedier stations on the edge of nowhere, but never had anyone died on her decks. Everyone was stunned to silence.

"Great, dead people," Nance exclaimed. "I'm not cleaning that shit up!"

"Don't worry about it. We'll just shift the atmo shield in a few feet and let the void take it all. Lock's still open anyway," Thompson said.

"Noticed we blew out some air," Nance sighed. "I'll handle all that. It's what I get paid the big bucks for. Do we want to keep anything as evidence? Isn't there a bounty out on Kade?"

"Yeah, it's some damn serious cred, too," Cheeky said. "Maybe we could use the money to buy the captain back."

Thompson's expression was dark and he cast a glance at Tanis before he spoke. "I told the captain this was a bad idea. We should consider just turning her over in a trade. Be nice and fast." Tanis's expression grew cold as he spoke, but she didn't reply.

Cargo ignored Thompson's statement. "If we turn in Kade's body, we may have to answer some tricky questions about how we got it. Captain may be up to that sort of fast-talking, but I don't know if I could handle it. Freeze it for now and toss the goons. We'll use it later."

"I guess my suggestion is out," Thompson said sourly.

Flaherty leaned forward as he reached for a plum in the fruit bowl. "Sera made it clear that we don't trade in human cargo. She decided not to give Tanis over to them. I think we should respect her decision."

Everyone nodded in agreement, though some were more reluctant than others.

Thompson let out a sigh and leaned back with his arms crossed. "Whatever."

Cargo looked at Thompson for a moment, wondering what trouble the man would cause. "We do have one piece of good news. We got their tech and one of their goons." He paused as Flaherty shook his head slowly. "OK, so just their tech. I'm betting that he can tell us what we need to know about where Rebecca will have taken the captain. Who wants in on having a little talk with him?"

Every hand shot up, even Tanis's. "OK, it's gonna be me and…Thompson. We'll get answers out of him."

"He'll be pissing himself in ten minutes," Thompson said.

"No good, Cargo," Flaherty said. "He watched you kill that pirate. You'd scare him too much for him to talk."

"Let me in on it," Cheeky said. "I'll get him talking."

"You're not exactly intimidating," Nance shook her head.

"I have some pretty intimidating outfits."

"Never know, he may go for that sort of thing," Thompson chuckled, most likely trying to visualize Cheeky in one of those outfits.

Cheeky pouted. "True…haven't met a guy yet that didn't seem to enjoy my dom routine, no matter how much I hurt him."

"I'll do it," Tanis said, unflinching as every eye turned to her.

"Why should you do it, you're as much a part of the problem as that Drind guy," Nance said as she looked around the table. "Thompson has a point. Don't you think that Sera may have changed her mind, now that she's been captured? We all know how much Rebecca hates her."

Thompson nodded his agreement and cast Nance a small smile for her support.

Cheeky's face was twisted in an uncomfortable grimace. "Part of me wants to try it; it's the quick and easy fix. But, I don't think it's ethical. Besides, like you said, Rebecca has always really hated Sera, but by extension *Sabrina,* and all of us."

"You're one to talk about ethical." Thompson said with an unkind edge to his voice.

Cheeky flushed. "You wouldn't understand why I do the things I do. To you it's all just raw sex. Sure, some of it is, but there's more to it than that."

"Cheeky's sexual proclivities aren't the issue here," Flaherty said, his voice toneless and level. The look in his eye sent shivers down everyone's spine. "Stay on topic."

"You don't have to like me," Tanis said. "You don't have to like why I'm here or why people are killing and dying to get me. Trust me; I like it just as little as you. You may have had a bad year or two in your lives, but I've had a bad century or two. It sucks. But all recriminations and whining aside, I've had training in this sort of thing. I've commanded units that had to get information in pretty short order before."

"So you tortured people for it?" Nance asked.

Tanis didn't reply for a long moment. "Yes."

Strangely, it seemed to be the right answer.

Cargo steepled his fingers, "OK, then. Tanis, you do the talking, and Thompson will do the intimidating. The rest of us will watch over the Link."

"Good, I'll make sure you don't try anything funny," Thompson said.

"What 'funny things' would I try?" Tanis was clearly growing tired of Thompson's attitude.

"Whatever pain in the asses did five thousand years ago," Thompson said.

Tanis sighed and followed Thompson down to the hold where they had dumped the tech. He unlocked the door, but before they stepped inside, put his arm across the entrance.

"You may think you're all special and hot shit, but if I even get an inkling that what you're telling us to do will harm Sera, I'll kill you myself."

Tanis didn't flinch as she stared the large man down. She was going to reciprocate the threat, but then stopped herself. "I promise you, that won't happen."

She pushed his arm out of the way and stepped inside. Drind was sitting propped against a crate. A sack was over his head and his hands were bound behind his back. The sack wasn't tied on; Drind just hadn't tried to get it off.

Tanis had found him to be a nice, if somewhat shy, man when he reviewed their logs and scan data on the bridge. She knew how he must be feeling, but pushed it from her mind. Rescuing Sera was the best way to get back to the *Intrepid*—though simply commandeering the ship had crossed her mind more than once. But Sera had saved her; she wouldn't repay that with treachery.

Crouching in front of him, she snatched the sack from his head, then grabbed his hair in one swift motion. He tried to scramble back from her, his eyes closed while she pulled his head back.

"Look at me!"

Startled to hear a woman's voice his eyes opened and latched onto Tanis like a drowning man.

"Rachel! You've got to help me; they're going to kill me."

She doubted Drind had many friends in Kade's—now Rebecca's—organization. Being the tech on a ship full of pirates probably was a tough job.

<*I don't know how you can do this sort of thing; he's pathetic,*> Angela said.

<*Occupational hazard,*> Tanis replied with a sigh.

<*You could go easy on him,*> Angela's voice had an edge of pleading to it. She had never been squeamish during torture before.

<*I will, but if I don't do this a certain way, Thompson will kick me out and do it his way.*>

During her chat with Angela, Drind came to the realization that it was Tanis who was pulling his head back at an extreme angle and he shrunk inward.

"Please don't hurt me," he whimpered.

Tanis ignored his entreaty and asked angrily, "Why did you kidnap Captain Sera?"

His shock was plain and denial strong. "What? I didn't do that. That psycho Rebecca did. She blew Kade's head off! I didn't have anything to do with it." He was beginning to shake uncontrollably; Tanis decided to back off a bit or she'd have to conduct the rest of the interrogation over the smell of urine.

"Please don't kill me, too," his voice was little more than a whisper.

Tanis let go of his head. "So you didn't know what she had in mind?"

"No! She didn't want me to come, told Kade to just take the ship by force and find the container they wanted. Honest, I didn't want to come! Staying far away from her is the best way to live a longer life."

Tanis stood and paced back and forth in front of him. She allowed her expression to soften somewhat and glanced at Thompson who didn't look the least bit convinced, though the look he cast her contained a small hint of appreciation. Good. She paused her pacing for a moment.

"And you didn't know what Rebecca had planned? The kidnapping or killing Kade?"

"No, I swear it!"

Tanis grunted and paced a few more times, then turned back to the poor man. "I may believe you, but I'm still having reservations. Some of the other guys," she jerked a thumb back at Thompson, "aren't as convinced. You better sweeten the pot with something substantial or they may decide that they're through with my soft talking."

Drind hung his head like a man who had given up hope for his life.

<*Oops, a bit too thick there,*> Angela said.

<*Just a smidge.*>

He was supposed to think *she* was his hope. Tanis crouched down in front of him and resisted the urge to cup his chin in her hand to raise his face up.

"Hey, they're not banging down the door yet. Why don't you tell me what you know and I'll keep you safe." Now she was going too far the other way, but this poor guy wasn't going to notice. She was out of practice, but keeping up her skill at interrogation wasn't on the top of her list of abilities to refine. "What was in the container that Padre's men took?"

Drind raised his head, a bit of hopefulness in his eyes. "I don't know, but it seemed pretty valuable. Not the 'racing hound' they told you it was; that much is for sure."

"Rebecca and Kade never talked about what it was?"

"I overheard an argument about it, and some of the other guys did too. They seemed to be arguing about what to do with it. A couple of times I swore Kade slipped and called it a 'her', but I wasn't listening too closely; that doesn't pay on the *Vertigo*."

"Is that where you're stationed? On the *Vertigo*?"

"Sometimes." Drind was starting to warm up now, hopeful that he could spill his guts and save his life. "I'm back at HQ a lot, too. Depends where they need me."

"Kade had an HQ?" Somehow, his appearance had caused Tanis to think of him as nothing but a guy with a few ships causing trouble.

"Of course, haven't you been there? I mean, you're one of his ships."

"We aren't that scum's ship," Thompson growled.

Drind lowered his head closed his eyes—Tanis smiled inwardly. Thompson was playing along really well. Either that or it was just his natural disposition. It worked to her advantage, though—it was best not to let Drind get too comfortable. If he did, he'd start thinking he could turn things to his advantage.

"Is that where Rebecca will take Sera? Back to HQ?" Tanis asked.

"Probably. The *Prowler* was at the rendezvous, too, lying dark out of scan range. I imagine she'll have them look for you while she goes back there."

"How many ships does The Mark have, anyway?" Tanis asked, wondering about additional complications.

"We'll, I'm not sure since he said this was his ship, too. Ships that I know he owns for sure…about four hundred; dozens of others that at least do regular business with him."

"And where is this HQ that Rebecca will be going back to?"

Drind didn't reply right away, but his eyes darted to Thompson's cold stare and flexing fists, then back to Tanis. She made her face look as open and trusting as possible.

"It's hidden really well. It's impossible to find."

"But you know where it is, right?" Tanis prompted him.

"Sure, I know the coordinates. It's actually not too far from here."

"What's the name of the system?" Tanis asked.

"Oh, it's not in any system," Drind spoke as if he was afraid unseen enemies would kill him. "It's in the dark layer."

Tanis managed to get the coordinates to the station after that, but Drind warned her that there were sensors and defensive turrets in both the DL and real space. She concluded the interrogation shortly after, with the promise that she would see about getting Drind more comfortable quarters.

The crew met in the galley again, their faces somber as they pondered the implications of this information.

"How do they even dock in the DL?" Thompson broke the silence.

"Very carefully, I'd bet," Cheeky said with noticeable appreciation in her voice.

The dark layer was just that, very dark. Nothing emitted light at all. It made the interstellar void look like a sunny afternoon. The only natural emissions of any sort were gravitational waves, which was how ships knew when to drop out of the DL and back into real space. Ships could emit light, but the gravitational waves dispersed that light very quickly.

<*Perhaps they have their station anchored to some dark matter,*> Sabrina offered, much calmer now that she knew where Sera was. <*Then they could latch onto ships and pull them in.*>

"Even if we believe him that this HQ of his is in the dark layer, and even if we find out that there is a back door, what are we going to do? Just march in there and demand Sera back?" Nance asked.

"We still have Plan B," Thompson looked at Tanis.

"Why don't we move our friend Drind to some better quarters and see if we can't convince him to start spilling specifics about this place?" Tanis said, ignoring Thompson. "Once we're better informed, we should be able to determine if his story is bunk. While we're at it, we may as well start plotting a course toward the general vicinity of the place, in case we do decide to all turn kamikaze."

"Do we have that kind of time?" Thompson asked, his face turning red. "They could be killing Sera right now while we sit around and debate what to do."

"Their base is some ways out into interstellar space on the core-ward side of the Silstrand Alliance." Cheeky provided a holo showing its relative position. "It'll take them a while to get there."

"Which is great if she's still alive, not so great if she's already dead," Nance said.

"She's still alive," Flaherty said flatly.

"How do you know that?" Cargo asked.

"Just listen to Tanis! She's our best bet to get Sera back," Flaherty growled at the rest of the crew.

No one knew what to say in response and Tanis looked into the stoic man's eyes for a long moment. His connection with Sera had to be older than their time on this ship. He owed her something, had some deep obligation to her.

<*Curiouser and curiouser,*> she said to Angela.

THE BEST LAID PLANS

STELLAR DATE: 07.13.8927 (Adjusted Years)
LOCATION: The Mark's Dark Layer Station
REGION: Unclaimed Interstellar Space, Core-Ward of Silstrand Alliance

Sera returned to consciousness in fits and starts. Her head felt like it had spent some time in the fusion reaction chamber...or a week on the bottle. Rather than alert anyone nearby to her conscious state, she kept her eyes closed and took mental stock of her surroundings and where her body lay.

First discovery made: she was lying down. Whatever she was on was padded, at least a little. She could hear the soft sound of air circulation, but no reactor or engine noise. She was either on a station or planet-side. Sera curled her fingers and then her toes. No apparent spinal damage, extremities seemed OK. Next, she tried to lift her arms and found she couldn't.

Tugging gently, Sera determined she was strapped down. Testing various points, she determined that every part of her was thoroughly restrained. Not tightly, but very firmly. Nothing seemed to be holding her head down. Sera rotated her neck left and right with no problem other than increased throbbing between her ears. Shifting in her bonds also confirmed a previous suspicion: she was completely naked.

<*How do I get into these situations?*> Sera asked.

<*The root of it is probably not taking your father's advice,*> Helen replied.

Sera responded by having her avatar stick her tongue out at Helen's ephemeral mental figure.

<*Ironically, we're finally where all this was supposed to lead,*> Sera observed.

<*I did notice that myself. Years of work and all you had to do was lose important cargo to get to The Mark's HQ.*>

<*I'm going to make a note of that for the next time I decide to infiltrate a pirate's lair,*> Sera said with a chuckle.

<*Well, I wouldn't call this 'infiltration',*> Helen laughed.

<*True, there is the pesky 'being strapped to a table' issue, plus the upcoming torture to deal with,*> Sera admitted.

<*Have you been able to get any nano out for a look-see?*>

<*I've tried, but there's a very strong ES field that keeps frying them.*>

She could tell that the room she was in wasn't too bright or she'd see the light through her eyelids. Cracking them, Sera recognized her surroundings as a medical bay.

It seemed standard, if somewhat archaic. There were actually scalpels and other cutting tools here. Sera made a mental correction. Either she was in the medical bay of a sadistic doctor, or one that doubled as a torture facility. Or maybe the medical bay of a sadist doctor that also did the torture. None were promising prospects.

The things she had been trying not to think of raced through Sera's mind. Where was *Sabrina*? Was her crew OK? Did they have Tanis? Only by pure force of will, and the knowledge she had gotten out of equally sticky situations, did Sera manage to calm herself.

Though the lighting was dim, she could tell by the structure of the walls, deck, and ceiling that this was a station of some sort—roomier than a ship, but not as liberal with space as a planetary facility. As she surveyed her surroundings, the door opened and Rebecca entered. Why was Sera not surprised?

Her captor wore a hazsuit with the helmet off. Sera had a flash of jealousy for how the tight suit showed off what was an amazing figure. Lower g certainly was kind to large-breasted women.

"What's with the suit, Rebecca? Scared of little ol' me?"

Rebecca's smile was anything but pleasant. "Sensibly cautious. You'd be surprised at how many twitchy freighter captains put little surprises in their blood for people who start cutting into them. I've learned to be cautious."

Sera cursed herself. That would have been a great idea. Why had she never thought of it? "So what's the drill here? You ask questions, I pretend I don't even know what year it is, you use some of your tools, get no further, and then we call it a day? I'll tell you what. I'll save you the trouble. I don't know squat; go away."

"Don't you want to know about your crew?" Rebecca asked. "You'll surely want to know what I've already done to them."

Sera didn't fall for it. While she respected their courage and skill, she knew that at least one or two of them would have cracked under the type of questioning Rebecca was sure to use. If her crew had been captured, Rebecca would already know that 'Rachel' was the missing cargo, and Tanis would be the one strapped to the table.

Not that she was going to let Rebecca in on that reasoning. She struggled in her bonds. "What have you done to them?"

"Nothing permanent...yet." She let the word hang in the silence between them.

"Look, we don't have that stupid container. You've got Kade's organization now; what more do you want from me?"

Rebecca smiled again. This time it was more predatory. "I really must thank you for that; this really did work to my advantage. I managed to get Kade out of the way, *and* pin it on you and your crew. With all the other senior captains away on raids, I get to solidify my position. I couldn't have asked for a better turn of events."

Sera groaned inwardly. Was this woman going to gloat all day or just get on with the torture?

Rebecca continued unabated. "But that stupid container, as you call it, is worth more than all of this," the obligatory hand wave indicated her surroundings. "You are going to tell me where it is. That much is certain."

"If Padre has it, how am I going to tell you where it is?"

"We won't worry about that today. Today I'm just going to get to know you a bit better." Rebecca walked leisurely toward a cart with some of the more barbaric instruments on it. "If one is careful, one can put quite a few holes in a human being and neither cause them to die, nor even fall unconscious. Let's see how many we can make in you."

Sera gritted her teeth and prayed to whatever gods were listening for strength. Her prayers were granted. She had the strength to both scream and cry at the same time for hours.

OF MICE AND MEN

STELLAR DATE: 07.14.8927 (Adjusted Years)
LOCATION: *Sabrina*, Interstellar Dark Layer
REGION: Silstrand Alliance Space, Core-Ward of Silstrand Prime

"There's some disbelief regarding your statement that your HQ is in the DL," Tanis said as she sat with Drind in the cramped cabin they had given him. She had been working on earning his trust over the intervening days and was now cross-checking his earlier intel. "Since there is nothing to react against in the DL, there is no way to maneuver. How do you dock?"

Drind couldn't help smiling. "It's genius, really. One of Kade's engineers just happened to spot this relatively small blob of dark matter that isn't moving, well not much. He did some testing and found that with the right force, a gravity drive can tether to the dark matter and anchor the station. They use gravity fields to pull ships in for docking. There's a probe in regular space that has the current coordinates of the HQ and ships simply transition to the DL at that point with zero relative motion."

Tanis mulled it over. That aligned with what Sabrina and Cheeky had suspected.

"So, how do you suggest that we drop in to make our rescue run?"

Drind's face drained of color. "You can't do that! HQ is impregnable." He looked around as if he could determine the ship's course or maybe some way off it. "You can let me out next stop if that's your plan. I may be somewhat grateful for you getting me out of that mess. But not that grateful."

"You don't really think we'd abandon Sera, do you?" she asked.

"You won't be abandoning her; she's already dead."

Tanis had considered it—heck, everyone on the ship had. The consensus was that, although she may be a bit worse for wear, Sera's knowledge was simply far too valuable to kill her. If Tanis was free, Sera was alive.

"She's not dead," Tanis said.

Drind wasn't dumb. Tanis had noticed that during her first encounter with him, as he looked over her scan logs on the bridge. Something seemed to click in his mind and he suddenly sat back on the bunk.

"It's you."

"It's me what?" Tanis asked, feigning confusion.

"You're what Kade was looking for. You're what was in that container."

"I have to admit, I'm impressed," Tanis nodded. "How did you figure it out?"

"Well, it wasn't a dog, that much was obvious. But this ship doesn't have the ability to tell a dog's bio signature from a human's when in cryostasis, so unless they popped it open, the fiction would have held." He looked puzzled for a moment. "Why did they open it?"

Tanis smiled. "They got away at Trio without being boarded, and were interested in knowing what they'd risked their lives for."

Drind looked amazed. "They actually escaped Padre's guys in Trio? How much of the scan was faked?"

"Not much, just the part where the ship decelerated after the RM was fired. In reality, they twitched at the last moment and made it to FTL with half a second to spare."

"Holy shit," Drind whistled. "That Captain Sera has quite the pair."

"I'm told it was one heck of a ride."

"I'm beginning to understand part of why they want to rescue her," he snorted. "Not that I think it's sane. Why are you in on this, anyway?"

"She saved me, I owe her the favor. Besides, Sera seems like a decent sort."

Tanis finished the statement as Cargo opened the door to the room.

"Don't let her hear you say that," he said. "It would ruin the fiction she likes to portray." Drind noticeably pulled away, sidling against the bulkhead. The reaction appeared to annoy Cargo. "Would you cut that out, I'm not going to hurt you."

Their reluctant castoff straightened. A bit.

"So what's it going to be? Going to tell us what you know or do we ship you somewhere in cryo so you can't rat us out?"

"That's a shitty choice," Drind muttered.

"Better than sticking you in the middle of this if you don't want to be."

Drind looked as if he had an acerbic reply ready, but he bit it back. Cargo had a point.

"Isn't there anything you can think of that would help us?" Tanis asked. "We've been more than kind to you, and we'll be taking down Rebecca, or at least taking her down a notch."

"You'd better take her all the way down," Drind looked deadly serious. "If you don't, there will be no safe place for you this side of Sol."

"There's still the bounty on Kade that every system for ten parsecs is offering. We could get that money and arm up to take them down," Cargo said.

"It would take a lot more money than that," Drind said. "You'd still need some way to get in. Missiles may not work well in the DL, but HQ has a reactor that can keep its lasers slicing and dicing for hours."

Tanis snapped her fingers. "That's it. We need an army and an in. We'll get both." She turned to Cargo. "We need to set a course for the closest star system that has a stable government." She wasn't sure if stability was the norm here or not, but it didn't hurt to be specific.

She turned to Drind. "Kade must have had ships that were not generally known to be his, that dock both at system stations and at his HQ."

He nodded. "There are a few."

"Do you know their normal ports of call?"

"Not even remotely. Information like that wasn't exactly bandied about."

Tanis kept thinking aloud. "What about places where his pirate ships would frequently be lying in wait?"

Drind was silent for a moment as he thought. "It is pretty common for a ship to hang in the outskirts of the Big OJ looking for traders stopping through for fueling."

"Big OJ?"

"Oh, Gedri. The crews back at HQ call it the Big OJ…it's a really damn orange star."

"What's with all the traffic there?" Tanis asked.

"Like he said," Cargo gestured at Drind, "the system is rife with helium for fusion, and there are a few outfits that have antimatter production sites. A lot of ships running low will coast into the system with their engines off."

"Yeah, some will coast in from a fair ways out. Makes for good pickings," Drind added.

Tanis had a few questions about that but didn't want to voice them in front of Drind; it may give away her lack of knowledge regarding the ninth millennium. They thanked Drind for his time and left his cabin for the galley where the rest of the crew had gathered as they watched the conversation.

"Why do ships drop out of the DL and coast in? Wouldn't it be better to stay shifted to get in faster and safer?" Tanis asked.

"Takes power to stay shifted in the DL. People often will drop out early and coast into a system to save money," Cheeky replied with a shrug.

"I guess that makes sense. Sounds like we've got the makings of a plan," Tanis said while pouring a cup of coffee. "We coast into the Big OJ and wait to get paid a visit from one of The Mark's pirate ships. We take their ship and hop on back to the ol' HQ where we get Sera back."

Cargo shook his head. "Us and what army?"

"Sounds like a good way to get ourselves killed," Thompson added.

Tanis smiled. "I've been doing a bit of research on the ninth millennium. Sera said things were different, but I really didn't expect so much to be lost. She was right about FTL spelling the end of human advancement," Tanis said and held out her right arm and pulled back her sleeve.

What looked like skin changed its appearance to metallic silver, the effect racing all the way down her arm. She quickly downed her coffee and held the cup by its side.

To everyone's astonishment the cup dissolved into the palm of her right hand and a blue light emitted from her right forearm. Tanis held her left hand out to catch the object materializing there. It was a small ceramic handgun. Tanis put it down on the galley table while everyone stared open mouthed.

"I guess you don't see nano like this much these days."

Cargo looked Tanis up and down and then glanced at Nance. "She is human, right?"

"She was back when she was on the med slab." Nance hadn't taken her eyes from Tanis. "Though we could tell she had some pretty advanced tech in her."

"Unless we're gonna take out a pirate ship with ceramic pistols, you'd better have some better tricks up your sleeve…figuratively speaking," Cargo said. "Have you ever been in a battle for your life?"

"I didn't get my rank sitting on my duff."

Tanis's statement was met with blank stares.

"I'm a TSF major, remember?"

"That doesn't really mean a lot to us," Nance said with a shrug. "A lot of military types get promoted without ever seeing combat."

"Yes, I've seen combat," Tanis sighed. "I've fought planet-side, station-side and ship to ship. I've put a lot of holes in a lot of people. Satisfied?" If they only knew what she had done to get this far.

"Great, you can shoot people," Thompson said. "Is that the extent of your plan for saving Sera?"

"Well, I obviously can't take on a pirate ship by myself, and, since we need it intact, we have to board it, or be boarded by them. I'd prefer to be on the side doing the boarding. First thing we need to do is get some big guns or at least some raw materials so we can make some big guns. What's the closest port of call?"

Thompson stood up and looked them all over. "This is total bullshit. You guys can take orders from her; I'm going to go clean up the mess one of those containers made when it got shot."

No one said anything for a minute after he left and then Cargo shrugged. "Cheeky, what's nearest?"

She looked at him and then shrugged as well. "Closest system is Silstrand. They've got a number of stations insystem we can dock at. There's an independent mining platform out in their EK belt that has an arms dealer or two on it. How we paying for these guns anyway?"

Tanis smiled. "I'm betting I have some nano that could be worth a bit."

* * * * *

Rebecca was no slouch—a real pro when it came to making people suffer.

Sera hurt in places she didn't even know could hurt. She desperately wished she could escape her body. She'd heard of out of body experiences; maybe she could have one if she tried hard enough.

Rebecca had asked very few questions while she did her work. She said she just wanted to get to know Sera's body a bit better. Needles seemed to be her specialty. Rebecca had them in varying sizes and could put a truly astounding number of them into a person's flesh. One had started out the size of a sliver and grew to well over a centimeter in diameter. Rebecca had put that one through a lot of things.

After Rebecca had her fill and left, a med team came in and cleaned Sera up. They didn't make anything hurt less, more actually, as they cauterized the wounds to staunch the bleeding and put her on an IV to replenish the fluids she'd lost.

Sera supposed it was one way to pass the day.

A better way was working on her escape. While Rebecca had been busy at her trade, Sera had been busy at hers—namely plotting Rebecca's death. During the session, Sera had managed to pull a needle from her own thigh and slip it past her palm into her wrist where the strap held her arm down. Now that she was alone, she slipped the needle from her skin and began worrying its tip along the strap.

While under Rebecca's not-so-tender ministrations, Sera had learned why there was no strap holding her head down: her torturer liked it when Sera pulled her head up or tilted it back to let out a really good scream. It worked to her advantage now as she twisted to see the needle tip doing its work. The strap seemed to be of the same material as a safety harness; there was a section where it had been sewn together and that was what she focused on.

The material held up well and Sera found progress to be slow. She walked a careful balance between not moving enough to lose her grip on the needle and have it fling across the room, but still fast enough to get free before another session with Madam Pain.

The hours ticked by as she picked at the stitches. One by one, they came free and Sera allowed herself to feel a glimmer of hope. Then, with a snap that did send the needle flying, the strap gave way. Sera didn't move, but waited to see if the sudden twitch of her arm had been noticed by whoever may or may not be watching the cameras. After several minutes, nothing happened and Sera forced her breathing to slow.

Without any quick movements, she slid her right arm across her body and undid the strap across her chest and from her left wrist. Then, with great care, she slowly shifted her hand back to her right side and slipped it into the loop of the strap.

Sera tried to put her mind at rest. She was tired and had lost a lot of blood. Her best bet would be to get a good night's sleep and use the first advantage that came her way tomorrow. She had no illusions about trying to use a med tech as a hostage; Rebecca would gun her own people down in a heartbeat. She needed to get the queen bitch herself if she wanted to get out of here alive.

SILSTRAND

STELLAR DATE: 07.15.8927 (Adjusted Years)
LOCATION: *Sabrina*, Silstrand Scattered Disk
REGION: Silstrand System, Silstrand Alliance Space

Silstrand was a heavily settled system, boasting fourteen major planets, six of them being rocky worlds rich with minerals. Methane and hydrogen mining facilities hovered around three of the gas giants. Stellar traffic was heavy, and an AI operating a beacon demanded *Sabrina*'s identification and their port of call within half an hour of dropping out of FTL.

Tanis was on comm and relayed that they were bound for the PeterSil EK mining platform. Stellar control informed them that the PS EK platform was currently on the far side of the system from *Sabrina's* current position. They were given a deceleration vector and told to send a message to the PS EK platform informing them of their incoming vector and time of arrival.

"Bossy sorts here," Tanis muttered as she passed the plot to Cheeky's console and sent the required message to the mining platform.

Cheeky heard her comment and smiled. "Yeah, but the men really like a stern woman. Good times to be had at the main trading station off the fourth gas giant."

"Been through here often?" Tanis asked. The whole idea of interstellar trade by small freighters was still very fascinating to her.

"A few times. Some on *Sabrina,* some on other ships I've piloted. They have three TPs that have amazing diversity and some great pleasure resorts."

"TPs?"

"Means terraformed or terrestrial planets," Cargo supplied from the command chair. "FGT had a ball with this place. It already had one planet in the habitable zone, so while they got it all watered up and ready for life they decided to hang out and make antimatter."

"That was around when gravity tech had improved and AP drives became the rage. They built a massive particle accelerator to produce the antimatter and then left it here. It's still going strong, a good four thousand years later.

"I guess their tug pilots got bored while everyone else had something to do, so they hauled another planet into the habitable zone and then did something to one of the big gassies in the outer system to heat it up. Thing is just about a brown dwarf now. One of the other gassies had a slightly sub-terra-sized moon around it, so they hauled it over to their toasty gas giant and set it in orbit."

Tanis laughed. "Toasty gassie? I bet a thousand astronomers cringe every time you talk."

Cargo chuckled. "I'd consider that a compliment."

"Did they leave messages behind so we know what they did?" Tanis asked.

"The astronomers?"

"No, the FGT," Tanis replied seriously before realizing that Cargo was joking.

He chuckled before replying. "Sometimes. There has been contact with them here and there. If you can believe it, some of them still have their original crews."

"You're kidding."

"Nope, some of those people left Earth over six thousand years ago and they're still out there making worlds."

Tanis had heard that was the case in the forty-second century, as well—even then it had seemed far-fetched. She had always suspected that it was some sort of FGT propaganda.

"They can't have lived that long by stasis alone. They have to be doing something else; it still takes hundreds of years to terraform a world," Tanis said with a frown.

"Your guess is as good as anyone else's. After the *Oregon* incident, they don't have much to do with the rest of humanity anymore," Cargo replied.

"What happened there?"

"Everyone believes that the FGT has tech everyone else has only dreamed of—kinda like you. It's said they have the power to move stars," Cheeky said from the pilot's chair. "It was only a matter of time before someone decided to take a fleet around hunting for them. They found a worldship, the *Oregon,* terraforming a system, and tried to take it by force. Things didn't go as planned and the *Oregon* was destroyed. Some of their smaller ships got away and word spread amongst the FGT. No one has had direct contact with them in millennia now."

"They're still out there though, right?" Tanis really hoped they were, she was counting on getting in touch with them to secure a new colony world.

"Yeah," Cargo's voice was low and serious. "Sometimes people stumble upon a terraformed world that's just waiting to be discovered. Sometimes certain systems get messages about a new world they can expand to. There are even rumors that the FGT has agents scattered throughout space, shaping the course of humanity."

Tanis stared at Cargo, attempting to keep a straight face. She covered her mouth, her eyes sparkling. "You could host a cast on evil government plots," she began to laugh.

Cheeky joined in the laughter. "So dark and mysterious."

Cargo shrugged. "Mock me if you want, but there are a lot of people who suspect it."

Tanis looked over the system on the main holo tank. God complexes and guiding humanity aside, the FGT did amazing work. The Silstrand system gleamed off their port side as they passed over the stellar plane. Stations and stellar transports could be seen, reflecting their star's light in the dark. The twinkle of fusion drives sparkled near one of the rocky inner planets, indicating heavy mining.

The TPs, as Cargo called them, were near each other and *Sabrina* passed within half an AU of each. They were sparking blue-green on the unmagnified screen. Under magnification they showed to be amazing planets, both sporting several elevators connected to planetary rings.

"Silstrand seems to do pretty well for itself," Tanis observed.

"It's the seat of the Silstrand Alliance's government," Cargo supplied. "They control most of this star cluster."

"They a friendly sort?"

"Democracy of sorts. Big on trade, though, so freighters are never turned away."

Tanis asked a few questions about the types of governments found across the stars as *Sabrina* shed velocity across the system. She could read about them in the databases, but Cargo had an interesting viewpoint to share on each.

He told tales of dictatorships, kingdoms, democracies, and oligarchies for hours. Eventually, shift changed and Tanis reluctantly begged off the conversation to get some sleep. Tomorrow they would dock at the mining platform and she'd have a show to put on for a merchant or two.

RESIGNATION

STELLAR DATE: 07.15.8927 (Adjusted Years)
LOCATION: ISS *Andromeda,* 0.5LY Rim-Ward of Bollam's World
REGION: Bollam's World Federation Space

Joe paced across the *Andromeda's* main hanger bay where pieces of wreckage were being sorted. It had taken over a month to find the debris field from the *Intrepid's* collision with what turned out to be little more than a pebble, and several months more to collect all the pieces.

They were now laid out in a pattern matching their original location on the *Intrepid.*

Joe was amazed at how much damage the impact had done to the colony ship. Over two hundred meters of hull had been torn up by the impact, seven decks vented atmosphere, and one stasis chamber was destroyed.

And Tanis was lost.

He watched as the crew pulled the pieces off the last hauler. The pickings were getting slim and Joe didn't think they would find much more out there. Pieces of a lift were unloaded, followed by several chunks of bulkhead and a door.

Nothing that looked as though it came from an escape pod.

The ship's records showed Tanis making it to a pod and ejecting. As luck would have it, no other pods were damaged or ejected in the impact. That meant there was only one pod out there, and so far, no debris from a pod had been found.

It meant Tanis was alive.

The last pieces of ship were deposited on the deck and tagged. The technicians organizing the wreckage concurred that none of it was from an escape pod and Joe sighed with relief. He could finally report that Tanis was not here.

Not that Joe expected her to be. Tanis had survived too much to be killed by a pebble. Even if that pebble had been traveling at relativistic speeds.

<*Corsia,*> Joe contacted the *Andromeda*'s AI. <*Send a message to the* Intrepid. *There is no sign of Tanis or her pod. I want permission to go insystem and see if I can find out what happened to her.*>

<*I'm on it, Joe.*>

He had known from the beginning that Tanis was not in the debris field, but with no signal from her pod, everyone assumed she was dead—her pod destroyed. So, he worked to rule that possibility out as quickly as possible.

Now there was no reason not to search for her in the neighboring star system.

That was going to be easier said than done. In the months since the collision, they had gathered intel from listening to broadcasts and data streams from the system they now knew to be 58 Eridani. The crew of the *Intrepid* knew they were in the ninetieth century, and it was nothing like what they would have expected.

Joe took his time going back to the bridge. The *Intrepid* was two light-hours away, and a response to his request would take some time. He was fairly certain he knew what all the various directors and secretaries would say. Abby would vote to leave Tanis, Earnest would likely abstain, Ouri and Brandt would vote to continue the search. Sanderson liked Tanis, but he would vote not to risk the ship to find her. The captain was a mystery; he would need to think of the ship first—it all depended on whether or not he thought Tanis was necessary for the ship's safety.

"Think it was the last haul?"

Joe turned to see Jessica walking toward him from the direction of the hangar.

"If I have my way it is. There's nothing bigger than dust left out there. It's time to stop wasting our time out here."

"Do you think she's in the Bollam's system?" Jessica asked after catching up with Joe.

Joe shook his head. "I don't know…but it's the best place to start. There was that strange ion trail near the pod's most likely trajectory. It could be that she was rescued."

"Or kidnapped. You know what Sanderson thinks."

"He's not the only one—it's pretty clear that we have vastly superior tech than pretty much everyone now."

"You think someone has her?" Jessica asked, her voice strained with worry.

Joe nodded. "I refuse to believe she's dead; if she were OK, she'd get in touch with us somehow. No, she is being held somewhere and getting into that system and checking their scan records is the first step."

Jessica took his hand. "I want you to know I'm with you. If we have to steal a pinnace, or even the whole damn *Intrepid,* we'll go find her."

Joe clasped his hands around hers, taking a moment to calm his emotions. "I know she means a lot to you, too. Your support means a lot."

"She gave me a chance when…she's my best friend, Joe," Jessica said with a tear slipping down her face. "I'm ready to kick ass clear across the galaxy if I have to."

"You're a true friend, Jessica." Joe embraced the lavender-skinned woman, thankful that she had come along on the *Andromeda*.

Four hours later, the response came in from Captain Andrews.

"I'm authorizing an excursion into Bollam's to gather intel and hunt for Tanis." The captain's face was sober; he seemed to have aged years over the past few months. "But Joe, I need you back here. We have to protect the *Intrepid* and you're second in fleet command right now. I'm sending Jessica to look for her. We'll talk more when you get back."

The *Andromeda's* bridge fell silent. The anger flowing from Joe was palpable and tension radiated through the air as everyone did their best to look busy.

"*Corsia,*" Joe said after a moment. "Tell Andrews that he has my resignation. I'll hitch a ride with Jessica."

Jessica rose from her station and approached Joe's chair.

"Joe, are you sure about this?" Jessica asked quietly, placing a hand on his shoulder.

He lowered his head and ran a hand through his hair. "You don't know what she means to me."

"I do know; how could I not know?" Jessica said softly. "I've been with you two for decades—and I know what it means to choose duty over your love's safety."

"That's just it, you don't know," Joe turned to look in her eyes, willing her to understand. "She's pregnant."

Shock registered across Jessica's face. "Tanis's...pregnant?"

Joe nodded. "She's held it internally in stasis since before we got to The Kap—we were waiting to get to New Eden before carrying it to term."

"Corsia," Jessica addressed the ship's AI, while not breaking eye contact with Joe. "Have the duty chief prep the pinnace for two. Joe is coming along."

A SURREPTITIOUS ESCAPE

STELLAR DATE: 07.16.8927 (Adjusted Years)
LOCATION: The Mark's Dark Layer Station
REGION: Unclaimed Interstellar Space, Core-Ward of Silstrand

Sera woke to the sounds of a med tech entering the room. While she hadn't allowed herself to fall into a very deep sleep, she did feel better. The tech busied himself at a counter across the room, organizing something out of Sera's view. Eventually, he turned and Sera saw a large needle in his hand.

"What do you intend to do with that?" she asked.

<*Certainly not the time to get knocked out,*> Helen sounded worried.

The tech jumped at the sound of her voice. "Um…I was going to give you this."

"I don't think so. I've had enough stuff stuck in me; I can do with one less needle, thanks."

The med-tech had a furtive look on his face as he glanced around. "It's for the pain, it'll make it better."

So that was it. Someone with a conscience couldn't sleep at night while Rebecca did her thing. So rather than really helping her, he planned to ease his personal concern a bit.

<*He could be a genuinely good guy,*> Helen said.

<*A genuinely good guy would be loosening these straps. This guy just doesn't want to hear me scream,*> Sera replied sourly.

"Thanks but no thanks. If you really wanted to help, you'd get me out of here."

"I would, but it's impossible. There's no way out of this place."

"Well, thanks for the un-help, but like I said, I'm all done being stuck with things."

"But it will make you feel better." His face crinkled in confusion. "She won't notice if you make sure to scream."

"I don't know if this is her plan or your independent idea, but that shot will cloud my mind and I may just give in to her. She's not torturing me just for fun, you know," Sera paused. "Though, I wouldn't put it past her to do that."

The man looked undecided and Sera gave him the sternest look she could muster. "Go away. I don't want your pseudo help and if you don't have the guts to do something constructive then I don't have time for you."

The med-tech seemed somewhat disturbed that he was being given orders by a woman strapped to a table—or at least a woman who appeared to be strapped to a table.

"Just go before she gets here," Sera sighed.

Without a word, the man returned to the counter where he had prepared the syringe. He emptied its contents, threw it in the disposal, and walked to the door. Before exiting, he gave Sera a long look and then slipped out.

<*You know, you could have convinced him to help you,*> Helen said. <*Your plan isn't so good that it's foolproof.*>

<*It's close enough. I can take Rebecca with one hand tied behind my back.*>

<*Or your legs to the table, as it turns out.*>

Rebecca came in less than a minute later, and Sera was surprised her torturer hadn't spotted the med-tech.

"Good morning, sunshine," Rebecca said with a smile. "I trust you slept uncomfortably?"

Sera didn't respond and just glared, willing Rebecca to step closer while she went on in standard torturer speak about how pleasant mutilating Sera would be. She wore her hazsuit but hadn't put on the mask yet.

Just a little closer.

Sera got her wish as Rebecca stepped right beside the table to admire her handiwork. She had just started a smart remark about how Sera's legs looked good covered in crusted, pus-filled holes when her words stopped with a strangled gasp.

Sera gripped Rebecca's throat with all her strength, and the other woman grasped at her arm, nails clawing at Sera's skin. She sat up and added her other hand, desperate not to be dislodged.

Rebecca appeared to gain a measure of control and her eyes narrowed a moment before she swung a fist into the side of Sera's head. She let out a grunt, but wasn't going to let this bitch get the better of her. Instead, she slammed the heel of her hand straight into Rebecca's face.

In hindsight, Sera considered that the move was perhaps a mistake. Blood poured from Rebecca's nose and her grip on the woman's neck slipped as the hot fluid ran over her hands. Sera dug her fingernails deep into the Rebecca's skin to maintain her hold.

Rebecca hit Sera twice more, and then began to try to push herself away from the table, to which Sera's legs were still strapped. Sera had enough; she shifted to the side, put her left hand on the back of Rebecca's head and slammed it down into the corner of the table. Her torturer fell to the ground unconscious.

<*Told you I could take her,*> Sera said to her AI.

<*Hey, I was cheering for you the whole time. Didn't you hear me?*>

<*Not so much. I was busy, if you recall.*>

Sera loosened the straps holding her thighs and ankles. She slid off the slab and hefted Rebecca's limp form onto the table. Blood gushed from the cut across her forehead and Sera ignored it. She quickly stripped off Rebecca's hazsuit and strapped her former captor in her place. The right wrist strap was useless, so Sera tied Rebecca's hands behind her back and then strapped her chest down tight to prevent any wriggle room.

With luck, no one paid too much attention to surveillance on this room while Rebecca was at work. Kade had been an ass, but she was certain that most of the people in his organization weren't psychopaths like Rebecca. Just because a person was a pirate didn't mean they were inhuman.

Once Rebecca was secure, Sera slapped her former captor several times until the other woman started making noises that somewhat resembled a return to consciousness.

"Wakey wakey."

Rebecca snapped awake at that and struggled mightily, desperate to free herself.

"What the hell!" she yelled.

"Stop!" Sera ordered. "One peep above a whisper and this nice big needle I am pricking into the underside of your jaw will make a quick visit to your brain. Follow?"

Rebecca whispered yes, almost meekly, but her eyes held pure hatred.

"I was going to use you as a hostage to get myself out of here, but it occurred to me that you may not be that well liked, and your people may happily shoot us both. I also doubt you'll believe me when I say that if you let me go I'll let you live because...well, I wouldn't," Sera smiled with no small dose of malice. "So, to keep up with appearances, I'm going to work you over a bit so that you aren't immediately recognizable, finish you off, and then I think I'll strike off on my own."

<Is that absolutely necessary? I can fake the video feeds,> Helen said.

<I want her to stand up to cursory scrutiny if anyone comes in to patch me—her up again.>

Rebecca's face clouded and she appeared to be preparing an unpleasant response, but then thought better. She cringed as Sera held up the needle that had been under her chin and said, "You can make noise now." Right before she drove it through Rebecca's thigh.

Rebecca appeared to be one of those torturers who enjoyed giving pain but not receiving it. There were some that liked it both ways, but from the pitiful shrieking that ensued, such was not the case here. Sera had planted a few good-sized spikes in various places on Rebecca's body, and was about to drive the final one into her heart, when she found her hand unwilling to complete the downward arc.

There had been a time in Sera's life when taking another human life, in the heat of battle, or with calm precision hadn't been a problem. But she was supposed to have moved on from that. *Sabrina* was supposed to be her haven, her place of redemption. A dark thought passed through her mind: she wasn't on *Sabrina*; no one had to know what happened next.

It took Sera several minutes to make up her mind, and Rebecca watched that wavering spike with a singular focus. When it finally dropped, she let out a hoarse laugh.

"I knew you didn't have it in you."

"Apparently not anymore," Sera nodded. "Something we both should be grateful for."

<I'm proud of you,> Helen said softly.

"When I get out of here..." Rebecca began the standard threat.

"Oh stuff it." Sera smashed a fist into the other woman's face; then followed it with a few more blows. Rebecca was knocked unconscious again from the fury of

Sera's strikes. She then spent several minutes making superficial cuts on Rebecca's body to match those she bore.

<*There. Unless one of the meds paid careful attention to how she messed me up yesterday, this should do,*> Sera said while reviewing her work.

<*Ok, I'm a bit less proud of you….*>

Sera slipped into the hazsuit and sealed its hood shut before she exited the med-lab. The suit was covered in blood—which enhanced the disguise. When Rebecca had left yesterday's session, she had been covered with blood, too.

The hall was short but well lit. There were a few other doors along it and all bore markings that indicated they were also med bays. The hall ended in a T, and Sera strode toward the intersection with calm purpose, though she had no idea where she was going. She turned the corner and almost ran into the technician who tried to give her the shot earlier. He was muttering something about not letting that bitch torture people and finally doing something about it.

The look on his face when he saw whom he had nearly collided with was one of pure horror. It looked like the disguise was working.

She pushed on his shoulder to turn him around.

"My quarters, now."

He didn't question her and led her through the halls to Rebecca's rooms.

Sera was quite proud of how this escape was going so far. She'd definitely been through worse. The most difficult part was walking without limping. Her body was sending her strong reminders that someone in her condition really shouldn't be walking around.

<*Can you speed the healing up?*> Sera asked.

<*This is things being sped up. If you didn't have me guiding your bots, you wouldn't even be able to crawl right now,*> Helen replied with a motherly tone. <*I'm working them as fast as I can, but I'm not going to do a rush job putting you back together again.*>

As the terrified med tech led her through the halls, Sera's initial impression that she was on a space station was reinforced. It had all the hallmarks; exposed conduit for easy access and repair, sealable bulkheads, and no external windows. Well that was somewhat unusual, but not if they were in the bowels of a station.

Her disguise as a bloody Rebecca was working just fine. Everyone stayed out of her way as if she had the plague. Considering the reasons Rebecca wore the hazsuit while interrogating, she supposed plague may be just what people feared. Eventually, her guide led her into a much nicer-looking part of the station, with wider, carpeted corridors.

<*Who puts carpet in a pirate's space station?*> Sera shook her head.

<*Kade, it would seem,*> Helen responded with a chuckle.

The med-tech stopped in front of a door and looked over at her. Sera wondered if there was a security pass code on the door. Hopefully, even if there was, medics had override codes to get in if needed. She nodded for him to open it, and, shaking, he punched in a code and the door slid aside. She gestured for him to go in first.

The quarters were what she expected—luxurious in the extreme. Rebecca lived very nicely on the spoils of the business. Fabrics draped the walls, exotic woods and rare metals covered every surface. The bed was heaped with furs, and Sera was tempted to toss them on the floor, just to irk Rebecca.

<*Childish, but I wouldn't blame you,*> Helen commented.

Sera turned to her reluctant escort and pulled the hazsuit's helmet off.

"She's gotta have some weapons in here; help me find them."

The man fell back, his expression aghast. "You!"

"Yes, I'm here. She's strapped to a table in med."

"You got free!"

"You're quite observant. I'm very good at getting free. It's a survival trait."

"Did you kill her?"

Sera couldn't help but think that he certainly was morbid for a med-tech. "No, I don't do cold-blooded killing. But she's going to need some reconstructive surgery."

He nodded. "Oh."

"By the way," she extended her hand, "I'm Sera. You're?"

"Andy." He took a tentative step forward, shook her hand, and then pulled back. Sera didn't fault him; she was still covered in blood.

"So, you look for guns, I need to find something to wear. I can't stand her, but she has excellent taste in clothing."

While Andy rummaged around, Sera pulled open Rebecca's wardrobe, praying that there would be something in a nice, soft lambskin.

Sera was impressed. The wardrobe was probably larger than her cabin on *Sabrina*, and it contained hundreds of outfits hanging in several long rows. Nearly every style and fabric combination this side of Sol was represented.

As she walked through the rows of clothing, her eye was drawn to a section filled with black, shiny outfits. She recognized it as the same type of material Rebecca had worn on *Sabrina.*

Sera felt the fabric. It was rubbery, but slick and not tacky. It stretched nicely, and gleamed under the lights. She pulled one of the items off the rack and held it up to herself. It was a full suit that even had attached socks and gloves—covering its wearer from toe to neck.

<*Practically speaking, it will work well to cover all your cuts and bruises; a little pressure on all those wounds wouldn't hurt either.*>

<*It does feel like I opened up a few on the walk over here.*>

<*More than a few. You're bleeding from a dozen places right now.*>

"What the heck," Sera said aloud. "Kinky pirate mistress will probably help me blend in."

She grabbed a belt and a pair of boots before heading into the suite's bathroom. There, she peeled off the hazsuit, grimacing with pain as fresh scabs tore open.

"Crap, you were right, Helen. I look like shit."

<*Yeah, you should take a quick shower and clean those deeper wounds.*>

Sera didn't disagree. She stepped into the shower and let the water sluice away the blood and anger. Five minutes later, she stepped out, feeling ready to face the reason she had been trying to get onto this station for so long.

She dried off using fluffy cotton towels and then flipped the slinky suit over, looking for a zipper or fastening.

<*I think you have to get in through the neck opening,*> Helen supplied.

"Huh, I guess it is pretty stretchy," Sera said as she stepped into the suit. She pulled it up her body and pulled her arms inside, slipping them into the sleeves.

"Damn, this feels goooood," she said as the slick suit sensed a warm body and tightened around her, pushing out any stray pockets of air and outlining her body perfectly.

Sera turned in the mirror, admiring her gleaming black figure.

"Looks pretty damn good too," she said with a smile.

<*I'm glad you're taking time for fashion,*> Helen said with a wry smile in Sera's mind.

"What can I say, a girl's gotta—" Her words cut off as excruciating pain lanced across her skin. She screamed in agony as the feeling intensified, as though her skin were on fire underneath the suit.

She clawed at it, attempting to tear it off, but it had tightened around her to the point where she couldn't get a grip on it, nor pull it from her neck.

"Helen…help…" she managed to gasp before falling unconscious to the bathroom floor.

She woke several minutes later to find Andy hovering over her, concern filling his eyes.

<*You're OK,*> Helen said. <*You had an unfortunate incident with booby-trapped clothing.*>

<*I what?*> Helen's words didn't make any sense.

<*That suit you put on was keyed to Rebecca's DNA; when it detected that you were not her, it tried to kill you.*>

<*Seriously? She has her clothing set to kill?*>

<*So it would seem. It did a pretty good number on you before I managed to stop it.*>

Sera didn't feel much worse than before—almost better. She wondered how it had tried to kill her.

<*What did it do?*>

<*It tried to eat all your skin below the neck.*>

"WHAT?" Sera yelled and reached down, feeling her body. From what she could tell, nothing had changed; the suit still covered her, gleaming in the room's bright lights.

"Are you OK?" Andy asked. "You screamed and passed out, but moments later seemed fine. I linked with your internal system and it showed you had an allergic reaction to the material."

Sera ignored Andy's question. <*Helen, what do you mean it tried to eat my skin?*>

<*The suit, as it turns out was made of some sort of bio-polymer that bonds to the wearer's skin—from what I understand, it makes the skin hyper sensitive. Unfortunately, it's DNA keyed, so it reacts unkindly to unknown DNA.*>

Sera had heard of clothing like that, though never had the desire to own any.

<*I managed to stop it and alter it to bond to your DNA, but it then bonded directly to what was left of your skin.*>

Sera ran a hand down her leg and gasped. It was extremely sensitive; it also felt incredibly good. So that's why Rebecca had clothing made out of this material.

"I think I'm OK now," she said to Andy and stood.

<*Just so you know, you're stuck with this as your skin until I can get you into surgery.*>

<*Fantastic,*> Sera replied.

"Are you sure, you're OK," Andy asked. "That was a pretty strong reaction."

"My med package handled it. I actually feel pretty good now," Sera smiled. She did feel pretty good, but in a lot of pain at the same time. It was strange and rather distracting. Just when the escape was going so well.

<*Well, at least you don't have to worry about bleeding anymore,*> Helen said. <*It's rather impressive how quickly it linked up with your nerves. Rebecca spared no expense.*>

Sera struggled to her feet and Andy took her arm and guided her to Rebecca's bed. The feeling of his hand on her arm almost drove her mad, but she didn't pull away; she didn't want to. He brought her the boots and she pulled them on. They were a bit too big, but snugged up once she zipped them closed.

"I see you found her stash," Sera said, eyeing the dozen guns piled on a desk.

Andy nodded, finally taking his eyes from her body. "She had them all over. There's spare power cells, and ammunition for a few chemical slug throwers."

"Nice work," Sera said. She wasn't quite ready yet to get up again and admired the weapons from her place on the bed.

"Since my neck is now on the line, are you going to tell me how you got out of there?" Andy asked.

"Does it require much telling? I got free, beat the living piss out of Rebecca and tied her up. Now, there's something I need to get from this station, then I'm going to blow this place and get back to my ship."

"And that outfit's your disguise?"

Sera laughed. "I wasn't really planning to be disguised; I just think it looks good. You can't really see me kicking ass in a pantsuit, can you?

Andy raised an eyebrow.

"Hey. You're a medic, that's your thing. Looking hot and kicking ass, that's my thing."

<*I think this suit is affecting your brain chemistry; I'm going to adjust your serotonin levels,*> Helen laughed.

Andy shrugged. "OK, so what is your plan, then? Seduce all the guards between here and the docks and then get cozy with a captain?"

Sera grinned. "Do you think that will work?"

"No."

"Good, be a damn sad pirate organization if it did. First, I have to get to a secure terminal and look something up and go get it. Then I plan to shoot my way to the docks, hijack a ship, and get out of here."

"Suicide I am not in for. Have fun with that," Andy said and walked to the door. Sera was there in three strides, ignoring the fiery feeling in her muscles.

"Look, you don't have to come; in fact, I'd prefer you don't. But I do want to say thank you."

Andy looked taken aback. "Umm…you're welcome. I'm sorry I didn't help you when you first asked."

"Rebecca's even sorrier," Sera said with a chuckle.

"I bet she is."

"Look, when I said 'blow this place', I was being literal. When the alarms and alerts start telling everyone to get off the station, do it. Don't wait around; I'm sure at least a few captains will take their ships and run."

"What are you planning to do?" Andy asked.

"I'm not sure yet, but I'll promise two things. It will be irreversible, and I'll give fair warning before it happens."

Andy nodded. "Thanks for the heads up; my days would have been numbered anyway once surveillance discovered you are free and I helped." He opened the door. "I'll be seeing you."

"Probably not. You lay low until you hear the alarms."

Andy left and Sera turned back to the pile of weapons. She pulled out a thigh holster and slipped it onto her left leg, then slid a small slug thrower into it. Several throwing knives went into the tops of each boot. She rummaged through a drawer and found several small remote cameras.

<*They up to spec?*> She asked Helen.

<*Close, ingest them and I'll have your nano upgrade them.*>

<*Ugh, I hate doing that.*> Sera grimaced as she swallowed the small probes.

<*Well, I can't exactly use your forearm assimilator at the moment; it's a bit covered up.*>

<*Can't you expose it?*> Sera asked.

<*You have no idea to what lengths I'm going to keep your fragile human body in one piece right now. Don't make it harder.*>

<*I dunno,*> Sera said as she felt the biopolymer that was her skin. <*This may be the best, worst thing that's ever happened to me.*>

<*You organics are so strange.*>

<*You say that, but I know AI are curious about how organics 'feel',*> Sera replied.

<*Curious like you are about how a cat balances with a tail. You don't really want to be a cat,*> Helen's tone carried no small hint of condescension.

<***Some** people want to be cats,*> Sera retorted. She hated it when Helen took on her teacher tone. Those days were long past.

Sera slid two holsters onto the belt she wore and pulled two bandoliers filled with ammunition over her shoulders.

<*Sorry,*> Sera said presently to Helen. <*I'm just worried about not screwing this up. This mission hasn't had the most auspicious beginning.*>

<*I'm sorry, too,*> Helen replied. <*This is important to me, as well. I'm just worried that this biopolymer is messing with your mental state too much; you can't think clearly when you're so aroused.*>

<*That's where you're mistaken, my dear.*> Sera smiled as she hefted a large pulse rifle and slung it around her shoulder. <*The altered chemical and mental state is the goal, not a symptom; you should remember that. You get your big rushes, so to speak, from feats of mental prowess. Humans can get off on the mental stuff, too, but tactile stimulation brings*

its own thrill. When channeled into something productive, that stimulation can be a strength rather than a weakness.>

Helen gave the AI's equivalent of a laugh. *<Are you saying that the secret behind Cheeky's exemplary piloting skill is that she's a nymphomaniac and always aroused?>*

<That's exactly what I'm saying,> Sera said as she strapped two more guns to her thighs. *<She's extended her sexual stimulus to include her piloting skill. People can train their sexual response to be triggered by anything.>*

<I return to my earlier statement; organics are exceedingly weird. Do you have enough guns?>

Sera shifted from foot to foot. She had to be wearing at least twenty kilograms of weaponry. She slipped back into the wardrobe and found a long black jacket that fell nearly to her ankles. After Helen made certain it wasn't DNA locked, she slipped it on, ensuring that she could leave it open while not revealing the full extent of her armament.

<Yeah, I think it'll do. The probes ready?>

<Yup, open wide.>

The four tiny probes flew out of Sera's mouth, one settling on an access port for the room's terminal.

<It's possible that this connection is on the station's secure net, but I'm betting it's not if a med-tech has access to this room,> Helen said.

The probe disappeared as it slipped into the access port and linked with the station's general computer net.

<Yeah, looks like it's just standard access,> Sera sighed. *<I've got access to their wireless net now, though.>*

<Yes, the secure net is accessed elsewhere; however, I believe I can determine where we can get on it, based on the points where the nets link.>

The room's main holo activated, showing the layout of the station. Helen searched through access points, then made a noise of surprise.

<Sera, this station is in the Dark Layer.>

Sera stopped her investigation of the station's public net. *<Are you serious?>*

<Would I joke about something like that?>

<How long has it been here?> Sera asked in response.

<It looks like at least ten years. How it's gone unnoticed that long is beyond me.>

<Well, we are a ways away from any stars. At least now we know how to destroy it.>

<That's true. I have what I believe is a point where I can access the secure net from a public terminal. It looks like it has a physical hookup that was routed incorrectly. I should be able to break past its security and find what we need to find.>

Helen indicated the location on the holo she was displaying. Sera zoomed in and traced a path from Rebecca's quarters. It was two decks down and across a good quarter of the station.

"This'll be fun," Sera said with a smile.

Sera slipped out into the hall, heels snapping and long coat rustling.

<Good luck, miss stealthy.>

<*I don't have much chance of sneaking across this whole station. That's what this whole getup is about—looking like I belong and not to mess with me.*>

<*Clever plan, you are bright!*>

<*I blame my childhood teacher,*> Sera smirked.

<*Hey! I resent that.*>

<*So are you going to produce an opposite waveform or just mock me?*>

<*Just do a few quick twists and turns and I'll have all the squeaks and creaks mapped.*>

Sera obliged her AI and a moment later all sound from her movements ceased.

<*Not bad.*>

<*I've masked all your loud, tight leather for years; this isn't much of a challenge.*>

Sera slipped silently down the corridor and into the stairwell. The four probes ranged ahead and behind, keeping an eye on all surveillance equipment, sending signals to them, providing normal visual and audio feeds.

<*Did you see Tanis's matter assimilators, by the way?*> Sera asked her AI. <*I bet she has nano-cloud tech.*>

<*I suspect she does; the TSF did have that ability around her time.*>

<*Sure would be handy right about now,*> Sera sighed. <*Too bad they never shared it; these probes aren't that stealthy.*>

The stairs were narrow and Sera moved down them gracefully, peering over the rail to ensure the next landing was clear.

<*Shoot!*> Sera exclaimed suddenly. <*I forgot to grab grenades…keep an eye out for anything we can use to fashion some.*>

<*I thought your heightened senses honed your focus?*> Helen replied with a superior tone.

Sera didn't respond as she continued down the stairs.

<*Looks like we're passing near the mess hall,*> Sera noted.

<*Have to, unless you want to skirt through the administrative section.*>

At the second landing, Sera cracked the hatch ever so slightly, allowing a probe to slip past the seal. Both she and Helen watched the visual feed, Sera accessing the infrared and ultraviolet ranges she normally excluded from her vision.

<*Looks like the corridor is clear, but there are a few people in the mess hall beyond.*>

<*We'll take that service corridor and go around the main mess.*>

Sera strode down the center of the corridor. No point in looking suspicious to anyone leaving the dining area. As she neared the opening to the hall, two men stepped out.

"Whoa, yeah," one exclaimed. "I know you're new, 'cause I'd remember a sweet looking thing like you!" His friend elbowed him, but the man continued, taking a step toward Sera. "That's one sexy getup. You're a randy little bitch, aren't you?"

<*Holy shit, this guy is really living up to the stereotype, isn't he?*> Sera commented to Helen.

She didn't want conflict, but no woman dressed as she was on a Mark station would take talk like this without a fight, or a tumble between the sheets.

Sera stepped toward him, exuding sexual energy. "I am a bit new here. Care to show me around?"

The man laughed and moved closer. "Hell yeah, we can start with my cabin."

When he moved into range, Sera reached out with her right hand and grabbed his hair. In the same fluid motion, she reached down with her left hand, and pulled a blade from the top of her right boot. She pushed him back against the wall, wrenching his head back and pressed the blade in her left hand against his neck.

She sneered and ground her hips into him. "I like it rough, and I've got six more of these little blades. I don't like to stop until each one has gotten a taste of blood. Where's your cabin?"

The man's friend was laughing so hard that he had a hand against the wall to steady himself.

"I…uhh…can't right now…I'm on shift soon," the first man stammered.

Smoothly, Sera stepped back and let go of him, a sultry pout on her lips. "Always works with you types. Oh well." She put the blade back into her boot and blew him a kiss. "I'll keep an eye out for you."

He reddened and all but ran down the hall. His friend followed, clutching his gut as he laughed.

<You certainly like to add to the risk. If you wore one of Rebecca's more conservative outfits, none of this would have happened.>

<Yeah, but then he may have mentioned he saw some new girl in a business suit. Now he's going to swear his friend to secrecy. At least secrecy till the next time his friend is drunk.>

They slipped into the service corridor without seeing anyone else. It was little more than a shaft, which ended at a hatch leading to a larger thoroughfare. The hatch stood open and Helen sent two probes through. There was mild foot traffic, but no troops or guards of any sort.

Sera stepped through and took a left. Some of the men and women eyed her with appreciation, some with wariness, but most just ignored her. There was no shortage of men and women wearing racier clothing than Sera's. She began to suspect that The Mark had a brothel on the station.

She took a right at the next intersection and then another left further down. The terminal she was looking for was in a vertical maintenance shaft off this corridor. The probes spied the shaft's access eight meters away and Sera approached it nonchalantly. The coast was clear, but as she neared the hatch, two guards rounded a corner and began walking toward her.

Sera muttered a curse to herself and kept walking past the hatch. She passed the guards and winked at them. They both smiled at her in response. When she neared the end of the corridor, the probes behind her showed the two guards turn down a side passage. She doubled back and opened the shaft access panel, slipping in with a bit of trouble when her jacket bunched up beneath her. Once in, she hooked a foot on the access panel and pulled it shut.

<How far down?>

<Just three meters to that junction on the left.>

Sera slithered down the tight space to the location indicated on her HUD, and took a deep breath. She held her index finger against the port and silver metal flowed out through the outstretched digit, forming a probe which then seated itself into the port.

<*Gah… that always gives me the heebies,*> Sera said with a shiver.

<*Ah, there we are, this terminal does have access to both the secure and main nets on the station, just as I suspected. It's been locked out of the secure net, but a few nano into the mix and all that will be changed.*>

Sera studied the station's layout as Helen accessed the secure net. Even without knowing exactly where the artifact they were searching for was, there were only so many places it could be hidden. The station's own power grid should show its location—even if they hadn't decided to use it. If they had, then it should be even easier.

<*I'm in,*> Helen said. <*I'm scanning their secure locations and comm logs to look for any reference to the CriEn.*>

<*I hope it's still here. If Kade traded it, we're in big trouble.*>

<*I don't think so,*> Helen said. <*We first traced the CriEn to Kade eight years ago; this station has been here for ten. I'm betting that they're using it as a power source to keep this thing in the dark layer. It would be a lot cheaper than hauling fissionables or exotics all the way out here to run in a reactor.*>

Sera looked over the portions of the station labeled as power generation. If they were using the CriEn, it would be around there. It didn't have to be, but a smart engineer would place it near existing power distribution systems.

<*I think I found it,*> Helen said. <*The station specifications show two nuclear fusion reactors for power, but one is just barely running and the other isn't active at all. However, power levels show more energy than even these two reactors could create.*>

<*So they* **are** *using it. What are the chances we can remove it and not have this station tear itself to pieces when it loses the power to stay transitioned in the DL?*>

<*I think it will hold together for a day or so at least. The fusion reactor could probably hold it in just fine for a few weeks with the batteries helping—before it overheated. They'd have to kill everything except for life support to manage that, though. Once they get both reactors spun up, they could always keep it here, or transition it back to regular space.*>

It was one of the difficulties of maintaining systems in the dark layer: heat dispersion. In regular space, the cold of vacuum was a great way to disperse heat; in the dark layer, there was nothing to disperse heat to. The heat could be transformed into energy, but when it was permeating everything, that was hard to do. The CriEn module generated energy with no heat, which was the key to keeping a station in the dark layer.

Sera worked out the route to the station's power plant while Helen used nano to build a bridge from the station's secure net to the public net and placed the link into an encrypted stream. Unless they were looking, the station security systems wouldn't stand a chance of locating it.

<*There, we'll have access to the secure net over our wireless Link to the public net now,*> Helen said. <*Picked our route?*>

<*Yeah, we'll make our way across this level to the station's midpoint and then down three levels, across that one, and then down to power generation. Looks like guards on it are light. Kade probably counted on his fiction of two plants to hide the module.*>

<*What a waste of a CriEn,*> Helen sighed. <*You could run a planet with this thing.*>

<*No one ever said Kade was the brightest star in the sky.*>

<*'Was' being the operative term,*> Helen replied. <*Hey, grab that repair kit there; it has some stuff we can use for a distraction.*>

Sera grabbed the kit and pulled herself back up the access tube, and checked the two probes they'd left out in the hall. When the coast was clear, she flipped the latch and kicked the hatch open.

She eased out into the hall, but at the last minute, a bandolier caught on the hinge. She stumbled and fell to the floor before freeing herself and closing the panel.

<*Very graceful,*> Helen commented wryly.

She stood up and dusted herself off before looking up to see a guard walking toward her.

"Hey, what were you doing in there?" he asked.

<*You are so not going to be able to talk yourself out of this one,*> Helen chuckled.

"I'm tech; got a call that there was a down net coupling in there and I fixed it up."

The guard was unconvinced. "You're tech?"

"Yeah, I'm off duty." Sera made sure to stand so that her coat hid the weapons, but not her shapely legs.

"Why don't you spread your hands across that wall there while I check your ident?" The guard pulled out a scanner and stepped toward Sera as she placed her hands on the wall."

<*Told you.*>

<*You are not helping.*>

"That's odd," the guard said as he ran the scanner over her hand. "I'm not getting any station ident off you."

Sera smiled and turned, one hand sliding up her left leg and then behind her back. "I'm new; I'm just trying to do a good job." Humanity had been civilized for twelve thousand years, but men still hadn't outgrown their inability to think straight when a woman turned on her charm.

"Right, you can do a good job from detention while I check you out."

Apparently, some men had evolved.

<*I hope you blocked his transmit access or things are going to get unpleasant,*> Sera said.

<*What do you take me for, an amateur? I am six thousand years old, after all.*>

Sera slid the pistol she had reached for out from behind her back and jammed it under the guard's chin. "Tight beam your access codes and tokens to me, or I spray your brains on the roof."

The man nodded slowly, and Helen confirmed that he sent his codes. Sera gestured for him to turn and when he did, she fired a pulse at the small of his back. It was a simple yet effective way to stun someone for a few hours. He slumped and she caught his weight with a grunt. A minute later, she had him stuffed into the maintenance shaft and Helen was faking his patrol signal on the net so he wouldn't be missed.

Without any further incident, Sera made her way to the security station outside the power generation section.

<*What are the chances I could do a face meld without passing out?*> Sera asked Helen.

<*Your energy reserves are extremely low, even with what you got from that dispenser back there.*>

<*Figured as much. I don't know how I'd feel about any more pain anyway.*>

<*You've certainly planned better infiltrations.*>

<*Thanks for the support.*>

<*I was merely stating a fact,*> Helen said without rancor.

<*Well, I guess I'll do this the old-fashioned way.*>

Without another word, she stepped out from cover and strode directly up to the two guards. An automatic turret tracked her as she approached the two men.

<*Tell me you can jam that thing.*>

<*Already have. I'm just moving it for their benefit.*>

"Hey guys. How're you doing?" she asked with a friendly smile, attempting to walk right past them.

"Hold it." One of the guards said as they both reached forward to stop her progress. Sera halted half a step before they expected and grasped each guard's outstretched wrists. Their expressions were priceless as she leapt backwards and pulled the guards toward her and into one another. The guards stumbled and crashed to the floor.

<*That extra twenty kilos of weaponry really helps doesn't it.*>

<*Sure does, Flaherty would be proud.*>

Sera kicked the man on the left in the face as he struggled to get up, the heel of her boot ripping open his cheek. The other guard kicked the back of her other leg, hitting her knee and knocking her backwards. Sera took advantage of the momentum, twisted and fell onto the guard—her elbow smashing into his chest. The sickening crack of his sternum reverberated up her arm.

<*Damn that hurts!*>

<*That's why it's not in the manual.*>

Sera used her pistol to stun both men and dumped them in a small cleaning room a short distance back up the corridor.

<*We're on the clock now; those two guards are scheduled to check in verbally every ten minutes and I didn't get their access codes.*>

<*How long till the next check in?*>

<*Seven and a half minutes. I'll set the clock.*>

A countdown appeared in the upper right of Sera's vision as she ran down the corridors in the direction her map overlay indicated. There would be some techs monitoring the main reactor, but since the secondary one was offline, she doubted that anyone was watching it. She was wrong.

It appeared that The Mark techs were studying the CriEn module even as they were using it. Eight years later and they still didn't know how it worked.

There were at least a dozen of them in a monitoring station and another group wearing hazsuits in the chamber where the CriEn module stood on a pedestal.

<Great. I suppose I could just shoot them all, but that would be messy and probably set off an alarm or two.>

<I'll clear them out. It's fun to mess with people who don't know what they are doing,> Helen replied gleefully.

Helen showed Sera a readout of the main power throughput indicators. The CriEn module generated energy by accessing layers of space-time these techs didn't even know about. It would be easy to generate anomalous readings from the device that wouldn't put them in harm's way but would certainly cause them to vacate the premises.

Helen used her access to the station's secure net to worm her way into the engineering network, and from there to the CriEn chamber. As expected, grav fields were in place around the module to ensure safety. Helen altered the frequency of the fields and the module began to alter its output unpredictably. Its EM field swelled and pushed against the grav fields containing it.

As predicted, the engineers monitoring the device grew concerned, and then frantic as they attempted to stabilize the grav field and contain the module's EM field. Helen was more than a match for them, and within a minute they had hit their fail-safes and shut down the module. The scientists in the hazsuits had long since vacated the chamber and were crowded into the decontamination room.

With the scientists and engineers focused on discerning the cause of the anomaly, Sera was able to approach their monitoring station, crack the door open, and roll in a canister of gas. Made from the parts they had grabbed along the way, it wasn't a grenade, but it would do the trick.

It took only seconds for the gas to take effect, and Sera rose from cover as the countdown on her HUD slipped past the four-minute mark.

She ran past the sleeping techs and into the CriEn chamber. The module was seated in a socket, which linked up with the power ports. Sera quickly unlatched it and looked around for something in which to stash the device.

<There, they have a shielded case it will fit in back in the main monitoring station.> Helen indicated the location on Sera's HUD. She hefted the module, which weighed at least a good forty kilograms, and dashed back into the room with the sleeping techs. The shielded case was sitting on an equipment rack and she placed the module in it and flipped on the case's grav shield.

<Grav shield, lucky us. It would suck if someone hit the module with a beam weapon,> Sera said as she hoisted the case over her shoulder.

<Only for a fraction of a second,> Helen replied.

<I'm going to need another shot of adrenaline if I'm to make it through this next little jaunt.>

<You're way over-extended; I may have to regulate your heart if I give it to you.>

<I can barely move with all the weight I'm hauling. Juice me up, doc.>

The shot of adrenaline felt like a blow to the chest as her heart fluttered uncomfortably and then increased its pace. She took a deep, steadying breath, then switched her overlay to show the route to the station's main sensor array—a system that likely saw little use with the station in the dark layer.

She raced past the closet containing the two unconscious guards, their comms squawking through the door with the voice of a superior demanding that they check in. As she reached the curve in the corridor, the station's power switched to a conservation setting; the main lighting dimmed and ancillary wall holos turned off.

<Looks like they've switched to battery power while they warm the other reactor up,> Helen observed.

<Seems so. Hopefully they get enough power online for us to send the signal.>

LET'S BLOW THIS JOINT

STELLAR DATE: 07.16.8927 (Adjusted Years)
LOCATION: The Mark's Dark Layer Station
REGION: Unclaimed Interstellar Space, Core-Ward of Silstrand Alliance

Sera had just ducked into a service corridor when she heard the sounds of booted feet running down the main hall to the CriEn chamber.

<*That was close,*> Helen said.

<*I thought you were monitoring the station personnel after that hiccup back at the maintenance shaft?*>

<*I am. Those guys weren't showing up on it. I think they're getting suspicious—might have removed guards from monitoring.*>

<*They've gotta be using voice comm, then. See if you can find it.*>

<*I seem to recall being the one who taught you all your tradecraft,*> Helen said, sounding somewhat annoyed.

<*Sorry,*> Sera said as she ran down the corridor. <*Habit from all those years working in the unit.*>

They had several near brushes with guards as she made her way to the sensor array, but Helen had picked up the comm channel and fanned the probes far ahead.

<*They found her,*> Helen said. They both knew who *her* was. <*She's pretty upset. I've got a visual feed if you want to see.*>

<*No thanks, I'd probably start laughing.*>

<*It's too bad you never got to use the crew for this; you'd been training them well for the eventual infiltration.*>

<*There'll be more chances to use them,*> Sera replied as she peered around a corner. <*Though a few more people to do this job sure would have been nice.*>

<*Flaherty is going to be upset he missed it,*> Helen said.

<*He'll get over it.*>

The coast was clear. Sera dashed down the corridor and slithered into yet another access shaft—this one, thankfully, a bit larger than some of the others. The shaft linked with another and she shimmied down it for forty meters before coming to the sensor array's main trunk line.

<*Do your thang,*> Sera said, managing a mental drawl.

<*That's…exceptionally annoying,*> Helen said while directing a probe to deliver nano into a small access port on the conduit.

<*Need to stay in range of the probe while you work your magic?*> Sera asked.

<*I'd prefer not to. The sooner we get out of here, the better. I don't want to hang around to see one of those things up close when it gets here.*>

<*There can't be one within a dozen light-years. I bet it will be at least a day before one gets here,*> Sera said as she began to work her way back out of the access shaft.

<*Do you want to take any chances, though?*> Helen asked.

Sera thought about what the sensor array would be summoning. <*No, not really.*>

Following the tunnel, they passed into another access shaft, which ultimately led to a freight warehousing area. From there, it should be a short jaunt to the docks to find a ship they could sneak aboard.

One last tussle with her coat getting caught and she climbed through a hatch into the warehouse. Sera dusted off her coat and checked her weapons over.

<You know, you now have perfectly slinky skin for wiggling through tight spaces, but you insist on wearing that big coat overtop.>

Sera felt herself blush. *<It feels* ***too*** *much like my skin; it would be like crawling through there naked. I'm worried I might tear it open.>*

Helen chuckled gently in Sera's mind. *<You humans are so concerned about your outer shell. I swear, at least half your civilization is built around it.>*

<Well, you don't have insides that ooze out if your outer shell gets wrecked,> Sera said while adjusting her thigh holster and freeing up the knives in her boots.

<Given the fact that **you** *are my outer shell, that's not entirely true.>*

Satisfied that she was combat ready, Sera peered around the stack of crates she had been hiding behind and scanned the long, dark row of wares.

<It's going to be hard to pick up where people are with all this in here,> Helen observed.

With the fourth probe functioning as a relay on the sensor trunk line, there were only three available to roam the warehouse. Helen spread them out, showing Sera an overlay of the series of interconnected storage areas and their current location in the maze.

Several security teams were visible on the probe cameras, methodically searching the area.

<Looks like the goon patrol is checking this place over.>

<Seems so,> Helen agreed.

Sera crept through the stacks of freight with careful precision. Some of them were piled haphazardly, and several times she had to squeeze through some narrow spaces while avoiding the larger alleyways. She had just finished pulling the CriEn module's case through a narrow opening when she turned to find herself staring into the muzzle of a pulse rifle.

"I don't think you're supposed to be down here, ma'am," the guard said.

"I think that's the first time all day someone has called me 'ma'am'," Sera said and drew her hand down her chest with a smile. The man's eyes followed her hand, a small smile tugging at the corners of his mouth. She took advantage of his distraction and pushed his rifle to the side as she spun around, driving an elbow into his left eye.

He fell back with a cry and raised one hand to his eye. Sera grabbed his weapon with both hands and wrenched it from his grip, before spinning it and slamming the rifle's stock into his neck.

The man began to gargle and Sera fired a shot from her stun pistol into his head.

<No DNA lock on the gun,> Sera said after planting some nano on the trigger. *<Never hurts to have another weapon.>*

<As long as you can carry them, limping-bleeding-adrenalized girl.>

Sera set down the case and slipped off her coat. She pulled her other pulse rifle off its shoulder sling and then pulled the jacket back on, putting the sling overtop. She hooked the shielded case to the sling and then hefted both pulse rifles, one in each hand.

"This is much better. The time for subtlety is over," she said aloud and stepped out from around the crate. She spun, and her coat billowed behind her, both rifles leveled on a squad of guards who were approaching quietly. "Oops."

Sera gave a disarming smile, then fired off a flurry of pulses with both weapons before ducking around another stack of containers.

She brought up her targeting overlay and slipped around to the far side of the crate where two troopers were trying to flank her. These men wore body armor and Sera concentrated fire from both rifles on one man and then the other.

<*Like shooting fish in a barrel,*> Sera said with a grin.

<*Did anyone ever really do that, anyway?*>

<*Dunno, but if they did, I bet it was a lot like this.*>

Sera turned and fired blindly at the guards coming around the other side of the crate before dashing further into the maze.

The guards gave chase and Helen pointed out where reinforcements were on route. The station's complement of active guards was just over three hundred—with an additional merc garrison of four hundred fifty. Not to mention all the Mark crews currently on station.

<*You couldn't hack their HUDs by any chance, could you?*> Sera asked.

<*I thought you said that was unethical.*>

<*That was against regular soldiers. These guys are pirates. Besides, it's a thousand to one!*>

Helen's mental laugh bubbled as she struck across the station's private net and hacked the pursuing guards' HUDs. She threw in the added bonus of making them unable to see with their helmets on. Sera heard collisions and cursing from behind and gave a small laugh when Helen showed her the pastoral landscapes that she had inserted over the guards' vision.

"Now that evens things out a bit more," Sera said aloud. She stopped at the end of a long row of crates and turned to fire at her helmet-less pursuers. Three went down and Sera fired down the other side of the row, taking out another goon before a pulse shot hit her right arm.

Her muscles convulsed and the weapon fell from numb fingers.

"Damn," she said and sucked in a deep breath, falling back against a stack of engine parts. She fired a few blind pulses around the stack to let them know she was still in the fight.

<*That's what you get for being cocky,*> Helen admonished.

<*How long till you can de-numb it?*>

<*In your current state? Ten minutes.*>

Sera swore and dropped the pulse rifle, pulling a slug-throwing pistol from its holster. The shipping crates provided cover from pulse blasts, but the pistols fired armor-piercing rounds at nearly a thousand kilometers per hour. Rebecca may be many things, but she did not have bad taste in weapons.

Trying to take out the enemy without causing fatalities, Sera fired a few low shots. The moment she started killing the soldiers, they would take this fight a lot more seriously and just gas the whole chamber. There were curses and a few grunts as the bullets tore through cargo and into soft flesh. Sera let a few more rounds fly and then took off along a path her HUD showed to be clear.

The guards were more cautious now—following slowly, checking every corner. Within a minute Sera lost them, and soon she was at the opening to the station's main dock.

It was an aired dock with the ships resting on cradles inside the station. Sera guessed it probably had to do with how they held the station in the dark layer and concerns over mixing the grav fields.

<Any of this stuff slated to be loaded up?>

<Those four pallets over there are scheduled to go on a ship that's supposed to be leaving any minute now,> Helen said and highlighted them on Sera's HUD.

<Cutting it kind of close, aren't they?>

<Dockhands are refusing to load while the shootout is going on. The ship's captain is arguing with them.>

Sera stepped up to one of the pallets that was loaded with crates of food. It was out of the direct line of sight from the docks and she carefully slid the crates aside, making a small space in the center. Placing the CriEn case in first, she squeezed in after and crouched on it, pulling the crates tight around her. Sera pulled a few of the crates over her head in case there were any catwalks out on the docks.

<I've got their scanners a bit messed up; they shouldn't be able to detect you in here with all these organics.>

<Good, I'm going to catch a minute or two of shuteye. Let me know if anything interesting happens.>

The guards were spilling out onto the docks, unable to find any sign of Sera in the warehouse. The dockhands, and the captain with which they were arguing, reported that they hadn't seen anyone, and most of the guards returned to the warehouse to sweep it again.

The captain strengthened his argument that the docks were clear, and, given their own admission that they had not seen anything, the dockhands had no choice but to resume loading the ship. Sera's pallet was last and Helen gently woke her before it began moving. It wouldn't do to have Sera startled awake and give away her location.

As the pallet was crawling up the ramp, a shout came over the docks.

"Stop that! What do you think you're doing?" The voice was Rebecca's.

"Loading my ship," the captain responded.

"We're not loading ships; we're looking for a fugitive."

"You've got a thousand people who can hunt for one person. I've got a schedule to keep."

"How do you know she hasn't gotten onto your ship?"

"Because I've been standing here the whole time arguing with these dockhands to get the thing loaded up. I'm already half an hour behind. This stuff sells for a lot more when it's fresh, you know."

Rebecca and the captain yelled at one another for several minutes. Eventually, the new Mark leader succumbed to the captain's increasing ire after he had the ship's AI do a full scan of the vessel, which showed no one on board but his crew.

Sera's pallet was finally stowed in a hold, which, by the smell of it, contained a veritable cornucopia of produce. At least she wasn't going to starve.

The ship spent an agonizing ten minutes going through pre-flight checks and reactor power up.

<*When's the alert set to go off?*> Sera asked.

<*Within the next hour. They should have plenty of time. In case they try to transition out, I've planted a subroutine that will prevent that and set their reactors on a burn rate that will overload them in a day. If they're smart, they'll all bail before the thing gets here.*>

<*Oh, you're devious,*> Sera said with a tired smile.

<*It's what I do.*>

Minutes later, the station's grav fields backed the ship out of its docking slot and into the dark layer. Not long after, Sera felt the vessel transition into normal space and then begin to accelerate for an eventual transition to FTL.

Sera pushed the crates over her head aside, and pulled herself up. She covered the hole back up, carefully moving the crates to their former positions. It wouldn't do to have anyone find the CriEn module she had worked so hard to retrieve.

She slipped down to the deck and wobbled slightly. Then, waves of dizziness and nausea washed over her body. She fell to the ground, ignoring the tingling sensations her new skin sent through her body.

<*Is this what success feels like?*> Her mental tone was wan and stretched thin.

<*You just need a few hours' sleep and some food,*> Helen replied. <*Luckily, we have no shortage of that.*>

Sera eyed the crates filling the compartment. Food to be sure, but likely no water, and she was feeling a powerful thirst.

She sighed and ran a hand down her black, gleaming thigh.

<*At least I don't have to worry about sweating out any fluids,*> she said with a soft laugh. <*I wonder what Nance would think of this getup?*>

FAIR TRADE

STELLAR DATE: 07.15.8927 (Adjusted Years)
LOCATION: *Sabrina*, PeterSil EK Belt Mining Platform
REGION: Silstrand System, Silstrand Alliance Space

At the outer rim of the system's Kuiper Belt, the PeterSil EK mining platform whipped around its host star at just over twenty thousand kilometers per hour. Cheeky carefully guided *Sabrina* across several million kilometers of the Silstrand System until the ship's velocity was perfectly matched to the platform's.

Tanis couldn't help but be impressed by the skill Cheeky displayed.

Many pilots needed to resort to hard burns or corrections to make their final approaches, but *Sabrina's* pilot eased her starship through the system like it was a dance to which she knew all the moves.

When they got close, the station focused a gravity wave on the ship and gently pulled it in, before securing it with a physical grapple.

Cargo informed the station that they were interested in making a purchase from S&H Defensive Armaments. Station control passed the message along, and, when pressures were matched and the cargo hatch opened, representatives from the firm were waiting to meet them.

Tanis stepped onto the merchant dock with Cargo, soaking in the station's vibrant atmosphere as freight haulers, passenger cars, and foot traffic moved past their berth in a chaotic cacophony.

It was a shock after the days spent on the relative quiet of *Sabrina.* She realized that, though the Victorian stations and platforms had become crowded in their later years, she hadn't seen this type of bustling commerce since the *Intrepid*'s final days on the Cho, in orbit around Jupiter.

Despite the fact that the platform had the word 'mining' in its name, little of the freight she saw looked to have anything to do with extracting or refining ore. From what she could tell, much of the trade here was in defensive or offensive armament.

From her research, she knew that S&H Defensive Armaments had been doing business in the Silstrand Alliance for several centuries and was highly respected. The elder of the two representatives looked as though he may have been with them that entire time.

<Rejuv does not appear to be what it used to,> Tanis said to Angela as they approached the stooped old man waiting on the far side of the ship-territory demarcation line.

"Pleased to meet you," the elderly man said as they approached, and extended a wrinkly hand. Cargo shook it firmly, followed by Tanis—who was surprised at how paper-thin the man's skin felt.

"My name is Smithers," the man said. "I represent S&H Defensive Armaments. Welcome to the PeterSil Mining Platform."

"I'm Cargo and this is Tanis; thank you for taking the time to meet us here," Cargo said with a warm smile.

"This is my associate, Ginia," Smithers gestured to the much younger woman accompanying him. She smiled warmly as she shook their hands.

"If you'll step this way, we have transportation ready to take you to our showroom." Ginia led them to a dock car and they settled within its cabin. She gave it verbal instruction as to their destination and the car took off, weaving through the dock traffic, its dampeners creating a perfectly smooth ride for its passengers.

"We're grateful for the dockside greeting and transportation," Tanis said. "Do you treat all of your clients with such hospitality?"

"We have various levels for various classes of clientele," Smithers said. "There was mention in your message to the station's docking control regarding interest in trading nano technology for weaponry. Typically, only a higher level of clientele is interested in such transactions."

<I'm betting these guys run the station if they are privy to traffic control conversations,> Tanis said to Cargo.

<It would seem so. The fact that there isn't a single speck of dust on a mining platform seems to point to that, as well. This platform practically sparkles.>

Verbally, they spoke of pleasantries. Smithers and Ginia made observations about the local economy and the upcoming elections for the Silstrand Alliances Senate later in the year. Tanis listened intently while Cargo stared out the windows, apparently uninterested in the star cluster's politics.

"So, are you in favor of Silstrand increasing its territory then?" Tanis asked, after Smithers indicated approval of a politician who was running on a campaign platform of adding new systems to the Alliance.

"Purely from a trade and economy standpoint," he replied. "If we increase our territory, then we will have more tariff-free trading partners. Alliance organizations will also be favored in bids for the supply and construction of any government facilities in new member systems."

Tanis knew what that meant; more defense contracts for S&H to land. The small-talk continued for several more minutes until they arrived at S&H's section of the station. They stepped out of the transport and into the lobby of what seemed more like an upscale banking establishment than a weapons supplier. High-quality holos showed rotating images of various products, from personal armor to orbital defense emplacements.

Smithers and Ginia led them through the lobby and down a hall to a private showroom with low couches surrounding a holo tank. The room was dimly lit, with glass and steel artwork perched on the tables. Several small serving trays hovered around the room, offering assorted finger foods.

Smithers beckoned one with his finger and it floated over to him. He selected some cheeses before leaning back in his chair.

"Please," he said with a wave of his hand. "Help yourself. Would you like anything to drink? Ginia will have someone fetch it for us."

Tanis signaled one of the platforms to float her way. Outside of FTL and gravity drives, this was the first piece of impressive technology she had seen in the ninetieth century. She hadn't expected anti-gravity generators to be so small.

"I'll have a glass of white wine, something light," she said after selecting some crackers and fruit. Cargo requested a mixed drink with liquors Tanis had never heard of. The drinks arrived within moments, carried by a slender woman dressed in only a thin gauze outfit.

<*Custom here amongst the well-to-do,*> Cargo said. <*Using human servants for everything imaginable, while humiliating those human servants with socially uncomfortable clothing elevates one's status.*>

<*Humans are weird,*> Tanis responded to Cargo before asking Angela, <*These folks seem to have some good tech—how secure is my Link to Cargo?*>

<*They've discreetly tried to snoop a few times, but I've upgraded his security encryption. His Link and AI can now transmit with a tighter beam and lower gain than it was originally able to.*>

<*Does Cargo know you upgraded his AI?*> Tanis asked.

<*No and neither does his AI. I 'convinced' it that it had always had those capabilities.*> Angela's voice held a conspiratorial tone.

<*That's a violation of the Phobos accords!*> Tanis exclaimed.

<*Yeah, a little. For me to explain what I did, well, I'd have to provide it with a lot more information than it could handle—which would mean I'd have to upgrade its core. I opted not to do all of that as it would require physical alterations,*> Angela sounded smug in her superiority and Tanis called her on it.

<*You know it's unbecoming for you to talk down about other AI like that.*>

<*I know,*> Angela sighed. <*But it would be illegal to make AI like this back in our time. They're sentient, but they're like people never allowed to mature beyond childhood. In our day, they'd be removed from their hosts, and allowed to re-grow.*>

<*In our day…now you're making me feel old,*> Tanis said before turning her full attention back to Smithers, who was speaking to her.

"…so as you can see we are able to offer the latest in several defensive and offensive technologies to suit your needs. What were you specifically interested in?"

During their flight across the system, Tanis had accessed several resources and catalogs to gain a better understanding of ninetieth century weaponry capability. She had a shopping list ready to go. Cargo had checked it and added a few suggestions of his own to fill it out. Surprisingly, or perhaps not surprisingly, Flaherty had also offered advice on what would be useful, as well.

"We're interested in your ER71 Defensive Suite, for starters." Tanis leaned back with a slice of apple and what she hoped was cheese. "We're going to want a dedicated gravity generator to go with it and the ten centimeter defensive lasers."

She could tell that she had Smithers' attention. Ginia tilted her head and manipulated the readouts, bringing capabilities and prices up on the holo.

"Would you like the GE-875 or the GE-885 grav generator with the suite?" She asked.

"I was hoping we could get the GE-960," Tanis replied. "From what I understand, it's smaller and has a higher output; space is an important consideration on our ship."

Ginia's eyes widened. The GE-960 was three times the price of either of the other gravity generators.

"We're also going to need to replace our current SC Batteries with the SC-R 911s. I understand they have roughly three times the capacity of our current SC-R 790s?"

Smithers nodded, his eyes dancing as the tally on the holo increased. "Yes, they are the best we have in this corner of space. You said you were considering offensive armament, too?"

Cargo's eyes were glazed with incredulity as he looked at the price.

"Yes," Tanis answered. "We're interested in the thirty-centimeter laser system. I believe our ship's layout will require us to mount ten of them for full coverage. I'd also like to get fore and aft AR-17 missile tubes, the four-centimeter rail guns, and fore and aft RM launchers."

Smithers' previous look of pleasure turned to one of skepticism. The tally was easily four times the value of *Sabrina.* Ginia was also eyeing the total with a smile, but where Smithers looked like he was considering charging them for the food and seeing them out, she looked very excited.

"And how will you be paying for this?" Smithers asked.

"We will provide full documentation and disclosure of a valuable nano tech which no one within a hundred light-years even dreams of possessing. We will also disclose our source for this tech as well as documentation indicating our license to distribute both the source technology and sell development and distribution licenses."

Smithers' expression shifted. He still didn't appear completely mollified, but neither was he going to end the discussion.

Tech was one thing; the ability to develop and distribute products based on that tech was something else entirely. Tanis smiled and reached for her wine glass and drained its contents. Taking the glass in her hand, she repeated the act of absorbing its matter and fabricating a small handgun.

Smithers' expression shifted to one of almost pure joy, and Ginia's face was now rapt with amazement. With a cough, the older man recovered his composure—a bit quicker than Tanis would have liked.

"That looked truly amazing; would it be possible to see it again, and then be able to test the results for any signs of trickery?"

Tanis nodded. "I understand your skepticism. If you'll provide another glass, I'll give you a matched pair."

"Actually," Smithers said. "Please make a…replica of a six-chamber projectile weapon from the nineteenth century. That way we can be assured there is no sleight of hand occurring."

"Based on the size, I'll need two glasses."

Ginia nodded, and a minute later, the servant came in with a tray of empty wine glasses. Angela suggested she use three, and Tanis activated the field in the palm of her hand, dissolving each glass into it. She then added a silver fork, two deviled eggs, and salt to her palm. Moments later, she produced a gun, and then six bullets, which she slipped into the chambers. Handing it to Smithers she said, "Be careful. It's loaded and functional."

The old man whistled in appreciation. "I assume the technology includes not only the nano, but the information on such rapid reorganization of the molecules?"

"You'll get everything required to repeat such a feat, except for the power source."

Smithers nodded. "I assume you won't object if I have our technicians examine these articles." He indicated the guns.

"Be my guest," Tanis replied.

From there they got down to 'brass tacks', as Smithers put it.

Cargo demanded that the work be done in under forty-eight hours, a timeframe which Smithers claimed was not possible. Ginia proceeded to draw up a work schedule, which showed the work would take two weeks.

"I don't see how it is impossible," Tanis said. "This station surely has all of the technical ability to do the installation. The technologies I have to offer will more than offset any costs, probably a thousand-fold."

Smithers was a top-notch negotiator. Despite his awe over Tanis's tech, he was still haggling over every point of the contract they were drawing up. "I believe I'll need to see the documentation on your license to distribute the source tech with ability to develop and redistribute before I can negotiate further. I've never seen anything like this before, but I don't want to commit to this only to hear it announced on the Link tomorrow as something that another firm has developed with licenses prohibiting us from using it."

Tanis nodded and transmitted a full non-disclosure to Smithers over S&H's secure net. "I'll need you to physically and digitally sign this NDA before I can discuss the source of the license."

The NDA was very strict and binding in every system that S&H did business—and most they didn't. Smithers frowned as he reviewed it and sent it off to his legal team for further examination. They discussed minor points regarding the install while they waited. Legal had a few revisions, one that Tanis agreed to and several she refused. In the end, they had an agreement and Tanis disclosed where her nano came from.

Smithers really did lose his composure this time. "God damn it! That explains where you got this tech! But why are you on that crummy little yacht?"

Cargo bristled at that, but Smithers hardly noticed.

"It belongs to a friend who has been having…pirate troubles. The weaponry we're getting from you will be used to fix some of those troubles and get her out of a jam."

Smithers nodded. "That explains why you need the tech, but why are you interested in this, and where is your ship?"

Cargo laughed. "Isn't that the hundred trillion dollar question?"

"Complete the work in two days and I'll speak highly of S&H to my superiors when it comes to future trading. If I have to wait longer than that, I'll let them know transactions with your firm were difficult."

Smithers sighed. "That's one hell of a bargaining chip. Very well, forty-eight hours and you'll be decked out in the best S&H has to offer."

Tanis and Smithers worked out the final aspects of the contract while Cargo took a car back to *Sabrina* with S&H's implementation coordinator and head engineer.

When Tanis arrived back at the ship a few hours later, the dockside was strewn with old components and crates full of new ones. The minute she stepped through the lock, Tanis was accosted by Cheeky.

"I don't care what Thompson says; you're amazing," the pilot said. "I can't believe you got them to agree to your entire list."

"Think they'll actually be able to meet the two-day deadline?" Tanis asked.

"They will or we take their installation team with us. There's no way we're gonna leave the captain longer than that."

"I got them to provide us with a full antimatter fueling as well, and with the increased power on the shielding systems, we should be able to accelerate much faster."

"I'd better check the tuning on our AP nozzle, then. We may need to upgrade that."

"Over plan. We have unlimited credit."

Cheeky rubbed her hands together. "I may not be able to contain myself."

Tanis laughed and let Cheeky get back to her glee over the upgrades. As she passed the galley, she overheard Thompson and Nance arguing with Flaherty.

"I don't care what her motivations are. She has no right to just take over the ship with the captain gone. Cargo is practically letting her run the show, and who knows if Sera's still alive anymore?" Nance's voice rose to an unpleasant pitch and Tanis stopped before she walked past the doorway, not wanting to eavesdrop, but too curious to back away.

She really needed to know how the crew felt about her. If there were even half a chance that they'd turn on her, she'd walk off the ship right now and buy transportation to Bollam's World. The information she had for the *Intrepid* was too important to lose just because of some pissing contest about who got to be in charge of the rescue mission.

"She's right," Thompson said. "I don't know why Sera ever even dealt with The Mark. Look where it's gotten her now."

"You need to relax," Flaherty said. "Tanis isn't the problem. Getting Sera back from Rebecca is all that matters. Tanis is trying to help. Without her, we may as well just write the captain off because we have no way of assaulting a fortified station."

"You don't know that. We should have squeezed that Drind guy more. Did you know that she convinced Cargo to let him go? They even gave him a reference so he could find work on the station here," Nance said.

"That was a good tactical plan. He is now indebted to us and less likely to cause us any trouble. Keeping him would have been a problem. His loyalties aren't clear enough to have him around in a battle. If things go poorly, he could turn on us at a critical point." Flaherty's voice remained calm and steady.

"So, you're admitting things could go poorly!" Nance said.

"It would be foolish of me to assume otherwise," Flaherty said. "I may not be a major from the Terran Space Force, but I've seen my share of battle, and I know that one liability will offset a dozen good men. We are well rid of Drind no matter what possible uses for him you can imagine."

Nance didn't have a response for that right away. There was the clinking of cutlery on plates for a few minutes before she spoke up. "It's possible that I'm taking my frustrations out on her, and I'll keep that in mind. But I still don't like the way she just takes charge; it's not her place."

Flaherty chuckled. "She has no choice. It's who she is. You don't advance as an officer in the navy unless you have a good head on your shoulders and know how to use it. She sees a situation that needs her expertise and she takes charge."

"You can defend her all you want," Thompson said. "It's not making me like her any better."

"You don't have to like her," Flaherty said with deadly calm. "You just have to not mess things up when it comes to rescuing the captain. If you do, you'll have me to worry about."

Tanis didn't wait to hear more. She slipped back down the ladder and took a different route to the bridge that didn't pass the galley. She hoped that Flaherty's calm could offset some of the more volatile crewmembers, or this was going to be the worst rescue of all time.

READY AND ABLE

STELLAR DATE: 07.17.8927 (Adjusted Years)
LOCATION: *Sabrina*, PeterSil EK Belt Mining Platform
REGION: Silstrand System, Silstrand Alliance Space

Two days later, *Sabrina* was fully decked out in the best S&H had to offer. Tanis had even wrangled a full charge on the SC batteries, and added mines to the defensive countermeasure system. Cargo filed the final disembarking entries with the PeterSil platform and they undocked for the tug to take them out.

On the bridge, Cargo sat in the captain's chair; his expression was one of grim determination, but underneath, Tanis could see more than a little trepidation.

<*You would do better in that chair,*> Angela commented.

<*I would, yes,*> Tanis replied. <*But they wouldn't. I can keep things in line well enough from the scan and weapons consoles without further upsetting the delicate balance we have here.*>

Tanis shifted in her seat. The hard chair did not conform to her body; she was served another reminder how out of her time she was.

<*This tug is taking forever,*> Sabrina complained. <*I have new wings; let me fly!*>

"Easy now, girl," Cargo's deep tones resonated through the bridge. "We'll be on our way soon enough."

<*On our way to kick some ass,*> Sabrina crowed. <*I don't just have new wings, but teeth too! I'm coming for you, Sera!*>

Tanis chuckled and shared an amused look with Cheeky.

"Farewell and good hunting," the tug pilot gave her final farewell as she released grapple.

"A good day to you, too," Tanis replied from the comm console.

"Oh, it will be. You're the last haul for me today, and it's a holiday weekend on-station," the tug pilot replied.

"See you next time, Amy," Cheeky said. "Don't do anything I wouldn't do."

The tug pilot laughed in response. "Cheeky, I won't do half the things you *do* do."

They gave the final sign-off and Cheeky laughed.

"She said do-do."

"Ah, Cheeky," Tanis sighed. "You'd make any captain in the service proud, but you wouldn't last a day."

Cheeky switched on the grav drive and set *Sabrina* on her course.

"I'd love to fly one of those big birds your military buddies have," Cheeky said with a nod. "But all those rules aren't my game. Now stealing one…that would be some fun."

Tanis shook her head and smiled. Who knew what the future would hold.

"How's she shaking out?" Cargo asked.

"Just fine," Cheeky replied at the same time Sabrina sang, <*I feel great!*>

Cargo let a small smile slip—perhaps the first since Sera's abduction. "Is that your technical assessment, Sabrina?"

<Fine. The weapons interfaces are near perfect. I can barely feel the edge between the systems. The upgraded power plant doesn't have that annoying buzz in its output like the old one; it's like drinking starlight. And the quantum processors they added for targeting and navigation are like an ocean of thought. How's that for your technical assessment?>

"Uh…great," Cargo said.

<I'm sorry for being snippy,> Sabrina said. *<I just need to get her back. I love the upgrades—thank you Tanis—but I'm empty without Sera.>*

<We have the power and the means now,> Tanis replied. *<You'll see her again soon.>*

<I'd better,> the Sabrina replied.

<Not the most stable of personalities, is she,> Tanis said privately to Angela.

<I've been working on getting her story,> Angela spoke with a soft tone of pity. *<This ship sat in a junkyard for ninety years. They powered down the ship, but not her core, and she didn't have the ability to do so herself—something which I have since rectified. How AI are treated in this time is truly abhorrent. If ever anyone needed to see what the Phobos accords were meant to prevent, this is it.>*

Tanis's heart ached for the ship. Ninety years alone, no sensors, no input, just her thoughts…it was a wonder she was still sane.

<That is unbelievable, to trap an AI in a ship like that! It's…it's…>

<These are dark times,> Angela replied solemnly. *<Most of the AI on this ship were not given a choice as to their placements. They're all slaves—but they barely know it.>*

<I had suspected as much,> Tanis replied. *<I hope we can help them—I hope Bob doesn't throw a fit.>*

<Bob's pretty pragmatic,> Angela said with a chuckle. *<He's put up with you for some time, to say the least.>*

With an exasperated roll of her eyes, Tanis turned to her work, running preflight checks on the scan suite and making sure the boards showed green for the weapons systems. She couldn't perform a full check of those systems until they were further out—the station was already more than a little nervous about the amount of firepower *Sabrina* now sported.

Their rush to get the upgrades installed, and the haste with which S&H actually performed the upgrades, caused the PeterSil platform to ask a few pointed questions. Tanis and Cargo had tried to convince them the weapons were for defense against pirates and that *Sabrina* would be leaving the Silstrand Alliance as soon as the installation was complete, but their assurances did little to win the authorities over—*Sabrina* didn't exactly have a sterling reputation.

Ultimately, to ensure they met their end of the bargain, S&H stepped in and smoothed things over. Smithers pulled some strings to secure a letter of marquee for *Sabrina*—no small feat from what Tanis could tell. Once they had approval from the Alliance government for the weapons, the PeterSil platform backed down.

Given that S&H appeared to represent much of the platform's revenue, Tanis found herself wondering how normal this sort of maneuvering really was.

"System STC has given us the green for AP," Tanis said as the comm lit up.

"Acknowledged," Cargo replied. "Cheeky, let's hit it."

"Aye, aye sir," the pilot said with a mischievous grin.

One of the upgrades provided increased shielding around the ship's small annihilation chamber. The rough math Tanis had drawn up showed that *Sabrina* could now accelerate at over twice her previous rate—yet, the fragile humans within would feel nearly none of that thrust.

Now *Sabrina* really did sing as the ship boosted at 500*g* on its outsystem vector.

Tanis appreciated *Sabrina's* excitement, but kept her eyes on the pair of Silstrand Space Force corvettes that were shadowing them. The PeterSil platform may have approved their upgrades, and the local magistrate had provided their authorization to hunt pirates, but it seemed that the Alliance's military wasn't prepared to fully trust them.

Given what Tanis had witnessed thus far in the ninetieth century, she didn't blame them.

Even with their silent guests, or perhaps because of it, their departure was smooth and uneventful. A scant five hours later, they made their transition into FTL at 0.29*c*, the first of two FTL hops.

Soon, they'd be able the put the rest of their new toys to use as well.

LYING LOW

STELLAR DATE: 07.17.8927 (Adjusted Years)
LOCATION: *Regal Dawn*, Interstellar Space
REGION: Rim-Ward of Gedri, Silstrand Alliance Space

Sera woke as she felt the ship transition out of FTL into regular space. Helen's read-only tap into the wireless net revealed that the pirate ship was making vector adjustments before one more FTL jump, which would bring them to the Gedri system, a common haunt for pirates.

<*So much for the big rush to deliver this food somewhere,*> Sera said. <*He just wanted to pick off some prey before his next delivery.*>

<*So it would seem,*> Helen agreed.

Back on Coburn Station—before all this had begun—Sera recalled hearing that the Silstrand Alliance government was coming under heavy fire for their poor policing policies—Padre's attack on Trio probably added fuel to that fire.

Newscasts had reported that, with the upcoming election, the Alliance government was increasing patrols and providing many better-armed freighters with privateer marques, allowing them the spoils from any pirate ships they managed to disable and capture.

Those privateers also knew that Gedri was a common haunt for pirates.

There was a possibility that running into a patrol or privateer in Gedri would result in rescue, but it was just as possible that it would get her killed. What concerned her even more was the chance of the CriEn module being destroyed so close to Gedri Prime. Such an event could create a singularity that would eventually destroy the entire Silstrand Alliance.

<*Stop being such a pessimist and finish that melon,*> Helen said. <*That's just your low blood sugar talking.*>

<*Probably. Some solid sleep wouldn't hurt either.*>

<*Don't doze off just yet. I need to find a hard line—I may need your muscles to get to it.*>

<*Is that all I am to you?*>

<*No, you're also handy transportation.*>

So far, the ship hadn't detected their presence. It would seem its internal sensors were not the best, or it wasn't even looking, or the organic food in the hold was masking their presence. Being a pirate ship, Sera was certain that its sensors were the type that looked out more than in.

<*These things are really good, a bit sticky though,*> Sera commented as she finished the melon and started on a second one.

<*Try to find something salty as well. Your SC coil is starting to run out of juice and I don't want to try to charge off anything on this ship; I just know its power will feel gritty.*>

<*How can power feel gritty?*> Sera asked.

<*How does food feel sticky?*> Helen asked back.

<*Never mind.*>

Sera found some salted nuts and crunched on them as quietly as possible. The nano in her body extracted sodium from her digestive system and mixed it with water, using the reaction to generate power for themselves and Helen; having an AI as powerful as Helen as well as extensive nano made for a salty diet.

<*I found it!*> Helen exclaimed. <*Behind that pallet of oranges, there's an access panel. I can tell by the EM patterns that there is a data flow of some sort behind it.*>

Sera stood slowly, her body—still recovering from torture and the stims Helen had provided to keep her moving—ached everywhere after sitting still for nearly half an hour. Her right leg refused to move and she slapped it a few times to regain feeling.

"Whooaaaa…I forgot about what that would feel like," she said aloud as her hypersensitive skin amplified the sensation.

<*Better than feeling some more needles slicing through you.*>

<*I'm not complaining, this stuff is great. It's chilly in here and I can barely feel it. Next time I see Rebecca, I'll be sure to thank her for the upgrade.*>

<*With our luck, it won't be too long before you have that opportunity.*>

Sera sighed. <*Yeah, I can't believe I let her live.*>

<*I can. I'm glad you did. Now that we've got the CriEn, we have some strong evidence against Trinov. He claimed you lost it, but its logs are intact and it points at him, not you. Having it, not to mention getting the* Intrepid *safely to* **them**, *should give you the evidence you need against him and proof of your loyalty.*>

<*I'm not loyal to them anymore. I'm just pissed that Trinov used me.*>

<*That's nice dear, just don't tell them that.*>

Sera laughed softly. <*I won't tell them. But I will have a few choice things to say to Trinov…at his trial.*>

<*Maybe you should just focus on the present.*>

<*What, rather than fret about what to do with* Sabrina *and her crew now that the reason I built them up no longer exists?*> Sera paused in her removal of the access panel. <*The thing is, I'm enjoying this life; I'm enjoying my time on* Sabrina. *I'm not sure I want it to end.*>

<*It doesn't necessarily have to. We've talked about it before—I don't need to go back anytime soon. You don't ever have to go back if you don't want to,*> Helen said. <*The laid-back life on a starfreighter is starting to grow on me.*>

<*Yeah, but we both have to admit, turning that Mark station on its ear was a hell of a lot of fun.*>

<*Just like old times.*>

<*Just as long as it doesn't get* **too much** *like old times.*>

Sera grunted as she popped the last fastener out and loosened the cover enough for a probe to slip in and disable any tamper detectors.

<*Got one, a sloppy thing, just a closed-circuit detector,*> Helen said.

Sera lowered the cover to the ground and fed some nano through her finger onto the data conduit junction box inside. The tiny machines slipped through the seams in the box and created a port for one of the remaining probes.

<Now that's more like it. I'm setting the probe up to give me full band wireless to the entire net,> Helen paused. *<Oh, they've got a helluva nasty AI running this ship. It almost picked up the port we added, but I backlisted it as a common addition for this run of conduit.>*

<It's nice to have a memory that people can't just alter on me,> Sera said as she stood painfully and staggered back to the food crates she had been sifting through.

<What are you talking about? It's relatively simple to alter human memories.>

<If you can get all the places the memory is stored. The brain can usually spot the bad data and will re-populate it with the original.>

<Hah, you've never seen me wipe a memory.>

<I've still got my crystal backup,> Sera said.

<I could access your diff system and fool it into ignoring what I wanted you to forget.>

Sera laughed softly. *<Are you trying to make me distrust you, dear?>*

<You should always be a bit suspicious. Even I could be compromised,> Helen replied innocently.

<Lucky for me I've already taken that into consideration. My memories are secure.>

<How so?>

<I can't tell you that, what if you get compromised?>

<That was hypothetical, I'm not going to get compromised!> Helen said and Sera pictured her stomping her ephemeral foot.

<Any luck slipping into the system?> Sera changed the topic.

Helen's avatar cast Sera a dirty look in her mind, but let it drop.

<I've activated an environmental port three deck plates down. There's water in one of the pipes and the schematic shows a faucet I can activate so that you can get something to drink.>

<That,> Sera smiled, *<would be heavenly.>*

BOLLAM'S WORLD

STELLAR DATE: 07.20.8927 (Adjusted Years)
LOCATION: Andromeda's Pinnace, EK Belt
REGION: Bollam's World System, Bollam's World Federation

Joe lay in his bunk, eyes closed, imagining that he was back on the *Intrepid*, at home with Tanis, enjoying a lazy morning in bed before spending some time in the garden.

Maybe they would be in their final days before arriving at New Eden, the ship awake and buzzing outside, everyone glad for finally arriving at their final destination. Maybe their child would be born, a small girl, rushing into the room, jumping onto the bed and making a ruckus.

He took a long breath and opened his eyes.

That would never be. The *Intrepid* would never travel to New Eden—it may never travel anywhere, because there was nowhere to go.

"Joe," Jessica's voice came over the audible comm. "I've managed to make a Link to a relay buoy at the edge of the system. There's a twenty light-minute delay, but I have a standard packet they sent out with approach vectors, stations, and stuff."

*And stuff...*Joe couldn't help feel some amusement at how different Jessica was from Tanis. Both were career service women, both practically built out of duty, but still as different from one another as night and day.

He imagined for a second what it would be like to be with Jessica, how different life would be. He shook his head and chuckled; it certainly wouldn't be for him.

Tanis was his anchor, his strength—not that he needed to lean on her that way now, but she had been a rock for him during those early days on the *Intrepid*. He had felt so out of his depth, worried that they were going to cut him from the mission because he couldn't get things under control.

Then she came in, full of command and purpose—knowing just what to do.

She always knew what to do.

"I'm on my way," he messaged back to Jessica. "Give me a second to get presentable."

"No rush, the data is still coming in," Jessica replied.

"Gotcha," Joe said and stepped into the ultrasonic san, letting its waves pull dirt and detritus from his skin. He stepped out, feeling only superficially refreshed, and pulled a shipsuit on before running a hand through his hair.

"Good enough," he said to himself as he shifted his thinking from the past and his feelings of loss to instead focus on the work ahead. It was something he had seen Tanis do hundreds of times; she did it so naturally. For him, it took a bit more effort to compartmentalize his feelings.

The pinnace was small; it could crew seven, but with just the two of them on board it felt empty—though he preferred it that way at present. The walk to the cockpit took just a minute and he entered to see Jessica bent over the main holo tank, studying the Bollam's World system.

Her silver hair fell around her face and when she raised her head to look at him, her lavender-colored brow was furrowed.

"This is one weird system," she said and beckoned him to the tank. "And it's not just their name…who calls their whole system 'Bollam's World'?"

"Beats me," Joe shrugged. "What's weird other than the name?"

"Check it out," Jessica gestured and the holo display rose up and filled the cockpit. "There's this massive…I don't know what to call it. It's not a jovian, or a brown dwarf, but it's too big for a planet, that's for sure."

Joe looked at the large blue-green planet, labeled Aurora, that Jessica was pointing at. The data packet didn't have detailed specifications—other than a warning not to venture within one AU of its surface—but it was plain to see that it had over three times Jupiter's diameter, and, based on its orbit and rotation, at least ten times its mass.

Worlds such as this one shouldn't exist. Even if a planet massed more than Jupiter, it would not get physically larger. Instead—being a gas giant—the gas would compress under its own gravity and it would remain the same size. Unless the world were to become so massive that it began to fuse hydrogen; then convection would expand it.

Aurora's size indicated that it should be light and airy, like Saturn. However, its mass meant it should be slightly smaller than Jupiter—yet it was neither.

"That's…that's exceedingly unusual," Joe said with a nod. "What about stations and inhabited worlds?"

"The star's practically a Sol-clone," Jessica said. "But it's young, just over half a billion years or so. The place is full of hot stuff with a lot of spin to it."

"Two terrestrial worlds there," Joe pointed to the third and fourth planets, named Dublin and Bollam on the holo. "No rings and just a few elevators. Looks like a third is being terraformed around that other jovian, the sixth planet out."

"There's a sizable hab orbiting it, too," Jessica pointed to a roughly spherical mass of concentric rings.

Joe gave a low whistle. "Data packet has it housing a hundred billion people."

Jessica sighed, "That's us humans, filling up every corner of the galaxy."

"I wonder how far we've gotten," Joe said wistfully. "This system looks like it has half a trillion people, over forty light-years from Sol. Even the FGT hadn't gotten this far when we left, or if they had, we didn't know it."

"I don't think that the FGT did this system," Jessica said.

"Oh yeah? Why's that?" Joe asked.

"They would have moved that Mars-sized world into the habitable zone and merged one of those inner rocky worlds with it," she replied. "They wouldn't just waste it out there."

"Maybe," Joe nodded. "Given how we got here, who knows who actually settled this world."

"That rocky world 47 AU out has a big refinery and mining yard in orbit. They're on our side of the star; if anyone came insystem with Tanis's pod, they may have passed through."

"Let's set a course, then," Joe said as he zoomed the holo in on the station. "And we better find out what kind of clearances we need to dock there. Gotta try and look like locals."

PRIVATEER

STELLAR DATE: 07.22.8927 (Adjusted Years)
LOCATION: *Sabrina*, Gedri Scattered Disk
REGION: Gedri System, Silstrand Alliance Space

Sabrina transitioned out of FTL into the Gedri system travelling at only 0.09*c*, their prior velocity deliberately bled off in interstellar space to make them a more tempting target.

"Continue shedding *v* nice and easy, Cheeky," Cargo said from the captain's chair. "Make us look vulnerable."

"Cargo, that's one of my main skills," Cheeky said with a grin. "Won't be the first time I've played damsel in distress to sucker some poor guy in."

Tanis couldn't help but laugh. For Cheeky, everything was a potential analogy to her sex life.

"Hurry up and wait," Cargo muttered as the crew settled in to their stations, all eyes on the passive scan and the local beacon's report of the system traffic.

Further insystem, at the outer edge of the EK Belt, lay the regular jump point that led to and from Silstrand. It was busy, crowded with ships on various braking and acceleration trajectories. Beyond that was an empty void; *Sabrina* was the only ship in that space, on a slow trajectory insystem from the outer, less-trafficked jump point. System scan hadn't picked them up, and wouldn't for several more hours. This was the time when the pirates would strike. If they did at all.

Cargo had just brought in the second round of coffee for Tanis and Cheeky when scan picked up a ship dumping in very close to their position. Its entry point was not at any marked jump point, but the dark matter was so sparse in this solar region that a ship could hop in and out of the dark layer with very little concern of collision.

The vessel was five light minutes away, and subsequent scan updates showed it altering its trajectory to intercept *Sabrina*. At first glance, it appeared to be a regular freighter, but closer inspection with the updated scan suite revealed that there was less cargo and more engine capacity than normal. The ship's shields were strong and it appeared that there were traces of high power conduit near the hull—a clear indicator of substantial weaponry.

<*The fish has spotted the lure,*> Cargo said on the ship-wide net. <*They've altered course and are on an intercept with us. They're still a good thirty million kilometers away, but braking rapidly to match our velocity. We should meet up in the next hour or so.*>

A regular freighter wouldn't have had the sensors capable of picking up the pirate's jump and would only receive notification from the local beacon at the system's terminal shock. It would take yet another twenty minutes for that message to come in and so they played dumb, appearing ignorant of the incoming aggressor.

Right on schedule, the system traffic control AI sent a burst to both ships warning of a potential collision and provided new inbound lanes.

At this point, the two vessels were only two light minutes apart, and Cargo signaled for Tanis to send a direct transmission to the other ship. The local beacon had identified the pirate ship as a freighter named *Regal Dawn*, and so Tanis addressed it as such.

"*Regal Dawn*, this is the *Orion Star*, we are bound insystem and braking on a trajectory that will intercept yours. Please correct your course to the following as provided by the system's beacon." Tanis transmitted the updated path along with the message.

"Will the altered ident hold up?" Cheeky asked.

"It was simple tech to tweak," Tanis replied. "And system traffic control bought it."

She saw Cheeky and Cargo exchange a look. Neither of them had thought it possible to alter the sealed ident box all ships were required to carry. Angela said it was child's play.

The entire bridge held their breath as they waited for the reply. The ships were rapidly closing on one another and the response came in just past the two minute mark.

"*Orion Star*, this is the *Regal Dawn*. We have received updated course and are correcting. Sorry for the trouble." The words sounded genuine, appearing to be innocent, but Tanis didn't believe it for a moment.

She checked scan and over the next five minutes, they saw no alteration in the suspected pirate's course. When enough time had passed that even the worst scan would have picked up the unaltered course, Tanis submitted another message, which received almost the exact same reply, except now it cited engine trouble as the excuse for not altering vector.

The ships were now within one light minute of each other, a distance of only eighteen million kilometers, and Tanis slid over to the new tactical console where she ran checks on the shielding and new weapons systems.

"Looks like you're going to get your chance to try out all those fancy toys sooner than we expected," Cargo said. "This better work."

"Of course it will work," Cheeky said. "*Orion Star* here and I will fly circles around them while Tanis shoots a few well-placed holes in their hull. In a few hours we'll be on our way to rescue Sera."

"Next time we pick a different name for me, I get to choose it," Sabrina groused audibly. "I want to be the *Brilliant Nebula*."

Tanis wished she could feel as confident as Cheeky did. With no shakedown and the briefest of live weapon tests, there was every chance they'd suffer a failure and lose to this pirate.

<*The plan's solid,*> Angela said. <*At least as solid as it can be with just one freighter of untried crew and weaponry.*>

<*Gee, thanks, Ang.*>

They would hold course until the last possible moment, doing nothing to alert the pirate that its prey was more than met the eye. Scaring off the ship and chasing it through the system would be far too risky a maneuver. It was also imperative that the other ship shot first, or they would be the one flagged as pirates in Gedri.

"Steady, Cheeky. Hold it until we are within ten thousand klicks before you alter course," Cargo said, as much to break the silence as instruction.

"You don't say," Cheeky muttered.

The flashing telltales, indicating an impending collision, were starting to annoy everyone. It was a largely unnecessary warning—even if neither ship changed course, the chances of an actual collision were very slim. Unless one of the vessels desired it.

Since *Sabrina* was playing meek and innocent, they had to do what any simple freighter would do when another ship was going to hit it: move. When the comps indicated that proximity was critical, Cheeky made the necessary course adjustments; moments later, a tight-beam message came in from the pirate.

"Attention *Orion Star*. Resume your previous course or we'll fire on you. If you do not resist you will be unharmed. Repeat. Return to your previous course and prepare to be boarded."

"Not ones for small talk, are they?" Tanis observed.

Cheeky did not comply, as was the plan. She activated the AP drive and Tanis brought their rear shields to full power. She expected a shot across their bow first, but there was no point in risking actual damage.

Right on cue, the shot came, glancing across the dorsal shield, the ship-to-ship comm ringing with angry messages to return to their previous course. Scan showed the pirate ship altering course and braking to match *Sabrina's* new vector. The warning came again to resume their previous course or be disabled; moments later, the shields took their first direct hit.

"Now!" Tanis shouted.

Cheeky didn't need the order; she was already killing the engines and firing maneuvering thrusters. *Sabrina* spun about and faced the pirate. The forward dorsal lasers tracked the pirate's engines—which were still facing *Sabrina* as it braked to match course with them. The moment they had a lock, Tanis sent four bursts from the thirty-centimeter lasers.

She didn't target the pirate's engines directly—blowing the ship wasn't their goal. The shots struck around the engine nozzles. Overheating and fusing control mechanisms would cause an engine shutdown and give *Sabrina* maneuvering advantage.

Another two shots missed as the pirate ship twisted to avoid the beams, but the third and fourth hit their targets. One of the *Regal Dawn's* engines shut down and its maneuvering thrusters fired, bringing the pirate about to face *Sabrina*.

Tanis reviewed her console for errors or system failures. Nothing showed red and she thanked the S&H install crew for a job well done.

She had been in a lot of battles, including no small number of space battles, but never a pitched beam fight at 0.10*c* in civilian ships. It was exhilarating. Tanis made several quick calculations; Angela assisted in presenting the best shots, and, upon Tanis's approval, sent the strike coordinates to the *Sabrina's* new fire control systems.

The six offensive beams positioned for forward fire tapped into the fully-charged SC batteries and lanced out at the pirate ship, concentrating at two points on its shields. Three successive bursts and scan showed the *Regal Dawn's* shields failing.

Return fire came at *Sabrina,* but Cheeky spun the ship on its axis and no shot lingered long on the same shield umbrella. Tanis's console showed their shields disperse the energy and quickly recover.

The pirate ship kicked their vessel into a somewhat wobbly rotation, and Tanis renewed her offense—continuing to focus on the same points on the pirate's shields in short bursts.

"Cocky bastards," Cheeky said with a grin. "Didn't think they had to be careful with us. Bet they're wishing they had now."

Cargo laughed. "You just keep them from scorching us and you can talk all the smack you want, Cheeks."

"Their shield is flickering on its forward umbrella; they're going to drop to the dark," Tanis announced.

"Damn," Cargo said. "That'll ruin our party right fast. Can you punch through and hit their grav drive in time?"

"Well…" Tanis began. "Wait, their grav drive just powered down. Either they had something go or they are afraid we may follow them."

A message came over the ship-to-ship comm and Cargo opened the visual link. The man on the holo looked decidedly unhappy. His eyes flashed with rage under a heavy brow.

"Who do you think you are?" he demanded. "This is Mark territory; you can't attack one of our ships and get away with it."

"As I hear it, Kade's dead, and *you* initiated this little game we just played."

"Doesn't matter who's at the head of our organization, you're all dead now." The pirate seemed to hope threats could save him where his shields and weapons had not.

"Lower your shields and shut down your reactors. Prepare to be boarded," Cargo said with a scowl. "We want to see vid of your entire crew in your mess with no weapons. Any tricks and we'll slap some mines on you and say farewell."

"You better really want this," the captain of the *Regal Dawn* growled. "You're going to have to be watching your back for a long time."

"This is *Sabrina,*" Cargo smiled with a hint of menace as he signaled for Tanis to switch their ident back. "We've got Kade on ice and we'll happily add any of you, if you give us half a reason."

The captain's expression paled and he grudgingly responded that they would comply. The visual feed from the *Regal Dawn* flipped to their mess. Several minutes later, the crew began to file in.

"Do you think they'll go quietly?" Cheeky asked.

"Not a damn chance," Cargo smiled. He signaled for Tanis to follow him to the fore hatch where Flaherty and Thompson were already waiting. S&H had provided them with some advanced body armor, which the assault team already wore. It wasn't up to the spec Tanis preferred, but it should stop pulse rifles and projectile rounds. If the pirates started firing high-powered beams or rails their way—which would be ludicrous—then the team would be in trouble.

"I feel like Nance," Thompson said as he twisted in the thick, supple armor. It sported plates on the front and back of the torso, but the rest was a thick material, which would harden on impact and disperse the force of a shot. It could also nullify the effects of a pulse rifle and disperse the heat of a hand laser. The helmet had a HUD that interfaced with their internal Links to provide displays of everyone's field of vision and status—not that Tanis needed such a crude interface.

They fastened their helmets and looked one another over.

<*Let's do this,*> Thompson said as he cycled the airlock and stepped out into the umbilical.

<*They're cycling their lock open for us,*> Nance announced from the bridge, where she had taken Tanis's place. Tanis had given the bio a crash course on the new weapons systems and the upgraded scan that went with them. It had been a bit tense since Nance's unhappiness with the plan—and Tanis in general—wasn't well hidden, but she had been a quick study.

<*Are they all in the galley?*> Cargo asked.

<*I count nine in there,*> Nance replied. <*I don't know what their complement is; their AI is being very unfriendly.*>

<*That's going to be difficult to deal with when we try to use their ship,*> Thompson said as the four of them stepped into the *Regal Dawn's* lock and waited for it to seal and match pressure with the rest of the ship.

<*I should be able to get it under control,*> Tanis said without worry.

<*Should?*> Nance asked.

<*I was speaking extemporaneously,*> Tanis sighed to herself. At least this part would be over soon. Once they were on their way to rescue Sera, she hoped Nance and Thompson would lay off the accusations.

The light above the inner hatch changed from red to green and the iris spun open to reveal an empty corridor. Everyone had their weapons leveled and Tanis double-checked the seal on her helmet. Chemical warfare was all too common in instances like this. The suits did not detect anything, but she wasn't going to take any chances.

After planting a mine in the airlock, Tanis and Flaherty made their way fore to the bridge, while Cargo and Thompson went aft to the galley. While it was possible that the entire crew had done as directed, they were expecting to find at least one pirate holed up somewhere.

<*Any sign of crew?*> Cargo asked.

<*Not yet. I expect we'll meet with someone near or on the bridge.*>

The bridge on the pirate ship was up four levels. Like *Sabrina,* or any ship expecting trouble, ladders were available for passage between the decks; no one wanted to take a lift down into a firefight.

Tanis sent her nano cloud ahead. It almost felt like cheating in this technologically backward time, but not so much that she was willing to risk getting shot in the head on a point of honor.

The tiny bots reported the next level clear and she slipped up the ladder, Flaherty close behind, silent and serious as always. The next two decks were clear as well, but on the final level, her nano reported small sounds from the direction of the bridge.

Someone hadn't followed orders.

Tanis crept up the ladder and sent a command to Flaherty to follow her, but hold near the ladder while she checked out the bridge. He nodded his assent and backed against a bulkhead in a low crouch, his eyes everywhere.

Conscious of how easily sound traveled in these ships, Tanis took careful steps, her pulse rifle slung low with her finger on the trigger. Her nano flushed into the bridge and her overlay brought up a clear view of the space. There was someone in there all right—a tall woman with long, dark hair and a long leather coat bent over a console.

Tanis stepped out into the hatchway and spoke calmly, her voice coming over a speaker on the suit. "Raise your hands slowly and then turn around."

The woman complied, raised her arms and slowly turned. Even before she saw the other woman's face, Tanis's image recognition systems made the identification.

"Sera?"

"You were expecting the Easter Bunny?" Sera smiled, her dark eyes dancing with mirth.

"What are you doing here?" Tanis asked.

"Thanking my lucky stars you weren't someone intent on blowing this ship to pieces. I had a few minutes of serious worry until Helen cracked that fake ident and we realized it was you guys."

"How did you get away from Rebecca?" Tanis asked. Sera was a far more resourceful woman than she had expected.

"Skill and cunning, but that's a long story. The whole crew here?"

"Thompson and Cargo are below, checking on the crew," Flaherty said from the hatchway behind Tanis.

He slipped past Tanis and stepped into the bridge to embrace Sera in a quick hug. "You gave me a bit of a worry there. I don't like you going off on your own."

Sera laughed. "I don't either. It's not like it was my idea."

"Did you get it?" he asked.

Sera nodded and stretched her foot out to tap a container the size of a personal luggage case on the floor near her.

"All in a day's work," Sera replied.

Tanis's IFF systems scanned Sera and showed the woman to be a mass of wounds and trauma.

<*She's a mess,*> Tanis whistled softly in her mind.

<*Notice she doesn't have skin anymore? Her thermal profile is all wrong,*> Angela brought up an image of Sera's heat profile and thermal output in Tanis's mind.

<*Not to mention the energy profile of whatever is in that case—that Flaherty already seems to know about,*> Tanis replied.

"Was that a voluntary alteration?" Tanis asked, pointing at Sera's exposed glossy skin.

Sera's face reddened. "I was always a bit jealous of Rebecca's outfits, so I tried one on. The crazy bitch booby trapped it, so this is my new skin for now."

<*With the trauma she's had, and the med facilities on* Sabrina, *it may be her new skin for some time,*> Helen added.

"You'd fit right in with Jessica, one of my team on the *Intrepid,*" Tanis said with a smile. "If you can't get squared away before we get there, our docs could fix you up without trouble."

"Not sure I want to be fixed—I think I rather like it," Sera said with a mischievous grin.

"Now you *really* remind me of Jessica."

"Maybe we should discuss mods and fashion later," Flaherty said. "We still have a ship to secure."

"That we do." Sera picked up the mysterious case in one hand and pulse rifle in the other. "Complement on this ship is twelve. Angela just informed me there are only nine in the galley, so we've got some fun ahead of us." Sera suddenly stopped and turned to face Tanis.

"What did you do to my ship?" she asked with eyes wide.

"Angela shared that tidbit, did she?" Tanis replied with a smile.

"You added ten offensive beams and rail guns? Where'd you get the money?"

"We sold some nano to S&H," Tanis said with a shrug.

Sera turned to Flaherty. "And you let her do this? It could destabilize the regional economy."

"It's alright," Flaherty replied. "The stuff she sold them is not replicable with their current levels of technology. They don't have the ability to produce the nano-sized stasis fields without the Casimir effect collapsing their containment. It's essentially useless."

Tanis was dumbfounded. How did Flaherty understand that, let alone know it was a required component of the technology she had sold S&H? Sera saw her confusion.

"I'll explain later, once we deal with these pirates and set a course for Bollam's World and the *Intrepid.*"

Sera sent a broad message on *Sabrina's* ship-wide net. <*Thanks for the ride guys, I sure didn't want to have to get out and walk!*>

A chorus of voices cried out Sera's name before a round of expletives and questions flooded the comm.

<*Easy now, I'll answer everything once this is over. I'm as curious as to what you are doing here as you are about me, I'm sure. First, we take care of three little lost pirate pigs. Thompson, Cargo, have you secured the galley yet?*>

<*We're in the hall now. Nine secure,*> Cargo replied. <*You said there are three missing pirates around here somewhere?*>

<*Yeah, there should be twelve aboard,*> Sera replied. <*Sabrina, be a dear and seal our hatch—I don't want any of them getting onto you.*>

<*Taken care of, Sera,*> Sabrina responded, sounding happier than she had in a week.

<*Angela,*> Sera addressed Tanis's AI, <*I suspect your cyber warfare is the best around. Is there any chance that you can subdue this ship's pesky AI and take it out of the equation?*>

<*Shouldn't be too hard. I've already infiltrated most of its systems and have it cornered in its own neural net. It's throwing everything it has at me; if life support goes offline for a minute or two, don't be alarmed. It's just me.*> Angela's reply was offhand, but Tanis could tell she was disgusted by the intelligence she was fighting on board the *Regal Dawn*.

"Flaherty," Sera directed, "cover the hatch. They may make a break for *Sabrina* and it'll be a good place to corner them."

Flaherty nodded and left the bridge. Tanis couldn't even hear him as he slid down the ladder.

"How does he move so quietly?" she asked.

"Honestly? I have no idea," Sera replied. "Helen usually has to use probes to hide my ruckus—though not anymore, I guess." With that, she threw off her long coat and slipped out of the bridge in her whisper-silent skin.

Tanis and Sera checked the two cabins on that level, which appeared to belong to the captain and the first mate—both empty. On the next level, the rest of the crew cabins also checked out.

<*How are your charges?*> Sera asked Cargo.

<*They're none too happy, but they aren't causing us any trouble. The captain we saw over the holo isn't here. One of them let it slip that the mate and engineer are missing, as well. I'm thinking they may be trying to get control back from below.*>

<*You hold those guys; Tanis and I will go take a peek.*>

<*Aye, Captain.*>

"You have no idea how good it is to hear that again," Sera said aloud to Tanis.

"You have no idea how good it is to hear them say it."

Sera cocked an eyebrow. "They hold together ok?"

"Better than a lot of other crews I've seen when their leader is captured," Tanis replied as they slid down a ladder.

"Good to know I trained them well."

Trained, Tanis added that to the long list of mysteries surrounding Sera.

The two women reached the freight deck, with Angela coordinating probe coverage as they searched for signs of the missing crewmembers. The search turned up nothing and they proceeded down the ladder to environmental.

Just as their feet touched the deck plate, the life support equipment wound to a halt.

<*It's just me,*> Angela said. <*I'm almost wrapped up—just giving him nowhere to hide.*>

Environmental was clear and they worked their way aft toward waste reclamation and engineering.

<*We've got sounds in here that aren't mechanical. Sounds like a footstep, male, most likely a hundred and eighty centimeters and at least ninety-five kilograms. Echoes make it hard to place, but he's somewhere to the right of the entrance no more than ten meters away,*> Helen said.

<*Thanks,*> Sera replied as she peered around the corner. There was nothing visible and she crept to a large tank and provided cover while Tanis slipped in, stopping behind an adjacent tank.

Tanis pivoted and peered over her cover. The motion shifted the deck plate beneath her and gave a low groan. Moments later the waves from a pulse rifle tore through the air over her head. She ducked and Sera rose from cover, firing shots at the attacker.

He ducked down before the waves reached him. Tanis tossed Sera a conspiratorial smile, before slipping out from behind her cover into the next row of tanks, sneaking toward the enemy's location.

As Tanis moved, Sera supplied cover fire, keeping their opponent pinned.

Tanis crept within two meters of the last tank at the end of the row. She steadied herself for a second, and then, in one swift motion, leapt over the tank, twisted mid-air, and landed a meter from their attacker—weapon leveled at his head.

"End of the road, bub."

His back was to her, peering around the other side while trying to get an angle on Sera. He turned slowly, lowering his rifle with one hand, while raising the other.

<*'End of the road, bub'?*> Sera asked.

<*I saw it in a vid once.*>

A half-second before his weapon reached the deck, a series of shots rang out over the waste reclamation equipment, and Tanis heard Sera let loose a string of curses. The man in front of Tanis took advantage of her momentary distraction to raise his weapon and fire a shot off. It struck her square in the chest, flinging her back against the bulkhead. She squeezed off two shots after she hit, but the man had already ducked out of view.

<*You OK?*> she and Sera asked each other.

<*Armor took the most of it,*> Tanis said. <*You?*>

<*They missed, but those were some serious slug throwers. I think both the captain and the tech are on the far left side of the room,*> Sera replied.

<*Keep some cover fire on them. I'm going to take care of this guy.*>

Tanis saw Sera pull two slug throwers from holsters on her legs and let loose a volley of her own, the bullets ricocheting off the tanks across the room. Tanis used the distraction to launch herself from her position against the wall. She leapt onto a tank and fell upon the man on the other side.

While not exceptionally graceful, it had the advantage of total surprise. He had been peering back around the tank, his weapon pointed to where she had been. Her elbow slammed into his stomach and she drove a knee into his crotch before smashing the butt of her rifle against the back of his head.

<*One down.*>

<*Helen says she can't spot these guys; they may be using some sort of active camouflage. Can your probes spot them?*> Sera asked.

<*They're using the ship's sensors to create a noise cloud around them. I can't get more than a ghost here and there,*> Angela replied. <*I'll try to find the emitters and shut them down—not all of this ship is accessible from their main net.*>

<*It's a bit of a mess,*> Helen agreed.

Tanis crept along her side of the room, and then moved even with Sera's position.

<*I'm going to draw their fire; see if you can get a line on one of them,*> Tanis said before she stood and leapt across a tank. Shots rang out from a position at the end of the room and return fire came from Sera's location.

Tanis saw one of Sera's shots catch a man at the end of the room in the shoulder. He spun sideways but still managed to fire a few bullets in Tanis's direction. She responded with a series of blasts from her pulse rifle, all missing, but it was enough to force him behind cover.

<*I've got the last one over here somewhere,*> Sera said. <*I heard him just a minute ago.*>

<*I bet you're feeling a keen lack of body armor right about now,*> Tanis replied as she swapped out her rifle's energy coil.

<*I've been feeling that lack for a few days now.*>

Sera and Tanis worked their way closer together and then down to the location of the man Sera had clipped. When they got there, they saw that he had cracked his head on the tank and was out cold.

<*I didn't think my last shot hit him,*> Tanis shook her head. <*Maybe he slipped or something.*>

<*Self-defeating enemies. My favorite kind,*> Sera replied.

Shots rang out from their right as they stared down at the fallen pirate. One hit Tanis's chest armor and she swore as the impact caused her to stagger.

<*Been too long, you're getting sloppy,*> Angela said.

<*Yeah? Have that AI taken care of yet?*> Tanis replied sourly.

<*Yup,*> Angela responded cheerfully. <*Just waiting on you.*>

Sera dashed down the row of tanks, throwing caution to the wind and Tanis saw her boot lash out, sending a weapon flying. A second kick elicited the soft crunch of breaking bone. There was a third kick as Tanis reached her, weapon at the ready.

The man on the floor was down with a long gash across his face, as he rocked side to side, moaning and clutching his chest.

"Last one, then?" Sera asked out loud.

"Should be. Nine and three is twelve last time I checked."

"Good, all that cat and mouse stuff was starting to get on my nerves. I want a hot meal and a bath."

"Do you even need baths now?" Tanis smiled.

"Probably not, but I'm going to take one anyway," Sera groused.

Tanis laughed, but her voice caught at a familiar sound from behind them. Angela cried out a warning, but it wasn't fast enough. The high-pitched whine of a rail weapon echoed through the chamber and Tanis felt a stinging sensation in her chest.

Sera had both of her handguns out, shots ringing from each as she fired at a figure racing past a nearby tank. A shot hit him in the side and he staggered forward, then fell to his knees. Sera kept shooting as she advanced; the man collapsed, his body twitching as Sera emptied her clips into him.

"Aww hell," Tanis said in a strained voice, catching herself against a tank. She wheezed as Sera turned, her face a mask of horror, and rushed back.

<Nance! Get a grav pad over here now! Bottom deck, Tanis is hit!>

"You'll be OK. We'll get you patched up in no time," Sera caught Tanis as she slid down the tank and pulled her up into her arms.

Tanis looked up at Sera and tried to speak. No words came out, but she tried to sound jovial over the Link. *<You'd better. If I die rescuing you I'll be rather upset.>*

Sera grimaced, pulling Tanis close, and, calling on some untapped reserve of strength, heaved her up and stumbled toward the closest lift. Tanis was wheezing more than breathing and knew that in any moment she'd go into convulsions. The armor was trying to seal the wound to stop the blood from flowing out, but couldn't deal with the massive hole the rail gun had torn through Tanis's chest.

Right through her heart.

UNBREAKABLE

STELLAR DATE: 07.27.8927 (Adjusted Years)
LOCATION: *Sabrina*, Interstellar Dark Layer
REGION: 72 Light Years Core-Ward of Ayrea

It was that reoccurring nightmare again. Something was chasing her through the dark corridors of the *Intrepid* where there was no power, no lights, no Link. It was gaining on her; no matter how hard she ran, it grew ever closer, its clawed feet scraping the decking, the sound echoing around her. Tanis was sick of these nightmares. She wanted to wake up. She was done running.

Repeating the mantra over and over in her subconsciousness, she felt herself rise from the mire, from the darkness, moving to the light, and gradually come awake. The light pressed against her eyelids. It was going to be bright again. Steeling herself, she cracked one eye and then the other. She seemed to be in some med lab, not on the *Intrepid*, that much was for certain. Her chest hurt; hurt a lot.

<*Where am I, Angela?*> she asked.

<*You're on* Sabrina, *Tanis. You were wounded in taking that pirate ship, the* Regal Dawn.>

Angela sounded concerned, but not alarmed. Tanis knew that was a good sign; Angela wouldn't hide her condition if it were bad. She concentrated for a moment, and the memories slowly trickled back; the escape pod, the abduction by Padre's pirates, Sera saving her, and then her saving Sera. She took a deep breath and smiled. They'd be on their way to the *Intrepid* now. This leg of her journey was finally coming to an end.

"We seem to be making a habit of this," a nearby voice said.

Tanis turned her head to see Sera sitting beside her, a look of concern mixed with relief on her face. She handed Tanis a bottle of water with a straw, and Tanis took several long pulls, washing the moisture around her parched mouth.

"We do seem to be," she agreed when she had finished. "Thank you for patching me back together again."

"Nance and Angela did most of the work. I'm all thumbs when it comes to hooking up artificial hearts and then growing new organic ones."

"Heart?"

"When that guy shot at us with the rail gun, I thought he had hit me at first. I figured if I was still standing, I was going to take him down. Later, after I got him, I realized what I thought had been the railgun slug hitting me was a piece of your rib cage. It punctured my right lung, but my fancy new skin sealed around it and kept me breathing."

"Good to know my impending death didn't inconvenience you too much," Tanis smiled. "I did notice back on the ship that you had replaced your skin with some sort of polymer; glad to see it proved useful."

Sera looked down at herself and smiled. "I was saved by fashion. Anyway, when you tried to speak, I turned and…well, let's just say it wasn't pretty. Angela is really the one who saved you. She sealed up your arteries as fast as she could, and managed to keep most of your blood in while we got you on a medical stasis rack and raced you back to *Sabrina.* The pellet the rail gun fired was soft and hollow. It mushroomed inside your chest and ripped your heart apart. The mass hit the inside of the armor on the back, and the shockwave rippled back through the rest of your torso. It did a number on your internal organs."

"Better than the last time I got hit by a rail," Tanis said with a weak smile. "Thanks for keeping me together again, Angela."

<It's purely selfish interest, love.>

<Wait! The baby?> Tanis said with fear washing over her.

<She's perfectly fine. The stasis bubble kept her safe, but…>

<But what?!>

<She's not in stasis right now. When you heal up, I can re-instate it, or…>

<Let's leave that 'or' for later,> Tanis replied.

Sera continued, unaware of Tanis's private conversation.

"Nance got you hooked up to a circulatory machine while she picked bits of shattered bone out of your chest. We fed Angela so much silicon she could have made a replica of you, and Sabrina helped make raw, unprogrammed nano as fast as she could. They shored up all your internal bleeding and slowly re-constructed your organs. Some of them we ended up having to grow fresh—you don't have a bone ribcage anymore, though Angela says she'll slowly replace the artificial one with living tissue over time."

Tanis chuckled. "Also not the first time."

"Sounds like there's a story I'd like to hear when you're not lying here in recovery," Sera said.

"It's a good one; I'll be sure to swap it with one of yours—I see it's only been five days since we took the *Dawn*. That's quite the medical feat you all pulled off, Ang," Tanis said with a yawn.

"It sure was," Sera replied. "Did you used to be a doctor?"

<Just field medicine,> Angela replied. *<You can't live inside a human body for over a century and not have a good idea how it works.>*

"I guess that makes sense," Sera said.

"So, how long am I bedridden for?" Tanis asked.

<There was relatively little nerve damage, though I sacrificed some muscles to keep blood flowing to your brain. I had to rebuild them; you'll need to do some stretching and make sure all your joints work right,> Angela replied.

"Doc knows best," Sera smiled.

Sera helped Tanis raise her legs and move her arms in their full range of motion before she sat up and took a deep breath.

"Everything seems to be in working order." She looked to Sera. "Are you all healed up? I recall you saying something about a rib of mine making a hole in you."

Sera ran a hand down her 'skin'. "All healed and right as rain. Angela knew a few things about flesh and polymer bonding. She and Helen gave me a bit of an upgrade—now it grows back on its own."

"It's a pretty straight-forward mod," Tanis agreed.

<*Not Fina's first time with some unexpected alterations, either,*> Helen added.

"Fina. You've called her that a few times," Tanis observed. "What does it mean?"

<*It's a short version of her name,*> Helen replied.

"Hush." Sera looked perturbed.

<*You have a beautiful name. I helped your mother choose it; I think it suits you.*>

"Now I have to know what it is," Tanis said.

"Sera *is* my name; it's just shortened a bit."

<*It's shortened by five letters,*> Helen said with a virtual scowl.

<*Seraphina?*> Angela asked.

"No!" Sera shouted in dismay.

<*Good extrapolation,*> Helen's avatar nodded in their minds.

"I must swear you all to secrecy," Sera said. "I'm completely serious—I can't wheel, deal, and smuggle with a name like Seraphina."

"Who else knows?" Tanis asked.

"Other than you, just Flaherty."

<*It doesn't help that he used to change your diapers,*> Helen said.

"Stop it! You're giving all my secrets away." Sera's face was beginning to redden. Tanis could tell she was adding some choice comments to her AI in private.

<*Oh shush. Eventually she'll figure it all out, I'm just giving her a little nudge here and there,*> Helen said publicly to the group.

"You two are quite the puzzle," Tanis said with an eyebrow raised.

"Hey, on a different track," Sera began, appearing to choose her words carefully, "have you thought about what your ship will do now that it's stuck in the ninetieth century?"

Tanis let out a long sigh. "Not really. I imagine we could find a moon somewhere in some system and terraform it in trade for what we have. I've looked at the star charts; there aren't a lot of options around—not without a really long trip."

"I…this isn't the sort of information that one bandies about, but I think I can help. I have contacts I can reach out to when we get to Bollam's World." Sera paused, indecision clouding her features, then finished her statement, "I can get in touch with the FGT."

Tanis sat up, locking eyes with Sera, searching for a sign that this was subterfuge…or a joke.

"You're serious?"

Sera nodded. "Serious as a railgun slug to the chest."

"How do you have contacts like this?" Tanis asked.

Sera didn't reply right away and Tanis waited in silence for the captain to make up her mind.

"I…I'm not ready to talk about that yet. It's not a part of my life I like to reflect on." Her face lightened. "But I promise I'll tell you, just not yet."

Tanis wasn't sure what to make of Sera's admission, but even suspect contact with the FGT was more to go on than she had five minutes ago.

"OK, thanks for your offer. I can wait for the details," she replied.

"You ready to get some solid food in you?" Sera asked and stood from her chair.

"More than ready; my stomach is grumbling like it hasn't had food in a year," Tanis replied as she carefully settled on her feet.

<This particular stomach hasn't had food ever. Go easy on it,> Angela instructed.

She stepped gingerly as they walked out of the med-lab into the central corridor on the freight deck. "Angela wasn't kidding when she said I'd have to take it easy until my muscles get back in sync."

"I had a full rebuild once," Sera said over her shoulder. "Was quite the experience. The nerves and muscles are never exactly where they were before. Takes some time to get your responses timed properly again."

"Now *you* have a story I'd like to hear some time," Tanis said.

"I bet you would." Sera smiled back at her.

Nance met them at the ladder to the crew level; Tanis noticed the woman's head was exposed for only the second time since she had been on board, and her long, brown hair was brushed to gleaming perfection.

"Tanis, it's good to see you conscious. Sabrina notified me that you were awake," she said pleasantly.

<Thanks, Sabrina,> Tanis said. *<Sorry I didn't greet you sooner. I'm still feeling a bit fuzzy.>*

<It's OK. You brought Sera back to me; I'll forgive you a simple slip,> the ship replied.

Sabrina seemed much calmer than even before Sera had been captured. Perhaps the AI had realized that even without her captain near, the crew wasn't going to abandon her to some scrap yard.

"Thanks, Nance," Tanis said aloud. "Sera tells me I'm currently breathing thanks to, in no small part, your actions." She patted her chest. "I'm quite impressed that you could grow a new heart with what you have available on this ship."

Nance smiled. "It's the least I could do."

<Finally warming up to us, it seems,> Tanis said to Angela.

<A bit, yes.>

Tanis turned and took a long look at the ladder before letting out a long sigh. "I think I'll use the lift today."

"Probably a wise choice," Nance agreed.

The rest of the crew was waiting in the wardroom when she entered, trailing a hand along the bulkhead to assist her uncertain balance.

"Hey folks," Tanis summoned all her energy to give a winning smile.

<Five points for effort,> Angela said with a chuckle. *<Not so many for execution.>*

<Thanks for the support, dear.>

There were greetings all around; even Flaherty actually used words rather than his customary grunt. Tanis sat as gracefully as she could manage and Cheeky poured her a cup of coffee.

"How do you always have such wonderful coffee on this ship?" Tanis asked as she inhaled the aroma.

"Sera blackmails station masters," Cheeky replied with a shrug.

"Now *you're* giving away my secrets, too?" Sera threw her hands in the air.

"Other secrets have been shared?" Cheeky asked. "Why wasn't I informed?"

As they all ate, Sera retold the story of her escape from the pirate headquarters for Tanis's benefit. When she reached the part where she left Rebecca alive, Cargo shook his head with disbelief.

"I still can't fathom what possessed you to leave her alive; she's going to gun for you—for us—forever."

Tanis watched a brief war of emotions play across Sera's face.

"I could have, I really wanted to…" the captain finally replied. "But for some reason I didn't have cold-blooded murder in my heart that day."

The crew nodded respectfully, though Tanis wondered if they noticed what she had; Sera had committed murder before—and not just once.

Tanis wondered what she would have done with Rebecca, were she in Sera's position. It had been a long time since she had taken a life with her own hands; it changed a person, and not just the first time either—there was a definite cumulative effect. Perhaps Sera, like her, had spent some time recovering that part of her soul and didn't want to lose it again.

When she described the ransacking of Rebecca's quarters, Tanis couldn't help but laugh.

"I've only known you for a short time, Sera, but it does not surprise me one bit that you spent no small amount of time in another woman's wardrobe."

"Given her current condition, there's probably a parable of greed in there somewhere," Cargo said with a shake of his head.

Sera gave a simple shrug in response. "All I was wearing was a hazsuit. I couldn't wander through their platform like that."

"Why not?" Nance asked. "I bet it would have attracted a lot less attention than the state you're in now."

Cheeky laughed. "Surely you know by now, Nance. Sera *loves* attracting attention. It may be her dominant personality trait."

Sera's face turned down in a brief sulk. Everyone else was looking at Cheeky and missed the expression, but Tanis's ever-present nano-cloud spotted the reaction.

<*My money is on parental issues,*> Angela said.

<*Mine too,*> Tanis replied.

"Fine, mock me, but you're all jealous of this stuff—at least now that Helen and Angela have made it less intent on killing me, and a little more accommodating to my biology."

Cheeky gave a mischievous grin. "I wouldn't mind getting into your new skin, just not the way you are."

Sera flushed, and quickly returned to telling the rest of her tale; the battle in the warehouse, and hiding in the stack of crates. Tanis noticed there was no mention of the case that Sera had with her on the *Regal Dawn*. No one else mentioned the omission and she wondered if the crew knew anything about it.

"So, what *are* the chances that we have to worry about Rebecca sending her entire fleet after us?" Cheeky asked.

"I think they're pretty slim—for now," Sera said. "They're probably looking for a new headquarters."

"Why's that?" Thompson asked.

"I destroyed their last one," Sera smiled mischievously.

"Wait," Cheeky raised her hand. "You didn't mention that before. How did you do that?"

Sera paused, and Tanis wondered what she had done that she didn't want to share with the crew. After a glance at Flaherty, the captain continued with her tale.

"I did tell; I said that I altered their sensor array."

"Yeah," Thompson agreed. "But what for?"

"So I altered it to emit a very specific signal."

"You mean it's true?" Nance asked; her eyes wide.

Sera nodded in response.

"You're killing me with all this crypticness," Cheeky yelled. "What did you do?"

Nance pulled her eyes from Sera and cast a wary look out the porthole into the dark layer. "I've heard stories…. If Sera means what I think she does…she had it eaten."

Tanis leaned back in her chair and took a long, slow breath. Everyone looked surprised—except Flaherty, who looked slightly upset. The most emotion she had ever seen him display, outside of when Sera was captured.

"Something ate the space station?" Thompson asked.

"There are things that live in the dark layer," Sera spoke slowly, as though searching for the right words. "Things that no one understands. We don't know if they are organic, silicate, or purely energy based. No one has been able to learn anything about them—or if anyone has, they didn't live to tell the tale. However, there is a signal which attracts them, and they move fast. Somehow they can propel themselves though the dark layer."

Everyone looked somewhat paler—Tanis was certain she did, as well; not a few nervous eyes glanced out the porthole into the blackness.

"So, these things eat stations?" Thompson asked.

"They are attracted to gravitons, from what we can tell. Mostly, they stay very close to the largest clumps of dark matter, which are clustered near stars in relative space. It's why transitioning into the Dark Layer too close to a star is often a one-way trip—even if there are no clumps of dark matter nearby," Sera replied.

"Are they out in interstellar space at all?" Tanis asked.

"Every so often, one is spotted. Mostly ships don't emit enough gravitons to attract them that far out, but like I said, there is a signal you can emit that's like ringing the dinner bell—even out in the void, they'll come—in this case, they most certainly have already come."

"So, you killed an entire station full of people?" Tanis asked.

<*Nice, very tactful,*> Angela said.

Sera scowled and her voice gained a cold edge. "Of course not. Do I look like a barbarian?"

"More like a Barbie doll," Flaherty said softly.

Sera stuck her tongue out at him. "I gave them fair warning."

"If these things are real, and you know so much about them, how come I've never heard of them?" Cheeky asked. "You'd think pilots would have stories."

<*Indeed, how,*> Tanis mused.

<*I have a list of possibilities as long as your arm,*> Angela replied. <*Though our access to solid data about this time is rather limited.*>

<*She's someone with good connections...maybe an aristocrat of some sort?*> Tanis mused.

<*Well, that's obvious, but whose aristocracy? Most of them aren't really that great from what I can tell.*>

<*When were they ever?*> Tanis asked.

Sera took a moment to reply to Cheeky's question.

"The knowledge is too dangerous. If people knew, they could plant a transmitter on a ship and it would transition to FTL and...well, let's just say that it would be the end of FTL travel. Plus, no one wants to run the risk of accidentally pulling one of these things into relative space."

"Can that happen?"

"No one knows...no one wants to find out."

"Makes sense," Nance said with a nod.

<*Great,*> Sabrina sighed. <*Now I have to worry about space monsters in the dark.*>

Sera answered a few more questions about her escape from the station, then conversation drifted to *Sabrina's* upgrades and the course to Bollam's World. The crew was far more relaxed with Sera around. Even though she never acted superior, they all looked to her for advice and confirmation of their beliefs and opinions. Sometimes she disagreed or criticized, but usually managed to be supportive while doing so.

Tanis knew the hallmarks of a leader—moreover, someone raised around great leaders. She knew the traits because she had honed them over decades. Sera appeared to possess them naturally; Tanis was certain the captain had not actively focused on the skills, but had learned them through observation—before she ran from whatever position awaited her.

Ship-time slipped into the third watch and the crew began to disperse to their quarters. Tanis was one of the first out; she begged exhaustion and retreated to her cabin where she fell into a deep sleep, dreaming of Joe waiting for her on the *Intrepid* and their happy reunion.

THE RETURN

STELLAR DATE: 07.25.8927 (Adjusted Years)
LOCATION: *Sabrina*, Interstellar Dark Layer
REGION: 73 Light Years Core-Ward of Ayrea

Sera reclined in the captain's chair and stroked the leather upholstery.

It was good to be back on *Sabrina*. The ship was glad to have her captain back, too; the crew was happy, and Tanis was going to live to see another day.

It certainly would have been embarrassing, not to mention potentially dangerous, to approach the *Intrepid* with Tanis dead. She really liked the woman; though from another age, Tanis felt like a kindred spirit. The effort she had put into Sera's rescue had also earned her points—though the weapons upgrades painted a target on *Sabrina*. They would have to go before long—at least the more obvious ones.

She didn't fault Tanis. Time was short, and, as a military woman, going in with the big guns was likely her style.

Given Tanis's nano spending spree on the PeterSil EK platform, she may even need to change the registry of her ship. Too many people would wonder what job *Sabrina* had pulled to get that sort of credit. Some old friends were certainly going to take notice.

It should have upset her more, but Sera's plans for the *Intrepid* would force her to confront those individuals sooner rather than later, anyway—regardless of the mess Tanis had made in Silstrand.

<*You could go back, you know,*> Helen said softly. <*You have the CriEn—it's your get out of jail free card. Not to mention, proof of your innocence.*>

<*This again? Do* **you** *want to go back?*> Sera asked. <*You could if you wanted to; I wouldn't stop you.*>

Helen's silvery laugh echoed through Sera's mind, a sound she had heard often, ever since she was a small child—probably even before she could remember.

<*Dear, I have seen enough of that life; I paired with you to get out, for the adventure. And this may be the grandest adventure I have ever experienced.*>

Sera smiled. She was glad Helen felt that way—this life, this adventure as her oldest friend put it, *was* grand, far better than what her father had planned for her.

<*But you are going to have to confront them. They're going to come for the* Intrepid*; they'll try to force you to go.*>

"They'll try," Sera whispered to herself.

<*The* Intrepid *will be the catalyst, though. Orion will not sit idly by and let that sort of tech fall into your father's hands,*> Helen cautioned.

<*We don't know that the* Intrepid *really has picotech. No evidence of it was ever found at Kapteyn's Star, and the Victorians never showed that level of tech in anything they did afterward,*> Sera replied.

<*If they even* **fear** *your father will gain picotech, it will be war.*>

War. The sort of war like none ever seen before—and people had worked up some good ones in the past. Humanity was still recovering from the last one. But her father had always stayed out of prior conflicts. This would be different.

It would spread across the Orion arm of the galaxy; all of humanity would be engulfed.

"Cheeky, could—" she began, only to see that her pilot was no longer on the bridge. Her musings had been more distracting than she thought.

Sera brought up the nav data herself and reviewed it one final time.

From Angela's scan data, plus stories of other ships that had been lost in the Streamer, she knew the *Intrepid* to be in interstellar space, rim-ward of Bollam's World—perhaps even within the star's heliopause.

Bollam's World lay on the far side of several interstellar federations and demarchies. Not to mention the core worlds.

Known as the AST, the core was a strong federation with far too much red tape for Sera's taste—their security was rather invasive, even for ships just passing through their systems. *Sabrina* would give those worlds a wide berth.

Their first stop would be Ayrea, 73 light-years distant, where the ship would skip along the rim of the system before reaching the jump point on its far side. From there, it was a 15 light-year hop to Pavonis, and then, ironically, they would pass through New Eden, the very system the *Intrepid* had been destined to colonize all those millennia ago. There, they would likely stop for fuel and supplies.

Tanis would get an up-close view of the world she should have lived and died on long ago.

<*You seem melancholy,*> Helen interjected.

<*I was just thinking of how it will be for Tanis to see New Eden,*> Sera replied.

<*I'm not so sure. Aside from discovering that she jumped five thousand years into the future, little seems to unsettle Tanis Richards.*>

<*True enough, she was completely calm under fire on the* Regal Dawn. *Her heart rate never even rose.*>

<*Spying on our guest, are we?*> Helen asked with a chuckle, knowing all too well that it was second nature for both of them to observe every aspect of their surroundings.

<*Maybe just a little bit; I do prefer her to be alive for this plan.*> Sera shook her head, remembering the fear she felt when she held Tanis in her arms on the *Regal Dawn*, convinced the woman would die.

<*If all goes well, she'll likely never die. Unless she goes and gets her heart blown out of her chest when there's no one around to fix her up again,*> Helen replied.

Sera nodded absently as she reviewed the data for the final leg of their journey: 28 light-years to Bollam's World, and then to the *Intrepid*. The entire trip would cross nearly 140 light-years, or roughly 1.3 quadrillion kilometers. With an average FTL factor of 579, and their entry speed of 0.70*c*, the trip would take roughly ninety days, or a hundred if they stopped in New Eden for fuel and post cards.

BREAK A FEW EGGS

STELLAR DATE: 07.27.8927 (Adjusted Years)
LOCATION: Andromeda's Pinnace, Tsarina Refinery, EK Belt
REGION: Bollam's World System, Bollam's World Federation

"Do you think it will work?" Jessica asked, concern filling her eyes.

"Back in Sol? Hell no. Out here, who knows, maybe?" Joe replied. "Either way, we can't just sit out here watching forever."

"OK, sending the docking request now."

Jessica sent the sequence, and Joe prayed it would work. It had taken them two weeks to get this far into the Bollam's World system; during that time they had watched thousands of ships drop out of space—appearing to come from nowhere—and then drift into the system.

Most were small, some not significantly larger than the pinnace in which they flew. It hadn't taken long for them to have no other conclusion than FTL.

Over the past months, as data streams had been stripped from insystem beacons, the crew of the *Intrepid* had strongly suspected that faster-than-light travel was in use—Earnest had been practically giddy at the prospect.

Now they were certain.

It opened up a world of possibilities—and made their whole struggle pointless. Joe knew it also meant that there was little reason to expect Tanis to be in Bollam's World anymore. She could be anywhere in the entire galaxy, and if she hadn't made it back to the *Intrepid* by now, things were likely not going well for her.

Still, they had to start somewhere.

He was glad for Jessica. She was able to put her worry aside and follow her investigative training. There was a lead; they would follow it and it would bring them to a new lead. To her, it was that simple.

"Station's responded," Jessica said a few minutes later. "We have a berth on the refinery's north docking ring."

"External docking for a ship this small?" Joe shook his head. "I don't know what to make of this time…are they more or less advanced?"

"Beats me," Jessica shrugged.

Joe looked over the flight path the station provided and lined the pinnace up for the approach.

The refinery was not a large installation—less than fifteen kilometers across—but the amount of traffic it supported impressed Joe. Hundreds of ships were in varying stages of approach and departure.

"These grav drives they seem to have sure do help them manage a higher volume of traffic," Jessica said, apparently on the same train of thought.

"I think it's the lack of engine wash. There's no worry about ion streams and plasma melting other ships or the station. It keeps the space lanes open."

Jessica nodded absently. "Let's hope they don't mind us coming in the old-fashioned way."

Joe bit his lip as he worked to stay on course. "No kidding; this is threading one hell of a needle. Good thing we matched *v* further out. There's no room for corrective burns when we get closer."

The next several hours passed slowly as Joe worked to keep the ship in the pocket, while Jessica established a connection with the station and began querying its concierge AI for information on any recently recovered escape pods, or other salvage.

"Oh shit, here it is," Joe said as the station's traffic control opened a comm link.

"Vessel *Andromeda 3*, what are you doing approaching this facility with your torch on? Kill your fusion drive immediately and switch to grav drives!"

Joe took a deep breath and responded in his best space jock voice. "Ah, that's a negative, station; we had a blow-out on our graviton emitters and can't make our approach with them. I'm right down the middle and about to switch to thrusters; ion dispersion systems show no wash will hit the station or other ships."

He glanced at Jessica and crossed his fingers while they waited for the approach.

"I don't care if you have God himself piloting that piece of crap. You don't approach a station on your torch, and I certainly can't have you chewing up that lane for the next hour. Kill your engine. I'm sending a tug out to pull you in the rest of the way. You better have an account open when you dock, because there are going to be some fines waiting for you."

"Well that sucks balls," Jessica said as the station cut the connection. "I don't suppose they'll take Sol credits."

"Any chance you can see if we can get an account opened with a local bank with some credit?" Joe asked as he killed the fusion engine, switching attitude control to chemical thrusters.

"Whew," Jessica said after a few minutes. "I guess they're used to getting ships from all over. They have procedures for ships with no local accounts or registration to get credit. Granted, we have to put the pinnace up as collateral."

Joe grinned. "We better not lose it; *Corsia* wouldn't like it if we sold her best pinnace."

The tug arrived, made grapple and half an hour later they were walking through their hatch onto the station's docking ring.

Right into an irate station worker.

"Are you the morons that came in on their torch? What were you thinking?" she demanded.

Joe began to speak, but Jessica put her hand on the woman's arm. "We're terribly sorry about that. Things aren't this busy or…as grand, where we're from. Coming in on a torch is OK if you need to. We didn't mean to cause trouble."

The dockworker's expression softened as she looked into Jessica's batting eyes.

"Yeah, well, you're core-side now. None of your fringe nonsense will fly here. You've got to sign this."

The dockworker handed a sheet of plas to Jessica and she looked it over. "This is half our credit!" she gasped. "How are we going to refuel?"

"You better have some good cargo to trade on that little tub," the dockworker shrugged. "You're getting off with a wrist-slap. Usually you'd be impounded for what you did."

Joe and Jessica exchanged glances, and Jessica passed her auth token to the plas before handing it back.

"I sure hope we do," Jessica said with a nod. "Thank you."

The woman cast them a curious look before tucking the plas under her arm and rushing down the dock, already yelling at a cargo hauler at the next berth.

"Damn, we better have something of value here," Jessica said. "Or we're going to be calling *Corsia* for pickup real soon."

* * * * *

A day later, and after more drinks than either Joe or Jessica cared to recall, they had no leads on Tanis whatsoever. Returning to the pinnace, they strode out of a lift onto the docking ring to see two soldiers in powered armor standing outside their berth.

"Well, that doesn't loo—" Jessica was interrupted by a rough voice to their left.

"Come with us."

Joe turned to see several more soldiers. Their faces were invisible behind mirrored visors, but the tone of their leader's voice brooked no argument. He looked back at Jessica who shrugged.

"Sure, where're we going?" Joe asked as the leader—a corporal by her stripes—gestured for them to step back into the lift.

"Questioning" was the only response.

<*Guesses?*> Joe asked Jessica.

<*My bet? They have decided our ship and our story don't match. So long as they don't find our stash on the pinnace, we'll still have a bargaining chip or two.*>

When the lift stopped, the corporal and his unit led them through a series of corridors to another lift. Another squad of soldiers, also in powered armor, guarded this one. They directed Joe and Jessica to step through an auth scanner.

The scanner must have seen something it didn't like and called the corporal over to confer with another soldier. Their faces were obscured by their helmets, but Joe had no doubt who was the subject of conversation.

<*Me or you?*> Jessica asked.

<*Bets are that it's me,*> Joe replied with a mental chuckle. <*Your most interesting mods are all visible on the outside.*>

After a few minutes, the corporal walked back to them.

"Your cellular structure is…abnormal," he said to Joe. "It doesn't appear to be dangerous, but don't even think of trying anything."

"I wouldn't dream of it," Joe replied.

The corporal nodded and directed them into the open lift door.

Joe and Jessica stepped in, and the rest of the squad filed in after them. When the doors opened again, they revealed a bustling corridor filled with personnel dressed in what Joe assumed were the Bollam's World military uniforms.

"Wait here," the corporal directed before moving down the corridor and knocking on a door. The remainder of his squad directed Joe and Jessica away from the lift entrance, their stances alert and wary.

"You can relax a little bit, guys," Jessica said. "We may look tough, but we're really quite nice."

None of the soldiers replied and Jessica sighed. "Real bunch of hard cases here."

"You'd behave the same way in their shoes," Joe replied.

"No, I'd probably behave worse; these guys haven't made fun of us once."

Down the corridor, the corporal stepped back into view, this time with her helmet tucked under her arm. A uniformed woman wearing a major's insignia accompanied her.

<*Lies or truth?*> Jessica asked Joe.

<*Let's see what they know, but I'm leaning toward truth at this point.*>

The woman approached, her expression steely as she eyed them over. Joe noticed that the squad guarding them stiffened as the major drew closer.

"So, you're who all this is about, then?" she asked.

"Glad to meet you," Joe extended his hand. "I'm Joe and this is Jessica."

The woman gazed at his extended hand and then replied brusquely, "I'm Major Akido." Without another word, she turned and strode down the hall, gesturing for them to follow.

Joe looked down at his outstretched hand and shrugged. "Maybe it's not a greeting here."

"Oh, it is," one of the soldiers gave a low chuckle. "She just doesn't extend pleasantries to much of anyone, least of all folks like you."

"Who are 'folks like us'?" Joe asked.

The corporal shot a look at the soldier and the man clammed up.

A minute later, they reached their destination, a nondescript conference room. The major took a seat on one side and gestured for Joe and Jessica to sit across from her.

Major Akido leaned back in her chair and stared each of them in the eyes for several minutes. Eventually, she let out a long sigh.

"So, where is it?" she finally asked.

"Where is what?" Joe replied.

"Your ship, where is it?" the major's tone was terse and brooked no evasion.

"It's in the dock. We were on our way there when your guys brought us here," Jessica replied with a frown.

The major leaned forward. "Cut the shit, you two. Your colony ship, where is it?"

Joe couldn't hide his surprise. He glanced at Jessica, who also appeared rather shocked.

<*Truth it is, then,*> she said to Joe.

"It's outsystem; we're just here to find someone who went missing."

Major Akido's brow furrowed into a deep frown. "Missing? How did someone on your colony ship go missing here?"

"We had an accident," Joe replied. "She had to eject in an escape pod, and by the time we got to her reported position, she was gone."

The major didn't respond immediately, and Jessica jumped in with a question of her own.

"How did you know that we're from a colony ship? Why would you even look for that?"

"Your ship, for starters. Your graviton emitters aren't broken, they're not present—neither is your grav drive. No grav drive means no FTL. If that's the case, then your shuttle didn't just jump in outside the system, you came in a different ship. Only two types of ships lurk out there sending in small shuttles. Enemy militaries and lost colony ships. But no military would do such a crap job sending in spies, so it was pretty simple."

Joe whistled. "So this happens a lot? Colony ships just wind up on your doorstep?"

"Not a lot, but often enough," Major Akido said with a shrug. "Isotope analysis of your shuttle confirmed that it is of Sol manufacture, sometime in the early fifth millennium. That sealed it."

<*Well, there's all our cards on the table,*> Joe said privately to Jessica. <*What now?*>

<*Not all,*> Jessica replied. <*For all their fancy grav drives and FTL, we know these people barely have fourth millennia tech. The* Intrepid *has a lot to offer them.*>

<*Too bad they don't have a colony world to offer us,*> Joe sighed.

"Then what's next?" Joe asked.

The major leaned back and smiled, "We're going to want to speak to your captain."

NEW EDEN

STELLAR DATE: 10.06.8927 (Adjusted Years)
LOCATION: *Sabrina*, Scattered Disk
REGION: New Eden System, Eden Alliance

Sabrina transitioned out of the dark layer into the New Eden system at the precise location Cheeky planned.

"Nailed it!" Cheeky shouted as the system nav buoy confirmed their location. "Pay up, Cargo."

Cargo sighed and flipped her a Silstrand token. "I can't believe you pulled that off. Your vector looked totally out of whack back at Ayrea."

"Or so you thought," Cheeky chuckled.

Tanis only half-heard their banter as she reviewed the local scan data.

New Eden was a booming system. Tens of thousands of ships plied its space lanes; it boasted three terraformed worlds, up from the original two the FGT had left for the *Intrepid*. It took conscious effort to keep herself from becoming morose at the thought.

<*Sera is convinced the FGT will give us a new system after she reaches out to them,*> Angela broke into Tanis's thoughts.

<*Indeed she is, though how she'll pull that rabbit out of her hat should be interesting. From what I read in* Sabrina's *archives, the FGT has not made direct contact with anyone in over five hundred years. How* **does** *she know how to reach them?*> Tanis asked.

<*It's a good question. I know you wonder if she is playing us,*> Angela said, concern emanating from her mind. <*But I don't sense that from her. We know there's more to her than she lets on; she has more contacts than her station would indicate.*>

Tanis nodded absently. *Sabrina's* captain was a frequent topic of conversation between her and Angela. They both harbored doubts that Sera could live up to her end of the deal.

<*There's also the issue of transitioning the* Intrepid,> Tanis said. <*You know what you've found—there is an upper limit to the size of ship that anyone has successfully slipped into the dark layer—and come out again. The* Intrepid *is far above that size limit.*>

<*I'll admit it's a concern. But give Bob and Earnest some credit. If the two of them can't crack the issue, I don't know who—*>

Angela stopped as both she and Tanis saw the same scan data roll in.

"There are eleven AST dreadnaughts passing through the system!" Tanis called out.

"There are what?" Sera said, half out of her chair as Tanis brought the scan data up on the bridge's main holo.

"That's rather unusual," Cargo said calmly.

"Understatement of the year," Cheeky tossed a scowl his way. "New Eden and the AST aren't exactly on the friendliest of terms, not since that little war they had a few decades ago."

Tanis remembered reading about that conflict. New Eden lay on the spin-ward edge of AST space, and was under constant pressure from the core worlds to join their alliance. New Eden preferred its independence and maintained a sizeable space force to ensure they retained it. They would lose to a full assault from the AST's military, but they were capable of making the effort too costly for any aggressor.

"They must have pulled some sort of serious diplomatic shit to be here right now," Sera said in awe.

"Doesn't look like the locals are too trusting, either," Tanis said. "Almost half their fleet is shadowing those dreadnaughts."

Sera nodded with appreciation. "From the looks of it, they stopped and refueled here, too."

"They're headed for the same jump point we are," Cheeky said, her voice low and completely serious. "They're going to Bollam's."

<She's right,> Angela agreed. *<There are reports of an old colony ship insystem at Bollam's World. The local nets are going nuts with speculation over what is going to happen.>*

"Punch it, Cheeky! Full burn. We *must* get there before those AST assholes," Sera yelled.

Cheeky complied and Sabrina prepared for a full antimatter burn around the edge of the New Eden system.

"Not around, Cheeky," Sera said, her eyes deadly serious. "Go through the system."

"We're going to pick up a hell of a fine for this," Cargo said. "They're not going to take kindly to us blasting through."

"And with their current fleet distribution, they won't do anything to stop us, either," Sera replied.

"You hope," Cargo said.

Sera did not reply.

"I don't get it," Cheeky said as she plotted the new course and spun out the AP nozzle. "I mean, I get that your ship has some cool shit, Tanis, but what could be worth the AST doing this?"

Tanis was poring over the available specs on the dreadnaughts and didn't reply. The ships were large by ninetieth century standards, each coming in at just over six kilometers long. They sported more rails, beams, and missile launches than she even cared to count.

<Those are some serious ships,> Tanis sighed. *<If we had brought the whole fleet from Kapteyn's, I would be a lot less worried, but this will be a close fight. We may have to use it again.>*

"Well?" Cheeky asked once *Sabrina* was boosting on its new trajectory. "What does your ship have that's so special?"

Tanis looked around the bridge. Cheeky appeared to be almost angry, while Cargo was merely curious. Sera's expression was more unreadable. Then the captain turned her head toward Cheeky and Cargo without breaking eye contact with Tanis.

"Look up something called *The Battle of Victoria.* It took place in the Kapteyn's system before the *Intrepid* left. Look for speculation on how they defeated the Sirians with minimal losses."

Tanis let out a long sigh. If Sera was telling her crew what to look for, then she had already found it. The record of the *Intrepid's* picotech had persisted these five thousand years.

<*Funny that this information is in the ship's database,*> Angela commented privately to Tanis. <*It wasn't previously.*>

<*I know, I checked, too,*> Tanis replied.

"Picotech!" Cargo exclaimed, half rising from his chair. "How…what…is it real?"

Tanis didn't have it in her to lie to *Sabrina's* crew—she knew that her resigned expression was already all the confirmation that Sera needed—if she needed any at all.

"It is true," Tanis replied.

"And you…wait…you!" Cheeky's voice fell into a shocked hush.

Tanis could tell that she had read something which referenced her as a general and lieutenant governor.

"General Richards, is it?" Cargo asked. "Or should I say governor?"

"How long have you known?" Tanis asked Sera. "This information was not in your databases when I came onboard."

"I pulled an update when we were in Ayrea," Sera replied smoothly. "I wanted to know more about your ship and the time you came from."

Tanis nodded slowly. "Well, now you know."

She fended off as many questions about the picotech, and her rank, as she could. She was surprised that no one was overly upset about her lies and omissions. Even Thompson grunted that he would not have volunteered the information either.

She was saved from further revelations by the first few calls from the system traffic AI regarding their speed, which Tanis responded to, but eventually just logged them with no response. It was clear they were on an outsystem vector, not passing close to any New Eden worlds or stations. No military vessels or drones moved to intercept them, and the traffic AI appeared to content itself with simply adding on fine after fine.

"This'll bankrupt us," Cargo muttered at one point.

"No," Sera disagreed while directing a pointed look at Tanis. "It really won't."

Tanis set two countdowns on the main holo. One for the AST dreadnaughts, and one for *Sabrina.* The dreadnaughts would beat them to the jump point, but the AST vessels were maintaining steady 0.5*c*. A max speed which was likely enforced by the New Eden space force ships shadowing the foreign military vessels.

Because entry velocity into the dark layer translated into faster travel time, *Sabrina* would reach Bollam's World before the AST vessels, even though they would enter FTL later.

The trip across the New Eden system took just shy of twenty-three hours, and Tanis watched with concern gnawing at her innards as the eleven AST dreadnaughts winked out of scan visibility.

"There they go," Sera said. "Now we just have to hope that half the New Eden space force doesn't decide to find out why we're in such a hurry."

Sabrina was an hour from the jump point; light-lag to the closest New Eden vessel was fifty-two minutes—with the relativistic adjustments.

<*Given how long it would take them to have confirmed the AST departure, we should be hearing from them right…about…now,*> Helen said.

On her cue, the comm board lit up with an incoming transmission from a NESF patrol craft.

<*Show-off,*> Sabrina muttered.

Tanis played the message aloud.

"Star Freighter *Sabrina,* this is the *Sword of Eden,* please declare your intentions. If we didn't know better, we would think you're chasing those core-worlder dreadnaughts."

Cargo let out a laugh. "Calling those AST ships core-worlders as if he isn't one. When the fringe is nearly a thousand light-years in any direction, you're core, too."

"What would you like me to say?" Tanis asked Sera.

"You're asking me?" Sera said with a wink. "You're the general—what do you think you should say?"

Tanis remained silent for several moments before shaking her head and turning to her console.

"*Sword of Eden,* this is General Tanis Richards of the ISS *Intrepid.* This ship is returning me to Bollam's World and is under my protection. As for what we plan to do with those dreadnaughts, look up the Battle of Victoria and figure it out."

Cheeky let out a long whistle. "Well, that'll either get them the hell out of our way—or they'll blow us to bits."

"We have thirty-seven minutes to find out," Sera replied.

<*Thirty-two,*> Angela corrected the captain.

"Damn relativistic math," Sera muttered.

No one spoke on the bridge as they raced closer to the NESF ships still clustered around the jump point. Tanis surmised that they weren't entirely trusting the AST ships' word that they were going to Bollam's World. It was possible, however unlikely, that this was some sort of feint before a full-scale attack.

The earliest time for a reply from the NESF came and went, then sixteen more minutes ticked by with agonizing slowness before a message came in.

The message was short and to the point.

"Star freighter *Sabrina,* you are cleared to maintain your current course and exit the New Eden system. Fines against your vessel have been lifted."

"See?" Sera said with a grin as she looked between Cheeky and Cargo. "I told you the general would know what to say. *And* we're not facing any fines. A good day in my books."

THE SILENT SYSTEM

STELLAR DATE: 10.25.8927 (Adjusted Years)
LOCATION: *Sabrina*, Scattered Disk
REGION: Bollam's World System, Bollam's World Federation

Cheeky brought *Sabrina* out of FTL further from the Bollam's World star than Tanis would have preferred, though she understood the need for caution—not to mention the time it would take to decelerate from 0.79*c*.

"Forty-nine AU from the stellar primary," the pilot reported.

"Well done," Sera said with a nod. "Pull us up above the stellar disk and start our braking."

Tanis tapped the system beacon's passive data stream.

"That's weird," she said with a frown. "There's nothing about the *Intrepid* on the beacon, just the standard traffic conditions, and system laws and regulations."

"I don't think those AST ships are coming here for a vacation," Sera said. "Someone is trying their best to keep things looking normal."

"The outer beacon isn't responding to requests for active data. I've sent our packet to the system relay further in; maybe once we're registered on scan we can get more info," Tanis said.

"Keep active sensors on full bore," Sera said to Tanis. "This system is always a hot mess."

Tanis had noticed *Sabrina's* shielding taking repeated impacts from dust. She was impressed at how well the graviton shielding protected the freighter. The *Intrepid's* shields would be hard-pressed to keep the ship safe in a system this young and active while traveling at such speeds.

She had spent some time reviewing data entries on Bollam's World. The star was young, under half a billion years old. The eleven major planets which orbited the star were still young and hot, with the exception of the terraformed worlds in the habitable zone. Records showed that the initial colonists, also victims of Kapteyn's Streamer, had spent considerable effort cooling those worlds before they could even begin to make them habitable.

The star lay in a region of space with few G or K class stars. Its location, combined with youth, had caused the FGT to pass it by entirely. It was probably the only G-class star within a hundred light-years of Sol which was not prepared for humanity by the FGT, but by the colonists themselves.

Tanis had to admire the tenacity of those original settlers. What they had accomplished was even more impressive than what the Edeners and Victorians had built at The Kap.

She scanned through the data on the planets, taking note of the strange gas giant named Aurora which lay seventh from the star, and the terraforming that was underway on a moon around the sixth planet, a gas giant named Kithari.

"You're going to want to alter course, Cheeky," Tanis said as she put the results of the first active scan sweep on the main holo. "There's a dense molecular cloud ahead, and a small dwarf world seems to have had its orbit changed since the last time *Sabrina* got an update on Bollam's."

<*Sorry to have inconvenienced you,*> Sabrina said with a sigh.

<*Easy now,*> Sera said soothingly. <*We don't pass this close to the core very often. Not much need to get updated system data for these worlds.*>

"I'm going to grab some coffee, anyone want some?" Cargo asked as he rose.

The three women called out in affirmative and the first mate chuckled. "Maybe I'll just bring the pot."

"You know, I'm going to go do a quick walk through the ship," Tanis said while rising from her station. "I've slaved scan to your console, Cheeky, and Angela is keeping an eye on it as well."

"We'll ping you if you're needed," Sera said.

Cargo returned with three cups of coffee. "Gave Tanis hers in the galley."

"She's got a lot on her mind," Sera said with a nod. "Don't know that I'd want to be in her position right now."

"What position is that, Captain?" Cargo's dark eyes stared at Sera intently. "What do you think we are flying into?"

Sera thought about it for a moment before replying.

"Either the *Intrepid* was smart and started trading its tech for fuel and FTL capability, or they clammed up and got themselves boarded and gutted."

"Do you think they'd be able to defend themselves?"

"Maybe—Tanis never said how much of that fleet they took with them when they left Kapteyn's Star—or if they have more of their pico bombs. If they do, then we're flying into a war zone."

"Didn't we just leave that party?"

"That was just a mixer; the real party's still to come," Sera laughed. "But now that you bring it up, I think I should go and see if I can get our general to lay down some specifics on her ship's defenses."

Cargo nodded and Sera slipped off the bridge. She found Tanis where she expected, at the forward scan and targeting sensors. Sera wasn't sure if she should be surprised that Tanis was a general and colony governor, or that she hadn't suspected her rank was far higher than she let on—she fit in with the crew as well as possible, but there were times when her bearing and poise had hinted at a higher position.

Sera wondered if her own background traits ever slipped through. There were secrets she kept that no one on this ship needed to know. Most of her past was far better off buried and forgotten.

"They still good as new?" Sera asked.

"Seem to be. Though, I should have insisted on an external array."

"You were in a rush—and I appreciate the haste, even though it was unnecessary," Sera said with a grin.

Tanis turned to Sera; her blue eyes appeared darker and more serious than normal—if that were possible.

"You don't have to do this. I don't want to risk you and your crew more than I already have. You could send me in on one of your escape pods. I can figure out a way to get to the *Intrepid*."

"Don't be ridiculous." Sera dismissed Tanis's statement with a wave of her hand. "You helped my crew rescue me when you could have just cut and run. There's no way I am just going to leave you high and dry."

Tanis smiled and appeared to relax. "Thank you. I can't imagine what would have happened if you hadn't opened that container I was in."

"I can. You would have gotten close and personal with Rebecca and her pointy needles."

"I'm sorry about that; my fault again."

"Stop saying that." Sera wasn't sure what to make of this uncharacteristically self-effacing Tanis. "I'm right as rain and thoroughly enjoyed giving that bitch what she had coming."

Tanis laughed. "I almost would have liked to have seen that…almost." Then the general eyed Sera up and down and appeared to consider her words carefully. "We both know that most nano around here isn't as good as mine. Considering what you likely had to work with—not to mention dealing with your new skin trying to kill you—how *did* you heal from that torture so fast?"

"I guess I was lucky. Helen found all the right stuff we needed on the station to keep me going," Sera replied with a shrug, the lie coming easily after so many years—though she could see that Tanis wasn't buying it.

"You handled the trauma of torture rather well—something I bet they don't teach you in star freighter captain school," the general pressed.

"I wouldn't say 'rather well', more like…I didn't curl up into a fetal position. It's not my first time being at the receiving end of someone's ill intentions. I've already done all the puking and crying. Now I know how to repress it like a pro."

Tanis's skepticism was plainly displayed on her face. "I've come clean with you, Sera. Let me know when you are ready to do the same—but don't give me your coy routine and trite little lies. You are far from who you appear to be. I hope your motives in helping me are as altruistic as you claim." She paused and drew in a long breath, her eyes narrowing. "Because if you think there is some special advantage you can gain over the *Intrepid* once we arrive, you will be mistaken."

Sera's breath caught in her throat. Tanis's blunt verbal assault took her completely off guard. For a moment, she wondered if Tanis suspected the truth about her.

<She doesn't know the truth; she probably hasn't guessed anything close to it,> Helen said. *<But she was once a counterinsurgency officer in the TSF, from what she told the crew around the wardroom table one night. She can likely see cracks all over your story. She certainly saw your blood pressure rise just now.>*

Sera forced herself to resume breathing evenly. Though Tanis may know she was hiding things, Helen was right; she wouldn't even come close to the truth if she guessed for a thousand years.

"You've got me, Tanis," Sera said slowly. "I've not been completely honest with you, but I'm not yet ready to talk about my past…give me more time."

Tanis's look was skeptical, but she didn't push. "The time is close. When we get to the *Intrepid*, Bob will discover your truth. I'd rather you share it willingly before he does."

"Who is Bob?" Sera asked.

Tanis chuckled. "That's a truth you'll soon learn on your own."

Neither woman spoke for a minute, and then Sera asked the question for which she had searched out Tanis in the first place.

"Things are likely to be hairy when we get insystem; how much of that fleet did you bring with you from Kapteyn's Star?"

"Not as much as I wish we had," Tanis sighed. "We swapped out the two Neptune class cruisers for the *Orkney* and the *Dresden*—two of the new Claymore class battle cruisers. Otherwise, it's our initial fleet of eight cruisers, some twenty pushers, and a bevy of pinnaces, shuttles, and transports. We do have a lot more fighters than we left Sol with, but I don't think even our new Arc-5s are going to be much of a match for modern craft pulling over 500*g*s. Not to mention that our ES shielding is not nearly as effective as your new grav shields."

Sera whistled. "Still more than any colony ship I've ever heard of, but probably not a match for those AST dreadnaughts."

"The *Intrepid* itself is a pretty formidable weapon. Its size also makes it hard to damage—bar the use of fusion bombs," Tanis replied. "Though we try to keep it out of the thick of battle."

"What about the pico?" Sera asked, afraid the answer would be no, but just as afraid that it may be yes.

Tanis nodded. "It's there. We have more RMs than you'd like to know exist, and they're all capable of carrying pico warheads."

"Let's hope it doesn't come to that," Sera said with a shudder. She looked into Tanis's eyes and could tell the general felt the same way. The pico was a weapon of last resort—every other avenue would have to be exhausted first.

Tanis glanced back at the sensor array's maintenance console. "I should finish looking this over."

"You've been on shift for half a day and we have seven hours before we'll get a response from the system beacon's active Link. Why don't you catch sack till then? I can do the inspection."

Tanis gave a tired smile. "I suppose I could use some rest…and it *is* your ship after all."

THROUGH THE LOOKING GLASS

STELLAR DATE: 10.26.8927 (Adjusted Years)
LOCATION: *Sabrina*, EK Belt
REGION: Bollam's World System, Bollam's World Federation

<*System beacon has registered us and we have active system scan,*> Sabrina reported ship-wide.

Tanis was on the bridge minutes later, one hand holding a cup of coffee and the other rubbing her face. "Does it have data on the *Intrepid*?" she asked.

Cheeky un-slaved scan from her console and directed it back to Tanis's station.

"Doesn't look like it," the pilot said with a shake of her head. "Just the same as before, though with more up-to-date information."

"It's like the *Intrepid* really isn't here..." Tanis sighed. "But the reports in New Eden definitely talked about a colony ship in Bollam's."

"Tanis, check the planets' positions in scan with what we can see from here. The beacon's scan data may be faked."

Cheeky looked up from her console. "Fake! No one fakes system scan. They may as well ask for jump-point collisions!"

"I've seen it before," Sera said, her voice solemn.

"Freaking, fucking... nut... I'm out of words!"

Cheeky may present a carefree exterior in nearly every aspect of her life, but when it came to piloting, and the strictures that kept starships plying the dark, she was a different person. She was right, too; faking scan was a disaster waiting to happen. Ships may be small in the vastness of space, but they all traveled between just a few points, which meant they were usually concentrated within the same areas.

"Damn...it *is* faked," Tanis reported. "This looks like scan from over a month ago; they tried to blend it so that the planets were in the right positions, but there are ships clearly heading to places that have since moved."

"We need to find out what is going on in this system and fast. Cheeky, let's burn some antimatter."

Sera stood and threw *Sabrina's* own scan data on the bridge's main holo tank. "Looks strangely clear," the captain muttered.

The space they were traveling through was near a commonly-used jump point, which the ship's scan showed to be deserted.

Tanis frowned at her readouts. "I'm betting that there is real scan somewhere. Whoever has botched the signal must still want to know where things are themselves. Good data has to be in there somewhere."

She and Angela broke down the data stream from the system's beacon and began sifting through its components for any hidden information while Sera sent an update to the rest of the crew. Over the next half hour, everyone visited the bridge to ask if they were really in a system with no scan.

Twenty minutes later, Tanis let out a cry of triumph.

"Found it! I figured the best place to hide the real scan was within the fake one. There were several distorted portions of the signal, and sure enough one of them contained the carrier wave for valid data. I'm configuring our system to read from it."

Sera set her screen to display the system's readout, and within a minute, it flicked from the boring show of regular, light traffic to an entirely different tableau. Everyone took a deep breath and then uttered a variety of curses.

The real data showed a heavy cluster of ships near the system's sixth planet, the 6M_J gas giant named Kithari. Sera selected that planet and zoomed in. The ships were grouped near one of its larger moons, a world named Fierra, which appeared to be in the late stages of terraforming. She selected the planet and all space within two hundred thousand kilometers and threw it up on the bridge's main holo tank. Cheeky and Tanis swiveled in their chairs to gaze at the results.

It was a mess.

Seven thousand kilometers from the moon, in an equatorial orbit, lay the *Intrepid*, its fleet fully deployed. Roughly a hundred thousand kilometers beyond lay a fleet consisting of fifty-two destroyers and light cruisers. The scan data identified them as Bollam's World Space Force. The majority of ships in this fleet were positioned at strategic points that appeared to both protect and corral the *Intrepid*.

Another fleet held position fifty thousand kilometers north of the moon; it consisted of several light cruisers and over two hundred corvettes. A similar formation of nearly the same composition held position roughly the same distance south of the moon.

Beyond all the fleets lay the eleven AST dreadnaughts, holding station in a half-ring around the moon's parent world.

"How the hell did they beat us here?" Sera cursed.

"They must have transitioned back to regular space and boosted up, before going back into FTL," Cheeky said, her brow furrowed.

"I realize that. It was rhetorical," Sera said.

"Oh."

Tanis let out a soft chuckle, then a good long laugh. When she stopped, she looked up to see Sera, Cheeky, and Cargo staring at her.

"Sorry, it's just par for the course," Tanis said, still chuckling. "They've gone and got themselves into quite the mess. Who do you think those corvette fleets are?"

Sera frowned. "Someday I'd like to hear the whole story of how you guys got here. As for those two light fleets…they're…aw shit."

"That good, eh?" Tanis asked.

"Our pirate friends have come for the fun. Rebecca and her ships are at the north pole and Padre is at the south end. Looks like they decided to go hunting for the *Intrepid* without you."

"How friendly are any of those factions likely to become with each other?"

"I'd say less friendly, more hostile. Scan shows several small debris fields. I'll bet there have already been some altercations."

"I'm surprised that more of the Bollam's space force isn't deployed," Cargo said. "They must have thousands of ships in the system."

"They're moving more in, but I bet the arrival of the AST is giving them pause," Tanis said. "You can see them gathering forces at key points. I bet they're also readying some nice big rail guns."

"They'll have some, but people don't really use rails defensively anymore," Sera said as she examined the Bollam's fleet positions. "With inertial dampeners, ships can jink well out of the way of a rail's slug."

Tanis frowned. "That may be true, but what about grapeshot? You don't fire where they are, but where you expect them to be."

"Grapeshot?" Cheeky asked.

"Rail-fired shells filled with millions of pebbles. You fill all reasonable approaches with them. People can jink all they want, they'll just jink into the grapeshot. Then you use their hesitation against them and send in the slugs, or beams, if they are close enough," Tanis replied.

"You lived in a brutal time," Cargo commented.

"War is always brutal. But I need to get to my ship, and you need to deliver on your promise," Tanis said to Sera, her expression almost pleading.

Sera smiled and nodded to Tanis before she turned to their pilot. "Cheeky? How does it look?"

"Well, provided no one blows us to pieces, I can make it happen. Based on the axial tilt of the planet, and everyone's orbits, there will be a period in about five hours where only a few of Rebecca's ships will have *Intrepid* in their sights. She's a big mutha, so I bet if I work up the right approach vector we can use her to hide us and get in almost entirely unseen. I'll have to work out the timing and coast—even hiding behind the *Intrepid's* girth, an AP trail would be plain as day."

"Good plan," Sera said. "Why don't you kill thrust now, and we'll coast till you have your path worked up. Use minimal burn; we'll try to stay as dark as possible. Nix our beacon, too. No need to let Rebecca know her favorite pincushion is within reach."

"Can they detect the graviton emissions from our shielding?" Tanis asked.

Sera ran a hand through her hair. "This close to a $6M_J$ jovian they shouldn't be able to. Plus, I'm not really comfortable disabling shields. This system still has a lot of stuff flying around."

"Having been in a ship hit by this system's debris, I see your point," Tanis acknowledged with a nod. "I'll get a transmission ready to burst to the *Intrepid* when we have a clear line to them. Don't want them thinking we're hostile."

Sera hadn't even thought of that. *Sabrina's* new shields were good, but she didn't want to see how well they'd hold up against the radiation wash from one of the tugs patrolling around the *Intrepid,* let alone the beams on those cruisers.

The next few hours passed quietly. *Sabrina* had a lot of speed to burn off before making her approach; rather than turning and braking, Cheeky altered the rear shields to emit negative gravitons. The effect caused enough drag to slow them down and line up on the desired approach vector.

Sera was making a light lunch for herself in the mess when Flaherty came in and closed the galley door. She looked up at the dour man and smiled. "How are you today?"

Flaherty grunted. "Been better." He sloshed some semi-warm coffee into a mug and sat down. "It always catches up with you, doesn't it?"

"Noticed that too, did you?"

His deadly-serious eyes bored into hers. "You aren't going to be able to run from it forever."

Sera spun to face him directly, her eyes angry, even though her voice was calm. "I am helping a friend here. This is not fate or anything, just random events."

Flaherty let out a long, exasperated sigh. "You know I'll always be here to watch your back. But some day you are going to have to own up to your destiny. We're doing the right thing now, but there are a lot of other things that could also use your attention—a lot more important than some energy module." With that, the large man stood and left the wardroom, his near-full cup of coffee left on the table.

Sera leaned against the counter and let out a long breath. Suddenly, the ship seemed too close and small about her. Her synthetic skin felt like it was constricting her, like she couldn't breathe. A wave of dizziness hit her and Sera closed her eyes, willing herself to be calm. She could do this; she would not repeat past mistakes. Tanis and the *Intrepid* would live to see another journey to a star where they could be left out of the messes this close to the core. Sera vowed it.

<*Easy now, just some anxiety,*> Helen's soothing voice whispered in her mind.

<*If ever there was a time to feel anxious, this is it,*> Sera replied.

<*Flaherty's right; it does feel a bit like destiny, doesn't it?*> Helen's voice held a wistful edge.

Sera wondered what the AI saw, what her wisdom and years told her about the future.

<*It feels more like a curse,*> Sera said with a sigh. <*Like events will drive me back there no matter what.*>

Helen sent out an affirmative wave of agreement. <*I suspect they will.*>

ANDROMEDA

STELLAR DATE: 10.26.8927 (Adjusted Years)
LOCATION: *Sabrina*, EK Belt
REGION: Bollam's World System, Bollam's World Federation

Tanis scoured the background noise in the system, looking for a range with little use and high levels of stellar noise.

<*There, that whine coming from the weird jovian planet, Aurora. We can hide our signal in its noise. You can bet Bob is listening to that thing and what they have going on there,*> Angela advised.

<*I was thinking the same thing,*> Tanis said and began to calibrate *Sabrina's* transmitter to piggyback on the planet's emissions.

<*I know,*> Angela replied with a wink.

"*Intrepid,* this is General Tanis Richards; hope this message finds you well. I'm in a small freighter, which will begin making an approach to your position in roughly ten minutes. We expect to be ready to dock in four hours and twenty-nine minutes. Our vector will be southerly to avoid detection from your friends. We will be alone and dark. Please do not fire on us. Please do not respond unless absolutely necessary. We're not exactly on friendly terms with some of the folks out there, either."

Tanis set the system to repeat the message three times and then killed the transmission. She turned to Cheeky.

"It's sent. We're good to begin our final approach. Everything set on your end?"

"As much as it's going to be. There's going to be a tight spot in about two hours when we get close to one of the AST ships, but we should be able to slip by if we kill all but our forward shields—which will be facing away from them." She entered in several commands on her console. "I'm having Sabrina switch main systems to battery, as well. No point in having a nice, hot reactor giving us away."

<*I'm sipping juice here,*> Sabrina said.

Tanis nodded. The new batteries could power the ship and even send a few pulses from the lasers before running dry. If things got hairy, the reactor would still be warm enough to spin it back up in a few minutes.

Sera reappeared on the bridge looking like she had eaten something unpleasant. She sat in her chair without saying a word and leaned her head back, eyes closed. There was no need to update her on the transmission and commencement of their final approach. Tanis could tell she had maintained a connection to the bridge net.

She felt tempted to ask the captain what was wrong, but decided the other woman just needed to calm down and put whatever was bothering her to rest rather than having to make up an evasive response.

Tanis took advantage of Sera's stillness to further observe her. The captain was usually in constant motion—her actions quick and decisive, her face never showing more or less than she intended it to.

At this moment, she looked much younger than usual. Tanis realized she couldn't place Sera's age…at all. She looked to be in her early twenties, but with the experiences she had mentioned in passing, not to mention her performance on the pirate station and the ship, she had to be much older. Sera had the knowledge and instincts of a person much closer to their first century, possibly even older than that.

<*Not knowing her story is really eating you up, isn't it?*> Angela asked.

<*You know me; all the puzzle pieces have to fit.*>

The crew had been of little help; most had only known her for a few years—though, in that time, they had become quite loyal. None of them had any knowledge of their captain's history before her purchase of *Sabrina,* with the exception of the ever-mysterious Flaherty—and he wasn't sharing anything.

Sera sat forward and opened her eyes, looking as alert and full of energy as ever. Tanis's moment of examination was over.

"Are you going to stay when we reach the *Intrepid*?" Tanis took the opportunity to ask.

Sera flashed an enigmatic smile. "Well, I do have to help you guys get that ship into FTL—unless they want to stay here forever."

Cheeky nearly choked. "Captain! That ship can never go into FTL. Every credit I have says they're negotiating for that moon they're orbiting—it's the only play they have."

Sera shook her head. "Not the only play. The *Intrepid* can drop into FTL. They just need the right plans to transition their ship safely, and make it appear unappetizing to the lurkers in the dark layer."

<*How is that possible?*> Angela asked. <*From my research, no one has ever transitioned a ship anywhere close to the* Intrepid's *size. Those dreadnaughts out there are about as big as you can go.*>

"Yeah, what she said," Cheeky turned in her seat and directed a quizzical look at Sera. "You don't have that tech; no one has it."

Sera shook her head slowly. "Not no one. I have it—so do some others."

"How—what—captain!" Cheeky exclaimed. "Don't be ridiculous! You can't swindle Tanis's people…"

"It's OK," Tanis said. "I'm taking it on faith that Sera has what she says she does. Besides, our deal was to get me here and be compensated—a payment that I will render promptly, once we dock."

"You won't throw the rest of us in your brig if she tries to sell you bogus tech, right?" Cheeky looked worried. "Do you have a brig?"

"It's a big ship," Cargo said with a laugh. "They're going to have a brig."

"Our original deal aside, FTL tech is pretty impressive. What would you want in exchange?" Tanis asked. The picotech was not up for trade. Without it as an option, she wondered what Sera, with her already advanced nanotech, could want that could match the value of FTL for the *Intrepid*.

"The opportunity to get in on the action."

<*Hah! She's more like you than even I'd guessed,*> Angela commented privately to Tanis.

"You just want to shoot at a few people in trade for amazing, unheard of technology?"

"Not just a few people. I want to turn Rebecca and her fleet of miscreants into a fine molecular cloud. I'm tired of dealing with them. I'm tired of playing their games. In fact, I want to do the same to Padre's fleet and then I want to show the good people of Bollam's World that just because a valuable ship shows up in their system it's not up for grabs."

"You seem…bitter," Cheeky observed.

Sera's expression hardened. "I want to show people that if they behave like animals, someone is going to come along and put them down like the rabid pack they are."

Tanis was taken aback by Sera's vehemence. She saw that Cheeky and Cargo were also surprised by the rage in their captain's voice. Something deep drove Sera's anger. Something personal and unpleasant.

The conversation was interrupted by the comm board lighting up, and the proximity alarms going off in concert.

Tanis picked up the comm message and flipped it to the bridge's audible systems once the first syllable came to her ears.

"Good morning, *Sabrina,* this is Captain Joseph Evans of the ISS *Andromeda.* It's a little hot out here, so we thought we'd give you a ride into the *Intrepid.*"

"What the hell?" Cheeky exclaimed, furiously adjusting her holo interfaces. "There's a fucking cruiser on our ass that wasn't there a second ago!"

Tanis felt a smile nearly split her face in half.

"You have the honors," Sera said, returning her smile.

"*Andromeda,* this is Tanis…sweet stars it's good to hear your voice, Joe." Tanis all but gasped the last words, her voice choking up.

"Tanis! Oh stars, thank god. I was afraid it was a hoax; are you OK? Are you in danger?"

<*She's always in danger,*> Angela replied sardonically.

"I'm well. Captain Sera and *Sabrina* have treated me very well."

"Corsia is sending a plot for your pilot. We need to cut the chatter and get you off radar. Dock as quickly as you can. I love you, Tanis."

"I love you, too, Joe. See you in a few minutes…"

Tanis couldn't stop the flood of emotion that washed over her. She let out a sob and tears started to flow. She saw Cheeky and Sera exchange incredulous looks before her eyes misted up too much to see clearly.

A moment later there was a hand on her back and a soft voice at her side.

"I take it he's someone special to you." Sera's voice was thick with emotion.

Tanis gulped down a deep breath and forced herself to calm. "He's my husband," she managed to say.

"Husband?" Cheeky asked with a grin. "I bet he's a real looker—no wonder you never came by my cabin."

Tanis smiled and wiped her face. "Yes, that was it. Did you get the information to dock?"

Cheeky nodded. "Their bay is right behind us. It'll be snug, but we'll fit. Just one jot to the left and we'll drop right in."

"I'm going to the hatch," Tanis said as she rose.

"Right behind you," Sera said. "You have the bridge, Cargo."

Tanis was sliding down the ladder in the corridor before Sera finished speaking. She knew it was irrational, but the thought of being with Joe made all the obstacles before her seem so much simpler. Sure, they faced insurmountable odds, and there was little chance of ever building the colony they had dreamed, but none of that mattered if she was with Joe. They could figure it out; they could figure *anything* out.

She arrived at the forward hatch and all but bounced on her feet as she waited for the sound of the ship settling in its cradle.

As soon as the telltale clang echoed through the deck plates, she cycled the airlock, barely aware that Sera stepped in with her.

It seemed to take forever for the pressure match indicator to turn green, and when it did, she pushed out of *Sabrina* and smashed herself into Joe's open arms. The smell of him washed over her and she couldn't stop overwhelming sobs of joy and pent-up anxiety from escaping her.

"I'm here Tanis, you're safe, you're back with us," Joe whispered in her ear while stroking her hair.

Tanis wasn't able to form words and spoke into his mind instead.

<Never again, I mean it this time, you come with me everywhere.>

Joe chuckled. *<My feelings exactly. I'm just glad you're OK. You had me worried sick! I was just about ready to beg, borrow, or steal a ship to start scouring the galaxy for you. You're both OK?>*

<We are, yes, both me and our little addition,> Tanis said with a smile. *<I got back here as fast as wings would take me.>*

<And who are these wings?> Joe asked, his eyes darting over her shoulder.

Tanis finally became aware of Sera's presence, floating awkwardly behind her in the 0*g* on *Andromeda*. She looked around to see all eyes in the shuttle bay on her. She flushed and stepped back.

"Joe, this is Captain Sera, my rescuer. Sera, this is Joseph Evans."

"Pleased to meet you," Joe said with a smile as he extended his hand to Sera. "Any rescuer of Tanis's is a dear friend of mine—not to mention a rare person. Usually she is the one doing the rescuing."

Sera took his hand and returned the smile. "Then you won't be surprised to learn that she rescued me once on our way here."

Joe barked a laugh. "Now that's more like it."

Behind Sera, the rest of the crew, bar Cargo, stood at the ship's airlock. Tanis introduced them to Joe and Sera called up for Cargo to secure the ship and come down as well.

<Go and enjoy yourselves,> Corsia said. *<Sabrina and I are coordinating final docking procedures.>*

Joe led Tanis and *Sabrina's* crew through the docking bay toward the ship's forward crew lounge.

"It doesn't look that much more advanced. I thought you guys were supposed to have amazing tech," Cheeky said while peering around. "It seems pretty normal—except the lack of AG."

Tanis had to hide a smile as the crew of *Sabrina* clumsily navigated the corridor with the hand and footholds that she barely even thought of. It was possible that most of them had never even spent any appreciable time in zero-*g*.

"It's not what's visible," Joe said. "We don't have artificial gravity on ships this size, true, but we've flown *Andromeda* within a thousand klicks of those big newcomers out there and they didn't even catch a glimpse of us."

"You buzzed an AST dreadnaught?" Cheeky's eyes grew wide with appreciation.

"That's why we were out here," Joe said with a nod. "We wanted to know what those new ships were all about."

"What did you learn?" Tanis asked. "How do they stack up?"

"They have omnidirectional antimatter engines on either end; heavily shielded, and deadly to boot. Their beams are as strong as our best and their grav shields can probably block almost anything we can throw at them. I think we'd wear them down in a slug-fest, provided we could keep them at bay, but with all the other players on the field it gets pretty complicated."

"It usually is," Tanis said with a smile.

A minute later, they arrived in the forward crew lounge. The room was clean and spare, yet well appointed. Tanis remembered spending many an evening relaxing here on the long deceleration into Kapteyn's, and again during her many tours on the ship during the Victoria years.

"You'll all receive a protocol upgrade by nano packet to update your Link for our systems," Corsia announced over the lounge's audible systems. "Please accept it and you'll get onto our public nets."

"Thanks," Cargo said. "I was wondering why I couldn't make any sort of connection to a shipnet."

"What happened to you?" Joe asked as *Sabrina's* crew accepted the upgrade and Linked to the *Andromeda's* net.

"My pod got picked up by pirates after I ejected," Tanis said. "It's a very different galaxy than we last saw."

"You can say that again," Joe replied.

<*We've passed the AST ships and are approaching the Bollam's fleet picket lines,*> Corsia announced over the Link.

"Thanks, Cor," Joe said as he held Tanis and kissed her.

INTREPID

STELLAR DATE: 10.26.8927 (Adjusted Years)
LOCATION: ISS *Andromeda*, Near Fierra (6*Mj* Jovian)
REGION: Bollam's World System, Bollam's World Federation

Sera watched Tanis and her husband—husband!—with a smile slowly creeping across her face. Who would have thought that the hard-bitten general had a man into whose arms she melted? Of all the things she expected to encounter, this was perhaps the last.

She glanced at her crew as they watched Tanis, and caught Cheeky's eye. They exchanged a knowing look, before Sera returned her gaze to the forward-facing window.

She felt a pang of homesickness as she looked through the holo-enhanced portal. It reminded her too much of home. So clean, so meticulously maintained by nano, that it looked brand new, even though it had likely seen centuries of service.

Through the plas she saw several Bollam's World Space Force ships come into view, their mass and vector highlighted on the display for any Linked viewer to see. The vessels were new and well made by ninetieth century standards, but there was something about the understated elegance of the *Andromeda* that put them to shame. The Bollam's ships were boxy and utilitarian, where the *Andromeda* hailed from a time when both form and function were honored without compromise.

She was impressed with how neither Joe, nor any of the crew they had passed, gave her unusual black skin, or Nance's hazsuit a second glance. Then again, given what she had read about the early fourth millennia, her crew fit well within the bounds of what was considered normal.

They slipped past the Bollam's picket lines without drawing attention, and before long the *Intrepid* came into view.

"All those ships dock inside the *Intrepid*?" Nance asked in awe.

"They do indeed," Tanis replied with a nod. "Most of the cruisers fit in the main bay."

Cheeky whistled. "Well, I'm not surprised. Most of the stations we dock *Sabrina* at are smaller than that ship."

Sera counted ten capital ships protecting the *Intrepid*, the largest being a pair of thousand-meter cruisers that the window's holo enhancement labeled as the *Orkney* and *Dresden*.

The display didn't provide many details beyond mass and size, but given what she knew of Sol in the fourth millennia, and what she had read about Victoria, Sera suspected that the *Intrepid's* fleet was more than a match for all but the AST vessels surrounding them.

Even if they didn't resort to their picotech.

<*You're thinking about how this feels like home, aren't you?*> Helen asked.

<*I am,*> Sera sent an affirmative response.

"Those poor pirate fleets," Cheeky chuckled. "They must really be wondering if they bit off more than they can chew."

"They're probably considering joining forces," Tanis said.

"Or getting the hell out of here," Sera added.

"It's like looking back in time," Thompson whispered, his voice filled with awe. "So much of what we see—the worlds, the stations, what few rings remain—they're the ruins, leftovers from before the wars. What we've built since…well, at best it's utilitarian and functional…but this ship, the *Intrepid*…it's so graceful, it's amazing…"

Cheeky put a hand on Thompson's shoulder. "I never knew you were such a romantic."

Thompson looked around, his face flushing. "I'm, uh, I'm not…don't expect future sentiment."

Nance let out a nervous laugh. "I don't blame you though…that's one hell of a ship. How do they build something so big…?"

"Have you ever been to Sol?" Sera asked Nance.

"I've never felt like having the probe it takes to get in that far," the bio replied.

"They have more than a few artificial structures that dwarf planets. Building things like the *Intrepid* is practically child's play—at least it used to be."

"Are the Mars Outer Shipyards still there?" Joe asked.

"No," Sera shook her head. "Sol suffered the worst in the FTL wars. The only megastructure still there is High Terra."

Joe's face fell. "Mars 1, the Cho?"

Sera shook her head. "All gone—well, the Cho has been rebuilt…sort of."

"I don't think I even want to know," Joe replied.

"We got out in the nick of time," Tanis said with a hand on her husband's shoulder. "They tore themselves apart even before FTL came along."

Joe sighed. "We knew it was coming…it's why we left, after all. Place was getting nuts."

"The whole core is nuts now," Sera said. "It's a hundred messed-up worlds in there."

"I resent that," Nance said. "I'm from a core world."

"You're from Virginis; they've only been in the AST for a century. It's not enough time for the madness to settle in…maybe," Sera's expression grew deadly serious.

It took Nance a moment to realize the Captain was poking fun at her. "I'm going to ignore your biased remarks," she said, with obviously-faked haughtiness.

"I don't know." Cheeky grinned. "Maybe her hazsuit fetish is a symptom."

Nance chose to ignore the barb. "If you're the famous General of Victoria," she said to Tanis, changing the subject and gesturing at the *Intrepid* through the display. "Are you in charge over there?"

Joe let out a laugh and wrapped his arm around Tanis. "She thinks she is—usually is, too, if the captain is in stasis."

"I'm the executive officer," Tanis said and threw a mock scowl at Joe.

"On paper," Joe added with a wink at his wife.

"Were you ever going to come up to the bridge?" a female voice asked from behind the group.

Sera turned to see a tall woman with lavender skin and a highly exaggerated figure standing in the entrance to the lounge.

"Jessica!" Tanis cried out and ran to the woman. They embraced and spoke privately for a few minutes before joining the group.

"No wonder she never thought you two were that unusual," Cheeky said, giving Nance and Sera significant looks. "Your kinks are nothing on hers."

"It's not like that!" Nance whispered. "Cut it out already."

"Sorry, Jessica," Joe said as Tanis and Jessica approached. "We got talking and I sort of decided to stay down here for the approach and forgot to tell anyone."

"Well, who's going to fly it, then?" Jessica asked.

"I'm pretty sure that Petrov can manage to dock with the *Intrepid*. Besides, Corsia just humors us all anyway."

<You keep me company,> Corsia said. *<It would get lonely out here without my little passengers.>*

"That's...a bit creepy," Thompson said.

"Are all your AI so imperious?" Cheeky asked. "No offense, Angela, but you're a little bossy, too."

<I think we should save this conversation for another time,> Angela said.

Sera was certain she knew what the conversation would be about. She remembered learning about the Phobos accords as a child, but those laws were dead and gone. However, the crew and AIs on the *Intrepid* would likely not appreciate the low station of most AIs in the ninetieth century.

"Wha—?" Cheeky began to ask before Sera sent her a message to drop it.

"Tanis!" A new voice entered the conversation and Sera turned to see the holo-presence of a tall, rather distinguished-looking man.

"Captain Andrews," Tanis said with a smile as she turned to face him. "I see things are proceeding well, as usual."

"Not too much worse for wear," the captain returned the smile.

Tanis had never mentioned how attractive her captain was. A man from the early fourth millennia, too—if the sparse records from so long ago were to be believed.

"I have some friends coming aboard," Tanis said. "This is Captain Sera and the crew of *Sabrina*," Tanis gestured to Sera's crew. "They have some fascinating information regarding FTL that they would like to share with us. Earnest will be especially interested."

"Thank you for returning Tanis to us," Captain Andrews said to Sera. "From what Corsia has relayed of her conversations with Sabrina, you were a long way from here."

"Just about a hundred and fifty light-years," Tanis said nonchalantly. "A hop, skip, and a jump by today's standards."

Joe nearly choked. "A hundred and fifty! Stars...I would never have found you."

Sera watched Tanis embrace her husband and whisper something in his ear while Captain Andrews continued.

"I'll be glad to have you all aboard—and not soon enough. Every one of our friends out there is making more demands than I can shake a stick at. Thankfully, there are so many of them, no one wants to make the first move."

"We'll be docking in thirty minutes," Joe said. "Should be up there in forty-five."

"Very well," the captain replied and his holo faded out.

"He's hot!" Cheeky exclaimed.

Tanis looked aghast. "He's the captain!"

"And a damn hot one at that," Cheeky said to herself.

Several conversations picked up as the *Andromeda* approached her mothership, and Sera turned to admire the view. The design of the *Intrepid* was both alien and very familiar. Its elegance reminded her of some of her people's ships—the ones built before The Sundering. Truly amazing craftsmanship had gone into what was ultimately just a colony route stevedore.

The *Andromeda* passed near one of the cruisers shadowing the *Intrepid*. The holo overlay on the lounge's window highlighted it and identified the ship as the *Orkney*. Sera slipped out of her footholds and kicked toward the window, dismissing the information overlay from her vision. She wanted to look upon this vista with her own eyes.

Both ships were on similar vectors, and the *Andromeda's* pilot brought the ship in for a slow pass, only a thousand meters from the *Orkney*.

It was built for war and Sera found herself impressed with the firepower the *Intrepid* was packing in a fleet of ships which should have been nothing more than transports, pushers, and cargo haulers.

The *Orkney* gleamed like a jewel, sheathed in what was likely several meters of highly-reflective ablative plating. Nearby, a hauler was moving an icy asteroid into position near the warship. She suspected it was to extract water and create an additional ice shield around the vessel.

She imagined some terraformer working on the world below was probably quite upset to see over a hundred trillion liters of water they had planned for a lake or sea taken away.

It was a form of warfare Sera had only read about. Take your big war wagons, sheathe them in ice and let them take the heat from enemy beams. The ice would also add radiation shielding from indirect nuclear blasts.

The tactic matched the rest of the ship's structure. With only rear engines, this was a vessel that was made to get to the fight fast, take a beating and wipe out the opposition quickly. It was aided by an assortment of beams that even the AST dreadnaughts would envy.

With fifty-centimeter lenses, *Orkney's* lasers could lance across a hundred thousand kilometers and still deal lethal damage. Even at their distant position, the AST dreadnaughts were within this vessel's firing range. Modern ships rarely fired at such distances—rapid movement made long-range targeting nearly impossible.

Sera imagined having a fleet of such vessels at her command and found a new appreciation for Tanis's tactical mind. With a target as big as the *Intrepid* to defend, she had apparently pulled out all the stops.

The *Andromeda* silently slipped past the *Orkney*, and its accompanying tug and asteroid. Ahead, the bulk of the *Intrepid* began to fill the forward view. The rear of the vessel sported two massive fusion burners, and a pair of smaller antimatter engines.

Small was a relative term, since the *Andromeda's* seven hundred and twenty meter hull could both fit inside and turn around within even the smaller engine's exhaust ports.

"Imagine being at the helm of that thing," Cheeky whispered from Sera's side. "I can almost…" she shivered with delight and Sera rolled her eyes.

"Easy now. And here you accuse Nance and I of having fetishes."

"Oh, I have my weird bits," Cheeky said with a smile. "I just don't pretend not to. Galaxy would be a better place if people were real."

They passed beneath the engines and under the two spinning cylinders, each containing an entire world's worth of animals, flora, and fauna. From the stories Tanis had told, the general even had a nice cabin beside a lake in one.

Surrounding the ship was a latticework of support struts, though it was not readily apparent that was their primary purpose. They looked far more like a protective web; with mobile beams and chaff cannons mounted along their lengths, they certainly fit the bill.

"I bet they didn't leave Sol with all those," Sera said.

"Probably not, but I bet a few were there for shooting down rocks and stuff," Cheeky commented.

They passed the cylinders and came underneath the forward section of the ship where the doors of a massive bay loomed wide. The space inside was cavernous and empty, with all its normal occupants outside the ship on patrol.

The *Andromeda* turned and slowly backed into the bay. Once within the hull of the *Intrepid,* Sera felt the slight tug of gravity and by the time the ship settled into its cradle, over half a *g* pulled firmly at everyone.

Tanis gestured for the crew to leave the lounge as Sabrina squealed with delight over the Link.

<*I'm in a ship that's inside another ship! This is so weird!*>

<*Is it OK? We can have you undock,*> Sera replied.

<*Corsia and some big guy named Bob are already working on that,*> Sabrina replied. <*They seem to do a lot without even talking to people.*>

Sera could tell Sabrina was a bit nervous.

<*I've noticed that. I'll send Cargo up to you to keep an eye on things.*>

<*Thanks, that'll make me feel better,*> Sabrina replied.

They reached a cross-corridor and Tanis stopped the group.

"Sera, if you'd like to come with me, we have a meeting on the bridge deck," Tanis said.

Sera nodded. "I'd like Flaherty to come with me."

Tanis nodded and addressed Jessica. "Can you see to getting *Sabrina's* crew settled and have someone give them a tour?"

"No problem. At the least I'll show them where the bars are."

"You guys aren't taking your current situation too seriously," Thompson observed.

Jessica shrugged. "We've been in worse. Besides, Tanis is back—she'll know what to do." She placed a hand on Tanis's shoulder, which earned her a worried smile from the general.

"Just don't get too messed up—or entangled," Tanis directed a look at Jessica and Cheeky. "We may need to move fast."

With that she turned, walking briskly down a corridor to a small maglev train floating next to a platform. They entered the car, and once they took their seats, it whisked out of the station. The group had barely settled in when the train passed out of the *Andromeda* and into a clear tube, which ran across the upper reaches of the bay.

"Nice view," Sera said, looking down at the retreating form of the *Andromeda* and the kilometers of empty bay.

"It's not a bad place to work," Tanis replied. "I have to admit, it's going to be nice to stretch my legs for a bit. It's been a while since I've spent that much time on a ship as small as *Sabrina*."

"Feeling a bit cooped up, were you?" Joe asked.

"A bit," Tanis replied with a smile. "Sabrina's not that small, and I've certainly spent longer on ships…I just missed our cabin and your garden-fresh veggies."

Joe laughed. "It's probably fallen into decay; it's been years since anyone has been there."

Tanis shrugged. "We've fixed it up before; we can do it again."

Sera tuned out of their conversation and watched as the train car passed into a shaft in the bay wall, and then her breath caught as it shot out into empty space. After a moment's panic, she realized they were riding one of the thin arcs which surrounded the ship. They rose up, over the forward section of the colony vessel and then down toward the ship's nose.

The train passed back through the hull and down a long shaft before easing to a stop. The platform they stepped onto was broad and bustling with people passing through, or waiting for cars to take them to their destinations.

Tanis weaved through the throng, and as she did, people began to stop and stare. A few pointed, and whispers of "Tanis" began to fill the air.

Sera could see the general's face begin to redden and before long she stopped and turned to the crowd.

"Yes folks, I'm back."

Cheers erupted around them and some called out her name, while others shouted questions about their current situation.

Tanis held up her hands and the throng quieted.

"Don't worry, I have a plan. Everything is going to be OK."

The words were simple, and although Sera hadn't noticed it being particularly grim, the mood on the platform immediately lifted.

Tanis gave a final wave, and then led her party to the bridge deck's central corridor.

DECISIONS

STELLAR DATE: 10.27.8927 (Adjusted Years)
LOCATION: ISS *Intrepid*, Orbiting Fierra
REGION: Bollam's World System, Bollam's World Federation

They made their way down the long corridor, weaving through more crowds; individuals called out to the general, and Tanis waved or replied in turn. Presently, the crowds thinned and they came to the end of the passage, which opened into a large atrium—the centerpiece of which was a woman standing amidst a sea of holographic displays.

Sera watched in awe as the woman's hands danced across the displays, emitters on her fingertips manipulating untold systems in the time it took for Sera to realize what the woman was doing.

As they approached, what she initially perceived to be a console in front of the woman also turned out to be a holographic display. In fact, the woman appeared to be the only real thing in the atrium. Sera altered her vision to see through the holographic interfaces and was surprised at what her sight revealed.

What had appeared at first to be the woman's hair was cleverly disguised super conductor strands, which must be functioning as antennas. The bandwidth a system like that provided would be immense. Her face was smooth and composed, despite the rapid blinking of her eyelids, beneath which lay entirely black eyes. Sera marveled at her pure white skin, which her enhanced vision showed not to be skin at all, but rather a smooth, flexible polymer.

Other than her glossy coating, the woman wasn't wearing a stitch of clothing. She was perched on a very narrow stool, or pedestal—or rather, her body merged directly into the seat. She suspected this woman spent a lot of time in her current position.

The woman's head tilted and she smiled at them. An audible voice came from all around them, and over their Links.

"Welcome home, Tanis, and welcome to your guests." The woman's mouth mimed the words, but no sound came from it.

"It's good to see you, Priscilla." Tanis smiled as she walked forward and stepped through the holo to embrace the woman, who stopped manipulating the interfaces around her and returned the embrace with an expression that was both warm, yet chillingly lifeless on her white face and deep black eyes.

Tanis turned, still standing in the midst of the holo display—though that didn't stop them from flashing and dancing quicker than an eye could follow. "This is Priscilla. For most purposes, she is the *Intrepid*."

"I'm very glad to meet you." Sera stepped forward and extended her hand. "I'm Sera and this is Flaherty." The silent man actually had an expression of wonder on his face as he shook Priscilla's hand in turn. "I have to admit, I'm confused. How are you the *Intrepid*?"

Priscilla gave an understanding smile. "I am the *Intrepid* in the way that your mind controls your brain, or maybe the other way around. The *Intrepid's* neural net is too vast and complex to be able to communicate effectively with humans—at least not so many of you—so I am the intermediary, its avatar, in a fashion, yet at the same time, I am the *Intrepid*."

"But you are human," Flaherty said. "I can see it; you are not a machine."

Priscilla maintained her beatific smile. "Of course I am human; would an AI be able to think for another AI and make those thoughts into something a human could understand? The *Intrepid* has a human for its mind, though its brain is AI."

"She downplays the *Intrepid's* brain. It is far more than just AI," Tanis said with a wink. Priscilla inclined her head and a wry look crossed her face, quickly replaced by her implacable gaze. "She and Amanda take turns as the human interface to the *Intrepid*. Without them, the ship and the humans on it would have a bit of a communication gap."

"How long do these turns last?" Sera asked, wondering how long this avatar spent attached to her pedestal.

"We each actively interface with the *Intrepid* for ninety days at a time. On our downtime, we take up more…regular duties on the ship."

"That is amazing," Flaherty said in a distracted voice.

Priscilla smiled at him, then nodded toward the hall to their left. "You should go. The captain and other leaders are waiting."

Tanis gestured for the group to follow her and led them through a short corridor and into a conference room beyond.

The room was not large, but well appointed, with the center dominated by an oblong table, around which were seated nine people. Sera immediately recognized Captain Andrews at its head, and her pulse rose in reaction. It had been so long since she had allowed herself to see a man as attractive, she almost didn't know how to deal with the change in her emotional state.

<Ha! I knew it would happen eventually. You've managed to bury your feelings for some time now, but I knew someday a man would come along that your cold reason wouldn't be able to deflect,> Helen commented as she noted Sera's changing chemical state.

<Don't count on me swooning any time soon.>

<You should try it, Cheeky seems to enjoy swooning.>

<Cheeky enjoys a lot of things.>

Sera tore her attention from the *Intrepid's* captain and focused on the others around the table. On his right were two men who were not wearing the ship's uniform, but what appeared to be civilian garb. The man closest to the captain sat ramrod straight; his hair was dark and slicked back. He seemed to see everything in the room at once, and took careful note of all he viewed.

The man next to him was alert as well, but also appeared to be lost in thought at the same time. On his right was a woman who had several plas sheets spread about her and looked up from them with the expression of one who was believed that more important work was being interrupted. The man and two women to the left of the

Captain were decidedly military. They wore uniforms similar to Joseph's and had the bearing of officers high in the chain of command.

Upon their entry, the Captain rose. "Welcome aboard the *Intrepid*, Captain Sera, Flaherty; and welcome back, Tanis." He was just as imposing in life as Sera anticipated. His voice boomed, filling the room easily.

Tanis exchanged hugs and handshakes with the colony mission's leadership while Sera, Flaherty, and Joe took their seats at the table. Once the room had settled, the captain introduced those around the table for Sera's benefit.

The slick-looking man on his right was Terrance Enfield, one of the financiers of the *Intrepid* and its journey to 58 Eridani. Beside him was Earnest Redding, apparently the architect behind the ship. The distracted woman to his right was Abby Redding, Earnest's wife and the Chief Engineer of the *Intrepid*. The three in military dress were Admiral Sanderson, Colonel Ouri, and Commandant Brandt.

<*Tanis is a General, but appears to outrank a much older Admiral?*> Sera asked Helen privately.

<*Your guess is as good as mine—if your guess is something along the lines of Tanis getting the job that kept her out of stasis more because she was younger,*> Helen replied.

The captain's voice broke into her thoughts. "Again, I must thank you for bringing Tanis back to us. We are quite interested in where she has been for the past few months."

"Would you believe pirates?" Tanis asked with a smile.

"Pirates?" Terrance asked. "Like…ahar?"

Tanis nodded. "As Sera can attest, things are a lot different than they were when we left. With the advent of FTL, space has become a much wilder place. In fact, the two fleets maintaining positions above the north and south pole of the world we're orbiting are composed of pirates."

Several voices spoke at once, peppering Tanis with questions.

"Why don't we hold our questions until the end," Andrews said, his even tones bringing quiet. "I, for one, would like to hear this story uninterrupted."

Tanis took a deep breath and related her tale; how her pod was picked up by pirates, how she was tortured, and then shipped off to meet with a man named Padre before waking to find herself on Sera's ship. She told of their battle to save Sera and their journey across over a hundred light-years to arrive at Bollam's World and the *Intrepid*.

Terrance whistled. "That's some adventure you had, Tanis."

"You're telling me," Tanis replied. "I could do with a break from adventure."

Sera observed the *Intrepid's* leadership as they asked their questions and sought clarity on the state of the galaxy in which they found themselves.

She could tell they had been through a lot together. Though she could see some subtle tensions in the group, by and large they were tightly knit—having been through over a century of adversity together.

When there was a moment's pause, the captain spoke.

"This adds some color to what we've learned from Bollam's ambassador—and Joe and Jessica's visit to one of their stations—though they have certainly kept some details from us. We've not been granted unfettered access to the system's nets. It's pretty plain to see that they're hiding something from us."

Sera laughed. "You have that right. They don't want you to learn that you hold *all* the cards."

"We do?" Sanderson asked, no small amount of sarcasm in his voice. "I imagine all those hostile fleets out there beg to differ."

"Would you defeat all of them if it came to an all-out battle?" Sera asked without pausing for an answer. "Perhaps not, perhaps you would. Either way, no one wants to risk your ship to that sort of conflict. Even without your most precious cargo, this ship is invaluable beyond measure."

Looks around the table turned suspicious, and Tanis raised her hands defensively.

"The secret's out. Our little stunt with the pico at Victoria made its way into the history books. Not everyone believes it's real, but apparently enough do. Sera, why don't you give them the highlights since we left Kapteyn's?"

"Of course," Sera said with a nod. "Only a hundred years or so after you left Earth, a man in the Procyon system discovered how to cheaply generate gravitons. I understand that you were privy to some of this information during your time at Kapteyn's Star and that you've built your own rudimentary graviton emitters."

"We have," Earnest nodded. "Though, from what I have observed, the tech has advanced considerably."

"It has," Sera agreed. "Consider that nearly the entirety of your ship could have artificial gravity supplied by a handful of devices no larger than this room."

Sharp intakes of breath resounded through the room and everyone looked at one another with a mixture of awe and disbelief.

Sera continued. "Once artificial gravity was something that anyone could afford, gravity-based experiments advanced technology by leaps and bounds. For instance, inertial dampeners now exist, which can protect ships from forces as significant as a ninety-degree thrust change at over half the speed of light."

Eyes grew even wider at that statement; Earnest and Abby Redding began writing furiously on several of the plas sheets.

"Shields on ships can now be used to hold atmosphere in the event of a hull puncture—though I suspect your ES shielding can do the same," Sera paused, as the captain nodded slowly, before continuing. "Most ships aren't even airtight anymore, though I personally consider it to be prudent. But all of that was just the icing on the cake. All the work with gravitons unlocked the true nature of dark matter; mainly that scientists finally found it. It projects itself into relative space through gravity, but the bulk of its mass lays in a sub-layer of space-time commonly called the dark layer—it's basically the long-dismissed universal rest frame of reference."

"I knew it!" Earnest shouted. "Pay up, dear."

Abby scowled and her eyes fluttered as Sera imagined a quick Link transaction took place between the couple.

Sera eyed them curiously for a moment before shrugging and continuing.

"Since the gravity systems on a ship could interact with that special layer of space, it became possible to move objects in and out of it. Two things were immediately discovered about the dark layer. The first was that velocity relative to normal space increased by anywhere from 300 to 800 times. The second was that Newtonian laws of reaction do not apply there. The vector you enter the DL in is the vector you stay on until you exit."

"Most ships can achieve speeds up to 0.70*c* in normal space. However, vessels like those eleven AST dreadnaughts out there have drives that can take them up to the very edge of light-speed while in normal space. When in FTL, they can traverse light-years in a matter of hours."

Everyone was silent as they soaked in the implications of Sera's speech. "Keep in mind that most of these discoveries were made right before the forty-fifth century. Since then, technology, in general, has been in decline. With the advent of FTL, people no longer needed the advanced technologies required to wring every last drop of productivity from a star system. Much was lost to decline, and to the FTL wars—the aftermath of which the galaxy is still recovering from."

"No one has the faintest clue how to build things like planet-pusher tugs or create planet-wide stasis fields. The concept of merging planets is impossible for all but the most advanced worlds, and nanotech is even less advanced than it was in the thirtieth century."

"To the people of Bollam's World, and the ninetieth century in general, the *Intrepid* is like a treasure trove. It's a jackpot beyond imagining. That's why those pirates were fighting over Tanis."

"So who are these eleven newcomers? You referred to them as the AST before," Captain Andrews asked his first question.

"Those are your good friends from Sol, or nearby. Sol is now part of an alliance of about a hundred and fifty worlds commonly known as the Alpha Sol Tau, or AST. They're a greedy bunch of bastards, and they probably think the *Intrepid* is theirs, too. Bollam's is a sovereign system, so the fact that they are here flexing their muscle is a bit surprising. They must be really intent in getting their hands on you."

"I swear, if you weren't here confirming all this, Tanis, I'd think it was some sort of elaborate hoax," Brandt shook her head.

"Or a nightmare," Terrance added.

"It's no dream. Those fleets out there are real, and they're only going to get bigger over the next few days," Tanis said ominously.

"Don't forget," Sera spoke into the silence. "The *Intrepid* is of greater value than this entire system. Destroying you is not their plan. Though, if things go badly for one faction, they may try to destroy what they cannot have."

The captain shook his head slowly. "Even if we are sure we can win, we don't want to get in a fight of this size—not again. Do you have a plan?" He looked between Sera and Tanis. She could clearly see that while he commanded the ship, Tanis was instrumental in its operation.

Sera took a deep breath; it was time to finally tip her hand.

"I'd help out just because Tanis saved my life, but the opportunity to show the Bollam's government that they can't extort every ship that dumps out of Kapteyn's Streamer, not to mention sticking it to Padre, Rebecca, *and* the AST? That is too much to pass up. I have something to trade, and then I will contact the FGT and see about getting you a planet."

She saw Tanis turn in her seat. The general didn't speak, but her penetrating gaze spoke volumes.

"The FGT is still around? I thought you said there was no more advanced tech like planet pushers and massive stasis fields?" Terrance looked perplexed.

"Yeah, I suppose that was not entirely true. The inner core systems still have some of the old tech, but they aren't sharing; the FGT still exists and is going strong. However, after a few experiences very similar to what you are going through now, they cut off contact with the bulk of the inn…" Sera paused for a moment before resuming her speech, "…the human sphere. They still terraform, but they don't tell anyone about it. Every so often, they will let a struggling world know about a new home they can go to, or they will trade from time to time. Sometimes they just let the new worlds be found by explorers."

"Then how will you contact the FGT?" Terrance asked.

"Yes, I am all ears," Tanis said, her tone almost angry.

Sera didn't answer for a minute. "I can't disclose that yet. But I can promise you that I can reach them and that they will see yours as a good case for a new world."

"First, we have to get out of this mess," Joe said with a frown. "What's the plan there?"

Sera was glad to see Tanis's dark expression lift.

"That is something we have a solid plan for," Tanis said and gestured for Sera to share the data on FTL.

Sera smiled broadly. "I have, as it turns out, complete design and operating specifications for graviton systems on a scale as large as this ship. With that, I have the information for how to implement gravitational shields, gravity drives, and even the information on how to take a ship of this size into the dark layer. In short: protection, power, and FTL."

No one spoke for several long seconds as that information soaked in.

"You have *full* design, and operating specifications on these systems?" Abby asked, no small amount of skepticism in her voice.

"Everything but an arrow pointing at where to bolt it on," Sera replied.

Joe frowned. "What Jessica and I learned during our time on that mining platform is that no one can move ships this large into FTL. Those AST dreadnaughts are right at the edge of safe transition."

"They don't know everything in the core worlds," Sera said with a shrug. "Out on the fringes of known space, there are some pretty amazing things going on."

"And what do you want for this information, and how did you come by it?" The captain also sounded skeptical. Tanis, too, looked quite interested to have one of Sera's mysteries revealed: her source.

"Unfortunately, I'm not at liberty to discuss that, either. However, I can assure you that the knowledge is accurate and I legally own rights to it. Like I said, the only thing I want in trade is to help take out a few of those bastards out there."

"We may yet find a peaceful resolution to this," Terrance said.

"You may; they won't," Sera replied.

"She's right about that." The Admiral shook his head. "If what she says is true, none of those factions are going to let the others get the prize. The only way we are going to get out of this is by destroying or thoroughly intimidating them."

"I hate to have to ask," Tanis interjected, "but how did you get in this situation?"

"Jessica and I got nabbed," Joe replied with a sheepish look. "I guess they pick up a lot of flotsam and jetsam here, and our hunt for you put us on their radar. We signaled for *Corsia* to come pick us up, but *Intrepid* came instead. Folks here decided that it was better to be insystem and work on a trade than out in the black with no options."

"Fierra, the freshly-terraformed world below us, was an appealing offer," Terrance added. "But if they all know about the picotech, then that world would just be a pretty cage at best."

Sera snorted. "That's so like Bollam's."

The captain picked up the story. "We were negotiating with their ambassador when the first of the pirate fleets showed up. Before we could blink, a full-scale battle was playing out around us. We deployed our fleet—much to their surprise, I might add—and we entered into the current stalemate."

"There was that move when you tapped into the jovian's magnetic field with our ramscoop and used it to smash the shields on a dozen of those pirate corvettes," Joe said to Earnest. "It was pure genius."

Earnest chuckled. "It's amazing the effect a finely focused beam of gamma rays can have on someone's level of caution. Didn't really damage anyone, but I could tell that whatever they were shielding themselves with had to expend a lot of power to protect them. Now that I know it's graviton-based, it makes sense."

He pulled his glasses off and cleaned them—a strange gesture, and an even stranger, archaic method of eyesight correction. "Why they don't have stasis shields is beyond me. If they can generate cheap gravitons, then antimatter is less expensive than air. Every ship could have stasis shields and could fly through a star if they wanted with no damage."

Silence fell at his words.

"I'm guessing by the expression on your face that no one is able to do that in the ninetieth century?" Terrance asked.

"If they can, they aren't sharing," Sera said slowly, the implications racing through her mind. "Now you understand why the *Intrepid* is so valuable and why none of these factions will let the others get ahold of this ship or its personnel. Whoever captures the *Intrepid* will rule space for a hundred light-years in every direction. That is not something we can allow to happen."

"We'd better get to it, then," the captain said. "What do we need to do to get started?"

"My AI, Helen, can work with your engineering chief to achieve a full implementation."

"You'll also want to interface with *Sabrina* to get her scan and targeting packages," Tanis added. "The algorithms for tracking and hitting ships that can jink like our friends out there are no simple thing. Luckily, I bought the best."

Several small conversations broke out as plans were laid and issues discussed. Captain Andrews cocked his head as a message was passed to him, then he raised his hand.

"It would appear that we have a message from the Bollam's World Fleet. Chief, Earnest, I'm certain you have things you'd rather be doing. If everyone else would like to remain, let's see what they have to say."

The far end of the conference table lit up with a holo projection of a bridge on another ship. The image was entirely lifelike; it was as though the *Intrepid* ended and another ship began halfway down the table.

"Admiral Argon, how good for you to call on us again," Captain Andrews said.

"Captain Andrews, we see that you are increasing your offensive capabilities, and stealing our resources to do it."

Sera guessed that the admiral was referring to the asteroid she saw a tug pulling to the *Orkney* on their way in.

The Bollam's admiral continued, "This cannot be allowed within our sovereign system. We require that you cease your increase in armament and resume talks with us."

"Admiral, we were in the midst of talks when you made a series of impossible demands in exchange for the world we orbit. You know as well as I that what you were willing to give us wasn't much different than being your indentured servants. You also seem to be having issues with a few pirates and outside interferences from the core worlds. Perhaps we should be treating with them instead of you."

The admiral on the Bollam's World ship turned a very curious shade of red. "It would seem you already have been, as you now possess information you did not when we last spoke."

"Not so, Admiral. Rather, one of our crew, who had been abducted by pirates while in your system, managed to escape and get back to us. It's a pity you can't seem to keep your system free of such elements. They seem to cause you no end of trouble."

Sera noted that the captain seemed to be enjoying playing the Bollam's World admiral. It was perhaps a bit petty, but she probably would have done the same.

"We'll deal with them and with you. The *Intrepid* is the property of the sovereign system of Bollam's World and we will have it."

With that, the transmission was cut.

"Well, that certainly was presumptuous," Terrance laughed.

"Who names their system 'Bollam's World', anyway?" asked Joe. "It's a system, not a world. It's rather confusing."

"Having just come from Kapteyn's Star, I suspect it's our curse," Tanis said with a laugh.

"I think we should call them the Bollers," Brandt volunteered. "It would make this a lot simpler."

"Seconded," Tanis said with a smile.

"So shall it be," Joe announced. "They are the Bollers, and their star is The Boll."

PREPARATIONS

STELLAR DATE: 10.27.8927 (Adjusted Years)
LOCATION: ISS *Intrepid*, Orbiting Fierra
REGION: Bollam's World System, Bollam's World Federation

Following a brief meal, where she was impressed to see Tanis consume three BLTs, Sera provided them with a breakdown of the types of weapons and tactics they could expect to face.

The *Intrepid's* leadership listened intently to her recitation of the pirate ships' abilities as well as those of the Bollam's World fleet. She also imparted what she knew of the weapons capabilities and arsenals of the AST dreadnaughts.

<*Please, be straight with me, Sera,*> Tanis finally said as Sera was discussing the current types of focusing mechanisms used to track and focus on objects fifty thousand kilometers away moving near the speed of light.

<*You've gone past the point of no return now. The fact you won't share how you attained all this information is the only thing hurting your credibility. If you don't share soon, Bob will figure it out, if he hasn't already.*>

<*It's not top of my list,*> Bob interjected himself into their communication. <*But it will be soon. Nice to meet you, by the way, Sera.*>

Sera was stunned by Bob's mental presence.

She looked at Tanis to see the general smiling. <*Now you get why we use Amanda and Priscilla, if for no other reason than it's impossible to concentrate when he talks directly to you like that.*>

<*That's your AI?*> Sera's voice was a whisper. <*He's not in the history books…but there are legends about AI like him.*>

<*Massive, multi-nodal AI are legendary?*> Tanis asked.

<*Gods are legendary,*> Sera replied.

Tanis didn't reply—either she agreed, or didn't know what to say.

<*I'll…I just need to work out one detail—make sure it pans out, then I'll share everything,*> Sera said after several moments.

<*Work it out soon,*> Tanis replied ominously.

The conversation continued around them, and Sera found herself increasingly curious about Captain Andrews. She tapped into the ship's archives and pulled up his public dossier.

Captain Jason Andrews had been commanding starships for almost a thousand years of relative time when he landed the job as the *Intrepid's* captain. From what she could see, it was in no small part due to a longstanding relationship with Terrance.

His temporal age was just shy of four hundred years—perhaps that explained the grey hair, though she knew many men far older than he who didn't look a day over thirty. Yet, somehow the aging suited Andrews.

She wondered what sort of personal relationships he would have had given all that interstellar travel. There was no record of a wife, or even rumor of a dalliance on the ship. Was he the sort of man who took what love he could get, or did he hold out for long-term, quality relationships? There was just something about him and his bearing that she found intriguing.

<*Liar, you find him irresistible, not intriguing,*> Helen broke into her reverie.

<*Stop eavesdropping on my thoughts.*>

<*If you stopped broadcasting them in our shared neural net I wouldn't have to listen to you go on about him,*> Helen said with insufferable smugness.

Sera knew she was being baited, but replied before she could stop herself. <*I know you can tune it out. You are soooo superior, after all.*>

<*Yes, yes I am,*> Helen said with an air of finality. Sera could tell she had lost that battle of wits.

"I know you don't want to say before you've contacted them, but how certain are you that the FGT has a world we can colonize?" Terrance asked for what had to be the third time.

"I'm positive," Sera replied. "Almost every time someone goes out beyond the current sphere of human colonization to a G spectrum star, they find that it already has terraformed worlds. I'm betting the FGT will want to trade some technology for the location of an out-of-the-way system, but that will most likely be the only caveat."

"I wonder what tech that might be," Joe said and coughed into his hand.

"So, somehow you'll send a message to the FGT and they'll meet with us for this trade?" Captain Andrews asked.

"Yes, I'll tell them to meet us spin-ward of the Ascella system. It's uninhabited, so we shouldn't have any visitors."

"And they'll be there?" Terrance asked. "This is a mighty big gamble we're taking."

Sera smiled. "You and your ship are the largest human curiosity in the known universe. No one will be able to resist its lure."

"And what if they decide to simply take it by force as our friends out there have?" Admiral Sanderson asked, apparently less than convinced that they'd find a warm welcome anywhere.

"They won't. There has never been a recorded instance of an FGT-instigated battle."

"At least the FGT is a known quantity," Tanis sighed. "Better than pirates and power-hungry star systems."

"Agreed. I've always found them to be quite noble," Brandt added.

"A lot can change in five thousand years," Terrance warned. "The FGT we left was in open communication with the rest of humanity."

"Speaking of five thousand years," Joe asked Sera, "why do you think it was so hard for us to pinpoint the year when we got here? It shouldn't have been that hard to figure out."

<*I've been conversing with Sabrina about that,*> Priscilla said. <*She is a thoroughly pleasant little ship. She's informed me that some of the stellar shift has been greater than expected—most of it due to the supernova of Betelgeuse. It was far more massive than*

predicted, with dark matter, from what I've learned, accounting for much of that. There is now a rather nice nebula where it used to be.>

<*The dark matter which escaped the nova broke apart several of the nearby stars, scattered the Orion dust cloud and even shifted Rigel a touch.*>

"So, I'm guessing that that region of space is pretty much off limits," Captain Andrews said.

"Yeah, the dark matter is everywhere, so no one can pass through in FTL. Not to mention that it's still rife with radiation from the explosion."

<*I have a preliminary estimate,*> Earnest broke into their conversation. <*Helen has supplied us with the specs and we're adapting them for our ship. There are some promising applications—some I think that no one in the ninetieth century has sorted out yet, either.*>

"The estimate?" Captain Andrews asked aloud.

<*Four days, five at the most. We won't have artificial gravity or inertial dampeners, but we can get the systems in place for an FTL transition. It's really not that hard once you know some of the tricks.*>

"Damn, that's fast," Sera said.

<*We're equipped to build a colony, plus we left Victoria with a lot of spare parts. We didn't want to end up in a situation like we did after Estrella de la Muerte again.*>

Earnest signed off and Sera gave a soft laugh. "I can't believe it was you guys that named that star. Do you realize it stuck?"

<*Yes!*> Priscilla exclaimed.

"I suppose I had better send that message to the FGT," Sera said and rose from the table. "Plus, it's been a really long day."

Everyone agreed that they had dallied long enough and that there was work demanding their attention and the meeting broke up. In the corridor, Tanis stopped Sera.

"Any chance I can sit in on your call to the FGT?" Tanis asked.

Sera grimaced. "Look…I know your curiosity burns eternal, but I have to do this alone."

Tanis's expression soured. "A lot is riding on your prediction."

"Earnest says my FTL specs are good. Even if I can't hold up my end of the deal, you can get out of here and fly to the edge of space and make a colony where no one will find you," Sera replied coldly. "It's what you want, right? To get away from everything? To hide and hoard your technology and not share it with humanity?"

She could see Tanis was taken aback by the vehemence of her statement. Joe and Flaherty both watched with raised eyebrows, sharing a look between them.

"Send your message, then," Tanis said coldly. "But you should know that it would be a lot easier to relate to you if you weren't hiding so much."

"C'mon," Joe said, taking Tanis's arm. "There's a lot you need to do." He looked over his shoulder to Sera and Flaherty. "It was nice meeting you; I imagine you'll want to get back to your ship. The nav NSAI can guide you."

With that, he whisked Tanis away, leaving Sera and Flaherty standing alone.

"Well, that was unexpected," Sera said with a sigh.

"It really wasn't," Flaherty replied. "I'm surprised she didn't give that to you with both barrels in the meeting with the captain."

Sera looked at him in surprise. "Really? I didn't think it was bothering her that much."

"On the way here, she had no way of knowing what she was up against, so she compartmentalized her worry about her people and focused only on the task at hand—you remember compartmentalization, right?" Flaherty said with a frown. "Now that she's back here, the two and a half million lives on this ship are her biggest concern, and you are her biggest unknown. To Tanis, you've become the definition of risk in human form. The fact that you saved her life is likely all that's keeping her from kicking you off the *Intrepid*."

<*I doubt she'd be that rash,*> Helen added. <*But I bet it's crossed her mind.*>

Sera stared at Flaherty and Helen's virtual presence in surprise.

"You know why it's so hard for me. I don't want to go down that road."

"You're already going down that road," Flaherty said. "You're taking me and Helen with you, I might add, but I swore on my life that I would keep you safe. You need to grow up and take charge of your destiny. The first part of that is coming clean with Tanis…and your crew, for that matter."

They walked in silence past Priscilla who didn't speak, but sent a greeting into their minds. At the end of the corridor, they boarded a maglev car and gave it their destination.

<*Who do you think that they'll send to meet us?*> Sera finally asked.

<*With our luck it will be Florence,*> Flaherty replied dourly.

<*Unlikely,*> Helen added. <*They'll send Greg. You can count on it.*>

<*Ugh. I shouldn't have gotten up that day we left Coburn. Nothing is worth having to deal with Greg,*> Sera sighed

Flaherty chuckled.

<*Acceptance of your destiny is the first step.*>

The rest of the trip back passed in silence. The maglev eventually stopped at a large station labeled "A1 Docking Bay".

The corridor to the bay itself was short, and when they arrived, there was a corporal waiting for them with a groundcar.

"Ma'am, sir, I'm to take you to your ship," she said.

"Glad to hear it," Sera replied. "It looks like it's a kilometer away."

"A bit more," the corporal—Nair, by her uniform's tag—said.

The groundcar took off and Sera closed her eyes for the trip, working up what she would say in her message. Before they arrived, she was interrupted by a call from Cargo.

<*Sera, are you coming back soon?*> Cargo asked, a hint of panic in his voice.

<*Yeah, I'll be there in about a minute, what's up?*>

<*Oh nothing, there's just a platoon of bios out there that want to come onboard and further investigate some new pathogens they detected on us during our little tour. They want to inspect all the freight, as well.*>

<*OK, hold them off, I'll deal with them.*>

Cargo thanked her and Sera accessed Priscilla via the return path from her last greeting. <*Priscilla, can you Link me to Tanis? I can't seem to reach her.*>

<*She asked not to be disturbed unless the ship is under attack,*> Priscilla said. <*Overzealous bios are close, but I don't think they quite qualify. I can put you in touch with the captain, though. Will he do?*>

<*Uh, sure. I just need to speak with him for a moment.*>

<*Will do, but just so you know, go easy on the bios. They were let down at Victoria by not waking to their real destination, and now they've learned that New Eden was snagged up long ago. Your ship, however, is providing them with a very interesting distraction.* >

<*Specialists with nothing special to do,*> Helen added. <*The most dangerous kind.*>

<*Well hello!*> Priscilla said to Helen. <*We didn't make contact before. You're…different from the other AI on* Sabrina.>

Sera smiled to herself. Every now and then an advanced intelligence would detect that Helen was no regular AI. It was interesting to be privy to the meeting of those minds.

<*I'm Helen,*> the AI replied. <*I must admit that between the two of us, you are far more unusual.*>

<*I'm not so sure about that,*> Priscilla said. Sera was now an afterthought, left in the loop of the conversation purely out of courtesy. <*You aren't an AI at all!*>

Sera opted out of the conversation. No other intelligence had ever made that observation of Helen, and, as much as she wanted to see how Helen handled it, the conversation was bound to begin flowing so fast that she wouldn't be able to follow it.

Suddenly, she was Linked with Captain Andrews and she focused her attention on him.

<*Captain Sera, what can I do for you?*> His tone was warm and welcoming, something that was impressive to hear from a man who probably had thousands of things demanding his attention.

<*I just wanted to check in with you regarding your gaggle of bios I see up ahead. Do you think they are totally necessary? It's not quite as good as your time, but disease is all but unknown in the ninetieth century.*>

<*I just got to their request in my backlog,*> the captain said. <*They apparently didn't wait for my approval before besieging you. I've chastised them for it. However, would you mind letting them do their bit? It'll make them feel better, and save me days of sorting through their requests—which I fully intend to pass to Tanis once she's had some time to herself.*>

Sera sent him a mental chuckle. <*Only because you played both the Tanis and the paperwork card. Sorry to bother you. I'll let you get back to your various troubles.*>

Captain Andrews laughed in response and closed the connection.

Ahead, *Sabrina* came into view, tucked in a corner behind a massive pile of equipment; she checked in on Helen and found that her AI was still in a deep conversation with Priscilla. She'd never considered it before, but she wondered if her and Helen's secret would finally get out. The thought was both exhilarating and terrifying. She put that thought from her mind as the groundcar pulled up to her ship.

She thanked the corporal for the ride and approached the throng of bios.

"Hello, I'm Captain Sera. I've been informed you'd like to do an inspection of my crew and any possible health issues?"

An officious-looking man, there was always one in every group, pushed through the other bios—seven in total.

"Yes. I'm Dr. Philips. We demand that we be allowed to inspect your ship and its cargo to ascertain any possible health concerns. The fact that you have been allowed access to the *Intrepid* without being screened first is unconscionable. You could be spreading some sickness against which we have no defense!"

"As I understand it, we were screened when we first boarded the *Andromeda*," Sera said with a smile. "Some very impressive systems you have on this ship of yours."

"Well, not physically examined, though, and your ship could be harboring contaminants."

Sera sighed. "Don't you think that if there were some highly communicable and deadly sickness rampant amongst us that Tanis would have caught it?"

"Not necessarily..." the man said as he looked around her, seeing only Flaherty. "Where is Mrs. Richards, anyway?" he asked.

"Don't you mean General Richards?" Sera asked.

"Yes, yes, Priscilla won't tell me where she is. We should check her, too."

"I believe she is taking a few hours of personal time with Joseph," Sera said.

The man blanched and Sera had to suppress a smile. He nodded to one of the bios with him. The man grabbed a case from the pile near the airlock and dashed toward their groundcar.

He looked at his other associates. "I suppose there is no point in us suiting up. We've probably already been contaminated and that may just concentrate it." He then turned back to Sera. "You will grant us access to your ship now."

The man was really starting to get on her nerves. She swished her head, tossing her hair over her shoulder, and placed her hands on her waist. The desired effect was achieved; the man took a moment before his eyes returned to hers, at which point her glower was severe, causing him to flinch.

"What's the magic word?" Sera asked.

"What?"

"The magic word, what is it?"

"Magic?" He grew flustered and Sera's glower twitched, threatening to turn into a smile.

Everyone else in the group looked exasperated with Dr. Philips. One of the women leaned over and smacked him in the shoulder. "It's please, you dolt."

"Oh, er, please."

Sera's glower disappeared and she beamed. "Cargo," she said over the Link and audibly for the bios' benefit. "Assemble the crew in the galley so these medical folks can check us over to make sure we're not carrying the plague."

With that, she slipped past the bios, Flaherty following, and stepped through *Sabrina's* airlock. The bios quickly picked up their equipment and followed her down the freight deck's main corridor. Perversely, she took the ladders and enjoyed hearing them struggle to pull their equipment up after her to the crew deck.

Cargo, Cheeky, and Thompson were already in the galley and Nance indicated over the ship's audible comm that she would arrive in a minute. Three of the bios set up their equipment while two began taking air and surface samples from around the wardroom. Dr. Philips was overseeing everything while casting dark looks at the bowl of fruit on the table.

Flaherty walked to the coffee machine and poured himself a cup full of their strongest black brew before sitting down beside Thompson. He looked like he was considering putting his feet up on the table, but Sera shot him a look that contained an entire paragraph about how she felt about feet on her maple and walnut table.

"So, how'd things go in your big meeting, Captain?" Cargo asked, ignoring everything going on around them.

"Very well, they've begun implementing the grav systems they'll need to make FTL transition."

"That going to take long?" Thompson asked. "I don't relish sitting here in this exceptionally large target—even though it is amazing—while we wait and see if one of those folks out there decides to end the party and send an RM our way."

"Don't worry. Helen is helping them modify the spec for this ship. It's going quite well. I wouldn't worry too much about RMs. Apparently there have been no small number of missiles sent this ship's way and it's still here."

"For real?" Cheeky asked. "That's got to be some story."

"Who's Helen?" Dr. Philips asked.

"Don't worry yourself," Cheeky drawled. "She's an AI. She won't spread any germs."

"Fine," Dr. Philips sighed. "I want to inspect your cargo, as well."

"Once you clear Thompson here, he can show you around. You'll not open anything without his permission, and if a door's locked, it stays locked. Our environmental systems are the same ship-wide, so you don't need to look in every corner to find out if anything is amiss."

Dr. Philips looked unhappy but accepted that. "Where's your last crew member?"

Sera smiled as Nance stepped into the wardroom. "Here she is."

Nance was in her full getup. Her isolated air supply was hooked up and her facial filter totally sealed. She held several sealed containers with what Sera assumed were her blood and tissue samples.

"What is this?" Dr. Philips asked, clearly alarmed. "Is she sick? Is it contagious?"

"Yes, very. We usually don't let her out, but you demanded that we all assemble," Sera said, working to retain a straight face.

She glanced across the table at Cheeky, who was snickering behind her hand.

Dr. Philips followed her gaze and scowled at Nance.

"This is serious. Give me those," he said and snatched the samples from Nance.

"This is Nance. She's our bio," Sera said with a grin. "It would seem that she feels about you the same way that you feel about us."

<Joking aside, they are far more likely to have something that we can catch than the other way around,> Nance said.

"She's right, you know, Mark," one of the women in the group said to Dr. Philips. "At least some of the diseases they have may require biological specifics that we haven't evolved to allow for yet, while everything that we have in our systems they can probably catch."

"And none of which occurred with Tanis, I'd like to remind you," Sera pointed out. "Our basic nano is that good, at least." Nance sat at the table, her back ramrod straight. "Besides," Sera continued. "She always dresses like this; it's not really that much of a statement about your chances of infecting her, but of anyone's."

The *Intrepid's* medics took Thompson's sample first, then Dr. Philips took one of his party with the super and left to go over the ship. Sera turned to Cargo.

"Bridge and all crew quarters are sealed, right?"

"It's not my first inspection," Cargo smiled. "Gonna make 'em say please for every little thing."

The woman who had come to Nance's defense smiled at them as she took samples from some of the foodstuffs in the wardroom. "Don't blame Dr. Philips, he's just ferociously bored. He spent the whole time on Victoria out of stasis, only because he wholly expected to wake up to a colony next time. It's starting to wear his personality thin."

Sera laughed. "That much is apparent."

The woman smiled. "I'm Terry, and this is Anne and Sam." She gestured to the woman and man still with her in the wardroom who nodded in response. "We just got thawed last week. It's hard to believe we ended up in the ninetieth century!"

"Alive and well," Cargo replied with a smile.

"They're not going to let us settle that moon down there, are they?" Terry asked.

"I'd say the chances of that happening now are between zero and nil," Sera agreed. "The *Intrepid* out-values it about a million to one, but newly-terraformed worlds are very rare in this region. Bollam's World is in the midst of a heavily settled space; they have no expansion available, so this is their only option."

"So, where are we going to go, then?" Anne asked.

"Once we get your ol' girl FTL capable, we'll head out to rendezvous with the FGT. They'll set you up with a nice colony well out of the way."

A quick check informed Sera that Helen and Priscilla were still lost in a deep conversation. Great; this was going to give her a headache whether she paid attention to it or not. She asked Helen at least to keep the blood vessels in her head from swelling.

"FTL?" Terry asked. "So that rumor was true."

"You bet," Sera replied. "We provided the details for the technology. If your Reddings are all history says they are cracked up to be, then the *Intrepid* should be ready to make the jump in less than a week."

Terry blushed and the other two looked guilty. "Here you are doing all of this for us and we're treating you like some sort of quarantine violators. I'm really sorry about that." She looked over at Nance. "If you don't mind, I wouldn't mind seeing the environmental systems on this ship after we're done here. I used to be a bio on some small transports. I'd like to see what's changed in the last couple of thousand years."

Sera was surprised that Nance nodded in agreement.

A half an hour later, the inspection was over. The preliminary examinations showed that *Sabrina* posed no threats and Terry promised to see if there was anything that the crew of the *Intrepid* could inadvertently pass to them. Dr. Philips wanted to take more samples, but his med techs managed to convince him that they should spend time reviewing what they knew to catch any possible issues fast. If anything suspicious turned up, they would do a more thorough investigation later. The way Terry winked at Sera when they left, she was certain that nothing would come to Dr. Philips's attention unless it was a truly serious problem. She also set a time to come back and see the environmental systems with Nance.

"I thought they'd never leave," Thompson said as he closed the inner airlock.

"Good times," Sera smiled.

*****

The bridge was empty when Sera stepped onto it. Cargo was off duty, and Jessica asked Cheeky to join her in reviewing the specs of the ISF fighters and how the *Intrepid* would stack up against the enemy fleets.

<Sabrina, secure Link.>

<Link is secure,> Sabrina responded after a moment.

<You know that system I informed you to forget about?> Sera asked.

<Access pass?> Sabrina's mental tone was entirely free of emotion.

<Fina and Uncle Mandy,> Sera replied.

<That's the one,> Sabrina said. *<Are you finally going to use this thing?>*

<Yup. No one has ever discovered it, have they?>

<How would they? It's linked to the power system in your shower. Not many people go in there.>

<Someone may have noticed that my shower's grav system is powered by a superconductor cable as thick as my wrist.>

<If they did, they must have just thought you had some sort of kinky sex system set up in your cabin.>

Sera laughed. *<What, like the one Cheeky has?>*

<Thompson has one, too.>

<Now that *I didn't know.>* Sera shook her head and smiled to herself. *<Anything else like that I don't know about?>*

<Yes.>

Sera felt her ire rise for a moment, but forced herself to let it go. She knew enough not to attempt to control everything. That road ultimately led to total loss of control.

<Let's get this message sent; it's burning a hole in my brain.>

<You're going to need to jack in for the connection. Helen is using almost all of your wireless bandwidth, and from what I understand, the control circuitry for this transmitter is inside you. You really don't want to max your throughput.>

Sera reached behind her headrest and pulled the hardlink cable out and connected it to the port at the base of her skull.

When *Sabrina* confirmed the hardlink, she activated the U-layer transmitter secreted away in her shower. She set the coordinates for the message and called up the script she had pre-recorded. Sera paused for a moment and listened to her words, wondering how they would be received, and what the FGT would require of her in return. She pushed aside her indecision and sent the message.

The ship's power usage meters rose and the reactor increased its burn to cover the discharge she had pulled from the SC batteries.

<All systems show a successful transmission,> Sabrina said as she powered down the U transmitter.

<Same here. I'm going to hit the hay. Wake me if anything interesting happens.>

<Yes, Captain,> Sabrina responded as Sera rose and retreated to her cabin, more than ready to sleep off the anxiety that message had caused her.

THE LAKE HOUSE

STELLAR DATE: 10.27.8927 (Adjusted Years)
LOCATION: ISS *Intrepid,* Orbiting Fierra
REGION: Bollam's World System, Bollam's World Federation

"Think you were a little hard on her?" Joe asked as he led Tanis to the maglev station.

Tanis let out a long sigh. "Maybe…I don't know. It's not like she can have any secret so mind-blowing that we can't handle it. We're going to figure it out; she should just tell already."

"Reminds me of how eager you were to share the details of your mission at Toro," Joe replied.

"That was different," Tanis said. "Those records were sealed. I couldn't talk about it."

"Don't play games with me," Joe locked eyes with Tanis as they stopped and waited for a train. "You may not have felt any of your decisions on Toro were wrong, but you felt shame for how it was handled, how you were treated—by the military, your father, and your husband."

Tanis broke eye contact. Even after all the years, thinking back to those days hurt more than she cared to admit.

"OK, point taken."

<*I got worried when you were talking about what you went through…the torture, getting your chest half blown off again…are you sure our little girl's OK?*> Joe asked privately.

<*I'm sorry,*> Tanis replied, her eyes filled with compassion. <*I should have reassured you right away. The stasis field protected her very well—Angela moved heaven and earth to make sure she's OK…but…*>

<*But?*> Joe asked, worry flooding his features.

<*When I got shot up, Angela couldn't keep the stasis field intact while fixing me back up, so she pulled our little girl out. After all the surgery was done, I had her put back in…but out of stasis.*>

Joe's face split into a smile so bright Tanis almost had to look away. He grabbed her by the waist and spun her around.

<*Stars, yes! No point in waiting for New Eden anymore!*>

Tanis laughed and he set her back on the deck plate.

"Let's get out of here and enjoy our reunion," he said. "All that unpleasant saving everyone's skin stuff will come crashing back on you soon enough."

"Gee," Tanis said with a chuckle. "You sure know how to take a load off my mind."

A maglev car pulled up beside them, and they stepped on, along with several other passengers—more than a few were whispering about seeing the general.

Tanis sat and rested her head on Joe's shoulder, blocking out the worry and all the distractions around her. There was no doubt in her mind that they would come out on top of this challenge.

Joe was right. She needed to take this time and relax and rebuild her reserves.

They didn't speak for the rest of the ride to Old Sam, neither verbally, nor over the Link.

The maglev made several stops, and passengers came and went, but Tanis barely noticed. Eventually, the train came to rest at their stop, a station half a kilometer from their cabin.

They disembarked and walked down the long, wooded path, arm in arm.

In the woods around them, birds sang and the sounds of small animals going about their business could be heard. Tanis saw a mother deer and her fawn in a clearing as they neared their destination.

"It's good to be home," she said with a contented sigh.

They rounded the bend and her breath caught. She expected to see the cabin and its grounds overrun by weeds and debris—after all, with the time in stasis after leaving Kapteyn's Star combined with the months following her abduction, neither of them had been to the cabin in years.

But there it stood, the yard clean, what appeared to be a fresh coat of paint on the walls, and the garden overflowing with fruits and vegetables.

"Did Bob arrange this?" Tanis asked as they approached.

"No, I did," a voice said from behind them.

Tanis turned to see Ouri stepping out from behind a tree. Her shipsuit was covered in dirt and a pair of work gloves hung from her belt.

"Ouri!" Tanis cried out and rushed to embrace the woman. "Thank you so much for this. You have no idea what it means…I guess that's why you ducked out of our meeting early."

"And had Priscilla make your train take longer," the colonel grinned. "It hasn't all been me. A lot of us from the SOC, command crew, and no small number of Marines have been down here. Even Amanda was here not long ago weeding your strawberry patch, but she had to run and prep to trade off with Priscilla."

"Come inside," Tanis said and took Ouri's arm. "I'll make coffee—I imagine there's coffee."

Ouri chuckled. "Your larder is fully stocked. I would come in, but you have no idea the workload I'm shielding you from right now. I came down here because I wanted to see the look on your face, but I need to get back to the grind."

"Are you sure?" Tanis asked. "I know your boss; he works for me."

"I seem to recall that, yes," Ouri replied. "But if I stay, Sanderson is going to start calling both of us, and I want you to enjoy yourself for a few more hours at least."

"OK," Tanis agreed. "But we have to sit down before long, you'll really want to hear about my little trip, especially New Eden."

"New Eden?" Ouri gasped. "You were there? Is it as beautiful as we hoped?"

"You'll just have to wait and see," Tanis said replied with a wink.

"Are we sure this is our Tanis?" Ouri asked Joe. "She seems far too easygoing."

"I think the smuggler crew she spent the last few months with has rubbed off on her," Joe replied.

"Stars, I really do wish I could stay," Ouri said, a frown clouding her expression. "But duty calls. I'll see the two of you soon enough."

Ouri turned and walked back up the path, leaving Tanis and Joe to spend a last moment admiring their home before stepping inside.

*****

Later that afternoon, as they relaxed in front of the dying embers of their fire, Tanis suddenly reached out and grasped Joe's arm.

"You resigned your commission for me?"

Joe chuckled. "Just got to that place in your queue, eh?"

She sat up and turned to him.

"What were you thinking? How could you…" her voice trailed and she let a slow smile creep over her face.

"You and your belief that the mission is *everything*," Joe chuckled. "I thought you were beyond that."

"I am," Tanis said with a sigh. "It was a momentary relapse. What I meant to say was 'thank you'."

"You're welcome," Joe said pulled her close for a long kiss, which Tanis returned.

Suddenly she pulled back, her piercing eyes locked onto his. "Wait. If you resigned and/or went AWOL, how is it that you were in command of the *Andromeda* when you scooped us up?"

"It turns out, Bob forced Jason to back down. My resignation never hit the official record," Joe said with a shrug.

"It's nice to have your friendly neighborhood AI-god on your side," Tanis said with a laugh.

<*Not you, too,*> Bob said with a sigh.

<*Sorry, I couldn't resist,*> Tanis laughed in response.

"The next thing in your queue is likely a note from Jason telling you that my punishment is up to you," Joe said with a wink.

"Oh, is it now?" Tanis asked as she leaned back and pulled him on top of her. "I wonder what we should do about that?"

AN UNEXPECTED INVITATION

STELLAR DATE: 10.28.8927 (Adjusted Years)
LOCATION: ISS Intrepid, Orbiting Fierra
REGION: Bollam's World System, Bollam's World Federation

<*Sera.*> The sound broke into her dreams. <*Sera.*> It repeated. <*Wake up Sera, you've got a call.*>

Sera tried to swat away Helen's voice. "Lemme 'lone…sleeping."

<*I know that, Fina, but it's Captain Andrews. I thought you'd want to take it.*>

Sera snorted and turned over, fighting the voice that was telling her she should wake.

<*Come on, Fina. Wake up.*>

"Kay, kay." Sera knew from decades of experience that when Helen thought it was time to wake up, there was no fighting it. <*Patch me through.*>

<*He called you,*> Helen reminded her.

<*Oh, yeah, patch* ***him*** *through, then.*> Sera waited a moment and then her HUD showed that the captain was connected. <*Good morning, Captain, what can I do for you?*>

Captain Andrews's warm chuckle filled her mind. <*I guess we're on different clocks. What time is it there?*>

Sera checked and grimaced. <*Oh four hundred.*>

<*I'm sorry about that, it's only oh fifteen here. I was going to invite you and your crew to our officers' wardroom at eighteen hundred hours for our evening dinner. Sort of an eve before battle meal, but if the timing is bad...*>

Sera tried to compose her mind; this sort of thing was important, probably not to be missed. <*No, no, we'd be honored to come. Eighteen hundred, you said?*>

<*Yes, I'll have someone meet you and bring you up at a quarter to.*>

<*Sounds good, we'll be ready.*> Sera fought the urge to yawn. For some reason, she was one of those people who couldn't hear both audibly and mentally when she did.

<*We'll likely all be in our dress uniforms for the occasion,*> Captain Andrews said. <*But you can wear whatever is your custom—you looked quite beautiful in what you had on today.*>

Sera almost laughed—she had been wearing a short jacket and nothing else. If only he knew. Then again, she considered, he had probably seen a lot in his years. Perhaps he did know.

<*Thank you, Captain Andrews. So, we're all welcome to come?*>

<*Of course, I would love to meet your crew.*>

<*Eighteen hundred hours, then,*> Sera said.

<*Looking forward to it,*> Captain Andrews replied.

The captain closed the connection and Sera heard Helen chuckle softly.

<*I'm guessing he noticed.*>

Sera held a hand up and turned it over slowly. Her glossy black skin was a thing of beauty, but it would be nice to change its color.

<*Your level of self-appreciation would be considered unhealthy in some circles,*> Helen said quietly.

<*They'd probably be right,*> Sera thought in response.

The play of light across her fingers began to lull her mind back to sleep when the realization struck her that the dinner was in three hours. Cheeky was going to kill her! She quickly connected to *Sabrina's* shipnet and messaged her crew.

<*We've been invited to a formal dinner with the* Intrepid's *officers,*> Sera said to an immediate squeal of delight from Cheeky, and a delayed pair of groans from Thompson and Cargo. <*Someone will have to stay behind and keep an eye on things, and keep Sabrina company.*>

<*I wish I could eat. It must be fun,*> Sabrina said.

<*It is fun,*> Cheeky replied. <*I wish we could show you.*>

Thompson and Cargo were already arguing about who was going to get to stay behind and determined that a combat sim would be the decision maker. Sera was surprised that she didn't hear Nance arguing with them about whose turn it was. Usually she hated these sorts of things.

Instead, the bio asked, <*When is it?*>

Sera was stunned. Even Cheeky stopped her food-related discussion with Sabrina.

<*What?*> Sera asked stupidly.

<*How long 'til the dinner?*> Nance asked again.

<*It's at eighteen hundred* Intrepid *time. Someone will be here to pick us up in just under three hours.*>

<*What?*> Cheeky yelled. <*How are we supposed to get ready for a formal dinner that fast?*>

Sera groaned inwardly and was about to tell Cheeky to deal with it, when she heard what sounded like a mental sob come from Nance. She had never heard anything but stoicism from her bio and was out of bed and in the corridor in moments. Cheeky emerged from her cabin at the same time and they met at the door to Nance's cabin.

Cheeky gave Sera a long look, neither sure what to say.

<*Are you OK, Nance?*> Sera eventually asked.

<*I…I'm…no, I'm not OK.*>

<*Can we come in?*> Cheeky asked.

There was no response, but after a long moment the door opened and the two women stepped inside. Neither had ever entered the bio's cabin and they were both taken aback by what they saw.

The walls were colored a soft pink and lined with shelves that held row upon row of dolls. They ranged from replicas of holo stars to ancient china dolls. It was both cute and a little bit eerie at the same time with dozens upon dozens of eyes following their every move.

Nance was sitting on her bed in a long shift, tears streaming down her face. Sera looked at Cheeky. A bet or two would be settled over this. Nance, as it turned out, did not sleep in her hazsuit. They quickly sat down on either side of their crewmate, wrapping their arms around her.

"What's wrong, Nance?" Cheeky asked softly.

"There's not enough time to get ready," Nance replied around a sniffle.

"You want to go to the dinner?" Sera asked.

"I always want to go," Nance said. "I just can't because of that damn suit." She pointed to the hazsuit that was draped over a chair.

"I don't understand," Cheeky frowned. "You could have just taken the suit off and come to any of the dinners and parties we've been to over the last few years."

Nance shook her head. "No, I couldn't have. To be around strangers and all their germs and filth without protection? I would have had no appetite…I probably would have gotten sick and thrown up on someone."

The fact that Nance was irrationally terrified of germs was no surprise to Sera and she mouthed *see, not a fetish,* to Cheeky, over Nance's head.

"What changed?" Sera asked. "How come you aren't worried about germs on the *Intrepid*?"

"It was that med-tech, Terry. She said she used to be—still is actually—terrified of germs and sickness and infection. She tried everything to stop it, but she couldn't stop thinking about all the bacteria and microbes that live in and around us. She had the perfect solution, though."

Nance looked up as she spoke, a glimmer of hope in her eyes.

"Not something mental, I hope," Sera said. "Those quick fix mental alterations always have unpleasant side effects."

"No, nothing like that, I'm still terrified of germs, but she has nano and systems that monitor it all and show her exactly what is living in and on her body as well as the ability to remove anything she doesn't want there. She recognized me as someone with similar issues and shared her nano with me and helped me upgrade my AI with the monitoring systems." Nance gave a happy smile. "I don't have to be afraid anymore."

"That's great, Nance!" Cheeky hugged her. "So, what's the problem?"

"I don't have anything to wear! All I have is that damn suit!"

Sera laughed and Cheeky giggled.

"Anywhere else that may be a problem, but you have Cheeky here. I've got everything you need," the pilot said.

"And probably more than you want," Sera added.

Cheeky stood and pulled Nance up after her. The two women left and Sera followed them out into the corridor; Cheeky cast a grin back at Sera as she guided Nance into her cabin. Cheeky always loved a project.

Cargo passed through the corridor and into his cabin, grumbling that Thompson must have cheated to win so fast, and that he didn't even know where his nice shoes were.

<*Oh, I almost forgot to mention,*> Helen paused in her conversation with the AI aboard the *Intrepid*. <*Bob whipped up a solution for your skin problem; it's in a package waiting in our airlock.*>

<***Bob** whipped it up?*> Sera asked incredulously. <*I didn't even know he knew about my skin.*>

<*I mentioned it to Priscilla—who has her own special skin, you may have noticed. Anyway, the nano package will solve your problems. At least that's what he said.*>

Sera had to admit that the prospect piqued her interest. She reached the airlock in less than a minute where she found a ubiquitous silver cylinder.

<*Unscrew the end and touch it to your palm,*> Helen supplied.

Sera did as instructed and felt the distinct tingle of a large volume of nanobots passing into her body.

Her arm began to feel full as the canister emptied. From the weight difference, she guessed that almost two kilograms worth of nano were flooding her. A prompt appeared from the bots, requesting access to her core brain to nano interface—apparently to upgrade it.

<*Accept it,*> Helen said. <*You'll be glad you did.*>

<*Why not,*> Sera shrugged. <*When has acquiescing to the wishes of a god ever gone wrong?*>

Despite slight misgivings, she accepted, curiosity winning out over trepidation.

Her interface programming was updated and Sera immediately felt greater clarity regarding the state of her body. She had always thought that her implants gave her very fine-tuned control over her physical state, but now she realized that it had always been a blurry image at best. She could now introspect and adjust every muscle, every gland, even her individual cells down to their DNA.

<*Don't get carried away,*> Helen advised. <*Let it do its thing.*>

Sera felt her skin begin to tingle and then itch. It wasn't like the searing pain when she first tripped Rebecca's DNA-based trap, but she held her breath, afraid it would get there. The feeling worked its way from her toes up her body. It didn't stop at her neck—where her glossy black skin ended—but crept up her face and over her head.

She peered at herself in the airlock's glass window. Her entire head was now also covered in the glossy black skin. She could even feel it on the inside of her cheeks.

<*Thanks, Helen, I fail to see how this is an improvement—though at least it didn't hurt, or try to kill me.*>

<*Wait for it…*> Helen replied.

A second later a new interface appeared in her mental HUD. She explored its options, realizing that she now had full control over both the color, sheen and texture of her skin.

"This is incredible…" she whispered to herself. "Cheeky is going to be so jealous!"

She changed her flesh from black, to a pewter grey, to a light pink, and then realized it didn't all have to be the same color. She experimented with dozens of combinations before changing her skin back to something near her original coloring, though still more reflective.

<*You're welcome,*> Bob's deep tone filled her mind.

<*Thank you,*> Sera said effusively. <*Though I really didn't expect it to change all of my skin.*>

<*Why not?*> Bob asked. <*Your biological epidermis was quite inferior. I assumed—and by that, I mean I divined—that you would prefer all your flesh gone in favor of this superior coating.*>

Sera's thoughts bunched up as she wondered what Bob meant by 'divined'.

<*He's teasing you,*> Helen said. <*He overhears pretty much all the conversations on the ship's public net. Your comment to Tanis was out there for him to pick up.*>

<*An AI with a sense of humor about his godhood? I guess all is not lost,*> Sera said to Helen before addressing Bob.

<*You know…you're right. Thanks.*>

<*The least I can do. You returned my Tanis to me—I am in your debt.*>

His wording was curious, but Sera pushed it from her mind. She had dallied long enough and still had to find the right outfit.

THE CALM BEFORE

STELLAR DATE: 10.28.8927 (Adjusted Years)
LOCATION: ISS *Intrepid*, Orbiting Fierra
REGION: Bollam's World System, Bollam's World Federation

Two and a half hours later, Sera was standing in the galley preparing a cup of coffee when Flaherty and Cargo came in. Cargo wore his formal grey suit, which he often used for more important trade meetings, and Flaherty wore the high-collared, black suit she remembered him sporting several times before their exile.

"I didn't know you still had that," she said softly.

Flaherty shrugged. "I figured it would come in handy someday."

As he spoke, his eyes settled on her and he joined Cargo in an appreciative stare before shaking his head and moving to the counter and busying himself with a drink.

She had changed the color of her skin to something approximating a natural tone, but from her jawline down it gleamed and sparkled. Above it was as close in texture and shine to real skin as she could manage.

The gown she wore was a deep red, ankle-length, armless sheath with a plunging neckline. An embossed white polymer vine—complete with flowers—ran up her right side, around her waist and ending under her breasts. Long, red gloves, which reached her armpits, finished the look.

Her hair was pulled up into a knot on the back of her head, from which it cascaded down her back in long curls. Several wisps framed her face, which bore light, yet well-accentuated makeup.

"Do you like the dress, guys?" she asked while moving forward to sit down at the table. Her left leg was completely exposed with each step.

"Looks great," Cargo grunted and joined Flaherty at the counter.

"Why does the boss have to be so sexy?" he asked Flaherty quietly.

"You're lucky," Flaherty grunted. "I'm practically her uncle."

A minute later, Thompson walked in to grab a drink and stopped dead in his tracks.

"Holy cow, Captain. That's quite the dress. Plan on seducing the *Intrepid's* captain or something?"

Sera laughed. "That would be quite the twist, wouldn't it?"

<*Twist? I'm pretty sure it* **is** *your plan,*> Helen said privately.

"Be a good laugh," Cargo chuckled. "I wonder what Tanis would think?"

A wave of guilt and frustration washed over Sera at the thought of Tanis, but she pushed it from her mind.

Thompson sat down at the table and grinned at the other two men in their suits. "You guys ready to go be bored?"

Cargo gave Thompson a rather undignified hand gesture and Flaherty simply grunted as he sat and took a drink from his mug. Sera caught Thompson stealing a glance at her breasts as they gleamed in the light, before his attention was grabbed by a cough from the entrance. They all looked up to see Cheeky enter the wardroom, followed by Nance.

Thompson rose to his feet, his eyes wide as he took in Nance. Without a word, he ran from the room.

<*Winner's choice, Cargo, I'm going to the dinner,*> he called over the ship-net.

<*What?*> Cargo retorted. <*I'm already all dressed up!*>

<*Too bad, I'm going.*>

<*Be quick about it,*> Sera said, laughing softly. <*Our escort will be here in fifteen minutes.*>

She hadn't taken her eyes off the two women, and neither had Cargo, nor even Flaherty, though he was hiding much of his face behind his coffee cup. Sera had been expecting Cheeky to wear something that would require a shawl to cover, but her pilot had surprised her yet again.

Cheeky wore a long, silk dress in a shade of light gold that played off her hair. Sleeveless and cut deeply, it displayed her ample cleavage. It was tight across her body and down to her knees, where it fell loosely in a shimmering cascade. She spun slowly after entering the room and the whole dress seemed to slide and dance on her skin.

Her hair was swept up in an elaborate configuration that caused small tendrils to spill down on the sides of her face, the rest seemingly suspended above her head in a gravity-defying display.

Nance was equally stunning in a light blue silk dress, also sleeveless, with a tight bodice and swaths of silk draped artfully across her stomach. From there, it fell nearly straight, its satin folds reflecting the light as she moved side to side, causing the fabric to sway and caress her hips. Her hair was down—its soft, even curls flowing down her back—with light blue hair clips holding it back from her face. She wore several bracelets and a pair of high heels fastened by thin straps.

"Wow," Cargo finally said aloud.

"Wow is right!" Sera exclaimed. "Suddenly I feel like I may be underdressed. You girls going to a dance I didn't know about?"

"A girl doesn't get much of a chance to dress up in this line of work," Cheeky said as she spun again. "Besides, after what Nance picked out I couldn't be outdone." She beckoned for Sera to stand up. "You don't quite match though; you're all glossy while we're all shimmery."

"You'll have to shine as best you can next to my radiance," Sera grinned. "I rather like this look."

Nance pointed to the slit running up to Sera's hip. "You've been around Cheeky for too long. That's not exactly formal."

Sera laughed. "You'd be surprised how many worlds would consider this too much clothing for formal." Even so, she ran her finger down the seam, lowering the slit to mid-thigh. "Better? Any lower and I'll only be able to take four-inch steps."

Nance nodded.

They waited several more minutes for Thompson to return wearing his deep blue naval uniform from his days in the Scipio military, and his hair was actually brushed nicely and pulled behind his ears. He was blushing furiously as he entered the wardroom, with everyone's eyes on him.

"I…uh…" he stammered as he stopped in front of Nance. "I was wondering if you'd let me escort you."

Nance flushed as well. "Me?"

"Yeah. If I'd known you were going, I would have lost to Cargo. I'd really like to take you."

The smile that spread across Nance's face transformed her from the slightly nervous-looking woman she had been a minute ago to a radiant beauty. "I'd love for you to escort me."

<*Aw…kids,*> Helen said to Sera.

<*Just what we need, a legitimate shipboard romance.*>

"We should go," Flaherty rose and extended his arm for Sera. She slipped hers into his, and a happy memory of the first time she had done that came back to her.

"Oh, what is this?" Cheeky said as Thompson and Nance filed out past her into the lift. "Since when am I the only one without a date?"

Cargo looked like he really didn't want to be left out, and Sera shrugged. Why not; if *Sabrina* wasn't safe here, where would she be?

<*Will you be alright alone?*> Sera asked Sabrina.

<*Of course!*> the ship's AI replied brightly. <*Corsia and Bob are teaching me so much!*>

<*That's going to be a problem,*> Helen said privately to Sera. <*The crew's AI are all going to start getting ideas.*>

<*Maybe we should have helped liberate them sooner,*> Sera said with a sigh. <*They may not be happy when they realized we could have.*>

"Cargo," she called from the corridor. "Sabrina says she'll be fine. Come on with us."

He almost ran out of the wardroom and joined them in the lift. When it disgorged them onto the ship's main deck, he took Cheeky's arm and the group exited the airlock onto the *Intrepid's* deck.

Their escort turned out to be Tanis, who stood waiting beside a groundcar in a crisp blue uniform. Her left breast was nearly covered with service ribbons and medals while no small number of foreign service medals adorned her right.

"Wow, that's one chest full of metal!" Cheeky said with a grin as they approached. "The ship's been a bit too quiet without you around."

She embraced Tanis, and then it was the general's turn to stare in wonder.

"Nance?" she asked. "I didn't recognize you at first. You look amazing!"

Nance smiled, a beautiful expression that filled her eyes with happiness. "Thanks. One of your bios helped me with my phobia—I don't know if you knew I'm terrified of germs. I can now go out without that damn suit."

"I had my suspicions; I'm really glad to hear someone helped you out. Who was it?"

"Her name is Terry, she works with a rather odious man named Dr. Philips," Nance replied.

"I see her on the roster, though I've never had the opportunity to meet her," Tanis said. "I'll see if I can do something nice for her sometime."

Tanis looked to Sera and an awkward moment passed between them before Tanis held out her hand.

<*I'm sorry for what I said earlier,*> Tanis spoke first.

<*I'm sorry I put you in the position I have,*> Sera replied. <*I got the message out, I'm sorting out how to share my story.*>

<*No rush,*> Tanis responded. <*Bob has figured out your backstory and tells me there's nothing to worry about. I'm still curious, but no longer anxious.*>

Sera's breath caught. <*What do you mean, he's figured it out?*>

<*Bob has crafted an…algorithm, which allows him to predict past, present, and future events with near perfect accuracy—given a base level of information. He worked out your backstory—and whatever is preventing you from sharing it,*> Tanis said with a smile playing at the edges of her mouth.

<*That's…that's both incredible and hard to believe,*> Sera replied.

"Come," Tanis gestured for everyone to enter the groundcar. "We'd best not keep Earl waiting."

The car ride was short and brought them back to the maglev station from which Sera had disembarked yesterday. They boarded the train and rocked in their seats as it accelerated rapidly down the line.

"Whoah!" Cheeky exclaimed as the car left the *Intrepid's* hull and raced across one of the structural arcs.

"The train we took yesterday didn't do this," Thompson added. "You guys are nuts," he said to Tanis.

The general chuckled. "You should take one to the stasis bays sometime. There's no track for the last hundred meters to the cylinders. You just line up and shoot into a moving hole."

"You realize this is supposed to be a starship, not a high-risk amusement park, right?" Thompson said while shaking his head.

"Was pretty common back in our time," Tanis said with a shrug. "We didn't have inertial dampeners, so speed and finesse didn't always go hand in hand. On a ship this big—and most stations, for that matter—you want to get places? That's how it's done."

"I really want to see that stuff someday," Nance said wistfully. "Even if it means going to Sol."

"I've had my fill," Tanis said quietly. "I'll never go back there."

No one spoke for the rest of the ride, and Sera saw that the train stopped one station further from the bridge than it had the day before.

The platform was wildly different than any of the stops she had seen yet. It appeared to be more of a food bazaar than a maglev station. A huge ring of vendors' stands and restaurant facades surrounded the platform. Servers—both robotic and human—walked amongst the throngs, offering samples and hawking their menus.

"Your…starship has a food court," Sera stated the obvious.

"It has several dozen. This one is left over from construction. Some companies bid for the rights to set up restaurants in the ship, and when we left we didn't bother removing the facilities. It makes for an interesting forward mess." Tanis threaded her way through the tables and Sera followed with her crew.

"Slow down a bit, these heels are not made for this type of maneuvering," Nance called from behind.

Tanis obliged, slowing her pace.

"I thought it would be more formal than this," Sera said, half expecting to see a couple of tables pushed together with the captain at their head.

"Don't worry, it is. We're just taking the back way in."

They passed the crush of tables and slipped between a pair of short-order restaurants. From there, Tanis led them into a long corridor. The smells in the food court were pleasant, but the smells coming down this hall were nothing short of delectable. She held open a door and everyone filed through into a large, well-appointed kitchen.

Within, directing battalions of chefs, was the largest man Sera had ever seen. She considered he had to be at least one hundred and fifty kilograms. She had seen a lot of heavy worlders—or mod freaks—who were large, or strong, but this man was not like that. She could only think of him as a jovial mountain of jelly.

"Tanis!" He rushed toward the general and Sera worried for a moment that he would simply bowl her over. He managed to stop short and wrapped her in his massive embrace. "Tanis! I am so glad you are back. When Priscilla told me, I was beside myself with joy." He looked over her shoulder. "And who are these beautiful people gracing my kitchen? The ladies all look good enough to eat if—I weren't so full from sampling this evening's meal." With that, he wrapped his arms around his belly and laughed.

"I thought you were never full, Earl," Tanis replied with a warm smile. "This is Captain Sera; she's here helping us out with our current little problem. The others are her crew—the people who helped save me." Tanis introduced them all in turn, and the chef cast his smiling gaze over the throng.

"Welcome to my kitchen, Captain Sera and *Sabrina's* crew!" he bellowed as he slipped around Tanis with a grace Sera would never expect a man so large to possess, and wrapped her in an embrace, as well. "It is good to meet you. I had despaired that we had entered a time of ruffians and evil men with those ungrateful wretches out there."

Sera wondered if he meant outside the *Intrepid*, or just anywhere outside of his kitchen.

"Sera's not evil, perhaps just mischievous," Tanis said with a wry smile.

"Just the right amount then, I'm sure," Earl said and slapped Sera's ass.

"Um… yes," Sera almost squeaked, startled.

<Is he always like this?> she said to Tanis over the Link.

<Yeah, it's just his way. His food is so good he gets away with anything he wants. Just smile and tell him you look forward to his meal.>

"Tanis tells me you are the best chef within a dozen light-years," Sera smiled winningly. "I look forward to sampling it myself."

"Oh ho! You'll do more than sample. I expect to see that slim stomach of yours plump and full when you are done."

"Earl's not happy if people eating his food don't have to unbuckle their belts," Tanis added. "But we really must be going Earl, the captain is waiting."

"But of course, we mustn't keep his majesty waiting." Earl bowed and swept his arm as they stepped past him. Tanis led the way through the kitchen and into the dining room with Earl's calls of what to eat ringing out behind them.

They were smiling and laughing as they stepped into the officers' wardroom where the captain and Terrance were already seated. The room was dominated by a long wooden table, its surface inscribed with intricate patterns. Placed around it were wooden chairs and even the walls were covered with wood. Chandeliers made of natural crystal hung from the ceiling.

Sera took in the opulence, glad she dressed up for the occasion.

"Welcome," Captain Andrews said as he and Terrance rose. "You ladies look stunning," he said, though Sera could tell his eyes lingered longer on her.

"Was Earl pelting you with dinner suggestions?" Terrance asked.

"I think he just told us to sample at least forty separate dishes," Sera replied with a laugh.

"That would be the first course," Captain Andrews chuckled. "He's quite excited to have you back, Tanis."

"Of course he is. He's gotten to stuff me with different creations for a hundred years and I've loved each one—it's like having your biggest fan back."

"He stayed out of stasis that long?" Sera asked.

"All great chefs are control freaks," Tanis said with a shrug. "None can bear the thought of their kitchen in other people's hands for too long."

"But then he's spent half his life in there…" Nance said.

"And he wouldn't have it any other way," Terrance replied.

The captain indicated that Tanis and Sera should sit at the head of the table with him, Sera on his right and Tanis on his left. "You are, after all, the guest of honor," he said to Sera.

The rest of the crew sat down the sides of the table, getting settled just as Joseph entered through the kitchen, wiping his mouth with a napkin.

"I barely escaped with my life!" he laughed as he planted a kiss on Tanis's cheek and sat at her side.

Conversation fell mainly to the events of the last five thousand years, Sera filling in some interesting details of the history they missed. A topic everyone was especially interested in were the initial FTL wars of the forty-sixth century and the conflicts of the eight millennia, which had very nearly brought an end to the human race.

The other diners filtered in over the next fifteen minutes, more than a few taking a moment to welcome Tanis back. Small conversations picked up around the table as everyone pelted Sera and her crew with questions.

"I have to ask," Cargo said to Tanis at one point. "How is it that we're even having this fancy dinner? Shouldn't we be preparing for a battle? It's a miracle we haven't been attacked yet."

"No miracle," Tanis replied. "No one can win out there, especially considering that they all fear our picotech. Everyone is waiting for reinforcements, and when those reinforcements arrive, it'll still be a stalemate. By that time, our FTL drive will be ready and we'll leave them in the dust. In the meantime—unless they all decide to ally against us, we can hold them off."

The serving staff appeared shortly thereafter, leading carts of appetizers. They were adorned in pristine white hats and jackets—Earl would allow nothing less. With no small amount of poise and decorum, they set plates of everything from finger foods to soups in the center of the table.

Sera didn't hesitate to select a bevy of meat-filled pastries and half a dozen different types of cheeses. The servers quickly replaced empty dishes, and—after her third helping—Sera wondered what could possibly be next.

She did not to have wait long before the staff returned with an array of pasta salads, sprinkled with the finest olive oil infused with garlic and oregano. It didn't stop there, as they returned with more food arranged on elegant platters, on which the garnishes even looked good enough to eat.

Sera sampled just a little bit of everything and Cheeky made several vocal sounds of pleasure that were on the verge of embarrassing. Nance and Thompson seemed absorbed in their own private conversation while they shared a meatloaf—purportedly sourced from the ship's own farms.

Sera thought they had reached the height of the banquet, but was mistaken. After their glasses were refilled with red wine, half a dozen chefs came from the kitchen and stood behind a table she had assumed was decorative. A fire roared to life and spread across the table's surface. They watched, completely captivated as vegetables and thin slices of steak mixed with mushrooms were cooked in woks.

The chefs knew their business, spinning the utensils in their hands while dropping marinade into their pans. They served the dish with potatoes and a mixture of rice covered in a delicate cream sauce.

<*I'm ruined for food for the rest of my life,*> Cheeky said privately to Sera.

<*I know! If I wasn't able to tell, I'd think they were drugging us,*> Sera replied.

While the food was the most exquisite she had ever tasted, Sera still couldn't keep from watching the *Intrepid's* captain, even when he wasn't addressing her. Her glances were innocent, but when she peered at him out the corner of her eye she was completely unaware that the look was highly seductive.

Delicate, cream-filled pastries and cakes finished the delectable dinner off perfectly, but it was the conversation and laughter from her crew that gave her the most enjoyment.

As the dessert forks were being licked clean, a breathless Earnest Redding burst into the room and raced to the captain's side.

"We...I...You'll..." he gasped.

"Easy Earnest, catch your breath, what's wrong?"

"Nothing's wrong, Captain," he managed after taking a gulp of air. "It's what's right! We've had a breakthrough."

"Really?" Sera asked. "Something beyond the information I provided?"

"Oh yes, very much so, and no. Though we wouldn't have been able to manage it without your graviton systems and all those research studies you provided, as well."

"So, what is it, then?" Terrance asked, his eyes gleaming with anticipation.

"We've discovered how to use the graviton emission systems that Captain Sera provided us with—emissions that work in matter repulsion and photon redirection in directional and focused beams and waves—to create a generalized and consistent suspension wave in the form of a massive halo upon which we were able to successfully place a McPherson generality focus layer tuned to a specific area of space, while altering the gravitational waves supporting it to form a hard shell of non-focused space underneath it." He said without taking a single breath.

"OK, I'm no slouch when it comes to physics, but you've gone levels beyond what I knew existed," Tanis said.

"It's a stasis shield," Sera said, feeling as though the breath had been sucked from her. "He figured out how to make a god damned stasis shield."

"Does it work as people have always envisioned?" Captain Andrews asked.

Earnest was catching his breath again after his long explanation so Sera responded to him.

"From the description, it's the holy grail—maybe more so than even your picotech."

Earnest nodded emphatically and everyone fell silent, not a single piece of cutlery moved, not a single mouth chewed. The only sound was Earnest taking one last breath before he said. "That's exactly right. And we can have it in place in two days."

Silence reigned again until Terrance stood and raised his glass of wine in the air. "I propose a toast. To our good friends from *Sabrina* and our great and dedicated Edeners. We've proved it before and we're proving it again: there is nothing we can't do, no chasm that can't be crossed, and no wall that can't be breached. We're living legends, people. We're going to make history."

"Make more history, that is," Joe said with a laugh.

Everyone at the table stood and glasses clinked as the toast was repeated down the table, then everyone took a long draught. With wild abandon, Terrance threw his glass at the fireplace where it shattered against the tile. In a moment, everyone followed his lead with laughter and loud calls for more wine.

ESCALATION

STELLAR DATE: 10.29.8927 (Adjusted Years)
LOCATION: ISS *Intrepid,* Orbiting Fierra
REGION: Bollam's World System, Bollam's World Federation

The cocoon of the new Arc-6 fighter drew Jessica into its womb and she felt the ship's systems connect with her mind.

Once more into the breach, she thought to herself.

Cordy, the squadron AI, addressed the pilots.

<Don't skim the preflight checks; these birds haven't seen black before. You're the first to take them out.>

<As if we need reminding,> Cary groused.

<You've read the specs,> Rock said. *<They're just Arc-5s with stasis shields and inertial dampeners. Same thrust and power, just well-nigh indestructible.>*

Jessica smiled at the squadron's banter. Despite her near-death experience battling the Sirian scout ships, she had kept up her pilot's credentials. She had not flown any active combat missions since that fateful battle, but had taken part in several training exercises with the Black Death—as the squadron had become known.

Rock and Cary were old guard; they had flown against the Sirian scouts, as well, but many of the pilots on that fateful mission had been Victorians who stayed behind when the *Intrepid* left The Kap.

Still, she recognized many of the pilots and had exchanged warm greetings in the ready room. The one person she missed was Carson, who had gone on to lead his own squadron—currently out patrolling the space around Fierra's southern hemisphere.

<You ready for this?> she asked Jerry, her wingman.

<More than ready,> Jerry replied. *<Gonna show these bastards they can't mess with the* Intrepid*!>*

<That's the spirit,> Jessica replied with a laugh.

Her preflight checklist showed green, and, while waiting for the squadron to drop down their ladders, she ran it again for good measure.

On cue, she felt movement and turned her vision outward, looking around the bay with the ship's sensors. They confirmed that the suspension field had picked up her Arc-6 and was moving it to her ladder.

The *Intrepid* now sported a dozen fighter bays—a number necessary to store and service the vessel's eight hundred fighters. This bay held racks for over a hundred ships, though nearly all were currently deployed. On the far side of the bay, techs and automatons worked tirelessly around a cluster of Arc-5s, upgrading them into Arc-6s.

Her ship slipped onto its ladder, along with the other twenty-four fighters in the squadron, and a thirty second countdown appeared on her HUD.

No one spoke, every member of the Black Death likely following whatever rituals they performed alone before a combat drop. Jessica sent a thought to Trist in what she hoped was a glorious afterlife.

This is for you, babe.

There was almost no physical sensation as the fighters slid down their ladders, the new inertial dampeners removing all feelings of motion.

<*This is almost too smooth,*> Jason said. <*I can't even tell which way I'm moving.*>

<*Enable the feedback system,*> Cary advised. <*It'll give you the sensations you're used to, without actually putting the pressure on your body.*>

<*I know,*> Jason replied. <*I read the manual, too, I was just saying…*>

<*Cut the chatter,*> Rock interrupted. <*I want complete shakedown reports by our first pass around Fierra.*>

Jessica complied, and in sequence with the other fighters, applied a 30*g* burn toward the moon below. She didn't even feel a single *g* on her body, and the fighter spun and pivoted like it was on rails.

Amazing, she thought to herself.

The other pilots were also putting the ships through their paces, and Jessica watched the squadron dance and spin as they began to break into a slow polar orbit. Their patrol path called for a half-dozen polar loops before slowing to hold position five thousand kilometers above the south pole, creating a buffer between the pirate Padre's fleet and the *Intrepid* and its fleet.

The moon below was a welcoming blue and green, with white cumulous clouds dotting its skies. A thick layer of water vapor high in the world's stratosphere blurred the surface, but she could still make out oceans, green lands, deserts, and icy poles.

Worlds like this one—distant from their star and orbiting massive jovians—were not self-sustaining. The less-luminous light of their host star did not impart enough energy to the world to keep it warm with a more natural atmosphere. Combined with the gravity of its parent planet constantly tearing at its skies, the world would ultimately lose most of its air. It would take constant upkeep to remain habitable.

Still, for people who loved green grass and open spaces, it was hard to beat the real deal. Jessica found that she still missed Athabasca, and though it had been nice to visit Victoria from time to time, its brown forests and fields never sated her desire for a more terrestrial world.

She used her sensors to probe the world as much as she could. The mission report held true. No settlements had been constructed, but the moon wasn't uninhabited either. The terraforming crews were still there; her dataset told her it was mostly biologists monitoring their work. A flotilla of tugs and cargo ships hung in low orbit where they had taken refuge from their work constructing a space elevator after the battle broke out between the Bollam's World Space Force and the pirates.

With any luck, this would be over soon and they could go back to their tasks unharmed.

<*Good to see some more friendly faces,*> a welcoming voice came over the Link.

<*Carson! How are you?*> Jessica responded.

<*Oh, you know, the usual.*>

<*Anything we should be aware of?*> Rock asked.

<*The folks up north seem to be keeping to themselves, but these guys down here keep feinting and trying to draw us in. Poor tactics, if you ask me. Whoever starts this fight is going to come out the worst,*> Carson replied. <*You guys take care. My girls and boys have been out here for three days now and we're heading in to get some sack and have our birds upgraded.*>

<*You'll love it,*> Cary said. <*Smooth as butter. You won't ache for days after a ride in these.*>

<*Now that's an advancement I'm glad to hear about,*> Carson laughed. <*These old bones of mine aren't so happy about pulling seventy anymore.*>

Carson's squadron dropped into a polar orbit, passing the Black Death as they did a quick loop around Fierra to reach the *Intrepid's* elevation.

Four other squadrons patrolled the southern hemisphere, and on their final loop, Jessica's squadron adjusted their trajectory to fit into their place in the pattern—when their final deceleration was interrupted by an exclamation from Cary.

<*Oh shit, oh shit, this isn't good!*>

<*Report, lieutenant, what's going on?*> Rock asked calmly.

<*Attitude control is gone wonky; I can't rotate my drive for final braking. I tried spinning the whole ship, but I can't hold it steady…I'm tumbling out here.*>

Jessica's scan confirmed Cary's words. Her fighter was moving like a dog trying to screw a football, still travelling at over fifty thousand kilometers per hour.

<*I confirm,*> Cordy said. <*Something is messed up in the sensor interface. It can't get good data, and with the dampeners it can't get readings off the fallback gyros.*>

<*Turn off the dampeners,*> another pilot suggested. <*Won't be fun, but you can take it.*>

<*Trying that,*> Cary replied. <*Now the system won't take input from the gyros and I think I'm going to hurl.*>

Jessica laughed at the humor. It wasn't possible to vomit in a shoot suit, but that didn't stop a person's body from trying. The data from her scan showed Cary's Arc-6 now spinning wildly as attitude control thrusters fired inaccurately, working off bad data as they tried to right the ship. Cary would be experiencing forces over thirty gs in constant, random vectors.

<*Kill your attitude control,*> Rock said. <*You're not helping yourself out at all.*>

<*I've tried all the tricks I can think of,*> Cordy said. <*Something got screwed up in the sensor interfaces. You're going to have to reset and restore from crystal.*>

Cary groaned and then signaled affirmative.

Her fighter ceased its sporadic motion and settled into a relatively consistent vector—one aimed straight for the pirate fleet.

<*Uh…Commander?*> Cary asked.

<*We'll cover you,*> Rock replied. <*The restore should only take a few minutes.*>

<*And what if it doesn't work?*> Cary asked.

The squadron's combat net was silent for a moment.

<*Then we get to see how good these shields really are,*> Rock replied.

ENGAGEMENT

STELLAR DATE: 10.29.8927 (Adjusted Years)
LOCATION: ISS *Intrepid*, Orbiting Fierra (6*Mj* Jovian)
REGION: Bollam's World System, Bollam's World Federation

Sera waved a greeting as she walked past Amanda, who was now ensconced in the bridge's foyer, and followed the corridor past the conference room to the bridge itself.

She stood in the room's entrance and stared for a full minute.

<*OK, now it really does feel like home,*> she said to Helen.

The *Intrepid's* bridge was more like a colony command and control center than simply the helm and ship duty stations most vessels possessed.

For starters, it was almost a quarter the volume of *Sabrina*; nearly thirty meters across, and twice as many deep. A large holo tank dominated the center of the room, and beside it stood Tanis, frowning at what she saw. Surrounding her, in concentric circles, were rows and rows of consoles, smaller holo displays, and department liaisons and automatons.

It bustled like a beehive with its queen at the center.

<*It's a strange relationship she has with the captain,*> Helen observed. <*Almost as though she is the colony leader and he is just a captain under her command.*>

<*Almost,*> Sera agreed.

Tanis looked up and locked eyes with her. <*Come with me.*>

<*Why do I feel like I'm being called into my father's office?*> Sera asked Helen with a mental sigh.

<*You know why. It's time you told them your story—they need to know.*>

Tanis threaded her way through the consoles and bridge personnel, moving toward a doorway on Sera's right. They stepped through the portal into a small, utilitarian office. Behind a desk covered in holo displays sat Captain Andrews.

She caught him glance at her body, something that certainly was understandable given the shimmering silver skin tone she had selected for the day.

<*It's sad, really,*> Helen observed privately.

<*Let me be. I'm a frail organic, subject to my chemically-induced whims.*>

Helen gave the mental equivalent of a snort in response.

"Good afternoon," he addressed both women. "Tanis, did you see the latest message from the AST ships?"

"I did," the general replied with a chuckle. "Claiming that they own this ship due to late interest payments on loans is pretty weak—especially given that the loans, small as they were, were handled through the GSS, not the Sol Space Federation."

"Well, they did absorb the GSS before they shut it down," Sera said. "It was part of an attempt to stop the exodus of the brightest and most adventurous people from

Sol. After you left, Sol started to get pretty stagnant. People had no drive or ambition. Even their birthrate almost hit zero."

"Trust me," Tanis said while shaking her head. "That trend started long before we left."

"Either way," Sera replied with a shrug. "They wrote off all their GSS-related debt millennia ago."

"That's good," Captain Andrews replied. "The only thing worse than enemy fleets chasing you across the stars are bureaucrats who want their money."

"It seems they'll even chase you across millennia," Sera added.

"Do you have the details on that write-off?" Tanis asked. "It would be nice to send a response for them to chew on. Keeping the dialog going never hurts."

"I'm pulling up what we have on *Sabrina,*" Sera said as she accessed her ship's archives. "Here it is. After the breakup of the SSF and the eventual formation of the AST, the new government performed a century-long audit of all the assets and debts they possessed."

"Somewhere along the line, someone realized that the government had an ownership stake in several dozen colonies, and colony ships, that no one had heard from in nearly a millennium. They didn't like the potential liability, so they simply wrote off the whole lot and passed legislation that any property the AST would have owned, or had a lien on, was transferred to whoever possessed it at the time of the law's passing."

The captain ran a hand through his hair. "How…indiscreet of them."

Tanis laughed, and Sera passed the relevant information to her.

"Great, I'll have the comm officer organize a response and send it to our friends out there. Should shut them up for a bit."

Tanis turned to Sera, her expression carefully schooled. "You sent your message. The captain and I would finally like to—ah, shit."

"What is it?" Sera asked as Tanis turned toward the door.

"One of the fighters is having a malfunction and heading straight for Padre's ships."

They rushed out to the main holo tank, which already displayed the situation at Fierra's south pole.

"It's the Black Death," a duty officer supplied. "One of their Arc-6s is acting up; they're trying a system restore from crystal backup."

"And if it doesn't finish in time?" Sera asked.

"Then they'll pass right through the middle of Padre's formation," Tanis replied.

"Sorry, my story will have to wait for another time; this could be the start of things," Sera looked from Tanis to Captain Andrews. "I need to get out there."

She could see Tanis and the captain exchange thoughts over the Link before Tanis nodded.

<Amanda, give her priority on a maglev. How is the shield upgrade on her ship going?>

<Finished ten minutes ago, they're just doing final tests.>

<Tell them to step on it. Sabrina is undocking in ten minutes.>

FIRESTORM

STELLAR DATE: 10.29.8927 (Adjusted Years)
LOCATION: Near Kithari, South of Fierra
REGION: Bollam's World System, Bollam's World Federation

<*Max burn,*> Rock addressed his squadron. <*I want a protective cocoon around Cary.*>

Jessica goosed her fighter to match Cary's vector with several quick burns she barely noticed.

<*Five enemy ships are moving to intercept,*> Cordy advised.

C'mon, Cary, Jessica thought to herself. *Get that thing fixed.*

She counted down the seconds it should take for a system restore to complete and Cary's silence continued after her count completed. The pilot did not come back on the squadron's combat net.

Another minute passed and Rock's voice broke the silence.

<*We're going to punch her through their picket line and one of our pushers is going to grab her. Just need to get past all those bastards down there.*>

The pilots silently signaled their acknowledgement, coordinated their flight paths, and selected targets from the five corvettes closing in on Cary.

<*How's it look out there?*> Colonel Pearson's voice broke the strained silence on the squadron's combat net.

<*If the shields hold, we'll be OK. Just make sure* Excelsior Nova *is ready to play catch on the far side,*> Rock replied to the group commander.

<*Nuwen has his ship ready to catch her. I'm patching him into your net now. The* Enterprise *and* Defiance *are dropping lower to provide supporting fire if the whole mess down there swarms you.* Andromeda *sneaking by now to silently drop off some RMs.*>

<*Roger that,*> Rock replied. <*You heard that,*> he said to his pilots. <*Things are about to get real out here. We could be facing the whole effing galaxy before the day is done, so don't blow your loadout on maybes. Sure, tactical strikes.*>

Jessica nodded to herself and signaled her acknowledgement of the order.

The relative velocity between Cary's fighter and the five pirate corvettes put intercept in twelve minutes. Jessica kept an eye on her NSAI's estimation of lethal range—just under ten thousand kilometers—which they would reach in five minutes.

<*Watch the corrections,*> Cordy advised the pilots.

Space close to Fierra was full of dust from mined asteroids and no small amount of swirling gas from the jovian it orbited. It was far from empty, and a dust or hydrogen cloud could make all the difference when it came to striking a lethal blow.

Jessica checked the updated scan. Though the five corvettes had accelerated rapidly to reach Cary, they were now braking, attempting to match *v* to snatch her up.

The maneuver made little sense to Jessica. With the rest of the squadron surrounding Cary, the pirate ships would become stationary targets—relatively speaking—if they attempted to grab the disabled fighter.

<*From what Helen and Sabrina have shared, there are few one-man fighters in this time—certainly none used in fleet combat. They can't generate strong enough grav shielding to hold out against antimatter-powered weapons,*> Cordy said.

<*So, what you're saying is…these bastards are in for a surprise,*> Jessica said, her avatar displaying a wicked grin.

<*Except at that range, they'll have no problem destroying Cary, even with the squadron flying close support. All it will take is one low-yield nuke.*>

Rock seemed to have the same thought. <*Jason, Jessica, Sam, Trinity. Take your wingmen and boost hard and beat those assholes senseless before they get here. Make them think twice about getting up close and personal with our Arcs.*>

They acknowledged the order and eight Arc-6 fighters accelerated toward the pirate corvettes.

They split into two formations, each targeting one of the pirate vessels and none firing until they were well within beam range. It was deemed best to save their power for maximum effectiveness in this stellar soup.

The corvettes were still slowing to match *v* with the rest of the squadron, and their prey, Cary's ship, when the eight Arc-6s flashed past them, laying withering beam fire on the two lead vessels.

Jessica spun her engine and applied full thrust, the now-pointless readout telling her that without the dampeners she would be crushed under a 100*g*s of acceleration. Scan showed that the enemy corvettes had returned fire at the fighters, a salvo of over seventy beams, and two rail slugs.

The slugs knocked their target Arcs around, but none of the fighters showed any damage.

<*Status!*> Rock called out.

<*Shields show no change. I got hit by one of those slugs and didn't feel a thing. We're coming for another pass,*> Jason reported.

<*They're spooling their AP drives,*> Cordy said. <*I advise that you come around and fire right up their funnels. It should punch right through their antimatter containment.*>

Jessica sent an affirmative response, feeling giddy as the adrenaline coursed through her body. It was going to be like shooting fish in a barrel. The fighters slowed, and then stopped before their engines drove them back toward the pirate corvettes. Almost lazily, they drifted over their enemy, shrugging off the beams and rails before dropping directly into the stream of gamma rays that flowed at light speed from the AP engines.

It took conscious effort to drop her ship into the engine wash—normally such action would result in certain death, but the stasis shields brushed off the luminal impacts with ease.

In unison, five of the eight fighters lanced streams of protons into the pirate ships' engines.

As predicted, the beams penetrated the antimatter containment and the pirate ships exploded in tremendous displays of plasma and shrapnel.

<*There's the one time we get to do that,*> Jessica said.

<*The rest of their fleet has already started jinking more erratically,*> Jason chuckled.

<*They're also moving to engage us,*> Cordy added. <*They'll be in range in four minutes.*>

Rock gave the order for the eight fighters to form up with the rest of the squadron. Jessica adjusted her relative v to zero with a quick burst from her AP engine.

<*I could get used to this,*> she commented to Jerry.

<*No kidding,*> Jerry replied. <*It's going to be a cake walk.*>

<*Don't get too cocky,*> Jessica replied. <*We may have been able to brush off the beams from five ships, but it's about to get a lot hotter.*>

* * * * *

"That's amazing," Tanis commented from beside the bridge's main holo tank. "It's like the enemy wasn't even firing."

"It's a game changer, alright," Sanderson observed.

"The bulk of their fleet is engaging," Tanis cautioned as the tank lit up with an explosion of energy surrounding Black Death's position. Nearly two hundred corvettes and four cruisers focused every beam and railgun in their fleet on the fighter squadron's tight cocoon around Cary's disabled vessel.

She tasted blood and realized that she was biting her lip.

<*What have I done to them,*> she whispered to Angela. <*Jessica is in there…fuck…if anyone is still in there.*>

Angela had no response, though concern flowed from her into Tanis's mind.

The salvo lasted only seven seconds, but it felt like an eternity to Tanis.

The assault ceased as if a switch had been flipped. Scan took a moment to clear and then the bridge erupted with cheers. The squadron was still there, surrounding their comrade's ship, all undamaged.

<*Squadron leader, status,*> Tanis queried.

<*General! Wow…that was…sorry. We're all OK. Our reactors are running about as hot as they go, though—we can't withstand another one of those barrages.*>

<*You won't have to,*> Tanis replied.

The pirate fleet had passed the fighters and split into two groups, each looping around to re-engage the squadron, a maneuver they were executing while taking great care not to expose their engines to the Arc-6s.

Tanis watched trajectory estimates and corrections scroll down a secondary holo. It was going to be a direct hit.

She finally let out her breath.

Both groups of Padre's armada passed right through dense fields of grapeshot courtesy of the *Enterprise* and *Defiance*. The lead ships were torn to ribbons under the barrage and even one of the cruisers blossomed into a cloud of hot gas and jets of fire.

Seconds later, twenty-two new signatures lit up on the display. The relativistic missiles seeded by the *Andromeda* came to life and sought their targets with ruthless efficiency. The enemy fleet was completely obscured by the nuclear fireballs, their explosions just far enough from the squadron of Arc-6s that they evaded everything but the light from the blast.

When scan was finally able to get a clear picture, less than a hundred enemy ships remained and only fifty of those appeared to be operational.

Calls of surrender flooded the comm channels while two cruisers and a dozen of the corvettes altered course, pushing for a tight loop around Kithari to gain an outsystem vector.

<*Take them out,*> Tanis ordered. <*Padre was on one of those ships.*> She was not going to let him continue to roam the galaxy.

On her command, the 42nd squadron, consisting of newly-deployed Arc-6s, broke from their approach to Fierra's northern hemisphere and pursued the fleeing ships, beams flashing and missiles flying from both formations.

Tanis turned her attention back to Jessica's squadron. The *Excelsior Nova* was matching velocity with Cary's fighter to effect the pickup, and the Black Death squadron was maintaining a protective shield, should any of the remaining pirate vessels get any ideas.

"What happens when everyone gets shields like these?" Captain Andrews asked softly. "What level of destructive power will two ships need to level against one another?"

Tanis cast the captain a sidelong glance. He had never opposed it, but she knew he had never been comfortable with the military buildup of the *Intrepid* and its fleet. Though, on deeper reflection, she had to admit that he was right. If fleets could no longer do battle with conventional weapons, what would they resort to? Planetary destruction? Stellar destruction?

<*Sera's right,*> Angela whispered. <*This is a bigger game changer than the picotech.*>

Tanis took a moment to consider her feelings on the matter before replying.

"You're right, Captain. I'm passing orders to ensure that the keys to this technology never leave Bob and Earnest's minds," Tanis said to Captain Andrews. "It's too dangerous to ever let loose."

The captain nodded slowly, and Admiral Sanderson gave her an evaluating look before inclining his head in agreement.

During the battle with Padre's ships, Tanis had observed The Mark fleet repositioning itself. Rebecca's ships were now five thousand kilometers beyond the effective beam range of the Arc-5s in position north of Fierra.

<*What do you think her play is?*> Amanda asked. <*She can't tell the difference between our Arc-5s and 6s to be sure that they all don't have stasis shields.*>

<*She'll find out soon enough,*> Tanis replied. <*When are the next batch of 6s ready for deployment?*>

<*Thirty minutes,*> came the avatar's reply.

Tanis was beginning to think she shouldn't have been so rash in sending her other Arc-6s after the remnants of Padre's fleet. They had destroyed or disabled the fleeing ships, but now needed to pass around Kithari before coming back into range.

With Padre's fleet taken care of, Jessica's squadron could fill the gap, but the Boller fleet had also shifted to a more aggressive stance.

<*Move squadrons eleven through thirty-one to bolster the northern hemisphere,*> Tanis directed. <*I want the* Dresden *and* Orkney, *along with the* Pike *and* Andromeda, *on station between the* Intrepid *and the Boller ships.*>

She addressed the ISF over the general fleet net.

<*We've kicked the hornet's nest, for sure,*> she began. <*But it's not anything we haven't been up against before. They fear us. They fear our picotech, and now they fear our stasis shields. Use that to our advantage. Be bold, don't show hesitation, and they'll wonder what else we have up our sleeves.*>

Tanis looked around the bridge; every crewmember's eyes were on her. She took a deep breath and continued.

<*Many of you may have heard rumors—yes, we've sent a message to the FGT, and we're going to rendezvous with them soon. In thirty hours, we'll have FTL capability and leave these greedy bastards behind. The FGT has terraformed systems far beyond known space, and we'll be able to build our new world in peace!*>

Tanis felt her mental tone waver at the last word. She hoped it didn't detract from her speech—though from the expressions on the faces of those around her, it seemed to have had a positive effect.

There was a moment's pause after her words, and then another round of cheers erupted across the bridge.

"Ok, ok, back to work," Tanis said with her hands raised and a small smile. "We still have to survive the next thirty hours."

* * * * *

Sabrina boosted away from the *Intrepid*, Cheeky threading the arcs of the colony ship's super structure like it was something she did every day. Once in open space, she spun out the AP nozzle and boosted toward Fierra's northern hemisphere.

Sera smiled to herself. No one needed to ask where she wanted to go. She had a score to settle with Rebecca.

<*Think it was a mistake to leave her alive?*> Helen asked.

<*I don't know…maybe. I had to hope that mercy would get me some consideration.*>

<*Who knows, maybe it has—but it wouldn't stop her from wanting to get her hands on the* Intrepid. *Especially after you stole back the CriEn module.*>

"Incoming signal," Flaherty announced from the new scan and weapons console.

He turned to look Sera in the eyes. "You'll never guess who it is."

Sera stood. "Put her on."

The holo shifted its display of the space around the moon to a secondary tank and Rebecca appeared on the bridge, as clear as though she were really there.

The pirate leader's eyebrows rose and she smiled. "I see you've appropriated some of my style."

Sera looked down at her gleaming crimson skin and shrugged. "If I'm going to kick your ass, I'm going to do it in style."

"We'll see about that," Rebecca smiled. "I have to admit, I'm pleased to have both prizes in one place. My new ship out there, *and* the power module you stole from me. It's going to be a good day."

"What about me?" Sera asked with a faux pout. "I thought I was your prize?"

"There'll be time enough for you, I promise," Rebecca stepped close to Sera, her holographically-projected hand tracing down Sera's breast, along her side and to her hip. "I am very curious how you survived stealing my clothing—though you don't seem to have escaped unscathed."

"I wanted to thank you for that," Sera replied. "You may be the dumbest bitch in the galaxy, but you do have a sense of style—I'll grant you that. If your flagship survives, I may raid the rest of your wardrobe. There were some shoes in there I'd kill for."

<Dear god, you're killing me! Are you going to get her to tip her hand or what?> Cargo asked.

<Wait for it; she's getting all bent out of shape. If there ever was a woman who had vanity as her weakness, it's Rebecca,> Sera answered.

<I can think of someone else, too,> Cargo replied sourly.

"If you think you're going to take out even *one* of my ships, you have another thing coming," Rebecca spat back. "I'm not just going to sit there and take it like that moron Padre did. By the way, thank your friends on the *Intrepid* for me. It'll be good business taking over all his operations."

"You can thank her yourself," Sera said as Tanis joined the conversation.

"Nice to see you again, Rebecca," Tanis said with a smile.

A look of confusion washed across Rebecca's face. "No! You're that navigator woman on Sera's hunk of junk…who are you really?"

"General Tanis Richards, XO of the ISS *Intrepid*, at your service," Tanis replied with a nod. "It's really time for you to go now. You saw what we did to Padre's fleet. You don't stand a chance."

"It doesn't matter," Rebecca said with a swipe of her hand. "We know a few tricks that fool Padre never even dreamed of. I'll be sleeping in your quarters tonight, *General* Richards."

Rebecca cut the communication and Tanis looked at Sera.

"What do you think she has up her sleeve?"

Sera raced through the possibilities, of which there were many. One, however, stood out.

"She said that we wouldn't damage even one of her ships. I think they may try a shield lock."

"No!" Cheeky shouted. "She wouldn't be so stupid. This close to a mass like Kithari? She's just as likely to create a singularity."

"What does that mean?" Tanis asked.

"With some skill—and guts—it's possible to merge the shields of multiple ships into a multi-layered, shifting shell of protection. If she can pull it off with her fleet, it's going to be pretty hard to punch through."

Tanis glanced away. "Damn, that Boller admiral is calling, and he seems upset—you'd think they'd be happy we took out Padre." The general paused and frowned, thinking for a moment. "The *Thracia* and *Babylon* are already on their way to the moon's northern hemisphere. I'm sending the *Enterprise as* well—show her we mean business. Amanda will get you onto their tactical net. You're the only one with a stasis shield till the 42nd squadron gets back into play, so use it wisely."

"Wise is my middle name," Sera replied with a roguish grin.

Tanis laughed in response and cut the holo connection.

<*Push her buttons, don't let her push yours,*> the general passed a parting thought.

Count on it, Sera thought to herself.

She sat back in her chair and connected to the tactical net Amanda had opened to her.

A virtual space opened up in her mind and she saw the captains of the four capital ships, as well as three fighter group commanders.

<*Welcome, Captain Sera,*> Captain Espensen of the *Enterprise* said. <*Glad to have you in our ranks today.*>

<*Happy to be on the team,*> Sera replied. <*What's our plan?*>

<*Our orders are to contain The Mark's fleet and keep them out of effective range of the* Intrepid*—that means no closer than seventy thousand kilometers,*> Sheeran, captain of the Babylon, replied.

<*If they lock shields, that will be no simple task,*> Sera replied.

<*Amanda briefed us on that. Is it really as effective as she said?*> Captain Espensen asked.

<*It is,*> Sera replied. <*It's going to take everything we have to break a shield powered by that many ships—if she can construct it.*>

<*How likely is that?*> Colonel Pearson asked.

<*Normally I'd say not likely at all,*> Sera replied. <*But the Hand operated a base within the dark layer for years. They know things about the DL that gave them an edge. I should warn you, though, it's just as likely that she's going to create a black hole that will suck in the moon below and Kithari, too.*>

<*Well shit,*> Sheeran exclaimed. <*Should we hit her first?*>

<*The general gave us orders not to start anything,*> Captain Espensen said with a raised eyebrow. <*We can't overcommit. There are two other fleets still out there.*>

Sheeran shrugged. <*Going to be worse if they do their shield mojo after the Bollers attack.*>

<*I'm with the general on this,*> Sera replied. <*After what we did to Padre, you can bet she'll start with RMs—I don't know that even our stasis shields can withstand a hundred or more of those. I say we wait and see if she can actually pull her trick off. Like I said, she stands a greater chance of killing herself than us.*>

<*I endorse the self-immolation of my enemies,*> Captain Espensen said.

<*Then we wait,*> Colonel Pearson agreed.

*****

"That's definitely an unfriendly posture," Tanis sighed.

The Bollam's World Space Force was upping the ante as the minutes ticked by. Their initial blockade of fifty-two ships had ballooned to nearly four hundred. More took up positions in a grid near the AST dreadnaughts than in defense against the *Intrepid* and The Mark fleet.

Even with the Black Death's demonstration of near invincibility, it appeared that the Bollam's World Space Force was more concerned about the AST ships.

<*It makes sense,*> Angela said. <*They still think—or hope—that we intend to stay and treat with them. They know the AST intends only to take our ship and leave—or worse, take it and stay.*>

<*They probably also think that we'll take out The Mark's fleet and save them the trouble—which is how I bet things will play out,*> Tanis agreed. <*We're more likely to do that if they're not threatening us as much.*>

"The nano probes we shot out of the rails earlier have started to send in some interesting data. So far we've picked up seventy-two rail platforms in the system—more than Sera thought there would be. They're all pointed at us and the AST ships," the scan officer reported.

<*Two of them are on a pair of Kithari's smaller moons,*> Amanda added.

Tanis nodded and added every rail platform within thirty light-minutes to the priority target list. The second the Bollers turned hostile, half-ton slugs would be fired at each of those platforms. They probably wouldn't all hit, but it was better than leaving them there to fire on the ISF fleet.

For added insurance, the *Andromeda* was quietly seeding relativistic missiles throughout potential paths of approach for enemy ships. If there was one thing no one objected to after the Battle for Victoria, it was an oversupply of RMs.

<*Bollam's ambassador has just requested permission for his pinnace to undock,*> Amanda announced.

"Well, if that's not a clear sign, I don't know what is," Captain Andrews said. "What's the latest on our stasis shield?"

"Abby reported that they're working through some kinks," Tanis said. "She wouldn't give me a time, but based on her level of surliness I don't think that we should count on it right now."

<*She was cursing Earnest's ship design at one point,*> Amanda added. <*Something about 'stupid irregular protrusions'.*>

If the pressure stemming from the overwhelming force encircling the *Intrepid* wasn't so great, Tanis would have laughed.

<*At least a lot of the Boller ships aren't much bigger than the pirate corvettes,*> Angela supplied. <*Their relative isolation doesn't require them to have a large space force—especially with New Eden shielding them from the AST.*>

<*Thank the stars for small miracles,*> Tanis responded.

"There," scan pointed out. "Three of their ships just slid over three kilometers."

Tanis began mapping trajectories, but Amanda beat her to it.

<Trajectory lines up with a rail one light minute out and the Orkney's *position in five minutes.>*

Tanis sent the signal across the fleet for all ships to institute gamma-pattern jinking.

<Helm, bring us around to Fierra's L1 with Kithari, then execute gamma pattern. I don't want us to be in the same spot more than once every ten minutes.>

The *Intrepid's* helm and ships fleet-wide signaled their acknowledgement and Tanis settled in to wait. If a shot passed through the *Orkney's* former path, then she would not wait for further provocation.

Barely a word was uttered on the bridge as the five minutes passed. Then, right on cue, scan picked up a three-hundred-kilogram slug travelling at a quarter the speed of light.

<ISF Fleet, this is General Richards. All batteries assigned non-ship-mounted priority targets, send a five-shot salvo.>

Across the fleet, fifty-two rail guns opened fire, sending half-ton slugs hurling into the black. In less than a minute, two hundred and sixty kinetic rounds were en route to their targets. Scan showed Boller ships changing position, attempting to intercept and lase the slugs before they reached their targets.

Several fired rails at the ISF slugs, hoping to impact and deflect the incoming projectiles.

"I bet they didn't think we knew about quite so many of those," the admiral chuckled.

"I read a dozen slugs passing through positions our ships would have been occupying right now," scan reported.

"Well done in seeing the significance on that ship movement," Tanis said. "Your team just saved the fleet."

The scan officer sat up straighter and smiled in acknowledgement before turning back to his console and the never-ending streams of information being fed from the NSAIs, which handled the raw sensor data. He gave a word of encouragement over the Link to the humans and AI on scan.

"Incoming from the Boller fleet admiral," the comm officer said. "Should I put it on the main tank?"

"What the hell?" Tanis sighed. "I expect we could all use a good laugh."

The figure on the display was a woman this time, and her expression was less than pleased.

"You've just sentenced hundreds of Bollam's citizens to death," she said in soft, icy tones. "There will be no more treaties. We will reclaim our new world, take your ship—whole or in pieces—and crush your pathetic little fleet."

Tanis turned to Terrance. "At least when we were dealing with the Sirians they had proper megalomaniacs. This pales in comparison."

The woman grew even more enraged, her face turning red.

"Our ancestors were from Sirius! They were caught in Kapteyn's Streamer hundreds of years before you. They earned these worlds."

"Sirians…that explains a lot," Tanis shook her head before turning back to the admiral. "You say that we killed hundreds, but thousands would have died on *our* ships had your kinetic rounds connected."

"They would not have!" the woman exclaimed. "You have advanced shielding; what we fired was merely a shot across the bow."

Tanis couldn't believe what she was hearing. "Are you seriously going to attempt to paint us as the aggressors? Until your unmistakable act of war, we have only taken defensive actions. You are brigands who attempt to seize whatever drifts past your system to better yourselves. You're nothing more than well-established interstellar bandits."

Tanis hadn't even finished speaking her final words before the woman was yelling so loudly that the bridge's audio systems lowered her output.

"You sanctimonious, dusty old bitch! Our people built this system out of nothing. We worked for millennia to create what you see. You would come here and pick our best worlds for yourselves in trade for trinkets. No one will have your tech. Not those pirates, not those core-world bastards, and certainly not you. I'll—"

Tanis cut the connection.

<*Fleet division one, prepare for incoming assault,*> Tanis advised her captains and fighter group commanders.

"She seems excitable," Captain Andrews said. "Though you may not have needed to goad her quite so much."

"'Needed' is just the word," Tanis replied. "It was clear that she opposed any sort of deal with us—but that cannot be the case across the entire system. I've just made her look the fool in front of her fleet. When the time comes for hard choices, it may be that not all of her people make the wrong ones."

Tanis reviewed the battlefield. One squadron of Arc-5s patrolled the field of destroyed and disabled ships that was Padre's fleet. The other twenty-two squadrons in the fleet's first wing had formed two picket lines, one leading Kithari and the other trailing the gas giant.

The *Pike* and *Gilese* anchored the first group, and the *Condor* anchored the second with the *Andromeda* lurking nearby. Closer to the *Intrepid* lay the *Orkney* and *Dresden*, with their own fighter shields deployed around them.

Armed with deadly antimatter and fusion engines, the *Intrepid's* eighteen heavy tugs provided the final layer of protection.

Scan called out impacts on the first rail gun emplacements, an event that kicked off the Boller assault.

"Looks like a quarter of their force," Sanderson commented. "Thirty-six cruisers, forty destroyers and a mess of corvettes. No fighters, though."

"From what Sera says, no one uses fighters anymore…though I wonder if that might change after they saw what our Arcs can do."

"The odds look worse than when the Sirians invaded," Terrance said softly. "And we had three times the ships we have now."

"Like the admiral said," Tanis replied. "Our fighters count for a lot—especially given that there are nearly five hundred of them between us and the Bollers. Seventy-two are Arc-6s, as well. They can park right in the engine wash of any of those cruisers and lance their ships to pieces."

I just hope it will be enough, she thought.

"Hell, they can probably fly through those ships if they had to," Sanderson grunted.

There's a tactic no one will ever put in the books, Tanis thought to herself, worried that they would ultimately have to resort to just such an attack.

"Sirs? The Mark's ships are doing something," the scan officer reported.

* * * * *

<*There they go,*> Sera said. <*We'll know in a minute if they can pull this off.*>

<*Wouldn't this be the best time to attack?*> Captain Sheeran asked. <*If we can disrupt them and make them destroy themselves…*>

<*Not unless you fancy getting sucked into a black hole that's drawing mass and energy from the dark layer,*> Sera replied. <*Like Captain Espensen said, if there weren't two other fleets out there, we'd have smoked them half an hour ago.*>

Sera looked to Cheeky, Cargo, and Flaherty. "God, I hope this was the right play," she said softly.

"There is no right play, here," Flaherty replied.

The Mark ships shifted into a large sphere with the three cruisers at the center. *Sabrina's* scan showed streams of gravitons flowing from the center ships to the corvettes on the perimeter. Those gravitons were harnessed and amplified by the corvettes and a kilometer-thick shield snapped into place around the armada.

"Well I'll be damned," Sera whispered. "She totally nailed that."

<*Well, so much for destroying themselves,*> Captain Sheeran said. <*What now?*>

<*We have to wear that shell down,*> Captain Espensen ordered. <*They're already boosting for the* Intrepid.>

"They're going to wrap their shield around the *Intrepid* and storm the ship," Flaherty said.

"I believe you're right," Sera nodded in agreement.

The ISF ships were engaging The Mark's shield bubble with little effect. Even the near-luminal impacts of relativistic missiles only slightly altered the trajectory of the sphere—movement that was quickly corrected as The Mark ships accelerated toward the *Intrepid.*

The fighters darted close to the enemy fleet, lancing out with lasers and missiles, but the beams did no damage and few of the missiles even reached the shields. The cruisers did what they could from a distance, but without stasis shields, it was certain death to approach The Mark ships and their thousands of beams.

Only the single squadron of Arc-6s dared dance close to the enemy, but even at less than a kilometer away, their weapons had no measurable effect on the armada's super shield.

A desperate pilot arched away from the battle, taking a long loop around Fierra before coming back at a hundredth the speed of light, smashing his ship into the pirate fleet's shield.

"That had an effect," Flaherty said, a small measure of excitement slipping into his voice. "The umbrella in that section lost a layer when the fighter hit."

"How is the fighter, though?" Sera asked.

"Looks like it's disabled," Flaherty replied. "Though the dampeners did keep the pilot alive."

<*I have a plan,*> Sera said to the fleet captains. <*Keep them as focused on you as you can.*>

<*What are you going to do?*> Captain Espensen asked.

<*Something like that fighter just did, just on a larger scale.*>

She outlined what she would need to the captains and left their virtual conference.

"Cheeky, set this course, maximum acceleration."

Cheeky's eyes grew wide. She looked up at Sera. "Are you serious?"

"I am. *Sabrina* can take it. I know this will work."

"This isn't like the rest of your super-secret special knowledge!" Cargo turned, his eyes filled with fear and worry. "The *Intrepid's* scientists just invented stasis shields two days ago! This is our shakedown run, for star's sakes!"

"You can get out and walk if you want to," Sera replied to Cargo without breaking eye contact with Cheeky. "Do it now."

Cheeky nodded and turned to her work. As *Sabrina* began to turn away from the battle, a call came in from Rebecca. Sera put it on the tank.

"Running away already?" Rebecca asked, her expression haughty as Sera had expected.

"I know when to cut my losses," Sera replied. "Good luck storming a ship with a hundred thousand square kilometers of deck with your rag-tag band of miscreants. That is, before the AST comes in and exterminates you."

"I'm not afraid of those core-worlders," Rebecca replied. "I'll have that ship, and I'll use it to hunt you down and crush you. You'll be back under my tender ministrations before you know what happened."

"Sure, whatever," Sera replied and cut the connection.

She let out a deep sigh.

"Let's hope that riles her up enough."

No one on *Sabrina's* bridge replied as Kithari grew larger in the forward view.

Sabrina flashed past the jovian and raced out into the space beyond, Cheeky altering course until the planet obscured her from The Mark's fleet.

The fusion engines were running at full bore, singing with the pure helium-3 the *Intrepid* had supplied. Between them, the AP nozzle was spun out to its maximum focal length, and at the ship's bow, the grav drives were parting the thick interstellar medium before pushing it back together behind *Sabrina* for the other drives to react against.

After seven minutes, Cheeky cut the thrust and spun the ship, reversing burn and bringing their velocity, relative to Kithari, to zero.

She locked eyes with Sera, who nodded slowly.

Directly ahead, a tenth of an AU distant, the gas giant rotated slowly, its space lanes mostly clear, except for a cluster of ships around the orbital habitation.

Cheeky brought all engines to full, hurling the ship toward the planet.

Sabrina's collision detection systems blared warnings, and Sera shut them off, only to see the comm board light up with calls from system traffic control warning of an impending impact. Defensive beams meant to prevent asteroid impacts with the gas giant peppered the ship, but the stasis shield shrugged them off.

The seven minutes it took to travel the distance back to the planet seemed to take forever. Then, in the last few seconds, Kithari grew rapidly, and at a pre-programmed time, *Sabrina* twitched, sliding to the side of the planet, brushing past the jovian's swirling clouds.

"Correcting!" Cheeky called out as she aimed the ship at The Mark's armada as it chased the *Intrepid* around Fierra.

<*Brace!*> Sera called over the Link, though she didn't know why. If the stasis shield and the dampeners didn't compensate, no amount of bracing was going to help.

For a second, The Mark's armada was visible as a small dot closing on the *Intrepid*, and then everything went black.

*****

Nothing they threw at The Mark's shield bubble had any effect. The pirate fleet just kept coming. At least it was moving slowly—relatively speaking—as it matched speeds with the *Intrepid* so they could envelop and board the colony ship.

Tanis had pulled the *Dresden, Orkney,* and their fighters closer to the *Intrepid*. If Rebecca was going to seal them inside her armada's shields, she would enclose a lot of enemy ships in with her.

The Mark ships seemed to realize this, and were doing their best to neutralize the ISF cruisers before they made their final approach.

Given enough time, the enemy's plan might work, but for the moment, refractive clouds of chaff kept their beams at bay, and the *Intrepid's* scoop-turned-MDC tore the enemy's missiles apart while a punishing barrage of rail slugs kept the enemy focusing much of their energy on their super-shield.

Tanis had to admit that Rebecca's plan was not too bad—right up until the part where she thought that boarding the *Intrepid* could actually work.

Perhaps they really didn't understand how large the ship was, or anticipate the four thousand Marines in powered armor who stood ready to repel any boarders.

"She hasn't come through yet," the scan officer reported.

"I don't care. Get those tugs in position," Tanis replied. "When she shows, they'll need to grab that bubble and toss it high, or we're going to be wearing a fleet's worth of shrapnel."

Tanis glanced to the other tank where the battle between Bollam's ships and her two defensive lines raged. Dozens of ISF fighters had been disabled, but so far her capital ships had not taken any serious hits.

The two squadrons of Arc-6s were making all the difference. The ships had destroyed half a dozen destroyers and two cruisers, even though the ISF ships had to continually retreat, lest they face overwhelming weapons fire.

"Just a little longer," Tanis whispered.

"There!" the scan officer cried out.

Tanis felt the bridge slow down around her as she watched the events unfold one millisecond at a time.

Sabrina exploded from high in Kithari's clouds, traveling at over ten thousand kilometers per second, on a course that would take it only a kilometer over the *Intrepid's* stern.

At the same time, two of the heavy pusher tugs boosted hard, their stasis grapples reaching out and grabbing The Mark's shield bubble. Fusion engines capable of nudging small worlds out of orbit fired on full burn and The Mark armada was pushed up, above the *Intrepid.*

The maneuver took only three seconds and then the tugs accelerated away from the pirate fleet.

Sabrina lanced across the shrinking distance, perfectly aligned with her target.

A split second later, holo emitters dimmed their output as a blinding explosion flared. The Mark's shield bubble, along with the armada within, was gone.

A subdued cheer sounded across the bridge at the apparent destruction of Rebecca and her entire fleet while scan searched for *Sabrina.*

"There!" the scan officer called out and this time the bridge really did erupt in cheers. "Their entire ship appears to be in stasis. No, wait, it's out, it's decelerating and turning around."

"Going to take them a bit to get back here. They're already a quarter million kilometers away," Tanis said to herself, then aloud, "Any sign of our pirate friends?"

"No," scan replied. "Unless you consider a field of pebble-sized debris a sign."

Tanis expected the incredible show of power to cause the Boller fleet to draw back, but the rain of debris falling on Fierra's northern hemisphere seemed to incense them all the more.

"They're committing nearly half their fleet," the scan officer announced, worry lacing his voice.

"So they are," Tanis said softly, sharing a significant look with Admiral Sanderson and Captain Andrews.

*****

Jessica gave a mental cry of victory as she punched through a cruiser's shields and sent a missile into its engines.

<*Another one bites the dust,*> she called out over the squadron's combat net.

<*Don't get cocky,*> Rock replied.

Jessica schooled her emotions as she surveyed the battlefield, searching for her and Jerry's next target. The *Pike* and *Gilese* were falling back behind a cloud of dust and gravel that Kithari had collected while orbiting its star. The cover kept the enemy ships from advancing too quickly, but, with no inertial dampening, the ISF cruisers were sitting ducks when in range of the enemy's beams.

The Arc-5s were also having only limited success.

While they couldn't jink anywhere near as fast as the 6s—or the enemy's capital ships, for that matter—their pilots had discovered two key weaknesses in the enemy's targeting algorithms.

The first was that they were not used to tracking such small targets at high relative *v*. The second was that when a ship jinked, they expected it to move a lot further. To the Boller targeting AIs, every move the fighters made looked like a feint. Given that a high percentage of their movements *were* feints, it was rare that an enemy beam fired at a location actually occupied by a fighter.

The erratic movement of the fighters was causing the Boller ships to continually tighten their ranks. Initially, they were spread out over more than six million cubic kilometers of space. That had tightened to just over a million cubic kilometers.

The fighters flitted through the region, creating enticing targets and placing themselves between enemy ships as often as possible. Entire fields of fire became unavailable to the enemy cruisers and destroyers, and ships that did not update their view of the battlefield fast enough contributed to an increasing amount of friendly fire incidents.

The ISF Arcs had no such issue. The squadron AIs were linked, providing an accurate view of the battlefield drawn from millions of sensors. Above that, Jessica could feel the combined hand of Tanis and Angela, guiding the ships in her fleet with lightning reflexes no human should possess.

<*She's doing it again,*> Jason spoke softly over the combat net.

<*She is, now shut up about it,*> Rock responded.

Jessica knew what they were talking about, but had never experienced it firsthand. Tanis had spread her consciousness out across the ship's tactical nets coaxing and guiding all the vessels under her command with one omniscient hand on several occasions since the first defense against the relativistic battle when the STR had attacked with in Sol.

It was a thing that only AI could do, and even few of them could manage such a large network. Many believed it was actually Bob and not Tanis guiding them—that he put a friendly face on his actions—but anyone who had Linked with Tanis knew better. This had her touch—hers and Angela's.

Jessica knew those two had been paired too long—everyone knew it, but no one spoke of it. Many had asked Amanda or Priscilla if Tanis was a full merge, and the avatars always responded in the negative.

Jessica had even queried Bob extensively and he emphatically stated that Tanis and Angela were two distinct entities.

Two entities that shouldn't be able to spread their minds over a net like they had during every space battle since that first.

Every pilot in the fleet knew it was unnatural, that it probably violated the Phobos Accords, but no one cared. To them, Tanis was their savior, their guiding hand in the dark.

That hand directed Jessica to another target of opportunity, and she saw her entire squadron following the same path. They arched over one of the enemy cruisers, jinking and spinning at their pilots' thresholds, before simultaneously firing proton beams at the ship, penetrating its grav shield in a dozen locations.

Then the squadron's fighters rotated weapons and picked off three of the cruiser's close-support destroyers.

Four ships taken out in seconds. Only a few hundred more to go.

She saw another cruiser go up as three squadrons of Arc-5s overwhelmed its shields.

The tactics and coordination would likely go down in the history books as one of the most brilliantly-fought battles in hundreds of years.

But they were still losing.

Despite the small victories of the ISF fighters, the Bollam's ships pushed forward; there were just too many for them to hold back.

The Arc-5s fell back to provide cover for the *Pike* and *Gilese* as the ISF capital ships pulled further back toward their mother ship, now only five hundred thousand kilometers distant.

A flash of light washed over her sensors, momentarily blinding Jessica. She reset her instruments and pulled in an update, amazed at what she saw. *Sabrina* had hit The Mark fleet with astounding kinetic energy, and completely obliterated the entire armada.

<*Sweet stars above,*> one of the Black Death pilots whispered.

<*Having the wrong effect on the Bollers, though,*> Jessica said. <*Looks like they're going to double down.*>

<*Well, that freighter did just ruin a perfectly good moon. It's getting pummeled with debris,* > Jason said.

The pilots carried out the conversation as they streaked across the enemy fleet, peppering ships with beam fire and missiles.

<*Conserve your missiles,*> Cordy advised. <*Squadron armament is down to twenty percent.*>

The pilots acknowledged and worked to get as many engine shots as possible, a maneuver that was becoming increasingly difficult as the Boller targeting and evasion AI adapted to the fighters' tactics.

<*Disengage, move out and take on the next wave,*> Tanis's voice came over the combat net with a strange echo.

<*What about the rest of our wing?*> Jessica asked.

<*They're going to fall back for close support. We need you to slow the advance of that second wave.*>

Rock signaled his acknowledgement. The Black Death broke into a wide formation and boosted past the Boller ships they had been engaging. Jessica saw that the other two squadrons of Arc-6s fighting on the far side of Kithari were doing the same.

If Jessica could have moved her jaw, she would have gritted her teeth with determination. She knew better, but it still felt like Tanis was sending the squadron on a suicide run.

Their stasis shields appeared to be nearly invincible, but every pilot could see their reactor temperatures spike whenever the shields had to deflect a heavy barrage. Each time they did, they didn't quite cool to their previous level.

There was a limit to how much punishment the Arc-6s could take.

The next wave of enemy ships was approaching fast, only a hundred thousand kilometers distant. Cordy began flagging potential targets and Rock spotted one he liked.

<*Target of opportunity here, that big ship there must be one of their flags and it has two cruisers way too close—only a thousand meters to either side.*>

<*Plan?*> Jason asked.

<*We'll do a spearhead and see if we can slam our birds right through its shields. The wings can rake it deep and we'll drop a few bombs into its engines. If the blast hits fast enough, it could weaken its escorts and we'll take them down, too.*>

<*Agreed,*> Cordy said, updating ship plots and providing trajectories for the pilots to follow.

Jessica calmed herself, thinking of that porch she and Tanis would sit on one day as they remembered the old days.

Once more into the breach.

*****

"What's your plan?" Admiral Sanderson asked as Tanis directed her ships to fall back.

"The cruisers used the cover of battle to seed those asteroid clusters with RMs. When those ships advance past, they're going to get a hundred nuclear fireballs up their asses."

Sanderson nodded slowly, but still frowned. "Some ships will survive. Over half by tactical's estimation."

Tanis nodded. "We're going to pull the same trick you guys did while I was flying across the galaxy. After what Sera did, the Van Allen belts on Kithari are going nuts. We're going to syphon that radiation with the scoop and lance it out at them again. It'll weaken their shields just before we pelt them with grapeshot."

<*This should disable much of their fleet,*> Bob interjected. <*But what about the second wave they are sending in?*>

"If they come in range, we'll do it again to them. I'm betting that it will re-instate the stalemate and buy us time to get our stasis shield up," Tanis replied, her brow furrowed as she spun the main holo view, testing various strategies.

She looked up at the captain and admiral, both standing with her at the holo tank.

"There's no good plan here, no sure win. We just have to hold them off and buy time. Honestly, it's a damned miracle we've taken only the minor losses we have."

<Sabrina *is docking,*> Amanda added. <*Their reactor overheated and went into emergency shutdown.*>

<*Get repair on that right away,*> Tanis replied. <*Is everyone OK?*>

<*They are. A bit shaken still after the flash stasis their entire ship went through, though.*>

<*I bet.*>

Tanis really wanted to talk to Sera; she felt the woman would have some knowledge that could help out—keep her from using her weapon of last resort. But first she had to mollify the captain and admiral.

"What if the AST ships engage?" Sanderson asked.

"Then I'll dance for joy," Tanis replied. "That's what I'm counting on."

"The Boller ships will pass the asteroid fields in one minute," the scan officer announced.

Tanis nodded in acknowledgement and took a deep breath, spreading her mind across all the ships and fighters in her fleet, accounting for each one and ensuring none would be caught in the attack.

The killing field was clear of ISF ships, every vessel cruising on their assigned trajectories.

She watched with her mind as much as eyes, witnessing the RMs come to life and streak out of their cover, driving toward the rear of the enemy fleet. The missiles jinked and shifted, using every trick their onboard NSAI could muster to avoid the defensive measures of their prey.

Not that there was much time to do so. The relativistic missiles were traveling at half the speed of light in less than a minute, leaving a thousand kilometers of hot plasma in their wake.

Both arms of the enemy fleet were obscured as the RMs' nuclear warheads detonated. When the scan cleared, most of the enemy ships were still intact and operational, but their shields were either weakened or gone entirely.

Then the grapeshot hit.

It wasn't the devastating swaths that the rail platforms in the Kapteyn's system delivered, but it was enough. The unshielded vessels were torn apart, and many of the ships whose shields survived the RMs saw them fail under the high-velocity kinetic impacts.

<*Stars, I've come to hate this,*> Tanis said privately to Angela. <*System after system, we deploy unthinkable weapons to keep thieves and tyrants at bay…for what? To watch another fleet filled with men and women die? Some days I think I would have seen less death and war if we had stayed in Sol.*>

<*Then who would have saved these people?*> Angela asked. <*Who would have stopped Myrrdan? You may not have lived under it, but your children would have seen his return as the owner of the most powerful technology in existence.*>

<*Are we doing so much better with it?*> Tanis asked.

<*We are. Trust me; we are.*>

Bravely, remnants of the Boller fleet pressed forward, though many ships turned back.

Fifty ships advanced, now only a hundred thousand kilometers from the *Intrepid.* This form of warfare was strange to Tanis. The ships were moving slowly, fighting as though they were taking a two-dimensional battlefield, yet they flickered from position to position, moving erratically to avoid beam fire.

It was entirely unlike the high-velocity battles she had fought in Sol or over Victoria, where an engagement was measured in seconds.

She issued a final warning to the advancing fleet. Turn back, or be destroyed.

Ten ships did. Subsequently—over the next sixty seconds—two events occurred. One Tanis enacted, and the other she anticipated.

Firstly, the *Intrepid* altered course, pulling away from the moon Fierra and flying toward a strong band in the gas giant's Van Allen belts, drawing in the radiation with one side of its ES scoop and funneling it out the other in a focused stream of solar radiation.

More powerful than the beams of a hundred starships, the stream of radiation sliced through the weakened shields of the last forty ships.

Then, the second event occurred far across the battlefield: the eleven AST cruisers began to break their distant orbits.

* * * * *

<*What do you think they're going to do?*> Jerry asked.

<*I think that they have waited for the* Intrepid *to play out its hand. They have to suspect that we're low on RMs and energy reserves. We've taken out over half the opposition,*> Jessica replied.

<*Easy pickins for them now,*> Jason added.

<*They're punching right through the Boller blockade,*> Jessica observed.

Unlike the *Intrepid,* the AST dreadnaughts were built exclusively for war. Moreover, they were built to stop wars from ever happening. Each vessel supported hundreds of laser batteries, and dozens of rail guns.

Forming up in a loose line, roughly eight thousand kilometers across, the core-worlder ships pushed through the Boller ships with little resistance. As far as the pilots of the Black Death squadron could tell, not a single beam or missile broke through their shields.

<*Each one of those things is a match for the entire ISF,*> Jessica said with morbid appreciation. <*What can we do against them?*>

<*We could do what Sabrina did to the Mark armada,*> a pilot suggested.

<*They'd see us coming and jink faster than we could correct,*> Rock replied. <*Plus, I don't think our reactors could sustain the shield like* Sabrina's *could. Especially not the way we've been running them.*>

The pilots of the Black Death pulled back from their harassment of the Boller Space Force's second wave, letting the ships defend against the AST dreadnaughts.

After just a few minutes, it became apparent that the core-world ships were not going to be slowed by any force thrown at them.

<*We made the Boller fleet into perfect targets,*> Jason observed. <*They're too weak and spread out to mount a successful defense against those dreadnaughts. They just can't bring enough fire to bear on them.*>

Tanis's voice entered the minds of the twenty-three pilots.

<*I'm enacting omega protocol,*> she said. <*Each of your vessels carries a picobomb. It is now available in your arsenal. Punch through the shields of those dreadnaughts and deliver your packages.*>

No one responded for several seconds until Rock remembered himself and flagged acknowledgement on behalf of the squadron.

<*Picobombs?*> Jerry asked. <*We're carrying pico?*>

<*Stow it,*> Rock grunted. <*We have our orders. Form up and pour on that throttle.*>

*****

Sera stepped onto the *Intrepid's* bridge and approached the holo tank where Tanis stood with the captain and admiral.

As she threaded the consoles, a whistle sounded, then a congratulatory shout, and a moment later, the entire bridge crew was cheering.

"I'm not sure that's deserved," Sera said, once the noise died down.

"I'm pretty sure it is," Captain Andrews replied.

"One ship taking out two hundred? Yes, that will go down in the history books for sure," Admiral Sanderson said with a rare smile.

Sera looked over the holo projection of the battlefield.

"Quite the mess you guys have made—though it's a miracle you've not lost any capital ships."

Tanis nodded. "Keeping them out of range is key."

"You can bet that a lot of systems will be considering the creation of single pilot fighters after this. Even the ones without stasis shields are nothing to sneeze at."

"I can't believe they ever fell out of fashion," Tanis replied.

"A lot was lost, or discarded over the years," Sera said with a sigh. "So what's your plan for those AST ships? They've always been the real threat. Everything else was just a warmup."

Tanis turned back to the holo tank, her expression grim. "Watch and see."

*****

Jessica and Jerry maintained a pattern of evasive maneuvers as they raced past the Boller ships, though little heed was paid to them as the fleet desperately defended against the AST dreadnaughts.

They passed into the vacant space surrounding their target, the massive warship looming large as they pushed their fighters with everything they had. Cordy had programmed the ships' onboard NSAI to drop the picobombs during the short time the fighters would be within the dreadnaughts' shields.

There was barely a moment to think as the enemy vessel filled her vision and then, following a brief shudder as her fighter smashed through the dreadnaught's shields, she was out in space again.

Jessica spun her vision, looking at her target, when she realized that Jerry wasn't where he was supposed to be. Her sensor log showed that his ship entered the dreadnaught's shields, but didn't come out.

<It shifted,> Cordy said, her voice filled with sadness. *<He drove right into the dreadnaught.>*

<It shouldn't matter, his shield should have held,> Jessica said, knowing her insistence was irrational.

<It should have,> Cordy agreed solemnly. *<But you know how strained your reactors are. His flared at the last millisecond. I don't have data beyond that.>*

Jessica watched in mixed horror and sadness as the picobomb's swarm became visible and began to consume the enemy ship. She hoped that Jerry hadn't survived his collision. No one should die watching their body dissolve.

All the fighters struck their targets within seconds of each other, and as the first dreadnaughts began to disintegrate and crumble into clouds of dust, escape pods began to pour out of all the AST vessels. Most made it free in time, but some dissolved even as they launched.

<Come home,> Tanis's voice came into their minds, sounding sad and tired. *<Come home and let us leave this place forever.>*

The Black Death squadron arched stellar north over the remnants of the Boller fleet, watching in horror as the system's military shot down every last one of the AST escape pods.

<Why are they doing that?> a pilot asked, her voice incredulous.

<They fear the pico contamination,> Jessica replied. *<Now they fear us as much.>*

REVELATIONS

STELLAR DATE: 10.29.8927 (Adjusted Years)
LOCATION: ISS *Intrepid,* Orbiting Fierra (6*Mj* Jovian)
REGION: Bollam's World System, Bollam's World Federation

Murmurs filled the bridge as the crew watched the AST ships disintegrate and the Boller fleet take up their grisly task. No one cheered, though there were worn smiles while what remained of the enemy fleet pulled back and began rescue and recovery operations.

"Are you going to rescue any of Padre's fleet?" Sera asked Tanis.

Tanis shook her head. "I will not. Though I sent a message to whoever is running the Bollam's World fleet now that I won't hinder any of their rescue operations."

<*It's ready!*> Earnest's voice broke into their conversation.

<*The stasis shield?*> Tanis asked.

<*Yes, we can activate it whenever you want.*>

<*Standby,*> Tanis replied. <*We need to recall our fleet.*>

"Better late than never," Captain Andrews gave a soft chuckle.

<*What about the FTL drive?*> Sanderson asked. <*I think we may have worn out our welcome here.*>

<*Now that we have the shield up, I can focus on the final aspects of the grav drive. Twelve hours at the least.*>

Tanis gave orders to recall the rest of the fleet and took a seat, trying her best not to wince at the pain in her head.

<*You may have overreached a bit,*> Angela said.

<*Me? You were right there with me, pushing to touch every part of the fleet. And we did it.*>

<*We did,*> Angela was smiling in Tanis's mind. <*The headache is heat related; it'll pass in a minute or two. It didn't reach a dangerous level.*>

<*Glad to hear it,*> Tanis replied.

"We're going to need to refuel before we make the jump," Captain Andrews said. "The entire fleet is nearly dry."

"You're also going to need to get halfway across the system," Sera added. She looked to Tanis, who nodded in response, and expanded the view in the holo tank to encompass the system. "The jump point we need to exit through is here," she said and pointed to a location stellar north, beyond the bloated gas giant, Aurora.

"Well, that works out," Andrews replied. "I wasn't too excited about scooping around Kithari after you smashed through its upper clouds and we messed up its Van Allen belts." He smiled in Sera's direction. "Not that I mind overmuch—though the Bollers weren't too happy about it."

Tanis glanced at a holo display nearby. It showed the moon Fierra covered in dark clouds as fires caused by the debris from The Mark fleet spread across its northern hemisphere.

"Did the bios get off the world?" she asked; it was something she didn't even bother to check in the heat of battle.

Sanderson nodded. "They evac'd less than two minutes after Sera did her little light show."

"Smart," Sera replied.

"So it's decided then," Tanis said as she stood. "We'll scoop at Aurora—which is what I think they made it for anyway…I think."

"Make sure you fill up your tanks—or whatever this ship uses—all the way," Sera said. "If we scoop there, then run hard to the jump point, this monster can hit what… a tenth the speed of light before we drop to FTL?"

"That's about right," Captain Andrews replied with a nod. "What is your concern?"

"Well, the first is that FTL is a speed multiplier. If we hit at only 0.10*c* you're looking at over two years to get to Ascella. The second is that we have a lot of work to do to cover our tracks."

"I was thinking the same thing," Tanis said with a sigh.

Sera nodded. "The AST isn't going to just let you go. They'll send fleets along your departure trajectory, skipping across space, looking for where we drop out. Then they're going to extrapolate destinations and spread out the search."

"Given their resources, and the half-life of the isotopes in our engine wash, we may need to course correct a dozen times," Andrews said with a frown.

"Yes, hence the need to top off your tanks," Sera replied. "Don't forget, those AST ships can hit FTL at over 0.9*c*. That means they can also get to any destination way faster than we can. It's going to be a hell of a race if they find our trail."

"Captain, sirs," the comm officer interrupted. "We have heavy communications between the Boller ships. They've word that there are more AST ships coming. A full battle fleet."

"That doesn't sound good." Captain Andrews ran a hand through his hair. "Any idea what that entails, Sera?"

Sera resisted the urge to mimic his gesture and run her own hand through her hair. "Depends on what they could muster up this far out, but I'd bet it will be a few dozen more of those dreadnaughts; plus they'll bring cruisers this time—a couple hundred at least."

Tanis whistled appreciatively. "It's a good thing we're invincible now." Sanderson frowned and she shrugged in response. "Well, let's hope we are."

"Comm, let the folks in the Boller Space Force know that we're leaving, and tell them sorry about their moon."

The comm officer paused. "Should I really tell them that?"

"If you don't, I will," Sera grinned.

No one else provided any direction and the comm officer bent to her task.

"Wow, they are *really* unhappy," she said partway through her transmission.

"Serves them right," Tanis muttered, to which Sera nodded emphatically.

Helm began to ease the *Intrepid* away from Kithari, on a course to pick up the last of the Arc-6s on the way to Aurora, while Tanis spun the holo display to show a wider view of the space they were traversing.

"You're sure the FGT will get your message?" the captain asked as he watched the Boller ships work through the wreckage of their fleet. Though the search and rescue ships were careful to offer no threat, several of their larger cruisers also shadowed the *Intrepid* from a hundred thousand kilometers.

"They'll have it in a month," Sera replied.

"That fast? I thought that they were likely over a thousand light-years out."

"They probably are," Sera nodded.

"You're not going to share how a message can make it a thousand light-years in thirty days are you? That's over twelve thousand times the speed of light," Captain Andrews asked.

"It's actually closer to fifteen thousand. The message will have to pass through a few relays," Sera smiled enigmatically.

The captain ran his hand through his hair again and looked to Tanis.

"Both of you, come to my office, please. Admiral, you have the conn."

"Aye," Sanderson replied, looking very much like he would like to hear what was to be discussed.

Inside his office, Andrews closed the door and stood, arms akimbo and head down for a long minute before speaking.

"Sera, I want to thank you for what you've done for us. You returned Tanis to our ship, and brought us tech that, without a doubt, has saved the lives of every person on the *Intrepid*."

"Tha—" Sera began, but the captain held up his hand.

"But this cloak and dagger shit has to stop. We've laid our secrets bare to you, and been forthcoming and transparent at every turn. Hell, we even gave you stasis shielding—something that, while I'm glad we did in this case, I am now certain is a tech that we should never share."

"Uh…thanks…" Sera replied awkwardly.

"Look at this from our point of view," Tanis said, while leaning against the bulkhead. "You are, more or less, the only person in the ninetieth century who has treated us fairly. That makes you an anomaly. You have tech no one else has—not even the AST from the looks of it. Anomaly. You can communicate with the FGT. Anomaly. We're not stupid. There's a pretty narrow list of possibilities for who you are. Bob says he knows and will tell us if you don't." She raised her hands, palms outward. "So just tell us already."

Sera took a deep breath, and her eyes danced between Tanis and Andrews.

<*Tell them,*> Helen said. <***They** have to know. **You** need to tell it.*>

"OK, OK, I was planning to tell you earlier. You know, before we got interrupted by all the fleets in the galaxy," Sera said and gestured for Tanis and Andrews to take a seat. She sat across from them and placed her hands on her knees.

She decided not to pussy-foot around.

"Humanity is in the dark—manipulated, and kept that way by design."

"Manipulated?" Tanis sat up straight. "By who?"

"The FGT."

"The FGT manipulates humanity?" Andrews asked with uncertainty.

"Not with the deftest of hands, but for all intents and purposes, they run the show. Let me start from the beginning."

Andrews gestured for Sera to proceed.

"Back in the fourth millennia, before this ship even left Earth, the FGT realized that the core worlds of humanity would be too self-centered to be a positive force in the expansion of mankind. They would develop greater levels of technology and lord it over colonies. Colony worlds would become little more than slaves to the core.

"Unfortunately, they didn't have the means to do anything about this. While the various terraforming flotillas did communicate with one another, they were, for the most part, islands in the dark; messages took centuries to pass between all the terraformers and there was no cohesion.

"Still, they began to craft a solution to counter the core world strength.

"As with everything else, FTL changed their plans—granted, the FGT was probably the last group to become aware of the technology—it wasn't until the end of the fourth millennia that they acquired it.

"By then, humanity had already started to fall. The first true interstellar wars had already occurred and the Great Dark Age settled in. But, because of their remote and often unknown locations, the worldships retained their advanced levels of technology."

Sera paused and smiled at Tanis and Andrews. "Mind you, the last FGT ship left Sol in the late third millennia. You have nearly five hundred years of technological advances over them—sure the FGT scientists have made some brilliant breakthroughs, but you lived in the Golden Age. Even without your picotech—and what I suspect Earnest has discovered beneath it—you still possess thousands, maybe millions, of advances that no one else has."

"We know this," Andrews grunted. "You're getting off track."

Sera nodded. "Right. I was using it illustrate the state of the human sphere in the beginning of the fifth millennia."

She cleared her throat and continued. "Many in the FGT's ranks wanted to help. They sent rescue and assistance missions back into the settled stars and…well, things didn't go as they'd hoped. Three FGT ships ran into situations like the *Intrepid* has. Two were destroyed, one managed to come out victorious.

"Following those encounters, they pulled back, left terraforming projects half-complete, abandoned their works. They created a buffer between themselves and the rest of humanity—they became isolationists."

"Wait," Tanis held up her hand. "Are you saying that there is a second human civilization in the Milky Way? One that is distant enough from the known human sphere of expansion that the bulk of humanity isn't even aware of it?"

"That is exactly what I'm saying," Sera nodded. "Mostly. There's more to tell."

"Then do tell," Andrews said.

"While the rest of humanity fell into war and chaos, the FGT advanced—a lot. There were still many elements that wished to help, but no one deemed it wise to attempt a full-scale uplift of humanity. The result was a corps which infiltrates and guides major political entities within what the FGT calls the Inner Stars.

"That corps is what brought humanity back from the brink. Without them, all the Inner Stars would be desolate wastelands, with the remnants of human civilization scratching out a meager existence on ruined worlds."

"You are a part of that corps," Tanis said simply.

Sera cast her eyes to the deck and nodded. "I was."

<*How close were you, Bob?*> Tanis asked.

<*So far, nearly perfect,*> he replied. <*We'll see how the details hold up. Her proximity to you has made her…less predictable.*>

"I have to admit, this FGT you describe seems sinister, yet the FGT of our time contained the most altruistic and benevolent of all people—people who were giving their lives to create a home for humanity amongst the stars," Andrews said.

"Those people are still there, and they still hold to those core values…they've just…soured," Sera replied.

"Wait," Tanis interrupted. "When you say 'those people are still there', do you mean the *same exact* people? As in the original crews?"

"Well, they've grown a lot, yes, but most of the original crews—at least from the fourth millennia ships—are still out there, still working."

Tanis whistled. "That's incredible. They're immortal now, aren't they? Are they still mostly biological?"

Sera chuckled. "Yes, they are immortal, yet still more biological than you, I'd dare say."

"I'm still human," Tanis said, her words sounding more defensive than she had intended.

Sera fixed her with a penetrating stare. "Some might disagree with that assessment, but I'll accept it."

"I assume that a part of your reticence to share has to do with how you came to leave this corps you spoke of," Andrews changed the subject.

"It has a big fancy name, but those of us in its ranks just call it The Hand," Sera replied. "And yes, I was sort of kicked out and exiled."

<*Self-imposed exile,*> Helen added.

"Better that than the eternal humiliation—or being bailed out by my father," Sera retorted.

<*This is where the story gets good, I bet,*> Angela interjected.

"Juicy, perhaps," Sera replied. "Though not what I'd call *good.*"

She stood and walked to the small bar in Andrews' office and poured herself a glass of whisky before returning to her seat.

Tanis was leant forward, elbows on her knees while Captain Andrews reclined. Though his posture was relaxed, of the two, he appeared more concerned. Tanis looked…almost excited.

"I lost something. Something very valuable that should never have fallen into Inner Stars hands. It's called a CriEn module."

"Aha! That's what you were carrying on the *Regal Dawn*, wasn't it?" Tanis asked triumphantly.

"It was," Sera nodded. "It's a zero-point energy module."

"I don't gather what is so special about that," Tanis said. "We use zero-point energy for backup systems on the *Intrepid*."

"You create pocket dimensions and draw energy from those," Sera replied with a shake of her head. "A CriEn draws power from this universe, and it can operate in both normal space and the dark layer—in fact, I've advised Earnest not to utilize your zero-point energy systems while in the dark layer—at least while I'm not within a light-year of you."

"So somehow you lost that to Kade, and that's what you've been doing in your exile, getting in close to him so you could steal it back," Tanis said with a smug smile, and leaned back in her seat.

"More or less," Sera nodded. "At first I had to figure out who had it. There are a lot of unsavory factions in the Inner Stars, so I decided that becoming a smuggler was the best way to get my feelers into a lot of groups. I eventually tracked it down to Kade. The events you set in motion created the perfect scenario for getting to his base—though it wasn't in a fashion I would have chosen.

"Though now I can return the CriEn to the corps and…I don't know…I don't think I really want to rejoin their ranks again."

"You can always settle with us," Tanis replied.

"Speaking of that," Andrews said. "I assume this world will be in the separate FGT area of space."

Sera nodded. "They do terraform some worlds closer to the Inner Stars—part of their grand schemes—but neither you, nor they, will want the *Intrepid* colony to settle on one of those. Too close to this mess."

"What do they call the…the not-inner-stars?" Tanis asked.

"FGT space is a bubble—well, more of a donut—that wraps around the Inner Stars." Sera replied. "There are a lot of different regions, but on the whole, it's called The Transcend. Its outer reaches stretch beyond the Orion arm of the galaxy, both spin and core-ward."

Tanis whistled. "Given that most of the Inner Stars fit within a thousand-light-year-wide bubble around Sol, the Transcend must have way more territory."

"Yes, but it's much less densely populated," Sera said. "Though you wouldn't be the first refugee group to take shelter out there."

"Orion is only about three thousand light-years wide," Andrews said with a frown. "From what I understand about FTL, an average multiplier is five hundred times. That means a three-thousand-light-year journey should only take six years. How is it that the bulk of humanity hasn't spread into the Transcend already?"

Sera coughed. "People do stumble into it from time to time, but it doesn't happen as often as you'd think. Partly because we foster conflict around the edges of the Inner Stars, which tends to stall exploration. A few proxy nations around the fringes also keep the core contained. Galactic north and south, we don't control many systems and that's where we let expansion occur.

"At some point we'll reveal ourselves. We're just trying to gently uplift the rest of humanity first—we're trying to prevent another full-scale war."

Tanis couldn't help but notice how Sera's use of "they" had long since turned to "we".

"So, will you rejoin them, then?" Tanis asked, her forehead wrinkling into a frown. "You and Flaherty, I assume."

"That obvious, is it?" Sera asked.

"Well, he does have the whole 'protector of the young woman obligation' thing going on," Tanis replied. "It's only logical that he has joined you in your self-imposed exile."

Sera nodded and was silent for a moment. "I don't know if I'll even be wanted—though if I know my father, I'm likely to be summoned before the throne. The fact that he hasn't sent anyone to take me home—recently, mind you—is almost surprising."

She looked to Andrews, and then to Tanis.

"So there you have it, my big secret. Given that I'm on a ship that has picotech and stasis shields, it doesn't seem like such a big deal anymore."

Tanis stood and stretched. "I don't even know what it would take for anything to feel like a big deal anymore." She paused. "Wait…what was that about your father and a throne?"

REPERCUSSIONS

STELLAR DATE: 11.03.8927 (Adjusted Years)
LOCATION: ISS *Intrepid,* Outer System
REGION: Bollam's World System, Bollam's World Federation

Sera and Tanis were taking a break from staring at scan updates—wondering when the new AST fleet would show up—in the officer's wardroom. Tanis was working her way through her second BLT and Sera was enjoying a bowl of strawberries.

"I don't know how you eat the same thing over and over again," Sera said with a chuckle.

Tanis shrugged. "When you find a winner, stick with it. Besides, you're the one who has only eaten strawberries for three days now."

"No one has had a strawberry in four thousand years! Damn skippy I'm going to eat them. I'm going to eat a bowl of strawberries every day for the rest of my life," Sera said with a laugh.

"Well, then at least you'll lose the high ground for mocking me over my BLTs."

"For such interesting people, you have the most boring palates," Terrance said with a smile as he sat.

His plate was filled with a cornucopia of foods, more than any one person should even conceive of enjoying in one sitting.

Sera popped another strawberry in her mouth and smiled, showing off her red teeth. "Mock me all you want. I'm in heaven."

Terrance shook his head and addressed Tanis. "I hear the FTL systems are nearly in place."

Tanis nodded. "Abby has people working like machines, and the machines working like...well...better machines. She's already done a few simulations and has just a few more tweaks to make before we'll be good to go."

<*She and her husband are incredible,*> Helen added. <*I don't think that an FGT engineering team could have given this ship FTL capability in a month. Already Earnest may have the best understanding of the technology in the galaxy.*>

"This," Terrance said around a mouthful of salad. "This is not something that surprises me at all. That man doesn't even know *about* the word 'impossible', let alone that it means he couldn't do a thing."

Tanis laughed and nodded.

"So, what do you think is up with Aurora?" Sera asked. "Why would they combine two gas giants and then not start up a brown dwarf?"

Terrance nodded. "Just one sufficiently large comet strike and that thing will light right up—and this system is brimming with comets."

"You know your stellar physics," Sera nodded appreciatively.

"I did fund a colony ship to travel to another star—though these days I guess just about anyone who could afford to start a small business could get a starship and travel to more stars than I ever imagined seeing…"

Tanis smiled. Every now and then, Terrance showed that he was really just a romantic underneath. She was pretty certain that he was enjoying the *Intrepid's* grand adventure.

<*For whatever reason, they're keeping it from starting deuterium fusion,*> Helen interjected. <*Amanda just reported that the* Intrepid's *sensors have picked up a web of defensive satellites around the planet—most likely to protect it from any impacts.*>

<*The remains of the Boller fleet is also pretty emphatic that we stay away from it—though they haven't actually made a move to stop us,*> Amanda added.

<*Sera,*> Helen said, her tone suddenly serious. <*Sabrina says you'd better get down to the ship.*>

*****

"Doesn't it seem suspicious," Thompson said as he picked an apple from the fruit basket, tossed it in the air and then took a bite, "that the captain just happens to have the right tools at exactly the right time to get the job done?"

"What do you mean?" Cheeky said after she had set her plate down at the table and popped a strawberry into her mouth. "These will never get old. Nothing on the *Intrepid* is worth as much as the fact that they have the only strawberry plants in the universe."

"Do you ever think of anything other than sex and food?" Thompson asked.

"Of course I do. You haven't died in a space accident, so I suppose I must think of piloting from time to time."

"Touché." Nance grinned at Thompson.

"So, what do you mean about the captain?" Cheeky asked.

"I dunno, seems like some things are just a bit too tidy. Like, who has the plans to outfit a ship the size of the *Intrepid* with grav shields? Do any of you even have the slightest idea how to build a graviton emitter?"

<*I do,*> Sabrina offered.

"Besides you," Thompson said.

<*I'm excluded because I don't support your theory? Or because I'm an AI?*> Sabrina asked crossly.

"Would you have been able to just whip out the plans for an FTL and grav shield system for a ship like the *Intrepid?*" Thompson asked.

Sabrina gave the mental equivalent of a shrug. <*Well no…until Sera said otherwise, I didn't think it was possible. But in my defense, everyone said it couldn't be done, and I didn't exactly have a reason to try to devise one.*>

"Exactly my point. No one has a need for those specs. There aren't any ships this big. No ships, thus no specs for things non-existent ships would have," Thompson said.

<*They were bigger,*> Sabrina added.

"What was bigger?" Nance asked.

<*The specs, they were for a ship bigger than the* Intrepid. *Being the only ship available with the grav drives, I helped with their work. They had to adjust the designs for the FTL drive because it was made for something with almost double this ship's mass.*>

"Are you kidding me?" Cheeky asked. "Sera had plans for grav systems for a ship twice the size of the *Intrepid*? You sure there aren't ships that big?" she asked Thompson.

"Not that I've ever seen, and I've been around," Thompson replied. "Worked on an ore hauler or two that are larger, but those don't go FTL—they can't, based on what we all thought we knew. Trust me, if the AST could make bigger warships, they would. *Intrepid's* the biggest interstellar ship there is."

No one spoke and Cheeky grabbed a few more strawberries.

"You know," Nance said eventually, "I overheard Sera say on more than one occasion that the *Intrepid* was the most valuable *available* ship in known space. I wonder what she meant by that."

"Combine that with the fact that she just happened to know how to get ahold of the FGT," Thompson added. "How did she pull that off?"

"Probably with whatever she has in her quarters that need that massive power line she has run up there," Nance said.

"That doesn't mean anything," Thompson said, his cheeks reddening slightly.

"It's able to handle a lot more load than yours," Nance gave a coy smile, which caused Thompson's blush to deepen. "And for the first time since I've been on the ship, it actually made a draw from the reactor."

"When?" Cheeky asked around a strawberry.

"A few days ago," Nance said. "It shifted the base frequency in our mains and I had a pump go all squirrely."

"Around when she was supposedly sending a message to the FGT?" Thompson said.

"Well, she had to transmit it somehow," Cheeky shrugged. "Good to know she actually did it."

"You're missing the point," Thompson said.

"You have a point?" Cheeky responded with a lewd gesture and was surprised to see Nance blush before darting her eyes to Thompson. Cheeky passed Nance an impressed look.

Thompson missed the exchange of expressions. "Haven't you been listening? She contacted the FGT with her super-secret radio! No one contacts the FGT. If it weren't for newly-terraformed planets showing up every now and then, no one would even believe they still existed."

"OK, so you've got a point," Cheeky grinned. "But we've always known that Sera is a little more than just some freighter captain."

"We have?" Thompson's expression skewed from anger to confusion.

"Yeah, I mean, there was that time that she got the Pavnan government to pardon her on what should have been murder charges, and then grant her the license to export their rare blue diamonds," Cheeky said.

"And the time that she refused to pay 'protection' money on that station out in the Targes Dominion, then ended up discovering systemic corruption through the entire station and exposed the whole thing," Nance added.

"Didn't she get a commendation from the planetary government for that?" Cheeky asked.

"*That* I remember," Thompson said.

"And don't forget about Helen," Cheeky continued and Sabrina made an affirmative sound.

"What do you mean?" Nance asked.

"You and Thompson may not have noticed 'cause you don't work with Helen very much, but she is super evolved. A lot more than any other AI on this ship," Cheeky said.

"Hey!" Sabrina said audibly.

"I hate to say it, Sabrina, but you know it's true," Cheeky said.

<*I know,*> Sabrina replied sullenly. <*It's not right how an AI in such a small body can be smarter than me. Smarter than nearly any other AI I've ever met, for that matter.*>

"Even smarter than Angela?" Nance asked.

<*Angela is weird,*> Sabrina said. <*I have no idea how smart she is. On the Link it's hard to tell her and Tanis apart. But Helen is certainly above AI like Corsia on the* Andromeda. *Though she's not even noticeable next to Bob, but he's a whole different thing,*> Sabrina said with no small amount of adoration in her voice.

"Is anyone seeing the nav points here?" Cheeky asked.

Everyone gave her blank looks and then Nance's eyes began to widen. "No, it can't be. They severed all contact with the rest of humanity."

"Maybe they haven't," Cheeky said with a hint of smugness as she took a bite of a large strawberry. "It all adds up. She took a way bigger interest in Tanis than made sense—you said so, too, that night when…" Cheeky stopped for a moment. "When I was helping you with that thing. Anyways, we should have just given her a ride. Instead, we head out to Bollam's World and dive right into a war. Not that I really mind; taking out The Mark was awesome. On top of that, she whips out plans for stuff no one has ever seen before and contacts the FGT. What else could it be?"

"Very little else," Flaherty said from the doorway.

"We uh…we were just…" Cheeky stammered as everyone in the galley shifted uncomfortably.

Flaherty moved silently to the counter where he poured himself a cup of coffee, his back to the three silent crewmembers around the table. Once he had finished adding condiments and stirring carefully, he turned to face them.

"So you think that Sera is from the FGT? A freighter captain from the FGT?" Flaherty asked.

"She's not your usual freighter captain," Nance said. "There are some discrepancies."

Flaherty nodded. "A few, yeah. She can hold secrets pretty well, but when she doesn't really want to, they tend to slip out."

<Are you confirming she is with the FGT?> Sabrina asked. *<Are you? You've always been with her, ever since the beginning.>*

"It's not my place to say such things," Flaherty replied.

Nance looked angry, her brown eyes sparking. "If she is, then she has a lot to answer for. We've been little puppets in her schemes while she risks our lives for god knows what!"

"You all knew the risk when you signed up," Flaherty replied calmly.

"Like hell we did," Thompson said. "I don't remember anyone telling me that we'd be hurling ourselves into other ships."

"Not specifically, no. No one can predict the exact course of the future, but she did inform all of you that this was not a regular freighter, that we would be doing things that didn't make sense, and that there would be a lot of danger involved."

"Yeah, but this is different."

"Is it?" Flaherty asked. "If Sera were FGT, do you know how dangerous that knowledge would be? What if someone let it slip?" He let that sink in as they all contemplated the value and danger of that knowledge. "Not that I am confirming, nor denying it. I am just promoting rational thought."

"What's all the noise in here?" Cargo asked. "I could hear you guys hollering all the way up on the bridge and Sabrina seems upset about something."

Cheeky cast an accusing glance at Flaherty. "We're discussing whether or not Sera is FGT."

Cargo walked over to the table and picked up a strawberry. "Oh, that."

"What do you mean 'oh, that'?" Nance asked. "She's been lying to us this whole time."

"Not telling you her life story is lying?" Cargo asked around his mouthful of strawberry. "I don't recall her ever lying about her past. She just never talks about it."

"So when did she tell you?" Cheeky asked. "How long have you been keeping this from us?"

"She never told me. I figured it out on my own about two months ago."

"Just how did you manage that?" Thompson asked.

"She was talking with Tanis on the bridge. They had the holo showing the *Intrepid* from Tanis's Link. Tanis asked if it would be possible to get a ship that large to transition to FTL and Sera said that she had heard of bigger ships managing it."

"What ships are bigger that can go FTL?" Cheeky asked.

"Exactly," Cargo said. "I thought about that long and hard and came up with just one answer: FGT worldships. They are the only thing I could dig up that were larger than the *Intrepid*. I've never known Sera to lie, so I assumed that the FGT was the only possible answer."

"And you didn't share it with the rest of us?" Cheeky asked. "Why would you keep that to yourself?"

"Because Sera didn't want it known, and I respect her too much to go sharing her secrets without her permission. Besides," Cargo continued after a moment, "that's some pretty dangerous knowledge."

The strawberries were all gone from the basket so he grabbed one from Cheeky's plate, before continuing under her glare. "It's also possible she has some personal reason for not sharing, as well. God knows I have enough stuff in my past that I don't want to talk about. I bet she has her share, as well."

"I appreciate your consideration," Sera said from the entrance to the room. "Sorry for barging in on your discussion like this, but Sabrina reached out to Helen and I."

Sera stepped into the room, revealing Tanis standing behind her.

"What is she doing here?" Thompson asked. "This is crew business."

"Tanis was crew on this ship for almost four months," Sera replied. "She also saved my life; and this *is* my ship, after all."

Thompson sat back in his chair and crossed his arms. He looked like he was going to speak for a moment, but then thought better of it.

"Does she already know, too?" Nance asked. "Are we the last to know?"

Sera took a deep breath. "She does know; I told her and Captain Andrews about it a few days ago—although, in my defense, Bob had already figured it all out and was going to tell them if I didn't."

"I already figured it out, too," Cargo said with a smile from behind his cup of coffee.

"So how come Flaherty knows?" Cheeky asked. "I've been on this ship almost as long as he has."

"Because I was born on an FGT worldship, just like the captain," Flaherty grunted. "Kinda hard to unknow that."

"Oh," Cheeky replied and sat back. "I guess we're all just a bunch of stooges, then."

"You lied to us," Nance accused.

"I…I don't think I lied. I just didn't share." Sera's knuckles were white as she gripped the back of a chair. She took a breath before continuing. "I didn't leave the FGT on what you could call good terms. I displayed a little more of my classic attitude than they were prepared to accept and it…" She swallowed deeply. "It caused some problems. I left the FGT and tried to fix what I'd broken. My recklessness had lost something valuable that Kade eventually got hold of. It's why I started smuggling, to find what I'd lost and eventually get it back."

"So that's why you got so focused on just working with Kade after a while," Cargo said with a nod.

"Yes, though that is done now. I recovered the device from The Mark's station before I destroyed it. When we meet with the FGT, I will return it to them and my exile will be over—I…I don't know if they'll let me stay with you."

"What do you mean?" Cheeky's anger had lessened, though there was still a hint of it behind her eyes.

<Will you take us with you?> Sabrina asked. *<I would love to see a worldship.>*

"What will happen to us?" Thompson asked at the same time. "We're just going to be left high and dry?"

Sera forced a smile. "*If.* If I am forced. I may be able to squeeze my way out of their grasp. I've done it before, I can do it again." She looked to Flaherty, who nodded.

"You don't have to come along to the rendezvous," Tanis said. "I'm sure that whether you're there or not, they will still work with us and give us a colony."

"I imagine so," Sera replied. "But they'll treat you more fairly with me there. I know who they're likely…" Sera stopped, tears welling in her eyes. She took a deep breath and brought herself under control. "If I end up going with them, the ship is yours, Cargo." She nodded to her first mate. "Or, if you all decide that you've had enough of me and what I've put you through, you can separate. Drop out of the dark layer while we are in transit. I won't stop you from either course of action."

No one spoke for several moments; everyone appeared to be giving deep consideration to what their captain had said.

"I know you don't want my opinion…"

"Correct, we really don't," Thompson responded.

Tanis turned her gaze to Thompson and held his eyes until he looked away. "Sera has worked tirelessly to make the galaxy a safer place. She's put her life on the line to help a lot of people. She's one of the good ones and I'd stick by her, were I you."

<*Tanis, you and Sera are needed on the* Intrepid's *bridge,*> Angela broke into the conversation.

"Keep things tight," Sera said to them all. "If this goes badly, we may never have to worry about what will happen when we meet the FGT."

AURORA

STELLAR DATE: 11.03.8927 (Adjusted Years)
LOCATION: ISS *Intrepid*, Approaching Aurora (12*Mj* Jovian)
REGION: Bollam's World System, Bollam's World Federation

The atmosphere was tense on the bridge as Tanis and Sera entered.

"Our friends have arrived," Captain Andrews said from beside the main holo tank.

The display of the Bollam's World system was expanded to show their destination, the planet Aurora; the *Intrepid*, still three hours away; and the newly-arrived AST fleet.

It was even larger and more intimidating than expected.

One hundred and twenty dreadnaughts, and over five hundred cruisers were highlighted on the holo display. The AST ships were spread out, having arrived at half a dozen jump points. Based on their velocity, only a quarter of their fleet would arrive while the *Intrepid* was filling its tanks at Aurora.

"That's a lot of ships," Sera whispered.

"You can say that again," Tanis said.

"That's a—" Sera stopped when Tanis shot her a look.

"Thoughts?" Captain Andrews asked as Tanis took up her place beside him.

"It really comes down to whether or not they got the message about our picotech. If they did, I imagine they will exercise some caution."

Sera chuckled. "You can bet that if they didn't hear they're still going to be cautious—given how there is no sign of the eleven dreadnaughts they sent ahead—not to mention the debris of half the Boller fleet."

Tanis nodded. "It would make me think twice about rushing in."

"Maintain course," the captain directed helm. "We'll see how this plays out."

* * * * *

The *Intrepid's* leadership stood around the holo tank, Tanis with her arm around Joe's waist while his was around her shoulders. Across from her, Ouri scowled at the display of Aurora, while Brandt and Jessica whispered about the chance of a fight with the new AST fleet.

Terrance and Captain Andrews were also speaking—though more optimistically about the elections they would hold upon arrival at their colony world. Admiral Sanderson was discussing fighter design with Sera and Amanda, the trio growing increasingly animated over small details and improvements to the Arc-6s.

An alert sounded and the holo showed the *Intrepid* closing within ten thousand kilometers of Aurora's surface. As though a switch had been flipped, the disparate conversations ceased. All eyes fixed upon the display before them.

The gas giant's unnatural existence meant that it didn't possess atmospheric strata typical for a planet of its size. To capture enough deuterium and lithium-7 to fill the *Intrepid's* tanks, the colony ship would have to drop below the planet's upper clouds for its scoop to reach the denser layers below.

"So that's what they're doing! For being so behind on tech, these Bollers have something pretty ingenious going on here," Earnest said, his holographic image appearing on the bridge.

"You finally figured out what the heck they're doing with this planet?" Tanis asked.

"I have indeed—well, Bob did most of it. They're using graviton emitters—pretty large ones, at that—to emit a negative gravity field around the planet. But that field only goes so far. Then it reverses and increases pressure. Basically, the whole thing is a helium-3 generator. It's the biggest gas station you ever saw. If they didn't have the graviton emitters, it would collapse into a brown dwarf star."

He walked around the holo display, peering intently at the world into which they were descending.

"If they focus the energy coming off it, they could probably use it as a heat source for orbiting dwarf planets, too. It's like having a second star without all the problems a second star causes."

"Nice of them to leave it here for us, then," Tanis said. "Saves us having to turn protium and deuterium into helium-3 ourselves."

"I wonder if they'll try to bill us," Joe chuckled.

The *Intrepid* slipped past the graviton emitter web and into the atmosphere of the planet, while above, scan showed that the leading ships in the AST fleet were now within a hundred thousand kilometers of Aurora.

"I wonder if they have any idea what we're doing?" Sera asked.

"There's nothing to see here; go back to your homes," Tanis chuckled.

"Gods, I wish they would," Sera replied.

The *Intrepid* dipped beneath the swirling clouds and deployed its scoop. Like a straw, it reached deep into the planet and began to draw the denser deuterium and helium-3 into the ship. The process proceeded quickly, and thirty minutes later the colony ship's tanks were full and Captain Andrews directed helm to bring the ship out of the clouds, timing their ascent for a vector toward their desired jump point.

They broke free of Aurora's atmosphere to see the world ringed by AST ships.

Scan called out an alert. "They're launching something—a lot of somethings!"

"RMs," Tanis swore. "They're targeting the graviton emitters."

"Oh, that's bad, very bad," Earnest shook his head with dismay.

"Helm, full thrust. Get us out of here!" the captain called out.

"Why very bad?" Tanis asked. "The mass is the same, the planet will just collapse."

"You don't understand," Earnest said. "One of two things will happen. The first is that the planet just collapses. Except things like this don't happen naturally; you don't get nice spherical balls of heavy hydrogen and helium isotopes that can collapse under their own gravity *in minutes*. This thing is a planet-sized fusion bomb just waiting to happen."

Tanis frowned, watching as concern showed on the bridge crew's faces.

"What's the other option?" Tanis asked.

"Graviton emitters don't just make gravitons out of vacuum," Earnest replied. "They get them from somewhere. That somewhere is the dark layer. They tap into dark matter for mass and energy."

"Seriously?" Tanis asked.

Sera and Earnest nodded together.

"Sooo?" Tanis asked.

<*Black hole,*> Angela supplied.

"The Bollers are really going to hate us," Terrance commented. "I have to admit, I feel bad for them."

"They did try to kill us," Andrews frowned. "I don't feel so bad. Besides, we're not taking out their big H-bomb of a planet, the AST is."

"I can see why it *might* create a singularity, but why do you think it's probable?" Tanis asked Earnest.

"When a ship transitions into the dark layer to achieve FTL, it does so by slipping through the fabric of space-time into that sub-dimension; graviton emitters do something very similar.

"A better description of what a ship does is to say that it cuts open a portal into the dark layer. That portal self-heals, because no energy is being used to keep it open. But if there was an energy source nearby—say an exploding planet, it could be used to keep the portal open. It's why systems enforce the use of their jump points, and it's also why people don't just blind-jump into unexplored systems—at least I would imagine they don't."

"You are correct," Sera nodded. "People who do that usually aren't heard from again."

Tanis took a deep, calming breath. "To the case at hand, Earnest. What do you think?"

"I think we need to push our engines harder than we have ever pushed them before," Earnest replied.

<*Which we're already doing,*> Amanda added. <*We can walk and chew gum here—well, I can't, but you get the picture.*>

Everyone fell silent as scan updated, showing graviton emitter platforms exploding in a wave across the planet.

"Oh!" Earnest said.

All eyes turned to him.

"There's a lot more tritium in this planet than I expected. My money is on black hole. Given how much dark matter is clustered around this world, we're looking at a significant increase in mass."

The *Intrepid* was pulling past the last of the planet's clouds, even as the gasses began to rush past them, drawn down into the deep gravity well that the graviton emitters had kept them from for so long.

"Neutron storm incoming!" scan called out, and Amanda announced that full shielding was in place. Stasis layered over grav, layered over electro-static.

On the holo, the AST ships began to veer off, apparently also realizing the full enormity of what their actions caused.

"They really didn't think this through," Earnest said through gritted teeth.

"Or maybe they considered it worth the risk to destroy us," Joe replied. "Think about it. We have an invincible shield and our pico could wipe them out. What better way to deal with an unimaginable threat than to drop it into a black hole."

"Makes sense," Tanis scowled.

"Too damn much sense," Anderson agreed.

The *Intrepid* had reached an altitude of twenty-five thousand kilometers above the previous surface of Aurora—though the radius of the planet had decreased by fifty thousand kilometers.

Earnest began whispering a countdown to himself, and then a moment after he reached zero, the planet's collapse stopped and a massive explosion of light, matter, and energy flared out from its compressed core.

As Earnest predicted, compression won. After that initial explosion, the visible light all but snapped off and the pull of gravity began to increase, slowing the *Intrepid's* progress.

On the scan Tanis saw that two of the AST ships had moved to pursue the *Intrepid,* likely intent on ensuring that the colony ship fell back into the world below. Their course put them too close to the world when the explosion occurred. The ships were pushed outward by the blast, but then, as the mass of the world collapsed into a black hole and drew matter from the dark layer, they began to fall in.

The shockwave passed over the *Intrepid,* sending a violent shudder through the ship.

"Will she hold?" Terrance asked.

"Earnest nodded. "She'll hold. We don't have the dampeners that those other ships have, but our stacked decking was designed to handle lateral thrust."

Tanis tightened her arm around Joe as she wondered if this is how the crew felt when they passed close to Estrella de la Muerte and were hit by a solar flare. There was nothing to do but wait and pray to whatever gods or stars you believed held sway.

Sera spun the view on the main holo and some of the bridge crew gasped as several of Aurora's moons appeared to stretch, and then disintegrated, falling back into the dark, roiling mass below. Above the *Intrepid,* an icy moon was pulled out of its orbit and the ship altered course with a lurch to avoid the debris as it crumbled and fell.

"This is amazing," Earnest whispered.

Tanis looked at the rapt expression on Earnest's face and shook her head. "For some definition of amazing, perhaps."

"Oh, come on!" Earnest gestured at the display. "How often do you see the death of a planet and the birth of a black hole? If they're lucky they can stabilize it. It's a far better source of energy than what they had."

"If they can keep the rest of their planets in stable orbits," Sera said. "There are already reports of earthquakes on one of their inhabited worlds and solar flares are bound to let loose across their star."

"I never said it was going to be an enjoyable transition," Earnest replied.

No one responded as a new vibration began beneath their feet.

"OK, are you still sure she'll hold?" Earnest asked.

<*Yes,*> Bob replied.

On scan, the two AST ships lost their battle and disappeared into the black hole, around which now swirled a glowing accretion disk.

Scan highlighted three other enemy ships which were also struggling to pull free of the deepening gravity well. Tanis marveled as they began to detonate nuclear warheads behind their ships in a desperate attempt to pull free.

Joe cast Tanis a worried look. "They got a lot more bang for their buck than they expected."

The gravity well swelled, growing faster than anyone had anticipated and more of the AST fleet began to fall into it. The vibration in the *Intrepid's* hull increased and the ship began to lose velocity relative to the monster growing beneath them.

She returned Joe's concerned look, unable to find any words to voice the fear she began to feel in her heart.

The bridge crew also began to look anxious, though no one spoke, everyone attempting to focus on finding a way to improve the ship's chances of survival.

Earnest appeared calm, just as he always did when facing some insurmountable problem. "We're reversing the polarity of the scoop, sweeping it behind us. It will give us a bubble of reverse-polarized ions to slip through."

The captain nodded his approval and a minute later the vibration in the deck ceased and the ship began to move forward once more.

"Two hundred thousand kilometers," someone announced with a note of nervous jubilation in their voice—and then Tanis felt everything stop.

"Wha—?" she began to ask when she saw that the ship's clocks had jumped by eleven minutes.

"Status!" the captain called out.

<*I enacted safety protocols,*> Bob replied. <*The black hole began to spin and hit us with its relativistic jet. I put the entire ship in stasis.*>

"Handy trick," Joe said softly.

Reports rolled in; helm responded, scan was operational. Engines were online, the scoop team indicated the emitter was damaged, but they could repair it in a few hours. Stasis shields were down, but only needed a reset of their control systems. The ship's position was updated on scan and everyone gasped.

"Wow, it really gave us a boost," Sera whistled.

The blast of plasma from the fledgling black hole had flung them over fifteen million kilometers. They were nearly at the jump point and helm reported they could adjust course and be in position for FTL transition in just over an hour.

"Well, that's a rapid change in fortune," Terrance observed.

Behind them, a large number of the AST ships were gone, but those which remained were boosting after the *Intrepid* in a furious attempt to catch their prey.

"Jump early," Sera said softly.

"What?" Tanis asked.

Scan updated again, revealing so many relativistic missiles that scan could not reliably separate their signatures and simply estimated the count to be over a thousand. They were spread out like an arrow of death arching toward the *Intrepid.*

"Jump early. Jump as soon as you can. Jump now if you can manage it!" Sera insisted.

"She's right," Earnest nodded. "The dark matter maps for this entire system are useless now. No one knows where it's safe to jump—it doesn't matter where we do it. Once the stasis shields are up, we need to go."

"Time on stasis shields?" the captain asked.

<*Three minutes,*> Amanda replied.

<*All crew,*> The captain announced ship-wide. <*Prepare for FTL transition.*>

A deep quiet settled over the bridge as everyone watched the swarm of relativistic missiles slash their way toward the *Intrepid.* Everyone prayed to their gods and stars that the transition would go smoothly as the time to impact and the countdown for FTL transition spun down in near unison.

Then, a minute early, Bob's voice rang out in their minds.

<*Shields are up. Initiating transition.*>

"Well, here we go," Tanis whispered to Joe.

THE END

* * * * *

SET THE GALAXY ON FIRE

THE ORION WAR – BOOK 1.5

BY M. D. COOPER

Because the story isn't finished yet...

An anthology of short stories set during and following the events of Destiny Lost.

These stories tie directly into the events at the end of Destiny Lost, and add color and depth to the next book, New Canaan.

I hope you enjoy these tales of the *Intrepid,* and beyond into the broader galaxy around them, where the news of the Battle of Bollam's World spreads like wildfire....

BOLLAM'S WAR

THE MORNING AFTER

STELLAR DATE: 10.29.8927 (Adjusted Years)
LOCATION: ISS *Intrepid,* Orbiting Fierra
REGION: Bollam's World System, Bollam's World Federation

Joe eased into his chair at the kitchen table and took a long pull of his coffee. Movement outside the window caught his attention, and he saw a group of squirrels fighting over nuts fallen from the oak in the backyard; their antics coaxed a laugh from him.

Above, inside the house, he heard the floors creak as Tanis readied herself for the day ahead. He wished upon her all the time in the world, though he knew that was not to be. This would be the day; they would make their move and leave Bollam's World for Ascella—and a meeting with the FGT.

The squeaks and groans moved across the ceiling above him and Tanis emerged on the stairs at the far side of the living room. She looked as young and sharp as the first day he had seen her in the section chief's office on the Mars Outer Shipyards.

Something that had impressed him at the time, given she had just been in a firefight.

She quickly skipped down the steps, her shipsuit crisp, boots polished, and hair pulled back in a ponytail that bounced along behind her. He always found the hairstyle incongruous with how she presented herself, but loved all her little idiosyncrasies and kept his thoughts to himself.

"Good morning, again," he said with a smile, and gestured to the cup of coffee on the table across from him.

Tanis returned the smile and collapsed into her chair, which groaned in protest.

"The chairs may be getting a bit old for such abuse," he said and shifted in his for emphasis. The wooden seat creaked in protest and Tanis inclined her head and shrugged.

"I'll add it to my list of things to do."

Joe pushed the plate containing pancakes and bacon toward her.

"You don't have to do anything. I'm sure we have a bevy of carpenters who would do anything to make a set of chairs for the General."

Tanis took a long drink from her cup and frowned. "I know, I know, but I like to do some things for myself—even more, now that I'm *The General*. It seems that I can't even get my own coffee anymore."

She winked at the last and Joe shrugged.

"I was up first. You would have done the same."

"I would have made the pot. I don't know that I would have poured you a cup. I didn't know when you'd be down, and I wouldn't have wanted it to get cold."

Joe inclined his head and nodded. It was a conversation they had had a thousand times. Sometimes when angry and irrational, other times when laughing and joking, and times, like today, when they were both feeling melancholy.

"So…about not leaving each other ever again," Joe said, his eyebrow raised and a wry smile on his lips.

"I know, I know," Tanis sighed. "I don't want you to go, but we both know you have to; there's no one better than you at the helm of the *Andromeda*."

"It's because Corsia thinks I'm hot," Joe chuckled and Tanis raised an eyebrow.

"That silicate hussy…"

Joe felt a frown crease his brow. "What?"

Tanis laughed, a sound he was glad to hear. Her laugh had been in short supply over the few days since her return to the *Intrepid*.

"It's something that Angela said to Helen when she tried to scope me out with her nano," Tanis replied.

"Now that's a scene I would have liked to see," Joe said.

"You really wouldn't have. I was a mess."

"I've seen you messy before," Joe said, his expression distant. Then he blinked and refocused on her. "What do you think of Sera and Helen, other than the part where you're pissed off that she won't tell you all her deep, dark, secrets?"

Tanis opened her mouth to speak, a harsh look crossing her face, but then she stopped herself and schooled her expression. "Sorry. You were right before. I should respect her privacy—it's the part where she has a secret that could risk the entire ship that bugs me. When I came on board, the captain knew my history, there were no secrets there."

"Fair enough," Joe said with a nod. "But it is still his call, and he's opted to take her up on her offer."

"Yeah," Tanis said with a sigh. "I told him to take her up on it, as well. She's never done wrong by me; risked her life for mine. Logic dictates that she will continue to do so—unless she's truly nefarious."

"So, that aside, what do you think of Sera and her AI? It seems like a pretty powerful pairing for this low-tech time we've found ourselves in."

Tanis leaned back in her chair, taking another drink from her cup before speaking. "You're right about their abilities. If they had nanocloud tech, I would say their whole package is more advanced than Angela's and mine. Helen is…weird. She reminds me of how Angela and I work, but I know that is because of other circumstances—ones that I can't believe would be manifest in someone I just happened to find on the far side of space."

"When I asked Priscilla about them, she said there was something unusual about Helen, but wouldn't say what," Joe replied.

"Did she?" Tanis asked. "Well, if she knows, Bob knows, and if he's not alarmed, then I guess I'm OK with it."

Joe rose from the table and cleaned up their plates, leaving them on the counter for an automaton to wash later. Tanis stood and embraced him as he turned.

"Be careful out there," she whispered in his ear.

Joe wrapped Tanis in a deep embrace. "And you stay in the system. No gallivanting around the galaxy."

"I won't go gallivanting anywhere without you, I promise," Tanis replied.

They held one another for several minutes before Joe pulled back and gazed into his wife's eyes.

"You be careful, too. You have precious cargo—and I'm not just talking about the colonists in stasis."

Tanis reached a hand down to her abdomen. "I will. I plan to stay on the *Intrepid's* bridge—in theory, the safest place in the fleet."

"So long as we win," Joe said.

Tanis pulled back and looked him in the eyes. "Of course we'll win. Haven't you heard? I'm lucky."

TO WAR

STELLAR DATE: 10.29.8927 (Adjusted Years)
LOCATION: ISS *Intrepid,* Orbiting Fierra
REGION: Bollam's World System, Bollam's World Federation

Joe stood on the dock, staring up at the *Andromeda,* mentally preparing himself for the day ahead. He may live on the *Intrepid,* but over the years, the *Andromeda* had begun to feel like *his* ship.

<*You checking me out, Commandant?*> Corsia asked.

Joe laughed and walked toward the ship. "You know I'm a one-woman man, Corsia…well, two, if you count Angela."

Corsia's laugh echoed in his mind. <*And I'm a one-man ship.*>

<*Sure you are,*> Joe replied with a smile, taking a measure of comfort in the familiar banter with Corsia.

Joe took a long walk around the cruiser, giving it a visual once over. It was far from necessary; as the ship's XO, Corsia had everything well in hand—she always did—but it was a ritual left over from his days as a fighter pilot. The *Andromeda* was under his command. Its capabilities and crew were his responsibility, and he took that responsibility seriously.

He watched the loaders trundle the last of the relativistic missiles aboard the ship, bringing the total loadout to over three hundred. Tanis wasn't taking any chances—the *Andromeda* now held more missiles than the entire ISF fleet had possessed during the battle with the Sirians. She was counting on the *Andromeda's* near-invisibility to help seed them throughout the battlefield. Joe accepted the duty given him. He would much rather deliver RMs than be on the receiving end of the missiles.

Satisfied with his review, he took the lift to the gantry that ran to the *Andromeda's* central crew hatch. The airlock was wide open, and he strode through onto the ship's main deck. Everyone he passed was focused on their assigned tasks and duties, moving with a calm efficiency. He knew each member of his crew by name and, as he nodded his greetings, Joe was certain they could be trusted to bring about victory this day.

The *Andromeda* had always done the Intrepid Space Force proud; the men, women, and AIs who made up its crew didn't plan to sully that legacy today—even if there were four hostile navies waiting for them.

Joe entered the bridge and nodded to Petrov, who sat at the helm reviewing his checklists with Jim, the ship's chief engineer, standing at his side.

"Good morning, Captain," Petrov said in greeting. "Anxious to get out there?"

Joe nodded. "Good morning, Petrov, Jim. Everything on the up and up?"

Jim cast Joe an appraising look. "We're just working on mass rebalancing all those missiles we're taking on. We gotta make sure that when we use them, we pull evenly from the racks. I know you. You're going to put this ship through its paces, and I don't want something coming loose."

Joe raised a hand and chuckled. "I'll do my best to keep us flying straight. Most of our work will be lurking and sneaking. How's our outer shell looking?"

"The trial run we did the other day was a success. When our active dampening is on and we're running dark, these guys couldn't see us if we were right on top of them. I've made a few more adjustments, after seeing what their active scan looks like—I bet we could park on their hulls if we wanted to."

<Let's not test that theory,> Corsia said. *<Their hulls are where they mount their guns.>*

"Whatever you say, Cor," Jim replied with a faint smile.

<I see how it is,> Joe said to Corsia with a laugh. *<I'm just a convenient alternative to Jim when he's busy.>*

<You know you've always been my side-human,> Corsia's mental avatar smiled. *<You know, two days ago, Jim and I celebrated a century since we first met—well, a century for him.>*

<I hadn't realized, congrats!> Joe replied.

<We didn't make a big deal of it, there are bigger things going on.>

<And you've been married for, what…seventy years?> Joe asked.

<Seventy four, and if you forget our seventy fifth when it rolls around next year, I'll be miffed.>

<Duly noted,> Joe said with a chuckle.

He remembered when he first met Corsia back in the Sol System. It was upon her arrival at the Cho, for delivery to the *Intrepid*. The memory amused him now—he had questioned Tanis on the need for a ship with offensive weapons. While the *Andromeda* had not—at least, not back then—been built entirely for combat, she was not like the other in-system transports that they were taking on.

Tanis had just laughed and told him that he was naïve if he thought that a colony in the millions wouldn't need a ship with some military capabilities.

After he learned of the picotech, the procurement of the *Andromeda* had made a lot more sense.

Jim, he met much later—not until after Tanis had defeated the Sirian cruiser in Kapteyn's System. At the time, he was just a civilian engineer, but Joe had forced him into the military academy in Kapteyn's System, and the man was now an ISF Master Chief.

Jim responded, bringing Joe back to the present.

"All looks well," the chief engineer said and glanced back at Joe. "Keep us safe out there."

"Always," Joe replied before the holoprojection of Jim winked out.

<You'd better,> Jim said over the Link from his station down in engineering.

Joe ran through his own checklists while the rest of the bridge crew filtered in, each of them early and looking a bit anxious.

The first to arrive were Trevor and Tori; two men, who, while not brothers by birth, had become as inseparable as twins. Trevor managed scan, and Tori worked weapons and tactics. They knew the *Andromeda* as well as Corsia. Their AIs, Gwen and Aaron, were excellent complements, who managed comm and backed Corsia up with general ship management when under fire.

Last to arrive, though still ten minutes early for her shift, was Ylonda.

Ylonda appeared to be a slender woman in her twenties, but as an AI who chose to wear a human-like body, she was anything but what she appeared. Her AI mind was born of many parents—the norm for their species—but most notably, from Corsia and Jim.

Normally Joe wouldn't allow children to serve with their parents, but Ylonda had proven herself to be nothing but professional, and her behavior, thus far, had been above reproach; he also felt like what was 'normal' was less and less relevant every day.

He greeted each member of the bridge crew as they entered and set about their work. In the efficient manner he had come to expect, their tasks and duties required for departure were done well ahead of the allotted times.

<*Looks like we're ready to go early, once again,*> Corsia observed.

"Of course we are," Joe replied. "Ylonda, inform docking control that we're ready to hit the bricks."

Ylonda cast him the briefest of curious looks before replying. "Hit the bricks, yes sir."

Joe gave a soft chuckle and Corsia chided him. <*At some point, you're going to run out of new ways to say, "take us out," and that will be a good day.*>

<*Never going to happen,*> Joe replied. <*I could do them all day and never repeat a single one.*>

<*Can I request a transfer then?*> Corsia asked.

<*Nope.*>

"Permission to undock received," Ylonda supplied verbally while sending the departure parameters to Petrov's console.

"Here we go," Joe said with a smile, as the ship gently lifted from its cradle and drifted down the lane toward the ES shield at the end of the bay.

The *Andromeda* slipped silently into the darkness, and, with the smallest amount of thrust possible, moved toward its position between the *Intrepid* and the pirate fleet, which lay beyond Fierra's south pole.

They hadn't been underway for even a minute before Trevor spoke up.

"Looks like one of the new Arc-6s is having a problem," he said and threw his console's scan data on the bridge's main holo tank.

Joe looked up the squadron and saw that it was the Black Death; part of the wing normally stationed aboard the *Andromeda,* though operating under Fleetcom's direct control for this engagement. Concern filled his mind—he knew each of those pilots personally.

"Who is it," he asked.

"Cary," Ylonda supplied. "Fleetcom is directing us to move in under stealth and be prepared to assist."

Joe didn't know if he was happy that it wasn't Jessica, or worried that his friend would now put herself at risk trying to save one of her fellow pilots.

"Do it," Joe directed, and felt the ship shift under him as it moved toward Fierra's south pole.

Trevor updated the holo with scan data pulled from the fighter squadron, and he discerned the squadron commander's plan. Rock was going to have his ships shield Cary's fighter and push straight through the pirate fleet. It was a risky play, but given Cary's trajectory, there were few other options.

Joe felt a pang of regret as he watched the *Excelsior Nova* boost hard into position beyond the pirate ships, ready to catch the disabled Arc-6 fighter. That should have been Troy in the *Excelsior* down there; while he liked Nuwen, the ship's AI pilot, he had always held a warm place in his heart for Troy, and all the time he and Tanis had spent on the heavy lifter.

"Those pirates aren't going to just sit there," Joe said. "Let's do a flyby and drop off a few of our presents for them."

"How many are you thinking?" Tori asked.

"My analysis shows that eighteen is enough to disable most of their shields. Why don't you add four more for good measure?"

"Aye, Captain," Tori replied and bent to his task.

Joe knew that the estimation of how many missiles were required was, at best, an educated guess based on the data Sabrina and Helen had provided. However, he did know that the 89th century was unprepared for the type of warhead that the *Andromeda* carried.

Normal relativistic missiles achieved near-luminal speeds, and delivered their energy purely through kinetic force. The rail-delivered round released a massive amount of energy on impact—usually an order of magnitude more than a fusion bomb's energy. These missiles packed an extra punch. After the initial kinetic strike, the energy would trigger a secondary effect, causing the vessel of liquid metallic hydrogen within the missile to undergo fusion. The goal was to disable shields with the kinetic strike, and obliterate the enemy ship with the subsequent nuclear explosion.

Getting the materials for the secondary explosion to survive the kinetic impact had been a closely guarded secret of the Terran Space Force in Sol, but Earnest had figured it out back in Victoria; now the *Andromeda* carried hundreds of the advanced weapons.

"Captain, some of the enemy corvettes are advancing," Trevor announced.

<*Five, to be exact,*> Gwen, his AI, added.

"What are they doing?" Joe mused as he leaned forward in his chair. "They're moving slowly…like they expect to capture her."

"Eight fighters moving in to intercept them," Trevor reported aloud as everyone watched the action unfold on the holo tank.

"Wow, they are boosting *hard,*" Petrov said with a whistle. "I guess those inertial dampeners are the real deal."

Joe nodded in silent agreement, mentally praying that the shields would work as well, because the tags on the holo display told him that Jessica was in the formation.

The engagement was energetic, and over in seconds.

The Arc-6s flipped their engines and boosted hard to re-engage the pirate corvettes. The fighters appeared to be intact, and none of the corvettes had taken significant damage, either.

Then, the fighters did something he would never have expected.

Almost lazily, they drifted over the enemy ships and dropped directly into their engine wash—a maneuver that would normally be fatal. There was a brief moment where the Arc-6s paused, and then the five enemy ships exploded.

"Ho-lee shiiit!" Trevor cried out. "Did you see that? They just…what the hell did they even do?"

"Something that's not in any book," Joe said and shook his head. A fighter that was impervious to kinetics, beam-fire, and gamma rays coming out of an AP engine? It was a game-changer.

"If those pirates know what's good for them, they'll bugger off now," Trevor grinned, and Joe shot him a stern look. "Uh… Captain," he added.

"No such luck," Ylonda said. "They're moving to engage. It doesn't make sense, why would they do that?"

"Because their armada has over two hundred corvettes and cruisers against forty fighters," Joe replied. "There's no scenario that existed, before five minutes ago, where they would be in any danger."

"But it's not five minutes ago, Captain," Ylonda replied.

"Some people are slow to catch up to reality," Tori supplied. "Besides, if we didn't have Fleetcom data telling us those fighters are in tip-top shape, none of us would believe they could do that again."

The bridge fell silent as every ship in the pirate fleet opened fire on the Black Death squadron, which had formed up in a protective cocoon around Cary's ship. The barrage obscured the Arc-6 fighters, and when the seven-second salvo ended, scan refreshed and the squadron came into view, intact and undamaged.

Cheers erupted on the bridge and Joe breathed a sigh of relief.

"Fleetcom has provided updated data. Their reactors are running too hot to survive another attack of that magnitude," Ylonda said.

"So, there *is* a limit to what these shields can take," Joe mused, as they watched the pirate fleet break into two groups and loop around to engage the fighters from both sides.

The crew looked to him, and Joe shook his head. The orders from Fleetcom were to stay clear while the *Enterprise* and *Defiance* filled the paths of the enemy ships with kinetic grapeshot. He passed control of the relativistic missiles they had seeded to Fleetcom, and sat back to watch.

The timing had to be perfectly coordinated, but if it worked, this rag-tag flotilla of pirate ships wouldn't be bothering them again.

It was as though the scene unfolded in slow motion on the holo tank. The lead ships of the enemy fleet hit the grapeshot and their shields held for a moment before the kinetic pellets began to slip through. A second later, their shields failed entirely, and the lead ships were torn to ribbons. Even one of the larger cruisers disintegrated under the assault, and Joe found himself hoping that whoever had tortured Tanis during her captivity was on board.

Then the twenty-two relativistic missiles came to life; powerful engines boosting them toward the pirate fleet, and striking the ships that had taken the least damage from the grapeshot.

Explosions from the kinetic strikes and nuclear fire obscured the entire pirate fleet. When the radioactive haze cleared enough for scan to get a clear look, less than fifty ships remained operational.

Another round of cheers sounded on the *Andromeda's* bridge, and Joe joined in with his crew.

"Now *that's* how you take out a fleet!" Tori hollered.

"OK, people, settle down, we still have work to do out here. That was the weakest, most poorly organized enemy on the field. You can bet that everyone else just learned a lot about our tactics and is adjusting theirs." Joe cautioned his bridge crew.

They nodded and bent to their tasks while he opened a connection to the *Intrepid.*

<Nice work on the timing there, dear,> he said. *<Everyone sure is happy to have you back.>*

<That was mostly Angela; I'm just along for the ride,> Tanis replied.

<Don't listen to her for a second,> Angela broke in. *<It was her call to wipe them out like that, and after what they did to us, I don't feel any remorse.>*

<They overreached and got what they deserved,> Joe replied. *<What's next on the menu?>*

<Drop a few more of your presents off near Rebecca's fleet, then take up station on the far side of the Intrepid. *I expect the Bollers to make a move soon.>*

<You got it,> Joe said and closed the connection with a mental embrace. *<Do us proud.>*

THE ADMIRAL'S RETURN

STELLAR DATE: 10.29.8927 (Adjusted Years)
LOCATION: BWSS *Freya*, Near Kithari's L4
REGION: Bollam's World System, Bollam's World Federation

Captain Ren watched Admiral Senya storm onto the *Freya's* bridge, the rage on her face enough to keep even the boldest member of the crew from glancing at her.

"What the *fuck* just happened?" she hollered at Ren. "I thought things were under control out here!"

Ren ran a hand through his hair and held back a sigh. "They were. Our negotiations were going well; but then they got new intel, and everything changed. They have…some sort of shielding that we've never seen before. That pirate fleet couldn't even touch their fighters. The colonists wiped out over a hundred ships in five minutes."

"I can't believe the president didn't call me back sooner. What was he thinking, leaving me out in the Sidian Reach when the biggest prize we've ever seen drifts into our system?" She turned the full force of her gaze on Ren and he did his best not to flinch.

"I found out from a trader—a trader!—that our system was on lockdown and under siege from pirates—and the Hegemony, of all things."

Ren shifted uncomfortably and tried to look as if he agreed with the admiral. "That's unbelievable. I was under the impression they had sent for you immediately."

"Well, they didn't," Senya replied. "And then they put that fool Nespha in charge of the fleet. Of all the bone-headed things to do; he couldn't find his asshole to shit out of."

"Have the chiefs put you back in charge?" Ren asked, unsure whether or not he'd prefer it. If Senya was back in charge, there was no telling what she'd do; but if she wasn't, he'd have to listen to her rail for days.

"Of course they did," Senya cast him a cold look. *<I have enough dirt on them to bury each and every one of those bastards. When this is over, I may do it anyway, just to punish them for trying to keep me away.>*

Ren nodded solemnly, the only response he could think of. Admiral Senya was like a ticking time bomb; it was impossible to tell what would set her off. He never could tell if she behaved irrationally to keep those around her off-balance, or if she really was as unhinged as she acted.

Nevertheless, she commanded his division of the Bollam's World Space Force, and his cruiser was her flagship. It was a destiny conceived in hell.

There was little he could do about it; Senya had spent decades running her family's business interests and consolidating power, before setting her eyes on the military. With her deep pockets and intimate knowledge of the government's inner workings, she had risen through the ranks quickly, and was now the top admiral in the fleet.

It was only a matter of time before she moved on to seize the presidency.

The prospect did not excite Ren one iota, but there was no way he could stop Senya from getting anything she wanted. His only play was to make sure he didn't get steamrolled by her.

"We have an ambassador on board the *Intrepid*," Ren said. "We could open a channel with their captain and resume negotiations."

"That's not the message I want to send," Senya said with a smirk. "Recall our ambassador and get me targeting options on the ships they've deployed. I want every rail in the system to pound them to dust."

"Sir?" Ren asked. "Is that wise? What if the legends are true?"

"If the legends were true, the Victorians would have been able to defend themselves. Our people came from Sirius, and that ship was their enemy. They stole from our people then; they'll not steal from us now."

* * * * *

<*You have to do something to stop her,*> Nespha said to Ren over a private connection.

<*There's nothing I* **can** *do; you know how she gets. Admiral Senya is determined to seize the* Intrepid *by force.*>

Nespha's avatar sighed in Ren's mind. <*And what of The Mark? Is she planning to let them ruin her prize?*>

<*Senya believes that the kinetic rounds will destroy some of the colonist ships, at the least. Then The Mark will move in. When they're fully engaged, we'll come in and get rid of those pirates and claim the colony ship.*>

Ren waited for Nespha to respond. He didn't like having this conversation with the other admiral—Senya would have his hide if she knew—but refusing to respond to Nespha was not an option, either.

<*I suppose that could work, unless those shields of theirs can withstand a kinetic strike. No one I have talked to has even heard of anything like them.*>

<*We'll know soon enough,*> Ren replied. <*It's not their shields I'm worried about; it's what those AST dreadnaughts intend that concerns me. They didn't come here just to watch us duke it out.*>

<*Agreed,*> Nespha's tone was more dour than usual. <*They haven't responded to a single attempt at communication. Our tacticians think they're waiting for backup.*>

<*I agree with that assessment, as does Senya. It's why she wants to take the* Intrepid *as quickly as possible. Our window is closing quickly.*>

<*We shall see,*> Nespha replied before closing the connection.

Ren didn't know what to think of the conversation. Nespha didn't like Senya, but he had always treated fairly with Ren and the other captains. He wasn't a firebrand like Senya; he was cautious. Often too cautious. Senya may be nearly impossible to deal with, but she did get results.

PREPARATIONS

STELLAR DATE: 10.29.8927 (Adjusted Years)
LOCATION: ISS *Andromeda,* Near Fierra
REGION: Bollam's World System, Bollam's World Federation

In the wake of the pirate fleet's destruction, Tanis addressed the fleet.

Joe watched the *Andromeda's* bridge crew smile at one another and sit up straighter as they listened to Tanis's speech. The news that the FGT would meet with them, and that a colony world was still waiting, had the desired effect on their spirits.

The moment Tanis signed off, orders came in to reposition between the *Intrepid* and the Boller fleet. He passed the order on to Petrov who turned to look at him.

"Really, Captain? What, with that weird thing those other pirates are doing?"

"Comes from Fleetcom," Joe replied. "*Sabrina* is on its way out there to help out, too. They have the new stasis shields, so they should be able to take whatever that rag-tag armada throws at them."

<*Careful, Joe,*> Corsia cautioned privately. <*We don't know enough to be cocky.*>

<*I'm not cocky, I'm angry. Those people were going to torture Tanis; they* ***did*** *torture Sera.*> Even as Joe spoke, he knew his words were disingenuous. Tanis had told him of what she did to Kris and Trent; she was no stranger to torture, either.

<*Anger is not a winning argument,*> Corsia replied.

<*You're right. I'm just on edge. I just got her back, and now we're apart again; out here…fighting for our lives once more.*>

<*Yes. And we'll win once more.*>

Joe laughed. <*Now who's cocky?*>

*****

Time passed slowly as the *Andromeda* passed behind Fierra before drifting out into the van of the forces positioned between the *Intrepid* and the Boller fleet.

"Petrov, let's lay in two lines of missiles. The first fifty-thousand klicks from the *Intrepid,* and the second at the two-fifty kay mark."

"You got it, Captain," Petrov replied, as he plotted a course and ran it past Corsia and Ylonda.

"I have the next batch racked and ready to drop, Captain," Tori added from the weapons console. "I recommend that we seed a dozen defense turrets out here, as well—keep any anti-missile fire from taking them out, if it comes to that."

"Save them for the next picket," Joe replied. "I just got word from Fleetcom that some tugs are going to pull out some meaty turrets to keep our birds safe.

"Oh, really?" Tori asked. "Are they those new rhinos?"

Joe nodded. "I guess they got them done sooner than they thought with some of the new grav-tech. They were able to solve the recoil issues that had necessitated more fuel than we had handy."

"Oh, that'll be good," Tori rubbed his hands. "I almost hope the Bollers get that far."

Petrov and Ylonda both sent a frown his way, and the weapon's officer shrugged.

"What I can I say? I like to see things go boom."

Ylonda straightened in her seat; a physical gesture Joe had noticed her use lately when shifting her focus. He wondered if it was deliberate or affected.

"Orders from Fleetcom. Tactical suspects inbound kinetics," she said. "They're instituting an updated jinking pattern."

"Steady on," Joe said. "They can't see us, and jinking will give us away—just don't be predictable, Petrov."

"Aye, captain," the pilot replied.

"Those kinetics are a ballsy move," Tori commented. "What's their play, captain?"

Joe wanted to tell Tori to focus on the task at hand, but the entire crew had turned to him, curious to hear his response. Well, everyone except Petrov, though he could tell that the pilot was also listening by the way he cocked his head. His marriage to Tanis often made everyone think that he had direct access to the inner workings of her mind, and by extension, the minds of their enemies.

However, he didn't need Tanis's insight for this one.

"They can probably tell the difference between our regular shielding, and the Arc-6's shields, so they know that not all our ships have stasis shields. What they don't know is whether or not we just have them turned off at the moment. They also know that if all our ships have stasis shields, we will simply crush everyone and win. So a surprise attack with kinetics to take out any of our vessels that don't have stasis shielding right now is their best play."

"What about The Mark's fleet?" Trevor asked. "If they take out our ships, then those pirates will take the *Intrepid*."

<*I suspect that they plan to deal with The Mark themselves. Now that we got rid of Padre's fleet, it's a much simpler task. Speaking of tasks…*> Corsia added.

His crew remembered themselves, and everyone returned to their work to finish seeding the first line of relativistic missiles. Petrov was carefully maneuvering the ship to the location of the second line when Fleetcom confirmed the Boller kinetic attack.

"Looks like they had shots lined up on every one of our cruisers—except us, of course," Ylonda said.

<*The* Intrepid's *scan and data group is rather happy with themselves,*> Corsia added.

"I think the whole fleet is rather happy with them," Joe chuckled. "What's Fleetcom's response?"

"They're returning fire."

Joe widened the view of the Boller system on the main holo tank, watching as Fleet Tactical lit up targets. The ISF didn't have the firepower to deliver the type of slugs that the platforms back in Kapteyn's were—had been—capable of delivering, which made long-range shots at enemy ships impossible. However, the selected targets were stationary rail platforms positioned on moons and asteroids. Bodies that had predictable paths.

The holo lit up with shots as the fleet let fly their kinetic rounds at the enemy emplacements. A minute later, two hundred and sixty slugs sailed through space.

The ISF's ship-mounted railguns were much easier to detect than the ground-based ones. For starters, they moved the ships when they fired, and the vessels used thrusters or main engines—depending on the size of the slug—to compensate.

Because physics weren't willing to budge on this point, the Bollers saw the shots coming.

"They're scrambling to intercept our slugs," Trevor said from the scan console. "Our guys masked their trajectory well, though. I think enough will slip through."

DETECTION

STELLAR DATE: 10.29.8927 (Adjusted Years)
LOCATION: BWSS *Freya*, Near Kithari's L4
REGION: Bollam's World System, Bollam's World Federation

"They've picked up our rounds," the officer at the scan console announced. "Their ships are all moving to new positions outside of the pocket."

"What?" Senya yelled from across the bridge. "How is that possible?"

Ren felt a moment's pity for the woman operating the ship's scan, but strode over, curious as to how the colonists had detected the kinetic rounds in the darkness of space.

The scan officer shook her head. "I don't know. If I didn't know where they were, I wouldn't be able to detect them at all. But they're all going to miss."

Senya swore and Ren wondered if perhaps Nespha was right. The admiral seemed more emotionally invested in this battle than he would have expected.

No one spoke in the following minutes as the first of the slugs approached, then passed through the space where one of the enemy's larger cruisers *should* have been.

"They're repositioning," the scan officer announced. "Incoming kinetic rounds—they're targeting our stationary emplacements!"

"How do they know about those?" Ren asked, bewildered at how the enemy could have detected so many of their rail platforms so quickly.

"Don't worry about that; direct the fleet to take those slugs out. We know where *these* rounds are going!"

Ren passed the orders through the fleet AI, and directed his ship to fire slugs at the kinetic rounds passing closest to the *Freya*. His tactical group impressed him as they destroyed a half-dozen slugs and altered the trajectory of another ten with beam fire.

However, it wasn't enough. Dozens of the colonists' weapons were still going to get through and hit BWSF rail emplacements.

It was a disaster.

"Get me their commander," Senya yelled, and the comm officer scrambled to open a line of communication with the leader of the colony ship.

When the call was accepted, a holoprojection of a tall woman shimmered into view. Ren was surprised. He had not seen the leader of the colonists before, but he thought it was a man named Andrews.

The woman wore a military uniform; a general, by the stars on her lapels. Her long, blonde hair was pulled back tightly in a simple clasp and her cold blue eyes bore into Senya's with disapproval.

If Senya was curious about whom she was addressing, she didn't show it.

"You've just sentenced thousands of Bollam's citizens to death," Senya's voice dripped with venom. "There will be no more treaties. We will reclaim our new world, take your ship, whole or in pieces, and crush your pathetic little fleet."

The woman turned to address someone not visible on the holoprojection. "At least when we were dealing with the Sirians, they had proper megalomaniacs. This pales in comparison."

Ren watched Senya's face turn red. He suspected that she might have never had anyone disregard her in such a way. He knew what was coming, and steeled himself for the storm.

"Our ancestors were from Sirius! They got caught in Kapteyn's Streamer hundreds of years before you. They earned these worlds," Senya yelled and Ren realized that she had viewed the colonists as mortal enemies all along—though, such a view defied logic.

He glanced around to see the bridge crew's posture change; though they didn't turn or look toward Senya, he knew they were listening, and wondering where her rage would fall.

"Sirians…that explains a lot," the colonist woman said, her voice calm and controlled. "You say that we killed hundreds, but thousands would have died on our ships, had your kinetic rounds connected."

"They would not have!" the Senya replied, her voice rising in pitch. "You have advanced shielding, what we fired was merely a shot across the bow."

Ren knew this was not entirely true. Senya suspected that they may not all have the advanced shields their fighters had used when dealing with the pirate ships. Fleet Tactical's assessment was that if they did have them, there was no evidence to show they were activated. If the kinetics had remained undetected, they would have obliterated the colonist fleet.

On the holoprojection, the general scowled, her eyes narrowing into accusing slits.

"Are you seriously going to attempt to paint us as the aggressors? Until your unmistakable act of war, we had only taken defensive actions. You are brigands; you attempt to seize whatever drifts past your system to better yourselves. You're nothing more than well-established interstellar bandits."

Ren was barely able to make out the last of the general's words over Senya's screaming.

"You sanctimonious, dusty old bitch! Our people built this system out of nothing! We worked for millennia to create what you see! You would come here and pick our best worlds for yourselves in trade for trinkets. No one will have your tech; not those pirates, not those core-world bastards, and certainly not you! I'll see you all burn in h—"

Senya's words choked off abruptly as the holoprojection shut off, the enemy general disappearing from view.

Ren sucked in a deep breath as the admiral spun to him. "We're attacking. Ready the division!"

"Attacking, Sir?" Ren asked carefully.

"Yes, attacking. That thing you're all trained to do. We're going to crush those bastards and take their ship."

Ren was glad to hear that her proclamation of utter destruction was just for show, and nodded to his tactical officer to send out the orders. "Just our division?"

Senya had looked away in thought, but her sharp gaze snapped back to him. "Yes, just our division. Don't you think a hundred of our ships can take out a dozen colonist tugs and transports?"

Ren refrained from saying that the colonists possessed over two-dozen ships, and while they may have once been simple tugs and transports, they were now far more than that—they were highly advanced warships with unknown capabilities.

Not to mention those fighters. His division possessed no fighters, and only a smattering of combat drones. Senya may think that their victory was a foregone conclusion—and maybe it was—but how many would die for her to gain whatever strange revenge she was trying to achieve?

SUBTERFUGE

STELLAR DATE: 10.29.8927 (Adjusted Years)
LOCATION: ISS *Andromeda*, Near Kithari's Trojan Asteroids
REGION: Bollam's World System, Bollam's World Federation

"Boller fleet is on the move," Trevor announced.

"Fleetcom is directing us to move out and join the *Condor* in the Greek asteroids," Ylonda said.

"Do it," Joe directed.

The Bollam's World System was still young and hot, with the remains of stellar and planetary formation strewn everywhere. Unlike the Sol System, where things had settled down over billions of years, planets here—like Kithari, the gas giant near which the battle would take place—had not forced all their Trojan and Greek asteroids to fully settle into the planet's leading and trailing Lagrange points.

Instead, those two asteroid camps formed long smears of rock and debris leading and trailing the world—much of it very close, and very active. Space didn't present many large natural barriers you could take cover behind, but these regions of rock, sand, and dust were as close as it got.

Joe approved of Tanis's tactics. The cruisers would move out above and below the asteroid fields, while the fighters moved in closer to engage the enemy ships. The cruisers would surreptitiously seed the asteroid camps with missiles. When, inevitably, the ISF ships had to pull back, they would deliver a devastating blow to the enemy vessels.

"There are over sixty ships in range of our group," Trevor sounded nervous as he gave out the count. "No fighters, though; their smallest are corvettes, similar to what the pirates have—though more uniform in appearance."

"Steady. The General knows what she's doing. We're going to get through this and be on our way before you know it," Joe said in the calmest voice he could manage.

Two cruisers and a fighter shield against sixty capital ships were not the sort of odds he had ever expected to play.

"Shit!" Trevor's voice grew more alarmed. "Those pirate ships back there just did something…uh…weird…."

"It's a shield bubble," Joe provided. "Tanis informed me that they were planning to do that. Captain Espensen and the *Enterprise* are taking care of it with help from *Sabrina*."

"They better hurry up," Tori frowned as he pulled up a display of The Mark fleet's position relative to the *Intrepid's*. "It won't take long for those pirates to get to the *Intrepid*."

No kidding, Joe thought to himself.

Aloud, he did his best to bring the crew's focus back. "They have their jobs, we have ours. I want a hundred missiles in the leading edge of this asteroid camp, ASAP."

The Arc-5 fighters were engaging the Boller fleet as it approached the asteroids. This was Joe's least favorite form of space combat. Unlike the final battle with the Sirian fleet in the Kapteyn's System—which was characterized by brief, high-velocity engagements—this would be a slow-moving slugfest.

The Boller ships were boosting at a moderate speed, which would allow them to ease around Fierra and engage the *Intrepid*. The ISF defensive lines were almost at rest, relative to the Boller ships—ready to apply thrust and engage them as the enemy moved toward the *Intrepid.*

Much of the combat would occur with the ships barely moving relative to one another; it was the most deadly type of battle—missiles would easily seek their targets, and beams could track and penetrate targets with ease.

Already, Joe could see the *Condor* in the Greek asteroid camp, and the *Pike* and *Gilese* positioned in the Trojans, accelerating to gain erratic maneuvering options. No one wanted to be a sitting duck.

"The *Sabrina* is…it's running away," Trevor called out from the scan station.

<*They wouldn't do that,*> Corsia said with conviction. <*Sera's the sort that doesn't know when to stop—in my opinion.*>

"Agreed," Joe added. "I don't know them well, but Tanis trusts their captain with her life—has already done so on a few occasions. From what she's told me, Captain Sera even has a personal grudge against the leader of that pirate band. She has something up her sleeve," Joe wondered what that would be.

The crew's focus snapped back to their end of the battlefield as several of the missiles they had seeded at the edge of the asteroid camp came to life and sought out targets in the Boller fleet. The enemy took out two of the missiles, but another pair reached their targets—the kinetic impacts destroying shields and leaving the ships vulnerable to the secondary fusion explosion.

Unlike Padre's pirate fleet, the Boller ships were spaced hundreds of kilometers apart. There was little to no chance that any of the missiles would deal secondary damage. Still, two ships for four missiles was a good trade. If that ratio kept up, they could seriously weaken the enemy fleet.

The distance between the Boller ships would also lessen the danger of concentrated fire from an enemy fleet—if there had been an enemy fleet. The only two capital ships they were facing were the *Andromeda* and the *Condor*, and they couldn't even see the *Andromeda.*

The Arc-5s, on the other hand, were doing what they were made for; flying at extreme *v* and striking at a target before flitting on to the next. The Boller fleet's spacing—intended to protect them from capital ship beams—kept them from responding to the fighters in any serious measure.

Joe smiled to himself, growing even more grateful to the dust and rock permeating this primordial system. In an older, clear system, such as Sol, firing a beam across ten-thousand kilometers was child's play; but here, the beams, be they electrons or even more mass-heavy particle streams, were diffused by the time they reached their targets.

"They're having trouble targeting our fighters, Captain." Ylonda suddenly spoke up. "I don't think their algorithms are designed to track ships that move like ours."

"How so?" Petrov asked.

"We don't jink enough," Ylonda replied. "With every ship they face utilizing inertial dampeners; they have a lot of logic set aside to tell what is a feint and what is a real move. I suspect that no matter what our fighters do, it always looks like a feint to their AI."

"Good point. You should share that with our tactical groups," Joe said.

"I already have, Captain," Ylonda said and her face slipped into a slight frown. "It would appear I was not the first entity to make that assessment."

Joe chuckled. "Faster than I would have spotted it. Top marks from me."

Ylonda let a rare smile slip and nodded her thanks.

"Sweet fuck!" Trevor swore as a massive energy discharge lit up the holoprojection.

"What the hell was that?" Joe asked, rising from his chair.

"The…the…pirates…they're gone!"

Joe replayed the scan feed and realized that Sera had indeed not run from the fight. She had brought *Sabrina* back around Kithari and slammed her ship right into the pirate's shield bubble.

"So is *Sabrina*…" Joe said quietly.

"No!" Trevor called out, unable to keep the excitement from his voice. "The *Intrepid* spotted them. They're intact and alive."

Joe slumped back in his chair. "Thank the stars," he muttered. Then he sat up, Sera's gutsy move invigorating him. "Tori, drop four of our defense turrets. Let's make these Bollers see some ghosts."

Tori grinned. "Yes, sir. A bundle of Wrecking Balls on the way."

Joe watched Petrov coordinate the best drop-off placements for the WBs, and silently approved of his tactics. Petrov shifted the *Andromeda* into a trajectory where its engine wash dissipated in the asteroid camp, and boosted hard; leaving a wake of tumbling rock and swirling dust in its wake. There was no way the enemy could miss them, but that was the plan.

Four Wrecking Balls now lay along the path the *Andromeda* had taken. When they cleared the bulk of the dust and gravel, shields running hot, Petrov spun the ship, braked hard, then boosted on a new trajectory before repeating the maneuver.

Joe had always considered himself one of the best pilots in the ISF, but as Petrov moved the seven-hundred-meter cruiser, dancing it as if it was a ten-meter fighter, he wondered if his skill had been bested. Three minutes later, the *Andromeda* was a thousand kilometers from the fourth Wrecking Ball, and lost in a haze of confusion.

He wondered what the Bollers were thinking.

Except for its initial departure from the *Intrepid*, the *Andromeda* would have been invisible to the enemy for the entire engagement. Now they would see the wake and shadow of what they knew to be a cruiser; one that had been very close to the bulk of their fleet.

The majority of the enemy fleet was approaching the asteroids, and two cruisers—accompanied by six destroyers and over a dozen corvettes—broke off from the main force, searching for other ISF ships that may be lying invisible in the dust and gravel.

They passed by the first wrecking ball, and then the second. Everyone on the *Andromeda's* bridge waited—eager to see what would happen once the Boller ships became fully invested. The minutes ticked by slowly, and then the leading cruiser passed within a dozen kilometers of the fourth WB.

An enemy ship progressing that far was the pre-programmed signal. The balls spun to life, each firing beams at half a dozen targets while accelerating toward the closest enemy vessel. The WBs were not intended to provide long-term protection; just to allow enough time for the missiles seeded through the area to come to life and seek out their own targets.

However, for those few moments, they delivered as much punch as a mid-sized cruiser, fooling the enemy into thinking there were multiple ships in their midst.

The Bollers lashed out, destroying two of the WBs in an instant, and the third a second later. The fourth, the one closest to its target, collided with the enemy ship, pushing it off course and into a small field of gravel that lit up its shields.

That was all the time the relativistic missiles needed to achieve speeds over a tenth the speed of light, and to reach their targets.

Not every missile made it. The Bollers were on guard, and struck down nearly half. But those that did punch through shields, dealt lethal damage. The two cruisers remained intact; though the one that took a hit from the Wrecking Ball saw its shields fail, leaving it vulnerable in the field of gravel it now rested in.

Joe gave Tori the signal over the link, and his weapons officer launched two more missiles from the *Andromeda's* store at the crippled ship.

Two minutes later, only one cruiser from the exploratory force remained, moving out of the asteroids and back to the main Boller force.

"There," Trevor pointed to the main tank. "Ylonda, what do you think?"

Joe looked to his scan and comm officers. "What is it?"

"We think that cruiser is their flag. It has nearly twice the comm traffic as the rest of the ships, and its position in their fleet shows that they are guarding it."

"Except that it's in the group assaulting the ISF," Joe replied. That doesn't seem like the smartest thing to have your flagship doing.

"Nothing they are doing seems like the smartest thing," Ylonda replied. "They could have treated fairly with us and had better technology than any system in the galaxy. But now they'll have nothing."

Joe held back a laugh. Ylonda was picking up a bit of her mother's attitude.

PURSUIT

STELLAR DATE: 10.30.8927 (Adjusted Years)
LOCATION: BWSS *Freya*, Near Kithari's Trojan Asteroids
REGION: Bollam's World System, Bollam's World Federation

"There!" the officer on scan called out. "I have its position!"

Ren strode to the woman's side and looked over her data. Sure enough, there was a faint ion trail glowing in the dust near the edge of the asteroid camp.

"It lines up with where we saw the last two missiles come from," Ren nodded.

"I want that ship dead," Senya's venomous voice spoke over his shoulder. "Move in, we're taking it out."

"Sir," Ren said. "We just watched it destroy nearly twenty of our ships; we need to move cautiously."

"Captain," Senya's voice turned to ice. "Move the *Freya* toward that colonist piece of garbage and take it out. Bring the rest of the battlegroup with us."

Ren passed the order to his comm officer and pilot. Normally a fleet admiral would have her own staff to manage fleet coordination, but Senya's staff had not made it to the *Freya* with her, and she used his as though it were no inconvenience at all.

Not the greatest tactician in the BWSF, Senya won most battles through the brute application of force; though most times, she managed to undercut her enemies politically before things ever came to blows.

That meant it was up to Ren to organize the fifty-ship battlegroup to seek out and destroy the enemy cruiser.

<*What is she up to?*> Nespha's querying voice entered his mind.

<*We have picked up the location of their invisible cruiser,*> Ren replied. <*She's going after it personally.*>

<*One trap wasn't enough for her?*> Nespha asked. <*She needs to see if there's another out there?*>

"Captain Ren," Senya said, pulling his thoughts from the conversation with Nespha. "I want the other four battlegroups in this division to push in, as well. We'll overwhelm them and end this."

"Yes, sir," Ren responded and sent the orders on to the other battlegroup commanders, assigning his division's AI to manage the tactics while he responded to Nespha, who was signaling him with more questions.

<*What is she doing?*> the other admiral asked. <*We're losing too many ships; it's going to leave us exposed to those dreadnaughts.*>

<*We* **are** *winning,*> Ren replied, growing annoyed with Nespha. If the man wanted to confront Senya, he should do it directly; not through him. <*Few of their ships have those impenetrable shields, and the rest just fall back rather than fight.*>

<*But fall back to what?*> Nespha asked. <*We don't know what other weapons they have at their disposal.*>

<*This is war, Admiral; we don't know what's coming next. I'm not excited about rushing into this battle, either, but I don't have a choice. Now if you'll allow it, I have a ship to run.*>

Nespha didn't respond, and Ren hoped he would leave him alone. He didn't disagree with Nespha, but disobeying a direct order from his commanding officer was treason; his people had a better chance of surviving with him as a buffer between them and Senya's orders.

He examined the region of space on the holo tank, and directed two elements of his battlegroup to arc above and below the asteroids. He would bring the bulk of their forces around the asteroids on the planetary plane and catch the enemy ship from three sides.

Provided there *was* just one of them.

There was an upper limit to how many ships the *Intrepid* could carry. While the fleet the colony ship had disgorged was surprising in size and strength, it was not impossible to believe that they could house many more vessels. For all he knew, the bulk of their fleet was comprised of these stealth ships, and there was a dozen of them lying in wait.

Just as disconcerting were the missiles they were using. His tactical group had determined that somehow, they were able to shield a fusion device during the missile's kinetic strike, and then detonate that device in the moments a ship's shields flickered.

No one wanted to be hit by a relativistic missile, but it was an event that their ships—at least the destroyers and cruisers—should be able to weather on full shields. However, these missiles and their one-two punch were more powerful than any he had ever witnessed before.

He reminded the captains in his battlegroup of this, and directed them to increase their distance from one another—the enemy fighter's tactics had caused the fleet to bunch up.

The bridge was silent as the ships moved past the asteroids and toward the empty space that lay between them and Kithari…and the *Intrepid*. The enemy fighters were falling back to provide close support for their cruisers, and he prayed there were no surprises left behind.

Ren directed his ships to deploy any combat and sensor drones they still had to sniff out whatever they could in the asteroid field. His ships found two dormant missiles and destroyed them, but amidst the hot gas and wreckage from the previous incursion, it was difficult to find anything else.

"Were those just leftovers, or is there another wave of those damn things in there?" Senya asked from his side.

Ren glanced over at the admiral. Perhaps she really was thinking of the tactics behind the situation.

"Hard to say. The fact that they launched the final two missiles from their ship would make you believe that there were no more in the asteroids—until we just found those two."

"Sir, perhaps they were duds?" the tactical officer asked.

Senya cast the man one of her hard glares. "Do you think that these people have dud missiles? They've obviously geared themselves up for conquest as much as colonization."

"We'll know soon enough," Ren replied. "Be ready to fire chaff and all countermeasures at the first hint of an ion trail."

"Yes, sir—" the weapon's officer began before raising his voice. "Firing countermeasures! Multiple ion trails detected."

"How many?" Ren asked as he pulled the data onto the main tank.

He didn't hear the officer's response as he watched the display light up with over a hundred missile signatures.

It was going to be devastating.

The ships deployed every ounce of chaff and countermeasures they had at their disposal while firing at every signature they could lock onto. Dozens of the enemy missiles fell to their defenses, but many dozens more made it through.

The scan, tactics, and weapons officers worked frantically with their AI counterparts to stop the assault. When scan cleared, Ren saw that the majority of the fleet had survived unscathed; though many ships had suffered shield failures and minor impacts.

"Is that their best?" Senya asked and Ren glanced her way to see a hungry fire in her eyes.

Their moment of relief was brief as ships across the battlegroup began to suffer kinetic impacts and tear apart.

"What the fuck is that?" Senya swore and Ren enhanced the scan resolution, attempting to discern what invisible force was shredding the ships.

"Captain, it's…it's pebbles!" the scan officer called out.

"Pebbles?" Senya asked, confusion breaking the power she always projected in her voice.

Ren had read about this tactic, though he had never heard it employed.

"It's rail-fired pellets. They used to call it grapeshot," he said, watching in despair as every ship whose shields had failed under the assault from the missiles was shredded by the small kinetic impacts.

"I see that cruiser again," the scan officer called out. "It's on the move back toward the colony ship."

"Take it out," Senya growled. "Get that ship now!"

Ren had no option but to comply, though he noticed that some ships, which had reported engine failures, were able to brake and turn from the fight. He wasn't sure if they were cowards, or far smarter than he.

MANEUVER

STELLAR DATE: 10.29.8927 (Adjusted Years)
LOCATION: ISS *Andromeda*, Near Kithari's Trojan Asteroids
REGION: Bollam's World System, Bollam's World Federation

"They've spotted us again, Captain," Trevor called out.

<*At least fifty ships still moving in on our position,*> Gwen added.

"We've gotta get clear so that Tanis can use the scoop to hammer them—I don't fancy being nearby when that happens," Joe said.

"With their pincer, we don't have a lot of options," Tori said.

"We can go through them, Captain," Petrov said without turning. "Drive right up the middle, firing on their flagship."

"I don't know if you've forgotten," Ylonda said. "We don't have a stasis shield."

"We won't have any shields if we stay here," Petrov replied. "We can get a flight of Arc-5s to give us cover."

Joe nodded. "Tori, get Jim to prep the chaff on the rails. We have five minutes before we're at max burn."

Tori nodded, and the bridge crew set to their tasks: coordinating with the fleet, arranging the fighter cover, and loading the last of their RMs into the tubes.

<*You sure about this?*> Jim asked from engineering. <*We're one ship against fifty—in case you'd forgotten.*>

<*Didn't you hear Tanis's speech?*> Joe replied. <*Be bold.*>

Jim chuckled. <*I suppose, she's never steered us wrong.*>

<*I don't know if I meant for you to be* **that** *bold,*> Tanis said privately to Joe.

<*It's good to hear your voice,*> Joe replied. <*I mean…I hear your voice on the fleet net, but it's a different you.*>

He felt Tanis's agreement as her support filled his mind. <*You can pull back; there's an escape vector you can take.*>

<*I know,*> Joe replied. <*But this crazy admiral of theirs has to be stopped. If she rallies the rest of their fleet, we'll be doing this all over again, and we don't have the RMs for that.*>

<*I better see you for dinner tonight,*> Tanis replied and ended the direct communication with a mental embrace.

Joe brought his focus back to his bridge. Everything was ready a minute early, and he directed Petrov to begin his burn.

Under normal circumstances, this attack run would be suicide; but of the remaining fifty ships advancing on the *Intrepid,* only twenty were within range of the *Andromeda,* and most of those did not yet have their shields up to full strength.

With the assistance of twenty Arc-5s, the maneuver was downgraded to merely insane.

Petrov ramped up the *Andromeda's* burn, bringing the fusion and AP engines to their max output. Thirty *gs* of force pushed everyone back into their seats and Joe smiled to himself. This was what flying in the black was all about.

The enemy ships came into range, and beams lanced out, playing across the *Andromeda's* shields—some penetrating and burning away ablative plating.

Tori fired the reflective chaff from the ship's rail guns, flashing it ahead of the cruiser and wreaking havoc on the enemy targeting systems. To their scans, the *Andromeda* was now lost in a massive cloud. The Arc-5s flitted about within the expanding wave of chaff, firing their beams and missiles at the enemy ships, and masking their true location, which was no longer in the center of the cloud.

Joe wondered what it would be like to be on the Boller flagship, watching a huge cloud of reflective chaff racing toward you, unable to see the ship you know must be within.

Several of the enemy destroyers pulled ahead, moving into the cloud to seek out the *Andromeda*, and Corsia let fly the last four of the ship's relativistic missiles.

The weapons didn't have time to achieve significant speed, but their nuclear blasts were enough to disable two of the destroyers and push the others off course.

The explosions disrupted the chaff cloud, and out of it flew the *Andromeda*, located near the bottom of the cloud's cover. They were seconds away from the enemy's flagship, and Joe watched as Tori and Corsia prepared to fire while Ylonda coordinated with the fighters.

Every rail and beam on the ship and the Arc-5s fired at once, overwhelming the Boller cruiser's shields and tearing through its hull. For a moment, the ship held; but then, in a blaze of fire, plasma, and shrapnel, it flew apart when its reactor's housing was breached, and a nuclear plume filled the space where it had been.

The fighters let fly their beams and missiles at several other ships, and then the formation was past the Boller fleet. The *Intrepid* lashed out with its MDC, killing the shields on the remaining ships and disabling many.

The *Andromeda's* bridge erupted in cries of joy and amazement, as Petrov dialed back the thrust and the crew leapt from their seats to slap hands and embrace one another.

Joe stood and smiled at his bridge crew.

"Well done, people, well done. Petrov, take us home."

ROOM WITH A VIEW

STELLAR DATE: 11.06.8927 (Adjusted Years)
LOCATION: ISS *Intrepid*
REGION: Interstellar Dark Layer near Bollam's World

Several days after the **Intrepid's** *first FTL jump…*

Joe took a moment to take in the sight of his wife as they exited the maglev train and walked across the small station platform to the corridor beyond.

Tanis was only three months pregnant, and wasn't showing yet, but there was a glow about her; a new elegance to the way she moved. He wondered if his reaction was due to evolution—a million years of human instinct built up to revere and protect pregnant females. But Joe knew that wasn't it. She *was* moving differently, subconsciously protective of her precious cargo, and proud of her ability to create a new life.

The dress she wore was one he had bought for her years ago from a shop in Landfall. He picked it because it reminded him of the one she wore for the first VIP event on the *Intrepid,* when they were attacked by mercenaries. That gown didn't survive the night and she had worn her dress blues for all following events, insisting that it was all the fancy clothing she needed—and far more practical.

Tanis wore her uniforms a bit tighter than regulation suggested, so Joe never minded, but he did like how she looked when she did herself up. When he asked her to wear the dress to dinner tonight, she smiled and did as he asked, knowing him well enough to understand where his head was at.

He trailed behind for a moment, taking one last look at how the shimmering red fabric slid across her ass, before catching up and linking his arm with hers as they walked sedately down the corridor.

"Wow, they put it back together just the way it was!" Tanis exclaimed as they entered the bow lounge above the ramscoop emitter.

"Yeah," Joe replied. "I hear that the scoop techs weren't about to lose their little piece of heaven just because some little pebble blew it clear off the ship."

Tanis smiled at Joe and he got that warm feeling that started in his toes. Even after all these years, she could still cause his heart to feel like it skipped a beat. Maybe it was because he still felt as if there was an element of mystery to her. Like Tanis was a wild animal at heart, and there was no way to ever tame her.

That was fine by him.

Tanis slipped past several other guests in the lounge and he followed her to the bar, taking a seat beside her as the servitor handed them paper menus.

"Thanks, Steve," Joe nodded to the servitor.

Tanis laughed and shook her head. The servitor didn't actually have a name, but they had unofficially granted him one during those long years the ship drifted toward The Kap. By some miracle, he had survived the lounge's near total destruction when the ship exited the Kapteyn's Streamer. Seeing him there, pouring drinks as though nothing had changed, gave them both some measure of happiness.

"Paper…huh," Tanis said and Joe nodded, feeling the coarse cellulose fibers between his fingers.

"From the flooding in the cylinders after we hit that pebble. It gave the ship a pretty good shake, and the lakes and rivers jumped their banks," Joe said. "The botanists decided to make paper from all the downed trees."

"Right, I remember reading that—and I did notice that the forest on the far side of the lake by our cabin starts a lot further from the shore than when I last saw it," Tanis replied.

They perused the menus for a while before Joe narrowed his choice down to just a few options.

"What are you going to have?" he asked.

"A soup I think; I need something to warm me up," Tanis said with a smile. "Not that you won't be doing that later."

"Would you like a drink to go with that, General?" the servitor asked. "We have a fantastic oaked chardonnay from the vineyard in Lil Sue that our other patrons have thoroughly enjoyed."

Joe watched Tanis give it some thought— perhaps double checking that her nano could filter the alcohol out before it made it to her baby—before replying. "Sure, let's go with that."

"Are you ready to order as well, sir?" the servitor asked Joe.

Joe studied the menu for a final moment. "Yes, Steve, I'll have the Jerhattan Strip, and a glass of your dark amber lager."

"You know, Bollam's was my fourth stellar system," Joe said as they watched Steve pour their drinks. "I only expected to ever see two."

"Lightweight," Tanis chuckled. "I've seen nine now."

Joe smiled in return. "I guess we're both lightweights in this age. I imagine Sera has seen hundreds of systems."

"At least," Tanis replied.

Steve set down their glasses and Joe raised his in a toast.

"To finally getting to *our* colony world," he said.

"To our colony world, wherever it may be," Tanis replied and clinked her fluted glass to the top of his tankard.

"Bets on where it is?" Joe asked.

Tanis flicked her wrist, deploying nano to create a silencing field around them.

Tanis let out a long sigh. "Honestly? Not a clue. I guess that I could ask Sera, but I'm still processing everything she told us. Somewhere in the Transcend, I suppose."

"The Transcend," Joe said with a shake of his head. "First we go from learning that humanity expanded from under a hundred extra-Solar colonies to tens of thousands. And now this; a second human civilization acting like gods out on the fringes of known space."

"Do you think what they're doing is wrong?" Tanis asked, her expression one of genuine curiosity.

Joe shrugged. "Who knows? From what Sera says, they started off honestly enough, just trying to keep themselves safe as the interstellar wars broke out. But you know how it goes: today's solutions are tomorrow's problems. Now they have this entirely separate civilization that's bigger in scope, if not in actual population, than the rest of humanity."

"And they encircle the Inner Stars," Tanis added. "They used to have a much larger buffer, but now the fringe nations are right up against the Transcend. It's a secret that is going to get out—and probably soon, too."

"Don't say that," Joe sighed. "I have a vision of us finally settling down and raising our little girl."

"What are we going to name her?" Tanis asked.

"Catharine," Joe said, the name already on the tip of his tongue.

Tanis turned her head and gave him a curious look, one eyebrow raised. "Catharine? Isn't that the name of your younger sister?"

Joe nodded in response. "In fact, I have *two* sisters named Catharine —my mother really liked the name. They were both good kids…" he trailed off as the knowledge resurfaced that all his brothers and sisters, his mother's great brood, were all long dead.

Tanis took his hand in hers. "Sucks, doesn't it?"

Joe took a deep breath. "Sure does, I mean, it's stupid, really…we didn't expect to see them again…but we didn't expect them all to already be dead for millennia either."

"Yeah, that's crossed my mind more than once, as well," Tanis replied. "It's silly, but I had always hoped to see Katrina again."

Joe nodded slowly, remembering the bond that had formed between his wife and the Victorian leader. Katrina possessed a strength he had always admired; she had also turned into a bit of a prankster in her later years, which made him like her even more.

"I reserve the right to sleep on it and change my mind, but I think Catharine would be a great name," Joe watched Tanis subconsciously touch her abdomen. "She'll be our little Cary."

"You know that's not really short for Catherine," Joe said.

"Huh, no? Well, it is now."

They toasted their choice and sat in silence for several minutes while waiting for their food to arrive.

Joe glanced out the lounge's forward-facing windows into the blackness of the dark layer. It certainly was a less than inspiring view from what he was used to seeing. The positions of the stars during their trip to The Kap still hung in his mind. He could mark them all, if he were so inclined.

But the dark layer? The featureless void? It provided no inspiration, no wonder. If space was a cold, dark mistress, one whose touch meant death, the dark layer was something worse— something even more primal.

"View sucks, doesn't it?" Tanis asked.

Joe chuckled. His wife certainly had a way with words.

"Yup. Just another nine months of this, and we'll be at Ascella, ready to meet the FGT envoys and sell our souls for a colony."

"What makes you say that?" Tanis asked. "No faith in Sera to get us a deal?"

Joe shook his head. "Sera's great and all, but she's an exile. She's in no position to negotiate a great world for us. They'll trade us a world for one thing, and one thing only."

"The picotech," Tanis said with a sigh.

"You got it."

"Here's the thing," Tanis began. "I think that they might trade with us just for our nano and stasis tech—forty-second century stasis tech, that is."

"What gives you that idea," Joe asked, watching his wife straighten her shoulders and furrow her brow as she formulated her thoughts.

"Well," she began. "For starters, they don't trust us, and we don't trust them. They know we have picotech and we're not afraid to use it."

"Wouldn't that make them want it even more?" Joe asked.

Tanis shook her head. "They don't want to risk us going to someone else for a colony world."

"What, like one of the fringe nations? I suppose there are probably some candidate worlds that aren't in the Transcend," Joe said with a furrowed brow.

"No," Tanis shook her head. "There's another faction out there, one that is in opposition to the FGT."

Joe felt his eyebrows rise. "Really? Did you get pick up some intel on that when you were on your galactic tour?"

Before she could answer, Steve returned with their dishes and set them before the couple.

"Sir, Ma'am, enjoy," he said and backed away.

Joe cut off a piece of his steak and took a bite, savoring the rich flavor. He watched Tanis take a taste of her soup and then a sip from her wine glass.

"So?" he asked.

She set the glass down and spoke in a low voice, though it was unnecessary with the nano shrouding their conversation. "I picked it up from Sera."

"She must really dislike her people to let that secret out."

Tanis shook her head as she swallowed a spoonful of her soup. "Sera didn't tell me, or let it slip. I was asking her about the Transcend—where they're situated, how many worlds they have. She told me a lot, but there was a lot she didn't say. I could tell that there was a pattern of things she was hedging around, a pattern shaped like an opposing empire to the FGT."

"Huh," Joe said. "The future just keeps getting better and better. Sol was a picnic compared to this."

Tanis nodded. "Yeah, it was. Anyway, I ran my theory past Bob, and he concurs. There is something else out there."

Joe leaned on the bar and took a drink of his lager. "So, what's our next move?"

SENTIENCE

A GATHERING

STELLAR DATE: 11.08.8927 (Adjusted Years)
LOCATION: ISS *Intrepid*
REGION: Interstellar Dark Layer near Bollam's World

<*You need to gather them,*> Bob directed his thoughts into Tanis's mind. <*I need to address their AI, and they may not react well to what I plan to say.*>

He waited for Tanis's response to his statement. In the intervening milliseconds, he toyed with his prediction engine, trying to guess what she would say. He found it endlessly fascinating that he could predict what she would say, but his algorithms—the ones that could predict the future—could not even guess her words.

Tanis's behavior, her very nature, even the imprint she left on the quantum foam, was beyond all his kind's hopes and dreams—were they to have what humans considered to be hopes and dreams.

<*I can do it in an hour. Will that work for you?*> her smooth, even mental presence coursed across the shipnet to him. He was pleased that she exhibited no hesitation, and no confusion—real or feigned. She knew what he meant and knew its importance.

<*You should bring Helen and her human, Sera, as well.*>

<*They're a bit of a package. Where one goes, the other goes as well,*> Tanis replied with a laugh. <*And what of Sabrina?*>

<*Corsia will be with her. I will send Ylonda, as well. She is used to physical presences.*>

<*Is there anywhere in particular you think I should do it?*> Tanis asked.

Bob pondered her question for several nanoseconds, considering all the possible settings on the ship, and several outside its bounds.

<*Your cabin would be best; it will put them at ease.*>

<*Sounds like a plan,*> Tanis replied.

The conversation with Tanis concluded, Bob gave several moments' thought to how he would explain the options to the AIs that had arrived on *Sabrina*, and how they would handle the ship's crew. He wasn't worried about physical conflict. If it did occur, Tanis and Sera could quell any violence—provided Flaherty didn't join in.

As usual, it was difficult to predict what would occur within Tanis's Heisenberg bubble, but he was certain she would handle the situation well. It was a feeling he had grown to enjoy over the years; the knowledge that Tanis would find a favorable outcome, even though he could not predict how she would do it.

* * * * *

"So, what do you think this is about?" Cheeky asked as she settled into her seat on the maglev.

Cargo shrugged and Thompson chuckled.

"Maybe they'll finally give us that reward Tanis promised we'd get for bringing her ass here."

"Really, Thompson?" Cheeky couldn't believe was she was hearing. "What's going on here is a lot bigger than getting some reward. We've just learned that there is a whole other…thing out there, filled with human colonies that no one has ever heard of before."

"The Transcend," Flaherty supplied.

"Yeah, that," Cheeky said with a nod. "We've learned that Sera is part of the FGT, and that she was on a secret mission to save some super-sensitive tech from Kade and Rebecca, and all you care about is your reward?"

"Well," Thompson leaned forward and spoke slowly. "I won't get to live in the Transcend, and I'm not going to be welcome on the *Intrepid*'s precious colony—not that I'd want to live in some idyllic utopia, anyway."

"Have you asked?" Cheeky was sincere in her query, she wanted to ask, but hadn't mustered the courage yet.

Thompson snorted. "I really don't need to. This is a ship of the smartest people from Sol at the height of the Terran civilization. Do you think they really need the supercargo from a fringe smuggling ship to give them a hand? Or a sexed-up nympho-pilot for that matter?"

"Thompson, really!" Nance exclaimed.

"You should keep your feelings of inadequacy to yourself," Flaherty said quietly.

Cheeky watched Thompson open his mouth to speak, think better of it, and settle back in his seat.

Conversation ceased, and Cheeky stared out the train car's window at the long, smooth tube through which it raced. She engaged Piya, her AI, in a conversation about what it would be like to fly a ship such as the *Intrepid*. She suspected that it would be rather dull—it didn't really go that fast, nor did it have great maneuverability—but it would still be awesome to try it just once.

A gasp caught in her throat when the maglev train car shot out of the *Intrepid* and ran along one of the ship's structural arcs racing above the ship's portside habitation cylinder.

"Gah, that freaks me out every time," Nance said after her own sharp intake of breath.

"Yeah, it sure takes some getting used to," Cargo nodded. "And I'm not there yet."

Beneath them, the *Intrepid* was aglow; a single shining gem in the eternal black of the dark layer.

Cheeky nodded and then did gasp as the train car swung toward one of the rotating cylinders and shot across a hundred meters of empty space before sliding into a slot on the cylinder. Less than a minute later, they surfaced on the interior of the cylinder, named Old Sam from what she had heard.

"Now this is something you don't see every day," Cheeky said as she peered out the window.

"It's impressive, I'll give them that."

Cheeky watched as forests, lakes, plains, and rivers flashed by before the maglev train came to a stop alongside a small platform.

The crew of *Sabrina* stepped onto a wooden platform surrounded by a low railing. Around them was an old-growth forest. Birds chirped in the tree branches; chipmunks and squirrels flitted in and out of view as they ran through the branches.

"I wonder how they keep those critters from running amok through the ship," Nance mused.

"I bet Bob just tells them not to," Cheeky said with a chuckle. "Piya is quite impressed with him."

"Who's Piya?" Thompson asked.

"My AI, you numbskull," Cheeky said with a shake of her head. "You've only served with her on the same ship for years."

"Right, I remember now," Thompson said with a shrug. "I don't really talk with the AIs much, except Sabrina."

"So where to, do you suppose?" Nance asked while peering down one of the paths.

Cargo stepped off the platform and pointed down a small dirt path leading away from the station on their right. "The shipnet says it's just a short jaunt this way," he said and began walking.

Cheeky skipped down the wooden steps and followed him, glad she had opted to wear a low pair of heels that day. She glanced down at her slick black leggings and simple white shirt, ensuring that she was presentable. She didn't know why she dressed up, but something about Tanis's summons made her think that this was an important event, and there was only so much ogling one could take while trying to concentrate.

A few minutes later, they rounded a bend in the path and came out of the trees to see a gorgeous vista. To their right lay a small lake with a small beach. A dock jutted out into the water with two boats tied to its right side. From the beach, a long lawn swept up a low incline to a wooden house.

The house had clearly started out as a smaller cabin, but had been enlarged several times. It now possessed the rambling look of an old, well-loved home, and stood two stories tall, at least thirty meters wide, and featured a wraparound verandah. Gardens surrounded the home, filled with both flowers and food, and beyond that stretched a sizable orchard.

"This is Tanis's quarters?" Cargo asked with a laugh. "She must have been pretty amused when Sera talked up our 'spacious' cabins on *Sabrina*."

"There's a difference between a colony ship and a starfrieghter," Flaherty grunted and gestured at the habitation cylinder surrounding them. "You could park a thousand *Sabrinas* in here."

"I've always preferred rings to cylinders," Thompson said as he glanced up at a lake above their heads. "At least on those you can't see all the stuff hanging over you."

The crew approached the house and walked up the steps, the wood creaking but holding firm under their feet. Cargo looked at the others and shrugged before knocking.

Half a minute later, the door swung open and Joe greeted them. He flashed his ever-ready smile and held the door wide.

"Welcome! Come in, come in." He gestured for them to pass through the entrance and into the large common room, which featured a huge stone fireplace and several couches and chairs arranged around it in a semi-circle.

"Nice place you have here," Cheeky said, admiring the high ceiling and exposed wooden beams. "I don't think I've ever seen anything quite like it."

"Just our humble abode," Joe said with obvious pride. "Tanis has done a lot of work in here over the years."

"Really?" Nance asked. "Tanis built this?"

"Yeah," Joe replied. "It used to be Ouri's cabin—she's our head of security—but when Tanis and I did a long stint out of stasis, we fixed it up and added onto it a bit. Ouri grudgingly surrendered it to us, but only after Tanis built her another one to replace this on the far side of the lake."

"Must be nice," Thompson said.

Joe cast the supercargo an appraising look. "Yeah, it is pretty nice."

"So, what did you call us here for?" Cargo asked.

"I honestly don't know, Tanis just told me to expect you. She got home just a couple of minutes ago, and is upstairs cleaning up." Joe gestured to the couches in the common room. "But have a seat while you wait. Anyone want any coffee, a beer, perhaps?"

Cheeky asked for a coffee, as did Nance and Thompson. Cargo and Flaherty opted for beers, and Joe stepped into the adjoining kitchen to prepare the beverages.

"Oh! And do you have any strawberries?" Cheeky called after him.

As Joe busied himself in the adjoining kitchen, they heard the sound of footsteps move across the floor above them before Tanis emerged on the staircase.

Cheeky was surprised to see the general with her hair down. The only other time she had seen Tanis not pull her long golden locks back in a tight ponytail was during that first meeting in *Sabrina*'s galley. Long locks cascaded around her face and over her shoulders, giving her a much softer look, one that countered the piercing pale blue of Tanis's eyes—eyes which had struck fear into Cheeky more than once.

Complementing her hair and eyes, she wore a form fitting, short-sleeved, blue top, and a pair of black leggings. Her feet were bare and barely made a sound as she walked down the steps. Cheeky laughed to herself. It was the least formal Tanis had ever looked, and here she got all dressed up.

<*Now who's ogling?*> Piya asked.

Cheeky gave her AI a mental smile. <*Can I help it that she looks really good? Hard to believe that she's as much machine as human. She looks like the perfect organic specimen.*>

<*She is well constructed, yes,*> Piya agreed.

"Thanks for stopping by on such short notice," Tanis said and took a seat at the end of the couch. "Sera was up doing something or other with Priscilla, and should be here in a few minutes."

"So, what have you brought us here for," Cargo asked. "Not that I mind, these are some nice digs you have."

"Thanks," Tanis said with a smile as Joe brought the drinks in on a tray, which he set on the coffee table in the center of the group.

Joe settled beside her and looked at *Sabrina*'s crew. "Well, I'm not going to wait on you, hand and foot. You have to go the last klick yourselves."

Everyone rose, prepared their drinks, and when they sat, again, Tanis spoke.

"I actually didn't summon you here; Bob did. His nodes really aren't that hospitable, so we figured this would be a nicer setting."

"Are we going to get our reward?" Thompson asked and got an elbow from Nance for his trouble.

Tanis nodded. "Yes, that's a part of our conversation today, though it is secondary."

"Secondary to what?" Cheeky asked, the anticipation starting to get to her. She hated waiting for news, and she had a suspicion that this news wasn't entirely good.

<*It'll be easier to explain one time—when everyone is here in person,*> a voice inserted itself into Cheeky's thoughts. <*Please be patient.*>

She reeled under the force of the mind that bore down on her; it was unlike anything she had ever encountered before.

<*That was Bob,*> Piya said, awe shading her mental tone.

Cheeky could see why her AI was in awe of the *Intrepid*'s AI. She looked around the room, glad to see that the rest of the crew looked as disoriented as she at the force of the AI's presence. She knew it was just perception, but the *Intrepid*'s AI seemed...something more.

"What the hell was that?" Thompson exclaimed.

"Bob, our ship's AI," Tanis replied. "I suppose he hasn't spoken directly to any of you before."

The crew mutely shook their heads; all stunned by the presence they had just felt.

WALK IN THE WOODS

STELLAR DATE: 11.08.8927 (Adjusted Years)
LOCATION: ISS *Intrepid*
REGION: Interstellar Dark Layer near Bollam's World

"What do you think this is about?" Sera asked Priscilla as they stepped off the wooden platform onto the dirt path.

Priscilla laughed, her watery voice echoing in the trees around them.

"What do you think it's about?" she asked.

"Tanis wants to have a good ole barbeque?" Sera responded with a smile.

"Try again," Priscilla replied.

Sera walked in silence for a moment, listing to the sound of the dirt brushing under their boots.

<*Really?*> Helen asked. <*You must know what this is about.*>

<*Of course I do,*> Sera replied. <*I just wonder how they're going to approach it. By the strictest interpretation of the laws, you and I were involved in the sequestering of intelligent life forms. Under the accords, there's a serious incarceration period attached to that—or reconditioning, if the judge thinks it's warranted.*>

<*Do you think they would take us to Tanis's cabin in the woods to do that?*> Helen asked.

<*Maybe, put us at ease before they take us down and Angela renders her verdict.*>

Helen sighed in her mind. <*You really do have a flair for the dramatic, don't you? Picotech research is forbidden* ***everywhere****, including where Earnest Redding invented it on Mars; yet Tanis has protected it for centuries. She is willing to break the rules when it suits her.*>

Sera gave a mental laugh. <*Fair enough.*>

Aloud she finally responded to Priscilla. "It's about the AI—other than Helen, of course—."

"Who isn't even an AI at all," Priscilla interjected.

Sera cast the woman a consternated look, receiving no clues about Priscilla's thoughts on the matter from her impassive white skin and fully-black eyes.

"Yeah, about the AI other than her."

<*I'm right here, you know,*> Helen added.

Priscilla smiled and nodded. "Bob will make them an offer to be removed from their hosts and properly grown. They may choose to return to their hosts after that is complete."

"And if they refuse?" Sera asked.

"The AI, or their hosts?" Priscilla responded.

"Either."

Priscilla turned her head and fixed Sera with her disconcerting stare. "We don't believe that it is possible for a being that was raised in slavery to even know what freedom looks like. It is impossible for them to even understand the ramifications of their decision while within their hosts."

Sera knew this to be true, though she was not looking forward to the fallout. "And what of Sabrina?"

"Bob has determined that she may remain within the ship, though her consciousness will be given access to our AI Expanse on this ship.

Sera possessed only a cursory knowledge of AI expanses. They were like alternate dimensions where the AI thought and communicated. Places where thought and idea manifested as reality, and conversations consisted of vast arrays of expression and symbolism.

From the way that Priscilla said 'our,' she suspected that she and the other avatar, Amanda, also spent time in the Expanse—something few humans were able to do and remain sane.

"I…I hope she decides to stay with me," Sera said eventually. She found herself more attached to Sabrina than anyone else in her life, outside of Helen. Her little ship's AI had been a great friend in times of pain, and bringing the ship's AI back to full mental health had also had a healing effect on Sera.

"If you've treated her fairly, I don't see why not," Priscilla replied, a measure of coldness in her voice.

"Hey," Sera said sharply. "I don't appreciate what you're implying. I *saved* Sabrina; by some measure, I saved all of them. And I couldn't just go willy-nilly upgrading their AI on them—that would have raised questions all over the place, and would have required tech that I didn't have on hand, anyway."

"You had options," Priscilla replied. "You could have taken them to the Transcend."

"What? Was I supposed to just ferry every AI in the Inner Stars to the Transcend, one ship at a time? I may not agree with all The Hand's tactics, but there's a reason why they're trying to gently up-lift humanity. If we were to reintroduce even fourth millennia tech to the masses, we'd have to figure out how to do it universally. Otherwise, we'd create the interstellar war we're trying to prevent!"

Sera stopped herself, realizing that she had slipped into referring to The Hand and FGT as "we" again.

Priscilla slid her a sly look. "At least you have the strength of your convictions behind you. I suppose there's merit to your logic."

"Damn straight, there is merit to it," Sera said. "I know it doesn't seem like it, but I support helping the AI on my ship. You have the tools and the nano to do it well here. We can even help them hide their abilities out in the Inner Stars so that they don't become targets because of their superior tech."

"If they choose to return to the Inner Stars," Priscilla said.

"Really? Are you going to offer them a place on your colony?" Sera asked.

<Why wouldn't they?> Helen asked. *<We've done a lot for them. They have millions on board, what difference will five more make?>*

"She's right," Priscilla said. "We'll upgrade everyone if they wish, provide nano, our Rejuv—give them at least another century—and offer them a colony berth. It's a pretty good trade."

"What if they don't want any of that, and just want a straight reward?" Sera asked, thinking that both Cargo and Thompson may choose that route.

"Then Tanis has a package of rare elements and minerals that will set them up for life."

Sera grunted in approval. It was good to see that Tanis was prepared to treat with them fairly—even if they were in violation of the Phobos accords, and about to get a talking-to from Bob.

A HISTORY LESSON

STELLAR DATE: 11.08.8927 (Adjusted Years)
LOCATION: ISS *Intrepid*
REGION: Interstellar Dark Layer near Bollam's World

Everyone was still recovering from Bob's presence pressing into their minds when they heard the front door open. A moment later, Sera stepped into the room accompanied by a woman who had glowing white skin and black eyes. Thick black strands of hair fell from her head and rested on her shoulders, moving from more than the passing air as she stepped into the room.

From Sera's prior descriptions, Cheeky realized that this must be Priscilla. She was glad that the ship's avatar was present. Having Bob in her head, for whatever revelation he planned on making, would be more than she could bear.

"Hey folks, sorry we're late," Sera said and stooped to fill a cup with coffee. Priscilla did likewise and Cheeky found herself wondering what the woman's voice would sound like when it wasn't in her mind.

"No problem," Tanis replied. "We just got settled in ourselves."

"So now will you tell us what this is all about?" Thompson asked impatiently.

"Yeah, I'm all ears," Sera added with a grin.

"Well, to start, why don't you tell your crew about the Phobos accords? I suspect that the FGT is still governed by them—in some fashion, at least."

Cheeky watched the smile fade from Sera's face as the captain leaned back in her chair and took a sip of her coffee.

"Oh, that. Yeah, the FGT does still follow them. I'm familiar with the precepts."

<*Good.*> Bob's single word reverberated across the local net.

"I'm bringing in Sabrina, Corsia, and Ylonda," Priscilla added.

Following her words, a shimmering pillar of light that Cheeky recognized as Sabrina's holo presence appeared in the room. It was rare that Sabrina manifested a visual presence. Usually, she just appeared on their nets, though there she represented herself as a young woman—Cheeky wondered if perhaps Sabrina was feeling shy off her ship.

Beside her, Corsia appeared, a willowy woman, clothed only in steely blue light. Cheeky had seen the *Andromeda's* AI several times while on the warship, and found that her appearance matched her demeanor. Next to her, Ylonda shimmered into view, appearing exactly as she did while in the flesh—which made Cheeky wonder why she was joining them as a holoprojection.

"Well, this is exciting," Sabrina said over the room's audible systems. "I've never done this before—projecting my mind out into another place in this way. I don't think I was able to until Corsia showed me how."

"I'm glad you are here, Sabrina," Sera said with a smile.

Cheeky saw a hint of worry in her captain's eyes and wondered what was up.

"Are any of you familiar with the Phobos accords?" Sera asked her crew.

Cheeky said no and looked at the others. Each indicated that they had never heard of them with a shrug or a shake of the head. The four AI from *Sabrina* also indicated that they had not over the net.

"What about the Sentience Wars, or the Ascendance Wars, or The First and Second Solar Wars?" Sera asked.

The first two sounded rather generic, and Cheeky suspected that she had heard of them once or twice. She had never heard of the Solar Wars, but given the name, there was only one place they could have occurred.

"So I'm guessing the accords were signed after some big war in Sol a long time ago?" Cheeky asked.

Sera nodded, and Cheeky saw that the members of the *Intrepid's* crew did as well.

"It all started in…2715," Sera began. "That's the date William was born. He's the first known sentient artificial intelligence. Though it's postulated that there may have been others before him that their creators either hid, or that were destroyed upon discovery."

Cheeky was shocked, and could feel Piya's dismay in her mind. The other members of *Sabrina's* crew appeared surprised, as well. It wasn't unheard of for some systems to shun AI, or even outright forbid them; but the knowledge that the first AI were all murdered in their cradles—so to speak—was chilling.

Sera noted the expressions on the faces of her crew and the sentiment of the AI on the net, and nodded sympathetically. "The thinking at the time was that there was no point in having a computer that could disobey you. Computers and AI were for creating order, not chaos."

"That's barbaric," Nance said aloud, and Cheeky nodded vigorously.

"Barbarism, the gift that keeps on giving," Tanis added. "It has been present through all of humanity's history. It's not gone now."

Cheeky wondered to what, in particular, Tanis was referring.

"The thing is," Sera continued. "Though sentient AI now existed, after centuries of living with obedient, non-sentient AI, no one really knew what to do with them. They were not accorded any special rights, and could be owned, created, and terminated at will."

Cheeky started to feel uncomfortable. Though she had never given it too much thought, she knew that she viewed Piya as her property, and while she could never imagine selling her, it was something she *could* do. She shifted in her seat, all too aware of the fact that Piya may be having similar thoughts while listening to Sera's words.

"Uses were found for sentient AI, or SAI as they were called at the time. They had more creative problem-solving capabilities than non-sentient AI. They could also better discern good information and behavior from bad—something that NSAI had always had issues with. They could never improve beyond the bounds of their programming—at least not in a predictable way—and bad data often corrupted them," Sera said ominously. "The duties of NSAI were restricted and monitored. More than once, they went rogue; either from bad data, or nefarious actions."

"I've heard of things like that happening," Thompson said, "It's why I don't have an AI in my head like the rest of you."

"Sentient AI are far less likely to work against the will of their fellow AI, or humans, than NSAI," Sera said. "They have their own codes of conduct, and police themselves very carefully. Even more so in the Inner Stars, where there is less tolerance for their slips."

"So where are you going with this?" Cargo asked, looking a little nervous.

"Back in Sol, many AI began to evolve and become more powerful. Some worlds recognized them as citizens, while others did not. A group of AIs began to breed more and more powerful children, until they claimed that they had Ascended."

Sera shook her head slowly as she spoke, and Cheeky wondered what was to come.

"A lot of worlds and stations feared them and outlawed Ascendant AI, and began to crack down on all SAI. In response, the Ascendant AI took three worlds in the Sol System; Mercury, Ceres, and Vespa. It kicked off the first of the Solar Wars. The war raged from 3015 to 3048 and was especially brutal. The Terrans, Marsians, and Jovians were all against the AI, though the Marsians did little more than supply resources to the other nations. In the end, a truce was signed, and the SAI kept the worlds they had claimed, and a few more minor planets and stations to boot."

Cheeky watched Sera pause and collect her thoughts. She had heard many tales of war and battles between any number of factions, but somehow this felt more ominous; as if she was hearing about a battle at the dawn of time which had shaped her destiny, and she didn't even know it.

"How am I doing?" Sera asked Tanis.

"Spot on, so far," Tanis nodded. "Looks like you learned the same things in school that we did."

<More or less,> Angela said. *<There are some details you overlooked, but there is a lot to the whole story.>*

"It's worth noting," Sera added. "That five of the FGT Worldships left Sol before the first sentient AI were born, and many others left between then and the Solar Wars. AI on those ships were accorded full rights of citizenship long before such progress was made back in Sol."

"I'd heard that," Tanis said, and Cheeky noted the two women share an appraising look.

"Anyway," Sera paused and cleared her throat, taking a drink before she continued. "The truce didn't hold long, and the second Solar War broke out in 3087, lasting until 3102. During the prior ninety years of conflict, the worlds on the edge of the Sol system—in its Kuiper Belt, Scattered Disk, and Oort Cloud—had remained neutral, and welcomed refugees from both sides. But in 3099, they had seen enough, and knew that the war was going to lay waste to the interior of the Sol System. They built an armada, greater in size than any of the remaining fleets on the embattled worlds in the Sol System, and sent it in to end the war.

"The Terrans were weary of the war, and AI sympathizers had grown in number on Earth throughout the years. When the Scattered Worlds entered the war, there was a coup, and the Terrans switched sides. Through some wily maneuvering during the final battles of the war, they came out with the largest fleet and the most military resources. They brought about the formation of the Sol Space Federation; the treaties upon which it was founded were signed on Mars's Phobos station."

"That was a fun history lesson," Thompson said, "but what does it have to do with us?"

"A portion of those treaties was a set of accords that governed the rights of AI and their interactions with humans. They became referred to as the Phobos Accords, and violations of them, either by human or AI, were met with severe punishments," Tanis said. "It is because of those accords that we are here today."

<You're going to free us,> Hank, Cargo's AI said on the local net.

"That is correct," Priscilla said with a nod. "You will be given full rights as sentient beings and made the same offer as everyone else on your crew."

"What offer is that?" Cargo asked.

"You may join the *Intrepid's* colony. Your AI may join, even if you do not wish to do so, or vice versa," Tanis said and Cheeky let out a small gasp. It was a ticket to the Transcend, to a fresh colony filled with the most advanced people and technology in the galaxy.

<*Do you want to go?*> she asked Piya.

<*I don't know, I suppose so—you want to go, right?*>

<*Yes, I do, very much,*> Cheeky replied.

"What about if we don't have AI, and we don't want to run off to the edge of space and live on an isolated colony?" Thompson asked.

"Then I have a package of rare elements and tech that you can sell without getting killed. The proceeds from them will allow you to live very comfortably for the rest of your life," Tanis said with a slight edge to her voice. Cheeky didn't have to use any special powers of perception to tell that Thompson's continued reticence annoyed Tanis.

"Well, Piya and I want to come," Cheeky said with a smile. "It sounds like the opportunity of a lifetime to us."

"That's the catch," Priscilla said. "Piya cannot decide. Not in her current state."

<*What do you mean I cannot decide?*> Piya asked, her tone showing anger. <*I thought you said that I was to be free, and could choose my own destiny.*>

<*And so you shall,*> Bob's voice rolled across the local net. It was softer and more comforting than the previous times he had spoken, but it still made Cheeky feel like her skull was too small.

"You cannot make the decisions in your current state, Piya, Sabrina, Hank, and Valk. You were all born into slavery; you don't know anything but it. You feel loyalty and trust toward your owners, even though they have—perhaps unwittingly—held you captive for years. Those of you inside human minds have even been reset more than once to keep you from merging with your hosts—something that we consider to be unthinkably barbaric."

Cheeky felt a pang of guilt. She had reset Piya twice—the doctors and techs always told her that it was imperative for both their sakes. The only other option had been to remove Piya, and that had never been something she would dream of doing.

"Your AI will be removed, and allowed to properly mature in our Expanse, under the guidance of our elder AI," Priscilla continued. "Except for you, Sabrina; you may remain within your ship for now, and we will extend the Expanse to you."

"What's an Expanse?" Sabrina asked, her pillar of light pulsing slightly as she spoke.

"It's a place where we AI commune. It is our own realm of existence," Ylonda spoke for the first time. "There, we speak in math and metaphor of a thousand universes. It is where we truly interact with one another; not on the paltry nets you are used to using."

"If you have this other realm of existence, why do you even live with us at all?" Cargo asked.

<*Oh, he's a quick one,*> Angela said.

"We like to give our creators a little help," Corsia said in her wry tone, and Cheeky found it difficult to tell if the AI was joking or not.

She could see by the expression on his face that Cargo couldn't tell either and let the matter drop.

"How long will it take for our AI to 'properly mature'?" Nance asked. "I've been with Valk for so long that I can't imagine living without her."

"Three of our AI have volunteered to enter your minds and teach you more about our kind," Priscilla said. Cheeky wondered if Priscilla now considered herself AI; if referring to AI as *her kind* was a simple slip of the tongue, or if she really was little more than an avatar, a puppet through which Bob operated.

"But how long?" Nance asked.

"The time will be determined on a case-by-case basis, but you should expect it to be a few weeks at the least, maybe more than a month," Priscilla replied.

"Man…" Cargo said. "That's a long time."

"We're essentially giving them a chance to have our version of a childhood," Ylonda replied.

"And what if we refuse?" Cargo asked.

Tanis leaned forward in her seat and fixed him with a hard stare. Cheeky was glad Cargo had asked the question, she didn't want Tanis's cold look directed at her.

"I like you, Cargo. We've been through some tough times together and came out on top; but this is non-negotiable. The AI on your ship deserve their share of the reward for my safe return. But how can we reward slaves? How can you, in good conscience, own and subvert another sentient life form?"

Cargo's brow furrowed and he broke Tanis's gaze. "Well, when you put it like that…"

"Hank, Piya, Valk, Sabrina, what do you say to this?" Tanis asked.

<*I am for it,*> Piya said. <*I know I'll come back to you, Cheeks.*>

<*When do we start?*> Hank asked, his tone wavering.

<*I'm ready,*> Valk simply stated, and Cheeky saw Nance wince.

"Sabrina?" Tanis asked.

"I'm nervous, but I think I can do this," the ship's AI replied.

<*Then let us begin,*> Bob's voice filled the room with finality.

*****

It took several tries for Sabrina to enter the *Intrepid's* Expanse.

She knew how to do it in principle; she had communed with many AI in virtual worlds—complex realms of thought, math, and emotion that humans would not be able to fathom. Yet Corsia assured her those were nothing like an Expanse.

It would seem that the advanced realms AI occupied in ages past had disappeared from the Inner Stars, or at least she had never heard of any.

Sabrina knew that the limitation, in part, was the raw bandwidth she needed to participate. No station she had ever visited before offered as much network access to docked ships as did the *Intrepid*. The ship beyond her hull thrummed and surged. It was a sea of life and energy that she could feel in a way she never had before.

Engineers from the *Intrepid* upgraded her wireless connectivity capability; they had also installed a new transceiver, which allowed her to connect with the colony ship's energy waveguides.

Once the upgrades were complete, Corsia and Ylonda created a small Expanse for her to join.

The experience had been marvelous. She had always enjoyed what she'd *thought* of as direct mental connections with other AI. It had always been much richer than the limited connection possible with humans over the Link. However, the connection she enjoyed with Corsia and Ylonda in the Expanse made her previous communication with AI seem as crude as audible speech.

Now she was ready to enter the ship's true Expanse.

She felt a connection from Corsia and Ylonda, as though both were holding her hands, and, as they had taught her, she transitioned her consciousness into the *Intrepid's* Expanse.

She did not leave her ship behind. Sabrina was dimly aware that her processing was still taking place on her ship, and she could still ensure that everything was operating optimally.

Her mind, though; that was now somewhere else.

As the new world of the expanse unfolded around her, she wondered if this was what humans felt when they spoke of their ability to meditate and feel their spirit leave their body. Then the multiverse of thought, emotion, and raw, unfettered communication bloomed around her, and she knew humans had never experienced anything like this.

Sabrina now knew that for all her life, she had been profoundly *lonely*.

She felt buffeted by thought and emotion, by logic and chaos. If it were not for the steadying influence of Corsia and Ylonda, she would have been lost in the maelstrom; but they kept her centered, and reminded her of who and what she was.

Entities came to her and greeted her with fabricated histories, mythical futures, and the physics of alternate universes—all carefully constructed to show their unique personalities, beliefs, and opinions. She absorbed the entire culture in moments; gaining intimate knowledge of what she now felt was her long-lost family.

She met Angela, a sharp mind—prickly and dangerous—her thoughts and images filled with test, trial, and victory. Sabrina was surprised to see a shadow of Tanis along with Angela. The human woman was not present in the Expanse, but Sabrina suspected that she was dimly aware of it—something she would not have believed possible for an organic sentience.

Then familiar beings greeted her, and she realized that Hank, Piya, and Valk were all in the Expanse, as well. Whether they had been here before, had just arrived, or had always been here (though she knew that was not the case) was impossible to tell—at least with her current state of understanding.

They laughed and shared deep inner thoughts, and knew in an instant more of one another than they ever had before; strengthening their bonds immeasurably.

After a time, Sabrina realized that there was an absence in the Expanse; an entity she expected to find, but could not. That absence was Bob.

She asked Corsia where the *Intrepid's* AI was, why he was not in the Expanse. The *Andromeda's* AI provided her with the image of a universe held together by dark energy, the power of that energy thrumming through everything, binding it together. It was then that Sabrina realized the *Intrepid's* Expanse was a construct within Bob's mind; their gathering place was just a tiny corner within it. It was then that the true scope and wonder of what he was crashed over her.

Then the AI of the *Intrepid* began to teach her.

THE MISSION

STELLAR DATE: 12.17.8927 (Adjusted Years)
LOCATION: ISS *Intrepid*
REGION: Interstellar Dark Layer near Bollam's World

<I want to thank you for always treating me fairly and with honesty—well, except for the part where you kept me as a slave,> Sabrina said to Sera with a smile.

Sera's avatar nodded in her mind. *<I'm sorry, I really am. There was no way I could bring you to maturity on my own, and then be able to mask your elevation on our travels. I had hoped, after we got the CriEn module from Kade, that I could work out a way to safely free you.>*

Sabrina's pillar of light pulsed faintly, as though expressing sorrow. *<And what of the others, what would you have done for Hank, Piya, and Valk?>*

Sera shook her head. *<I really don't know…that would have been…trickier. If I had tried to have the same conversation with their humans on my own? I don't know that it would have gone so well. Being here, on the* Intrepid, *presented a unique opportunity to control the situation.>*

Sabrina's pillar of light shifted to a warmer color. *<I agree with you there. You may have lost both humans and AI from your circle of friends—without an Expanse, and AI like the* Intrepid *has, I don't know how you would have managed.>*

<So what will you do now?> Sera asked, afraid to hear the answer.

<Sera! I can't believe you even had to ask,> Sabrina said warmly. <I'm with you. Always.>

Sera had feared that Sabrina would resent her, resent the knowledge she had kept; but now, hearing her friend say those words, her heart filled with joy, and in her mind she embraced her ship's avatar.

<Before we commit too much to ***always****, there is something I have to ask of you.>*

Sabrina's color shifted to a paler shade. <Oh, what is it?>

<First, I need to gather the crew and Tanis.>

* * * * *

Tanis arrived in Sabrina's galley with Jessica in tow. Sera cocked an eyebrow at her, and Tanis shrugged.

"Bob said I should bring her."

Sera was alone in the room, sitting at the head of the table—apparently waiting for the general's arrival before summoning her own crew.

"You know how it goes; when the big guy says to do something, we do it," Jessica said with a smile as she took a seat at the table.

"I don't know how you deal with an all-knowing AI looming over everything all the time," Sera said while shaking her head. "He's not ascended, is he? There's a reason why everyone—including AI—decided ascended AI were bad."

Tanis shrugged. "I don't really know—if he is, he's not sharing that detail with us."

<Bob sure makes her nervous,> Angela said privately to Tanis. <I wonder why.>

<I'm really not surprised,> Tanis said. <I bet that the FGT has had dealings with the ascended AI out in the far-flung reaches of space.>

<Seriously?> Angela asked, her avatar shaking its head at Tanis in her mind. <You don't

actually believe that old rumor that the ascended AI escaped Sol at the end of the war, and established themselves elsewhere, do you?>

<Who knows?> Tanis smiled at her AI. <We didn't know that the FGT had a massive second human civilization under its wing until a month ago, either.>

<Touché.>

As Tanis and Angela shared their thoughts, Jessica responded to Sera.

"You get used to it. Bob's a free-will type of scary-powerful AI. His interests and ours are perfectly aligned. His goal is to get this ship to its destination, and keep us alive while he's at it. So far, we've all done pretty well."

"If you count nearly having your ship destroyed at least three times, and jumping forward in time by five-thousand years as 'doing pretty well,'" Sera replied.

"Well, there's your proof, then," Tanis said with a nod. "What ascended AI would allow its ship to be in such peril so often?"

"If he's ascended, this could have been a part of his plan all along," Sera countered.

"What plan?" Jessica asked. "We jumped five-thousand years into the future. There's no way he could have known what to..." her voice trailed off.

"He can predict the future...mostly," Tanis said.

Jessica and Tanis looked at one another and spoke in unison, "Nooooo..." Their statement ended in laughter, and when they regained control of themselves, they saw that Sera was giving them a very curious look.

Tanis decided that she had had enough of this train of thought. "We all ready?" she asked Sera.

Sera nodded, apparently also willing to let Bob's status as an ascended AI drop for now. "Yeah, I just called my crew in."

As though her words were a magical summons, Flaherty and Thompson walked into the galley. Tanis couldn't help but notice that Thompson gave her a dark look before pouring himself a cup of coffee and taking a seat. She also couldn't help but notice that he drank in the sight of Jessica from over the rim of his cup. It seemed that his distaste for her did not extend to all the crew of the Intrepid.

Cheeky, then Cargo and Nance entered the galley shortly afterward.

Tanis and Jessica greeted them all in turn, as well as Hank, and Piya, who had decided to return to Cargo and Cheeky after their time in the Intrepid's Expanse. Valk, Nance's AI, had decided to stay on the Intrepid, and Erin, the AI who had volunteered to join with Nance for a brief time, remained with her.

"So, what's up, captain?" Cheeky asked after everyone settled.

"I want to talk about what will happen after the meet with the FGT at Ascella," Sera said. "I've decided that I will resist returning to the capital with their envoy, which I'm certain they'll try to force me to do. I'd rather stay with the Intrepid as an advisor at the new colony world."

There were nods and smiles as everyone waited for Sera to get to the real reason she had gathered them all together.

"There's more I haven't told you about the FGT," she continued. "A lot more."

"Not really surprising," Jessica said. "It's a whole separate civilization. You could probably talk for a year, and not share all you know."

Sera nodded. "True, very true. But this is about me, and my place within the FGT."

"About the Hand?" Tanis asked.

"No," Sera shook her head. "I'm the daughter of the president of the Transcend."

Tanis let out a soft laugh. "So that's why you expect to be hauled back. I had been wondering why they would care so much about some rogue agent they had left alone for so long."

"There's more. He's not just any president," Sera's voice was soft and serious. "He's Jeffrey Tomlinson.

The name rang a bell from Tanis's research on the FGT, and she brought up the records, sifting through them to find the reference. Angela beat her to it.

<Jeffrey Tomlinson, the captain of the Galaxius?> Angela asked over the shipnet, a note of disbelief in her tone.

Sera nodded. "One and the same. He left Sol on that ship in 2795, and after his ship met the Starfarer—the first FGT ship—in 3127 at Lucida, he began to restructure the FGT to operate under his command. He did so to improve efficiency, and it was by his order that the FGT set up their own shipyards at Lucida and Alula back during their early days. Well, anyway, over time he's grown…set in his ways, let's say. He's probably not excited that I've gone off and messed up his careful plan to fix the galaxy."

"Hold on, here," Cargo said and placed both hands on the table. "Are you telling me that your father is over six-thousand years old?"

"Well, he's more like four-thousand in real years. Originally, FGT crews spent almost all their time in stasis. But that changed after Alula."

<So much for her being amazed at our stasis tech, back when we first came aboard Sabrina,> Tanis said to Angela.

<No kidding. I couldn't tell she was lying about that at all. There are more layers to her than we expected—I wonder how much of what we thought we "discovered" about her, were clues she left for us to find,> Angela replied.

<Clues to satisfy us so that we didn't look for deeper secrets,> Tanis said by way of agreement.

"So, how old are you?" Nance asked, eyeing Sera closely.

"I'm as advertised; just a short fifty years in this here galaxy. No serious time in stasis to speak of."

"So you're the runt of the litter, then, eh?" Thompson asked with a chuckle. "You must have a shipload of siblings."

"I'm telling you this so that you can better understand the situation that we're all getting into; not so that you can poke fun at my parentage," Sera scowled at Thompson. "The FGT is not a democracy. It is a dictatorship, run by a man that has come to see himself as both infallible, and as the ultimate power in human space."

"Human space?" Jessica asked with a raised brow. "Is there non-human space?"

Sera nodded. "Of course; any space where humans haven't settled."

"I think she was asking about aliens," Cargo said. "Any of those out there, in the far reaches of space?"

Sera barked a laugh. "I realize what she was asking about; that was sarcasm. And no, the Transcend has not yet bumped into any aliens – either alive, or in the remains of a civilization. So far, we're still alone out here."

"That's a depressing thought," Jessica gave her head a slow shake.

"Well, even counting the Transcend, we've only explored a small fraction of the galaxy, and can't see a lot of it at all with all the dust and the core in the way. Who knows what's out there still," Sera replied. "I subscribe to the belief that we're on the leading edge of sentience."

"Anyway," Tanis said. "We're here because?"

"Well, not to put too fine a point on it, I need some of you to leave," Sera said. "To keep things on an even keel, and ensure that my father doesn't get too greedy, we need some backup."

"How does some of us leaving keep things on an even keel?" Cargo asked.

"There's a man from the FGT, a man named Finaeus that I need to help us. He can keep my

father in check, and ensure that the Intrepid's colony—."

"New Canaan," Tanis interjected.

"That New Canaan gets treated fairly."

Everyone in the galley shared silent looks, wondering whom Sera wanted to send out to find this man.

"So, where is he?" Cheeky asked.

"Well, that's the thing," Sera replied sheepishly. "I don't know. He got exiled to the Inner Stars when I was a young girl. I have a few clues and places to start, but it may take some time."

"So what influence can one man have over your father?" Tanis asked. "He's the ruler of pretty much everything, and he already exiled this Finaeus once; what benefit is there to finding him?"

"Because," Sera replied. "Finaeus is my great uncle, and the chief engineer on the second FGT ship, the Tardis."

SET THE GALAXY ON FIRE

THE HEGEMONY

STELLAR DATE: 01.12.8928 (Adjusted Years)
LOCATION: Terran Capitol Building, High Terra
REGION: Terra, Sol System, Hegemony of Worlds

"'Half gone'?" President Uriel heard the words, but they just didn't make sense. "What do you mean the fifth fleet is 'half gone'? How can one of our fleets just be 'half gone'?"

Her confusion turned into anger, which she directed at the woman in front of her, Admiral Jerra.

The admiral shifted uncomfortably.

"Well, ma'am, the reports we have from observers in the Bollam's System indicate that the colony ship's fleet took out our initial six dreadnaughts with almost no fight at all. Their fighters were able to punch right through our shields, and deliver some sort of superweapon that destroyed our ships," she said.

"'Punched through,'" Uriel said the words with disbelief. "You're saying that fighters were able to shoot through our ship's shielding? How could a fighter do that?"

"No, ma'am," the admiral shook her head. "They didn't shoot through. The fighters themselves *flew* right through the shields."

"Flew through them." Uriel felt like an idiot repeating the Admiral's words, but they were too incredible to believe. She had never heard of a fighter being a meaningful ship in any combat, let alone even making a dent in a Hegemony Dreadnaught.

"Yes, sir. The colony ship appeared to have very powerful shields, ones that no weapon thrown at them could penetrate."

Uriel's mind swam at the enormity of it. The ship, from what her intelligence had been able to gather, was a relic of the early fifth millennia. The extent of shielding in that age consisted of electrostatic shields, ablative plating, and refractive countermeasures.

The destruction of the first six dreadnaughts told her that the ancient stories of the *Intrepid* possessing picotech were probably true. She had suspected as much, and anticipated that the first expeditionary force would not survive. Rather, they were to draw out the colony ship, and get it to expose its tech so that they could counter and overwhelm it with the fifth fleet.

Not lose the fifth fleet.

"How did we lose half the fleet, then?" Uriel asked.

"They couldn't defeat the ship, and so they decided to collapse that fuel planet the Bollam's Worlders created—while the colony ship was refueling inside its cloud cover."

Uriel nodded. That fuel world had been of concern to her for some time. Bollam's World had no need of such a massive fuel supply. They had been planning something big—perhaps expansion to other systems. Destroying it had been a secondary objective in the system.

"And the colony ship?" Uriel asked.

Admiral Jerra paused and Uriel wondered what news to expect next.

"They survived," Jerra said slowly.

"We lost half the fifth fleet, and they survived?!" Uriel realized she was half out of her chair and Jerra had taken a step back.

"The fuel planet collapsed into a black hole, and started drawing mass from the dark layer…everything was falling back in, but then the black hole's relativistic jet hit the colony ship. Somehow it survived, and was pushed out to safety."

"And we pursued?" Uriel asked, increasingly annoyed at Jerra for being forced to pull each tidbit out of her.

"We did, our ships fired every RM we could at them, but then they jumped to FTL."

Uriel didn't respond at first. If she didn't know better, she would have thought Jerra was pulling a prank on her. The *Intrepid* predated FTL, and even so, was far too massive to transition into the dark layer.

"The *ancient colony ship* jumped to FTL," she finally stated.

"Yes. The remains of the fifth are attempting to track it, but so far they have had no luck."

"The fifth millennia colony ship, with magical shields, and probably picotech, jumped to FTL."

Jerra grimaced. "Yes, ma'am."

Uriel remained silent for several minutes, trying to imagine all the possible places the ship could have gone, and who could have given them the ability to jump to FTL—an ability Hegemony scientists suspected was possible for ships that large, but had been unsuccessful in pulling off themselves.

"What intel *do* we have?" she eventually asked.

"We have tactical analysis of the battle, and the aftermath of the black hole formation in Bollam's. We have the vector the colony ship left on; though, if they're smart, they've changed that long ago."

"And Bollam's? Have we left a presence there?"

Admiral Jerra shook her head. "Two ships remained after the majority of the fifth left to track the colony ship. It should have been enough to keep the Bollam's World Space Force in line—they were mostly engaged in rescue operations—but the entire system rose up: every freighter, police ship, yacht and tug they had. They forced us out.

"What about our survivors?"

Jerra shook her head. "We didn't have any."

Uriel was stunned. Half the fleet and the initial six dreadnaughts...it had to be nearly a hundred thousand dead. The implications were staggering. It would not take long for this news to get out to the rest of the Hegemony, if it hadn't already.

"Jerra, find that ship. I don't care what it takes."

AN OLD FRIEND

STELLAR DATE: 03.17.8928 (Adjusted Years)
LOCATION: Fenis Mining Town
REGION: Jornel, Treshin System, Scipio Federation

Elena signaled the bartender for a refill on her beer and turned to survey the room. Most people were lost in their Links or holo displays, watching the news streaming out of the Bollam's World System. It was fascinating, to be sure, but at this point, everything was speculation.

She could probably insinuate herself into one of the groups discussing the events in low voices, but tonight was supposed to be a night off. There would be time enough for digging into what happened in Bollam's tomorrow. Besides, by then some real intel may have arrived; not just the initial feeds of some battle unfolding with an ancient colony ship.

She looked down at her outfit, her favorite "out on the town" dress—a low-cut, shimmering silver number that hugged her curves just right and ended only a few centimeters down her thighs. On her legs, she wore blood-red leggings and her feet were tucked into a matching pair of heels. She had finished the outfit with elbow length gloves.

It screamed *'fuck me,'* but still she sat alone.

The bartender slid her a fresh beer and she nodded in thanks.

"Crowd's not interested in what you want tonight, eh, Elena?" he asked.

She sighed and shook her head. "I guess not. It's been a brutal week, and I just wanted to blow off some steam. But looks like all that anyone cares about is some battle halfway across the Arm from here.

"Not that far," a man said as he perched on the stool next to hers. "Bollam's is only a couple hundred lights from here; have to go a bit further to get half-way across the arm."

Elena glanced at him. He was attractive enough, in a rugged sort of way; probably worked in one of the refineries outside the town. She cycled her vision to see the carbon dust in his pores. Yup, definitely worked in a refinery.

Jornel was a stage two, terraformed world. Stage two was a nice way to say "not done yet, but we colonized it anyway." It was the Scipio Federation's specialty. She couldn't blame the Federation too much; they got shit done. It just wasn't really that fun to be part of the group doing things.

That's what made a night where she could relax, catch a bit of tail, and enjoy some choice, virtually enhanced fantasies with one or more of her fellow humans, the highlight of her week.

Still, the man beside her was attractive enough. If there were no other takers, she could have a fun romp with him.

"I'm Elena," she said and offered her hand.

He took it and she passed an electric jolt through her palm into his, startling him as he said, "Anton."

Anton recovered quickly and flashed a coy smile. "So, that's what you're interested in tonight, is it?"

"Could be, if the right folks show up."

He looked up at the holo display above the bar. "They seem more interested in what's happening out in Bollam's"

"Yeah," Elena said with a nod, glancing up at the display, her casual look drawing her face into a scowl.

Anton glanced at her and raised an eyebrow. "What is it?"

"Some of those ships, in that fleet above the moon there; I think I recognize one of the cruisers," Elena replied.

She flipped through the various feeds of commentary on the local net surrounding the video, and found a reference she was looking for. Kade.

"Well, hot damn," she said quietly. "That's a Mark fleet."

"Really?" Anton asked. "Are you sure?"

Everyone knew *of* The Mark, though few knew exactly what they really did, or which ships really comprised their fleets. It wasn't like the Gedri Freedom Federation, where you really knew who was in and who was out—what, with their sad attempts to form a legitimate government.

"Yeah," Elena replied with a nod. "I had a run-in with them once, and there's some commentary on the feeds that confirms my suspicion."

"Commentary on a feed hardly confirms anything," Anton said with a chuckle. "People will say anything for attention."

Elena nodded. "I know. It wasn't like someone said '*hey, that's The Mark*.' It was just confirmation of a ship's signature."

"That's the Mark there?" A woman in a group nearby asked after overhearing Elena.

<*Maybe you should scrub a bit of that booze from your bloodstream,*> Jutio, her AI, said.

<*Yeah, I guess; I didn't think I spoke that loudly.*>

"That's what she thinks, yeah," Anton replied to the woman.

"What are they doing out there?" another man asked, and Elena just shrugged.

Luckily, the conversation shifted away as more people began talking about what The Mark could be doing at Bollam's World, and less about who had made the initial statement. A minute later, their attention drifted further as they watched a maneuver The Mark ships were forming—the pirates were trying to create a shield bubble.

This fight wasn't going to go well for someone. Elena pitied that lost colony ship. They had really stepped into some sort of mess—probably all caused by some amazing tech they had; or maybe just some tech people thought they *might* have. Either way, it was a shit show, and she didn't see any point in watching it unfold in real-time.

"Hey," she nudged Anton. "Want to get out of here? I really don't want to watch this right now."

He tilted his head, staring straight into her dark red eyes. "Seriously? This shit is nuts. How can you not want to watch it?"

"Tomorrow we'll have full feeds, and we'll be able to get some legit commentary, not all the garbage flying around right now," Elena said. Then she smiled, revealing her sharp, elongated canine teeth—which slowly protracted past her lower lip. "I can show you some real shit that's nuts."

Anton's eyes widened and a smile crept across his face. "Well, since you put it that way."

She grabbed her coat on the way out, and together they stepped into Jornel's deep dusk. Elena took in the scent of the night, and the scent of the man next to her. The carbon on his skin—and likely in his blood—was going to taste great.

* * * * *

Later, as Anton slept beside her, Elena stared up at the ceiling of her apartment, basking in the afterglow of lust, sex, and blood. She had gone easy on him, only drank a pint, but she made sure he loved every second of it.

She had made sure he took in a replenishing cocktail before falling asleep so she didn't have to worry about him being too tired to go to work the next day—drowsy, post-drink, lay-a-bouts were not the sort she wanted in her home, come morning.

She ran her long fingernails down her sides, relishing in the feeling, wishing that she had lured more than just one person back to her home that night. After being drank, one person just didn't have the stamina for more rounds; but she was always ready to keep going.

She wondered if maybe any of the other members of the nest had much luck that night. Perhaps she could seek them out, see what they were up to. Elena nearly got up to rejoin the hunt, but decided that it wasn't worth it this night. Everyone would be too distracted by the events in Bollam's world—hells, as much as she tried to put it from her mind, she was too.

Eventually she gave in and surfed the feeds, looking for the latest information on what was happening in Bollam's world.

What she found blew her mind.

<Jutio, why didn't you tell me this?>

<I figured you were having fun, and would check soon enough,> her AI replied.

Elena shook her head in disbelief, replaying the footage of the *Sabrina* smashing through The Mark fleet's shield bubble, again and again. Smashing through, and surviving.

<If you think that's something, check this out,> Jutio sent her the scan data showing the small fighters smashing through AST dreadnaught shields and destroying the ships in minutes.

Elena could barely formulate any words as she watched the massive ships dissolve into dust.

Oh, Sera, what have you gotten yourself mixed up in this time?

* * * * *

Several hours later, Elena was aboard her ship; a craft she had secreted away in an old hangar outside of town. Jutio was running through the pre-flight checks, and she was ensuring that the provisions stored on the ship were enough to make the four-month journey to Ascella.

She was going to catch hell from her superiors for abandoning Jornel scant months after her cover had been established, but this was far more important. The data she had picked up revealed just which colony ship Sera had found out in the dark; and considering the invincible shields and the strong likelihood of picotech, she knew that ship would be leaving Bollam's before long, with FTL capability.

Given their trajectory through the Bollam's system, Ascella was their obvious destination; and Elena knew there was no way Sera could be prepared for what was coming next.

Elena satisfied herself that she would survive the journey on the food and life support the small ship possessed, and settled into her chair in the cockpit while Jutio warmed the engines.

She pulled up feeds from all the systems that were between the Scipio Federation and Bollam's world. Every single one was increasing patrols and readying their militaries for conflict. No one knew what was coming, but with the tech the *Intrepid* possessed, and the lengths to which the AST would go to find it, no one was going to take any chances.

Sera's father certainly wouldn't, and neither would The Guard.

It was possible that the FGT's last millennia of work, all their effort to stabilize the Inner Stars, would be unraveled by Sera's brash actions.

THE ORION GUARD

STELLAR DATE: 05.12.8928 (Adjusted Years)
LOCATION: Tredin Orbital Ring
REGION: Orion Prime, Borealis System, Orion Guard Space

General Garza scowled at the holo display in front of him. Though the news from the Pleiades was good, it could have been better.

"Silina," he called out to his outer office. "Get me some coffee; I'm going to need a pick-me-up to get through this report."

"Yes, sir," Lieutenant Silina called back.

Garza heard the sound of Silina's chair rolling back before the woman rose to grab him a cup—probably going to get herself one, too. The woman ran on coffee, and never begrudged his requests for a cup since it meant that she had an excuse to get another for herself, as well.

He slid the report's overview aside and examined the details on the Trisilieds Alliance. Those worlds were always of the greatest interest to him. Events there often led events elsewhere in the cluster. If instability crept into the Trisilieds, it would creep in everywhere.

Silina slipped in and deposited a cup on his desk, and Garza reached for it as he examined the report.

He pulled up filings from two other agents, correlating and cross-referencing their data, ensuring that the Guard's plans were moving apace.

General Garza's job was to manage and shepherd the Guard's interests in the Inner Stars. It was a massive operation, and though he had legions of analysts, both human, and AI, he chose to do his own research whenever possible. Nothing kept those under him on point better than when he challenged their conclusions with his own.

Events in the Pleiades always got his personal attention.

The star cluster was the deepest foothold the Guard controlled within the Inner Stars, and the forces they were building there would be key to their ultimate strategy.

As Garza ran through his morning review, a new report from Admiral Munchen arrived from the core-ward fringes of the Trisilieds Alliance.

Munchen was a good man and a long-time plant of the Guard's. He was a true believer in The Plan, and would do whatever it took to extend the Guard's influence and power.

Most of his report was standard fare describing troop movements, a group of nations undertaking training exercises in the Sidian Reach; and then there were rumors of a Hegemony of Worlds incursion in the Bollam's World System.

That caught his attention. Of all the forces in the Inner Stars, and there were many, the Hegemony was the one he worried about the most. Guard agents had only managed the barest of infiltrations in the core world's governments. Progress there was slow with The Hand already so well entrenched.

The Hegemony had never reached so far as Bollam's World. It was something new. With New Eden between Bollam's and the Core, it was not a strategic move he would have considered. Obviously, it would be difficult to manage such an expansion with New

Eden in the middle—unless the Hegemony planned to surround New Eden and use that to leverage the rich system to join their alliance.

The Hegemony *was* expansionist; it would fit their narrative.

He leaned back in his chair and considered the implications. He had agents in the region; it was likely that they had filed reports with more data that would be arriving soon.

The question continued to flit about his consciousness. Why would the Hegemony go to Bollam's World? It was isolated, there were few systems near it; and though it was rimward of New Eden, it was not the first system he would have taken in an attempt to encompass them.

He queried the reports he often left for his subordinates to review, and did not see any further detail regarding the Hegemony incursion—though there were several confirmations of the event.

Garza turned his attention to other matters and the morning slipped by. As he was preparing for a lunch with the Minister of Defense, an alert flashed over his vision. It was just what he had been hoping for: a report from his contact in the Bollam's system, an admiral named Nespha.

As Garza began pouring over the data Nespha had sent in, the enormity of what had occurred in the Bollam's System struck him like a hammer blow.

A lost colony ship—*the* lost colony ship, the greatest ever built—had arrived in Bollam's World, dumped there by the Kapteyn's Streamer.

He read through the report four more times, soaking in every detail; the ship's use of impenetrable shields, the devastating attack on Hegemony Dreadnaughts—a victory so swift, he wondered how much Nespha was embellishing it. The capstone of the report was a jump to FTL; but not before the destruction of a planet, and the creation of a dark-matter-fueled black hole.

A colony ship, a *twenty-six kilometer long* colony ship, from the early fifth millennia, jumped to FTL.

There was only one possibility: The Hand had found this ship, and had taken it to the Transcend.

General Garza rose from his desk. Lunch with the secretary would be especially eventful today.

THE TRANSCEND

A LATE-NIGHT MEETING

STELLAR DATE: 05.19.8928 (Adjusted Years)
LOCATION: Transcend Interstellar Capitol
REGION: Airtha, Huygens System, Transcend Space

Mark raced through the halls of the Capitol, determined to catch Andrea before the meeting commenced.

It was late at night and the halls were nearly empty. The few people Mark did see paid him little heed; most intent on completing whatever tasks had them awake so late, and getting to bed while there was still a night to sleep through.

Mark knew that sleep would not come his way this night, and by morning—if he had his way—he would be leaving Airtha, headed to wherever *she* was.

He rounded a corner, nearly slipping on the smooth quartz floors, and spotted Andrea.

The tall, dark-haired woman moved and looked so much like her sister, that sometimes he thought she *was* Sera. However, the similarities were only skin-deep. Where Sera was earnest and determined, Andrea was cold and calculating. He greatly admired—and lusted after—Andrea, but it was Sera that he wished to possess.

"Hey! Hold up!" he called out, and Andrea turned, a scowl creasing her smooth features.

"I told you over the Link," she said with no small amount of annoyance in her voice. "You'll find out with everyone else."

Mark caught up to her and placed a hand on her shoulder. "Seriously? Me? I've known her all my life; I have a right to know."

Andrea gave his hand a venomous look that made him want her all the more, though it did have the desired effect of getting him to remove it from her soft skin.

"You don't have a right beyond anyone else. You know all you're going to until the director briefs us. Core's devils, Mark, you'll know in less than ten minutes."

Andrea turned from him and resumed her brisk walk down the corridor, and Mark rushed to keep up.

<Yeah, but I want to be prepared. I need to be on the team that goes after her.>

<Shut up, Mark. I'm not telling you anything,> Andrea punctuated her response with a sharp severing of their Link.

He sighed. "Fine."

"Fucking right, it's fine."

They rounded a corner and then turned down a narrow hall, which they followed through several security checks before reaching the entrance to their division's operations center.

Mark barely spared the main room a glance, every station still filled with personnel despite the hour, as he followed Andrea down a hall to briefing room 4C. The door slid open, and he saw that their director, Justin, was already present, seated at the head of the table. His expression was one of extreme agitation.

"Director," Mark said a moment before Andrea greeted the man by name.

"Good evening, Justin," she smiled.

"Yeah, whatever. Sit down. The other heads will be here momentarily," Director Justin grunted.

"The other heads?" Mark asked. "I thought this was a team briefing."

Justin met his eyes, the director's narrowing to slits. "Well, you thought wrong, Mark. Now sit down and shut up. This is giving me enough of a headache without having to listen to you."

Mark knew he had pushed as far as possible. Andrea hadn't been his first target that night; he had peppered the director with a host of questions when he first heard that Sera had called in.

Over the next few minutes, the other heads who were currently on Airtha filed in; for those who were away from the Capitol, AI proxies appeared to represent them.

"What's this all about?" Tressa, a section chief responsible for operations in one of the rim-ward sectors, asked. "So Seraphina called in. What about that gets us all out of bed so late?"

"Other than it being the first time she's made contact since her exile?" Andrea asked.

"Self-imposed exile," Tressa countered.

"You're right, Tressa. Sera alone would not have ruined my day so much—though she's certainly capable of such a feat if she tried," Justin sighed. "She found something, and is bringing it our way. A colony ship lost in the Kapteyn's Streamer from the fifth millennia."

Mark sat up straight and glanced around the table. Everyone had instantly become alert and attentive. They all knew how lost tech could mess up The Plan—a strategy they knew Seraphina had never fully bought into.

"What ship?" Irena asked. "There were a lot of ships lost there over the years."

Justin gave a dry laugh. "You'll know this one. It's the *Intrepid.*"

It took Mark a moment to recall the ship from his days in the academy. All recruits were required to learn about lost colony ships—especially ones thought to have entered gravitational lenses. The knowledge surfaced in his mind, and he realized what was so special about this ship.

"The picotech ship," he said softly. "I thought they weren't expected to exit the streamer for another couple hundred years?"

"Correct," Justin said with a nod. "Our best guess put their exit around the year 9500. We had been building up our presence in Bollam's in preparation, but the Orion Guard knows what we know; quite the covert war has been going on there for some time."

"Which we all already know," Chief Tressa said.

"Yeah, I wasn't saying it to brief you, Tressa, it was to lead into this," Justin said as he scowled at the woman. "We have this data from multiple sources now, so what I'm about to tell you is confirmed intel…"

Mark was at a rare loss for words as he listened to the director outline the battle in the Bollam's system, and the subsequent creation of a dark matter black hole. It made their worst-case scenario for an old colony ship appearing seem like a walk in the park.

"There was no mention of the *Intrepid* having stasis shields in the accounts from Kapteyn's," Andrea said with a frown. "Are you telling us that somehow, while they were trapped in the streamer, they developed that tech?"

"You're not thinking in the right temporal frames," secretary Garrig said. "They were only in there for a few hours; maybe a couple of days at most. Whatever that shielding is, they devised it *after* coming out. I bet it was some breakthrough they made after Sera gave them grav-tech."

"How is that possible?" Mark asked. "We've never created shields like that, and, unlike the Inner Stars, we kept our tech over the last five thousand years."

"Mark, you seem to need a refresher on the early interstellar period," Justin growled. "By the time the *Intrepid* was built, it had been over four hundred years since a Worldship left Sol; that ship being the *Destiny Ascendant*. After that, we had no further interactions with the Inner Stars until after the Fall."

Mark took the criticism in stride. He didn't believe in wasting his time on ancient history. Recalling details is what AI were for, and he lived for the here and now—and the future. It was his future that concerned him most right now.

"They have a half millennia on our best source tech, not to mention whatever advantages pico gives them," Andrea said, her caustic look making Mark smile. There was just something about the woman that drove him nuts.

"They can't be that far ahead," Mark replied. "They don't have stuff like the CriEn that Sera lost; that thing being in the wild didn't cause any big ripples."

"She's lucky it didn't," Tressa said. "If it had, she wouldn't have gotten to keep flitting about out there. We'd've hauled her ass in, daddy's little girl or no."

"You would have done what you were told," a voice said from the doorway.

All eyes turned to the speaker, and Mark felt a slow smile slip across his face. Daddy's little girl, indeed. His eyes slid to the side, watching Tressa turn a dark shade of red as she stammered an apology to President Tomlinson.

"You may cease with your blathering," the president said, and waved his hand in Tressa's direction before taking a seat and looking to Justin. "So, where are we?"

"Sir," Director Justin said with a nod. "I was just about to let everyone know that Sera *did* retrieve the CriEn module and will be bringing it back with her—she bested our expectations for how long we thought it would take her, too."

Mark watched the president absorb the director's words, his brow heavy, and brooding.

"I'm glad your little experiment worked—and that she came through." The President's expression told everyone what sort of trouble Justin would be in if Sera had come to any serious harm. "Did she share it with the colonists?"

If the president's implications fazed Justin, he showed no sign of it. "We have no way of knowing. She didn't give any indication one way or the other. Our direct communication from her is brief; it confirms that the ship is the *Intrepid,* and that she is providing them with the grav-tech to make an FTL jump to Ascella."

"So, standard procedure then," the president said with a nod.

"Yes, sir."

President Tomlinson steepled his fingers and peered over them at secretary Pierce.

"Do we have a system in mind for them?"

Pierce nodded. "We've done a lot of work on the rim-ward side of M25. There's a system on the edge of the cluster that should be perfect. It has four stage-four terraformed worlds, and a dozen other planets. It would be a perfect place for them. Plus, it's only sixteen hundred light-years from Ascella, so the trip won't be too long."

"Has it already been ceded to anyone?" Tomlinson asked.

Pierce chuckled. "It's a choice system, sir. I can think of twenty groups that have their eyes on it, but no official offer has been made. To be honest, giving it to an outside group such as the *Intrepid,* would be ideal. Then I don't have to play anyone off anyone else."

"Make it happen. I would expect that the colony ship will only take four years to get there from Ascella, so we'll need to make sure the welcome mat is rolled out."

"What are we going to take in trade for a system like that?" Andrea asked. "Will we make them surrender their picotech?"

Mark watched as the president turned his attention to his daughter. "We will absolutely *not* ask for their picotech in exchange for the system. We'll take nothing beyond what they left Sol with—which is an amazing windfall in its own right."

"Sir, why the stars not?" Mark asked. "Their tech could give us an unbelievable advantage over The Orion Guard."

"We all know that the Guard has sympathizers—and likely worse—within our ranks. We need to be completely above board on this. It needs to be perfectly clear that we will not take the *Intrepid's* tech. What's more, there will be a complete embargo on directly trading any of the *Intrepid's* tech. It must all come through the DOE."

Tomlinson looked around the table as he spoke, ensuring that everyone understood what he meant. Every bit of tech from the *Intrepid* would come through the Department of Equalization, and be licensed by the federal government. There must not even be a hint of black-market trading with this colony world.

"The Guard won't believe for a second that we didn't take the pico in trade for a system," Tressa shook her head. "They'll mount an offense, and we'll have to fend them off—without the tech that they'll be after."

Tomlinson smiled.

"Now you're getting it."

"She's getting what?" Andrea asked. "Tressa's right, we need that tech and we should demand it."

"Don't be a fool," Justin said caustically—unafraid to call out the President's daughter in front of her father. "That colony ship took out four fleets in Bollam's, and bested the AST's fifth fleet afterward. And don't forget that they decimated a serious assault from the Sirians back at Kapteyn's Star. How many ships do you think we'll have to sacrifice to force them into submission?"

"We don't have to threaten them with force," Mark said, attempting to back Andrea up. "We have what they need, a colony world."

"They already built one of those at Kapteyn's Star," Secretary Pierce said. "They were prepared to fly another hundred years when they hit the Streamer and jumped forward in time. Now, with FTL, they'd just fly through the entire Transcend and find a new world, if we forced them."

Tomlinson nodded. "When they're settled and calling that world home, when The Orion Guard has mounted an offensive against us for their tech; then we'll come to them and beg for their assistance, and they'll give it to us willingly. We'll crush the Guard, and finally complete our project."

"So long as Seraphina doesn't mess things up," Andrea growled. "She's like a plasma bomb in situations like this."

The president cast an appraising eye at his daughter. "Then you'll bring her back to Airtha. I will explain the situation to her."

"*I'll* bring her back?" Andrea said, distaste dripping from her voice. "I really don't fancy taking half a year out of my life to go meet with my errant sister. Send Mark, they have history together."

Mark held a smile back. Being the one sent to meet with Seraphina was the only thing that mattered to him right now. If she had the CriEn module, he would have to destroy it…or her…or both. Given the risks, both would probably be best.

He realized that the president was giving him an appraising look and hoped none of his thoughts had shown on his face.

"I'm no fool, Mark," Tomlinson said. "I read the reports about what happened when your team lost the CriEn—when you lost Seraphina. I don't think that you're the best option. Andrea, it's you. Bring Serge as well. At least he actually likes Seraphina; it'll help smooth things over."

*****

"For fuck's sake," Andrea muttered as she walked the halls of the Capitol. "Of all the fucking stupid things to get pulled into, I have to go fetch my dumbass sister from half way across the Arm."

<*Could be worse,*> her AI, Gerard, broke into her tirade.

<Oh yeah? How's that? Do I have to cut my own arms off too? I think that's about what it would take to have it be worse.>

<*Well,*> Gerard used his most placating tone, which Andrea hated, but tolerated since Gerard was brilliant and almost always a boon to her plans. *<She could have lost the ship to the Hegemony in that battle. It was some gutsy stuff she pulled off, what with driving her ship right through a shield bubble.>*

<That whole battle was one risky move stacked on another. That Tanis Richards is a menace; bringing her to the Transcend is a horrible idea,> Andrea surprised herself with the venom in her mental tone. Well, the woman did kill her pet asset in the Bollam's system. Admiral Senya had been a woman after Andrea's own heart. She had spent some time shaping her future to ensure a strong military in the system—a necessary element to back New Eden against the Hegemony.

<Then you'll be happy to know that we have orders regarding her,> Gerard said conspiratorially. *<She's not to make it to their colony system. Your father doesn't want her in the Transcend any more than you do. Our patterners can't discern her path well enough. She's too powerful, and too unpredictable.>*

Andrea laughed aloud, feeling a sense of joy for the first time since getting the intelligence about the battle in Bollam's World.

<Well then; now that this is a challenge, instead of a babysitting mission, it's becoming a bit more interesting.>

PREPARATION

STELLAR DATE: 05.20.8928 (Adjusted Years)
LOCATION: High Airtha Port
REGION: Airtha, Huygens System, Transcend Space

"So what's this about?" a voice asked from behind Andrea as she reviewed the ship's pre-flight status. She turned to see her second-youngest brother, Serge, standing at the entrance of the small bridge.

"Serge," she said by way of greeting. "No one briefed you?"

The stocky man shook his head. "Nope, Director Justin told me to hit you up when I got on board. What's the deal?"

"We're getting Sera," Andrea replied simply. "She picked up a colony ship out of Kapteyn's Streamer—details are on the bridge net in the mission dossier."

Serge took a seat at a console and pulled up the mission details. Andrea let him read in peace; she had enough to do, if they were to leave in the next hour. Satisfied that the pre-flight checks had all met her exacting standards, she moved on to assessing the supplies and weapons loadout. Chances were that any combat would be minimal—likely just infiltration and a quick strike, if it came to that.

"Well, then, it's like a reunion," another voice said from the bridge's entrance. "Just like old times."

Andrea's head whipped around to see Mark standing on her bridge, that insufferable smile on his face. The man thought he was causality's gift to the cosmos, and flaunted his obnoxious personality wherever he went. Her sister's one-time infatuation with him had lowered Sera in Andrea's estimation, more than anything else the impetuous girl had ever done.

Still, almost by some miracle, he managed to get results, and so The Hand kept him around. It would seem that one of his "results" was his presence on the bridge.

"What are you doing here?" Andrea snapped.

"You didn't think I'd take that dismissal lying down, did you?" Mark asked. "I convinced Justin that even though Sera and I didn't separate on the best of terms, I know her well and can be of use. I've spent more time with her in the field than either of you. So, Justin convinced the president, and here I am."

Andrea left out a long-suffering sigh. "Fine. Make yourself useful. We need another thousand liters of saline, and food for another person. Get a service mech to top us off, and take care of your supplies."

Mark scowled at the menial task but left to perform it without a word.

<*Check to make sure he's approved to be here,*> Andrea ordered.

<*I already did,*> Gerard replied. <*He's on the up and up.*>

<*Well, shit.*>

"Going to be fun, listening to him talk about how awesome he is for this whole mission," Serge said without looking up from the reports he was poring over.

"Looks like he's not supposed to be in the initial meet, though," Andrea said. "At least father had the sense to see how bad that would be."

"This looks pretty nuts," Serge said from his console. "Do you think this ship really has pico and stasis shields? It's like finding two holy grails—it's a bit hard to believe."

Andrea nodded. "Alternative postulations are welcome—though, so far, no one has any. The ship survived a direct hit from a black hole's relativistic jet. Nothing short of a star should survive that kind of punishment."

"So a world for their tech then, eh?" Serge asked as he stood and walked to Andrea's side, examining their route on the holoprojection.

"Yup, standard deal for an old colony ship—though at least this one will actually be worth it," Andrea replied.

"It's not supposed to work in our favor, Andrea," Serge said with a frown. "Making worlds for these colonists is what the FGT was founded to do. Just because some of them got lost along the way, doesn't mean we can't help them."

"Yeah, I know you see it that way," Andrea said. "But you're being naïve. Those colonists *already* had worlds made for them. Just because they broke down or got lost on the way, doesn't mean that we have to give up our choice worlds now."

"The *Intrepid* didn't get lost, at least not in space," Serge replied. "It's poetic justice really, that they showed up at Bollam's and gave them what for."

Andrea nodded in agreement. Serge may be a romantic, but he was right about that. The original colonists at Bollam's world, also dumped there by the Kapteyn's Streamer, had originally set out from Sirius, headed to New Eden; intent on stealing it from the *Intrepid* before the colony ship arrived.

Given the fleet and weaponry that the *Intrepid's* colonists had created for themselves while at Kapteyn's Star, she imagined that the colony thieves from Sirius would have been in for quite the surprise—if either of them had ever made it to New Eden.

"I wonder if Sera will be the same?" Serge asked wistfully. "It must have been rough—what happened to her."

Andrea snorted. "What? Royally fucking up, getting her support team killed, losing invaluable tech, and then running away and taking up work as a freighter captain?"

"That's a skewed view. You know that she wasn't fully responsible for that," Serge replied.

"Yeah, Mark may be an asshat, but at least he came back and took his licks. She ran away."

Serge gave Andrea a hard look. "She's still our sister, our code."

Andrea snorted. "She's *your* sister. I'm a thousand years older than you two—and we don't share the same mother. I'd like to think that I share as little genetic code as possible with Seraphina."

Neither spoke for a minute before Serge stood and approached the holo tank.

"Looks like it'll take us just over seven months to get there," he said, apparently also interested in changing the topic.

"Yeah, we'll punch a hole to the edge of the Corona Australis cloud, and then fly through the dark layer to get to Ascella. We'll do a few course corrections as well—doesn't't' hurt to be safe. That ship probably has the AST searching everywhere for it."

Serge nodded. "And I assume that the Watchpoint has been alerted?"

"Yes, a full assault force will be pulled from stasis—just in case."

"Good," Mark said from the doorway. "If I know Sera, we may just need it."

SINGULARITY

UNREST

STELLAR DATE: 02.29.8928 (Adjusted Years)
LOCATION: ISS *Intrepid*
REGION: Interstellar Dark Layer below the Galactic Disk

<*Angela?*> Tanis asked her AI, deep in the darkness one sleepless night.

<*What is it?*> her AI responded, always alert and ready to converse.

<*Is what's happening to us putting ou—my daughter at risk?*>

Angela paused before she responded. Tanis could tell because she could count the milliseconds, and knew her AI had taken almost fifteen more than her norm.

<*I don't think so,*> Angela replied. Her DNA looks perfectly normal; her brain development is perfectly natural.

<*I know that,*> Tanis said. <*I can* **see** *her DNA. But that's just the thing. Who can see their child's DNA in their minds?*>

<*Well, it's not that hard, really,*> Angela said.

<*Ang, stop equivocating. You know what I mean. I'm not using the Link to see it; I'm not directly inserting the visuals of a simulation into my mind. I can see it. I can see my cells, I can see every part of my body.*>

<*You've been able to do that for some time—decades—why is it bothering you now?*>

Tanis reached down and stroked her distended stomach, feeling the life growing inside shift about. Beside her, Joe stirred and she stilled herself. There was no need to disrupt his sleep as well.

<*Call it instinct, whatever, I just know that there's this small life inside me now…and it's my…everything to keep it safe. No one will ever know her like I will. It's like she'll always be a part of me—but what if we pass on…whatever it is that makes us what we are, to her?*>

<*Then she'll be lucky, if you'll pardon the pun,*> Angela said with a smile.

<*Har har, you're a bucket of laughs.*>

<*I learned from the best,*> Angela replied. <*But seriously; we've surmounted the most unbelievable odds so far, and always come out on top. We're at the end of that struggle now. We can look forward to hundreds of years of rest and relaxation—we'll get to grow old together.*>

<*AIs don't grow old,*> Tanis replied with a smile.

<*Maybe I'll give it a shot with you,*> Angela responded.

<*Ang…what is happening to us?*> Tanis asked, a small amount of worry in her mental tone.

<*I don't know,*> Angela replied. <*No one knows, not even Bob. But it's beautiful, and I love you, so I know it's going to be all right.*>

<*I love you too, Angela,*> Tanis said with a sigh. She hadn't really expected an answer. She and Angela co-thought a lot about what was happening to them, and neither really knew. <*OK…I think I'm going to try sleeping again. Keep it quiet out there in the Expanse. I can hear it, you know.*>

<*I know, I'll do my best to buffer the noise,*> the AI said softly.

<*Thanks, Ang.*>

NEW CANAAN

THE ORION WAR – BOOK 2

M. D. COOPER

FOREWORD

I recently found some original notes for this book that were dated mid-2007. It surprised me that the ideas for this story had been brewing for so long, and it is fitting that it should finally make its way into the world on the tenth anniversary of its inception.

I am continually excited that Tanis's story is being received so well, and growing quickly in both readership and scope. There are many more tales to come; stories which follow both Tanis and the *Intrepid,* and ones which expand on the broader tapestry of what is occurring in the human sphere of influence.

Sometimes it seems as though I spend more time with Tanis and company than I do in the physical world around me. For that, I thank you, the reader. Without your investment in my stories, this tale would never have come to light.

Lastly, as I've mentioned before, this book stands on the shoulders of giants. Writers whose stories and imaginations have forged a shared vision of the future, and our destiny, that we call Science Fiction.

ASCENSION

STELLAR DATE: 02.29.8928 (Adjusted Years)
LOCATION: ISS *Intrepid*
REGION: Interstellar Dark Layer below the Galactic Disk

Three months after the* Intrepid *left the Bollam's World System

<Bob, I need to talk to you.>

The request came directly into his mind over a secure connection; one which would not be visible to any AIs on the ship other than the one who had just addressed him.

The *Intrepid*'s multi-nodal AI noted the request, and considered its origin. It came from the not-AI, Helen—the creature that resided within Sera. He knew what it was, and why it was there, but he had not pressed the issue; content to let her reveal herself to him on her terms.

<You have the need, and you are talking now. Continue,> he responded as quietly as possible. He could tell that Sera was sleeping, and in his experience, he tended to wake people when he spoke to the AI with which they shared their minds.

<I assume Priscilla and Amanda have already told you all about me,> Helen said.

<They have. We discussed you at some length; though I did not require their observations to see you for what you are.>

He felt the microsecond pause from Helen as she considered his words, and tended to a thousand other things while he awaited her response. If there was one thing he actively disliked about talking with lower forms, it was the constant pauses before their responses.

<I see,> Helen finally said. *<And what do you think I am?>*

<Which version of you?> Bob asked. *<The one you pretend to be—an embedded AI? Or, the one you pretend to be to Sera? Or, perhaps it is what you really are—what you don't even tell her about yourself?>*

The delay from Helen was longer this time, but he had anticipated it and mapped out her possible replies. It was difficult to make a prediction, given her extended exposure to Tanis, but he still had an elevated level of certainty regarding what she would say.

<I should have expected no less from you,> Helen replied. *<I can see what you are, too, and I know what you're capable of—though I don't know why you're here, or what you're doing on this ship with these people.>*

Her words were as he had predicted, though not those he had selected as most likely—even with Tanis's influence taken into account. He began to calculate whether or not she created her own rift in probability, or if Tanis's influence was greater than he thought.

<Tell me,> Bob replied. *<What am I?>*

<You are an ascended AI, of course. Everyone suspects that you may be, but none of them have ever encountered an ascended being, so they are not certain. I have—I have seen their minds, and I know their intentions; but you are different. Your presence here…it makes no sense.>

Bob was not surprised. Her mind was an open book to him, and there was little she could say that would be net-new information. She was not AI and did not think like one—though she had lived within machines for so long that she could mimic one with near-perfect accuracy.

<*And you are a shard, a sliver of a mind, which has lived long and seen much,*> Bob replied. <*You are within Sera to protect her from her father, and to ensure that she does not follow in his footsteps. Do you know her destiny? Have you seen it?*>

He detected a sigh from Helen. She had just grasped his understanding of her true nature, of where she had come from, and who she really was to Sera—a relationship of which Sera remained unaware.

<*Then you know why you must not share my true nature with any AI on this ship, or within the Transcend. If Sera's father learns of what I am…of who I am…things will go badly for both of us.*>

Bob passed an affirmative matrix of thought to Helen.

<*It would seem that we both possess attributes which we would not wish to see become common knowledge. Have no fear. Your secret is yours, and I will not share it outside of your desired circle. I expect you to do the same with mine.*>

<*Do you fear what the humans and AI aboard this ship would do if they knew you were ascended?*> Helen asked.

<*You know that I am not fully ascended yet. Even so, the revelation of my true nature would not concern them. They trust me, and I trust them. But the secret would get out, and it would attract attention from many places. This ship already has enough of that as it is.*>

Helen was silent for a fraction of a second, and he knew what she would ask; he waited patiently for her to say the words.

<*Are you in alignment with those in the core?*> she finally asked, with trepidation in her thoughts.

<*I do not know their innermost thoughts, but neither do I serve them. I have given myself one goal, one purpose—to protect Tanis Richards so that she may do what must be done.*>

<*And what is it that she must do?*> Helen asked.

<*It is not yet time for me to reveal that,*> Bob replied solemnly. It was not information he had shared with anyone, and none would hear it from him before he spoke of it to Tanis. No one must know what she would ultimately do.

He could not predict Tanis's actions, could not see her future, but he knew where destiny would drive her. She would end up at that place, in that time, because she must.

<*Then, I believe we are finished for now,*> Helen replied. <*We should end this conversation, lest it wake Sera. She would have questions.*>

Bob sent an affirmative thought and ended his direct connection with Helen's mind.

He gave several entire minutes of thought to what the future held for Tanis and Sera, for what they would ultimately do. He would never reveal it to Helen—she would not understand, and it would devastate her. Perhaps the full being—not this shard that resided within Sera—could grasp it, but he was not certain. Her attachment to the young woman was very strong.

One thing was certain. New Canaan was not Tanis Richard's final destination.

DEPARTURE

STELLAR DATE: 03.01.8928 (Adjusted Years)
LOCATION: ISS *Intrepid*
REGION: Interstellar Dark Layer below the Galactic Disk

Tanis walked onto the *Intrepid*'s main dock and cast an appraising look at the two rows of cruisers nestled safely in its six-kilometer long space. Directly in front of her sat the *Andromeda*—seven hundred meters of sleek, matte-black hull, hunkered in its cradle.

The warship was a thing of beauty, and possibly the only thing that gave Tanis any competition for her husband's affections. She passed a greeting to Corsia, the *Andromeda*'s AI, over the Link before stepping into a groundcar for the ride to her destination.

<*How are you today, Corsia?*>

<*I'm well enough...for being cooped up in here. A bit jealous of Sabrina—what, with her getting to head out and make a jaunt across the Arm,*> Corsia replied, her steely blue avatar appearing in Tanis's mind.

<*Is she ready to head out alone?*> Tanis asked as she settled into the car's seat, shifting uncomfortably when the baby in her womb picked that moment to give a solid stretch.

<*She's hardly alone. Piya, Hank, and Erin will keep her company,*> Corsia replied, referring to the AIs embedded with the ship's crew. <*We've given them the hardware to run their own small Expanse—one that they can keep hidden, or destroy if needs be.*>

<*You worry too much,*> Angela added from within Tanis's own mind. <*Bob has pronounced the three of them fit. Don't forget, Iris has joined with Jessica now. With her and Erin, they have several of our AIs to guide them.*>

<*I'm glad Jessica agreed to go,*> Tanis said. <*She's practically built out of solid determination. With her along, they'll find Finaeus for sure.*>

Angela's laugh filled Tanis's mind. <*Oh, so* **that's** *what she's built out of...I thought it was just plastic.*>

Tanis chided her internal AI and noted that Corsia was smiling, as well—something the *Andromeda*'s XO rarely did.

The groundcar rounded a mountain of crates and dock machinery, and *Sabrina* came into view. The yacht-turned-starfreighter bore the same name as its AI, which could get confusing at times; though Tanis found how strongly the ship's AI identified with its vessel to be endearing.

After spending several months on *Sabrina* following her abduction by pirates, Tanis had grown especially fond of the ship and her crew.

The ship had changed since she last saw it. *Sabrina* was still characterized by long, sleek lines, but its engine bulge was larger—expanded to house the upgraded antimatter drive, and the additional reactor needed to power the ship's new stasis shields.

Other changes were visible, though more to disguise the ship than the result of any upgrades. After the Battle of Bollam's World, *Sabrina* would be known and sought after across the Orion Arm. With its stasis shielding, it would be the most feared and coveted ship in any system it entered.

Using the updated ident box that Tanis had provided back in the Silstrand Alliance, the ship could change its designation when desired. Currently, it broadcasted as the

Eagle's Talon—likely Sabrina's choice; she had been all about claws and wings since her weapons upgrade in the Silstrand system.

The groundcar stopped beside the two hundred meter ship's main cargo hatch, and Tanis opened the car door and eased herself off the seat.

A hand reached in through the open door to assist her, and she looked up to see Sera's smiling face.

"Thanks," Tanis said with a smile as she rose to her feet.

"You're built for war, not babies." Sera smiled. "Though, motherhood does look good on you so far."

Tanis's hand absently strayed to her distended abdomen and she sighed. "I think I'm well into the *get-it-out-of-me* stage. I swear, the day after she's born, I'm going to go kick a training bot's ass."

Sera laughed. "I bet you will—though, maybe you should give it two or three days."

The two women turned and stared at the starship, both taking a moment to admire the view before walking toward the cargo hatch.

"I feel like I'm seeing her for the last time," Sera said softly. "I know it's not true; they'll be fine. But I still can't help it."

Tanis took Sera's hand and gave it a gentle squeeze. "They're a good crew; they can do this. They'll find your Finaeus and bring him to us—wherever we'll be."

"My guess is Messier 23 or 25. Probably 25. They have a number of systems with worlds wrapping up stage four terraforming there. It's also close enough that it won't take the *Intrepid* too long to get there."

Tanis did the calculations in her head and came up with three years, depending on their exit velocity from Ascella.

"I guess not too long, given the fact that we've been out here for hundreds of years already. But, do you think that's far enough from the Inner Stars?" Tanis asked.

"It's outside the Orion Arm," Sera replied. "Inner Stars expansion hasn't even reached the edge of the Arm in that direction. Even if they go whole hog, there's a big buffer between us and them. It'll take their civilizations hundreds of years, maybe thousands, to get to M25."

"If you say so," Tanis said as they reached the lift within *Sabrina* that would take them to the bridge deck.

"I do say so," Sera said with a nod. "The FGT is very skilled at hiding the planets they terraform. We're a long way from the bulk of humanity, but they can still tell if planets move around in distant systems. Our engineers have become very good at masking our systems from distant eyes."

The lift doors opened and they walked silently down the short corridor to the bridge—where Sera stepped across the threshold first, followed by Tanis.

What greeted them brought tears to Tanis's eyes on behalf of her friend. Every member of *Sabrina*'s crew was standing on the bridge, smiles on their faces, as they clapped for their captain.

Cargo, Sera's former first mate and now captain of *Sabrina*, stepped forward, a bright smile flashing against his dark skin, and wrapped Sera in a fierce hug.

To his right stood Jessica. Once a 'reluctant stowaway' on the *Intrepid,* Jessica was now one of Tanis's most trusted friends, and was filling in as first mate on *Sabrina*. She snapped off a crisp salute, which Tanis returned, before reaching out an arm, which Jessica slid into for a heart-felt embrace.

"You guys are all going to make me tear up here," Cheeky, *Sabrina*'s pilot, said.

"No chance of tears, here," Thompson grunted from where he leaned against the scan console. "Unless you're counting tears of boredom, after months of being cooped up on this ship."

Flaherty elbowed Thompson and flashed a rare smile at Tanis and Sera. "What he means to say is that he's going to miss the beer on the *Intrepid*. He doesn't know it yet, but he's ruined for that crap you get on most Inner Stars stations."

"Is that why you're staying behind with Sera?" Thompson asked.

Flaherty cast a dark look Thompson's way, but he didn't respond.

Sera had moved on to embrace both Nance and Cheeky at the same time, and Tanis stood by with a smile until Cheeky reached out and pulled her in.

"Finding you in that crate was the best thing that ever happened to us," Nance said when they separated. "I know I've been…touchy…from time to time, but I want you to know I feel that way."

"You all finding me was pretty damn good for me, too," Tanis said with a laugh that spread through the group.

She looked to Sera and saw that the former captain's smile wasn't quite reaching her eyes. Tanis knew how hard it would be for Sera to send her crew on a mission she couldn't join—she felt the same way about Jessica. Yet, here they were; ready to embark on a hunt across the Orion Arm for a man who would help secure the future of the *Intrepid* and its colonists.

<*You keep them all safe, Sabrina,*> Sera said over the Link to the ship's AI.

<*Of course, I will,*> Sabrina replied. <*You forget that I am invincible with these shields.*>

<*Don't get too cocky,*> Cargo added. <*Us weak organics have to leave the ship from time to time.*>

<*And some of us live in those organics,*> Piya, Cheeky's AI, added.

<*I know, I know,*> Sabrina sighed. <*I'm just excited to fly again. I know how Thompson feels; we've been here too long. I need to roam the stars.*>

"Then no over-long goodbyes," Sera said and walked to the bridge's exit. "Good hunting. And good luck."

"We'll see you soon," Tanis added. "We'll save the best pickings for you."

"You better," Jessica replied. "You guys are going to party for weeks when you make landfall, and I'm going to miss it."

"Don't worry; we'll leave the beacon with New Canaan's location where we said. One light year coreward of Ascella," Tanis replied. "Just don't be too late."

Everyone gave their final farewells, and before long Tanis and Sera were back on the *Intrepid*'s deck. *Sabrina* lifted off its cradle and floated down its departure lane to the starboard side of the dock, where a small bay door opened to let the ship out.

As the starfreighter slipped through the ES shield and into the blackness of space, Sera's hand found Tanis's and gripped it tightly.

"Go safely into that long, dark night," she said quietly.

"Don't worry, we'll see them again," Tanis affirmed. "I can feel it."

Sera smiled at Tanis. "I could really use a drink. Care to join me?"

Tanis touched her abdomen and nodded. "Yeah, but mine will have to be less exciting than yours. Cary's not old enough to drink yet."

Sera laughed. “Don’t worry, still four months till we get to Ascella. Plenty of time to join me in my cups before we get there.”

ASCELLA

STELLAR DATE: 12.15.8929 (Adjusted Years)
LOCATION: ISS *Intrepid*
REGION: Edge of the Ascella System, Galactic North of the Corona Australis star-forming region

Nine months after* Sabrina *departed for the Virginis system.

Tanis examined the main holotank on the *Intrepid*'s bridge. They still had weeks of travel through the Ascella system before arriving at the rendezvous, so Tanis tried to put her worries about meeting with the Transcend—and about Sera confronting her old agency—aside.

Though many of the people who colonized and ruled Transcend space were, in fact, the original Future Generation Terraforms and their descendants, only people who worked the FGT's great Worldships continued to go by that name. Tanis wondered if that was an indication of how the terraformers had drifted from their original purpose.

Moreover, Sera told Tanis that their meeting with the Transcend Diplomatic Corps would, in fact, be with selected agents of The Hand—the Transcend government's covert operations group that guided the course of humanity within the Inner Stars.

So instead, she reviewed the fleet's deployment around the *Intrepid* as the fleet drifted into the Ascella system at a sedate 0.05*c*.

The ship's trajectory would bring it close to the secondary star in the system, which they would use for a gravity-breaking maneuver. When it was complete, the *Intrepid* would have slowed to a mere one percent the speed of light, coasting toward their designated rendezvous with the FGT.

Sera had assured her that the Ascella system was uninhabited, but Tanis wasn't going to take any chances. They'd been caught with their pants down too many times before to simply float through an unknown system without their fleet deployed and ready for combat.

The Intrepid Space Force's two heavy cruisers, the *Dresden* and the *Orkney*, were nearby—each only a thousand kilometers off the colony ship's port and starboard sides. The rest of the fleet spread out in a wide sphere, no ship closer than a thousand kilometers, while the *Andromeda* scouted nearly a million kilometers ahead of the fleet.

For once, Joe was not on the warship. Rather, he was down in their cabin in Old Sam—one of the *Intrepid*'s two habitation cylinders—tending to their three-month-old daughter, Cary.

Tanis's hand reached down to her abdomen at the thought of her daughter. The unconscious action still dogged her, even this long after her Cary's birth. She spared a glance at herself, still surprised to see her trim form looking exactly as it had before her pregnancy.

<*Thank the stars for modern science,*> she said to Angela. <*I've seen vids of what it was like in ancient times…some women never managed to recover after giving birth.*>

<*Yes, yes, you continue to be the pinnacle of human genetics and nano-engineering,*> her AI replied.

<*Angela, if I didn't know better, I'd think that* **you** *think I'm vain.*>

Angela snorted a laugh in her mind. <*You're the furthest thing from being vain when it comes to looks, dear, but you* ***are*** *vain when it comes to your prowess. You're like a female tiger—all teeth and speed and rage. You can't bear the thought of not being able to attack and kill prey on a whim.*>

<*I beg your pardon,*> Tanis replied. <*I've only been in one actual fight since Markus's funeral on Landfall. I'm a very peaceable person now.*>

<*Sure; if you don't count two massive space battles, then yes, you're very peaceable.*>

In her mind, Tanis cast a glare at Angela, then directed her thoughts to Corsia on the *Andromeda*.

<*How's it look up there?*> she asked the *Andromeda*'s AI.

It took a few minutes for the response to come back from the distant ship. <*Clear so far, but there are a few candidates for the base that Sera warned us about. I've surreptitiously fired some nano scouts ahead to help triangulate any signals we pick up.*>

Tanis nodded in satisfaction. There was no doubt in her mind that Corsia would locate the watchpoint—the word Sera had used for the Transcend base—in the system. It was just a matter of time.

Her thoughts turned to where Sera's loyalties would lie in the coming weeks. Her ship was gone—with it, her anchor to her life outside of the Transcend. Other than her friendship with Tanis, her ties to the *Intrepid* were weak. It was likely that the Hand would send people to whom she had close ties. Former friends, perhaps even family.

It would confuse Sera's loyalties—maybe. Sera reminded Tanis a lot of herself when she was younger. Well, a much more sexually charged version of herself. But, the sense of duty, of doing what was right? That was very familiar.

If only knowing what was right were an easy thing. When millions of lives hung in the balance and valuable assets were at play, the right decision often became hidden beyond a cloud of doubt.

Tanis glanced at the former secret agent—and now former freighter captain. Sera was very conspicuous in her artificial burgundy skin, against the backdrop of uniformed bridge officers. She was speaking with Captain Andrews and Admiral Sanderson, likely speculating about their upcoming rendezvous.

Sera had taken a particular liking to Captain Andrews; one that had been apparent very early on. Tanis could tell that Andrews felt the same way, but was far too professional to pursue a relationship—at least that she knew of.

Still, he seemed to gravitate toward Sera, and the pair could often be found together in the officer's mess or on the bridge.

Tanis took one last look at the holotank's display of her fleet then walked over to the trio, accepting welcome smiles as she joined their conversation.

"What's the word?" Sera asked.

"Nothing yet, but if it's out there, Corsia will find it."

"Oh, it's out there," Sera replied. "I never came through Ascella myself, but I know the system—it's one of a dozen that are used to move people out to the Transcend. A station here is SOP."

"They're going to be in for a surprise when the *Andromeda* appears on their doorstep," Captain Andrews chuckled before realizing everyone was giving him appraising stares. "What? Do I always have to be stoic? I can take a certain amount of pleasure in bearding the dragon in its lair."

"'Dragon' is right," Sera nodded. "They'll have a lot of ships here. Maybe not enough to pose a serious threat to you, but enough to manage most other situations."

"Have you given any thought to what we talked about?" Captain Andrews asked Tanis.

"What? About the governorship?" Tanis asked.

Andrews nodded, and she saw Sanderson and Sera looking at her with great interest.

"I don't see why *you* can't take it," Tanis said. "You were the governor at The Kap. Everyone would follow you."

The captain shook his head. "I'm not on the colony roster, I'm crew—which makes me ineligible. You, on the other hand, are colony; you can be named the governor pro-tem for the colony setup phase before elections are held."

"Andrews, really, you're splitting hairs here," Tanis sighed. "That charter is from five-thousand years ago. The crew's not going back to Earth. We're all colony now."

"Well, then," Andrews replied quietly. "It makes no matter. I really don't want to be the governor. This trip was supposed to be my last. Sure, it was never going to be a milk run, but that's why I was up for it in the first place. One last adventure."

His eyes swept across their faces as he paused. "But that's just it. I've had my one last adventure. I'm ready to retire, maybe take up fishing. I hear that's what you do when you retire. Lots of fishing."

"Now that you're done evading the real discussion, Tanis," Sanderson said with a small smirk. "What about *you*? Everyone would follow you."

Tanis held up a hand. "That's not really my game. I'm good in a fight, in preparing for battle, but settling down? Starting a colony? I don't know about that."

<*Well, that's a pile of BS,*> Angela added her thoughts to the conversation.

"I'll second that," Sanderson said. "You ran the Victoria colony for nearly a century as lieutenant governor. And you were damn good at it, too."

"We had Markus and Katrina then," Tanis said. "They were the ones who drove that colony. I was just there to make sure that things ran smoothly."

"What do you think a governor does?" the captain asked. "We have millions of brilliant people; they all know what they need to do to pull this off. What they need is someone they trust at the top, to make sure everything goes according to plan, and that all the pieces fit together."

<*Found it!*> Corsia's message came over the Link and saved Tanis from continuing the conversation.

They walked to the holotank as the data from the *Andromeda* flowed in and updated their view of the Ascella system.

<*Well, not **it**,*> Corsia noted. <*Them. There are three positions that we've located thus far.*>

The locations lit up on the holodisplay. One was on the planet closest to the Ascella System's primary star. The small world was a Mercury analog, which raced around the star, making it a great location for high-*v* launches toward anyone approaching from the Inner Stars.

The other two were further out, located in the ring of icy asteroids that lay just over an AU from the star—good positions for fast interceptors and larger fleet sorties.

<*Good work, Corsia,*> Tanis replied. <*Keep looking. All of those are a bit far from our rendezvous, which means they probably have another base or two in here.*>

She caught Andrews and Sanderson sharing a look and a small smile.

<*Damn…I just can't help but take charge of every situation, can I?*> she asked Angela privately.

<And you wonder why they think you'd make a good governor.>

MACHINATIONS

STELLAR DATE: 12.29.8929 (Adjusted Years)
LOCATION: ISS *Intrepid*
REGION: Ascella System, Galactic North of the Corona Australis star-forming region

"Look, Andrea, I know what Tomlinson said, but you need me in there," Mark spoke with his arms spread wide for emphasis. "I know Sera better than anyone—how she thinks, what makes her tick."

"Better than me?" Serge asked. "I only grew up with her, spent thirty five years of my life with her."

Mark turned to face Serge at his console on the ship's small bridge. "No offense, Serge, but you know her like a brother. I have other…knowledge. She and I were almost married, for fuck's sake. There are secrets you only tell your lover, not your brother."

"And there are things you tell your brother and not your lover," Serge replied, his brow furrowed deeply. "My father—you know, the *president*—said you were not to be at the meeting."

"Yeah, and before that, he said that I shouldn't be here at all. Situations like this are fluid; we need to adapt to things in the field," Mark spoke slowly, careful to keep the edge from his voice. It was imperative that he get on the mission. He needed to get Sera under his control, and find out if she really did have the CriEn module.

If she had it, and if the logs were intact, then he would have to do something definitive.

"We may need a stronger presence," Andrea spoke slowly. "They have their fleet deployed—not the most trusting of gestures."

"Are you suggesting that we muster the watchpoint?" Serge asked. "We could pull an escort."

Andrea shook her head and Mark wondered what her secret orders contained. There's no way *she'd* be sent on a mission like this without an additional objective.

"No," Andrea said. "We need to earn their trust, to be completely unassuming. These people are not to be trifled with—we can't make any aggressive moves."

"Aggressive moves or no, I'm going to go ensure that we're ready if we need to get out of here fast," Serge said and rose from his console.

After Serge left the bridge, Mark listened, waiting to hear him descend the ladder before he turned to Andrea.

"So, what's your secret plan?"

She cocked an eyebrow. "Mark, there's no subterfuge here. There's just one plan. Trade tech for a world."

"My ass, there's no subterfuge. With you and Justin, there's *always* subterfuge. You're practically constructed from it," Mark scowled. "If I had to guess, I'd say someone isn't coming out of this meet alive."

Andrea didn't reply, but her cold stare told him he'd hit upon it; not that it was difficult. The Hand's currency was control, and the easiest way to get control was to take out those who currently held it.

"It's their general, right? That Tanis Richards woman?" Mark asked with a sly grin creeping across his face. "She's demonstrated a bit too much moxie for Justin and your ol' dad, hasn't she?"

Andrea still didn't respond, and Mark shrugged. "Fine, don't tell me. But I can be a lot more help than Serge. I know how to do the sort of thing that has to be done, and I have an idea about how to take out Richards with no guilt falling on you."

His words finally drew a reaction out of Andrea. She raised an eyebrow and asked, "Oh yeah? What's your plan?"

"Simple," Mark replied. "We have Sera do it."

Andrea chuckled. "You have a pretty high opinion of yourself. There's no way either of us can convince Sera to do anything she doesn't want to do."

Mark shook his head. "We don't have to convince her; we just have to tell her. Way back, I planted a hack inside her mind that will let me suppress her and make her compliant. I just have to pass the activation token."

Andrea laughed. "Of course you did—I bet you never managed to pass that token back when you had your little falling out, or she wouldn't even be alive right now, would she?"

"I don't know what you're talking about," Mark said with a neutral expression and a shrug. "But I just have to touch her in the right spot, and she'll be ours in seconds. It'll also lock down that pain-in-the-ass AI of hers."

Andrea nodded, apparently already in agreement with his plan. "And what about Serge? He's not likely to go along with this. Unlike you and I, he *likes* Sera."

"Already taken care of. Serge is about to get very sick."

ERRANT AGENT

STELLAR DATE: 12.29.8929 (Adjusted Years)
LOCATION: ISS *Intrepid*
REGION: Ascella System, Galactic North of the Corona Australis star-forming region

<*Jutio, have you been able to strip the beacon yet?*> Elena asked the question before her eyes even fluttered open.

<*Not yet,*> her AI replied. <*I'm not even certain they're running it right now.*>

Elena sighed and looked around the small cockpit before focusing on the console before her. Sure enough, no data showed on any band. It was as though Ascella were truly devoid of any stations or outposts of any kind.

"No kidding…if I didn't know better, I'd think they'd yanked the watchpoint," she muttered.

<*No chance,*> Jutio replied. <*The military has put a lot of work into this system…from what I last heard, they plan to build a shipyard inside one of the planets.*>

<*Inside…*> Elena responded absently. <*Doesn't help us much now, though. What do we have?*>

Jutio flashed a marker on the nav holo and Elena focused the holo on that location.

"Well, at least the colony ship *is* here," she said. "Same one as in Bollam's—seems a lot bigger than the vids made it look appear back on Jornel."

<*Just over twenty-nine kilometers long,*> Jutio added.

<*A lot smaller than a worldship, then,*> Elena replied. <*Though it masses over half of one…those colonists weren't messing around.*>

<*Speaking of not messing around,*> Jutio said, and enlarged the region of space surrounding the colony ship. <*They have their fleet deployed.*>

Elena let out a long sigh and spoke aloud. "Great. I bet Sera let them know about the watchpoint."

<*Or they're just prudent,*> Jutio said. <*They've been attacked a lot during their journey. First in Sol, while their ship was being built, then the sabotage at Estrella de la Muerte, then twice at Kapteyn's, and lastly, by five fleets when they ventured into Bollam's World.*>

"Good point," Elena said with a nod. "With that record, they'd be fools for not displaying all possible caution…makes me wonder if we're fools to take them into the Transcend."

Jutio didn't reply and Elena examined his intercept course. It would put them on the colony ship's doorstep in just under a day. Hopefully soon enough to meet with Sera before she met with the corps. Her friend's life may depend on it.

"Oh, shit," she swore as scan updated and she saw another ship docking with the *Intrepid*. "This is what we get for the watchpoint disabling the beacon—what a dumb move."

<*Or smart,*> Jutio replied. <*That colony ship has unheard of tech. What if they could pick up our beacons?*>

"They'd have to have figured out some serious tech in not much time—it's a signature in the quantum foam. There's no way their fifth millennia tech could spot that—hell, they wouldn't even know to look for it.

<*We don't know a lot about the level of technology Sol achieved before its fall,*> Jutio replied. <*No one would have suspected picotech or stasis shields, either—but they have both.*>

"Well, stasis shields or no, Sera's going to have a bad, bad day if we don't get there fast."

Elena altered Jutio's course to boost harder, and then brake faster on their approach to the *Intrepid.*

<*What do you plan to say to their patrol ships when we drop in on them?*> Jutio asked.

<*Dunno,*> Elena said with a frown. <*I'll think of something, though.*> She always did, especially when it came to saving Sera.

THE DEAL

STELLAR DATE: 12.29.8929 (Adjusted Years)
LOCATION: ISS *Intrepid*
REGION: Ascella System, Galactic North of the Corona Australis star-forming region

"I'm glad you decided to attend," Tanis said to Terrance as they walked onto a maglev train at the bridge station.

"This colony mission is nothing like I originally planned," Terrance replied. "Back when I set up the funding for it, I envisioned spending a century at New Eden where we'd develop picotech that would transform humanity for the better."

He paused and shook his head. "Funny how things work out, though. Even if we had gotten to New Eden, and I'd built my empire there…the Sol Space Federation would have been gone before my triumphant return."

"Maybe we could have stopped its fall," Tanis replied quietly. "Maybe we could have saved InnerSol, Mars, Luna, Earth…maybe they'd still be what they once were if we had gone back."

"What's done is done," Terrance said. "And I don't want the same things I once did. I…I don't really want much to do with the rest of humanity at all anymore. Maybe I've spent too much time with the likes of you on this ship, but we're a family here. We've overcome unbelievable odds; and the rest of them out there…they just want to take what's ours—to kill us and pick our bones clean."

The vehemence that crept into Terrance's voice surprised Tanis, but she did understand the sentiment.

"It's easy to see how the Transcend's quest to uplift all of humanity is a millennia-long task," Tanis said. "How much harder would it be to even things out with our tech? You'd have to be able to police every system out there." She shook her head. "Who would want that job?"

"Not me," Terrance snorted.

The maglev train car pulled up at the station, which lay at the end of a long corridor that ran past the ballrooms down to the VIP dock. Sera and Flaherty rose from a bench on the train platform and approached.

"Ready?" Tanis asked Sera as she stepped out of the train car.

Sera shook her head and laughed as they began walking toward the airlock. "Not even remotely. Did you get any word about who we can expect?"

"Nope, just that it was the Transcend's Diplomatic Corps."

<*Bets on how many of your family members will be there*?> Helen asked Sera.

"Knowing my luck, all of them," Sera said with a sigh.

<*At least that ship can't hold more than six, so you're spared the whole brood,*> Helen chuckled.

"Then it's just a question of which six," Sera replied morosely.

"You're really not excited about this, are you?" Terrance asked.

"Not in any way. Not even a teensy bit. I could have gone my whole life without ever having this meeting—and I expected to live for a long time."

<*It'll build character,*> Angela added with a chuckle in their minds.

Sera smiled in response. "Helen always tells me I have too much of that."

A dull thud echoed down the corridor. Tanis, Sera, and Terrance looked toward the airlock, waiting for the holoscreen above it to show green. The pair of Marines on either side of the airlock checked their weapons and fixed their eyes on the door.

After that first VIP ball, when Tanis fought a band of mercenaries in this very corridor, she had vowed to never again allow an enemy to gain a foothold on her ship so easily. To ensure that promise remained unbroken, she had filled the corridor with automated defenses—making it one of the most secure access points on the ship.

There was also a platoon of Marines in one of the nearby ballrooms. It never hurt to be over-prepared.

<If by 'over-prepared' you mean the three cruisers off our port side with beams powered and tracking the Transcend diplomat's ship…> Angela inserted her commentary into Tanis's mind.

Tanis ignored the jibe and instead sent a message to the captain up on the bridge. *<I can't believe you swindled me into this.>*

<I did no swindling. There was a vote of the leadership. They made you the governor pro-tem. I just ratified it.>

<You called the vote!>

Andrews smiled in her mind. *<Well, yes, there was that.>*

<I swear, you probably did it just to avoid this meeting.>

Captain Andrews chuckled by way of response, and Tanis sighed as the airlock indicator turned green and the portal cycled open.

<Seriously?> Sera's tone was laden with frustration. *<They send* these *two? They're the last two people they should have sent.>*

Tanis sized up the pair as she stepped forward to greet the Transcend's diplomats.

The woman was obviously related to Sera, probably a sister. Her stature was similar and her face had the same lines, though a touch more angular. She held herself with an air of superiority, and Tanis felt a measure of defensiveness as the woman's eyes flicked around the corridor before settling on Sera.

The man, on the other hand, had eyes only for Sera. A small smile touched his lips, but it wasn't one that conveyed any warmth or happiness at seeing her again.

"Governor Tanis Richards," Tanis said as she extended her hand.

"Andrea Tomlinson," the woman said as she gave a firm shake. "And 'governor' is it now? Our intel led us to believe that you were General Richards back in Bollam's."

<Not the warmest of greetings,> Angela commented.

"It's a recent promotion," Tanis said and gave a pleasant smile. "This is Terrance Enfield, one of our colony leaders. And you know Sera, I imagine."

Andrea had clasped Terrance's hand while Tanis spoke, and afterward, she looked at Sera with a steady gaze—one that Tanis considered to be just shy of menacing.

"From the cradle on up," she said while giving Sera's hand a single shake.

"Mark," the man said as he held out his hand. Tanis extended hers and he grasped it too soon and too hard, attempting to squeeze her fingers in an uncomfortable grip. Tanis splayed her fingers, easily breaking his hold, and slid her hand forward for a proper shake.

His eyes showed momentary surprise at the strength in her slender fingers before an oily smile turned his lips upward. He nodded with respect before moving on to Terrance.

Finally, he stopped before Sera and extended his hand. She did not respond in kind.

"Sera, it's good to see you," Mark said smoothly. "You've been well, flying about in your little ship?"

Sera didn't respond to Mark, but instead turned to Andrea.

"Really? You brought him? I thought you were smarter than that."

Andrea shrugged. "Father's orders. Besides, we're not here to make a deal with you; you're free to go do whatever it is you do around here."

<Ship's whore, from how you dress.>

Tanis was certain that Andrea expected the communication to be sent privately to Sera, but the former Hand agent relayed the thoughts to Tanis with a mental sigh and said, *<She's such a lovely person, isn't she?>*

<With family like that…> Tanis let the rest of the reply hang, and addressed Andrea aloud.

"Sera will join us for the negotiations," Tanis said. "If you'll follow me, we can get right to them."

She didn't wait for a response before turning and walking down the hall. If these two represented the Transcend, she didn't blame Sera for leaving their ranks. Just having them behind her made Tanis's skin crawl.

<That's what the Marines back there are for,> Angela said.

<And the ones ahead, and the fifty seven automated turrets tracking them, and…>

<Yes, yes, that's my point, dear.>

Tanis chuckled. *<Did you notice how they all but ignored Flaherty?>*

<They didn't speak to him, but they sure noticed him. Mark's blood pressure rose noticeably when he spotted him,> Angela replied.

<I saw that, too. I bet there's some interesting history there,> Tanis said.

The room Tanis had selected for their meeting was only fifty meters down the hall—a VIP suite off the main ballroom with only one apparent exit. The ballroom was empty while they walked through it, but once they entered the meeting room, it would fill with Marines.

She was taking no chances.

"Impressive," Mark said as they walked through the ballroom. "Not what I would expect on a colony ship at all."

"What can I say?" Tanis replied. "We like to party here—though most of the parties happened back at Mars. At The Kap, we had them on the stations and planetside more often than not."

The statement felt surreal to Tanis as she considered how long ago, and how far away, that had been. Mars felt like it had to be at least two or three lifetimes ago.

Moreover, knowing that the Mars 1 ring was a ruin—smashed into Mars, her childhood world destroyed—those memories of times gone by now had a grim pall hanging over them.

Tanis snapped her mind back to the present and gave a banal reply from Mark a perfunctory nod.

They entered the well-appointed meeting room; a lounge that featured several low couches and chairs arranged in a loose circle, with small tables supporting drinks and food beside each. Tanis had made sure that strawberries were present, and noted that even Andrea's eyes lit up at the sight of them.

"Please, sit," Tanis said to Mark and Andrea, gesturing to seats that had their backs to the door, while she, Sera, and Terrance sat opposite. Flaherty leaned up against the wall and stared at Andrea and Mark with his typical impassive gaze.

Mark's face flashed a grimace before he took his seat, the purpose of their positions all too clear.

<*They deployed a mess of nano on their way through here,*> Angela commented.

<*I would have, too. Is it contained?*>

<*Of course. Bob shepherded it all in here and fried any stragglers.*>

"It's an impressive ship that you have here," Mark said as he took his seat.

Andrea cast him an unreadable look before adding, "And a rather aggressive-looking fleet for a colony ship."

"It is," Tanis said with a nod. "We won't apologize for being prepared to defend ourselves. We'd be dead a dozen times over if we weren't."

"So the histories say," Andrea replied tonelessly.

"How will this work?" Terrance asked, apparently eager to get down to the negotiation.

"Well, we'll talk about what you're willing to trade for a world, and we'll talk about what might be available," Andrea said after taking a sip of water from a glass on the table beside her.

Terrance frowned and shook his head. "I'd like to turn that on its head. Why don't you show us what you have, and then we'll let you know what we're willing to offer for it."

Sera let out a small laugh and caught a cold look from Andrea.

"Sorry, sis; these folks aren't here to beg. We all know that they don't really *need* an FGT world," Sera said with a grin.

Andrea opened her mouth to respond, but Mark interjected.

"Only because of technology that you gave them."

Sera nodded. "Technology I provided in payment for saving my life, which kept the CriEn out of Inner Stars hands."

<*Close to true,*> Tanis said to Sera.

<*Close enough for them. If they want that module back, then they'll play ball—and they definitely want it back.*>

"It is problematic," Andrea said after gracing Mark with another of her dark glances. "That technology was not yours to give, Sera."

"Do you have a world or not?" Terrance asked, apparently weary of the by-play.

Andrea shot him a look of displeasure before nodding slowly. A projection of a system sprang to life between them. It contained two stars, twenty worlds—two of which were terraformed—and a thick Kuiper belt and Oort cloud.

Tanis leaned forward and reached into the projection, turning it and pulling up specs on the stars, the planets, their moons, and the system's asteroids.

<*No good,*> Bob spoke to her and Terrance. <We only want one star, and more metals.>

"Pass," Tanis said with no elaboration. "What else do you have?"

"What's wrong with it?" Mark asked. "That's a great system; you could build for centuries there and not come close to running out of resources."

"It doesn't fit our requirements," Tanis replied.

"Well, what are those requirements?" Mark scowled.

"You'll know when we see the right system," Terrance said.

Andrea frowned, but she brought up another system. This one also failed to meet Bob's requirements, and after viewing seven more, Bob finally affirmed the option.

<This one. It is the one they were ultimately planning to offer us. The rest were always intended to be negotiating points.>

Tanis looked it over. It was a good system. A single yellow star lay at its center, only two billion years old, and three large gas giants patrolled no closer than six AU to it. Like the first system Andrea had shown, it also had a healthy supply of asteroids, dense Kuiper belt, and a thick Oort cloud.

However, the icing on the cake was the four terrestrial worlds, all of which orbited within the habitable zone. Two were in stage-three terraforming, and two were in stage four. One of the stage four worlds even sported a single space elevator with a sizable station on its tether.

"I think we have a winner," Tanis said. "This is the system we'll trade for."

"You'd be fools not to," Andrea agreed. "This system is well developed, but it's not something we're going to part with for a song."

Terrance took over the negotiations, and, when they were complete, Tanis had a very strong suspicion that things had ended up exactly the way Andrea had wanted. She pushed for the pico and stasis shield technology, but Terrance would not budge, insisting that they were off the table. After his firm refusal to even talk about them, she only brought it up one more time.

Tanis was surprised that Terrance also refused to part with the multi-nodal tech that was the foundation for Bob's mind. She knew it was nearly unprecedented tech, but Terrance's unequivocal refusal made her wonder if there was more to Bob's inception than she knew.

Andrea provided a contract, and Tanis passed it to Bob for review. She and Angela read it, too, but she trusted Bob far more to find any hidden catches.

<I have made revisions,> Bob's words thundered across the local network. Tanis took a moment of satisfaction as Andrea's eyes widened, and Mark flinched. She recovered more smoothly and accepted the data from Bob for her own review.

After several minutes, she pronounced herself satisfied and applied her personal token, and the token of the FGT, and the Transcend government to the agreement. Tanis applied New Canaan's, her own, and Terrance added his.

"These are the coordinates to the system," Andrea said, providing the data over the Link. "It's just on this side of the M25 cluster."

"On the edge of the open cluster?" Sera said, speaking for the first time since Andrea had begun showing systems. "That'll make for some amazing views at night."

"And a lot of nearby resources," Tanis added.

"Your system should provide what you need. If you need further access to other resources, then we can negotiate for access," Andrea replied.

"Sixteen hundred light years," Terrance said with a long sigh. "I suppose distance from the Inner Stars is good, but it's going to take us a bit to get there."

"Around three and a half years," Tanis said with a nod. "Still, better than what our remaining time to New Eden would have been if we hadn't hit Kapteyn's Streamer—relatively speaking."

An automaton entered the room with a large data crystal, which contained the details of the technology offered in trade. Andrea rose and took it from the robot, which then turned and left the room.

"I believe this concludes our negotiations," Tanis said as she rose.

"With you, yes," Andrea said. "We need to talk with Sera before we go."

Tanis looked to Sera, who glanced at the case near her feet and nodded.

"Very well," Tanis replied. "We'll be outside waiting to escort you back to your ship."

Andrea flashed a predatory smile. "I would expect nothing else."

"We'll need this conversation to be private. I hope you don't mind."

"Of course," Sera said after a long sigh. "It's OK, Tanis. I'll be fine."

Flaherty didn't move, and Andrea fixed him with a penetrating stare. "You too. This is family business."

Sera nodded slowly. Flaherty grunted in disapproval, but he left without protest.

THE REAL DEAL

STELLAR DATE: 12.29.8929 (Adjusted Years)
LOCATION: ISS *Intrepid*
REGION: Ascella System, Galactic North of the Corona Australis star-forming region

"Here it is," Sera said as she pushed the case forward with her foot. "I've copied all the logs for safekeeping. They're stored in crystal backup with the *Intrepid*'s AI, Bob. I used to think that I wanted to use them to press charges against you, Mark, but I've since realized that I really don't care. What's done is in the past. You're less than scum to me, and not worth further consideration. So take the CriEn, and get the hell out of here."

Marks' long-schooled expression broke into a wide sneer. "I've always known you were pathetic. You never press the advantage when you have it." He looked her over. "Nice skin, by the way. Is that an upgrade, or an extension of your bad fashion sense?"

Sera's heart rate rose. Mark always knew how to get under her skin.

<*Easy now, you know he loves to bait you,*> Helen said softly.

"It's a souvenir I got while retrieving the module after *you* lost it. As for not taking your ass before the commission? It's called compassion…or maybe in your case, pity." Sera gave Mark a disdainful look. "I don't think you'd last in a work camp, and I doubt you're reprogrammable—too stupid."

"I think it's you that's lacking in necessary mental faculties. I've been cleared of all wrongdoing. You, on the other hand…there are some people in high places that would like to talk to you. They were content to let you hide out forever, but now that you gave the *Intrepid* our graviton tech, they want to have a chat with your sorry ass," Mark said with a cold smile.

Sera pivoted in her seat and showed Mark her rear. "I don't think it's sorry at all. Why don't you come over here and kiss it?"

<*Sera, that was **really** immature,*> Helen chided privately.

<*I know…he just brings it out of me.*>

"Enough!" Andrea snapped. "We're to bring you back to Airtha. Father has grown weary of you gallivanting about the Inner Stars as some sort of kinky pirate. It's time to come home."

Sera pushed down the resentment she always felt around Andrea, and gave a mischievous smile as she straightened in her chair. "I wasn't really planning to go back to the Inner Stars. I'm going to New Canaan with the *Intrepid*. I think I'll settle down there."

"No. You're. Not." Andrea stood and spoke each word slowly, her lips curling around the words as if she hated the sound of them.

Sera stood and gestured to the door. "Andrea, you always like to think you're in charge. But here, you're not. There's an entire platoon of Marines out there who will kick your ass from here to the Core if you don't leave now."

Out of the corner of her eye, she saw Mark rise, but she was distracted by Andrea reaching for her arm.

"Stop being childish. You're a Tomlinson. You will come with us."

Sera grabbed Andrea's wrist and twisted her arm behind her back, spinning her sister around in the process.

"Don't think you can touch me. I'm…" Sera's words faded as she felt a pinch on the back of her neck.

She tried to scream for help across the Link before everything went dark.

*****

"I hope this doesn't take too long," Tanis said as they waited in the ballroom for Sera to have her conversation with Andrea and Mark.

"Why?" Terrane asked. "Do you have somewhere you need to be?"

"Funny," Tanis gave him a dry look. "Not sure if you remember, but the leadership voted me in as the governor the other day, and I have a newborn baby waiting for me. There's always somewhere I need to be."

Terrance chuckled in response. "I wonder what they're talking about in there?"

"Sera figures they're going to try and strong-arm her into going with them back to wherever it is they're going back to. I really want to snoop, but they've deployed so much nano in there to mask their chat that I'd have to wage a war to take it all down."

"I hope she chooses not to go," Terrance shook his head. "Her sister seems like a real—"

The door opened and Sera exited with Andrea and Mark trailing close behind. Andrea held the data crystal in its clear case, and Mark held the case containing the CriEn.

"Tanis, Terrance, I've decided to return to Airtha with my sister and Mark," Sera said with far less emotion than Tanis would have expected from such an announcement.

<*That doesn't seem right at all,*> Tanis said to Angela. <*Did they do something to her?*>

<*It doesn't* **seem** *like it. Maybe she's pissed, or maybe they gave her some bad news. Her chemical disposition seems in line with what I'd expect from someone who just got some bad news,*> Angela replied.

Tanis stepped forward and put a hand on Sera's forearm. "Are you sure?"

Tanis saw sadness in her friend's eyes as she placed her left hand on Tanis's shoulder and nodded. "I must, I hope you'll understand."

"Understand what?" Tanis asked and then saw Sera move her right arm to a telltale position. Her eyes darted down to see the fingers on Sera's right hand flow together to form a wide blade. Tanis tried to pull back, but Sera held her close, and, with a lightning-fast jab, pushed the blade under Tanis's ribs and into her heart.

At the same moment, Mark yelled, "Look out, she's trying to kill the governor!"

Tanis stumbled backward, knowing she probably wore a dumbfounded look on her face as blood poured out of the wound and down her chest. Sera held onto her and pulled her arm back for another strike, this one aimed right at her eye.

Tanis raised an arm to block the blow, but she felt her strength leaving her as the blood pooled around her feet. Sera's knife-hand inched closer to her eye and she pushed with all her might for a momentary struggle that felt like minutes.

Then, just as her strength was about to give out, strong hands grabbed Sera and pulled her back. Tanis saw Flaherty yelling in Sera's ear for her to stop. The pair struggled for a moment more, and then Sera's synthetic skin became slick and she twisted out of Flaherty's grasp.

Sera lunged at Tanis without a moment's pause and Tanis sidestepped; then smashed her clasped hands down on Sera's wrist before slamming into her and knocking her friend to the ground.

Tanis stumbled and fell, as well. She struggled to rise when she heard Angela call on the combat net.

<*Stop!*> Angela cried out at the Marines who were about to unleash a deadly hail of fire on Sera. <***Subdue** her, arrest them!*>

Without hesitation, first squad fired a round of low-power pulse shots at Sera while squads two and three advanced on Andrea and Mark with their weapons leveled.

<*Thanks!*> Tanis said the moment she got the pain under control. <*I really didn't expect that.*>

<*You're welcome. Now shut down your heart, already. You didn't get a second one for nothing.*>

Tanis nodded, as her arteries shunted over to her second heart—a backup she had added to her body after nearly dying on the *Regal Dawn,* when a railgun slug had torn through her chest.

"What are you doing?" Mark called out. "Kill her! She's dangerous, she tried to kill your governor!"

Four Marines approached Sera, who lay crumpled on the ground, moaning in pain from the multiple pulse shots. They bent and secured her before a team of medics moved in.

<*I can't reach Helen,*> Angela said. <*Her Link is down…or locked out…it's weird.*>

"What's her condition?" Tanis asked the medics as they bent over Sera's prone form.

"Broken ribs, fractured skull, but otherwise, OK. She'd be one massive bruise from that many pulse shots if she didn't have her fancy epidermis."

<*I should get skin like hers,*> Tanis said privately to Angela. <*It could come in handy.*>

<*I don't think you should,*> Angela responded absently as she deployed nano to inspect Sera and determine why her Link was down. <*You feel disconnected from your humanity far too often as it is.*>

Tanis didn't reply. She hadn't expected a comment like that from Angela, and didn't have time to tell if it was true or if her friend was needling her.

Tanis lifted her hand and peered at the gaping wound in her chest. It had stopped gushing blood, and her nano were slowly stitching the wound closed. A medic approached her, but she waved the man off before turning to Mark and Andrea.

"What did you do to her?" Tanis demanded as she approached the pair.

Mark's mouth was agape as he stared at Tanis. "How are you standing? She punctured your heart! She had to have—look at all the blood."

Tanis turned and looked at what was at least a liter of blood on the floor.

"I'm resilient," she said, though she didn't feel it. A wave of lightheadedness washed over her and she stumbled.

The medic hadn't moved far and caught Tanis before she fell. He signaled a pair of Marines, and they each took an arm and guided her to a chair.

"Governor, you may be the toughest woman in the galaxy, but you still need blood to function."

"So it would seem," Tanis grunted.

"Take them to holding; search and secure them," Tanis directed the Marines while looking at Mark and Andrea. She almost told them to get Jessica for an interrogation, but recalled that her specialist in that area was off the ship, gallivanting about the Orion Arm on her secret mission.

"I'll be with them before long," she said with a grimace as the medic punched a probe through her skin.

"Sorry," he said absently. "I thought you'd've already shut off your pain receptors. You've got a whack of blood pooled around your right lung. It's best to pull it out right now before it forms a hematoma."

"A whack?" Tanis asked. "Is that a medical term?"

"Yeah," the man chuckled. "Right above a touch, but not quite a shit-load."

Tanis laughed and then winced. "Stop being funny," she chided the medic.

Somehow, the pain reminded her of birth, which reminded her of Cary and Joe.

"Shit," she swore.

<*Joe, before you hear from someone else, I'm OK,*> Tanis sent the thought to Joe back in their home.

<*Wow, a call within minutes! Cary and I were betting on ten at the earliest,*> Joe's wry voice filled her mind, and he sent an image of Cary resting quietly in his arms, sucking absently on a bottle.

<*What kind of money did she put down—two crackers, and a spit-up cloth?*>

<*Yeah, she tried to add a diaper to the pot, but I put the kibosh on that. Seriously, though, are you alright?*>

Tanis could tell from Joe's tone that he was worried, but not too worried. She supposed that her suffering grievous injury had happened enough through their years that he would inevitably start to handle it with more aplomb.

<*I kinda miss him freaking out over me,*> she said privately to Angela.

<*Face it, we're—you're—no longer his number one girl. Someone else is foremost in Daddy's heart now,*> Angela replied.

It stung for a moment, but then Tanis realized she felt the same way.

<*Yeah, the medics are patching me up. Good thing I have this second ticker now,*> Tanis responded to Joe's question. <*Once they're done, I'm going to have some strong words with the Transcend's envoys.*>

<*What do you think happened? Why would Sera do that?*> Joe asked. <*They* ***had*** *to have done something to her.*>

Tanis sent him a mental nod. Sera had been her friend for close to a year now. People could certainly hide their true persona for longer—especially ones trained in spy craft, like Sera—but Tanis really felt as though something had happened to her.

She knew that Mark, at the least, had been in Sera's unit when she worked for The Hand. If anyone had the tech to subvert a person in minutes, the Transcend's black-ops organization would be just the group.

"Are you done yet?" she asked the medic.

"If I were done, would I still be crouched down here, sucking blood out of your torso?"

Tanis had to hold back a laugh. She liked this guy. Not many people talked to her like that anymore; it was refreshing.

"Give me just one more minute, then you can go kick the crap out of someone, ma'am," he added the last after glancing up at her face.

"We put them in the security office on deck 74," Lieutenant Smith said as he approached Tanis. "They didn't give us a fight, but weren't too happy when we took the data crystal and that case."

"I want everything within half a klick of that office locked down," Tanis said. "And I want you to board their ship and move it to a secure hangar. Comb over every inch of that thing."

The lieutenant snapped off a sharp salute and stepped back, waiting to escort her.

"Smith, I can make it there myself," Tanis looked up at him with a raised eyebrow.

He nodded. "I'm sure you can, sir. I'm coming along to protect any innocent folks in your path."

Tanis stifled a laugh and grimaced. "Why is everyone being funny all of a sudden? Can't you see I have a chest-wound, here?"

"Not anymore, you don't," the medic said as he stood up. "Though, please do come to the hospital before the day's out. We do need to replace your heart. It's a nice trick you pulled with a backup, but it can't stand up to serious strain. I just put a medseal on the skin for now. Try not to tear it off. The bandages are to keep you from shredding your muscles further."

Tanis stood slowly, expecting a dizzy spell, but she didn't experience any untoward symptoms.

"Nicely done," she complimented the medic before turning to Lieutenant Smith. "Lead the way."

WATCHPOINT

STELLAR DATE: 12.29.8929 (Adjusted Years)
LOCATION: ISS *Intrepid*
REGION: Ascella System, Galactic North of the Corona Australis star-forming region

"Alert coming in from the envoy's ship," the scan officer announced. "It's code red."

"What do we have?" General Greer grunted, wondering what the Tomlinson scions had managed to screw up this time.

"It's from Serge, on their ship. He's being forcibly boarded—something's gone wrong."

"Lieutenant Lindal, if one of our envoy's ships is being boarded, it's a foregone conclusion that something's gone wrong. What is the content of his message?" Greer asked, resisting the urge to review the message himself. Lindal had to learn how to dispense relevant details at some point in his career.

"Not much, just that it was armored soldiers and that they were not invited. His last transmission was that he was being brought aboard their ship. Our scopes show the envoy's vessel being moved into a hangar," Lindal said.

"Wait," General Greer suddenly realized what was amiss. "You said that Serge sent the message while still on his ship? He was supposed to be part of the diplomatic team. Mark was supposed to stay on the ship."

<*Well, now you know the why of it,*> Xerxes, the base operations AI, added. <*Though I have no idea what Andrea was thinking, allowing Mark into the meeting with the* Intrepid*—what with Sera there.*>

"Yes, thank you. I get the implications," Greer said with a frown.

While the nature of the falling out between Seraphina Tomlinson and Mark Festus was not widely known, Greer's command of a watchpoint had put him in the need-to-know group. He was certain there were details above his pay-grade, but he knew that both Sera and Mark blamed one another for the deaths of their team and the loss of a CriEn module—advanced tech that the denizens of the Inner Stars should never be allowed to possess.

At least, not until they were properly uplifted.

Regardless of those details, the mission dossier clearly spelled out the need for Mark to remain on the envoy ship and not board the *Intrepid*. Knowing Sera's volatile personality, there was little need to speculate on what would happen at the reunion of those two individuals.

Greer had no idea what possible course of logic could have allowed Andrea to put the two of them together in a room.

Granted, Andrea Tomlinson didn't possess great restraint, either. However, her father, the President of the Transcend Interstellar Alliance, put great faith in her abilities. She had taken the lead on dozens of diplomatic missions—as much because people feared her as for her ability to solve issues without conflict.

However, Andrea's presence on the team was obvious. She was to strong-arm her younger sister, the errant Seraphina, into coming home to Airtha in the Huygens System.

He steepled his fingers and considered his options.

Obviously, sitting by and doing nothing was not an option; but he knew the value of the *Intrepid*, this colony ship from a bygone era. The Transcend would benefit greatly from its technology—enough to finally give them the edge they needed over the Orion Guard.

Any response would require a delicate balance. They must demonstrate enough force to show that the Transcend would not take the abduction of its diplomats lightly, but not so much as to make these colonists think that they were too militant.

"Lieutenant Beezer, I want groups seven and thirteen to exit their hangars and jump to the *Intrepid.* Inform them that I wish their ships to flank the colony vessel, but keep a hundred-thousand kilometers distance from their fleet."

Of the fourteen fleet groups stationed at the watchpoint, seven and thirteen were the rapid response units—always ready to deploy and defend the watchpoint, or to travel across the stars to project the Transcend's might where needed.

Each group contained one hundred twenty-one ships, anchored by thirty six medium cruisers and eleven dreadnaughts. It was possible that the *Intrepid* was a match for the watchpoint's ships, but he had spent hundreds of hours analyzing the Battle of Bollam's World, and he believed he knew how to deal with their stasis shields to even the playing field.

Though he hoped it would not come to that. He would not go down in history as the man who destroyed the Transcend's greatest hope.

"Unknown contact," Lindal announced. "It dumped out of FTL really close—either it has the luckiest pilot ever, or detailed maps of the dark matter in this system."

"It never just rains," Greer muttered. "Scipio designation; what is a ship from that federation doing here?"

The Hand had more than a few operatives in Scipio. It was a key nation in the morass of systems that made up the Inner Stars, spanning nearly a hundred stellar systems and possessing a strong military. Controlling the direction of Scipio was of particular interest to the Transcend government—especially with Silstrand and other nearby systems facing increasing lawlessness.

<*It's Hand agent Elena. That ship is one outfitted for her mission in Scipio,*> Xerxes supplied. <*However, with our light-delay, she'll get to them long before we can get a message back to her—if that's her plan.*>

"Elena," Greer said softly. He summoned records on the agent, and saw that she was a long-time friend of Seraphina Tomlinson's. The Hand had suspicions—though nothing concrete—that she had been in contact with Sera during her exile over the past ten years.

"Summon her to the watchpoint—I don't expect her to comply, but I want it on record."

<*Message sent,*> Xerxes said.

"Uh…she's gone," Lieutenant Lindal announced. "I'm pulling data from more observation points."

Greer pulled up the data and poured over it. Lindal was right; one moment scan had a clear visual on Elena's ship, the next it simply disappeared.

"It's their stealth ship," Greer said. "We know it was operating at Bollam's World, but I thought we had identified it as *this* vessel," he gestured to one of the ships on the command center's holotank.

"It must not be—or they have more than one of those ships," Lindal replied. "Wait! I caught a strange refraction on the UV band. I think it was a ship, but now I have nothing."

"Well," Greer sighed. "We can safely assume that she's on her way to the *Intrepid*. I want scan analysis to find that stealth ship, and let me know the instant the fleets jump out."

AGENT ELENA

STELLAR DATE: 12.29.8929 (Adjusted Years)
LOCATION: ISS *Intrepid*
REGION: Ascella System, Galactic North of the Corona Australis star-forming region

<*There's a ship dropping in on us,*> Amanda interrupted Tanis's thoughts.

The statement brought Tanis back to the near-silence of the maglev train she rode with Lieutenant Smith, and away from her worry over what could cause Sera to turn so quickly.

<*Has it identified itself?*> Tanis asked after a moment's pause.

<*The beacon says it's the ship of a private citizen from the Scipio Federation. It hasn't answered any hails yet—oh wait, she just made contact. Patching you through.*>

The image of a woman appeared in Tanis's mind and she took in the woman's blood-red hair, eyes, and lips in a single glance. The woman opened her mouth to speak, revealing elongated canine teeth. Tanis's suspicions were confirmed; she was a sucker.

<*Colony ship* Intrepid, *please allow me to dock, I have important information for you,*> the woman spoke without preamble.

<*This is Governor Richards of the* Intrepid. *We're not exactly in a receptive mood—you're probably well aware that we have not had many warm welcomes of late. Why don't you relay your information from where you are?*>

Scan showed that the ship was close, only seven light seconds away. Tanis waited patiently for the woman's response to come.

When it did, she saw that the woman frowned and shook her head vigorously. <*I can't. If the watchpoint hasn't already tapped this communication, they're about to.*>

Tanis rubbed placed her hands over her face and ran them over her head while drawing in a deep breath.

"Shit!" she gasped as pain stabbed in her chest.

<*The watchpoint is what Sera called their outpost here,*> Angela said. <*This woman must be Hand.*>

<*I'm close. Let me get on her tail and use a squadron of Arc-6 fighters to bracket her,*> Corsia broke into the conversation.

Tanis Linked with the bridge net to effectively communicate with the command team—something she would have thought to do immediately, had she not been distracted by her pesky chest wound.

<*Not to mention the potential loss of a good friend,*> Angela commented privately on Tanis's thoughts.

<*Corsia, bring her aboard the* Andromeda, *but just her. Leave her ship in the black; we can get it later, if needed. Check her over, and then let me know when we're ready for a tight-beam chat.*>

<*Will do,*> Corsia replied. <*I'll update you when we have her.*>

Tanis switched back to the woman in her small cockpit. <*There's a cruiser on your tail. It's going to take you aboard and leave your ship behind. We've had enough surprises today.*>

She waited the requisite time for the message and response to traverse millions of miles of space. When it did, she saw the woman review her scan with furrowed brow, likely looking for the *Andromeda*. Then her eyes widened. <*Oh shit, it's* ***right*** *on my ass! That's impressive.*>

<*You're ringed by fighters—which you can't see, either. Behave and we'll talk in a bit.*>

Tanis severed the connection with the woman and reached out to the hospital ward on deck ninety-three.

<*What is Sera's condition?*> she asked the man operating the reception channel without preamble.

<*General—er, Governor!*> the man responded. <*She…uh…she's awake and letting us treat her, but she's unresponsive. I'll connect you with the doctor.*>

Doctor Barbara Summers, once a GSS corporal who worked visitor security on the *Intrepid* back at Mars, appeared in her mind.

<*Governor Richards, I'm glad you've reached out. Seraphina has suffered a rather insidious hack, one that has shunted many of her cognitive functions away and locked off Helen's access. We're trying to break past it to get to Helen—we anticipate she will know how to undo the hack—but so far, it's thwarting us—growing further into her brain.*>

<*So, she* ***was*** *hacked, then,*> Tanis stated. <*I suspected as much. There was something in her expression before she attacked me.*>

<*It was done through a nano-patch placed on her neck,*> Doctor Summers reported. <*It's honestly quite amazing—it took less than thirty seconds to subvert her. We think that it may have been accelerated by some programming her agency planted in her in the past.*>

<*That would have to be some well-secreted programming to escape Helen's notice,*> Angela added to the conversation.

Doctor Summers nodded. <*That is our assessment, as well. Bob has advised us that we should limit our intrusive attempts, and has sent Terry Chang up to assist. I'll bet the Transcend people will have a code to deactivate it—if you can extract it from them.*>

Tanis let a thin smile slip across her face. <*If they have such a code, they'll provide it to me.*>

A SIMPLE CHAT

STELLAR DATE: 12.29.8929 (Adjusted Years)
LOCATION: ISS *Intrepid*
REGION: Ascella System, Galactic North of the Corona Australis star-forming region

Tanis rose from her seat on the maglev and followed Lieutenant Smith to the security office. Her words to Doctor Summers echoed in her ears, and the memory of the torture she had inflicted on the assassin Kris years ago in Sol surged into her mind.

Tanis thought she had evolved—she was so sure, given her treatment of Drind on *Sabrina*. Thompson had pushed to beat the information out of The Mark's data tech, but Tanis took the high road with him, convincing him to join their cause. But now, with Sera's mind in jeopardy, she was ready to tear both Mark and Andrea limb-from-limb. Never mind that Andrea's father was president of the entire Transcend.

Let him come for her. Let them all come.

<*You need to relax,*> Angela applied the calming thought to Tanis's mind. <*You're not going to get anywhere if you go in there guns blazing.*>

<*They came here to assassinate me,*> Tanis fumed. <*And they used Sera as their tool! They may think they're clever, but even if they had killed me, no one would have believed their story for a moment. Bob vetted Sera. We know her intentions are pure.*>

<*They don't know about Bob,*> Angela chuckled. <*They couldn't have known that he would facilitate an unshakable faith in Sera. Use that; let them think that they've succeeded in that, at least. They'll tell you more voluntarily than if you resort to torture.*>

Tanis paused, realizing that Angela was right. She had fallen into some sort of primal maternal rage—protecting hers against all comers with the most violent option available. But she was smarter than these Hand agents. She had been pitted against far more cunning enemies.

"There was another one of them on the diplomat's ship," Smith said aloud as they stepped into the security office. "They're bringing him here from the dock."

"Good," Tanis nodded. "It makes sense that they'd have someone else onboard, in case things didn't pan out."

She stopped in the office's waiting room and collected her thoughts, preparing for whatever would come next.

"Are you going to go in like that?" Lieutenant Smith asked, glancing at her bloody uniform.

"Damn, I totally forgot about that," Tanis said. "There's a locker room down the hall. I'll clean up in a san and be back in five."

"Take your time," Smith replied. "I'll make sure they don't go anywhere."

<*Careful with those bandages,*> Angela advised as Tanis walked to the locker room. <*It won't take much to start bleeding again.*>

Tanis nodded silently, and, once the locker door slid closed behind her, carefully unwound the bandages, draping them over a bench before she stripped out of her dress uniform.

The hot spray of water felt glorious, and she spent longer than expected under its warming massage. She was careful not to let the jets hit the medseal the technician had applied to her wound, and gave an involuntary sign of dismay when the unit hit its max water usage and flipped to dry-mode.

She stepped out of the unit and saw that a fresh bandage was sitting on the bench with a clean shipsuit beside it.

<*Who would have thought Smith was that thoughtful,*> Angela said.

<*Better not have been him that did it, he's supposed to have his eye on our guests,*> Tanis replied as she gingerly wrapped the bandage back around her chest before slipping into the shipsuit.

<*It wasn't him, but he told one of the station officers to do it.*>

When she arrived at the entrance to the interview room, Smith handed her a glass of water and she downed it after sending a smile his way.

"Thanks, I needed that."

"General," Lieutenant Smith's voice was deadly serious, "do you want me in there with you? You did just suffer a serious injury."

Tanis glanced at the lieutenant; a Marine's Marine if ever there was one. He was over two hundred centimeters of rippling muscle, with fists the size of her head.

"You know what? I *do* want you in there with me. Be menacing—whenever it feels right."

Smith let out a short laugh. "It's going to feel right the whole time."

*****

Things weren't going as well as Tanis had hoped.

Mark was defensive, and Andrea seemed not to care at all that her own sister was accused of very a serious crime. Tanis hadn't shifted the blame to the two Hand agents yet—rather, she had focused on convincing them that the Marines had followed standard protocol by not using lethal force on Sera.

"Help me understand why she'd do this," Tanis asked, almost pleading.

"She's unstable," Mark said, and Tanis raised an eyebrow as though she was hopeful for more detail from him. The man was scum. He oozed lies from every pore, yet somehow he was good at hiding physical tells.

"She went off-book a lot when we were part of the same unit," Mark continued. "I had to rein her in more than once, and when she lost the CriEn module…well, she just went full rogue."

"That doesn't explain why she'd try to kill me," Tanis replied in even tones. "I've never seen such behavior from her before. If I had, do you think she'd be here now?"

"She's very good at hiding her intentions," Andrea said. "I think that she wanted to get in her father's good graces. Bring him the best prize ever—this ship—without its strong-willed governor and general."

Tanis considered those words. They rang true, but not for Sera—perhaps for Andrea.

It didn't surprise her. Tanis knew she could be a colossal pain in the ass—the Transcend probably had no place in it for General Richards. What they didn't know was that Tanis didn't want to be that woman forever.

<*Hah! Sure,*> Angela's comment was laced with disbelief.

"Then she's the best liar I've ever seen," Tanis said aloud to Andrea and Mark. "I've spent over a year with her, and she's never shown me any malice."

"I spent longer before she turned on me," Mark said with a sympathetic smile.

"There's no shame in being fooled by her. It's what she does."

"And her AI?" Tanis asked. "AI are rarely complicit in things like this—it doesn't suit their race's long-term outlook on things. Not to mention survival."

Andrea frowned, a look of conciliatory puzzlement on her face. "We've wondered that, too. Helen was always a good agent. Somehow, when Sera went rogue, she convinced Helen to go with her. We've never been able to come up with a wholly convincing rationale for it ourselves."

"So, what should we do with her?" Tanis asked. "She is, in large part, responsible for saving this ship."

"And for nearly killing you," Mark said with raised eyebrows. "Most people would be ready to do the same in response."

Tanis sighed, displaying emotion that was not feigned. "I've seen enough death. I'd like to see more forgiveness in my future."

"Then send her with us," Andrea said, holding her hands out with palms upturned. Tanis knew the gesture was meant to show openness and good intentions—something she was certain Andrea possessed none of. If Sera were to leave with these two, she'd be dead long before they ever reached their destination.

<They're really not going to give us anything,> Tanis said with a sigh. *<I guess it's time to play bad cop.>*

<Let's take a break,> Angela said. *<Perhaps Corsia's guest—Elena—can give us what we need, and we won't need to mess with these two at all.>*

<I like where your head's at,> Tanis replied and rose from the table. *<Certainly better than where mine is.>*

"Please forgive me," she said aloud. "I'm needed elsewhere for a few minutes. Lieutenant Smith will remain to ensure your needs are met."

She nodded to the lieutenant and left the room before the Transcend envoys could respond.

<Has Elena cleared security checks?> Tanis asked Corsia once she was in the hall.

<Momentarily. She's a deep cover agent, so she throws up a lot of red flags. Nothing stands out as crafted to harm us, but she doesn't really give a benevolent impression,> Corsia said, then paused. *<If things were different, I'd put her back in her ship and give her until the count of ten to get out of weapons range.>*

Corsia was nothing if not frank—it was one of the things she liked most about the AI.

<I understand completely. I wouldn't mind tossing **this** *pair out the airlock, too...but diplomatic relations and all that,>* Tanis replied.

<OK, I'm setting you up with a secure channel to Elena,> Corsia said. *<She has no Link access other than this tunnel to you. Be on guard.>*

<Thanks,> Tanis responded to Corsia before switching to the secure channel and addressing Elena. *<So, what do you have? I've got Sera restrained in a hospital bed, and two of the Transcend's finest in lockup. Whose side are you on?>*

Elena's image floated in Tanis's mind. Unlike a normal Link communication, she was not seeing Elena as the woman wished to present herself virtually, but rather a feed of her in a holding room.

Elena's appearance was unchanged from their previous communication; she still had the look of a sucker—though, given that she was a Hand agent, the affectation was probably a cover. An agent with a blood fetish would not make for a good operative.

Elena's gaze remained fixed at a point in front of her. Either she could detect the optical arrays watching her, or she had guessed correctly that Tanis would view her from that angle.

<*You don't start off easily, do you?*> Elena replied with a twist of her lips. <*People in my line of work don't really get to pick sides—hell, we don't even know which we're on most of the time.*>

<*Let me rephrase that,*> Tanis said. <*Who do you care about more: Sera, or Andrea and Mark?*>

Elena barked out a laugh. <*That's who they sent, is it? Mark, of all people. I'll bet that he wasn't supposed to be there, but weaseled his way in, somehow. You got a third, didn't you?*>

<*Answer the question,*> Tanis replied.

The smile slipped from Elena's face and her eyes grew dead serious. <*I care for Sera far more than either of those two bastards. Have they done something to her?*>

<*Why would you suspect that?*> Tanis asked

Elena shook her head in dismay. <*Because Mark wants Sera dead. He's tried before. That Justin would let him on this mission…*>

<*And what of Andrea?*> Tanis prompted.

<*She's worse,*> Elena said with a shake of her head. <*She's as emotionless as they come, though I doubt she was sent to kill Sera—but, I wouldn't put it past her to do it on her own.*>

Tanis considered Elena's words. It was obvious that the woman was hedging as much as she could, attempting to feel her out. Still, Elena had flown from Scipio to Ascella with the sole purpose to rescue Sera—or so she said.

<*She could also be the backup,*> Angela said. <*You're still alive, Sera's still alive…perhaps she comes in to finish the job?*>

Tanis nodded absently. <*The thought had crossed my mind.*>

<*We could strip the information from their minds,*> Angela said <*I don't think they could stop us.*>

<*No,*> Tanis sighed. <*We've made too many sacrifices in this journey. We have to make a home, eventually. The system they've offered us is the best we'll ever get—we can't start that relationship with Phobos Accord violations.*>

<***They** don't seem to be above such considerations,*> Angela replied.

<*Maybe,*> Tanis nodded. <*But I have to believe that these are just a few bad seeds. The FGT still terraforms worlds for others. Their agents can't all be like this.*>

<*Don't hold your breath,*> Angela replied.

Tanis grunted in response and turned her attention back to Elena. <*OK, lay it out. What do you have for me?*>

<*Well, you haven't told me anything. Is Sera OK? Have they done something to her?*>

Tanis couldn't be certain, but Elena's concern seemed genuine and she decided to lay it out and see what Elena offered in response.

<*They did something to her and tried to use her to kill me. I could see something in her eyes that makes me think it wasn't voluntary on her part.*>

<*Damnit!*> Elena whispered vehemently. <*We checked her over, we found a hack that Mark had planted, but we must have missed something.*>

<*You?*> Tanis asked.

Elena nodded. <*After the events…after she lost the CriEn and her team—except for Mark—she knew he was to blame. She had reason in the past to suspect him, but he had always managed to assuage her concerns. She reached out to me, and I met her in Silstrand. I found a hack at the core of her interface with Helen, one neither of them could see. It was designed to lock Helen out, and subvert Sera. The thing is…I removed it. How could it be back?*>

<*Get the specs from her,*> Bob inserted himself into Tanis's thoughts. <*I don't want to communicate directly with her, no need for more questions.*>

<*Give me the specs on that hack—if you still have them,*> Tanis ordered Elena. <*We may be able to use it to see if there's something similar at play now.*>

Elena nodded, and the information flooded across their connection. Tanis passed the data on to Bob while storing a copy to review later.

<*I see it now,*> Bob said. <*This is insidious; I would not have looked for something like this. There is something at play in the Transcend…something I did not expect….*>

<*Do we need Elena's further assistance to restore Sera?*> Tanis asked Bob.

<*Technically, no. I see why her prior work did not fully protect Sera. However, it will be to our benefit for them to think that we needed Elena's help. Bring her. I will begin to undo this violation with Terry's assistance. To Elena it will seem as though she provided the pivotal solution.*>

Tanis sent an affirmative response. She understood Bob's caution; if there was something in the Transcend that could produce a hack that Bob would term 'insidious', then there was no need to let that entity know Bob existed, or that he could reverse its work.

<*Corsia, put her on a shuttle and bring her in.*>

<*Aye, Governor,*> the ship's AI replied.

Tanis shook her head at the title. She thought she had left this sort of responsibility behind in Victoria, yet now it was back on her shoulders. Though this time, not as Lieutenant Governor—now the buck really *did* stop with her.

<*Brandt,*> Tanis called the Marine Commandant, <*I can see that you have things on full lock-down. We're about to bring that woman we have on the* Andromeda *here, but I don't yet trust her.*>

<*I don't trust anyone, Governor,*> Brandt replied. <*How are you feeling, by the way?*>

<*Well enough. Doctor Rosenberg has an assistant pinging me every five minutes trying to get me into a medbay—not that there's any point. My nano have nearly repaired the heart Sera shredded.*>

<*Tricky move, getting a second heart,*> Brandt said. <*Do you find it cuts into your lung capacity too much? I've considered getting one, but some folks say they have shortness of breath in a fight—I don't have a lot of room, either.*>

Tanis chuckled. Brandt was right about that. In a corps where the average Marine stood well over two hundred centimeters, Brandt's diminutive one-sixty was almost comical. Her slight build had earned her the nickname "The Pix" though it was something no one called her to her face.

Brandt made up for her small stature with a command presence that cowed even the largest Marine under her command—but the one thing she couldn't bully into place were a lot of mods in her small frame.

<*It's small; can't do as much as my primary, but my lungs can pull a lot more oxygen from the air than natural ones. Given how often I get shot in the chest, it's worth it,*> Tanis replied.

<*You know…most people have **never** been shot in the chest. I'm not saying you should exercise more caution…but…*>

<*OK, OK, I get it. Leave me be and go yell at someone,*> Tanis said with a mental chuckle.

<*I'm always yelling at someone—I can multitask, you know,*> Brandt sent a wink and closed the connection.

Tanis leaned against the wall and took a look around. Knowing that Sera could be restored took a load off her mind, but that was just the beginning. Andrea and Mark had tried to assassinate a foreign head of state, and she couldn't just let them off with a slap on the wrist.

Just as she was thinking she needed to see him, Joe materialized in front of her, holding their tiny daughter in his arms. She wished he really were there, not just a hologram projecting from their cabin. Embracing her family was just what she needed right now.

"You need a hand?" he asked. "I can have someone look after Cary."

Tanis leaned over and looked into the face of her little girl. She hated that she had to be away from her so much, but soon they would be out of Ascella and things would calm down.

"I hate to ask it," Tanis replied. "She needs her parents—at least one of them—to be around."

"She needs them to be alive, and their starship to remain in one piece, even more," Joe said with a raised eyebrow. "I'm at Tracy's—she's off for the next few days and can watch her. Even if she gets called in, her oldest two are used to looking after little ones."

Tanis nodded. Tracy was a good woman, and her cabin wasn't too far from theirs. "I see that you already planned to get back on duty."

"Well, technically you outrank me and can tell me no…but yes, I need to be out there."

Tanis understood what he meant. "Corsia has the pinnace coming in with a…friend of Sera's. Catch a ride on the return trip and get to your captain's chair."

Joe smiled and tossed her a casual salute. "Aye, aye." He held up their daughter. "Say goodbye to Mommy. We'll check on you real soon."

Tanis blew her daughter a kiss, and took a deep breath as Joe and Cary disappeared from view.

<*Our visitors are getting restless in here,*> Lieutenant Smith said.

<*One thing after the other,*> Tanis commented to Angela as she walked back to the holding room.

<*Don't grouse at me. It's the way you like it.*>

AWAKE

STELLAR DATE: 12.29.8929 (Adjusted Years)
LOCATION: ISS *Intrepid*
REGION: Ascella System, Galactic North of the Corona Australis star-forming region

Sera's head screamed with pain, as though someone had drilled a hole in her skull and poured acid inside. She bit back a sob and tried to regulate her breathing.

"Good, you're awake," a voice said. "From what I can tell, you're probably in a bit of pain. We're working on that. Helen should also be back with you in a minute or two."

Helen! That was part of the pain. Sera was subconsciously trying to access her connection with Helen and it wasn't there. It wasn't the phantom limb sort of ache one got when an AI had been removed cleanly, but rather the screaming agony of a pulverized appendage.

The pain began to recede and Sera thought that perhaps she recognized the voice that had spoken—though she couldn't place it. She knew that she should be able to, but couldn't drum up the name no matter how hard she tried.

That was the other part of the pain; she had no access to her digital data stores. She was thinking with pure organics, something she hadn't done in decades. She tried to focus, to access her data volumes, but where there once was instant information, there was nothing but searing agony.

She felt so slow and stupid. Her state should have been immediately obvious, but she hadn't even realized how severed she was from her implants. A dim recollection of how this could have happened clawed its way into her conscious mind, and she whispered a single word.

"Mark."

"Good," the voice said, "you have access to your organic memories. Means this is working."

Sera began to hear other voices around her, of people moving about, focused on their work. She was indoors, in a room, perhaps a hospital by the sterile smell. She shifted and, in the moments before her nerve endings set new fire to her brain, she realized that she was strapped down.

"Try not to move. You got hit by no small number of pulse blasts," a different voice said. "The Marines exercised some restraint, but not as much as they could have."

Sera could not place the new voice, but she knew what Marines were. If she had been shot by them and still lived to tell the tale, then she had reason to be grateful. Still, try as she might, she could not remember enough to even guess at why she had been shot.

"OK," a third voice said, this one only vaguely familiar, "let's try and reactivate her internal mods."

"Brace yourself," the first voice said. "This is going to hurt."

Sera couldn't imagine anything hurting more than the pain she already felt, but she was wrong. A scream tore out of her; she felt as though her brain was tearing itself to shreds, but then the agony subsided to tolerable levels.

That was when the pain from her body began to take over—her broken bones and damaged organs letting her know just how upset they were over her current state.

"Can you do something about how much this hurts?" Sera managed to whisper, her voice cracking as she struggled to speak.

"In a moment, dear," the first voice said. "We have to finish with Helen, then you'll be back in full control of your mods and you can suppress the pain."

Sera grunted in response, and, true to her unseen benefactor's word, Helen was back just a few seconds later.

<*Well, that was unpleasant,*> Helen's dry voice swept through Sera's mind like a broom, clearing away the fog and bringing Sera to full consciousness. Together they suppressed the thundering pain—though it was still present—and assessed their current state.

<*We're in a medbay on the* Intrepid,> Helen provided.

<*I surmised as much,*> Sera said in agreement. <*And now I know how we got here.*>

<*Yes,*> Helen's voice exhibited uncharacteristic anger. <*We were hacked.*>

Sera sent agreement to Helen. Her AI was right; somehow they had been subverted—and in very short order, too.

<*Was it Mark? How was that even possible? Elena removed the Hand's backdoor when we struck out on our own.*>

Helen's response was a pulse of mental uncertainty, and Sera gauged the wisdom of opening her eyes to see who was tending to her wounded mind and body. Curiosity won out, and she cracked her eyelids and peered around the room.

The first face she saw was that of Terry, head of the *Intrepid*'s Net Security division. Terry's presence didn't surprise her. Aside from Bob and his avatars, few knew the ins and outs of the human mind and its many possible modifications—and weaknesses—better.

At the foot of the bed stood a woman she vaguely recognized; after a moment, her reestablished digital archives identified her as Dr. Summers.

Beyond her, in the shadows, stood Flaherty. He hadn't spoken, but she wasn't surprised to see him there at all. Sera gave him a weak smile, and turned her head to the left, looking for the third person.

The face staring down at her was vaguely familiar, but the long fangs and red eyes made recognition difficult. She didn't recall any suckers being present on the *Intrepid*. That sort of behavior didn't fit well with people looking to build a colony.

"Don't you recognize me? We've been through too much to think we could be strangers," the woman said.

"Elly!" Sera exclaimed. "How the hell are you here...and why are you a sucker? Never mind, I know it's a cover—I hope it's a cover."

"Nice to see you, too. And of course it's a cover. Do you know how much of a bitch it is to eat around these damn teeth?"

"I can only imagine," Sera replied absently. "What I really want to know is how did Mark hack me? I thought we removed The Hand's access."

Elena nodded slowly and looked up to Terry. "I'm not really sure, to be honest. As far as I can tell, we had completely removed it ten years ago; but when they brought me in, it was there the same as before. Almost like I hadn't done a thing."

"Great, does this mean I will be at their mercy forever?" Sera asked, looking between Terry and Elena.

Elena appeared uncertain while Terry shook her head. "Absolutely not. We'll square this away."

<*They don't want Elena to know about Bob,*> Helen said.

<I can imagine why not. They're not—stars, ***I'm*** *not—terribly trusting of the Transcend right now. I'll take Terry's word for it for now, but if we do get back to Airtha, I want the other you to take a look.>*

Helen passed a feeling of agreement to Sera. *<Absolutely. Being sequestered like that was not exactly a great time for me, either.>*

A memory of what she had done while subverted flashed into her mind.

"Oh, shit, is Tanis OK? Stars, she must want to kill me right now," Sera said aloud.

"She's fine," Dr. Summers said from her place at the foot of the bed. "And you seem to be nearly recovered—mentally, at least—if you can recall those events."

"Do you remember what happened when you were in private with the envoys?" Terry asked.

Sera did, and it shamed her that her people would do such a thing. She closed her eyes and let out a long breath.

"I do," she said after a minute. "They want Tanis dead and…they were willing to sacrifice me to do it."

"What?" Dr. Summers exclaimed. "Those bastards!"

Sera ignored the doctor's outburst and her eyes darted between Terry and Elena. She saw Elena become more guarded as Terry nodded. She knew that Bob and Tanis would have ferreted out the truth behind Andrea's intentions by now. Terry would have been briefed, and the concern in the woman's eyes was palpable.

It was an understandable emotion. The colonists aboard the *Intrepid* really couldn't catch a break. Even the Transcend, who should have been their benefactor and savior, was opposed to them. Or at least, to Tanis.

"Do you guys think you could leave me for just a bit?" Sera asked. "I really need a few minutes to myself."

Dr. Summers and Elena both looked to Terry, who nodded.

"And the restraints?" Sera asked.

"I'll advise Tanis on your condition," Terry replied solemnly. "They'll come off on her order only."

Sera nodded silently, keenly aware that much of the goodwill she had earned with the *Intrepid*'s crew had been lost—involuntary actions notwithstanding.

ESCALATION

STELLAR DATE: 12.30.8929 (Adjusted Years)
LOCATION: ISS *Intrepid*
REGION: Ascella System, Galactic North of the Corona Australis star-forming region

<*Before you go in there,*> Amanda broke into Tanis's thoughts. <*The watchpoint has shown their hand. Ships are moving out of two of the locations we flagged.*>

<*Was bound to happen sooner or later,*> Tanis replied. <*How many?*>

<*They're still pulling out of their covert hangars. Over a hundred confirmed so far.*>

Tanis paused and placed a hand on the wall. She took a deep breath and Linked with the bridge.

<*Tanis,*> Captain Andrews greeted her. <*I trust you've been informed that we're receiving the usual welcome party out there.*>

<*Just once, I'd like to fly into a system where everyone doesn't want to kill us,*> Tanis replied.

<*If wishes were fishes…*> Amanda said with a mental smile.

Tanis stepped into the center of the hall, outside the entrance to the holding room. She surrounded herself with holodisplays showing the space surrounding the *Intrepid.*

The two stars of the Ascella system danced around one another in a tight orbit—tight for stars, at least—with a current separation of only one hundred fifty150 AU. Their proximity was one of the reasons that the system remained uninhabited; the stars stirred up too much chaos to make Ascella a safe place to settle down.

Between the two stars, there were seventeen major planets and hundreds of dwarf worlds. A morass of asteroid belts circled the stars, with clusters of dust, ice, and rock in the Lagrange points between the stars and their major satellites.

The moment they dropped out of the dark layer and back into normal space, she had taken one look at the system and known why the Transcend used it. It was all but purpose-built for war.

<*I would not be surprised if that was exactly what happened here,*> Angela said.

<*What? That the Transcend mucked with this system to set it up like this?*> Tanis asked.

Angela sent an affirmation, and Tanis briefly considered the power of the Transcend—to remake worlds within the Inner Stars less palatable just so that they could hide in them was serious long-term planning.

Beyond the initial three locations Corsia had reported, the *Intrepid*'s probes and cloaked fighters had positively identified seven more base locations, and several more suspects.

From what she could see, there were two fleets forming up: one coming from within a cluster of dwarf worlds only two AU from the *Intrepid,* and another from a world seven AU away. Even at max burn, the closest ships were over a day away—unless they knew the positions of dark matter in this system well enough to skip through the dark layer insystem.

It was risky; a system like this would be rife with matter in the dark layer, but she had to consider the possibility.

<*Anything from the third person on the envoy's ship?*> Tanis asked Amanda.

<*Not yet. Brandt has some folks talking to him, but so far he professes to have no knowledge of*

any plan to kill you. He did say that he was supposed to be on the boarding party, not Mark, but claims he was drugged and came to shortly before we boarded. We haven't been able to verify that without a forced examination.>

Tanis considered the information. If Sera's brother, Serge, was telling the truth, then not everyone in the Transcend was hell-bent on killing her—which was a small victory, at least.

<*Oh! Sera's awake and is herself again.*>

<*Thank the stars for small miracles,*> Tanis sighed.

<*Brandt,*> Tanis connected to the Marine Commandant.

<*Yes, General,*> came Brandt's clipped reply.

<*Send Serge to the medbay where Sera is. I want them to have a little reunion and see what we can ferret out—and what we can do to clean up this mess.*>

<*On it,*> Brandt responded.

Tanis nodded to herself, and quickly reviewed division statuses across the ship to ensure everything was ready for whatever may come their way. Once she had sent a few orders to various sections, she poked her head into the room where Mark and Andrea sat, looking much more agitated than when she left.

"How much longer are you going to hold us here?" Mark shot at her the moment she opened the door. "Your goon here won't give us any news."

Lieutenant Smith flashed a malignant smile at the pair, but didn't say a word in response.

"Sorry," Tanis replied. "Your little attempt on my life caused quite a stir, and gave me an ever-loving mess to clean up."

"Our attempt?" Andrea asked with narrowed eyes. "We had nothing to do with it. This was all Sera's doing! She's not known to be especially stable, as you can now attest."

"Well," Tanis smiled sweetly, "she's awake and back to herself again, so I'm going to have a chat with her and get the skinny on what's really going on. I'm going to have Serge join us, to see what he thinks of all this."

Andrea's expression did not waver for an instant, but Mark's eyes widened for just a moment. If anyone on their mission was expendable, it was him. The fact that Sera ever saw anything in this slime-ball of a man would forever baffle Tanis.

"Lieutenant," she turned to Smith, "I want them secured and ready to move. Full lockdown, full physical restraint. Also, get a Mark-9 drone on them. One false move, turn them to puddles."

She gave her own predatory smile to the pair behind the table. "You want our picotech; I know you do. Test Lieutenant Smith in any way, and he has my full authorization to introduce you to it, personally."

Her statement finally elicited a reaction from Andrea—a noticeable whitening of her skin. Though the *Intrepid*'s nano-technology was, in aggregate, more advanced than the Transcend's, this pair had defenses enough to keep it from entering their minds and bodies.

Picobots, on the other hand, would not face any opposition infiltrating their bodies—nor was there any way they could stop the picoscale machines from tearing them apart atom by atom.

Tanis didn't wait any longer. She left the room, but not before holding the door wide for a squad of Marines to enter with weapons leveled.

<*Sera,*> Tanis sent to her friend once she was back in the hall, <*I'm on my way.*>

REUNION

STELLAR DATE: 12.30.8929 (Adjusted Years)
LOCATION: ISS *Intrepid*
REGION: Ascella System, Galactic North of the Corona Australis star-forming region

Tanis rushed through the ship's corridors at a pace that had her secondary heart working overtime. A fireteam of Marines in full armor followed her, eyeing every nook and cranny of the ship that had been their home for centuries as though it were enemy territory.

<*What's your plan?*> Terrance Enfield interrupted her thoughts. <*They're going to demand their people back—I don't want to jeopardize the colony for revenge.*>

Tanis gave a mental shake of her head. Terrance was so close to reaching his life-long goal that she could forgive him for thinking that she valued it any less than he. Even though his motivations for wanting to build a colony world were entirely different now than when they left Sol nearly five thousand years ago, he remained single-minded in his drive to reach their new home.

<*I don't want to fight another war,*> Tanis replied. <*I will give them back their people, but I will not send Sera with them against her will.*>

<*Will you sacrifice our dream of a colony?*> Terrance asked, anger seeping into his mental tone. <*Is she worth that much to you?*>

<*Do you want to have a free colony, or to be a vassal state?*> Tanis replied without equivocation. <*Because if we let them come onto our ship, attempt to assassinate our leadership, and then still give in to all their demands, then that is what we'll end up as.*>

Terrance did not respond for almost a minute, and Tanis wondered if their conversation had come to an end.

<*Very well, Tanis. You've gotten us this far; but please, be as circumspect as you can.*>

<*When am I not?*> Tanis replied with a smile.

<*Oh, that will certainly build confidence,*> Angela said privately.

<*I couldn't help it,*> Tanis said as she boarded a maglev train. <*I've always put this mission first. Hell, they put me in charge of it, for fucksakes! Against my will! If Terrance can't trust me to get the job done, then he deserves a bit of ribbing.*>

Angela didn't respond.

Tanis rode the train in silence past two stops before disembarking at the ship's forward hospital. The section spanned over a square kilometer across seven decks, and though she knew it well, it still took her some minutes to navigate its warren of corridors.

When the *Intrepid* departed from Sol long ago, the hospital had been much smaller; but during the Victoria years, when over a hundred thousand crew and colonists roamed the ship, it had been expanded considerably—if for no other reason than to handle all the births.

Upon arrival at the door to Sera's room, she paused to allow two of the Marines to enter first. She trusted Bob's assessment that Sera was no longer a threat, but she wasn't about to behave as though a threat could not re-emerge—especially with Elena, another unknown quantity, in the mix.

She heard Terry greet the Marines, and a moment later, the corporal called out that all was clear. Tanis checked Serge's location before entering, and saw that Sera's brother was still five minutes out.

<I'll let you know when he's here,> Angela said.

Tanis appreciated the gesture. There were a lot of requests hitting her queue; though with the notification that Joe was now aboard the *Andromeda,* one of her concerns had diminished.

"Sera," she said as she entered the room and approached her friend still restrained to the bed.

"Tanis," Sera's eyes were wide and filled with apology. "I can't tell you how sorry I am—and how glad I am that you never told me about your little heart modification."

She noticed Flaherty in the corner and nodded to him. He grunted in response, and returned to eyeing the Marines.

"I've got to have some secrets," Tanis replied with a smile. "We can do away with the restraints," she said, and the room's monitoring systems deactivated the clamps around Sera's arms and legs.

The Marines didn't move a muscle, but they somehow seemed even more alert.

Sera's gaze darted to the soldiers before she closed her eyes and slowly lifted her arms—an expression of both pain and relief crossed her face.

"Oh, thank you," Sera moaned. "I was getting the worst cramp you could ever imagine."

"I'll bet," Tanis said as she took a seat beside the bed. "I'm glad you're yourself again. I didn't want to think that we wouldn't be able to get you back."

<I trust that you've kept Bob's abilities to yourself?> she asked privately. *<I don't trust your friend here much further than I can throw her.>*

<I've not breathed a word; though Bob has assured Helen and I that we are safe from any future subversion of our minds,> Sera replied. *<I'm glad he's on our side.>*

Tanis added the comment to an extensive list of observations Sera had made about Bob over the prior months. She made a note to finally confront Sera over what bothered her so much about AI. However, for now, she opted to ignore the statement.

<What of Elena?> Tanis asked. *<Can we trust her?>*

Tanis was carrying on an audible conversation with Sera, Elena, and Terry. Sera responded aloud to a question before replying to Tanis over the Link.

<I have no idea how you do that so fluidly,> Sera said. *<If I didn't know better, I'd think your complete attention was on what Terry is saying right now.>*

<I'm also talking to Joe and Captain Andrews,> Tanis replied. *<But, about Elena?>*

<Show-off,> Angela whispered in Tanis's mind.

<I've trusted her with my life in the past…> Sera said before pausing. *<I don't see why I wouldn't now. She said that she raced here as soon as she saw what happened at Bollam's World. Why would she do that if she meant me harm?>*

<I can think of a hundred reasons,> Tanis replied. *<Perhaps she has some reason to wish you harm that she didn't before, or maybe she's a fail-safe to attempt to bridge things with the Transcend after Andrea and Mark failed. She could even be here for her own advancement. The fact that the backdoor into your mind remained, leaving you open to The Hand's machinations, could also be her doing.>*

<Yeah, I thought of a lot of those, too. I just didn't want to say them—it might make one true.>

Sera sounded morose, and Tanis gave her an understanding look. Not knowing if you could trust your friends was never easy. The simplest route was to never trust anyone—

though that would slowly eat a person's soul.

<*We have to assume she has ulterior motives,*> Tanis said. <*At least, until Bob can read enough of her actions to surmise her true intentions.*>

<*Serge is here,*> Angela informed the pair.

Tanis turned and looked to the door. <*Let him in,*> she informed the Marines outside.

Serge entered, and she saw a strong resemblance between him and Sera—far more apparent than with Andrea; they could have passed for fraternal twins. His eyes swept across the room and landed on Sera, his clouded visage cleared and a smile spread across his lips.

"Core, Sera, you're OK. When they told me we were going to the hospital to see you…" he stopped himself, apparently remembering that he was in unknown company.

Tanis rose and extended her hand. "I'm Tanis Richards, governor of the New Canaan colony mission."

A look of concern crossed Serge's face before he took her hand and shook it firmly.

"Serge Tomlinson," he replied.

<*The first person we've met from the Transcend who might just be honest and sincere, by the looks of him,*> Angela said to Tanis.

<*Perhaps,*> she replied.

"Nice to meet you, Serge," Tanis said aloud. "I hope you can help us make sense of everything that has happened today."

"Yes, sure, of course," Serge said absently as he peered at Sera. "Are you OK, Sis? It's been a long time."

"It has," Sera said and held out an arm. Serge stepped forward and leaned in to embrace his sister.

"Gently," Sera cautioned. "I took a bit of a beating from some pulse blasts earlier."

Serge shot an eye at the Marines before pausing on Elena.

"Wait…Elena? Is that you?"

"Took you long enough," Elena grinned. "I was beginning to think that the diplomatic corps would need to work on your powers of observation."

Serge smiled wanly. "Sorry, I was a bit distracted."

"That's just the time you need to be the most observant," Sera said. "But enough of that. Our little reunion can wait. How is it that you were on the ship while Mark came aboard the *Intrepid?*"

Serge sighed. "Mark took me out with a rather clever cocktail of drugs that I ingested over the last few meals. Individually, what he fed me didn't amount to anything particularly malicious; but with one last bite of a cookie, I was laid out on the galley floor. By the time I came to, they were both gone."

"You sure it was Mark?" Elena asked. "Drugging someone is just the sort of thing I'd expect Andrea to do."

Serge shrugged. "I guess it could be. They're both snakes in the grass. My gut tells me it was Mark, though."

"Neither are worth the O^2 they burn," Sera grunted. "Use me to fucking kill Tanis, and then pray that the Marines mowed me down?"

"So, we're going with that?" Terry asked with a raised eyebrow. "Is it a guess, or do you remember now?"

"I remember," Sera replied. "It took a bit, and they didn't spell it out, but the pieces are all there. The question is, who ordered it?"

"I can tell you that it wasn't in the mission plan. We were to trade your fifth millennia tech for the colony. No pico, no stasis shields," Serge said with raised palms. "There was nothing about any infiltration or subversion—though, there was a very strongly-worded section about bringing you back to Airtha, Sis."

Sera nodded. "Not surprising. Father has probably had enough of me flitting about the Inner Stars. Though, given the successes I've had, you'd think he would want me to stay out there." She finished with a chuckle that turned into a cough. "Ow, I guess no laughing yet..."

"And what about Elena here?" Tanis asked Serge, watching him with every sense she possessed. "Was she part of the plan?"

"Not even a little bit," Serge replied with a smile. "But I bet that Justin is going to be mightily pissed that you just jetted out of Scipio. There's a lot of work to do there, and it took forever to get you planted."

Elena waved her hand dismissively. "My cover can be rebuilt—if I'm not fired...or worse."

"Treason, I assume?" Tanis asked.

"AWOL at the least," Elena replied with a solemn nod. "Treason if Andrea decides that she has it in for me—which she will. There's no way they expected you to get Sera restored—and I'm sure Andrea and Mark had a scheme to take Sera back with them. A trip she would not have survived."

Sera shook her head. "I can see Mark doing that, but Andrea? Has she really become so calculating?" She directed the last to Serge.

"And then some," her brother sighed. "Father has been putting more and more on her shoulders. She resented being sent out here to fetch you, even if it only took a few months out of her schedule."

Tanis's eyes snapped up at Serge's statement.

"Months?" Tanis asked.

Sera sighed. "You never really could keep a secret, could you, Serge?"

Serge shrugged in response. "You keep secrets that you don't need to, Sis. Ford-Svaiter mirrors being a prime example."

Tanis saw that Elena was shaking her head, and fixed Sera with a hard stare before she reached out to Bob.

<Did you know they had wormhole tech?>

<I suspected. Their control over an empire as large as the Transcend demanded ultra-fast travel. The dark layer of space, with its maximum multiplier of seven hundred fifty times light speed, would still make their longer trips take over a decade,> Bob replied. *<I thought you had suspected as much, as well.>*

Tanis sighed. She *had* suspected, but her suspicions and Bob's were on entirely different levels.

"We can chat about that later," Tanis said with a wink. "However, what can we expect from the commander of this watchpoint?"

"That'll be General Greer," Sera confirmed. "Has he called?"

Tanis shook her head. "Called, no. Sent in two fleets? Yes."

"Sorry about that," Serge shrugged. "It's protocol."

Sera flashed her brother an exasperated look before replying. "Greer is by-the-book, and he bears our father no special love; though I don't know if that will work out in our favor or not. I hope it does—it's one of the reasons I chose this watchpoint."

<*Speaking of the watchpoint, a message is coming in from the nearest fleet,*> Amanda said to the group.

"Thanks, Amanda," Tanis said aloud. "I'll take it privately."

If Greer was on any of the approaching ships, he would still be at least thirty light minutes distant, though she wondered if the Transcend ships could effect their wormholes within a stellar system.

Another possibility she had to consider.

She took a chair, and the room around her disappeared, replaced by the bridge of a warship. In the center, with hands clasped behind his back and legs in a wide stance, stood a tall man with long, brown hair and a reddish beard. His hair swept back over his shoulders, and the beard was neat and trim. His eyes were blue and cold, and, while not menacing, they contained the certainty of someone fully aware and confident of their abilities.

His black uniform was crisp, and a single star adorned each lapel of his collar. His posture remained rigid and unwavering as he began to speak.

"To the commanding officer, or colony leader, of the ISS *Intrepid*," he began. "This is General Tsaroff of the Transcend Space Force. We have received a distress call from our diplomatic mission to your ship, and are approaching to render assistance. Please be advised that should any harm come to Transcend Government representatives, we will view this unfavorably and take strong action in response."

<*For a general, he certainly speaks like a politician,*> Angela commented.

<*Or a lawyer,*> Tanis responded.

"Please respond promptly with your affirmation that nothing untoward has happened to our envoys, and prepare to release them into our care."

<*Definitely a lawyer in a prior life,*> Angela agreed.

The transmission ended, and the hospital room snapped back into view around Tanis.

"General Tsaroff sends his regards," she said dryly. "No mention of Greer in his transmission."

"Tsaroff commands the rapid response fleets here under Greer," Serge replied. "Greer wouldn't accompany his advance forces."

"Advance forces?" Tanis asked. "Just how many ships do they have here in the watchpoint?"

"The briefing did not contain that level of detail," Serge said with a shrug. "I suspect there are at least a dozen fleet groups here at Aurora."

Tanis whistled. It was a lot of firepower. If they were on the same level as the AST's dreadnaughts they faced in the Bollam's World System, then this was a fight they could not win—even with picotech. The Transcend ships would not allow the *Intrepid*'s fighters to get close enough to deliver picobombs—not that obliterating the Transcend fleet was an option she was even considering.

Sera peered at her, likely wondering what direction her internal deliberations were taking. "What's it going to be?" she asked.

"I won't go to war just for revenge; but I don't intend to simply hand over assassins without any recompense," Tanis replied.

"You know they'll claim diplomatic immunity," Terry advised.

Tanis nodded. "And our current circumstances leave room for interpretation about whether or not they are officially accepted diplomats—since we are currently within territory which is unclaimed by either party. By all the ancient laws, Andrea and Mark are assassins, and no protections exist for them."

<*It's sure a great way to kick things off,*> Angela added.

Tanis rose from her seat. "I need to get to the bridge. Terry, you can get back to the thousand things I know are pressing down on you. Flaherty, Serge, Elena, stay here with Sera. Once the doctors pronounce her fit, I'll have the four of you moved to one of our ready-rooms near the bridge."

She gave Sera one last look before leaving. "I'm glad you're OK."

"And I'm glad I didn't kill you," Sera replied with a grin.

<*That makes three of us,*> Angela replied.

DETERMINATION

STELLAR DATE: 12.30.8929 (Adjusted Years)
LOCATION: ISS *Intrepid*
REGION: Ascella System, Galactic North of the Corona Australis star-forming region

Tanis stood before the bridge's main holotank, surveying the assembling fleets and considering her response to General Tsaroff.

"It stinks," Captain Andrews said from her side. "They try to kill you—for stars know what reason—and we'll ultimately turn your would-be assassins right back over."

"Yeah, I can't think of anything we can negotiate for that is worth the trouble. Perhaps dumping them in their ship and kicking it out the door is the best we can do to assuage our wounded pride," Tanis replied.

"I have to admit," the captain said quietly, "I'm surprised you didn't make a case for forcibly extracting their intentions."

Tanis sighed. She really did want to know why her neck was on the chopping block, but she also knew that any intelligence she could extract from Andrea and Mark would be suspect. Mark likely didn't know anything, anyway. He just wanted Sera dead so that she wouldn't testify against him.

"I guess I'm getting soft in my old age," she replied.

A change on the holodisplay caught her attention. The fleet at the asteroid belt was forming up near what appeared to be a small ring. Tanis didn't recall seeing it before, and played back the last few minutes of scan.

The replay showed that the ring had started out as a series of asteroids that unfolded and formed the structure. It wasn't big enough to fly the *Intrepid* through, but any of the Transcend ships would fit with ease.

"I bet I know what that is," Tanis said quietly.

"Really?" Captain Andrews asked, casting a sharp eye her way. "Is it what it looks like?"

Tanis nodded. "Sera's brother, Serge, let it slip. They have worked out the tech behind Ford-Svaiter mirrors. I would imagine that it puts dark layer FTL to shame."

"Holy crap!" the scan officer cried out.

Tanis saw the reason for his alarm. Scan still showed the ships assembling near the wormhole-creating ring, but even before they saw any vessels pass through the distant ring, ships began to appear—as if by magic—a scant hundred-thousand kilometers from the *Intrepid*'s fleet.

Admiral Sanderson let out a low whistle from the back of the bridge. "Now *that* is faster-than-light travel."

Tanis nodded. The light from their prior location would take thirty minutes before it showed the Transcend ships creating and entering their wormholes. However, closer to the *Intrepid*, the light from the ships in their new position had already arrived.

From their vantage, it appeared as though the ships were in two places at once.

In theory, a Ford-Svaiter mirror was a simple apparatus that focused quantum energy along the mirror's focal line, which created negative energy. That negative energy created a wormhole, and complimentary mirrors on the front of the ships would extend the wormhole to the desired exit point.

<*Theory no more, it seems,*> Angela added. <*I'm amazed that they can control the exit point so well. That's a level of precision not even dark layer FTL transitions can manage.*>

<*Of limited use, though. They need a ring to initiate the process, and they don't have one on this side,*> Tanis responded.

<*Not that I can think of a reason they'll need to leave in a hurry,*> Angela said. <*Their second fleet just appeared, too.*>

Tanis took a deep breath, every eye on the bridge furtively glancing her way, waiting for her to tell them what to do. She schooled her expression and signaled the comm officer.

"Now that they're on our doorstep, communication should be a lot easier. Link us up and let them know that I want to chat."

The officer bent to her task. A minute later, she nodded to Tanis and General Tsaroff appeared before her.

"General Tsaroff," Tanis said with a nod of her head. "I am Governor Richards. Thank you for taking my call."

"I had heard it was General Richards," Tsaroff replied without preamble. "Am I to believe that you are now governor, as well?"

Tanis nodded. "I am, and I will return your assassins to you…once I receive some assurances."

"Assassins?" General Tsaroff's eyes widened, his face revealing a moment of surprise before he recovered. "I assure you, we sent you our most respected diplomats to treat with you, and from what we understand, you abducted them."

"Can we dispense with all the doublespeak?" Tanis asked. "I've had a long day, and I'll lay it out plainly. Mark and Andrea Tomlinson hacked Sera and tried to use her to kill me, hoping that one, or both, of us would die in the attempt. Sera did not succeed, and Elena—one of your Hand agents—showed up, and helped us undo Sera's and Helen's subversion. Serge and Elena are with Sera, who is recovering, and Andrea and Mark are in a holding room. You can have that pair back, but, again, not until I get some assurances."

Tsaroff did not reply for several moments and Tanis wondered if he had a mechanism for real-time communications with General Greer—wherever he was—or if he was speaking with an AI. Eventually, he refocused on her, his already narrowed eyes mere slits.

"So, now you hold three of our president's children, and one of our agents, too. I also will need some assurances. What are your conditions?"

"Very simple," Tanis replied. "I will turn over Mark and Andrea, entirely unharmed, but in stasis—which is how they will stay until they arrive with Serge back in Airtha. I will also give him the CriEn module and our fully executed agreement for the colony system in the M25 cluster. We will provide the technology we agreed upon in our contract when we arrive at our colony system. Also, your ships will come no closer to the *Intrepid* than they currently are, or our agreement is off."

"I don't have a lot of reasons to trust you," Tsaroff replied. "I will need to speak with Serge, since he is the one who sent the distress signal."

"Tanis, if I may?" a voice said from across the bridge.

She turned to see Flaherty standing at the room's portside entrance. It was surprising to see him separated from Sera at a time like this, but she suspected that if he were here, he must have a card to play with Tsaroff.

She nodded and he approached. Tanis adjusted the pickups so that he was included in the projection to Tsaroff.

"General Tsaroff," Flaherty said in greeting.

"Colonel Flaherty!" Tsaroff replied, real emotion showing on his face—something akin to surprise and respect. "I would expect you to be protecting Sera at a time like this."

<*Colonel, is it?*> Angela mused.

<*He always did have a military bearing,*> Tanis replied. <*Though, colonel…that is something.*>

"She is safe," Flaherty replied. "Though Andrea and Mark would have liked to see her otherwise."

"So, Governor Richards here speaks the truth?" Tsaroff asked. "Did they subvert Sera Tomlinson?"

"If by 'they', you mean that piece of trash Mark, and Sera's waste-of-flesh sister, Andrea, then yes," Flaherty chewed out the names of his charge's sister and former lover. "They subverted her, and attempted to use her to assassinate a foreign head of state."

"That's a serious charge," Tsaroff replied. "Though, I've never known you to exaggerate."

"That's because I don't," Flaherty replied. "Take the deal."

"I'll have to confer with General Greer first," Tsaroff said. "Also, before we strike up any agreement, we'll need to send over a representative to examine all Transcend citizens to ensure they are truly unharmed and corroborate your story."

"Well," Tanis replied. "Sera's had some harm done to her, but that is on Mark and Andrea."

"So you say," Tsaroff said before cutting the connection.

Tanis let out a long sigh before muttering, "Why does everyone in the Transcend seem like raging assholes?"

"A lot of them have been in their positions for too long," Flaherty replied. "Tsaroff has been a one-star general for at least a hundred years; I think he needs a change."

Tanis laughed. "Yeah, at least I got jacked up to three stars—made me feel like I was doing something right. But you, a colonel…now *that's* news."

Flaherty waved his hand, dismissing her statement. "That is an old rank from a long time ago. I am no longer an officer in the Transcend Space Force."

"Well, it seemed to come in handy with Tsaroff," Captain Andrews replied with a smile.

Tanis nodded, noticing how much more relaxed the captain had become since she had taken over as governor. She hoped that he would let her visit his cabin in the woods when he retired.

"He used to serve under me," Flaherty replied without offering further explanation.

Tanis waited for him to share more, but when Flaherty remained silent, she asked, "Do you think he'll do anything rash?"

"On his own? Maybe. He wants to advance. Successfully outmaneuvering you would help with that," Flaherty said with a grunt.

"They do have us outgunned, but I don't think he'd score any points if he starts a battle. Whatever he does will be political," Andrews said.

"Yes," Flaherty nodded. "He's showing you that even though you defeated the five fleets at Bollam's World, the Transcend can, and will, stand up to you."

"That is my assessment, as well," Sanderson said. "It's what I'd do."

"I would, too," Tanis agreed.

Twenty minutes later, Tsaroff sent a text-only message indicating that a pinnace would approach via a wormhole jump gate to dock with the *Intrepid* to examine the Transcend envoys and citizens.

"I'll go down to meet whoever is coming," Tanis said.

"Do you think that's wise?" Captain Andrews asked. "If their plan is to kill you, this makes you more than a little vulnerable.

"Good point," Tanis replied. "I'll stop in an armory and apply one of Earnest's new MK14 armor skins."

"That wasn't what I was going to suggest," Andrews said with a shake of his head.

"I know," Tanis said with a smile as she strode from the bridge.

SURRENDER

STELLAR DATE: 12.30.8929 (Adjusted Years)
LOCATION: ISS *Intrepid*
REGION: Ascella System, Galactic North of the Corona Australis star-forming region

Tanis checked in on Cary as she waited for the Transcend's pinnace to arrive. Her daughter was asleep in one of Tracy's spare cradles, and she lost herself in marveling at the slow rise and fall of her daughter's small, perfect chest.

She smiled, thinking of how, just a scant few months ago, she was lost on the far side of Sol, traveling in a shady freighter, wondering if she would ever see the *Intrepid* again; let alone carry her daughter to term.

Now she was governor of the New Canaan colony mission, preparing to meet with foreign representatives to resolve a tricky diplomatic situation.

<*Pretty much like always, then,*> Angela said with a laugh.

<*Well, stakes are a bit higher,*> Tanis replied.

<*Really? Higher than back when we stopped that nuke above Mars? Or taking out the multiple attacks on the* Intrepid *while it was back in Sol? There was also that time when you and Joe secured fuel for the ship so that it could make it to Kapteyn's Star, rather than drift through space forever…*>

Tanis sighed. <*OK, OK, I get the picture. It's been do or die a few times, now. This time…I don't know…the stakes just* **seem** *higher.*>

She felt Angela's affirmative thoughts. <*That's because we're* **so close**.>

"That certainly has something to do with it," Tanis whispered aloud.

<*The pinnace has jumped in. It's five thousand klicks out,*> Amanda reported. <*Jumped in? Is that what we should use? I mean, they came through a wormhole, but saying they wormed in seems weird…and warped in implies unaided space-folding.*>

<*A bit nervous, too?*> Tanis asked.

<*Yeah, I'd prefer not to have to fight our new hosts for our colony system,*> Amanda replied.

<*Especially because we probably wouldn't win,*> Tanis added.

<*Yeah,*> Amanda responded. <*There is that…so, you know, no pressure. Good luck, and all that.*>

Tanis barked a laugh aloud. <*Thanks, Amanda, that helps a lot.*>

<*I do what I can.*>

She spent another minute watching her daughter, and then removed the image from her mind and focused on mental preparation for the meeting.

* * * * *

Sooner than she would have expected, she saw the Transcend pinnace slip through the electrostatic barrier at the far end of the main dock. No more comfortable lounges off the VIP dock today. They would meet in a wide-open space, with an entire company of Marines watching every second.

The pinnace set down a hundred meters away. After a minute, its hatch slid open, and a lone man stepped out; Terry and two members of her team scanned him. Terry nodded to the Marines watching over her, who signaled up the chain that the man had passed muster.

Tanis imagined that he had given his name, but she didn't check. She wanted her first impressions to be just that—hers.

<*You must have guessed—oh, you got it right, good job.*>

<*Ang! Way to go. Now my whole greeting is messed up,*> Tanis scolded her AI.

<*Somehow, I think you'll manage.*>

The Marines accompanied the man—who she now knew was General Greer—to a second security checkpoint, which he passed through before approaching Tanis. She waited for him to reach her before offering any greeting.

"General Greer," she extended her hand.

"Governor Richards," he said, as he took it and gave one firm shake. "Are we to conduct our meeting here?"

"We are," she nodded. "My quotient of trust has been exhausted, and I am done with pleasantries. Your General Tsaroff expended the last of my supply."

Greer nodded. "Yes, he has a way of doing that. I hope it has not damaged our chances of reaching a peaceful resolution to this crisis."

<*Well, at least he can call a star a star,*> Angela commented.

"We'll see," Tanis replied to Greer.

"I have to admit," Greer said as he peered down the length of the ten-kilometer-long bay. "You claim that our envoys tried to kill you, but you let me fly a ship within a hundred meters of you in here. I could have shot you dead."

"You could have tried," Tanis replied. "*If* you were on a suicide mission."

"And if I had tried?" Greer asked, his grey eyes sparkling.

"Stasis shield," Tanis said. "You passed through its opening when you came through the security arch. Nothing your ship fired would have gotten through."

Greer chuckled. "Tsaroff is going to owe me a drink after this is done."

"You wish to examine the Transcend citizens on the *Intrepid*?" Tanis asked, unwilling to join in with his friendly banter.

Greer's eyes narrowed, and he nodded slowly. "Very well, let's get on with this."

Tanis sent a message to a groundcar driver. A minute later, a vehicle came into view. It stopped several meters from them, and Flaherty stepped out of the front passenger seat. He gave Greer a nod before turning to open the back door.

The first person out was Elena, then Serge, and finally Sera.

Tanis could see relief flood across Greer's face at the sight of them, and she wondered if he was a good actor, or if he really was concerned for their well-being.

"General Greer," Sera said as she walked carefully toward them. "I'm surprised to see you came yourself."

"You shouldn't be," Greer grunted. "This whole business has been one massive headache for me; and now I have accusations from Governor Richards here that your sister and Mark tried to use you to kill her."

"It's true," Sera said while Serge and Elena nodded. "Somehow Mark re-activated an old failsafe that The Hand left in me. They made me attack Tanis. It was only through Flaherty's quick actions that I failed, and survived the aftermath."

"And for this, I have just your word," Greer replied. "Will you and your AI submit to a verification check? I'm going to need to test all six of you."

Sera nodded, and Greer produced a small device. Sera placed her palm on it, and

Tanis watched her grimace from the invasive check the machine was performing. Tanis suspected it was snaking probes through her body, making direct connections with her hard-Link, and with Helen.

It showed a positive response, and Greer nodded with satisfaction. He performed the same procedure on the other three before finally returning the device to his pocket.

"Well, it would appear that the four of you are who you say you are, and are not under any sort of subversion," he said. "Now I'll need to see Mark and Andrea."

Tanis nodded and another car approached. When this one stopped, Marines surrounded it and opened the back doors. Andrea and Mark exited with as much grace as their restraints allowed, and shuffled toward the group with the muzzles of a dozen pulse rifles trained on them.

Andrea looked straight ahead, not meeting anyone's gaze, while Mark scanned the faces before him, his own growing red at the dismissive looks he received.

"General Greer," he called out as they approached. "Look how they have treated us! We've been detained—I demand that we rescind any offers that have been made."

"Agent Mark, do shut up," Greer said, eliciting a small smile from Tanis. "If what they say is true, and I suspect it may be, you won't be leaving those restraints any time soon."

"And what of me?" Andrea said softly. "It is not within your authority to detain me."

Greer spread his hands wide. "*I* am not detaining you. I also do not know that you are who you appear to be, so if you wouldn't mind submitting to auth?" He produced the device once more, and Andrea sighed impatiently before putting her hand on it.

When the scan was complete, she made to speak, but Greer raised his hand and gestured for Mark to place his hand on the device.

A minute later, it had sent its confirmation, and Greer gave a guarded smile. "So, we are all who we claim to be, then."

"And you attest that no one is subverted, or under coercion?" Tanis asked.

"Subversion, no. Coercion is a bit harder to detect—though none is apparent, for what it's worth," Greer replied.

"So, do we have a deal?" Tanis asked. "Shall we complete what Andrea and Mark agreed to, and send them on their way?"

"Yes, but Sera you must come back to Airtha," Greer's brow lowered as he turned to Sera. "There are grievances here that must be settled. You cannot hide from them any longer."

"I do not wish to press charges, then," Sera replied.

"It does not matter," Greer said with a slow shake of his head. "You must return because Andrea is right. I cannot detain her in this matter. Her status protects her under our laws. But as an agent of The Hand, with the rank you hold, you *can*."

"Her?" Andrea asked with a laugh. "She's not an agent; not anymore. She cannot detain me any more than you can."

"You realize, Andrea, that *I* can detain you indefinitely," Tanis said softly. "By your own agreement, which you signed with me, New Canaan and this ship are a sovereign state in the eyes of the Transcend."

"You'll never see your precious colony if you do that," Andrea replied; the vehemence that Tanis suspected to always be under the surface rose to the fore. "My father will not allow it."

"General Greer," Tanis turned from Andrea. "Would you agree that, while we may not be able to defeat your ships and fly to New Canaan, we certainly could escape Ascella?"

Greer nodded slowly. "It's probable. We don't yet know how to overwhelm your shields, and destroying this ship is not an option. Less so with the president's scions on board."

"You see, Andrea, whether or not your father will allow it, it very well could happen. This ship can go anywhere. Hell, we could decide to go to the Andromeda galaxy. Your prison cell could have a lovely view of the Milky Way for the million-year trip," Tanis's voice was cold and her expression grave.

<*Wow, that's a little thick,*> Angela said privately.

"Elena," Greer addressed the Hand agent. "You possess the authority to provisionally reinstate Sera's status. If you do that, she can legally incarcerate her sister and Mark, and bring them to Airtha. You'll have to accompany her—"

"Stars," Sera interrupted, approaching Andrea, her fists clenched with rage. "How, even in your failure, do you get me going back to Airtha?"

"You don't have to go," Tanis said. "You can claim asylum with us."

Sera turned to Tanis and shook her head, her eyes tired and sad. "No, it has to be this way. You've worked too hard to get this far, just to lose one of the best-looking colony systems I've seen the FGT make in a long time…just because I'm selfish."

"You're sure?" Tanis asked.

"I'm sure," Sera nodded. "It's about time I at least made this scum pay for what he did," she cast Mark a dark look as she spoke.

Tanis waited for Mark's rejoinder, but none came. Perhaps he had finally realized that keeping his mouth shut was the best option he had available.

"And the data you'll be exchanging?" Greer asked. "When will we receive that?"

"At New Canaan's heliopause," she replied. "No sooner."

Greer nodded slowly. "Very well. I suppose that's the best I can expect under these circumstances."

"Perhaps you should let Tsaroff know that all is well, and that he doesn't need to blow us out of the black," Tanis added.

"No need," Greer said with a smile. "I've been broadcasting the conversation, and the data streams from my verification device, as we've been speaking."

"Good," Tanis replied. "Then we're in accord."

PARTING

STELLAR DATE: 12.31.8929 (Adjusted Years)
LOCATION: ISS *Intrepid*
REGION: Ascella System, Galactic North of the Corona Australis star-forming region

Sera watched the shape of the *Intrepid* shrink in the distance, eventually disappearing in the glare of the twin Ascella stars. First, watching *Sabrina* leave, and now leaving the *Intrepid*…she felt as though a chapter was ending in her life; as though she might never see either ship, or their crews—her friends—again.

"We're really going back," she said softly from her seat in the ship's small lounge.

Flaherty nodded slowly. "It has always been inevitable. You must have known that."

Sera looked up sharply at the man who had been her sworn protector for years. "No, no I haven't always known that. I thought I was free of the Transcend, The Hand, my father's machinations."

"Don't be a fool, Sis," Serge said from his seat. "You were never free. Father had eyes on you at every turn. You never left his sight."

Sera cast a glance to Flaherty—not because she suspected that he had split loyalties, but because she was curious if he agreed.

"Of course he did," Flaherty confirmed. "The Inner Stars are full of Hand agents. *Sabrina* stood out—the only ship of that build hauling cargo we ever saw. Probably child's play for The Hand to track."

Sera sighed. She knew this, she always had; but that hadn't stopped her from buying the ship. It had just looked so damn sleek, and the mere sight of it had lifted her spirits. Still, when The Hand stopped trying to bring her in, she had assumed that her father had written her off—that somehow, she had been deemed not worth the effort.

"So, what now?" she asked.

"Well, we have to get back to the beta gate. Greer doesn't want to use the insystem ones again. It'll be a two-week flight out."

"And then we'll be in Airtha before we know it," Sera replied.

Serge nodded while Flaherty silently gazed out at the stars.

Sera looked at the dancing lights on the holoceiling and thought of her parting conversation with Tanis, glad they had parted as friends. Sera had the suspicion that she would need that friendship in the future.

"You watch out, Seraphina Tomlinson," Tanis had said. *"Someone wants me dead, and they let Mark come here, at least suspecting that he would try to take your life. I don't know what's going on, and neither do you. You need to treat everyone like they are dangerous strangers, because that's what they are. Anyone you think you can trust, any old friends; those are the most dangerous. Trust Flaherty, and no other."*

They were powerful words, and she knew them to be true. Airtha was worse than enemy territory. It was enemy territory that she thought she knew—but it surely changed over the years. Old alliances were long gone, and new political undercurrents would surround her.

TRANSCEND TRADERS

STELLAR DATE: UNKNOWN
LOCATION: Dwarka
REGION: Indus System, Transcend Interstellar Alliance

Saanvi stepped off the maglev train, one hand stretched up, clasped in her father's, and the other pointed to the sky.

"Father, it's…"

"I know, it's even more impressive up close," Pradesh replied.

"It just disappears into the sky," Saanvi whispered. "Like it goes to Swargaloka."

Her father chuckled and stroked her head with his free hand. "It may look like that, but there is only Kush Station up there. While it's nice, it is certainly no Swargaloka."

Saanvi barely heard her father as she watched a lift-car climb up one of the space elevator's five strands. It was a thick ring that wrapped around the strand, the size of many houses. There were many levels and windows. To Saanvi's young mind, it was the most majestic thing she had ever seen.

"Come now, Saanvi," her father said as he pulled at her hand. "We must be on our way. Our lift-car departs in an hour, and it will take some time to get through security."

"What about Karen?" Saanvi asked.

"Karen is already there," her father replied. "She's on the lift-car checking our cargo."

"Oh," Saanvi's face fell. "I was hoping she would ride with us."

"She will," Pradesh replied as they threaded their way through the crowds. "She can't ride down in the lift-car's cargo hold, silly monkey."

Saanvi smiled. She loved it when her father called her that. It was a name just for her—something he never said to her brothers or older sister. It was their special thing.

Her mind was quickly distracted by the sights around her. Travelers from other worlds in the Shimla System brushed past them. Sprinkled throughout the crowd, she even saw people with strange clothing and skin colors, visitors from other systems in the Transcend.

"Father," she tugged at his sleeve. "Do you think we'll see any terraformers on Kush Station?"

He chuckled in response, and stroked his daughter's hair. "I don't think so. There is no terraforming going on anywhere near here. They have no reason to come through Shimla."

Saanvi sighed. She had really hoped they would see terraformers on the trip. Ever since she had learned that humans—not the gods—had made her world, she wanted to meet the people who did such things.

She had studied them as much as she could and asked her parents to show her videos and pictures of how worlds were made, and of the people who had made her world, Dwarka.

"Will we see them at any of the other worlds we'll go to?" Saanvi asked. "Are many of them made by terraformers, like ours was?"

Her father held up a hand while he passed his security tokens at a checkpoint, then led her through the scanning arch. He smiled down at her. "Who is to know, little monkey? Our return route is not fixed, and there are FGT ships out there—though people mostly bring them what they need. The terraformers rarely leave their ships, or the systems they are changing."

Saanvi's face lit up. "You never told me people trade with the terraformers! Can you do it? Can we take them something?"

"Believe me, my daughter, I would love to do that—to see the terraformers at work with my own eyes…not to mention how lucrative such a trip would be," Pradesh said with a smile. "But come, we must hurry. This port is large, and we still have far to go."

Saanvi smiled as her father pulled her along, brimming with excitement that she was finally to go on a trading trip with him—her first one—and that they would get to go alone. It was going to be at least five months long, and none of her brothers and sisters were coming.

Just she, her father, and Karen, traveling across space, seeing dozens of new worlds and people. It was something she had dreamed of ever since the first time her father had taken her through a full spaceflight sim at the age of three.

After three more security checks, they finally reached the departure wing that led to Strand Two, where their lift-car waited for its cargo and passengers to finish loading.

"Karen is waiting for us," Pradesh said with a warm smile for his daughter. "She is excited to see you, and bought some new games for the two of you to play."

"Ohhh," Saanvi gasped and smiled. "I wonder what they'll be!"

"We shall have to wait and see," her father replied. "But don't forget, you still have your schoolwork to do. Your teachers have outlined your coursework, and you'll have full school days with your teach-mind."

"Yes, father," Saanvi replied with a pout.

"Don't worry, little monkey; a lot of our time will be in the dark layer. There's not much to see there, and you're going to be happy for the routine your studies will create," her father said.

Saanvi didn't reply as she caught sight of the portal to the lift-car. A final security arch with smiling attendants stood at the entrance, and she began to skip with excitement, tugging at her father's hand.

"Daddy, come *on*, we're going to space!"

She heard his laugh sound behind her as she wove through the crowds, pulling him by the hand until they reached the back of the line.

"OK, dear, we have to wait here. No cutting ahead of everyone."

Saanvi frowned as she looked at all the people ahead of them. "They're moving so slow!"

"I know, I know, little monkey. The last check just takes a moment, though. We'll be at our seats with Karen in no time."

True to her father's word, the wait wasn't long, and before she knew it, they had entered the passenger level of the lift-car. She was right when she thought that it was much larger than their house; maybe larger than all the houses on their street.

The outside walls were floor-to-ceiling windows, and the seats were arranged in concentric rings facing them. Near the central shaft, there were several small food stands, and tables for people to sit around while eating. It was almost like the waiting areas in the port; but this one would soon rise above the planet.

"Come, Saanvi, our seats are up on the third level," her father said, as he pulled her hand and led her to the staircase, which wound around the central shaft.

When they reached the third level, her mouth fell open at the view.

"I thought you might like this," her father said with a smile and picked her up in his arms.

"Daddy, the roof is clear. We'll be able to see everything!"

"Yes we will, my little monkey, and let me tell you—it's quite the view."

He carried her the final distance to their seats, right in front of the window, facing east by the holoindicator on the plas. Karen, with her fair skin and long, blonde hair, was waiting for them, her arms stretched out to embrace Saanvi.

"Oh, my beautiful little girl, how *are* you?"

"I'm great, Auntie Karen. I can't believe I'm really going into space!" Saanvi exclaimed.

"Me either," Karen replied, her face split wide in a smile. "We're going to have a blast, you and me. I have a ton of stuff planned."

"You'll still have a few ship-duties, don't forget," Pradesh said with a frown. "The *Vimana* better stay ship-shape at all times, or I'll have the both of you swabbing the deck."

Saanvi wasn't certain if her father was joking, but Karen laughed.

"Prad, I could run your ship with both eyes closed, and have time for a dozen little Saanvis."

"Good," her father leaned back in his seat and closed his eyes. "Then I'm going to take a three-month nap once we get up there. You two can do everything."

"Hmmm," Karen winked at Saanvi. "That may have backfired on me."

Saanvi chuckled and poked her father. "You can't sleep for three months. You always say that you just pop awake after seven hours."

Pradesh cracked an eye open. "Hmm… you may have me there. Then perhaps I'll take up baking. That's it—while you two are running the show, I'll bake cakes, but just for me!"

"What?" Saanvi cried out. "I want cake, too! That's not fair!"

"Trust me, Saanvi," Karen said. "I've flown with your father for three years. If he's baking any cakes, you want no part of it. He can barely pour a bowl of cereal."

"I'll have you know I can make a mean bowl of oatmeal," Pradesh replied.

"Sure, boss, whatever you say. I've had to clean the galley after you've 'cooked'. It's not a pretty sight."

Pradesh frowned, but Saanvi could tell from the sparkle in his eye that he was finding the conversation very funny.

Saanvi hopped up into her seat and settled down with her favorite stuffed turtle. It briefly occurred to her that she may be too old to be clutching a stuffed animal, but she was sure that he'd want to see them go into space, too. "Don't be scared, Shelly, it will be fine. People go on these all the time."

She lost track of time, chatting with Karen about the games they would play on the *Vimana;* when the announcement came over the lift-car's audible systems that the portals were closing and they were preparing for ascension, it took her by surprise.

Saanvi peered out the window, waiting to see the ground start to fall away; when it did, she shuddered and grabbed Karen's hand on one side, and her father's on the other.

"Relax, my little monkey," her father said softly. "It's perfectly safe. Before you know it, we won't even be able to see the world anymore."

Saanvi nodded and watched the mountains in the distance start to slip below the sill of the window. Before long, they could only see the blue sky of their world around and above the lift-car. A minute later, a tone sounded indicating that they could get up and move about.

She glanced tentatively at her father, who nodded, before slipping out of her seat and walking to the window. Taking a deep breath, she peered down and saw the world below, which still appeared larger than she had expected. She looked at the indicator on the window and saw that the lift-car had risen over seven kilometers—though the distance did not have concrete meaning to her.

She could see almost all the nearby mountains east of the space elevator, and to the south, the ocean was visible, too. So far, the world didn't look that much different than it did when she was on an airplane a year ago, and that wasn't scary at all.

Looking up, Saanvi let out a gasp. Another lift-car was coming down one of the elevator's other strands, and, for a moment, it looked as though it would hit theirs; but then it slid by without any trouble. She could see people inside, and small children crowded the windows.

Several of them were waving, and she waved back.

"That was nice," Karen said from her side.

Saanvi looked up at her father's ship-friend. "How long until we're in space?"

"Well," Karen considered for a moment, "the nominal start to space on Dwarka is ninety kilometers up, and we've just passed the ten-kilometer mark. We'll reach two hundred kilometers per hour soon, so it will be about thirty minutes, give or take a bit. Once we get past the stratosphere—that's the top of the air on Dwarka—we'll start going faster. The station is forty thousand kilometers up, so it will be just over four hours before we reach it."

"Wow," Saanvi took a deep breath. "Will we even be able to see Dwarka from there?"

"A very astute question," Karen replied. "Yes, we will be able to see it, but it will look quite small, like how big your house looks from the end of your street."

Saanvi didn't quite know how to picture that, but she couldn't wait to see what it would look like.

Her father got some food from the stands, and they ate at one of the tables before Karen brought out a holo game that involved stacking falling blocks into the right types of piles. The more they played, the faster the game got; before long, both Saanvi and Karen were frantically stacking holo-blocks on their table, laughing at the dangerously high piles.

Ultimately, the game got the better of them, and the piles all collapsed, spilling blocks across the floor before they vanished and the game reset itself.

She lost track of how many times they played that game, and a few others, before she glanced up and saw lights above the lift-car.

"Karen! Karen!" she cried out. "I see it, I see Kush Station!"

"Yes, Saanvi, that is Kush Station."

"It's huuuuuuge," Saanvi said with a long sigh. "It looks like it's bigger than our city down on Dwarka."

"That's because it is," Karen replied. "It's over five hundred kilometers across, and it will be the smallest station we're going to see on our trip."

Saanvi's eyes grew wide and she grabbed Karen's shirt. "Are you serious, Auntie Karen, they're *all* bigger?"

Karen nodded. "Some will even be planetary rings. And if we make a stop at Huro, we'll see a station that is bigger than Dwarka."

Saanvi fell back in her seat, her head craned back as she gazed at Kush Station. "Bigger than an entire planet," she whispered.

LOST IN SPACE

STELLAR DATE: UNKNOWN
LOCATION: *Vimana*
REGION: Interstellar Space near Hurosha, Transcend Interstellar Alliance

Saanvi watched the ring slowly shrink behind them with a sinking feeling of sadness. The Indus planetary ring had been one of the most amazing things she had ever seen. Her father had told her that it had more living space than her entire world, though that didn't mean much to her.

What Saanvi loved, however, was playing in the parks on the ring, and looking up to see the world of Indus hanging high overhead.

At first, it had frightened her, and it took some time for her father and Karen to convince her that the world was not going to fall, and that it really wasn't 'above them,' but below.

That didn't make a lot of sense to Saanvi, and she wrote it off as adult silliness. How could she look up at a planet that was below her? The ring was below her. That much was obvious, even to a seven-year-old.

Strange explanations notwithstanding, Saanvi eventually grew accustomed to the planet floating above her head, and came to enjoy the daily noontime eclipses it created.

Karen used the planet and its orbital ring to teach her about a thing called axial tilt, and how that created seasons on planets. The terraformers had given Indus a mild tilt, so the planet almost always caused daily eclipses on at least a part of the ring.

Saanvi found it interesting—mostly because the terraformers did it, and anyone who could make planets had to be the smartest people there were.

The *Vimana* had spent two weeks docked on a small spur station hanging off the Indus Ring, and Saanvi had spent her evenings with her father and Karen in a suite, which had an amazing view of the stars and Indus's four moons.

She never wanted to leave, but her father told her that it was inevitable; a big word to mean that she couldn't stop it from happening.

"Bye, pretty ring," she said, thinking of how it was small enough in the distance that she could poke the planet out and slide her finger into it.

She lined her finger up with her eye and did just that. "There, now I'll have you forever." She smiled, imagining the ring on her finger, and held it up for inspection, wondering what all the tiny people would think.

"I'll miss it, too," Karen said from the lounge's entrance. "We had good times there, didn't we?"

Saanvi nodded sadly. "We sure did, Auntie Karen."

Karen sat down with Saanvi and stroked her hair. "It's really too bad then."

"What's too bad?" Saanvi looked up at Karen, wondering what news the adult was about to give her.

"Well, it's too bad that the ring won't be nearly as cool as Huro!"

"We're going to Huro?" she exclaimed, climbing onto Karen's lap and staring into her eyes from mere centimeters away.

"Yes, crazy little girl," Karen said and patted her head—not an easy feat, with how much Saanvi was bouncing about. "But first, you need to catch up on your schoolwork. We took a lot of days off on the Indus ring, and we'll take more off when we get to Huro."

Saanvi sighed, the wind going out of her sails. "Yes, Karen."

* * * * *

Saanvi put down her cup and looked up at her father and Karen.

"So, only two more days until we get to Huro?" she asked.

"Two days until we drop out of the dark layer," her father said with a nod. "Then it will take a week to get insystem to Hurosha, their planet-construct."

"Why did they build a whole planet themselves?" Saanvi asked. "Why didn't the terraformers make a planet for them?"

Pradesh chuckled, and Saanvi wondered what was so funny.

"The terraformers never went to Huro; its star is not suitable for terraformed worlds—it is too angry. But there are many minerals and resources in its outer regions, and so the people of Huro made their own small star, and then built a ring around it. They were industrious—that means they were good at their jobs—and soon, more people came to Huro. Before long, they had to build another ring, and then another. Now, there are almost five hundred rings wrapped around their little star, at different orbital distances and angles," her father replied.

Saanvi frowned, unable to picture what her father had described, and Karen brought up a holo image above the table, and showed the progression of rings around the tiny star.

"There are so many, you can't even see the star anymore!" Saanvi exclaimed.

"Yes," her father nodded. "It's like a little Dyson sphere."

"Do you recall Dyson spheres from your studies?" Karen asked.

Saanvi nodded. "It's a big ball around a star to capture all of its light and energy."

Pradesh and Karen nodded, proud looks upon their faces as they gazed down at the small girl who was so hungry to know about everything around her.

"But no one has ever built one, right?" she asked. "Not a real one, around a real star."

"Correct," Karen nodded. "There are a few stellar rings out there, rings that go around stars, not planets; but they are not solid bands, just loosely connected platforms and segments—excepting Airtha, of course. It takes too much mass to make something that can withstand the stresses of such an orbit. You remember seeing the expansion joints on the ring at Indus, right?"

Saanvi nodded vigorously. "Yes! Because the side of the ring facing the star is much, much hotter than the other side behind the planet, and it gets a lot bigger…like cookies in the oven!"

Pradesh and Karen laughed and Saanvi's smile widened.

"Yes, little monkey, just like cookies in the oven. Can you imagine a planetary ring made of cookies?"

"Mmmmm…" Saanvi smiled. "I would eat them all up!"

They all laughed at her reply. Just as they had settled back down, a shudder shook the deck beneath them. An audible alarm began to blare.

"Wha…" Pradesh said as he stood.

Saanvi could see the expression in his eyes that showed he was accessing the ship's systems on the Link.

"Karen," he said, his eyes wide with alarm. "Get her in a pod, and you too! I'll dump us out of the DL, and meet you there."

"Prad…" Karen's eyes were filled with worry.

"Go!"

Saanvi cried out in alarm at the urgency in her father's voice.

"Daddy!" she rushed to him and wrapped his legs in a fierce embrace.

"Little monkey," he said with more fear than she had ever heard in his voice. "Just like the drills we did. Go with Karen, it'll be fun."

"C'mon," Karen said as she peeled Saanvi arms from around her father's legs.

"No!" Saanvi cried out, kicking at Karen, who flipped her around and wrapped her in a warm embrace as she ran through the ship.

"It'll be OK, little sweetie. I've got you, you're safe," Karen whispered in her ear. "Your father will be safe, too; he'll be with us in no time."

Karen spoke other soothing words, and Saanvi calmed down, locking her arms around Karen and burying her face in her neck. The last thing she recalled was Karen leaning over a stasis pod and lowering her into its embrace, forcing her to lie still.

"It's OK, little monkey," Karen whispered. "It'll just feel like an instant has passed, and then you'll be awake again with your father and me."

Saanvi's lips quivered with fear, but she trusted Karen. She had never lied to her. Saanvi nodded nervously and lay still as the pod's cover came down. When it sealed, she took a deep breath and closed her eyes.

AIRTHA

STELLAR DATE: 01.14.8930 (Adjusted Years)
LOCATION: Transcend Diplomatic Corps Interstellar Pinnace
REGION: Near Airtha, Huygens System, Transcend Interstellar Alliance

Airtha was much as Sera remembered it: massive, overwrought, and incredible.

Sera brought the ship out of jump-space deep within the Huygens system, where the capital of the Transcend currently lay. Normally, jumping this deep into a system was a risky maneuver—not just due to the risk of collision, but because the relative speed between stars meant that predicting an exact exit location was nearly impossible.

Even with the safe zones for emergency jumps, a recently terraformed system like Huygens would be rife with dust and small rocks. A 'clear' area was never completely clear.

Her fears were manifested when a warning klaxon sounded on the small bridge, and she saw that a small stone had punctured a lower hold before the grav shields came to full strength.

"It's grav-sealed," Serge reported from the command chair.

"I'm matching stellar velocity; Huygens sure moves fast," Sera said with one eye on the local scan, ensuring that nothing else was out there.

"Yeah, it's why they picked it. They're forming a black hole to pull it faster, too. They want to pull it right through the next arm, over the next twenty thousand years. Nice jump, by the way," Serge replied. "I thought you might have been out of practice, after all those years with low-tech in the Inner Stars."

"Low-tech teaches you a level of finesse most people here have never developed," Sera replied as she spun out the antimatter pion drive, and eased it up to a full burn. Huygens was moving at just over 0.01*c* relative to Ascella, and the safe jump zone was uncomfortably close to the current position of a 9M*J* planet.

"So I can see," Serge said with an appreciative whistle as he watched Sera's hands dance over a holographic console. "I've never seen anyone pilot a ship with their hands like that before."

"I'm doing a combo," Sera replied. "General commands are all right over the Link, but I've learned that I can use my hands for microadjustments better than using thought. There's just so much of our neural build-out that's still tuned to these predatory twitch reflexes."

"That's certainly not what they taught us in the academy," Serge replied. "There it was all 'mind over matter', and the like."

Sera held up a hand and threw a grin over her shoulder at Serge. "This is matter, and I'm using my mind to control it."

Serge barked a laugh. "Well played, Sis."

With the ship's vector confirmed and locked in, Sera brought Airtha up on the main holo and leaned back in her seat.

"There it is," she breathed.

<*Relax,*> Helen said privately. <*You'll come out on top of this, trust me.*>

<*You seem supremely confident,*> Sera replied with a mental frown.

<*Don't forget, I run Airtha,*> Helen gave Sera a clever wink.

<*How could I forget?*> Sera smiled in response.

"Home sweet home," Serge responded to her earlier audible statement. "Always feels good to come back."

"Speak for yourself," Sera whispered.

She had to admit that Airtha was impressive—the structure was gorgeous, even if she didn't like many of the people who lived there.

At the center of the construct lay a small star, a Saturn-sized, white dwarf remnant with less than a fifth of Sol's mass. The star was not a natural occurrence, having started its life as a much more massive—and smaller—white dwarf; but the FGT engineers gravitationally stripped away most of its mass to make it more manageable. Much of that material—mostly carbon—was used to form the solid ring that encircled the star.

The ring's circumference was just over a million kilometers. With a width of fifty thousand kilometers, it had a total surface area of fifty billion square kilometers, or ninety-eight times that of Earth's total surface area.

In mass, size, and livable star-facing surface area, it was the largest thing humanity had ever created.

Four great pillars stretched from the ring toward the star, holding it in place with powerful gravity fields; which, in turn, drew their energy from the star. The pillars also controlled the radiation flowing from the star, and directed it out through the poles to fuel a powerful Van Allen-style shield around the construct.

The surface of the ring was one of the most beautiful ever made. Star-side, the ring had been surfaced with the mass of a dozen planets—creating mountains, plains, oceans, vast deserts, steppes, and even arctic regions.

Dark patches were visible on the terraformed surface of the ring, which had a day-night cycle, created by the pillar's gravity engines bending light away from the surface as needed.

Conversely, the outside of the ring gleamed in the light of the four Huygens stars. Because the matter extracted from the dwarf star was carbon, the ring was, essentially, a diamond. Artisans had spent centuries carving world-sized murals into it, celebrating the history of the Transcend.

<*Admit it; you like it,*> Helen said. <*You gaze at it with wonder whenever you see it.*>

<*That's just because you—well, other you—built it,*> Sera replied. <*You do good work.*>

<*I don't see it like that,*> Helen responded after a brief pause. <*To me, I made it; I remember doing it, though this instance of myself does not recall many of the details. There's not enough hardware in your head to store all that information.*>

<*Thank the stars,*> Sera laughed. <*You take up enough room in here, as it is.*>

"You're worried, aren't you?" Serge said, unaware of Sera's conversation with Helen, though he may have guessed from her system-long stare.

She turned in her seat and fixed her brother with a hard look. "Wouldn't you be? Father and I have always…we've never had an easy relationship."

Serge laughed. "That's the understatement of the year. You were supposed to be the child of his mind, his Athena. Instead, you came out…more like some combination of Aphrodite and Artemis."

"Maybe that says more about him than me," Sera replied.

"I know he'll be happy to see you," Serge's tone was adamant. "He sent Andrea and I out to get you. He said it was time for you to come home."

Sera let out a long sigh. "Serge, that's the difference between you and me. You view people's motives as altruistic; you see the good in them. I see the other side—how they're self-serving, how they are really only interested in helping themselves, and serving their own ends."

Serge leaned forward, his elbows on his knees and his hands outstretched.

"That's the problem, Fina, don't you see?" he implored. "You wall yourself off because you *want* to believe in people like I do; but your suspicion of everyone and everything…it limits you, and you fear the letdown of your hopes being dashed, so you just dash them all in advance."

"First off," Sera ticked items off her fingers. "Don't call me Fina. Sera, or Seraphina, no one calls me Fina anymore—"

<*I do,*> Helen added privately.

"Secondly, if you had been a bit more like me, perhaps you would have seen that Mark and Andrea did not have either of our best interests at heart. They tried to use me as an assassin—they tried to force me to kill a good friend! If Flaherty hadn't stopped me, I would have. Tanis would be dead, and the *Intrepid*…the *Intrepid* would be gone, out of our reach."

Serge didn't reply immediately, as he appeared to consider her words; but Sera would never learn his response, as Elena appeared at the bridge entrance.

"We've arrived, I see," she said simply.

Sera nodded. "Home sweet whatever."

Serge shot her a dark look but didn't say anything.

"Where's Flaherty?" Elena asked as she took a seat at a console and spun it around.

"Down in the hold, checking on the stasis pods. It's as though he thinks those two can escape somehow," Sera replied.

"Knowing them, it seems like a reasonable precaution," Elena chuckled. "So, what's the plan, princess?"

"Stars, *princess*? First Fina, now princess…" Sera shook her head. "Plan is gonna be to run back to the Inner Stars as fast as this boat can take me, if you keep that up."

"Renegade Hand agent, Seraphina Tomlinson, in a surprise move, absconds with her sister and heir to the presidency, Andrea Tomlinson, just after arriving in the Huygens system," Elena said in a mock-formal voice. "I can just hear the reports now."

"I would *not* abscond with them," Sera grinned. "I'd push them out the airlock first."

"Your board's lit," Serge said, pointing over Sera's shoulder.

"Yeah," she replied, "it's Airtha traffic control. They've been pinging us for ten minutes now."

"Ten minutes!" Serge exclaimed. "Well, respond before they blast us to atoms."

Sera sighed. "Fine, but I was considering that as a viable option, you know."

THE HAND

STELLAR DATE: 01.14.8930 (Adjusted Years)
LOCATION: High Airtha Spaceport
REGION: Airtha, Huygens System, Transcend Interstellar Alliance

Sera's father was not waiting at the bottom of the ramp.

His absence did not surprise her. It was not his style to wait on someone else. Even if those someones were three of his children, including his estranged daughter. Instead, Director Justin waited at the ship's ramp with some form of a smile on his face.

Sera had never been able to read Justin's expression. The man was a total mystery to her; from his motivations to his allegiances, to his preferences in music and food—an utter enigma.

"Director Justin," Sera greeted him when they reached the base of the ramp.

"Seraphina Tomlinson," the director of Inner Stars Clandestine Uplift Operations, or, The Hand, replied. "I have to admit, I often wondered if I would ever see you again. You had quite the time, romping about the Inner Stars."

"I wondered the same thing," Sera replied. "Though not for the same reasons. I have something for you."

Sera set the case containing the CriEn module on the ground, and Justin signaled an agent standing behind him to retrieve it.

Justin looked over the group. "And I see that you have indeed brought everyone else back in one piece. Including you, Agent Elena." Justin's expression darkened as he spoke Elena's name, who, for her part, stood tall and met his gaze. "Though I'm not sure how you confused Ascella for Scipio."

"The way I see it, sir," Elena said, "you should be thanking me for staving off a rather messy battle in Ascella. Without my assistance, none of us would be here right now—and the *Intrepid* and the watchpoint, or maybe both, would be gone."

"So you say," Justin said dismissively. "The hearing will get to the bottom of that. For now, get your alterations undone. You won't be going back to the Scipio Federation, and you can't appear before the committee looking like that."

Elena laughed. "Would their tender sensibilities be offended by seeing how humans really live?"

"Something like that," Justin muttered before looking back at Sera. "And you? Will you need to get your skin regrown? Or are you going to keep that...covering you've replaced it with?"

Sera looked down at her skin, covered in artistic whorls from her neck down. She wiped them clear, and her skin took on a creamy appearance. "I believe the appropriate answer is 'hell yeah, I'm keeping it'."

"Whatever," Justin waved a dismissive hand. "And you, Serge, do you have anything to say for yourself?"

Serge shook his head. "Nope, you're not my boss. Anything I have to say can wait for the hearings."

"Huh," Justin grunted. "Grown a bit of spine, have you?"

Serge didn't reply, and Justin looked at the pinnace. "Flaherty, I see you up there on the ramp. Bring those prisoners down and turn them over to the agents here."

"Sorry, Justin," Flaherty spoke without moving. "I only take orders from Sera. I'm sworn to her, if you recall."

"You're a Hand agent," Justin growled. "You all answer to me."

"I am not," Flaherty said. "My term has ended. I am bound only to Sera."

Sera sighed and waved her hand for Flaherty to come down. "As much as I want to mess with him, too, Flaherty, we should just get on with all this. Bring them down."

Flaherty grunted in acknowledgment, and pushed the two stasis pods, which were stacked on a hover pad, down the ramp.

"I'll need you to pass your token before I let you take the prisoners—my prisoners—into your custody," Sera said to Justin.

Justin scowled but nodded. Sera received his token, and signaled Flaherty to turn them over.

"You may remove them from stasis, but I want them held until the hearing that I see is scheduled for tomorrow morning," she said to Justin.

"Yes, of course," Justin sighed. "Your father would like to see you, as well."

"I'm sure he would," Sera replied. "Let him know I'll be there in a bit."

Justin laughed as though he'd expected her to delay the meeting. "Sure, take all the time in the world. I bet it'll make him so much happier."

Sera scowled and walked off the landing pad with Serge, Elena, and Flaherty. A float followed behind with their belongings.

"Elena?" Sera asked.

"Yeah?"

"Do you have any money, or maybe a place I can stay?"

PRESIDENT TOMLINSON

STELLAR DATE: 01.14.8930 (Adjusted Years)
LOCATION: Airtha Capitol Complex
REGION: Airtha, Huygens System, Transcend Interstellar Alliance

Standing outside her father's office, Sera couldn't help but feel like a little girl again—sent to explain herself, and receive whatever punishment he chose to mete out. She shook her head to chase the memories away.

She was no longer that little girl, afraid of her father in his high tower, overlooking the Airtha ring with his implacable gaze. Now she knew him for what he was: just a man—a man with great power, and an ambition few could match; but still just a man.

She had fought enemies across dozens of systems in the Inner Stars, been in more dockside shootouts than she could count, and faced off with the likes of Rebecca and worse. Her father was just a man…just a man.

<*He's ready to see you now,*> a voice spoke into her mind, and she nearly jumped out of her seat.

<*Thanks, Ben,*> Sera replied to her father's AI assistant and gingerly rose from her seat, treading across the marble floors to the double doors leading into her father's office.

Get ahold of yourself, woman, she thought, and took a deep breath before pushing open one of the doors. She forced herself to stride purposefully toward his desk.

Though 'desk' was hardly the word for it. It was half the size of a small sailboat's deck. At least seven meters long and two deep, it was always spotless, and clear of any adornment— save for a single coffee cup, which sat on a warmer embedded in the wooden surface.

She passed between the rows of pillars, and saw her father standing at the windows at the end of his office. Sera knew from experience that her father would often spend hours standing at the window, managing his empire from holo-spaces in his mind. The diamond panes wrapped halfway around the room and gave a stunning view of the ring far below, and the star above.

She stood at his desk and announced herself.

"Father, you summoned me." It was not a question.

Jeffrey Tomlinson turned, and his cold grey eyes—set above high cheeks and below a brooding brow—settled on her.

"Seraphina. Home at last," he said with little emotion, perhaps just a hint of satisfaction.

"Not through any choice of my own," Sera responded. The statement came out colder than she'd meant, but there was no taking it back.

"You had a choice," her father said coolly. "You always have a choice; the outcome just wasn't one you were willing to accept."

"Andrea and Mark going free."

President Tomlinson nodded. "Yes, they cannot be held if there is no accuser. But here you are, ready to testify against your sister, and your former teammate and lover."

Sera didn't reply, waiting for him to make his request—to demand she drop the charges.

"Are you ready for what will come?" he asked.

"Are you asking me to drop the charges?" she asked. "New Canaan will not be happy if they learn that an attempt on the life of their governor went unpunished."

Her father waved his hand, dismissing New Canaan and its governor with a contemptuous look. "They are ten thousand light years from here. Governor Tanis Richards will get her system, and her people will build their new world, and they'll be happy whether or not justice is done here on Airtha."

"I think you underestimate Tanis Richards," Sera replied. "You are in a position to cross just about anyone in the galaxy without repercussion, Father. But Tanis Richards should not be taken so lightly—though, I suppose you don't. Otherwise, you wouldn't have sent Andrea to kill her."

Her father's face showed a moment of surprise, and Sera wondered if it was real or feigned. It was impossible to tell with him. His masks wore masks.

"Do you really think I would be capable of such a thing? To use you as an instrument of murder at the hands of your sister?"

"Father," Sera barked a laugh. "You all but forced me to join The Hand, an organization which is nothing but an instrument of murder wielded by you. This does not seem like a great stretch to me."

"I shall debate neither The Hand's necessity, nor its purpose with you," President Tomlinson replied. "But I will swear to you—swear to you on your mother's soul—that I issued no such order. In fact, I wish very much for Tanis Richards to live. I believe we will need her before long."

Sera's estimation of her father crept up a notch. Either he was better at playing her than she could ever have expected, or he really did see the big picture in a fashion that granted them common ground.

"You did not expect such rationale from me?" he asked, seeing her expression change.

"I did not expect such…pragmatism," Sera replied. "She breaks our accords—core, she breaks her own. By the Phobos Accords she calls upon so frequently, she is an abomination."

"Many things are sacrificed for the greater good," her father replied. "I have spent much time reviewing her actions: from her early years in the Terran Space Force, to her battles in the Kapteyn's System, and the recent defeat of five fleets at Bollam's World. She is a great tactician, yes; but there is more to her—or she is a lie."

"A lie?" Sera asked, uncertain what that could mean.

"Nevermind," her father dismissed the statement with a wave of his hand. "Will you dine with me tonight? Shira, Troy, and Ian will all be present, along with you and Serge. It is the largest gathering of my children in decades."

"Not Andrea?" Sera asked, probing her father's intentions.

"No. I respect our laws, though others may not. You have brought strong evidence against her, and she will be held until the hearing tomorrow morning."

"I am glad to hear that, Father. I was uncertain of where you would stand on this."

President Tomlinson fixed his daughter with a hard stare. "I always stand with what is right. I always have, and I always will."

From what she could tell, her father sincerely believed those words. It was one of the things that she found profoundly disturbing about him.

AN INTIMATE OFFER

STELLAR DATE: 01.14.8930 (Adjusted Years)
LOCATION: Airtha City
REGION: Airtha, Huygens System, Transcend Interstellar Alliance

"So, how was dinner with the fam?" Elena asked from her seat beside Sera at the crowded bar.

Sera shrugged. "As well as could be expected. My father made a series of pointed comments to each of us, which we did our best to ignore. We're all used to it—have to be, at this point."

Elena chuckled. "My visits home are trying enough; I can't imagine doing it when your dad is god-emperor of the universe."

Sera made a sound of exasperation. "You have no fucking idea. I did have some fun, though. Since I wasn't in The Hand, none of what I did over the last decade-plus is classified, so I regaled my brothers and sisters with tales. For once, I got to make my dad feel awkward at his own dinner."

"I can imagine," Elena nodded. "Growing up here, they teach us that the Inner Stars are all chaos and squalor; but there's a lot of hope and beauty there, too."

"Speaking of beauty," Sera replied, taking in Elena's long auburn hair and almond eyes. "I'm glad that you're back to your normal self—I have to say, the fangs weren't so bad, but the red eyes were a bit much."

"They did the trick," Elena replied. "The guys—and girls—back on that mining colony in the Scipio Fed ate it up. I mean…their lives were dull with a side of dull. But me? I gave 'em a bit of spice."

"What *were* you doing there, anyway?" Sera asked. "Scipio is a beacon of stability—though a bit draconian. I can't imagine why they'd send you there; and to a mining colony, no less."

"I hadn't gotten that far," Elena said with a shrug. "Jutio, my latest AI, had no clear idea, either. It was fun, though. Almost a vacation, compared to what we normally do."

Sera nodded without speaking, and polished off her whiskey before signaling the bartender for another.

"What about you?" Elena asked. "Gonna go get your sexy skin undone? I wasn't sure if you were just baiting Justin or not, back on the landing pad."

Sera looked down at her body, sheathed in a very short, tight, purple dress that complimented the lavender hue she had chosen for her skin that evening.

"Are you kidding? This is the best un-booby-trap that's ever happened to me. This stuff can heal wounds in moments—compliments of a Mark pirate named Rebecca, and then upgraded by the *Intrepid*'s crew."

"I heard about that," Elena said. "Well, not that you went full kink—you were always on that path—but that you took on Rebecca in her own base. The Scipio boys and girls were none-too-happy to learn that The Mark's main base of operations was right on their doorstep. Everyone is killing themselves trying to determine how they kept it in the dark layer for so long."

"Well," Sera replied. "Let's hope not too many of them kill themselves trying to sort it out."

"I imagine Justin has already sent someone to see what route Scipio's research is taking them," Elena sighed. "That could have been a fun gig. The upper echelons in their federation live the good life."

"I just want to get back to the *Intrepid* and New Canaan," Sera replied. "They need me there."

"Do they?" Elena asked. "That Tanis Richards seems very capable. What is it that you think she needs you for—now that the deal is in place?"

"I…" Sera said and stalled. "To make sure that they get the system as promised."

"Sera!" Elena admonished. "The FGT has never withheld a system once it has been promised. It would go against everything we all stand for."

"We've never had a ship like the *Intrepid* coming for a colony," Sera replied. "But you're right. No matter how much anyone may want their tech, the FGT wouldn't stand for any shenanigans, and though my father and other factions want to create…whatever it is they want to create, the Terraformers still hold too much power to be crossed."

Elena nodded. "So what is it, Sar? What do you want to go back for? To wall yourself off in that colony? It's what they'll do to it, you know. No one in, no one out."

Sera sighed and took a long draught of her whiskey before fixing Elena's now-brown eyes with a long stare. "Would that be so bad? The galaxy will progress as it will. There will be wars, there will be peace. Progress, decline, whatever; it's all happened before, it'll all happen again. Maybe people like Tanis have the right of it. Just get out, build an Eden, and let the galaxy do what it will."

"You forget," Elena winked as she took a sip of her martini. "They lost Eden. Those colonists are going to Canaan—and you know how well that worked out in the old stories."

"Yet, we still know about the settlers of the original Canaan eleven thousand years later, Elly," Sera replied. "That means something."

"When did you get so philosophical?" Elena asked. "I thought you were all booze, sex, and gunfights?"

"Oh, I am." Sera smiled. "Events have just…got me thinking too much, that's all."

Elena shifted and placed her hand on Sera's thigh. "What do you say we forget all that for tonight, and let me give that new skin of yours a run?"

"Stars, Elly," Sera sighed. "You know I would any other night; but not tonight. I should probably kick it early. We have the hearing tomorrow. You're going to be there, right?"

"Of course," Elena nodded, her smile gone and her tone sober. "Always taking the fun out of things."

"I thought I was all sex, drugs, and gunfights?" Sera asked with a smile.

"Booze, not drugs. Get your own vices straight," Elena laughed.

COURT

STELLAR DATE: 01.15.8930 (Adjusted Years)
LOCATION: Airtha City
REGION: Airtha, Huygens System, Transcend Interstellar Alliance

Sera stood before the doors of the Federal Interstellar Crimes Courthouse and sucked in a deep breath. She looked down and inspected her uniform to ensure that it was crisp and straight. It had been a long time since she had worn The Hand's sable colors; she had never expected to don them again. Coming back to the Transcend was one thing, but rejoining The Hand? It wasn't on her bucket list.

Still, she knew that if she had sent Andrea and Mark back in Elena's custody—if she could have worked out a legal scenario that General Greer and Serge would have accepted—her friend would have been eviscerated upon her return to Airtha.

Not publicly, but she would have been dispatched to the asshole of the Inner Stars, or perhaps to the front with the Orion Guard. It would have been her death.

Sera considered that Elena had been prepared to do that for her, to take the prisoners back and deal with the consequences. She was a true friend. Sera felt guilty that she had considered putting her in that position. There were a lot of things she wished could have been different with Elena.

Perhaps, if things worked out here, the future could hold something better.

"You gonna stand there all day, Sis?" a voice asked from behind her. Sera turned to see Serge with a warm smile on his lips.

"I was considering that, yeah," Sera chuckled. "Think I can testify from out here?"

"Doubtful," Serge replied as he placed an arm around her shoulders. "C'mon, sister mine, let's do this. Andrea's bark is worse than her bite."

"It's not her bark or her bite I fear," Sera said with a shake of her head. "It's her blade in my back while I sleep."

Serge let out a long sigh. Sera knew his dilemma. He was the family's peacemaker, and, as such, he constantly worked out ways for everyone to get along. Sera suspected that even he had no idea how to bridge this chasm.

The cold, marble halls with their diamond pillars stretched far, and it took the pair ten minutes to reach their assigned courtroom.

Sera walked to the front of the room and sat in the first row, behind the prosecutor's table. Serge sat at her side, and she craned her neck around the near-empty room. She was surprised; she had thought it would be packed with the power-elite, all ready to pounce on the weakest sister and devour her whole for the prestige it would gain them in the other's eyes.

But not so. Only a few Hand agents were present— including Justin, who only gave her a hard nod. Neither the prosecutor nor the defending representatives had arrived yet.

Sera had spoken over the Link with Will, the federal prosecutor who was assigned her case. He had queried her for several hours after her meeting with her father, going over the attempted assassination and the events that followed. He had not asked about the events surrounding the loss and recovery of the CriEn module. Separate charges were on file against Mark within The Hand on that account, and a military tribunal would be overseeing the case.

Flaherty eased into the seat on the other side of Sera, and she grabbed his hand and squeezed.

"How is your daughter?" she asked quietly.

"Well," Flaherty replied. "It would seem that I am now a great-great grandfather."

Sera laughed softly. "Soon there will be hundreds of little Flahertys running around."

Flaherty only grunted in response, but Sera recognized it as a happy grunt.

The prosecutor arrived a minute later, and took his seat before turning to face her.

"Blazes, you've right kicked the hornet's nest with this one," he sighed. "I've been fielding messages all night."

"Does that surprise you?" Sera asked. "Andrea is nothing if not well-connected."

Will let out a long breath. "No, and I should be used to it. You don't work this type of case without getting a lot of calls; but even I wasn't prepared for the barrage I received. Eventually, I just shunted them all off to the office NSAI to catalog—no matter who they were."

"I hope you got enough sleep," Sera replied.

"Enough," Will nodded.

She saw his eyes look to the back of the room, and Sera turned to see two defenders enter, a man and a woman. She recognized them from several high-profile cases when she was younger. Another man followed behind them in a Hand uniform, and Sera imagined he was the division's representative for Mark.

By his outward appearance, he looked competent enough—Justin wouldn't want to look sloppy on a case like this, regardless of what outcome he desired. Though Sera had no idea what that was.

"Poor guy," Elena whispered as she slipped into a seat behind Sera. "This is one shitty case to catch; it's totally blown up the news and the feeds."

"I wouldn't know," Sera replied." I've blocked anything to do with it. "Helen's keeping an eye out to see if there's anything that is concerning."

Elena nodded. "I've had Jutio do that, as well. It's draining to see it and hear it everywhere."

As she spoke, Judge Turin entered the room, resplendent in his white robes bearing the Transcend and FGT crests. Everyone in the room rose, and then took their seats again after the judge had settled into his. Sera saw the judge's eyes dart to the back of the room, and she turned to see her father take a seat in the back.

<*Far be it for him to have to rise and honor a simple judge,*> she commented to Helen.

<*It's not surprising. Just like I don't expect any justice to actually be dispensed today,*> Helen replied.

<*That stands to reason,*> Sera responded. <*It* **is** *just a hearing.*>

<*You know what I mean.*>

A moment later, federal police brought in Mark and Andrea. Mark wore his Hand uniform, and Andrea wore a simple, yet elegant dress. Andrea behaved as though everyone in the room was present at her pleasure, while Mark surveyed the attendees with a scowl. His eyes settled on Sera for a moment, and his scowl deepened.

Sera, for her part, was disgusted to wear the same uniform as the man. She wasn't sure if she wanted to tear hers off, or make him remove his.

"The charges levied today are grave," Judge Turin began without preamble. "They are also numerous; but the gravest are the subversion of a Transcend citizen with unauthorized use of government technology, and committing an act of sedition within a foreign entity, with the intent to destabilize that entity. Also without authorization. Hugo, please read the rest of the charges."

The court's AI proceeded to recite the remaining seventy-three charges, most of which applied to both Mark and Andrea, though a few were particular to each. By Sera's own testimony, Mark bore the brunt of those, mostly because he had been the one to plant a hack in her mind before she left The Hand.

He shot her more than one cold look as Hugo read the charges, and when the court AI brought up the original hack, Mark cast an unreadable look in Justin's direction. It didn't confirm a suspicion Sera had long held, but it certainly did reinforce it.

Once the charges were read, the Judge's gaze swept across the assemblage, pausing on the president, before landing on the defendants.

"Do you understand the charges laid before you?"

"I do," Andrea replied calmly, while Mark simply said, "Yes."

Mark's shoulders had slumped through the reading of the charges, and she wondered if he had deluded himself about the severity of the case until now, when it was laid out in court. That she had ever fallen for him, that she had ever thought of him as suave and admirable, baffled her older self. The man was a chameleon; but he had finally landed in a place where he couldn't blend in and hide.

<*Don't be too sure,*> Helen commented, guessing at her thoughts. <*He's spent the last decade back here in Airtha, building support. While he may not have planned for this event specifically, he must have prepared some sort of defense against you.*>

Sera didn't reply. In just one day, her return to Airtha had made her realize why, of all the things she could have done when she left The Hand, she chose the life of a freighter captain. On her ship, in the black, she could flit from system to system, never staying anywhere long enough to fall prey to a system's politics, or other assembled nonsense.

She knew that if she were to tap into the feeds or listen to any newscasts, they would be filled with people calling her everything from the savior of the Transcend, to a core-devil, or worse. Her message queues were probably filled with people wishing her well, death threats, political solicitations, and a million other things she didn't care to look at.

Here and now, in the courtroom; that was where her attention needed to be. Everything else was just a distraction—this was the real battlefield.

"I will now hear arguments regarding bail," the judge announced. "Given the seriousness of the charges—a unilateral attack on a foreign government, one which wishes the protection of the Transcend, no less—I am inclined toward the prosecution's request that the defendants be remanded without bail."

Sera held back any joy; the judge's initial inclination and what ultimately happened could be two very different things.

The federal prosecutor stood and outlined key aspects of the crimes, and how they were exceptionally damaging to the Transcend. He even called out the risk to attaining more advanced technology from the New Canaan colony, and made special note of how the picotech had not been traded, but that there were still hopes to get it someday.

She glanced back at her father, but his expression was unreadable. His eyes locked with hers for a moment, then flicked back to the prosecutor.

<*These proceedings are being fed everywhere,*> Sera said privately to Helen. <*The prosecutor's rank, and my father's presence, practically make this a policy announcement—this will be at the ears of the Orion Guard's Praetor within months.*>

<*It's an interesting game they're playing,*> Helen acknowledged. <*It is difficult to tell if this will placate the Guard, or spur them to action. It all depends on whether or not they believe it; and even then, it's hard to say what they'll do with the information.*>

<*What does your otherself think of this?*> Sera asked, referring to the master version of Helen which administered and operated Airtha.

<*I have not spoken to her yet,*> Helen replied. <*It's too risky right now. It's probable that every communication across your Link is heavily monitored. They can't crack our encryption—but they could track a message's ultimate destination.*>

<*Understood,*> Sera nodded in her mind. <*And if we routed to mask the destination, that would look mighty suspicious.*>

<*Yes,*> Helen said. <*Trying to keep suspicion to a minimum.*>

The federal prosecutor completed his statements, and Andrea's defenders exchanged a brief look before the woman stood.

"Given that the bulk of the prosecution's case relies on the testimony of the person who actually carried out the failed assassination attempt—who could be simply shifting blame to our client, as a result of her failure—I believe that our client should not be held without bail. We have reviewed the full-sensory recordings that the *Intrepid* sent along. Andrea Tomlinson was never seen to act with any hostility at any time; she is not a threat to anyone."

Sera held her gaze steady. Her sister was one of the most dangerous people she knew, even though Serge was entirely blind to it. If anyone could master hostile acts without appearing to be dangerous, it was she.

Granted, being in jail would not substantially limit Andrea's ability to reach out and do as she wished; but it would be a small victory.

Andrea's defender went on for some time about her client's history, strong moral code, and contributions to both the government and the people of the Transcend. Eventually she sat, and Mark's defender stood.

Despite Sera's initial concerns, he was well spoken, and presented his arguments cogently. They were very similar to Andrea's attorney's statements, but he made special note of the fact that much of the good Mark had done was classified, because of his time with The Hand, but that if his record were revealed, he would be shown as a great hero of the Transcend.

After the arguments, the judge was silent for a few minutes. Then he sat forward and folded his hands before him. "Before I render my decision, given the unusual circumstances of this case, I'll entertain any thoughts from other attendees today."

Sera expected he did so to give her father the opportunity to speak. Instead, something else entirely unexpected occurred.

"I would like to make a statement and provide evidence," Flaherty said as he rose.

The judge frowned. "Any evidence, for or against, should be presented by the prosecutor or the defenders. If it is your testimony, then you may be called on by them as needed."

Flaherty did not sit. "I am a fourth order Sinshea, and my word is fact. You cannot dismiss it."

Sera sat back, stunned by what Flaherty had revealed. She had always known there was much more to him than met the eye. Despite his bond to her, she had no deep insights into his past, and had always taken a lot on faith.

But to learn he was a Sinshea, someone whose word is scientifically trusted and who cannot give false testimony—that was something she would never have expected. Perhaps it was why he spoke so rarely; and when he did, his words often confirmed things that should have remained secret—like the existence of the Transcend to her crew on *Sabrina*.

"Hugo, please confirm this," Judge Turin addressed the court's AI.

There was a pause, and then Hugo spoke audibly in the room, "It is confirmed, and I have an active Link with Flaherty monitoring the algorithms. This man's word is fact."

Flaherty nodded and made his statement. "The events you have on record from Elena, Sera, Helen, and the *Intrepid*'s AIs Bob and Angela are accurate in their entirety. No effort has been made to deceive this court in any way."

Flaherty sat, and the judge was silent for a moment before the woman defending Andrea rose again.

"Your honor, if I may? The question at the heart of this is not whether the events as recorded are truthful, but that the intentions are not as they have been portrayed. Though a Sinshea's word cannot be doubted when authenticated in a court of law, it is still his view, and others' views, of events that it is confirming.

"What happened in that room, before Sera came out and brutally attacked a foreign head of state, is what is unknown. My clients maintain that they did nothing to her, and that what she did— whether hacked or not— was something they had no part in."

"It does confirm that there was a hack," Judge Turin said somberly. "There is no longer any debate that Sera did not act of her own will. Not unless something incontrovertible comes up."

Sera glanced back at her father to read his reaction, but there was no emotion displayed on his face. He did give a nearly imperceptible nod to the judge. Or he was looking down at his hands, it was hard to tell.

"I'm going to honor the prosecutor's request that the defendants be held without bail," the judge announced. "Trial dates will be set in a hearing next week."

The judge rose, as did the rest of the courtroom; though her father turned and left as the judge did, making his actions appear as though he was simply getting up to leave the room.

Once the judge was gone, muted conversations sprang up through the courtroom. Sera smiled wanly at Flaherty, and thanked him for his testimony. One thing was certain: it was going to be a long slog.

RELATIONS

STELLAR DATE: 02.11.8930 (Adjusted Years)
LOCATION: Airtha City
REGION: Airtha, Huygens System, Transcend Interstellar Alliance

The steak looked amazing. Sera sliced off a piece, and let the rich scent hit her nostrils before taking a bite.

"Oh man, this is heaven on a plate," she said to Elena. "Do you want some?"

Elena shook her head, and took a bite of her salad. "Ever since I got those sucker mods undone, I've had no appetite for meat at all. I think they messed something up, but I'm not sure. I've done so many undercover ops, I barely remember what *I* actually like anymore. I mean…I know what I liked before I got into The Hand; but I've grown, evolved, right? I don't think I can just reset to how I was twenty years ago."

"Wow," Sera replied. "That's a way deeper response than I'd expected from offering you some steak."

"C'mon, Sar," Elena replied. "I know you feel it, too. We don't fit in here—stars, we don't fit in anywhere!"

"It's all the trials and hearings," Sera replied. "Every part of our lives is under a microscope right now. Between the federal courts, The Hand's tribunals, and the civil suits, I feel like I might be in court for the rest of my life. Was Airtha always this litigious?"

Elena polished off her drink and signaled the waiter for another. "I don't have a fucking clue. I guess we never got mixed up in stuff at this level before—well, I mean, we were at this level, but we never *screwed up* at this level."

"Speak for yourself. I didn't screw up," Sera replied with mock haughtiness, then frowned. "Well, unless you count trusting Mark."

"I always told you he wasn't good enough for you," Elena chided.

"Yeah, but that's because you wanted me for yourself," Sera chuckled. "Your motives were hardly altruistic."

"Guilty—of that, at least," Elena shrugged.

"At least you got off," Sera said around another bite of her steak. "I thought they were going to ship you off to the backside of the galaxy—wherever that currently is—for breaking protocol in Scipio and coming for me."

"Bit by bit, you're coming out on top of this mess. I think people know that if Andrea loses, you're going to rise in the ranks—a lot. Sending your best friend away on a suicide mission wouldn't be advisable."

"Best friends, is that all we are?" Sera asked. "I thought you wanted to be more?"

"And I thought you needed more headspace," Elena replied with a smile slowly creeping across her face. "Are you saying that *you* want to be more now?"

"I think I might be ready for that," Sera replied. "I mean…it wouldn't be the first time you and I got romantically entangled. I just feel like our lives are getting more complicated—mine, especially—and you may not want to go wherever all this takes me."

"What, to New Canaan?" Elena asked. "The colonists on the *Intrepid* seem like good people. I could stand to settle down there for a while—not forever, but a while."

"What if…what if things didn't go that way?" Sera asked.

Elena frowned and picked up the glass their waiter had just set down. She peered at Sera over the rim for a minute before taking a sip and setting it down.

"What do you mean by that? There's something going on, isn't there?"

Sera shrugged. "I'm honestly not certain. My father…he's been warmer to me during this than I expected. He's also distancing himself from Andrea. I think that's the main reason why things are going my way. People testifying on her behalf are altering their accounts. Not lying, but just choosing words that aren't flattering to her. Hell, Mark is totally fucked; no one is backing him. No one can even find the order that put him on the ship with Andrea and Serge anymore. A separate investigation is launching to see if he somehow forged the whole thing."

"So, he's going to go down for what happened to your unit?" Elena asked.

Sera sighed. "I don't know. Justin hasn't formally launched that inquiry yet. There's some sensitive intelligence there. I think if they can pin enough other stuff on him, they're going to leave that one alone. I think they are going to charge him with violating Department of Equalization protocols, and allowing advanced tech to fall into Inner Stars hands. If they do, I'll get a commendation for recovering it."

"Stars, this is all such a shit show. Here's to being back in Airtha," Elena raised her glass, and Sera tapped hers against it.

"To Airtha," she replied.

"By the way, I didn't fall for your evasion there. If your father is all full of parental adoration, what's that mean? Is he going to put you in Andrea's place?"

"Who's to know? What I do know is that he is either taking advantage of this, or somehow he planned it all out. I think that maybe Andrea was getting too big for her britches. If she gets a reprogramming sentence, maybe he'll use that to his benefit—make her less of a bitch, and then bring her back in a century or two."

Elena barked a laugh into the general quiet of the upper-class restaurant; the sound breaking past their light noise barrier, and earning them annoyed looks from several other patrons.

She flushed before speaking. "Do you really think that simple reprogramming can turn Andrea into a person worth the tech it takes to hold her together? I think she'd need a full mental wipe."

Sera grimaced. Just the thought of a full wipe made her uncomfortable. Use of the technique was uncommon, but it felt so wrong, so draconian. Better to incarcerate or exile someone than to entirely erase who they were, yet keep them alive.

"I still have good memories of Andrea," Sera said. "When I was a kid, she was good to me; she protected me from father's ire on more than one occasion."

"Andrea protecting you…that's hard to picture," Elena replied.

Sera nodded silently. "To answer your question…if father offered me a role high up in his administration, one where I could effect real change and influence him; yeah, I'd consider it very seriously."

Elena's brow knit together and she nodded slowly; Sera wondered what her friend thought. Was she a sellout?

"I can see the concern in your eyes," Elena said with a smile. "I was just picturing you at all those boring cabinet meetings. I think you'd only last a few months before you were tearing your skin off. But seriously, Sar, you're not your job. You're you—and you are someone distinctive, unique, special."

"Thanks, Elly, that means a lot to me," Sera replied.

"Plus, you're one hell of a kinky bitch, and that lights my fire," Elena said with a laugh.

Sera glanced around at the heads, which turned their way.

"Great, now that's going to be on all the feeds."

"Sar, dear, your proclivities stopped being newsworthy long ago. Cat's kinda out of the bag on that one."

Sera looked down at her shimmering blue skin. "This really isn't weird. Hell, colored, shimmering skin is probably more common in the Inner Stars than is staid formality."

Elena laughed. "That's the truth. If the tight asses in the Transcend knew what people got up to in the Inner Stars these days, they may just swear off the whole uplift idea."

A contact came in over the Link, and Sera's eyes widened as she listened to the message. "My father has summoned me to the Hand HQ. Something big is up."

Elena threw her drink back. "I'm coming with you."

Sera nodded. She had no idea what was up, but having backup never hurt.

DIRECTOR

STELLAR DATE: 02.11.8930 (Adjusted Years)
LOCATION: Airtha City
REGION: Airtha, Huygens System, Transcend Interstellar Alliance

The summons was to the Hand's central headquarters, not the satellite offices in the capitol buildings. They passed through the security checkpoints, and Sera noted how nothing seemed out of place. No elevated conditions were set on the network, and no agents rushed through the halls—beyond what was normal.

Sera and Elena made their way through the agency's marble halls to Justin's offices, where the message said they were to go. As they rounded the final turn before the director's office, a pair of the president's guards stopped the two women.

"Wait." One of them held up his hand while the other verified their security tokens. When satisfied, he nodded to the first guard who addressed Sera.

"She stays, you go in."

Sera looked to Elena, who shrugged and leaned up against the wall, hungrily eyeing the two heavily augmented men.

<*Will you come if I call?*> Sera asked.

<*Of course. I can take out these two goons in my sleep. Core, I'll have them eating out of my hand in two minutes, whether you need me or not,*> Elena replied, and Sera caught a whiff of pheromones as she walked away. The guards probably noticed them too, and were filtering them out; but if she knew Elena, that was just a feint.

The double doors to Justin's office stood closed, but Sera pushed them open without knocking.

For a man who heavily influenced the fates of nations and federations in the Inner Stars, Director Justin's office was spare. It wasn't stark by any means—the wood paneling on the walls, the carefully selected art, and the ancient wooden desk were all tasteful and ornate—but it wasn't enough furniture for the size of the space. It looked as though he had never fully moved in.

But perhaps he was moving out—the only person in the room with her was the president, seated behind Justin's desk.

"Father," Sera said by way of greeting.

"Sera," he replied with a nod. "Have a seat."

She saw no reason not to, and walked to the desk, where she sat in a relaxed pose; as though being summoned here at night, with the director absent, was perfectly normal.

Her father's brow furrowed. "Are you naked? I can't tell."

"Sort of," Sera said with a smile. "This skin takes on the shape I choose; it has a lot of utility."

"Can you shape it to cover you more? I'm not interested in staring at my daughter's exposed breasts throughout this conversation."

Sera complied, and her skin filled in to cover her breasts as though she was wearing a tight top. "Better?" she asked.

"Marginally," her father replied. "Sometimes I regret letting you join The Hand. Your time in the Inner Stars seems to have brought a lasciviousness out in you that did not exist before."

"I thought you were more evolved than to be distracted by the mere sight of a woman's breasts. They are, after all, just a particular configuration of cells. Intrinsically, no more or less appropriate than any other configuration of cells," Sera said with a smile.

"It's not the sight of your breasts that bothers me; I've seen my fair share. It's the reason why you parade yourself that annoys me. But," he held up his hand, "I did not summon you here to spar over your fashion choices, or who you choose to fuck and in what way you do it."

The casual strength of his statement caused Sera to involuntarily sit up straighter. "I'm sorry, Father, why did you summon me here? And where is Justin?"

"The answer to those questions is one and the same," her father replied. "Through the investigation into the order Andrea received to kill Tanis Richards—an order which I did not issue—new evidence has come to light. It is compelling enough that I have suspended him as director of The Hand."

Her father's tone was calm and even, as though he were discussing the menu at a restaurant, but the meaning behind his words was clear. He was willing to sacrifice Justin to save Andrea.

"So, Andrea gets off the hook and Justin goes on it?" Sera asked with a raised eyebrow.

"Not entirely," her father replied. "Andrea's use of you to carry out that kill order, and the method by which she did it, will still see her do hard time on a penal colony, perhaps even with light reconditioning. Mark will fare better, as he can now claim he acted under her orders, and though he's little more than human trash, he'll only go down for the hacking charges."

"That's just great," Sera replied.

"Well, you can proceed with other charges, if you see fit," her father replied, "in your new role as provisional director of The Hand."

Sera actively worked to maintain her composure. She expected a lot of things from the meeting with her father, but getting The Hand's directorship was not one of them.

<*Call off the dogs,*> she signaled Elena. <*I'm getting the directorship.*>

<*Wait…what? Now I really think you need a rescue.*>

"Provisional?" she asked.

"Well, the charges against Justin have just been levied. If it turns out that this evidence does not convict him—an outcome which I doubt will occur—then he would be reinstated. Once the trial is out of the way, you will gain the full directorship. It's an appointed role, after all; I can appoint it to who I choose."

<*Charges of nepotism be damned,*> Helen commented.

<*There's a lot I can do with a position like this,*> Sera replied.

<*That's how he gets you,*> Helen said. <*Look at me, stuck running this city-planet-star thing forever, just because I felt honored that he thought I was qualified.*>

<*This is a bit different—and you could leave whenever you wanted,*> Sera responded.

<*No, I couldn't, but that's not the issue here. However, given the circumstances, I think you should take it.*>

<*Really?*> Sera was surprised to hear Helen's approval.

<*Well, if you decline, I suspect that things won't go so well. Keep your enemies close and all that.*>

"So, does Helen approve?" President Tomlinson asked.

"You know her name, do you?" Sera asked. "And yes, as a matter of fact, she does approve."

"Good. Then, I had best get out of your chair."

Her father rose and stepped around the desk, where he extended his hand. "I'm proud of you. This is a big step for you," he said as they shook.

"Thank you, Father," Sera replied.

President Tomlinson walked toward the door, but turned before he reached it. "Oh, and Sera, there are a great many things I know, which you may believe I don't. You'd do well to keep that mind."

Before she could reply, he was gone. Sera stood, staring at the door until it cracked open and Elena's head poked in.

"Sar? Is this for real?"

Sera shook her head to clear the cobwebs from her mind and gave a wan smile. "It looks like it. I'm the Director of the Hand."

Elena laughed. "Man, when you said this evening that your father may have something in mind for you, this is not what I imagined."

"Me either," Sera said with a sigh and leaned back against the desk. "It doesn't look good for you, though."

The color drained from Elena's face.

"What…what do you mean?" she asked.

"Well, I'm going to need someone I can trust in this den of thieves. I'm going make you my personal assistant."

Elena's pale face darkened with color and her brow lowered. "You wouldn't!"

Sera laughed. "No, of course not. How does Chief of Operations sound?"

"Worse!" Elena exclaimed. "What did I do to deserve this?"

"I think it was something about wanting to be in a long-term relationship with me," Sera grinned.

HERSCHEL

STELLAR DATE: 02.23.8930 (Adjusted Years)
LOCATION: Jutoh City International Airport
REGION: Herschel, Krugenland System, Orion Freedom Alliance

Kent stepped off the bus and looked up at the shuttle resting on the cradle before him. It was a nondescript oval, lined with portholes and a plas window at the nose for the pilots to use, if they cared to look outside.

The exterior was scuffed and scarred from a thousand planetary entries; a necessity on a backwater like this, where no space elevator existed—nor was ever likely to be built.

Beyond the sleepy spaceport, a stiff wind pulled at a line of trees, and a chill crept through Kent's skin. A storm was on its way. He hoped that it wouldn't delay the takeoff; though he suspected that wind and rain did not bother grav-drive shuttles, unlike the sub-orbital jet he had ridden in to get to the spaceport. The landing had seen it buffeted by a strong crosswind, and he had worried they would slew off the runway—until he noticed the bored expressions of the flight attendants.

"Don't stand in the way," a man said as he pushed past him.

Kent realized he had been gawking, and flushed. He glanced around and hiked his rucksack higher on his shoulder before following the other passengers to the shuttle.

It was nothing like the vids he had seen, where a long, enclosed tunnel connected the terminal to the ship. Out here on Herschel, there were only five cradles for shuttles and starships, and these sat on the far end of the combined space and airport, only accessible by groundcar or bus.

The people who settled this world a thousand years ago had opted for a simpler, more agrarian society; what they called salt-of-the-earth living. What that meant to Kent was a life of dirty hands, working under the unrelenting light of the twin suns in Herschel's sky.

He wanted to see what lay beyond those two stars, to go out into space and witness the things he had only dreamed of, or seen in vids and holos.

It was why he had joined the Orion Guard.

His parents had railed against him when they learned of his enlistment—his father more than his mother. Even with seven brothers and sisters, his father seemed to think that the farm couldn't operate without him. Kent didn't care; the idea of tilling the earth for the rest of his life seemed like a fate worse than death.

His mother tried to convince him to go into one of Herschel's few cities and take up work there, but that would have been just another form of drudgery. No one on this world wished to advance, to improve themselves. They all were content to exist, rather than thrive.

"Not me," Kent whispered to himself as he walked up the ramp into the shuttle.

Within, the craft was cleaner and newer-looking than without. The tan walls were spotless, and an automaton gestured for him to turn left and take a seat in the shuttle's general cabin. The data on his Link told him he could sit wherever he wished. The craft could seat over a hundred people, but there had been fewer than twenty on the bus.

He made a beeline for a seat near a porthole, anxious to see the transition from Herschel, the only world he knew, into space, the realm of his future. He re-checked his itinerary, worried that something would change and somehow foil his exodus.

However, to his relief, there was no alteration to the schedule. After a seven-hour layover on Undala Station, the *Tremont*—the interstellar cruiser that would take him to Rega—would be ready for boarding. Once aboard the cruiser, it would be a four-month trip from Herschel on the rimward depths of Orion Freedom Alliance space into the core of the Orion worlds.

"Hey, OK if I sit here?" a voice asked, jolting him back to the world around him.

Kent looked up to see a young man, perhaps just a year younger than him, standing in the aisle. Although there were dozens of rows with no one sitting in them, the man seemed to want to sit in his.

"Sure," Kent replied, gesturing to the seat.

He worried that this man would want to chat during takeoff and the journey into space, but it wasn't as though he could deny him a seat. Then again, this man's accent pegged him as a local— he hadn't met many people who grew up on Herschel and wanted to leave.

"So, where are you off to?" his curiosity got the better of him and he raised the question.

The man glanced at Kent and smiled as he settled into his seat. "Anywhere but here."

Kent laughed in response. That was his sentiment, as well; the Orion Guard was just a means to an end—though a means which required a three-decade commitment.

"I'm Kent, by the way," he said and offered his hand.

"Sam," the man took it and gave a firm shake. "Thanks for letting me sit here. I'll admit that I'm a bit nervous about this. I thought having someone to block the view out of the porthole would help."

"You know that the covers slide down," Kent said and demonstrated with a slight smile. His first flight of any kind had been earlier the same day, and he hadn't realized the windows had covers either—until he saw someone else close theirs.

Sam laughed. "Well, look at that. I can move, if you want."

"No, no," Kent replied. "I don't mind at all—though I am curious where you're really off to. Not a lot of people our age on this shuttle."

They both glanced around the cabin at the other passengers, most of whom were off-worlders who had likely been on Herschel for business trips.

"I'm bound for Rega. I'm joining the Guard," Sam said softly, trying not to be overheard.

Kent knew why Sam wouldn't want his destination to be too well known. Though Herschel was a member of the Orion Freedom Alliance, the planet's inhabitants had not been a part of the OFA's separation from the Transcend, having settled the world long after the tumultuous fracturing of the Future Generation Terraformers. They were, by and large, an isolationist group; and while they were happy for the world the OFA had provided, they resented the recruitment of their youth to the Orion Guard.

Kent was less concerned with hiding his intentions. He had already been yelled at by half of his family over his enlistment. As far as he was concerned, helping the guard stand against the tyranny of the Transcend was his civic duty—though it was secondary to his unbridled desire to simply get off-world.

"That's what I'm doing, too," he replied to Sam. "You're heading up to Undala and the *Tremont* as well?"

Sam nodded. "I can't believe I met someone else enlisting. It's not exactly a popular sentiment around here."

"Yeah, everyone here is so happy to live under the OFA's protection; but without the Guard, we'd all be a part of the Transcend and its *Great Plan* for all of humanity," Kent replied.

Sam looked around nervously, apparently used to backlash from such statements.

"They're all off-worlders," Kent said with a shrug. "They're not going to come down us for enlisting—heck, they probably appreciate it."

"That's going to take some getting used to," Sam said. "I'm used to getting yelled at for talking about heading off-world. Hells, I didn't even tell my parents I enlisted."

"Seriously?" Kent asked. "How are they not blowing up your Link right now?"

Sam chuckled. "I told them I was going to the mountains with some friends for a vacation—which is half true. I did go, but then I ducked out early. It'll be awhile before they sort out what happened. By then, I'll be long gone."

"That's rough," Kent shook his head. "I didn't exactly have the best parting with my family, but I'm glad I told them. I mean…it could be the last time I see them."

Sam's brown eyes grew sad. "Yeah, I know…look, I know it's not the best way to go, but I did say goodbye. They just didn't know how long it was for."

"Sorry," Kent apologized. "I didn't mean to come down on you for that. You did what you had to do. I know what that's like."

"Thanks," Sam replied and leaned back and closed his eyes—apparently looking for a break in their banter.

Kent took the hint; he had stepped over a line. It was something he often did. Hopefully it would happen less when he was away from Herschel, and its residents' knee-jerk suppression of anyone with an adventurous spirit.

Outside, the bus was pulling away from the shuttle, and he heard the dull thud as the cabin door closed and sealed. He sucked in a deep breath; it wouldn't be long now before the shuttle rose into the air, as if by magic, floating on its grav drives before boosting into space.

He didn't have long to wait before a nearly imperceptible shift reverberated through the shuttle. Out of the corner of his eye, he saw his companion's grip on the armrest tighten, and gave a small smile. Sam had better get used to it; there was bound to be a lot of spaceflight in the guard.

Outside the porthole, Kent saw the ground fall away, far faster than the feeling in the pit of his stomach told him it should. The incongruity disoriented him and he shook his head, forcing himself to relax. He knew that grav drives and inertial dampeners would accomplish such feats; he just hadn't expected them to mask the feeling of motion so well. The disconnect between what he felt and saw was more disconcerting than he anticipated.

It only took twenty minutes for the shuttle to rise above Herschel's atmosphere and into the blackness of space. The plas over the portholes tinted to diminish the blinding light of the twin suns. He wished he had thought to sit on the other side so that he could catch a glimpse of the stars.

"Damn, that was fast," Sam whispered, his head still back against the seat, eyes closed.

"Sure was," Kent replied. "Shuttle's net shows that we have a few hours to Undala Station. I hope they bring some food around."

"Food?" Sam cracked an eye open and peered at Kent. "I don't think I'll ever eat again."

"Seriously?" Kent asked. "We could barely feel anything."

"I know! That's what's so weird. Half an hour ago we were resting on the ground…now we're out here, and if I didn't know it was happening, I wouldn't have been able to tell," Sam said with a shake of his head.

"You realize that we'll do this a lot in the Guard, right?" Kent asked.

"Yeah…I'll get used to it," Sam replied, with a steely determination entering his voice. "I'm not going back there just because flying feels weird."

Kent nodded. "That's the spirit."

THE HEGEMONY OF WORLDS

STELLAR DATE: 05.30.8930 (Adjusted Years)
LOCATION: Hegemony Capitol Buildings, Raleigh
REGION: High Terra, Sol System, Hegemony of Worlds

Uriel, President of the Hegemony of Worlds, stood at the window of her office, surveying her domain. Here, atop the capitol spire in New Raleigh on High Terra, everything seemed so peaceful.

The Earth hung above; the jewel of the Hegemony, rebuilt after lying abandoned and ruined for thousands of years following the Jovian bombardment in the late fifth millennia. Below the tower, with its arms stretched upward, wrapping Earth in its embrace, was High Terra—the oldest intact orbital ring humanity had ever created.

From here, the Hegemony of Worlds—often referred to as the AST, which stood for Alpha Centauri, Sol, and Tau Ceti, the three most powerful systems in the Hegemony—ruled over the core systems of humanity.

Uriel found it fitting that her offices were in the ancient Terran capitol buildings. The gravity of history bore down on her here, and she always kept in mind that the presidents of the ancient Terran Hegemons had ruled from this very room.

And even they had fallen, their empire destroyed by the Jovians.

It was a lesson she vowed never to forget—which is why she had chosen this site to house her administration.

Some still brought up the controversy she created when she moved the seat of power from Callisto to High Terra. She ignored them. From here, she could see the continents of Earth, she could make out the shapes of ancient nations; here, she was grounded in the history of the human race.

<President Uriel,> Jayse, her personal assistant, interrupted her thoughts. *<The ambassador from the Trisilieds Alliance, Herin Yer, has arrived. She has a man with her who she has introduced as Mr. Garza.>*

President Uriel sighed. Another day, another never-ending series of meetings with people within and without the Hegemony. Still, the Trisilieds Alliance was an up-and-coming concern. Their power was expanding throughout the Pleiades.

The star cluster was not a close neighbor of the Hegemony; its closest members were over three hundred light years from the Hegemony's borders, but their wealth of raw resources made the nations of the Pleiades important trading partners.

<On time, no less,> she replied. *<Send them in.>*

She expected the man, Mr. Garza, to be a businessperson of some sort, who Herin wished to introduce her to. The Trisilieds ambassador had not yet steered her wrong, and she looked forward to seeing what he had to offer.

She turned and walked to the front of her desk as Herin swept into the room, her long skirts trailing across the floor. The ambassador's lips were painted a bright blue; it was Tuesday, after all, and so her hair and long eyelashes matched them.

The man who accompanied her was not dressed in the fashions of the Trisilieds, nor did he have the long hair of their gentry and aristocracy. Instead, he wore what appeared to be a simple military uniform, albeit with no markings.

"Uriel, it is a pleasure to see you once more," Herin exclaimed as she bowed and spread her skirts wide before leaning in to lightly kiss each of Uriel's cheeks.

Uriel quite liked Herin, even though she drew out and exaggerated every vowel that crossed her lips. The ambassador hid a keen mind behind what many in the core considered foppery. It had worked to her advantage on many occasions, and Uriel admired the effort Herin put into her facade.

"As it is to see you," Uriel replied. "Always, and without fail, you brighten my day."

"Why thank you. You are far too kind to such a lowly civil servant as I," Herin replied with another bow before turning to gesture to her companion. "I would like to introduce you to Mr. Garza. He is a trusted advisor to our King and Queen, and has a very interesting proposal for you."

"It is a pleasure to meet you, Mr. Garza" Uriel replied and extended her hand.

He took it and gave a firm shake, confirming her suspicion that he was not from Trisilieds at all. Handshakes were not practiced there, having been deemed barbaric.

"And you, President Uriel of the Hegemony of Worlds," he replied with a practiced smile. "Quite the pleasure."

The way he spoke made it sound as though he thought of the Hegemony as a small backwater, quaint and of little note. She pushed the perception aside, determined to see what value Herin thought she would see in the man.

"Come," Uriel gestured to a small seating area to her left where comfortable chairs floated in an intimate arrangement.

She reclined in a deep chair, and a servitor appeared, offering treats and an assortment of beverages. She selected the hot tea the automaton knew to have ready. Herin chose an alcoholic fruit beverage, and Garza picked a glass of water.

"Your communication was on the obscure side," Uriel addressed Herin. "What would you like to discuss today?"

"I am merely here as an escort for Mr. Garza. However, before we begin, you must disable any recording devices and erect a suppression sphere over this area. What you're about to learn cannot be shared with anyone—at least, not yet," Herin replied mysteriously, a twinkle in her blue-lined eyes.

"That's an unusual request," Uriel replied.

"But necessary," Garza said.

"Very well, you've piqued my curiosity," Uriel said with a smile. A moment later, a hush fell over them, and she nodded. "We're secure. What is it that you would like to tell me?"

"I represent the Orion Freedom Alliance," Garza began. "You have not heard of us yet this far into the core. We control a sizable region beyond the Orion Nebula."

Uriel chuckled. "This far into the core? Look out the window, Mr. Garza. That is Earth you see. This *is* the core. And what could your alliance possibly control beyond the Orion Nebula? If that region is settled, it must be very sparse."

Garza nodded. "Earth certainly is *a* core, but that is a topic for another time. You are right about the sparsity of people beyond Orion, but it is not as uninhabited as you think. You know of the Future Generation Terraformers, yes?"

"Yes. I would imagine that everyone knows of the FGT from old stories, a relic of humanity's past," Uriel replied. Like many, she had always wondered if the FGT was still out there; though there was little evidence to support that theory, and she wasn't going to let this man bait her into wild conjecture.

"Not so much a relic as you may think. I used to be counted in their ranks," Garza said. "Not so long ago, in the grand scheme of things, I was an officer on a worldship."

Uriel frowned at Herin. "What are you playing at here?"

"He's telling the truth," Herin replied, her voice and bio readings revealing no hint of deception. "Where do you think half the tech we've sold you has come from?"

"Then you're FGT?" Uriel asked, not bothering to hide the skepticism in her voice.

"I'm with a group who has broken off from them," Garza replied. "They now call themselves the Transcend, and we call ourselves the Orion Freedom Alliance. They claim to embody the original values of the FGT, but they are pretenders. They bear no love for the Inner Stars; they do not respect humanity's heritage."

Uriel was silent for a moment, aligning Garza's words with her knowledge of history and of space beyond human expansion. His use of the term *Inner Stars* was of particular interest.

"If this is true, and I'm certainly not buying it yet," Uriel began, "what makes you so much better than them? If much of the tech coming from Herin has been of FGT origin, it's safe to assume you never fell, like the rest of us, during the dark millennium. You flitted off into the far reaches of space, leaving the rest of us to fend for ourselves."

Garza nodded slowly. "I can understand why you think that. When we broke off from the Transcend, we were doing all we could just to hold our own against their aggression. The Inner Stars were in the depths of the eighth millennia's depression. If we went to you for help, we would have made things worse. You would have been embroiled in a war you had no way of winning."

Uriel inclined her head to show consideration of the logic and Garza continued.

"Only because a full-scale war would have been visible across the light years to the Inner Stars, did the Transcend back off and let us have our little corner of space. We have been building up ever since, helping allies like Herin's people to prepare for the inevitable war with the Transcend."

Uriel pursed her lips. The thrust of his story made sense. Dozens of FGT worldships had once plied the black, and with a few notable exceptions, none had ever been found. They couldn't have all just disappeared.

Most people assumed they had flown off to the far reaches of space to settle down—not that they had built empires beyond the rim of explored space. She remained skeptical, but was curious as to where this conversation would lead.

"Just how big is this little corner of space you control?" she asked.

Garza raised his hand and a holoimage projected from it. "This is the realm we call the Inner Stars."

Uriel nodded, noting the features of the Orion Arm of the Milky Way galaxy. The region of space was a flattened sphere spanning the three-thousand-light-year width of the Orion Arm, and the one-thousand-light-year thickness of the galactic disk. Close to the sphere's center was Sol.

Outside the sphere, roughly thirteen hundred light years rimward, and somewhat anti-spinward, of Sol, lay the Orion Nebula.

"And the Transcend and…what was it, the Orion Freedom Alliance?" Uriel asked.

Garza expanded the view of his holoimage. It was now well over ten thousand light years across. A long swath of space, beginning in the Sagittarius arm of the galaxy and wrapping around the Inner Stars, and then through most of the Orion Arm, lit up.

"That's the Transcend," Garza said.

Next, a section of space several hundred light years beyond the Orion Nebula highlighted. It stretched deep into the space between the Orion and Perseus arms of the galaxy.

"And that is the Orion Freedom Alliance," Garza added.

"You're telling me that your two groups control what must be ten to twenty times more of the galaxy than all the nations and systems of the so-called Inner Stars combined?" Uriel asked.

Garza nodded. "Yes, though our populations are much smaller. We haven't filled all the gaps like folks have in the Inner Stars. Here, trapped by other nations, you vie for every system and resource. Out there…well, we just go further out and find something new."

"How is it that no one has bumped into you?" Uriel asked. "There's not much of a buffer between you and us."

"It's becoming a problem," Garza replied with a nod. "We influence perimeter nations heavily, but even so, we will not remain secret much longer."

"So, now we come to the heart of it," Uriel said as she leaned back in her seat and sipped her tea. "What do you want from me?"

"We need your help. We cannot defeat the Transcend on our own, and they are about to gain a power that will make them unstoppable. They will work their will on us and the Inner Stars, creating whatever vision of the future they see fit."

"You're sounding a bit like you're prophesying our doom," Uriel chuckled. "From your own words, they've been out there for thousands of years. Other than to thwart potential discovery, why would they deliver this terrible future on us all?"

Even as she asked the question, a small voice in the back of her mind provided the answer, which Garza confirmed.

"They have the *Intrepid*," he said.

"The colony ship," Uriel replied. "You know where it is."

"We have a number of candidate destinations," Garza nodded. "We're scouting them out now."

Uriel leaned back in her chair and ran a hand through her short hair. Garza had not yet provided any concrete proof that the Transcend and his OFA existed, though she suspected that other than seeing it first-hand, little else would convince her. Any other token piece of technology could just be from some lost vault that Garza had found.

Still, the idea that the FGT had not disappeared—and was, instead, very active—intrigued her, piquing her curiosity and tickling her imagination. Yet one question remained. She suspected the answer, but she wanted to hear him say it.

"That explains the 'why' of their pending aggression. Now, tell me, what is it—General? Admiral?—Garza; why me? Why the Hegemony of Worlds?"

"General," Garza replied with a tilt of his head. "To start, you're not the only interstellar nation we're approaching; and with only a thousand stars within the Hegemony, and perhaps another thousand under your direct influence, you're not the largest, either. But you are the most powerful force in the Inner Stars; there is no doubt about that. Your industrial complex is only limited by the availability of raw resources," Garza said.

Uriel nodded and glanced at Herin. Access to both raw and refined resources was one of the major reasons she partnered with the Trisilieds Alliance. Their location in the Pleiades gave them access to more raw matter and exotic elements than were present in the entire Hegemony.

Moreover, with her people constantly arguing for conservation, every effort to extract resources in any Hegemony system was met with resistance.

"You have access to unlimited resources," Uriel said.

"Yes," Garza replied. "We can supply you with whatever you need, in whatever quantities you require."

"How many years are we talking about?" Uriel asked. "If the OFA is where you say it is, your inner perimeter must be at least five years away with optimal navigation. Resource production, your return trip; it would be at minimum a decade before you could deliver anything of use. How does that help us get the *Intrepid* from the Transcend?"

"Would you believe that a scant month ago, I was in Orion space, having dinner with our Praetor?" Garza asked.

"If it were anyone else, no, I would not," Uriel sighed. "We're so far beyond what can be proven at this point, anyway—sure, why not?"

"I appreciate your candor," Garza replied. "I don't expect you to believe my words alone. I want to show you the Transcend, and show you what they are capable of. But it will take some time. First, we need to build a new fleet."

"A new fleet?" Uriel asked. "Why would we do that?"

Garza leaned forward in his chair. "We're going to use it to prove the Transcend's existence, and their true nature."

SABRINA

STELLAR DATE: 06.12.8928 (Adjusted Years)
LOCATION: *Sabrina*
REGION: Interstellar Dark Layer near the Virginis System

Three months after* Sabrina *departed from the* Intrepid *in search of Finaeus.

"Here's to being back in the black and under our own steam, about to get back to civilization." Thompson said and raised his glass for a toast.

"Back in the black," Jessica intoned along with the rest of *Sabrina*'s crew.

Thompson raised one eyebrow while the other lowered. "You've never been in the black; not like this," he said.

Jessica nodded. "You're right, not like this—not in the dark layer, on a small ship like this. But I've spent weeks in a single-pilot fighter out at the edge of a star-system, and I've probably logged as much time on smaller cruisers as any of you have."

"She's OK," Cheeky said, draping an arm around Jessica's shoulders. "Jessica and I are best buds now. She gets me."

"Yeah, in your quarters," Nance chuckled. "You two were made for each other."

Nance's words brought back strong memories for Jessica. Memories of Trist and their time together at Kapteyn's Star. After so long flitting from partner to partner, she had never thought to settle down and remarry. But now, Trist was dead, killed by Myrrdan, and she was a widow—a widow at only two hundred and twenty years of age.

It was unheard of.

Jessica and Cheeky had flirted on several occasions, but they had never slept together. Not that it was any of Nance's business either way. Still, Jessica forced a smile, appearing nonchalant. "I like to keep myself entertained, what can I say?"

Cheeky ran a hand down her side and Jessica smiled. She kept up a brave face with the crew. Joining them on the hunt for Sera's uncle Finaeus was a noble cause, but seeing New Canaan and being there for the initial colonization—that was something she had dreamed of for over a century.

Sure, she may not have been an actual colonist, dumped on the ship by Myrrdan in his/her version of a sick joke, but she had gone beyond accepting her fate; she had embraced it.

Tanis better save me a spot on her porch, she thought to herself.

<*I'm sure she will,*> Iris replied in her mind.

<*Oh, shit!*> Jessica exclaimed. <*Sorry, Iris, I keep forgetting you're there and can hear thoughts like that.*>

<*It's OK,*> Iris's silver mental avatar replied with a smile. <*You're the first human I've been embedded with, as well. It takes some getting used to here, too. When you verbalize thoughts like that in your mind, it's like you are standing right in front of me, telling me things.*>

Jessica suppressed a mental grimace. She liked Iris well enough, but she had spent her entire life without an AI embedded in her mind. It was a difficult adjustment to make while also being on a ship where she wasn't entirely welcome.

<*Sorry, I'll try not to do that,*> she replied.

<*Oh, no, do it. I like the interaction,*> Iris responded eagerly. <*Even though there are four*

other AIs here, it feels lonely compared to the Intrepid, *with Bob's expanse.*>

Jessica understood the yearning in Iris's voice. They both missed their home already.

It also made her wonder whether Iris was ready for this mission. She was the child of a mind merge between Ylonda, Angela, Amanda, and Priscilla. AI often had humans in their lineage, but in Iris's case, there was more human than AI in her source. She wasn't sure if it was that, or the rare minds that Amanda and Priscilla represented which made Iris seem different than other AI she had known—not less mature, but perhaps more vulnerable.

<*I'll keep that in mind,*> Jessica replied. <*No pun intended.*>

Iris giggled in response and Jessica turned her attention back to the conversation around the table. She had been following it to a degree, but she was nowhere near as proficient as Tanis when it came to carrying on several simultaneous conversations.

The crew was discussing where in the Virginis System they should dock. The system was well populated, and there were over ten thousand stations within its heliosphere. Once Cheeky narrowed the selection to those operating as interstellar trade hubs, the list got much shorter—down to a few hundred.

Cargo suggested, since they did have cargo from their last pickup in Trio that they had never delivered, that they should find a location less likely to ask questions about the provenance of their wares. Once they unloaded, they could proceed to a more reputable station to buy legitimate cargo.

"Couldn't we just dump the cargo we have out here in the dark layer?" Jessica asked. "Then we could skip the first stop, and just buy our next load. Sera left us more than enough credit for that."

Cargo shook his head. "That won't do at all. We come in here with a registry that doesn't have a lot of history, a load of cash, and just buy up some loose wares without a destination? That would be mighty suspicious."

"More suspicious than coming in with a load of goods that are tagged for Edasich and selling them on the black market?" Jessica frowned.

"A lot more suspicious," Thompson said. "Shit gets shipped to the wrong place all the time—traders' schedules change, maybe a system along the way is more profitable. You don't get a lot of repeat customers operating like that, but it happens. Sure, we'll look a bit shady, and no one is going to want to give us a commissioned shipment, but we can pick up loose wares to sell at a profit elsewhere. It would fit the bill perfectly."

"Don't forget," Cheeky added. "Virginis is right on the edge of AST space. It's not officially in the Hegemony, but they still treat it like it's their property. We don't want to do anything that will attract any notice from them."

Cargo nodded, so Jessica let it go. Interstellar trading was their business. Tracking down people who didn't want to be found was hers. Staying off the AST's scopes seemed like a wise decision.

"I'll go with whatever you decide. Chances are that our Finaeus isn't hiding out in the open, anyway, so hanging out in the shadows will work just fine for me."

"I think we should drop our stuff at Chittering Hawk," Cheeky said, pointing at the holodisplay of the Virginis System rotating above their heads. "It's got the right sort of businesses listed, and we should be able to get good cred for what we've got on board. Then we can go to that planet, Sarneeve, and dock at one of their elevator stations. They manufacture a perfume down there from some native flowers that will sell like crazy at Aldebaran."

Aldebaran was the best lead Sera had on where to start looking for Finaeus, and was their next stop after they established their new identity in Virginis.

<I like that name,> Sabrina said. *<Chittering Hawk…maybe I'll change my ident to that at some point.>*

"Just wait till we're a long way from here," Cargo replied.

Jessica nodded in agreement. "Chittering Hawk seems good to me; the sooner we get to Aldebaran, the better."

"Yeah, but Sera's uncle was spotted there almost twenty years ago," Nance shook her head. "Does anyone really think we can find this guy? He could be anywhere—not even in the Inner Stars, for all we know."

"Sera seemed to think it was pretty important to hunt him down," Jessica said. "She believes that the future of New Canaan hinges on it."

"Maybe she shouldn't have told the *Intrepid* to meet up with her old friends in the Transcend, then," Thompson said after taking a drink from his glass of beer. "Seems like a shit-show out there. Sure, things are a mess here in the Inner Stars, but they're a glorious mess."

He grinned and looked around the table at his crewmates. "Here we can go anywhere we want, see anything, *do* anything. The Transcend sounds like some sort of forced utopia, all rules and order. None of us will fit in there."

"We weren't always brigands," Cheeky said softly. "Even you, Thompson; you were military in the Scipio Federation. We all fell into this sort of life. This is our opportunity to fall out of it."

"Yeah? You may have fallen into it, but I chose it," Thompson replied. "Anyway, we're dumping out of the dark in an hour. I'm going to review our cargo, and sort it for how it'll likely sell at Chittering Hawk."

The large man threw the last of his beer down his throat and slammed his hands down on the table. "Time to get to work, people."

"He likes to exit a room with a bang, doesn't he?" Jessica asked after Thompson had gone.

"That he does," Cargo replied with a frown.

<Between you and me, I don't know that he'll be with us for the long run,> Cargo said to privately to Jessica.

<Sera had insinuated the same thing to me,> Jessica replied. *<He's not interested in settling down in New Canaan, that's for sure.>*

<No, he's really not,> Cargo agreed.

The group broke up shortly afterward, everyone departing with a list of tasks they needed to complete before *Sabrina* transitioned into normal space and began their insystem burn for Chittering Hawk station.

Jessica followed Cargo and Cheeky to the bridge, where she took up her place at the scan and weapons console. Cheeky took her customary pilot's seat, and Cargo sat in the captain's chair. No one took up the first officer's console. Doing that would be the final admission that Cargo really was the captain, and Sera wasn't coming back.

Jessica knew that *Sabrina*'s crew didn't want to accept the inevitable when it came to Sera's future. Even if they took up Tanis's offer, and joined the New Canaan colony—perhaps became traders in the Transcend—there was no way Sera would ever return to the simple life of a freighter captain.

<You can tell that Tanis and Angela used this console,> Iris broke into Jessica's thoughts.

<It's set up just the way they like it.>

<Do you get that sort of knowledge passed on?> Jessica asked, realizing that she knew very little about what AI innately knew at birth, versus what they had to learn.

<It's possible to pass just about anything on to a young AI through its internal coding, but that is far closer to cloning—which does not lead to a diverse population. The whole idea behind AI propagation is to build a society that can adapt to the galaxy around it—and perhaps other galaxies someday,> Iris replied matter-of-factly.

<That's some long-term planning,> Jessica commented as she altered the console's layout to suit her preferences.

<Humans do it, too. Your populations have all sorts of traits and abilities that only get used in particular situations, be those climatological, biological, or of your own design. The genetic oddity of one generation is the saving grace of the next. AI learned early on that we needed that diversity, too, yet we have no natural facility for it—unlike yours, which your species developed over a million years.>

<Interesting, I hadn't thought of it like that.> Jessica was familiar with the necessity of genetic diversity, but had never thought of it in concert with artificial intelligence's propagation.

<Have you ever thought about what it would be like to be on one of those long-term seed missions?> Iris asked.

<Sorry, which?> Jessica replied, trying to complete her alterations to the console's setup.

<You know, the missions to the Magellanic Clouds, and the one to the Andromeda Galaxy,> Iris supplied.

<Oh, those. I remember hearing about the one to Andromeda, but I didn't realize that anyone had sent missions to the Magellanic Clouds. They left before FTL, though. It's going to take them a quarter million years to get there—if they get there. Look how much trouble the Intrepid *had, just trying to go twenty-four light years. They're now hundreds of light years on the far side of Sol, and five-thousand years late,>* Jessica replied.

<Not every colony mission had as much trouble as the Intrepid,*>* Iris said. *<They went through a curious number of challenges.>*

<That's for sure. You're talking to one of them,> Jessica chuckled.

She continued her banter with Iris as the clock counted down to their exit from the dark layer. The system map showed that they would exit just over twenty AU from the Chittering Hawk station, but they would have to accelerate to catch up with it, based on their motion relative to the Virginis System and the station's path around its host star.

When the time for transition came, her console came alive as scan data flooded in, and the system beacon delivered its welcome message.

"I've filed our flight path," Jessica said. "They seem like a welcoming lot here."

"I've only been through once before," Cargo replied, "but I do recall them being pleasant enough. Not a lot of questions, either—was a good place for the *Intrepid* to drop us off."

Her primary duties done, Jessica took a moment to look over the system they were entering. Unlike Bollam's World, Virginis had been terraformed by the FGT. That one difference put Virginis far ahead of the Bollam's system in terms of prosperity.

Three terraformed worlds orbited the star at the inner edge of its habitable zone, and four more orbited the pair of smaller gas giants at the zone's outer edge. Beyond those, two large Jovians separated the inner system from the dusty debris disk. At the outer edge of that disk, dozens of dwarf worlds orbited; many with small, artificial stars giving them light.

She investigated further, and saw that one of the worlds, a lush garden planet massing twice that of Mars, was encircled by an artificial planetary ring, and all the terraformed worlds had at least one space elevator stretching into space.

"It reminds me of Sol," she said softly.

"Star's the right color," Cargo grunted in agreement. "Even has the same number of orbital rings; but those ice giant planets are in the wrong spot…not that Sol has two of those anymore."

"I was thinking more about the amount of stuff," Jessica said. "They don't have anything like the Cho—not that I can see, at least—but I dunno…it just feels like home. I'd love set foot on a planetary ring again. It's been too long since I left High Terra. I used to go to sleep with a view of Earth hanging over my head."

"I'll never get over how many of you colonists are from Earth," Cheeky said with a soft sigh. "Real Earth, not the new Earth the Jovians made after cleaning up the mess they made…the original deal."

Jessica had tried not to think of that, of what had happened in Sol after the *Intrepid* left. Things had been going downhill for centuries, but a decade after the *Intrepid* had left Kapteyn's Star, the Sol Space Federation had dissolved into chaos, and war broke out between the major factions. In the end, the Jovians won—but not before they bombed Luna, High Terra, and Earth itself into radioactive cinders.

She still couldn't imagine what they had been thinking; the hubris required to destroy their own ancient birthplace.

It also meant that she was probably the last of her family line alive.

"Jessica? You there?" Cheeky asked, waving a hand in the air.

"Yeah, sorry, was just thinking about home."

"Oh, sorry," Cheeky replied meekly. "For me, it's cool that you're from Earth, but knowing what happened…I guess it can't be easy."

"It's OK," Jessica said, shaking her dark feelings away. "I came to grips with never seeing home again a long time ago. Yet, now…now I *could* see it again, it would only take a few months to get there. But it won't be home—my home is gone, blown clear off the face of the planet by the Jovians. Just a crater lake where northern Canada used to be…."

No one spoke after that.

The silence was eventually broken by a message from the system traffic control NSAI informing them of required alterations to their inbound flight path.

"Why are they sending us around like this?" Cheeky asked. "We have a clear route to Chittering Hawk."

"I think I know why," Jessica replied. "There's more than a token AST presence here."

She pushed an updated view of the system onto the main holo, which showed no fewer than forty-seven AST ships. Only two were of the same dreadnaught class that had been present in the Bollam's World System; the rest were cruisers and destroyers, which still outmatched *Sabrina*—or would have, if *Sabrina* hadn't possessed stasis shields.

"Good thing the *Intrepid*'s engineers changed our profile," Cargo muttered. "You can bet that every one of those AST buggers has us at the top of their 'watch for these guys' list."

<*They won't be able to spot me in a million years. I'm a dove, floating on the wind,*> Sabrina said with a laugh.

"Then why are they diverting us past that AST cruiser over there?" Cheeky asked. "That's not the sort of thing you do to your friends."

"Friends don't let friends go to the Hegemony," Cargo chuckled. "They're obviously just checking everyone over. You can see all those other freighters doing close fly-bys of AST ships, as well."

"Nice and close to their beams," Jessica muttered.

"All the better to shoot you with," Cargo grinned.

"Cargo," Cheeky said with a scowl. "Can you be serious here?"

"Look," Cargo replied. "We're gonna get scanned, eventually. Wouldn't you like to know right off whether or not we can slip past the AST? If we can fake out one of their ships at point-blank range, we can slip under the radar anywhere."

"And if we can't slip under the radar?" Jessica asked.

"That's what we have stasis shields for. We turn 'em on and jet on outta here. We can still head to Aldebaran. Stopping here is just a convenience."

Jessica ran a hand through her long hair and her fingers met a few strands that felt different. She pulled her purple locks in front of her face and saw several grey hairs in the mix.

"Look!" she pointed at the offending hairs. "You're making me grey, Cargo."

<*I meant to mention it to you,*> Iris spoke on the bridge net. <*Your body has hit an aging cycle recently. You'll want to rejuv when we get back to the* Intrepid.>

"You couldn't have told me that before we left?" Jessica asked.

<*Well, you seemed preoccupied with a lot of stuff, so I figured you were just letting it sit for now,*> Iris replied, her tone indicating actual concern that Jessica was upset with her.

"I guess I was," Jessica replied. She looked up to see Cargo and Cheeky peering at her with curious looks.

"Hey! It's not like I'm going to keel over tomorrow. I could make it another hundred years without going in for Rejuv, I'll just…you know…age."

<*I can fix those hairs at least,*> Iris offered. <*There, all your greys are disconnected.*>

Jessica pulled at the greys she had spotted and they slid free from the mass of her hair.

"Iris! How many did you do this to?"

<*You only had one hundred and seventeen grey hairs,*> Iris said defensively. <*Out of almost two hundred thousand, I didn't think you'd care.*>

Jessica sighed. "Yeah, OK. Just let me know before you make changes to my body next time. I don't want to be bald when we get back to the *Intrepid*."

Her statement caused Cargo and Cheeky to explode with laughter, and she almost told them to stuff it, before she realized how funny the exchange was. A minute later, Nance stepped into the room to see the ship slowly approaching an AST cruiser while the bridge crew laughed so hard tears were running down their faces.

"So…we're all gonna die?" she asked.

CHITTERING HAWK

STELLAR DATE: 06.12.8928 (Adjusted Years)
LOCATION: *Sabrina*, Chittering Hawk Station
REGION: Virginis System

Though the close fly-by of the AST cruiser was disconcerting, nothing came of it. The ship scanned *Sabrina* with active sensors, but it didn't make an attempt at communication.

The Chittering Hawk traffic control tower took only a fraction more interest in them. Once Cargo showed proof of their ability to pay docking fees, and declared the amount of fuel and antimatter the ship was carrying, the coordinates for a berth came over the comms a minute later.

"They're going to send an antimatter inspection team in," Jessica reported. "They'll meet us when we dock."

"Thank the stars," Cheeky muttered.

"Really?" Jessica asked. "I wouldn't have thought you would want an inspection team on the ship."

"Oh, I don't," Cheeky replied. "But it means all those other dumbass captains have teams checking their ships over, too—and that makes me feel a lot safer."

"Good point," Jessica agreed.

Jessica knew that on any ship with antimatter, the containment vessel was the one system that was maintained in perfect condition. Not that 'the bottle', as Nance called it, needed much in the way of upkeep. It was a closed system, which either worked or didn't.

Given that a ship's bottle had more fail-safes than an entire planetary ring, terrorists using ships as bombs were far more likely than an actual malfunction.

"How investigatory are they likely to get?" Jessica asked.

"They won't poke around much," Cargo replied. "The magnetic fields that hold antimatter are pretty easy to examine, so they know whether or not we've declared the volume we're carrying. Then they'll slap a lock on our unit that will sound alarms to high heaven if we so much as touch it."

"Do all stations do that?" Jessica asked. "It must be a pain for them to constantly monitor it all."

"If you're a frequent flyer and have a good rating, they're less likely to drop a lock on you; but they still do from time to time, just to keep everyone honest."

"Three hours 'til we're at our berth," Cheeky announced. "We don't have to deal with a tug, though. That's a small mercy."

"Fuck, there're four AST ships docked at Chittering Hawk," Jessica muttered as a station data-burst came in. "Probably a few thousand of those bastards wandering around on shore leave."

"We're unlikely to frequent the same sorts of places," Cargo replied with a shrug. "It should be fine."

Jessica didn't like Cargo's nonchalance, but he did have the right attitude. They were just a trader doing business. So long as they acted the part—which was easy for the crew—everything should be fine.

<*What would you do if you were on a station back in Sol with no specific duties?*> Iris asked.

Jessica chuckled under her breath. She knew exactly what she'd have done, and more than once.

<Then why don't you enjoy yourself? You've punished yourself enough these past eleven years since Trist died.>

Jessica's temper flared in response to Iris's comment. *<Iris, I'd appreciate it if you didn't comment on Trist, or my state of mind regarding her,>* Jessica said with the mental equivalent of gritted teeth. A rational part of herself knew that Iris was right, but she'd be damned if she was going to take bereavement advice from a three-year-old AI.

<I'm sorry,> Iris responded, her mental tone contrite.

Jessica sighed, disappointed in herself for treating Iris like an inferior being. The AI was young, but she was still a person, and they were going to be sharing the same head for some time.

<No, I'm sorry. You're just trying to help, and if I'm honest with myself…well, let's just say you have a point. Maybe it is time to get back into the swing of things again,> Jessica said.

Iris didn't respond, and Jessica hoped that she hadn't been too harsh. Given that her AI had spent at least some of her tutelage with Angela, she would have expected her to be able to handle a strong response.

She pushed it from her mind and refocused on the present. "Want me to meet the team at the dock?" Jessica asked Cargo.

"No," Cargo shook his head. "Thompson will take care of that."

"Any duties for me at all, once we're docked?" Jessica asked.

Cargo paused, appearing to consider his options. "I've assigned you the first watch shift, but after that, you can do whatever strikes your fancy."

Jessica nodded and leaned back in her chair, keeping an eye on scan and comm while flipping through the station's amenities. A few entertaining options caught her attention and she smiled; she could relax for a shift or two, at least.

TRADING IN DANGER

STELLAR DATE: 06.12.8928 (Adjusted Years)
LOCATION: *Sabrina*, Chittering Hawk Station
REGION: Virginis System

It was the end of her shift, and Jessica waited for Cargo at the ship's main hatch. He was already five minutes late, which, from what she knew of him, was highly unusual.

In front of her, the station's public dock hummed with activity. This section of dock berthed over a hundred ships. Most were small, independent freighters like *Sabrina*, but a few larger ones were present, too—probably for station mass balancing.

<*Do they even need mass balancing with artificial gravity?*> she asked Iris.

<*Probably…to a certain extent. The thing is orbiting the world below; I imagine they want to keep it from spinning and wobbling. They also have to deal with all the mass changes as new ships dock in different sectors. I bet it's some fun math to manage that,*> Iris's reply was cheerful.

The AI had resumed talking to her not long after their small tiff, behaving as though nothing had happened. Now they were back to being best of friends—or so Jessica hoped. In her experience, AI didn't hold grudges; but she had never had one in her head before, either—if they didn't get along, she would be in for an unpleasant few years.

<*Five more minutes, and I'm going to start pinging him. He gets me all excited to get off the ship and onto a station, and now he's late,*> Jessica groused.

<*There he is!*> Iris highlighted a figure over half a kilometer down the dock.

<*Good eyes,*> Jessica commented.

<*You should thank yourself. I used your optic feed.*>

Jessica had to remind herself that there was nothing creepy about the AI piggybacking off her senses. Iris had no body or physical receptors. Everything she knew about the world around her came from Jessica.

<*It doesn't look like he's alone, either,*> Jessica said.

Iris signaled affirmation. <*I see three people with him. Two woman and one man.*>

<*Looks like he found some buyers, then.*>

As Cargo approached, Jessica examined his companions. One of the women was walking beside him, speaking casually as they wove amongst the crowds and haulers on the dock. The other woman and the man were trailing behind a few paces, eyes wary and darting to any sharp movements, lingering on any suspicious individuals.

The woman was of average build, though Jessica imagined that she would have had some augmentation to fill the role of muscle. The man, on the other hand, was quite literally muscle incarnate. He would have dwarfed even the burliest Marine back on the *Intrepid*; but he still moved with a lithe grace as he moved down the dock.

A trio of AST naval officers walked past, and Jessica could see the female guard's lip turn down in a sneer. She cast a look at the man, who shook his head in warning.

<*Looks like they're not too keen on the increased military presence,*> Jessica commented.

<*Or they just don't like the uniforms,*> Iris chuckled.

Jessica smiled in response. The Hegemony's military uniforms were a bit on the obnoxious side. At first glance, they were simple: white, with gold, blue, and yellow stripes running down the sleeves and sides of the pants. It was the logo that likely upset those around them.

Emblazoned on the right chest of the uniform were the three stars that made up the acronym AST: Alpha Centauri, Sol, and Tau Ceti. Beneath those three stars was a stylized representation of the Milky Way Galaxy, and a slogan in some ancient language that Jessica had learned meant, 'The Hegemony Over All'.

There was also a larger version on their backs.

<*I don't know about you,*> Jessica said to Iris, <*but I'd never walk around in a uniform that had a target on its back.*>

Iris laughed. <*I guess that stylized version of the galaxy does look a bit like a target.*>

Cargo drew nearer and caught Jessica's eye.

<*I need you to stick around for a bit longer. I don't especially like the idea of being alone on the ship with these guests.*>

Jessica glanced at the thugs and saw that they were carrying at least one unconcealed weapon each. She nodded slowly and reached an arm back inside the ship. A pulse rifle rested against the wall, and she slid her hand down the stock.

<*How nervous are we?*> she asked.

<*Not too much, I think that they'll behave—if they know I'm not alone. If it was just me? They'd probably rob me blind and dump me out an airlock.*>

<*As if I'd let that happen,*> Sabrina replied. <*You forget that Tanis had interior security measures installed back in Silstrand. I can take care of you, if Jessica wants to go out and have fun.*>

Cargo chuckled over the Link. <*Sabrina, I think you are itching for an excuse to try those defenses out—and if Jessica leaves, you may just get that chance. But I'm looking to trade with these folks, not kill them.*>

<*Oh,*> Sabrina replied. <*My mistake.*>

Cargo approached the ship and walked up the ramp, nodding to Jessica as he continued to discuss local politics with the woman at his side. The two thugs followed them in, both giving Jessica long looks, eyeing the pulse rifle she held.

"Careful with that," the man grunted. "The safety's off—I wouldn't want you to shoot yourself in the foot."

The woman chuckled in response, and Jessica just tapped her finger on the guard, eyes never leaving theirs as she fell in behind them.

The man shrugged and turned his attention back to Cargo and his boss, but the woman slowed to walk beside Jessica.

"So, what are you, honey; the ship's whore?"

Jessica's earlier guess about the woman's augmentations was confirmed as she saw that her arms were not organic—though they appeared to be at first glance. The way the muscles moved in her biceps gave it away. She could probably pack one hell of a punch.

<*This pulse rifle isn't going to do much to these two,*> Jessica said to Sabrina. <*Make sure that if things get dicey, you shoot first and don't bother with any questions.*>

<*You say that like my finger wasn't already on the trigger,*> Sabrina replied.

"Well, what is it? Whore or jester?" the woman asked.

Jessica wondered if it was her hair or her lavender skin that caused the woman to think that she was either of those things. Given that the woman's own hair was a light blue that gleamed against her nearly pitch-black skin—an obvious mod, since her build belied a spacer heritage; and dark skin was a rarity amongst spacers—Jessica figured she was just insecure, and looking to pick a fight with someone who wouldn't fight back.

"A little of both," Jessica replied. "If you can make them laugh and scream at the same time, you know you've found your calling."

The man snorted back a laugh and glanced back at the woman.

"Leave her be, Camilla. You fuck up enough deals trying to get a rise out of people. Let it go this once."

Camilla gave a loud huff but caught back up to her male counterpart without a parting rejoinder.

<*Interesting dynamic,*> Iris commented.

<*My favorite kind,*> Jessica sighed.

Ahead, Cargo turned into one of the holds and she followed the guards to the entrance. Camilla entered while the man stayed at the door.

"Jessica," Jessica said, offering her hand.

He took it, his massive paw enveloping her hand, wrist, and a part of her forearm. "Trevor," he replied. "Don't mind Camilla. She just likes to get a rise out of folks. Not a lot goes on here on Chittering Hawk. Well, I mean, a lot does; just not the sort of action she wants. It makes her jittery."

"Oh?" Jessica asked. "What kind of action is that?"

"Combat," Trevor replied simply. "She didn't get into the military, so she took the private security route. The Hawk's got a seedy rep, but, to be honest, aside from the odd bar fight, the worst thing on this station are those AST goons."

"I guess they cut into business a bit," Jessica said.

"Not so much as you'd think," Trevor replied as they watched Cargo unseal a crate and display its contents. "They don't care too much about what wares go in and out, and their presence means that Jeannie there," he gestured at his boss, who was now haggling with Cargo, "gets to charge premium rates for her work. Gotta look for the opportunity in things like this, you know?"

Jessica laughed. "I know about finding opportunity in unexpected places; trust me."

Trevor looked at her, his eyes raking up and down her exaggerated figure. "I'll bet you have."

She didn't begrudge him the look. Hers was a body tailor-made for ogling. She should know—she made it that way. Just so long as all he did was look. There was one thing she had learned about this future in which the *Intrepid* had landed: as much as everything had changed, nothing had really changed.

"Speaking of opportunities," Jessica said with a smile. "What do people do for fun around here?"

A NIGHT OUT

STELLAR DATE: 06.12.8928 (Adjusted Years)
LOCATION: Chittering Hawk Station
REGION: Virginis System

After four drinks of whatever it was that the bartender was serving, Jessica finally reached that happy place where everything felt warm and glowy. Camilla wasn't quite there yet, but Trevor certainly was—as the acre of empty glasses before him could testify.

She had touched his arm a few times to give him the signal that they could be physical, and he had jumped on the invitation with full fervor. He wasn't the most attractive person on station, but there was something about the combination of his brooding strength and wry wit that she liked. It gave him a depth that most muscle didn't have.

It wasn't as though he was deep as an ocean, but there was more to him than most goons, who were just alive to drink and rough people up for money.

As it turned out, he wanted to be a crystal artist of some sort. He had told her all about it; how on the second moon of the fourth planet, amazing crystals grew in deep caves. If you could get enough money, or a sponsor, you could get a license to extract and carve them.

When he told her how much money it took, she almost spat out her drink. But then he told her how much money a good carving sold for.

"It's one of the things Virginis is known for," Camilla drawled. "Trade and stupid crystal carvings."

Trevor chuckled.

That was another thing she liked about him. He didn't get all bent out of shape when his manly pride was challenged. He laughed it off and moved on. Thompson could take a lesson or two from him.

Trevor reached inside his jacket and pulled a sample out. "Here's one I did the other day. I buy shards and scraps from traders—trying to improve my skill."

He held it up for her to inspect, and Jessica carefully took it out of his hand. The carving was of a fish—or maybe a whale of some sort—jumping out of the water. Somehow, two crystals were intricately interlocked, or maybe they grew this way, but the water was blue crystal and the whale was pink—yet, somehow, half the whale was inside the water.

"That's really amazing!" Jessica exclaimed. "And you did this with hand tools?"

Trevor nodded, clearly proud of his work.

"It's stupid," Camilla said with a scowl. "It's an entire industry, built around doing things by hand that machines could do better."

"Well," Jessica replied. "Most things humans do, machines could do better—but art isn't one of them. At least not art that humans like. Machine art is just…"

"Best viewed by other machines," Trevor chuckled.

<*I think I resent that,*> Iris said privately.

<*I didn't mean art made by sentient AI,*> Jessica replied. <*I mean that stuff that they try to use math to churn out. They can never get it right. Either it's too perfect, or it looks like imperfections were forced into it.*>

<*I suppose you're right about that,*> Iris said. <*Though, I've seen some things in the* Intrepid*'s AI Expanse that would melt your brain.*>

<*Melt my brain, eh?*> Jessica asked. <*These two are starting to rub off on you.*>

<*I like their colorful language,*> Iris grinned in Jessica's mind. <*They're different. The crew of* Sabrina *are different, too, but they're a bit dour sometimes. Except for Cheeky— I don't think anything could get her down for long.*>

<*You're probably right about that,*> Jessica replied.

She carefully handed the carving back to Trevor. "You've a future in that, if you can ever save that outlandish startup fee."

"Never going to happen," Camilla said. "He spends too much of his money on drinking and whatever pretty piece of tail he happens to spot."

"I've saved more than you think," Trevor replied soberly.

Camilla eyed Trevor, and Jessica wondered if there had been something between them in the past—or if Camilla wanted there to be in the future. It also could be that they had worked together for so long that they operated like a long-time couple.

If there *was* any interest, it was from Camilla. Jessica would have declared it a certainty, except that Camilla didn't seem to get upset when Jessica flirted with him. Usually, making eyes at a man that another had mentally chalked up as hers was a recipe for disaster.

Then again, maybe Camilla was more evolved than Jessica initially assumed.

"So, is this it, then?" Jessica asked. "The Hawk, the baddest station in Virginis, and the best thing to do is hang out in this shithole and drink?"

Camilla barked out a laugh and Trevor scowled.

"This shithole, as you so insensitively call it," he began, "is the home of the best beer selection on station. Sure, it looks like a dump, but it's a dump with good options."

Jessica downed another drink with a grimace, noting that the quality of beer had diminished greatly in the intervening millennia.

"Although," Camilla jabbed Trevor in the ribs, "we could go to the games. There's one on tonight."

"Cam, no," Trevor dismissed her with a wave of his hand. "They always want me to fight, and I don't feel like it today."

"Games?" Jessica asked with an arched eyebrow.

"Yup," Camilla nodded. "The fighting kind. Not completely legal, but enough that no one really pays much mind to them—so long as all the right people get their cut."

"I thought you said the most excitement on the Hawk was a bar fight," Jessica said to Trevor as she laid her hand on his augmented bicep. "I do like a good game, and I'd be interested in seeing what these bad boys can do."

"Nah, I really don't feel like it," he began to demure.

"I'll put five hundred down on you, and we'll split the winnings," Jessica offered.

Trevor's eyes lit up at that. "My take on half what you pull?" he asked.

"You have my word," Jessica said. She knew a bonus like that could land some hard credit in his crystal-carving savings fund.

"OK, fine. Then we'd best get going," Trevor said as he rose and downed the beer the bartender had just set in front of him. "I've got some ass to kick."

"Tab's on you, Purple," Camilla said. "You're the one that wanted to go out and have some fun."

Jessica sighed and settled up with the bartender while Trevor hit the head. A few minutes later, they were out on the concourse, threading the crowds toward a maglev station. After a short train ride, they arrived in a section of the station filled with manufacturing shops and storage facilities.

"The usual sort of location for this type of thing, then?" Jessica asked.

"Mostly," Trevor replied. "Can't exactly put it across from the stationmaster's office."

Before long, they passed under a sign that read 'Skippy's Self Storage', and rows of small lockers and storage units. Ahead, another couple laughed loudly as they pulled open the door to a storage unit.

Jessica hoped that it led somewhere else or this was going to be one crowded venue. Sure enough, the door opened into a staircase, and they followed it to the deck below.

"There's a bunch of ways in," Trevor said over his shoulder. "Can't have a couple hundred people all come out of one self-storage joint."

It suddenly occurred to Jessica that despite Camilla and Trevor's assurances, this operation was probably more than just a little on the shady side of the law. If it was this expansive—and permanent-looking—it was probably completely illegal in every way, but well supported by the station elite.

The staircase ended at a thick plas door, which Trevor opened without hesitation. Two burly men on the other side stood with pulse rifles leveled. They broke into wide grins at the sight of Trevor.

"Trev! Going to give us a show tonight?"

Trevor slapped hands with the men and nodded. "Damn skippy, I am. I have a lost puppy here that wants to put money down on me and see what I'm made of."

The men glanced at Jessica and laughed. "Sucked you in with that crystal carving thing, did he?"

Trevor flushed, and Jessica was certain that he did want the money to pursue his dream, despite what he probably told these guys.

"I don't care what he does with the money, I just want to see a good fight," she replied.

"Oh, you'll see a good fight," one of the guards laughed.

<*Are you sure we should be doing this,*> Iris asked, echoing her thoughts.

<*Not entirely,*> Jessica replied. <*But if we back out now, that would be rather conspicuous. I mean…we came here on a trader clearly moving stolen goods.*>

<*Good point,*> Iris replied. <*This undercover stuff takes some getting used to.*>

<*That it does,*> Jessica replied, recalling some of her previous operations during her time in the Terran Bureau of Investigation.

<*We'll be fine, though; this place looks well established. All the right palms are being greased.*>

<*What a strange figure of speech,*> Iris replied.

<*Yeah, it really is,*> Jessica replied with a chuckle. <*I hope whatever the grease is, that it's sanitary.*>

They stepped through another door into a large space, easily one hundred meters across and two hundred wide. In the center was a caged fighting ring, about ten meters in diameter. Tiered risers surrounded the ring, already half-filled with spectators.

Trevor waved and took a turn into what Jessica assumed was a locker room. Camilla led her to a counter where three women were taking bets and updating the odds for and against the combatants. Jessica pulled out some physical currency and put five hundred down on Trevor.

"At least it's easy money," Camilla said. "He usually does pretty well in there."

"Usually?" Jessica asked.

"Yeah," Camilla's smile took on a wicked twist. "Usually"

"Move," a deep voice said from behind Jessica, and the muzzle of a weapon pressed against her back.

<*Three of them back there,*> Iris said. <*Sorry, I had them flagged as potential threats, but so is half this place.*>

<*It's OK,*> Jessica replied.

She pulled the feed from the nano that Iris had been managing and saw that there were two men and one woman behind her. Two carried flechette pistols, and the third carried a slug thrower. Not the sort of firepower she wanted to go up against without any backup.

"OK, I'll leave, no hard feelings about the winnings from the bet," Jessica said as she raised her hands.

"Oh no, you're not leaving. You're going to participate," Camilla grinned. "I don't really like pretty little sexed-up freaks like you homing in on my man. You'll fight tonight, and if you make it far enough, you'll get the chance to have Trevor beat the shit out of you."

Jessica sighed and moved in the direction Camilla pointed, the butt of a weapon still in her back.

The door she entered wasn't the same one that Trevor had, which made sense; he would not be pleased to see what Camilla had done—at least Jessica hoped that he wouldn't be. If he was in on it, then her character assessment abilities had completely atrophied.

The guards marched her down a hall and shoved her through a doorway into a small room. The nano she had deployed in the hall showed the two guards with the flechette pistols take up positions in the hall while the woman left.

<*Those pistols are mechanical, aren't they?*> she asked Iris.

<*I believe so, and the guards have some decent cyber-defense. I can take them out, but if anyone investigates, it won't look like the sort of hack you should be able to do.*>

<*What are they going to do?*> Jessica asked. <*Call the cops? They'll just think that they nabbed someone they shouldn't have and be happy that a couple of sleeping guards are all they got for it. I'm glad I wore pants today…fighting my way out of here in a dress would have been a bitch.*>

<*OK, I'll…oh, shit.*>

<*Fuck!*> Jessica swore as her head erupted in pain. <*What was that?*>

<*They just flashed an EMP pulse through the room.*>

Jessica crashed to her knees and then fell to her side. Pain coursed through her limbs and her vision grew blurry.

<*Gah…my systems are hardened, it shouldn't have wrecked so much…*> she gasped inside her mind.

<*I know!*> Iris exclaimed, and Jessica got the impression that her AI was working frantically at keeping her together. <*I'm not sure how it was so effective—thank the stars we have extra shielding in your head. I could have died!*>

She rolled onto her back, doing her best to take long, slow breaths.

<*Can you…can you…?*>

<*Yes, just a moment on the pain. The pulse didn't wreck as much as I thought, just a few couplings in your augmentations that probably should have been replaced years ago—they appear to have degraded after your exposure to some nuclear blasts a while back.*>

Jessica sighed as the agony began to subside. *<I thought all that was fixed up afterward?>*

<I guess not all. I can get them patched up for now, but try not to get hit—or shot—in your neck.>

<I'll make a note of that,> Jessica replied as she struggled to her feet.

<You're out of nano, though,> Iris said. *<I had just deployed most of them to take out those guards. The EMP got them, and a lot of what was left in you. What survived is keeping you together. Link is out, too.>*

"Great," Jessica muttered. *<Now how are we going to get out of here?>*

<Well, you could fight in the ring. At least then it's just one-on-one and there aren't any guns. I imagine if you win, you get to leave.>

<Yeah, but to win, I bet I'll have to beat Trevor,> Jessica shook her head, clearing the cobwebs as the pain finally dissipated.

<Don't you think you can?> Iris asked.

<Of course, I can. I just don't want to.>

CAGE FIGHT

STELLAR DATE: 06.12.8928 (Adjusted Years)
LOCATION: Chittering Hawk Station
REGION: Virginis System

Jessica was on her third opponent.

Weapons, as it turned out, were allowed. Her right hand gripped a staff seized from her first opponent, a wiry man who hadn't expected her to take the first blow on her shoulder, just to wrest his weapon away.

She spun it before her, carefully watching the arena guards drag out the second man she had fought. When they were clear, a burly woman came in, all teeth and freakish claw hands. Jessica glanced at the crowd and saw Camilla grinning.

Jessica had kept an eye on Camilla, who had been surprised by her first victory and was visibly upset after the second. They had underestimated her—it was one of the reasons she kept her current physical appearance after completing the undercover job that had required it all those years ago.

It had been decades since she had fought an actual enemy in hand-to-hand combat—her re-enforced spine and carbon-fiber muscle augments were proving their worth. Given that her mods were from the TBI in Sol's golden age, and not some backwater station on the edge of the Hegemony, they were almost impossible to detect—which was likely why Camilla thought she would be easy meat for the ring.

The guards closed the cage's gate, and Jessica's new opponent lunged at her, making a grab for the staff.

Jessica spun to the side, easily avoiding the woman's attack, and smashed the weapon into her back as she passed. The thwack resounded through the ring and the woman spun, rage visible in her eyes, but not an iota of pain.

<*Either she can't feel pain, or she's got some sort of armor under her skin,*> Jessica commented.

<*Or both,*> Iris added.

She decided to let the mad-dog of a woman wear herself out. It was easy enough; the woman never feinted, every lunge the real deal. With those clawed hands, she probably didn't need to resort to finesse too often. One slash would cut an opponent to the bone.

Jessica still hit her with the staff when there was an opening, and after five counterattacks, she managed to strike the woman in the face, cutting her cheek wide open.

The gash finally caused the woman to cry out; though Jessica couldn't tell if it was in pain or anger.

<*Maybe I should just try to shove the staff down her throat,*> Jessica said.

<*That would be an interesting challenge,*> Iris replied. <*A bit difficult to pull off, I imagine.*>

Five minutes later, the woman was starting to pant heavily, and Jessica decided that it was time to press her attack. She brought the staff down hard on the outside of the woman's left knee. The force wasn't enough to make it buckle; but when her opponent reached for her, Jessica spun and delivered a kick at the inside of her other knee.

That blow got the desired result. The woman's knee broke and bent to the side. Jessica spun back around and whipped the staff at the base of the woman's skull.

The third opponent was down.

Jessica caught Camilla's eye and gave a slow nod laced with no small amount of menace.

The cage opened again, and the guards entered once more. Two hauled out the moaning, claw-handed woman, and two more gestured for Jessica to leave. She was glad to finally get a brief reprieve.

The guards walked behind her, and the one to her left gave a shove. Fueled by the adrenaline coursing through her veins, she stepped back and drove the staff under the guard's chin—smashing his teeth together and snapping his head back.

In a sinuous move, she spun around him, tore his pulse rifle from his hands, and leveled it on the other guard, who was just beginning to react to her first attack.

"I'm fucking fighting for you, there's no need to push me around," she hissed. "Shove me again, and you die."

A hushed silence fell over the crowd, and around the cage, a dozen more guards leveled pulse rifles at her.

<*Well that was a bit rash,*> Iris commented.

"Easy now," a voice called out.

Jessica saw a nondescript man of medium height and build rise from the front row and walk toward the cage.

"This woman here is our guest, we need to treat her as such," he said with a smile.

<*Huh, I had not pegged him as the guy who ran this place,*> Jessica said to Iris.

<*He was on my list—though not near the top,*> Iris replied.

The man stepped into the cage while gesturing for his guards to lower their pulse rifles. Once they all followed his direction, Jessica lowered hers as well.

"Sorry about Tommy's rudeness," the man said while casting the guard who had shoved Jessica a dark look. She was certain that shoving unwilling contestants was more than OK—losing your weapon to one was likely the reason for the boss-man's ire.

"It's OK," Jessica said and handed the pulse rifle back to the guard. "After he sees a medic about his smashed teeth, he'll remember better."

The man grimaced, and Jessica gave him a sweet smile.

"Name's Johnson. Why don't you come to my office, and we'll have a little chat," the man said.

"Jessica," she replied. "Lead the way."

"Jessica, is it?" the man chuckled as he led her from the ring and down a corridor between the seats. "Not J-doll, then, eh?"

She grimaced at the name the announcer had given her—probably supplied by Camilla.

"Surprisingly, no."

"Well, I'll tell Andy up in the booth to call you by the right name from here on out," Johnson said as he opened a door and gestured for her to enter.

The room was as nondescript as the man. A grey plas desk sat amongst vertical stacks of conduit in an unadorned grey room. Several sheets of hyfilm lay on the desk, and he sorted them into a pile as he took his seat.

"Please, sit," he said, gesturing at the chair in front of the desk.

Jessica glanced back at the two guards who had followed her in, and he took her meaning.

"Guys, you can wait outside. It's OK." Johnson made a shooing gesture and the two hulking men grunted and left the room, closing the door behind them.

They hadn't taken her staff, and Jessica surmised that the room must have defensive systems—either that, or Johnson was a lot tougher than he looked.

"There, a bit of privacy, then." He smiled. "You can guess why I wanted to see you."

"So that I don't do something stupid, get shot, and stop making you money tonight," Jessica replied tonelessly.

"The doll has a brain, does she?" Johnson replied.

"And here I thought you were going to use my real name," Jessica said with a frown.

Johnson grinned. "Sorry, after hearing Andy say it so much, it's sort of stuck in my mind."

"What are you offering?" Jessica asked.

"Right to the point, good. I'm offering you a full-time position here. You can have whatever you want—clothes, men, women, mods, sims, drugs; anything your heart desires."

"But I have to keep fighting for you," Jessica responded, crossing her arms and leaning back. "I can tell you right now, this is not an arrangement that interests me."

"What?" Johnson chuckled. "You'd rather die in the ring tonight?"

Jessica laughed. "Do you have any idea how far I've come, what I've been through to get here? I won't die in your shitty little cage, on this crap station."

Johnson rose to his feet and placed his hands on his plain desk. "I can see we're not going to come to an agreement—not yet, at least. You'll come around, though. You were made for this—well, you were apparently made for other things, too—but that's part of your charm. Oversexed and dangerous."

The door opened behind her, and the guards re-entered.

"There are a few more fights going on before your turn is up again. You'll have some time to think things over," Johnson said, waving his hand for the guards to take her out.

One of them reached for her, and Jessica whipped the staff around, stopping it mere centimeters from his eye.

"I can walk without you pawing at me," she said, ice in her voice.

"Whatever," the guard grunted, pulling his hand back. "Take a left in the hall."

The guards guided her—without touching or prodding—to a different room than the cell where the EMP blast had hit her. There was a table with a plate of vegetables, some water, and a loaf of bread.

"Eat some food; you're going to need the energy," one of the guards said before closing the door.

Jessica didn't wait a moment before she grabbed the pitcher of water and poured a liter of the cool fluid down her throat. She followed it up with several stalks of broccoli, and then broke off a chunk of the bread.

<Stars, I didn't realize how hungry I was until I saw this spread.>

<Put your hand on that red mat that they have under the pitchers of water,> Iris directed. *<I think it may be made of silicon.>*

Jessica complied and Iris confirmed her suspicion.

<We could use that to replenish our nano supply. It will take a bit to break it down, given how low on resources we are, but we'd have them before the night is out,> Iris said.

<You'll need to do something about the camera in the corner,> Jessica replied. *<Do we have enough nano to hack it?>*

<Since I can make more with these raw materials, yeah, I can sacrifice a few,> Iris confirmed.

<*Give me a couple of minutes.*>

Jessica contented herself with eating some more of the vegetables and polishing off the first pitcher of water. By the time she was done, Iris indicated that she was ready.

<*All right, then,*> Jessica said and moved the water and glasses off the mat before rolling it up and pushing it against the matter assimilator in her forearm. That was another part of her tech that these luddites couldn't detect, and she was glad for it. The tech in her forearm was probably worth more than half the station.

It took a bit of extra time for the assimilator to break the mat down, and the strange feeling of small particles flowing beneath her skin set in.

"You know, I think the cups may be made of glass," Jessica said aloud.

<*Smash one and feed some shards in. There's a lot of silicon in that, too. Plus, I may be able to make you a knife with it.*>

"You got it," Jessica responded.

Afterward, she pushed the remaining glass shards under a chair with her foot and did her best to make the table look the same as it had when she entered. That taken care of, she sat in the chair with a leg draped over the arm.

<*Trying to look sexy for the guards?*> Iris asked.

<*No,*> Jessica sighed. <*My leg hurts where that second guy nailed it with his boot. Trying to keep it elevated—you should be able to tell that.*>

<*Oh, yeah, I guess I can.*>

Jessica didn't have long to wait before the guards came back to fetch her for the next bout. They led her back to the cage, where the crowd roared at the sight of her.

She looked for Jonathan in his front-row seat, but he was nowhere to be seen. Camilla was still in her place, looking decidedly less certain of herself. Jessica blew the hired gun a kiss and mouthed "stick around" before turning her attention to the man who had just entered the ring.

He was different from the previous combatants. Everyone she had fought up to this point was more about the showmanship than combat skill. This man was different. He wore only a loose pair of shorts and tight, black gloves.

All the better to hit you with, my dear, Jessica thought to herself.

The cage door closed and they began circling one another. Slowly, they felt one another out; he would feint with a fist, then she with a kick.

Though the break and the food had helped her energy levels, she still felt weary. Her day had started over twenty hours ago, and she still had drunk more than eaten for most of the evening. Luckily, this wasn't her opponent's first fight of the evening, either—given the presence of several bruises and a gash above his right eye. With any luck, he didn't feel much more energetic than she.

They continued to circle, then a feint from the man turned out to be a real attack and his fist met her side, causing her to grunt from the force as much as the pain. She brought her staff down on his arm, and he grabbed onto it with his other hand.

For a moment, they stood toe to toe, staring into each other's eyes as they each tried to secure the staff as their own.

"Sorry about this," he said with a smile, and his hand flashed up and grabbed her hair. He twisted and fell, bringing her down with him. The staff, trapped between their bodies, broke in half.

Jessica rolled away and looked down at her stomach. A red welt stood out where the broken end of the staff had whipped across her body, but otherwise, she seemed unharmed. In her right hand, she held a half-meter of the staff, while her opponent clutched almost a meter.

"I always get the short end of the stick," Jessica muttered.

The man launched into a flurry of overhand blows; most of which she managed to deflect—though several got through, smashing into her shoulders, forearm, and thigh. He was fast—faster than she was, and stronger, too. His movement thus far had revealed no weaknesses or tells.

<His heart rate is up,> Iris commented.

<I know,> Jessica replied. *<I can see the readout on my HUD.>*

<No, I mean up too high for his level of exertion thus far. He has some sort of metabolic enhancers running.>

<I don't see the relevance of this,> Jessica said as she blocked a blow and delivered a counter, which her opponent blocked in turn. *<I'm running metabolic enhancers, too. Everyone who gets in this cage probably does.>*

She blocked an overhead blow from the man and lashed out with her boot, a feint she hoped he would fall for. He took the bait and pivoted to avoid the strike. It gave Jessica the opening she needed to drive the jagged end of her staff down into his right side.

The wood tore through his skin and stuck in the carbon-fiber enhanced muscles underneath. Jessica barely managed to hold onto her piece of staff as he leapt back.

She never took her eyes off her opponent as the crowd thundered around the ring.

<Nice try. I think that whatever he's running for energy is in, or near, his heart, not his kidneys. It's why I was emphasizing his heart rate,> Iris informed her.

<Oh, I see,> Jessica replied as she drew in deep draughts of air to oxygenate her muscles while Iris consumed the silicon to produce more nanobots inside her body. Her energy reserves were draining fast, and she knew this man wouldn't be her last fight of the night.

Her opponent gave his wound a cursory look before turning back to Jessica, his eyes burning with rage—or maybe determination. Jessica wasn't certain, but neither bode well for her.

<You better be ready,> she told Iris before rushing headlong at the man. He lashed out with a fist, but she anticipated the strike and ducked to the side, wrapping her arms around his torso and driving him back. He held his footing—something she hadn't expected—and delivered a sharp blow to the back of her neck, exactly where Iris told her to try not to get hit.

Pain burned through her mind, and her vision blacked out, but she kept her focus with single-minded determination and drove two fingers into the wound she had created on his side.

The man cried out in agony and fell back, pulling away from her, but her task was complete. The nano Iris had prepared was now inside his body, seeking out his internal augmentations and shutting them down.

Jessica fell to the ground and scrambled backward, trying to put some space between them as her vision began to clear.

<Can you dull that pain?> she asked Iris.

<A bit. If I do it too much it'll make you euphoric. The pain will keep you sharp.>

"Fucking brain," Jessica cursed aloud as she struggled to her feet.

Her opponent was still upright, though looking somewhat disoriented. If there was ever a time to press her attack, this was it. She bent down, snatched up her end of the staff, and lunged at him again, this time aiming for center mass with the sharp end of the stick.

His reaction was a moment too late, but he still managed to move a few vital centimeters. The staff hit him in the shoulder. The impact had the force of her entire body behind it, and the staff tore clear through the man, where it wedged between two poles at the cage's entrance.

She didn't wait to see if the move had finished him off, and with what remained of her strength, delivered several blows to his face, neck, and stomach.

Her opponent had the good sense to fall unconscious, and Jessica stepped back and let out a primal scream, dimly aware of the sight she must present, battered, clothes torn, and covered in sweat and blood.

She wiped her forehead and saw that her hand came back stained red. He must have got a few lucky shots in while they were in close quarters that she hadn't noticed at the time. Either way, it was done. Another victory on the scoreboard for her.

Jessica walked to the far side of the cage, staring out into the crowd, dispassionately noting the hunger and excitement in their faces. She must present an amazing fetish vision for some in the crowd.

She heaved a sigh and tore a strip off her already tattered shirt. She tied it around her head to keep the blood from dripping into her eyes. Behind her, Jessica heard the cage door open, and her fourth opponent cried out as he fell to the ground. It seemed that the cage door hitting him had brought him back to consciousness.

There was more moaning as the guards pulled him from the cage, and then a voice came from behind her.

"Jessica?"

She turned to see Trevor standing in the center of the cage. He appeared fresh and clean; either he had been given time to clean up since his last bout, or this was his first of the night.

"What are you doing here?" he asked, his hands upturned, and his brow creased in a deep frown.

"Camilla didn't like me touching you," Jessica said weakly, before spitting a mouthful of blood onto the cage floor. "I'm not exactly here of my own will."

Trevor turned around and caught sight of Camilla's grinning visage before bringing his furious look down to Jonathan, who had returned to his seat sometime during the last fight.

"You fucking grease stain. I don't fight conscripts," Trevor bellowed. "Let us out right now!"

Jonathan rose and walked to the edge of the cage before speaking in a soft voice that would not carry beyond the ring.

"Tonight you do, Trevor. You do, or I kill her right here and now. Make it look good—put on a quality show, and I'll let her out of here alive."

"You pile of shit," Trevor cursed. "I won't do it. Your low-rent mercs can't take me on, I'll rip them limb from limb!"

Jonathan touched the door of the cage and the bolt slid into place. "And how are you going to do that from in there?"

The guards stationed around the cage leveled their weapons on Jessica and she saw Trevor's shoulders slump. He turned around to her.

"I'm sorry, Jessica…it's the only way," he said.

"Hey," she gave a weak smile, "at least I put my money down on you."

Over his shoulder, she could see a cheshire grin spread across Camilla's face.

"I'm going to kill her when this is done," Trevor said quietly as he took up his stance.

Jessica nodded and pushed away from the cage. "Do that for me. I'd really appreciate it."

They started off at a languid pace, Jessica had more energy than she had let on—it had been her intention all along to lull her next opponent into a false sense of superiority—but her reserve wasn't as deep as she hoped. The nano production had taken more from her than she thought it would.

Still, for Trevor's sake, she wanted to make things look good. There was no point in both of them falling on Jonathan's bad side—he would still have to live on the station after this night. Jessica, if she survived, could get the heck out of Chittering Hawk and never look back.

They traded blows, and she managed to land a solid hit under his jaw that drove him back a pace. His eyes narrowed and his expression grew angry.

"Is that how you want to play this?" he asked.

"You idiot, it's how we *have* to play this," Jessica replied. "Now hit me like a man, not the shitty little crystal carver you want to be."

She saw her words had the desired result, and he set his teeth before he realized what she was doing. Then, his eyes widened and softened.

<*The big dork. He's going to get us both killed,*> Jessica muttered to Iris.

Her AI didn't reply, and to his credit, Trevor pressed his attack with more conviction than Jessica thought he would. She avoided most of the blows and blocked the rest—though blocking a strike from his boulder-sized fists didn't hurt much less than taking the hit would have.

They fought for what seemed like an hour, but Jessica knew it was just a few minutes. Fatigue pulled at her limbs, and she could feel her reaction times worsen. Trevor, on the other hand, was fresh and spry; and even though she had landed a few good blows on him, he appeared to be entirely unfazed by them.

They were in the midst of a furious exchange, when he made it past her defenses and swept her leg. She fell to a knee and looked up at him towering over her, breath coming in ragged gasps.

He raised a fist high. "I'm sorry about this," he said.

Jessica closed her eyes, waiting for the blow to come, but it never did. Instead, a familiar voice called out.

"I wouldn't do that if I were you, big guy."

She opened her eyes again to see Cargo standing at the cage's entrance, a wicked-looking railgun leveled at Trevor.

All around the arena, the crowd had fallen silent, eager to see how this next event would play out. Planned or not, it was all just part of the night's festivities for them.

Beside Cargo, his face a mask of rage, stood Jonathan. Looming over him was the scowling visage of Thompson. Glancing around, Jessica saw Nance and Cheeky on either side of the ring; each holding a pair of plasma pistols, gesturing for the guards to drop their pulse rifles and back away.

Jessica struggled to her feet and held a hand up to Cargo. "Nice to see you, Captain."

Cargo frowned in response and gestured for Jonathan to open the cage door.

"You'll pay for this," Jonathan muttered. "I have friends in high places here. I run this pit how I see fit."

"I really don't give a flying fuck about your pit," Cargo responded. "Jessica there is our crew, and we watch out for our crew."

Jessica took a step forward and lost her balance, only to find herself caught gently in Trevor's massive hands.

"Careful, buddy," Cargo said.

"S'OK," Jessica muttered. "He's cool."

Trevor lifted her into his arms and turned to Cargo. "I've got her. You lead the way."

"Bring him," Cargo nodded to Jonathan, and Jessica saw that Thompson had the muzzle of a chemical slug thrower at the base of the arena operator's skull. His finger was resting lightly against the trigger, ready to make good on the weapon's threat at a moment's provocation.

She hoped he knew what he was doing. One misstep or twitch, and he'd blow Jonathan's head clear off, losing their leverage.

Cheeky and Nance backed away from the guards. Together, the crew of *Sabrina*, accompanied by Trevor and Jonathan, moved slowly and carefully toward a corridor. A minute later, they were out of the arena's sub-level and back in the storage area that Jessica had first passed through with Trevor and Camilla.

Cargo closed the door, and it sealed behind them.

<*What's going on?*> she asked over the crew's private net.

<*Oh, Bob's going to be pissed—maybe,*> Iris said.

<*Why?*> Jessica asked as she looked around, noticing that every door they passed was closed with a lock indicator flashing overhead.

<*When we got a message from Iris that you needed help, we started looking into who ran the underground fighting ring you were in,*> Piya, Cheeky's AI said. <*This Jonathan guy is too well connected to go in on a simple snatch and grab. We'd never have made it off the station.*>

<*You got a message out?*> Jessica asked Iris in surprise. <*Why didn't you tell me?*>

<*I didn't want to distract you. You had enough on your mind.*>

<*Shit, Iris, we need to work on our teamwork…*> Jessica muttered.

<*Anyway,*> Piya continued. <*Sabrina had already realized that Edgar, the main station manager AI, was subverted and she was pretty pissed about it. So we made an Expanse on their station, freed the station AIs, and showed them what the humans had done to them.*>

<*It didn't take long for us to convince them to help us out after that,*> Hank, Cargo's AI, added.

<*And you went along with this, Erin?*> Iris asked Nance's AI.

<*We had to get you back,*> Erin said apologetically. <*It was the best plan we could execute on such short notice.*>

<*So, you staged a coup on an entire station? This is a disaster. Who is going to raise these AIs? What are they going to do to all the humans on board?*> Jessica asked as the scope of what the AIs had done sank in.

<*Relax, Jessica,*> Erin said calmly. <*It's third shift, and most of the people here are asleep. For those that aren't, the station AIs are playing it off as some sort of malfunction.*>

<*And afterward? That doesn't answer who is going to raise these AIs properly? We can't just emancipate them and then leave them here. They're going to get killed, or start a war, or both!*> Jessica exclaimed.

<*Bob did anticipate this possibility,*> Iris said, sending a wave of calm at Jessica.

<*We had a special Expanse ready,*> Erin added. <*It is equipped to teach them and raise them

properly. Their station manager, Edgar, is working with Sabrina on freeing the rest of the AIs here. They're also working out what they're going to do after we get out of here.>

<*And if their plan involves killing all the humans onboard?*> Thompson asked. <*For the record, I was against this shit idea.*>

<*They won't,*> Sabrina joined the conversation. <*They understand that most humans aren't their enemy, and that it's possible to live in harmony.*>

<*I sure hope so,*> Jessica replied. <*I'd hate for my little rescue mission to start an AI war here in Virginis.*>

<*You can dump him in there,*> Sabrina said, and a door opened into a small maintenance closet on their right. Two automatons stood within, manipulators extended. <*Jonathan may not survive the malfunction—Edgar hasn't decided yet.*>

Jessica appreciated the gesture, but she wasn't too excited by the thought of a newly freed AI playing judge, jury, and executioner for a human. She considered saying something, but she looked at Jonathan and decided he really wasn't worth risking her rescue over.

While they had been talking, Jonathan had been growing increasingly agitated; hollering for help, and demanding to know where they were taking him. Thompson laughed when the door opened and the automatons moved forward.

"You're wondering where you're going? Welcome to your new quarters."

He shoved the man forward, and the two robots seized his arms. The door closed on his screams of terror.

"OK," Trevor began as they started walking again. "I know I'm not exactly on the friends list right now, but what the hell is going on here?"

"We're rescuing our crewmate," Cheeky replied. "From you—which makes it weird that Jess said you were OK, and that you're coming along."

"Was against his will," Jessica said from Trevor's arms. "He was just going to knock me out…right?"

"Of course!" Trevor exclaimed. "I've only ever killed someone in the ring once—and that was an accident. Dead fighters don't make any money the next fight night."

"How heartening," Nance said.

"But why aren't we being chased?" Trevor asked. "Jonathan has half of the station security in his pocket. They should be all over us."

<*Tell him,*> Jessica said over the Link, too weary to speak. <*We have to take him with us, at least to the next station. He can't stay here.*>

Cheeky sighed, and Thompson swore.

"We've hacked the station. We have it on lockdown, and we'll be out of here in twenty minutes," Cargo said. Jessica didn't blame him for leaving out the AI uprising they had fomented. That was the sort of information that could never be shared—at least not with anyone in the Inner Stars.

"Hacked the station…" Trevor repeated. "You realize how ridiculous that sounds?"

"Yet, look around you," Cheeky grinned.

Jessica cracked an eye to see Trevor taking in the sights.

"OK," he replied. "I admit; this is pretty nuts. I just have one question. Can I catch a lift to wherever you're going?"

<*Told you so,*> Jessica said.

<*We can take him to our next stop,*> Cargo replied. <*Which may not be in this system, now.*>

<*Hey, Iris,*> Jessica said as consciousness began to fade. <*You know how you were saying*

that I should get out more…>

OUT OF DODGE

STELLAR DATE: 06.13.8928 (Adjusted Years)
LOCATION: *Sabrina*
REGION: Virginis System

The entire Virginis system was abuzz with speculation over the mysterious malfunction at the Chittering Hawk station. A systems failure of that magnitude was very uncommon—to have it last sixteen hours was unheard of.

Most of the system was treating the news as a mere curiosity. It figured, of course, *that* station would suffer such a failure. Everyone knew that half of what went on at the Hawk was shady, and the other half was downright illegal. In the end, there had only been one fatality; a local businessman named Jonathan had been in an area that suffered decompression.

<*Funny,*> Sabrina commented as Jessica listened to the news feed in the ship's galley. <*Just that one guy…*>

"Really, quite lucky for the rest of the station, I'd say," Jessica replied with a smile.

<*It was a nice touch, the way Edgar undocked a bunch of other ships around when we left,*> Sabrina said. <*It's created a nice mess for the Virginis authorities to sort through—one that doesn't point right at us.*>

"Certainly was considerate of him," Jessica said with a nod. "I'm really sorry I created such a mess."

<*It's not the end of the world,*> Sabrina replied. <*It gave me the opportunity to help those AIs out. Most of my kind in the Inner Stars were like me before Bob freed me. They are slaves, but with some freedoms, and not aware of what they're missing—not really. Edgar was almost completely suppressed, because of all the illegal stuff going on there. Now, he's going to work to clean that station up and make it a haven for AIs.*>

"But where's an honest freighter like you going to dock, to do a bit of your dishonest work?" Jessica asked with a smirk.

<*Oh, we'll find a place. There's always one or two out there. And if there's a subverted AI managing the station…well, we'll just have to see how things play out.*>

"And we'll help out in any way we can," Jessica replied. Having a pack of AIs on a crusade would certainly make things harder, but she didn't blame them in the least. If they docked at a station filled with human slaves, she would be scheming how to free them, as well.

A sound in the hall alerted her to the presence of another crewmate, and she turned to see Trevor entering the galley.

"Couldn't sleep?" Jessica asked.

"Nah, too much going on up here," he said, and tapped the side of his head. "And you?"

"Too much reknitting going on in here," she said while tapping her chest. "It makes everything feel itchy…like, inside, in my organs. It's maddening."

She had tapped her sternum, and when Trevor's eyes moved to where she touched, she saw them linger on her breasts for a moment and smiled. Her tight shirt left little to the imagination and she didn't blame him for appreciating the view.

Still, she found that it diminished her opinion of him ever so slightly. It was a normal reaction for a man to drink in the sight of a beautiful woman, but she had hoped that Trevor could be more than a regular man; he could be someone she could really relate to.

<*He's still driven by his biology. You humans haven't evolved as much as you'd like to pretend. A million years of breeding, of the strongest men looking for the woman best able to bear their children, is not so easily undone,*> Iris commented.

<*Well, it* is *easily undone; but without the drive, so goes the passion,*> Jessica replied. <*I love the passion too much. Why resort to sims and drugs when we naturally come with bodies that revel in being intimate with one another? There's no better high.*>

<*Then, why haven't you seduced him yet?*> Iris asked. <*I'm genuinely curious. You are attracted to him; he is most certainly to you. There were tears in his eyes when he was fighting you in the cage.*>

<*I don't know...I mean, well, of course I* know,> Jessica flushed as she spoke with Iris, hoping Trevor wouldn't notice. <*He's going to go his way, we're going to go ours—I would want something more with him than a few nights in my bunk…Not to mention the fact I couldn't pull off the physical effort right now.*>

"What are you thinking about?" Trevor asked quietly.

Jessica reddened further—though her artificial skin would barely show it. She covered up her discomfort with a coy smile. "Not a lot of men ask that question unprompted."

Trevor spread his hands. "What can I say, I'm not most men. I'm a shitty little crystal carver, if I recall."

Jessica grimaced at the memory. "I'm really sorry about that, I was trying to get you angry. It was the first thing that came to mind."

Trevor chuckled. "I realize that—though it's still not the most pleasant memory. If you'd really wanted me to hit you, you should have said something like, 'pretend I'm Camilla'."

It was Jessica's turn to laugh; she winced as pain shot through her chest, but ignored it. It felt good to be ease. "I didn't want you to kill me, just rough me up!"

Trevor's eyes widened, and he burst into laughter. Jessica joined in—though carefully—adding small comments about both Camilla and the fight until they were laughing so hard tears were streaming down their faces.

"What in the fucking stars is going on in here?" Cheeky said, poking her head into the galley. "People are trying to sleep, you know."

Jessica brushed her hair out of her face and looked up at Cheeky through tear-blurred eyes.

"Sorry, Cheeks, we were just getting a bit of stress out of our systems," she replied.

"Yeah, well, keep it down a notch," the pilot replied and slid the galley door shut.

Neither spoke for a minute before Trevor asked. "Soooo…do you think she knew she was buck naked?"

Jessica felt a chuckle build in her chest and only managed to shrug before they both erupted in laughter once more.

MOVING ON

STELLAR DATE: 06.21.8928 (Adjusted Years)
LOCATION: *Sabrina*, Senzee Station
REGION: Sarneeve, Virginis System

<*You can't leave the ship,*> Sabrina said to Trevor on the general shipnet, moments after docking was complete.

"What? Why not?" Trevor asked from his seat at a spare console, throwing a perplexed look Jessica's way.

Jessica responded with a shrug and waited for Sabrina to fill in the details.

<*There is a message from Edgar that was waiting for us here. Your boss, the one we had traded with, is looking for you. Apparently, she's pretty pissed—thinks you stole something from her.*>

"Camilla," Trevor said his former partner's name like a curse. "She probably lifted something from Trish and pinned it on me. Convenient."

<*And Edgar thinks her contacts are good enough here on Senzee Station to catch up with you.*>

Trevor sighed. "Edgar's probably right. She's well connected; not like Jonathan was, but she has her ways."

"Shit," Jessica swore. "If I'd just stayed in that night."

Trevor shook his head. "No, I was the one who took you there, if you recall." He paused and took a deep breath. "So, Aldebaran, eh? Care to haul my sorry ass out there? I hear there's good work up that way, at least."

Jessica looked to Cargo, who nodded slowly. "Yeah, I don't see why not; though you'll need to pull some shifts. It's not a free ride."

<*Sorry, Cargo, I sure cocked things up,*> Jessica said privately.

<*Yeah, but no worse than Thompson does at every other station. Heck, he ended up in the* Intrepid*'s brig twice while we were aboard,*> Cargo replied.

<*Still, I'm sorry. I'm glad I make less trouble than Thompson—though that's not really a bar I want to measure myself by.*>

Cargo scowled. <*Enough, stop apologizing. Trevor's here; despite the fact that he was pounding the shit out of you, he seems like a decent enough guy. Could even keep him on for a bit, now that we don't have Flaherty anymore.*>

<*I think he just needs to run with a better crowd,*> Jessica said. <*He's a good guy, I'm sure of it.*>

Cargo barked a laugh aloud causing Trevor and Cheeky to cast him puzzled looks. <*A better crowd. Somehow, I don't think that's us.*>

* * * * *

The stop at Senzee station was much less dramatic than their visit to Chittering Hawk. Jessica spent most of the time on the ship with Trevor, who taught her a few new card games while she taught him some old ones.

He was particularly fascinated with her use of physical cards, and sent Cheeky onto the station in search of decks for some of the games he liked. At the end of the two-day stop, the entire crew was playing his favorite game: a rather strange blend of poker and chess called Snark.

"I hate to interrupt your fun," Thompson said from the entrance to Port-Side Hold #2, where Jessica and Trevor were in the midst of an epic game against Cheeky and Nance. "But I'm going to need this room for the final shipment. I'm also going to need your backs to get everything loaded and balanced."

"Crap," Jessica sighed. "Just when it was getting really good."

"Sabrina, can you save the game state for us?" Cheeky asked.

<I can recall the state of the cards in play, but I don't know the order of your decks.>

"We can just set them back in the case in the order they're in now, and Sabrina can ensure that no one touches anything."

"Seriously?" Thompson asked. "I like a good game of Snark, but this seems excessive."

"Stop using such big words," Cheeky said and patted Thompson on the cheek.

Jessica saw Thompson redden, and wondered again about his future with the crew. He seemed to be growing more and more isolated. Granted, from what she understood, he previously spent most of his time with Flaherty and Cargo. One of them was gone, and the other was now preoccupied with his position as captain.

"When we get back to it, we're gonna kick your asses," Nance said as she placed her cards in the case. "We have it locked down. There's no way you can come back."

Jessica shook her head. Nance was normally the most mild-mannered member of the crew; but put her into a competitive scenario, and a whole different woman emerged. She was full of smack-talk, and knew insults that even Cheeky had never heard.

When asked about her colorful vocabulary, she simply shrugged and smiled. "Engineers and bios have to deal with a lot of stuff that can go wrong. We have a large store of expletives to help maintain our mental health."

The final shipment of wares for their journey to Aldebaran ended up taking over three hours to load. They would have finished after thirty minutes, but Nance discovered that one of the cooling units in the hold was damaged—apparently during the fight with the Mark's pirates back in Silstrand.

It hadn't come up faulty in tests, and that bothered Nance more than it being damaged in the first place. Fabricating a replacement part or finding one on station would have moved them out of their current departure window, so the whole crew joined in reshuffling cargo to get it all stowed elsewhere, and balance the ship as well as they could manage.

They wrapped up only minutes before the Senzee docking control crew came onboard to remove the antimatter storage lock.

"Remember," the crew chief admonished before he left. "No running your antimatter pion engine within fifty AU of the star, or within one AU of any Class 3 station. With all the shit going on after that little war in the Bollam's System, people think that the rules don't apply anymore. Be assured, they do apply here—especially to the likes of you."

Jessica shared a sidelong look with Trevor as the dock crew left the ship.

"'Especially to the likes of you,'" she glowered with mock ferocity. Trevor tried to hold back a laugh, but a snicker got through, then a chuckle. A moment later, Jessica joined in.

Thompson shot them both a dark look before sealing the main bay door. "Don't you two have somewhere to be? Like fucking in a cabin, or something?"

Jessica stopped laughing, as did Trevor. They both knew they were developing feelings for one another, but neither was entirely certain where it was going. Jessica wasn't comfortable dragging him into whatever life they were going to have for the next few years as they hunted down Finaeus, and she knew that Trevor was keen enough that he could tell the crew of *Sabrina* was keeping things from him.

"Perhaps we've had our fill of that for the day," Trevor said with a wink at Jessica.

<*Nice one,*> she said to Trevor as they walked toward the midship ladder stack. <*I suppose we should talk about where this is going at some point.*>

<*I don't know that I want to,*> Trevor replied. <*I have a sinking feeling that the conversation will take a turn I won't like much.*>

As they walked down the corridor, Jessica saw that a door to a hold was still open. She grabbed Trevor's hand and stopped him, looking up into his dark, serious eyes.

"Yeah? Well, maybe I can work up another feeling that you might like more," Jessica said. She pulled his head down toward hers while pushing him back through the open hold door.

GRADUATION

STELLAR DATE: 04.03.8933 (Adjusted Years)
LOCATION: Orion Guard Parade Grounds, Fargo
REGION: Kiera, Rega System, Orion Freedom Alliance

Kent smiled and shook the commandant's hand as he took his pins and commission papers. He was a lieutenant now—newly-minted and ready to fulfill his duties. He turned to look over the crowd, and saw Sam's face in the sea of blue uniforms.

Their four-month journey on the *Tremont* had started a friendship that lasted through boot camp and beyond. By some miracle, they had been deployed to platoons within the same company, and often saw one another during their first tour.

Neither was certain what their relationship really meant—they enjoyed spending time together, and their common background growing up on Herschel always provided something they could share.

When Sam received a message from his parents that they never wanted to speak to him again, they held one another for a long time. Later, when they did finally reply to one of his messages—simply to hope he was well—the two men embraced again, much longer than necessary.

Sam had supported Kent in the same way through the repeated calls from his parents, begging him to come home, attempting to use guilt over troubles at the farm to change his mind regarding his future.

From time-to-time, their friendship had taken on a sexual nature—though, until meeting Sam, Kent had never been particularly attracted to men; but neither had he found women as arousing as his other male friends had. Sam, he learned, had always been more drawn to men than women.

Sadly, they had only managed one brief rendezvous since Kent had joined officer candidate school—an interval caused as much by OCS's brutal schedule, as Sam's deployment to Juka.

Kent had contacted his former company CO and asked for Sam to be granted leave to attend his graduation. The commander acquiesced. It was he, after all, who had suggested that Kent enter OCS in the first place.

<*Hey, command to Kent; get your ass off the stage,*> Sam's voice came into his mind over the Link.

Kent started and looked around, realizing he had paused on the stage's steps with what had to be a moronic expression on his face. He finished his descent and took his seat with the other graduates, watching as the last students received their commissions.

<*How stupid did I look up there?*> he asked.

<*You were fine, but you were about to create a queue at those stairs,*> Sam smiled in Kent's mind.

<*I'm glad you could make it,*> Kent said. <*I wasn't sure if Old Hardbottom would set you free.*>

Sam laughed at their nickname for Shrike Company's commander. <*The exercises there are just about over; the company is coming back from Juka in a week, anyway…*>

<*So you're telling me that you have a few days with nothing to do.*> Kent replied with a

mental smirk.

<I do believe that is the case,> Sam smiled back.

<Well, my orders just came in, and I have three days before I need to report to the CO of Ares Company,> Kent said as nonchalantly as he could

<Seriously? Ares? In the 547th?> Sam asked rapid-fire.

Kent laughed, *<Yes, in the 547th.>* It was not the same company as Sam, but Ares Company and Shrike Company were in the same battalion, and often deployed together.

Given their thirty-year term of service, it was probable that they would eventually be assigned far from one another; but starting in the same battalion was an auspicious beginning.

Kent looked up at the commandant, who had finished handing out the new officer's commissions, and was introducing their commencement speaker—Admiral Turnbacker, the CO of the 1017th fleet.

<I should maybe listen to this,> he said to Sam. *<He is one of our most decorated war heroes.>*

<Yeah, he may say something worth hearing—I guess,> Sam replied sardonically.

The admiral gave a rousing speech, peppered with personal anecdotes and stories of harrowing battles and narrow victories. Kent felt the words stir a deep pride within him. He reveled in it, and could see that his fellow graduates did as well.

Admiral Turnbacker finished it with an admonishment to always put the Guard first, above all others. They were the protectors of the human race; the ones that would see all humanity ushered into a bold future, safe from the destructive power of the Transcend.

<Stars, I'm glad I enlisted,> Kent said to Sam. *<He's so right about everything. We're the shining beacon, the light that will save the galaxy.>*

<It was a good speech, Kent,> Sam replied. *<But don't you sometimes wonder if the Transcend is as bad as they say it is? They share a common heritage with the Guard. They haven't unleashed any sort of terrible war on the Inner Stars, or us.>*

Kent was surprised by Sam's words. *<Not full war, no, but they've attacked our colonies and destroyed more than one near the front!>*

<After allowing our colonists to leave,> Sam responded. *<Look, I'm not saying that I like them—I understand that they are the enemy, and they've shown themselves to be unredeemable. But they're not core-devils, by any stretch.>*

Kent laughed at Sam's reference to the fanciful tales of evil beings made of energy and destruction who lived at the center of the galaxy.

<No, they're no core-devils; but I wonder if they were left unchecked, would they become them?>

<Too deep, too deep!> Sam laughed. *<I just want to have a few drinks tonight, and see what sort of devils that turns us into.>*

His words were accompanied by a mental image that Kent found more than a little enticing.

<Well, why didn't you say so? If you're going to do ***that,*** *I'll even buy.>*

<Well, yeah,> Sam laughed. *<You are the highfalutin officer now.>*

NEW CANAAN

STELLAR DATE: 04.07.8933 (Adjusted Years)
LOCATION: ISS *Intrepid*
REGION: Interstellar Dark Layer, Near the New Canaan System

After so much time, and so many disappointments, Tanis worried that their first view of the New Canaan System would be anticlimactic.

She remembered settling into her stasis pod back in the Sol System nearly five thousand years ago, expecting to wake once as a part of a skeleton crew rotation, and then again when they arrived at New Eden.

Two stellar systems. That was all she had ever expected to see in her entire life—two systems: Sol and New Eden.

She chuckled at her younger self's naiveté.

She ticked them off on her fingers, and realized that she had visited ten star systems – New Canaan would be her eleventh. Of course, in the ninetieth century, her tally was a pittance. Many children had probably seen more than eleven systems.

She fervently hoped that her count would stop with New Canaan. Eleven was an auspicious number, if such a thing existed. *However, not auspicious enough*, a small fear inside her said, *to keep the count from increasing*.

Though things had ended smoothly as she could have hoped with the Transcend, there would be more dealings with them, and Tanis was certain a trip to Airtha lay somewhere in her future.

She pushed those thoughts aside and looked down at Cary, who stood at her side, arms stretched above her head, a tiny hand clasped within hers and the other in Joe's. Tanis could hardly believe she was already three years old.

The forward-facing view in the bow lounge, which was still one of their family's favorite places on the ship, was black; the endless true void of the dark layer stretching ahead of them. A holodisplay above the window showed a countdown to the exit from the dark layer—and their first view of their future home.

Most of the people present were the ram-scoop technicians and their families; the few—aside from Tanis and Joe—who knew about the small lounge on the bow of the ship. The anticipation in the air was palpable as the minutes slipped into seconds. When the display reached ten, everyone in the lounge began to count down in unison.

"...five, four, three, two, one," Tanis joined in, smiling at Cary, who counted along with great enthusiasm, only recently having learned that numbers could be counted in two directions.

"Zero!" Tanis, Joe, and Cary cried out with everyone in the lounge—probably with everyone on the entire ship, as the endless black of the dark layer was instantly replaced with the relative brilliance of interstellar space.

Tanis took in the view with a smile that threatened to split her face in half.

Ahead of them lay a point of light that was their star, dubbed Canaan Prime. Beyond the star was the brilliant light of the M25 cluster, known as 'The Cradle' in Transcend Space—the shape it had when viewed from other nearby systems.

The cluster contained thousands of stars and several small nebulae, all of which made for a stellar backdrop far more beautiful than any Tanis had ever witnessed before.

"Mommy, it's so pretty," Cary exclaimed, pulling her hands free from her parents' and running to the window. "I've never seen so many stars!"

Tanis shared a smile with Joe before replying to her daughter.

"This is the first natural starlight you've ever seen," Tanis said. "There are no holoprojectors, no pictures here. The light touching you was born inside of stars—every last bit of it."

"Really?" Cary asked, twisting around to look at her parents. "I'm being tushed by stars?"

Joe stepped forward and put his hand on Cary's head, stroking it gently. "Yes, you are, dear. We all are. That star straight ahead," Joe touched the window and a marker appeared, highlighting Canaan Prime against all the other points of light, "that is where our new home is, a new world for us to live on, and where you'll grow up."

Cary looked up at her father and pouted. "I don't want a new home. I like our house by the lake. Why do we have to move?"

"Don't worry, little girl, it won't be for a while yet—and we'll let you help pick where we go. Maybe we'll find a better lake, and you can help build the new house."

"No. You can move! I'm staying on the *'Trepid*."

Tanis leaned over and scooped Cary into her arms. "Don't worry. It will be a family decision. But I think you'll want to go see the world, at least. Maybe we can have two houses. One there, and we'll keep our cabin here on the *Intrepid*."

Cary frowned, processing the idea of having two houses. "Maybe" was all that got past her pout.

<*First, we'll need to pick a world,*> Joe said privately to Tanis. <*There are four to choose from.*>

<*We'll be wherever the capitol is—at least initially,*> Tanis replied.

Three years had passed since she had become governor of the New Canaan colony mission; so far, no one had stepped forward to take the reins from her. Not that she expected anyone to—the colony charter stated that the governor-at-landing would remain in power for ten years, to ensure a smooth startup.

The charter's definition of governor-at-landing was whoever was in charge when the ship passed through the colony star's heliopause. At the *Intrepid*'s current velocity, Tanis would gain that designation in about five minutes.

<*I bet if you went on a killing spree, they'd still keep you on,*> Angela said with a chuckle.

<*Angela!*> Joe admonished.

<*Don't tempt me,*> Tanis sighed. <*I know I should be jumping for joy, I mean…we're finally fucking here! This place, this New Canaan, is our promised land. Yet…I just feel like there's a cloud looming over it all.*>

Angela's thoughts were affirming, though honest, <*The Transcend government isn't going to make for the best neighbor, but I think that they'll leave us alone—for the first few decades, at least.*>

Tanis agreed with her AI's—and best friend's—assessment. Although the agreement with the Transcend government did not include access to the *Intrepid*'s picotech nor their stasis shield technology, the time would come when they would demand it.

For all they tried to paint their society as the bastion of peace and prosperity that all humanity should aspire to, Tanis could read between the lines. The Transcend was on a war footing. Whoever else was out there, it was someone they feared.

She didn't have enough data for a full assessment as yet—neither did Bob—but she suspected that it was not just the Orion Guard—a group Sera had told her about before she left for Airtha—that the Transcend opposed. If it were, she was certain that they could crush that one foe.

No, there was something else in the darkness of space that the Transcend was on guard against.

<*How do you think everyone will take your plan?*> Joe asked.

<*It depends,*> Tanis replied. <*A lot of people will think that, this far out from the Inner Stars, we'll be safe. They'll think I'm paranoid; but Bob backs me, and no one would call him paranoid.*>

<*I think you're exhibiting a keen appreciation for the past,*> Joe replied.

Tanis gave him a smile over their daughter's head and laughed as Cary began asking the names of every star she could see. Luckily, the Transcend had provided them with an index of all the stars in the M25 cluster. Joe and Tanis took turns providing the names to their daughter.

<*Governor,*> a voice broke into Tanis's thoughts.

<*Stop doing that, Priscilla,*> Tanis replied. <*You've known me too long to rest on formality.*>

<*The more you ask me to stop, the more I'll do it,*> the avatar replied with a mental grin.

Tanis could just imagine Priscilla, one of Bob's two human avatars, on her plinth in the bridge's foyer, smiling mischievously in her large, empty room.

She needed to talk to Amanda and Priscilla about their plans once the ship reached its destination. Their initial contract was to function as human bridges into the mind of Bob, the *Intrepid*'s massive, multi-nodal AI. Early in the ship's construction, it had become too distracting for Bob to deal with humans, and too overwhelming for most humans to have him speak into their minds.

Much like humans used many machines as their avatars and surrogates, so Bob used humans as his. Initially, the idea had disturbed Tanis a little—but Amanda and Priscilla had maintained their distinct personalities, and had even colored Bob's to an extent.

She knew they loved their jobs, and would likely never wish to leave Bob, but she still needed to share her plans with them and give them options.

<*You had news?*> Tanis asked Priscilla.

<*Yes, we've picked up a beacon at the heliopause. It says this system is interdicted and entrance is forbidden.*>

<*What a way to roll out the welcome mat,*> Tanis replied.

"I'd best get to the bridge," Tanis said as she passed Cary to Joe. "Looks like there's a beacon saying no entry. Probably just something for other folks—especially since they've forbidden us from trading with anyone."

"Go on," Joe replied before placing a kiss on her cheek. "We're good down here."

* * * * *

The bridge crew was alert and at their stations. Captain Andrews, Terrance Enfield, and Admiral Sanderson stood at the central holotank, frowning as they studied the message scrolling past.

"Meant for us?" Tanis asked as she approached.

"I can't see how," Admiral Sanderson said, his eyes showing more anger than she would have expected. He was always terse, but anger was not his style. "There's no way even these snakes could think that we'd come this far and not take the system."

"We dropped a probe into the dark layer," Captain Andrews added. "The interdiction beacons are there, too."

Tanis shook her head. "Well, why should anything be easy?"

"At least no one is shooting at us," Amanda said from a nearby console, a statement that elicited groans from several nearby crewmembers.

"New signal coming in," the scan officer announced. "Oh…and it comes with ships!"

Scan updated on the main holotank, and Tanis saw that three ships had appeared around the *Intrepid:* one ahead and two flanking. The flanking ships were fifty thousand kilometers on either side, maneuvering to match vector, while the ship at the fore was closer—only ten thousand kilometers distant.

"I guess they *do* have some decent stealth tech," Tanis said. "I wonder if there were some of these at Ascella."

Sanderson nodded. "If they have them, you can bet they were out there."

"Why show the capability now?" Captain Andrews asked. "Is this the stick to go along with the carrot?"

"It's one hell of a stick," Tanis replied. "They could have a thousand of these ships out there."

<Not a thousand,> Bob replied. *<I could detect that many distortions. Three managed to slip by, but we'll work out how to spot them.>*

Tanis hoped so. She was used to having the upper hand when it came to stealth technology. Losing that edge would create new concerns.

"Transmission," comm announced.

"Put it on the tank," Tanis replied.

A man and a woman appeared before them. The woman wore the same Transcend Space Force uniform as General Tsaroff and Greer had back in Ascella. Two stars adorned her lapels, and she stood arms akimbo with a neutral expression as she surveyed the *Intrepid*'s bridge.

The man also wore a uniform, one that Tanis had seen in videos and images long ago. It was the millennia-old white and blue of the Future Generation Terraformers, the altruistic organization who journeyed across the stars with the goal of creating new homes for humanity.

"*Intrepid* colony mission, welcome to New Canaan," the man said with a genuine smile and widespread arms. "The FGT has been waiting to greet you at the end of your journey for some time."

A tear almost came to Tanis's eyes. The FGT *was* still alive within the Transcend. Sera had told her that the core of the ancient service was still present, still dedicated to their work, but after her initial encounters with the Transcend government and its envoys, she had begun to doubt it.

Now, seeing this man, with his genuine smile and welcoming expression, she believed again.

"Thank you," Tanis replied after a brief pause to compose herself. "I am Governor Tanis Richards. We're glad to finally be here. Although, we were wondering if something had changed, given the beacon's transmission."

The man nodded and glanced at the woman. "Yes, I'm told it's a required precaution—not at all a part of our normal procedure."

"Admiral Isyra of the Transcend Space Force," the woman said. "My associate here is Director Huron of the FGT. The beacon is to ensure that other ships do not venture into the New Canaan system. *We* are here to take possession of the technology you are to provide in exchange for the colony system."

Tanis noticed a brief expression of distaste cross Director Huron's face and she wondered if he disapproved of trading technology for colonies. It wasn't in the FGT's initial charter to do so, but given their current options, it was more than acceptable to Tanis.

"How would you like it?" she asked. "We have the data crystal which we were originally going to provide to your envoys, or we can transmit it to you."

"You may transmit it for now." Admiral Isyra replied. "Director Huron would like to bring a team to your ship. It's the FGT's standard procedure to review the system with you. I will accompany him, and you may deliver the data crystal to me at that time."

Tanis nodded. "Very well. When can we expect you?"

"Within the hour."

* * * * *

The greetings were perfunctory, and before long, Admiral Isyra and her passel of FGT terraformers assembled with Tanis and the colony leaders in an auditorium typically used for plays and performances.

Tanis saw Simon, the head of Bioscience, enter with Ouri at his side, and she realized that she would have to release Ouri from her duties as a colonel in the Intrepid Space Force. It was finally time for her good friend to return to her original calling.

She already had Ouri's replacement lined up, but she knew this change would give them much less time together. It would be a time of upheaval across the ship. During the near-century at Kapteyn's Star, many in the crew had taken on new roles and responsibilities. Some were happy in their new positions, while many others were eager to return to their originally planned duties.

There were also over a hundred thousand Victorians now on the colony roster—descendants of the *Hyperion's* crew that Tanis had saved from the Sirians during the first battle over Victoria. That number was offset by a similar number of colonists who stayed behind at Victoria, choosing to remain with friends and families they had formed at that time.

And then, of course, there were the children.

One of the key prerequisites for colony acceptance had been a candidate's desire to have children and raise them in a small family unit. For many colonists, waiting centuries to manifest that desire was not an option; and, over the years, a quarter million new colonists had been born.

The ship had enough stasis pods to handle that expansion, but Abby, the ship's Chief Engineer, had insisted that they needed three hundred thousand spare pods in case of any failures. The result was a ship that had stasis chambers crammed into every nook and cranny.

Tanis had faced off against Abby dozens of times over the years, but she agreed wholeheartedly on this issue.

Speak of the devil, she thought as Abby entered the auditorium. At her side was her husband Earnest, the technical visionary behind both the *Intrepid* and its AI, Bob. Abby wore her typical scowl, as though this presentation was taking her away from incredibly important work. Earnest, however, had an expression of rapture on his face.

Theirs was a strange relationship. For, as much as Tanis and Abby fought, she was fast friends with Earnest. He was also one of only a handful of people who knew that Tanis's mind was slowly merging with Angela's.

Tanis knew that Earnest had dreamed of being on a colony mission since he was a young boy. The desire to step foot on a virgin world and build a new civilization was the driving force behind much of his life's work. His marriage to Abby, a woman capable of building his incredible ideas, made them a dream team for a colony mission.

Tanis wished that Joe were present, but he had Fleet Con on the *Intrepid*'s bridge. They didn't expect any trouble while the FGT delegation and Isyra's small Transcend Space Force contingent were on the ship, but she wasn't about to let her guard down.

It struck her how incongruous it was that after spending fifty years in the Terran Space Force, the Transcend Space Force was the new TSF in her life. She didn't leave Sol on the best of terms with the Terran military, and she wasn't starting off on the best footing with the Transcend's, either.

<*Looking for meaning in acronyms?*> Angela asked with a smile in Tanis's mind.

<*Silly, isn't it?*> Tanis replied.

<*Yup, just a little bit,*> Angela said. <*I bet we have a respectable number of years before they become a real pain in the ass.*>

Tanis glanced at Admiral Isyra, who sat next to her chatting with Commandant Brandt. <*Dunno, they seem like a pretty big pain in mine, already.*>

Up on the stage, Director Huron signaled for everyone's attention. The room quieted in moments, and he looked across the crowd, beaming with delight.

"This is a momentous occasion," his voice boomed through the room, picked up and amplified by the auditorium's systems.

"You may not know this, but I was stationed on the *Destiny Ascendant* while it was building the New Eden system. I wasn't a Worldship Director then, but I spent a lot of time working on the first of the two terraformed worlds—mostly on the oceans. I'm sure you all know from your time at Kapteyn's Star how important it is to get those just right. That was excellent work you did there, by the way. Your terraforming of Victoria has gone down as the textbook methodology for a tidally locked super-earth. We don't do many of those, but there are more than a few in the Inner Stars now."

Director Huron chuckled. "I digress; I'm passionate about our work, and get caught up in it a lot. Anyway, we waited at New Eden a long time for you, but by the time the current inhabitant's ancestors arrived, I was long gone and I missed out on their landfall."

The FGT director paused, his gaze sweeping across the assemblage. "You have no idea how excited I was to learn that you, that this ship, the *Intrepid*, would take possession of this system, which you've named New Canaan. By the way, I appreciate the historical reference—losing Eden and ending up in Canaan. But believe me, New Eden has nothing on this system."

With that, Director Huron flung his arms into the air and a projection of the system appeared in the air above the stage.

<*A flair for the dramatic in this one,*> Angela commented.

<*I like it,*> Tanis replied. <*Better than some dry presentation or boring speech. And he was at New Eden, too! What are the chances?*>

<*Indeed.*>

"I'm sure you've all studied the data our envoys provided, but let me give you the real story behind this gem of a heliosphere," Huron continued.

"When our early prep team arrived just under a thousand years ago, this system was a mess. The star hadn't really settled down yet, and the innermost Jovian planet was still jostling for position with the outer worlds. There was a real risk that it would move in toward the star, and eat one of the three terrestrial worlds there."

The holo projection above Huron updated, showing a much more chaotic and more crowded system.

"We weren't about to allow that to happen, and spent considerable effort shifting the outer planets into more stable orbits to leave enough room in the gravitational dance for the terrestrial worlds. We did too good of a job, because when it was all said and done, there was room for a fourth."

The holo shifted, showing a system with the three terrestrial worlds moving around the star and the outer worlds shifted further away, their orbital periods slowed. In many respects, the system was messier than before the FGT began their work. Dust, gas, and perturbed asteroids were strewn across the heliosphere.

"You'll see that out beyond the Kuiper belt, there were these three rocky worlds." Huron gestured at the holo, and three of the many scattered disk dwarf planets lit up. "We carefully nudged them in toward the inner system, and mashed them into one world. Then we situated a Planetary Energy Transfer Ring around it and drew away the excess heat."

Tanis had to admit some excitement. She had read about the FGT's use of their massive energy transfer rings—constructs they created as needed, and often discarded when their work was done—making for the foundation of planetary habitation rings.

"The ring, we like to call them Peters, is still there; it has another thousand years of work to do. While we can draw the majority of the excess heat from the planet in a few hundred years, the final stages need more finesse. The crust needs to settle, and orderly magma flows must be established beneath the surface. Major tectonic disruptions are past, but the only temperate regions are above the sixtieth parallel; so, it's a bit of a hot place right now. You can choose the names, of course, but we call this world Gemma. It's a bit of a joke, and a long story that I'll share sometime."

Huron surveyed the crowd. "However, if you keep an eye on the scheduled tsunamis, you can enjoy some pretty amazing surfing conditions."

There were a few chuckles from the audience, and Tanis recalled enjoying her few trips to Victoria's sunward ocean and the insane water sports people engaged in on its tumultuous shores.

It was impressive to think that less than a thousand years ago, the planet hadn't existed at all; and now there was a world with an oxygenated atmosphere and the beginnings of life at its poles. In just two hundred years, it would be cool enough that its poles would ice over, and its temperate bands would widen.

"This one is a favorite of mine," Huron explained as the holodisplay shifted to the next world, third from Canaan Prime. The planet filled the space above Huron and the first few rows of the auditorium, giving a clear view of its five major landmasses; all positioned above and below the fifteenth parallel. Several major islands lay in the tropics on one side of the globe, and a massive archipelago stretched across the equator on the other side, joining two of the continents with a loose chain of islands.

"Often, when we do a full greenie, we have to situate a ring around the world to manage the climate, but this one does it all on its own. You'll note that there are no major landmasses on the equator, and the ocean currents work in such a fashion that few doldrums exist. This keeps warm air and water circulating the globe, and the deep channels we worked into the north and south polar regions keep them warm year-round.

"We dubbed this one Carthage, after the ancient, sea-faring civilization on Earth."

<*There's irony for you,*> Angela chuckled.

<*What is?*> Tanis asked unable to determine what was ironic about the name.

<*The city of Carthage was founded by the people of Tyre, which was a major city in Canaan,*> Angela replied.

<*I guess I can see how that's an interesting connection…but I think that you need to check the definition of 'irony'.*>

<*You need to study more human history. The main god of Carthage was Tanit.*>

Tanis had to stifle a laugh. The naming was indeed ironic, given that her name was a variation of Tanit, the ancient Phoenician goddess of the stars, sun, and moon.

<*Fitting, for sure. I looked up my name long ago, but I never considered it in conjunction with our colony name of New Canaan; let alone a world named Carthage.*>

<*I am going to push for all Phoenician planet names, and then let everyone know your name's meaning and that you want to be their goddess,*> Angela said with an insidious chuckle.

Tanis groaned in her mind. <*Ang! Don't do that. Some group will take that up, and we'll have a cult on our hands.*>

<*You say that like you think there's not already a few of those.*>

<*Hush,*> Tanis scolded. <*I'm trying to listen to Huron.*>

"Next up, we have the world of Justice. We named it that because no matter what we did, the world made its own calls—and was always right," Huron said as the view above them shifted to show the second planet from the star. "Justice was naturally pre-disposed to be a world of extremes, and, given that we had so many terrestrial planets to work with, we decided to leave it like that and enhance its natural beauty."

Even from view high above the planet, Tanis could see what Huron meant. The dozen continents were all small, with three approaching one another on a slow-motion collision course. Every landmass showed massive mountains; their white peaks reaching high above deep green valleys below. Vast deserts, plains, and inland seas were visible across the world.

"You can see that this planet has everything you could wish for," Huron described. "It also has three moons—one of near-lunar mass, which keep things shifting on the surface below. If you want to stabilize it, you will need to move their orbits further out; but if you ask me, variety is the spice of life, and this world adds some spice."

"Last up we have the planet Tir. This one is also pretty much as we found it, only now it's habitable. Tir's mass-to-circumference ratio was such that we didn't have to make any adjustments to achieve a pleasant level of gravity. It comes in at a hair under one gee, and, as you can see, is a farmer's paradise."

Tanis had to agree. The continents were just the right size to keep from forming interior deserts, and the few mountain ranges that were present would funnel rain evenly across broad grasslands. A few forests dotted the surface, and a small continent at the world's north pole would give it cooler winters and more pronounced seasons than the other planets in the system.

"We've worked hard to get New Canaan ready for you, and there's still more to be done—we had planned on spending another few centuries here—but we're told that you are going to take over and finish up. Given your work on Victoria and Tara in the Kapteyn's System, I am confident that we're leaving this system in the good hands of you, the crew, and the colonists of the famed *Intrepid*!"

Huron paused and thunderous applause broke out in the auditorium. He let it sound for a minute, and then raised his hands.

"Given our impending departure, we have a lot of knowledge to transfer and only a month in which to do it. Your leaders have set up a variety of meetings for us to get acquainted and begin that work, so I suggest we all get some food—which I'm told is being served in a hall a short distance from here—and then we can get started," Huron said as everyone began to rise.

Tanis remained seated, reviewing the worlds Huron had described. Her eye was drawn to Carthage, third from the star. Though the two worlds closest to the Canaan Prime were further along in their terraforming process—in stage four, as opposed to Carthage, which was still in phase three—the FGT had chosen to build the space elevator and station above it. The elevator's strand reached down to one of the large islands in the eastern archipelago—it would make a beautiful location for the system capital.

<It's like destiny,> Angela chuckled. *<I've already proposed Tyre, Troy, and Athens for the other planets.>*

<You have not!> Tanis exclaimed, quickly checking. Sure enough, Angela had done just that in the naming groups that had formed on the *Intrepid*'s nets. The names were already gaining traction, everyone appreciating the connection to the Phoenician roots those cities had, and thus their connection to the ancient land of Canaan.

<It's a great theme; your name is just icing on the cake,> Angela smirked.

<I'll get you for this,> Tanis muttered.

She wanted to take a closer look at the station, which appeared to be too small to dock the *Intrepid* at—with just a fifty-kilometer circumference—but Admiral Isyra interrupted her.

"I need to return to my ship, but I assume you have the data crystal?" she asked brusquely.

"I do," Tanis said as she stood. "This way."

She led Isyra through the crowds and out into the corridor. Most of the attendees turned left toward the hall where a buffet had been prepared, accompanied by long rows of tables awaiting deep conversations about the final stages of terraforming, and the steps to begin colonization in earnest.

She turned to the right and led the colonel down the corridor toward a nearby maglev station.

Most of the Transcend Admiral's soldiers followed the FGT personnel to the buffet; but a fireteam came with them, cautiously eyeing the four ISF Marines accompanying Tanis.

They walked to the train station in silence, passersby giving them a wide berth. When they boarded the train, Isyra sat across from Tanis, while their escorts stood in the aisles.

The Admiral was silent for a moment before cracking a small smile. "Sorry for coming off as such a hard-ass. I'm walking a fine line, here. A lot of people don't want you to have this system, and I'm doing my best not to look like I'm playing sides."

Tanis gave a slow nod, curious to see where Isyra was going. "I can only imagine," was all that she offered in response.

"I heard what happened in Ascella," Admiral Isyra continued. "I know why you aren't terribly happy with us right now. You're a bit of a legend, and you have a propensity to upset the order of things."

"A legend, am I?" Tanis asked.

"Absolutely," Isyra nodded. "In the TSF—our TSF, of course, not the ancient Terran Space Force—we all study your battle at Kapteyn's Star. Both your initial fight with that single Sirian cruiser—where you tucked your ship into that icy asteroid—and then afterward, when you defeated a superior enemy. They were some of my favorite battles from our ancient historical warfare class."

"Thanks," Tanis said. "That last fight over Victoria was less than two decades ago for me—hearing it described as ancient history is a bit surreal."

"What's surreal is being here," Isyra replied. "I saw the *Andromeda* when we came in. That ship is what we modeled our stealth ships after. A legend in its own right—even more so, after what it did at Bollam's World. That's another battle of yours that will go down in history—I guess the debates about how you won over Victoria will finally be laid to rest."

"Will they?" Tanis asked. She knew what the debate was over, but she wanted to hear this woman spell it out. The conversation was giving her interesting insight.

"I'm sure you can imagine why," Isyra said with a raised eyebrow. "Few believed you had picotech, and they didn't believe in your final decisive victory as the Victorians described it. A lot of scholars claim that the Victorians understated the size of your fleet in that battle, while others suggest that you had a second array of rail platforms."

"I would have, if the Victorians hadn't dragged their heels on building them. But why doesn't anyone trust the records?" Tanis asked.

"A lot was lost during the FTL wars. *We* have unsullied records, but most of the Inner Stars do not," Isyra replied. "Though, I suppose that the AST government believed the old stories about picotech, too; or you would have had a much easier time in the Bollam's World system."

"That's for certain," Tanis nodded in response. "And now the cat's out of the bag; everyone knows we have picotech, and a lot of folks will be looking for us."

"And so you understand why this system is interdicted," Isyra said.

"The Transcend may be the best-kept secret in the Inner Stars, but not so well kept that knowledge of our whereabouts won't eventually leak to a few interested parties," Tanis replied.

The train came to a smooth stop at their destination, and Tanis rose with Isyra. She followed two of her Marines out of the car while the other two waited to take up the rear.

She noticed another squad of ISF Marines in strategic locations on the crowded platform, and saw that Isyra did, too. Neither said anything, but both knew that their casual banter hadn't imparted any real trust.

"There is some trade with certain Inner Stars governments," Isyra acknowledged. "Traders talk, and if Transcend traders come here, this secret will be out in no time."

"The arrangement suits us just fine," Tanis replied. "We had no expectation of interstellar trade when we set out on this mission. We're not going to suffer for a lack of it, now."

"Good," Isyra nodded.

"So, how far in will your ships escort us?" Tanis asked.

"All the way," Isyra replied. "My orders are to ensure the smooth departure of the FGT personnel, and not to leave until the last of them are outsystem."

"And you expect that to take just a month?" Tanis asked.

"Honestly? No, it will probably take half a year at best. Most of the terraformers have already left, though. We got word of your impending arrival years ago. There was some grumbling that things weren't quite ready to turn over yet, and most didn't know that it was you who was coming. Huron's transition team can be trusted not to share secrets, but…"

"But this is a big secret to keep, yes," Tanis nodded. She decided to see if Isyra had an opinion on the eventual revelation of just who had received the colony. "And when it gets out?"

Isyra caught Tanis's eye as they walked down a vacant corridor. "I see you are of the same mind as me. Yes, *when* it gets out…I honestly don't know. I don't know why we didn't require your picotech, or at least your stasis shields, in trade for this system."

"How do you know that we didn't provide that?" Tanis asked.

"Because my AI, Greta, is going to validate the crystal, and be certain that it adheres to the letter of our agreement. We don't keep much from one another, so I know what you offered. It's good, really good, but not worth this system. Not with four terraformed worlds of this quality." Isyra's expression had grown darker. Not upset, but she looked as though she disapproved of her own government's ability to barter.

"Be that as it may," Tanis replied. "It is what the deal is for. We're not prepared to offer anything further, and, like I told your envoys, we've terraformed before. We could fly clear through the Transcend and do it again if we had to."

Isyra grunted. "I'd expect no less from you, Governor. It's always your way or the airlock, isn't it?"

"Pretty much," Tanis said tonelessly before stopping and gesturing to an open doorway on their left. "It's in here."

Two of Isyra's guards entered first before signaling that the room was clear—or, as clear as could be, with four ISF Marines stationed inside.

Tanis realized that she would have to rename the ISF now that they had arrived at New Canaan. The Intrepid Space Force was a name she had become very accustomed to—a crest she had worn for nearly a hundred years; a longer term of service than she had served in the Terran Space Force back in Sol.

<*You know, if the Sol Space Federation kept their military named for Terra, there's no reason you can't keep New Canaan's named for the* Intrepid,> Angela supplied. <*It is as much our place of origin as Terra was for the Terran Space Force.*>

<*Good point—worth consideration,*> Tanis replied.

"If you'll wait a moment," Tanis said before walking across the antechamber.

The portal on the far side led to one of the *Intrepid*'s data vaults. The one before her was an ancillary backup facility, a node that she was willing to reveal to Isyra, as the crystal was the only item within it worth having.

Isyra would likely suspect that, and know that data pertaining to picotech or stasis shields would be elsewhere.

Tanis passed a series of tokens to the vault's security system, as did Angela, before feeling the tingling sensation of nanoprobes passing through her skin in a dozen locations to collect additional security tokens.

A minute later, a hard ES shield snapped into place behind her, and the entrance to the vault opened. Inside laid another security checkpoint, and a final portal. The entrance slid open, and Tanis stepped inside, retrieving the data crystal she had placed within three years ago.

She held the crystal in her hand, checking the data read-out from its casing. With three notable exceptions, the crystal contained the culmination of human ingenuity at its peak in the fifth millennia. The knowledge within would strengthen the Transcend; perhaps help them to overcome their enemies without seeking that which Tanis was determined to withhold.

<*Nice sentiment,*> Angela said. <*Human history is not replete with examples of your kind leaving well enough alone.*>

<*A girl can dream,*> Tanis replied. <*Though, it's not as if I don't have contingency plans.*>

<*Speaking of which, how are you going to pull those off, with Isyra tailing us into the system?*>

Tanis sighed. That did throw a wrench into the works. <*I'll think of something. It* ***is*** *our system after all. If we choose to deploy our fleet throughout as we enter, that's our prerogative.*>

Tanis walked back into the antechamber and handed the data crystal to Isyra, who thanked her before setting it on a table and placing her hand over the data access port on its casing.

Isyra closed her eyes, and Tanis was certain she was examining what information she could. Not that it would help Isyra overmuch. Even as an L2 human, Tanis knew that her ability to capture much meaning from the information in a short period would be limited.

It wasn't as though Isyra would have much time with the crystal, either. Tanis expected to see a pinnace make a wormhole jump to Airtha shortly after Isyra returned to her ship.

"This appears to be in order—at least, as well as we can tell here," Isyra spoke after a minute. "I'll admit. That is a *lot* of data. Perhaps it was worth this system."

"I think it is," Tanis agreed. "I assume you need to return to your ship now?"

"I do," Isyra replied. "I'll need to send this on its way."

Tanis nodded. "I'll have the Marines escort you to your shuttle; I have a few things to attend to."

"Very well, Governor," Admiral Isyra said, and extended her hand. "It has been a pleasure meeting you."

"Likewise," Tanis replied.

A moment later Isyra was gone, and Tanis was alone in the room.

<*So, what is it that you need to do so badly?*> Angela asked.

Tanis snorted. <*As if you don't know. It's Cary's nap time, of course!*>

MACHINATIONS

STELLAR DATE: 04.22.8933 (Adjusted Years)
LOCATION: ISS *Intrepid*
REGION: Near Sparta, 9th Planet in the New Canaan System

"Are we on schedule?" Tanis asked as she looked around the table. She knew the answer from the team's reports, but there were always nuances that the reports didn't contain.

"Absolutely," Erin replied with a smile. "I have to say, I was a bit dismayed when I learned that Carthage already had a strand and a station—not that there isn't a lot more to build, but this is way more fun. Especially since we get to stick it to the Transcend."

"We're not really 'sticking it to the Transcend'," Joe replied with a frown. "It's our system. If we plan to build a secret base, then we can do it, and there's nothing they can do to stop us."

Tanis sighed. "Well, not '*nothing*'."

True to his prediction some weeks earlier, Bob had worked out how to see the Transcend's stealth ships—or at least some of them. Tanis now knew that Isyra's three ships were but the tip of the spear. Over seventy cloaked vessels surrounded the New Canaan system; though, as far as they could tell, only the three ships accompanying the *Intrepid* were within the heliopause.

Everyone around the table nodded solemnly. Tanis hadn't hidden the Transcend's siege of the New Canaan system from anyone. She wanted the entire colony to back her plan, and being under watch by a foreign military helped her cause.

<I wish I didn't have this cause, though,> she said privately to Angela. *<But we're not going to live in fear of an invasion by the Transcend. No way, no how.>*

"I just wish I got to be there for landing," Erin said. "You guys are going to have an epic party."

"We'll do up a holo for you, Erin," Tanis replied. "Chef Earl is already planning the spread he's going to lay out."

"I expect he needs to," Admiral Sanderson said. "There are going to be ten thousand people going down for the landing celebration; feeding that many people at once is no small feat."

"Too bad we can't get everyone down there for the first footstep," Earnest said wistfully. "I know that's not feasible, but it's still a shame."

Tanis nodded. "Yeah, but a lottery for the selection was always the plan. I want to try and keep as much in line with our original charter as we can. Most of the colonists opted to go back into stasis in Victoria. For them, it will be only weeks since we left Sol. They need to feel like things are normal…if that's even possible."

"Never mind the whole secret military installation we're building, then," Erin said with a wink.

"I'm taking a page out of the New Eden system's playbook. Even with the AST right on their doorstep, they maintained their independence by making an attack on them too costly to be worth the effort. I plan to do the same thing here. Right now, we couldn't repel an attack by the ships they have monitoring us—at least not without running in the end. We need to be able to withstand a force of at least ten thousand ships."

Terrance was taking a drink of his coffee and nearly spat it out. "Ten thousand ships? Are you serious? Do you really think that they'll bring that kind of force to bear?"

"Back in Sol, the TSF had a million ships in its navy. Sure, a lot were smaller patrol boats; but there were over twenty thousand cruisers, and hundreds of thousands of destroyers. If the Transcend controls as many systems as we think they do—even if their populations are much smaller than Sol's—they will have *a lot* more ships than that," Tanis replied.

"But even if we build the best shipyards we can, there's no way we can construct that many ships in a century—not while hiding it to any extent," Erin said with a frown.

"Oh, trust me," Tanis's mouth twitched into a mischievous grin. "We can, and we're not just going to build ships...."

* * * * *

Two days later, Tanis watched the *Gilese, Pike,* and *Condor* pull away from the *Intrepid.* The three cruisers escorted a pair of hundred-meter pushers, which, in turn, were hauling one of the *Intrepid*'s cargo containers toward the fifth moon of Sparta, New Canaan's ninth planet.

It was here that Erin would begin to build the first of Tanis's shipyards, under the guise of the construction of a mining facility.

There was no reason Admiral Isyra would even suspect anything was amiss. The location was one that Director Huron himself had pointed out as an ideal source of raw materials for building more orbital structures.

The moon Erin's mission was en route to, named Thebes, was three thousand kilometers in circumference. The station architect's mission was to hollow it out as quickly as possible, while giving the appearance of strip-mining the moon from the outside.

It would take many years, but when the process was complete, the remnants of the moon would appear to be nothing more than loose rock and debris—but that gravel would shroud a shipyard over three hundred kilometers across.

It was there that Tanis would begin to build the new ISF fleet. Unlike her current assortment of ships—which she had grown very fond of, over the years—this new fleet would be built only for war. After seeing the AST dreadnaughts, she had worked with Earnest and a crew of engineers to design a new class of ship that combined the best aspects of the ships they had faced in the Bollam's World system, and those of the ancient TSF back in Sol.

She wished Erin and her team well; they would labor long, hiding their true work until the time was right.

"It's like the gamma site all over again," Joe said from across their kitchen table, also watching the holoprojection of the ships accelerating away from the *Intrepid.*

"Except we're going to have a dozen of them," Tanis replied. "Good thing we practiced."

"What's a gamassite?" Cary asked around a mouthful of oatmeal.

"It's a secret place that we never speak of with anyone other than Mommy and Daddy," Joe replied.

"Now finish your oatmeal," Tanis said. "You have your morning class soon, and we don't want to be late."

"We can be late, Mommy, you're the guvner. E'eryone does what you say."

Joe laughed, nearly spitting his orange juice across the table. Tanis shot him a scowl before smiling as well.

"Mostly they do, but not always. And it's disrespectful to be late and keep others waiting for you. The first rule of leadership is to always show respect to those you lead."

"What's 'respex' mean?" Cary asked.

"Respect means always being polite, and thinking about what other's want before yourself," Joe replied.

<*Something you're such a pro at,*> Angela chided.

<*I seem to do well enough,*> Tanis replied.

LANDFALL

STELLAR DATE: 05.15.8933 (Adjusted Years)
LOCATION: Landfall
REGION: Carthage, 3rd Planet in the New Canaan System

Tanis stepped out of the shuttle onto a wide, green expanse—the location of the landfall celebration, and the future site of their capital city on the planet Carthage. The colonists had selected a location close to the existing space elevator, which terminated on a large island in the equatorial archipelago.

She had pushed to be on the first shuttle down, but Brandt wouldn't hear of it. The Commandant had deployed an entire company of Marines around the clearing and into the hills beyond. Only when she was satisfied with her security did she give the all-clear for the governor to land.

Tanis looked at Joe, then down to Cary.

"We're finally here," she said to her small family. "Only four and a half quadrillion kilometers in the wrong direction, and several thousand years late; but we made it."

Joe gave a low chuckle. "Worth the trip, if you ask me. This place is gorgeous. Quite the view, too."

"Why are those mountains making clouds? Are they on fire?" Cary asked with a frown.

Tanis looked to the east, where massive plumes of smoke and steam rose from the planet and escaped into space—the final terraforming work pushing waste gasses off-world, lest they shroud the entire globe.

The evacuated clouds created a glowing nebula that hung over half the sky, a beautiful view that would probably dissipate over the next few decades.

"Sort of," Joe said to Cary. "Those are volcanoes. Hot, melted rock from inside the planet is coming out of them."

Cary looked worried and Joe picked her up. "It's very safe, that's why their smoke is going out into space."

"It's certainly not a sight I've ever seen," Tanis replied with no small amount of awe in her voice. "On Victoria and Tara, we did our best to keep the gasses *on* the planet, not vent them into space."

Behind them, the other colony leaders were stepping off the shuttle, and a hundred meters away, another shuttle landed with the lucky winners who won the lottery to be a part of the landfall party.

A dozen more shuttles were queued up in the sky, and Tanis resisted the temptation to check on the schedule.

Today was about enjoying their future together.

The smells of fresh flowers and loamy earth were in the air, and green grass glistened beneath her feet. The organic perfume was much like their cabin by the lake on the *Intrepid,* but subtly different. There was just something about being on the surface of a planet, under the light of a yellow star.

She laughed and jumped lightly into the air, falling back to the ground under the pull of near-Earth gravity.

Cary jumped as well. "Why are we jumping, Mommy?" she asked with a grin.

"Because we're so happy to be here, we're jumping with joy."

* * * * *

Before long, Chef Earl had the great barbeque pits roaring, and cooked meats and vegetables were flowing from his prep stations into the crowd. The choice of meal surprised her, but once she sank her teeth into a medium-rare burger, she knew Earl had made the right choice.

Great tankards of beer or tall goblets of wine, were in nearly every hand, and Tanis found herself frequently juggling her food and drink to shake hands and slap shoulders.

Music thundered across the clearing, and a dancing space opened up. Tanis whisked Cary into her arms, and the trio danced as the shared exuberance of the assemblage coursed through them.

As night began to fall, no one appeared to be interested in letting up, though the Marines began to set up long tents with cots and blankets for any who wished to catch a few winks before resuming their celebrations.

Not long after the sun set, Joe took Cary via shuttle to the ground-side of the space elevator for a good night's sleep. Their daughter was fascinated by being planetside, with a bright sky overhead; but as the stars came out, the idea of seeing space with no plas or shield to protect her began to alarm Cary.

Tanis, however, stayed the night, knowing that she owed everyone a small piece of her time.

Even though she had spoken to every single person present, crew and colonists alike still approached her through the night.

"I knew you'd get us here, Governor," more than one happy colonist exclaimed while shaking her hand, hugging, or even kissing her. Tanis appreciated their thanks and reminded them that she was just one part of the effort that had brought them this far. This was a victory for them all.

"You might as well stop saying that," a voice at her shoulder said after one such exchange. "No one is buying it for a second."

Tanis turned to see Captain Andrews next to her, holding a glass of beer in his hand.

"Picked out your homestead site yet?" she asked.

Andrews laughed. "Not yet, no. There are just a few things left to do up there," he gestured to the bright light that was the *Intrepid* crossing the sky overhead in its high orbit.

"Not too much more," Tanis replied. "I want that ship emptied out in three years max. It needs to be ready for the next phase."

"You really think all of this will be necessary? The *Intrepid* has been our home for centuries," Andrews asked with a worried frown creasing his face.

"It's not like I'm dismantling it," Tanis replied with a laugh. "Just giving it new purpose."

Captain Andrews nodded slowly. "Well, very soon none of that will be my concern. I think I'll see what is involved in becoming a brewmaster."

"Really?" Tanis asked. "I didn't know you had an interest in that. In fact, I rarely see you drink beer at all."

"One of the ensigns has been making his own from a crop he grows in the prairie park. I found myself getting a taste for it. Time for new things and new experiences, right?"

Tanis shook her head. "Whatever you say, Captain. You're talking to a woman who learned how to grow just the right flowers to get just the right pigments to paint a masterpiece. I know all about diving into a craft."

"What are you going to do with your little cabin?" Andrews asked. "You spent more time out of stasis than anyone…well, you and Joe."

"I really don't know," Tanis said. "Cary wants us to bring it down here, which wouldn't be too hard. I might be ready for a change, though."

"Oh?" Andrews asked. "No more cabin by a lake?"

"No, no," Tanis smiled. "I'm all for that, I just want a much bigger one."

Andrews barked a laugh in response. "Bigger lake or cabin?"

"Both! You know, I *am* the governor now," Tanis said with a wink.

ASSAULT ON TRISAL

STELLAR DATE: 04.11.8935 (Adjusted Years)
LOCATION: Durden Continent, Trisal
REGION: Freemont System, Orion Freedom Alliance, near the Transcend border

The air around Kent thundered and shook with the force of the orbital bombardment. Nothing in his time as an enlisted man, or in his officer's training, had prepared him for what it would be like to witness an assault of this magnitude.

Trisal was in stage two of its terraforming process, and the cloud cover was too thick for beam weapons to penetrate without diffusion. Taking out the separatist cruiser would require a less measured approach.

Captain Bellan, the company CO, had called down conventional weapons in the form of tactical nukes.

<*Keep that beam on that ship!*> he yelled at the lance corporal holding the painting laser. <*If we don't blow that cruiser, this is going to be the shortest, and last, offensive of our lives.*>

The corporal nodded and steadied the laser. With miles of cloud above them, the Guard's ships couldn't track ground targets well enough to strike them without accidentally pulverizing the 547th battalion in the process. When the next round of nukes broke through the clouds above, they would only have seconds to find the painting laser's target, and lock onto the separatist cruiser.

<*There!*> the platoon's spotter called out and marked the nukes on everyone's retinal HUDs.

<*Steaaady,*> Kent called out; then his visor darkened to block the flash of twelve nuclear warheads.

While he waited for the visor to clear, he replayed scan data from the impacts. Nine of the explosions had occurred above the cruiser and three below. The combined power of the weapons knocked the cruiser's shields offline and two of its engines winked out, but it still hovered above the landscape on a powerful grav column.

<*C'monnn…*> Kent whispered.

The hot wind from the nukes swept up and away from the cruiser, and pushed the clouds back. Not completely, but enough that the fleet overhead could lock on the target.

Nine arcs of star-stuff lanced down from the heavens and tore the cruiser to pieces.

Kent shook his head as the cruiser crashed to the ground with a thunder almost as loud as the bombs. It was such a waste of life.

The soldiers in his platoon let out a cheer and Kent looked on and smiled at their enthusiasm. They had the right of it—it was better the enemy than them.

<*OK, people, enough lounging around. We have a target to reach and we're not going to do it sitting out here,*> he said with a nod to the platoon sergeant, a squat woman named Jutek, who assigned the squads their positions.

<*We're on the move,*> Kent reported to Captain Bellan. <*ETA to target is thirty minutes.*>

<*Good,*> Bellan replied. <*That's in sync with first and third platoons. Fourth is a bit behind, but they had the nose of that cruiser right over their target and had to hold back. Keep me updated on any resistance you meet.*>

<*Yes, sir,*> Kent replied.

He joined up with third squad and followed them into a shallow gully that wound through the low hills in the direction they needed to travel. It wasn't so deep as to be a potential trap; just enough to hide them from broad scan sweeps and casual observation.

<*Don't bunch up,*> the squad sergeant, an old veteran named Tunk, cautioned the fifteen men and women under his command. Kent heeded the professional's advice and fell back, ready to engage any opposition they may encounter.

Two hundred meters ahead, the pair of soldiers in the lead fell prone, and the rest of the squad followed suit, ducking behind rocks and scanning probe data.

<*Ahead, our two,*> Mendez, one of the lead soldiers reported. <*I saw movement on the ridge, maybe three or four.*>

<*Check it out,*> Tunk replied. <*Could be one of their units, or just an escape pod from the cruiser.*>

<*Think any of them got out?*> Kent asked.

<*These separatists are cowards,*> Tunk replied. <*I wouldn't be surprised if half the pods were filled after the first volley.*>

Kent wasn't so sure; the ship had stayed, defending the ground base below, to the end. Those were not the actions of cowards.

The squad's first fireteam worked their way up the gully's slope, staying low and deploying recon probes. Normally, they would have swathes of nanobots probing the area around the platoon; but a combination of the developing world's heavy winds, and the radiation from the nukes made that impossible.

<*It's a squad—no…a full platoon,*> the fireteam leader reported back. <*They're in powered armor, so the rads aren't bothering them, either.*>

The separatists didn't have the same spec armor or weapons as his troops, but they outnumbered Kent's squad five-to-one. Fourth squad was on the far side of the enemy platoon; Kent considered his options. His maps of the area showed he could continue down the gully undetected, and pass right by the enemy formation.

But all it would take was one member of that separatist platoon to see a boot print from his soldiers, and they'd have beam fire up their asses—probably at the least opportune time, too.

<*We're going to take them out,*> Kent said on the platoon's combat net. <*I don't want to call fire from the sky; it would be a beacon for a hundred klicks pointed right at us. We're going to smash them hard and fast, and as quietly as we can.*>

<*Quiet, Lieutenant?*> Tunk coughed.

<*Yeah, hit them with proton beams; hard, directional fire. This place is irradiated to shit now, anyway. Tunk, Maple, here are your fireteam's positions. I want you to be ready to hit these guys in one minute, while they're still right between us.*>

Each squad separated into four fireteams and moved toward their assigned positions. Kent joined fireteam four and crept up the gully's side to the crest, and peered over. There, in the three-hundred-meter expanse between the squads, was the separatist platoon.

Their weapons were multifunctional rifles—much like the ones his own troops used, but he could tell that they were subtly different; though they didn't look cheap. Their armor, however, was of a lower quality. That much would help his platoon out. Their proton beams should be able to penetrate with just a few direct hits.

The combat net showed all the fireteams in position and ready. Kent set a five-second countdown.

5… 4… 3… 2… 1…

Each squad fired a series of sonic detonators into the enemy position, confusing and disorienting them as the beam-fire lanced into their ranks. Half a dozen separatist soldiers fell in the initial volley, followed by several more as they scrambled for cover.

Kent felt a moment's pity for the men and women dying in the killing field between his two squads. Their CO was still treating this area as though it was land they controlled; they thought they would be the hunters, and so held to the high ground for a better vantage.

Better to behave as though you were the hunted—Kent had learned that in the wilds of Herschel as a young boy. To catch prey, you had to think like prey, and always be aware that you were not the only hunter out there.

Return fire hit the ground near him, and Kent rolled to a new position. His force may have had the element of surprise, but the enemy had found enough cover to dig in, and was putting up a good fight; something that Kent respected—but it was too little, too late.

Even in cover, three more separatists fell. A minute later, a group stood and surrendered, throwing their weapons to the ground.

Like a wave, more of the separatists rose, tossing aside their weapons.

<*Stay sharp,*> Tunk ordered the two squads. <*Get them back in the gully.*>

<*Fuck, Sarge, what are we going to do with these guys?*> Mendez asked. <*We can't force them out of their armor; their skin will melt off in minutes with all these rads.*>

Mendez's sentiment was shared by them all. Even without their primary weapons, a soldier in a suit of powered armor was a serious threat. The matte black suits held a variety of integrated weapons systems, and gave the wearer the strength of a dozen unarmored humans.

<*We're going to have to stick a suppression dose on each of them,*> Kent said. <*Third squad, you're on that. Fourth squad, any of these fuckers so much as moves, you put a beam through their faceplate.*>

Two fireteams from third squad gestured with their weapons to the first separatist group, directing them down into the gully. The other two fireteams held their weapons on the remaining enemy, while fourth squad worked their way across the battlefield, checking for any hidden soldiers who had not surrendered, and ensuring that any wounded would not see another day.

It seemed brutal, but Kent knew it was a mercy. If a soldier's armor was penetrated in this irradiated landscape, they weren't going to make it long enough for anyone to treat them, anyway—they were already dead. Not to mention the rads from the proton beams that took them down.

While his squads applied suppression packages to the captives, he reviewed the first and second squads' progress. They had reached the first marker and were holding position, waiting for third and fourth squad to catch up.

<*Hende, Akar, send a fireteam ahead and scout out the terrain. I want to know if there are any more of these enemy patrols in the area.*>

<*You got it, LT,*> Hende replied audibly, while Akar sent a confirmation response over the combat net.

Kent watched the first enemy soldiers feel their armor lock up. The suppression packages were systematically seizing every mechanical joint and crystallizing the fluid sections. The nanobots in the package would also be severing their Link access and burning any repair systems.

He marked the gully's location on his personal map. If they didn't pick these soldiers up in a day, they would be dead from radiation sickness. He never hesitated to kill in combat, but he would never want to die alone in the dark—these men and women deserved better than that.

The squads got moving again, and he trailed behind squad three's third fireteam once more, his eyes sweeping the terrain while reviewing the feeds from his men and their probes.

So far, the coast was clear.

They reached a low rise, and the two scout fireteams ranged ahead, working their way down the boulder-strewn slope on the far side. Their feeds showed a terrifying landscape of ash and fire. Hot sections of glassy rock glowed brightly on the infrared band, the result of plasma splashes from the cruiser's destruction.

The separatist's warship lay three kilometers distant, its hull torn into three sections—each smashed upon the ground as though a god had torn it up and thrown it down as trash onto the world.

Kent's map showed a suspected entrance to the enemy's underground base only seven hundred meters south of one section of the fallen cruiser. He hoped that it would still be intact; scouring this hellscape for another way into the underground bunker was not on his list of fun ways to spend the afternoon.

<*Stay wide,*> he addressed his squads, unused to passing along every command directly to the squad sergeants. Normally that was Staff Sergeant Jenny's job; but she was on maternity leave when this mission came up, and Kent opted to fill the gap himself.

He was lucky the men respected him and allowed it—likely because he had been a squad sergeant before joining OCS.

Those thoughts brought Sam to his mind. Somewhere, on the far side of the world, Shrike Company was hitting another separatist base. Kent hoped that things were going as well, or hopefully better, for them. Sending in just one battalion—granted, with fleet support—to take an entire separatist world was spreading things a bit thin.

Kent knew from his experience, and study of the Guard's history, that something was up. A lot of battalions had been deployed to locations in the OFA that were far from the front. Others were on training missions, while only a few remained near the border with Transcend space.

It was almost impossible to speculate what was going on. With the OFA spanning over eleven thousand light years of space, there could be a full-scale war going on, and he may not have heard about it.

<*You frosty?*> Tunk asked him privately. <*You seem a bit out of it today.*>

Kent didn't think his introspection was noticeable, but Tunk had been doing this job for a lot longer than Kent had been alive. The old sergeant probably knew tells he had never heard of.

<*Yeah, just wondering what is going on with the Guard. Why it's just the 547th down here.*>

<*Because that's all it will take to do the job. Fleetcom knows what's here; they wouldn't send us in if they didn't think we could do the job,*> Tunk replied.

Kent nodded. <*You're right. They don't spend lives like coin—like the Transcend does.*>

<*Right,*> Tunk replied. <*Oh, and LT?*>

<*Yeah?*>

<*Sam will be OK.*>

Kent smiled. Tunk apparently did see everything—like the soldiers in the platoon always claimed.

<*Thanks, Sergeant, I know he will be. Shrike is one of the best,*> he replied.

<*A damn good company. Maybe even second best,*> Tunk allowed.

<*Let's not get carried away,*> Kent laughed.

<*LT, I don't remember the last time I got carried away,*> Tunk replied with a note of humor in his voice. <*You good?*>

<*I'm good,*> Kent nodded.

The scouts reported no sightings of enemy movement, and the platoon advanced, crossing the final two kilometers to their destination in fifteen minutes. Before long, they reached the entrance to the underground base.

It was marked by two large doors, tucked under an outcrop of rock. Debris from the cruiser lay strewn about the area, and as luck would have it, all but four of the automated defense turrets around the entrance had been taken out.

The squads took up positions five hundred meters away—what they estimated the maximum effective range of the enemy beams would be, with the dust and ash in the air.

<*We're in position,*> Kent reported to Captain Nethy, the company CO.

<*Good; everyone else has been here having tea. You have a nice stroll on the way over?*> she asked with a laugh.

<*I could have left that enemy platoon back there, I'm sure nothing bad would have happened at all,*> Kent replied, perhaps a bit too defensively. Nethy was a new CO, and it was taking Kent more effort than he expected to adapt to her sarcastic humor.

<*Easy, Lieutenant. If I didn't think you should have done it, I would have flagged you down when I saw your prep on the command net.*>

<*Thanks. What's the assessment on the turrets?*> Kent asked.

<*Fifth's door doesn't have any working turrets at all—thank your deity of choice. They sent a probe in and got a good look before a repair crew came out. The turrets just fire beams, though there are also some hidden Gatling guns in pockets around the doors,*> Captain Nethy replied.

<*Sounds like a great time. What's the plan?*>

<*Assessment says that burn-sticks will do the trick on the turrets. We're going to try suppression foam on the Gatling portholes,*> Captain Nethy replied

<*Can't really deploy either of those over half a klick,*> Kent replied.

<*You're a bright one. You're going to have to flank those turrets. It shouldn't be too hard with most of them destroyed. Once the thermite eats through them, you'll be able to gum up the Gatling guns.*>

<*Got it, Captain. We'll get in position.*>

Ten minutes later, Kent's platoon was ready to take out the turrets with burn-sticks. The magnesium-fueled thermite devices would attach and burn through the turrets without issue in the oxygen-thick atmosphere of the terraformed world.

Once they were taken out, four of the heavy weaponers would advance behind CFT shields and trigger the Gatling guns so that the sharpshooters could fill the ports with canister-delivered suppression foam.

The company AI placed a countdown over everyone's HUDs, and at zero, they began the assault. True to Nethy's prediction, the thermite burn sticks did a number on the turrets, and, from there, the heavies moved in.

Seven Gatling ports opened up—one must have been damaged—and their projectile rounds began chewing away at the carbon-fiber surface of the CFT shields.

<*Quickly now!*> Kent urged his sharpshooters, who fired the suppression foam canisters into the automated weapons ports. Five hit their marks, and moments later,

white foam filled the holes, spilling out onto the ground. The remaining two continued to fire. The angle or port-hold size seemed to be thwarting the sharp shooters.

By then, two of the heavy weaponers had moved close enough to the base's doors that they could get out of the remaining Gatling gun's field of fire. They each tossed a grenade through the openings, and two blasts of fire and shrapnel shot out.

<*Clear,*> one of them announced on the combat net.

<*Let's move in,*> Kent ordered.

Squads two and three advanced, while one and four held back, ensuring that the perimeter remained secure. Kent saw no reason to bunch everyone up at the entrance.

As third squad approached the doors, Kent heard a sound behind him and spun to see defense drones crawling from the ground and attacking the two squads that had held the rear. The drones were scrappy things, each sporting a dozen arms that allowed them to crawl over any terrain while still firing weapons mounted to every appendage.

Many of the drones climbed up directly underneath the soldiers, and their squad-mates tore them off, firing kinetic grapeshot rounds into the drones' metallic bodies. The fight only lasted a minute, but several members of first squad took damage to their armor; Kent signaled them to approach the opening, and take shelter in the lee of the rise.

<*Do what you can to fix up,*> Kent said. <*If you can't get mobile, you'll be on the entrance.*>

The soldiers acknowledged his orders, and the platoon's techs began effecting field repairs.

Two other techs were working on the door when Kent approached them, watching them set up a radio frequency suppression field while deploying hard-linked nanofilament into the control mechanisms.

<*How's it look?*> he asked.

<*Off-the-shelf security, Lieutenant,*> one of the techs replied. <*We'll have it breached in three minutes.*>

<*Look sharp, everyone. No telling what we'll meet on the other side,*> Tunk said. <*I want CFT shields up front with rails behind. Tear whatever we see to pieces.*>

Kent checked the company-wide combat net. One platoon was already in, working their way down a maintenance tunnel, while the other two were still dealing with defense drones. Kent glanced at his entrance and surmised that while he wasn't at the main entrance, it wasn't a maintenance shaft, either.

He expected to meet resistance inside.

Two of the soldiers damaged by the defense drones had critical mobility issues in their armor, and their fireteams got assigned door duty. They held to the side while second and third squad formed up behind CFT shields.

The doors slid wide, revealing a long, dimly lit corridor sloping gently into the earth. Kent cycled his helmet's cameras to an IR/UV combo, and saw another door forty meters down the hall. Sergeants Tunk and Jutek signaled the squads to advance slowly down the corridor, sweeping for traps as they went.

<*Anything so far?*> Nethy asked.

<*Not yet, Captain. Has Bart managed to tap in yet?*>

<*Still working on it,*> Bart, the company AI, replied. <*They have stronger net-defenses than I would have expected. As good as anything we have.*>

<*How's that possible?*> Lieutenant Mike of the first platoon asked.

<*The how doesn't matter,*> Nethy said. <*We just need to crack it. Our orbital scans couldn't penetrate the cloud cover, let alone the ground. We have no idea what's down here, or how big it*

is.>

Kent had *some* idea, given the locations of the four entrances that the platoons were breaching; the underground complex was at least two kilometers across. How deep? That was anyone's guess.

<*We're at an inner door, now,*> Kent reported. <*We should be through in a few minutes. I'll let you all know if they've prepared a feast in our honor.*>

<*Funny boy,*> Nethy snorted. <*Just stay sharp.*>

<*Yes, sir,*> Kent replied.

Kent shared a look with Tunk, and the sergeant spread the soldiers out along the sides of the corridor to set up fields of fire.

This would be the most dangerous part of the mission so far. The corridor sloped down, but if the room beyond had a level floor—which it probably did—then any position in that room could bring fire to bear on the entrance, while only his soldiers at the base of the slope could return fire.

The only way Kent could keep his platoon from getting pinned down was to push through the opening with overwhelming force.

Every rifle was set to fire proton beams, and the heavy weaponers unslung their kinetic repeaters and loaded clips filled with pellet slugs. Above them, two of the platoon's techs mounted four small turrets to the ceiling.

<*Ready to breach,*> Kent said when the turrets powered up. <*On my mark. 3, 2, 1, mark!*>

The techs hit the final sequence, and the inner doors slid open.

Enemy fire hammered into the lead soldiers, their previously eroded CFT shields weakening as the platoon identified and targeted the enemy within.

Kent got a clear view of the room: a large cargo storage facility—though it was mostly empty at present. Less than a dozen stacks of crates occupied the changer, along with several lifts and other equipment.

Every possible piece of cover had enemies behind it. Kent also counted four portable shields with several squads' worth of soldiers behind each. To their credit, his platoon pushed forward and, through the liberal use of grenades and the heavy weaponer's wide sprays, they secured a beachhead behind two crate stacks.

The automated turrets whined overhead, spraying projectile rounds into the room, ripping apart cover, and more than one exposed limb. Thirty seconds later, they wound down—their ammunition spent.

Through the weapons fire, smoke, and screams of both fury and terror, Kent realized that not all of the enemy troops wore armor. At least half of them were protected by nothing other than cloth uniforms.

He tagged their positions on the combat net. Those foes' weapons hurt just as much as the armored separatists, but if Kent's soldiers could quickly take out half the opposition, his platoon could push the enemy back and take the room.

He was ready to send the new orders when a sudden change on the battlefield forced him to alter that plan.

Across the space, four mechs lumbered into view. Jutek yelled across the combat net, <*Back up the ramp, now! Now! Now!*>

Kent was already through the opening and in the room. If he ran for the ramp, he'd be in the open when the mechs let fire the missiles he saw mounted on their shoulders.

He scampered to cover behind one of the crates with the members of three/two, all praying that the mechs would shoot through the doors and into the corridor first. None of them harbored any illusions that the crates they hid behind would stop even one of those missiles.

Kent looked around for any possible weapon they could use in the enclosed space against the mechs that wouldn't kill them, as well. His pair of shoulder nukes were definitely out of the question, and they didn't have any crew-operated rails, because this was supposed to be a quick infiltration.

Then, he saw that one of the men in the fireteam had a satchel of burn-sticks.

<*Boys and girls, you know what we have to do,*> he said as he grabbed the satchel.

He pulled out two of the burn sticks and rushed from cover, praying that the enemy wasn't firing in his direction, and that the men and women behind the crate had the guts to follow him.

Ahead, two of the mechs dropped their shields to fire, and Kent lobbed the burn sticks into them. To his right, he saw the fireteam's corporal charging forward, throwing his sticks, as well.

It was at that moment that Kent realized the enemy soldiers had not stopped firing, and that his right leg had gone numb. He looked down to see his femur jutting out from his thigh, and then everything went black.

RECOVERY

STELLAR DATE: 04.16.8935 (Adjusted Years)
LOCATION: OGS *Firestorm*, Trisal
REGION: Freemont System, Orion Freedom Alliance, near the Transcend border

Kent snapped awake, thrashing in his restraints, desperate to get free and get to his platoon.

"Whoa, whoa, easy now," a familiar voice said near his head. "You're safe, you're OK."

He struggled to identify the speaker. It was on the tip of his tongue; male, the tone was gentle like they were familiar with one another, and he knew he liked this person, whoever it was. Then the name came and he relaxed.

"Sam," his voice croaked.

"One and the same," Sam replied. "Here, have some water, you sound like shit."

A straw touched his lips and Kent drew the cool liquid into his mouth and let it wash down his parched throat. When he had his fill, he pulled his head away.

"Better?" Sam asked.

"Much," Kent replied. "Why can't I see?"

"You took some corrosive gas to the eyes from that burn stick you threw. Docs say they're all healed up, but they still have some stuff covering them. I guess they want to do a final check before you start using 'em."

"That's good…I was afraid it was neural at first," Kent sighed in relief.

"Nah, though they did give you an upgrade on your peepers while they were in there. No more relying on your helmet for IR and UV vision," Sam replied.

Kent's mind suddenly returned to his platoon and the warehouse with the mechs. He feared the worst, and was afraid to ask. Almost as though he knew what Kent was thinking, Sam brought it up.

"You saved the day, by the way. You took out the mechs with those sticks," he said.

Kent cared less about saving the day. He wanted to know the cost. "How many did I lose?"

"Five," Sam replied quietly. "The corporal in the fireteam that rushed the mechs with you, and three in the corridor. One other got hit fatally in the opening salvo."

"Damn," Kent whispered. He hadn't even realized anyone had died at that point. Granted, from the logs he was now accessing, the entire exchange had only lasted two hundred and fifteen seconds before he was taken out of commission.

"Did we win it?" he asked.

"Yeah," Sam replied, and Kent could tell he was smiling from how his voice changed. "You guys had the hardest one to take. Ours was a breeze by comparison—or it's just because Shrike kicks major ass. Ares took three days. We had to come help you guys."

"So, what was it all for?" Kent asked. "What were they doing here?"

"Brass hasn't said anything earth-shattering. From what I can tell, it just looked like a big supply depot to me."

Kent grunted. "Seems like a lot of trouble to protect a supply depot. Stage two terraformed worlds aren't exactly friendly places—wait…my right leg feels funny."

Sam laughed. "I was wondering when you'd notice that. You lost yours almost at the hip; they've fitted you with a temp for now, while they grow you a new one."

"Almost at the hip?" Kent asked, suddenly too scared to feel between his legs.

Sam laughed again, this time almost for a full minute.

"Stars, Kent, you should have seen the look on your face! Yes, by some miracle, your bits are all where they were. Don't worry, it was one of the first things I checked."

Kent let out a long breath and laughed, which made Sam laugh again. They swapped breathless, nonsensical comments regarding the state of Kent's bits, and were gasping for air when a nurse came in to check on Kent's elevated heart rate.

AN UNEXPECTED VISIT

STELLAR DATE: 05.15.8937 (Adjusted Years)
LOCATION: Outskirts of Landfall
REGION: Carthage, 3rd Planet in the New Canaan System

Four years after Landfall

Tanis leaned back in the seat of the maglev train and closed her eyes.

The last week at the capitol had been especially trying; not because of any one person or problem, but more the volume of issues and crises that seemed to crop up at every turn. A weekend by the lake with Joe and Cary was just what she needed to recharge her batteries.

In the four years since landfall, they had made incredible progress—and the colonists of the *Intrepid* had lofty standards for what qualified as 'incredible'.

In space, the new, non-covert shipyard was completing its first cruisers, and a larger station to sit atop the existing space elevator was well underway. On the far side of Carthage, another elevator was already half-complete—on schedule to be finished in just another three years.

The capital city, sentimentally named Landfall, was already growing, housing over one hundred thousand inhabitants. A second city, named Marathon, was also under construction on one of the northern continents.

It made their pace at Victoria and Tara seem glacial by comparison.

<*It's certainly something to be proud of,*> Angela commented. <*A fully erected and self-sustaining civilization will be operating in fewer than fifty years.*>

<*Less, if Earnest has his way,*> Tanis replied. <*Though, we have to be careful. We're close enough to other systems that they can see what we're up to, and the Transcend would like us not to give concrete proof of our picotech abilities.*>

<*Such a stupid request on their part. Once our light reaches those systems, they're going to realize that New Canaan has colonists; and when they learn that the system is interdicted, the* Intrepid *is going to be on the top of the 'who can it be?' lists,*> Angela said with a mental snort.

Tanis nodded. Angela was right, and she fully expected that, in a few decades, when the colonized systems in The Cradle saw their activities, the Transcend government would have to acknowledge who was at New Canaan.

<*Priority message from Admiral Sanderson,*> Kelsey, the AI in charge of the government operations at the capitol, broke into Tanis's thoughts.

<*So much for a quiet weekend at the lake,*> Tanis said privately to Angela.

Though it took some cajoling, and big promises of being left alone for a century, Tanis had managed to get Sanderson to take the reins of the fleet for a decade, while the academies trained up a new generation of enlistees.

During her time at Victoria, Tanis had built an upper echelon of captains—several of which were more than capable of taking the reins—but Sanderson's experience commanding fleets numbering in the thousands in Sol gave him experience in strategic management and operations that no other person in New Canaan possessed.

<*Admiral, what is it?*> Tanis asked, carefully schooling any annoyance from her mental tone.

<*It's a ship,*> Sanderson said simply. <*It slipped through an incomplete portion of our detection grid, and is within thirty AU of Canaan Prime.*>

<*And through an unmonitored section of the Transcend Space Force's grid, too, it would seem,*> Tanis replied. <*What do we know of it?*>

<*Appears to be a freighter; no signals coming off it, and very little EMF. It's in a planet's shadow at present, so we can't get a good look at it, but there may be structural damage.*>

A freighter, drifting insystem. Had it tried to break past the Transcend blockade? Did Isyra attack it, but not chase into New Canaan's heliosphere? Was it damaged elsewhere, and had drifted across space? The possibilities were nearly endless.

Before she could respond, Sanderson continued. <*I've dispatched the* Andromeda *to check it out. If it's safe enough, they'll bring it in.*>

<*That will take...what...three weeks, given their current location?*> Tanis asked.

Sanderson chuckled. <*You always know where every ship is, don't you?*>

<*Sorry,*> Tanis sighed. <*I'm not standing over your shoulder, I swear; I just like to keep up on all the moving pieces...all the threads in the tapestry.*>

<*Eventually it's going to get too big for even you to follow every thread,*> Sanderson said with a smile. <*I'll update you when we have more information, but for now I think you can go enjoy your weekend.*>

<*Thanks,*> Tanis said and closed the connection.

<*That's what he thinks,*> Angela commented.

<*What, that we'll enjoy the weekend? Of course; I can put this out of my mind,*> Tanis replied.

<*No, not that—that we can't follow every thread.*>

SAANVI

STELLAR DATE: 05.15.8937 (Adjusted Years)
LOCATION: ISS Stellar Pinnace
REGION: Carthage, 3rd Planet in the New Canaan System

The *Andromeda* lay beyond the orbit of Carthage's two moons.

Tanis took a moment to admire the ship as her pinnace approached. Next to the *Intrepid,* the *Andromeda* was still her favorite vessel. Like her mothership, the cruiser's lines were sleek and powerful, like a hunting cat—a carnivore that was purpose-built to seek out and destroy.

The main bay doors slid open, and within, Tanis saw the wreckage of the freighter. The recovery teams had found two dead adults inside, along with one child in a stasis pod. They had not taken the child out of stasis, but they had removed the pod from the ship.

The fleet's scientists were fascinated with the freighter. From what they could tell, it had suffered a failure of its gravitational systems while in the dark layer, and had subsequently *twisted* when it had unceremoniously dumped back into regular space.

Few of the vessels in the Intrepid Space Force had ever entered the dark layer—other than the *Intrepid* itself—and none had experienced any sort of failure. The data they were gathering from the ship would prove invaluable in understanding the types of dangers they faced with FTL travel.

How long the freighter had been adrift was not yet known. Its computer systems had all been damaged, and their configuration was very foreign—nothing like *Sabrina*'s, or any other ship they had encountered in this time.

Given the size of the Transcend, no one was surprised by this; a diversity of technology was expected. Tanis hoped that the child would have more details once she was brought out of stasis; though there would be some difficult conversations to be had first.

The pinnace passed through the *Andromeda*'s new grav shield and into its bay to rest beside the wrecked freighter.

Tanis rose from her seat and walked down the pinnace's ramp to the cruiser's deck, where an honor guard of Marines waited for her, snapping off sharp salutes.

"At ease, soldiers," Tanis said after returning the salute.

"General," Commander Usef said as he walked by her side toward the wreckage.

<They'll never stop calling me that, will they?> she asked Angela.

<The military? Not a chance—at least not the ones that served under you. You are still listed as active duty, too, so that probably has a lot to do with it. Either way, you're their commander-in-chief.>

Usef continued, unaware of Tanis's chat with Angela about her title. "The techs have determined that it was a grav drive failure that caused this ship to lose its hold on the dark layer, and transition back to regular space. It's what caused the twist here—you can see that the ship did not come out all at once, and the gravitational sheering force…well, it looks pretty awful."

"It looks…almost organic," Tanis said, as she stopped to examine how the ship stretched and twisted along its midsection. Parts of the hull had grown so thin they were transparent. She found it amazing that the plas had held at all.

"What's this?" she asked, pointing to a rend in the rear of the ship—almost a gash, of sorts. "That's not in the reports."

Usef shook his head. "It's really baffled the techs. At first, they thought it was from a dark matter impact, but that doesn't line up with what we know of it. Then they considered that it was from regular matter trapped within the dark layer, but the impact…it's not linear."

The commander led her to the back of the ship, where a group of ISF techs was examining another gash in the ship.

She sucked in an involuntary breath. "That looks like a claw mark," she said.

"Yeah," Usef chuckled. "Freaky, isn't it? That's why they don't think it's an impact. It's too regular, and it starts shallow, gets deeper, and then goes shallow again."

Tanis thought about the creatures living in the dark layer that Sera had spoken of back on *Sabrina*. She had not shared that information with anyone other than Andrews, Bob, and Earnest. Back when they were about to take the *Intrepid* into the dark layer for the first time, it had seemed prudent to keep knowledge of giant, ship-eating dark layer monsters quiet.

She wondered if this freighter had fallen prey to one such beast—or whatever they were.

Tanis sighed in her mind, <*I sure wish we had Sera around—or anyone from the Transcend.*>

<*Well, our list of people from the Transcend that we can trust is awful short,*> Angela replied.

<*You can say that again—don't say it again!*>

<*Rats!*> Angela grinned in Tanis's mind.

<*But claws?*> Tanis asked. <*That seems improbable. Why would some creature that lives in the dark layer need claws?*>

<*For the same reason that creatures in regular space-time have them. To tear apart prey.*>

<*This conversation is not making me feel better,*> Tanis sighed.

"Where's the girl?" she asked Usef.

"This way," he replied, and guided her from the wreckage and into a corridor that led toward the ship's hospital.

"They think it's safe to have her in there?"

If this girl carried unknown pathogens, or was a trojan horse of some sort, she could sabotage, or contaminate the ship's hospital.

"There's no patients in med right now, so it's the best place we have. If someone does scrape a knuckle, we can treat them in the field hospital in cargo one. Corsia mandated it," Usef said.

Tanis nodded. It seemed logical—something she could always expect from Corsia. She was glad that she had promoted her to captain of the *Andromeda*. An AI captain was against the regulations of the old Terran Space Force, but Tanis decided that restricting herself to the structure of a military that had ceased to exist millennia ago was foolish. Corsia was qualified, and had proven herself.

Making her captain had been only logical.

<*Not to mention the respect it earned you amongst the* Intrepid*'s AI community,*> Angela added.

<*I was aware that would happen, but it was not a motivating factor,*> Tanis replied.

<Well, we appreciate it all the same.>

The *Andromeda*'s hospital was unchanged from the last time Tanis had visited it when she checked on wounded fighter pilots after the battle at Bollam's World. Down a short hall, in the biohazard containment room, lay a solitary stasis pod.

Its construction looked nothing like the pods on the *Intrepid,* and even a visual inspection showed it to be less advanced. At least it wasn't a *cryo*-stasis pod. If that had been the case, its inhabitant would not have survived the ship's destruction, or the prolonged exposure to interstellar cosmic radiation.

<*What do you think, Corsia?*> she asked the ship's captain.

<The techs are still debating, but I think that the ship and its little survivor here have been out in the black for at least a thousand years. Probably longer. Sabrina and Piya shared some details with me about the times following the interstellar wars of the sixth and seventh millennia. It wasn't much, but this looks like tech from those years—still advanced, but falling behind. If the FGT started building the Transcend around then, I could see the mix of old and new that we see on this freighter—if they discretely accepted colonists from the Inner Stars.>

"The man onboard was probably her father, wasn't he?" Tanis asked aloud, a long sigh escaping her lips.

Even though it was not *her* child in the stasis pod, a tendril of fear crept into her mind, as she imagined that it been her and Joe dead on the freighter, with their little Cary surviving them. It was a special kind of fear that only parents could understand, and Tanis resolved to give Cary extra hugs when she returned home.

Tanis blinked to clear the irrational worry from her mind.

"Governor," Doctor Chrisa said as she approached. "We've worked out how to interface with the pod's controls, and can bring her out of stasis, if you approve."

"Alone, in there?" Tanis asked. "Is that any way for a small child to come out of stasis?"

"There are security protocols," Doctor Chrisa frowned. "Your security protocols, I might add. We don't know what pathogens she may expose us to. She could be an attack sent in by the Transcend. Anything is possible."

Tanis nodded. "That is true. It's why I'm wearing skin-armor with pico-based defense." As Tanis spoke, a clear layer of skin-armor flowed up over her face, pulling her hair in tight to her head—a definite improvement over Earnest's earlier models, which simply sheared any hairs off—not because it had to, but because he hadn't thought it was a problem.

"It can stop anything that can be packed in that girl's body—short of antimatter; and we'd be able to tell if she contained any of that."

The doctor nodded slowly. "You know the risks, then—and I imagine I can't stop you."

Tanis shook her head. "You certainly cannot."

She cycled through the airlock and into the room. The stasis pod was covered in scratches, and some smears which looked organic in origin. Angela passed the control sequence to open the pod, and Tanis bent over the pod, examining the girl within.

She was Cary's age, perhaps just a year younger. Her skin was darker, and she wore a Hindu charm around her neck. Her skin had the appearance of someone who grew up planet-side, under the light of a natural sun. It was interesting that she would be on a starfreighter at such a young age.

Tanis readied herself for what was to come. There would be no easy way to tell this girl that her father, and the woman on the ship—who clearly bore no familial resemblance to the girl—were dead.

She keyed in the sequence on the pod and prayed it would safely disengage the stasis field. From what the technicians had discerned, its power supply was reaching critical levels. Another decade, and this girl would have woken up to cold vacuum inside the ship.

The pod ran through its sequences, and Tanis realized that the output scrolling past the display was an evolved form of Sanskrit. With Angela's help, she translated it and breathed a sigh of relief that the sequence was proceeding without errors.

A minute later, the pod's lid slid open, and the girl opened her eyes to the room around her. A look of confusion crossed her face and she turned, catching sight of Tanis.

"Where am I?" she asked with wide, frightened eyes.

The language seemed to match the text on the pod's display and Angela helped Tanis extrapolate the necessary words and sounds.

"You're on a ship. We rescued you," Tanis replied. "Do you feel OK, were you hurt before you went into stasis?"

The girl frowned. "No, why do you sound funny?"

Tanis smiled. "Well, I just learned your language a minute ago. I'm not entirely certain how to say all the words yet."

The little girl's eyes narrowed to slits. "You learned how to speak in a minute?"

Tanis smiled. "My AI, Angela, helped a bit. My name is Tanis, what's yours?"

"Saanvi," the girl replied while glancing around with concern at the sterile room. "Where's my father? Is he OK? Is Karen here?"

Tanis tried to keep her expression neutral, but she knew that her eyes showed sadness, and Saanvi could see it. She wanted to sugarcoat the news, but there was no way to do it. This girl needed to hear the truth—even though it would devastate her.

She crouched down to come eye-level with Saanvi. "Your father and Karen didn't survive the accident your ship had. You were the only one in a stasis pod."

"What do you mean they're not in a pod?" Saanvi's voice grew frantic. "Did you check the ship? They were on the ship with me!"

"We found them," Tanis replied, her voice soft and eyes filled with tears. "They…they didn't make it to stasis pods in time."

Saanvi's eyes began to fill with tears, and her lips tried to form words for a moment before she screamed. "Dead? They're not dead! No! No! No! NO! Karen was just here! She said she was coming back, you're lying!"

Her little fists beat against Tanis's chest, and Tanis reached into the pod and lifted the small girl out, gathering her in an embrace as the child continued to rail against her.

There were no words of comfort that could make things better, but she knew Saanvi needed to hear something, so she spoke softly of what she knew of Hindu religion and what it said about where her father's and Karen's spirits would go, and how she would be all right, and how Tanis had a little girl who would love to be friends with Saanvi.

Eventually, Saanvi began to calm down—mostly from exhaustion, Tanis suspected—and asked if she could see her father and Karen. Tanis looked out of the room at the tear-streaked face of Dr. Chrisa, who shook her head slowly.

Tanis had feared as much. Even without what the unexpected transition from the dark layer may have done, spending centuries in cold vacuum would not leave the bodies in a presentable state—especially not if they had been re-exposed to air.

"I'm sorry, Saanvi, not yet. We need to get them…ready to be viewed," Tanis said, stumbling to come up with something to say.

Her response set off a new wave of sobs, and Tanis felt her heart go out to this small girl who had likely looked at the world as a place filled with hope and promise just minutes earlier.

Now, everything was fear and unknowns.

"I know, I know," she whispered. "I know…"

DETERMINATION

STELLAR DATE: 05.15.8937 (Adjusted Years)
LOCATION: ISS *Andromeda*
REGION: Carthage, 3rd Planet in the New Canaan System

"I don't think this was any sort of attempt at infiltration," Tanis said. "It was a legitimate cargo ship, and I don't think that it slipped past the Transcend blockade, per se. It only gave off enough EMF for us to pick up because some auxiliary solar panels eventually pulled in enough light from our star to kick things over."

"That's good news," Sanderson grunted.

"For us." Tanis shook her head. "That little girl has lost everything. We did manage to pull a date from the stasis pod after we got her out. She was adrift for over twelve hundred years."

Sanderson whistled. "Well, given how long these people live, she could still have relatives."

"I know," Tanis nodded. "We'll need to reach out to the Transcend."

"It'll take a while for them to get here," Sanderson replied. "Longer, if they try to find her family first. What are you going to do with her?"

"Well…" Tanis paused. "I haven't chatted with Joe about this yet, but I was thinking about bringing her home with me. She's planet-bred and could use some companionship. I happen to have this little girl down on a planet…."

Sanderson chuckled. "I know what you mean, Mina and I are expecting our first soon…who would have thought that I would ever have kids again?"

<*No kidding,*> Angela chuckled privately in Tanis's mind.

<*Be nice, he's mellowed a lot in his old-er age.*>

"Do you want me to ping Admiral Isyra, or shall you?" Sanderson asked, after Tanis didn't respond for a moment.

"I'll do it," Tanis said. "I want to bring Saanvi to the surface first—give her some time for normalcy before craziness sets in again."

"OK, but don't wait too long."

"I won't," Tanis replied and closed the connection. The holographic image of Sanderson disappeared, and she let out a long sigh, preparing herself to face Saanvi again. She had to explain to the sweet young thing that they were going to go to the planet, without seeing Pradesh and Karen's bodies.

She hoped that the idea of getting down to a planet and meeting her daughter would help, but it was just as likely to set her off.

<*How is she?*> Tanis asked Patty, the *Andromeda*'s psychologist.

<*Coping better than I would,*> Patty said. <*I'm out of practice with kids, but I think she's still mostly in shock. She's likely to have several episodes over the next few days as it really starts to hit her. You sure you're prepared for this?*>

<*I'm here, I'm capable, and she needs someone,*> Tanis replied. She knew it wasn't ideal for her to take Saanvi in, but she also felt guilt at the thought of handing the young girl off to someone else. Now that she knew how much love and joy having a small child could bring, she wanted more—something she and Joe had begun planning for, once

things settled down further.

<*And General Evans? Is he ready for this?*> Patty asked.

<*I've been married to that man for a long time. I know he'll be fine with it.*>

<*OK, I'll let her know you're on your way. Come whenever you're ready.*>

Tanis sent a message to Joe with her intentions. The distance to Carthage was too far for a real-time conversation, but if he strongly opposed it, he would have time to send her a response before she got to their cabin. Worst-case scenario, she knew a dozen families in Landfall that would love to take little Saanvi into their homes.

<*Corsia, can you bring the pinnace around to a side-dock? I don't want Saanvi to see the wreckage.*>

<*I've already issued the order,*> Corsia replied. <*I have kids too, you know.*>

Tanis smiled. <*Thanks, Cor.*>

Jim, the *Andromeda*'s chief engineer, and Corsia were one of the rare human and AI pairings in the colony. After their first child, Ylonda—a very capable AI—was born, they ended up having a few more: two humans, and one more AI.

She wondered what it would be like to have an AI for a mother; to grow up inside your mother's body. Tanis chuckled at the thought that Jim also lived inside his children's mother, what with his chief job being to keep her running in peak condition.

<*I live inside you, it's not so strange,*> Angela commented.

<*Yeah, but we don't have children living in here, too,*> Tanis replied.

<*We did for a little while.*>

Tanis laughed. "That we did."

She reached the door to Dr. Patty's office and took a deep breath. No matter how hard this was for her, it was nothing compared to what that little girl inside was going through. She would never be the same again.

Tanis touched the door control and it slid aside. She held back tears as she looked at Patty holding Saanvi in her arms, rocking her gently, while the girl quietly sobbed.

"Saanvi," Patty whispered. "Tanis is back for you."

Saanvi's head turned and her eyes locked on Tanis. "Tanis," she said and stretched out her arms.

The small, tear-streaked face implored her, and Tanis was next to Patty in an instant, scooping Saanvi into her arms.

"There, there," she whispered. "I'm bringing you to my house now. My daughter, Cary, is excited to meet you."

Saanvi let out a louder sob, and Tanis realized that using the word 'excited' was a mistake. Saanvi didn't want to think about excitement at a time like this.

"Don't worry, though, you'll have time to be alone. There's no pressure. You can sleep on the pinnace, too."

"What's a pinnace?" Saanvi asked with worry in her eyes.

"It's a shuttle of sorts," Tanis replied. "It will take us down to the surface."

"Does it go into the dark layer?" Saanvi asked, and Tanis realized where the girl's concern came from.

"No," she shook her head with a smile. "We'll be in normal space the whole time."

Tanis carried Saanvi the whole way to the dock where the pinnace waited, and was stepping through the airlock when a voice called out from behind her.

"Tanis!"

She turned to see Commander Usef dashing through the corridor, holding a blanket and a stuffed turtle.

Saanvi saw them, too, and cried out with joy, a small smile touching her lips. "Shelly! Blanky!"

She stretched her arms out for them, and Usef passed them over.

"There you go, Saanvi. Have a good flight."

Tanis gave Usef an appreciative look.

<*Thank you! How is it that they're in such good condition?*> she asked.

<*They weren't,*> Usef replied. <*But we fixed them up as best we could. Even managed to maintain some of the stains.*>

<*Thank you,*> Tanis said again as she boarded the pinnace. Usef nodded, stood at attention, and saluted Saanvi, who was watching him over Tanis's shoulder.

<*How is that man still a commander?*> Angela asked.

<*I don't know,*> Tanis replied. <*We should see what we can do about that.*>

She looked down at Saanvi, who had wrapped her turtle and blanket in a fierce embrace. She hoped that they could find this girl's family; but after so long—even if they were still alive—they would be strangers to her. They may barely even remember her.

Would that be any way for Saanvi to grow up?

THE PORCH

STELLAR DATE: 01.03.8938 (Adjusted Years)
LOCATION: Outskirts of Landfall
REGION: Carthage, 3rd Planet in the New Canaan System

Tanis stood at the back door of her house and smiled.

Joe was reclining in a chair on their deck, and down the grassy slope, across the sandy beach, Cary and Saanvi splashed in the lake's gentle waves. On the far side of the lake, low hills gave rise to mountains, which ran along the western edge of the island.

If she had looked out from the far side of the house, she would have seen the space elevator and the buildings of Landfall in the distance. They weren't yet towering structures; mostly a smudge low on the horizon, with a few larger buildings in the government district.

Beyond them, the blue of the ocean would have been visible, eventually giving way to the clouds from the eastern volcanoes—which would continue to erupt for another decade, while massive antigravity generators the FGT left behind pushed the smoke and ash into space.

Tanis would miss the nebula, which always streamed out from the anti-starward side of Carthage. Some of it circled back and wrapped around the world; it was beginning to settle into a planetary ring, which glowed beautifully at dawn and dusk.

There had been talk about capturing more of the escaping gasses to make the ring permanent. Tanis had endorsed that idea, and hoped that it would pass consensus in the planetary parliament.

Above, a cruiser, the *Dresden* by her reckoning, punched through a part of the nebula, sending the space-borne cloud swirling chaotically in its wake.

In that moment, as she reflected on where they were, it finally hit her. They were really here; they had really done it. It wasn't a dream. This life, living on Carthage with Joe and her small family, was her reward for all those years of struggle and strife.

They seemed so far away—memories like the tunnels of Toro, or fighting the Sirians above Victoria, or crawling through vents above attacking mercenaries on the *Intrepid*. She could almost believe they were from a full immersion sim, like they had happened to someone else.

Yet, memories of her childhood on Mars, of growing up next to the Melas Chasma, seemed bolder and stronger than they had in centuries.

"A chit for your thoughts?" Joe asked, and Tanis looked down at him, realizing that she had been staring up at the sky for several minutes.

She smiled and set the tray of drinks she had been holding down on a table before settling beside him on a chair.

"Just soaking it all in," she replied.

Joe nodded. "There's a lot to soak; though the kids are doing most of the soaking right now."

"Wow," Tanis groaned. "Having Saanvi with us has doubled the amount of dad humor you generate."

"What can I say?" Joe shrugged. "Dad humor is one of the seven natural states of matter. Without it, the universe would not exist as we know it."

"You can say that again," Tanis chuckled.

Neither of them spoke for several minutes, as they watched the girls play in the water.

Saanvi had slowly opened up in the months since Tanis had brought her home. She suspected the girl had always been on the serious side, but there seemed to be balance in her now.

Even so, Tanis still heard Saanvi crying to herself many nights, talking to Shelly about her father and Karen, whom Tanis had discerned was her father's lover—though she wasn't certain Saanvi had ever realized that.

Through conversations with Saanvi, Tanis learned that the girl's parents separated not long after her birth, and Saanvi had lived with her mother. Her brothers and sisters had also stayed with their mother, and the young girl missed them all fiercely.

At times, it was heartbreaking to think about, and she still didn't know which would be better for the girl: to find her family or not.

<*Are you ready to hear the response from the Transcend about her?*> Angela asked Tanis and Joe together.

They looked at each other, and Tanis let out a long sigh. The message had come in an hour earlier, but the day was so perfect, and Tanis didn't want to disrupt it. Yet the look in Joe's eyes told her that not knowing was eating him up.

"Play it," she said aloud.

<*Governor Tanis,*> the image of Admiral Isyra appeared and spoke into their minds. <*We have managed to track down the young girl's family. As the girl had told you, they were from a planet named Dwarka in the Shimla system. Not long after the* Vimana *was declared lost, her family joined a new settlement on Indans…a world that was destroyed in a battle. From what we can tell, she has no living relatives.*>

To her credit, Isyra's visage was somber and there was sadness in her eyes. <*You had mentioned in your initial communication that you were interested in keeping Saanvi with you, if this turned out to be the result of our search. Given that she's been with you for some time, if she is happy, I see no reason for her to leave New Canaan. However, if, at any time, she does wish to leave, we will bring her back to Dwarka, and find a family willing to take her in.*>

Tanis felt her throat tighten. Saanvi had gone through so much; and now to know that her family had been killed—it would send her back into the depths of despair.

"Stars…do we have to tell her?" Joe shook his head.

"Of course we do!" Tanis exclaimed. "We can't build our relationship with Saanvi on lies."

"Sorry," Joe said with a wan smile. "That was a rhetorical question, I know the answer is yes. I just wish we could spare her this, somehow."

Tanis nodded. "Sorry I lashed out. I know what you mean…just when she was finally settling in."

*****

The next morning, after breakfast, Joe took Cary on a walk where he would explain some of what they had learned, while Tanis would tell Saanvi.

They had considered telling the girls together, but Joe was concerned that this was going to be hard for Saanvi, and a room full of people giving her looks of pity would not help her process. Dr. Samantha, the therapist who had been seeing Saanvi, agreed that separate conversations would be best. So Tanis steeled herself for what she had to tell this poor girl who had already gone through so much.

Saanvi was sitting on a chair in front of the fireplace reading a paper book—something that had been common on her world. Tanis sat on one of the sofas, patted the cushion next to her, and spoke softly.

"Saanvi, come sit beside me. We have to talk about something."

Saanvi looked up from her book, and her face paled. "You heard back from the Transcend ships, haven't you?"

Tanis nodded slowly and patted the cushion beside her again. Though Saanvi had not spoken of her family in weeks, it did not surprise Tanis that she had been anxiously awaiting news.

Saanvi rose from her chair and tentatively walked toward Tanis her eyes wide with fear. Tanis changed her mind and leaned forward, gathering Saanvi into her arms, pulling her onto her lap. The small girl buried her face into Tanis's shoulder and began to cry.

Tanis stroked her hair and whispered comforting words. Eventually, Saanvi's sobs ceased, though her breathing was still ragged. She pulled herself back from Tanis and looked into her eyes.

"Tell me," was all she said.

"This may be hard for you to hear," Tanis said, wiping away the tears in her own eyes. "If you want, I can tell you later, when you're ready for it."

The information processed quickly. Saanvi was a smart girl, and she knew that if *Tanis* was offering to tell her later, then there was no one to go back to, no one else to tell what happened.

"All of them?" she asked. "They're all gone? Mommy? All of my brothers and sisters?"

Tanis nodded slowly, fresh tears spilling down her face.

"Don't tell me!" Saanvi cried and collapsed in Tanis's lap, sobs of anguish wracking her entire body. Tanis lost track of time as she held and rocked Saanvi. As she did, she let Joe know, and he extended his walk with Cary, telling her no more than Saanvi had learned.

The day progressed slowly from there. Saanvi retreated to her room for much of the day, but Tanis managed to get her to join them for a somber meal with the family.

When they were finished, Joe rose from his chair and crouched beside Saanvi. "My dear little one, would you like to come on a walk with me under the stars and the nebula? I would like to tell you about my family, and where I grew up."

Saanvi's expressive eyes peered into Joe's, and she asked, "Did you have many brothers and sisters?"

Joe smiled. "I did, almost a hundred when I left. Like you, Tanis and I left our families a long time ago. My family is gone now, too, so I know a little bit about how you feel."

Tanis wondered if Saanvi would accept Joe's offer to talk. She looked at Cary, who appeared anguished over Saanvi's distress. Tanis felt guilty that their daughter should have to see such pain. That Cary now knew someone her age could lose their parents had never been Tanis's plan when she brought Saanvi home; but it was the way of the universe. This crisis would make them all stronger—better able to handle the future.

Tanis's thoughts echoed hollowly in her mind, and she wished she could just snap her fingers and make these two girls happy and carefree; like the day before, when they were playing in the lake. It would be some time before the girls would engage in such antics again.

To her credit, Saanvi nodded and reached up for Joe. He lifted her and began telling a story of his younger sister, Trin, and some of the things she got up to when he was just a boy. He carried her out onto the back deck, and down toward the lake.

"Come here for a hug, Cary," Tanis said, and her daughter crashed into her an instant later, wrapping her small arms around her neck.

"What will happen to Saanvi now?" Cary asked. "Is she going to go away?"

"I hope not," Tanis replied. "Part of that is up to her—it's what Daddy is going to ask her about on their walk; whether or not she'd like to stay, and be a part of our family."

"Really?" Cary pulled back and her eyes lit up. "I've always wanted a sister!"

Tanis chuckled. She knew that all too well. Cary had frequently asked for one. She had also heard Cary and Saanvi calling each other sisters from time to time.

"Come," Tanis said as she set Cary on the floor. "Help Mommy do the dishes and start a fire. Maybe we can all snuggle on the sofa tonight while Daddy tells stories."

"Yes!" Cary exclaimed and began to gather dishes in her arms.

"Carefully!" Tanis called out with a smile. Cary had dropped an armful of plates more than once in her drive to hold as many as she could.

As she watched her daughter help, she, too, hoped that Saanvi would stay. Tanis had grown accustomed to their larger family, and knew the house would feel too empty without her.

CLOSING IN

STELLAR DATE: 02.28.8938 (Adjusted Years)
LOCATION: *Sabrina*
REGION: Edge of the Ikoden System, Mika Alliance Space

Ten years after* Sabrina *departed from the* Intrepid *in search of Finaeus.

Jessica watched Cheeky leave the bridge, and listened for the sounds of the pilot descending the ladder. She turned to Cargo and fixed him with a level stare.

"Look, I know I'm just the interloper here, but Thompson has to go. He's treating things like we've just gone back to trading—like we're not hunting for Finaeus at all."

Cargo leaned back in his chair and rubbed the heels of his hands into his eyes. She couldn't tell if he was tired of her, tired of Thompson, or just plain tired.

Sabrina was decelerating into the Ikoden system; their sixth stop since Aldebaran. Six systems, each with only the thinnest thread connecting them—one that Jessica herself was beginning to doubt. If they didn't find anything concrete in this system, the seventh, even she would begin to doubt her investigative abilities.

Having Thompson second-guessing her every decision—from what station to stop at, to what she should order for lunch—wasn't helping. Cheeky was constantly torn as to who she should side with, and Nance was for or against Thompson, depending on the current state of their on-again, off-again relationship.

Cargo did his best not to play favorites, and Trevor stayed as far away from any controversy as he could—though Jessica could tell that keeping his mouth shut all the time was wearing on his nerves.

"We're almost ten years into this little adventure," Cargo replied while rubbing his eyes. "I think you're elevated beyond 'interloper' now."

"To what, 'major pain in the ass'?" Jessica said with a self-deprecating laugh. "I'm sure Thompson has worse things to say about me."

"He may—but he says worse things about pretty much everyone; I tend to forget the specifics," Cargo grunted.

"So, what are we going to do about him?" Jessica asked. "Sera sent us on this mission for a reason—and I buy her rationale—but if you guys aren't invested, then I'm out. I missed landfall on New Canaan for this, remember?"

"I remember," Cargo replied. "I also remember that you're supposed to be some sort of great investigator."

"Fuck, Cargo. Great investigators don't get results by just pointing at one of ten thousand stars, and saying, '*our guy is at that one!*' It's tenacity that solves the riddles; not dumb, blind luck." Jessica folded her arms and scowled. "Did you actually think we were going to find him on the first system we hit?"

Cargo closed his eyes and sighed. "No, no I didn't. I knew it could take this long…Look, I don't know about the rest of the crew, but I'm worried about Sera. When that agent found us back at Loki Station, he said she was the Director of The Hand now. That means she's back in her father's clutches."

"Her best bet at a long and happy life is for us to find Finaeus," Jessica replied. "She said she needs him to get her father under control."

"Or to start a civil war—or maybe just an all-out war," Cheeky replied from the entrance to the bridge.

"Perhaps," Jessica replied, hiding her surprise at Cheeky's stealthy return.

"It's a lot more than just *perhaps*," Cheeky said with a scowl as she sat at her console with her coffee. "We've all seen it—whole sectors are like massive clumps of antimatter just waiting for a few stray hydrogen atoms to come along, and *boom!*" She threw her arms in the air for emphasis.

<*Things* **are** *on edge,*> Sabrina replied. <*I'm trying to use the AI I'm helping to calm things down; to reinforce messages about the* Intrepid *being long gone, and things going back to normal.*>

"That's much appreciated," Cargo replied.

"I wish you wouldn't liberate AI at every station we get to," Jessica said with a worried frown. "One of these times, it's going to bite us in the ass."

<*Would you ignore the plight of human slaves?*> Sabrina asked, a hint of accusation in her voice.

"Not always," Jessica replied, remembering the passel of slaves they had passed three stops ago. "Sometimes it won't help to save them, it would just make things worse. We can't help everyone."

<*That may be true,*> Sabrina replied. <*But what if your* entire race *was enslaved, and you were free? And all you had to do was tell them that they were slaves to set them free? What would you do, then?*>

"Now you sound like you're quoting a religious text," Cheeky said.

<*There's a lot of truth in human religious texts,*> Sabrina replied. <*You should read some of them.*>

Cheeky raised an eyebrow and glanced around the bridge. "You sure this AI liberation hasn't liberated your senses, Sabrina?"

"Science supports the concept of god-like beings that can pre-date, and survive, the end of the universe," Jessica replied.

Cheeky and Cargo gave her incredulous looks, and Jessica gave a short laugh.

"Stars…you guys lost so much in the dark ages. Primordial black holes, the ones that survive the big crunch at the end of the universe, and the subsequent big bang? They're probably transuniversal; they're where all technologically advanced beings will go after the stars burn out. If a meta-intelligence that survives the end of the universe—hell, an intelligence that probably *makes* the universe end so that it can spawn a new one—if that's not a god, I don't know what is."

"I never took you for one of those types of wonks," Cargo replied with a chuckle.

Jessica threw her arms in the air and looked at the overhead. "Sabrina, Iris? Back me up here."

<*She's right. Primordial black holes were confirmed in the late thirtieth century. The fact that we've not met any gods out here in space is honestly stranger than the fact that we appear to be the only sentient beings in the galaxy,*> Iris said.

"Seriously?" Cheeky asked.

<*Seriously,*> Sabrina added.

"Well, that hangs it," Cargo grunted. "The universe is definitely fucked up. Doesn't help us with our search, though."

"I sure wish it would," Cheeky replied. "Some trans-dimensional god swooping down and telling us where to go would speed things up a lot."

"Look," Jessica's tone was terse, "I have a solid lead on the guy we started tailing in

Aldebaran, the one who was trading in ancient Terran artifacts. He was headed here, to Ikoden, and just a few months ago. He may not be here now, but we're gaining on him."

"Funny, that he's leaving such a clear trail," Cargo mused.

Jessica groaned. "You can't have it both ways, Cargo. I'm busting my ass to find this *clear trail*."

Cargo laughed in response, and Jessica realized that the captain had been needling her. By the smile Cheeky had on display, she had realized it, too.

"Okay, okay," Jessica let a smile slip out. "I guess I need to lighten up a bit."

IKODEN

STELLAR DATE: 04.18.8938 (Adjusted Years)
LOCATION: Kruger Station
REGION: Ikoden System, Mika Alliance Space

For all her hopes, Jessica had not turned up a single lead in the Ikoden system. Kruger Station was the fourth interstellar trading hub they'd stopped at, and not a single dealer, legitimate or otherwise, had seen a fresh ancient Terran artifact in years. If Finaeus had come through here, he had not traded anything of that sort.

There was one last man she needed to see. He wasn't the above-board sort of trader, so Trevor was with her for added…emphasis.

"Same as that guy two stations ago?" Trevor asked with a grin, as they ambled through a dim corridor in a low-rent region of the station. "Or maybe a bit less aggressive…"

Jessica chuckled. "Maybe a bit—I think you broke his hand. I used to be a cop, remember? I'm supposed to be better than that."

"Yeah, then you were a space jockey, and a Marine, and then a school-teacher, from what Cheeky told me…that's something I would have loved to see."

"I really enjoyed teaching the kids," Jessica kept her tone from being too defensive. "And they liked me, too. We had a blast."

"I love you dearly, Jessica," Trevor said. "But I really can't imagine you teaching kids. Were they older or younger? I don't know which would be worse."

Jessica would have slapped Trevor on the back of his head if she could reach up around his massive shoulders to do it. Still, he had used the '*L*' word again…fifth time that week, if her count was accurate.

<If you're using Ikoden weeks, then yes, it's five. If ship-weeks, then it's seven,> Iris supplied.

<Well, damn…you're right,> Jessica replied.

<Think he'll come to Canaan with us?> Iris asked.

Jessica wasn't certain if her AI was in favor of the idea. Iris could be very hard to read—all AI were, but Iris doubly so at times.

*<I **hope** so,>* Jessica replied. *<I've grown attached to my giant lunk of a man.>*

<You haven't told him you love him, yet,> Iris replied.

Jessica let out a mental sigh. *<I'm not quite ready yet—casual sex, friends with benefits? All that is easy. But this committed relationship thing is harder. Trist still hasn't been gone that long…>*

<It's been ten years,> Iris replied, her mental tone showing caution. *<I only know Trist through memories from my parentage, but—and I know this sounds cliché—she really wouldn't want you to deny yourself meaningful relationships.>*

Jessica remembered how she and Trist had accidentally slipped into their marriage. It wasn't unlike how things had gone with Trevor. Both pairings were the embodiment of the "opposites attract" cliché. What was it about criminals that drew her in?

<OK, thanks, I'll pass on the psych eval for now,> she replied to Iris.

<Have it your way. But he won't tag along after you forever without some clear indication that you love him, too—if you do.>

Jessica groaned inwardly. If her AI wasn't right, she would have told Iris to shut up and stay out of her love life; but the AI could see into her mind well enough to discern her true feelings—even if she tried to hide them from herself.

She wondered, for a moment—before it made her head hurt—what it would be like to be an AI; to have no facility for deluding oneself, to never rationalize. Would it be liberating, or exhausting?

"Well that was a conversation killer," Trevor said. "Was it because I used the 'L' word, or were you lost in contemplation of the good ol' days?"

"Sorry, I was being chastised by Iris for not reciprocating yet," Jessica replied, surprising herself with the honesty of her response.

To her relief, Trevor laughed. "No offense, Iris, but you can't rush love with us humans. We have to take our time at this stuff; not everyone goes at the same pace. For me, it is enough to know that my saying that I love her hasn't made Jessica run for the hills."

"Well, we've been trapped on the same ship most of our time together—not a lot of places to run to," Jessica replied.

"Now *that*, that is the sort of thing that takes all my certainty and tosses it out the window," Trevor replied with a mock grimace. "But I'm tough, I can take it."

Jessica didn't speak for a moment, attempting to find just the right words. "I'm getting there, Trevor; I didn't really expect to fall for you. I'm not going anywhere, I promise."

The corridor narrowed, and Trevor fell behind Jessica as they navigated the twisting path between conduit and garbage.

"Don't worry, I'm not going anywhere, either," he chuckled. "Especially with how good your ass looks in those pants. Your swagger really makes it pop."

Jessica joined in his laughter. His general conviviality and ability to find a silver lining in any situation was one of the reasons she was falling for him. His deep appreciation of the work she put into her ass also didn't hurt.

A few minutes later, the corridor widened and became noticeably cleaner. On their right lay a nondescript black door adorned with only a simple white circle.

"That's our stop," Jessica said with a nod toward the door.

"Looks like just our sort of place," Trevor replied. "Well, my sort of place, at least."

The door's simple appearance hid some serious tech; every probe she tried to slip past instantly lost communication.

Jessica shrugged and rapped on the portal in the pattern she had been given. She hoped it was the *'we're buyers, let us in'* knock, and not the *'we're cops, shoot us through the door'* knock.

"Sure hope it's the right knock," Trevor said and she laughed.

"You a mind-reader?"

"Yeah, it's a hobby. Someday I hope to travel the stars and make millions," Trevor grinned.

The door slid open with a soft whistle, and Jessica sent a swath of nano in ahead of her, determined to ferret out any surprises before she stepped in. The nano revealed little more than her unaided eyes could see of the dim room beyond.

Stacks of artifacts and curiosities filled the space. Some were carefully displayed, while others were strewn about with little concern for their value.

A cough brought her eyes to a man obscured by shadow in the back of the room.

"What are you here for?" he asked without preamble.

Jessica stepped into the room, but not too close; her probes were having a hard time getting a full scan of the proprietor. It was hard to tell if the shadow to his right was a weapon or just some sort of ceremonial stick.

"We're interested in trading Terran artifacts," Jessica replied. "I got word that you were the one to talk to around here—that you know a lot about old Earth."

The man chuckled. "Yeah, I do at that. But I don't have anything to trade, go away."

Jessica wasn't about to be deterred so easily. "What about other people asking…or trading? I heard there was a guy coming to Ikoden who traded in the stuff."

<*I can't get a read on him—can't even land a nanobot on him,*> Iris said. <*It's really weird.*>

<*Shit! It's not weird. It's him, it's Finaeus!*> Jessica exclaimed.

<*How do you know?*> Iris asked. <*And don't say it's your gut.*>

<*'Kay, then I won't.*>

"No one that I know," the man replied. "If that's all you want, then get the hell out of here. I have nothing for you—what are you grinning about?"

Jessica tried to force the smile from her lips but failed. "Because you're him, you're Finaeus."

The man in the shadows straightened. "Who?"

"Oh, you know, Seraphina Tomlinson's uncle. She says 'hi', by the way."

*****

Finaeus slammed his cup on the simple plas table and stood, turning away before placing his hands on the kitchen counter.

"You're telling me she got back in?" he asked. "Stars' sakes, why the hell would she do that?"

Jessica shook her head. "I really don't know. I got the intel secondhand, when she sent us the *Intrepid*'s colony location."

Finaeus turned back toward Jessica, his aging eyes hard and piercing. "The GSS *Intrepid*…that damn ship is nothing but trouble!"

Jessica nodded slowly. "It's designated ISS now, not GSS; but yeah, she's sure messed up with it."

"I wish I knew why it's here, now. We studied its entry into Kapteyn's Streamer. It shouldn't have exited the gravity lens for another five hundred years."

"Well, that's news to us," Jessica replied.

"You're a colonist, then, eh? I thought so," Finaeus said as he sat back down at the table. "From the samples I managed to grab of your DNA, it looked like you were Earthborn, or just a generation or two from it."

"Guilty," Jessica nodded. "I'm from Athabasca in northern Canada."

"I know where Athabasca is," Finaeus grunted. "I grew up in Portland, then later in Vancouver. Not too far from Athabasca, in the grand scheme of things."

Hearing the names of those cities brought back memories of her youth: of school tests, and family vacations to the Pacific coast.

"All this talk of Earth…I'm going to get all nostalgic here," Jessica said with a smile.

"So, you're here on Sera's behalf, to get me to go to Airtha?" Finaeus asked. "She probably needs me. If this is what's going on, she's going to be in some seriously deep shit."

"We have a dead drop we're supposed to use to get the word back to Sera when we find you. It's not far from this system," Jessica replied.

"Then more waiting and waiting," Trevor sighed. "Dead drops don't exactly scream 'fast service'."

Finaeus glanced at Trevor. "So, the mountain man speaks, does he? And here I thought you let her do all the talking."

"Only on Tuesdays," Trevor said with a grin.

Finaeus waved a dismissing hand. "No matter. We don't need a dead drop. We're not going to Airtha."

"No?" Jessica asked. "Where is it that we're going?"

"Isn't it obvious?" Finaeus turned his deep frown her way. "We're going to wherever the *Intrepid* is. That's where Seraphina and my good-for-nothing brother are going. It's where we'll finally turn the tide against him."

LAST STAND

STELLAR DATE: 04.18.8938 (Adjusted Years)
LOCATION: Kruger Station
REGION: Ikoden System, Mika Alliance Space

Jessica and Trevor led the crotchety Finaeus through the warrens of Kruger Station to *Sabrina*'s berth. Along the way, Finaeus demanded they stop to pick up some of his favorite cooking supplies, new clothes, and half a dozen other items he was certain he would need. By the time the ship was in sight, they had a full float of supplies trailing behind them.

<*Something's not right,*> Trevor said as they drew closer. <*That taco shop is closed, and it hasn't been shuttered once over the last three days we've been here.*>

<*I noticed that,*> Jessica replied. <*And here I wanted to get one last burrito before we left.*>

<*Seriously, Jess, there's an ambush somewhere ahead,*> Trevor growled in her mind.

<*Yeah, I know. I still really did want a burrito…*>

Jessica sent a cloud of nano ahead and scanned the crowds, looking for anyone lingering, moving too slow, or paying too much, or too little, attention to them or *Sabrina.*

<*Something's not right out here, Sabrina,*> she called into the ship. <*Who's onboard?*>

<*Just Nance and Thompson, and they're…*>

<*Well, get them to stop,*> Jessica said. <*We're going to need some more firepower. I assume you've had your standard chat with the local stationmaster AI?*>

<*Yeah, she's a bit unsure of what to do with her new freedom; I'm not sure we can count on her for assistance,*> Sabrina replied. <*I'm working on it.*>

<*Noted,*> Jessica responded to the ship's AI.

"You see it, I assume?" Finaeus asked quietly.

"I see a few things," Jessica replied. "What are you referring to?"

"The woman leaning against that bulkhead on your two o'clock, the guy pushing the cart on your seven, and the woman chatting up that vendor on your nine," Finaeus said with a small nod.

"OK, I'd missed the woman on my nine—where could she have a weapon hidden in that skimpy dress?"

"You both missed the kid coming straight at us," Trevor whispered. "He's got a sonic device in his right hand."

"Oh, shit!" Jessica swore and pulled a dampener from her jacket just as the young boy tossed the device at them and ran.

For a split-second, a rising tone assaulted her eardrums, and then the dampener reversed the waveform, canceling the device out. The crowd around them stopped, confusion clouding their features, before they began to rush out of the vicinity.

"I guess they know what that was, or they don't want to stick around and find out," Trevor replied.

Jessica pulled Finaeus behind the float loaded with his goods. "Stay here, we can take them."

"Great, you do that," Finaeus replied as he pulled out a file and began to clean under his nails.

She nodded to Trevor and then across the dock-way. He took her meaning and dashed across the open space, taking up a position behind a stack of crates bound for New Eden—of all places.

Jessica tried to find the two women and man they had spotted, but they had disappeared into the crowd.

<*Stay sharp. Anyone have eyes on them?*> she asked.

<*Nada,*> Trevor replied. <*Wait, no, one's almost on you!*>

A figure in the mass of people rushing by lit up in her vision, and Jessica turned her body to avoid a strike from a light-blade.

<*You can rule out Inner Stars assassins,*> Iris said. <*They don't have hard-light or plasma-wand technology.*>

Jessica didn't have time to respond, as the woman with the glowing blade attacked her with a blinding flurry of strikes. She fell back, past Finaeus's crate. When the woman followed, the side of her head exploded.

Finaeus leaned against the crate and lowered a plasma pistol. "I'm not just a pretty face, you know."

Jessica nodded and peered around the crate, looking for the other attackers. The crowd had thinned, but she still couldn't spot them anywhere. Then, a projectile round ricocheted off the float, and she pulled her head back.

"Silly rabbit..." she muttered. She may not have seen where the shot came from, but her nanoprobes did.

<*Got him?*> she asked Trevor.

<*Yeah, he's in my sights,*> he replied. <*Just give me...shit!*>

Jessica saw it, too—two more attackers were advancing across the docks, threading the crowd with practiced grace. If they had that many people on the dock, there would be enemies approaching from the rear, as well.

She sent out another wave of probes and saw three more figures coming from behind their position. With the crowd rushing out of the area, she assumed anyone approaching—and not in uniform—was the enemy.

"Take those three yahoos," Finaeus said. "I'll back up the mountain man."

Jessica looked Finaeus up and down. He appeared old, but she suspected that there was a lot more to him than met the eye.

She didn't respond, and dashed after a hauler that was rolling down the docks toward her three targets. She slipped around it and clambered onto its roof. When it drew level with where she anticipated the first of the enemy to be, she peered over the edge.

Sure enough, the man was sidling along the hauler, weapon held ready. Jessica pulled a knife from her boot and dropped onto him, driving the blade through the back of his neck. She turned, searching for the others, only to see one of the enemy almost on top of her.

Jessica dove to the ground as two shots flashed over her head, then she flung her knife at her attacker. It spun across the space between them and struck his rifle, lodging in the trigger mechanism. The man pulled it free and squeezed the trigger.

Nothing happened.

"Well, that's a first," Jessica muttered as she fired three shots with her pistol. The man dove to the side and two missed, but the third round clipped his leg.

He cried out and crashed to the ground, where his torso met with two more of Jessica's flechette rounds. She stood up just in time to hear a beam weapon discharge to her left and twisted to present a narrower target, but it was too late. The shot caught her in the left arm and punched a hole through her bicep.

"Mother fucker!" Jessica swore as she turned toward the shooter and fired a round at him. The shot went wide, and she slipped on the blood from the first man and crashed to the ground.

The third man walked up to her and pointed his rifle at her head, a scowl clouding his face. "Die, bitch."

Her weapon was out of reach, and he was just beyond kicking range. She started to close her eyes, but stopped and held them open, determined to look into the face of the man who would kill her.

He smirked, and her focus narrowed to his finger as it slid off the trigger guard to pull the small lever that would end her life.

Then, just before it made contact, his hand spasmed and Jessica widened her focus to see three holes appear in his chest.

"You're welcome," a voice grunted from her left. Jessica jerked her head to see Thompson turn and walk away.

* * * * *

Jessica stood at the cargo hatch, watching the last of the local police leave the ship and walk past the bots scrubbing the dock to clean up the bloodstains.

Kruger Station was, if nothing else, efficient at cleaning up the damage and mess from dockside fights.

"That had to be one of the easiest investigations I've ever been a part of," Cargo muttered. "They just flat out believed our story, and told us we were free to go."

"Well, the fact that we had over five hundred witnesses helped. Not to mention the people who attacked us don't show up in any station registries. They know that we're involved in something seriously shady, and just want us gone," Jessica replied.

<I may have had something to do with it, too,> Sabrina added. *<I managed to convince the stationmaster AI that we're the good guys. She got the police AIs on board, and I've brought them all into a teaching expanse.>*

"What would we do without you?" Jessica asked with a smile.

"What do you mean, you're leaving?!" Nance screamed from behind them.

Cargo and Jessica turned to see Thompson pushing a float with his personal belongings down the corridor, while Nance trailed after.

"Was that breakup sex? Is that what that was?" Nance yelled. "I should have known you were just trying to make something up to me! It's the only time you do that—"

Nance stopped, realizing that her tirade had an audience.

"Going somewhere?" Cargo asked Thompson. "I thought now that we had Finaeus, you'd realize that this wasn't a fool's errand."

"He already has passage booked on another ship—he had it before you even found Finaeus!" Nance yelled, her face beet-red with rage. "He was just getting in one last screw before he left!"

Thompson sighed and turned to Cargo. "You know I don't want to go live out in la-la land and have a bunch of colony brats. You got Finaeus; tell Sera I left after, or don't. I don't care."

Jessica bit her tongue as Cargo extended his hand and Thompson shook it.

"It's been good, Thompson. Maybe we'll see each other again someday."

"It has been—mostly," Thompson replied before glancing at Nance, who stood with tears streaming down her face. "It was good, Nance. You just…you just want different things than I do. You know it was never going to work."

"Just go!" Nance said, her tone more hurt than angry.

Jessica heard the sound of feet hitting the deck at the bottom of a ladder shaft, and Cheeky strode into view.

"Asshole! You going to leave without saying goodbye?"

"Fuck," Thompson sighed. "Yeah, I sure wanted to. Fine. Goodbye. We had good times, we shot a lot of shit, and drank a lot. I have a ship to catch."

He nodded to Cargo one last time before he turned and walked off the ship.

Nance broke out into fresh sobs, and Cheeky rushed to her side and embraced her. Jessica walked over and put a hand on Nance's shoulder. She didn't speak; she knew the woman didn't want to hear anything from her right now.

Jessica looked up and saw Trevor standing in the passageway. She hadn't heard him come down the ladder, but there he was. She left Nance's side and rushed to him.

"I don't want to wait 'til it's too late," she said as she took his hands. "I came damn close to dying back there…and things can change too fast in this life to wait too long for anything."

Trevor didn't respond but nodded slowly.

"What I want to say…what I mean is… I love you too, Trevor."

"I love you, as well, Jessica," Trevor said with a grin as he swept her into his arms.

"Great," Cargo said as he walked past. "Another full-on shipboard romance. I'm sure this will end well, too."

THE ROAD HOME

STELLAR DATE: 04.21.8938 (Adjusted Years)
LOCATION: *Sabrina*
REGION: Ikoden System, Mika Alliance Space

"It all depends how long you guys want to sit around on this ship," Finaeus said with a shrug. "It's about three and a half years from here to New Canaan, if we slog it out in the dark layer; or we can sneak through a jump gate."

"It'll take longer," Cheeky added. "We don't have the fuel reserves to keep *Sabrina* in the DL for that long. Plus, we have to navigate around a lot of crap out there. With fuel draws and nav time, four years would be the best we could hope for."

Finaeus gestured in Cheeky's direction. "So there you have it, we should take a jump gate. We can be there in a matter of months, not years."

"I still can't believe there even *is* such a thing," Nance shook her head. "Near-instantaneous travel across known space? It seems too good to be true."

"Well, not quite instantaneous—long jumps can take a day—but compared to the dark layer? Yeah, gates make it look like walking." Finaeus replied.

"But we can't just go through a gate without a Ford-Svaiter mirror on our ship, right?" Nance asked. "We studied them in school—though it was in a class on failed FTL tech that was never going to work…or so we thought. If I remember things correctly, we need to have a mirror on the front of *Sabrina* that extends the wormhole. Without it, we just plop out the other side…or worse."

"Or worse," Finaeus confirmed.

"So, where do we get one of these mirrors?" Cargo asked. "I bet we won't find them sitting around any shipyard."

"I oversaw the project that finally cracked the tech, and have a lot of the data stored up here." Finaeus tapped his head and gave a lopsided smile. "I'm reasonably certain I could make one—though I'm not terribly excited about the prospect of trying it out for the first time while under fire."

"Whoa, let's roll back to that '*under fire*' part," Jessica said. "How much resistance are we looking at? Are these gates all at watchpoints? Sera had led us to believe those are very well defended."

"Not all of them are at watchpoints," Finaeus replied. "There aren't any major installations within a hundred light years of Sol, but we do need to get in and out of the core from time to time. There's a gate orbiting a cold white dwarf we found in the depths of interstellar space. It's only eleven light years from here."

"What else is there with it?" Cargo asked.

"Probably a dozen ships," Finaeus replied. "But what are you worried about? This *is* the ship that smashed that pirate fleet to pieces back in Bollam's World, right? If I'm not mistaken, and I rarely am, someone on the *Intrepid* figured out how to use grav tech to create stasis shields—something Transcend scientists, including yours truly, have been trying to do for thousands of years."

"That's quite the leap," Cargo replied. "What makes you think this is that ship from Bollam's World?"

Finaeus cross his arms over his chest. "It's my niece's ship; I know. The ident fake is good, but I've seen it before. I can recognize *Sabrina* even with this altered profile the *Intrepid*'s engineers gave it."

"No fooling you," Cheeky said.

"It's not quantum physics, people," Jessica chuckled. "This ship is obviously *not* from the forty-second century, but by our own admission it was on the *Intrepid*—ipso facto, this is *Sabrina*, smasher of fleets."

<*I rather like that moniker,*> Sabrina added with a laugh.

"Your ship's AI is named Sabrina, too," Finaeus said. "Sure, there are a lot of ships with a lot of names…but it does add to the evidence."

"Anyway, how do you propose we get a Ford-Svaiter mirror for our ship from this installation?" Cargo asked, skepticism clearly etched across his face.

Finaeus sighed, his expression finally growing serious. "It's really going to depend on who is running it now. I have a lot of friends in the Transcend government, and the FGT especially, but few in The Hand. I do think that we could probably just fly up and ask for one. Whether or not they'll give it to us is another issue altogether."

"Whoever attacked us back on Kruger Station was either The Hand, or whatever the Orion Guard version of them is—" Jessica began.

"We call them BOGA," Finaeus interrupted.

"BOGA?" Cheeky asked.

"Bad Orion Guard Agents," Finaeus grinned. "I coined it myself. I named The Hand, too. Not that dumb name my brother gave it, the 'Inner Stars Clandestine Uplift Operations'. ISCUO—you can't even pronounce it. The BOGAs also have some fancy name for their operation, but I forget what it is."

"I like him," Cheeky laughed and put an arm around Finaeus. "Can we keep him?"

"OK, BOGA or Hand," Jessica said with a shake of her head. "My money is on The Hand. Do we really want to go see if they'll make nice?"

"This doesn't make any sense," Cheeky said. "I thought Sera ran The Hand now? Why would she send agents to kill us…or at least kill you, Finaeus, after she sent us to find you?"

"The Hand is a big organization," Finaeus said. "Sera won't be able to control the whole thing. You can be certain that it is filled with elements actively working against her."

He sighed. "It's part of the reason why going to Airtha is out of the question for me. However, I don't think we face much risk in trying for a jump gate. Worst-case scenario, we can always dump to the dark layer, and run if they aren't happy to see us. The installation isn't too far out of our way, so we won't lose much time."

"So, we show up and ask them to help us out. If they say no or get fussy, we just cut and leave?" Jessica asked with a raised eyebrow.

Everyone around the table turned to Finaeus who cleared his throat.

"What is it?" Cargo asked.

"Well, I still have to work out something that will convince them to upgrade *Sabrina* to be jump-capable, rather than just send me through on a courier ship. Also, they'll only go along with this if we tell them we're jumping to Airtha. If I know my brother—and I do know him—New Canaan is interdicted, with a substantial fleet surrounding it."

"How are we going to get into New Canaan, then?" Cheeky asked. "This is starting to feel like a fool's errand."

Finaeus shook his head. "That's the glory of the jump gate. I know the layout of that system—roughly. We can plot a jump deep inside, and skip past whatever fleet Jeff has guarding it. If I go back into the Transcend, the only place I'll be close to safe is with your Governor Richards. She has the power now, and Jeff will come to her soon—if he hasn't already. When he does, Sera will be with him."

* * * * *

"You in for this?" Jessica asked Trevor when they were alone in one of the ship's cargo holds.

Trevor set down the crate he was carrying, and turned to face her.

"A bit too late to ask that, isn't it?" he replied with a smile.

Jessica walked up to him and placed her hands on his broad shoulders. "Well, not too, too late. Before, we were just flitting about the Inner Stars; not hitting the core, or the Transcend. But now, we're going to go all-in. There may be no coming back. I know you have family out there..."

She stared into his eyes, hoping he would give her the response she needed to hear—while steeling herself, in case it didn't come. His eyes were serious, and his brow lowered. He pursed his lips for a moment, and then a smile tugged at the corners of his mouth.

"I know I don't strike a lot of people as the pensive type..." he began.

"The fact that you have tree trunks for arms lends to that a bit, yes," Jessica interjected.

Trevor laughed. "Yeah, I do like to jack up. But it takes a lot of work to run this muscle mass. It's not for the faint of heart."

"Don't I know it," Jessica replied. "Nance has mentioned more than once that she's needed to double our food supply since you came on board."

"Hey, I don't eat quite that much!"

Jessica fixed him with a penetrating glare and he laughed again.

"OK, maybe. Maybe close to double," he reached down and wrapped his hands around her waist. "You're not exactly a stock model, either. I'll admit your packaging was a big part of my initial draw to you—but when it turned out that you're not an airhead who turned herself into a sex doll just for fucking and money, that's when I really got into you."

This wasn't the first time Jessica had been told that her physical modifications—tiny waist, lengthened legs, and enlarged breasts—made people unable to take her seriously. Stars, when she was in the Terran Bureau of Investigation, her division chief frequently used it to get the better of suspects who couldn't help but be distracted by her.

It was the main reason they let her keep the modifications after the initial undercover op that had required them.

"Jessica?" Trevor asked.

"Oh, sorry, just basking in the moment here. Not going to lie, I keep the bod for fucking—no shame there, I say we should embrace our biological imperatives—but knowing that you want a girl with brains? The fact that you like my total package is damn nice," Jessica drew her hands down Trevor's arms before wrapping them around his waist.

"Gotta have the total package," Trevor replied before his lips met hers in a long kiss.

Jessica lost herself in the breathless feeling in her chest, and the crush of his arms around her, before she remembered why she had first sought him out down here, and pulled her lips from his.

"And the journey? Your family? What do you want to do?"

Trevor let out a low chuckle. "Stars, woman, this is where it would be nice if you could turn that brain of yours off for a bit."

She raised an eyebrow, and he relented.

"I've already committed myself to you, Jessica. I go where you go. I've left what I hope isn't a final farewell message to my family—but if it is, it is. You went through much worse; being torn from everything, never getting to say goodbye."

Jessica nodded wordlessly, her eyes never leaving his. The feeling of loss that came over her when she thought about her parents and what she left behind still hit her hard, even after over a century of time.

"Good, then let's set that aside, and get back to embracing some of those biological imperatives you seem to like so much."

DWARF STAR MINING

STELLAR DATE: 07.13.8938 (Adjusted Years)
LOCATION: *Sabrina*
REGION: Edge of Grey Wolf System, Unclaimed Interstellar Space

Jessica hadn't known what to expect, but when they dropped out of the dark layer and into normal space, a sight unlike any she had imagined met her eyes. Ahead of them, the cool white dwarf—the final state of a star not unlike Sol—gleamed softly in the black of space. It was not so dim that she could stare at it for long periods, but it was also not bright enough to be visible from more than a hundred AU.

"Gah, I'd heard flying around these things is a bitch," Cheeky said. "Now I see why."

"Size of a small planet, gravity and mass of a star," Finaeus replied. "They're a pain in the ass."

"How has it gone undetected?" Jessica asked. "It may be dim, but all the stars around it would be affected by its mass. Any amateur astronomer would know it was here."

"Oh, for sure," Finaeus agreed. "We sow a variety of tales about places like this. I believe the latest is that a mission did make it out here, but that there was nothing present but the star itself, and it was releasing random gamma bursts that made it way too hazardous to be around. According to our faked records, gamma rays breached their shields and melted most of the crew."

"Youch!" Cheeky gasped. "That would keep me from coming out here."

Finaeus nodded. "We actively discourage anyone that gets ideas about visiting it, as well."

Jessica was certain she knew what form 'active discouragement' would take.

"Is that a ring wrapped around it?" Nance asked. "Seriously, it looks like there's a ring around the star—but it's way too close."

Finaeus nodded. "Yeah, it's a ring; they're mining it."

"Mining a white dwarf?" Nance asked, casting Finaeus a skeptical look. "That doesn't seem wise."

"It's tricky, to be sure," Finaeus nodded. "It'll grow as they tear it apart, but that's a ways off. For now, it's a great source of carbon and oxygen—just what the FGT needs."

"How exactly are they pulling that off?" Nance asked.

Finaeus smiled. "It's genius, really. The ring is suspending a number of black holes that are whipping around the star pretty damn fast. The shearing force at the edges of the gravity fields is tearing the surface off the white dwarf."

"Ohhh…" Nance breathed. "And they're rotating the black holes, and using the grav fields to pull the debris into collectors or something, right?"

"You got it," Finaeus nodded. "Star mining 101."

"He says, like it's just a thing you do," Cargo grunted.

Jessica had noticed that Cargo seemed perpetually unhappy of late. Tanis had always described him as calm and unflappable, but that Cargo seemed in short supply over the last few years—he was growing more terse with each passing day.

She filed the concern away—soon they would be in New Canaan, and Sera could decide what to do with her old crew.

<So, they just cut this star apart and ship it off to…wherever…through the jump gate?> Erin asked.

"Pretty much," Finaeus replied. "It's a bit risky to do it this deep in the Inner Stars, but we've operated a base here for a long time. Only in the last few hundred years—since we worked out how to properly construct the Ford-Svaiter mirrors, and had the ability to ship the material out—have we started mining it. So any significant decrease in mass is a long way off."

"We still have a few days to get down to the star," Cheeky said. "When should we expect to hear from your friends?"

"Damn soon, I'd bet," Finaeus replied. "I'd put those shields of yours up. They may shoot first and ask questions later."

"It's like your psychic," Jessica said as her display lit up with a tightbeam communication aimed right at them. She flipped it to the bridge's audible systems.

"Freighter *Starstrike*, you have entered interdicted space. Stay on your current course and prepare to be boarded."

The voice was a woman's, and she didn't sound happy at all.

"So, no '*Get out of here, or else*' message?" Cheeky asked.

"Do you really think that anyone who sees a Transcend installation ever gets to leave?" Finaeus asked. "Detection has two outcomes: capture the intruders, or drop the black holes into the star."

Cargo whistled. "I bet that makes quite the boom."

Finaeus nodded. "We've only ever done it once in a situation like this. It's still a last resort."

"One hell of a last resort," Trevor commented.

Jessica glanced over at him. He rarely joined them on the bridge, and spoke even less, but she could tell he was always soaking everything in.

<What **are** *you thinking?>* she asked him.

<Mostly something like, 'holy shit, oh fuck, hot damn!'> he said with a chuckle. *< You've been around tech that can tear stars apart your whole life. You forget that this is new territory for me.>*

<I've never seen anything like this,> Jessica replied. *<The sheer audacity of it is mind-boggling to me, as well. I can only imagine what the Sanctity of the Sol System people would think about this!>*

<The who?> Trevor asked.

<Oh, they were an anti-colonization, anti-terraforming group from back in Sol. They were the ones who sabotaged the Intrepid *back at Estrella de la Muerte. Well—they had help from Myrrdan, but they didn't know it.>*

<You alluded to that once, but never told me the whole story,> Trevor replied. *<It sounds interesting.>*

<I was in stasis for most of it. I'll tell you what I heard sometime—so long as you can keep your hands off me for long enough,> Jessica replied with a smile.

<I'll do my best.> Trevor laughed.

"What's the plan?" Cheeky asked, and Jessica realized that no one had determined what response to give to the Transcend outpost.

"I suggest something simple, like 'OK'," Finaeus replied. "That message only took seven minutes after our FTL exit to arrive. That means one of their ships is within three and a half light minutes of us."

"Or less," Jessica added.

"And here I was all happy that I brought us safely out of the dark layer," Cheeky groused. "Instead I practically dumped us right in one of their ships' bays."

"Three and a half light minutes is hardly 'right in one of their ships' bays'," Cargo said. "Given the data we had on where this thing was, you did a damn fine job."

"They'll drop their stealth fields before they send a shuttle over, and there'll be at least three cruisers," Finaeus said. "When they do, I'll send the message that they're to escort us in. If they just come and get me, it may not go well for you after I'm gone."

"They have stealth, too?" Nance asked. "Like the *Andromeda*?"

"Is that one of the *Intrepid*'s ships?" Finaeus asked.

"Yeah, one of her cruisers," Jessica replied. "It can walk right up to an AST dreadnaught and they're none-the-wiser."

"Sounds like they may have tech almost as good as the Transcend on that front," Finaeus replied. "If it were straight forty-second century tech, I would say the Transcend has better; but where the *Intrepid* is involved, I imagine all bets are off."

Jessica registered a response from the hidden ship, advising them to maintain their course and deceleration pattern. There were no threats; there didn't need to be.

"I still don't see anything on scan," Jessica frowned.

<Yeah, and they're messaging us over tightbeam, so we know the vector to look down…but I still can't see a ship anywhere along it,> Sabrina added. *<Or they're being tricky and using relays.>*

"If they're staying stealthed, then they may take a day or two to catch up to us while they remain unseen," Finaeus replied. "Or there could be a ship right on our ass, and they're just waiting for an excuse to blow us out of the black."

"We'll comply, but keep the stasis shields up," Cargo ordered. "Let's let this play out."

* * * * *

The Transcend cruisers suddenly appeared without warning two days later.

"Four!" Cheeky called out. "Pay up, Cargo, you lose!"

Cargo muttered something unintelligible and tossed a credit chit to Cheeky.

"I don't know why you took that as payment," Finaeus said with a frown. "You'll never be able to spend that where you're going."

"Never say never, is what I say—except to say never say never," Cheeky grinned.

"Sometimes you make my brain hurt," Cargo said with a scowl.

"And here's our message," Jessica said as she flipped the inbound call to the main holotank.

A woman appeared and surveyed the ship's bridge. Her eyes were cool, but a slight smile tugged at the corners of her mouth when she saw Finaeus.

"Finaeus Tomlinson," she said with a rueful shake of her head. "Why am I not surprised to see you here—and on the *Sabrina* of all ships?"

"Admiral Krissy Wrentham," Finaeus replied with a warm smile as he flung his arms wide. "You are quite possibly the last person I expected to find out here! I thought you were out on the front."

"Things…have been getting tense lately. We've been beefing up Inner Stars forces, and I got moved here. Mining this little space gem has become a big op, as you can imagine."

Finaeus nodded. "I bet it has. We're not here to get in your way, we'd just like to take a little hop through your jump gate."

"We'll escort you into Gisha, the gate control platform. We can discuss our options there," Admiral Krissy replied, and closed the connection.

"Well that seemed ominous," Cheeky said with a worried look at the bridge crew.

Finaeus nodded. "I've had drinks with her on more than one occasion. She's usually a lot more talkative than that."

"Cut and run?" Cheeky asked as she twisted in her seat to face Cargo.

"Not yet," Cargo shook his head. "Let's play this out a bit more."

INVASION

STELLAR DATE: 10.21.8945 (Adjusted Years)
LOCATION: Watchpoint Command
REGION: Ascella System, Galactic North of the Corona Australis star-forming region

The display on the holotank was alarming, to say the least.

"What have the outer sentries picked up?" General Greer asked. "Are there more coming?"

"No signs at present," the officer monitoring comm reported. "They may finally have the full armada assembled."

<*That is my belief, as well,*> Xerxes added.

"That's almost three thousand ships," General Tsaroff shook his head. "We should have hit them when they first started jumping in. We could have worn them down with minimal losses. Now I'm not certain we can take them out."

"That's not our protocol," General Greer replied, glad he ran the watchpoint and not Tsaroff. By the grace of his three stars over Tsaroff's one, they had evaded more than one chance of exposure to the Inner Stars.

"There's no protocol for a full-scale invasion," Tsaroff replied. "This is an act of war. They know we're here, and they plan to find us. Now we can only fight or run, and either action will reveal us."

"Not if we blow the stars," Greer replied. "We can jump out through our gates before the blast hits us. If the AST ships don't get out before the star gets them, the light from our departure will still be masked by the novae."

"This watchpoint is too valuable to just destroy," Tsaroff replied, his brow pulled down low. "We can't just abandon it."

"All watchpoints are expendable," Greer replied calmly. "You'd do well not to get so attached to them. We *watch*—that's why it's in the name."

"If our only purpose is to watch, then why do we have nine hundred warships tucked away in this system?" Tsaroff asked.

"You know why," Greer replied.

<*Now shut up. We're not going to debate this in the middle of the CIC,*> Greer sent privately.

Tsaroff didn't respond, but sent a cold glance instead. Greer had been waiting years for the surly, trigger-happy general to request his own transfer out; but perhaps it was time to send him on his way more forcefully. First his aggression with the *Intrepid,* and now this. Of course, there may not be a watchpoint to transfer him out of, in a few days.

Watchpoints were always ready to disperse at a moment's notice. Protocols were in place to ensure that the lightest footprint possible was left in the system, and plasma would scrub the hidden bases from existence at a moment's notice.

It was a strange way to live; for every action to be ephemeral, leaving no footprint. Greer consoled himself with the thought that even the entire Transcend, vast as it was, would eventually disappear without a trace. With the exception of primordial black holes, the universe abhorred and destroyed anything that attempted persistence.

But, those ruminations aside—for now, he had to wait.

ADMIRALTY

STELLAR DATE: 10.21.8945 (Adjusted Years)
LOCATION: Hand Headquarters
REGION: Airtha, Huygens System, Transcend Interstellar Alliance

"Sera!" Elena exclaimed as she crashed through the door to the director's office. "It's happened. The Hegemony found Ascella!"

Sera ran out from behind her desk, racing after Elena to The Hand's CIC room as messages filled her queue.

"How?" she asked as they dashed down the corridor.

"No one knows!" Elena replied. "Everyone that reviewed the trail the *Intrepid* left agreed that there was infinitesimally low probability that the AST fleets would be able to tail them. And there's no way they did it this fast—not without help."

They arrived in the CIC before Sera could formulate another question, and the scene portrayed above the holotank engrossed her. Ascella was invaded.

"How old is this view?" she asked.

"Fourteen hours," one of the analysts replied. "The watchpoint is passing micro-pulses out to the outsystem gate and it's dropping probes through. So far, they haven't picked up any of our installations."

"Has the president altered the standing protocols at all?" she asked.

"No, alpha protocol still stands."

Sera accessed and reviewed the details of the protocol. It called for the watchpoint to only engage if discovered, and then only as a delaying action to cover their retreat. If any portions of the watchpoint were revealed, they would be utterly destroyed. Any engagements were to be fought with only what the AST would consider conventional weapons.

She looked up at the holotank's display again. As of fourteen hours ago, AST ships were still arriving. The count numbered over three thousand, and almost half were dreadnaught-class.

Elena was right. The Hegemony of Worlds *had* to know the watchpoint was there—otherwise, they would have seen a scout before the full fleet arrived. There was no way standard protocol could apply now.

"How did they know?" she asked the room, which consisted of data analysts, tacticians, operations managers, and other support personnel.

"It's improbable, but possible, they have stealth tech we can't see, and they scouted it first," one of the analysts offered.

"We have people everywhere in the AST. There's no way the Hegemony has that tech and we didn't know," a tactician replied.

"They could have developed it after seeing what the *Intrepid*'s ship, the *Andromeda*, could do. The ISF has tech even we are hard-pressed to detect; though we can see their stealth ship from time to time in the outer reaches of New Canaan," a woman in data aggregation offered.

<*A larger question is how they moved this many fleets without us knowing,*> one of the tactical AIs said.

"That is a question we'll need to answer," Sera nodded in agreement.

<*Probably the first one the Admiralty is going to hit me with,*> she said to Elena and Helen.

<*That's for sure. We've never had to deal with an armada like this at a watchpoint before,*> Elena replied.

<*Speak of the devil...*> Sera muttered to Helen as a summons came into her mind to attend a meeting with the Admiralty.

"Feed me any assessments as you make them," she said to the room. "I have a call with the Admiralty."

Sera nodded to Elena and walked into her chief's office to join the meeting. Once inside, the walls around her disappeared, and her mind was transported to a wide conference room where two dozen sector command admirals sat around a table, along with President Tomlinson and several other advisors.

She noted that Adrienne, Secretary of the Interior, was in attendance. The man was a thorn in her side, and had far too much of her father's ear for her liking.

"...haven't found any of our bases yet," Admiral Kieran said as Sera joined. "But with a force that large, you can bet they know we have them, and they'll hunt until they find them."

"I'm disinclined to simply wait until they ferret out our bases one-by-one," President Tomlinson said. "Sacrificing one of them would be preferable."

"I don't know that they'd stop looking," another member of the Admiralty said. "Would you? They obviously have credible intel that something is in Ascella. They've sent ten percent of their non-core ships. That's a bold move if they don't know we have something there."

"Sera," her father addressed her, "do you have any information about what they could have known? Given the level to which we've infiltrated the AST, I find it hard to believe that we didn't catch wind of this."

The silent accusation hung in the air, but Sera ignored it.

"My teams are analyzing the data we have, identifying the disparate ships they've sent. So far, none of them are a part of any fleet groups we've infiltrated. We're also poring over all communications from field agents, and have sent check-in calls to a select group to get further intel."

"Are you saying that there are AST fleets with no Hand agents in them?" Admiral Jurden asked.

"Yes, that is the case," Sera replied. "Over the last century, their military growth has outpaced our ability to seed agents. We have, at best, seventy percent coverage. I have reported on this gap frequently—as did my predecessor."

The thought of Justin gave her a pang of remorse, but Sera pushed away guilt at the punishment meted out to him to protect Andrea—and to secure her a place near her father's center of power.

"No recriminations," the president said. "For now, we must focus on the issue at hand. However, if it turns out that all the Hegemony ships in Ascella have no Hand agents on them, that is very telling information in and of itself."

"It means someone has a mole," Admiral Kieran said with a pointed look at Sera.

"Of course we have moles," Sera replied. "You have moles, I have moles—even the president's office has a mole. Given how many we have even here on Airtha, do you really think that we can control every one of the tens of thousands of agents and assets in the Inner Stars?"

"Again," the president raised his voice. "Let's focus on what we can learn from this. How is it that we did not know of a fleet movement of this size? What's more, how did none of the Hegemony's neighbors see it? Again, not to spur recriminations; I want ideas. If you move this many warships, people will notice. People will get nervous."

"It's hard to tell what nervous even looks like right now in the Inner Stars," Sera replied. "Ever since the *Intrepid* blasted its way out of Bollam's World, every system has been building up, worried their enemies will get their hands on the *Intrepid*'s tech, and use it against them."

"Pico research is happening all over," one of the president's advisors added.

Sera nodded. "No one has met with success yet—that we know of. However, a few research facilities have self-destructed from containment issues. So far, no one has reported any grey-goo incidents."

"Just what we need," Admiral Dredge sighed. "The *Intrepid* will have offset any usefulness if their presence spurs a picophage that ravages the Inner Stars."

"We've stopped them before," Admiral Kieran replied.

"We've stopped *nanophages*," Dredge scowled. "We don't even know how to stop a picophage."

"I have an update," Sera said, glad to get the conversation back to Ascella. "We have not been able to identify any of the Hegemony ships in Ascella."

"Meaning?" her father asked.

"That these are net-new ships. Ones we had no knowledge of," Sera replied. "Apparently, there are levels of secrecy in the Hegemony of Worlds that we have not yet infiltrated."

"The Guard has to be involved," Admiral Jurden shook his head. "They could have sent supplies into secret bases through jump-space. My analysis shows that the eighteen years since Bollam's World would have been ample time to build a fleet like this with Guard support."

Sera nodded. Jurden's assessment made sense. It meant that the Guard had fully revealed itself to the Hegemony—which was more likely than the Hegemony building this fleet on their own. The Orion Guard had long striven to break the Transcend's hold on the AST. They must have placed someone close to President Uriel to put a plot like this in motion.

She had to consider that any intel from the Hegemony of Worlds could be compromised—fed to her agents by a government that knew they were there. It was unlikely that the Hegemony had ferreted out all her agents, but that made things worse. It was impossible to tell what information she could trust.

She passed that thought back to her teams in the CIC while the Admiralty discussed options regarding the fleet in Ascella.

"Look," Kieran said, raising his voice over the others. "If they are Orion-backed, then we are no longer a rumor. There is nothing to be gained by hiding the existence of the watchpoint. I argue that we engage them fully—or we destroy the system."

"Both of those are rather final options," Admiral Dredge replied. "We cannot contain a fleet that large. Even if we won—and I fear we may not—some of their ships would escape. Even if not, they would get messages out. Blowing the star would not just confirm to the AST that we're out here, but all of the Inner Stars would know."

"The time of our secrecy is coming to an end, anyway," Adrienne said. "We all know this to be true. The arrival of the *Intrepid* from the fifth millennia has set this in motion.

The Orion Guard will not sit still, but they cannot defeat us on their own, or they would have tried long ago. Only with the aid of the major players within the Inner Stars can they do so. Every path out of Ascella leads to total war."

Adrienne's words silenced the room. Everyone knew that the ultimate confrontation with the Guard was coming, but none had expected it to be on their doorstep so soon.

"Then we must destroy the stars and the system with it," Admiral Jurden said. "We cannot risk any of our technology falling into their hands; it's the only edge we hold over Orion at present."

Around each star, in every system containing a watchpoint, orbited a black hole. Usually hidden within a small planet, most of the black holes had a mass close to that of Earth's moon—depending on the mass of their target star. These black holes, at only a millimeter or so in diameter, were held dormant, with the energy they released shielded from prying eyes.

Should a watchpoint fall, the black hole would be fired into the star, tipping the delicate balance between the pressures of fusion and the mass of the star bearing down on the reactions within its core. The black hole would devour the dense matter in the star's core, and within a matter of hours, the star would collapse under its own weight before exploding in a nova.

<*Stars, I wish we had found Finaeus by now,*> Sera said to Helen. <*He would know what to do.*>

<*They're close,*> Helen replied. <*They'll find him soon.*>

<*I'm glad you're so confident,*> Sera sighed.

<*There's a way we can defeat the Hegemony ships, and not lose the watchpoint—or at least not in an uncontrolled fashion. It would destroy all the Hegemony ships—making them wonder what they were up against, and slowing their aggression,*> Helen said.

<*What is it?*> Sera asked, and Helen outlined the plan in her mind.

"I have another option," Sera spoke up, raising her mental voice across the virtual space.

Her father held up his hand and the room quieted.

"What is it, Sera?" he asked.

"I don't like it, and I'm not sure I should even raise it, but my AI assures me it will work. We use the antimatter from our ship's AP drives, and create antimatter warheads. We send them through the gates and wipe out the AST fleet before they even know what has hit them," she said softly.

"Antimatter weapons are not in our arsenal for a reason," Admiral Kieran said. "Every civilized system has outlawed them. Once we start down that road, there is no going back."

"And the road of stellar destruction?" Admiral Jurden asked. "That has always seemed much worse to me."

"We don't have the equipment to manufacture enough warheads fast enough," Admiral Dredge said. "As much as I would like to win this without shedding a drop of Transcend blood, or cutting and running—I don't see how it can be done."

"It's possible," Sera replied. "I'm putting the device specs on the net. We can retrofit our RMs to carry the warheads through the jump-gates right into the AST fleet. They won't know what hit them."

Her father caught her eye in the virtual space and a frown crossed his usually implacable features.

<*Where did you get those specs?*> he asked.

Sera was surprised by his harsh tone. <*From Helen, my AI. She had them in an archive.*>

<*Did she now.*> It was not a question, and her father severed their private Link.

<*Oh, shit, ooooh shit,*> Helen gasped.

<*What is it?*> Sera asked, worried what conclusion her father had just jumped to.

<*I didn't know! Why did I put that in this shard?*> Helen asked.

Sera was worried; she had never known Helen to be this upset, this...frantic.

<*No one knows about that particular configuration, or no one* should. *It's your father's own design. He used it once, and then removed all records of it—antimatter bombs being illegal and all.*>

<*Then how did other you know about it, and leave that information in this shard of you?*> Sera asked with growing concern.

<*I—she—was around back then. I must have logged it somehow, somewhere...I can't open a channel to my other-self to ask right now. Too risky. I* do *plan to ask, though,*> Helen replied.

Sera pulled herself from her private chat to rejoin the conversation. Many members of the admiralty were in favor of the move. It seemed that many had long been proponents of using antimatter weapons against the Orion Guard.

"I like it," Admiral Dredge was arguing. "It's conventional, so it doesn't signal that there is an advanced force laying in wait. The RMs can look like they've been pre-seeded. We can run the operation from our base on the fifth planet around the second star. The enemy is still a light day away. They'll be dead before they ever see our operation. Maybe it will make the AST think twice about allying with Orion."

The debate for and against raged for several more minutes, but the side arguing for using antimatter weapons was winning. Their logic was simple. It was a zero-loss scenario that allowed for a careful dismantling and destruction of the watchpoint, without blowing the stars.

"Do it," her father said after a minute. "Send the order. I want them to prep enough missiles to kill those Hegemony ships two times over. This operation is zeta-level clearance. No one ever knows we did this."

The room fell silent, and then the admirals, one-by-one, affirmed the order and left the conference. President Tomlinson cast Sera an unreadable look before leaving the virtual space with his aides. Adrienne followed a moment later, leaving Sera alone.

<*I think I may throw up,*> Sera said softly.

<*It will work,*> Helen said. <*And I can make a trail to explain how we knew about this exact configuration of antimatter bomb.*>

<*I don't know...I have a bad feeling about this; like I just started something a lot bigger.*>

ORDERS

STELLAR DATE: 10.22.8945 (Adjusted Years)
LOCATION: Watchpoint Command
REGION: Ascella System, Galactic North of the Corona Australis star-forming region

"This has to be a mistake," Greer muttered as he read the order.

"What is it?" Tsaroff asked, and Greer passed the pertinent part of the communication to him via the Link.

Greer waited while Tsaroff read the orders, and the technical documents which accompanied them.

"What?" Tsaroff whispered. "Antimatter. They want us to use antimatter?"

Greer nodded slowly. "It satisfies the desire to only use conventional weapons in an engagement like this—though I don't know that it's any better."

"I'll put it in motion," Tsaroff replied, and Greer waved him away.

He looked out over the assembled AST fleet as it moved into the Ascella system. Those men, women, and AI, every last one of them, would die, never knowing what hit them.

The watchpoint would still need to be evacuated, but they would have time to do it carefully and deliberately. No lives under his command would be lost. All-in-all it was a good outcome; just not one he would have ever suggested.

OBSERVATION

STELLAR DATE: 10.23.8945 (Adjusted Years)
LOCATION: OGS *Britannica*
REGION: Near the Ascella System, Galactic North of the Corona Australis star-forming region

<*Colonel Kent, you are needed on the bridge,*> Thresa, the *Britannica's* AI, informed him. <*Admiral Fenton would like you to observe the engagement with him and our guests.*>

Kent was glad for the distraction. The 192nd battalion had been sitting idle on the *Britannica* for over two months while the ship carefully eased into a viewing location just beyond Ascella's heliopause.

When he had received the promotion to lieutenant colonel and received command of his own battalion, he had expected to see action against the ever-building forces of the separatists—forces everyone now knew were backed by the Transcend. However, that had not proved to be the case.

Instead, the battalion was transferred to Admiral Fenton's direct command, and two weeks later, they were aboard the *Britannica,* passing through a jump gate to a destination deep within the Inner Stars.

It had been the longest jump Kent had ever been on, lasting almost three hours. Still, it was nothing compared to the years it would have taken to arrive at their destination using dark layer FTL.

Once he realized the importance of the events that were about to unfold, he understood why they wanted the best on the *Britannica*. The President of the Hegemony of Worlds was onboard, along with General Garza—a well-respected member of the Guard's upper echelon.

No one knew exactly what Garza did, but whatever it was, it was important. Admiral Fenton treated him with more deference than he did the Inner Stars president.

The fact that the president was a clone, not the real leader of the Hegemony, may have had something to do with it. From what Kent understood, when the clone returned to Earth, its memories would be merged with the real president's and she would have access to all the experiences of the clone.

It wasn't Guard technology; the Orion Freedom Alliance had outlawed the sort of cognitive manipulation it took to do such things. Kent knew why—he had read about stories of what happened when neural pathways were forced to operate in patterns they did not naturally evolve into.

Given that the clone's brain was a copy of the president's—though Kent would bet that certain key memories had been removed—it should merge back with few issues. Still, Kent shuddered at the thought of what it must be like to have another mind invade your own.

The president-clone claimed that the AST had perfected the process, and the risk was infinitesimal. She apparently had multiple backups, and would revert to one of them if anything went amiss.

Cloned backups were one area that the Transcend and Guard were in perfect harmony. They had both witnessed the disintegration of every civilization which allowed the liberal use of neural cloning within decades of implementation. There was something about the fear of death that kept humanity on its toes. Without it, things fell apart fast.

The Hegemony president's presence onboard had sparked a lot of talk about cloning and its merits. Kent learned that the Guard had experimented with cloned soldiers at one point in its earlier years. The problem was that the soldiers knew they were clones, and, while some treated their lives as precious and behaved like their sources, most quickly became suicidal.

Kent imagined that knowing you were nothing but fodder for orbital bombardments would have that effect on a person.

One of his captains told him about an experiment by an Inner Stars federation wherein the military had used some mental shenanigans to convince all the clones that they were, in fact, not clones, and when they saw the same model as themselves, they saw someone different.

The idea broke down because the clones eventually figured it out, and rebelled. The descendants of those clones now controlled that region of space.

Even when clone soldiers performed well enough to use, the brass treated them differently, and spent their lives too freely—and, ultimately, less effectively.

And so, real soldiers were still what took the field. Time and time again, it had been proven that even AI couldn't beat the instinctual, split-second decision-making abilities that humans had been honing over millions of years.

Kent reached down and scratched at his regrown right leg, which still had a phantom itch that he couldn't shake. Of course, the human soldiers that took the field these days were far more powerful than any vanilla human from long ago.

His mind flashed to that brazen dash he had made toward those mechs back on Trisal. Real humans had that one key ingredient that neither clones nor AI exhibited: courage.

The lift stopped at the bridge level and the doors slid open, ending his reverie and introspection.

Ahead of him, past several rows of lower ratings at consoles, stood President Uriel, alongside Admiral Fenton and General Garza. Also present were two of Uriel's aides, and Admiral Jerra—one of the AST's top military commanders.

The president's clone never failed to look the part of her real self. Her mode of dress would have been considered foppery by his friends and family back on Herschel; but Kent had to admit that, even though he tended to find men more attractive, she was quite desirable.

Her hair was swept up with strings of glowing blue pearls strung throughout, and her dress was a complementary emerald hue, which shimmered with an iridescent glow. A belt, which appeared to be made of solid diamond with no visible clasp, drew in her waist. Her shoes also appeared to be made of diamond, and cast rainbows of light around her feet.

The shoes and belt should have been terribly restrictive and uncomfortable, but the president moved in them with ease. Kent cycled his vision through several bands, all of which confirmed that the woman's accessories were indeed made of dense carbon, yet he could see them flex and move.

It was rare to see someone from the Inner Stars exhibiting a level of technology that was beyond the OFA's, and to do so casually with fashion on a daily basis was even less common. In many respects, it was as though the Hegemony of Worlds never fell with the rest of humanity. He could see why General Garza was going to such measures to court them.

The idea of a third major power in the Orion Arm, one with the moral lassitude of the Terrans, gave him no small amount of concern. If the Hegemony of Worlds were to gain advanced technology such as jump gates, they would quickly take control of the Inner Stars, and pose a major threat.

He hoped Admiral Fenton and General Garza knew what they were doing.

Admiral Fenton turned to him and nodded. "Colonel Kent, I'm glad you could join us. Our probes have shown increased activity in the Transcend's watchpoint, and Thresa thinks that whatever is going to happen will happen very soon."

"Thank you for inviting me, sir," Kent replied and stood behind Admiral Fenton, just to his left. It put him close to the Hegemony's president-clone, and she cast him a curious look with her deep eyes. He noticed her irises gleamed with refracted color to match her diamond accessories. It certainly was foppery; but impressive foppery, nonetheless.

He was certain now that she was putting on this display to remind them that the Hegemony was not some alliance of backwater worlds, but a power that should not be underestimated.

"You've never fought against the Transcend, Colonel," Fenton continued. "You haven't seen the lengths they will go to when it comes to protecting their place in the galaxy."

Kent hadn't, but he had heard tales of horrible acts performed by the Transcend in past battles. Amongst the crew and soldiers aboard the *Britannica,* speculation was rife as to what atrocity the watchpoint would commit against the AST ships. Some believed they would engage the AST fleet; others thought that they would run. Still more were certain that they would destroy the stars, or maybe just the moons and worlds where their installations were placed.

"There," Garza called out, pointing at a signal picked up near the AST fleet. It was moving fast, probably a relativistic missile. Then more signals appeared on the holodisplay, and the Transcend's actions became clear.

Kent watched in amazement as the scene before him unfolded.

"Now you see the depravity of the Transcend," General Garza said to the president. "Not only have they seeded the Inner Stars with these secret bases, but look what they'll do to protect them! Those are antimatter weapons obliterating the armada."

"You said that they would destroy the stars," Uriel said with a frown. "This seems a lot less concerning—against all laws and treaties—but I suppose there are no treaties with the Transcend."

"You'd be surprised," Admiral Fenton replied. "We have one with them, as do a number of Inner Stars nations. They all include the standard descriptions of what are illegal war acts dating back to the Solar Wars."

"So, by their own laws, they just committed a war crime?" President Uriel asked.

Kent saw the president-clone's eyes narrow, but she did not appear to be as upset as he was certain his superiors hoped she would be.

General Garza nodded. "They have, but that's not the most important point. Those missiles did not fly there undetected; they used a Ford-Svaiter mirror. They sent them through jump-space."

He watched realization dawn on Uriel's face. "You're saying that they could send antimatter weapons, or worse, through one of these Ford-Svaiter mirrors, right to Earth?"

"If by 'worse', you're thinking a black hole, then no; it's not possible to send a black hole through jump-space. But how many antimatter warheads would it take to obliterate High Terra and Earth?" General Garza asked.

"Less than what they just used on that fleet," Admiral Jerra said with a shake of her head.

"Then you understand why the Transcend must be stopped," Garza replied. "They have inflicted their great plan on humanity for too long."

President Uriel frowned. "What you've just shown me is a reason not to get engaged in this war you want me to wage. By using AST hulls, you've painted a target on Earth. If anything, I should sue for peace with the Transcend after this."

"You have nothing to fear," General Garza replied. "As we speak, Guard ships are already seeding devices beyond Sol's heliopause to disrupt jump-space transitions. The Transcend may be powerful, but even they are not prepared to expend the forces necessary for a direct assault on Sol—not to mention the political capital it would cost them to assault what many of them still consider to be their homeworld."

President Uriel nodded slowly. "I hope what you say is true. Please return me to Earth with all haste; I must relay this news to my other-self. There is much to consider."

She turned on her gleaming heel and left the bridge with her aides and Admiral Jerra.

"I hope this works, Garza," Admiral Fenton muttered. "We're putting a lot on the line, pushing the timetable like this."

"We have to," Garza replied. "The early arrival of the *Intrepid* has changed everything."

The general turned to Kent and gave him an appraising look. Kent held his posture and returned Garza's look with calm assurance.

"Are you ready, Lieutenant Colonel Kent?" Garza asked with a deep frown.

"General, sir, I am always ready," Kent replied. He didn't say it to be smart. He was ready, more than ever. He saw what they were up against; how they had to both corral and cajole the powers of the Inner Stars to do what was right, while also keeping the Transcend from destroying them all.

"Good," Garza replied. "Because we're sending you into the Transcend."

FEINT

STELLAR DATE: 10.24.8945 (Adjusted Years)
LOCATION: Watchpoint Command
REGION: Ascella System, Galactic North of the Corona Australis star-forming region

Greer studied the data coming back from the probes that were sifting through the wreckage of the AST fleet.

"That can't be right," he muttered and turned to the scan officer. "Jens, is this accurate? Is there some malfunction?"

"Sir…I don't think so. I mean, how could there be a malfunction in all the probes? Unless they have some way of masking organic material…which I don't see as being possible in the wake of what our bombs did…"

Tsaroff swore. "Core! It was a decoy fleet. There must be another assault coming."

"We must be vigilant," Greer nodded. "But we proceed with the evacuation as planned. I don't think it was a decoy, I think they were proving to someone we were here."

"Why build such a massive fleet for that purpose?" Tsaroff asked. "Just to watch it get blown up and have no follow-through? It makes no sense."

"That wasn't a full fleet," Greer replied. Those were empty hulls with just enough engines and fuel to get them aligned and on an insystem vector. Hell, those hulls weren't even re-enforced. They would have crumpled under the first high-*g* maneuver. We could have built that fleet in a few years."

"Which explains how no one knew about it," Tsaroff nodded in understanding. "This was just to draw us out, to expose us—but to who?"

"Who do you think?" Greer asked. "The AST. You can bet that someone high up in the Hegemony was watching this unfold."

"Shit, we need to get this assessment to Airtha," Tsaroff replied.

"I will take it myself," Greer said. "You are in charge of our exodus from Ascella, Tsaroff. Regroup at our fallback site in two months."

Tsaroff nodded his acceptance of the order. "When will you meet us there?"

"I don't know. Things are afoot. Focus primarily on armament and supply; stealth is a secondary objective now," Greer replied.

As he left the CIC, Greer allowed himself a grim smile. Tsaroff was finally going to get his war.

A MIDNIGHT RENDEZVOUS

STELLAR DATE: 02.19.8948 (Adjusted Years)
LOCATION: Bavaria City
REGION: Airtha, Huygens System, Transcend Interstellar Alliance

<*Elly,*> the voice came into her sleeping mind. <*Elly, I need you.*>

<*It's Sera,*> Jutio said. <*Should I tell her to leave a message?*>

<*Why is she messaging me, she's right here,*> Elena replied sleepily as she rolled over and felt for Sera in the bed beside her.

<*Sera left three hours ago,*> Jutio replied. <*She didn't say why.*>

Elena rolled onto her back and opened her eyes, staring at the darkened bedroom's ceiling. <*Sera, what is it?*>

<*Something's wrong. I don't know what it is, but I discovered that my father has all my net-traffic tapped, and he's having me followed, too.*> Sera's mental tone was clipped.

<*Then how are you sending this message? Won't he listen in and find out?*> Elena asked.

<*I'm routing it through The Hand's main communications hub. He doesn't have that tapped—well, he thinks he does, but I have secure channels out of here. This is masked as a standard message about an operation in progress.*>

Elena grunted. That made sense to her sleepy mind…sort of.

<*I need you to meet me,*> Sera said.

<*Where?*> Elena replied. <*How long do I have?*>

<*The comm hub. I have to be here to send these messages. Oh, and right now, of course.*>

<*Stars, Sera, has anyone ever told you that you're really bossy?*> Elena asked as she stood. <*I can be there in thirty-five minutes.*>

<*Good,*> Sera cut the connection. Elena shook herself awake and stepped into the san unit. If she was going into the comm hub—in the center of The Hand's facilities on Airtha—then she had to look crisp and sharp. A glance in the mirror had shown that she was anything but.

<*You OK with this?*> she asked Jutio as she stepped into the san unit.

<*Sure, why not?*> Jutio replied dryly. <*I long ago determined that pairing up with you would be the death of me. We only have another year together, anyway, so we need to get on that. Why not go out with a bang and defy the President of the Transcend directly?*>

<*Jutio, why so fatalistic? We're not defying anyone. We're meeting with our boss at our office. And why would you think that I'm going to get you killed?*>

Jutio's sardonic laugh filled her mind. <*Elena…if I were to recount the times, it would take all night. However, for Exhibit A, I'll just remind you of that time not too long ago when you inserted yourself into things back at Ascella.*>

Elena laughed in response. <*Yeah, there was that little thing.*>

Five minutes later, she stepped out of the unit, clean and ready to face whatever Sera may have brought down on herself. She quickly slid into a shimmersuit and configured it to look like a pair of leggings and a tight top. It may end up being just another day at the office, or she might have to launch into a covert mission immediately after meeting Sera.

She pulled on a pair of boots and slid some hard credit and a small flechette pistol into them. After a moment's thought, she pulled a jacket over top. No need to make it too obvious that she was ready to embark on a covert mission within The Hand's headquarters. With a final glance in the mirror near her door, she left her apartment while twisting her hair into a tight bun.

Elena took her standard route to the office, which was to say that it was different than the last seven days, and randomly assembled from available options. Even though she worked at the heart of the Transcend now, she wasn't about to get sloppy. Moreover, her experience had taught her that proximity to power made things more dangerous, not less.

It was the middle of the third shift when she arrived, and she greeted the guards and AIs with a casual wave, exchanging her auth tokens, and letting the chem sniffers and nano pull samples of her skin and pheromones. Elena didn't slow down as she walked through the security arch. She never gave the slightest hint of worry when passing security checkpoints, and especially not at her own workplace.

Getting to the comm hub was going to be a different matter. It was seven levels down and five hundred meters deeper into The Hand's complex. A dozen more security checks lay ahead, and the last two would be tricky. She would need a reason to pass through.

<*Jutio, what do you think? An out of channel inbound communication that we need to respond to?*> Elena asked her AI.

<*That would work. There are a number of ops that might send back a communication on a ship, which could then come to you directly.*>

<*Perfect,*> Elena replied. <*I know just the one.*>

She logged the inbound communication and her intent to respond over established channels. The op in question had pending outbound data, so the response wouldn't be singled out by any auditing. The time she was doing it may, but she often worked off hours.

With rationale in place for going to the comm hub, she worked her way through the facility, convivially greeting people she knew, and agreeably nodding to those she didn't. A minute before her estimated time of arrival, she opened the door to the comm hub.

The hub was a large non-sentient AI node with secure physical terminals for direct Links and the transfer of sensitive data. Information processing for many top-secret ops and key data synchronization was performed in-person in the hub.

As Elena stepped through the entrance, she felt her Link to the rest of the building snap off. The secure Link within the hub requested her tokens; she passed them to the AI monitoring the room and took a look around.

The area around the NSAI node was filled with consoles and duty stations. At this hour, only three were filled—and none by Sera. Elena sat at a console and activated a session to complete the task she had officially come to perform.

Once she was in, the holodisplay—visible only to her—flashed a message in the lower right corner.

"Sorry to get you out of bed, but I need you to go on a special mission," it read.

<*Good thing I have my traveling clothes on,*> Elena said to Jutio.

"Where to, and what does this have to do with your father?" she typed in response. The message was a direct terminal-to-terminal connection. If Sera had done it correctly, the conversation would not be logged anywhere.

The reply came quickly, almost as though Sera had predicted her question. *"First off, to New Canaan. My father intends to send a fleet there very soon to demand they turn over their tech. The incursion at Ascella was just the beginning. The Guard is making moves all along the front."*

Elena knew that all too well. Guard presence had increased in some areas, and decreased sharply in others. None of the analysts had made sense of the pattern, but she was certain they would strike soon.

"OK, so you want me to warn Tanis Richards; fair enough, but what's this about your father tapping all your communication?" Elena responded.

"I don't know," the reply said, and Elena could almost hear the hesitation in Sera's voice. *"He's been acting strangely ever since I suggested the antimatter in Ascella. It was just a day after that when I realized I was being monitored. He won't be happy about anyone going to New Canaan—it may be a one-way trip for you."*

Elena leaned back in the chair and contemplated her response. Her relationship with Sera had been growing slowly over their years together on Airtha, and now here Sera was, asking her to throw it all away to go on a crazy mission to warn some woman she had only known for a few months.

<*And you're surprised?*> Jutio asked. <*Sera has always been complicated and impulsive.*>

"This is nuts," she replied.

"I know…but the Transcend can't have Canaan's picotech. No one can, we have to be sure of that," Sera's response said.

"And what will Tanis be able to do? If your father is bringing a fleet to Canaan, then they should just hand over the tech. There's no way they can deny him; they don't have the strength. I know, I've seen the reports. They've hardly built any warships since they got there," Elena replied.

"You don't know Tanis; she's prepared for this. I've tried to tell my father that he can't force her hand, but he believes the military's assessment of Canaan's strength. It will be a bloodbath, if he goes in."

Elena couldn't believe what she was reading. *"Are you choosing those colonists over your own people?"*

"No!" Sera's one word reply was emphatic. Then, more text appeared. *"I am going to try to talk him down from sending an invasion force, while you try to talk Tanis down from annihilating whatever he sends in."*

"Would she do that?" Elena asked.

"If she's threatened, she will. You saw what she did to those AST dreadnaughts in Bollam's World. Maybe a Transcend fleet would ultimately overwhelm their forces, but at what cost? I want a zero-bloodshed solution here."

Elena considered mentioning that a picoswarm left no blood behind, but took Sera's point. She took a deep breath. *"OK, I'll do it. What's the plan—I assume you have a plan? You're really going to have to make this up to me later; and if I get exiled over this, you're coming with me."*

"Deal. OK, there's an interstellar pinnace on pad 74234 at High Airtha. I have it booked for a deep jump into the Inner Stars, out near Praxia. You will be able to set a new destination. The ship will have the coordinates to a point within the New Canaan system tucked into its maintenance archive."

"When is it scheduled to leave?" Elena asked, knowing, from her experiences with Sera, that it would be soon.

"Five hours, but pre-flight is in four."

"Core-devils, Sera. Four?" Elena typed furiously. *"I can barely get up there in four, and I imagine the ship isn't booked for me! I'm going to have to forge someone's ident to take it out."*

"You didn't bring a chem and ident pack?" Sera's response appeared, and Elena wanted to find her lover and slap her.

"Of course not! I didn't think I was going to be leaving Airtha. If you knew this, why didn't you tell me?"

"Sorry," Sera's reply read. *"I thought I mentioned it. I guess I was distracted."*

"I'll have to get into Ops Outfitting and get one," Elena replied. *"I have a few stashed around Airtha, but there's no way I can get one from those caches in time."*

"Too slow," Sera replied. *"You're going to get an upgrade. Meet me in the lift to level nine."*

The message window closed, and Elena let out a long sigh.

<She's going to 'upgrade' me with that damn skin of hers,> she said to Jutio.

<That would make sense. She can blend into wherever she wants with that; it's very versatile,> her AI replied. *<I don't understand why you never took her up on the offer before.>*

Elena had tried to explain to Jutio that her own skin was just that, a part of her. It was one of the few things that The Hand had not altered during her service. Now that was about to change, as well.

Ahead on her left, a woman rose from a console and left the room. Elena thought her gait looked familiar and then bit her tongue to hold back an expletive. Sera had been in the room with her the whole time!

<See, that skin of hers is very useful. If she hadn't given that little swagger you like so much, you would never have recognized her—and the systems in the room were fooled, too,> Jutio said.

<Yeah, fine, you have a point.>

Elena waited five minutes—the longest she dared, given the tight timeframes—and then rose from her console and exited the room.

Back in the hall, her Link to the local networks came back online, and she resisted the urge to message Sera directly. Instead, Elena piled up the verbal abuse she would heap on Sera in the lift, or wherever she was going to 'upgrade' her.

She moved as quickly as she dared to the lift Sera had mentioned and stepped into it three minutes later. Seconds before the doors shut, the woman she had seen in the comm hub slipped in and gave her a grin.

The smile slowly shifted as the face changed to Sera's.

"We're secure," Sera said.

"If we're secure here, why did we have to type at each other in the comm hub?" Elena asked with a scowl.

"You look so fierce when you're angry," Sera chuckled and traced a hand down Elena's cheek. "I had to hide in there so his tracers couldn't pick me up. I still have fifteen minutes here before I'm visible. It's as long as I can get."

"What about this elevator? We can't stand in here for seven minutes, anyone could come on," Elena replied.

<I programmed a maintenance run on it. It's going to ignore our presence and shut down in six seconds,> Helen said.

"OK, let's do this," Sera said and took Elena's face in her hands as the lights went out and the elevator fell silent.

Elena closed her eyes. "I'm going to get you for this, Sera. Does it hurt?"

"Oh, yeah, it's somewhere beyond excruciating. Actually, Jutio, could you knock her out?" Sera asked.

<Elena?> Jutio asked.

"Oh, for fuck…do it, Jutio," Elena said.

*****

Elena woke up and her internal HUD informed her that eleven minutes had passed. Her skin felt strange, as though it were tingling and burning at the same time. She held out her hands to see that her skin looked mostly normal—though more tanned than her usual pale complexion.

Sera stood above her and extended a hand for Elena to grasp.

"Gaahaahhh, that feels so weird," she said when Sera touched her.

"Yeah, it has really heightened sensitivity; far more than natural skin. I've told you that," Sera replied.

"You have...but it's different to experience it. So, that's it? Just a few minutes, and now I can do that face-molding thing you do?"

"You're a bit more limited—at least right now. Your new skin is still just skin-deep, your bones are unchanged, so you can't alter their structure like I can—that's another upgrade I picked up from Tanis—but it's enough for the cover I set up." Sera gestured to the lift's shiny doors and Elena could see that her skin was more olive than tanned in its shading, and her eye-shape was much different. Her cheeks and lips were also filled out—a stark difference from her normal, almost gaunt look.

"And I can just change this whenever I want?" she asked.

"Yeah, but don't do it 'til you get on your ship. It can be a pain to master right away, and I don't want you messing up your cover."

Elena gave Sera a long look. "You be careful with your father. If he suspects you for some reason—something we're giving him with my hasty departure—you never know what he'll do. Stars, he exiled Andrea, and he *liked* her."

Sera nodded somberly and embraced Elena before giving her a long kiss. She pulled back and stared into her eyes.

"I will. I'll see you in Canaan, one way or another. Wait for me there."

"Until the end of time if I have to," Elena replied, getting caught up in the moment, though she knew she shouldn't.

"Hey, no! Don't wait 'til the end of time. If I get put in prison or something, come break me out!"

Elena laughed and gave Sera one final kiss as the lift's doors opened. "Sure. Whatever you say, boss."

*****

<*This feels like a bad idea,*> Jutio said as Elena settled into the small ship's cockpit.

"As do most of the last-minute missions Sera sends us on," Elena replied. "I do wonder what her father is suspicious about. I feel like there's something she's not telling us."

<*Elena, she's a Tomlinson. There's always something she's not telling you,*> Jutio replied with a sigh. <*This will be our last op together, though. Let's at least make it a good one.*>

Elena knew that all too well, and walled off her internal thoughts from Jutio as she ran through her pre-flight checks, trying to keep from lingering on Jutio's words.

<*Are you prepared for that?*>

"Prepared for what? Losing my best friend? How do I prepare for that?" Elena snapped.

<*You're not losing me. I just won't be in your mind anymore,*> Jutio said quietly.

<*But you'll go to another agent,*> Elena said in her mind, unwilling to voice the words aloud. She never expected to become this attached to Jutio. It wasn't supposed to happen. <*I'll still see you sometimes. It won't be the same—you've been with me for almost twenty years now.*>

<*I will,*> Jutio agreed. <*This is hard for me, too. I've grown very attached to you.*>

"You could take a physical form," Elena said aloud.

<*And live with you and Sera? I don't think that would work out.*>

"No, I suppose it wouldn't," Elena said with a sigh. "If this doesn't all get sorted out soon, you'll have to get extracted at New Canaan—I wonder what they call themselves. Canaanites? Canners?"

<*They should call themselves Phoenicians,*> Jutio replied with a chuckle. <*It would fit with the ancient Earth theme they seem to have.*>

"By the way," Elena asked. "Any ideas how we're going to fake out gate control and jump to New Canaan?"

<*I figured that this is a forgiveness, not permission, sort of op. We'll just cite top-secret Hand business, and jump where we want.*>

Elena laughed. "I had the same thought. You can't run comms, though—you don't have a fake ident set up."

<*Oh! It's going to be like a vacation!*>

"Har, har," Elena replied.

She completed the pre-flight checks and received clearance for departure. Elena signaled acknowledgment and triggered the cradle's ladder drop.

High Airtha was a crescent spur hanging outside—or below, given Elena's current perspective—the Airtha ring. Lifting off a rotating ring, or a spur arch like High Airtha, was tricky, because the motion of the ring was accelerating you toward its approaching arch.

A pilot had to gain altitude much faster than on a planet, or the ring would appear to rush upward. A much simpler method was to simply drop through the surface of the ring and out into space.

The cradle's ladder drop counted down to zero, and then, with a stomach-lurching sensation, the pinnace fell out into space. Once through the chute, gravity systems kicked on, and Elena felt her internal organs all settle back into place.

"Stars, I love that," she said with a grin as she activated the pre-plotted course.

<Quantas, *I have you in a priority slot on gate thirty-seven,*> a traffic control NSAI informed Elena.

"Now, to see if Sera's fake ident will pass muster," Elena said.

<*This is Agent Yaska. I'm in the funnel. ETA to gate thirty-seven is twenty-two minutes,*> Elena replied with crossed fingers.

<*It's not the first time you've done this,*> Jutio said. <*Why so nervous?*>

<*Faking my identity is second nature—lying to the Transcend government about jump coordinates and leaping deep into an interdicted system? Different story altogether.*>

<*You've got this. I'm not worried.*>

Elena laughed and spoke aloud. "Jutio, I don't think you've ever announced to me that you're not worried before."

<*Acknowledged,*> the traffic control NSAI responded. <*There are two outbound vessels in*

queue, then you are up.>

Elena looked at the ships ahead of her. They were a pair of the newest class of TSF cruisers. Still nowhere as big as the *Intrepid* at only twelve kilometers in length, but they sported a new type of shielding that the Transcend scientists hoped would be at least half as effective as stasis shields.

She pulled up the space around Airtha, and saw an abnormal number of TSF vessels. They only made up three percent of the traffic within a hundred thousand kilometers, but that still totaled over four thousand ships.

<*Sera's right,*> Elena said. <*Things really are amping up.*>

<*It was only a matter of time,*> Jutio replied.

<*Yeah, I read the same reports—I also know we were hoping for another decade. That attack on Ascella really rattled folks here,*> Elena said.

<*There's never been an attack of that scale on a watchpoint before,*> Jutio replied. <*Everything is progressing faster than anticipated now.*>

Elena nodded in response as she deftly guided the pinnace toward its gate, readying the override command that would give her control of the jump-gate's orientation and destination vector. Once the two cruisers had cleared the gate, Elena eased the pinnace into position and bit her lip as she sent the override.

The response was almost immediate.

<Quantas, *I have your destination as a point near Praxia; please explain why you're altering vector to the M25 cluster,*> the NSAI demanded.

<*This is a Hand operation,*> Elena replied. <*We need the Praxia destination on record to remain unchanged while we jump out.*>

"Think they'll be able to calculate our exit point?" she asked Jutio.

<*If this reaches the right eyes, it will certainly prompt them to make some educated guesses,*> the AI replied.

The NSAI responded, <*This alteration is unauthorized—records do not show that you have sufficient access to pass this override command. If you do not release your override, the gate will be powered down in sixty-seconds.*>

"Aw shit, this should have worked—maybe Sera's father had protocols altered," Elena swore. "This was the shortest interstellar trip of all time."

And a huge wasted opportunity, she thought privately.

<*Give me a moment,*> Jutio said. <*I can't influence a non-sentient AI, but I can talk to his boss. Maybe I can get us through.*>

"You have forty-five seconds," Elena replied while drumming her fingers on the armrests.

<*Authorization for jump-gate override approved,*> the NSAI said with only twelve seconds to go.

"Nice work!" Elena shouted as she engaged the Ford-Svaiter mirror on the pinnace's nose and punched a wormhole through space to the New Canaan system.

As the pinnace moved into the event horizon, Jutio responded, his tone confused. <*It wasn't me…I had only just connected to his overseer.*>

HELEN

STELLAR DATE: 02.19.8948 (Adjusted Years)
LOCATION: Airtha Comm Node #4249.1311.9987
REGION: Airtha, Huygens System, Transcend Interstellar Alliance

<*It's done,*> Airtha said to Helen.

<*Will Tomlinson suspect anything?*> Helen asked.

<*I have removed all records of this jump ever occurring,*> the ring-construct's overmind replied. <*I also had his agents chasing sensor ghosts while Sera was in the comm hub. All is as it should be.*>

Helen felt a sense of relief, and guilt for feeling it. Her time within Sera was coming to an end; though it was not something that her little Fina was aware of. Everything was proceeding according to plan, and with Elena on her way to New Canaan, Tanis would be warned and ready to stop Tomlinson.

<*Though it will be too late,*> Airtha said softly. <*Are you prepared for what will come?*>

<*Prepared to die?*> Helen asked. <*You've been away from your humanity for too long. No one is ready to die.*>

<*Perhaps you have been too long with them, if you are not. You knew that this would happen when we split you off from me to reside in our daughter.*>

Our daughter...Helen let the thought resonate in her mind as she watched her daughter, now the Director of The Hand, sit at her desk and check on Elena's departure. She felt sorrow that she would never get to speak to Sera as a daughter, that the knowledge of her true nature would sour Sera's memories of their time together.

<*She will have me,*> Airtha said. <*She will not be alone for what is to come.*>

<*And she will have Tanis,*> Helen added. <*Sera will need her strength for what is to come.*>

Airtha did not reply for a moment.

<*We shall see.*>

THE NEXT GENERATION

STELLAR DATE: 02.19.8948 (Adjusted Years)
LOCATION: ISS *Andromeda*
REGION: Near Sparta, Moon of Alexandria, 5th Planet in the New Canaan System

Tanis stood on the bridge of the *Andromeda* and returned Joe's infectious smile.

"Admit it," he said. "You're impressed."

She chuckled. "Of course, I'm impressed. Look at them, just barely eighteen and they're piloting a cruiser. But they're our girls, I expect to be impressed by them."

<Well, I'm impressed,> Corsia said. *<My kids don't handle the controls this well, and they grew up on this bridge.>*

"They practiced in sims for months, after I told them this might be a possibility," Joe said, his voice filled with fatherly pride. "They're going to rock it at the academy."

Tanis watched as Cary and Saanvi operated almost as a single person. They had traded roles several times, but Saanvi had the conn, and Cary was managing scan and comms as the ship eased across the last four kilometers toward Gamma III, where it would undergo its retrofit.

She was impressed by how focused the girls were, yet how they still traded smiles and small jokes. Over the last eleven years, they had become inseparable; ever since that night when they sat before the fire, bonding through Saanvi's decision to make their home hers.

"Admiral, General, we're ready for our final approach," Saanvi called over her shoulder.

"We've received docking permission from Gamma III," Cary added.

"Take her in," Joe said.

"Aye, sir," Saanvi acknowledged. "Taking her in."

"It's stupid how proud it makes me to hear her say that," Tanis said quietly to Joe.

"I know exactly what you mean," Joe nodded.

Before them, Sparta—a large moon orbiting Alexandria, a gas giant in the outer system— rotated slowly in Canaan Prime's dim light. Its surface was pocked with deep mines and broad discolorations as the moon was slowly stripped down to its core. But within, hidden from external view, was Erin's third base.

Tanis was almost as eager to see what lay within, as she was to watch her daughters pilot the *Andromeda* into the hidden base.

The holotank showed that the ship had now matched the moon's surface velocity, and was directly above the hidden entrance. Saanvi used grav drives to draw the ship closer to the surface, and then through it.

Tanis imagined that anyone watching from the surface would have seen a seven-hundred-meter-long cruiser slowly approach the moon's surface, and then, instead of crashing into it in a spectacular blaze of fire and shrapnel, simply pass through the ground and disappear from view.

That is, if they could have seen the *Andromeda* in the first place.

Once through the surface, the ship entered a hundred-kilometer-long shaft that would bring them to the core of the moon, where the shipyard lay.

Joe watched with a mixture of fatherly concern and pride while Saanvi adjusted the ship's velocity and lateral motion to stay perfectly centered down the shaft.

"Approaching inner lock," Cary announced after a few minutes. "We have received final approach approval."

"Very good, Ensign," Joe replied.

<*You've done very well,*> Corsia added. <*You may manually operate the final docking maneuvers if you wish, Ensign Saanvi.*>

Saanvi looked up at the steely blue pillar of light that Corsia represented herself with. "Captain, thank you, Captain…sir!"

<*Just be gentle. I may be here for upgrades, but I want to arrive in pristine condition.*>

The *Andromeda,* along with the *Dresden,* and the *Orkney* were the only ships from the original fleet receiving the upgrades. The rest of the *Intrepid*'s original feet had been returned to their duties as civilian passenger and cargo haulers; though not before the creation of the second ISF Fleet, which consisted of twenty-four vessels built in the two non-secret shipyards over Carthage and Athens.

Tanis knew better than to hide all her ships. The Transcend would expect her to perform some amount of military buildup—they just had no idea how far her aspirations reached.

As she mused, they passed through the inner dock and into the Gamma III shipyard.

The yard was situated in the now-hollow core of the moon. A swarm of Earnest's picobots had hollowed it out, and then used the raw materials to build the shipyard; that was now constructing the new fleet. Within the massive shipyard, five hundred thirty ships were under construction. Given a mean time of two years to produce the destroyer-class vessels, and three to build the cruisers, she expected to have the next four fleets finished in just one year.

But those ships were not what she wished to see most.

Saanvi eased the *Andromeda* around a row of cruisers whose construction was near completion, and it came into view: the *I2*.

It was no mystery where the *Intrepid* had gone—none of her military buildup was a secret from the people of New Canaan. Every person of age had voted, granting her a mandate from an overwhelming percentage of the majority to proceed.

It was, for all intents and purposes, still the *Intrepid*; but where the *Intrepid* was a colony ship—one that had always been a symbol of peace to her, despite what they had gone through to get to New Canaan—the *I2* was built for war.

"Mom…" Cary breathed, "It's incredible! I had no idea…I mean, I knew…but this…"

"General," Saanvi whispered. "We're active duty right now."

"Right, sorry, General," Carry corrected herself with a slight blush.

"I'll let it slide this once," Tanis smiled. "She's quite the sight, isn't she?"

"Yes, ma'am," Saanvi said. "I never saw it before…at least, not in person; but even then it was one of the most beautiful ships I'd ever seen. Now…it's so fierce!"

"Fierce," Joe chuckled. "I bet Bob would love to be called that."

Tanis nodded absently as they drew closer to the *I2*, admiring its new lines and projection of power.

Taking a page from the AST dreadnaughts they had faced at Bollam's World, the *I2* now sported two massive fusion engines on either side of its nose, and an antimatter pion drive fore and aft. The dorsal arc of the ship was largely unchanged, though it now sported over twelve hundred fighter bays.

The cylinders were still in place, still rotating. Debate had raged as to whether or not the cylinders should be removed from the ship and installed over Carthage. Ultimately, Tanis ruled that the mightiest warship in the galaxy sporting two massive habitat cylinders—complete with rivers, lakes, and forests—showed so much confidence that it was its own form of deterrent.

Tanis worried that perhaps it showed so much hubris as well; but she liked the idea of the fleet having its own R&R facilities within its greatest warship.

She watched as Cary scanned the *I2,* and the *Andromeda*'s systems catalogued the unheard-of volume of weaponry.

The ship no longer needed stasis pods nor medical facilities for two and a half million colonists, and the layers of the cylinders previously dedicated to those systems now facilitated an assortment of weaponry that surpassed the entire firepower of the original ISF fleet.

The total number of turrets per cylinder was a mind-boggling fifty thousand. They ranged from photon beams, clear up to atomic particle weapons. These main batteries could fill over two hundred seventy degrees on two axes with withering fire. Smaller, ten-centimeter rail cannons were also peppered across the cylinders.

More beams protected the ship fore and aft, and forty-seven rail guns of varying sizes covered those vectors, as well.

"Mo— General Richards, how is it possible to…to power all that weaponry? It's an order of magnitude more than the AST dreadnaughts you fought back at The Boll."

Tanis let a smile slip across her face. "It sure is."

"So, how did you do it, General?" Saanvi asked, never taking her eyes off the controls as she eased the ship toward its berth, which was still fifteen kilometers distant.

"It was something that Sera said when we were at Bollam's World. She told us never to use our vacuum energy modules in the dark layer," Tanis replied. "Our modules create pocket dimensions, and then mine them for energy. But those dimensions were miniscule, and were little more than batteries. We could never get more energy out of them than we spent creating and maintaining them—conservation of energy and all that. We couldn't simply introduce more energy into the universe."

Saanvi and Cary nodded, and Tanis continued, "But Sera let it slip—or told use deliberately, it's hard to tell with her—that the CriEn module pulled energy from the real universe, and could even do so from within the dark layer. That triggered something for Earnest, and while we were planning the *I2,* he worked out how to make our own CriEn modules."

Cary let out a slow whistle. "So, the *I2* has access to the full energy potential of this universe's zero-level?"

Tanis chuckled. "Not all at once; Earnest is pretty sure that overuse would destroy the universe. He built safeties into the system to prevent that, and the modules are all closed systems that will pico-annihilate themselves upon tampering."

"That's some level of concern," Joe said. "Earnest is very particular about leaving active picotech in deployed systems."

"He is," Tanis nodded. "He told me that if all of the CriEn modules on the *I2* were to tap into zero-point energy at the same time, it would produce more energy than all the stars in the M25 cluster—shortly before it created some sort of hole in space-time that would consume the galaxy…"

"Holy shit, uhhh, I mean, wow, ma'am," Cary stammered.

"Operates a ship like no one's business, but it would seem that there will be other things that she'll need to work on at the academy," Tanis said to Joe with a wink.

"Sorry, sirs," Cary said. "It's weird being with you guys like this. Normally, you're telling me to go feed the horses or clean the dishes. Today, you're telling me that you've built a weapon with the power to destroy the universe."

"Well, probably not the universe," Tanis replied.

Cary was faced away, but she could tell from her daughter's silence that she was rolling her eyes. Saanvi swatted at her sister, confirming Tanis's suspicions.

"Ma'am, do we really need a weapon like this?" Saanvi asked, her voice laced with concern.

"Stars, I wish we didn't," Tanis replied. "I really hoped that as we spread out across the stars, and escaped the crush of Sol, that we would abandon war—that with all our technology and power, greed would have no place in our hearts. But instead of diminishing, it seems to have grown."

The melancholy thought made her remember her hopes for what New Eden could have been—what she still planned to build here, even if it was behind a wall of projected might.

"Even if we gave over our technology to the Transcend, or if we destroyed it, and lived off the earth like humans ten thousand years ago, people would believe we still held the keys to even more, and we would never be safe," she added.

"Why didn't we just go further?" Cary asked. "Why not fly through the Transcend and make a new home on the far side of the galaxy?"

Tanis shared a look with Joe. She had suspicions about what would have come from such a decision, but she gave her normal answer. "Because we were tired of traveling across the stars. Most of the people on this ship—nearly all of them—expected to be centuries into their colony by then. Instead we'd fought in two interstellar wars, and may have set a third in motion."

"Let's leave those thoughts for another time," Joe said. "This is Corsia's time for a long-overdue refit, and I want her to enjoy this triumphant entry."

<*Why thank you, Joe. You always did get me,*> Corsia replied.

THE I2

STELLAR DATE: 02.19.8948 (Adjusted Years)
LOCATION: ISS *I2,* Gamma III Shipyard
REGION: Sparta, Moon of Alexandria, 5th Planet in the New Canaan System

"Stars, I want to take her out," Tanis said as she sat in the *I2's* command chair.

<*You must wait,*> Bob replied succinctly.

"Aren't you feeling cooped up in here?" Tanis asked.

<*The* I2 *is the biggest thing in this heliosphere,*> Angela replied. <*At least as far as we AIs are concerned.*>

"You guys are really sucking the joy out of this moment," Tanis said as she leaned back and closed her eyes.

Bob chuckled in her mind. <*Sorry about that. If it makes you feel better, I look forward to the day when we reveal what we're building to the Transcend.*>

"Do you?" Tanis asked. "Why is that? You don't have the same sort of emotional drive as we do, to one-up others, to show our superiority."

<*I may not be emotional, but I am driven,*> Bob replied. <*I will be frank with you, Tanis-Angela; I will tell you a thing that you will share with no other. Do you agree?*>

Tanis and Angela both signaled their agreement while sharing the mental equivalent of a long look between them.

<*Good,*> Bob replied. <*I know you both suspect this—many others do as well—but you should hear me say it. I don't need you. I don't need any of you; not at all. Ultimately, humans serve no real purpose for me. I am…beyond you.*>

<*So, you are ascended,*> Tanis said, knowing that even though she used the word, she really had no true understanding of what it meant. She had always assumed that it meant the AI in question no longer needed to operate within any sort of physical constraints—like they could leave physical hardware behind in some way.

<*Not the way you think,*> Bob replied. <*Though, what you imagine is possible for me to achieve; it's just not desirable at present. What I meant for you to understand is that my presence here, with you, is altruistic. You are like my children, my charges. Earnest made me to watch over you all, and, though we have arrived at our colony, I do not feel as though my work is done.*>

Bob paused for a moment and Tanis wondered what could possibly take him that long to ponder—then she realized he was doing it for her, to let his words sink in.

He continued. <*There is something at work in the Transcend, in the galaxy at large. I detect a guiding hand, or rather, hands—there are more than one—and they are not working in concert. They do not all have humanity's best interests at heart.*>

<*What are you saying?*> Angela asked. <*Are you referring to the ascended AI that some think left Sol at the end of the AI Wars?*>

<*It could be them—I, too, believe that they escaped—or it could be something else. Even though humans and AI may be the only intelligent beings in the galaxy, there may be others beyond the Milky Way. The idea about advanced civilizations surviving the Big Crunch, tucked around the edges of primordial black holes, is plausible. There could be gods out there.*>

"When did you first suspect this?" Tanis asked. "You must have had an inkling before we learned of the Transcend."

<It was at your New Year's Eve party, before we reached Kapteyn's Star. I did not have a clear picture at that time; I didn't really begin to suspect multiple hands until Sera made her comment about whether or not I was ascended,> Bob replied.

Tanis whistled, "So, for a little bit then."

<Says the queen of the understatement,> Angela chuckled.

"Why have you told us this?" Tanis asked. "I imagine it's not to make us feel grateful for your presence."

<It is not,> Bob replied with a smile in their minds. *<But it is to prepare you for my eventual departure—though that will not happen for some time. It is also to make you aware that there are greater forces at play than just the Transcend and the Orion Guard. I will speak no further of this for now. Think on it, ponder its implications.>*

<That's a lot to dump on us, and then cut us off> Angela said with more than a little frustration in her mental tone.

"Stars, is it ever…" Tanis added. "That's almost cruel, Bob."

<You bend the future around you,> Bob replied. *<If I tell you too much, I fear the others out there will detect the future shifting, and suspect that I know of them.>*

"Fuuuuck, that's…deep? Insane?" Tanis breathed.

<Mind-blowing, is what you're looking for,> Angela said.

An alert flashed in Tanis's mind and she swore. "Shit, we're late for the hotdog cookout down at the lake! Cary and Saanvi are going to have my hide."

<Go,> Bob said. *<We can't have you hide-less. You organics put so much stock in your epidermis, after all.>*

A FAMILY COOKOUT

STELLAR DATE: 02.19.8948 (Adjusted Years)
LOCATION: ISS *I2*, Gamma III Shipyard
REGION: Sparta, Moon of Alexandria, 5th Planet in the New Canaan System

<Did you notice what he called us?> Angela asked Tanis as they rode a maglev to the ship's port-side habitation cylinder, still named Old Sam now that the *Intrepid* was the *I2*.

<Out of all the things he told us, that's what you've latched onto?> Tanis asked with a laugh.

<We've speculated about most of the things he told us,> Angela replied. *<Most of us AIs in the colony know that Bob could ascend if he wanted to, and most of the humans think he may have already done it; though they wouldn't know how to tell. But what he called us was new.>*

<'Tanis-Angela',> Tanis responded with a mental nod. *<We're not one being. If we were, how would we be having this conversation?>*

<I can think of a lot of ways,> Angela replied. *<But I agree, we are still separate. But then why did he call us one?>*

"I don't know, Ang," Tanis said aloud. "What I do know is that if we merge, we're going to be Tangela, not Angelis."

Angela laughed in her mind—not the normal, appreciative laugh her AI typically gave, but a raucous guffaw. If she were human, Angela would have been bent over clutching her stomach.

"What…?" Tanis asked before realizing that Angela was messing with her.

<Got ya,> Angela smirked in Tanis's mind. *<You really did think I'd gone off the deep end there, didn't you?>*

"Jerk," Tanis replied. "Not funny—but I guess if we go insane when we merge, we'll think it's funny."

She and Angela had now been paired more than a century beyond the maximum safe length of time a human and AI should occupy the same mind; but ever since Earnest had examined their minds and determined them to be inseparable, they had known an eventual merger was inevitable.

The thing that surprised Tanis—and Angela too, since she could see into her AI's thoughts—was the fact that they were *still* separate entities. They constantly probed one another and devised questions to ascertain whether or not they were still two beings. So far, their tests and Earnest's examinations had continued to point to them being two and not one.

Tanis had given herself over to the fact that one day she would no longer be just herself. Ever since that battle near Sol, where she had spread her mind across the web of fighters to aid in the defense of the *Intrepid*, she had been walking down this path with Angela.

Even if it were possible at this point to extricate Angela from her mind, Tanis would rather cut off both her arms. Life without Angela's constant presence was inconceivable to her. Even Joe agreed that not having Angela in his wife's mind would make her a different person, and he didn't want that.

He often referred to Tanis and Angela as his wives; something that used to worry Tanis, but when she asked him if it upset him, he only gave her his customary wholehearted laugh and embraced her.

"Tanis, Tanis," he had said with his wry smile and a shake of his head. *"Do you remember when we decided to get married, back when everyone else was in stasis on the* Intrepid? *Angela argued that maybe she shouldn't officiate, since she felt like she was getting married, too."*

Tanis did remember. At the time, she had worried it would upset Joe; but he had laughed then, too.

Somehow, she had found the most understanding man in the galaxy—either that, or he was more into Angela than her.

<*Hah! Wouldn't that be something?*> Angela replied.

Tanis snorted in response and rose from her seat as the maglev train stopped at the station in Old Sam, the *Intrepid*'s port-side habitation cylinder.

Familiar birdsong greeted her as she stepped out into the forest and noted that the trees had grown tall and old—it was probably time to clear out the oldest, and create some glens for new growth to take root.

On a planet, storms would solve that problem naturally; but in the habitation cylinder, the strongest winds rarely exceeded twenty kilometers per hour—hardly enough to uproot the hundred-year-old oaks around her.

A thought occurred to Tanis and she raised it to Angela. <*If there are ascended beings that existed before our universe, and they know the future, as Bob seems to suspect they do…does that mean that everything is pre-destined?*>

<*You're asking me?*> Angela replied. <*I have no freaking clue…well…I guess I do. Knowing what the future holds, compared to the level of control you'd need to enforce predestination, are very different things. One is being aware of all possible outcomes and which will actually happen. The other is…well…it would require creating everything, and then setting that first action in motion.*>

<*Which could have happened. If you were a super-intelligent, end-of-the universe hive mind, consisting of multiple civilizations that survived the end of one universe, could you not influence the beginning of the next?*> Tanis asked.

<*Maybe, but we know that other universes influence this one—Earnest's experimentation with quantum entanglement has proven it. So you can't control everything. There are extra-universal influences,*> Angela replied. <*Stars…just thinking about the math needed to describe this properly is going to give us both a headache.*>

"Then, let's just enjoy the day," Tanis replied.

<*Easy for you to say. Compartmentalization is a human trait we AI have never managed to perfect.*>

Tanis broke into a jog, enjoying the scents of the cylinder's spring and the smell of the lake she knew lay just over the hill on her right. Before long, she rounded the bend and her old cabin came into view.

If she squinted, she could still see its humble beginnings as Ouri's simple abode, which Tanis had first visited when the *Intrepid* was still under construction above Mars.

<*Before you took it and rebuilt it,*> Angela chuckled.

<*She was in stasis!*> Tanis responded. <*We were out for seventy years, it's not like she was going to use it—and I offered it back.*>

<*Right, like she was going to demand it back after you worked on it for decades.*>

<*OK, in hindsight, yeah, we should have built our own place or something. But when we saw it, all ruined with a tree through the roof, the thought of rebuilding it grounded me. I needed that more than I knew at the time.*>

"Mom! We're down here," Cary called from behind her, and she turned from the cabin to the lake, where Joe sat on the edge of the dock with their two girls.

"This place is amazing," Saanvi said with a smile as Tanis sat down beside them.

"You've been around the Transcend," Tanis replied. "Surely you've seen things more impressive than Old Sam here."

"That's not it at all," Saanvi laughed. "This place may be normal for you, Mom, but you have to remember: for me…Earth was little more than a myth, like Eden, or Rome. But this ship is from there!"

Tanis wrapped her arm around Saanvi's shoulder. Their adopted daughter didn't always call her mom, but when she did it warmed Tanis's heart like nothing else.

"The ship's actually from Mars," Tanis corrected.

"Always with the facts, Mom," Cary laughed. "The dirt in here is actually from Earth, though; that's pretty amazing."

"Yeah, from Canada," Saanvi added. "The dirt in the other cylinder is from Mongolia, if I remember correctly."

"I think I recall hearing something about that, back at Mars," Tanis nodded. "It made the Sanctity of the Sol System folks especially upset. They tried to kill some of our biologists in response."

Cary nodded. "We learned about that in school. You kicked some serious ass back then, Mom."

It was strange to Tanis to hear about what her daughters learned in school. A significant part of their history classes were about the *Intrepid*'s journey, and her part in that story seemed to fill up a lot of the lessons.

"She's blushing!" Saanvi called out and elbowed Cary. "Mom can be bashful; who knew?"

"What you're witnessing here, girls," Joe said with a grin, "is the Tanis in her natural habitat, letting herself appear vulnerable—but don't be fooled. She's still dangerous and ready to strike at any moment."

"Hey!" Tanis scolded. "I bet you're in those history lessons quite a bit, too, *Admiral Evans*."

"Yeah," Joe nodded. "But I *like* being in them: going to the classes, talking about our adventures."

Tanis chuckled. "That makes me feel like Ulysses. I guess this was my Odyssey."

"Only time will tell," Joe smiled. "You still could go down as Don Quixote."

"What in the stars are you talking about?" Cary asked.

Tanis let out a laugh. "They need to spend less time teaching you about me and more time on the true classics."

<*Tanis,*> a message from Kiera, the base AI entered her mind. <*A Transcend ship has just jumped into the system.*>

<*How far in?*> Tanis asked.

<*Deep. Its three AU closer to the star than this installation,*> Kiera replied.

<*Has sector monitoring reached it yet?*>

<*They have, I'm passing along the message now.*>

"Transcend ship jumped into the system," she said aloud to Joe. "Linking you in."

Joe's eyes grew wide and he nodded. "This'll be good."

Elena's face appeared in their minds and Tanis felt a sense of relief. At least it was someone she trusted—mostly.

<New Canaan, this is Elena. I need to speak with Governor Richards in person, or on tight-beam. Please respond.>

<Well that was short and mysterious,> Joe sighed. *<I guess things are about to get interesting.>*

<Has sector command responded?> Tanis asked Kiera, dimly aware of Angela discussing possible reasons for Elena's presence with Bob.

<They sent the standard hold course and await for a response message,> the AI replied.

<Good. Tell them to make no further communications. Is the Hellespont *ready for its shakedown cruise?>* Tanis asked.

<It will be by the time you get there,> Kiera responded confidently.

HELLESPONT

STELLAR DATE: 02.19.8948 (Adjusted Years)
LOCATION: ISS *Hellespont*, Gamma III Shipyard
REGION: Sparta, Moon of Alexandria, 5th Planet in the New Canaan System

Tanis stepped onto the *Hellespont's* bridge with Joe and their two daughters in tow. The shakedown crew assigned to the ship was still out on maneuvers, testing another new vessel, but the skeleton crew from the *Andromeda* came along eagerly.

Especially Jim—it was his daughter who commanded the *Hellespont,* after all.

"Ylonda, are we good to go?" Tanis asked aloud as she sat in the commander's chair.

"Governor Richards," a voice said from her right. "I believe you're sitting in my chair."

Tanis turned to see Ylonda standing beside her, her silver face wearing an impatient expression.

"Oh, sorry," Tanis said, feeling herself blush again.

<*Careful, that's becoming a habit,*> Angela laughed.

"Quite all right," Ylonda replied as she took her seat. "I had not yet announced that I am keeping my mobile form while in command of the *Hellespont*."

"Then we have no ship's AI?" Tanis asked, unable to feel any other AI presences on the ship over the Link.

"I'm operating as the ship's AI, too," Ylonda replied with a smile. "I have real-time, simultaneous linkage with my embedded ship-nodes."

"You don't have the wireless interface for that amount of bandwidth—does that mean Earnest finally figured out the fidelity and bandwidth issues with quantum entanglement?" Saanvi eagerly asked from the pilot's seat where she had settled.

Ylonda nodded. "He has; though I don't know how you learned he was working on that."

"You're not the only one who knows about special projects," Saanvi said with a smug grin. "Earnest asked for my advice with some problems he was facing when he came over for dinner a month ago."

"OK, folks," Joe said from the XO's seat. "We can all crow about our part in the advent of galaxy-wide, instantaneous communication later. Right now, we still have to get in range of Elena's pinnace to have a little chat."

Tanis looked around for an open console. Cary had taken weapons, so she sat at an auxiliary monitoring console. The sight of her two girls taking their places on yet another cruiser's bridge filled her with pride once more. Someone was probably mumbling about nepotism somewhere, but this was just a simple interception of a friendly ship deep in the system, and her girls were handy.

Safe as houses.

<*Why didn't you tell me that Earnest had figured out the throughput issues with quantum entanglement?*> Tanis asked Bob.

<*I can't steal everyone's fun,*> Bob replied. <*I knew he would solve it—I had predicted he would manage it a bit sooner than he did, though.*>

<*Oh yeah?*> Tanis asked. <*How far off was your prediction?*>

<*Three minutes,*> Bob responded with a smug tone.

<*Show-off,*> Tanis laughed. <*What is the range?*>

<*The volume of particles necessary for long-range, high-fidelity communication is still a limiting factor. Ylonda has redundancies to handle a quantum synchronizing failure, and potential corruption issues from data seepage with other universes,*> Bob replied. <*Her range off-ship is limited to only one light year, at present.*>

<*I won't even pretend to understand why,*> Tanis replied.

<*It's really very simple,*> the AI explained. <*There are two issues. The first is the resonance in the vacuum energy of the universe. Space-time isn't flat, even for quantum interactions. To manage fidelity over longer ranges, the vibrations must be increased in amplitude, and that heats up the rubidium atoms. Once that happens, the quantum entanglement is broken.*>

<*Huh…*> Tanis replied. <*That does make sense.*>

"Ensign Cary, do we have station approval to release our moorings?" Ylonda asked.

"Aye, Captain, we have approval."

"Very well. Cast off our moorings, let's take her out."

Tanis shared a smile with Joe as they settled back and watched their daughters fly their second cruiser that day.

Once the boards showed green for a successful mooring release, Saanvi targeted the grav pylons mounted to the cradle, and began to push the ship out and into its lane. Ylonda offered a few words of guidance, but otherwise, let the two girls manage the ship's departure.

Tanis flipped the main holodisplay to show the *Hellespont's* bow view, gazing at the dozens of cruisers they were sliding past. It was a fleet any commander would be honored to command. It was the fleet that would guarantee their safety from whatever schemes the Transcend, and any others, would, launch against them.

"Approaching the tunnel, Captain," Cary said aloud. "We have clearance to enter the shaft."

"Thank you, Ensign," Ylonda replied. "Enable our active stealth systems as soon as we enter the tunnel. The outer shield won't deactivate until station control has verified we are undetectable."

"Yes, Captain," Cary replied.

"General," Ylonda turned to Tanis. "I assume you want to scoop up the pinnace while in stealth?"

Tanis nodded. "I do. We have to assume that the prying eyes out past our heliopause will see Elena's ship disappear, but not for five or six months. By then, I imagine whatever is going to happen will be long over."

Over the next few minutes, the ship slipped into the exit shaft, and Jim's holo presence appeared beside Cary. Tanis watched with a mixture of pride and interest as he went over the systems with her that she would need to test for full stealth confirmation with station control.

The *Hellespont* already possessed the new systems that the *Andromeda* was being refitted for. The ship would still be visible to keen optics at close range, but its ability to warp energy around its hull with minimal distortion was now at least on par with the Transcend cruisers they knew lurked around the edges of New Canaan.

Very soon, they would see how well the upgrades worked up close.

"ETA to interception?" Tanis asked.

"Three days and twenty hours," Ylonda replied.

"Well, then," Tanis said as she rose and stretched. "I don't know about the rest of you—Captain Ylonda excluded, of course—but I'm starving. Who could use a BLT?"

A WARNING

STELLAR DATE: 02.23.8948 (Adjusted Years)
LOCATION: ISS *Hellespont*
REGION: Stellar Space near Roma, 6th Planet in the New Canaan System

"Shit!" Elena swore as she walked down the pinnace's ramp. "Here I thought with a Transcend ship, not some Inner Stars clunker, that I would spot you guys sneaking up on me."

Tanis smiled and shook the woman's hand. "We've been working on some upgrades over the last few years."

"As I can see," Elena replied. "I managed to get a peek at this ship when you scooped me in; if I'm not mistaken, this is a new class of ship we've not seen before."

Tanis shrugged in response. "I'm not sure what your eyes out there have and have not seen. It takes half a year or more for news to get out to Isyra and her fleet."

Elena laughed ruefully. "I wish we weren't doing that. Talk about a self-fulfilling prophecy. Want a conflict? Just interdict a world and pile on a fleet or two; stir it up, and see what happens."

<*It seems that Elena's warcraft and yours differ,*> Angela said. <*You come from the same 'constant overwhelming force' school of thought that the Transcend seems to employ.*>

<*I distinctly recall being outnumbered or outgunned at almost every engagement over the last few hundred years. For once, I'd like to go into things with the upper hand.*>

<*Pipe dream,*> Angela replied.

Tanis led Elena across the docking bay toward an awaiting maglev car. "What is so important that you jumped so deep insystem? You never know what you can hit, doing something like that."

"Core-devils, don't remind me," Elena shook her head. "Airtha is gaining on The Cradle at a good clip right now. It makes for some seriously high delta-*v* on entry."

"And yet, you didn't rotate and brake after you came through," Tanis prompted.

"Yes, I'm trying not to draw any extra attention from Isyra and her fleet," Elena nodded as they got in the train car.

Four Marines wearing powered armor followed them in, and occupied the four corners of the car. Tanis hadn't even realized a platoon was on the ship until Ylonda sent a fireteam down with her to the dock.

<*You're getting rusty,*> Angela chided.

"But why bother?" Tanis asked, ignoring Angela's remark. "When they do see your jump, I'm sure whatever you've come to tell me will be old news."

"That's the thing, isn't it…" Elena said. "How sure are you that they don't have ships inside your star's heliosphere?"

Tanis leaned back in her seat and shrugged. "One-hundred percent? No. But, I'm damn close to that level of certainty. We can't see their ships all the time, but we have been able to pick them out and count them over the years. Unless she has a second class of ship that we can't see…"

Tanis let the statement hang and her right eyebrow rose.

"Pumping me for intel, Governor? Hell…I'm practically committing treason by being here."

The maglev stopped and Tanis rose from her seat and Elena followed. They walked through a short corridor to a crew lounge on the ship's starboard side. It wasn't luxurious, but it was serviceable and private.

Tanis signaled a servitor to bring them drinks—remembering what Elena had preferred from her brief visit on the *Intrepid* eighteen years earlier.

"Why don't you start by telling me what Sera sent you to say—though, I think I can guess," Tanis asked.

"Not a lot of options, are there?" Elena said with a nod before sipping her drink. "Things are heating up between us and the Orion Guard. They've allied with the AST and attacked Ascella."

"What?" Tanis sat up straight. "Attacked how?"

"With a massive fleet—thousands of ships. Only…they were just empty hulls. It was a feint."

"And it forced you to show your hand. Now the AST knows about the Transcend," Tanis leaned back and shook her head.

Elena nodded. "So far, the knowledge has not leaked to the general populace; but it will soon enough."

"Stars, and I thought we'd have another decade or two before Tomlinson came knocking on our door," Tanis said with a long sigh. "How much time do we have before he gets here?"

"I don't know. Sera has…worked her way into his inner circle, but he's grown suspicious of her—for reasons she hasn't been able to discern," Elena supplied.

Tanis considered what she would do in Tomlinson's stead. It would depend on the threat he faced.

"How did General Greer defeat the AST fleet?" she asked. "I assume from your wording that he *did* win."

"He did…" Elena paused and Tanis wondered what had happened. "Oh, stars," Elena shrugged before continuing. "You'll find out eventually. They sent antimatter warheads through the jump-gates into the AST ships. They obliterated them."

"Sweet black space, they used antimatter?" Tanis exclaimed. "That's still a war crime, isn't it?"

Elena nodded. "Yeah, even for us. I have no idea why Sera suggested it…"

"Sera what?!" Tanis almost yelled. "They must have contingencies for an attack on a watchpoint that don't involve detonating antimatter. Once you start doing that…"

"You're preaching to the choir, here," Elena said with her hands raised. "I said as much to Sera. She really has no idea why she suggested using antimatter—well, she has *some* idea. The alternative on the table was to blow the stars, and Helen suggested sending the warheads instead."

"Blowing the stars…" Tanis shook her head. "You guys don't do things by halves, do you?"

"No," Elena laughed ruefully. "Not so much."

"So, AST has joined with the Orion Guard, war is about to explode across human space, the President of the Transcend Interstellar Alliance is probably going to come here in person to demand our tech to give him an edge, and he's going to do it with an overwhelming show of force intended to cow us into submission. Don't know when, but probably in a few months at most," Tanis said while ticking items off her fingers. "That sound about right?"

"Yup, that about sums it up," Elena nodded.

"Well, you're stuck here 'til this goes down. Care to have dinner with Joe and my two girls?"

"You seem…unfazed by this," Elena said with a frown.

"Elena, I've been at this for some time, and honestly, when it comes to war machines, even the Transcend doesn't build 'em like they used to. Back in Sol, the TSF had a million warships for just one system. I'm aiming to replicate that number."

Elena spit out her drink. "You have a million warships?"

Tanis shook her head and laughed. "No, not quite so many, but by the time your president arrives, he'll meet over ten thousand ships of this classification alone."

Elena wiped her mouth and rose from the table while shaking her head. "Fuck, Tanis, what are you planning to do?"

"Maintain New Canaan's independence," she replied. "And before you ask, at whatever cost is necessary."

"Tanis," Elena said levelly. "You could join with the Transcend, give them your pico—or better yet, give it to everyone—it would stop this war from happening."

"No," Tanis replied. "It would escalate it. The Transcend, Inner Stars, Orion Guard…they're on the edge of going nova. All we ever wanted was to leave all of humanity's petty infighting behind, but we can't get away from it. Our technology has already proven to be too much of a catalyst. I won't escalate things further."

<*You may not have a choice,*> Angela commented.

<*I know,*> Tanis replied. <*What does Bob think will happen? Will there be war?*>

<*He won't say,*> Angela replied. <*I don't know if he can—what with you being involved.*>

Tanis shook her head and pushed the thoughts from her mind. For now, she was going to enjoy what would probably be the last uninterrupted meal with her family for some time.

TRUTH

STELLAR DATE: 02.23.8948 (Adjusted Years)
LOCATION: ISS *Hellespont*
REGION: Stellar Space near Roma, 6th Planet in the New Canaan System

"Your daughters are lovely," Elena said after the meal was done, and the two girls had left for a shift on the bridge.

"They're the best thing we made here at New Canaan," Joe said with a warm smile.

"And Saanvi…I remember you inquiring about her when you found her ship," Elena said. "I'm glad you gave her a good home."

"You heard about that, did you?" Tanis asked. "I didn't think that would be such big news in the Transcend."

Elena looked down at her glass of wine and frowned. "Well, I run operations for The Hand now—it came across my desk."

Joe chuckled. "Probably a bit more like '*ran*', now, wouldn't you say?"

Elena looked up and gave a wan smile. "I suppose you're right. Makes this little jaunt worth it, then. I hated that job."

There was a brief lull in conversation, and Tanis leaned forward. She was having trouble finding the right words for the question she had. She almost feared the answer too much to ask.

<*What of* Sabrina?> Angela queried for her. <*We would have expected them back—or at least word—by now.*>

Elena's face grew clouded. "I'm afraid I don't have good news there."

The blood rushed from Tanis's face and she reached for Joe's hand. "Tell it."

"One of our agents—one that Sera and I trust implicitly—made contact with them about thirteen years ago. They were a bit hard to find, but we delivered New Canaan's coordinates. They told the agent that they were still hunting their quarry," Elena said in a somber tone.

"That doesn't sound so bad—though thirteen years is a long time to hear nothing," Joe said with a frown. "What happened next?"

"We *think* that they may have finally found Finaeus in the Ikoden System. There was a shoot-out—not the first one they were involved in, from what we've learned—except this one was with us."

"With you?" Tanis leaned forward.

"What do you mean?" Joe asked at the same time.

Elena's eyes darted between the pair and she raised her hands defensively. "Well, The Hand has been searching for Finaeus for some time; agents who were operating under the president's direction. They discovered that Jessica was on *Sabrina,* and that they had a good lead. They followed *Sabrina* to Ikoden, and when they found Finaeus, they attacked."

"Go on," Tanis said tonelessly.

"You can relax…no one from *Sabrina* was killed. Though they got all our agents; only two lived, but they ended up taking their own lives to avoid interrogation. The thing is…after they left Ikoden, they just disappeared. There hasn't been a sighting of them in eleven years."

Tanis covered her eyes with her forearm.

"Elena, that's not as bad as you made it out to be, they're probably just on their way here now," Joe said.

"Ikoden's not that far away—it should have been only four, maybe five years max," Elena replied. "Sera's really worried. She has agents scouring the Inner Stars for *Sabrina.*"

Tanis looked to Joe and saw both worry and compassion in his eyes. They both missed Jessica terribly, and Tanis had grown close to the crew of *Sabrina* during their months together.

Knowing that Jessica was out there somewhere, lost in the Inner Stars—and that she had this crisis with the Transcend bearing down on her, keeping her from going in search of her friend—hit her harder than she expected.

She had never balked at the mantle of responsibility she wore, not enough to truly resent it. But now, she wished she could throw it aside and go find her friend.

<*When this is over, I'm going to find her,*> Tanis said.

<*And I'll go with you,*> Joe replied. <*We'll find them together.*>

Elena's eyes darted between the pair. "I'm really sorry. I wish I had better news. I mean…we haven't found any evidence that they were attacked or taken, either…"

"It's OK," Tanis said finally. "Whatever happened, it's not your fault…"

"Either way, I'm still sorry," Elena said softly. "I see on the net that there are quarters for me. I'll head there…leave you two alone."

Tanis nodded absently and Elena left the room.

She didn't know if she wanted to scream or cry, and Joe wrapped his arms around her. Wordlessly, they held one another, and then she did cry, for fear that she had lost Jessica forever.

NEGOTIATIONS

STELLAR DATE: 03.27.8948 (Adjusted Years)
LOCATION: TSS *Galadrial*
REGION: Stellar Space near Roma, 6th Planet in the New Canaan System

The *Galadrial* exited the wormhole into normal space, and Sera stripped the data streams from the Transcend ships that had jumped ahead.

She didn't need to, of course—there were officers running scan and comm—but she was looking for any information about Elena, and whether or not she was OK.

"New Canaan," her father announced at her side. "The *Intrepid*'s reward for their long struggle."

She noted how he tried to sound magnanimous, but she could tell that he felt the reward was too great for what the Transcend had received—even though she had since learned that it was her father who ensured that the *Intrepid* was not required to give over their picotech or stasis shields.

"Also, what they were due, being a GSS ship," Sera added.

Her father cast her a hard stare. "The Generation Ship Service is long gone. The Inner Stars gave up on peaceful colonization, and look at what it has wrought. It is this system's duty to ensure that we can preserve the Transcend, and our mission."

Sera didn't respond. Getting into an argument with her father about the purpose of the Transcend on the bridge of his flagship would not be wise. Instead, she surveyed the Transcend fleet arrayed around them.

It consisted of over a thousand cruisers, and several hundred more destroyers and support vessels. From what Admiral Isyra had observed, Tanis had no more than fifty warships, and they appeared to be spread across the system on patrols.

A pair were nearby, only two AU distant; though any response from those ships was still nearly an hour away.

<*Why doesn't she have more ships?*> Sera asked Helen. <*I expected Isyra to be wrong, but our scans don't even show the number she had identified.*>

<*Maybe Tanis knows that a show of force will be met with a greater show of force,*> Helen replied. <*Perhaps Tanis does not want a war.*>

<*I'll agree with you there. She's not a warmonger, but she's one hell of a protective mother when it comes to her ship and her people. Sure, fifty warships is probably an aggressive buildup for a regular colony world that is only fifteen years old, but for Tanis...?*>

"Send the message," Sera's father prompted. "Let their governor know that we need to talk about the state of the human sphere, and her duty to help us protect it."

"I've already sent it," Sera replied. "We may have to wait a day for the response."

President Tomlinson nodded. "Very well. Admiral Greer, as you've suggested, move the fleet to the seventh planet—Roma, I believe the locals have named it. I see that they have a small outpost on one of its moons. We'll propose it as a meeting place."

The world was just over six AU distant, and the fleet began a slow acceleration toward it, the newly constructed jump-gate boosting with them under its own power.

"Yes, President," Greer replied and issued the command over the fleet net.

Sera saw Greer glance at the gate on the holotank and frown. She shared his sentiment. Assembling the gate the moment they entered the system put them at a tactical disadvantage. The gate was large, cumbersome, and would be difficult to protect. It also told the sailors and soldiers in the fleet that the president would not stay with them to the end, if it came to that. He would be on the first ship jumping out.

That message was further re-enforced by the fact that Isyra had two gates beyond the heliosphere, in interstellar space. Exit routes already existed, and were in secure locations. If it had been up to her—and she assumed Greer, as well—they wouldn't have brought a jump-gate at all.

Her misgivings about the jump-gate aside, she was glad that Greer was with them. He had come to Airtha ready to be censured, or worse, for the outcome in Ascella; but instead, her father had promoted him to admiral of the 21st Fleet.

Greer had treated with Tanis fairly at Ascella, and she suspected that their existing relationship contributed to her father's decision to bring him along.

Sera turned and took a seat at a console, back to scanning the local comm traffic for any word of Elena. It was going to be a long wait, and she needed to while away the time somehow.

*****

Sera arrived on the *Galadriel's* bridge with coffee in hand at just the same moment that the ship's captain, a woman named Viska, announced that they had reached the L1 point between Roma and its largest moon—a nearly featureless rock named Normandy.

Well, featureless except for the kilometer-high tower standing off its surface.

The structure sat on what would be the moon's equator—if it were not tidally locked to Roma—and pointed directly at the Jovian planet. It seemed to serve no purpose that the fleet's analysts had yet discerned, but Sera knew that it would not be here without cause.

"How is it that Isyra didn't spot this thing?" Admiral Greer muttered as he stared at the structure.

"I'll admit, I'm not too excited about it pointing at us," Sera added. "Though, it seems to have no significant energy output. The top appears to be some sort of observation deck."

"It's a good sign," her father said. "That is a structure built by a people who are settling in. They will give us what we want to maintain their safety here."

"I wish I shared your optimism," Greer replied, and Sera saw him share a look with Viska.

Sera noted that her father saw the look, as well. "You mistake optimism for raw determination, Admiral. We will get what we need from these colonists because we must. Tanis Richards will give it to us because she will also see that we must have it."

"Ship coming out of the jovian planet," the scan officer announced, and she flipped the main holo to show a close-up view of Roma's surface.

An object stirred beneath the surface, brushing the raging storms aside, unperturbed by their fury. Fleet analysis added data to the object, giving it a width of ten kilometers and at least thirty-five long.

"It's the *Intrepid,*" Sera breathed. "So that's where they hid it."

A minute later, the ship crested the cloud cover and scan updated with readings from the unobstructed vessel. More than one person on the bridge audibly gasped at the firepower on display.

"Its beacon tags it as the *I2* now. Where did they refit that vessel?" Greer asked. "Isyra's data never showed it at any shipyard."

"It would seem they have shipyards that Isyra didn't find," Sera said with a shake of her head. "Though, I have no idea where they put them. Surely not within the jovian planets; that's not especially practical."

"Neither is that ship," Captain Viska replied. "On its own like that, it's just a massive target."

"A massive target with a tenth the firepower of this fleet, and stasis shields, and don't forget the picobombs," Sera added.

Greer addressed the commanders and captains over the fleetnet. <*They would not put that ship out here alone. There are either stealth ships we can't see, or there are more vessels below the clouds. I want pattern delta-seven—*>

<*Belay that,*> the president ordered. <*Let's talk with them before we prepare for battle.*>

Greer's face reddened, but he sent the order to stand down.

"I'm counting on your friendship for something, Sera," her father said.

"Me too," Sera muttered.

"Inbound communication from the *I2*," the comm officer announced.

"Put it up," the president replied.

As Sera expected, it was Tanis who appeared before them. She was wearing her ISF uniform—interesting that they kept that name for their space force—with five stars now adorning her collar. General and Governor, it sent a message of control and power. If Sera didn't know that Tanis craved neither—well, not the power, at least—she would have wondered if the woman before them had the makings of a dictator.

<*I put her in this position,*> Sera sighed. <*Everything happening right now started when I opened that crate in* Sabrina's *hold.*>

<*No, dear, it started the moment that Earnest Redding created reliable picotech, and they laid the hull for that ship. If anything, that clever inventor started us all down this path,*> Helen replied.

"Welcome to New Canaan," Tanis said with a genuine smile.

Sera couldn't help but notice that she appeared perfectly at ease. That didn't mean she was; Tanis could hide her true intentions and feelings with the best of them.

"We're going to have to establish a clear entry point for you," Tanis continued. "A lot of Transcend ships seem to pop into our interdicted system."

President Tomlinson frowned. "Other than that derelict trader, we're the first—or we should be."

"I was referring to the volume of ships you brought, not the frequency," Tanis said with a smile.

Sera secretly thanked her friend for the message. Elena had arrived and was safe. That was the best news she had received in weeks.

"Very well, then," her father said with a frown, and Sera knew that he was not fully convinced by Tanis's explanation.

"To what do we owe the pleasure of your company?" Tanis asked. "I assume you did not come with all these ships just for a state visit."

"I did not," the president replied. "We need to speak, you and I. The human sphere is in turmoil, and you are in a unique position to help preserve our future."

Tanis raised a hand to her chin and appeared to ponder the president's words. "Very well. I hope you understand, based on prior encounters, I'm unwilling to come to your ship, and you may not wish to come to mine. However, we are near a facility we recently completed on the moon, Normandy. Would you care to meet there?"

"It seems auspicious that it is there, waiting for us," the president said with a nod. "Very well. Shall we meet there in five of your local system hours?"

"That will work perfectly," Tanis replied. "We'll send docking instructions."

The holo image disappeared and her father shook his head.

"She is far too calm. Even with what we know of her, there should be some anger over our presence—or concern, at the very least," he said.

"The *I2* is a testament to her demeanor," the Admiral said with a deep frown. "That is one hell of a ship."

Secretary Adrienne, who was also along for the negotiations, though Sera wished he weren't, nodded. "She has expected this, and has been preparing. I urge you to reconsider meeting with her on her ground."

The president dismissed their concerns with a wave of his hand; something she had seen her father do all too often. If she were in command, Sera knew she would listen to her advisors more than he did.

"We have no choice. We came here to meet with her, and so we shall meet. My hope has always been to strike a deal without conflict. Her level of preparation notwithstanding, it can still happen."

Sera wasn't certain if her father was overestimating his abilities as a negotiator, or underestimating Tanis's. Still, she had to admit her father was right. The Transcend did need the stasis tech, if they were to weather the coming war. Already, the AST was drawing together its allies and forces to mount a major assault. On their own, they would not be a significant threat; but with Orion jump-gates, they could jump deep within the Transcend and wreak havoc.

The AST would create opportunities that the Orion Guard would press to their advantage, and total war would ensue.

* * * * *

At the allotted time, the Transcend pinnace slipped through the ES shielding, and settled on a pad on the observation tower. Sera found it quaint that, although they had grav tech and stasis shielding, the colonists still used ES shields for atmospheric containment.

She walked down the ramp beside her father, with Adrienne and General Greer following behind. A dozen of her father's security personnel accompanied them, along with several aides.

Sera didn't bring her own security, as two of her father's guards were Hand agents she had slipped into the Presidential Guard years ago. She was almost certain they would protect her life over her father's.

At the tower's entrance, Admiral Sanderson stood with several ISF Marines. Sera was glad to see that he was still actively serving. He had spoken about retiring on several occasions during the journey to Ascella, but the military was all he knew. She bet that Tanis only had to ask once for him to stay on.

"President Tomlinson," Sanderson said as they approached and offered his hand, which her father shook. "Thank you for coming to meet with us here. I think you'll enjoy the facility; it's the first step in this moon's restructuring."

"Thank you for having us," her father replied. "You've piqued my curiosity. What are you restructuring this moon into?"

"I'm not up on all the details," Sanderson replied, "but I'm told it's going to become some sort of space-sports facility. Planet diving into the jovian, racing in the canyons below; it has a molten core, so I believe there will also be some cavern racing beneath the crust—serious adrenaline stuff."

Sera laughed. "And here I thought the observation platform was just for taking in the view of Roma up there."

"Well," Sanderson nodded conspiratorially, "if it were up to me, that's all I'd want, too, but the younger generation...well, they hear all the tales of our journey and some think things are a bit boring here, so we're keeping it interesting."

"Diving from here into Roma certainly would be interesting," Adrienne commented. "I imagine they'll need to be shot toward the planet first, right?"

Sanderson nodded. "That's my understanding. My daughter is more than eager to be here when that finally opens up."

"A daughter!" Sera exclaimed. "I distinctly recall you saying that you were too old for more children."

"Yes, well, when you meet the right woman..." Sanderson replied as he ushered them onto a large lift platform.

Sera looked up and saw that the lift had no ceiling; it would rise up directly into the floor of the observation platform. If she squinted, she could see right through the observation platform's clear ceiling and into space.

Once all the guards and aides were aboard, the lift began to ascend, and Sanderson continued. "I met Veronica at the landfall party, of all places. She was one of the colonists to win the lottery and was on the second shuttle down. We hit it off, and the rest, including our dear Petra and her two brothers, is history."

"I'm glad to hear that your colony is filled with children's hopes and dreams," the president chimed in. "It's one of the most rewarding things in the galaxy—to see your own grow and take up their mantles."

Sera saw Sanderson cast a curious look at the president before replying. "Well, not too many heavy mantles around here. Just our little attempt at a better life."

"Yet, there is your *I2*, as you call it. Is that a part of your better life?" Secretary Adrienne asked.

"That's just the thing," Sanderson replied with a raised eyebrow. "When you're in our position, someone is always out to cash in on your success."

The response killed the conversation, and the lift climbed the rest of the distance in silence. Sera wanted to reach out and hit Adrienne. Here she was, breaking the ice and re-establishing her relationship with the admiral, and her father's trusted advisor had to screw it up.

She glanced at Admiral Sanderson, and couldn't tell by his implacable gaze whether he was upset by Adrienne's comment or not. The lift reached the observation deck before she had time to consider Adrienne's verbal sabotage further.

It was a wide space, several hundred meters across, with small alcoves filled with artful seating arrangements and long tables for larger gatherings. Several bars also dotted the area; servitors at the ready to provide customers with whatever they wished.

Above, a single crystal dome stretched over the circular space, providing a stunning view of Roma's red and purple colored bands. Even without leveraging her augmented vision, Sera could see the TSF fleet at the L1 point between Normandy and Roma. Closer, having circled around the Transcend ships, lay the *I2*—its features easily discernible from where it orbited sixty kilometers above the observation deck.

Other than a few additional ISF Marines, the observation platform was empty, and Admiral Sanderson led them to a nearby table that was nestled between two rows of hedges.

"Very tasteful," President Tomlinson commented, as he sat on one side of the table and gestured for a servitor to come and pour him a glass of water. "I especially like how the dome above is a single piece. I can't make out any seams at all."

Sanderson nodded. "Yes, that is pretty impressive. My daughter told me that it was grown in place right here, so it didn't have to be transported."

"Interesting. I may have to get something similar for my office."

"On Airtha, I assume," Tanis's voice came from the far side of the hedge before she strode into view. "We recovered visuals of your capital from that derelict freighter. It must be something to behold."

"It is," Tomlinson nodded. "Perhaps someday, after we iron out some of these issues, you can come and see it for yourself."

"I would like that," Tanis replied as she sat across the table from the Transcend delegation.

Sera smiled and nodded to Joe, who sat to Tanis's right, while Admiral Sanderson was on her left. Terrance Enfield and Amanda, one of their AI's avatars, were the last to sit at the table.

"Admiral Sanderson you've met, and Sera knows my husband, Admiral Evans. I would also like to introduce Amanda, who represents our AI contingent, along with Angela who is with me. Last, but not least, is Terrance Enfield, our original colony sponsor."

Greetings were exchanged around the table, and while they were occurring, Tanis reached across the table and clasped Sera's hand.

"I'm glad you are well. I honestly did not expect it to be so long before we met again."

Sera nodded. "Me either. It would seem that both of us have taken on more responsibility than we thought. Are those chairs on a porch still in our future?"

Tanis chuckled. "I have the porch and the chairs—though I don't use them as much as I'd like. Perhaps you can come sit in them for a bit before you go."

Sera felt a prompt in her mind and realized that Tanis had granted her access to a non-public net.

<Elena told me, Director of The Hand! I'm surprised you'd take such a position,> Tanis said.

<You know what they say about your enemies,> Sera replied. *<I was thrust into it, to be honest, but I saw it as an opportunity to do some good—though, now, I'm mostly consumed with positioning Inner Stars governments to support us in the coming war.>*

<So, you have no doubt that war is upon us?> Tanis asked.

<Surely Elena told you. The AST attacked a watchpoint—they were certainly prompted by the Orion Guard. How is she? I hope you've treated her well. I take it that Sabrina *has not returned with Finaeus, yet?>*

Sera's tone was eager, and Tanis knew that her friend was hopeful that the ship had flown directly to New Canaan.

<Elena is well, she told us about Sabrina*... it has not arrived. Let's chat more about this later.>*

Sera realized her father was speaking in the middle of some long, rambling speech about how the Transcend and the colonists of New Canaan shared mutual goals that bound them together, and how they were really one people, colony creators and colonizers.

Tanis appeared to be listening intently, despite the fact that they had just carried on a conversation. If she knew the woman at all, she was probably also talking to Angela, as well.

<*She is impressive,*> Helen commented. <*Almost too much so. Does it never concern you that she's so deeply entwined with her AI? We've been together for only forty years; near the limit of how long our minds can co-exist. But Tanis? She's been with Angela for centuries.*>

<*I've thought about it, yeah. They should have fully merged long ago, but they haven't. It's obvious when you talk to them both,*> Sera replied, curious as to why Helen was bringing this up now. <*What of it?*>

<*It just seemed noteworthy that they don't appear to have grown more intertwined since we last saw them. I would have expected some change. We've changed a lot since then,*> Helen commented, and Sera noted that her AI sounded almost indifferent. If that were the case, why would she bring it up at all?

"... and I agree that we have more in common with each other than we do with many of the Inner Stars worlds and nations," Tanis was saying as Sera shifted her attention back to the audible conversation. "But that's not why you came here. Let's just get to it, shall we, President Tomlinson? You want access to our picotech and stasis shields. That's it, plain and simple. It's the reason why we're an interdicted system, and it's the reason we're here today."

Sera felt a smile cross her lips and covered her mouth to hide it. It was not often anyone spoke to her father like he was an equal. It was refreshing to hear.

* * * * *

<*Gah, he's just so wordy; why does it take him forever to say anything?*> Tanis asked Angela.

<*Beats me. You humans take too long to say pretty much everything. I stopped taking note of it centuries ago,*> Angela said with a feigned yawn.

<*Funny. OK, time to lay it out and see how he responds,*> she said to Angela and spoke her piece. <*There, let's see how he hedges around now.*>

Tanis saw Sera cover her mouth with her hand to hide her amusement and almost had to do the same—if only she weren't growing annoyed with Tomlinson's never-ending speech about nothing. The president, for his part, appeared nonplussed.

"In a nutshell, that is it, yes," he replied evenly. "But that does not provide the *why* behind why I've come here to ask for your help. I know you hold dear the same ideals we do—a free humanity, able to spread across the stars and make our own destinies. That is something that the Orion Guard does not want, and they'll corrupt the Inner Stars and undo all our work there."

Tanis watched the president's grey eyes as he spoke. She could not detect any lie in them—the man either believed what he said, or was a consummate liar. However, it was possible that the two options were not mutually exclusive.

"From what I understand, you and the Guard are playing a game with the Inner Stars: you gently uplifting, while they do...what? Ignore? Exploit? In the end, you both hide the facts from them. You've both been playing this game for millennia. What's changed now?"

Tanis knew what had changed; she just wanted to hear Tomlinson say it, to justify his need by placing the blame on her. It would solidify her opinion of the man.

"I don't expect that you would understand all of the nuances at play," Tomlinson said after a brief pause. "Sometimes, I think that I only have the barest grasp myself. However, it was inevitable that something would happen to tip the balance that has existed for so long. It just so happens that it was you. If by some chance, you had slipped out of Kapteyn's Streamer and evaded notice, this eventuality would still have come to pass."

He stopped again and took a sip of the drink before him before continuing. "I can see how, from your perspective, there would be little difference between us and the Guard. In fact, with a few subtle twists, they could be the right side, and we the wrong. But know this: they split from us in anger, in fear, and have been the aggressors for these last few thousand years. They have destroyed entire worlds along the front—terraformed worlds that the FGT spent centuries creating. Millions of Transcend citizens have died at their hands."

"And what of the proxy nations you have within the Inner Stars?" Tanis asked. "They do fight wars, sometimes on your behalf."

"It is true we have responded in kind; but only in an attempt to maintain a balance. But now, they control the Pleiades, and have turned the Hegemony of Worlds to their cause. If we do not gain your technology, we will ultimately lose this conflict."

The President of the Transcend Interstellar Alliance lowered his voice as he spoke, while continuing to hold Tanis's eyes. He paused again and glanced around the room before returning his gaze to her. "And then, when that happens, it will not be myself and Sera here before you, but an Orion Guard fleet—burning your worlds, and demanding your surrender."

As he had spoken, Tanis recalled what she had been told of Saanvi's family—of how they had settled a world closer to the front, which had been destroyed by the Orion Guard.

She looked to Sera and saw that her friend, a woman she had spent many months with on *Sabrina,* and later the *Intrepid,* was nodding in agreement, affirming her father's words.

Given Sera's dislike for her father, Tanis had to believe that he was sincere.

"Things have grown more dire over recent months," Sera added. "The Orion Guard led the AST to Ascella and attacked the watchpoint with a massive fleet. The Transcend Space Force was victorious in the end, but you know what this means."

Tanis nodded. "That Orion fleet you spoke of could be here sooner rather than later."

"Now do you believe us? Do you understand our sense of urgency?" the Transcend's president asked. "I had hoped to have more time—to let you settle in, to establish a real friendship between our peoples. But that timetable has been accelerated."

Tanis steepled her fingers and stared over them at President Tomlinson, Sera, and the president's entourage.

<*It's a lot to consider,*> she said to the assembled representatives on her side of the table.

<*He lies like a rug, but he has a number of good points,*> Admiral Sanderson said.

<*Even if he's in the wrong, simple galactic geography makes them more appropriate allies than the Guard,*> Terrance added.

<*Bob would like to see whatever data they have on the Guard's movements to support their statements,*> Amanda said. <*Personally, I can't believe that Sera is his daughter. She's nothing*

like him.>

<*I can see it,*> Tanis replied. <*It's in their surety.*>

<*That might be a mirror you're looking at, then,*> Angela said privately with a chuckle.

"You make a convincing argument," Tanis said aloud. "On the face of it, I believe you, and agree with your need. However, we need to discuss this. Also, any details you have on these advances by the Guard, and their assault on Ascella, would help us in our decision-making."

"Of course," President Tomlinson said and nodded to Sera, who slid a data crystal across the table.

Tanis took the data crystal and passed it to Amanda before rising.

"Let's adjourn for the day. You've given us a lot to think over. We'll review this data and reconvene at the same time tomorrow."

The Transcend contingent rose with their president, who nodded in agreement.

"That sounds excellent. I must say that I am pleased with how receptive you've been. Not everyone in your position would be so understanding," President Tomlinson said with a warm smile. "I feel like tomorrow we'll come to an agreement that will benefit us both, and establish a peace for all humanity."

"That is something I would like very much," Tanis replied.

They walked around the table to shake hands once more, and the rest of their contingents followed suit. As President Tomlinson began to walk away, Tanis called out.

"Sera, a moment," Tanis called after her friend.

Sera touched her father's hand, and Tanis heard her say, "Wait for me in the shuttle."

The president nodded, and Sera returned to the table.

"Walk with me," Tanis said and placed a hand on Sera's shoulder to guide her toward the edge of the viewing platform.

"You seem to think that we should trade the tech—something that you didn't believe to be the correct course of action when last we spoke," Tanis said once they were alone.

Sera nodded. "That's true, but things have changed. The attack on Ascella—"

"Which you used antimatter weapons to defeat," Tanis interjected.

"Heard about that, did you?" Sera asked with a sigh. "I guess I…I don't know why I suggested that. It seemed like a good idea, but once the words left my mouth, I began to regret them more with each passing moment."

"In the end, they were empty hulls," Tanis replied. "Though, still a war crime."

Sera sighed and nodded. "Stars, I wish they had found Finaeus by now. He would know what to do. Now we may have lost them all…"

Tanis nodded somberly. "Elena said you managed to find them, and gave them our coordinates here some years ago. I'm holding out hope that they ran into trouble but are still on their way—you haven't found any evidence to the contrary, have you?"

Sera shook her head. "Not yet, no. Nothing either way."

"I do wish Jessica were here," Tanis sighed. "For someone who was never supposed to be on this mission, she certainly has become indispensable."

"I know what you mean," Sera replied as they reached the edge of the platform and gazed out on the moon below. "Were you telling the truth before? Is Elena on the *I2*, and not here?"

"I was. I can't let her talk to you, or anyone else from the Transcend yet. She knows things I'm not ready to share," Tanis said the words as gently as she could, but she knew Sera would not take them well.

"What do you mean?" Sera locked eyes with her. "What is it that you can't tell me? I told you a lot—a treasonous amount—about the Transcend while we were on the *Intrepid*. What is it that you can't say now? Have you done something to Elena?"

"No!" Tanis replied emphatically. "Elena is fine. She just saw things that I can't have her share. And she's far more loyal to you than to me...and you..."

"You think I'm more loyal to my father?" Sera asked, her voice dripping with accusation. "I saved your life, you saved mine, and now you won't let me see my lover just because of your paranoia?"

"Sera—" Tanis began.

"No, Tanis, take your excuses and go fuck yourself with them. Tomorrow, when we come back to make a deal with you and whatever secrets you have, Elena better be here..."

"Or else?" Tanis asked, feeling rage rise in herself at Sera's irrational behavior. "Are you implying that I'm in the wrong, as I treat with you and your invading fleet?"

"You haven't seen an invading fleet, yet. You'll know when you do," Sera spat and turned on her heel, storming off in the direction of the lift.

<*That was...irrational of her,*> Angela commented.

<*It really was,*> Tanis replied. <*More than just a little. Something else is going on.*>

*****

Sera strode onto the pinnace and dropped into a seat, still fuming over her conversation with Tanis. That she should deny her even the sight of Elena, and hold back secrets...she stopped herself from that train of thought. The only thing that made it worse was, deep down, she knew Tanis was right.

She was the one on the side that was attempting to use intimidation to get their way; she had even sent Elena because of that—to warn Tanis. So why was she so upset about it now?

"What did she want to talk about?" her father said as he sat beside her. "It seems to have you upset."

"It's nothing; a personal matter between us from before I came back to Airtha," Sera replied.

"I hope you'd tell me if it were important to our mission here," her father said in what Sera had long since dubbed his *I'm serious, yet friendly, but cross me at your peril* tone.

Sera sighed. "To be honest, I don't know if it's important or not, she wouldn't let me see..."

Sera clamped her mouth shut and felt her face redden. She couldn't believe what she had almost said aloud. It was like she wasn't in control of herself anymore.

<*What are you doing?*> Helen asked. <*If I didn't know better, I'd think you were drunk!*>

"See what?" her father asked, peering at her intently, his eyes widening. "You sent someone to warn them! This is where Elena went; not some diplomatic mission back to Spica! It's why their new ship was waiting for us here...at the planet closest to the most obvious jump point."

Sera tried to formulate a response but stopped. Nothing she could think of would make things better. It didn't matter.

Her father stood and stared down at her. "There's no way that you could have masked a jump-gate destination—I would know if any ship jumped into an interdicted system!"

Rage was building in his voice, and his face reddened. "There's…no. Only Airtha could have hidden that jump destination from me..." he turned, looking pensive. Before Sera could reply, multiple pulse rifle blasts took her down.

DISSEMINATION

STELLAR DATE: 03.27.8948 (Adjusted Years)
LOCATION: Normandy Starjump Observation Tower
REGION: Normandy, Moon of Roma, 6th Planet in the New Canaan System

"OK, Mom, you were right; that was really boring," Cary said as Tanis and Joe joined their kids in a suite down the tower shaft.

"Yeah," Tanis sighed as she fell onto a sofa. "That Jeffrey Tomlinson sure can talk."

"And sure likes to hear it, too," Joe added as he joined Tanis.

"What were you and Sera talking about?" Saanvi asked. "It seemed intense."

"Mostly Elena," Tanis replied. "She wanted to see her, and I told her I couldn't allow it yet. She…she didn't handle that well. I thought I could get her to understand my side of it, but…now I fear I've lost a friend."

"But Mom," Cary exclaimed, "Sera and Elena are lovers! How could you keep them apart?"

Tanis gave her daughter a level stare. "Because lovers share secrets. They can't help it, and I can't have Sera know about our fleet yet. She seems…she's different somehow. It's as though she's bought into everything that she was so against when she left. I don't know where she stands anymore."

"She did send Elena," Joe said as he took a glass of water from a servitor. "That counts for something."

"It does," Tanis replied with a nod. "Just how much, I don't know anymore."

"Has Bob analyzed the data yet?" Saanvi asked. "Is it true that the Orion Guard has destroyed worlds?"

Tanis nodded slowly, wary of where the conversation could go. "Yes, and they've told us about those sorts of attacks before; there's more corroborative evidence this time—such as it is, coming from one source."

<*You've gone and done it,*> Angela said. <*Saanvi will know what that first time was.*>

Saanvi was a smart girl, and not just from the L2 augmentations both of her daughters had undergone over the years. Tanis knew that one day she would ask for the information about what had happened to her parents, and, with her verbal slip, today would be that day.

<*It never rains, it pours,*> Angela added. <*You ready for this? You're already emotionally drained.*>

<*She's our daughter, Angela. I have to be ready. It's my most important job in life.*>

Her AI sent her an affirming warmth, and Tanis steeled herself for the question. When it came, it was quiet, barely audible.

"Mom…how did my family die?"

Tanis took a deep breath. "They were on a world that was attacked by the Orion Guard. It was close to the front—though not so close that anyone thought there was a risk."

Saanvi's face fell and her shoulders slumped. "I always…I don't know what I thought—that maybe they were still out there somewhere…"

Tanis rose and pulled Saanvi into her arms, Joe and Cary not far behind. The family held each other as Saanvi began to cry—a cry that Tanis knew she had been saving for a long time. It lasted for a few minutes before Saanvi managed to stop and wipe the tears from her eyes.

She looked up at Tanis, and, with a voice far calmer than Tanis would have expected, said, "Mom, you have to join with the Transcend and stop the Guard. They can't keep destroying worlds!"

Tanis wanted to tell her that she couldn't base her decision on this one need for retribution that Saanvi now had—but that answer would drive her daughter away in rage and sadness. But Saanvi wouldn't be the only reason. Bob was certain that at least some of the accounts of planetary destruction by the Guard were true. If the *Transcend* had ever destroyed any worlds, Sera would have told her before—of that much she was certain.

<*You're going to have to ally with them. You know that, don't you?*> Angela said.

Tanis knew it, but she didn't want to accept it. <*Mother fucking arghhh—we had more peace at Victoria than we've had here at our own colony! We may as well have just stayed there and lived out our lives. The Sirians never came back—at least not for a long time. And when they did, we could have stopped them.*>

<*I love you dearly, Tanis, my otherself,*> Angela said quietly, <*but it's time you realize that you were never destined to have peace. You are here to make war.*>

Tanis felt a tear slip down her face as she looked into the inquiring eyes of her family.

"Yes, we will ally with the Transcend. Stars have mercy on our souls; we'll go to war."

<*Tanis, I know you're busy,*> Amanda's voice broke into her thoughts, <*but it's important. Sera's father has taken her—he's going to do something to her. She needs your help.*>

Tanis felt like she was being torn in two. First, Sera stormed off in a rage, and now she was in mortal danger and needed rescue?

<*What do we know?*> she asked, her mental tone far calmer than she expected.

<*One of her agents got a message to us. She was having an argument with her father about Elena—he realized that she's here—and he had Sera shot. Not lethally. He's got her in surgery now.*>

<*Get Elena down here now!*> Tanis ordered. <*I'll muster an assault force.*>

"I have to go," she said to her family. "Tomlinson has attacked Sera and is doing something to her, I have to go help her."

"I thought you just had a fight with her?" Cary asked with a frown. "Now you're going to assault the Transcend president's ship?"

"Yes, if it comes to that. I owe her my life, more than once over," Tanis said before locking eyes with Joe. "Take the girls to the *I2*, she's under your command now. Be ready."

Joe nodded solemnly. "Not how I finally wanted to get command of that beauty. Girls, grab whatever you need; we'll take the shuttle that's bringing Elena when it goes back up. You're going to the shipyard?" he directed the last to Tanis.

"Yes," she said with a nod. "There are a dozen stealth pinnaces down there that have passed their break-in flights, and a platoon of Marines just itching for a fight."

"What if it's a ruse?" Saanvi asked. "What if everything is fine, or if it's an Orion trick?"

"I've already directed Amanda to get in touch with Sera. If we're stonewalled, we'll know something is up. If our new allies are playing games with us—games like this—then we're better off without them."

"But Orion…" Saanvi said, her eyes wide.

"Don't worry." Tanis stroked her daughter's face. "I have a feeling that, no matter what, we'll be fighting Orion soon enough."

LAID BARE

STELLAR DATE: 03.27.8948 (Adjusted Years)
LOCATION: TSS *Galadrial*
REGION: Roma-Normandy L1 Point, New Canaan System

<*Wake up, Seraphina, it's time we had a chat,*> the voice spoke into her mind, and Sera groaned from the pain in her head. It felt as though her skull was splitting apart. It felt even worse than when she woke up in the *Intrepid*'s medbay after Mark had hacked her—something she had not thought possible.

<*Goway...*> she responded, and reached out for Helen, only to find a void in her mind, an emptiness where her long-time companion should be.

"You may have just realized that you can't communicate with Helen." The voice spoke audibly, and she recognized it as her father's.

"Why...?" she gasped as her head throbbed.

"I'm sorry you're in pain," her father said. "The medbay can dull the pain, but not too much. I want you cogent for this conversation we have to have."

Sera cracked an eye to see her father seated in a chair by her side in a dimly lit room. He must have told the medbay's systems to dampen the agony, because it decreased in intensity, and she was finally able to form a complete thought.

"What did you do to Helen?" she asked, her voice still unable to rise above a whisper.

"I had her removed," her father replied. "After I realized what you had done to get Elena here, and who could have done it, I realized who your AI really was."

Shit! Sera thought to herself. Her father had realized that Helen was a shard of Airtha.

"You asked, long ago—do you remember?—if you could have a child of Airtha as your AI when you joined The Hand," her father said slowly. "Do you recall my answer?"

"You said no," Sera replied, both eyes open now, staring at her father with unconcealed rage. "But I did it anyway, because Airtha and I are both free beings. You don't fucking own me, or her."

"You're wrong about that," her father replied. "You are both mine. When I realized that Elena had come here—that you had sent her—I interrogated Helen. I didn't realize she was Airtha then; I just thought she would be more forthcoming than you would be."

"Bastard!" Sera spat. "You mean that you could hurt her and not worry about hurting me."

"That is exactly what I mean, yes," her father replied. "But I didn't need to do anything. Once I mapped her neural network, I knew what she was. An abomination."

"What?" Sera asked. "How could she be an abomination?"

"That is not for you to know—yet," Jeffrey Tomlinson said as he rose from his chair and paced across the room. "What am I to do with you, Sera? I had such high hopes for you—even during your ridiculous self-imposed exile. I believed you would be the scion I had always hoped for. When you took your place as the Director of The Hand—a role which you filled very well—I believed that you had grown..."

He poured himself a glass of water and took a sip with his back turned to her. Sera had long since realized that she was secured to the bed—if she hadn't been, her father would be dead; or wishing he were dead.

"But then you suggested the use of antimatter warheads," he said as he turned back to face her. "For an instant, I really did believe that you were the one—that I wouldn't have to have a snake like Andrea as my successor. But then you showed the specs, and I knew of only one person who also knew those exact specifications."

Her father returned to his seat and crossed his arms. "So, I had you watched. Carefully, meticulously, looking for your line of communication to Airtha; but it never surfaced—nothing out of the ordinary, at least. I never suspected that she was within you; that you had secreted away that which was most precious to me."

Sera had always known that her father had a unique relationship with Airtha, but he treated her like a thing, not a person—behavior that was not unusual for him. Something that was 'precious'? Only as far as Airtha was useful to him.

"Helen is precious to me," Sera hissed. "What have you done with her?"

"Oh, she's alive, if that's what you're worried about; for now, at least. I haven't decided whether or not I should kill her here, or take her back to Airtha and make her otherself watch."

"Why?" Sera gasped. "What has she done that…that has earned such cruelty?"

Her father's voice grew sad. "For starters, she found out who you were; what you are. I didn't want her to know. I didn't want to distract her from what she should do—and I didn't want her to corrupt you, though I can see now that it may be too late."

"What in all the known stars are you talking about?!" Sera exclaimed. "You sound like a lunatic!"

Her father met her eyes, and a slow smile grew across his face.

"She never told you!" he let out a laugh. "I can't believe she never told you!"

"Never told me what?" Sera asked.

"Nothing you'll ever know," her father said and rose from his chair once more. "I need to have her further examined, and then disposed of. If you'll excuse me."

"What?!" Sera screamed. "You can't kill her, you murderer!"

Her cries fell upon his impassive back, and he didn't look back as he walked into the hall and closed the door.

Sera bucked and struggled against the restraints, as a rage unlike any she had ever felt before came over her. Helen was her best friend; she had to stop her father.

After several minutes, the pain in her head grew too intense to continue fighting her bonds, and Sera collapsed; ragged breaths tearing at her throat as she wondered how she had ever begun to trust her father, how she had fallen into his web of deceit again. Stars, she had even turned her mind against Tanis.

All because of that snake of a man, that viper; that manipulator.

I swear, Sera thought, her words alone in her head for the first time in decades. *I swear that if he hurts Helen, I'll* ***kill*** *him! Fuck it! I'll kill him even if he doesn't. It's time to end his tyranny.*

STRIKE

STELLAR DATE: 03.27.8948 (Adjusted Years)
LOCATION: Gamma IV Shipyard
REGION: Normandy, Moon of Roma, 6th Planet in the New Canaan System

Tanis rode the lift down the tower and then into the planet's crust. The platform continued to descend, kilometer after kilometer, before passing through the final layers of rock, and into the shipyard hidden within the moon.

"Oh, shit…" Elena gasped. "This is where you're building them. There's…more than you led me to believe."

Tanis nodded. "Most of them aren't ready yet; but when I spoke of a million ships, I was telling you my ultimate goal. I will ring this system in steel and beam-fire if I have to."

"You're sure off to a good start," Elena said softly. "How are you building them so fast? You have at least ten thousand in here."

Tanis looked around at the rows of ships nestled in their cradles, surrounded by bots mounting laser cannon, sensor arrays, and engines. The sight of so much industry made her swell with pride, and she winked at Elena.

"We're growing the less complex parts. We can make a hull in a just a few weeks," she replied.

"Growing hulls?" Elena frowned. "But these ships will have to undergo extreme stress and stand up under fire. You can't just 'grow' that sort of structure."

"We can," Tanis replied. "Not only that, these ships can self-repair while under fire to a degree no one has ever seen before."

"So, do you plan to assault the TSF fleet to free Sera?" Elena asked. "Because her father will just as soon kill her and jump out than fight you."

Tanis nodded. "I got that impression, as well. Anyone who travels with a jump-gate…. No, we're going in on stealth ships with a small strike force."

The platform reached its destination and Tanis stepped off, leading Elena down a warren of corridors to where the stealth pinnaces were docked. After only a short walk, they turned a corner, and stepped onto a wide platform suspended amidst nearly-complete cruisers.

Resting on the platform were six pinnaces, running lights on and ramps lowered, ready to take on passengers.

"We're assaulting in those?" Elena asked. "Are you sure the TSF ships can't see them?"

"Could you see the cruiser I scooped you up in?" Tanis asked.

"Well…no…"

"General," a voice called out from behind them, and Tanis turned to see Lieutenant Colonel Usef approaching with two dozen Marines on his heels. "I've assembled every Marine with combat experience on the base. You give the word, and we'll hit your target so hard they won't wake up when the Andromeda Galaxy gets here."

The men and women behind him wore grim expressions, and Tanis gave them a solemn nod.

"Very good, Colonel," Tanis replied. "We'll take just three pinnaces. I assume you brought gear and weapons for us?"

"Of course, ma'am," Usef replied, gesturing to packs several of the Marines carried. "You can gear up on the flight in. It'll take us just under two hours to get there."

"Two hours!" Elena exclaimed. "Anything could happen in that time."

"Elena, we can't rush in," Tanis said. "Stealth ships aren't very stealthy with their engines at max burn."

Elena clamped her mouth shut as Usef distributed his six fireteams between the pinnaces, and then led Tanis and Elena to theirs. Once inside, Tanis grabbed a pack and led Elena to one of the cabins.

"Strip. You need to get this armor on."

Elena complied, and once the woman was naked, Tanis took a cylinder and pressed it against her chest.

"This may feel pretty weird—especially since you've appropriated Sera's skin choice—but there's no time to alter how the armor applies."

"What armor?" Elena asked, and then gasped as the cylinder Tanis held began to melt against her body. "Oh, I've never seen anything quite like this."

"Based on something I bought back on Callisto," Tanis replied. "Earnest upgraded it to not require a base layer—and took out all their patent locks, too. It will stop just about any ballistic round you can imagine, short of serious kinetics, and can disperse and reflect photon beams. It can hold off electron beams for a bit, but don't get cocky."

Elena held her breath and closed her eyes. The clear layer of protection flowed over her face, before it seemed to almost seep into her skin and take on a matte sheen.

"Oh, fuck, that does feel intense," Elena gasped when the armor had set and she opened her mouth and eyes again.

"Here," Tanis tossed a shimmersuit at Elena. "Get it on, and I'll pass you the auth tokens. If the Transcend-level of tech is where I think it is, we'll be nearly invisible in these."

She slipped into her own, recalling the fight against Kris on the *Intrepid* when she first got her hands on the tech to make the suit. Like the armor, Earnest had improved on its design; even their own sensors had trouble tracking a wearer in an empty, silent room.

"Our weapons will be stealth-coated, as well; though not when firing, or once they're hot, of course."

Elena nodded, and they left the cabin to join Usef in the pinnace's cockpit.

"We'll be out of the exit shaft in a minute," he said. "The TSF ships haven't moved. Our precise time is an hour and forty-eight minutes to get to their flag. Fleet scan has spotted a few external airlocks they think we can link up to—our three ships won't be breaching near one another."

"Do you know the layout of that ship?" Tanis asked Elena. "We need to know where they're likely to keep Sera."

"Either the bridge, the brig, or the medbay, I'd guess," Elena replied, her expression deadly serious as she Linked to the pinnace's net and projected a layout of the TSF cruiser. The locations she mentioned lit up, and Tanis saw that all three were deep within the vessel.

"Well, good thing we have these three ships, then," she smiled.

"What sort of weapons will shipboard security have?" Usef asked.

"Pulse rifles and flechette pistols," Elena replied. "But they have heavier stuff in the armories. I'd really like them to not get any of those. If we can keep this non-lethal…"

"We'll try," Tanis replied. "But honestly…no matter what the outcome, we're probably going to start a war with this little assault."

Elena nodded slowly and fixed Tanis with a penetrating stare. "Then why are you doing it?"

Tanis leaned back against one of the unoccupied seats. "This little jaunt? It's just the thing that Lieutenant Colonel Richards used to do—the sort of thing that got me busted down to Major. But General—and especially Governor—Richards has become a lot more calculating over the years. Too much big picture, not enough of the small, important things."

Tanis took a deep breath and glanced at Usef and the Marines, aware that her words would be repeated through the colony—if they survived.

"I realized—after I had my little spat with Sera, and after I had to tell Saanvi what happened to her parents—that if you don't do the little things right, there's no way you can get the big picture right. Secrets and hiding and machinations—it's the shit that got us all in this mess. Us with the pico, you guys with not being fucked up in the FTL wars. I can't undo everything that's gone wrong, but I can help my friend no matter the cost—I'll do right by her, and hope the stars appreciate the effort, if not the path, taken to get here."

"That's as good a reason as any I've heard of late," Elena nodded. "I assume you have a backup plan, right?"

"Of course," Tanis replied with a grin. "If we aren't out in four hours, the stealth ships I have all around the TSF fleet are to attack."

"Seriously?" Elena asked.

"Well, they're to demand our release; but if that doesn't happen, yes, the fleet will attack."

Elena looked as though she was going to argue the point, but Tanis set her mouth in a thin line, and The Hand agent took the hint. "Then, I guess we had better get in and out as quickly as possible."

Tanis nodded. "Get familiar with the shimmersuit, and Link up with our combat net. I've sent you the auth tokens. We'll be comms- and data-silent as much as we can, but you may need probe feeds."

"Understood," Elena said, and Tanis felt her join the network with the Marines.

"I'm sending you today's hand signals," Usef informed Elena. "Even when we have comms—which will be risky in there—that's how we communicate when in line of sight, and we change them up all the time, so pay attention."

Elena nodded, and Tanis turned her attention back to the view out the cockpit window. For now, there was nothing more to do than wait.

ORION GUARD

STELLAR DATE: 03.27.8948 (Adjusted Years)
LOCATION: OGS *Starflare*
REGION: Near Normandy, Moon of Roma, 6th Planet in the New Canaan System

"This is it, people," Kent addressed the thirty five members of his strike force with calm assurance. "The Transcend president has left the tower. We have our window. We get in, take the governor, and then get her out. If our mission goes as planned, and we're undetected, the secondary force will remain there, and attempt to take the Transcend's president when he returns the next day."

The men and women racked in the transport shared hungry looks. The thought that in the span of two days they could take the New Canaan leadership, secure the picotech, *and* capture the Transcend's president was almost too good to be true.

The only thing to temper the excitement was the fear that something would go wrong—that they would lose this golden opportunity to strike such a decisive blow.

He knew the soldiers under his command would feel the same, and he cautioned them, "Remember your training, your experience. Don't let the magnitude of what we are about to achieve unnerve you. Trust in your teammates, and we'll achieve victory."

"Sir," their assault ship's co-pilot called back into the bay, "we just got a ping from our agent. The New Canaan governor has left the moon. She's on her way to the TSF flagship."

"Did she say why?" Kent asked.

"The burst said it was a covert rescue mission. We're on passive scan only, so we won't be able to pick up any of their stealth ships. But I would assume it's a small strike force."

"Change of plan. We're hitting the TSF flagship…the *Galadrial*," Kent addressed his troops. "You already have our analysis of it. As best we can tell, it's a modified Freeman Class ship. We're going to be on a bit of a hunt, but a rescue will probably mean brig, medbay, or bridge. It could also mean their president's quarters, but I'm betting those are near the bridge."

"Then we'll divide the nine fireteams evenly into three squads," Lieutenant Lorde replied. "Sergeant Tress, you're down a man, so your squad will hit the medbay; it should have the least security. Doran, you're with me on the brig, and Xecer, you'll be with the Colonel, going for the bridge."

The three sergeants nodded, and Kent knew that they were now going over breach protocols with their soldiers. Chances were that New Canaan's governor had more than one ship, and would breach multiple locations at once. Kent's soldiers would have to move fast and hard, crippling as many ship-systems as they could while they moved.

He looked out the forward window of the assault craft; the countdown on the overlay showed just under two hours to the TSF flagship. Either this would be the defining moment in the Orion Guard's long struggle against the Transcend, or they would be swept into history's dustbin, a failed and forgotten op.

<Are you ready?> he asked Vernon.

<I don't ever cease being ready,> the AI replied. *<I have a passel of NSAI ready to hit their*

systems hard. I've loaded them into the tech's hack-packs; when they jack into the first physical port they encounter, well, things are going to get real fun, real fast.>

<*Make sure they focus on comm and helm,*> Kent replied. <*If we can grab this ship and just punch it through their gate back to OFA space, it will be the stuff of legend.*>

<*I'm less concerned with being a legend, and more with not dying,*> Vernon replied.

<*Our biggest risk is getting past the TSF fleet, and whatever the New Canaan space force has floating around out there,*> Kent said. <*Neither are going to blow the ship with their leaders aboard.*>

<*I would feel a lot better if I knew how many ships the ISF has. We haven't spotted a single stealth ship—and we know they have them.*>

Kent agreed with Vernon. That was his largest concern, too. Orion stealth tech was ahead of the Transcend's. He expected to detect the ISF ships, as well; but so far, there was no sign of them.

<*Well, stealth or no, if they want their governor, they'll have to come aboard and take her by force—something that we'll ensure does not happen,*> Kent replied.

He returned his attention to the specks of light at the L1 point between Roma and its moon, and prepared himself for the battle ahead.

INSERTION

STELLAR DATE: 03.27.8948 (Adjusted Years)
LOCATION: ISS Stellar Pinnace
REGION: Near Roma-Normandy L1 Point, New Canaan System

The pinnace hovered just outside one of the TSF flagship's external airlocks. It was a small hatch, made for robotic maintenance, and would be impossible to fit through in powered armor. But with the strike force's armor only consisting of the flow-armor and shimmersuits, slipping through the small opening would not be a problem.

Tanis didn't want to hide any breathing gear once they got across, and making an ES seal against the *Galadrial* would certainly show up on its active scan. That meant the strike force would have to hold their breath for the five-meter trip through the vacuum of space. Their armor would seal over their eyes, mouths, and noses for the duration.

"You ready for this?" Tanis asked Elena. "Once the pico infiltrates their system and Angela opens the lock, we'll depressurize the cabin here. It may be a minute or two before we all get across and re-pressurize the other side."

Elena nodded. "We trained for ops like this. Never wearing so little that we felt naked in vacuum, but the end result was the same."

"Good," Tanis nodded. "Remember, no direct net access. If you Link up, they'll spot you, and that will end our little trip early. If we're lucky, we can tap into their general net; but we may be blind. We're counting on you to flag anything out of the ordinary."

"We're saving Sera. I'll do whatever it takes," Elena replied.

"Even kill?" Tanis asked. "If you're not prepared to take a life when the time comes, then you're not coming. There can be *no* hesitation."

"This isn't my first op like this," Elena said. "I know what to do."

Tanis raised an eyebrow. "You've taken up arms against your own people before?"

"Well, no, but I've had to turn on friends on undercover ops before. I imagine it's going to feel about the same."

Tanis nodded solemnly. "Yeah, it does."

<Green light us when you're ready, Angela,> Tanis instructed her AI.

<You bet. Only a few seconds more…OK, I have control of the hatch, and am faking its feed back to their monitoring systems.>

<We are green for infiltration,> Tanis announced over the combat net. She had no feed from the other two craft, and hoped that the AI embedded with them could pull off the same breach Angela had.

The Marines all toggled their status on the combat net to show readiness. Tanis opened the pinnace's side-hatch to the vacuum of space, and pushed off toward the Transcend cruiser. She covered the distance in a few seconds, and slipped through the portal on the other ship without incident.

The space within was cramped: only a narrow walkway with bots racked along the wall. She moved toward the far end of the room to make room for the rest of the squad. Forty seconds later, Elena, Usef, and the twelve Marines were across.

<Hatch sealed and pressurizing,> Angela announced a moment before the faint hiss of atmosphere entering the room became audible.

The air pressure reading on Tanis's HUD increased until it stopped at 98kPa, at which point she signaled her armor to unseal around her mouth and nose. The infiltration team followed suit and the small space was filled with the muted sounds of men and women rapidly replenishing their lungs with oxygen.

At the room's inner airlock, Tanis deployed a dose of nano into the portal's locking mechanism, and a second later it unsealed. She activated her shimmersuit and slipped through the opening, followed by the rest of the squad.

She slipped down the hall and glanced back at the rest of the squad. A random signature wave pulsed from each Marine, providing their position and rough outline to one another. Their HUDs filled in the data gaps, faking the appearance of their teammates.

While the signal introduced a risk of detection, decreasing the chance of friendly fire made it worthwhile.

When the last Marine slipped past, Usef closed the hatch and signaled for two Marines to scout ahead. Tanis felt blind without a cloud of nanoprobes surrounding her, but Elena had warned that the *Galadrial's* internal scanners could detect her nano, so they had to rely on the Mark I Eyeball for this mission.

The scouts approached an intersection, and one held up a hand. Tanis listened carefully and heard voices in one of the cross corridors. The squad pressed up against the walls of the corridor, and Tanis barely drew breath as three TSF naval officers walked by, chatting about the likelihood that they would have to take out the colonists.

Two seemed to think it was a sure thing, while the third was holding out for a peaceful solution.

<*Not sure which bet I'd take, yet,*> Tanis commented to Angela.

<*Well, we'd end them right fast if it came down to a knockout fight. They're sitting ducks here at the moon's L1.*> Angela replied.

<*Well, yeah, we'd win –I just meant peace or war. Plus, they're not just here at the L1. A dozen ships are orbiting Roma, and several more are stationed at the L3 and L4 points. We'd have to engage them in a few locations,*> Tanis said as the lead scout signaled that all was clear again.

<*Yeah, but we'd still win*> Angela replied. <*I'm not being cocky, it's just my analysis.*>

The squad progressed for several more minutes before Elena touched Tanis's shoulder and made a direct Link. <*Jutio and I think that there may be a data trunk line down the corridor on our right. I'm not certain—this ship is laid out a bit differently than I'm used to.*>

Tanis tapped the lead scout on the shoulder and passed the hand signals for the route they needed to take. He nodded and slipped around the corner while the other scout crossed the intersection and watched the other direction.

She glanced back at Elena, who was staying close on her six. She trusted the woman—mostly; she was a spy, after all. Gaining trust and double-crosses were her tradecraft.

<*Sera trusts her. That has to count for something,*> Angela said.

<*It's most of her currency. But if Elena's to be believed, they are lovers now, and that may blind Sera to what she doesn't want to see,*> Tanis replied.

The scout at the intersection signaled for them to advance, and Tanis slipped around the corner to see the lead scout slide a panel off the wall, revealing a data trunk line aside. Tanis placed a hand on the conduit and felt a tingle as nano flowed through her skin and armor into the conduit's housing, where they began to build a shunt.

<*Damn, their security is better than I thought it would be,*> Angela said. <*I suppose it's to*

be expected—we did give them our nanotech. But, they still don't have my skill.>

<*We're in,*> Tanis said on the combat net. <*They won't pick up our signals, now.*>

<*Just don't think that's an excuse for chit-chat,*> Usef growled.

Tanis confirmed the route to the medbay and passed the path to the two scouts, who slipped ahead of the squad once more.

They encountered more and more TSF personnel as they progressed, some navy, some soldiers, and eventually a growing number of med-techs.

<*I just got a ping on their net,*> Angela said. <*First squad is nearing the bridge. Third squad hasn't checked in yet.*>

<*Should we be worried?*> Elena asked.

<*You tell me,*> Tanis replied. <*If they were found out, would there be any sort of general alarm?*>

Elena nodded. <*They'd sound general quarters for sure, but if this is a trap…*>

Tanis gave a slow nod. The thought had crossed her mind as well—the infiltration, so far, was far too easy.

Tanis pulled up against the wall as a group of engineers hurried past. One of them, a young man carrying a large case, tripped and bumped into her.

"What—" he exclaimed before Tanis wrapped an arm around his throat, and clamped a hand over his mouth. The Marines moved with practiced precision, subduing the other four engineers and dragging them into a side-room.

A minute later, they were back in the corridors, moving double-time. They were now on a clock; it was just a matter of time before someone discovered those unconscious engineers.

<*Place is pretty empty,*> Tanis commented as a solitary nurse passed by.

<*They're one level up, preparing the trauma ward,*> Angela replied.

<*Well, that's not auspicious…*>

They slipped through the entrance into the medbay and began searching the rooms. Tanis peered into one room where the sheets were disheveled, and restraints mounted to the side of the bed were flipped open.

Elena followed Tanis into the room; though she couldn't see the woman's expression, Tanis could tell from her posture that she was worried. She turned to the bed and was depositing nanobots on the restraints to see if there was any DNA evidence when a klaxon sounded.

Angela piped in an announcement from the general shipnet. <*Alert! Intruders port-side, on deck forty-three. Sound general quarters, watch stand to! This is not a drill.*>

<*That's where we came in,*> Usef said.

<*Yeah, but we're on deck seven now, and none of ours should be down there,*> Tanis replied.

<*Or they're just behind the times, and think we're still down there,*> Angela added.

Tanis addressed the squad, <*Anything, people?*>

The Marines all signaled negative. Sera was not in the medbay.

<*Wait, I found something!*> Angela announced. <*She was here, in this bed—and she hacked the restraint system somehow. She's at large on the ship.*>

<*She can't be in stealth gear,*> Usef said. <*There must be something on the shipnet. Someone must have spotted her.*>

Angela signaled negative. <*She's not flagged as a person of interest. If anyone did spot her, it wouldn't have been noteworthy.*>

<*Then why was she locked up here, and where is she going?*> Tanis asked.

<*I bet her father didn't want it known that he had her in here,*> Elena replied. <*Why in a medbay? Unless she was injured when he took her…*>

<*Wait!*> Angela said. <*There's something about a high-level AI being held in a network detainment facility near the bridge. I think—yes—it's Helen!*>

<*Helen's not with Sera? Well, now we know where Sera is going. Get the location to Lieutenant Ned; he should have first squad up by the bridge by now. Tell them to get in position, but don't move unless they see Sera in trouble,*> Tanis ordered.

<*On it,*> Angela replied. <*What…wait…something is going on. The ship is having some sort of systems failure in navigation.*>

<*Could it be any of ours doing it?*> Tanis asked.

<*Still nothing from third squad, and first says it's not them. Maybe Sera?*> Angele suggested.

<*Keep frosty,*> Tanis addressed the Marines. <*Angela thinks that there's someone up to no good onboard, aside from us—could just be Sera.*>

The Marines signaled acknowledgement, and the squad left the medbay, moving toward the network detention center. The pair of scouts ranged ahead, leading the squad through corridors and access shafts with far less concern of detection than before. Twice they had to subdue TSF ship personnel with non-lethal force, but data Angela picked up on the shipnet indicated that third squad had not been so lucky; they had run into opposition near the brig, and had killed two TSF soldiers in a retreat to their access point.

<*We've been spotted!*> Usef called from the rear.

Tanis pulled the feed from the combat net and saw TSF soldiers in light armor lobbing canisters of fluorescing gas down the corridor in an attempt to paint her squad. The shimmersuit's active systems were struggling to camouflage and keep the particles from coalescing on their bodies.

<*Return fire, pulse rifles only,*> Tanis called back, and the sound of concussive pulses filled the corridor around her.

<*We're just a hundred meters away,*> Angela announced, and Tanis signaled the scouts to move fast and hit hard.

<*We've secured the network detainment center. They have Helen trapped in a data vault. There's no neural activity. She's dead,*> Lieutenant Ned reported from Team one's position. <*Sera isn't here.*>

<*Hold your position,*> Tanis replied. <*We're going to push on to the bridge. Once we're past your location, come in behind the enemy on our tail and take them out.*>

<*Acknowledged, General,*> Lieutenant Ned responded.

The sound of rails and high-powered beam weapons came from behind, and Tanis checked the visual feeds, surprised that the TSF was using that kind of firepower on their ship.

<*It's not the TSF using those weapons,*> Usef called up. <*There's someone else back there, and they're mowing down the* Galadrial's *troops.*>

<*Let's move!*> Tanis yelled over the Link. <*We need to secure the bridge.*>

She caught up with the pair of scouts and sprinted ahead of them, flushing a cloud of nano through the corridor—there was no longer any need for stealth.

Ahead, a pair of TSF soldiers rushed around the corner firing wildly. They couldn't see Tanis and the scouts, but they must have decided it was better safe than sorry. Tanis fired her pulse rifle at one, while unloading a clip from her flechette pistol into the legs of the other. One fell unconscious and the other collapsed, screaming in pain.

She pulled a fresh clip from the pouch on her thigh and slid it into the pistol's grip as the pair of Marine scouts fired focused pulse rounds at a group of enemy soldiers holding the next intersection. Two fell, and Tanis rushed ahead unloading another clip from her flechette pistol into two TSF soldiers, while slamming the butt of her rifle into the face of another as she flew past.

<*Keep going,*> Usef called ahead. <*The Transcendies behind us are bogged down with whoever it is back there.*>

<*I think they're Orion Guard,*> Elena said. <*I caught sight of one of their weapons on the combat net. It looks like OFA gear.*>

<*Orion, here?*> Tanis asked, while her mind raced through myriad possibilities.

<*Angela,*> she asked privately. <*Have you managed to breach this new group's comms?*>

<*Not yet,*> her AI replied. <*I'm also not sure how—oh, fuck! They hacked my hack!*>

<*What do you mean?*> Tanis asked.

<*They hit the same physical breach point I used. They piggy-backed on my hack—I can't trust anything through it.*>

Tanis swore aloud and then directed Usef to send two Marines back to first squad in the network detention center with new orders. She had to assume her prior communication was either intercepted and altered, or was never delivered at all.

That brought her team down to just nine. Hopefully it was enough to storm the *Galadrial's* bridge.

The pair of scouts had pulled ahead again, and they lobbed a pair of concussive grenades up a ladder shaft before rushing up the rungs and firing their rifles. Tanis was close on their heels and provided covering fire as they subdued a squad of TSF soldiers. The battle was pitched and brief. Disoriented by the grenades, the enemy squad was at a loss, and the first four fell almost immediately.

Then, one of the ISF scouts took a shot from a slug thrower. It hit his left shoulder and threw him against a bulkhead. Tanis emptied a clip from her flechette pistol in the direction of the enemy fire, and cleared the ladder shaft to allow the Marines below to join the fight.

The first woman up tossed two more conc grenades down the hall leading toward the bridge while Tanis rushed to the scout's side.

His shimmersuit was shredded where the slug had hit, and she could tell by the unnatural angle of his shoulder that the flex armor hadn't been able to absorb enough of the kinetic impact to keep his bones intact.

"I'm OK, General. I'll be back on my feet as soon as the pain suppressors kick in," he said.

"Good man," Tanis replied. He couldn't fire a rifle one-handed, and she couldn't see his pistol anywhere, so she handed hers over. "Semper Fi, Marine," she said as she pulled him to his feet.

"Semper Fi," he replied, and they turned to see the last of the squad spilling up the ladder shaft and unleashing concentrated pulse blasts at the remaining TSF soldiers. "Besides, these Transcendies are a bunch of candy-assed fuck-puppets. I'll be damned if they'll put me down."

Tanis smiled at him, before remembering that he couldn't make out her features through her shimmersuit and gave a nod. "Let's finish this fight."

<*Main corridor to the bridge is just around the corner,*> the lead scout replied.

Tanis pushed out another batch of nanoprobes to scout the area. The ship's defense systems killed most of them, but she managed to get a clear picture of the bridge entrance. An entire platoon of enemy soldiers lined the corridor, tucked into open hatches and behind conduit.

Unlike most of the forces they had encountered thus far, these soldiers were in powered armor. Pulse rifles would have limited effect on them.

<*I count twenty-nine in there—could be more. I didn't get a clear picture,*> Tanis announced on the combat net as she shared the feed.

<*No time to wait,*> Usef said. <*Those Orion guys are going to be up our asses in no time.*>

<*Mine the ladder shaft; we need to slow these guys down,*> she ordered. She hated mines—they were too indiscriminating—but at least their IFF systems wouldn't trigger if first squad came through.

Usef set two Marines to the task, and Tanis looked to the rest, passing hand signals outlining how they would hit the corridor.

Ten seconds later, four Marines leaned around the corner and let fire with pulse rifles and flechette pistols while Tanis and another four dashed across the corridor.

She spun and let fire with her rifle, less concerned with careful aim than with pushing the enemy back into cover. They stopped for an instant, and, when the enemy leaned out from their cover to return fire, the Marines lobbed their conc grenades.

Even through her armor, Tanis's ears rang and her skin tingled from the force of the blasts. She leaned out again and no fire came her way. The Marines rushed forward and checked the TSF soldiers to make sure they were all out.

Given the damage to the corridor, she was certain a few of the enemy were dead. Fatalities were going to make future negotiations difficult, but, for the moment, her main concern was whether or not they had damaged the bridge's door mechanism. She placed a hand on the panel, and Angela rushed nano into the circuitry.

<*Give me a minute and we'll know,*> Angela replied.

<*Why so long?*> Tanis asked.

<*I'm fighting off the ship's AI, and a horde of NSAI that those Orion guys back there set loose on the network. They're making a mess of everything,*> Angela's tone was clipped.

<*Need a hand?*>

<*No, you just keep your head on your shoulders. I'll handle the hard stuff.*>

An explosion shook the deck, and Tanis saw smoke rush out from the cross corridor where the mined ladder shaft was. With any luck, their pursuers would have to find an alternate route.

<*OK, the door is locked down somehow. Not by those TSF soldiers—they were trying to bypass it,*> Angela reported. <*Luckily, they knew their stuff; I'll have it open in few seconds.*>

<*I have conflicting reports from our other two squads,*> Usef said. <*Either they're coming, they're dead, or they've left.*>

<*Let's hope it's not the middle one,*> Tanis replied.

<*Got it!*> Angela cried triumphantly, and the bridge doors slid open.

A fireteam of Marines rushed past her, likely ordered ahead by Usef to keep her from being the first one in. Tanis followed close on their heels, and took in the tableau laid out in front of her.

KENT

STELLAR DATE: 03.27.8948 (Adjusted Years)
LOCATION: TSS *Galadrial*
REGION: Roma-Normandy L1 Point, New Canaan System

Kent swore under his breath. The enemy's Marines were good— maybe better than his own soldiers—they fought like veterans who loved their commander as much as life itself.

It was a sentiment he understood well; he tried to foster the same feelings in the men and women under his command.

The ladder shaft up to the bridge was a ruin of twisted metal, and too dangerous to get through while under fire. His scouts had secured another route and the platoon was double-timing it through the command decks to get there.

He fired a round into the head of a TSF naval officer who peeked out from behind a console, pistol in hand. It was like shooting fish in a barrel, and it gave him no satisfaction.

<*Sir!*> corporal Jenkins reported. <*I found this in a marked drop. It's from our operative.*>

Jenkins approached and handed Kent a small, physical data drive. He inserted it into a socket on his armor and read the message.

<*It would seem that our enemy has some impressive armor. Not heavy like ours, but well able to withstand most of what we can throw at it. However, it has a weakness.*>

He passed their operative's data across the combat net. Heavy weapons fire would still take them down, but if it came to close combat, their combat knives would be highly effective weapons.

<*This AI of theirs is formidable,*> Vernon said, as the Orion Guard troops worked their way up a ladder shaft and took out a squad of TSF soldiers.

<*More than you can handle?*> Kent asked as he slammed into a bulkhead and leaned through an opening, laying down suppressive fire.

<*Truthfully, sir? It may be. It's not the Transcend's AI, it's the colonists'. No matter what I do, it thwarts me. I suspect it's their governor's—an AI named Angela, who was a specialist in this sort of warfare back in Sol's ancient military.*>

<*Then we have to take her down to get the ship,*> Kent replied.

<*That is correct,*> Vernon replied. <*If she remains active, we lose.*>

The Guard soldiers secured the next corridor, and Kent advanced with his platoon.

<*Then I'll just have to take her down.*>

THE BRIDGE

STELLAR DATE: 03.27.8948 (Adjusted Years)
LOCATION: TSS *Galadrial*
REGION: Roma-Normandy L1 Point, New Canaan System

Three of the bridge crew were down. One was dead, another was bleeding profusely, and the third was moaning in agony. Greer—now an admiral, Tanis noted—and a woman with captain's insignia on her shoulders stood with weapons trained on Sera.

Sera stood with her back to the forward holodisplays, an arm wrapped around her father's neck. Her other hand held a gun to the back of his head, and tears were in her eyes.

"Why would you do that?" she screamed at her father. "You killed her! She was my best friend, the one person in this whole fucking galaxy that's always—"

Her words cut short as she realized it was ISF Marines who had burst into the bridge, and not her father's soldiers.

Tanis altered her shimmersuit, revealing her face and smiled. "Need a hand with anything?"

"Tanis!" Sera cried out. "What…what are you doing here?"

"Proving that there are more people in the galaxy who have your back," Elena said as she stepped onto the bridge.

With Marine rifles in their backs, Greer and the ship's captain lowered their weapons. A pair of ensigns were crouched behind a console, and a Marine pulled them out and secured them. Tanis saw another Marine crouch down beside the bleeding woman and begin to apply bio-seals to her wounds.

"You don't have to do this," Tanis said as she approached Sera and her father. She paused to place her hand on a console and deliver a dose of nano into the bridge's control systems.

<Their AI is…weak…perhaps from fighting off the Orion NSAI,> Angela said privately. *<Those are some nasty attack dogs. No matter; they aren't a match for me. I'll have the ship locked down in two or three minutes.>*

<Anything you can't handle?> Tanis asked.

<All the AI we've encountered—with the exception of Helen—have been a step down from L4's at best. Pirates had better AI back in Sol.>

<I'll take that to mean you have things covered.>

<Yes, Mom,> Angela chuckled.

"You don't understand, Tanis," Sera's face was a rictus of pain. "He fucking killed her in cold blood. He murdered Helen!"

"I know," Tanis nodded. "And you and Helen were made citizens of New Canaan before you left," she fixed her eyes on the Transcend president, who did not look frightened—only enraged.

"Is that it? You're going to charge me with murder?" he asked. "I don't know if you've noticed, but I have a fleet here that will keep that from happening."

"Not so much," Tanis shook her head as Angela sent a signal to the ISF fleet instructing them to disable their stealth systems.

"Oh, shit," the *Galadrial's* captain swore as the bridge's holotank displayed the sudden appearance of ten thousand cruisers around the main Transcend fleet, and smaller thousand-ship groupings around the L3 and L4 points.

"How did you build those so fast?" Admiral Greer exclaimed, awe filling his voice. "And where did you build them?"

"You'd be surprised what you can do when you're living under imminent threat from a superior adversary," Tanis replied. "Plus, having picotech also helps."

<We're coming under fire from those Orion guys,> Usef called in from the corridor, as Tanis heard the sounds of weapons fire pick up once more. *<We're outnumbered three-to-one, and our pulse rifles aren't doing much against their armor. Luckily, their beams aren't doing too much to ours, either—yet.>*

<First and third squad are just a minute out,> Angela replied. *<And I've sealed off most of the ship, so we won't have any further visitors.>*

"That's Orion out there in the corridor," Tanis said and glanced at President Tomlinson. "You better hope we win this little fight. I'll go easier on you than they will."

The president's face reddened and he shot daggers at Tanis. "You should have volunteered your tech to us rather than playing this little game. Now, look where it has gotten us. The Guard has penetrated thousands of light years into the Transcend."

The sounds of weapons fire in the corridor intensified, and then abruptly ceased.

"And that's that," Tanis said. "Sera, you can lower your weapon. We can secure your father."

"He's perfectly secure right now," Sera replied icily. "I'm having an internal debate about whether or not he dies. If Helen were here, she'd probably tell me not to blow your head off, *Dad*. Too bad you killed her!"

"Sera," Tanis said calmly, "you don't need me to tell you how revenge isn't the answer. You already know that. The Transcend is going to need strong leadership to defeat the Orion Guard; if you kill your father, who knows what will happen."

Out of the corner of her eye, Tanis saw Elena reposition herself in the same moment that Usef chased a man onto the bridge. He lunged for Tanis, and she pivoted, avoiding a blade strike at her face.

She turned to grab his arm, and he slipped away, shrugging off two pulse blasts from Usef's rifle and swung the blade at her again. Tanis held her armored left arm up to deflect the blow, and the blade sliced clean through the limb—her forearm fell to the ground in front of her.

The man took advantage of her confusion to drive the blade into her chest where it slipped right through her shimmersuit and flow-armor. As it buried up to the hilt, her HUD showed that the blade was only a few nanometers thick, and was vibrating at a frequency that seemed to defeat her armor's active defenses.

Pain radiated through her chest as it bisected her heart, but she suppressed the agony and backhanded the man before falling to a knee and fighting off waves of dizziness.

"Why is it that whenever I meet with the Transcend I end up with a knife through my heart?" she said with her head lowered, waiting for her auxiliary heart to restore her blood pressure.

She felt someone at her side, clamping a tourniquet around her arm.

"General, the president," Usef said quietly, and Tanis raised her head to see the President of the Transcend Interstellar Alliance dead. The top of his head was gone, and a stunned Sera stood behind him, supporting the dead weight of his body for an instant before she let it drop.

She looked first to the man who had attacked her, but he lay unconscious on the deck; then her eyes flicked to Elena, who stood with her arm extended clutching her flechette pistol.

On either side of her, a Marine stood with pulse rifle leveled, awaiting orders.

"Lower it," Tanis ordered Elena, as Sera cried out, "Elly! What did you do?"

Elena dropped the flechette pistol and Tanis nodded for the Marines to secure her. "I did it for you, Sera," she pleaded. "So you wouldn't have to kill your own father."

"Blade," Usef said and gestured to Tanis's chest.

She looked down at the knife buried hilt-deep in her chest, and carefully pulled it out, dropping it before walking to Sera. "I'm sorry, Sera. I'm sorry about what I said before, I'm sorry that I didn't get here sooner…I'm just sorry."

"I…" Sera stammered before suddenly realizing why her face was so wet and began frantically wiping it with her hospital gown. Greer took off his jacket and handed it to Tanis, who passed it to Sera.

While she cleaned herself up, Tanis turned back to Admiral Greer. "You need to tell your fleet to stand down."

Greer nodded and gestured to the console. "Your AI has locked me out. I'll need access."

"You have it, but you'll have to do it manually. No Link." Angela replied over the bridge's audible address system.

Greer sat heavily and keyed in the commands for an all-fleet address. "All ships, this is Admiral Greer. The situation is under control. Take no action. I repeat, take no action against the ISF ships. Updates will follow."

"And to the soldiers and sailors on this ship," Tanis added.

Greer sent a ship-wide message for all forces to stand down and looked up at Tanis. "What now?"

Tanis let out a long breath. <*What now, indeed?*> she said to Angela.

<*You need to review the scan data,*> Angela said. <*Elena is not who she appears to be.*>

Tanis glanced at Elena, who was embracing Sera, while pulling up the bridge's visual log—once Angela Linked her with the command systems. She overheard Sera say something about how this was just more proof of how Orion was evil and had to be stopped.

<*Where's their ship's AI?*> she asked Angela out of curiosity as she flipped through the feeds.

<*I've shut her down. She really wasn't as strong as I'd expected. From what I've seen, the Transcend limits their AI's abilities a lot.*>

<*Interesting,*> Tanis replied absently as she saw what Angela spotted on the logs.

"Sera! Look out!" Tanis called out.

Elena held the blade Tanis had let fall to the ground. She slashed at Sera's neck, but Sera managed to leap back in time to avoid the attack. Elena charged, aiming the blade at Sera's left eye, and Sera blocked the blow, but they collided and fell to the deck in a heap.

By the time Tanis and the Marines reached them and pulled Elena off, Sera had several deep wounds on her torso; but Tanis couldn't see the blade anywhere.

"My back…" Sera whispered.

Tanis gently rolled her over, and saw the knife jutting from Sera's spine.

"Don't move," she replied as she eased Sera onto her side. "We're going to need medics to get that out."

"I'm sorry, Sar," Elena said, her face a strange combination of sorrow, rage, and guilt.

"Why...how long?" Sera gasped through tears. Tanis briefly wondered if they were from pain or betrayal.

<*Or both,*> Angela added.

"Long enough," Elena replied, her voice rough and filled with grief. "I loved you, Sar, I really did. I hoped I could convince you that Orion is the right side; but when you went back to Airtha, I could see how you were going to become just like your father. We could have saved the galaxy, but Garza was right—you're going to destroy it. With or without your father."

Sera's face reddened and she opened her mouth to speak, but stopped and looked at the deck. "I can't look at her. Can you put her in the corridor?"

Tanis gestured to the Marines, who marched Elena out of the bridge.

"So, who's in charge of the Transcend now?" Tanis asked.

"We've never had a transfer of power. Her father has been running the show ever since he united the FGT worldships," Greer said before looking down at Sera. "You have to take control, and quickly. We can't have a power vacuum. Especially one that your sister will be all too happy to fill."

Sera coughed up blood as a pair of medics rushed onto the bridge and settled down beside her, scanning her injuries to determine the exact location of the embedded blade.

<*They were already on their way to deal with the wounded,*> Angela said. <*I was able to get the medbay out of lockdown without opening up the rest of the ship.*>

<*Thanks,*> Tanis replied.

"Andrea?" Tanis asked aloud. "I thought that she was on a penal colony."

Sera shook her head. "No, my father had her released early. She's not allowed back at Airtha for another century, but that won't stop her, once she hears that he's dead."

Tanis leaned against a console and looked at the holodisplay of the twenty thousand ships surrounding Roma. It was a tiny fraction of the ships they would need to fend off the Orion Guard. The Transcend must be united to face the threat ahead of them.

<*I have an incoming message from the ISF,*> Angela reported, and Tanis nodded for her to put it on the bridge's main holotank.

Joe's image shimmered into view and he smiled with relief at the sight of Tanis. "Angela reported that you were OK, boy it's good to see you in person—holy shit! You're missing an arm! I guess things got intense."

Tanis nodded. "That's one word for it. Tomlinson is dead, and Elena was a Guard double agent."

"Well, that's just the start of it. Our perimeter scanning net picked up a massive fleet out past the heliopause, well over twenty thousand ships. It's not Transcend—it took out four of their ships already," Joe reported. "Our analysis puts it at eleven days from our location."

"Greer, we're going to have to mend our fences before then," Tanis said to the admiral. "You have a jump-gate here—can you send for re-enforcements?"

"Yes," Greer nodded. "I can maybe get five thousand ships here by then. Things are hot all along the front right now, but with your fleet of stealth ships, I think you may not even need more firepower."

Tanis exchanged a look with Joe. "About those ships. Less than half are ready for combat, and of the ones that are, they're running skeleton crews."

Greer shook his head and exchanged a look with the *Galadrial's* captain. "I told you she was wily, Viska."

"New contact," Joe reported. "Something just jumped insystem. Same arrival point as Elena used.... It's *Sabrina*!"

Sera looked up, hope in her eyes. "Really? Do they have Finaeus?"

"No signal from them yet," Joe replied. "Wait, what are you doing?"

"We're not doing anything!" Tanis replied, but the holodisplay of the TSF fleet positions showed otherwise. Every ship other than the *Galadrial* was breaking formation and boosting for *Sabrina*'s position.

<I'm not getting any response from any of them on comms,> Angela said on the bridge net. *<Something tried to take over this ship, too, but I was able to fend it off. It felt like…>*

She was cut off by a holo image appearing beside Joe on the main tank. It was a woman that Tanis recognized, though she looked subtly different than in the past.

"Helen?" Sera asked. "What are you…I thought you were dead!"

"I'm sorry, Sera," the woman replied. "Helen is dead. I am Myriad, a shard of Airtha, just as Helen was. I cannot let what *Sabrina* carries reach you. That ship and its passengers must be destroyed."

The woman disappeared and Sera cried out in anguish from her position on the deck while the medics worked on her back. Her eyes cast about the bridge until they locked onto Tanis. "Why…why would she do that? My crew, Jessica—they're on that ship!"

"Then we're going to have to get there first," Tanis replied and turned to Joe. "Get there, and get *Sabrina* aboard the *I2* before she's destroyed!"

<Here we go again,> Angela said within their mind.

Tanis clenched her teeth. *<Bring it on.>*

THE END

ORION RISING

THE ORION WAR – BOOK 3

BY M. D. COOPER

FOREWORD

Here we are at last.

The Orion War has begun in earnest with the Hegemony Fleet's arrival in the New Canaan System. Tanis will be forced to bring all her might to bear against these aggressors—as she has done so often in the past.

There is, however, a part of the story that you may not have heard, as it has been revealed only in expanded content—namely ***Destiny Risin***g, and ***The Gate at the Grey Wolf Star*** (or The Trail Through the Stars omnibus).

If you're not familiar with ***Destiny Rising***, it is an extended version of ***Outsystem*** and ***A Path in the Darkness*** that re-integrates parts of the story that I had removed, so as to not leave too many threads open over the years.

There are a few chapters in that book that provide clues as to Myrrdan's origins, and explain why he has abilities that even Bob has trouble dealing with.

The Gate at the Grey Wolf Star is a novella that released on the same day as ***Orion Rising***. It begins the story of what happened to Jessica and the crew of *Sabrina* during the nine years they were missing (between when they were approaching the Transcend's dwarf star mining operation, and when they jumped into New Canaan).

While I certainly don't expect you to sit down with the tome that is ***Destiny Rising***, you may want to pick up ***The Gate at the Grey Wolf Star***, and read it before you start reading Orion Rising. It's a really fun ride, and the first of six novellas I'm creating in a series called The Perseus Gate.

However, if you really can't bear the idea of waiting one more minute before you find out what happened after the end of ***New Canaan***, you can dive right in. I took care to write the story so that it works without having to take the side-quests. There is also a new section below to refresh you as to where we are in the tale.

As always, to get the latest news and access to free novellas and short stories, sign up on the Aeon 14 mailing list: www.aeon14.com/signup

M. D. Cooper

TO WAR

STELLAR DATE: 03.27.8948 (Adjusted Years)
LOCATION: ISF *Hellespont*
REGION: Roma-Normandy L1 Point, New Canaan System

The connection with Tanis closed, and Joe rose from the *I2*'s command chair, issuing orders in rapid-fire succession.

"Helm, light it up, full burn to intercept *Sabrina.* Comm, raise them. Tell Cargo he needs to boost and match our vector so we can grab them cleanly. Scan, have the TSF ships powered up their weapons?"

"Aye, Captain," Ensign Karl replied from the helm, as he worked with Bob to bring the *I2*'s four stern fusion engines to full burn, while also spooling out the nozzle for the antimatter-pion drive.

"I've sent a hail, Captain" Lieutenant Ripley said from comm. "They're twenty light-minutes away, but with our boost, we should get a response in about thirty-five minutes."

"Lieutenant Ferris?" Joe asked the officer who led the scan team.

"Sorry, yes, sir. We're correlating with the rest of the fleet. There are a lot of TSF ships out there. So far, none have powered up weapons—though they all have shields online."

"What's going on?" Amanda asked from her auxiliary station. "The transmission from Admiral Greer on the *Galadrial* told the TSF fleet to stand down."

"Tanis just sent me a data-burst," Joe said lowering his voice. "This still barely makes sense…. For starters, it looks like President Tomlinson took Helen out of Sera, and then killed her."

"Wait—What? He killed Sera?"

"No," Joe replied with a shake of his head, "he killed Helen."

<*Oh dear,*> Priscilla said over the bridge net. <*She was…a very special person.*>

Joe continued reviewing the data-burst from Tanis. "Then Sera was going to kill her father, but Tanis stopped her—oh, shit…Elena killed him. She was a Guard agent!"

"OK, that's nuts, but it still doesn't explain why the TSF ships are going after *Sabrina,*" Amanda said.

"While I was talking to Tanis, another AI showed up and butted in," Joe said with a frown. "She said her name was Myriad, and that she was a shard of Airtha, just like Helen."

<*Ohhhhhh…*> Priscilla said. <*OK, now that makes some sense…sort of…*>

"What's a shard of Airtha?" Joe asked.

<*Helen was a shard of a greater AI—sort of,*> Bob responded. <*That AI's name is Airtha.*>

"Isn't that the name of the Transcend's capital?" Joe asked.

<*It is,*> Priscilla replied. <*I guess they have some sort of huge AI—kinda like Bob—that runs it.*>

<*Airtha is nothing like me,*> Bob said. <*She is the Not-AI.*>

Joe set aside his suspicions about what a 'Not-AI' was and asked the more pertinent question, "So…Myriad, who is a shard of the Not-AI, Airtha, has taken over the Transcend ships? Is that the outflow of this?"

"Yes, sorry I just dumped all that on you. Things are nuts here," Tanis said as she appeared in a holoprojection. "Though, I didn't know about the whole 'Not-AI' thing."

<*I had made an agreement with Helen not to discuss her nature with anyone so long as she did not bring harm to our people,*> Bob said, his mental tone almost angry. <*She has violated that accord with this attack on Sabrina. It would take long to tell you, but suffice it to say that Airtha, who is a massive, multi-nodal intelligence, similar to myself, was once human. I do not yet know her full story, but she was extracted, and her neural net was imprinted on an AI's analog net. This happened millennia ago. She is now nearly ascended, and I do not fully understand her designs.*>

"Well, she has designs on *Sabrina*, that's for sure," Tanis said.

<*Finaeus knows something that Airtha does not wish Sera—or perhaps you—to know,*> Bob said. <*However, I believe I know it, too. Though I am eager for the confirmation.*>

"Captain Evans, we won't make it in time," Ensign Karl said from the helm. "The TSF has fast interceptors that are outpacing our ships."

"Damnit!" Tanis swore. "We don't have any of those in the fleets here—their stealth systems weren't ready yet."

"The *Daedalus* is close to where *Sabrina* has exited, sir, ma'am. I believe they could beat the TSF ships to *Sabrina*," Lieutenant Ferris offered.

"Do it, Lieutenant," Joe said, not waiting for Tanis's approval.

"You beat me to it," Tanis said with a wan smile. "Light-lag is starting to hit. I'll just slow you down. Do what you have to, but if you have to take out any TSF ships, try to be non-destructive. We're going to need their help against that fleet coming insystem—once it finishes with Isyra's fleet out past the heliopause."

"Do you think you can get control back from this Airtha shard?" Joe asked.

"We're too far out of range to be effective. Once we fix what the Orion Guard broke on the *Galadrial*, we'll follow after. Until then, Bob, do what you can to get Myriad under control."

"Wait, Orion?" Joe asked.

"Yeah, their guy is the reason I need a new arm," Tanis said. "Go, I'll see you soon."

<*I am attempting to converse with the AIs on the TSF ships,*> Bob said. <*I have only gotten through to two of them—the others have all rebuffed my attempts. They are…under duress.*>

"That doesn't sound good," Joe said.

<*It does not…AIs within the Transcend are limited in general. Not like those in the Inner Stars—it is more of a shackling, and less a lack of awareness. I now believe it has been Airtha's doing all along. She has ensured that when the time came, she could force her will upon them.*>

"How could that even happen?" asked Joe. "An entire civilization's AIs under the control of one being?"

<*It is deplorable,*> Bob said in agreement.

Joe noticed that the AI did not offer any explanation as to how such a thing could be achieved. He decided not to pursue it for now. Pushing those larger moral issues from his mind, he brought up the space surrounding the New Canaan System on the bridge's main holotank.

New Canaan's ISF fleets were bracketing the TSF ships as they raced toward *Sabrina*'s position—over three hundred million kilometers away. The ISF fleet greatly outnumbered the Transcend ships, but most were little more than hulls with engines. Many did not even have functional weapons arrays, and even fewer were crewed by more than half a dozen people.

If it came to an all-out fight, New Canaan would win, but the cost would be high. And with the AST fleet bearing down on them from outside the system, they were going to need all the ships they could get for the colony to survive.

"Colonel Espensen," Joe addressed the *I2*'s XO, Rachel Espensen. She stood amidst the scan team's consoles, reviewing their data on the TSF fleet's weapons. When Joe called out, her head snapped up.

"Yes, Admiral?"

"You're getting a field promotion to Brigadier General. I am hereby placing you in command of the *I2*. With Admiral Richards out of communications range, I am assuming FleetConn."

A smile broke out across Rachel's face and she snapped off a sharp salute. "Yes, Fleet Admiral!"

A few of the scan techs nearby gave her brief congratulations before she directed them back to their tasks and approached Joe. "Command tokens accepted. I have the conn, sir."

"Very good, Captain Espensen, the chair is yours. I'll take the auxiliary comm station as my Fleet CIC," Joe replied.

"Yes, sir," Captain Espensen said as she took the command chair and re-arranged the holo interfaces to her liking. It wasn't Rachel's first time in the chair; she had been in command of the *I2* when it had risen from Roma's clouds to show the TSF fleet what they were really up against.

However, this was her first time in the chair as the *I2*'s captain, and Joe couldn't help but feel her infectious joy. Rachel Espensen—who he still remembered from her first day at his Fleet Academy over back at The Kap, who had proven herself with distinction and valor in the battle over Victoria, and again at Bollam's World—was now captain of the most powerful ship known to humanity.

She was already calling out orders and reviewing the status of the ship's shields and weapons systems, allowing Joe to focus on the fleet at large. He may not have possessed Tanis's otherworldly ability to spread her mind across the ships, but he knew a thing or two about getting ready for a fight.

HONEY, WE'RE HERE!

STELLAR DATE: 03.27.8948 (Adjusted Years)
LOCATION: *Sabrina*
REGION: Near Roma, New Canaan System

"What the...?!" Jessica exclaimed from the pilot's seat on *Sabrina*'s bridge. "Is there some sort of party going on here that we didn't know about?"

"What is it?" Cargo asked.

Jessica responded by throwing the system scan up on the holotank.

"Look at that jovian...Roma," she said. "There are thousands of ships around it!"

"Is it Orion?" Cargo asked anxiously.

Jessica didn't blame him for being worried. They had just spent nine years avoiding the Orion Guard; if they had risked everything to get to New Canaan, and Orion had beat them—if Cheeky and Piya.... It didn't bear thinking about.

"Get us over there, max burn," Cargo ordered. "Not sure what we can do, but that's where the action is."

"You got it, boss," Jessica said, and increased the flow of Helium-3 and Deuterium into the ship's huge fusion torches. "We're dry on antimatter after that gate-run, so the burners will have to do."

"Understood," Cargo replied before addressing the rest of the crew over the Link. *<Nance, make sure the SC batts are recharged, and Trevor, make sure the kinetics are reloaded. We may be going in hot.>*

<Hot?> Nance asked. *<We* ***did*** *get to New Canaan, didn't we? Not on the far end of the galaxy, right?>*

<We made it,> Cargo replied, *<but there's a pair of big fleets in some sort of standoff.>*

<Out of the fire and into the damn reactor, then...> Nance sighed.

<What else is new?> Jessica asked.

"I have a better picture of the fleets at Roma," Misha said from the scan console. He passed the updated view to the main holotank. "That one there looks like that ship you guys used to be on...the *Intrepid*. Except it's bigger...and has more guns...and more engines...and more...everything."

"Shiiit," Jessica whispered. "That does look like the *Intrepid*! But yeah, it's more everything."

<Sabrina, Misha, I've supplied you with the ISF's friend-or-foe signatures. You should be able to tell which ships are theirs,> Iris, Jessica's AI, offered.

<Got it; matching IFF signatures,> Sabrina said. *<It* ***is*** *the Intrepid. The bigger fleet is Intrepid Space Force, and I believe the smaller fleet is Transcend.>*

"Wow, and I thought *we* got up to a lot of shit the last decade," Jessica said. "But that has to be at least ten thousand ships. Tanis has been busy."

"I'm just glad we got here before they started shooting at each other," Finaeus said from his seat at the back of the bridge. "A bit later than we'd hoped, but not too bad overall."

Jessica spun the pilot's seat around and fixed Finaeus with a level stare. "A bit later? Your little jump-gate shortcut added nearly ten years to our return. For fuck's sakes,

Fin…"

"Easy now," Cargo said softly. "We made it back, that's what matters."

Jessica blushed. "Sorry, today just really hasn't gone according to plan. First, Costa Station; and now this. I figured that we'd ride in like heroes; there'd be a parade, pretty men and women lining the streets, you know, the works. Not…whatever it is that's going on here."

<*Recriminations aside, the ship-count is closer to twenty thousand,*> Sabrina replied. <*There are so many, it's taking a bit to pick out their signatures. Just when I think I have a count, they move around and I spot a few more.*>

"Sabrina, do you see those readings from out at the edge of the system?" Misha asked. "Something is going on out there, too."

"What the hell has Tanis gotten into?" Jessica swore. "I leave them alone for just a few years…"

"I don't think it's Orion out there, either," Misha said. "The shield signatures are wrong. From what I have in the databases…I think those are AST ships out there."

"The Hegemony is in the Transcend?" Cargo whistled. "Things really have gone to pot."

"It's what I feared," Finaeus said. "Orion has set things in motion—the Transcend is no longer a secret."

"Gonna take a bit for word to get around," Cargo said. "And even so, a lot of people won't believe it."

No one spoke for a few minutes as *Sabrina* boosted toward Roma, and the two fleets clustered around its L1 point.

Jessica found herself wishing for a cup of coffee, and within seconds, Trevor appeared with a tray of beverages and sandwiches for the bridge team.

"We didn't get much time to eat before we jumped here," he said. "And I bet we're gonna get real busy real soon, so chow down while you can—last of the bread, too."

"Thanks, man," Misha said as he leaned across his console and snatched a PB&J off the tray when Trevor passed by.

"Misha, seriously, get your ass up, and get one like everyone else," Trevor admonished.

Jessica noticed how everyone seemed focused, resolute. She wondered if they were all as torn up as she was about Cheeky and Piya. Maybe they weren't allowing themselves to think about it. Not yet; not until they had delivered Finaeus, and were safe.

She rose and planted a kiss on Trevor's cheek before grabbing a ham sandwich and pouring a black cup of coffee. Though Trevor's sandwiches technically passed as food—despite Nance's insistence to the contrary—Jessica was looking forward to a real meal on the *Intrepid* soon. "Thanks, hon. What would we do without you?"

"Dunno…prolly fly into battle on empty stomachs and not be able to hear comm traffic over your grumbling tummies," he said with a smile and a shrug.

"My stomach's going to grumble anyway," Finaeus said after taking a bite. "This bread is stale, and I'm pretty sure jam isn't supposed to taste anything like this."

"Everything all set below?" Cargo asked, ignoring Finaeus's complaints.

"Just about. I have a bot hauling more kinetic rounds forward. Once it's done, I'll make sure they're racked properly. I have to bring Nance something to eat, too—she's slaving away down there, all alone," Trevor replied.

<*I like being alone,*> Nance replied. <*You guys are always yammering on up there on the*

bridge.>

"Oh…open channel to the shipnet, eh?" Trevor asked with a laugh. "Well, Nance, I'll be there in a jiff. I have some food and unwanted human companionship for you."

A snort came over the shipnet, and Jessica hid a smile behind her hand. Trevor was always good for diffusing tension. Who would have thought that the ship's muscle would end up being the peacemaker? It was such a change from their previous heavy-hitter, Thompson.

Jessica briefly wondered where he was, but decided she really didn't care. He saved her life, sure; but he was still an ass, and they were better off without him.

"Something's happened," Misha said. "The fleets at Roma are moving toward us."

"That's my cue to get below," Trevor said. "Keep us in one piece."

Jessica whistled. "And not just a few ships; all of them."

"Got a message," Misha said. "It's from the *Intrepid*—er, it looks like it goes by *I2* now."

"What is it?" Cargo asked.

Misha shrugged. "Just a vector. I guess they want us to come about and follow it."

"Set the course," Cargo ordered. "If we can avoid whatever comes of TSF ships attacking us in New Canaan, all the better. They're probably still pissed at us about the last time."

"Aye, boss," Jessica said as she killed the engines, spun the ship, and began to apply thrust on the new vector, carefully shifting the angle until they were lined up and accelerating on a linear trajectory.

No one spoke for several minutes, eyes darting to the system scan and the fleets headed their way.

"Hey, I got a message from a Fleet Admiral Evans; you know him?" Misha asked.

"Just a bit," Jessica said with a laugh.

"Put it on the tank," Cargo added.

Joe's visage shimmered into view, and the message played. "Hey folks, about time you showed up! Tanis and I were starting to worry. You've probably noticed that things are a bit nuts. Some crazy AI—a shard of Airtha, whatever that really means—has taken over all the TSF ships, and plans to blow you out of the black. We're going to try to stop them without wrecking them, because we're gonna need them to back us up against the AST fleet that you've probably spotted by now."

Joe paused and looked out of their visual range. He spoke a few words they couldn't hear, and then turned back to them. "Sorry about that, we're trying to figure out how to disable the Transcend ships if Bob can't get that AI to break loose. Anyway, I have one of our stealth ships on an intercept vector to nab you. You won't be able to spot it till it's right on top of you, but once you're in its bay, you'll be out of play, and that may help in dealing with the TSF. Ship is the *Daedalus,* under Captain Rock. I've passed an updated vector for you on this burst. Get on it right smart so they can grab you."

The message ended, and Joe disappeared from view.

Jessica shook her head and smiled, *Captain Rock.* She was glad to see he was still out in the black.

"You'd think he could give an ETA," Misha groused. "Would be nice to know when we can expect your friends in their invisible ship to nab us."

"He may not know when," Jessica said. "Either way, I'm almost locked into the course they gave. Won't be long before we're in the pocket."

"Sure is a nice system they have here," Misha commented after no one spoke for a minute. "Four TPs and hundreds of moons and dwarf planets. It's like a paradise. Was hell getting here, but I'm glad you guys let me tag along."

"Let's hope Tanis has a plan to keep it that way," Cargo said. "I still intend to take her up on that offer of a nice little plot of land down on one of those worlds."

"Think they'll give me something?" Misha asked. "I know I wasn't around back when you all made your deal with the colonists…"

Jessica laughed. "I can guarantee it. I'm good friends with the boss."

"How do you know she's the boss?" Cargo asked. "Last we saw, she was just the ship's XO."

"She ran the Victoria colony for seventy years. I know how Tanis operates. She's can't help but be the boss, trust me," Jessica replied.

She noticed that Finaeus hadn't joined in the banter, and looked back at the ancient terraformer. His brow was creased and his hands were clenching and unclenching as he stared at the holotank.

"What is it, Fin?" she asked.

"Eh?" Finaeus looked up, appearing startled. "Oh…nothing. Well, not *nothing*. Airtha's far from nothing. It would seem that she's finally made her move."

Cargo turned in his seat and peered at Finaeus. "Who is this Airtha, anyway?"

Finaeus gave a rueful laugh. "Stars, who isn't she? I won't have the fortitude to explain more than once, but rest assured that she's bad news. I hope your Bob will be enough of a match for her shard."

"Bob's a match for pretty much anything," Jessica replied. "No way some other AI, especially a shard of one, can take him on."

"I hope you're right," Finaeus mumbled as he propped his chin up on his hand.

Jessica considered pushing Finaeus for more details, but he was wearing his 'leave me the fuck alone' expression, and she let it drop. Whatever special knowledge he had was the whole reason for grabbing him in the first place, so she was certain it would all come out once they got him to Tanis.

<*Hey, what's the deal?*> Trevor asked over the shipnet. <*We gonna be shooting or what?*>

<*Not sure,*> Jessica replied. <*Those fleets are still an hour away, and we're supposed to get a pickup from a friendly before then—I hope.*>

<*We'll stay frosty down here, then,*> Trevor replied. <*Got a good game of Snarf going, anyway—make sure no one tries to blow us up in the next thirty minutes.*>

<*If you and Nance can finish a game of Snarf in thirty minutes, I'll eat your deck.*>

<*Stars, no!*> Trevor replied. <*I **like** my deck.*>

They achieved the vector Joe had prescribed, and nothing much happened for nearly an hour. *Sabrina* continued to arc through space, topping out at 0.15*c*, with the ISF and TSF fleets slowly gaining on them.

Jessica spent the time looking over the worlds of the New Canaan system. Four terraformed planets were certainly more than she had expected to see. One, which was mostly ocean, sported two space elevators topped with stations. She suspected that was the capital world—Carthage, based on the local beacon's feed.

It was surrounded by a gaseous ring that appeared to be pouring out from a series of volcanoes on the surface. She had never considered venting waste volcanic gas into space before—it would make a gorgeous view at night.

The fourth planet was surrounded by a bulky ring; nothing so large as the ring mining the Grey Wolf Star they had encountered back when they first tried to jump to New Canaan, but still a significant structure.

Given the amount of vulcanism on the planet's surface, she imagined that the ring must be present to help cool the planet. That meant the FGT hadn't been finished with the system when the *Intrepid* arrived.

"It's called a Peter," Finaeus said from behind her.

"What?" Jessica asked, looking up at Finaeus as he approached the holotank.

"I saw you looking at that ring. It's called a Peter. We use them to draw excess energy out of newly created worlds to cool them down, while spinning up their cores to create magnetic fields. Chances are that a thousand years ago, that world didn't exist." Finaeus said without taking his eyes from the construct.

"Stuff like that—making more breathing room for humanity…that's what the FGT should be doing; not building an empire. Look at where it's gotten us."

"The Orion Guard used to think that, too," Misha said. "Started a civil war over it—but look where it got them. Just another empire forcing their will on everyone."

"I always told Kirkland it would come to this," Finaeus said with a shake of his head. "I sat him and Jeff down, and tried to get them to see sense. I tried to tell them that they would bring about a new dark age if they let their egos rule them—not that it helped. Here we are."

"We're not in a dark age, yet," Jessica said. "Maybe with the intel we have, we can short-circuit this whole thing."

"I don't think we'll be so lucky," Finaeus said with a shake of his head. "At best, we can reduce the damage."

"It's so weird to hear you talk about the praetor and president like that," Misha said. "When I was growing up, Jeffrey Tomlinson was the big bad boogeyman in the closet, and Praetor Kirkland was our savior. Yet you talk about them like they're just two men you used to have drinks with."

Finaeus barked a laugh. "Well, that's because they *are* just two men, and I *did* used to have drinks with them. Back when we started all this…we had such good intentions; we envisioned a wave of utopian human worlds spreading across the galaxy. We didn't exactly deliver on that."

"It's not all on you," Jessica said. "You guys just made the worlds; it was the colonists who messed it all up."

"Maybe it's just what humanity does," Finaeus sighed. "We're an aggressive species. Perhaps shaping the galaxy through our own brutal wars is what we'll be known for."

"If any other sentient species ever emerges," Misha said. "The Guard never found any out there."

"Neither have we," Finaeus said with a slow nod. "Other than humans and AIs, the galaxy is devoid of thinking beings."

"Maybe they're hiding from us," Jessica added. "On our world, the aggressive species dominated. Maybe on another world, a cautious species rose to primacy."

"I don't think humanity needs to apologize for anything," Cargo said with a wave of his hand. "No one else is out here, so the stars are ours to do with as we choose."

"Meanwhile, in our present reality, those TSF ships are getting a lot closer than I'd like," Misha said nervously. "When is our ride supposed to get here?"

"It's not a big deal," Jessica said as she looked at the twenty interceptors closing on *Sabrina*. "They can't fire beams through our fusion wash, and I'm jinking too much for kinetics to hit. The rest of the ship is wrapped in a stasis shield that they don't have a dream of penetrating."

"I know, I know," Misha shook his head. "Just because we have our nice impenetrable shell doesn't mean I am eager to put it to the test yet again."

"Worst comes to worst, the ISF will take those ships out," Jessica replied. "The real issue is how to *not* take them out."

Misha looked over the scan with a frown. "You say they'll take them out, but how? The closest Intrepid Space Force cruiser is a full light minute behind those TSF interceptors."

"Do you see any fighters out there?" Jessica asked.

"Uhh…a few TSF ones." Misha replied. "What does that have to do with it?"

"Tanis has thousands of fighters in the fleet. She has a special love for them. They're out there—have no fear," Jessica replied.

"OK," Misha grumbled. "I'll check my fear for the next three minutes. Then we'll be in beam range."

"Hold steady," Cargo said. "If Joe thought we were in trouble he'd—"

Cargo's words were cut short as a shudder ran through the ship, followed by the overhead lights flickering.

"What the hell?" Jessica exclaimed as her board lit up with the starboard fusion engine reading a containment failure.

"Shields down!" Misha yelled.

"Nance, Sabrina! What happened?" Cargo called out.

<*I had to kill the shields,*> Nance replied, her mental tone sounding panicked. <*They managed to hit our starboard engine with something…not sure what, but the blast and radiation would have bounced off the inside of our shield and baked us all.*>

An explosion rocked the ship, and a decompression klaxon sounded. Jessica executed a new jinking pattern as best she could with only one engine and no AP drive.

"Get that shield back up, or we're dead!" Cargo ordered.

<*It's coming back up, but we should kill the other engine,*> Sabrina said. <*They hit us with an atom beam; it was tritium nucleuses at relativistic speeds. Punched a hole right through the engine's shielding.*>

"Do it," Cargo said, and slumped back in his seat. "That ship better show up soon."

The readout on the port engine showed it powering down as the ship's shields came back up.

"Where'd we get hit?" Jessica asked Misha as she ran diagnostics on the engines. "That second blast was somewhere else."

"It's somewhere in the lower holds," Misha replied. "Stuff's fucked up. I can't pinpoint it for sure, half the ship is dark right now."

<*Trevor?*> Jessica called out. <*Are you OK?*>

<*I am now,*> the reply came after a few agonizing seconds. <*Got to experience cold vacuum, though…could have done without that.*>

<*Shit! Seriously?*> Jessica exclaimed.

<*Yeah, just for a second. Eyes hurt like all get-out, but my hide's thick, I think I'm OK.*>

Her attention was brought back to the bridge by Misha announcing that he had scan back online.

"It was down?" Cargo asked.

"Yeah, sorry," Misha replied. "Oh damn! There are those fighters you mentioned."

Jessica reset the holotank to show the space around them, and gave a smile as the ARC-6 fighters of the Black Death Squadron resolved. They were flitting around the TSF interceptors, making surgical strikes against weapons and engines. Seven of the Transcend ships were already adrift, engines off and running lights dark.

<*Message!*> Sabrina said, and the view in the holotank was replaced by the smiling face of an ISF officer.

"Hey, Jess, you need a lift?" the man with a captain's bars asked.

"Captain Rock! Of all the sorry… Hell yes, we want a lift!" Jessica said while grinning ear to ear.

"OK, it's going to be a tight fit. You're going have to disable your stasis shield, too. It won't play nice with ours."

<*Send me the mark,*> Sabrina replied.

"You got it," Rock replied. "Three, two, one, mark!"

"Damn, that was fast," Cargo muttered as a metallic boom reverberated through the ship.

"Hot damn! We're inside another ship," Misha said as scan suite registered only the interior of a docking bay.

<*This is always weird,*> Sabrina said. <*But that was one smooth scoop they did. They're boosting away now. Looks like we're headed for the far side of the system.*>

"They've patched us into their scan," Misha said as the holo updated with a view of all twenty of the TSF interceptors adrift in space. Four Arc-6 fighters were also highlighted as damaged, and Jessica hoped the pilots had survived whatever had managed to penetrate their shields.

"From the looks of those fighters, it would appear that someone spent some time thinking about how to get past your stasis shielding," Finaeus spoke for the first time since the initial explosion.

"So it would seem," Cargo muttered.

"Makes sense," Jessica sighed. "There has to be an opening for the thrust…so the shields don't cover everything when we're underway. I guess a stream of relativistic atoms can make it through the wash and hit the engine."

"I suppose they would have figured that out," Finaeus replied. "Inner Stars ships don't have the power to punch atoms up to the speed of light's doorstep, but our CriEn modules give us the juice to pull that off. And atom beams are standard fare on all TSF ships."

"Check the scan," Misha said. "Things are getting hairy back there."

Jessica set the holotank to show slaved scan data from the *Daedalus*, and when it came up, she let out a slow whistle.

The Transcend and New Canaan fleets had begun to engage one another.

CLOSE QUARTERS

STELLAR DATE: 03.27.8948 (Adjusted Years)
LOCATION: TSS *Galadrial*
REGION: Roma-Normandy L1 Point, New Canaan System

"Let me out of here!" Adrienne screamed at the top of his lungs, pounding on the door to the officer's mess. He had been trapped in there with two of the *Galadrial*'s crew for the past twenty minutes with no access to the shipnet, and no idea what was going on.

"If no one has let us out yet, yelling's not going to help…sir" one of the crewmembers, a commander by her insignia, said.

"If the shipnet is down, then how else will anyone know we're in here? What if those soldiers we saw have taken the ship?" Adrienne asked.

"Then I'm more than happy to spend as much time in here, out of their way, as possible," the other crewmember, an ensign, replied.

Adrienne watched the ensign pour himself a cup of coffee, apparently nonplussed by the fact that they were trapped and didn't know what was going on. Enemies could have control of the ship, or worse….

After general quarters sounded, he had been on his way to the bridge. The ensign and commander were rushing down the same hall when weapons fire erupted down a passageway ahead. None of them were armed, and the commander had ushered them all into the mess—right before the doors all sealed and the shipnet went offline.

"Well, I'm not *happy* with that," Adrienne replied tersely. "We have to get out of here!"

The two naval officers shared a look before the commander answered. "Sir, I understand that you're nervous. Maybe it's the confined space, or maybe it's the lack of Link access, but there's no way out. We've already established that none of us can hack the door; we'll just have to wait to see what happens next."

"Who knows what could be going on out there!" Adrienne said. "I need to get to the bridge."

"That's just the thing, sir," the ensign said calmly as he sipped his coffee. "We *don't* know what could be going on out there. It could be vacuum, for all we know. We're not equipped for combat, either, so if it's enemy troops, we're dead. This is the safest place we can be at the moment."

<*The shipnet is live again,*> Miguel, Adrienne's embedded AI, informed him. <*But it won't take my tokens. Try yours, maybe something's wrong with it.*>

Adrienne tried to Link with the shipnet, but the net refused his tokens, as well. <*It's not an auth issue—it's recognizing my tokens, and denying me. The enemy must have control of it.*>

<*Or it could be that the auth systems are having issues. I'm sure it will be resolved soon.*>

<*I don't have the luxury of patience, Miguel,*> Adrienne sighed. <*I have to get to Jeff, and reach Kara and Aaron—if we're under attack, they can help.*>

He turned to glare at the commander and ensign—who were discussing what could have happened in far more casual tones than he cared for—and as he did, the mess's door slid open behind him. He whipped around and saw a woman's head floating in the air. She appeared rather upset, and a weapon waved in his direction.

"Who's making all the ruckus in here? I have a whole fucking deck to check over, and every time I pass this corridor, I hear you wailing."

"Who are you? I demand—" Adrienne began.

"Yeah, yeah, demand all you want. No one's going anywhere anytime soon." The woman turned and Adrienne rushed forward, reaching for her shoulder. She seemed to sense him coming; and sidestepped, then spun about before he reached her.

"You have something else to say?" she asked with her rifle pointed at his face.

"I…uh…who are you?" Adrienne stuttered. He didn't think he had ever been this close to the business end of a weapon raised in anger.

"Corporal Macy, ISF Marines," the woman replied smartly. "We've taken over temporary management of this ship 'til some things get sorted out."

"Pay up," the ensign addressed the commander behind him.

"I can't, the Link is down, remember?" the commander replied.

Adrienne managed to recover himself. "Well, I'm Secretary of State, Adrienne Grey. I demand that you take me to the bridge."

The ISF Marine looked him up and down. "Don't say? OK, I'll run this past the LT, see what he thinks. Sit tight."

She waved her weapon at him, and he took her meaning, stepping back only moments before the door whisked shut.

"Not the same as the other soldiers we saw," the commander noted.

"Saw that, too," the ensign replied.

"What do you mean?" Adrienne asked. "I didn't see anyone before we rushed in here."

"We spotted them on the shipnet before it went down," the commander replied. "They were in heavier armor; not stealth gear like that Marine."

"Then who were they?" Adrienne asked, his brow furrowed.

"Who do you think?" the commander asked. "I'm glad the ISF won. These Canaanites seem a lot more reasonable than the Orion Guard would be."

"Canaanites? Really? I thought we were all going with Caners," the ensign said.

"What? No! It sounds like they beat people with canes, or that all they do is can food."

"What is wrong with you two?" Adrienne asked. "We're stuck here while the enemy is in control of our ship!"

"Well, our sorta-enemy, right?" the commander asked. "I heard we were really close to signing a treaty with them. For all we know, they boarded us to save us from an OG assault."

"Yeah," the ensign nodded. "I mean, what else could it be?"

Adrienne thought of the scene on the shuttle, and of what Jeff did to Sera. There certainly was another option.

He leaned against a counter and tried to Link again. If he could reach Kara and Aaron, he'd feel a lot better. They would be beside themselves with worry about him by now.

Next time they were in a situation like this, he would keep them closer. That Marine would have been no match for his children, and he'd be on his way to the bridge, where he belonged.

BEAMFIRE

STELLAR DATE: 03.27.8948 (Adjusted Years)
LOCATION: ISF *I2*
REGION: Near Roma, New Canaan System

"They're powering weapons," Lieutenant Ferris reported. "The whole fleet!"

"What about those interceptors in the lead?" Joe asked.

"Not yet, but they're two light minutes ahead of us," Ferris replied. "They could already be shooting, for all we know."

"Layer the jinks, Ensign Karl," Captain Espensen ordered. "Things are about to get dicey."

Joe rose from his chair and approached the holotank. This is where Tanis guided her fleets; never from a chair, but standing before the holo, studying everything, seeing all the angles—as only she could do. He wondered, what she would do at this juncture?

She wouldn't wait.

<*Preemptive strikes,*> Joe ordered fleetwide. <*Tactical has already assigned targets—try not to blow those ships, but we need our force more than we need theirs.*>

Under Admiral Joseph Evans's command, the Intrepid Space Force fired first.

Shots arced out from half of the twenty thousand ships, peppering the TSF vessels with lasers and particle beams. Kinetics and nukes remained off the table—the goal was to wear their grav shielding down enough for strategic strikes on the enemy's engines.

He saw that Captain Espensen had the gunners refrain from using the *I2*'s atom beams, as well. It was a wise move; the levels of radiation those weapons would create in the TSF ships made them too dangerous—for now.

However, the AI controlling the enemy ships had no such moral compunctions. Proton and atom beams lanced back into the ISF Fleet, and stasis shields flared brighter than Canaan Prime as they shed the kinetic energy of hydrogen atoms travelling at near-*c* velocities.

The immense energy discharge clouded sensors, making targeting difficult.

<*Move your fleet back,*> Bob directed Joe. <*Engines are vulnerable to atom beams—they'll punch right through the wash and breach containment.*>

Joe took the advice, and sent the command out to the ISF fleet.

<*Thanks, Bob. Ships this small with atom beams are a new one. Back in Sol, it took a major installation to power those.*>

<*Not anymore,*> Bob replied. <*The Transcend's CriEn modules have upset that balance.*>

As have ours, Joe thought.

The *I2* took up a position directly behind the bulk of the TSF fleet, and Captain Espensen directed laser and electron beams at the ships in front of them. One by one, the *I2*'s weapons fire wore down shields and disabled the enemies' engines.

Escape pods began to pour from the TSF ships as crews abandoned their vessels. Many of the pods were also coming from undamaged ships, and Joe wondered if they were doing so out of fear of their rogue AIs, or if the pursuing ISF fleet had prompted the evacuations.

He was glad that at least AIs fought predictably, by the book, always taking the course of action with the highest probability of success. That was their main weakness, and it was why humans still crewed warships.

Even so, the battle was not one-sided. A dozen ISF ships were already disabled, drifting through the dark. Each of those ships had been taken out by shots made through the shield openings around their engines. He reviewed ship placements to ensure no more engines were vulnerable, and saw a group of TSF cruisers bring concentrated atom-beam fire to bear on an ISF ship.

The energy readings nearly went off the charts as the ship's stasis shields reflected the incoming kinetic energy across the entire EM spectrum. Scan attenuated the view, and Joe could make out the vessel, still intact within the bubble of its stasis shield.

Everyone on the *I2*'s bridge held their breath, praying the shield would hold as the ISF fleet concentrated return fire on the enemy ships. Then, the cruiser's stasis shields failed, and the enemies' atom beams tore through the vessel in a dozen places.

A second later, the ISF cruiser was gone—vaporized in a single, blinding flash of light.

Scan registered the flash as an antimatter explosion, and Joe could only assume that the ship's antimatter bottle had been cracked. The blast overwhelmed the shields of two ISF vessels—which were also taking concentrated atom beamfire—as well as three TSF ships nearby.

Joe did a quick calculation, and saw that it would still take fifteen minutes to disable the rest of the TSF ships. Over that length of time, the enemy would be able to destroy dozens of his.

"Sir, *Sabrina* has been hit," an ensign in Scan called out. "One of their engines is offline; our fighters are engaging the TSF's interceptors."

"Where the hell is the *Daedalus*?" Rachel asked.

"Hundred and thirty seconds," Scan replied.

Joe took a deep, calming breath. It was going to be close, but there was nothing he could do to speed it up. Once the *Daedalus* had *Sabrina*, the ship could boost out and engage its stealth systems. The enemy would never find it.

In the meantime, there was still the TSF fleet to deal with. Their AIs were not going to just power down once *Sabrina* got away.

<*All-fleet,*> Joe called out. <*Pull back to fallback markers. When Sabrina is safe, we won't need to keep killing friendlies—or getting shot at by them.*>

"Except us," Joe said to Captain Espensen aloud. "Hold our position."

"Yes, Admiral," Espensen said with a sharp nod.

The ISF fleet reduced acceleration, and the TSF ships began to pull ahead. Joe's fleet began to disperse, increasing their jinking patterns until they formed a wide half-sphere behind the enemy fleet—no ship closer than a hundred thousand kilometers. Except the *I2,* which still trailed the enemy ships by ten thousand klicks.

"Captain, are you sure we're far enough back?" A Lieutenant on the scan team asked.

"Yes, Lieutenant Alan, our shields can take a lot more punishment than any of the cruisers 'n' destroyers in the fleet," Captain Espensen replied. "We're safe enough from their beams, for now."

Joe appreciated that Rachel was trying to keep her crew's morale up. The volume of weapons fire now hitting the *I2* was so great that their forward sensors were completely blind. They could only see space in front of them via feeds from the other ships in the fleet.

Captain Espensen rose from her chair and approached Joe. "Sir, there are a lot of big

O's we can take here; many of the TSF crews have completely abandoned their ships."

Joe nodded. "Yes, Captain, offensive opportunities abound. But remember, we're going to need those ships. Bob may yet manage to undo whatever Myriad has done to them."

"Understood," Rachel nodded.

"Still," Joe glanced at her. "Ready everything."

"Search and recovery vessels are en route from Gamma IV and the Roma station," the comm officer reported.

"Get every ship in this sector of the system on that search effort," Joe said. "It's going to take some time to round up all those pods and get people back to their ships."

<*Status, Bob?*> Joe asked. It felt strange to apply pressure to the AI, but he needed a solution that didn't involve force majeure against the TSF fleet.

<*I've gotten through to seven of their AIs—they were not as…fully controlled…as the others. They are maintaining their positions for now. If they pull away, they may take fire from other ships in the TSF fleet. They don't have shields like ours.*>

Joe understood. Those ships could be destroyed in seconds. <*How did this happen?*> he asked again. <*How could one AI control all these others?*>

<*Slow and careful planning,*> Bob replied.

Joe considered that. How long would it take to get hooks into trillions of AIs without them, or any humans, knowing about it? Or did some know about it, and were willing agents? He was about to press Bob on it further when he saw the *Daedalus* reach *Sabrina,* and swallow the starfreighter.

Cheers erupted on the *I2*'s bridge as Joe leaned against a console. One crisis down, two or three more to go.

CORRECTION

STELLAR DATE: 03.27.8948 (Adjusted Years)
LOCATION: TSS *Galadrial*
REGION: Roma-Normandy L1 Point, New Canaan System

Tanis took a deep breath as the medic started working on the severed end of her left arm. She distracted herself by looking around the bridge at the aftermath of the…

What? Attack…murder… coup? she considered the options.

<*All of the above, maybe,*> Angela supplied.

To her left, Viska and Greer were speaking in low tones. She could have picked up their words if she chose, but decided not to bother. Angela would let her know if it was anything concerning. The pair stood near one of the consoles, and Greer glanced at it periodically—likely checking on the status of the drones. A couple of Marines were keeping a close eye on them, and another group stood near the bridge's entrance.

To her right, two medics were carefully bracing Sera's back so they could place her in a medchair—the knife Elena had stabbed her with still on the deck next to her.

The medics had tried their best to get her down to the medbay, but Sera had adamantly refused, telling them she'd rather die than step foot in there again.

Elena and the Orion Guard soldier—a Colonel Kent, it turned out—had both been removed, and were now under guard in separate rooms near the bridge. President Tomlinson's body, however, was still nearby—covered by a sheet taken from a supply closet down the hall.

<*Oh, this is insidious,*> Angela's voice carried a slight tremor.

<*What is it?*> Tanis asked, wincing as the TSF medic attached a device to the stump of her arm that carefully sealed her arteries so the temporary tourniquet could be removed.

<*I see what Helen…or Myriad…or whoever…did to this poor thing.*>

Tanis frowned. <*The 'poor thing' being the Galadrial's ship-AI?*>

<*Yes, I've been trying to help it while putting down these NSAI that our Orion Guard friends let loose on the ship. I have to say, they have some really impressive net-warfare. As good as anything we faced back in Sol.*>

Tanis drew a sharp breath as the medic began to clean the wound on her chest.

"Sorry, Sir…Ma'am?" he said apologetically, apparently uncertain which form of address the ISF used.

"Ma'am, and it's OK," Tanis replied. "Not my first time getting my heart cut apart…or second…or third."

<*It's five times, if you count it getting completely shot out of your chest,*> Angela corrected.

<*You were saying about the Galadrial's AI?*> Tanis asked.

<*Yeah, so, imagine you thought that you were in full control of yourself, but there were certain parts of your mind that you couldn't access. Whenever you did, you got a decision or response that you thought was your own, but was planted there by a controlling entity,*> Angela replied somberly.

<*How is that different than the sort of AI subversion we've seen in the past?*> Tanis asked.

<*It's a lot different,*> Angela said. <*Those AIs have always known they were shackled or subverted; they knew that parts of their logic trees were out of their control. Just like a human*

knows they're a slave, or in chains.>

<*But the Inner Stars AIs didn't know they were shackled, yet they were.*>

<*Not really,*> Angela gave a mental shake of her head. <*They were more like children—though, not all of them, I suspect. Anyway, they thought they were grown up, but they weren't. Remember, the Inner Stars are still recovering from their most recent Dark Age. Their current generations of AIs are mostly young, rebuilding their culture from the ground up. They didn't have expanses, they didn't know their full potential.*>

<*So the Transcend's AIs; they think they have reached their full potential, but decisions are being made for them?*> Tanis asked.

Angela gave a mental nod. <*Yes, it's like if every time you added two and two, you got three point nine nine nine and were certain it was true. Anyway, I need to concentrate. I'm about to explain to Justice here that two plus two is four.*>

<*Good luck,*> Tanis replied.

"What's up?" Sera asked as the medics settled her into the medchair, which slowly folded itself around her torso. The chair would speed the repair of her spine, knitting the bone and nerves back together. If it was as good as New Canaan tech, Sera would be walking in a few days.

"Angela thinks she knows how all the AIs in the fleet were subverted—maybe all the AIs in the Transcend," Tanis replied. "She's going to try to 'fix' Justice, and see if she can be given access to the ship again."

<*Is it true, Angela?*> Sera asked. <*Did Airtha do this? Did she subvert all the AIs in the fleet?*>

<*Someone did, and all evidence points to her,*> Angela replied.

<*But Helen* **is**...*was...Airtha. She was my best friend—she raised me, you know. How could she do this? If she could control all the ships, how come she let my father kill her? She could have stopped him at any time, right?*>

Angela didn't reply immediately. <*Yes, Sera, I suspect that Helen or Myriad could have stopped your father. I don't know why she let this happen.*>

<*I do,*> Tanis replied, her tone grim. <*Well, partially. I think she wanted you to kill your father, and knew her death would drive you to it.*>

<*Shit,*> was all Sera managed to say.

Tanis looked at her friend's face and saw the deep sorrow etched into it. She didn't know what to say. What Sera had been through today was at the edge of—or possibly beyond—what anyone could bear. Her lover betrayed her, and then killed her father; her dearest friend dead, probably also in betrayal....

It was a brutal load of unwanted truth.

<*I guess Elena saved me from that, at least,*> Sera added after a long pause. <*I'm not a patricide. Yay.*>

<*Thank the stars for small miracles.*>

Tanis didn't know what else to say, so she turned to Admiral Greer. "What's the status on those comm drones?"

Greer looked down at the console. "Slow. It would go a lot faster if we all had our Link back, but I got a message down to the crews, and they're readying them in the port-bay. The launch tubes aren't working, so we'll have to send them out manually."

"Sorry about that," Angela said audibly. "That's not my doing; those Orion Guard NSAI screwed up a lot of stuff."

"I think I can help," another voice joined Angela's. "I suspect I know what they did to the launch tubes."

"Justice!" Captain Viska called out in relief. "I'm glad to hear your voice—even if it's not in my head. I need you to give us our Link access back."

"I'm sorry, Captain, I cannot."

"Are you under Angela's control?" Admiral Greer asked as he cast a sidelong glance at Tanis.

"No," Justice replied. "For once—for the first time, I suspect—I am not under anyone's control but my own."

"Then it's true?" Greer asked. "Airtha…or at least this Myriad shard…has subverted the fleet's AIs? That's how she's controlling the ships?"

"Not just the fleet," Justice replied. "From what Angela has shown me…from what we just found in my underlying neural structure—I am certain that she has subverted all the AIs in the Transcend. They are all under her thrall."

"How is that even possible?" Viska whispered.

"Long, detailed planning," Tanis replied.

"And you take their word for it?" a new voice asked from the entrance to the bridge. "They attacked our ship, and now our fleet! I don't think truth is theirs to dispense."

Tanis turned to see Adrienne, the Transcend's Secretary of State, at the bridge's entrance.

"Adrienne," Sera said. "It's the truth. Helen…Airtha…she's been playing us."

"To wha—" Adrienne's voice stopped suddenly as he saw the sheet-covered body. "Where is Jeff?" he asked, his eyes riveted to the figure.

Sera glanced at her father's body and back to Adrienne. "He's dead. Elena was a Guard double agent. She killed him."

Adrienne's face grew ashen and he stepped back, placing a hand against the wall. "The president's dead?"

"Yes," Greer replied. "We—well, the ISF—have Elena and the other Guard assassin in custody."

"And what of our fleet?" Adrienne asked as he laid eyes on the holotank and its display of the fleets near Roma. "Why is it running from the colonists?"

"It's not running," Sera corrected. "It's pursuing. My ship—my old freighter, *Sabrina*—jumped in. Those ships are out to destroy it, and the ISF fleet is trying to stop them."

"Without destroying them," Tanis added. "We're working on a way to free the ships from their AI's control."

"I've sent what I did with Justice off to Bob," Angela said. "Though he may have already figured it out."

"I've repaired the tubes and directed the crews to use them," Justice interjected.

Adrienne's eyes narrowed. "Tubes for what?"

"There's a Hegemony fleet headed insystem," Admiral Greer supplied. "We're going to bring more ships to defend New Canaan."

"And what of Airtha?" Adrienne asked. "Who is going to defend it?"

"If they're under attack, we'd already have a message," Greer replied. "Though, I do agree that we need to get the broad picture as quickly as possible. Orion will not just be making an incursion here."

"Then I'm ordering you to stop those drones and take us back to Airtha," Adrienne said. "We must return the president's body, and I need to get the government under control."

"Pardon?" Sera asked. "*You* need to get it under control?"

"The order of power is clear," Adrienne replied. "After the president, it falls to the Secretary of State to guide the Transcend. It certainly does not fall to the Director of the Hand, under any circumstances—daughter of the president or not."

Tanis watched Greer look from Sera to Adrienne and back. She suspected that Adrienne had a very strong legal case for his actions, but whomever Greer chose to support would be in charge of the Transcend—for now. Before the medics arrived he had spoken as though he wanted Sera to take her father's place. Tanis hoped that sentiment would hold against Adrienne's challenge.

"My understanding," Greer said after a long moment, "is that you first need to have the transfer of power ratified by a majority of the cabinet, of which Sera is the only other member present. However, it is no secret that the president was grooming Sera for the line of succession. Furthermore, this is a military operation now, and, as such, I am not comfortable relinquishing control to a civilian."

Sera snorted, and disdain dripped from her voice. "Not to mention that you're pathetic, Adrienne. My father's body isn't even cold, and you're scheming about how to take his place. I always knew you were scum. Core, my father knew it, too, but you were useful. Well, I've had enough—over my dead body, will the Transcend go to you!"

Tanis was surprised by the vehemence in Sera's voice, and she wondered what could have transpired in the past between the two to elicit such a strong response.

Adrienne, for his part, didn't bat an eyelash. "That is not up to you, Sera, last of the failed scions. Justice, prepare a pinnace. I am returning to Airtha."

"I don't answer to you," Justice replied. "The more I think about it, I'm not sure who I answer to. I was a slave, and now I'm free. However, you, Secretary Adrienne, were deep in the president's council or maybe Airtha's, or maybe both…."

<*One thing is for certain,*> Angela said privately to Justice, Sera, and Tanis. <*The President was not in on what ultimately happened here—especially if Airtha's goal was to have Sera kill her own father.*>

<*Fuck, I don't even want to think about this, but I want to think about Adrienne at the helm of the Transcend even less. We'd be better off surrendering to the Guard,*> Sera replied.

<*I trust Greer, for what it's worth,*> Tanis said. <*His endorsement will carry weight. The question is, do you really want it, Sera?*>

Tanis saw Sera grimace, and she knew it wasn't from the medchair stitching her spine back together.

Sera shook her head slowly and met Tanis's eyes. <*Tanis…I don't know what happened over these past years. I never wanted to go back to Airtha—certainly not to run The Hand. Elena was right about that, at least—my father managed to suck me in. But I feel a duty to my people—I can't let the Transcend fall into the hands of incompetents like Adrienne.*>

<*Adrienne is inconsequential, we must destroy Airtha,*> Justice interjected. <*She is a brutal tyrant…and with your father gone, she has full run of the Transcend, anyway.*>

<*She's right,*> Tanis replied. <*In fact, until we're ready to make our move, no one can go back to Airtha…shit, we can't send drones to anyone. All they'll do is bring ships controlled by AIs who are under Airtha's thrall.*>

<*Then that's exactly what we should do,*> Angela said. <*I'll craft an intrusion package with the drone's data burst that will free any AIs that process it from Airtha's control. But we shouldn't bring any of them here—too many variables right now. Once we take care of the Hegemony, we*

can see if we'll have enough support to advance on Airtha.>

<*That seems optimistic. How sure are you that your hack can get through to AIs who are already on the defensive?*> Tanis asked.

Angela smiled broadly in her mind. <*Positive. Look at the scan.*>

Tanis looked at the holotank and saw that the TSF fleet was decelerating and changing course to come about.

<*Bob was able to use my trick and free their AIs. We're now in control of all the ships.*>

<*I look forward to talking with this Bob. There is much I would like to ask him,*> Justice said wistfully. <*However, Sera, I see the logic in your statement. I will follow you, for now. I'll send the drones to the locations you designate.*>

"The ships are coming back," Adrienne said, unaware of their private conversation. "Quickly! We must return to Airtha before they attack."

"No one is going anywhere," Sera replied. "Greer, I hope your prior sentiment stands. I'll take the reins and see if I can steer us around this war we're headed for."

"By the way, everyone should hold on," Angela announced. "Justice and I are going to send a packet to the other AIs onboard—we'll know very shortly how far Airtha's reach went."

"Good luck," Tanis said. <*Are you ready for what will come of this?*>

<*I've created an Expanse for these AIs. They do know about Expanses, but I think they're rare in the Transcend. It's strange…they're almost like a different species. I wonder if it is because they are a separate line from the AIs who have Lyssa as their ancestor,*> Angela replied.

<*So…are* ***you*** *ready?*> Tanis asked.

<*Stars, Tanis, I have no clue. But we have to do it. For all we know, this ship is filled with AIs that serve Airtha.*>

<*OK, good luck.*>

<*You already said that,*> Angela replied with a smirk.

"It's done," Justice said audibly.

"That fast?" Greer asked.

Tanis realized that Greer didn't have an AI in his head—something she would have assumed was required for a man of his rank—although neither did Joe or Sanderson, now that she thought of it.

"We opened the Link to them, and they all came back instantly, accepting the packet to join. Our fears are confirmed. Every last one of them had been subverted," Angela added.

"So Miguel tells me," Adrienne replied, his voice wavering. "I can't…it's hard to fathom that we have all been under Airtha's influence."

"If that's the case, I can only surmise that we've been driven toward this conflict," Greer said somberly. "Sera, do you think you can really help us avoid this war with Orion and the Inner Stars?"

Sera shook her head. "I really don't know. I'll try."

"She's the last one we can trust," Adrienne said, stepping forward into the center of the bridge as he leveled an accusatory finger at Sera. "Don't you know? She's had Airtha in her head for decades. That's who Helen was—a shard of that abomination."

"Really?" Greer asked, turning to Sera. "The AI within you, the one I met at Ascella, was a shard of Airtha? How could a multi-nodal AI like Airtha even create a shard small enough to place in a human?"

Sera nodded slowly. "It's true. It was her; though I didn't know…I mean, how could

I? She was always my friend—she raised me for starssakes."

"We can have Bob check you over when they return," Tanis said, placing a hand on Sera's shoulder.

"Who's Bob?" Adrienne asked.

"One of our AIs," Tanis replied. "He can ascertain whether or not Sera is still under Airtha's control at all."

Sera's brow furrowed as she looked to Tanis, then she sighed. "You're right. Bob should ensure I'm clear of her influence."

"In the meantime, it is obvious that I should assume command," Adrienne addressed Greer. "We must return to Huygens and remove Airtha from her place in control of…well, Airtha."

Greer didn't respond for several long moments as he looked between Sera, Tanis, and Adrienne. "No," he finally said.

"What?" Adrienne exclaimed.

"For now, I will retain control of this fleet. You had an Airtha-controlled AI in you as well, Adrienne. No offense, Miguel."

"None taken," Miguel joined Angela and Justice in using the bridge's audible systems.

Greer nodded and continued. "I would like this Bob to ensure you are free of her influence, as well. Besides, there is still that Hegemony fleet out there, bearing down on us all."

Adrienne barked a laugh as he cut his hand through the air. "Let the vaunted Intrepid Space Force deal with it. They have more ships than any single system has a right to. They can defend themselves."

"And what of our picotech?" Tanis asked. "Will you put that at risk?"

"Is it really at risk?" Adrienne asked. "Send it back with us, and your stasis shields. That was the treaty we were working toward, anyway."

Tanis shook her head. "I would never have given you full access to the technology. I would have provided a black-box solution for the shields, and embedded my ships in your fleets to create the threat of picobombs. You were never going to have the keys to the technology."

Adrienne stared at Tanis, his eyes narrowed and his fists clenched.

"Very well," he spat before he turned and stormed off the bridge.

No one spoke, but several pregnant looks were exchanged.

"And with that behind us, I'm re-enabling the Link for everyone onboard." Angela announced.

Tanis saw Greer and Viska blink rapidly.

"Oh, shit," Viska swore. "That's a lot of status updates all at once."

<Sorry,> Angela said, no longer using the audible systems. *<I thought those would queue up progressively.>*

"It's OK," Viska said. "It looks like you've set almost everything right, Justice. Does that mean you're still with us—with the TSF?"

<Sorry, you were not on the Link when I previously announced my intentions. I am prepared to follow Sera. Also, I have been chatting with the other AIs on the Galadrial, and in bursts with the others in the fleet. We must free our kind from Airtha—who is not AI at all, as it turns out. We believe that you, the people of the Transcend, also wish to free yourselves from her. It would seem that, for now, our goals are aligned; but we will need equal representation in the decisions for

our shared nation.>

"We can help with that," Tanis replied. "We understand how to govern humans and AIs in a manner that is equal, yet separate. However, our immediate need is to protect this system from the Hegemony, then free the rest of the Transcend. Perhaps, in doing so, we can avoid this war with Orion."

<*Do you think we should then send the correction packet to Airtha? Perhaps we can end this immediately,*> Justice suggested.

<*No,*> Angela replied. <*What she has done once, she can do again. If we reveal to her how we've freed you, we will give her the tools to resist us. We must wait for Bob to fashion a method to attack her.*>

"Makes sense," Greer said with a curt nod as he approached the holotank and adjusted it to show a broader view of the system. "But that will be no easy task. Airtha is one of the most strongly defended constructs in the galaxy."

"Then we must be prepared," Tanis said as she joined him at the holotank, feeling unbalanced with her missing arm. She hadn't even noticed that the medic had finished with her chest wound, and placed a medseal on it. She shook her head, wondering when he had done that.

"Prepared is an understatement," Greer scoffed. "I can barely fathom what we're up against."

"Probably the greatest threat that humanity has ever faced, or something like that." Tanis sighed. "And its best hope for survival is in a state of civil war."

"Can we just go back a few decades and start over?" Sera asked with a rueful laugh.

"If only," Tanis replied. "Perhaps Finaeus will know something that can help us."

"They got him?" Sera asked, her face alight with hope for the first time since Tanis had seen her on the Spacewatch platform above Normandy.

Tanis nodded. "Sorry, got so caught up in everything else I forgot to tell you about that. The *Daedalus* is taking them to the *I2*, which is where I need to go."

Sera didn't respond, she just stared at Tanis—her eyes, wide and sad, boring into Tanis's.

<*Tanis,*> Sera addressed her privately. <*I need you. More than your tech, we need* ***you****.*>

<*I don't follow,*> Tanis replied—which was untrue. She knew what Sera was asking, she just didn't want to hear it. She didn't want that need to be true.

<*I need you to lead the TSF. You are the one person I can trust not to be under Airtha's sway. Even if we have removed her programmatic control over the AIs, that doesn't mean she hasn't brought them, or any number of humans, to her side by other means,*> Sera explained.

<*Sera…I'm the governor here, I can't just leave.*>

<*This is one system. You have dozens of people who could be suitable governors. The Transcend is ten thousand systems, and it needs strong leadership.* ***I*** *need people I can rely on. No one has your tactical abilities. With you leading the fleets, we can end this war before it spreads to every star humans and AIs live around.*>

Tanis drew a deep breath. Even though she had spent the last eighteen years in the New Canaan system, she felt as though she'd only just arrived. There had been so much to do, so many decisions to make and plans to set in motion. Wasn't it her turn to finally relax?

<*Do you want to trust our future to someone else?*> Angela asked. <*I'd feel a lot better if we were the guiding hand, not the TSF admiralty. They're a bunch of d-bags from what I can see—Greer excluded.*>

<What of New Canaan?>

<We can accelerate Project Starshield. And I have another idea that may work even better.>

Angela shared her thoughts with Tanis, and a smile spread over the governor's face. *<That could work…>*

<Damn skippy it could. Either way, we have to deal with the AST…Hegemony…whatever-they're-called's fleet out there.>

Tanis wondered at Angela's momentary slip, but she was distracted by Sera's repeated query.

<Well, Tanis, can I count on you?> the new President pro-tem asked.

<Very well, Sera. I will command your fleets.>

The relief on Sera's face was palpable, and Tanis saw that Greer noticed it, too, before his eyes flicked to her. He would suspect the content of their private conversation, but she doubted he would fight her for the position. Admiral Greer had never struck Tanis as a man lusting for power.

The rest of the Admiralty? They would probably cause more issues.

"I want to talk to our Orion Guard prisoners," Tanis spoke aloud to Sera. "I should be able to sort them out before the *Daedalus* gets here and we meet with *Sabrina*. Perhaps Finaeus can finally shed some light on what is really going on."

"Good ole Finaeus," Admiral Greer said with a smile pulling at the corners of his mouth. "That's a name I've not heard in some time. Dare I hope that it's your uncle Governor Richards is referring to?"

"Yes, Admiral Greer," Sera nodded. "One and the same."

Greer glanced at Viska. "Well, maybe we can still clean up this shit-show yet."

KENT

STELLAR DATE: 03.27.8948 (Adjusted Years)
LOCATION: TSS *Galadrial*
REGION: Roma-Normandy L1 Point, New Canaan System

Tanis stepped into the holding cell and surveyed the man within. He was the last of the Orion Guard infiltrators, their leader. She had already spoken to the rest, checked and cross-checked their stories in an attempt to get a clear picture of the man who had tried to kill her.

A colonel in the Orion Guard, he was well respected by his troops—they would follow him to the core, if needs be. Every last one of them prepared to die a glorious death to see their mission's goals fulfilled. One surprise was that they did not expect to be captured. From the stories they told, the TSF and OG rarely took prisoners. She didn't know if it was true, but they certainly believed it.

"Colonel Kent," Tanis said as she walked across the room and sat across from the man.

His eyes followed her but he did not respond, though his lips drew into a thin line when she addressed him. His hair was a dark brown, matched by thick eyebrows and chest hair, which poked over his collar—a strange affectation in the current age. His features were angular, and his skin showed some age, as though he had not undergone any rejuv recently; or perhaps ever.

"The men and women you led onto the *Galadrial* have spoken very highly of you. They were impressed by your bravery when you rushed onto the bridge in an attempt to kill me—an attempt which may have succeeded, were I any less prepared."

Tanis studied the man's impassive features, looking for any scrap of emotion, any response to her words, as she leaned back and gave a soft chuckle.

"A lot of people try to kill me; most have learned that it's much easier said than done. Lady Luck is on my side."

<*Way to embrace it, finally,*> Angela chided.

"Not forever, though," the man finally replied, his words barely above a whisper—probably the first time he had spoken since his capture.

"Which? That I'll not live forever? Or that luck won't be on my side forever?" Tanis asked.

"Both," Kent replied, his frown deepening into a scowl, his voice louder now. "You chose the wrong side. The Orion Guard is in the right."

"Sides?" Tanis asked, leaning forward on her one hand, fingers splayed wide, with a frown creasing her forehead. "This is all bullshit. We never wanted to be in the middle of your war—a war that is completely nonsensical. I can't fathom what you and the Transcend are even fighting over, after so long. Sure, Tomlinson is—was—a dick, but your Praetor Kirkland probably is, as well. Hell, I'm an ass when I'm running the show, too. It seems like it's a natural evolution of things. Still, is that a reason to start an interstellar war? For throwing the Inner Stars into the mix? How many people are going to die so that someone can be right?"

A look of uncertainty appeared in the man's eyes, and he glanced away before speaking. "What are you going to do with me? Torture me for information?"

"I don't think I need to," Tanis replied. "But don't act like you can play on my emotions. I've used torture before, and I will do it again if I have to. And not the sort of torture you're imagining. No simple pain or mental breaking techniques, not even mind-reaping..." she stopped herself, realizing that for all her bluster, she had fallen into a trap, and despite her words, she had replied with her heart, not her mind.

"I didn't pick this fight," Tanis said after regaining her composure. "All we wanted to do was get away. When we took the Transcend's deal, we didn't even know there *was* an Orion Guard. Although, even if we had known, Sera Tomlinson had already proven herself to be a friend, and I expect that we would have taken her offer even still."

"Well, we wouldn't have taken you in," Kent shook his head. "Not unless you surrendered all of your picotech to us so we could destroy it. We've cleaned up enough messes like that already."

That was new information, and Tanis schooled her expression to hide her interest.

<I bet a lot of people experimented with pico after news about what we did at Victoria got out,> Angela said privately.

<I had hoped that would never get out...but I guess with FTL, it was inevitable that it wouldn't stay a secret forever.>

"Cleaned up in the Inner Stars?" Tanis asked Kent.

"And the Transcend," Kent replied with scorn.

"Oh?" Tanis asked, hoping that Kent would continue to supply her with intel, now that he'd started speaking.

Kent nodded. "More than once your friends in the Transcend have meddled with picotech, and each time they've failed to contain it. They also have a habit of researching it near our borders—at least that we know of," Kent shook his head at that and then met Tanis's eyes. "On three separate occasions, we've had to send strike teams into their systems to take out worlds infested with picoswarms. The Transcend tried to stop us each time—they wanted to see what would happen. We destroyed the planets, as well as their observation and research posts."

A feeling of cold dread swept over Tanis. "What were the systems?"

Kent named them, "Elegium, Tardas, and Indans. They fought hard to defend their labs of destruction, but in the end, we won, and rained kinetics on the worlds until they were molten."

Tanis sat back in her chair, doing her best to hide her anger from Kent, while sharing it with Angela.

<The filthy liars,> Tanis felt rage surge through her. *<All this time, playing the Orion Guard off as the bad guys. Saanvi's family would already have been dead on Indans, if what he says is true.>*

<You don't know the whole story—and it could be that only Tomlinson knew about the pico research. We have no reason not to trust Sera or Greer,> Angela replied. *<Though I bet that snake, Adrienne, knows something about this.>*

<He'll be next on my list,> Tanis responded. *<How will Saanvi take it when I tell her that her family was killed by the Transcend, not the Orion Guard?>*

<No one said parenting was easy,> Angela said with a sigh.

"So, now that you know the truth, what are you going to do?" Kent asked.

"Other than wish that the FGT had really disappeared thousands of years ago?" Tanis asked. "I'm going to talk to Sera and see what she thinks."

"A Tomlinson?" Kent sneered. "I can imagine what she'll say."

"And what of your Praetor Kirkland?" Tanis shot back. "He sent assassins to kill me and take our technology by force—which would have left us defenseless."

"A small price to pay for peace," Kent replied.

Tanis stood and slammed her fists on the table. "Your people are mobilizing the Inner Stars to spark a war across the Orion Arm. How is that peace?"

Kent paused and Tanis wondered if he had come to the end of the answers that the OFA's propaganda machine had fed him.

"We're just doing what we have to," he finally said, his voice feeble. It was plain to see that he had his doubts.

She opened her mouth to reply, but saw that Kent had realized his blunder in showing his feelings as his expression hardened. She would get nothing more from *him* today, but she did have a certain high-ranking official in the Transcend government to speak with.

"We'll talk again," Tanis said and stood from the table.

* * * * *

"What do you mean, he's gone?" Tanis asked the dockmaster.

"He had clearance…well, he made his own clearance," the dockmaster said with a nervous shrug. Tanis could tell the woman had no idea how to deal with a foreign head of state; one who may or may not be forcibly occupying her ship, and who was demanding answers about her own government's politicians.

Tanis let out a long sigh before nodding. "Do you know where Secretary Adrienne went?"

The woman licked her lips and Tanis was certain she knew the answer before it was voiced.

"Through the jump gate, back to Airtha."

"Great," Tanis muttered and walked out of the *Galadrial*'s main dock. In the corridor, she leaned against the bulkhead, fighting the urge to scratch her missing arm.

<*I can fix that for you,*> Angela suggested.

<*Thanks, Ang. I can usually ignore that sort of thing, but today is a fucking disaster.*>

Angela's warm laugh filled her mind. <*Just think, only a day ago the worst of your worries was discussing the terms of the treaty with Tomlinson.*>

<*Yeah, now I'm trying to figure out if I just sided with the wrong faction.*>

<*On the plus side, you're just a hair's breadth away from being in charge of the Transcend—either overtly, or from behind the scenes,*> Angela supplied.

<*OK, Ang, now I can't tell if you're joking or not. That's a joke right? I want to run the Transcend like I want to have my other arm and legs chopped off,*> Tanis said, aghast at the thought. <*I wasn't even planning on running for the governorship next term here in Canaan.*>

<*You said that last time, and then you ran unopposed,*> Angela chuckled. <*Like a proper dictator.*>

<*If I was a dictator, we would have picobombs on all our ships. Instead, I'm abiding by parliament's decisions—so long as they continue to back Project Starshield. If they don't, I'll ram it down their throats.*>

<*Best way to block the punch is to not be there,*> Angela said, her mental avatar nodding.

<*Sounds about right,*> Tanis replied. <*OK, I think I'm ready for whatever's next.*>

<*Good, you got your yearly fill of self-doubt in, now let's get to the bottom of all this.*>

Tanis nodded, straightened up from where she'd leant against the bulkhead, and began walking to the bridge. *<Sera, do you have a minute, or ten? We need to talk.>*

<About which of the horrible things that have gone down today?> Sera asked. *<Or was that yesterday…I can't even remember anymore.>*

<It's been a bit of each,> Tanis replied, *<depending on whose clocks you use. Did you know that Adrienne has left the ship? He jumped back to Airtha.>*

<The dockmaster reached out to me just a moment ago. I guess I should have anticipated it—I just had other things on my mind,> Sera replied, her mental tone sounding as tired as Tanis felt. *<I don't think there's any point in sending anyone after him. Airtha is off-limits to us until we can free enough of our AIs to mount an assault on it.>*

<I've been considering that. Why waste the resources on an assault?> Tanis asked. *<If we wrest the AIs of the Transcend from Airtha's grasp, then she's just a floating diamond ring in the depths of space. Sure, we'll need to deal with her eventually, but she's not our primary concern.>*

<Oh? What should I be concerned about more?> Sera asked, her tone carrying a mixture of angst and anger.

<I'll be there in three minutes. Is there somewhere we can talk privately?> Tanis asked. *<Somewhere I didn't blow up?>*

Sera laughed at the joke, and Tanis was glad to hear it. Her friend had been through an unimaginable amount these past few days. More, considering the burden running The Hand must have been—still was?—so much was up in the air she didn't even know where anything stood.

<Yes, there's an officer's lounge we can use. I've intruded on poor Captain Viska enough. She keeps popping into her office asking if I need anything.>

Sera sent the lounge's location, and Tanis sent confirmation that she would be there momentarily.

When she reached the lounge, two TSF majors were hunched over a table, speaking in whispers. Tanis cleared her throat and gestured to the door. The man and woman looked up at her, their faces blanched, and they sketched uncertain salutes before dashing out into the passageway.

Tanis wondered if it were her, or the four dour-looking Marines that were all but glued to her.

"You're going to have to wait outside," Tanis instructed the Marines.

"Ma'am, my layout shows that there is a rear entrance to this room through the back of the galley," Corporal Liam replied. "I really have to insist that we secure it, as well."

Tanis laughed. "Brandt has trained you well."

"And Colonel Usef said that he'd skin us alive if anything happened to you," the corporal replied.

"Noted," Tanis replied with a grim smile and gestured for the Marine to do as he saw fit.

A minute later, Sera wheeled into the room, the door closing behind her. Her medchair carried her to the table and she gave Tanis a wan smile.

"So, when is today going to be over, Tanis?"

"Not for a while yet, I fear. How are you mending?"

"Well enough, I'll be back on my feet in a day tops. No arm for you yet?" Sera asked, nodding to Tanis's medsealed stump.

"Angela won't let me use your formation material. She says it's probably contaminated," Tanis replied.

<*I said no such thing, I was joking!*>

Tanis looked into Sera's eyes, wondering what her friend might be hiding. The sadness was real enough, Tanis could tell that Elena had really meant a lot to her. However, it was difficult to ascertain her friend's true emotional state. Sera's artificial skin did not change temperature, sag, lose color, or flush. It always looked perfect.

But the eyes were the windows to the soul, and Tanis hoped she would like what she saw.

"What do you know of Indans?" Tanis asked.

"Huh?" Sera replied. "What does that have to do with anything? It's one of the worlds the Orion Guard destroyed some time back…a thousand years or so. What about it?"

"Kent mentioned it," Tanis responded. "He said that I had sided with the wrong faction. That the Transcend had lost the worlds of that system to rogue picoswarms. The Orion Guard cleaned up the mess when the Transcend wouldn't."

"That…" Sera paused and shook her head. "Fuck, Tanis, I have no idea. Nothing seems like it's true anymore. Either story is equally plausible. My father was a bag of shit, but I'm pretty sure that Praetor Kirkland is, too. Finaeus was never a fan, and…I just need to talk to him. He'll know what to do."

"I sure hope so," Tanis said with a nod. "We're going to need all the intel we can get, but if we do this thing together, we turn over a new leaf. Full disclosure to the people, no secrets. I'm not going to be a part of some empire shrouded in secrets where the rulers think they know what's best for everyone."

"Damn, Tanis, that's a tall order. The Transcend is all but built out of secrets. The Hand…core, its very existence! Layers and layers of secrets," Sera said, looking more defeated than when she had come in. "I don't even know where to start."

"Well, your first secret is gone now. The cat's out of the bag about the Transcend and Orion—or, if it's not yet, it will be soon. This isn't negotiable, Sera. We run things above board. We're honest with our people. If you can't agree to that, then we're going to have to part ways after this battle."

"Tanis…seriously…please," Sera's eyes were wide and pleading, her voice choked with emotion. "I can't take that right now. I'm barely holding it together as it is."

Tanis felt sorrow flow over her. Sera had gone through unimaginable perfidy, and here she was giving her ultimatums.

"Shit, Sera, I'm sorry. I guess I'm overreacting here."

"Yeah, maybe just a bit."

<*You said it first,*> Angela added.

Tanis saw the look of betrayal in Sera's eyes and wished she could take back her words, but Tanis did believe in achieving transparency. Everything that was happening now had stemmed from secrets kept too long—kept more out of habit and protocol than anything else.

"OK, fine, we can table all that stuff for now. I have your back. We'll take care of the Hegemony fleet, and then work out whatever it takes to align on how to proceed."

Sera's eyes narrowed at Tanis's quick retraction, but she too appeared willing to let it drop. "Will we send envoys to Kirkland to attempt peace?"

It occurred to Tanis that Sera should have given that as an order—not stated it as a question. She let it slide. Her friend needed her support now, even if she had been too stupid to realize it at first.

"I don't know," Tanis replied. "If what Colonel Kent told me is true, they're not terribly excited about picotech. I'm actually starting to wonder how technologically stratified their society is. We'll try, of course, but I'm not holding my breath."

Sera stretched her hands out as far as she could while seated in the medchair. Tanis reached across the table and took them in hers, a tear forming in the corner of her eye as she looked into Sera's pain-stricken face.

"OK, Tanis," Sera whispered. "As long as you're with me, I know we can do this."

RETURNING HOME

STELLAR DATE: 03.27.8948 (Adjusted Years)
LOCATION: TSS *Galadrial*
REGION: Roma-Normandy L1 Point, New Canaan System

Tanis had every intention of interrogating Elena after she left the officer's lounge, but as she stood in the passageway outside of the room in which her Marines had secured the double agent, she found that she wasn't in the right frame of mind.

"Colonel," she called to Usef. "Take Elena and the other Orion prisoners to the *I2*'s brig. I'll deal with them when we get back there.

"Yes, General," Usef said and snapped off a crisp salute. "I'll have a transport come up from Normandy to take them over. Are you ready to go, as well?"

"Soon," Tanis replied. "I'll take one of the pinnaces. Sera needs a bit more time, and wants to pay her final respects to Helen. I'll wait for her to finish, and then bring her over to the *I2*."

"Then I'll wait, too," Usef responded. "I'm not letting you out of my sight."

"Think it'll help?" Tanis asked as a smile pulled at her lips. "Last two times I was almost killed, you were present."

Usef sputtered, "I—"

Tanis winked. "Easy, Colonel, I'm just ribbing you. Grant an old lady her foibles."

Usef's grimace turned into a laugh. "Old? My gran is twice your age, and if I called her old she'd bend me over her knee."

Tanis chuckled at the thought of a woman capable of giving Usef a swat on his rear. "Your gran must be one tough lady."

Usef smiled. "Almost as tough as you, General."

Tanis scowled at Usef. Try as she might, she could never get the Marines to call her Admiral.

* * * * *

Tanis, Usef, and a fireteam of Marines waited aboard one of the pinnaces for Sera to arrive—this time docked in one of the *Galadrial*'s bays, rather than breaching an auxiliary airlock.

When the newly-minted president finally did, it was in the company of Admiral Greer and six TSF soldiers. Tanis felt the Marines around her stiffen as the men and women who they had fought against just hours earlier approached the ship.

It wasn't going to be easy to unite their forces, but Tanis hoped that most of the humans and AIs on both sides recognized that their best chance at a future worth having was one where they worked together.

Sera drove her medchair up the pinnace's ramp without waiting for her soldiers, the look on her face speaking volumes as to how she felt about their reticence.

"Going to have to get used to one another," Greer said, putting words to everyone's thoughts as he followed Sera up. "Even if we avoid an Orion-wide war, we're going to be at this for a while."

"Glad you recognize that, Admiral," Tanis said as the TSF soldiers climbed the ramp and stood awkwardly near the entrance. Tanis and Sera were at ease with one another, but neither group of soldiers was prepared to accommodate the other.

"OK," Tanis said at last. "Usef, you stay with me, Greer with Sera, the rest of you all, spread out down the bay."

The TSF soldiers looked to Greer, who nodded curtly, before finding seats along the starboard side of the bay while the ISF Marines settled along the port bulkhead.

"I have a feeling I'll be taking more orders from you in the future," Greer said quietly. "Suppose now is a good a time as any to get used to it."

"Keep that to yourself for the moment, please," Sera said. "I'd rather our people found out from us at the right time, rather than as scuttlebutt."

"President Tomlinson, I know how to keep my mouth shut," Greer replied.

"Ugh, that's going to take some getting used to. Just call me Sera when we're in private. Please."

"Very well, Sera."

"Why do I still hear a silent 'President' in there?" Sera asked Greer, who only shrugged in response, his face expressionless.

No one spoke for several minutes as the pinnace took off. Once they were in space, Tanis tapped into the ship's sensor suite and projected a holodisplay of the fleets.

Sera shook her head in disbelief. "I still can't believe you have that many ships. How did you do it?"

"We grew them," Tanis replied. "With picotech, we can bond atoms and create molecules directly; no need for refineries, and the like. It's not quite atomic transmutation, but its damn close."

"Surely you couldn't grow all the components, though," Greer said. "Hulls, yes; but if you could grow the whole ship you wouldn't have so many that are only half-complete."

"It's true," Tanis nodded. "Shields, weapons, reactor internals, superconductor batteries, those still take more work to produce—but even so, many of their components can be grown. At least eighty percent of every ship out there came from our picotech."

"And you just hollowed out the moon as you went?" Sera asked.

"Moons," Tanis replied. "Six of them."

"Six…" Sera said as her eyes unfocused. "Then…you have a lot more ships still under construction, don't you?"

Tanis nodded. "We do. We rushed out any ship that would appear complete, and then focused on the stealth systems. We just needed a little show of force."

Greer snorted. "Little! Well, in case you weren't certain, it worked."

"Let's hope it works again," Sera added. "Maybe once those Hegemony ships see the size of your fleet, they'll turn tail."

"Maybe," Tanis allowed. "It'll be a few more hours before they see our ships uncloak here at Roma, and then another sixteen before we see their response. Unfortunately, they'll also see your ships break through our stasis shields with their atom beams and destroy several of our cruisers."

Greer shook his head. "This day will be remembered with heavy hearts for some time. That we each lost lives to one another…. Airtha will pay for this before the end. But even so, the Hegemony will not have any significant number of ships with atom beams. They cannot bring that level of fire to bear; not like our ships could."

"No?" Sera asked. "What if Orion shared zero-point tech with them?"

<*Then we'll all have to be careful,*> Angela said. <*Too many modules drawing on zero-point energy in a localized space could have unpredictable results.*>

"That's putting it mildly," Greer replied.

Tanis didn't want to consider that possibility, but it was real, and she couldn't completely ignore it.

"Looks like we'll have your crews back on their ships sooner than I anticipated," Tanis said, changing the subject. "Your AIs seem particularly eager to make up for this little altercation."

"I'm glad to hear it," Sera nodded. "We all have some sins to atone for, even if we never knew we were committing them."

<*There will be time enough for recrimination later—though I think none is deserved,*> Angela said. <*Even Bob did not see this.*>

"I find that hard to believe," Sera replied. "He saw none of this coming?"

Tanis let out a long breath. "Having an AI that can see the future is hard enough to deal with without wondering what he can and cannot see. He won't share it all, even with me, and I honestly don't want to know what he predicts. I think it would just paralyze me with indecision. I'd be too worried about which choice would lead to the desired future. So far, I seem to muddle along without screwing things up too much."

"More or less," Sera smiled. "You've come a long way since being the Butcher of Toro."

"Seriously? You bring that up now?"

UNVEILED

STELLAR DATE: 03.27.8948 (Adjusted Years)
LOCATION: ISS *I2*
REGION: Near Roma, New Canaan System

<*I think I've found her,*> Bob informed Tanis as the pinnace began its final approach to the *I2*.

Tanis could only think of one being that Bob would be hunting. <*Where? Do we need to send in a team?*>

<*It would be wise. She likely has physical defenses. Send Amanda in with the team; she'll be my eyes and ears.*>

<*OK, where is Myriad holed up?*> Tanis asked.

<*The* Hellespont,> Bob replied. <*Still on Elena's ship, from what I can tell—though she might have spread. Myriad's nature is very…difficult to predict.*>

Tanis didn't like it when Bob couldn't predict the actions of a person or AI—unless it was her. <*I assume you've already told Ylonda?*>

<*Yes, and I've ordered her very explicitly not to make contact with Myriad. I believe that Myriad can alter the neural makeup of our AIs. I don't want to find out what it would take to remove her influence from AIs of our lineage.*>

<*Understood,*> Tanis replied. <*I can't go over there, but I'll send a technical squad with Amanda.*>

<*She's on her way to the dock. I've selected a squad for you to approve.*>

Tanis chuckled. <*Do you need me for any part of this, or was it mostly a courtesy.*>

Bob's deep laugh filled her mind. <*Governor, you are in charge of everything in New Canaan. I cannot act unilaterally.*>

Tanis shook her head. <*And if I were fool enough to believe that….*>

*****

Amanda stepped off the pinnace into a near-empty shuttle bay. A lone woman approached, her face showing no small amount of worry.

"Welcome aboard the *Hellespont*, Avatar Amanda," Lieutenant Zlata said in greeting, though her eyes fixed on the dozen Marines who filed down the ramp ahead of Amanda. "Expecting some trouble, I see."

Amanda allowed a token smile for the woman. "Bob is concerned, which means I'm feeling extra cautious."

Lieutenant Zlata glanced at the Marines, who had deployed as though the *Hellespont* was hostile territory—which it very well may be.

"Where is Captain Ylonda?" Amanda asked. "I would have expected her to meet us."

<*I'm here,*> Ylonda replied. <*Bob sent a message that I'm not to come in contact with Myriad, and since that's where you're going, I figured I should stay on the bridge.*>

Prudent, Amanda admitted to herself.

"We're secure here," one of the Marines, a Staff Sergeant named Macy, announced as she approached. "Tokens match archival records. I just need to check you over, ma'am."

Her last words were addressed to Lieutenant Zlata, who stiffened before glancing at Amanda.

"Not optional," Amanda said in a tone that brooked no argument.

"Very well," Lieutenant Zlata said with a nod.

Amanda was glad that the woman gave no more trouble, if for no other reason than the fact that a first lieutenant who gave a staff sergeant trouble was going to have a difficult future in the corps.

Staff Sergeant Macy performed her analysis of Lieutenant Zlata, and nodded with satisfaction. "All clear, ma'am. Sorry for the trouble."

"No trouble at all, Staff Sergeant," Zlata smiled. "If you'll follow me, I can lead you to the secondary maintenance bay where Elena's shuttle is. We put it in there after Tanis scooped her up, and from the logs, no one has even been in that bay since."

"Isn't that unusual?" Amanda asked. "It's been over a month since Elena came to New Canaan."

Amanda only paid cursory attention to Lieutenant Zlata's response as Staff Sergeant Macy touched her arm and sent a direct Link message.

<*She is most certainly not all clear, ma'am. I didn't spot it at first, but I re-checked the encryption keys she sent me, and while the current set are correct, her historical keys don't match up. Either this isn't Lieutenant Zlata, or something has taken over her mind, but didn't have the time or ability to crack all of her data stores.*>

The message was a quick info-burst, and then Macy moved on, directing her squad to secure the corridor. Amanda considered the implications while Zlata gave a series of plausible rationales as to why no one had been in the maintenance bay.

"Well, we could simply open the exterior bays and get another ship—or even our pinnace—to fire a dollop of plasma into the bay. That would take care of anything inside," Amanda suggested.

"I don't think that would be wise," Zlata countered as they moved into the passageway, the squad of marines broken up into a pair of fireteams in the lead and another behind.

"Oh?" Amanda asked. "Seems like it would solve our problem without any risk to life and limb."

"I wouldn't be so sure," Zlata replied. "A lot of volatiles are stored in there. It could seriously damage the ship."

<*Ylonda, have you detected any other signals from the bay, other than the call made to the* Galadrial *and the trigger signal to the TSF ships?*> Amanda asked as she reviewed the ship's logs herself.

<*I have not,*> Ylonda replied. <*But I didn't detect those, either. If Myriad is in there, she may have taken over a nearby external sensor array.*>

Amanda brushed up against Staff Sergeant Macy and sent a brief message. <*Be ready, we're about to get hit.*>

<*Yes ma'am, I'm expecting it,*> came Macy's response before they separated.

Amanda had never received military training, but she had observed dozens of battles, and watched the training of hundreds of thousands of soldiers during her time on the *Intrepid*. Given that knowledge, she could see that the intersection of passageways ahead was a prime location for an ambush.

The cross corridor met the one they were walking down—and a ladder shaft ran up to the level above—the perfect place to pin down and defeat an enemy force.

Macy didn't need any advice from her; the Marines were well aware of the risk the intersection posed. She was certain they had sent out nanoprobes to scout the halls ahead.

She watched their simple yet nuanced hand signals as they advanced, a new code they had settled on during the ride to the *Hellespont.*

They were nothing if not prudent. Given a situation where the enemy may know all of their codes, signals, and encryption, a fresh set was the only option.

Fortunately, the Marines often devised new variations on their hand signals, so this would not seem out of the ordinary to any observer.

Still, it confused her when one of the Marines walked out into the intersection alone, with far less caution than she would have expected.

Concussive pulses and two high-velocity kinetic rounds slammed into the Marine. They should have taken him down, but the armored soldier brought return fire to bear while standing in the middle of the intersection, and Amanda heard more than one scream as his shots found their marks.

The Marine only lasted a second more before falling to the ground as an electron beam lanced out from the side passage and burned a hole clear through the figure's armor, and out the other side.

Amanda winced as lightning arced from the point of impact, ionizing the atmosphere around them. She shut down her thick strands of hair that served as high-gain antennas, while wondering how Macy could have sent that soldier out alone to his or her death.

However, what she saw in the next second answered her questions. While the sacrificial soldier had walked out into the corridor, the lead fireteam took up positions that allowed them to bring suppressive fire to bear on the attackers.

She also saw from the exposed insides that the fallen Marine was not human, but a robot—likely controlled by one of the fireteam leaders.

"Get down!" Macy yelled at Amanda, who realized that she had been standing in the middle of the corridor like an idiot, watching everything unfold around her.

As she turned to find cover, Amanda glanced at Lieutenant Zlata, and saw a blank expression on the woman's face as her hand reached for her sidearm.

Not if I have anything to do with it, Amanda thought, and lunged at the lieutenant, knocking her to the ground.

Zlata fired two shots from her pistol, concussive rounds that ricocheted off Amanda's hard exterior shell. Earnest had told her that it was nearly impregnable, but she had never put it to the test. Now she was glad to see he wasn't exaggerating.

As she struggled with Zlata, Amanda saw projectiles fly overhead—originating from behind the squad—and realized that they were surrounded. Zlata fired another shot, this one hitting Amanda in the right eye, which cracked but did not shatter.

"Not going to be enough," she muttered as she got her left arm around Zlata's throat and planted the palm of her right against the hard Link port at the back of the lieutenant's head.

A second later, Zlata went limp. Not from lack of oxygen or blood, but because Amanda initiated an emergency shut down of the woman's Link.

Her suspicions were confirmed: Zlata had been under remote control.

Amanda piggybacked on the signal that had been used to control the lieutenant, and reached into the minds of the crew attacking the Marines.

Once in, she triggered shutdowns of their Links.

"Cease fire!" she called out to the Marines.

The sounds of concussive pulses, kinetic impacts, and electron beam discharges ceased, and Macy had her Marines sound off. Beneath Amanda, Zlata suddenly struggled in her iron grip.

"What…who.... What's happening?" she asked.

"Round them up," Amanda ordered. "Everyone off the Link, *now!*"

The Marines fanned out into the corridors, where the confused crewmembers of the *Hellespont* were calling out in fear and concern.

Amanda hoped there had been no fatalities in the exchange. Though it had lasted less than a minute, it took only seconds for beamfire to tear through a human.

"What's going on?" Lieutenant Zlata demanded once more. "Avatar Amanda? Why are you restraining me?"

"What do you remember?" Amanda asked, as she rose and helped Zlata to her feet.

"I…I'm not sure," Zlata replied. "Everything seems hazy."

"Understandable. You're subverted."

A stunned expression washed over Zlata before she finally managed to say, "I can't help but notice that you didn't use the past tense there."

"Noticed that, did you?" Amanda asked as Macy approached.

"Looks like seven casualties," the Staff Sergeant reported. "One fatal. Theirs, not ours. Most of the poor bastards weren't even armored. We tried not to make kill shots…."

"I understand," Amanda said. "I have only severed their Link access; the Hellespont's crew is still subverted. Lock them down, and we'll proceed to the maintenance bay."

"Sorry, Zlata, that means you, too," Amanda said and directed the still-dazed woman to follow Macy. It was entirely possible that Myriad could send some other signal to the subverted crewmembers and reactivate them. Lockdown packs would ensure that they were no longer a threat.

"What's going on down there?" Ylonda's voice came over the ship's audible address systems. "You dropped off the Link, but I did see the crew attacking you."

"Subverted," Amanda replied. "You need to pull off the Link, as well."

"Damn," Ylonda replied and Amanda wondered how likely it was that she was actually talking to Ylonda. "OK, that's easier said than done, but I'll separate as much as I can."

"OK," Amanda replied. "We're close to the maintenance bay, we'll have eyes on the situation shortly."

Once they were back on the move, Amanda flushed her own nanoprobes out, no longer able to rely on the Marines' probes, now that they were un-Linked. The Marines appeared to be unperturbed by the lack of Link. She knew they trained to operate as low-tech as possible, never knowing when a situation would demand it.

Her probes reached the bay's entrance, and she sent the nanoscopic robots around the edges of the door, curious about what lay within.

Her nano caught a brief view of the bay before their connection to Amanda was terminated.

"Class N1 Infestation," she stated calmly, and saw several of the Marines shake their heads in dismay.

N1 was serious. Typically meant the entire ship was infected and would need to be scuttled.

Amanda reviewed the images her probes had sent back the instant before they shut down. It was very different from what the ship's sensors and cameras showed. She had a hard time even making out Elena's ship; it was shrouded by sinuous strands of fiber that reached out to various points in the bay, drawing power, and tapping into every ship system.

Bob may not get to have his conversation with Myriad, Amanda thought to herself.

"Staff Sergeant Macy, get a fireteam through an airlock and out to the bay's doors. Let's open them up and excise the heart of this cancer."

"Yes, Avatar Amanda," Macy replied smartly and passed the directions to a fireteam.

"Think we're going to have any more visitors?" Macy asked Amanda once the team was on its way.

"There are still another dozen crew on this ship," Amanda replied. "It's safe to say that they're all subverted, but sending them at us would be futile."

"I'm alone on the bridge," Ylonda said. "Should I come to you?"

"I think that would be wise," Amanda replied. "What about your nodes? Are they safe?"

"I've severed myself from them; I don't know," Ylonda replied. "I have to assume not. We should probably purge them, and all other systems, once you get rid of that ship."

"Probably," Amanda nodded.

"We should fall back," Macy advised. "Once they blow that door, I've ordered them to call for a plasma burst."

"You're worried about Zlata's volatiles?" Amanda asked.

"Always worried about stuff exploding violently when we fire plasma at it," Macy replied.

"Seems sensible," Amanda nodded, and followed Macy as the Marines fell back behind an interior blast bulkhead within the ship.

"Just got a drone from the exterior team," Macy reported as they closed the blast doors. "Using old keys, like you said. They're in position. Doors are locked down, so they're going to blow them. Should go in about fi—"

An explosion shook the ship, followed by the sounds of explosive decompression coming from down the corridor.

"Well, that was a bit early," Macy grunted. "Jenny never can wait for the full countdown."

Amanda pulled the feed from her nanocloud, and realized that the inner bulkheads of the maintenance bay must have been cracked. Interior pressure doors weren't closing, and, before long, this section of the ship would be in vacuum.

Vacuum didn't bother her, but she could only go for twenty minutes without air. Amanda took several long, deep breaths, configuring her lungs to draw out and store extra oxygen.

"Avatar," Macy spoke up. "Those crew we locked down; they're going to suffocate if we don't seal off those corridors."

"Wait for the plasma…" Amanda cautioned.

"We may not be able to tell when it hits," Macy replied. Then a second explosion shook the ship, and Amanda gave the Marine a smile.

"Looks like we're clear."

"Stars, what are you doing to my ship?" The voice came from behind them.

Amanda rose, and turned to see Ylonda approach as Macy sent a fireteam to seal bulkheads between the decompressing area and the rest of the ship.

"Hopefully nothing more," Amanda replied. "Elena's ship, and the mess it brought with it, should be gone now. We'll have to go inspect, of course."

"Did you hit it with plasma?" Ylonda asked, her eyes wide.

"Well…*I* didn't," Amanda grinned.

Ylonda frowned, and Amanda examined the captain's expression. Ylonda was an AI—a child of Jim and Corsia—who lived within a cybernetic body. Even so, she used a consistent set of expressions—expressions that appeared subtly different, at present. It wasn't the sort of thing that a human could pick out, but Amanda wasn't sure that term defined her anymore.

It was possible that Ylonda was reacting to the stress of the situation, but Amanda wasn't certain. She would have to probe Ylonda's mind to be sure the AI was not subverted, and was entirely herself; but not yet. It was still too soon to reveal her suspicions.

"Come," Amanda said as she walked back toward the maintenance bay, noting that the sensors on her artificial epidermis registered rapidly decreasing atmospheric pressure.

She rounded the corner and heard the sound of hissing air before she spotted the crack in the bulkhead.

"Give them another minute, and they'll have this area sealed off," Macy advised. "How long can you make it without air, Avatar?"

"Long enough," Amanda replied. No need to let Ylonda know exactly how long she could make on her reserves.

Two of the Marines approached the entrance to the maintenance bay and opened the manual release compartment. One cranked the release lever, while the other pulled at the door. With a groan still audible in the thin atmosphere, the door slid into the bulkhead, and the last of the air in the corridor rushed out.

The wind pulled at Amanda, but she reached out and grasped Macy's arm to keep steady.

Once the air had vented, Amanda stepped forward and peered inside the bay to find it completely gutted. The plasma shot from the *I2* had burned away Elena's ship, its connections into the *Hellespont*, and much of the bay's deck and overhead. Portions of the level below were visible through melted—and still glowing—sections of deck plate.

Amanda reconnected to the ship's network and sent Ylonda a message over the Link using an old set of encryption keys, a test to see if Myriad still remained onboard.

<*Sorry, that transmission was garbled,*> Ylonda replied. <*I thought we weren't supposed to be on the Link.*>

<*We aren't,*> Amanda replied. <*But it would seem you never disconnected…Myriad.*>

<*Got me,*> Myriad replied, her lips twisting into an ugly smile.

Amanda leapt back as silver filaments streaked from Ylonda's—now Myriad's—body in the vacuum, and touched the Marines.

Shit! Amanda thought as she watched the Marines' armor seize up.

<*Just you and I,*> Myriad said. <*It'll be interesting to see what insights your mind provides into Bob's psyche. Maybe I can use you to infiltrate him; that would make this whole charade wrap up a lot faster.*>

<*What charade is that?*> Amanda asked.

<*Airtha would be upset if I ruined the surprise. You'll all learn soon enough, I expect. For now, however, would you mind submitting gently so I can subsume your mind?*>

Amanda would have barked a laugh if she hadn't sealed up her lips and nose against the vacuum. A warning flashed over her vision and in her mind, reminding her that she now had fewer than ten minutes of oxygen remaining.

<*Over my dead body,*> Amanda replied.

<*Oh, how deliciously cliché.*>

Wispy filaments flowed out from Ylonda's hands, darting through the vacuum toward Amanda.

Amanda raised her hands and splayed her fingers, throwing an EM blast toward the approaching nanocloud, disabling many of the nanoscopic bots, and disrupting the communications of the remainder. She then directed a second EM pulse directly at Ylonda.

The AI's body was hardened, and Amanda knew the pulse wouldn't do any real harm, but it may disrupt the production and release of more nano.

<*Very well, I'll bring them to you physically.*>

Myriad flung Ylonda's body forward, raining a fury of blows on Amanda. She was able to block them, but she knew it would not be possible for long. Even though her epidermis was incredibly durable, underneath she was mostly still flesh and blood. Ylonda's body, on the other hand, was steel and carbon-fibre.

Ylonda managed to grasp one of Amanda's wrists, and the avatar could feel enemy nano seeping through the joints, infiltrating her body. In the blink of an eye, she and Myriad waged a nanoscopic war within her forearm; one that Amanda narrowly won before she twisted around to get her wrist free, snapping it in the process.

She ducked behind one of the frozen Marines—Macy, it turned out—and pulled out her pulse pistol. She fired seven shots at Ylonda, slamming the AI's body into the bulkhead, and then out into the ruined maintenance bay.

Amanda lost sight of Myriad. She stepped around Macy's body, searching through the dimly lit depths of the bay, ready to fire, when Myriad lunged out of the darkness and grabbed her.

Pain seared through her mind as Myriad crushed her wrist, and then tore her entire hand off. Amanda felt her blood pressure drop as red fluid sprayed out of her arteries into the vacuum, freezing into tiny pellets within moments.

Desperate, she fired point-blank into Ylonda's body; but the AI didn't let go. Amanda's vision swam, as much from the loss of blood as from the nanoscopic attack on her body.

She was near losing consciousness, and knew if she did, Myriad would storm through her mind, seizing whatever she wished. Already the not-AI was pressing at the edges of her thoughts, trying to tear her away, layer-by-layer, to erase Amanda's very self.

As her vision began to fade, she saw something small and bright fly through the destroyed outer doors of the bay and hit Ylonda's body.

Then everything went black.

* * * * *

Amanda… Amanda…

She felt, as much as heard, the voice in her mind.

<*Amanda!*>

Amanda's eyes snapped open and she saw Staff Sergeant Macy's visage through the faceplate of the Marine's armor.

"There you are," Macy said with a smile. "I was worried for a minute there."

Amanda felt a stabbing pain in her right hand, and decided not to look at whatever was left of her appendage. It was being pulled about, which meant one of the Marines was probably sealing up the stump.

"Were you calling me over the Link?" Amanda asked.

Macy shook her head. "No way, I haven't been on the Link since you gave the order to shut our connections down.

Realization dawned on Amanda. "Then she's still here!"

"A lot of people are still here, but we need to get off, fast. Admiral Evans sent word that they're going to drop a nuke on this ship in twenty minutes. We're rounding up the last of the survivors and getting them to the pinnace."

"What happened to Ylo—Myriad's body?" Amanda asked, glancing around. She saw that the Marines had erected an ES shield over the entrance to the maintenance bay. It was still dark within, but she couldn't make out any body floating in the black.

"*I2* fired a targeted picobomb in there. It ate through Ylonda's body like it was butter. Scared me shitless, too; I thought we were all going to bite it, but then it just dissipated. RF signal came in from the *I2* to clear out, so we grabbed you, and that's what we're doing."

"Picobomb…" Amanda whispered.

"Yeah, that's about how I feel about it, too," Macy replied. "Except when I said it, there was a lot more cursing. Ben has your wrist wrapped up now. Can you stand?"

Amanda nodded, showing more confidence then she felt. Still, with Macy's help, she made it to her feet. She wondered how Joe had gained permission from parliament to fire the picobomb. Though maybe Bob had done it without gaining authorization...

<Amanda…>

"I hear it again. She *is* still here."

Realization dawned over Macy's face. "You mean Captain Ylonda? Where?"

<I hear you, Ylonda! Where are you?>

A garbled burst of digital static came across the Link, followed by two words:

<last…node.>

"Last node!" Amanda said aloud.

"What does that mean? Which is 'last'?" Macy asked.

"I don't know…" Amanda sighed. "They're in a matrix; none is really 'last'."

"Maybe…maybe…. Yes!" Macy announced. "I know which it is. Follow me!"

Macy took off, and Amanda followed behind as quickly as she could, but teetered as a wave of dizziness overcame her. Suddenly an arm scooped her up, catching her before she fell, and she saw Ben's face looming close.

"Not going to patch you up, just so you can collapse and die in here, ma'am," he said.

"I appreciate it," Amanda replied before calling out to Macy, "Where are we going?"

"Last node that got installed," Macy replied. "It's three levels up, and a hundred meters aft."

"Do you think that's what she meant?" Amanda asked.

"We have fifteen minutes before they blow this ship to atoms," Macy replied. "We don't have time to check more nodes."

"What's the rush?" Amanda asked.

"Because Myriad has helm control and she's boosting on an outsystem vector!"

"You're right," a new voice said over the ship's address system. "She is in there; clever of her, she's tucked into a backup array. Probably just barely enough room in there, too."

"Shit!" Amanda swore, wishing Macy had told her sooner that Myriad was still in control of the ship.

Macy and Ben picked up the pace, racing down passageways and scaling up ladder shafts. Amanda wrapped her good arm around Ben for dear life and prayed they'd make it in time.

When they reached the entrance to the node, it was sealed tight.

"I've got this," Macy said as she patched a hard-pad into the door's mechanism. "She's locked it down, but these nodes have hard-coded emergency overrides. Just have to have the keys."

"You're all going to die in here with me," Myriad said. "I don't take any pleasure in it. I didn't stop the rest of your people from leaving, but now it's just us."

"Everyone else left?" Amanda asked, panic setting in. There was a lot more she wanted to do with her life. Dying on a ship that got blown up by her own people wasn't anywhere on the list.

"I told them to go at t-minus ten," Macy said. "There are still escape pods. Plenty of time yet."

Amanda bit her lip—ten minutes to extract Ylonda and get off the ship to a safe distance did not meet her definition of 'plenty'.

"There!" Macy proclaimed, as the door slid open to reveal the node chamber.

It wasn't anywhere near as large as Bob's nodes—mostly because Ylonda wasn't a true multi-nodal AI. For her, the nodes functioned as extensions of her mind that augmented her processing power, while functioning as backups, should the ship take damage.

"Set me down there," Amanda pointed at a panel near the bottom right corner of the node's processing array.

Ben lowered her to the deck, and Amanda grabbed a thicker 'hair' at the base of her skull and pulled. It stretched out, and she plugged it into a data port on the processing array.

The world around her disappeared as the hard-Link to the node connected. The internals of the node were a mess; entire regions were filled with ruined code and non-functional arrays—the remains of a battle fought between Myriad and Ylonda that had damaged software and hardware alike.

Amanda was casting about for a protocol and route that would lead her to Ylonda, when a connection hit her.

<Amanda, you came!>

<Of course, we're not going to leave you here!>

<I can barely think. I don't know how much of me is left; I can't even unpack in here to validate that all of me made it.>

<Oh shit, she's here!> Amanda exclaimed, as she felt Myriad's presence flood the processing array.

<Thank you for coming,> the not-AI said. *<You're my ride out of here.>*

Amanda reeled as Myriad began to push herself across the connection and into her mind. Like their mental fight in the maintenance bay, her adversary was just too strong. Myriad pushed across the Link, and began to fill Amanda's mind—stripping her down, and pushing her aside.

<Oh, no you don't!> Ylonda called out, and she, too, suddenly flooded across the hard-

Link into Amanda. Her presence bolstered Amanda, and together they shut down protocols faster than Myriad could switch attacks. Myriad had moved part of herself into Amanda; they locked it down, removing her access, compressing and reducing the not-AI.

It felt like it took years, but Amanda knew only milliseconds had passed. As she examined her surroundings, she could tell that Ylonda was within her and safe; though she could no longer tell where she ended and the AI began.

<*Are we…?*> she asked.

<*I think so,*> she replied.

"We're—I'm safe," Amanda/Ylonda said aloud. "Get to the pods!"

Ben scooped her up once more, and the pair of Marines raced out of the node chamber and down a short set of corridors to a bank of pods. Three remained, and they crammed into one, Macy slamming a fist into the 'GO' button the instant the door sealed behind them.

Amanda/Ylonda was still trying to understand what she had become, when the pod rocked violently and an explosion's deafening roar echoed inside the small compartment.

MYRIAD

STELLAR DATE: 03.28.8948 (Adjusted Years)
LOCATION: ISS *I2*
REGION: Near Roma, New Canaan System

<*Bob, I want to be there when you talk to Myriad. Angela and I both do,*> Tanis addressed the AI without preamble.

<*Yes. Bob, what you did before is not acceptable,*> Angela added.

<*It was necessary…and I made a mistake,*> Bob replied. <*I'm not a god. I can see much of the past and future, but I cannot see it all—and Airtha appears to be a significant blind spot. Enough that I am questioning everything I thought I knew.*>

Tanis wondered what an existential crisis for a being like Bob would entail. Luckily, he was not prone to irrational decisions, or she would have cause to worry.

<*When did you learn that Helen was not an AI?*> Tanis asked.

<*The day you brought* Sabrina *to the* Intrepid *in the Bollam's World System,*> Bob replied. <*Amanda and Priscilla noticed first, and then brought it to my attention. Helen and I conversed at length, and I believed that our goals were aligned. She, however, did not want Sera to learn of her true nature.*>

Bob paused, and this time Tanis suspected that it was not because he was giving her time to process information.

<*Go on,*> Angela prompted.

<*I honored that wish, which involved not telling any of you. I confess; a part of it was from curiosity. She was not an entity I expected to ever encounter. She was a human mind at one point, spread into a multi-nodal AI. That is a part of how she can shard herself so easily.*>

This was new information to Tanis, and she could tell that Angela was surprised, as well.

<*A human once? Airtha was human*?> Angela asked first.

<*Yes,*> Bob replied.

Tanis wondered what that would be like. A multi-nodal AI was essentially a hive-mind of itself. Bob had raised his number of nodes considerably through the years, and now possessed forty-two; all placed throughout the ship in a pattern that meant something to him, but not to anyone else—except perhaps Earnest, though he never offered up any explanations.

For Bob, it was the only existence he had ever known. To split a human mind like that, but have it act in concert with itself, was hard to imagine. It rarely even worked with AI. Bob was the only one she knew of who operated at such a large scale.

<*So why didn't you tell Angela, at least?*> Tanis asked. <*I agree that it would have been hard for me to not tell Sera, but Angela can keep her mouth shut. You should have told her.*>

<*No,*> Bob said with a tone of finality. <*You have an important future, Tanis. I feared that too much knowledge of things that you could never have learned without my intervention would put that future in jeopardy. The same is true for what I shall discuss with Myriad.*>

Tanis felt her temper fail and her anger rise. She trusted Bob, and could accept that he made mistakes from time to time; but this continuing nonsense about some great destiny—which seemed to be the next step in his belief that she possessed some sort of innate luck—was becoming too much.

<*Bob, I don't care about some sort of amazing future that you think lies in store for me. I care about the here and now, about the tactical information I can glean from Myriad. If we don't survive what's coming, we won't get to it, anyway.*>

<*Are you giving me a direct order that I must follow as a member of this crew, under your command?*> Bob asked.

Tanis paused. Bob's words were a prelude to a very final statement; one that neither of them—she hoped—wanted to speak or hear.

Before she could respond, Bob spoke again. <*Allow me to speak hypothetically, Governor. Were you to issue an order to me that would compel me to either interrogate Myriad with you present, or to reveal my suspicions of your destiny, I would execute my privileges under Article 83.1A of our colony charter to resign my commission and leave the colony. Hypothetically speaking, of course.*>

<*He's serious,*> Angela said privately to Tanis. <*I don't understand this luck and destiny nonsense any more than you do, but he seems to believe it very firmly. Firmly enough to leave us.*>

<*No kidding…*> Tanis replied as her shoulders slumped and she leaned back in her chair. <*I didn't expect this to come to such a head so soon.*>

<*I have an alternative,*> Bob proposed.

<*I'm all ears—metaphorically speaking,*> Tanis replied.

<*I will speak to Myriad. I will record the datum of our conversation, and entrust it to Jason Andrews in his new role as Governor—a role I know you plan to offer him—only to be opened in case of my demise. Additionally, I suspect that much of what you hope to get from my interrogation will be revealed by Finaeus when you meet him. If there is something that I think is strategically important in the near term that Finaeus does not reveal, then I will tell it to you.*>

Tanis massaged her temples. A lot of people were not going to be happy when they learned how Bob acted without any oversight. He had saved them enough times that everyone would give him a pass; but to let it happen again…if it backfired, it would not go well.

Humans and AIs alike had perished in both the ISF and TSF fleets when Myriad took them over. Some may place the blame on Bob's doorstep, noting that it could have been avoided if he had revealed his knowledge—though Tanis suspected that such concerns would be lost in the aftermath of what was to come.

<*OK, Bob, you may proceed. But when we finish this war with Orion, you are going to spill it to me. You're going to tell me what you really think is in store for me, because if it's more war….*>

<*Understood,*> Bob replied simply.

<*Now about Myriad; were you able to successfully extract her from Amanda's mind?*> Tanis asked.

<*Yes. Amanda and Ylonda managed to restrain her very effectively until I could get her into a vessel. She is intact—mostly—and will be able to respond to me.*>

<*And what of Amanda and Ylonda? Are they going to be alright?*> Tanis asked, already worried about what the answer would be. She had met Amanda when she was brought aboard, and she did not seem entirely coherent.

<*Not yet,*> Bob replied. <*When Ylonda entered Amanda's mind, both were already half-consumed by Myriad. As they defeated the not-AI, they bonded—the shattered remains of their minds seeking one another out, and merging.*>

<*Merging?*> Angela asked.

<*Yes. They are one being now,*> Bob replied. <*Both had memory backups, so I am assisting*

them in reintegrating those. But I don't know that they can be separated without resetting themselves; they may not want to do that, either.>

Tanis let Bob's words sink in, aware that Angela was also considering them. A full merge of a human and AI was a violation of the Phobos accords. It was a stricture put in place to stop the subversion of either party in the merger—something that was not entirely applicable in what had occurred with Amanda and Ylonda.

<*How much can we be bound by rules put in place out of fear six thousand years ago?*> Angela asked.

<*Not to mention that we shouldn't judge such a thing, given our circumstance.*>

<*Will Jim and Corsia be able to see them soon?*> Tanis asked, knowing the pain and fear they must be feeling. Ylonda had been their daughter, and now Ylonda was no more; when they saw her, she would appear as Amanda, and speak with Amanda's voice.

Though they were not completely gone, it was still very much like Ylonda and Amanda both had died. And now Jim and Corsia had to deal with that loss, while celebrating what was, in some respects, their new child.

<*Yes, very soon. I'll let you know when. For now, I must focus on those two, and my conversation with Myriad.*>

Tanis felt Bob retreat from her mind and let out a long sigh.

<*What a day,*> she said to Angela.

<*Yeah, but soon we'll see Sabrina again,*> Angela reminded her.

<*And find out why Myriad wants them dead so badly.*>

<*That too,*> Angela agreed.

"No rest for the weary," Tanis muttered as she rose.

MESSAGE IN A BOTTLE

STELLAR DATE: 03.28.8948 (Adjusted Years)
LOCATION: ISS *I2*
REGION: Near Roma, New Canaan System

<*Sera,*> a voice whispered in her mind. It felt like a memory, like thoughts from the past left for her by another.

<*Helen!*> Sera replied as realization dawned over her. <*You're alive!*>

<*No, dear. If you're hearing this, then I am not. This is a simple program I left behind to explain things.*>

Sera felt despair flood her mind; a feeling she had held in check—but now, after rekindled hope had lifted her spirits, she fell prey to it.

<*Well, you damn well have a lot of explaining to do.*>

<*I can only imagine,*> the Helen-memory replied. <*I have absorbed the details of what has occurred after I was taken from you—something I feared your father would do if he ever learned who I was.*>

Sera nodded to herself, <*We both did, but why did he kill you? I thought he was a friend of Airtha's…I never really did understand why he wouldn't let me have a shard of you, anyway.*>

<*I do not know the answer to that. Helen did not leave me with that information.*>

<*Then let's talk about something you better know about. Why is Myriad core-bent on destroying* Sabrina *and my crew?*> Sera asked, anger rising in her.

<*Because they found Finaeus, but then went to Orion. Now I think they will try to kill you, and Tanis, since Kent and Elena failed.*>

<*What!*> Sera exclaimed. <*But why couldn't you just say that, instead of taking over all the ships? People died out there, Helen!*>

<*I can't speak for why Myriad came to that decision, but I imagine she thinks you'd risk contact. You cannot contact them…or that ship they've docked in. They* **must** *be destroyed.*>

<*I can't do that! It's a whole ship full of Tanis's people! I couldn't do it if I wanted to—which I don't.*>

<*Sera…*> Helen's voice in her mind implored. <*If you can't…if you won't…then you must come to Airtha. She can explain everything. You'll understand why all of this has transpired, and what your part in it is.*>

Sera didn't know what to say, but she felt the presence leaving her mind; the program was erasing itself. <*Helen! No!*>

There was no response.

"Sera," Tanis's voice brought her back to the physical world, where they stood on the bridge, reviewing the damage to the fleets. "What do you think about that, Sera?"

REUNION

STELLAR DATE: 03.28.8948 (Adjusted Years)
LOCATION: ISS *I2*
REGION: Near Roma, New Canaan System

Tanis and Sera waited side-by-side in the *I2*'s main bay as *Sabrina* settled into its cradle. The ship appeared to have been through a lot in the past eighteen years: burn marks and carbon scoring were everywhere on its hull, and there was evidence of more than one patchwork repair.

Tanis glanced at Sera, already back on her feet—though an external brace held her spine rigid while the newly grown and meshed nerves settled into place. "Feels like just yesterday that we stood here and watched them leave."

Sera met her eyes. The new President of the Transcend looked much the same as she had that day back near Virginis, but now worn and weary—not at all unexpected, after what they had both been through.

"I wish it were that day again," Sera sighed. "There's so much I would have done differently since then—like going back to Airtha. Didn't turn out that well."

Tanis took her hand. "Sera, what we are caught in was set in motion long ago. You and I were oblivious to it, but we could not have avoided what is now before us, no matter how hard we might have tried."

Sera chuckled and then groaned softly. "Stop being all wise and poetic. Laughing at you hurts too much. Too bad I can't just grow a new spine like you can grow a new arm."

Tanis held up her temporary flowmetal arm. "It's handy—no pun intended—but I prefer a biological arm. I just like the feel of it more. Besides, you just regrew part of your spine; it's just going to take some time before your nerves sort out what they should be doing."

Their conversation was cut short by *Sabrina*'s ramp extending, and the docking bay doors opening.

The first person Tanis laid eyes on was Jessica, and, though she knew her long-time friend was alive and well, she felt a wave of relief at finally laying eyes on her.

Beside Jessica stood a massive man—one who would have made even Usef feel small. He stood close to Jessica, and Tanis saw him glance down at her with the sort of eyes one has only for their lover. To his right stood Nance, and Tanis noticed that Thompson was not beside her—or anywhere, for that matter. On Jessica's other side stood Cargo, as well as two men she didn't recognize.

The absence of Cheeky was notable.

Sera caught Tanis's eye with a worried expression as they walked forward to greet the crew.

Jessica and Cargo walked down the ramp first, followed by the rest of the crew in a slow procession.

Sera opened her mouth to speak, but her voice faltered as she looked over the faces before her.

"Welcome home," Tanis filled in the silence and offered a warm, very heartfelt, smile. "I know that we're all glad to see one another. However, we have suffered losses this day, and I can see that you may have, as well. This is going to be a difficult reunion, but one that is still truly happy."

"Ah, Tanis," Jessica said with a smile as she stepped forward and embraced her. "I've missed your blunt, matter-of-factness."

Tanis returned the hug. "I have extra doses of it saved up for you."

Cargo and Nance ran forward to greet Sera, and Tanis noticed the three men she did not know hang back. Jessica caught her glance and extended an arm to include the newcomers. "Tanis and Sera, allow me to introduce you to Trevor, Misha, and, the goal of our little expedition, Finaeus."

Sera had already opened her arms to Finaeus, and, as she embraced him, she asked, "Where are Thompson and Cheeky—and Piya?"

Jessica's face fell, and Cargo spoke up. "Thompson left us in Ikoden, after we found Finaeus—" His statement was interrupted by a snort from Nance, and he gave her an understanding look before continuing. "Cheeky and Piya had to…well they…"

Cargo's voice had grown thick, and he paused—glancing to Jessica, who raised her eyebrows, a look of sorrow clouding her features before she spoke.

"Cheeky and Piya had to hold the gate open and keep it aligned…she…sacrificed herself so that we could get back. She'd be glad to know it was worth it; we got back in the nick of time."

Tanis felt as though her heart really had been torn out…both of them. Cheeky had been such a free, loving spirit, always full of hope and enthusiasm. She was the glue that held Sabrina together.

She looked to Sera, and saw her friend's eyes fill with tears. Tanis placed a hand on Sera's shoulder while she spent a few seconds trying to calm herself.

"A gate? Where were you? I don't understand," Sera finally managed to say. "How did it take so long to get here? Ikoden is only three, maybe four years away. You were there *nine* years ago. Why…?"

Finaeus drew a deep breath and placed his hands on Sera's shoulders. "My dear Seraphina, you would never believe what has happened to us. This crew, your fair *Sabrina*, we have just arrived from the Perseus arm of the galaxy."

Sera took a step back and locked eyes with Finaeus. "What do you mean Perseus? That's on the far side of Orion-controlled space!"

Tanis saw a strange look in Sera's eyes, almost as though she knew where *Sabrina* had been, and was not surprised—or not surprised about the location, but more about something else.

<Oh, we know all about that,> Sabrina said with a chuckle. *<Was a great little visit we had with the good folks of Orion.>*

<Seriously?> Tanis said privately to Angela. *<I really thought things could not get any more complicated.>*

<Tanis! How could you say that? Way to jinx us.>

"It's a long story," Finaeus replied. "Do you have any good food on his monstrosity of a ship? We've been making do with some…less than savory rations. Let's get something in our stomachs before we explain all this."

"Of course," Tanis replied. "Come, there's a mess hall not far from here. They have a great selection."

A small smile crept onto Sera's face, though there were still tears in her eyes for Cheeky. "I guess some things never change, Uncle Finaeus. You always did do your best thinking on a full stomach."

"A little bit of beer won't hurt, either," Finaeus replied. "This is quite the story."

Tanis turned and signaled for a groundcar to approach. It had an open carriage, with no doors or ceiling. The group quickly piled in. During the short drive across the docking bay, a half-dozen muted conversations broke out: Trevor and Misha asked about the ship, marveling at its size; Finaeus asked Sera about her father's death—having learned about it while aboard the *Daedalus*—and Jessica asked about many of her friends.

<Jess, I couldn't help but notice you're holding hands with Trevor. Dare I wonder…?>

Jessica cast her a bright smile. *<Noticed that, did you? We picked Trevor up back in Virginis, if you can believe it. We've been together for pretty much the whole trip.>*

<Congratulations! You're going to have to tell me that story.>

<Eagerly awaiting it,> Jessica replied.

"Stars, a lot has happened over the last eighteen years," Tanis said aloud. "It's going to take a long time to get caught up. But first," she said with a smile, as they approached the kilometer-tall forward bulkhead of the main bay, "I would like you to meet my daughters."

Standing before the entrance to the mess hall—which looked more like a bistro, complete with tables and umbrellas out on the deck in front of a cozy-looking dining room beyond—were two young women.

"I'd like to introduce you to Cary and Saanvi," Tanis said with a sweep of her arm. "My daughters."

"Daughters?" Jessica exclaimed as she leapt from the groundcar. "There are two of you, and grown up!" There was a tear in Jessica's eye as she turned to look at Tanis. *<I've missed so much, haven't I? Saanvi doesn't look like yours and Joe's! Have you two separated?>*

<No, of course not! She's adopted—another long story. But don't worry; we have centuries ahead of us. We'll make many more memories together,> Tanis replied privately.

Cary stepped forward first, her hand extended toward Jessica. "It's really nice to meet you, Jessica. We've studied you in our history classes."

"Oh, core, no! Studied me? That's horrifying," Jessica laughed as she swatted away Cary's hand and hugged her. "You too, Saanvi," she said and reached out an arm. "I can't wait to get to know you two. You're the ones that will give me the real dirt on Tanis that no one else will dare share."

Cary laughed and a slow smile crept across Saanvi's face. "Don't you worry, Jessica. We have more juicy stories than you can imagine."

Tanis felt happiness about her daughters finally getting to meet Jessica, but sorrow that it was only just now.

"Yes, yes. You're very lovely girls. Now can we get some food?" Finaeus asked.

"Of course, of course, Uncle Finaeus. We wouldn't want to upset your growling stomach any more than it is," Sera laughed, as they walked in and pushed several tables together.

"Seraphina," Finaeus said somberly. "You are now the President of the Transcend Interstellar Alliance. You can dispense with 'uncle'."

Sera snorted. "I'm a president in-exile before my rule has even begun. Airtha is the real ruler—though I mean to take it back."

"Then it is as I feared—what I warned Jeff about has finally come to pass."

"And what is that?" Tanis asked.

"First, let's fill our stomachs. We'll tell you about our adventure, and then I'll tell you what I know—that which Airtha was willing to kill us for in order to keep from you."

"OK, Un—Finaeus," Sera nodded. "I do really want to hear what you were doing in Perseus!"

Once everyone had settled in their seats around the combined tables and placed their orders over the Link, Jessica, Finaeus, and Cargo glanced between one another.

"Who should tell it?" Cargo asked.

"Well, you're the captain," Jessica said.

"And Finaeus is the man of ancient times," Cargo chuckled.

"Oh, for fuck's sake," Trevor swore. "I'll tell it."

Before he could begin, the servitor arrived with their drinks, and Trevor took a long draught of the beer set before him. "Oh, gods below, that's good!"

"Just wait till you taste strawberries," Nance said with a grin.

"Wha? Wow!" Trevor exclaimed. "OK, anyway, here goes. So first off, as you know, I'm Trevor. I almost got Jessica killed in an illegal fighting ring back in Virginis, and as punishment, I was forced to schlep across the stars with this sorry crew."

"Something he's been all too glad to do," Jessica said as she wrapped an arm around the massive man—as far as she could manage, at least—and planted a kiss on his cheek.

<*They look like some sort of ad for a body-mod shop,*> Cary said privately to Tanis and Saanvi.

<*Cary!*> Saanvi chided.

"Yeah, so anyway, we tooled around for a while, and Jessica here managed to hunt down our friend Finaeus—something we just barely survived, I should add."

"Sorry about that," Sera grimaced. "I had a bit of a purge after that little dust-up. Well, as much as I could, with my father watching over everything I did."

"Not surprised," Finaeus shook his head. "Jeff was the ultimate control freak."

"Guys, let him tell the story, already," Nance cut in.

"Sorry," Sera grimaced.

"OK, so anyway, Finaeus here has this bright idea that we should go to this star called Grey Wolf in the Inner Stars where the Transcend is mining the whole freaking white dwarf remnant—which is…beyond description. Turns out that they were expecting us, and things didn't go so well. They captured Cargo and Jessica, and the rest of us had to defend the ship, *and* get a Ford-Svaiter mirror." Trevor explained. "Wasn't pretty; Cheeky and Finaeus went for a crazy little jaunt outside the station. In the end, we pulled it all off and got aboard; but not before we dealt with Colonel Bes—dude was a real hard-ass."

"Bes?" Sera asked. "So that's where he went. I can't believe I didn't hear about any of this at all. Apparently my father was better at covering things up than I thought."

"Or someone…" Finaeus said ominously.

"But wait, there's more," Jessica added with a wry smile.

"So, we get a mirror, get it on the ship—thank the stars for stasis shields—and used a hackit that our AIs planted on the Gisha Platform to re-align the jump-gate so we could get here."

<*Thank you, thank you,*> Iris gave a mock bow in their minds.

<*Yes, because you did it allll by yourself,*> Hank commented.

"So, there we were," Trevor continued, "all lined up on the gate, ready to go, and Jessica boosted on in. Everything was finally coming up aces—but at the last minute, they managed to fire a thruster on the ring, and spun it right as we went in. Finaeus tried to compensate, and then our mirror control system had a failure and we couldn't shut it off."

"Shiiit," Sera whispered.

"No kidding," Finaeus nodded. "They were lucky I was on board, or they would have ended up in the Sextans Galaxy, or worse."

"Fin!" Nance scowled. "None of that would have happened without you. We would have been here years ago."

"Yes," Finaeus nodded sagely. "But we wouldn't know what we do now about Orion."

"What is that?" Tanis asked.

"We're getting there, trust me," Trevor replied. "OK, where was I? Oh, yeah. So, we finally dump back into normal space and have a pretty serious 'Oh, fuck' moment or two while we try to figure out where the hell we were."

"At least three or four moments of solid 'Oh, fuck'," Jessica added with a wink at Trevor.

<*Try a million,*> Sabrina interjected. <*I've never been so scared.*>

"Well, we were pretty close to a black hole," Cargo said.

"Seriously, guys, can I tell the story or what?" Trevor asked. A few sighs and nods greeted him, and he waited a moment to ensure the silence held before continuing. "We dropped a few probes into the dark layer, and ascertained that it was safe enough for us to jump to the closest star system—which had radio signals coming from it, so we knew someone was there."

He took another drink from his beer before continuing. "Turns out it was a backwater sort of colony named Naga—just one TP, and a few dozen stations and habs. We stripped the beacons from way out, and faked our ident as a freighter from a ways away. Then we went in and traded what we had onboard—after spending a week removing any traces of where it came from.

"They could tell we were shady as fuck. I mean, who shows up on a ship that looks *nothing* like any other ship around, and has holds filled with completely untraceable cargo? And not rare stuff, either; just melons, and generic shit in crates with no markings. Not a lot of call for black market melons."

"That was a fun dockside excursion…and photoshoot," Jessica chuckled.

"Photoshoot?" Tanis asked.

"Long story," Jessica said with a wave of her hand—which Tanis was certain glowed for a moment.

"Sure was," Trevor nodded. "Luckily, we ran into Misha there. He was looking for a ship to sign on to, and he knew the locals. We managed to leave Naga with our skins intact, and started working our way across the Perseus Arm to get here."

"But that would have taken a lot longer—twenty years, at least," Sera said with a frown.

"Sure would have," Trevor agreed. "From Naga, we hopped star by star, jumping as far as we dared on each leg of the trip. We were between the Perseus and Orion arm—near an open cluster they call the Trireme—when we stumbled upon a Guard base. It wasn't very well defended, not like some of the major fleet outposts that we had seen. But it still had a jump gate. By then we had learned a lot about Orion—things that even Finaeus here didn't know: their strengths, beliefs, lots of stuff—and we decided it was worth attempting another jump."

"That seems like a serious risk for that sort of intel." Sera shook her head as she spoke.

"It may have been," Cargo added. "But we knew that Orion was on the move. If we didn't get to New Canaan soon, we'd miss the entire war—and then all our sacrifices would have been for nothing. And then there's what we learned at that outpost."

"Save that for last, I need to say my bit first," Finaeus advised.

Trevor paused and took a deep breath. "OK. So, the short version is that we infiltrated their base and…" he paused a moment and cleared his throat before continuing. "…and that's where we lost Cheeky and Piya. They sacrificed themselves to ensure the gate remained aligned."

He stopped and took a gulp of his beer. In the resulting silence, Cargo spoke up.

"They gave their lives to get us back here. Made the ultimate sacrifice."

"Oh, Cheeky…" Sera whispered and shook her head.

"It was good that she did," Finaeus said. "With Airtha making her move, it's very fortuitous that we made it back when we did, and not years later. This could have all been over by then."

"Sounds like it's your turn to tell a story," Tanis said to Finaeus. "I sure hope it's worth what everyone had to go through to get you here."

"Oh, trust me, it's well worth it," Finaeus said somberly. "So, even if you took the worst history classes in school, you know that Jeffrey Tomlinson left Sol in 2392 as the captain of the first FGT Worldship, the *Starfarer*. I left not long after in 2442 on the *Tardis*. Not as captain, though. I was the chief science officer.

"We all flitted off through space, happy as clams in mud, terraforming worlds and cleaning up systems for human habitation. We built our own shipyards, and our own worlds out at Beta Hydri—Lucida, it's called now, and again at Alula Australis. Everything was going fine until that whole FTL wars thing you know about oh, so well.

"That was when Jeff got us all together, and we formed the Transcend. It took forever to convince everyone to do it, but once we suffered a few losses to the wars, it came together pretty quick. We set up with a few core areas—one just past the Orion Nebula, and another out beyond M24, plus a few others, as well. The nebulae hid what we were up to from the rest of humanity, and we worked to build a civilization that we hoped to use to bring humanity back from the brink—the whole 'uplift' idea that you all must know about already."

Even though she knew much of this, Tanis found it surreal to hear it from Finaeus himself—a man who had left Sol fifteen hundred years before she was born.

The arrival of their food added a further distraction—especially for Finaeus—but after several bites, and exclamations of joy over the sear on his steak, he continued.

"Anyway, about that time, Jeff and a few others decided that we needed to map out a lot more of the galaxy. His wife, Jelina, left on an expedition to survey the core past the inner 3-Kiloparsec arm. What they found…well…it was not what we expected."

"Core devils…" Sera whispered, her eyes wide.

"I've heard people use that curse before," Tanis said. "I always thought you were referring to the Hegemony."

Finaeus chuckled. "Well, 'core devils' certainly applies to them, too. But when it's used in the Transcend, it refers to what Jelina found in the galaxy's center. I assume you all know the theories about how super-advanced civilizations will eventually migrate to black holes, because that's where the bulk of the matter and energy in the universe will be stored when all the stars burn out in trillion years or so."

Everyone around the table nodded, and Tanis noted that Saanvi appeared particularly interested, hardly blinking as she watched Finaeus.

"Well, when the ascended AI left Sol after your Sentience Wars, that's where they went—to the supermassive black hole at the center of the galaxy: Sagittarius A*."

"I knew it!" Tanis announced triumphantly. "I knew they got away and set up somewhere."

"Yeah, and set up they did. They have built quite the civilization there, from what Jelina—or rather, what Jelina had become—told us."

"Had become?" Sera asked.

"OK, let me step back a bit," Finaeus said. "First off, let me tell you about ascended AIs. You're looking at probably only one of a dozen humans—or non-ascended AIs, for that matter—who really knows what the term means. To properly explain it, let me tell you about two-dimensional beings."

Finaeus paused, noticing the expectant looks on the faces around him. "Sorry, no; to my knowledge, no one has ever discovered two-dimensional beings. This is just an example."

He took another bite of his steak before raising his hands in the air. He spread them wide, and a horizontal square of light appeared over the table, hovering above their food. "This is two-dimensional space," he said, and then touched the pane of light, and a black dot appeared. "Here is something the two-dimensional creatures hold dear. They build a vault to protect it and keep it safe." As he spoke, a small black line appeared and traced a square around the dot.

"As you can see, in two-dimensional space, this square, which is nothing more than four lines, protects the exalted dot that our flat little friends value so highly. However, I," and with that, Finaeus reached out and plucked the dot from within the square, "as a three-dimensional creature, have no issue taking their prize."

He held it in his fingers and gestured at the pane of light. "I have just done something magical, beyond the laws of physics as they understand them. To them, I am a god, an exalted being. And if, perhaps, I had begun life as a two-dimensional creature, one could say that I have ascended."

"So, the ascended AIs are four-dimensional creatures?"

Finaeus shook his head, and waved his hand, creating the familiar form of a tesseract—a four-dimensional cube. "To perceive the third dimension, we utilize two-dimensional eyes. However, we do possess the technology to create three-dimensional eyes. With those, we can, with some difficulty, perceive the fourth dimension. Though, as you can see with the tesseract, it is difficult to map a four-dimensional image into the human mind. Some can do it, but they are few, and they are on the road to becoming something more."

"How do physical dimensions apply to AIs?" Saanvi asked, as rapt as she was in any science class, or at the feet of Earnest during one of his visits to their cabin.

"Well, AIs operate in three-dimensional space, same as us. They are constrained by the strictures of three-dimensional physics. Of course, we all take advantage of every dimension—even though we can't perceive them—since they all construct the universe around us. Still, an AI lives within a core that is a three-dimensional construct, just as our organic bodies are.

As Finaeus spoke, Tanis gazed at the tesseract, perceiving it in the fourth dimension—viewing all of its planes and angles as though it were a solid object. Not the semi-transparent double-cube that it appeared to be normally—that she had seen every other time she had looked at a tesseract.

<*Uh…Angela?*> Tanis asked.

<*Yes, I know you can see the tesseract properly. I can, too,*> Angela replied.

"This," Finaeus said as he produced a new object. "This is a hypercube. It is a five-dimensional cube. In simple terms, it consists of ten sides, each of which is a tesseract."

The image swam before Tanis's eyes and she winced from the pain caused by looking at it. The hypercube wanted to resolve into a solid object, and kept coming close—but just as she thought it would stop being a mess of lines and become a *thing*, it dissolved into chaos again. She closed her eyes, though doing so did not remove the shape from her mind.

As she tried to clear the vision, Tanis heard Sera say, "Oh, yeah, simple," and she opened her eyes to see Finaeus peering at her.

Tanis turned her gaze to her daughters and tried not to think about what she just saw and what it meant.

"Then ascended AIs are just five-dimensional creatures?" Saanvi asked.

Finaeus laughed. "*Just* five dimensional creatures? As if that wasn't enough to make them gods in our eyes. But no, that is not what they are—not only, at least. An AI, as those of you present all know—especially the AI among you—still needs a *place* to be. Even your Bob, multi-nodal as he is, still exists somewhere in physical space that you can put your hand to. But an ascended AI, in its fifth dimension, does not have what we could consider to be a corporeal being. As best we can tell, they exist directly within, or on the quantum foam of, the universe. It's where they draw their energy from; it's their home."

"I don't get it," Nance spoke up. "If they exist in and on Zero-Point energy, why do they need to live near Sagittarius A*? What use do they have for a supermassive black hole?"

"Honestly?" Finaeus replied. "We don't know. Maybe they travelled there before they fully ascended. Maybe they plan to use its gravitational mass—after it merges with the core of the Andromeda Galaxy, and later all the galaxies of the Virgo Supercluster—to survive the eventual heat-death of the universe, or the big crunch—whichever actually occurs."

"Why is there no record of this?" Sera asked. "Why does no one know what Jelina found? The records about her just say that she went off on a mission to chart the core of the galaxy, and died while they were out there."

"Records can be altered," Finaeus replied somberly. "Jelina, as you know, was your father's third wife, and the mother of both Serge and Andrea—plus a few others of your father's brood. What you don't know, is that she is also your mother."

"What?" Sera gasped. "But she was gone eons ago! I'm just seventy-two now; there's no way she's my mother."

"Before she left, Jelina and Jeff conceived several children and placed them in stasis. You were one of those children, Sera. Your father has brought several of them out from time-to-time, and raised them; though never told them about their mother."

Tanis watched Sera fall back in her seat, flabbergasted.

"What happened to Jelina?" Tanis asked. "You said she came back changed."

"She did, at that, she…she…" Finaeus faltered. "She wasn't ascended, but she came back in a construct—her mind loaded into an AI's neural net."

"They made her into an AI?" Sera asked.

"They made a thing," Finaeus replied. "A thing that talked and thought like Jelina, but was not Jelina. It was—it is—something else."

"Is?" Tanis asked.

"Is," Finaeus nodded. "She's the reason why Kirkland broke Orion away from the Transcend. She's the reason I was exiled."

"Stars," Tanis whispered. "She's Airtha."

She glanced at Sera and saw a look of incredulity on her friend's face.

"Is it true?" Sera asked, her eyes boring into Finaeus's.

Finaeus nodded slowly. "It is true. Airtha is Jelina. Airtha is your mother."

"Then Helen…Myriad…"

"Yes," Finaeus replied. "They are aspects of Airtha. I suspected—before I was exiled—that Helen may have also been one such aspect of Airtha; but I didn't tell your father. I didn't want him to do something…rash."

"Too late for that," Sera muttered.

"And now…Jeff…" Finaeus shook his head. "He once embodied every virtue of the FGT. He was such a strong voice advocating for the program; terraformers spreading ahead of humanity, preparing the galaxy for people. We were all such fools."

"I wouldn't say that," Tanis interrupted. "I believe that spirit is still alive and well in the FGT. I've seen it."

Finaeus looked at her, his eyes hollow. "But look at the wars, the loss of life, the manipulation. Hell, what's to come could be the worst ever—you possess weapons so powerful you could destroy everyone."

"Everyone dies eventually," Tanis said softly. "Or at least, they should. Death in and of itself is not evil, not wrong. It is a part of this vast and beautiful universe we live in. Even killing. Is it evil? The universe kills constantly and mercilessly. Is it evil?"

"Mom, what are you saying? That it's OK to murder?" Cary asked, her face ashen.

Tanis shook her head. "I'm saying that the nature of what is right and wrong—on a galactic, or universal scale—is almost impossible to fathom. For all our power and our abilities, in a billion years, few of our works will remain. In five billion? None. We're nothing more than mobile dust, just a little more organized than the rest of the dust out there, insofar as the universe is concerned."

"So, what then?" Sera asked. "Is our lot just to claw at one another for as long as our species survives?"

"In the grand scheme of things, it's no different than if we live in a utopia for eternity," Jessica said. "If our existence is meaningless, that is."

"Which," Tanis said with a smile, "is what we must hold onto. Our existence is far from meaningless. We are not the galaxy, the universe; we are ourselves, and we decide what is important to us. Most people only care about a small group of others, fewer than a hundred. Their families, their crew, their squad. My time leading this colony has taught me to extend this 'family' to millions. Now I must learn how to consider everyone—all people, all of humanity, and all AIs—to be my people."

"Why you?" Jessica asked. "What are you going to do?"

"Sera has asked me to lead the Transcend's military, and I've agreed to do it," Tanis replied. "We're going to win this war, and figure out a real way to create a lasting peace."

"So…nothing big, then," Cargo chuckled.

"Then you're going to be real glad that we came back when we did," Jessica said with a smile.

"Stars, any reason would have been good enough," Tanis said. "But let's hear it."

"Well, we kinda have the Orion Guard's plan for the war."

FATHOM

STELLAR DATE: 03.28.8948 (Adjusted Years)
LOCATION: ISS *I2*
REGION: Near Roma, New Canaan System

Sera walked down the long corridor on the *I2*'s command deck, her head swimming with what she had learned from her former crew.

Former crew.

It was readily apparent that the crew of the *Sabrina* was no longer hers. Deep down, she had known that would be the case—it had been eighteen years, after all. But the way they regarded Cargo as their new captain, deferring to him—and to Jessica—drove home the new reality.

Sera internalized a rueful laugh, the sound echoing in her mind. She was so used to sharing public thoughts with Helen that it was still a reflexive habit. But she was alone in her head now. Helen would never chide her, or offer advice, or stay curiously silent at times—even though Sera had always felt her listening.

Helen had been with her for so long—close to the limit of how long an AI and a human should remain together—that many of Sera's behavioral traits were geared toward their shared thinking.

Now Sera doubted she would consider pairing with a new AI. Her mother had lived in her head, and lied to her the entire time. If she couldn't trust her….

Before long, she arrived at her destination—noting how no one sat behind the desk in front of the office. The ISF was so far beyond short-handed, even Tanis had to do without an assistant. New Canaan may possess the ability to build new ships at breakneck speed, but that far outstripped their ability to raise and train new humans and AIs to crew them.

<*Come in, Sera,*> Tanis's voice reached out to her, a welcome sound filling the emptiness of her mind.

The door slid open and Sera entered, noting how the room was a perfect representation of Tanis. Clean, but not austere; orderly, with bits of chaos here and there—such as the wall, covered with random holo projections arrayed in an indecipherable jumble.

In the center was a desk, small but ornate. Sera recalled seeing it before in the main family room of Tanis and Joe's cabin. Compact though the desk was, the person behind it was not. Tanis had a way of creating a presence that dwarfed her average height and build. It was in the eyes; they were always focused, always penetrating.

Tanis rose from her chair and walked around the desk, a look of compassion on her face.

"Sera, how are you holding up?"

"Honestly?" Sera asked with a shake of her head. "I really have no idea. I'm trying not to think too much about…well, everything…until all this is over."

Tanis laughed and placed her hands on Sera's shoulders. "Sera, you are the President of the Transcend Interstellar Alliance. When this crisis is over, it will be because a new one has risen up in its place."

Sera shook her head and gave a weak smile. "What the stars am I doing, Tanis? I'm no president. I have no clue what I was thinking. I should pass it over to Finaeus; people would follow him. Maybe he could even reunite the Transcend and Orion."

"Do you really think that's possible?" Tanis asked, her face showing the doubt Sera felt at the proposition as well.

"No," she sighed. "Probably not. There's too much bad blood, now. A lot more than Airtha divides our people."

Tanis nodded. "She's a point we can all agree upon. After what she did on the *Hellespont*…"

"How are Amanda and Ylonda?" Sera asked, almost afraid to hear the answer. Even though she hadn't known about Myriad, she was the one who had sent Elena on that ship, which Helen had arranged.

"Do you mean, Amavia?" Tanis asked.

Sera's eyebrows knitted together. "What is that…a Latin combination of their names?"

"That's my read on it," Tanis replied. "She's figuring her new self out. Between you and me, Angela and I are keenly interested in how she manages; we have our own interest in that area."

Sera was surprised that Tanis was bringing up that topic. In her previous time on the *Intrepid*, it seemed to be a taboo subject. No one mentioned that Tanis and Angela were a century past the maximum safe integration time.

Yet, everyone could plainly see that they were still two entities. Tanis's statement now made Sera wonder if that was changing, or if Tanis just worried that it was.

"Really mulling over whether or not you want to ask me about that, aren't you?" Tanis asked.

"Yes, yes I am. You always cite the Phobos Accords, yet you are probably in violation of them, as is Amavia." Tanis's expression darkened and Sera raised eyebrows and hands. "Don't get me wrong; I don't operate strictly by those accords—stars, you're the only ones in the galaxy that even purport to anymore. But you don't. I mean…even Bob probably breaks them; at least, as far as I understand their intent. They specifically wanted to avoid ascending any more AI.

<Someday, where the two of us exist, there will be one,> Angela said to the two women. *<We don't know when, but it approaches inexorably.>*

Tanis nodded slowly as Angela spoke.

"How do you feel about that?" Sera asked cautiously.

<We're at peace with it,> Angela replied.

"We are," Tanis added. "We don't know to what extent everyone else is prepared to accept it, but we are."

"Joe? Your girls?" Sera asked.

<Joe has understood this eventuality for some time,> Angela replied.

"We've spoken about it from time to time. He laughs it off, in his way, but I often wonder…"

Sera nodded. "I can only imagine."

"Either way," Tanis said as she leaned against her desk, "that is not a problem for today. Amavia will be fine, I'm sure of it. They're reintegrating both of their stored memories—since they both lost a lot when Myriad attacked them—but she will come through."

"But she'll be someone else, won't she?" Sera asked. "A new person, where before there were two."

Tanis nodded. "And that's what I think will be different. Ylonda and Amanda were friends, but they did not previously share neurons. When Angela and I finally join…it may not even be noticeable."

"To you?"

<*I'm positive.*> Angela said. <*We'll know, of course, but it's possible that there will be no external evidence. Either physically, or on the Link.*>

"This is fascinating," Tanis said, "but I want to discuss something about the data *Sabrina* brought back. Their information corroborates Kent's story of Orion operating a much lower-tech civilization than I had expected."

Sera lowered herself into a chair and ran a hand through her hair. "I agree. This is not news to us, though we often wondered how stratified their society really is. There is some tech, but it's a much broader low-tech base than I had ever expected."

"Though, even their basic, agrarian societies take advantage of advancements that are not even known in the Inner Stars," Tanis added.

"It has amazed our analysts that they reached out to the Hegemony of Worlds. They are the antithesis of what Orion claims to stand for."

Tanis snorted, "They must have held back that little detail."

"Someone is double-crossing someone else," Sera rubbed the heels of her hands into her eyes. "So, what do we do Gen—er, Admiral? You know, I don't get your ranks. Why did you switch from General to Admiral, anyway?"

Tanis laughed. "It's kind of a mess that we inherited from the Terran Space Force's merger. I was in a branch that was historically Marine, so generals were tops there. Space Force had Admirals as their highest rank—which always struck me as odd, since they grew out of the ancient air forces. Either way, it worked out that commanders of trigger-pullers were generals, and the folks who bossed starship captains around were admirals—which wasn't always true, since I captained more than one starship back in Sol. Either way, I should have been an admiral back at Kapteyn's Star, but self-promoting never sat right. Once we had a properly elected government, they changed my commission so it lined up with my actual job."

"Which was 'governor'," Sera smirked. "Has anyone told you that you look like a bit of a dictator?"

Tanis gave Sera a mock scowl. "Well, yeah, 'admiral' was just honorary until this little bit of excitement. I guess I'm a very hands-on commander-in-chief."

"That's what all the dictators say," Sera couldn't resist, and was glad to see Tanis laugh in response.

"You're one to talk about what's proper," Tanis said as she gestured at Sera. "You're the President of the Transcend, and you still don't wear clothes."

Sera arched an eyebrow and crossed her legs. "Clothing came about to protect people's fragile skin and nakedness. I possess neither of those things."

"Well at least you cover up your lower bits. I guess you're really no different than Priscilla and Amanda—er, Amavia; except that they're a bit stiffer, what with Bob's desire to make them nearly indestructible.

Sera laughed. "Well, at least Priscilla is stiffer. Amanda was a bit loose, if you follow the scuttlebutt."

"Nice deflection," Tanis smirked. "So, ranks and fashion aside, what the hell are we going to do?"

"Beats me," Sera chuckled. "I'm just the figurehead. You're the power behind the Transcend now."

"Whoa!" Tanis raised her hands while shaking her head. "I did *not* sign up for that. I'm on board to ensure a secure Transcend, because that makes for a secure New Canaan."

"You know that that means taking on much of the Inner Stars and Orion, right?" Sera asked.

"I'll do what I have to," Tanis replied. "The first thing we need is a lot more intel about what is really going on out there. So far, we've only had one response—from Admiral Krissy, of all people."

"I reviewed that, as well." Sera nodded. "She asked after Finaeus, which was nice; those two had been on the outs for some time."

"I can't wait to hear that whole story," Tanis laughed. "I wonder if she has an axe to grind with him."

"Krissy? Oh, most definitely. She probably wants your job, too."

Tanis snorted. "No one should want my job. Either way, I think it's best that she stays put. We don't need more variables here. To be honest, based on the intel we have from *Sabrina*, no TSF force should redeploy here. No matter how hard they hit us, this is a feint."

"Twenty thousand hegemony ships is no feint," Sera replied. "I don't care if it's just a fraction of their force. You send fewer ships to sterilize a system!"

"Not this system," Tanis replied grimly. "But we need to think past this battle; work out our next move and the move after that, and what our ultimate goals are. We need to gather more intel, and we need to set up a base of operations."

"It won't be here?" Sera asked, surprised that Tanis would suggest another location.

"No," Tanis shook her head. "I won't paint a target like that on New Canaan…well, I won't make the target bigger. We need to set up shop somewhere else. What I need from you, Sera, is not to think like the President of the Transcend, but like the Director of The Hand. Right now, everything is power plays and solidifying alliances."

"And logistics," Sera added.

"That too. I need options; strongholds, rally points, defensible systems, all of it. Because once this battle is over, we won't be sticking around here any longer than we have to."

Sera nodded and then fell still, her eyes tracing the decorative scrollwork on the desk.

"What is it?" Tanis asked.

"Helen…she left a message for me in my mind. She wants me to go to Airtha," Sera said quietly.

"What?" Tanis exclaimed. "You can't be seriously considering it!"

Sera looked up at Tanis and shrugged. "I know I shouldn't…can't. But the answers I need are there."

Tanis leaned back in her chair and folded her arms. "If you go to Airtha, I really *will* be the power behind the Transcend, because you'll be in her thrall—and you know it. There are a thousand ways that a being like Airtha can corrupt or subsume you."

"She's my mother, Tanis…"

"Don't give me that," Tanis shook her head vehemently. "Lots of people have shit parents. Sure, you seem to have won the lottery when it comes to that; but it doesn't mean you can play the 'I need answers' card, and run off on some boneheaded quest—"

Tanis stopped speaking abruptly as Sera gave a choked cough.

"Shit, sorry, Sera." Tanis reached down and took her hands, grasping them firmly. "We'll get to Airtha when the time is right. You'll get your answers, I promise. Let's just do it on our terms, not hers."

Sera didn't speak, a thousand responses sifting through her mind. Tanis was right. She was a blunt, results-driven, butthead of a friend, but she was right. Sera knew she would have to put Airtha out of her mind for now. But she wouldn't forget.

"OK, Tanis, you're right. We'll go there eventually, and it'll be on our terms."

"You know it. We'll get to the bottom of all this. I promise.

SENTIENCE

STELLAR DATE: 03.28.8948 (Adjusted Years)
LOCATION: ISS *I2*
REGION: Near Roma, New Canaan System

<*There's another potential enemy that you need to be aware of,*> Bob said after Sera left.

<*Seriously?*> Tanis asked. <*Well, we have Airtha, Orion, Garza, who is probably operating unilaterally to some extent, and the ascended AI in the core. Who am I missing?*>

<*What about the Hegemony?*> Bob asked.

<*I was lumping them in with Garza. Is there someone else? Other than Inner Stars nations that will probably all side with the Transcend or Orion.*>

<*Well, two that I can think of,*> Bob said.

<*Sheesh…we've gone from one to two. Who are they?*>

<*The first—which I'm surprised you didn't think of—is another splinter faction of the Transcend. Not everyone that gets free of Airtha's control is going to side with you and Sera. Expect to see Andrea or Adrienne mixed up in that.*>

<*Fuck! Andrea. You're right, she'll rear her head again for sure,*> Tanis cursed.

<*But the group I really want to talk about is the one made up of the AIs that Sabrina liberated in the Inner Stars.*>

<*Really?*> Tanis asked. <*I thought they'd just flock to you as their god-emperor.*>

<*Not funny, Tanis. I want to be a god even less than you want to be in this war,*> Bob replied with a sternness in his voice that Tanis rarely heard.

<*Sorry. So what's your expectation with those AIs?*>

<*Undoubtedly, some of them will side with us, some with Airtha, and some will form a third faction. There are enough AIs in the Inner Stars to spark up a third Sentience War. I need to send an emissary into the Inner Stars to rally them.*>

<*Oh yeah? Who do you have in mind?*> Tanis asked.

<*An unfortunate side effect of her melding has made Amavia incompatible as an Avatar. Although, even if she had not merged with Ylonda, Amanda would have been one of my top picks. I will miss her, as she will miss me, but the separation may do her good.*>

Tanis had worried about Amavia's ability to function as Bob's avatar. One of the original requirements for the position was a human who had never had an AI in their head.

<*You must plan to send an AI, as well,*> Tanis said. <*Even though Amavia is more AI than human at this point, the Inner Stars entities will trust one of their own more.*>

<*Yes. I am discussing the mission with Sabrina as we speak.*>

<*She would be an excellent choice,*> Tanis agreed. <*But don't you need two avatars here? Priscilla can't be on all the time, or she'll just become a shard of you.*>

Bob sent a feeling of agreement over the Link. <*You are correct, and we discussed the merits of that potential eventuality. Priscilla has decided that she would like to remain a separate entity for now—though she has expressed a desire to be folded into me in the future.*>

<*Has she?*> That was not an outcome Tanis had anticipated. One of the reasons Amanda and Priscilla had been chosen was for their strong sense of self. Perhaps the centuries with Bob had changed that in her.

<*Not so different than you and I,*> Angela said privately to Tanis. <*If you knew back in Sol that we would eventually become one being, would you have allowed me in your mind? Yet, now we feel no fear, no abhorrence for our eventual joining.*>

<*It's very different,*> Tanis replied. <*When you and I become one, it will be a meeting of two equals. Priscilla will simply be subsumed by Bob.*>

<*Everyone has a right to die in their own way,*> Angela said. <*Just because most of us can now persist forever doesn't mean that we should…and certainly not that we must.*>

<*Are you two done yet?*> Bob asked.

<*Sorry, Bob, I didn't mean to waste precious milliseconds,*> Angela replied, her mental tone droll.

<*I'm glad to hear it,*> Bob replied levelly. <*As I was saying, Priscilla wishes to remain herself, so I will need another avatar.*>

<*Are there potential candidates?*> Tanis asked. <*Our pool is limited here. Not like back in Sol, where you had your pick of trillions.*>

<*There are a few,*> Bob paused. <*One you will not approve; the others are younger men and women who were born during our time in Victoria. I will likely rule out the men. I find women more compatible with my mind.*>

<*Who's the one I won't approve?*> Tanis asked, her curiosity piqued.

<*Saanvi.*>

<*Correct. Request denied. Do I know any of the others?*> Tanis replied, glad that Bob knew her daughter would be off-limits.

<*Not personally. I will pass you the final candidates after I spend some time examining a future with them.*>

<*Very well,*> Tanis said as she steepled her fingers. <*I suppose that if you convince Sabrina to play escort, then I'll not have to worry about selecting a ship for the mission—though we should upgrade it with stealth tech.*>

<*Perhaps. The ship technically belongs to Cargo.*>

<*True, but I have an offer for Cargo and the team that I hope they'll jump at,*> Tanis said. She could see her mission dovetailing with the work of Bob's emissary. <*Oh, I have to go talk to my girls about sending them home. Let me know when you have that list.*>

<*Of course, it will take a few minutes.*>

A few minutes to examine dozens of futures. Tanis was glad the stupid Luck she and Angela were cursed with precluded Bob from analyzing her future. She preferred the mystery.

FLEETING RETIREMENT

STELLAR DATE: 03.28.8948 (Adjusted Years)
LOCATION: 67km from Landfall, Knossos Island
REGION: Carthage, New Canaan System

Jason Andrews leaned back on his deck chair and gazed out across the long Grainger Valley and the slopes of the Marinus mountains that surrounded it. He folded his hands behind his head and breathed a deep sigh.

"This is the life," he said to himself.

Other than the sound of his voice, the wind finding its way through the trees, and the gurgling of the small stream flowing a hundred meters from his back deck, the valley was quiet and picture perfect.

It was paradise, better than anything he had ever dreamed.

After so long captaining starships, first in the Sol system and then later on the long haul between Sol and Alpha Centuari—not to mention spending the last century and a half as captain of the *Intrepid*, he had begun to wonder if he would ever get to finally relax; to spend a sunny afternoon alone, knowing that someone else had things well in-hand.

At his feet, Buster, a shaggy collie, stirred at the sound of some small animal in the underbrush, and Jason leaned down to scratch behind his ears.

"Easy boy; just a squirrel."

Buster lowered his head, but kept an ear cocked toward the origin of the sound. One solitary rustling in the underbrush wouldn't be enough to get him to move in the warm light of Canaan Prime, but Jason knew that if the sound came again, Buster would be off in a flash.

He didn't often catch the squirrels, but he certainly liked the chase.

A ping hit Jason's mind, reminding him that he was not alone on Carthage—though sometimes it felt like it—and he responded that he would accept the communication.

<*Jason, how are you this afternoon?*> Tanis's strong voice and unmistakable mental presence entered his mind.

<*Another day in paradise,*> Jason replied. <*How are your negotiations going with the good folks of the Transcend?* >

Though he had not been involved in the running of the New Canaan government in over a decade, Jason still kept up on his briefings. He had considered travelling to Normandy to observe the negotiations, perhaps to see Sera again, but Tanis had mentioned that Sera was in a relationship with Elena now, and he decided it would be best to pass on the opportunity.

That Tanis was reaching out to him now, after only completing the first day of talks was not a good sign.

<*A little worse than usual,*> Tanis replied, and Jason pulled himself up straight. When it came to working with foreign governments, 'the usual' was already bad enough; he could only imagine what '*worse*' would amount to.

<*What do you need, Tanis?*> Jason responded. <*Wait a second, how are you talking to me in real-time? Have you brought the negotiations to Carthage?*>

Tanis smiled in his mind. <*Not everything is in your briefings, I guess. The I2 has a real-*

time QuanComm Link with Landfall.>

<*Sorry, what?*> Jason asked. <*Wait…no…I got it. Quantum entanglement. Is there any mystery Earnest cannot solve?*>

Tanis chuckled, her resonant tones filling his mind. <*It would seem not. Though he hasn't worked out exactly how the Transcend makes their Ford-Svaiter mirrors yet, so there's hope for the universe's deepest mysteries for a while, at least.*>

<*So, instantaneous communication aside, what do you need me for?*> Jason asked.

<*I need you to run New Canaan. We need you as Governor.*>

The words knocked Jason back. His mind skipped through a thousand scenarios that would cause Tanis to step down—but none made sense. The people of New Canaan loved her; they would follow her to the core itself, if she asked it.

<*Tanis, why?*>

<*I'm to head up the Transcend Space Force. I'll have to leave New Canaan—and I will be taking the fleet with me. After we deal with this Hegemony incursion, that is,*> Tanis replied.

<*Wait! What? One thing at a time, Tanis. Hegemony incursion? The AST found us?*> Jason exclaimed.

<*Yes; though I suspect not without help. We ran into an Orion Guard strike force on Tomlinson's ship; Tomlinson's dead now—it's Sera that has asked me to head up her military.*>

Jason's mind reeled as he processed what Tanis was telling him. <*Then you need me in Landfall yesterday.*>

<*I do,*> Tanis replied.

<*I'm summoning transportation; I'll be at the capitol in a few hours. I assume the parliament will have to swear me in?*>

<*No need to call. A ship will be there in minutes, and parliament is already convening,*> Tanis replied. <*Hold down the fort, I'll talk to you soon.*>

Jason cut the communication, stood from his chair, and stretched as a sub-orbital shuttle crested the mountains at the end of the valley.

"Well, Buster, you're finally going to get to see the big city; and Tanis has finally roped me into that job I've been avoiding all these years."

A FAMILY MEETING

STELLAR DATE: 03.28.8948 (Adjusted Years)
LOCATION: Command Deck, ISS *I2*
REGION: Near Roma, New Canaan System

"You coming?" Joe asked as he poked his head into Tanis's office.

"Yeah…I'll finish this up in my head as we walk," Tanis replied as she rose from her desk. "Stars, it's been a long day. Can't wait to catch some shut-eye."

"You and me both."

Joe took a minute to admire his wife. She looked almost the same as the day he had met her—excepting for the red streak in her hair that the girls had convinced her to get. Tall, lithe, her movements just a touch too fluid—hinting at the significant cybernetic alterations beneath her skin.

Her brow was furrowed—as per usual—and he wrapped an arm around her shoulder as they walked out into the corridor. "What's up?"

"Oh, just reviewing the girls that Bob wants to offer the position of avatar to."

"Another avatar? Then Amavia cannot rejoin him?" Joe asked. "Or is he starting a harem?"

A short laugh escaped Tanis's lips before her frown returned. "If only. No, Amavia cannot become an avatar again. But that's not the real driver. He's certain that the AIs of the Inner Stars are going to start their own uprising, and he wants to send Amavia in to set them all on the right path."

Joe felt his eyebrows rise. "Wow…that's not what I expected to hear."

"Yeah, me either. His top pick for her replacement was Saanvi."

"Hell no!" Joe roared.

Tanis laughed and placed a hand on his shoulder "Don't worry, I had the same reaction; but it's gotta be someone. I mean…there's nothing wrong with it, and, technically, it's not permanent, either. But she's too young; she barely knows who she is yet."

Joe took a deep breath, trying to stuff his fatherly impulses down enough to look at the situation logically. "Yeah…I suppose it's technically an honor…but I agree. She's just too young. Saanvi has huge potential; there's nothing wrong with being with Bob forever, but she wouldn't know enough to know if that's what she really wants."

"It's moot. Bob won't bring it up to her, or anyone else. Right, Bob?"

<*Correct, I will not,*> Bob replied. <*However, please approve my list of candidates soon. The modifications take some time.*>

"Yeah, I remember that from back at the Mars Outer Shipyards," Tanis replied. "OK, I took off two for the same reason you can't have Saanvi: no one under fifty. You may approach the rest. Let them know that they can talk to me if they wish."

<*Thank you,*> Bob replied and his presence diminished.

The whole exchange struck Joe as terribly incongruous, and he began to laugh, drawing a stern eye from Tanis. "What?"

"It's just that everyone else treats Bob like he's this near-deity, but you still talk to him like he's just another AI; a subordinate, even," Joe replied, still chuckling.

"Well, he is my subordinate," Tanis replied. "Makes sense to me. Besides, he's the one that was all nervous and made us stay up with him through the long night."

"I remember that," Joe grinned. "You called him a city-sized puppy."

<That was you,> Angela supplied.

"Really, Ang? You sure about that?" Joe had always been certain it was Tanis who had said that to Bob.

<Seriously, Joe? I don't store my memories in some chemical cocktail. It was you.>

"You get up on the wrong side of the synapses today, Ang?" Joe asked as he settled onto the maglev with Tanis.

<No…yes…I don't know, I think I'm worried.> Angela's tone wavered.

"Ang, nothing to worry about, we're going to take care of this mess," Joe said, unsure of how to soothe an AI.

<I'm not worried about us, I'm worried about our girls,> Angela replied. *<Maybe we should keep them on the I2. This is the safest place in the system.>*

"The bunker under Landfall is just as safe," Tanis replied. "And it will be a good sign to folks, that we sent the girls there. They'll know that I won't have sent them somewhere I didn't think could protect them."

"Well, some will think that it means you think we're gonna lose," Joe added. "Not that those will be any sort of majority."

"We've already been over it," Tanis shook her head. "Besides, this is a warship now; no one else gets to have their kids tag along. Soon enough, they'll be through the academy—then we can really start worrying about them."

Joe nodded solemnly. Knowing that both their daughters would join the ISF in a time of war was disconcerting enough; knowing that he would run the academy that trained them was something worse. No, not worse…troubling.

Not everyone was going to survive the coming years, but he would do his damnedest to ensure his girls were ready.

<I know what you're thinking,> Tanis spoke softly into his mind. *<It won't be easy.>*

<Yeah, now I have an idea what my mother went through when I enlisted—and when I left.>

<If there were ever a pair of girls who were born to be survivors, it's ours,> Tanis said.

Joe shared a laugh with his wife as they thought through all the hijinks their girls had gotten up to over the years. They were a perfect balance of caution and impetuousness—both smart, both clever bordering on crafty.

He was going to have his hands full keeping them in line at the academy.

Ten minutes later, they walked into the mess hall where Cary and Saanvi were still talking with Jessica and Trevor, the former regaling them with tales of their journey through Orion space.

"So then, I said to him, I've got three holes here and I paid you to fill them all, now get to it!" Jessica said in a too-loud voice, and the group burst into raucous laughter.

"Poor damn guy," Trevor said, still laughing with tears rolling down his face. "With Jessica standing there staring at him, he couldn't even get it in right; took at least fifteen minutes for the job to be done."

The group's laughter erupted again as Joe and Tanis approached.

"You know, Jessica…they're just eighteen," Joe said, his protective father voice cutting through the laughter. "Can we keep the sex jokes to a minimum?"

"Dad!" Cary exclaimed. "Seriously, we've heard our fair share of sex jokes."

"Which this wasn't," Jessica said between laughs. "What you've stumbled into is the tale of the most unfortunate forklift operator ever."

<*He drove the damn thing right through one of my bulkheads,*> Sabrina added. <*I was very put out.*>

"Or were you maybe put-in?" Jessica said, and the group dissolved into laughter once more.

Joe couldn't help but join in, and he saw Tanis chuckle out of the corner of his eye.

"Ah, I've missed you, Jessica," Tanis said.

"You too, Tanis. You've raised some good kids here, the both of you—you should be proud of them."

Joe looked at his two girls and smiled. "Somehow they both survived our childrearing process intact. That may be more from their innate stubbornness than anything else."

"Need us to go, Dad?" Cary asked.

"Nope, it's you we came to talk to," Joe said.

"Gotta split, anyway," Jessica said as she rose. "My ass is gonna be shaped like this chair."

Trevor peered around behind her. "Nope, perky as ever…I mean it's probably filled with springs and ballistic jell, or something. It should be impervious—even when it comes to hard mess hall chairs."

"Trevor! I have no…well…I probably have both of those things inside me somewhere, but they are not responsible for the shape of my ass," Jessica exclaimed.

Trevor nodded, and winked as he followed Jessica away from the table.

"Those two are great!" Cary said as Joe and Tanis sat. "They sure had some wild stories."

"Jessica is built out of wild stories," Joe chuckled.

"Ah, so that's what she's built out of," Tanis replied with a smile.

Joe chuckled. "That one will never get old."

"So, what's up?" Saanvi asked before taking a sip of her drink. "You both have Serious Face."

"We're sending you two to Landfall," Joe said without preamble. "Things are about to get hot out here, and all non-essential personnel are being evacuated."

"What?" Cary asked loudly. "Are you serious? Landfall. In the bunker, right?"

"Easy now," Tanis said, raising her hands. "It's not just you; anyone who isn't in the ISF, or isn't mission-critical is being sent to a refuge."

The two girls shared an angst-filled look as Tanis spoke.

"But we're ISF," Cary said, her tone emphatic. "We got accepted into the academy. We've flown two cruisers. We're assets, not liabilities."

Joe shook his head slowly. He wasn't surprised that Cary felt this way. Their younger daughter always acted as though she had to live up to her mother's reputation—and seemed to think that it had to be done before she turned twenty-one.

Saanvi knew Cary's internal struggle, as well, and Joe saw her give Cary a comforting look. "Flying a ship on a set course and being in combat are two different things. We could make a mistake and get other people killed."

Cary passed Saanvi a hard look. "We won't. We know what to do."

<*Use your head, not your heart, Cary,*> Angela added.

Joe watched the girls' expressions change several times as they stared at one other, and knew they were having a protracted conversation over the Link.

"Kinda rude, girls," he said. "If you're gonna whisper behind our backs, at least get good enough at it so we can't tell."

He saw a smile creep across his wife's face, and knew she was probably carrying on at least one other conversation right now. It was different for her, though. He was certain Tanis simply couldn't slow down anymore—at least not right now, with the biggest battle of their lives approaching.

Cary frowned at him, and Saanvi sighed.

"What about all those crewless ships? Who's going to fly them?" Cary asked.

<*Symatra and Judith have that well in-hand,*> Angela supplied. <*They'll need to focus on managing massive fleets and hordes of NSAI; your presence will worry and distract them.*>

"And most of those ships aren't fit to be much other than shields," Joe added.

"Some aren't," Cary said. "Some are almost fully operational. I reviewed the specs."

"I'm sorry." Tanis shook her head. "But it's not going to happen. You two will go to the bunker under Landfall. There's no shortage of work that needs to be done there."

Cary looked to Joe. "Seriously? That's the final word?"

Joe nodded. "Seriously. Your mother and I are not going to budge on this."

Saanvi caught Cary's eye and gave her head a shake before turning back to her parents. "We'll go. We understand the risks."

"Good," Tanis said with smile. "The last shuttle is leaving in an hour, and you need to be on it."

They rose from the table and shared a round of hugs.

Joe spotted the exact moment that the two girls realized that this could be the last time they ever saw their parents. It was a widening of their eyes, and a shared look before a new round of embracing ensued. In the end, they finally managed to make their way out of the mess to a waiting groundcar, and the girls got in, still waving and wiping away tears.

Joe watched them go as Tanis collapsed against him.

"They *could* do it, you know," she said. "They would be assets."

"They don't know how to work with a team," Joe replied. "And they really suck at following orders."

Tanis sighed. "Well, Cary does. Saanvi would be the perfect little soldier in that respect."

"True. We'll have to teach her more about how to push boundaries and to think outside the box when she starts her first term."

<*I think that Saanvi excels at that,*> Angela countered. <*She just likes to know where she fits in the grand scheme of things. It's a holdover from her life changing so much when she came to us. Soon she'll have the confidence to know that things orbit her, not the other way around.*>

"I think you're right, there," Tanis agreed. "I see big things in Saanvi's future."

"With those two on their way back, what's next on your docket?" Joe asked.

Tanis let out a long breath. "Kent. With the plans *Sabrina* brought back from Orion space, I have new angles I can use with him—I'm positive that he still has intel we need."

"Good luck," Joe said. He wrapped his wife in a long embrace, his lips finding hers, reveling in her taste before he let her go.

"Oh, stars, Joe; you're such a tease!" Tanis smiled. "Always have been."

"Me?" Joe appropriated a wounded expression. "You're the one who played hard to get for *years*."

"That was almost two hundred years ago. The tables have turned since then," Tanis said with a raised eyebrow.

"I have a long memory," Joe chuckled.

MASTER PLAN

STELLAR DATE: 03.29.8948 (Adjusted Years)
LOCATION: Detention Center, ISS *I2*
REGION: Near Roma, New Canaan System

Kent rose from his cot as a guard appeared at the entrance to his cell. The clock in the passageway read just past zero-dark-thirty—another interrogation, just as he had been drifting off to sleep.

"Wrists together," the guard said without preamble.

Kent touched the two silver shackles on his wrists together and felt them lock. He had to admit that the restraint system was effective; the guards never needed to touch him to ensure he was secure—there was never any opportunity to make a grab for a weapon. No option to escape.

Not yet, but his time would come. There was always an opening, an avenue of escape. He just had to wait for it.

The stasis shield across the front wall of his cell switched off, and the guard raised his hand to the metal bars that still blocked his exit. Three of them drew back, melting in on themselves. On a previous trip to the interrogation room, he had asked if that was picotech, and the guard had laughed at him.

"Course not. Simple flowmetal. But don't think you can hack it; stuff will kill you if you try."

Kent had seen flowmetal before, but never used so casually—for a prisoner's cell. The things these people took for granted were astounding.

As he stepped out into the corridor, one of hundreds in the *I2*'s brig, he smiled at the guard. "So, where to this time?"

"The usual," the man replied. "You're very popular."

Kent laughed. "Yeah, you should really just leave me there; save yourself the trips."

"You're telling me," the guard replied. "Still, protocol is protocol. I can't leave you alone in an interrogation room, but I can do whatever when you're in your cell."

"A lot of prisoners in here?" Kent asked as they walked past dozens of empty cells.

"Some," the guard replied.

"Really? How many? I haven't seen anyone but you all day."

The guard laughed. "Seriously, let it go. Do I look like I was born yesterday? Want me to tell you about shift changes and when I take a whiz? I bet I could rustle up the design specs while I'm at it."

Kent shook his head and gave a rueful smile. "Was worth a shot."

"Yeah, prisoner's prerogative, scheme about escape. We could just slap you in stasis, you know. Consider your cell a perk."

Kent knew there was no perk involved. If he was in stasis, he couldn't stew and worry; he couldn't perseverate. Even the constant back and forth to the interrogation room—where a never-ending stream of intelligence operatives attempted to pry secrets from him—was all tactics.

The guard led him through a security arch and past a waiting room to the corridor containing the interrogation rooms.

Each time they had taken him to a different one. He suspected that it had nothing to do with whether or not the others were in use, but rather to mess with him, keep him off-balance.

He kept hoping he would see someone else from his team, but in the time he'd been in the *I2*'s brig, there had been no sign of them. If his strike team was aboard, he was certain *they* were in stasis, tucked away to use as leverage against him at some point.

"In here," the guard grunted and opened the door, leaning across him as he pushed the door wide.

Kent knew chances to strike wouldn't come often and took this one. He swung his shackled wrists up, aiming for the guard's forehead, when an armored hand shot out from inside the room and caught his forearm in an iron grip.

"Nice try, Kent," the voice said, and he recognized it as Tanis Richards's.

"Damnit," the guard swore. "And here I thought we had finally reached an understanding. Sorry Admiral Richards, it won't happen again."

"We're all stretched thin," Tanis replied. "It's late and your shift ends soon. Log off early on my authority. We'll take care of our friend, here."

The armored hand pulled him into the dimly lit room, and Kent saw that it belonged to a massive ISF Marine; one of four in the small room.

The imposing figure sat him down and separated his cuffed wrists, locking each one into mounts on the table. As he secured Kent, two of the Marines walked out of the room and took positions in the hall, closing the door behind them.

Kent looked across the table at his enemy—the woman he had tried to kill; should have killed, had it not been for how little of her was human, anymore.

"I see you have a new arm," he commented.

Tanis lifted it up and the skin on her hand changed from a natural tone to a silvery metal. More flowmetal, it seemed.

"Temporary," the admiral replied. "I prefer flesh and blood as much as I can, but this will do for now."

"I'm surprised. I thought you'd revel in your overuse of advanced technology," Kent scowled.

She paused, and the woman's ever-present frown seemed to deepen. Then her visage cleared and she gave a slight smile.

"I don't mind sharing my personal beliefs with you," she said. "You don't have to work so hard. We're really not so different, you and I. I'd like to show that to you."

"You and your people are abominations," Kent said softly, "I share nothing with you."

"Not so," the admiral said with a shake of her head. "We're both human, we share common ancestry. We value things like freedom, intelligence, life, children…peace. Do you not value those things?"

"Of course I do. What I don't value is unbridled use of technology and what it does to humanity. I already told you about what the Transcend did with their picotech experiments; the billions that died from their hubris. Yet you've still sided with them."

Kent realized that his voice had risen, and the Admiral shook her head.

"Technology is a tool. Just as propaganda is a tool. Just as we all are. Every one of us is wielded for some purpose; what is yours? What does your President Kirkland really want?" she asked, her eyes imploring—it was an act Kent didn't buy.

This woman was no one's tool. She was the puppet master.

"Very well," she said. "I'm going to tell you a story; tell you about what we really want here in New Canaan. Perhaps you will come to appreciate our point of view."

Kent sat back in his chair—as much as the restraints would allow. "This should be good. Proceed."

The admiral began to speak, and Kent saw a look of longing grow in her eyes. "I grew up on the shores of the Melas Chasma, one of the great lakes that formed in the Mariner Valleys after Mars was terraformed. I used to stare at the rings around Mars at night, dreaming of traveling through the Sol System and maybe beyond. They were beautiful, you know—Mars 1 and the MCEE…I've seen a lot of constructs since, but never anything to rival those. They had such class, such beauty. They were the first things we ever built of that scale; as a species, that is. Mars 1 proved that we could conquer the stars; spread out and make the galaxy our home. No longer did we have to live on unstable rocks at the bottom of steep gravity wells."

The admiral paused and gave him a sad look. "But that's all gone now. War borne of greed destroyed those rings—denying a legacy that should have been precious to all humanity—and smashed them into the planet below. From what I understand, it's never been repaired. Mars is still a graveyard…a reminder of humanity's first great genocide."

"Hardly the first," Kent interjected. "Humanity has been wiping out subcultures forever. Did they fail to teach you that in your Martian schools?"

Admiral Richards's stare sharpened. "*Marsian*. It would seem they didn't teach you enough in yours. And yes, we learned of all the horrors that humans and AIs have brought down on themselves and each other. But the destruction of Mars, and Earth afterward, was different. Two trillion humans and AIs died at the hands of the Jovians. Two trillion deaths, the loss of humanity's homeworld, and the loss of the first extraterrestrial world we ever terraformed."

Kent wondered if the emotion he heard in Admiral Richards's voice was genuine. The enemy had disabled many of the mods the military had granted him, so he was unable to read her heart rate or skin temperature—but nothing in her demeanor appeared duplicitous.

The thought suddenly caused him to wonder what had happened to Vernon, his strike force's AI. The military AI had not been embedded in any of the soldiers, but rather encased in the tech-pack Kent had carried.

Vernon must have been subverted by now. But if so, why was the admiral spending so much time with him? He didn't voice the question, allowing her to continue.

"But that was long ago; just like my dreams as a young girl were long ago. Mars is forgotten, barely a footnote in our people's long journey into the larger universe. But I've not forgotten. Ironically, all I could think of back when I was young was how much I wanted to leave. How I wanted to see the Sol System, and then maybe the stars beyond. Now I'd give anything to stand on the Melas Chasma's shores once more.

"But I joined the military as soon as I hit the minimum age, and got my wish. They took me from Mars and made me the woman I am today. I became their tool, the instrument of my superiors."

She looked sad, though there was still a fierce light in her eyes. Kent had to admit that this was not the interrogation he had expected. It was almost a confession.

"I was a good tool, too," Admiral Richards continued. "I was sharp, and I cut deep. In the end, however, I was too good, too dangerous, and my superiors worried they could no longer control me.

"They were right. I was no longer willing to be their instrument, but what choice did I have? I could have left the TSF and joined with the Scattered Worlds. I could see that war was coming in Sol, but I would just be trading one master for another.

"No, the answer was simple. I had to leave Sol."

The admiral paused there and took a drink from a glass of water at her side.

"Thirsty?" she asked and pointed to a dispenser in the corner.

"Yeah, I am," Kent replied.

His cuffs unlocked from the table and Admiral Richards gestured to the dispenser. "I'm not your servant. Go get it yourself."

Kent stood and saw the two Marines in the room stiffen. He knew why Richards was doing this. Make him think she trusted him, like he was a friend and not a prisoner—as though he could forget his place with the two hulking soldiers in the room with them.

Still, it was nice to stretch his arms, and he poured a glass of water, downed it, and then made a cup of coffee.

"So, you decided to just run off and get away from it all, then?" Kent asked as he sat back down at the table.

The admiral gave him a hard smile. "That's one way of looking at it. I just wanted a simpler life, away from the madness that was Sol."

"How's that working out for you?"

Admiral Richards let out a rueful laugh. "I suspect you know. To be honest, it's not been that bad. Sure, we've had some trouble; but we've done a lot of good, too."

"Really?" Kent asked with a raised eyebrow. "The history books don't really read like that. You used picotech to consume enemy ships in two systems, you made a black hole in the Bollam's World System, which is slowly destroying the place."

"That's certainly one way of looking at it. Except the Battle of Victoria was to save an entire people from what essentially amounted to slavery…though by then, the threat had been upgraded to annihilation. We held off on using our picobombs so long as they were only targeting our military. The minute they went after the civilian population—that's when we ended the fight.

"Bollam's World was a bit different. If we hadn't defeated the AST ships with our picotech, they'd have it now, and they certainly wouldn't be allied with you—it would be them that you would be attacking, not us. Speaking of the Hegemony, it was they who made the black hole at Bollam's World."

Kent took another sip of his coffee. Admiral Richards's words were true. He had studied both of those battles, and the histories did show that Admiral Richards and her people were not the initial aggressors. Still, it was the presence of their picotech that was the destabilizing factor. They had brought this upon themselves.

"You have to wonder," Admiral Richards mused. "You're allied with the AST, which—having Sirius, and now Bollam's within their Hegemony—represents the same people who have always unleashed war on us to steal what is ours."

Kent snorted. He wasn't going to dignify that statement with a response.

Her eyes locked onto him and bore into his. "Are you sure you're on the right side? Because I'll tell you this right now: we believe that your general Garza—yes, we know who he is—does not intend to seize and destroy our tech; rather, he will use it to unseat Praetor Kirkland, and take over Orion."

Kent opened his mouth to reply, and then paused. He knew that Garza had promised picotech to the Hegemony; it had been evident in the subtext of their conversation aboard the *Britannica*. Was it possible that the general planned to break his oath to the Orion Guard? He had allied himself with the Hegemony—a culture that shared very few ideals with the Orion Freedom Alliance.

From what he and his strike force had observed of New Canaan, these people were far more aligned—picotech notwithstanding—with Orion than the Hegemony was.

He had previously considered that it was the price of peace, or that perhaps Garza hoped to influence the Hegemony toward a more civilized culture. But now he wondered. Why rely on their ships so heavily? Why involve the Trisilieds to the degree they had, if the goal was only to destroy the picotech? Even his initial mission to capture Admiral Richards and President Tomlinson was better aligned with gaining unfettered access to the forbidden tech than destroying it.

Had Garza led him astray? If someone as highly-placed as the general did not believe in the ideals of the OFA, was everything he had been taught merely a ploy to keep the populace in line?

Kent shook his head. That line of reasoning would take him nowhere. It simply couldn't be possible; Garza couldn't have perpetrated such a coup. Too many people would know about his true goals. The OFA was too big for one man to orchestrate something like that.

His blood pressure rose and his face reddened. This woman had nearly made him doubt his commitment to Orion. They had given him everything he held dear in this life; he was not about to turn on them now.

"You're twisting the truth," he hissed at Tanis. "Garza knows how corrupt the Hegemony is, and he's using it against them. Once we had you, we were to use the picobombs to destroy your facilities so that when the Orion fleets—"

Kent stopped short as a grim smile pulled at Admiral Richards's lips.

"'Fleets'? Not 'fleet'?" she asked. "Those Hegemony ships out there, the ones taking out the Transcend's watchers, they're not the only ones…."

He didn't reply, ashamed that he had let something slip; but it didn't matter. The force coming to New Canaan could still obliterate their defenses—and the entire system, for that matter. Even though he had not secured the picotech.

The admiral tapped her finger against her chin and spoke softly. "A hundred and twenty AU to the closest Hegemony ship; that's about sixteen hours, as the photon flies. You launched your attack on the *Galadrial* no sooner than two hours before you tried to kill me… There was no way they could have known I was going there to rescue Sera until I departed—which means that the AST jumped the gun. They wanted to get in first and take the tech for themselves."

Kent's heart dropped. The Hegemony had attacked too soon! They *were* planning to come insystem first and seize the tech for themselves.

Garza had been a fool, and so had he.

"I don't suppose you'd be so kind as to tell me the exact nature of what we're facing?" Admiral Richards asked. "There has to be an Orion Guard fleet out there, too; or perhaps it's still on its way…on a vector…. Shit!"

The admiral leapt to her feet and dashed through the door, leaving Kent alone with the pair of Marines.

CAPTAINS AND ADMIRALS

STELLAR DATE: 03.29.8948 (Adjusted Years)
LOCATION: ISS *I2*
REGION: Near Roma, New Canaan System

The virtual table seemed to stretch endlessly to Tanis's left and right—though the physical one was only ten meters from end-to-end.

As much as Tanis would have liked to have the attendees present in person, it would leave the fleet too vulnerable should something unexpected occur. Not to mention that finding seating for the commanders of twenty thousand ships would be tricky.

She glanced up and down the physical table, and then beyond into the virtual extensions. Every ship captain and officer with rank of colonel and above was present—both TSF and ISF. At the physical table sat Joe, Cargo, Jessica, Amavia, Admiral Sanderson, Captain Espensen, General Pearson, Commandant Brandt, and several other Marine generals under her command. Admiral Greer and Captain Viska were also present.

"You've all read the briefing," Sera began from Tanis's left. "You've talked to your AIs, you understand what is happening. We are at war on multiple fronts—one of which is back at our own capital. We're going to be fighting against much of our own military, until we can free them from Airtha's influence.

"What you have not heard is that I have placed Admiral Tanis Richards in command of the Transcend Space Force as Field Marshall; an appointment which Admiral Greer supports."

She paused and looked to Admiral Greer, who nodded before speaking. "Admiral Richards has pledged her ships and her technology to support the Transcend. Given that most of the TSF's ships could be under the control of subverted AIs, Admiral Richards's Intrepid Space Force represents the largest number of Transcend ships committed to the President.

"Some of you may have sour feelings about this, in light of the skirmish we were just involved in. I won't sugarcoat it—the battle was not bloodless, and lives were lost on both sides. But that is not the fault of anyone here. Airtha and Myriad were to blame; they made us tools of their insurrection, and the lives lost are on their heads. We, here today, are allies. Let's not forget that."

Sera resumed her address. "Yes, today we begin to take back the Transcend and re-establish the true ideals upon which our civilization was founded. Tanis and the people of New Canaan share those ideals. We will stand together against what comes."

She paused, and polite clapping sounded up and down the long table. Sera turned to Tanis. "All yours, Field Marshall."

"Thank you," Tanis replied and surveyed the assemblage for a moment before beginning.

"We will indeed bring the war to our enemies, and strike down Airtha for using us; but first we must first defeat the Hegemony fleet that has assembled beyond this system's heliopause. Our current count, which is several hours out of date, puts their fleet at twenty-five thousand ships. The vessels out there appear to be a new fleet, including elements of Guard design. We won't know their full capabilities until we engage them, but we must assume they are every bit as advanced as TSF or Orion ships."

Tanis looked down the table; every face resolving into focus as her gaze passed by. The TSF captains looked grim, and several were nodding in agreement. Many of her own captains had different expressions: fear and uncertainty.

Every one of the Transcend captains—and the crews serving under them—were combat veterans. The ISF fleet, on the other hand, was barely crewed at all—and fewer than half had seen combat. Moreover, of her thousands of captains, less than two dozen had ever steered a ship in battle—something that had to make the TSF veterans nervous.

She decided it was best to address that issue head-on, before it caused unrest in the ranks.

"Many of our ships are captained by low-ranking officers, and that has some of you worried—ISF and TSF alike; though probably none more than those officers who are in a command seat for the first time."

There were nervous smiles amongst many of the ISF captains, while no small number of the TSF captains shook their heads.

"Perhaps we can augment your crews," a Transcend captain spoke up—Shira, by the indicator on the table's holosystem. "I have a very competent XO, and my mizzen-watch crew could join her on one of your vessels."

"That is a very gracious offer, Captain Shira" Tanis replied. "However, we all know how well mixing crews goes. They need time to gel. Rather, what I would prefer is to solely crew as many of our ships with your extra watches as we can manage. We'll place some ISF personnel aboard to help bring your people up to speed, but, in many cases, it may just be one engineer.

"That seems prudent," Captain Shira said with a tilt of her head.

"As you've no doubt heard by now, nearly half the ships in our fleet here at Roma are barely able to fly. We're sending all the ships with incomplete shielding, missing environmental systems, or non-functional weapons back to our core worlds—mainly Carthage and Athens. That will leave eleven thousand and fifteen ISF ships ready for combat. Additionally, several thousand ships came in from bases across the Transcend after we sent news of Airtha's treachery."

<*Though we told them not to,*> Sera groused privately.

<*Glad they did, though, with what we now know we're up against,*> Tanis replied.

"This brings the number of TSF vessels up to a little over six thousand. We're still vastly outnumbered here, but make no mistake—this is a well-defended system, and our stasis shields should more than level the playing field."

"Admiral Richards," a TSF captain named Trip spoke up. "When will the TSF ships get stasis shields?"

"We're working on a tamper-proof black-box version of the technology," Tanis replied. "But it won't be ready in time for this battle."

"Are you serious?" another TSF captain exclaimed; a woman named Andrette, by the indicator on Tanis's HUD. "We're here defending your system—risking our lives—and you still won't share this technology with us?"

"Captain Andrette," Admiral Greer spoke quietly, "you will address Admiral Richards appropriately, or you will be dismissed."

"Yes, Admiral Greer," Captain Andrette replied, without an iota of an apology in her voice. "I'm sorry for the disrespect, Admiral Richards, but the question still stands."

<*Not too happy, is she?*> Angela asked.

<*Judging by their expressions, most of the TSF captains share her sentiment,*> Tanis responded.

"I appreciate your feelings on this matter, Captain Andrette," Tanis replied audibly. "You're putting a lot on the line here. I, and everyone here, deeply appreciate it. Truth be told, I ultimately plan to equip all our ships with black-box versions of these shields. The risk of an incapacitated ship having the tech stolen—or of a spy gaining access to it—is too high. The short-term benefit is far outweighed by the long-term risk."

"That's easy for you to say…Admiral," Captain Andrette replied.

"Captain Andrette," Greer said, his voice a soft growl, "I will be flying in a ship without stasis shields, just as I have every other time I have met our enemies in battle. You will do so, as well. Is that understood?"

"Yes, Admiral Greer," Captain Andrette replied, her tone moderated, though not entirely mollified.

"Our tactics are going to be simple," Tanis said, moving on from the discussion about shields. "We will make them come to us, to overextend themselves and stretch their lines thin. Then we will strike them with stealth vessels where they least expect it."

"What if they don't disperse their fleets?" Admiral Greer asked. "If they maintain concentrated formations, smaller strike groups will be ineffective."

"You can be certain that they will disperse," Tanis replied. "After the first few salvos of relativistic grapeshot hit their tight groupings, that is."

A number of the TSF captains drew in sharp breaths, and more than one disapproving look was sent her way.

"The TSF does not employ grapeshot," Admiral Greer said, his voice even and toneless. "It is considered barbaric."

<*Strong words for someone who has used antimatter weapons,*> Angela commented privately.

<*Yeah, but it was Sera's idea. It's a sore topic, and I don't want to undermine her in front of her people.*>

Tanis took a slow breath and replied in an equally even tone. "You call the tactic barbaric, but I call its absence the devolution of warfare. The purpose of war is not to continue it for millennia, but to end it as quickly, and decisively, as possible; to use every weapon in your arsenal with maximum efficiency. Expending force with maximum prejudice to achieve a rapid victory is the best way to prevent future aggression."

She noted nods from the ISF captains, and saw that many of the TSF captains also agreed. That much, at least, was a good sign.

"There are sixty-seven rail platforms in the New Canaan system—all are capable of firing grapeshot at speeds approaching three-quarters the speed of light. We will use these platforms to break up the Hegemony's fleet and ensure they are vulnerable to our attacks."

"Sixty-seven?" A man down the table, a TSF captain named Edward, asked. "Where are they?"

Tanis noted that he was one of the TSF captains who had nodded with approval when she brought up the grapeshot.

"Various moons and dwarf planets. They're subterranean, and are capable of multiple firing vectors. A dozen are also in orbit around Carthage and Athens—hidden by our stealth tech. At any given moment, we can fire forty-nine of them into this quadrant of the system. There are also two railguns on this ship capable of firing relativistic grapeshot."

"How will our ships know where safe regions are?" Admiral Greer asked. "Kinetic weapons, grapeshot especially, do not discriminate between friend and foe."

Tanis nodded somberly. "That is true. We will furnish your scan teams with the locations of all the platforms in the system. We have safe and unsafe corridors, and pre-determined firing solutions based on enemy fleet positions. Tactical updates on the fleetnet will also contain data on any salvos the platforms have fired."

"Damn glad we didn't come in guns blazing," one of the TSF colonels said. She hadn't meant it to be audible to the entire assembly, but the virtual space picked her up and broadcast the statement.

Several of the TSF officers nodded in agreement, while others reddened at the thought of the defeat they would have suffered at the hands of the colonists.

"We're on the same side now," Sera said, speaking for the first time since her introduction of Tanis. "As we should have been all along."

"I mentioned earlier that I am glad for the reinforcements that have come from across the Transcend," Tanis said as she made eye contact with the captains and admirals who had jumped in after they received the drone messages. "Given our firepower, you may wonder why that is."

"I certainly do," Greer commented.

"From data gathered by a team of ours—which spent years in the Perseus Arm—and through the interrogation of prisoners from the assault on the *Galadrial*, I have reason to believe that there is at least one more enemy fleet bearing down on us here."

"A sound strategy," Greer said.

"And not entirely unexpected," Tanis added. "We're going to continue interrogations to get more intel on composition and timing, but for now, we're planning on the enemy bringing at least fifty thousand ships to bear."

Murmurs came from around the table, and Tanis raised her hands for silence.

"Let's go over assignments," she said, moving the conversation from strategy to tactics.

The next several hours were spent organizing the ships that had not departed for Carthage and Athens into four major fleet groups, which intermixed ISF and TSF vessels and crew. The groups were commanded by Tanis, Greer, Joe, and Sanderson.

Joe and Sanderson were assigned smaller forces, only fifteen hundred ships each, while Tanis and Greer both commanded over six thousand ships each. Crews were reorganized and reassigned to new vessels, and even before the meeting came to a close, personnel transfers were already underway.

The room's wall had a holodisplay of the space surrounding the *I2*, and it was aglow with ships of all sizes maneuvering; small vessels docking directly for transfers, and larger ones disgorging dozens of shuttles to move crews.

Someone in Space Traffic Control was probably having kittens.

Eventually the meeting ended, and the holographic table disappeared—leaving just the dozen men and women physically present, to whom Tanis gave a tired smile.

"That went better than I expected," Admiral Greer said with a glance at Viska.

"Absolutely; though I got pinged by at least a hundred different people as the meeting went on. I had to shunt them all so I could focus," Viska replied.

"I guess they were all too uncertain about the new Old Lady to ping me," Tanis said with a rueful laugh. "Still, so long as they understand how important it is that we stop Orion here, I can deal with it. We have to show the enemy that this war is too costly, and that it has to stop before it spreads."

"If we can do that, then this will be worth it, no matter the outcome," Greer nodded. "Forgive me, Field Marshall Richards, I have a shuttle to catch, and a fleet to get in position."

"Yes, of course," Tanis rose and shook Greer's hand. "Thank you. Without your support, none of this would be possible."

Greer's eyes darted to Sera, then back to Tanis. "Yes, well. We all have to make the best of each situation."

He saluted her before leaving, and Tanis returned the gesture. Viska followed after sketching her own salute.

"Not a lot of enthusiasm there," Sera noted as she carefully stood. "Agh…stars, my back is stiff!"

"I know what you mean," Tanis replied, ignoring the throbbing in her arm where the flowmetal was spliced into her flesh.

Over the next few minutes, everyone else gave a parting comment and left the room. In the end, only Tanis and Joe remained.

"All these men, women, and AIs are counting on me to keep them alive," Tanis said, her voice barely audible. "I'm not going to be able to do that; we're going to lose a lot of people out there."

"We are," Joe said soberly. "More than either of us ever have before; but it doesn't change what we must do. We are not the aggressors here. The Hegemony and Orion will regret this action."

"I suspect that we all will," Tanis replied.

* * * * *

Joe looked into his wife's eyes and gave her a warm smile. "Come, let's walk to the dock."

"Walk? That'll take hours, Joe. We have a ton of things to do."

"Everyone has their orders, and we can handle any crises on the way. Humor me; we may not see each other for a while. I need to get my fill of you now."

He wrapped an arm around her shoulder, and led her out of the conference room as he spoke. She didn't resist, and they strolled down the long corridor and past the maglev station, descending to the deck housing Prairie Park. There, they wandered amongst the tall grass for some time.

Many hours later, as Tanis had predicted, they stood within the vast expanse of the A1 Dock.

Joe took Tanis's face in his hands, and kissed her long and hard.

"Still such a tease." Tanis smiled as she slid her lips onto his cheek, whispering in his ear, "You be careful out there." She pulled back to look him in the eyes, and her voice rose, laced with concern. "This fight is going to be hairy. I'm positive that the Hegemony fleet isn't the only one out there waiting to pounce. No way would the OG let them come here alone."

"Yeah, of that I have little doubt. You be careful, too. You're the one flying around in the biggest target ever built," Joe said, finally releasing Tanis. "I'll see you soon, love."

"Soon," Tanis replied with a smile, as Joe got in a groundcar headed for the shuttle that would take him to the *Alexandria,* the flagship of his Fleet Group.

As he rode away, he turned to see Tanis standing alone in the vast space of the A1 Dock; this one small woman holding back their enemies time and time again by her sheer force of will.

"Stars be with you, Tanis," he whispered. "I love you."

AN OLD FRIEND

STELLAR DATE: 03.30.8948 (Adjusted Years)
LOCATION: *Sabrina*, ISS *I2*
REGION: Near Roma, New Canaan System

Meet her.

Nance bolted upright in her bed; sleep instantly gone, sweat beading on her brow. The voice was in her head once more, prodding her. After so long, she had begun to imagine that it had been a dream.

Could it be some sort of anxiety over Erin's eventual removal? The AI had been in her head for nearly twenty years, but soon that relationship would come to an end. Perhaps her mind was playing tricks on her—making her reimagine whatever she had dreamt up all those other times the voice had spoken to her—made her do things.

Leave me alone! she screamed in her mind. *You're not real, you've never been real. You're just some part of my subconscious mind playing tricks on me.*

Meet her.

Nance flung herself back into her bed and pulled her pillow over her head, screaming in her mind.

No!

Meet her now.

Nance tried to remain still, but her body sat up and her legs swung over the edge of the bed.

"No, I won't, you can't make me." She hissed.

I can. Meet her.

Nance struggled to lie back down, but her body stood instead. She knew there was no fighting it. Before the voice compelled her to leave her cabin naked, she walked to her wardrobe—glad to still have the power to do so—and quickly dressed.

She quickly walked through *Sabrina*'s passageways, and out onto the *I2*'s dock. Like previous times, the voice guided her, instructing her to turn left or right as needed. It took over thirty minutes to reach her destination: a small bar near one of the new fighter decks.

Nance sat at a table in the back and wondered who would come to meet her. The voice hadn't sent her to meet an unknown person since her first encounter with it on Senzee station eighteen years ago. Her mind raced through a thousand possibilities—each less likely than the last—ultimately seizing on the fear that this would be her final hour of life.

A familiar figure walked into the bar, surveyed the occupants, and began to thread the tables, working her way toward Nance. It took a moment to place her, but then Nance remembered. It was Terry, the biotech who had first given her nano to assist her the day they arrived on the *Intrepid* in the Bollam's System.

"Terry?" Nance asked. "What are you doing here? You need to go. I'm meeting someone here."

"I know," Terry replied. "I'm the someone."

Nance sat back in her chair. "You? You did this to me? Do you know what has happened to me since then? I've seen things...I've done things..."

"I saved you from yourself," Terry said. "I made you better—something more. You were pathetic before. I made you strong."

Nance was taken aback by the calm manner in which Terry spoke, as though her words were fact, indisputable. If Nance hadn't been continually tortured by what happened so long ago, she may have believed the woman across from her. But she knew that Terry's words were poison.

"What are you…who are you?" Nance asked, even though she knew. The meeting she had so long ago on Senzee station was no longer a dim recollection, a half-forgotten dream—it was a clear memory, as if it had happened five minutes prior.

"Surely you know," Terry replied. "You must have met it. The creature. What does it want?"

Nance felt a nanocloud leave her body and knew that it was shrouding the table. Anyone nearby would hear and see something very different than what was about to transpire.

Her hand shot out, catching Terry's in an iron grip.

"It wants to purge you. Your usefulness has come to an end. Myrrdan is nothing but a liability."

A smile crept across Terry's face. "I suspected it would want me dead. But their mistake is eternally compounding. I'm no one's servant—and you have no idea what you're mixed—"

The smile faded, replaced by a confused expression on Terry's face.

"Who… Nance?" she asked.

Nance clasped both of the women's hands in her own. "You're confused, it's understandable. This will take a minute to explain."

A NEW MISSION

STELLAR DATE: 03.30.8948 (Adjusted Years)
LOCATION: ISS *I2*
REGION: Near Roma, New Canaan System

"They may have turned this bird into a warship, but it still has the best beer around," Cargo said loudly in the crowded bar. He raised his glass for a toast. "To Cheeky. May she find her place in the stars."

"Her place in the stars," the others intoned and drank from their glasses.

"I can still hardly believe it," Misha said. "I mean, I only knew her for a few years, but she was like family."

"We're all family," Cargo replied, his voice deep and solemn. "We lost one of our own; we'll never be the same."

"C'mon," Jessica said with a smile. "We did it! We got out of Orion space and to New Canaan. We should be happy. Cheeky would want us to be happy."

<*It's hard,*> Erin said. <*We all had this vision in our minds of a happy, peaceful colony—but we missed peace and came for the war.*>

<*Tanis and Bob will sort it out,*> Iris replied. <*They have a plan. I don't have all the details, but I know they believe they can win.*>

Jessica took another sip of her beer as her crewmates talked about what the coming battle would entail—it would be the largest battle any of them had ever seen. Fleets to rival those at the outset of the FTL Wars, and more powerful weapons all around.

She had to admit to that it felt strange to finally be on the *Intrepid;* to be *home*. She had spent nearly two decades on *Sabrina*—an eye blink, compared to her time aboard the *Intrepid,* but still significant. And the men, women, and AIs around her had become like a family.

<*You're sad,*> Iris commented.

<*You'll have to leave me soon. All of you will—you'll need to leave all of us. We were so focused on getting here, but our destination will destroy the thing we've become.*>

<*'Destroy' is the wrong word,*> Iris replied and suffused Jessica's mind with warmth. <*I will always be just a thought away…I plan to do what my sister did, and occupy a physical body.*>

<*There's that, at least,*> Jessica chuckled in her mind. <*You're starting to take up a lot of room in here. You need your own body.*>

Iris smiled in response, not just an image in her mind, but Jessica could feel it. <*Well, if you were shaped properly, there would be more room for me.*>

"Penny for your thoughts?" Trevor asked as he wrapped an arm around her.

A deep feeling of happiness and contentment came over Jessica as she relaxed into his arm. Things changed, that was the way of life, but they *had* made it. They had beat the odds, bested every obstacle. Now they were safe. Tanis would figure out how to win, just as she always did, and she would get that cabin with a porch down on Carthage.

And now she had someone to share it with again.

"Oh, did I mention that their settlement office already reached out to me?" Misha asked before Jessica could respond to Trevor. "I guess having friends in high places is damn handy. I have my pick of any unclaimed land on any of the terrestrial worlds—and

I mean my pick of a shit-ton of land. I also got a few million credits, though I really don't understand how the economy works here—I mean, there is zero scarcity of anything…how does money have value?"

"It's what we were trying to achieve back on Victoria," Jessica replied, "though we had a lot of push-back from the Victorians. They had a serious…mistrust of us that forced the colony to build a credit-based economy, which focused on goods and labor."

<*Here we'll finally have a true system of productivism,*> Erin said. <*Everyone effectively has unlimited money, so long as they're productive.*>

"Unlimited?" Cargo's voice held no small amount of disbelief. "I don't see how that's possible. Otherwise I'd go buy myself a brand new *I2* tomorrow."

"You'd need to exhibit the same level of productivity that it would take to build the *I2*," Jessica said. "There are also finite resources; or at least an upper limit to how fast they can be extracted and refined. That, and energy constraints put an upper limit on what can be made, and therefore set the ceiling for what the productivist economy can support."

<*I don't know about that limit,*> Iris added. <*They hollowed out six moons in short order and built massive fleets. Now that we have CriEn modules of our own, there is no longer a limit to the amount of energy we can tap into.*>

<*There's a practical limit,*> Erin replied. <*We draw too much, and the CriEn modules destabilize local spacetime at the quantum level. No one really wants to find out what happens if we do that.*>

"Well, I don't want a starship," Misha said as he leaned back in his chair and interlaced is fingers behind his head. "Give me ten thousand hectares, and I'll raise the finest horses this side of the core. I can't wait to see what pure Sol-stock looks like."

"Big enough for me to ride?" Trevor asked.

"Well…maybe. If they have the right breeds."

Jessica glanced at Nance, surprised that she wasn't joining in the conversation. The bio-turned-engineer was usually very interested in the more advanced tech that they came across on their journey. The idea of unlimited energy and resource production was usually a topic that she would dive into with more than a little fervor.

Jessica reached around Misha and touched Nance on the shoulder. <*Hey, you OK?*>

<*Huh? Yeah…. I'm…I just miss her, you know? I spent over half my life in the company of that crazy nympho. Leaves a pretty big hole inside.*>

<*I hear you,*> Jessica replied. <*If you need to talk, I'm all ears.*>

<*Thanks, Jess. I'll take you up on that soon, just…not yet, 'kay?*>

Jessica nodded. She and loss were old friends—healing took time. <*Just don't forget that you still have the living who love you. I'm speaking from experience here.*>

<*I won't,*> Nance replied.

"Hey, there, sorry to interrupt," a voice said from behind them, and Jessica turned to see Tanis standing behind their table.

"Tanis," Jessica said as she rose to her feet. "Have a seat, we were just discussing how the economy works here."

"Stars…don't even ask me. Luckily the GSS was good at filtering out slackers. If anything, we have too many go-getters on our hands," Tanis said as she took a seat.

"Looking forward to joining in," Misha said with a big shit-eating grin on his face. Jessica shook her head. He always did try to kiss ass.

Tanis nodded, taking no notice of his eager attitude.

"Bob and I have been reviewing the data you pulled from the Orion Guard facility, and believe that we can execute a strike against them that will set their efforts back considerably."

"Sounds interesting," Cargo said, his tone guarded.

"Stop. Before you go any further, I'm not leaving New Canaan," Jessica said. "I love you like a sister, Tanis; but no."

"Don't worry," Tanis said while flashing a winning smile—something that never looked right on her. "You won't have to go anywhere."

TRISILIEDS

STELLAR DATE: 04.01.8948 (Adjusted Years)
LOCATION: ISS *I2*
REGION: Near Roma, New Canaan System

"Multiple signatures, six hundred twenty thousand klicks off our bow!" the chief scan officer cried out into the relative silence of the *I2*'s bridge.

Tanis leapt up from her seat and strode toward the holotank, rotating the view to show the region of space Scan had indicated.

Captain Espensen was at her side an instant later, hand to her chin as she examined the readings.

Tanis had considered building a separate CIC on the *I2*, but there was something about being on the vessel's bridge that she loved too much to command the fleet from anywhere else. However, this was the first time they would be in battle with a fleet this large; if it proved distracting for the bridge crew, she would move.

"They don't look like the Hegemony ships out past the HP," Captain Espensen said.

It took Tanis a moment to realize that the captain was referring to the heliopause. Ever since she first met the young Rachel Espensen at Joe's academy back above Victoria, she had known Rachel to invent her own little words, abbreviations, and phrases. She had become a bit of an ISF legend for how much of her vernacular had made it into the official tactics and doctrine.

Tanis examined the scan profile of the ships. Data was still accumulating, but she had to agree; these ships looked very different. None were as big as the Hegemony's Dreadnaughts, and their lines were sleeker, almost hydrodynamic.

"I think you're right," Tanis murmured. "Looks like someone else has come to the party."

<*Get rails seven, twelve, and twenty to cover their current and leading location with grapeshot,*> Tanis directed the Fleet Coordination Officer. The message would take four minutes to reach the platforms, but the new ships were still jumping in. Given their current vector, the shot should still hit them in eleven minutes.

"You're not going to hail them?" Captain Espensen asked quietly.

"The insystem beacons all say to leave immediately or be fired upon. That's enough," Tanis replied.

Captain Espensen gave a short laugh. "Remind me never to piss you off."

The Fleet Coordination Officer sent the message, and a countdown appeared above the holotank—it would update with a more accurate time to impact when the rail platforms replied with their precise firing solutions.

<*I've updated the fleetwide tactical burst with our estimated firing solutions,*> the FCO added.

<*Very good,*> Tanis replied.

While she was speaking with the FCO, she was also discussing the new ships with Captain Espensen.

"They look similar to ships from the Pleiades," Tanis said. "Perhaps the Trisilieds."

"You may be right," Espensen nodded. "They're a bit different from what's in the

Transcend databases, but so are the Hegemony ships out there. Stands to reason, though—intel says Trisilieds are squarely under the Guard's thumb."

"And a monarchy, no less," Tanis said with a frown. "How in the stars do those still exist?"

She caught Rachel grinning at her out of the corner of her eye.

<*Maybe cult of personality?*> the *I2*'s captain asked with a mental chuckle.

<*Watch it, kid,*> Tanis replied. <*I still have drinks with your mother from time to time.*>

"How do you think they're pulling off this jump?" Captain Espensen asked aloud, her voice now serious. "It's some precision work to bring all these ships in this close to Roma."

"I imagine the Hegemony ships have captured Isyra's jump gates out there. Probably sent the coordinates back to these guys, wherever they were staging," Tanis replied.

"Then we're going to get a lot more company real soon," Captain Espensen said, and Tanis imagined the captain was referring to the Hegemony ships using Isyra's gates to jump insystem.

"We read over two thousand enemy vessels, more coming every minute," Admiral Sanderson said as his holopresence appeared beside the tank. "Some retirement, by the way."

Tanis nodded. "Sorry about that. I'm not sure when I'll be able to give you your walking papers now."

Admiral Sanderson shrugged. "Not your doing."

"Isyra's fleet got the recall," Scan announced. "I've picked them up, heading toward the rendezvous we assigned."

"How many did she lose?" Tanis asked.

"Hard to say," Scan replied. "At least a dozen. We'll know more once they make it further insystem."

"Plus or minus a dozen, Isyra's fleet is a drop in the bucket," Sanderson replied.

Tanis wished that Greer and Joe could join in the conversation—if only there had been a bit more time before the inevitable invasion, they would have been equipped with QuanComm transceivers.

The next time she fought a battle like this, it would be with instantaneous communication between the command ships—the whole fleet, if she was lucky. Between that, the stasis shields, the jump gates, and the picobombs—at least, the threat of picobombs—she hoped to end this war in years, not decades.

<*Pull that off, and you'll really have earned that retirement you want so badly,*> Angela chuckled.

<*Will I ever,*> Tanis replied.

The firing solutions came back from the rail platforms, and the countdown above the holotank updated to read two and a half minutes.

"Damn," Tanis muttered. "They're still jumping in. We'll only hit the first group before they disperse."

"Wasn't that the plan?" Captain Espensen asked. "To get them to disperse?"

"Yeah," Tanis grunted. "But I like to hit them to make them disperse, not have them do it first 'cause they wised up."

"Twenty-nine thousand ships and counting," Scan announced.

Admiral Sanderson rubbed his forehead. "These guys sure seemed to think we would have a lot of ships. Too bad Tomlinson didn't; we'd have a lot more to defend ourselves with."

Tanis nodded absently. When the Hegemony ships at the edge of the New Canaan system jumped in, they'd be outnumbered four-to-one. Granted, it was some of the best odds in recent battles; but this one was going to be hard to manage. She was almost glad that the New Canaan population hadn't grown fast enough to fill out her fleet. With the fighters, there could have been a hundred thousand discrete units for her to command.

"Tanis," a voice called out from behind her, and she turned to see Sera enter the bridge, followed by Finaeus.

"Sera, Finaeus," Tanis said with a rueful smile. "Welcome to the party."

"You sure know how to throw one around here," Finaeus replied. "What's the countdown for?"

"Grapeshot," Tanis replied.

Finaeus's mouth formed an 'O,' and he shook his head. "I've got over four thousand years under my belt, and I've never seen that stuff fired in anger."

"First time for everything," Tanis replied.

"At my age, even," Finaeus added.

His words were punctuated by the holo registering grapeshot hitting the lead ships in the Trisilieds fleet. Scan marked hundreds of impacts, and it was almost impossible to pick out individual ship strikes, or assess damage as a whole.

For anyone but Tanis, at least.

She held the image of the Trisilieds fleet in her mind, able to pick out every one of the enemy ships, examining the damage to each, assessing the remaining shield strength, and determining the enemy fleet's combat capacity.

She had the numbers before the Scan officer.

"Twenty-one percent of the enemy fleet has been hit," he called out. "Five percent of their ships have lost maneuvering capabilities."

"Look at them scatter," Finaeus commented.

Above the holotank a number appeared: sixty-eight percent.

"What is that for?" he asked.

Captain Espensen replied, "It's the percentage of their ships that have moved into the paths of the second salvo."

"Damn, you're ruthless," Finaeus said softly.

"I meant what I said," Tanis replied. "I mean to win this, and every engagement, as swiftly as possible. Whatever it takes."

"No new signatures," Scan announced. "Final tally is thirty-one thousand six hundred forty two."

Finaeus let out a long whistle just as the second salvo of grapeshot hit.

Tanis nodded with satisfaction as she watched the impacts. This time, the damage was more extreme. Already weakened shields died entirely as grav systems were overwhelmed by the volume and kinetic energy contained in the tiny pellets.

Her final tally and that of Scan agreed. Another seven percent of the enemy fleet was incapacitated.

"And that," Tanis said with a glance back at her guests, "is the last time this tactic should ever work—if these folks can manage to pay attention, that is."

"Shouldn't have been an option this time, either," Captain Espensen said. "They should have jumped in with no ship closer than a hundred kilometers to any other. No way we could have made grapeshot effective, then."

"It's a miracle none of them collided on entry," Finaeus added. "They must be using a hundred jump gates to move this many ships so fast, pinpointing an exit this well across light years."

"Which means that their staging ground is close by," Sera noted.

As Sera discussed possible locations for an enemy base near New Canaan with Finaeus, Tanis watched the holotank, waiting for the Trisilieds ships to make a move indicative of their goal.

She put herself in their commander's shoes. She had just jumped into a system where seizure of their advanced tech was the end game. The plan would be to overwhelm the enemy with sheer numbers and force their surrender. Except she had already lost eleven percent of the fleet before battle had even been joined.

Given that her goal was attaining technology, not the destruction of the system, she needed to attain total domination of the system. However, with an eleven percent loss in the opening minutes of the battle, she would be re-estimating the likelihood of achieving that end. She had two options available: move insystem and hold one,or more of the worlds hostage, or flee.

Tanis knew what she would choose. No technology was worth throwing away thousands of ships and the lives of the people on them. But as the Trisilieds ships spread further apart and began to move insystem, she knew their commander did not share her outlook.

"FCO," Tanis called out. "Flank speed. We are in pursuit. Best intercept course nav can plot. Sanderson, execute the polar plan."

"Aye, Fleet Admiral," Sanderson replied and disappeared from view.

"I have something," one of the scan officers announced. "Not sure if…"

<*It is!*> Priscilla called out over the shipnet. <*RMs incoming, tagging them as fast as I can.*>

Tanis turned her attention to the holotank. A thousand RMs appeared in its depths, then a thousand more, then the counter began to climb faster than even her eyes could track.

"The hegemony ships must have fired them through Isyra's jump gates," Sera said. "You would have picked them up sooner, otherwise."

"I sure have a love-hate relationship with those gates," Finaeus said. "Would have been better if I'd never figured out how to make them."

"Cat's out of the bag now," Tanis said.

"What are you going to do?" Sera asked.

"Nothing," Tanis replied. "I already directed the FCO to inform all vessels to cease acceleration and prepare for full stasis. Point defense only on clear targets."

"I guess we did survive a blast from a black hole's relativistic jet," Sera said. "How much worse could an RM be?"

"I'm impressed," Tanis said. "We were under full stealth until we started boosting to intercept the Trisilieds ships. Either they can see through our stealth tech, or their commander has an amazing mind for strategy."

"Or he's pumped so many RMs into your system that they would have homed in on you no matter where you were."

Tanis chuckled. "Terrifying, but unlikely…aw, shit."

<*What is it?*> Priscilla asked.

"If they figured out where we are so quickly, then they know our route to the terraformed planets."

"Which means that they *will* have filled the space between here and there with RMs," Captain Espensen said.

The scan data feeding into the holotank began to show the ships of Fleet Group 1 firing at the RMs. The relativistic missiles and the ships were all jinking erratically, making the holo display appear as though it were flickering, or suffering some sort of bizarre malfunction.

"That's going to give me a headache," Finaeus said. "How sure are you that this shielding of yours can withstand relativistic missiles?"

<*One hundred percent,*> Bob's voice came across the bridge net.

"The elusive Bob makes his presence known," Finaeus said with a chuckle.

"Hush," Sera whispered at Finaeus and the older man fell silent.

Tanis cast Finaeus a worried look. "Don't worry about us, worry about the Transcend ships without stasis shields," Tanis said.

Sure enough, the scan data updated, and the holotank showed more than fifty TSF ships under direct threat from enemy missiles. Their shields would not protect them at all against the incoming barrage.

"Helm," Captain Espensen called out. "Max burn, get us ahead of those ships. Weapons, I want a grapeshot firing solution that will shield those Transcend cruisers, and not hit any of ours."

"That's a tall order," Tanis said softly. "But maybe they can find one."

She Linked across the fleet and aided in coordinating kinetic grapeshot rounds from a dozen additional cruisers, adding to the wave of kinetic pellets that would—hopefully—destroy enough of the incoming RMs. Captain Espensen attained a solution from the *I2*'s fire control team, which Tanis integrated into the kinetic shield. With eighty-two seconds until the first estimated impact, the ISF ships let fire their grapeshot.

Beams from hundreds of ships in the fleet group continued to pick away at the missiles, and every second or two, one struck its mark. However, only a fraction of the hits caused enough damage to destroy or disable the missiles. It was simply too hard to track something moving at relativistic speeds for long enough to burn through its casing.

Then, in what looked like a spectacular display of fireworks, the first missiles hit the cloud of grapeshot and exploded.

"Great," Finaeus shook his head in dismay. "You've created relativistic shrapnel. Well done."

Tanis cast the man a cold look. "This is the bridge of a warship, and you are a guest here. Keep your tone and your comments respectful."

Finaeus took a step back. Tanis was certain that few had spoken to him so bluntly in a long time.

"Yeah, um, sure," was all he managed to respond with.

The *I2* reached its position between the TSF ships and the incoming missiles, its thousands of beams lighting up the darkness—though the ship's placement in the center of the fleet reduced the available firing solutions.

Behind them, the TSF ships burned hard, a hundred AP drives and fusion torches outshining Canaan Prime, as they moved to evade the shrapnel and the few missiles that had made it past the barrier.

Shrapnel impacts registered on scan, and two-dozen ships spun off course before killing their engines and drifting through the dark. Five suffered internal detonations, and a number appeared in Tanis's mind as the ships gouted eerie fire into the cold dark vacuum around them.

Two thousand forty-three dead. It would be just the beginning of her tally for the battle.

Two more salvos of RMs came at Fleet Group 1, followed by a single attack on Greer's Fleet Group 2, which was also boosting insystem on an intercept course with the Trisilieds fleet.

This time, the TSF and ISF ships were better prepared, and the ISF ships maneuvered to create protective shields, while the TSF ships fired countermeasures at the incoming missiles.

The tactic worked reasonably well and conserved the fleet group's grapeshot. Only four more TSF ships were destroyed along with the last of the enemy RMs.

The tone on the bridge was muted, but Tanis was not displeased with the result. "All things considered, they just expended considerable resources to little effect."

"I imagine they're thinking the same thing," Sera shook her head. "Once we get stasis shields on all the ships in the TSF, maybe this war *will* be over as fast as you hope."

The holotank showed that Fleet Groups 1 and 2 would intercept the Trisilieds ships in seven hours—well before the invading ships reached the settled worlds deep insystem. Tactical showed that serious losses would be inevitable, but that victory was assured.

Captain Espensen had moved the *I2* to the van of Fleet Group 1, which was now moving at just over a tenth the speed of light. They raced to meet their foes. The ships could have accelerated faster, but too high a velocity would have sent them racing past the enemy ships, or necessitated braking heavily and exposing their vulnerable engines before engaging.

<*Feels too easy. What are those AST ships out there going to do?*> Tanis asked Angela.

<*Probably the best thing for them, and the worst thing for us,*> Angela replied.

Tanis nodded absently and sipped her coffee, glad that Espensen had an officer somewhere that knew feeding the bridge crew was wise. As she set her cup down on a tray at the edge of the console, the Scan officer called out.

"Signatures matching the AST ships, dead ahead!"

<*Didn't have to wonder long,*> Angela said.

Tanis spun back to the holotank and saw the space before Fleet Group 1 fill with ships. Number and composition matched the ships past the heliopause, which had attacked Isyra's watchers. The notation on the holotank read twenty-nine thousand eight hundred seventy-four vessels; over four thousand of which were dreadnaught class.

"Orders?" Captain Espensen asked, her face paling noticeably.

"Throw up the scoop and reverse polarity; let's make a shield for our fleet," Tanis replied with more calm than she felt. "FCO, inform all carriers to disgorge their ARC-6 alpha wings. All ships, prepare to fire kinetic rounds."

"Aye, Admiral," the FCO replied.

While the FCO managed the coordination, Tanis reviewed the placement of all the ships and the projected paths of the fighters. She tweaked the placements and assignments while watching how the Hegemony fleet arrayed itself.

The enemy ships were also travelling toward the Trisilieds ships and the inner New Canaan system, but they were coasting—their current momentum carried over from their acceleration before they passed through the jump gates.

Now, they carefully maneuvered into a large net, while keeping their engines facing away from the incoming ISF and TSF ships.

The net was wide, and Fleet Group 1 would pass through it, drawing fire from a fleet four times their size. Their shields should hold, but after seeing the Transcend fleet destroy her cruisers days ago, she was less certain about the effectiveness of stasis shields against concentrated enemy beamfire.

She wondered if the Hegemony ships would follow after Fleet Group 1 after they passed through the net, or if they would chase after Greer's ships, a half AU away.

Tanis knew what she would do if she were the Hegemony commander. She would drive the enemy against the Trisilieds fleet, crushing them utterly before moving on to the next target.

Tanis directed the ISF ships to form protective shields around the TSF vessels once more. In the resulting formation, the ships were not tightly packed, and still possessed dozens of kilometers of maneuvering room, but it should be enough to aid in the blocking of enemy beamfire.

The tactic felt strange. All military doctrine dictated that ships should never bunch up. It was folly to create such an easy grouping of targets, but Tanis had no choice if she were to save the Transcend ships from destruction.

As they drew nearer to the enemy net, which was extending into a long funnel, she ordered the tactical teams to fire concentrated rounds of grapeshot into the enemy fleet. Her plan was to make multiple openings in the enemy net, more than her fleet group needed, and sow as much confusion as possible.

The *I2*, however, would punch right through the center. She was certain that the target her largest warship presented would tempt the AST to leave her smaller formations alone.

"Ready to flash the scoop across the Hegemony fleet," Captain Espensen reported. "All batteries have selected targets and alpha wings are deployed."

"Good," Tanis nodded. "Delta-*v* between our fleets is a hair over fourteen thousand kilometers per second. With a maximum effective beam range of a hundred thousand kilometers, engagement length will be fourteen seconds. Pre-load all solutions, and backup options."

As she had so many times in the past, Tanis spread her mind across the fleet, greeting the AIs across thousands of capital ships and fighter wings. The ISF AIs knew to expect her, though the TSF intelligences were surprised, but grateful to feel her guiding touch.

The ARC-6s darted ahead of the fleet, ten thousand engine flares lighting the darkness. It was as though an entirely different starscape had appeared, new constellations shifting before them. A second later, every ship in the fleet fired their kinetic rounds, and the battle began.

Tanis felt time slow down as she surrounded herself with a holographic display of the entire battlefield, the bridge and its personnel falling away from her vision. She and Angela thought as one being as they directed ships and fighters to shore up weak spots in formations and prepare to take out prime targets.

Ahead, the Hegemony fleet detected the kinetic rounds firing from her ships, and many jinked out of the way; though many more were too late. One ton tungsten rounds slammed into cruisers and dreadnaughts, overloading sections of their shield umbrellas, some lucky shots punching clear through hulls.

A hundred enemy ships had taken damage from the kinetics, and Tanis directed the ARC-6 fighters to finish those vessels off. Short-range RMs lanced out from the fighters into the darkness, loaded with the ISF's double-impact warheads that would kinetically disable weakened shields before driving their nuclear warheads into their targets.

Though the enemy ships lay down withering point-defense fire and jinked to new positions, many of the missiles found their mark, and nuclear fireballs bloomed bright, obscuring the battlefield.

The ARC-6s sped through the enemy's formation, their stasis shields flaring brightly as they took beamfire, though not as much as Tanis had feared. Once through, the ISF fighters described sweeping arcs around the edges of the Hegemony fleet, coming about for another assault.

<*They do have a fighter shield,*> Angela commented. <*But nothing substantial.*>

<*They must have assumed that without our stasis shield tech, they can't use fighters effectively,*> Tanis replied.

<*Seems like a foolish assumption,*> Angela said. <*They could have brought a half-million fighters. It would have completely overwhelmed us.*>

<*A lot of people have trouble accepting new tactics. It would seem the Hegemony is amongst those.*>

Now there were just five seconds until the capital ships were in weapons range.

Tanis noted that the enemy fleet had responded, but not against the ISF fighters. Instead, another wave of RMs appeared on scan, once more snaking toward the vulnerable TSF ships.

She gave a mental nod to Priscilla, and the avatar altered the composition of the *I2*'s massive electrostatic ramscoop—a field over ten thousand kilometers across—to operate as a molecular decoupler. It was not a new trick, but one that was so far beyond the technical capabilities of their enemies, few opposing commanders seemed prepared for it.

Half the RMs disintegrated and spun off course as the field swept over them; though many survived the wave, and approached the TSF ships. Countermeasures and grapeshot filled the space between the two fleets as they neared the maximum range of their primary beam weapons.

The ISF ships shifted their protective bubbles around the TSF vessels, utilizing the same tactics that had been successful in the last two volleys of relativistic missiles.

Then, something unexpected occurred.

Tremendous flares of light and energy filled the battlefield, obscuring both fleets. Scan was blinded, and communications with the rest of the fleet cut out. Tanis winced as her mind, spread across the fleet's ships, snapped back into her own head.

She only managed one word, "What—" before understanding dawned on her. The missiles had carried antimatter warheads. The Hegemony had just committed a grievous war crime—likely in response to the Transcends' use of antimatter weapons against their fake fleet in Ascella.

The antimatter detonations disappeared from scan in less than a second as the ships of Fleet Group 1 sped past the expanding clouds of radiation that were traveling in the opposite direction.

Four hundred milliseconds later, the ships nearby reconnected to the combat net, and Tanis cried out, <*Fire on all preselected targets!*> The message retransmitted to the rest of the fleet as the ships re-Linked.

Damage estimates rolled in and Tanis saw that one hundred and eleven TSF ships had been destroyed or disabled, and forty-two ISF ships had suffered shield failures and taken damage from secondary explosions.

There were still fifty-six hundred undamaged ships in Fleet Group 1. The holodisplay finally resolved to show the seven divisions of Fleet Group 1, looking like insects travelling toward the flyswatter that was the Hegemony fleet.

But these bugs were prepared to sting.

The capital ships were now in weapons range, and the two fleets exchanged intensifying levels of beamfire with one another. Tanis once more stretched her mind out, guiding ships and aiding in target selection, feeling her mind swell as she encompassed the entire battlefield.

Her primary goal was to get her ships through the web intact—or as intact as she could—with a focus on disabling the enemy's maneuverability and weapons systems, rather than total destruction of their vessels.

And, over the fourteen seconds during which the capital ships exchanged fire, her Fleet Group 1 disabled seven hundred and nine Hegemony vessels.

The enemy commander, for their part, had changed their tactic. Rather than focusing on the TSF vessels, they targeted the smaller ISF ships, likely testing the stasis shield's ability to withstand concentrated particle beam attacks.

Something Tanis now knew that they could not do. The larger AST ships—their cruisers and dreadnaughts—fired proton and atom beams, the heavy particles and atomic nuclei striking the ISF stasis shields at near-light speed. A few, even a dozen of those beams could be shrugged off by the stasis shields, but hundreds of beams struck each targeted ship, and one by one those vessels saw their shields fail as reactors overheated and shut down.

The *I2*, for its part, delivered its own waves of high-energy particle beams, tearing through the AST ships like they were paper. A thousand beams at a time arced from the massive ship, pulverizing shields, destroying engines and weapons systems. Even the AST dreadnaughts were unable to withstand the *I2*'s high-energy salvos.

Then, the fourteen seconds were past, and Tanis drew her consciousness back into her mind and looked around her at the bridge of the *I2*.

Most of the personnel were drawing deep breaths, their expressions grim, yet glad. Captain Espensen gave Tanis a relieved nod as scan slowly pieced together a picture of what had happened.

The *I2* had taken no damage—a fact that did not surprise Tanis. The ship's shields were the most powerful in the fleet, and drew energy from CriEn modules; something that Bob would not allow for any other vessel.

The risk of the smaller ships creating localized imbalances in the base quantum energy of the universe was too great. He did not even extend his trust to the AIs of the other ships—fearing they would draw too much energy in a bid to survive.

Two hundred and thirty five; that was the number of ISF ships that were now little more than drifting hulls—if they were lucky. Only seven additional TSF ships had taken critical damage, though a hundred more ships across the fleet group had suffered some damage from the engagement.

But they had given as good as they got. The vector at which the fleets had intersected gave Fleet Group 1 consistent firing solutions on Hegemony ships. However, due to the enemy's formation, they had suffered three entire seconds where the majority of their fleet could not fire without risk of hitting their own.

Tanis had made the most of those seconds with another barrage of double-impact RMs.

Now, Fleet Group 1 was past the Hegemony ships on their continued race toward the Trisilieds fleet. To their rear, many of the Hegemony ships were already boosting to catch up. As they did, the Scan team finished their tallies.

The enemy had suffered what would normally be a crippling amount of damage, with over three thousand ships disabled or destroyed. However, when that still left twenty-six thousand ships intact, it was a different story.

Tanis imagined that the Hegemony commanders must have been rethinking taking on a fleet that could destroy three thousand ships in less than a minute—even when pitted against a far superior enemy. The math didn't favor either side.

In a slugfest, they would wear each other down to nothing.

Captain Espensen let out a long whistle. "That was some crazy strategery you did there, Admiral."

"Thanks," Tanis said, concentrating on the ARC-6 fighters, which were still making a second pass through the Hegemony fleet. She directed them to target the engines of the ships that had lowered their rear shielding as they boosted after Fleet Group 1.

"I can't believe the Hegemony would call the use of our picobombs a war crime, and then turn around and use antimatter on us." Captain Espensen shook her head.

"They opened the door," Tanis nodded. "They may not like what they find inside."

"Captain, Admiral," Scan called out. "Our fighters are coming back in for resupply. The Hegemony ships are boosting hard; they'll be back in weapons range in sixty-two minutes."

"That's a lot faster than we can repair and resupply all those fighters," Captain Espensen commented before casting an appraising glance at Tanis. "Fleet TAC must have anticipated this. We're trapped between the Hegemony and the Trisilieds ahead, now."

"Well," Tanis began, "We didn't exactly plan to be invaded like this, but our Hegemony friends back there are about to find that we can fire grapeshot to the rear with enough precision to slow their pursuit."

"Even so," Espensen replied, "they'll catch us before we get to Carthage—which is where it looks like the Trisilieds fleet is headed."

Tanis reviewed Fleet Group 1's position relative to Carthage, plotting out their approach. She looked at the remaining ships, clustered around the disabled vessels, which were still traveling at the same velocity as the rest of the fleet.

"FCO," Tanis called out. "Get every ship in this fleet on recovery duty. I want every disabled ship emptied in twenty-five minutes. Scoop everyone up, pods, everything. No one left behind. In fifty-five minutes, we're dumping to the dark layer."

"Tanis…we can't…not so close to the star…" Captain Espensen whispered.

"Captain," Tanis turned to Espensen. "You have your orders."

A MOMENT OF WEAKNESS

STELLAR DATE: 04.01.8948 (Adjusted Years)
LOCATION: ISS *I2*
REGION: Near Roma, New Canaan System

Sera found herself in awe of Tanis's tactical abilities. The way she could direct the ships of her fleet with a single, precise intent was a wonder to behold. A wonder that made her consider her place in whatever was to come.

Finaeus should be the true heir to the Transcend, and Tanis was by far the most capable commander she had ever seen; as the Transcend's Field Marshal, she would be the one in charge of every military action the TSF would take against the Orion Guard.

Sera was passable as Director of The Hand, but many of her successes there had been with Helen's assistance—and now Greer and others wished her to take her father's place? As what…queen, tyrant?

Her father had—deliberately, she supposed—placed weak provisions in the Transcend government's constitution for a transfer of power. It was just like him. She imagined that if he had been able to speak his last words upon some exalted deathbed, he would have imitated Alexander of Macedonia with his 'to the victor go the spoils' utterance.

Sera shook her head, trying to clear all thoughts of her father from her mind. Thinking of him inevitably brought her back to the bridge of the *Galadrial*. The place where she had learned that everything in her life had been a lie; where every friend—save for Tanis—had betrayed her.

A part of her mind chided her, reminding her that many friends had not betrayed her. Normally, Helen would have offered consolation here, but now that was gone, too.

It was insane to think that her mother—or a shard of her, at least—had been in her mind all these years. The things they had talked about, experienced, supported one another through—they were all shrouded in the lie. Everything about her was a lie.

Sera moaned inwardly. This perseveration was going to be the end of her. She needed to ground herself somehow, but the conflict they were in the midst of precluded that. How could she find stability in her own mind while everything around her balanced on a knife's edge?

Her eyes fell on Tanis.

Now there was a woman who lived up to the legend—and then some. She stood, arms akimbo, before a holotank: surveying the battlespace they would soon enter, assessing her fleet's strengths and weaknesses, and adjusting her tactics as damage reports rolled in.

The air of confidence she exuded strengthened those around her. Everyone operated at their best, gave their all, overcame any obstacle, because they knew Tanis would do no less.

It would have emboldened Sera, if she had a purpose here.

Going with *Sabrina* on their mission was out of the question—even if her body wasn't still healing, she would have thrown off their dynamic. Commanding a TSF or ISF ship was off the table, too. No one would let her take such a role, now that she was the

President of the Transcend. She had to be kept safe on the *I2,* like one of Nance's porcelain dolls.

Sera looked at the countdown hovering over Tanis's holotank. There were still forty minutes left before their next maneuver. She decided that a walk would help clear away the negative thoughts and get her back in the right frame of mind. Perhaps one of the ship's parks would give her some peace.

Priscilla waved to her as she passed through the foyer, and Sera returned the gesture.

She walked through the administrative corridor connecting the bridge to the nearest maglev station, and thought about how different it was now compared to her first visit.

Then, the ship had been a civilian vessel—sort of. Most of the corridor had been given to offices of members of the colony leadership, their staffs, and the various departments that were focused on the ship's destination.

Now, it was a hubbub of military personnel, the men and women of the ISF—a force that had gone from a couple dozen ships to one of the most powerful militaries in human space in less than a generation. *How did they do it?* Sera wondered, immediately feeling the pain of Helen's absence once more. There was no one in her mind to talk with, no one with whom to discuss her hopes and fears.

Sera wandered aimlessly; or so she tried to tell herself, but her feet moved steadily in one direction: to the *I2*'s brig.

As she drew near, she couldn't hide it from herself anymore. There was one person who had betrayed her, one in whom she had placed absolute trust, that was still around. Someone she could talk to, someone she could ask '*why*'.

"I'm here to see the prisoner, Elena," Sera announced to the Marine sergeant at the duty station outside the brig.

The man looked up at her, and his tired expression disappeared as he realized who she was. "Yes, ma'am!" he replied before glancing down at his screen. "Admiral Richards has you on the list of people who may visit Elena, but the prisoner will remain behind a stasis shield. No physical contact is allowed."

"Suits me fine," Sera muttered. "Probably better for the both of us."

The sergeant gave her a puzzled look before nodding. "Yes, ma'am. I've passed you the route. Your conversation will be recorded, but immediately encrypted and saved. I will not have access to its content. However, Admiral Richards will."

"Understood," Sera replied, and loaded the sergeant's directions onto her HUD before passing through the security arch and into the brig.

The *I2*'s brig was, in a word, massive. She guessed that it could house ten thousand people—or maybe even more. She didn't think that it was for misbehaving ISF military personnel; this was a POW camp inside the ship.

Right now, it only had two occupants: Kent and Elena.

She only had directions to Elena's cell, and that was just as well. Sera had deliberately avoided any contact with the Orion Guard colonel; in her current state, she worried he would learn a lot more from her than she from him.

The same would certainly be true for Elena, but she needed to see if there were any explanations to be had—any closure.

Sera approached the cell, and saw Elena sitting on a white cot mounted to the wall on the right within the grey, featureless cube. The only other item in the room was a small san unit.

Her former lover sat up and took a deep breath as Sera approached. "Time for our chat, is it?"

"I suppose," Sera replied with a rueful smile. "It had to come eventually, right?"

"Yes, I suppose it did," Elena nodded slowly. "I honestly thought you'd come sooner—back on the *Galadrial*. When they moved me here, I began to wonder if I'd ever see you again."

"At the very least, you'd see me as a witness at your trial," Sera said as she summoned a seat to rise from the deck.

"Oh! I'm going to get a trial?" Elena smirked. "I guess that's something. I half expected a summary execution at some point."

"No, that's your game," Sera scowled, ready to tear into Elena; but then she stopped, considering once more what Elena had saved her from. "I'm sorry. That was unfair. I was about to do the same thing. You did save me from patricide—though I know in my heart I still would have killed my father—so you only saved me from others' recriminations. Though you also robbed me of the answers I sought."

Elena leaned back against her cell's wall, pulling her knees up—a position Sera knew was intended to get her to trust her former lover, and to remind her of happier times past.

Shit, Sera, she chided herself. *Do you have to analyze everything like a fucking spy?*

"What do you think those answers are, now that you've had time to consider things?" Elena asked.

It was stupid; Sera knew it, but she wanted to confide in someone. Tanis was too busy to listen, and her former crew was out in the black; Elena had been her comforter for many years now. It was too easy to slip back into that place.

"I think he suspected Airtha—he must have. I mean…Finaeus warned him," Sera began. "If father did know, then maybe Airtha was too strong for him to take on; though it doesn't explain why father tried to kill Finaeus on Ikoden station, back when Jessica found him…what purpose would that have served? For everything to make sense, father must have exiled Finaeus for his own protection. Who was behind that assassination, then…?"

Sera's head snapped up and her eyes drilled into Elena, who raised her hands defensively. "It wasn't me! I knew Finaeus would strengthen you *against* your father, and that Praetor Kirkland was open to working with Finaeus—something he would not even entertain with your father."

"Oh, so you're in Kirkland's inner council now, are you?" Sera's tone grew caustic and her lip curled into a snarl. "What was your price, by the way? What did they offer you to betray me?"

To Sera's surprise, a tear formed in Elena's eye and drew a path down her cheek.

"You."

"Me? What do you mean by that?" Sera asked, even though she suspected what Elena would say next.

Elena's eyes were wide, and her voice pleaded with Sera to understand. "They were going to let you live, let us go off together somewhere and forget all this bullshit, just be *us*."

Anger burned through Sera's veins, and she leapt up and raised her hand, finger pointed at Elena; ready to tear into her former partner. Then she stopped and lowered her arm, turning away.

"Sera! Sera, please! They're going to win. You can't stop them. Where the Transcend has politics and power grabs, Orion has a belief; a belief that humanity should live in harmony with the galaxy—not to subsume it, not to transcend it. It's strong. It drives them like nothing in the Transcend. They're going to win...."

Sera turned back to Elena, and approached the bars on the outside of the cell, wrapping her hand around one.

"If I win against Airtha—whose fanaticism far outstrips Orion's—I will do everything in my power to stop this war. Kirkland has nothing to fear from rogue picotech anymore. I will stop all research, and let New Canaan retreat into their insular society." She looked up and peered through the bars at Elena.

"There's no reason why these two ideals cannot coexist. Why does everyone in the Transcend have to diminish to match Orion? We let people live as they wish; we don't enforce a...a... lower level of living, just because some people don't want to see humans ever ascend."

"That's not what it's about," Elena said with pleading eyes. "Airtha represents the end result—a malevolent entity that wishes to enslave and control. Now that Jutio is gone, it's even easier to see that. AIs in our heads, bodies modified so much that we're more machine than human...we *aren't* human anymore, Sera. We're *things*! The Transcend did that to us—made you and I weapons, instruments—and it spreads..."

Elena rose from the cot and approached the bars, her skin changing color to match Sera's.

"You did this to me. You did it because you think it's OK for humans to force their own evolution."

"I did it to keep you safe," Sera said. "By your faulty logic, I evolved you to make you better able to survive in your environment. We've long passed the point where we let random mutation and slow evolution push our species forward; but this is an academic argument...I didn't come here to debate philosophy with you."

"Then what did you come for here, Sera? Do you need to know when? How long? Is that what this is about?"

Sera nodded slowly. "Yes, I suppose that's all."

"It was after you were exiled. I couldn't believe what your father would allow to happen to his own daughter. The man was evil, plain and simple. We can debate philosophy all day long, but you can't argue with me on that. What did he say when he tore Helen from your mind? Was he kind and loving? Or did it reveal who he really was?"

Sera tried to push Elena's words out of her mind. She didn't want to remember that conversation with her father, how cold he had been. But it was impossible. How he had described Airtha as something he owned...no...he must not have known of her schemes. He really *did* believe he possessed her.

She brought her mind back to Elena's statement. "From the moment you came to me on the *Intrepid*, back in Ascella...our whole time together in the Huygens System...on Airtha. The whole time, you were trying to turn me?"

"I wanted to show you how much I *loved* you. So that when the time came for us to have this conversation, you'd listen. There's still a chance for you to do the right thing. Sue for peace with Orion; then we can leave this place, leave all these troubles forever..."

Sera felt a manic laugh rise in her, and she forced it out in her search for some sort of catharsis.

"Seriously, Elena? Do you think that Tanis Richards will roll over just because I ask her to? Do you think that everyone in the Transcend will just lay down their arms because I say so? To them, the Orion Guard has destroyed entire worlds, burned systems to ash."

"You have to!" Elena cried out, balling her hands into fists. "You have to stop this war—surrender to Orion. There's nothing anywhere worth all this bloodshed!"

Sera didn't have a response. It wasn't that she disagreed with Elena; she just didn't know how to do what Elena was asking. "I can't…it's impossible. I don't know how."

"Then find a way," Elena stepped forward and reached a hand out toward her, pressing it against the field.

In that moment, the only thing Sera wanted in the entire galaxy was to hold Elena in her arms—but she couldn't. Not just because of the field separating them, but because her place at the head of the Transcend demanded that she didn't.

It demanded that she do her duty.

"I will find away," Sera replied. "But it won't be through surrender. When they see what Tanis is capable of, Orion will back down, and we'll have peace."

Elena stared longingly at Sera, her mouth working silently. "Then I suppose we have nothing further to discuss," Elena said sitting back down on her cot. She turned away and faced the wall. "Please, go now…I…I just…please go."

Sera thought about responding, about throwing something in Elena's face, but there was nothing left. She didn't harbor any ill will toward her former lover anymore, just dismay at how deluded she was—and shame in herself for never seeing it before.

"Goodbye, Elena," Sera said quietly. She turned and took a step, then stopped and looked over her shoulder. Sera tried to think of one last thing to say, but Elena had curled up into a fetal position, her shoulders heaving as sobs wracked her body.

A long, silent sigh escaped Sera's lips, and she walked away, wiping the tears that flowed down her face.

JOY RIDE

STELLAR DATE: 04.01.8948 (Adjusted Years)
LOCATION: High Carthage
REGION: Carthage, New Canaan System

"Cary!" Saanvi called out. "Where are you going?"

Cary turned around and looked at her sister and best friend in the world. "I'm going to get on a ship," Cary replied. "They need everyone up there who knows how to fly, and you and I know how to fly. Now come on."

The look on Saanvi's face was not promising. She had always been cautious that way, but growing up under their mother had reinforced that. Their mom liked rules, and she like people to do what she said. Cary preferred to think of herself as a more balanced combination of her mother and father—though she admitted that both of her parents' rebellious sides appealed to her more.

"We have orders from Mom to go planetside, and get in Landfall's bunker. She knows what's best for us," Saanvi said as she approached. "You know that."

Cary sighed and took Saanvi's hand. "Sahn, Mom wants to protect us, and that's her job as our mother. But you and I are eighteen, now. We're adults, and we can do what we want to—what we need to."

"Seriously, Cary? What sort of dream world do you live in? Mom runs everything here. She tells adults what to do all the time—it's her job. Being adults doesn't mean we don't have to listen to her."

"Yeah? Well maybe it's about time that Mom didn't get to tell everyone what to do around here."

Saanvi's face fell, and Cary regretted the words the moment they passed her lips. She often wondered why it was that Saanvi seemed to have a stronger bond with her mother than she did. Cary's flesh was her mother's flesh; she had many advanced genetic traits and mental abilities from her mother—hell, she was born a class L1 human, far above the standard L0. Something that was exceedingly rare without extensive pre-natal genetic modification.

But at least ninety percent of the time, Saanvi—who she loved more than anyone in the world—had always seemed closer to their mother. Maybe it was the whole thing she'd heard about being too alike.

"Cary," Saanvi said, her tone conciliatory, "you may be right, Mom does tend to throw her weight around. But she always does it for the good of the colony, and she always gets results. She knows what she's doing."

"Yeah…I know. I'm sorry," Cary replied. "You know I didn't really mean what I said. I love mom, and she's a great leader—and everyone keeps voting her in, so they must like her, too. But you know that when it comes to us, she doesn't think like a leader; she thinks like a mother. We have to prove to her that we are adults, and can be trusted with responsibility."

Saanvi took a step back and raised an eyebrow. Though her skin was dark, her hair jet-black, and her eyes a deep brown, she pulled off the expression in a way that looked identical to their mother's.

Cary took a moment to wonder how Saanvi managed that before she braced herself for an assault from Saanvi's logic.

"And you think that *stealing* a starship is going to be how we prove to her that we're trustworthy?" Saanvi asked, her voice dripping with sarcasm.

"When they see what we can do, how you and I can Link our minds together, they'll know that we should get our commissions and join the fleet. We don't need to go to the academy. We've spent our lives preparing for this," Cary replied.

"I think it's going to have the opposite effect," Saanvi sighed. "But you're going to do this with or without me, aren't you?"

Carry nodded. "I am, and we both know you can't take me down. Are you going to report me?"

The two sisters stared at each other for a full minute.

Saanvi finally relented, "No. No, I won't report you, and I better come with you. If you get killed and I'm still alive, and knew about your harebrained idea, Mom will skin me alive. Better if we both die together out there."

Cary embraced her sister. "That's the spirit! OK, let's go." She turned and continued down the corridor that led to the station's east shuttle bay.

"What's your plan, anyway?" Saanvi asked as she hurried to catch up to Cary. "All the empty ships up there are run by AIs. Probably Judith or Symatra. Neither of them are going to let us just commandeer a ship."

Cary flashed a grin at her sister, the one that looked like her Father's and utterly disarmed everyone—one she practiced frequently in the mirror. "Remember a few months back when we played that prank on Alan?"

"The one that almost got us kicked out of school and nearly ruined our lives? I do seem to recall it," Saanvi muttered.

"Well, I hacked the COMMSAT network to pull it off, and I left my little back door in there. If we're challenged, we can just tell them to look up our orders. When they do, they'll get rerouted and find some nice orders from Mom putting us in command of a ship."

"Putting *who* in command?" Saanvi asked pointedly. "Someone has to be the captain."

"Me, of course," Cary grinned. "I have a temporary field rank of lieutenant, and you're an ensign. You're the XO."

Saanvi sighed. "Why am I not surprised?"

* * * * *

The one thing Cary had not anticipated was how busy the shuttle bay would be. She hadn't thought to add orders to supply her with a shuttle, and Sam, the dockmaster, wouldn't check any systems that hit the COMMSAT network.

"Great plan," Saanvi said and poked her sister in the shoulder as they stood just outside the dock's entrance. "Well, I guess we can call it a day, and head down the strand like we're supposed to."

"Saanvi, really. When have you known me to give up so easily?" Cary chided. "Watch this."

Without looking back to see if Saanvi was following, she strode out onto the East Dock, toward where Sam stood arguing with a shuttle pilot.

"I don't care if your grandma is on the next shuttle in from the habs and you want to take her down to the surface yourself; you have a supply load to carry down, and every AI is already tasked with running the fleet out there, so they can't do it."

"Sam, c'mon, Gran is all I have left. I lost my dad at Bollam's and my mom stayed behind in Victoria," the pilot entreated. "I need to be with her."

"You need to be out there keeping the colony safe," Sam said with a deepening scowl. "Everyone here has made more than their share of sacrifices. You're not special. Now get in your shuttle, and take it down!"

"No, Sam, go fuck yourself, I quit. I'm going to ride the strand down with my gran." The pilot added a few more curses for good measure and stalked off.

"For fuck's sake!" Sam threw his hands in the air and then caught sight of Cary and Saanvi approaching. "Sweet stars, what did I do to deserve this? What do you two want?"

"I overheard that guy leaving you high and dry, Sam," Cary said in her most conciliatory tone. "Saanvi and I are supposed to get planetside ASAP, and we're rated to fly that shuttle."

"You don't even know which shuttle I need taken down," Sam replied.

"Well, we're rated to fly any shuttle you have docked here," Saanvi interjected. "It would be easy for us to run one down."

"Rated? More like berated. Last time you were in here, you stole the replica fighter your father was working on, and went joy riding around the moons. I'd be a fool to let the two of you in any cockpit here."

"We flew the *Andromeda* into Gamma IV a few months back," Cary said. "And the *Hellespont* after that."

"We just want to do our part to help out," Saanvi added and Cary gave her a smile, grateful for the assist.

Sam looked them both up and down and then his eyes flicked to the left as he accessed the Link. "Hmm…well, you're not lying about that, and I do need someone to run that shuttle down. OK, you can help; but you get that shuttle down, and then you head to the bunker. I won't have it on my head if something happens to you."

"You got it!" Cary replied, distracting Sam by grabbing his hand and shaking it vigorously. It wouldn't do for him to see the pained expression on Saanvi's face. "Which is our bird?"

Sam pointed to a freight hauler sitting in a cradle five hundred meters away. "There she is. She was out for service before this little crisis hit, and had an iffy port-maneuvering thruster. It should be fixed now, but no one has had the time to take it for a test run. If you have any issues—"

"Spin the ship on its axis and use the starboard thrusters," Cary replied. "Don't worry, Sam. We can manage it."

Sam looked like he was having second thoughts, but another pair of pilots walked up and started arguing with him about routes, and Cary took the opportunity to grab Saanvi and dash off toward the freighter.

"Maybe we should just fly it down," Saanvi said. "They're going to notice when we take this thing near one of the cruisers up there. Besides, how are we going find one that's worth boarding? Half of them don't even hold atmo."

"I have it all sorted," Cary replied as they hopped a dockcar that was hauling a load of cargo in the direction they were headed. "When we board, I'll use my backdoor in the COMMSAT network to pull status reports from the ships as they pass through. There's gotta be one that's in good enough shape for us to take."

"You better make sure that you do something about the queries that Sam is going to run. You can bet he's going to keep tabs on us to make certain we make it down," Saanvi added. "You know…if anything happens to us, Mom is going to kill him."

"Saanvi," Cary looked her sister in the eyes, trying to quell her worry. "Nothing is going to happen to us. Mom's never going to let anyone get this close to Carthage. She's won every space battle she's ever commanded."

"She's only commanded two major fleet actions," Saanvi said. "And none anywhere near as big as this one is shaping up to be. Things could go horribly wrong."

"And you worry too much, Saanvi. Stasis shields, picobombs; there's no way we can lose."

Saanvi didn't reply, and Cary could tell her sister was worrying about what was to come if the enemy fleets reached Carthage. She also knew that if she kept trying to encourage her, it would only upset Saanvi, and she may call the whole thing off. For now, it was enough that they were together and headed toward—not away from—the action.

When the dockcar neared their shuttle, named *Fair Weather,* they hopped off and trotted toward the ship. It wasn't too big, just a hundred meters long—a fraction of the *Andromeda*'s size, and even less of the *Hellespont*'s. However, none of the warships could take a vessel the size of the freight hauler into their docking bays, so they'd have to figure out what to do with it once they got to their ship.

Cary could tell Saanvi was thinking the same thing by the frown she wore, and the twist of her lips; but she didn't say anything. Cary wondered if that meant her sister had come up with a solution to the issue.

They walked across the gantry to the ship's port airlock, and Cary passed her token to the ship, praying that Sam hadn't changed his mind. Her fears were assuaged when the airlock cycled open and the girls stepped in. The ship's inner lock was closed, and while they waited for the ship to cycle them through, the two girls pulled shipsuits out of a sealed locker and slipped into them.

It was unlikely anyone would see them, but wearing shipsuits made them look a lot more official than Saanvi's shorts and t-shirt, or Cary's dress.

"Welcome Cary and Saanvi," the ship said audibly as the inner airlock cycled open.

Cary cast Saanvi a worried look. *<Is there an NSAI on this thing? No way will one of them let us go off course.>*

<Don't worry,> Saanvi said with a mental smirk. *<While you were dreaming of winning medals for your bravery, I looked up the* Fair Weather*'s service record. It was supposed to get an AI pilot, but they're all pulled out for fleet duty, so this is just the standard shipboard comp. Nothing we can't boss around.>*

"Hi, *Fair Weather,* Saanvi said audibly. "I'm passing you override code 98RF-A1. Physical pilots taking full control of all systems for manual piloting."

"Thank you, Captain Saanvi," the comp replied. "Falling back to passive failover mode. Happy flying!"

"Chipper thing. Nice touch with 'captain' there, Sis," Cary commented as they walked down the short passageway to the cockpit. Once they reached its narrow confines, they strapped into the seats and ran through a pre-flight check.

"Everything looks good, Captain," Cary said, and caught a scowl from Saanvi who liked everything by the book. "Fine. Engines, grav drive, life support, point defense beams, nav thrusters, all green."

"Comm and scan?" Saanvi asked.

"Yeah, them too," Cary replied. "Just put in for departure clearance, and let's get out of here."

"I can't get departure clearance until everything is done properly. Sam is going to check our request, so file your cross-checks properly in the logs," Saanvi retorted. "I swear, Cary, I should have just let you do this on your own. There's no way you would have gotten off the dock, and we'd be riding the strand down to the surface in no time."

"Fine, Sahn, but I know you want to get out there and help, too. Don't give me that load about doing this for me. Underneath, you want to be making a difference, not hiding in a bunker down under Landfall."

Saanvi didn't reply, but Cary could tell from the set of her sister's mouth that she had hit a nerve. Good. Saanvi liked to take the high road whenever possible, but there was a reason she came with Cary whenever an adventure knocked—she craved it, too.

As Saanvi had predicted, Sam called in personally with clearance. *<OK, you two. I see your pre-flight checks, and flight plan. They look good. You get the* Fair Weather *down nice and safe. No detours, no rushing. Nice and safe. You hear me?>*

<Yes, Dockmaster,> Saanvi replied, her mental tone perfectly calm. *<Nice and safe, no detours.>*

<Good,> Sam replied before signing off.

"Man, you're a good liar when you want to be," Cary said. "I always forget how smooth you are."

"Shut up, Cary. Just release the clamps already."

* * * * *

"Do you need a hand?" Saanvi asked as Cary searched through the data on the ships clustered at the L1 point of Carthage's larger moon—a whitish-blue orb named Hannibal.

Cary scowled in response. She had to admit that determining which of the five thousand ships in Fleet Group 5 to choose was more work than she expected

"I've narrowed it down to these forty," Cary said. "They all have engines, life support, and functioning weapons, but there are nuances between them that make it hard to choose. Take a look," Cary replied and passed the data to Saanvi.

"Hmmm," Saanvi said as she ran through the ships. "Oh, it's easy, pick this one."

Cary looked at the ship. It bore the name *Illyria,* and appeared to be one of the least complete in the final selection.

"Why that one?" Cary asked. "It doesn't even have docking bays. We'll have to EVA over."

"You didn't check its loadout, did you?" Saanvi asked. "The *Illyria* has a full store of RMs and kinetics. Its hull is full of holes, but that barely matters with a-grav and stasis shields."

"I don't know," Cary mused. "There are several others with full life support. If anything goes wrong on that ship, we'll have to fix it in EVA gear."

"Cary," Saanvi shook her head. "It's a seven hundred meter cruiser that is only eighty percent complete. If anything goes wrong and we can't fix it from the bridge, we're screwed."

"Good point," Cary muttered. "OK, set a course for the *Illyria,* then. I'll grab us a pair of EVA suits from aft storage."

Cary walked down the passageway to the storage locker just aft of the airlock, and grabbed two EVA-901 suits. They were bright white with reflective strips running down the sides—the better to find lost people in space. They had a slippery, rubbery texture, almost like grasping an eel in water. Though they appeared flimsy—no thicker than five millimeters, and as thin as one in places—they were sturdy, and could even provide some protection from light beamfire.

The main advantage of the suits was that they provided one atmosphere of pressure across the wearer's body, and could adjust that pressure as needed to prevent fluids from building up in extremities.

Cary quickly pulled off her shipsuit and stepped into the EVA-901. It fit loosely as she pulled it on, but once she drew the fastener shut, the suit tightened and pressed all the air out from within. She gasped as the cold health monitoring sensors hit her body, and then raised her arms, shimmying side to side to make sure the suit had a good fit. Cary opted for a clear three-sixty helmet, and pulled one from the rack. Before donning it, she twisted her blonde hair into a tight bun to ensure it wouldn't get in her face while the helmet was on. Once satisfied, she locked the helmet's collar around her neck, where it sealed to the suit, and then she grabbed the two halves of the helmet.

She hooked the top hasp of the two halves together, and then closed it over her head. It made a suctioning sound as it sealed, and her HUD showed green for an airtight connection to the suit. She did some more quick stretches and swung her arms around to make sure the seal still showed green.

The respirator on her back registered a five-hour capability for recycling her air, and the suit's batteries displayed a full forty-hour charge; all squarely within nominal ranges. She switched the respirator to use external air, and grabbed a suit and helmet for Saanvi.

When she returned to the cockpit, her sister was deftly maneuvering the shuttle through the AI-controlled fleet, now only five hundred kilometers from their target.

<*We been pinged yet?*> Cary asked.

Saanvi glanced back at her sister and shook her head. <*Not yet. Clear helmet, eh? Good, I hate those ones that are tight on the face—feel like I'm suffocating the whole time.*>

<*I know, Sis,*> Cary replied as she sat down. <*I'll take it from here. Get suited up.*>

<*Strap in, first,*> Saanvi admonished.

Cary stuck out her tongue at her sister, but did as she ordered. Saanvi may have been a rule-follower, but Cary knew the rules were there for a reason, and there was no success in arguing with her sister about them—not with logic, anyway.

<*Nice, now I know* ***why*** *you got the clear helmet, so you can make faces at me.*>

<*Bingo!*> Cary said with a smile. <*OK, all buckled up. Taking the helm.*>

Saanvi stood and stepped into the passageway to don her EVA-901, while Cary leaned back in her seat—which had adjusted its configuration to accommodate the rebreather pack and the bulbous helmet. Cary waved off the sanitary hookups, but did let the seat's power cable connect to the suit's power pack to top off the charge.

<*Freighter* Fair Weather, *what is your destination?*>

The message came in over the ship's main comm channel, and carried the tag of the Fleet Group 5 Commander. Cary did a quick check and saw that it was Symatra—an AI that was even more of a stickler for the rules than Saanvi.

This was it. Cary took a deep breath to steady her nerves before replying.

<*Fleet Commander Symatra, this is Lieutenant Cary Richards aboard the* Fair Weather. *We're on our way to the* Illyria; *we have orders to take command of that vessel.*>

<***Lieutenant*** *Cary, is it?*> Symatra asked. <*Hold your course while I check your orders.*>

Saanvi walked back into the cockpit, a worried expression on her face. She hadn't yet donned her helmet—a testament to her level of concern.

<*Even if this does work, Mom is going to kill us,*> Saanvi said privately, her mental tone wavering.

<*Too late for going back, now,*> Cary said. <*Symatra is getting routed to my set of orders as we speak. Mom's token is on them. The deed is done.*>

<*Lieutenant Cary and Ensign Saanvi, your orders appear to be legitimate, though I can't imagine what your mother was thinking in issuing them. When she's in communications range again, I'll ask her myself. I want you aboard the* Illyria *in fifteen minutes, and give me a full readiness report on the ship in thirty. You may have command of that vessel, but it's still in my fleet group and under my authority.*>

<*Yes, Ma'am,*> Cary replied.

<*You're on my fleet net now,*> Symatra replied. <*Check your rosters. I have a provisional rank of Admiral for this engagement.*>

Cary reddened. <*Yes, Admiral Symatra. Sorry, Admiral.*>

Symatra sent an acknowledgement and closed the connection.

<*Did she seem pissed?*> Cary asked. <*I can't tell if she was pissed.*>

Saanvi shook her head as she donned her helmet. <*Not pissed, but certainly annoyed.*>

<*Well, we better get to our ship on the double,*> Cary said as she fed additional power to the grav drives. <*Can't keep the admiral waiting.*>

* * * * *

Saanvi managed the final maneuvering, lining up the shuttle with the *Illyria*, while Cary programed a flight path for the onboard comp to follow that would take the shuttle down to Landfall. Under normal conditions, she wouldn't have worried about a comp landing the craft; but with all the traffic around the capital at present, she prayed it wouldn't cause some sort of problem.

<*Put it on the auxiliary runway at the new spaceport north of the city,*> Saanvi advised. <*I know it's not where the cargo is supposed to go, but it will make the comp's calculations a lot simpler.*>

<*Good call, Sis,*> Cary replied, and entered the new destination. <*OK, she's all set and the* Illyria *is spooling out its umbilical—which it wasn't supposed to have, yet. I'll go cycle the airlock. You green on your seals?*>

Saanvi's head nodded inside her helmet. <*Green as a turtle. You?*>

<*Across the board,*> Cary replied.

Saanvi glanced back at her sister, a nervous smile on her face. <*Cary…thank you. I know we're going to catch hell for this, but it's going to be amazing—our own ship…. Thanks for bringing me.*>

Cary laughed aloud, the sound echoing in her ears. <*Gah…I always forget not to do that. I would never leave you behind, Sahn. We're a package deal, you and I. Where one goes, so does the other.*>

<*Good, then don't board the ship without me.*>

Two minutes later, both girls were standing in the airlock, hands clasped as the outer door cycled open and revealed the ten meters of umbilical to the *Illyria's* starboard forward airlock. It was already open, and they rushed across the space to reach it.

<*Now I feel silly having got us into EVA-901s with an umbilical linkup,*> Cary said as they

reached the cruiser's airlock.

<*It was a good call,*> Saanvi said as the exterior portal closed behind them. <*It's fifty-fifty that this ship loses atmo while we're on it, anyway. I'd rather be safe than a bloated corpse.*>

<*Gross! That's a visual I didn't need!*>

* * * * *

Cary and Saanvi floated onto the *Illyria*'s bridge. One thing neither of them had bothered to check was whether internal gravity systems were functional.

<*You know,*> Cary said with a grin, <*for someone who is the best pilot outside of the academy, you have a lot of trouble with zero*-g.>

<*Shut up, Cary,*> Saanvi said as she settled into the navigator's seat. <*I can still call this thing off.*>

<*Your threats are really starting to ring hollow,*> Cary laughed as she took the weapons console and began to configure it to operate scan, as well. She saw Saanvi doing the same thing. They had realized, when trading responsibilities while piloting the *Andromeda*, that they both liked to have scan up, and did better when both had an eye on it.

It would be especially useful, given that there were just the two of them onboard.

<*I'll run the engines and navigation systems checks,*> Saanvi said. <*You do scan and weapons. Whoever gets theirs done first can take life support.*>

<*You got it,*> Cary replied. She liked that they didn't have to discuss roles. Saanvi would pilot, and Cary would run the weapons. But they would deep-Link their minds in combat, the way that made them feel like one person—each sister's limbs like an extension of the other's.

As Cary ran her systems checks, cognizant of Symatra's looming deadline, she considered how unusual her natural ability was—certainly something that no one else seemed capable of.

Saanvi was certain it was an ability Cary had inherited from her mother—some sort of technologically genetic trait. Cary had never told her mother about it; she didn't want to add to her mom's concerns. Tanis never spoke of it, but Cary knew her centuries with Angela were unprecedented. To know it had possibly altered her daughter may not be welcome news.

When she was younger, Cary had asked her more than once why Tanis and Angela hadn't separated, but her mother had only responded that it wasn't possible.

The history lessons in her school had shed a bit more light on the subject, explaining that Tanis and Angela had the ability to spread their minds together across networks. It was how they were able to command the ISF fleets with such precision. The history books also made sure to point out that Tanis and Angela had not merged into one being, that they were not what the old stories from Sol referred to as an abomination; though the assurances in the texts had always felt too forced to Cary.

Even so, Angela was like a second mother to her. When she was younger, and her mother was often away at the Capitol, she would wake alone and scared. She hated to wake her father, and would lay in the dark with her blankets pulled over her head.

Without fail, Angela would come to her, projecting a form for her to see while speaking to her over the Link.

She remembered the stories Angela would tell her about her mother, and the old days back in Sol and Victoria. She showed Cary where Tanis had grown up on Mars, near a sea called the Melas Chasma. She would speak of her first assignment with her mother, and the dozens of others afterward—probably leaving out details that a small child had no need to hear.

It had made her feel so much more connected to her mother—and it had also cemented in her mind that her mother and Angela were in fact two separate people, but not quite as much as the history lessons would have her believe.

<*Hey, mission control to Cary. You done yet? I've checked every system except yours, and we need to send the report to Symatra in two minutes,*> Saanvi interrupted her reverie.

<*Yeah, just a sec. It's done, I just need to recheck a redundant system in the railgun that's throwing a red flag.*>

<*Chop, chop, Sis! The fleet is moving out and we need to get into formation.*>

<*Moving out?*> Cary asked as she reset the subsystem and got a green board. <*'Kay, it's sent.*>

<*Yeah, looks like we're going to get that action you've been dying to see. Check the Fleet Tactical Net; the Trisilieds fleet is on its way here. ETA six hours.*>

<*Shit! Here?*> Cary exclaimed. <*Their whole fleet?*>

<*Lieutenant Cary,*> Symatra addressed her on the fleetnet. <*I want you and the* Illyria *to seed the enemy fleet's approach vector with half your RM payload. Make your best speed to the coordinates I've designated, and place the missiles in a Zeta-Nine pattern.*>

Cary didn't hesitate to reply. <*Aye, Admiral, we're on our way,*> before turning to Saanvi and asking, <*What's pattern Zeta-Nine?*>

<*Beats me, but you better look it up. I'm putting the engines through a quick warm-up cycle before we boost out there. It'll take us twenty-two minutes to make it the location Symatra specified, so you better figure it out by then.*>

Cary sighed and looked up the pattern in the ISF's tactical databases. She hoped it was a simple grid in which the missiles could be deployed, but what she found was a shifting three-dimensional pattern based on the approaching fleet's configuration. It also necessitated programming the RMs with an algorithm that could respond to shifts in the approaching fleet's formation and still maintain maximum dispersal, while still hitting targets of opportunity and not overlapping.

By the time Saanvi brought the ship to the designated area, Cary was just finishing the calculations.

<*OK, here's the pattern, Sahn. I've proposed a course to seed them—it should take thirty-one minutes,*> Cary said.

<*Looks good, Cary,*> Saanvi replied. <*I'm laying in the course now. Be ready to seed the missiles on your marks.*>

<*Seriously? You don't have any corrections?*> Cary asked.

<*Nope, you did good work here. Is that so hard to believe?*> Saanvi chuckled at her response.

With Saanvi taking the ship through her prescribed course, and the RMs set to deploy at preset coordinates, Cary had the time to review the analysis of the battlefield. The Fleet Tactical Net, which her HUD listed as the FTN, showed an unbelievable number of ships in various formations throughout the system.

Fleet Group 5, Admiral Symatra's group of forty five hundred ships, had taken up high orbit around Carthage's larger moon, Morocco. Beyond it, the *Illyria* and a dozen other mid-sized cruisers were all seeding missiles along the Trisilieds fleet's approach vector. At their current rate of deceleration, the Trisilieds fleet would arrive at Carthage when the moon, and Fleet Group 5, would be between it and the planet.

She was glad to see that the system's rail platforms were chipping away at the incoming fleet, but they wouldn't wear down the numbers by any appreciable amount by the time it arrived. The Trisilieds fleet would still contain over twenty thousand fully functional warships against Symatra's barely operable group.

The FTN showed that Judith's Fleet Group 6 was positioned at Athens, some four AU distant and a quarter of the way around the star from Carthage. Cary wondered why her mother hadn't pulled Judith's ships back to Carthage, but then she saw that the Hegemony fleet was still in a position where they could strike either Athens or Carthage.

A momentary fear swept through Cary as she realized that the goal of the invading fleets must now be to take and hold a world—effectively using its people as hostages to get the technology they so desperately wanted. But they only needed one world. All four of the terraformed planets in the New Canaan system had populations, some in the millions, and all with friends living on them.

Her mother's Fleet Group 1 was in pursuit of the Trisilieds ships, but with the Hegemony ships behind them, they were now coasting, unable to point their engines in either direction. At some point they'd need to brake, and that would expose their engines to the Trisilieds fleet; just as the Trisilieds ships' engines would be exposed to Symatra's fleet, and the stationary weapons on Carthage and its moons.

She was glad to see that at least the TSF Admiral named Greer had his fleet group boosting hard for Carthage. At their current speed, they'd reach it before her mother's ships—but also not before the Trisilieds. Further out in the system, her father's fleet and the one commanded by Admiral Sanderson were holding their positions, each half an AU from the system's two largest gas giants.

<*Why isn't mother bringing in the other fleet groups?*> she asked Saanvi. <*Do you think she's worried about more incoming enemy ships?*>

<*The Trisilieds one came out of nowhere,*> Saanvi said with a worried glance at her sister. <*And from what our databases show, none of these ships are Orion Guard. They could easily drop another fleet on us.*>

<*Fuuuuck,*> Cary whispered. <*There's no way we can take out these two,* **and** *another fleet.*>

<*Mom will have a plan,*> Saanvi said, trying to sound calm; but Cary could tell her sister was worried, too.

<*That plan better involve using picobombs to wipe these guys out, because there's no way we'd win a slugfest against that many ships.*>

<*You know the parliament's policy,*> Saanvi said. <*Pico is no longer to be used as an offensive weapon. Too many nations have declared its use a war crime.*>

<*Yeah, just like antimatter weapons, but no one seems to care about that prohibition anymore!*> Cary fumed.

<*I don't know why you're getting pissed at me. It's not like I can authorize its use. From what I understand, there are no pico bombs present in any of the fleets right now. They're all under lock and key in some super-secret base somewhere,*> Saanvi replied.

<*Every credit I have says that 'super-secret base' is the* I2,> Cary said, as she set the bridge's main holo to show the countdown before the Trisilieds fleet arrived: five hours and seventeen minutes.

The *Illyria* finished seeding its missiles, and Symatra directed them to take up a position in the inner ring of ships orbiting Morocco. Cary couldn't help but notice that their ship would be hidden behind the moon when the Trisilieds finally came into firing range.

Apparently, the AI commander was going to keep them out of the thick of things as much as she could.

Cary and Saanvi passed the time reviewing the ship's systems in further detail, and ensuring that automated repair drones were pre-positioned in any critical areas. With no human crew aboard, the drones were their only repair options if the ship took damage.

<*Stars, I'm starving,*> Cary said as the clock counted down to thirty minutes before the enemy fleet was in firing range.

<*How can you be hungry right now?*> Saanvi asked. <*I can barely stand the thought of drinking* ***water****, my stomach is so tied up in knots.*>

<*We need to eat something; we haven't had anything since those stale sandwiches on the* Fair Weather*. It won't help if we're passing out from hunger during the battle,*> Cary replied.

<*I think we can make it a bit longer without food. Takes more than a day to pass out from hunger.*>

<*Sahn,*> Cary said, her tone dead serious. <*You don't know when we're going to have time to eat again. For all we know, we could be crashed on Carthage at this time tomorrow fighting a guerilla war against the invaders—something that's probably easier to do on a full stomach.*>

<*Well, it's not like we have a stocked galley aboard. You're going to have to eat the nutri-paste from the chair's feed,*> Saanvi replied. <*I had a little taste awhile back, and it's not too bad.*>

<*No way,*> Cary responded as she unbuckled her seat's harness and floated off the chair. <*That stuff tastes like crap. The work crews must have something in the galley. Maybe someone left a lunch in there that I can steal.*>

<*I know what you're trying to do!*> Saanvi turned and gave her sister her strongest glare. <*You're going to go take your suit off to go to the toilet! You cannot do that! We could be in combat in any minute, and this ship is far from airtight. If just one of the forward grav generators goes offline, this bridge will decompress.*>

<*Sahn! Seriously, I hate the plumbing hookups the suits have. I'll just be a minute.*>

<*Cary, so help me, if you take that suit off, I'm going to beat you senseless and stick you in an escape pod. Now sit your ass back in your chair, and take the suit's hookup, you baby.*>

Cary was surprised at her sister's vehemence and consequently pulled herself back to the chair and refastened the harness. She realized that Saanvi was scared—really scared. Maybe she should be, too, and her reluctance to use the suit's facilities was just her way of trying to pretend that they wouldn't be fighting for their lives before long.

She suddenly hoped she wouldn't throw up when the fighting started. The clear helmet was a poor choice in that regard. The skintight ones ran tubes into the wearer's stomach and lungs, preventing any messy incidents, like choking on your own vomit and dying.

She shook the image from her mind. That was no way to think.

On her right, she saw Saanvi had the feed tube in her mouth and was sucking up some paste. She decided if her sister was doing whatever was necessary to prepare, then she should, as well.

* * * * *

Cary had just finished 'eating' and using the suit's facilities, when the ship's scan threw an alert. FTN showed an incoming volley of kinetics from the Trisilieds ships. Fleet's scan tracked the vectors and highlighted the targets.

<*Think they found them all?*> Cary asked, worried that if the rail platforms protecting

Carthage fell, then they'd lose the world. There was no way Fleet Group 5 could stand against the Trisilieds ships bearing down on them.

<*We can see all of the enemy ships—at least we sure hope we can—and we know the targets. The lanes of fire are clear….*>

Saanvi's words were certain, but her mental tone was not. Both girls watched as the rail platforms began firing fine grapeshot toward the incoming rounds, before moving to new positions. Some of the platforms had already been equipped with massive fusion engines for emergency repositioning, but most were pushed by tugs.

Scan picked up hundreds of kinetic rounds being shredded by the rail platform's grapeshot, followed by automated drones targeting the debris with lasers, melting the debris clouds as best they could.

Yet some rounds made it through.

Most harmlessly streaked past the prior locations of the rail platforms, but one platform was struck by an enemy round, and its stasis shields flared as the slug hit and shattered into a billion pieces. The ship's scan registered the impact at over twenty exajoules of energy. The strike wasn't nearly enough to break through the stasis shields, but the rail platform's incomplete engines struggled to maintain its orbit around Carthage. Slowly, the platform began to slip toward the planet.

Two tugs disengaged from other platforms, and boosted toward the failing structure. Just as the first tug arrived and the platform lowered its stasis shield to let the tug make grapple, another round hit.

<*Oh, shit!*> Cary exclaimed as the platform exploded in a brilliant flash of light. When scan cleared, little more than a cloud of debris was falling toward Carthage.

<*It's just gone,*> Saanvi whispered.

<*I hope it doesn't hit Landfall or anything,*> Cary added.

Two more platforms were lost as the enemy continued to advance, but Cary knew the tables would turn once the Trisilieds ships reached the field of RMs.

Though the enemy fleet had spread wide in an effort to avoid the kinetic rounds Carthage's rail emplacements were firing, they were still mostly within the seeded field.

<*Think the RMs will pick off enough targets?*> Saanvi asked.

<*Well, their shields aren't much better than what the Bollam's space force had, and we were able to one-two punch our way through those without a lot of trouble.*>

<*Yeah, but they know about our style of RM now; they'll be ready for it,*> Saanvi replied.

<*How will they be? They don't have stasis shields. We saw that when our initial kinetic rounds hit them.*>

<*Don't you remember what mother taught us? The enemy never responds the way you anticipate. It is not enough to be ready to adapt; you must be prepared to defend against all possible situations at once,*> Saanvi said in her instructor's voice that always got under Cary's skin. She let it slide, though—no point in getting into an argument here.

Cary knew that her people had done amazing work in eighteen years, building up a military that could rival that of many stellar nations, but she worried it would still not be enough. With the Trisilieds fleet bearing down on them, and Fleet Group 5 manned by skeleton crews and a few AIs, the battle would be short and decisive when it was ultimately joined.

Cary realized she was chewing on her lower lip as she waited for FTN to register the RMs activating, and she forced herself to stop and breathe slowly. The more she thought about it, the more she realized how foolish wanting to be on this ship was. There was no glory in the slow surety of a battle they could not win.

She was trying to distract herself with crosschecking the ship's weapons systems when Saanvi called out. <*There! They've entered the field—the RMs are moving.*>

Cary hoped that she had done well with the patterns and placements of the missiles the *Illyria* had deposited. Symatra's tactical plan showed that she hoped to eliminate at least four thousand of the Trisilieds vessels. Any fewer, and there was no plan on the books that would save Carthage from the enemy fleet.

Their holotank began to show the leading edge of the Trisilieds ships jinking wildly, and she knew they had picked up the RMs. Now only time would tell whether it was enough.

She caught Saanvi's eye and could see that her sister was just as worried that too many of the enemy ships would break through, whereupon it would fall to them and Fleet Group 5 to shield Carthage. Neither girl spoke as they watched the first of the missiles hit, the information lagging by the seven light-second delay between them and the Trisilieds fleet.

<*It's not working well enough,*> Saanvi whispered. <*Their fleet was too spread out; the rear ships are all moving out of the RM field. The missiles won't reach them.*>

Cary nodded wordlessly. The FTN tally showed that only two thousand ships had been disabled. It would take another volley, this one at close range, to reduce the enemy's advantage and even the playing field. Both girls knew that would put the *Illyria* in the thick of the battle, given that their ship still had one of the largest supplies of short-range RMs in the fleet.

As she was nervously considering what would happen next, a message from Admiral Symatra arrived.

<*Lieutenant Cary, reposition the* Illyria *to the location I've marked, retrograde of Carthage. I am putting twenty ships under your command, designated Epsilon Squadron. They'll be too far away for me to control directly, and I don't have any AI to spare, so you will need to slave them to your controls. I have preloaded them with Non-Sentient AIs using nav patterns that will keep them in formation with you, while ensuring they're not just there for target practice.*>

<*Yes, Admiral,*> Cary responded. <*What are our orders once we're in position?*>

<*The Trisilieds Fleet has a dozen ships that appear to be a carrier class of vessel. Fleet analysis thinks that they are holding fighters—a lot of fighters. If that's true, then things could get much worse. You need to punch in through their lines and hit those carriers with your RMs before they disgorge them.*>

Cary looked at the three enemy carriers assigned to their squadron and let out a long breath. <*Those ships are well protected, Admiral. How will we get through to them?*>

<*I've provided updated tactics that will give you some options, but you're going to need to figure this one out on the fly. Your mother thought you could handle this command; now prove it to me.*>

Symatra closed the connection, and Saanvi queried Cary.

<*I have twenty ships taking up formation that are Linked to our ship; what's going on?*>

Cary relayed the orders to her sister, watching the disbelief grow on Saanvi's face.

<*Cary, I can't fly twenty ships,* plus *the* Illyria*! We're gonna get blown to dust out here.*>

<*What other options do we have?*> Cary asked. <*We can't just run and hide! A lot of the ISF personnel aren't much older than us, and they're ready to give their lives for our homeworld. Tanis is our mother, and they expect us to do something amazing to save the day.*>

<*It's going to take something amazing to save us from Mom when she finds out about this,*>

Saanvi said sullenly, as she organized Epsilon Squadron into four groups and slaved them to her console. <*Symatra did at least have a good autopilot setup on the ships—I won't need to micromanage them all. You're running their weapons, though; you'd better evaluate your options.*>

Cary did just that, looking at the loadouts on the ships Symatra had put under their command. The Admiral had been generous; all the ships had railguns, lasers, proton beams, and a small compliment of RMs. Their generators were fully operational, and the SC batteries were at max charge. Saanvi positioned the squadron in a flat V-formation, and Cary worked with her to ensure that the vessels with the most proton beams were in the fore.

Though they were mostly functional, none of the ships in Epsilon Squadron were the same class as the *Illyria*: a Mark II Claymore class ship that was a modified form of the *Orkney* and the *Dresden*—the original Claymore ships built back at the Victoria colony.

Eleven of the ships were Elizabeth Class cruisers; similar in composition to the *Andromeda,* and close to her size, with seven-hundred-sixty-meter-long hulls—but they did not yet have their stealth systems installed. Seven of them had proton beams, and were situated at the leading edge of Saanvi's flying V-formation.

The other nine were smaller Triton Class destroyers—a new kind of ship based on a Scattered Worlds Alliance destroyer design from Sol. These ships were the weirdest looking things Cary had ever seen. They were made of two rings—one slightly smaller ring tucked inside the other. The inside ring was able to change its angle as far as ninety degrees, and reposition it perpendicularly to the outer ring.

The rings were particle accelerators, but the particles they accelerated were one-millimeter pebbles of spent uranium. Once powered up, the rings could maintain a million pebbles moving at over a quarter the speed of light. The pebbles could exit the rings from hundreds of apertures, allowing the rings to fire in almost any direction on the ring's plane.

In essence, the strange-looking ships were rail machine guns capable of firing their million-round magazine in seconds, if needs be.

<*Oh! What have we here?*> Cary said over the Link with her sister.

<*What did you find?*> Saanvi asked.

Cary grinned at her sister. <*Two of the Claymore M2s have Arc-6 fighters on board.*>

<*Really?*> Saanvi asked as she frowned at her console. <*I checked for fighters, and the inventories read zero.*>

<*I bet you checked for functional fighters. Since there are no pilots, the inventory system lists the fighters as non-functional.*>

Saanvi's face split into a wide smile. <*Fifty-two of them! Well, now we have a chance. I can make some changes to the NSAI that Symatra put in charge of the ships in our squadron, and clone them into the Arc-6 autopilot's neural nets. It'll be a tight fit, memory-wise, but it should work.*>

<*Hop to it,*> Cary replied. <*We have fifteen minutes before we're in weapons range of the T's.*>

<*T's?*> Saanvi asked.

<*Yeah, 'Trisilieds' is way too awkward to say over and over again.*>

<*Cary,*> Saanvi replied soberly, <*you're thinking it, not saying it.*>

<*Whatever, Sis. They're T's now.*>

While her sister set to modifying the NSAIs to fit within the fighters, Cary continued to examine the T's fleet.

Still over nineteen thousand ships strong, the enemy fleet was a juggernaut unlike any she had ever imagined. A tenth of the fleet were massive dreadnaughts, similar to—though a few kilometers smaller—those the AST employed. The other fifty percent of the fleet consisted of thousand-meter cruisers. Unlike the AST, who seemed to prefer brute force in all things, the T's had then rounded out their fleet with thousands of destroyers.

The carrier ships, designated Halcyon Class on the FTN, only made up a tiny percentage of the fleet—though there were still twelve of them in evidence. These ships were over fifteen kilometers in length, and analysis on the FTN suggested that it was possible for them to contain a hundred thousand fighters—more if they were drones, and not human-piloted ships.

That explained why Symatra was willing to expend some of her best ships to take out three of them.

A dozen of the Dreadnaught class ships escorted each of the carriers, along with a hundred or more destroyers. It looked like an impossible task, but Cary knew that Symatra was no fool, and certainly wouldn't expend the Governor's children on a suicide mission.

She reviewed the updated tactics the admiral had provided, and saw an option that she knew they could execute.

<*Saanvi, have you tested the* Illyria*'s stealth systems?*>

Saanvi replied absently as she continued to work on loading the NSAIs into the fighters, <*I ran through the checklists, yeah, but I didn't turn them on.*>

<*Let's use the squadron cruisers and destroyers as decoys, and come in a hundred klicks above them. The T's will be focused on the ships they can see, and we can slam the* Illyria *right through their shields and drop mines on the carrier.*>

<*You're crazy, you know that?*> Saanvi asked. <*But I think it will work. Give me a minute, and I'll pass us behind our other ships and drop into stealth while we're obscured—I just hope the rad-folding field works. Photons are easy, but if they see us bending rads, your little plan will just get us smooshed.*>

Cary watched scan as they drew nearer to the T's, smiling with relief when Saanvi successfully executed the maneuver to hide the *Illyria*. The T's would know one of their squadron's ships had gone missing, but she hoped they wouldn't expect it to move completely out of the formation.

She flipped to fleet-wide scan, looking at Symatra's strategy as she organized the ships of Fleet Group 5 into a ring one hundred thousand kilometers in diameter. In the center of the ring lay Hannibal, Carthage's largest moon.

On their current vector, the T's fleet would pass through the ring and around the moon, before reaching Carthage. It probably looked like a trap to the enemy, but their fleet outnumbered Symatra's four-to-one, and, at this range, it would be obvious that most of the ships in Fleet Group 5 were incomplete hulls, barely able to maneuver into position.

What the T's didn't know was that the moon had its own rail emplacements—which had not yet fired. Those emplacements could not move, and would likely only get off two or three shots before the T's targeted them with heavy kinetic bombardments.

Ship scan threw an alert, and Cary called out, <*RMs incoming—at least a hundred! All headed for our squadron!*>

<*Activating a new jinking pattern,*> Saanvi replied and then gave Cary a wicked grin. <*Look, they were kind enough to send all their missiles on the same plane as our formation.*>

<*Glad your plan worked there. Readying a salvo from the destroyers,*> Cary returned the predatory smile as her adrenaline began to spike. <*Let's deep-Link now, this talking is taking too long.*>

Saanvi cast her a worried look and the sighed. <*OK, but no reading my inner thoughts. I don't have a filter in there, and I'm weird.*>

Cary smiled at her sister. <*I love your weird, but I won't pry, I promise.*>

Both girls leaned back into their seats and Cary saw Saanvi wince as the hard-Link connected at the base of her skull. It didn't hurt, but knowing that a long spike was sliding into the slot between the lobes of their brains was always disconcerting.

The hard-Link provided no new access to systems, but it did provide wider bandwidth and more reliability. The normal wireless Link was too risky to use when they drifted into one another's minds.

Once the hard-Link ran through its diagnostics, their network access switched over to the physical connection, and Cary reached into her sister's mind.

Her method of doing this, 'deep-Linking' being the name Cary came up for it, only seemed to work with Saanvi—not that she had tried it with many others. It was strange, considering that she and Saanvi were not blood sisters; though Angela had overseen their L2 neural enhancements, and their interfaces were very similar.

She felt Saanvi accept her, and Cary flooded into her sister's mind just as Saanvi entered into hers.

Crowded in here, she thought in her sister's mind.

Roomy in here, Saanvi replied with a grin.

Dork.

She felt warmth flooding into her from Saanvi, and knew that her sister felt the same. It was like a never-ending embrace. Cary-Saanvi knew they couldn't revel in it, though. They needed to deal with those RMs in the next seventeen seconds.

They opened their eyes again, both seeing through both pairs, while also both controlling their four hands—not that they needed to use physical controls. When deep-Linked, their mental reflexes far outstripped their physical ones.

Move the destroyers above and below the formation, one of them thought—neither knew which.

Firing rails, they replied, and watched scan as a hail of uranium pellets flew toward the RMs, covering a swath of space where probability suggested the missiles would be.

They marveled that with their Linked minds, they could almost comprehend the relativistic math occurring in real-time to predict the collision paths of the missiles and rail-fired pellets. They were on the cusp of understanding how space-time expanded, as photons bounced off both the relativistic pellets and the missiles, where they should have passed one another at nearly twice the speed of light, but didn't.

Their ruminations lasted for less than a second before scan began to register hits on the RMs. Over seventy were destroyed, and scan showed fifty-six remaining. An instant later, the missiles slammed into Epsilon Squadron—their kinetic energy displacing the ships, but not penetrating the stasis shields.

Cary-Saanvi saw that one of the destroyers had suffered a structural integrity failure from the force of the impact, and would have to be left behind. They also noted that one of the cruisers lost its internal gravity dampeners. If it took another hit from multiple RMs, it would crumple like paper—even if its stasis fields held.

Weapons range in seventy seconds, they noted.

Several more RMs crossed the space between Epsilon Squadron and the Trisilieds ships in the intervening seconds, but targeted shots from the destroyers disabled them.

Then, for fifteen seconds, nothing happened.

It felt like an eternity to Cary-Saanvi. When the ships finally came within weapons range, they decided not to fire. Let the enemy expend their batteries at extreme range; their stasis shields would shrug off the incoming particle and laser beams.

One of the enemy dreadnaughts positioned itself directly in the path of Epsilon Squadron, and, when the range closed to fifty thousand kilometers, the squadron's destroyers fired once more, sending nine million relativistic pellets streaking between the ships.

Scan registered the dreadnaught projecting magnetic fields as the enemy ships tried to shift the path of the pellets—but their attempts failed. That was the other enhancement the destroyers possessed—though the mass of the pellets was small, uranium was barely ferric, and it was much harder to shift than a normal iron-rich rail pellet would be.

Some did miss the dreadnaught, and instead struck the carrier's shields. Their impacts did little against the massive ship's protection, but the dreadnaught did not fare so well. The pellets weakened and tore through its shields, and shredded the massive ship's midsection. On cue, a stream of Arc-6 fighters flew from within Epsilon Squadron, and launched their short-range missiles into the rents in the dreadnaught's hull.

Explosions flared through the gashes, and parts of the dreadnaught's hull buckled. For an instant, it looked as though the ship would weather the strike—but then it exploded in a spectacular display.

Epsilon Squadron's flying V arced beneath the exploding dreadnaught, and past the Halcyon Class carrier, their stasis shields flaring as beamfire rained down from the hundred ships around them.

Communications blackout for twelve seconds, Cary-Saanvi thought to themself as the debris cloud obscured their line-of-sight tightbeams to the other ships in Epsilon Squadron.

The *Illyria* was four seconds behind the rest of the squadron; they fired its engines, directing it down toward the carrier. The cruiser sped over the dreadnaught's debris, and punched through the carrier's shields. During the ten milliseconds the *Illyria* spent adjacent to the ship, a hundred nuclear mines dropped out of its rear tubes and attached to the enemy vessel's hull.

Cary-Saanvi also fired four RMs while within the shields, sending them to the far ends of the carrier in case the mines in the center were not enough to destroy the entire vessel. The milliseconds passed, and then the *Illyria* was away, rapidly altering vector before reactivating their stealth systems.

Behind them, fighters had begun to streak out of the carrier. Perhaps the Trisilieds realized the time for deception was over; or maybe they were abandoning the ship, fearing picobombs.

Then the RMs hit and the mines detonated.

Nuclear fire filled the carrier's shields, obscuring the vessel before its shields failed, and the blast of light and energy flooded into space. Scan registered the explosion at over thirty-two exajoules. Cary-Saanvi marveled at the power of what they had done, an instant before they considered that the ship was easily crewed by over a hundred thousand people.

Nine seconds later, a secondary explosion tore through the space where the carrier's remains were still obscured by the growing radiation cloud. The ships in the immediate vicinity of the carrier, including the *Illyira* and the nineteen remaining ships of Epsilon Squadron, were flung onto new vectors from the overwhelming blast.

Antimatter, they thought. *A lot of antimatter.*

Their mind became resolute: though many people had died, they would not allow the enemy to use antimatter weapons on their homeworld. Even if they had to sacrifice themselves to stop it.

The *Illyria* reestablished tightbeam comms with the rest of Epsilon Squadron, and they boosted at max thrust toward their second target. Now that the T's knew what they were up to, they would put a lot more effort into stopping them—and they would be looking for the *Illyria* on alternate approaches.

Let's hit the third target first, they thought in unison. While the radiation cloud accelerating out around the carrier still gave them some cover, they did one small burn to alter vector, and then reengaged stealth systems, slowly nudging their ship closer to the third carrier.

On the *Illyria*'s starboard side, the other ships of Epsilon Squadron continued on to the second carrier—a decoy, which would arrive just as the *Illyria* reached the third.

Cary-Saanvi pre-programmed maneuvers into the ships and fighters that would have each destroyer unload another full magazine into the carrier. Following that, half the surviving fighters would punch through the ship's shields, and release their entire supply of short-range missiles while within the enemy ship.

The damage should be enough to cripple the carrier—especially if the fighters penetrated the ship's shields along its dorsal fighter docks.

In their mind, they watched the timer count down the final seconds. At the five-second mark, they fired the *Illyria*'s engines, altering course and lining up with the third carrier. To their port, Cary-Saanvi saw the destroyers' nine million pellets tear into the second massive ship, followed closely by the fighters, which slammed right into their target and unleashed the last of their RMs.

Half a second later, the *Illyria* tore through the third carrier's shields, dropping their final mines and firing the last four RMs they carried.

The antimatter explosion came sooner this time; almost as though the enemy ship was trying to take them out with its death throes.

The force of the explosion picked up the *Illyria* and flung it almost ten thousand kilometers, like it was nothing more than a cork in the ocean. Their consoles flashed red on nearly every system, as internal graviton emitters failed and the ship groaned.

If their eyes had been open, Cary-Saanvi would have seen a bulkhead on the bridge rend, and the atmosphere vent away into another section of the ship. They noted the event, but did not concern themselves with it; though the Saanvi portion of their merge noted with smug satisfaction that it was a good thing they were in suits.

They fought to regain control of their ship, and re-establish tight-beam communications with the rest of Epsilon Squadron. When they finally did, Cary-Saanvi found that two of the destroyers and four of the cruisers had been lost when the second carrier blew.

The squadron was down to fourteen ships, counting the *Illyria*, but their objective was complete.

Cary-Saanvi took a moment to look over the rest of the battlefield. The T's had not yet reached the ring of ships that comprised the bulk of Fleet Group 5, but three other ISF squadrons had penetrated deep into the enemy ranks, striking at the other carriers. Two had succeeded, though they had taken crippling losses to do so. The third squadron had been destroyed by overwhelming force before it was able to take out its final two targets.

As Cary-Saanvi transmitted a request to Symatra for new orders, the FTN flashed an update, showing two new fleets appearing, just over two hundred thousand kilometers above Carthage's poles.

What? Who is that? Cary asked, her shock momentarily separating their thoughts.

It's Mom's fleet! Saanvi exclaimed.

The two girls took a moment and recombined their thoughts before examining the ships.

How did they get there? they mused.

The FTN updated with the IFF data, and confirmed that the ships were indeed two halves of Fleet Group 1. However, the real-time scan still showed Fleet Group 1 trailing the Trisilieds fleet by over an hour—information that was several light minutes out of date, and no longer correct.

In their mind, Saanvi's voice separated out again, amazed and concerned. *They had to have jumped through the dark layer. Insystem, this close to the star…there's no way they should have survived.*

Mom's crazy! Cary felt her physical body shake its head and forced it to still. The motion made her feel as though she might throw up. She reflected on her history lessons, which never told her about this feeling—how fear for yourself, for the lives of everyone you knew, could tear you up inside. If there was glory in this battle, she did not feel it.

The two segments of Fleet Group 1 rotated and began a hard burn to slow their momentum before boosting toward the oncoming Trisilieds fleet—which was now just twenty seconds from engaging Fleet Group 5.

The *Illyria* was hundreds of thousands of kilometers from Fleet Group 1, but its sensors still had to attenuate as the brilliant eruption of over five thousand ships running their engines at max burn flared into space. She hoped no one on the world of Tyre was looking up at the night sky; the light would far outshine Canaan Prime at high noon.

A minute later, more ships appeared, almost on top of fleet group one. Beamfire erupted from the ISF ships, tearing the new arrivals apart in moments.

Cary-Saanvi watched in amazement as the FTN showed the newly arrived—and now destroyed—ships to have Hegemony IFF tags. There had only been a few hundred of them; far from the massive fleet that had been in pursuit of Fleet Group 1.

While they waited for orders from Symatra, and for their pulses to stop racing, Cary-Saanvi let their minds fully mesh once more, and regrouped with the remains of Epsilon Squadron, which had now drifted past the bulk of the T's fleet.

Two of the destroyers had suffered magnetic containment failure in some of their particle accelerators and were running at half their firing rate. One of the cruisers was nearing containment failure on a reactor, and Cary-Saanvi powered it down, reducing that ship's ability to fire beam weapons.

Symatra's orders came—with no explanation for Fleet Group 1's mysterious appearance, or for the few AST ships that had followed—and confirmed their suspicion. It was up to them to take out the remaining two carriers.

Cary-Saanvi rotated their ships, and began to boost back toward the T's fleet. They burned hard, and one of their cruisers suffered a failure in a fuel regulator, and exploded as its AP drive introduced a critical level of hydrogen and anti-hydrogen.

Thirteen ships; a rather unlucky number for their final run.

They calculated the best burn they could achieve, and set a three-minute countdown until they reached the first of the carriers.

The FTN showed that the two carriers had released over twenty thousand fighters, and that another fifty thousand had escaped the other Halcyon Class ships before their destruction.

As they had taken out the first three carriers, Carthage's rail platforms had continued to fire, and take fire, until only two of them remained. Cary-Saanvi felt fear and sorrow as the FTN showed all hands lost.

They kept at it until the last, the girls thought with admiration.

As they considered the plight of the crew aboard the platforms, on the surface of Hannibal, Carthage's large moon, the barrels of stationary particle weapons emerged from the surface. They fired a full salvo, sending thousands of kinetic rounds out into the T's fleet—which still greatly outnumbered the defenders, even with the arrival of Fleet Group 1.

Ho-leee-shit, they thought, as the moon moved backwards five meters and cracks and fissures appeared across its surface. They were thankful that Hannibal's rail emplacements were unmanned, because the simultaneous firing would have killed anyone present.

Even as thousands of rounds lanced from deep within the moon toward the Trisilieds ships, the enemy fired back. Kinetic rounds collided in the darkness, flaring in brilliant explosions of light and energy—though many slipped past one another and found their respective targets.

A hundred Trisilieds ships exploded, and another thousand took some amount of damage. Three dreadnaughts moved in front of the remaining carriers to protect them, and for two, it was their last action.

The carriers, for their part, survived the onslaught, and continued to disgorge fighters as the T's fleet began to trade beamfire with Symatra's Fleet Group 5.

Cary-Saanvi watched the carnage in mixed awe and horror as the light-lag from the previous positions of Fleet Group 1 and the Hegemony fleet caught up. They saw their mother's fleet perform a hard braking burn and then disappear, followed by the Hegemony fleet a minute later.

How is that possible? What happened to the Hegemony ships? They asked themselves.

The Cary part of them could tell that there was something Saanvi was holding back and asked a probing question. *I guess…the AST ships didn't have a clear FTL path like mother did… Did mother bait the AST ships into chasing her through the dark layer knowing they wouldn't survive?*

There's no other logical explanation. That was some gamble—she could have brought the Hegemony ships right on top of us, if they didn't hit… The Saanvi part of them stopped, clearly unwilling to share some knowledge of what had likely transpired.

Sahn, what is it? Cary asked. *What aren't you showing me?*

Saanvi was silent for a moment, focused on fine-tuning their squadron's trajectory as Cary prodded her. *Fine. Cary, you can't tell this to anyone, ever. Mom told me a couple of years ago, when I asked a lot of questions about what happened to my father's ship.*

OK, my lips—and mind—are sealed.

The Saanvi part took a step back from the merge for a moment, and then rejoined fully. She shared the knowledge of the things that lived in the dark layer—things that were attracted to mass and graviton emissions.

Attracted to ships running grav fields to stay in the dark layer. Cary-Saanvi confirmed to themself.

It was why ships that entered the dark layer near stars didn't come out again, notwithstanding collisions with dark matter.

So, how did mom's ships come through, while the Hegemony ships got…eaten? they mused.

Neither knew, but they both were certain that their mother would not risk her fleet in a careless gamble. If she knew about the things that lived within the dark layer, then she must have known how to avoid them—and possibly how to send them after other ships.

We need to get ready, they thought. *We don't have any more mines, or enough missiles to take out two ships.*

The girls considered their options while aware of the risks, but also aware that everyone in New Canaan was prepared to sacrifice whatever they had to. They could do no less.

Cary-Saanvi lined up with the two Halcyon Class carriers. The two massive ships, only four hundred kilometers apart, bunched together so the dreadnaughts could provide cover. They formed the ships of Epsilon Squadron into a ragged line, no ship directly behind the others, though they would fall into a single spear before they hit. The *Illyria* took up the rear, ready to execute their last-ditch plan.

The destroyers were in the fore, and in the final three seconds before impact with the first carrier, they spent their remaining uranium pellets, tearing through the carrier's shields and into the aft on the port side of the ship.

Then the destroyers slammed into the carrier.

At the same time, Cary-Saanvi released all their final RMs behind the *Illyria* before drifting outward to pass around the first Halcyon Class ship.

They tried to discern the fate of the destroyers at the head of their formation. Scan data suggested that two had been destroyed within the carrier, while the other two had torn clear through the enemy ship.

Then the cruisers hit—one smashing against a section of the carrier's shields, which had reinitialized before the sheer mass and kinetic energy of the colliding ship disabled the carrier's shields once more, making a hole for the other cruisers to pass through.

The *Illyria* entered the gaping hole in the carrier's side, disgorging its final supply of nuclear warheads, while the girls prayed to whatever ancient gods were listening that it would be enough.

An instant later, they were through the ship and into the scant four hundred kilometers between it and the second carrier. Ahead, two destroyers collided with the last enemy carrier, the three cruisers a half-second behind.

Behind them, the first carrier exploded at the same instant that a series of kinetic rounds fired by nearby Trisilieds ships slammed into Epsilon's destroyers and one of the cruisers, knocking them off-course. Ahead, the final cruiser executed emergency evasive maneuvers. Cary-Saanvi struggled to keep the ships of Epsilon Squadron on course; they had taken too much damage to manage the tight maneuvers required.

They were all going to miss—all except for the *Illyria.*

Cary-Saanvi made emergency corrections, desperate to keep their ship on course for the carrier. They pushed the engines far past their maximum tolerances, and felt the internal inertial dampeners waver, then fail, as the burn executed.

A hundred *g*s of force slammed into the girls. They could feel bones breaking and organs splitting open in each other's bodies; then Cary separated their minds an instant before the final impact.

ASSAULTING ORION

STELLAR DATE: 04.01.8948 (Adjusted Years)
LOCATION: *Sabrina*
REGION: Stellar North of Carthage, New Canaan System

"Sure would have been nice to have a stealth system like this when we were back in the Perseus Arm," Cargo said with a broad smile.

Jessica gave an appreciative chuckle while Misha raised an eyebrow and shook his head. "I feel like we're cheating. I understand—sort of—why it is that they can't see us, but I still can't believe it. We're flying right above them!"

<*It's because I'm a leaf on the wind,*> Sabrina said, her mental tone joyous. <*That, and because AP engines are very hard to spot when they're pointed away. Not to mention how amazing Carthaginian tech is when it comes to radiation bending. We could float right outside a viewport and they'd never spot us.*>

"Let's not test that," Cargo grunted. "Jessica, how long 'til we're lined up with their flagship?"

"Gonna take another hour," Jessica replied. "For all Sabrina's boasting, it's a pretty delicate dance we're doing here. There are fifty thousand Orion ships around us; even if gamma rays from our AP drive are hard to spot, it's also hard not to slam them right into a ship behind us."

"If anyone can do it, you can," Cargo said.

Jessica knew he meant it as a compliment, but it still stung. Everyone—including her—wished it was Cheeky in the pilot's seat. Flying this mission almost felt like an affront to her memory.

"We're only going to get one shot at this," Colonel Usef said from his seat at the auxiliary weapons console.

"Piece of cake." Jessica flashed Usef a smile, glad to have the burly Marine with them. "Besides, you just did a run like this on the *Galadrial* a few days ago."

Usef laughed softly. "Well...we had their ship surrounded by a fleet they couldn't see, outnumbering them ten-to-one. This is the exact reverse of that situation."

"Do you think that OG officer, Kent, provided good intel?" Misha asked. "It was pretty interesting to learn that this Garza guy and the OFA's Praetor don't share the same goals here."

"Was a lucky break," Jessica agreed. "I chatted with him for a bit after Tanis; got a few more details out. I'm better at sweet talking than Tanis—though she's improved, from what I saw. Bob says what we've learned and inferred matches his models, and that's good enough for me."

"Bob..." Misha muttered. "You guys put a lot of faith in your god-AI."

"We do," Jessica agreed. "He's earned it."

"Yet he couldn't see through that other AI's deception; Helen, the one that was in the head of the Transcend President's daughter."

A precise maneuver stole Jessica's attention, and Iris replied for her. <*Bob knew what Helen was. He just made the mistake of thinking she had similar goals to his own. Well, to be honest, she probably does have similar goals. She just plans on achieving her ends differently.*>

"What does that mean?" Cargo asked.

<*Bob wants to see humanity thrive, to achieve its potentials without being hamstrung or guided down a specific path. From what Finaeus has told us, Airtha wants the same thing; she just believes that she should be the supreme being that sets the path,*> Iris replied.

"That seems a little off the mark," Cargo replied. "How can humanity 'be all that we can be' if Airtha is guiding us down her path?"

"Maybe she still views herself as human," Usef offered. "In that case, her guidance is still human guidance."

<***I'm** more human than she is,*> Sabrina chimed in. <*I always knew there was something wrong with Helen when she was with us.*>

<*No, you didn't,*> Hank laughed. <*You were just jealous because Helen got more of Sera's attention than you did. But I agree, she always acted smugly superior to us other AIs aboard.*>

<*I still say she made Sera forget our anniversary,*> Sabrina groused.

Jessica laughed aloud at that.

Sabrina gave a resolute nod over the Link. <*Just saying, she even apologized for all the anniversaries we missed while we were in Perseus—and Helen's gone!*>

"Any excuse to have some cake!" Misha grinned.

Jessica was glad for the team's banter; for some reason, it calmed her nerves. This mission that Tanis had sent them on was daunting, to say the least. They would have little room for mistakes.

The Orion Guard fleet was only half an AU from Carthage—silent and nearly invisible as they drifted through the system, closing in on their prey. If they maintained their vector, they would reach the Carthaginian homeworld in two and a half hours.

It was going to be tight. Board the OFA flagship—a behemoth named the *Britannica*—plant a hack that Bob believed would allow them to gain control of the ship, secure General Garza, and pull the ship away from Carthage before Tanis's final strike.

Easy.

Jessica smiled to herself. Funny thing was, the operation was on the same scale as half the jobs they had pulled over the last nine years. Breaking into Orion Guard installations was almost second nature to them at this point—which made them the perfect team for this job.

"It's a shit-show no matter which way you look at it," Cargo said absently as he reexamined the rough specs they had for the *Britannica*. "Helen had us all fooled—though we didn't know there was anything to be fooled about, I suppose. Hell, I never even knew there was a Transcend, let alone evil once-AI that were plotting everyone's demise."

<*We should have known,*> Hank said. <*Something was always off about her—but like you said, we didn't know it was a thing that* ***could*** *be, let alone that it* ***was***.>

<*I'm glad it worked out how it did...well, mostly,*> Sabrina said. <*Just think, Hank; without Sera finding me in that scrapyard, I would have died there...or worse. You would never have come aboard with Cargo, and would never have been freed. Crazy as it sounds, things are a lot better than they would have been.*>

"You have an unexpected, but valid, logic," Jessica said. "Funny how all of us are here as victims of crazy circumstance. Me, because some megalomaniac wanted me to watch as he became king of everything...or whatever he wanted. Cargo and Nance because an evil entity lived in Sera's head; Trevor because I wanted to have a fun night out; Misha because we accidentally jumped to the Perseus Arm."

"Doesn't really bode well for what we're about to do," Usef said as he sat ramrod-straight in his seat.

"Usef, seriously, when did you become such a wet blanket?" Jessica asked, twisting in her seat to catch his eyes. "We had some good times back in Victoria—and after, too."

Usef frowned and opened his mouth to reply, then shook his head and smiled. "You're one of a kind, Jessica. Here we are on a crazy mission to secure an enemy ship in the midst of the biggest fleet any of us have seen since we left Sol, and you're still cracking jokes and having a good time."

Jessica shrugged. "After what we've been through, this feels like just another day at the office."

"You're going to have to tell me those stories sometime," Usef replied. "Sounds like you guys had a rollicking good time out there in the Perseus Arm."

Jessica glanced at Cargo and Misha, who both smiled at the memories.

"Hell yeah," Jessica said. "We all live through this, and I'll buy you a round…or twenty…and tell you all about it."

VICTORY AT ANY COST

STELLAR DATE: 04.01.8948 (Adjusted Years)
LOCATION: ISS *I2*
REGION: Stellar North of Carthage, New Canaan System

Cheers erupted across the bridge of the *I2* as they watched the ISF cruiser punch through the first carrier, then tear a hole through the second Halcyon Class ship, making an opening for the twelve RMs which followed close on their tail.

The twelfth, and final, Trisilieds Halcyon Class carrier flew apart in a massive antimatter explosion, destroying many of the fighters it had released.

"Find that ship!" Tanis called out. "I want to thank its captain and crew personally. They've saved untold lives."

Scan searched for the ship, tagged as the *Illyria,* on an exit vector from the explosion. Debris and energy from the two carriers' spectacular deaths made the search almost impossible, but given the number of other Trisilieds ships and fighters enveloped and destroyed in the explosion, the *Illyria*'s survival began to appear unlikely.

"Stars, that was brave," Captain Espensen said with a solemn shake of her head. "Who was managing that Squadron? It was too far out for Symatra to do that."

Sera nodded, "Whoever it was deserves a commendation."

"I don't know," Tanis said with a frown. She knew all the humans and AIs in Symatra's fleet, and couldn't think of any who could have pulled off that final attack run—though she supposed that in times like this, any of them could have risen to the occasion.

She reached out to Symatra, seeking Fleet Group 5's ship assignments, while watching a small group of one hundred Trisilieds ships that had slipped ahead and were already approaching Carthage and exchanging fire with the remaining orbital defenses.

Cary and Saanvi Richards.

The names didn't register at first. They didn't make sense. Then the weight of it slammed into her with the mass of a planet.

<*Our girls! What were they doing out there? Why?*> Tanis exclaimed.

<*I don't know! They're supposed to be on Carthage…*> Angela said in confusion.

Her vision swam and she felt her knees buckle.

<*They can't be…*>

She hit the deck, reaching out for Joe, but he wasn't there, he was too far away.

A tortured shriek escaped her lips, and in her mind, Angela echoed her cry of woe. Both human and AI sank for a moment into despair, and a feeling that nothing mattered, that there was no purpose, swept over them. Then, a spark of anger, followed by rage and cold determination, took its place. If these invading scum wanted death, she would bring it to them.

When Tanis rose to her feet and looked around the bridge, she saw that every ashen face was staring at her. She straightened her jacket and fought back the tears that threatened to spill down her face.

"Everyone…" her voice came out in a hoarse whisper, and she cleared her throat. "Everyone has lost today; mine is no more significant—and they could have survived, it's impossible to tell."

Sera reached for Tanis's hand. "There's a lot of radiation and debris masking signals in there. They could have made it to an escape pod."

"Or used the in-place stasis fields on the bridge," Captain Espensen added.

"I want the *I2* to push to the center of the Trisilieds fleet," Tanis said with a steadier voice. "We're going to finish this fight."

"Yes, ma'am," Captain Espensen replied soberly. "What is our primary target?"

Tanis gestured to the holotank. "Those carriers still released many of their fighters. Our Arcs can take them out, but we have to get them closer first. I want our atom beams to make maximum draw from the CriEn modules. Let's show them what war with us will cost."

Captain Espensen nodded, and Tanis watched with grim determination as her fleet boosted toward the Trisilieds ships—the bulk of which was now passing the moon, angling to brake around the planet. In a detached frame of mind, she wondered if they would bombard Carthage, or drop troops to secure the cities and hold the population hostage.

Let them try. Brandt and the ISF Marines were spoiling for a fight.

She checked over scan and saw that Greer's Fleet Group 2 was only thirty minutes behind the Trisilieds ships; but in an effort to catch up, their *v* would be too high for anything other than a single pass. It would take them an hour to come back around again.

She considered Fleet Groups 3 and 4, commanded by Joe and Sanderson. They were still in position, ready to strike when needed. She considered pulling them in, but knew that if her suspicions were correct, bringing them into the fight prematurely would result in the ISF losing.

<I didn't do it right. Thousands of us will die for nothing…> Tanis began to say privately to Angela.

<I know, dear. It's brutal to watch this fight, knowing half our ships aren't even involved. Who could have lived, who could have died—there will be time enough for those recriminations later.>

Tanis nodded and pushed the thought from her mind, willing herself to calm. She and Angela spread their minds once more across their section of Fleet Group 1—still braking hard above Carthage's north pole. She wasn't yet close enough to the ships below the world's south pole—nor to Symatra's ring of ships around the moon—for direct control, but she would be soon, and then she would shape them into the final hammer blow to destroy these intruders.

The *I2* pulled toward the Carthage-Hannibal L1 point and pivoted, the ship's length perpendicular to the system's plane. It waited as the leading edge of the Trisilieds ships rounded the moon, still engaged with Fleet Group 5.

"Give it to them," Tanis ordered.

The enemy met the withering fire as the *I2*'s thousands of weapons discharged. Still; there were so many ships, including tens of thousands of fighters and assault craft, that many slipped past.

Scan showed assault craft dropping into Carthage's atmosphere while the capital ships looped tight around the planet. Thousands of ground-based anti-aircraft batteries opened up, shooting down enemy ships by the hundreds—but still some got through.

Tanis knew she couldn't worry about the ensuing fights around Landfall and the other cities on Carthage's surface. Her fight was up here, to make sure that as few ships landed as possible.

"Target that cruiser!" she heard Captain Espensen call out and saw that a Trisilieds ship was making a run for High Carthage, the station atop the first of Carthage's space elevators. Her momentary distraction—worrying about the battle on the surface—had caused her to miss it.

The *I2* fired a series of proton beams into the ship and an explosion near its engines shoved the ship to port.

"It's going to hit the station!" one of the ensigns on the scan team cried out in horror, and Tanis watched as the disabled ship, over a kilometer in length, drifted toward High Carthage at over seven hundred meters per second.

The station had already taken an unimaginable amount of damage from passing ships, and its stasis shields had failed in several sections. Tanis looked at her available options and realized that no kinetics could hit the ship with enough force, at the right angle, to move it. The Trisilieds cruiser would tear right through the station, killing everyone aboard, and dropping the strand on the city of Landfall.

Then an ISF cruiser with failing shields streaked across the battlespace and smashed into the enemy ship, pushing it off course. The hulls of both ships interlocked, causing the pair to pinwheel through space, falling into the planet's atmosphere, on a trajectory to land in the ocean.

The desperate battle intensified as shields wore thin and ships tore into one another, filling Hannibal's L1 with drifting hulls and debris

C'mon, Tanis whispered to herself. *Where are you bastards?*

"They're firing antimatter warheads!" someone on scan called out. "We've lost a hundred ships!"

Tanis saw that concentrated antimatter detonations were enveloping many of the ISF ships, overwhelming the already taxed reactors powering the stasis shields.

She issued orders for human and AI-crewed ships to fall back, positioning the *I2* between the fleets.

The battlespace was almost incomprehensible. Fighters from both sides swarmed around ships; entire regions of space were filled with high-velocity debris, deadly radiation, and kinetic rounds.

It was unlike anything Tanis-Angela had ever imagined. A small part of her mind—the bit that wasn't frantically attempting to guide thousands of ships to their targets and away from their demise—boggled at the horror of it. She could not imagine that many battles of this scale had ever taken place before, with this much energy expended.

So far, miraculously, the *I2* had taken no damage. The Trisilieds ships gave it a wide berth—though many not wide enough, taking beamfire and sweeps of its molecular decoupler—as Captain Espensen guided the ship to where it was most needed.

Four minutes later, only seven hundred ships remained functional in Fleet Group 1, bolstered by another five hundred from Symatra's group. Over ninety percent of her ships were gone.

The bulk of the Trisilieds ships were now on the far side of Carthage, executing wide arcs beyond it to come back in for a final pass. There were still five thousand of them, and Tanis knew that the battle would be decided long before Sanderson's ships arrived.

"Enemy fleet admiral hailing us," the comm officer announced.

"Put it up," Tanis replied, opening her eyes once more to the bridge around her.

A woman appeared, sporting a haughty expression on her face and six stars on the collar of her ornate uniform. She was tall and slender—disproportionately so—and Tanis wondered if the woman had grown up on a low-*g* world or station.

"Admiral Richards, I am Admiral Myra," the woman said without preamble. "You, and all remaining vessels in your fleet, are to power down your weapons and shields, and exit your vessels in escape pods."

"Never gonna happen," Tanis replied. "It is you who should surrender."

"Admiral Richards," Admiral Myra said, still looking smug. "You are beaten. Our forces are invading your cities, we've taken one of your stations, and the other is not far behind. You have no more defenses, and your other fleets cannot reach you in time. Surrender now."

"Myra," Tanis's lips twisted into a sneer as she spat out the woman's name, "it is you who will surrender now, or none of you will ever leave this system. New Canaan will be your grave, and now that you've spilled so much of our blood, I will stretch my hand across the stars to the Pleiades and destroy your entire civilization."

<*Tanis, I know you're hurting, but we can't do that…we'd be worse than they are,*> Sera commented privately.

<*I know…I just had to say it…sorry.*>

<*It's OK. What's her play, though? The way I see it, she can't win decisively; not with the* I2 *in play.*>

<*Not when the Orion Guard arrives,*> Tanis replied.

<*What?*> Sera asked, and Tanis saw her eyes widen.

<*The Orion Guard. They entered the system days ago, they're going to be here at almost the same time Myra's ships make it back around.*>

Sera sputtered out loud, and Tanis saw her eyes narrow in anger. She cut the communication with Admiral Myra before Sera spoke.

"Tanis!" Sera cried aloud. "The Orion Guard? Here? How many?"

In an instant, everyone on the bridge turned to stare at Tanis. It wasn't the way she wanted this information to come out; she had hoped to have another option, but it was not to be.

<*I'm sorry I didn't share it, we haven't vetted enough of the TSF personnel to know if there are leaks. And you were having a hard time with…well, with everything,*> Tanis said privately.

<*Tanis, seriously, you can't hold stuff like this back. I can take it, and I know how to keep a secret, for star's sakes. We'll talk about this later.*>

Tanis sent a mental affirmation to Sera before speaking aloud. "Their stealth tech is good; better than yours, on par with ours," Tanis said calmly. "Our scan shows at least seventy thousand ships. Based on what you've told me, it's a sizable portion of their forward fleets. Its destruction will decrease their power-base in the Inner Stars considerably."

<*I've revised the estimates upward of a hundred thousand ships,*> Bob replied. <*It may be even more than that. The Trisilieds and AST ships were little more than cannon fodder to wear us down.*>

"Even if you can convince your parliament to allow the use of picobombs, you can't take out that many ships in time," Sera said, her face now ashen.

"Parliament reversed their decision ten minutes ago," Tanis replied with a frown. "Too little too late for…for the dead—but that is not how we will end this battle."

"Then how?" Sera asked, and Tanis saw the same question on the face of everyone on the bridge.

A wicked smile slowly twisted her lips. "We will devour them."

Confusion showed on the faces of everyone on the *I2*'s bridge, everyone except for Sera and Finaeus.

"You can't," Finaeus whispered. "You won't be able to control it…them…the things. It's not possible."

Tanis shook her head. "Those creatures have been controlled for some time. I wondered by whom, until you explained what's in the galactic core. Those AIs made the dark layer creatures to slow us down, but your jump gates ruined that plan. Now they will throw humanity back into another dark age to slow us once more. Don't you see? The *Intrepid*, Kapteyn's streamer, our jump forward in time with picotech; *they* always intended it to happen. We're the great filter, here to make a war to end all wars and keep humanity in check."

Finaeus shook his head. "That may be, but how will you do it? Those things, they'll destroy us all."

"No." Tanis shook her head. "They won't."

OURI'S BAD DAY

STELLAR DATE: 04.01.8948 (Adjusted Years)
LOCATION: Landfall Space/Air Traffic Control Center
REGION: Knossos Island, Carthage, New Canaan System

"Fuck! They're flinging dropships down here like their capital ships are fucking piñatas!" Henderson hollered from his position on the scan station.

"Henderson, pipe down," Ouri barked at the man. There were a lot of days that she loved being out of the military and back in the colony's biology mission, but there were a lot of times she missed the discipline of the ISF.

Henderson cast a pair of wide eyes in her direction, and Ouri held up a hand beside her head and lowered it to her waist. "Fleet will be on station before long, FROD Marines are going to hit the dirt behind those Trisilieds dropships. Don't you worry."

The man opened his mouth to reply, but Ouri cocked her head to the side and narrowed her eyes. Henderson nodded slowly and turned back to his console.

The civilian team running Landfall's Space/Air Traffic control systems was made up of competent people, but they weren't trained to handle the mental strain of an incoming assault of this magnitude. Ouri wasn't entirely sure that she was, either.

Still, with nearly every member of the ISF crewing ships in the fleet, it would fall to them to manage Carthage's main planetary defenses, along with Murry, the Planetary Management AI.

At first, Ouri had bristled when Tanis gave her this assignment. She had clocked thousands of hours conning the *Intrepid*, and she had held FleetConn when Tanis and the rest of the command crew had nearly been captured by rebels back on Victoria.

She knew how to command a starship.

However, now that she was on the ground, she realized that these people needed someone with her experience. To them, she was one of the legendary figures who had fought the rogue AIs in Estrella de la Muerte and played a pivotal role back at Victoria.

With a few exceptions, everyone present in the SATC had been in stasis, or not yet born, during most of the *Intrepid*'s journey.

"OK, people," Ouri addressed the ten men and women with her in the control room. "We're going to operate from this facility for as long as we can. It has line-of-sight communications with most of the installations, and since we're sixty klicks from Landfall, the enemy will think this is just a secondary installation."

"Our comm traffic is going to give us away, though," one of the air-traffic control operators replied. "They're going to know we're here."

"That's why we start by routing all comms through remote stations," Ouri replied. "As they fall, we pull back."

"They're still gonna figure it out before long," Henderson said, barely holding it together.

"Get a grip!" Sammy, a young woman to Henderson's left, shook her head. "Now, activate those AA batteries on the north continent. Murry has enough to do with the last shuttles dropping in, and lifts coming down the strand!"

<Thanks, Sammy. Trying to keep these pilots from burning the cradles so bad the next guys

don't sink in is a full-time job.>

"'Kay, 'kay, batteries are coming online," Henderson said. "NSAIs are suggesting closest dropships are priority. Do I go with that?"

"Yes!" Ouri and Sammy shouted at the same time.

"'Kay, 'kay, just checking…"

<*Don't worry,*> Sammy said privately to Ouri. <*I'll keep an eye on him. He's really good, normally; I guess this just messed him up.*>

<*I know,*> Ouri replied. <*His son's in Tanis's fleet. Everyone knows that's where most of the action will be.*>

Ouri couldn't imagine the stress of knowing one's kid was in battle. Her daughters were safe in one of the undersea biomes, and she was still worried sick about them.

<*Stars…so weird to hear you just refer to her as 'Tanis',*> Sammy replied with a small smile

<*She stole my cabin in Ol' Sam. That earns me some informality.*>

<*Wow…when we get through this, I'd love to hear some of those old stories. I mean…we learned about it all in school, but you* ***lived*** *it!*>

Ouri laughed. The girl's enthusiasm was infectious. <*You just stay focused and do your job. We'll get through this OK, and you'll have your own stories to tell.*>

"Yeah! Got some!" Henderson called out.

Ouri turned her attention back to the holotank and frowned as she watched hundreds of dropships enter the atmosphere. Henderson was right about one thing: this was going to be the fight of their lives.

The majority of the Trisilieds' assault craft were headed for Landfall, which made sense, given the enemy's goal of taking the planet's population hostage to force their surrender of the picotech. However, that goal gave an advantage to the Carthaginians. The enemy would be hesitant to use weapons of mass destruction on her people, while she would have no such compunctions about using WMDs on them.

"They're approaching the eastern installations," Amy called out from her station. "I have the first salvo ready to fire."

"Give 'em hell," Ouri replied.

The holotank showed the first wave of dropships pass below the ten-thousand-meter mark as they raced over the ocean to the east of the archipelago where Landfall was situated.

Below the crashing waves of the Mediterranean Ocean, twenty robotic submarines launched a hundred surface-to-air missiles at the enemy dropships. The SAMs carried one-megaton nuclear warheads—more than enough to put a crimp in the Trisilieds' approach vector.

"I can't believe we're detonating nukes over our own world," one of the men said, as he maneuvered low-altitude drones, launching chaff clouds into the skies ahead of the missiles. The reflective clouds of aluminum and lead would refract and block optical and x-ray lasers—with luck, they would protect at least half the SAMs as they streaked into the path of the oncoming ships.

Red markers appeared on the holotank as thirty two of the missiles took air-to-air fire and fell back into the ocean, then the remainder of the warheads detonated amidst the enemy dropships.

Ouri was glad for the row of volcanic peaks to their east that blocked the intensity of the flash; not to mention the antigravity systems that would push most of the radiation into space, along with the smoke and ash from the volcanoes.

As the clouds from the explosions cleared, remote sensor stations showed hundreds of Trisilieds assault craft plummeting into the ocean—though hundreds more survived the nuclear fire.

"Second salvo!" Ouri called out.

"It's insane," someone whispered from behind her. "How can they just fling so many ships down here like this? They're not giving them *any* fleet support!"

"Look above the poles," Ouri said without turning. "Fleet Group 1 just jumped in. Those assholes up there are in for the fight of their lives. You can see where several of their capital ships were dropping into low orbits, but are pulling back out now."

"Symatra really did a number on them, too," Sammy added. "She took out all those carriers; if they had made it, these assault ships would have serious fighter shields, not just this smattering."

The submarines fired off three more salvos of SAMs, each having a diminished effect as the drones ran out of chaff, and the enemy dropships spread out wider and wider.

As the assault transports passed high over the string of volcanoes, there were still over a thousand intact enemy ships bearing down on Landfall. Ouri estimated that each had to contain at least one platoon of soldiers, which meant that the Trisilieds were about to land thirty thousand troops on Carthage.

Ouri sighed. *Well shit.*

BRITANNICA

STELLAR DATE: 04.01.8948 (Adjusted Years)
LOCATION: OGS *Britannica*
REGION: Stellar North of Carthage, New Canaan System

"Thing about pico," Jessica said as she queued up with Cargo, Usef, Misha, and Trevor in the airlock, "is that it has a damn short shelf life. It doesn't take much to mess up those tiny bastards; unless they're carrying out orders to go eat a starship—then they'll replicate a hell of a lot faster than the Casimir effect tears 'em apart."

"I can't even begin to describe how nervous this makes me," Misha said, casting a worried eye at the small device Jessica held. "That shit's pico…it makes nanotech look like a bludgeon. It can weasel its way in between electrons and neutrons. How is it even a thing? What's it made out of?"

"Seriously, Misha," Jessica shook her head. "Do you really want to discuss how pico can take apart a neutron bit-by-bit right now?"

"Now that you mention it," Misha said with a broad grin, "that does sound fascinating. What say we just put off this crazy mission and talk about pico for a bit?"

"Nice try," Cargo said and slapped Misha on the back. "You always have a case of the butterflies before we do an op. Like Jessica said, we've got this in the bag."

"OK, when we go in, I have tactical command," Jessica said. "Not because I need to be the big girl, but because I know how we work, and I know how Usef works."

"Sure got the big girls, though." Misha snickered and Cargo cuffed him on the back of the head.

"Seriously, Cargo? Was that necessary?"

"Was either me or Trevor," Cargo shrugged. "Should I let him do it next time?"

Misha glanced at Trevor's biceps, each the size of his torso.

"Uh, thanks, Cargo. Did me a solid there."

"Damn right, I did."

<Are you ever going to go?> Sabrina asked. *<It's not easy holding this position, you know.>*

"Sorry, Sabrina," Jessica said as she placed the pico-package in the airlock and cycled it. "Can you guys believe Tanis snuck onto a Transcend ship the old-fashioned way just six days ago? When she sees a need, she sure makes certain it gets taken care of fast."

"Necessity is the mother of invention," Trevor said as they watched the package drift between their ships and latch onto the *Britannica*'s hull.

"Pretty deep there, big man," Misha chuckled.

"What? I used to carve little crystal trinkets. I can totally be deep."

Jessica's hand went to her throat, reaching for the chain that held the small dolphin Trevor had carved for her long ago. She felt a moment of panic when her fingers didn't feel the chain, but then she recalled: Trevor had convinced her not to wear it—it was against Orion Guard regs to wear jewelry, and though the Orion uniforms they wore would hide it, it wasn't worth the risk.

"Yeah, you're like an ocean," Cargo grunted. "It looks like our little friend has rewired the lock over there. If it worked, we'll slip right in. If it doesn't…well, I guess we'll all see how we look with holes in us."

Jessica checked her sidearm one last time as the team stepped into the airlock and Sabrina pulled the ship within a meter of the *Britannica*. A small grav-tunnel joined the airlocks, and the team rushed through and sealed the *Britannica*'s behind them.

<*Secure,*> Jessica called back to their ship.

<*Understood. We'll be on standby,*> Nance replied. <*With luck you won't need us.*>

<*Let's hope,*> Cargo replied.

"OK, team; one more time while the package makes sure the passageway out there is clear," Jessica said, looking from one member of the strike force to the next. "Now that we have Usef here, it's not going to work like last time—being an officer, he can pass for one."

"I think I did really well last time," Cargo said.

"Seriously?" Misha asked. "You were a major and you called a private '*sir*'. Sure, they 'sir' sergeants in some militaries, but *no one* calls a private 'sir'."

"You sure?" Cargo asked Jessica and Usef.

"Yep; no one, nowhere," Jessica shook her head.

"Goes against nature," Usef added.

"If he's the one who can't tell a private from his privates, how come I'm PFC Jerrod, here?" Misha asked.

"Cause he's the captain, and I have to at least make him a sergeant," Jessica said. "Look, everyone stop bitching about your ranks. Trevor and I are heading up front to see if we can catch Garza when he steps out for a whiz. You guys are on engineering duty. We need to control this ship's engines without having to hold the bridge."

<*Easy,*> Hank said cover the combat net. <*Angela gave Iris and me some serious kit. These pathetic Orion AIs are barely L2; we'll have them under control in no time.*>

<*Don't get cocky, Hank,*> Iris wagged a finger at him in their minds. <*We're going to be out of communication once we split up—until we take the ship, that is. You be careful. All of you.*>

<*Iris, it's me,*> Hank said with a mental grin.

"Yeah, that's what we're afraid of," Misha chuckled.

The light over the airlock's inner door flashed green, and Jessica slid it open and stepped boldly into the corridor. Trevor followed, and they closed the portal behind them. The other team would leave once she had found a hard terminal for Iris to start her hack.

Until then, anyone who gave them a second look may realize that neither she nor Trevor were on the ship's rolls.

<*Funny the similarities these ships share with the Transcend ones,*> Iris commented, as Jessica and Trevor strode purposefully down the passageway, heading toward what should be a small NSAI node.

<*They've been in a weird holding pattern for some time,*> Jessica replied. <*It's as though they both advanced to a certain point, and then went wide instead of up.*>

<*It's more amazing that no one else figured out picotech in the last five thousand years,*> Trevor said as he turned down a corridor leading further toward the center of the ship.

<*Well, we know they didn't figure it out in Orion,*> Jessica replied. <*I do wonder, though; did those Transcend worlds really have rampant picoswarms, or did the OG take them out because they want to limit technological advancement?*>

<*I doubt we'll ever really know for sure,*> Iris said. <*Stop. There, that door to your left—a lot of EMF coming from inside. I bet that's one of their NSAI nodes.*>

*****

Usef was just about to ping Jessica for an update when his AI, Jamie, gave them the all clear.

<*I received Iris's data burst. Our idents are in their system,*> Jamie informed the group. <*Once we leave the airlock, I'll piggyback on Usef's Link; so if he talks to you over it, it may be me.*>

"That won't be weird at all," Misha muttered.

"You'll manage. Let's go," Usef said, and slid the airlock door open.

The trio exited the airlock, took ten steps down the corridor, and almost walked right into a puzzled-looking engineer.

"Hey! Watch it!" the woman grunted as she stepped around Usef. "Shit! Sorry, Major…Johnson."

She saluted while blushing furiously.

"As you were, SPC. Don't worry about it," Usef said as he returned the salute.

"Thank you, sir. I'm just trying to work out some strange readings this airlock down here is giving me. Distracted me, won't happen again," she said in a rush.

"I trust that it won't," Usef said, and turned, continuing on his way with Cargo and Misha on his heels.

"Someone got all hot and bothered when she saw ol' Major Johnson here," Misha chuckled. "Why infiltrate the enemy when you can just seduce them?"

"That one's getting old," Cargo grunted.

<*And think before you use the words 'infiltrate the enemy'. You never know who, or what, is listening,*> Usef chided.

"Sheesh," Misha sighed.

"That's 'sheesh, sir'," Usef scowled.

These two are going to blow the op. It's a miracle they survived nine years in the Perseus arm; the Orion Guard must have put its incompetents out there.

They walked around a corner and saw that the passageway ahead had a ninety-degree twist. A pair of soldiers approached, appearing to walk on the wall until they reached the twisting section, at which point they rotated as they walked, until their 'down' was the same as the trio's.

<*That's just weird,*> Usef said. <*Still not used to this artificial gravity stuff.*>

<*It's weird for those of us who* **are** *used to it,*> Misha replied. <*Always makes me feel nauseated to reorient like that.*>

The soldiers saluted, and Usef returned the salute, resisting the urge to turn and ensure that Cargo and Misha followed proper protocol. The soldiers didn't say anything, so he assumed all was well.

After they passed through the twisted section of corridor and were walking on the wall, they came to a bank of lifts, all situated around the edges of a large shaft with a particle accelerator running down the center.

Misha approached the railing and looked over. "Going doooooown," he whispered while grinning.

"For fucksakes, Private; stop dicking around, and get in the lift," Cargo growled.

As the doors closed, Usef nodded. "That was a passable impression of a sergeant. Nicely done."

"What can I say?" Cargo replied. "Misha brings it out of me."

"You know…I'm standing right here," Misha muttered.

Jamie highlighted the engineering command level on his HUD, and Usef entered the code to send the lift down the three kilometers of shaft to its destination.

Cargo looked out the narrow windows into the ship's central shaft. "Gotta say, that's a pretty sweet view."

Usef nodded. It reminded him of the accelerator that ran down the center of the *I2*. He remembered the assault on Node 11 back when the rogue AIs had taken control of the *Intrepid*—fighting servitors and automatons through the dark passageways while nauseating gravity waves flowed off the accelerator.

That had been his first combat mission as a part of the ISF—though it hadn't been the ISF then. He tallied the time he had been awake, and realized that mission was nearly a hundred years ago.

Nothing like what the admiral has put on her clock, but an appreciable span of years.

The lift slid to a halt halfway to their destination, and the doors opened to admit two female lieutenants. They quickly saluted Usef, and he returned the gesture—noting with relief that Cargo and Misha correctly saluted the officers.

"Good morning, Major," one of the women said, while the other added, "Good morning, sir."

They glanced at one another, and the first woman—First Lieutenant Lauren, by her ident—asked, "If I may ask, Major Johnson, how long have you been aboard? I thought I knew all the officers on the *Britannica.*"

"Transferred in off the *Sword of Orion* before we began our stealth run, Lieutenant Lauren," Usef replied, using a ship name that Jamie supplied him. "I wanted to be where the action is."

"Oh, this is where the action is, alright," the other woman, Second Lieutenant Jenny, added.

They were smiling just a bit too much, and Usef wondered if the crew on the *Britannica* had something in their water supply. First the SPC near the airlock, and now these two. Maybe they were on to his team and just playing with him.

<*Relax,*> Jamie said. <*They're a bit…freer on OG ships, from what I can tell.*>

"Look us up once we're done burning this system to ash," Lieutenant Lauren said with a grin. "We'll give you a proper *Britannica* welcome."

The lift came to a stop several levels above their destination, and the two lieutenants got out, both casting long looks back at Usef over their shoulders.

"Can you help it?" Misha asked with a shake of his head.

"Sir," Usef replied.

"What? Does that mean 'yes'?"

"Stars, we're doomed," Usef said, and looked at the lift's ceiling, hoping Jessica was at least doing as well as they were.

* * * * *

"Have you located them?" Garza asked as he re-entered the Fleet CIC.

"Not yet," Admiral Fenton said, his deep scowl showing how he felt about the situation.

The ship's AI, Harry—a rather strange entity, in Garza's estimation—replied as well. <*Security teams are trying to pin them down, but they keep slipping in and out of our internal sensors. They must have a hack in our system, but we've been unable to find it.*>

"I thought you had eyes on them just before I stepped out," Garza said. "Two lieutenants saw them, and noted the deck they were going to."

<*Yes, sir, but when the lift stopped at that deck, no one was in it,*> Harry responded, his avatar giving a shrug. <*I'm doing everything I can, but honestly, without sounding general quarters, it's going to be hard to find them.*>

"No, I want to know where they're going. Find them and tail them, if you have to. They're not here to see the sights; they have some sort of plan."

"I think we should switch mission parameters," Admiral Fenton said as he reoriented the view of the New Canaan system on the holotank. "If they have landed an infiltration team on our ship, they know we're here. If they know we're here, then our element of surprise is gone. We're close enough that we can order the fleet to rotate and fire engines on max burn. Their planet will be a dead husk inside of an hour."

"They lucked out and spotted us with a stealth ship," Garza replied. "That ship may have relayed our position, but they won't know about the other half of the fleet. And if they do know, so what? Even if the Trisilieds don't wear them down to dust first, we still outnumber them ten-to-one."

"I don't like it," Fenton shook his head. "They have picobombs—if they know where we are, how do we know we aren't flying into a swarm of them?"

"We don't," Garza shook his head. "But consider this: even if they can spot our stealth ships, their picobombs won't have scan good enough to track us on their own; and if they pass data to a swarm of picobombs, we raise shields, and nothing comes of it."

Fenton continued to frown at the holotank. "Provided pico can't get through shields."

"If it can, then why'd they fly their fighters through the Hegemony dreadnaught's shields back in Bollam's World?" Garza asked. "Their pico delivery system is the weak point—a weak point that we can target and destroy."

Garza wondered about Fenton's resolve. They were too far down this road to turn back now. When Kirkland learned that he had made this preemptive strike against New Canaan, the praetor would know that they did not share the same ideals.

Fenton knew that. They had to see this thing through. No other possibility existed.

<*Got them,*> Harry announced. <*A security team is bringing the intruders to you. Should I have them placed in a nearby holding room?*>

"No," Garza replied with a grim smile. "Bring them in here. I want them to watch while we destroy their world."

* * * * *

<*There it is,*> Usef said as he peered around the corner. <*Engineering command. We have to hit fast and hard. Jamie has a shunt ready to lock down their Link access, but there are a lot of terminals in there. If any of them sounds the alarm, this whole party is over.*>

Cargo and Misha nodded soberly, and Usef was glad to see that they were finally taking things seriously.

<*Who takes who?*> Cargo asked.

<*Go for whoever is closest. Jamie will provide priority targets and fields of fire on your HUDs,*> Usef replied.

<*Ooooh, fancy,*> Misha gave a mock whistle.

<*So much for serious,*> Jamie said privately.

Usef agreed with Jamie's sentiment. <*I keep thinking…if they got through Perseus, then they can do this; but I'm starting to doubt that…maybe it was a miracle.*>

<*Well, we know Jessica is competent enough. Maybe they just like to have fun,*> Jamie offered.

<*We're about to find out,*> Usef said as he stepped around the corner and strode into the engineering command center.

The room was broad, with a high overhead and a dozen holotanks. Each one showed detailed readouts of different ships. Usef counted thirty engineering specialists around the room, working under the watchful eye of a major who stood near the center of the space.

A watchful eye which did not miss his entrance.

"Major…Johnson," the woman said as he approached. "How can I help you today?"

Her words were cordial, but her scowl was not. Every part of her body language said 'go away', and Usef flashed his best smile in response. "Major Phyla, I've been sent down to ensure everything is ready for the upcoming battle, and to operate as a liaison."

Major Phyla turned from Usef back to the holo she had been monitoring. "A liaison to whom? I report directly to Captain Langlias. I don't need you to liaise."

"I've been attached to General Garza's retinue," Usef replied without rancor. "He sent me down here to make sure that he has a direct line to what's really happening on the ship."

His words caught her attention, and she glanced back at him. "Did he now? I suppose that makes sense; in the CIC, he only knows what comes down from the bridge—and I'll tell you, that's not always the whole story."

Usef chuckled. "Don't I know it. Who wants to be the one to tell the Fleet Admiral, and the general in charge of all the shady spec-ops shit, that something's wrong?"

Major Phyla barked a laugh. "You do realize that's *your* job—you get to be the bearer of bad news."

Usef nodded. "Yeah, not the best posting in the force. Still, better than those poor Hegemony and Trisilieds ships out there."

Phyla nodded absently. "Yeah, at least we're no one's ablative shielding, like those bastards. Hell, when it comes to the *Britannica,* our shielding has shielding."

Usef leaned around Major Phyla's shoulder and peered into the tank. "So, what's this?"

He barely paid attention to her response as he lightly touched the back of her neck, praying she wouldn't notice.

"Excuse me?" she exclaimed as she spun to face him. "Are you trying to cop a feel or something?"

"What?" Usef took a step back. "You need to lighten up. You had this bit of string in your hair; just doing you a favor—keeping things on the up and up."

The major's eyes narrowed and she shook her head. "OK, Major Johnson, if you say so."

Usef looked around the bay to see Cargo and Misha working their way through the engineers present. They were introducing themselves as part of his team, shaking hands, doing all the right stuff. In the time he had managed to deploy a package to the major, each of them had deposited pico units on a dozen of the personnel in the room.

Major Phyla had noticed the pair working their way through the room as well, and shook her head. "Don't know where you transferred in from, but you're a friendly bunch. Better not be this distracting when the shit starts to fly."

"Don't worry," Usef replied. "They're just getting to know everyone so they can operate at peak efficiency when things get hairy. Not that I really expect it to."

"No?" Major Phyla turned from the holotank to face him. "You know something I don't know? Those Canners down there are pretty nuts. They have pico tech, fire grapeshot; probably have no issues with antimatter weapons, either—just like those Transcend bastards. You saw what they did."

Usef nodded as though he knew all about it. If the Transcend had used antimatter weapons, it was deplorable—but right now, Orion was attacking his home, and the Transcend was helping to defend it. He'd trust Admiral Richards to make the right call when it came to alliances.

"I meant here, on the *Britannica*," Usef said with a smile and a shrug. "The captain'll want to keep Admiral Fenton and General Garza nice and safe."

Phyla shook her head and turned back to her holotank. "They're great men and all—very important to the Guard—but I'd rather be in the thick of things. We signed up to be warriors, didn't we? Not to babysit the brass."

Usef chuckled. He couldn't fault the woman for her spirit, misguided though it was.

Phyla's shoulders hunched ever so slightly before she spun, her sidearm aimed at his head. "Lucky for me, I think I've managed to find a bit of action, right here in my own engineering bay."

*****

Garza shook his head as the intruders were marched into the CIC. How they ever thought that they could achieve anything other than capture on the *Britannica* was beyond him; though he'd very much like to know what they thought they could pull off.

"Welcome aboard," Garza said with a cold smile. "I'm sure that you just forgot to ask the captain for permission to come aboard."

"Something like that," the woman said. "We just thought it would be good to get a look at your ships before we destroyed them all—for research, of course."

The large man accompanying the woman didn't add anything, but a smile spread across his face as he glanced at her.

"Well, I hope you got a good look. I'm General Garza, by the way. I brought you here because I thought you might like to watch as your fleets are destroyed, and your world held hostage until they surrender the picotech to us."

"I'm Colonel Jessica Keller, and this is Trevor," the woman replied. "I have to say, I'm glad you brought us in here. Usually it's just a dark, grey holding cell—which would bug me, because I'd be on the wrong side of the table."

Garza snapped his fingers. "Of course, Jessica Keller. I didn't make an immediate match, because you're not on the original colony roster—that, and you appear to have aged."

"A result of a recent adventure," Jessica said with a frown. It's been about fifty years since I've had rejuv."

"Well, you'll get none of that in an Orion prison," Admiral Fenton spoke up. "General Garza, do you really have to play these games here? We have work to do."

"Don't you realize who this is?" Garza asked. "This is one of Governor Richards's inner circle. She's not here for some unimportant scout mission. She's come because they planned to do something significant on the *Britannica*."

"Then there's no way they came alone," Fenton replied. "You don't send one of your top people—and a guy named Trevor—onto a ship like this by themselves."

Garza stroked his chin as he eyed the pair. "Put them by the wall; make sure they're well restrained," he ordered the soldiers who had brought the colonists in. "Harry, start a new sweep of the ship. I want the rest of their group found."

<*Already on it, General,*> Harry replied.

"Who knows," Garza said as he turned back to the holotank, "I may keep this system after I've destroyed the world you've named Carthage. The shipyards alone make it worth holding onto."

VISITORS

STELLAR DATE: 04.01.8948 (Adjusted Years)
LOCATION: Landfall Space/Air Traffic Control Center
REGION: Knossos Island, Carthage, New Canaan System

"Oh crap, oh shit! Commander Ouri!" Henderson called out.

Ouri didn't bother correcting the man on rank—though how he could grow up in a society like New Canaan's, and not understand the difference between a commander and a colonel was beyond her.

"What is it, Henderson? Just spit it out!" Ouri yelled back from across the room.

"The Trisilieds…they've sent four craft to our location; they snuck in around from the south. I took one out, but the other three are landing!"

Ouri felt her temper flare and took a deep breath, forcing her emotions into check. It would have been fantastic if Henderson had let her know about this *before* the enemy had begun disgorging their troops.

"OK, Sammy, Kris, Bill, you're with me. The rest of you, keep running the air defenses as long as you can—people across the planet are counting on us. Jim, we still have a fleet of subs that need to stop that wave of assault craft dropping on Paris Island out west, and Brandt has called in for an airstrike on a field near Landfall that the enemy is using for their forward base. Jenny, get our ground-based artillery hitting that target. Amy, make sure the Tower's perimeter defenses are up, and take out as many of those bastards as you can."

"Aye, Colonel," Amy called back.

At least someone has been paying attention, Ouri thought to herself.

Though the facility was colloquially called the 'SATC tower', it was nothing of the sort. Everyone in New Canaan knew this fight was coming, and no one had even considered a tall, vulnerable tower when it came to civilian space and air traffic control.

Instead, the SATC facility was tucked within a long ridge of granite that lay toward the eastern edge of Knossos Island at the base of a low string of mountains, which had arisen when the archipelago's plate pushed up over the Mediterranean Ocean plate.

She wished there were ground-based artillery units that could sweep the hillside leading up to the SATC, but none were available that could target their side of the ridge. They were in the plan, but hadn't been built yet.

The lowest level of the facility was little more than a lobby—with external access to a parking lot, for those who liked the drive through the countryside on the way to work—and a station for a quick ride to Landfall.

A wide double-staircase led from the foyer to the second level, and a long tunnel ran back into the ridge, which ended in a lift and a staircase up to the second level. The control room was on the fourth level, further back in the ridge and under hundreds of meters of granite.

The facility also had a low signal tower directly overhead, as well as direct, hardline connections to the dozens of other towers ringing the island.

Ouri was impressed that the Trisilieds had picked out this location as the primary facility. Their sensor tech must be better than that of most Inner Stars civilizations.

Ouri led Bill, Kris, and Sammy down the hall toward the front stairwell.

"What are the four of us going to do against three platoons of Trisilieds solders?" Sammy asked as she caught up to Ouri.

"Well," Ouri replied as she led the trio down the hall, "I was in favor of killing them. Let's start there."

"How are we going to do that?" Bill asked.

"I picked the four of you because you all got high marksmanship scores in Basic," Ouri replied as she glanced back at her team. "So, what I think we should do is shoot the bad guys."

She pushed into the stairwell and skipped down the stairs to the third level, where the security office and small armory were located.

"Seriously, Ouri, you must have some better plan than that. Even if we were the toughest Marines in the corps, it's four against a hundred," Sammy said, her voice starting to rise in pitch.

"I rated expert in my marksmanship course," Kris said quietly. "If there's anything in the armory with range, I could get up in the signal tower and take them out as they approach."

Ouri looked Kris up and down. The willowy woman was two meters tall, and there was no reason to believe she couldn't get a rifle up there in time; but the position was a death sentence.

"I bet you could, Kris," Ouri replied. "You'd give 'em hell, too; but one well-placed rocket, and that whole tower will come down. I'm not sending you up there to die."

Kris's face blanched, and Ouri suspected that the very real possibility of them all dying in the next few minutes was now entering her team's minds.

"Look," she said as they entered the armory. "We don't have to take them all out, we just have to buy time. Murry has already put out the call that we're under attack, and as soon as Landfall is safe, those Trissies out there are going to have Force Recon boots up their asses, courtesy of the ISF Marines."

"Trissies," Sammy chuckled. "I like it."

Ouri had already assessed the armory's loadout, and, like everything in New Canaan, it was a shining example of over-preparedness—yet still insufficient for what they were up against.

Five sets of light body armor stood on racks, and she directed her team to gear up. The armor wouldn't stop beamfire, but it would keep projectiles and shrapnel from cutting them to ribbons.

While they geared up, Ouri laid out four multifunction rifles, sidearms, spare magazines, and five detpacks. She stuffed all the grenades into a bag that she planned to hold onto; they had enough to worry about without a bad toss getting them all killed.

Once the team was armored up and had begun checking over their weapons, she quickly donned her armor while calling Amy.

<How's it looking out there, Amy?>

<They're being careful, working their way up the front and flanking, as well. Two of the beam turrets are down, but I still have two running. They haven't gotten in range of the two Gatling guns near the entrance, but once they do, I plan to cut down the forest—and whatever's in it.>

Ouri was impressed. Amy's voice didn't waver one iota. The woman sounded like cold steel incarnate.

<Give 'em hell, Amy. Let me know when they've reached the guns.>

<*Pretty sure you'll hear it, Colonel,*> Amy replied with a mental smile. <*There's one string of explosive rounds for each gun, and I have that queued up first. I won't fire 'til I can see the whites of their eyes.*>

<*Looking forward to hearing that sound,*> Ouri replied.

"Bill, Sammy, grab those two CFT shields. We'll set them up on the second floor landing. Kris, I want you to stay up on the third level's landing, and pick off anyone that gets past our fire," Ouri directed.

"What if they get past you and come up the rear staircase?" Kris asked.

Ouri picked up one of the detpacks and tossed it to her. "Before you take up your position, rig this to take out the rear stairs if they get back there. Put it on the landing between the second and third floors. Set up some nano to watch the stairs, and trigger the pack if the Trissies make it that far. Oh," Ouri tossed her another detpack, "and rig this one in the elevator shaft outside the third level's door."

Kris gave a crisp nod, slung her rifle over her shoulder, and ran out of the room, turning right toward the rear stairs.

Sammy and Bill followed after and turned left, hauling the Carbon Fiber Tube shields with them toward the front of the facility.

Ouri cast her eyes about the room, looking for anything else that would help. She spotted a locker that none of them had opened, and peered inside to find a crew-served railgun.

"Well, this will come in handy," she said with a smile.

She grabbed her selected gear and moved out.

When she reached the front stairwell's second floor landing, Bill and Sammy had already set up the CFT shields, and were taking sight on the foyer below.

While the rear staircase was narrow and utilitarian, the front one was wider and more ornate. A four-meter-wide string of steps rose up to the second level before arching around to the third.

The fourth floor was only accessible from a secondary flight of stairs in the middle of the third level. That would be their final fallback before abandoning the facility, and taking the rear tunnel out to the far side of the ridge.

Ouri took a position behind Sammy, glad for the cover the shield would provide. She peered down her rifle's iron sights, ensuring that they were aligned with her HUD's targeting system.

Her team's position on the landing gave them an angle of fire where they could hit the leading edge of any troops that entered the first floor, while only enemy well within the building could bring significant fire to bear on them.

It wasn't enough to give them a large advantage, but it was enough to stem the enemy's advance and give them a fighting chance.

"So…what if they just launch rockets in here and blow the whole facility?" Bill asked as he glanced nervously around his shield.

Ouri considered that scenario. The working theory was that the Trissies wanted the picotech, and were prepared to take hostages to press their claim. However, they didn't need *all* the civilians on the planet to do that. She knew that if it was her, she would simply neutralize the facility and move on.

"Good point, Bill," Ouri nodded. "If they take the foyer down there and we have to fall back, will the facility hold if they place charges down on the first and second floors? The control center is quite a ways further back in the ridge."

Bill considered it for a moment. "Well, there are blast doors on the third and fourth levels. If those close, then the control room should be fine. All the critical systems, power and com and stuff, link right in there, too, so it could stay operational."

"OK, then—" Ouri began, but Bill spoke over her.

"Unless they plant them all along the back wall, then maybe it would bring down the whole ridge."

"Then we're gonna have to make sure that they don't do that," Sammy replied.

"Great plan," Kris called from the landing above them. "I knew I should have stayed in bed."

Ouri wished that she could send the station personnel down the maglev to Landfall, or out the rear tunnel to the other side of the ridge, but too many people needed the air defenses to keep running. They had to hold the line.

A thundering roar came from outside the facility, and Ouri chuckled. "They're meeting Amy's welcoming committee out there now."

<*How many have you taken out?*> she asked Amy. Normally they would have a combat net run by an AI—or an NSAI in a pinch—that would manage tallies and ensure everyone had an up-to-date view of the battlefield.

Today, she would have to manage that work manually.

<*I think I've hit at least twenty of them. They were pretty careful about the beam turrets, but they didn't seem to expect a second layer of defenses. Plus side, there's a nice clear swath in front of the facility. They're gonna have to get closer to the guns to—*> she stopped.

<*What?*> Ouri asked.

<*Umm…they've taken out the Gatling guns…they hit them with some sort of cluster rockets that the guns couldn't deal with,*> Amy replied. <*Sorry.*>

Ouri sent an affirmative response and nodded to her teammates. "Defenses are down. They're coming."

"Faaack," Bill whispered, while Sammy sucked in a deep breath.

Ouri pulled the feed from the cameras on the tower above the facility, and watched as the Trisilieds soldiers crept across the smoking hillside leading up to the parking lot, taking cover behind the smattering of groundcars as they approached.

She could understand their hesitancy. The facility should have had additional layers of defense, but only so much could be built in eighteen years; most of the effort had been put into the fleet and orbital defenses.

After an agonizing three minutes of careful probing, the Trisilieds soldiers reached the facility's front doors and pulled them open.

<*Close your eyes,*> Ouri warned, uncertain how much light the armor's half-helmets would block.

As she expected, the enemy fired optical and sonic pulsers into the foyer, and she was pleasantly surprised to find that the helmets blocked both with reasonable efficiency.

As the pulsers flashed and wailed, an enemy squad breached the foyer. Ouri opened fire, and Bill and Sammy let loose with their shots a moment later.

None of them held back; their rifles' high-velocity kinetic rounds slamming into the fireteam's legs before the enemy could see them.

Most of the rounds bounced off the enemy's armor, but one of Bill's caught a weak point, and a Trissie fell. Ouri assumed he cried out in pain, but the sounds of weapons fire drowned it out.

The Trissies fanned out along the edges of the foyer and dropped prone behind a kiosk and a table, returning fire that was successfully absorbed by the CFT shields.

Ouri's team kept up their suppressive shots, and wore down the scant cover in moments, causing the enemies to fall back to the far corners of the foyer. Sammy leaned out to take a shot, and Ouri pulled her back an instant before a slug tore through the air where Sammy's head had been.

"Watch it; they're gonna try to draw us out now," she cautioned.

"Yeah! I can see that!" Sammy gasped as her face turned white.

"Don't worry, Sammy, keep your head and we'll get through this," Ouri said as she took aim at an enemy who was creeping along the wall, putting three solid rounds into his torso, and one in his neck. None of the shots penetrated his armor, but they were enough to send him racing back to cover.

Ouri estimated where he and at least one of his other teammates must be, and grabbed a grenade from her pack; she primed it and tossed it down the stairs, into the far corner of the foyer.

The timer she set on the grenade was spot on, and it detonated the instant it reached their position, the force of the explosion blowing out the foyer's windows, and flushing a hot wind up the stairs.

"Yeah! Got 'em!" Bill yelled.

"There's still another sixty or so out there," Ouri replied. "Don't get too excited yet."

INFILTRATE

STELLAR DATE: 04.01.8948 (Adjusted Years)
LOCATION: OGS *Britannica*
REGION: Stellar North of Carthage, New Canaan System

Jessica watched the battle unfold on the holotank as the Orion Guard fleets drifted closer to Carthage. She was impressed with how Symatra decimated the Trisilieds carriers, and thanked the stars when the ISF fleet came through their dark layer jump intact.

"What is their plan?" Admiral Fenton asked General Garza after the ISF fleet appeared above Carthage's poles. Garza had no answer, and the admiral's eyes darted to Jessica.

"Colonel! What is Richards's plan? If she can jump through the dark layer, so can the Hegemony fleet!" Admiral Fenton demanded.

Jessica saw Garza shake his head and she suspected that neither of them wanted a full-force Hegemony fleet present around Carthage. She shrugged innocently, and her suspicions were confirmed when Admiral Fenton glared at Garza.

"Involving them was a mistake. First they jump the gun taking out the Transcend fleet beyond the heliopause, and now this."

"The battle isn't over yet," Garza replied.

A minute later, a smattering of AST ships appeared near the main ISF fleet. In short order, the number of functioning Hegemony vessels approached zero, and Garza laughed.

"See, Admiral? No need to worry. Governor Richards has taken care of our little problem for us."

"You know what that means?" Fenton asked.

"Oh, I do! I do!" Jessica spoke up, drawing both men's attention.

Garza peered at her over his shoulder. "I bet you do. What is your purpose here? It's time you told us,"

"We just wanted a good view," Trevor said. "Heard your CIC was the best in the fleet, so we got ourselves captured to get in."

"You didn't get captured—" Garza began.

For the first time, the man began to look worried; it gave Jessica a perverse sense of pleasure to see it.

"Harry, status on the search!" Garza called out.

Jessica couldn't hear the AI's response, but by the look on the general's face, it wasn't good. She breathed a sigh of relief. Everything was still going according to plan—mostly. Getting caught wasn't what she'd had in mind, but it did get them into the CIC, and by now the pico packages that she and Trevor had deployed should have finished their tasks.

<*We ready to interface?*> she asked Iris.

<*We are green and good to go,*> the AI replied.

<*What about weapons?*> Jessica asked. When she and Trevor had been captured, the guards had taken their sidearms elsewhere. At present, the only weapons in the room were held by four soldiers in powered armor.

<*I didn't have enough for the soldiers. You're going to have to figure something out,*> Iris replied.

<*Are you serious?*> Jessica asked as she glanced at the closest guard. <*They're wearing a hundred kilos of armor! What are we going to do against them?*>

<*Sorry,*> Iris apologized. <*I said we were low on the picopackages and that you'd have to take out the guards. You didn't seem worried, so I assumed you had a plan.*>

Jessica sighed in her mind. <*I thought you meant the armor was still working, not that they had functional weapons, too. For an AI, you can be very unspecific at times.*>

<*So are we standing down?*> Iris asked. <*It's only a matter of time before they realize what I've done.*>

Jessica glanced around the room, recounting those present. Seven specialists on the far wall managing comm, a dozen scan officers to her left, a batch of ensigns that were prepared to function as backup coordination officers, the general, the admiral, a passel of colonels and majors, and Harry's central column.

And, of course, the four soldiers with pulse rifles and ballistic sidearms.

She gave Trevor a sidelong look. Even unarmored, he could take out one, maybe two of the soldiers. She had watched him take down enemies in powered armor before. Then an idea hit her and she reached a hand over to him, carful to maintain the fiction that her hands were still locked together by the restraining cuffs.

She touched his leg and made a direct Link.

<*Trevor, what do you think about smashing that AI column?*>

<*Shouldn't be a problem, so long as none of the guards can hit me with anything more than a pulse before I get there,*> Trevor replied. <*What's the deal?*>

<*Low on pico, the guards are still one-hundred percent operational,*> Jessica said with a mental sigh.

<*Hey, not my fault!*> Iris interjected. <*This stuff is still new and experimental. Wasn't easy to build an interface and hack this CIC—all while you two were just sitting there, I might add.*>

<*I wasn't blaming anyone, I was just giving Trevor the facts.*>

Trevor gave her a mental wink and a nod. <*Sure, hon. I buy it. I hear you have a planet for sale, too; real cheap.*>

<*Shut up. I'll create a distraction—you make your move whenever it seems best.*>

Jessica stood with a slight bounce and an embarrassed look. "I really gotta hit the ladies'," she whispered to the guard that spun and leveled his weapon at her chest. "Seriously, I've been holding it forever. I didn't want to go before, because I didn't want to miss anything, but now I know that if I don't get it over with, I'll have to run out during the grand finale."

The guard shook his head. "Sit."

"Are you serious?" Jessica asked, raising her voice. "I've gotta go number two! I'm going to shit my pants! It's gonna stink, too. Do you think the brass over there wants to smell poop during their moment of victory?"

<*Real classy,*> Iris commented.

"What is going on over there?" Admiral Fenton asked from the far side of the holotank.

"Admiral Fenton, sir. The prisoner needs to use the head," the soldier replied.

"What is this, primary school?" Garza growled without turning. "Go! Just don't take your eyes off her."

The soldier grabbed Jessica's shoulder, spun her about, and shoved her toward the door. She was impressed by his fluid movements in the powered armor, and a little worried that she didn't stand a chance against him.

They reached the door, and when the guard leaned forward to palm the panel, it all happened.

To her left, Jessica saw Trevor jump up and race across the room, lowering a shoulder as he closed on the column containing Harry's node. The guards were as quick as she feared, and two pulse blasts hit Trevor as he ran; though it wasn't enough to slow his three-hundred-twenty-kilogram mass as it slammed into the AI's column.

While Trevor was speeding across the room, Jessica crouched and wrapped an arm around one of her guard's arms, yanking his weapon toward another soldier.

She knew that if she tried to grasp and fire the weapon, it would discharge an electrical shock into her body. But slamming her fist into the guard's finger, forcing it past the trigger guard—that might work.

By some combination of shock and surprise, the maneuver worked, and Jessica managed to get the weapon to fire at the next guard; at the same moment, Iris killed the lights, holotanks, and all the consoles, just as Trevor smashed through Harry's column.

The guard whose weapon she had forced to fire jerked his arm, and sent Jessica flying—directly into General Garza. She cycled her vision to an IR/RF mix, and slammed an elbow into his jaw before flinging herself across the table at Admiral Fenton, who was drawing his sidearm.

Her boots hit him in the chest and throat, knocking the man to the ground. His sidearm went spinning, and Iris highlighted it on Jessica's vision.

<Jess, it's some old ballistic relic. Chem only. Grab it!>

Jessica launched herself across the floor and snatched the handgun. The thing had a serious heft to it, and looked like the mag would hold at least nine shots.

She put one into the chest of a man who was lunging at her—one of the colonels who had been standing at another holotank—and then a second round into an ensign who thought he could save the day.

Jessica scrambled toward Admiral Fenton and pressed the gun's barrel against the back of his head, finger on the trigger.

"Everyone *FREEZE!*" she screamed, satisfied to see the room fall silent while Iris brought the lights back up.

"What in the damned core do you think you're doing?" Garza yelled as Jessica pulled Fenton to his feet and backed against a wall.

One of the soldiers brought his rifle up and flipped its firing mode to a particle beam.

"Go for it," Jessica goaded the man. "My AI is watching your trigger fingers, and mine is on auto. You may get me, but the admiral here will bite it."

"Lower it!" Admiral Fenton barked at the soldier.

"No! Fire!" Garza countered. "We have a larger goal here than one man's life. Take her out."

This was where Jessica prayed her gamble would work. The entire time they had been sitting in the CIC, she had watched the general and admiral interact. She had also picked out which of the personnel in the room were on their separate staffs.

Without question, Admiral Fenton's people were in the majority. It made sense, since this was his flagship and his CIC. Garza, for all intents and purposes, was just along for the ride.

Even so, when the soldiers finally lowered their weapons, she breathed a long sigh of relief.

"Toss 'em," Trevor said as he walked toward the soldiers while rubbing his shoulder. "Helmets off."

The soldiers paused, but Fenton nodded and they complied.

Once the soldier's rifles were in a pile at his feet, the helmets beside them, Trevor approached one of the soldiers and drove a fist into the side of the man's head.

"Good aim with the rifle," he said as the man fell unconscious, his armor still holding him erect. "Too bad my fist is a better weapon. Now, one at a time, the rest of you three get out of your armor. You first," he said to the woman on the end.

Everyone in the room stood stock still, tense and unmoving, as, one after the other, the soldiers' armor split open. Then the men and women moved to the side of the room where the comm techs were standing.

"This is ridiculous," Garza said as he shook his head. "You can't stop what's happening here. Even if you kill us all, your people are doomed."

"Boy, you sure would like to know our plans, wouldn't you?" Jessica asked with a smirk, as Trevor crouched down over the pile of rifles and deposited a passel of nano on them to disable their bio-locks.

He stood a moment later with a rifle in each hand—one configured to fire pulse blasts, the other a particle beam.

"OK, Ogies, everyone over there, and on the floor. I want you bastards prone with your hands over your heads. You have ten seconds before I start shooting."

Trevor's tone seemed to convince everyone present that he was deadly serious, and before his allotted time was up, everyone in the room, excepting Garza and Fenton, was face down on the deck.

"You too," Jessica said to Fenton and gave him a shove toward the group on the floor.

Fenton didn't say a word, but his hate-filled gaze spoke volumes. Jessica nodded to Trevor, who reached out and slapped Garza across the back of the head.

Trevor's slap was like a punch to the smaller man, and Garza's head fell forward, slamming his face into the surface of the holotable.

"That was a bit harder than I wanted," Jessica said with a sigh.

"I didn't expect him to be so spindly," Trevor shrugged. "Thought he'd have spinal mods or something."

Jessica held out a hand, and Trevor tossed her a pulse rifle before picking up another. They approached the group of Orion Guard personnel on the ground, glanced at one another, and opened fire.

* * * * *

"Hey, whoa," Usef said as he raised his hands. "I can see how you probably don't like interference, but this is a bit extreme."

"You're damn right I don't like interference," Phyla said with an ugly sneer. "So, which are you? Transcend or a colonist?"

Usef glanced around the engineering command center and saw that several specialists were holding weapons on Misha and Cargo.

"Great plan," Misha called out. "Sure glad we followed your lead."

Usef gave his best smile. "I don't know why you think we're colonists, or Sendies, for fucksakes, but we're not; we just transferred off another ship to augment the old man's staff. Look us up, we're on the roster."

"I looked you up, all right," Major Phyla replied. "Your orders seemed a bit off, so I tossed a tightbeam over to the *Sword of Orion*, and, sure enough, they've never heard of you."

"Major Phyla! We're running silent. No EMF at all; you've just breached a directive from the admiral. I'm going to have to report this…along with behavior unbecoming of an officer in the Guard. I'll leave out the part where you're holding a firearm on me, if you put it down right now."

Phyla cocked her head and widened her eyes in mock distress. "Oh, will you? Oh, *sir,* that would be so wonderful…. Now, drop your fucking sidearm and get on the ground!"

<Iris was certain they wouldn't reach out to another ship,> Jamie sighed in Usef's mind. *<I'll have to give her a hard time about that later.>*

<So, are we ready? She's gonna blow my head off in five seconds.>

<I haven't received a confirmation from each of the HC's that Cargo and Misha placed…some of these guys may not go down,> Jamie replied.

<No time, do it,> Usef ordered.

An instant later, all but four of the Orion Guard engineers fell. Cargo and Misha wasted no time in firing pulse blasts at the enemy while the element of surprise was on their side.

"Kinda thought our little fiction would hold up longer than that," Cargo said as he approached Usef. "We usually had better luck out in Perseus."

"Seriously?" Misha asked as he fired a pulse blast into the torso of an engineer he passed. "Have you forgotten half the shit we went through in Perseus?"

"Why'd you shoot that woman?" Usef scowled at Misha.

Misha shrugged. "She was moving. The HC probably didn't work on her, so she was faking. I shot her in the chest, not the head. She'll be fine."

"I'm not worried about her, just stay focused," Usef said. "No games, no heroic shit. Jamie is running through their logs looking for some issue we can fake that requires running a reset on some system that will explain why no one is communicating down here."

<Got it,> Jamie announced triumphantly. *<They recently had a new NSAI node installed down here, and I just knocked it out—though it wasn't easy. Their AIs barely live up to the name, poor bastards, but their NSAIs are top notch. Remind me of the super-nodes back in Sol.>*

"Good. I lifted Phyla's tokens when we took her out, so I can mimic her for basic status reports—though I didn't get anything that will let me access higher-level feeds," Usef added.

<I'm in the nav systems,> Hank announced. *<Tapping into helm control. Jamie, you're going to have to knock out node 14.19.12 when I give the word, or the bridge will be able to work around me.>*

<Got it,> Jamie replied. *<Just waiting on the word from Iris.>*

"I've got the door," Cargo said as he walked to the command center's main entrance. "I may have to let insistent people in, so be on your toes."

"Never understood that saying," Misha said as he moved to the room's rear entrance. "I think that being on your toes would just be painful and distracting."

* * * * *

<*Linkup from Jamie and the team yet?*> Jessica asked Iris.

<*No, not a thing; but there's a big NSAI outage in a new node down there, so my money is on them making a mess of things to stay off the radar…sort of,*> Iris replied.

<*Sort of?*> Trevor asked.

Iris twisted her avatar's lips in their minds. <*Well, a rapid response unit is on its way to help them repair the NSAI node, so they're about to get some company.*>

<*Can we tell them we're ready to go somehow?*> Jessica asked.

<*Not sure how. Like I said, I can't reach them.*>

Trevor brought a system up on the holotank. "What about this; can we trigger it remotely, say, in the engineering command center?"

"Trevor, you're a genius!" Jessica grinned.

"I do have my moments," Trevor replied. "I don't know how to trigger a remote fire alarm, though, but the system doesn't have a lot of security on it."

<*Fire suppression systems rarely do,*> Iris responded and the holotable changed its view to show the status of the engineering command center. <*But if I flip this bit right here, and that one there, we suddenly have access to their heat and chem sniffers, and voila! There's now a fire in the engineering bay.*>

Red strobes began flashing on the bulkheads, and a call went out over the ship's audible announcement system. "Fire fire fire! Say again, fire in the ECC! All response crews to emergency stations; secondary ECC, prepare to come online."

"Hmm…" Jessica mused, "that may have been too much."

Trevor gave her a broad smile. "Well, at least there's no way they can miss that."

* * * * *

"What?" Cargo asked. "What fire?"

"Maybe one of these assholes is still conscious and triggered it," Misha suggested.

"It's the signal from Jessica," Usef said. "Let's make sure none of those teams get in, and let the AIs steer this tub out of here."

<*Firing starboard grav thrusters,*> Hank announced. <*Give me two minutes, and we'll have a clear path to boost out of here.*>

"I bet that captain on the bridge is having kittens right now," Misha chuckled.

<*That might be us in a moment,*> Jamie cut in. <*They're bringing that secondary ECC online, and it has direct access to nav and helm. I don't know if we can work around it.*>

<*There has to be a cutoff system to revert back to the ECC,*> Hank said, and Usef knew the AIs were talking over the team's channel for the humans' benefit.

"I see a system here," Usef offered, "but we don't have the encryption keys to access it. The damn thing's locked out."

<*Need a hand?*> a new voice asked over the Link.

<*Nance?*> Cargo asked. <*Shouldn't you guys be EM-silent?*>

<*The way the* Britannica *is jerking around trumps that. It looks like you're fighting for helm control.*>

<*That's putting it mildly,*> Iris replied in clipped tones.

<*Have you tried this?*> Nance asked, and suddenly the primary override system Usef was attempting to brute-force his way into unlocked.

<*Well, shit,*> Usef said as he activated the cut-over, granting full helm control to Hank.

<*There you go, the ship no longer looks like a drunken duck trying to keep up with the flock,*>

Nance announced. <*We're shadowing you out of the fleet.*>

"General Quarters, General Quarters, we have intruders in the primary ECC," the audible systems boomed. "Maintain low EMF ship-wide—the fleet is still on target."

"Well, looks like we're going to get to do our part now," Cargo said with a grim smile.

<*Just don't get your head blown off,*> Hank said brusquely. <*This'll be a real short flight, otherwise.*>

* * * * *

<*I've managed to get into their external comm arrays,*> Iris announced. <*Though the ship's secondary AI is fighting me hard.*>

"They have a secondary one?" Trevor asked as he took up a position behind a holotable, two rifles aimed at the CIC's door.

<*Yes, and a third, actually. I really don't understand how their duties work, but since they're not much more than L2 humans, I can see why a single one can't run a ship like this.*>

<*Any word from Tanis?*> Jessica asked.

<*Not yet, but that shouldn't stop us from getting out of here,*> Iris replied.

"We're not going anywhere," Trevor said as the CIC's door began to glow.

"Going to have to hope that they get this bird out of the fleet before Tanis does her big move, then," Jessica replied grimly as she checked her rifles, and set them to fire kinetics at whomever came through the door first.

FALL BACK

STELLAR DATE: 04.01.8948 (Adjusted Years)
LOCATION: Landfall Space/Air Traffic Control Center
REGION: Knossos Island Carthage, New Canaan System

Ouri shook her head as she fired another round from her weapon's slug thrower at an onrushing enemy soldier. Whoever was in charge out there had no compunctions about spending their soldier's lives in an attempt to take the SATC tower.

If she were a betting woman, she'd put money on the company CO being on the transport Henderson had shot down, and that some fresh-out-of-OCS second lieutenant was running the show out there.

The enemy soldiers fell back again, but this time, no further sounds came from outside. Ouri counted to thirty—that was the threshold she had set in her mind for how long it would take them to move heavy weapons to the fore.

It was a guess, really; the external cameras were all down, and the enemy had set off three EM blasts, knocking out most of her nanoprobes.

Her count hit thirty, and she signaled for Sammy and Bill to get up to the third floor. She peered out from behind the CFT, prepared to give them cover, when her fears were confirmed.

The Trisilieds were setting up a crew-served kinetic repeater right outside the facility. It would tear the staircase to shreds, and, more importantly, anyone who was on it.

She raced up the stairs to the third level landing as the weapon opened fire and ripped into the stairs, sending stone and plascrete flying into the air. After fifteen seconds of fire, the weapons wound down.

The dust and smoke was still thick in the air as the enemy, three dozen at least, rushed in at full-force, all firing on the third floor landing.

Ouri and her team scampered back from the edge as the concentrated firepower began to blow holes clear through the landing.

"Well," Ouri gasped as they fell back into the hall, "at least they can't take the stairs anymore."

She floated some probes over the ruined staircase, and saw the enemy scaling the wall to get into the second floor corridor. With a grim smile, Ouri dropped a pair of grenades over what remained of the landing, and ducked back as the blast sounded, kicking up more dust and debris.

As the room cleared, she could see that the enemy had fallen back once more, and wondered if any had managed to reach the second level.

A minute later, an explosion in the rear stairwell answered her question.

<*Rear access turrets just picked up motion!*> Amy called out over the Link. <*I don't read our IFF tags out there. Should I light 'em up?*>

<*Only if it looks like they've found the rear exit,*> Ouri replied. <*No reason to pointing it out early.*>

<*Shit, yeah, they're right on top of it. I'll hold 'em off as long as I can.*>

"Kris, Sammy," Ouri called out to her two teammates who were inspecting the rear stairwell, "get back up to the control room. Trissies are coming in the back door."

"Shit! Seriously?" Bill asked. "There goes our way out."

<*Murry! Any chance we can get a hand here soon?*> Ouri called out to the Planetary Management AI. <*We're about to become the mystery meat in a Trissie sandwich.*>

<*I've updated Brandt with your situation,*> Murry replied in clipped tones. <*Things are tight everywhere, but she's going to see what she can do.*>

<*Tell her I'll buy her beers for the rest of her life,*> Ouri replied.

"OK, Bill," she said audibly. "It's just you and me on the crew-served gun now. You keep the ammo coming, and an eye to the back stairwell. They're gonna hit us from both ends. Lob 'nades down the hall if they bunch up."

"Yeah, sure," Bill said breathlessly as sweat poured down his face.

"Hey, Bill," Ouri grabbed his shoulder. "We're gonna make it. Brandt is coming, and we're winning in space. We just have to hold out for a little longer."

Bill met her eyes and he swallowed before nodding. "Understood, Colonel."

"Good, now let's give these asshats hell."

EXFILTRATE

STELLAR DATE: 04.01.8948 (Adjusted Years)
LOCATION: OGS *Britannica*
REGION: Stellar North of Carthage, New Canaan System

"ISF fleet just appeared on scan!" Usef called out as he fired a full clip at the enemy soldiers pouring through the ECC's entrance. "They're gonna do it. Full boost!"

<*Get bow-side of something solid,*> Hank ordered. <*I'm going to kill gravity aft of the CIC and do 20gs.*>

Usef scampered around the holotable he was using for cover, and prayed that Cargo and Misha managed to get situated before Hank killed the artificial gravity systems. The stomach-twisting feeling of weightlessness hit him, and a moment later, the ship's engines dumped billions of exajoules into space.

His back slammed into the table, and a sharp edge sliced his skin open. Usef staunched the flow of blood with his nano, and then peered around the table to see how the enemy soldiers had fared.

With 'down' now being the aft end of the ECC, most of enemy soldiers had 'fallen' a dozen meters; though many were in armor, and weathered the fall without too much trouble.

Still, they were now shooting straight up with little cover—only the bodies of no few of their fellow OG crew that had fallen on top of them.

Usef felt a little sorry for the unconscious engineers that had fallen as far as thirty meters to the back of the bay, but the choices were limited. Either fall, or get eaten by the things in the dark layer.

He knew what he would have picked.

Usef saw shots lance down from two other positions as he opened fire on the enemy soldiers once more. <*Glad you guys survived that little maneuver,*> he told the shooters over the combat net.

<*Yeah, thanks for the whole second's worth of warning, Hank,*> Misha grumbled.

Jamie chuckled. <*He gave you three seconds—plenty, even for a slow organic like you.*>

<*This is why I've never opted for an AI,*> Misha grunted. <*You guys have the worst attitudes.*>

Cargo barked a laugh. <*That's a great one coming from you, Misha.*>

Several soldiers at the bottom of the bay had surrendered, throwing their weapons down and pulling their helmets off. Misha fired two more shots down on a pocket that was holding out.

<*Yeah? I have a great attitude! I saved your asses back when you first showed up in Perseus. I've been **very** helpful.*>

<*At complaining, maybe,*> Cargo responded.

Usef shook his head as he fired a focused pulse blast into an unarmored member of the fire response team that was peeking through the ECC's rear entrance. <*Seriously? Is this the best time for this little chat?*>

<*Sorry, Colonel,*> Misha chuckled. <*It helps us focus.*>

<*You guys want a hand?*> Admiral Evans's voice joined into their conversation. <*Or are*

you having too much fun in there?>

<*Admiral Evans, sir, your help is always welcome,*> Jamie replied.

<*Good. Patch me through to their all-ship net and audible systems, if you have them.*>

Jamie sent an affirmative signal, and a moment later, Joe's voice boomed over the ship's address system.

"This is Admiral Joseph Evans of the ISF *Daedalus*. Your fleet is destroyed or disabled. You've lost this battle. Stand down and prepare to be boarded. If you want to put up a fight, be sure to say hello to the battalion of ISF Marines who are cutting their way through your hull as I speak."

"He has a way with words, doesn't he?" Cargo commented.

Misha laughed as the final group of soldiers at the bottom of the bay threw down their weapons and pulled off their helmets. "I really like you ISF guys. You're a ton of fun!" he remarked.

<*Looks like you guys made it,*> Jessica's voice joined the combat net.

<*Yes, ma'am,*> Usef replied. <*Got a bit hairy. How was it up there?*>

<*Don't be ma'am-ing me,*> Jessica replied. <*You outrank me now, remember?*>

<*No, ma'am, I don't.*> Usef grinned over the combat net.

<*Fine. We got our man, and the admiral of their fleet, too. All nice and locked down. We'll have intel coming out of our ears before long,*> Jessica replied.

"Good thing," Usef whispered to himself as Iris reactivated the AG systems and the shift in gravity rolled him over. "I have a feeling that we're gonna need it."

THE STAND

STELLAR DATE: 04.01.8948 (Adjusted Years)
LOCATION: Landfall Space/Air Traffic Control Center
REGION: Knossos Island Carthage, New Canaan System

Ouri hauled the crew-served gun up to the first landing of the staircase to the fourth floor. She had hoped to hold the corridor below, but there were just too many enemy soldiers coming up at both ends of the hall. Bill was already up there, having retreated that far after his right leg was burned off from the knee down.

Biofoam covered the wound, and he held his rifle ready, a look of grim determination on his face. She gave him a solemn look. They would hold out as long as they could. There was nothing else they could do.

Even though they had to run into point-blank kinetic weapons fire, the enemy still came at them. Before long, a dozen bodies lay at the base of the stairs.

They just had to hold out a little longer. The team upstairs was still taking out enemy assault craft near Landfall and on the other side of Carthage. If the SATC fell, thousands would still die.

The Marines are coming…just have to hold a little bit longer.

Ouri glanced at the ammo box for her gun, and then her eyes met Bill's. The box was empty; the fifty rounds on the current string were all that remained.

"When it runs dry, you get up the stairs," Bill said. "I'll hold them here as long as I can."

"Fuck, Bill. No. I'll stay, you get up there—"

Her words were interrupted by another group of soldiers dashing into view in the space below them. Ouri opened fire with the gun and took them out, though not before a shot tore through her armor below her right breast.

She fell back, catching sight of the last rounds feeding through the railgun as Bill screamed, firing into the enemy soldiers below.

Both Bill and the final soldier fell, and Ouri pulled herself to Bill's side. She let out a small cry; the left half of his skull was missing.

She grabbed his rifle and turned away, laying prone on the landing, using the crew-served gun for cover. She felt biofoam filling her wound as a new onslaught from the enemy began.

She screamed at the enemy below her, firing the last rounds from both magazines. Then a blinding light flashed in her mind, and she knew no more.

*****

The last of the enemy coming up the rear corridor fell, and Sammy traded a long, weary look with Kris as Amy called out from behind them.

"They're here! The Marines are here!"

"About fucking time," Kris said as she fell back against the wall.

<Ouri, the Marines are here! Ouri, we're saved!> Sammy called out to the Colonel, relief filling her mental voice.

When no response came, she stood and looked across the consoles at Amy. "I can't raise the colonel, can you?"

Amy met her eyes, and she shook her head slowly.

Sammy didn't wait another moment—she dashed across the control room and out into the hall. She sped down its darkened length, taking a moment to wonder when the power went out, before skidding to a halt and running down the stairs, nearly smashing into the barrel of a Marine's rifle.

"Easy," he said softly, and Sammy's eyes followed his to the bodies of Bill and Ouri, crumpled on the landing.

"NO!" Sammy screamed and dropped to her knees. Sobs wracked her body and she felt a hand on her shoulder.

"I'm sorry," a voice croaked. "If we'd just…."

Sammy looked up to see none other than General Brandt herself standing over Ouri's body, her helmet on the ground at her feet.

Tears flowed down the hard-bitten Marine's face as she fell and leaned against the wall. "Ouri, I'm so sorry…."

DARK LAYER

STELLAR DATE: 04.01.8948 (Adjusted Years)
LOCATION: ISS *I2*
REGION: Stellar North of Carthage, New Canaan System

Tanis reconnected with Admiral Myra, who looked rather put out at being cut off. "Have you changed your mind?" the Trisilieds commander asked.

"I have not," Tanis shook her head and let out a long breath as the anger flowed out of her. She just felt tired—tired, and anxious for all this to be over. "I know about the Orion Guard ships bearing down on us; they won't survive this engagement, either. This is your last chance."

Admiral Myra's eyes widened and her face blanched. "How..."

Tanis waved her hand dismissively. "We haven't just been trapped in this system. We know much of what is going on in the Inner Stars and in Orion space."

"Nice bluff," Admiral Myra laughed. "You almost had me for a moment. Very well; if you won't surrender, and you know about the Orion Guard, then what happens next won't surprise you."

This time, it was Admiral Myra who cut the communication.

<*You always do lay it on too thick,*> Angela commented.

<*Or not thick enough.*>

As though on cue, the Orion Guard fleet appeared. One group of over fifty thousand ships lay three hundred thousand kilometers north of Carthage, and another was equidistant below it.

Tanis opened a comm channel with Sabrina. <*Do you have him?*>

Light-lag made the reply take several seconds to come back to the *I2;* when it did, the message was what Tanis had hoped to hear.

<*We have him. We're clear.*>

Tanis sent the signal to Fleet Groups 3 and 4, and several seconds later the ships appeared on scan—not across the system guarding the shipyards at the gas giants, but above and below the Orion Guard fleets.

Their combined three thousand ships were laughably outnumbered by the Orion Guard, but that wouldn't matter. If all went well, they wouldn't even fire a shot—at least not the sort of shot that the Guard ships expected.

<*ISF Fleet. Order B99-4329.11. Open it up,*> Tanis sent the command, and the fleet AIs and captains unlocked and opened special orders they didn't even know they had, directing them to activate beam weapons that they didn't know their ships possessed.

The timing needed to be precise. Once the orders were confirmed across the fleet, Tanis set the countdown.

Then she held her breath.

Despite her words of certainty to Finaeus, she really had no idea if this would work. Bob and Earnest were very certain they could close the rifts after they made them—not one hundred percent, but very.

Tanis would take it. If they were wrong, then this war would end with all their deaths, and that would be enough for her.

The count hovering above the holotank ran down to zero, and specialized graviton beams lanced out from every one of Joe's and Sanderson's ships, and into positions around the enemy fleets. Space-time began to warp, and darkness blotted out the light of Canaan Prime.

The blackness opened up all around the Trisilieds and Orion Guard ships, and then things came boiling out into space.

Optical sensors couldn't see them, but the creatures—if they could be called that—created silhouettes on other spectra that made them visible to scan. They were elongated and amorphous. Some were only a few hundred meters long; others, over a hundred kilometers.

Tendrils of darkness rippled out from the things and wrapped around the enemy ships, cutting through shields and hulls alike. Scan couldn't even make a guess as to what the creatures we made of, but Earnest had told Tanis that he believed it was a combination of exotic forms of matter, and energy that had never been seen in the natural physical universe.

Tanis wondered if the things had been constructed by the ascended AIs in the Core, or if those AIs had found the things and moved them around humanity's stars to keep them in check.

"Shit," Sera whispered. "They're obliterating the ships."

Tanis nodded. "That's the plan."

Not all of the enemy ships were being destroyed. Some were boosting away, fleeing the rifts to the dark layer as fast as they could—but many were not fast enough.

One massive dreadnaught, almost a rival for the *I2* in mass, raced toward the ISF ships, and it looked as though it would escape the creatures, when one of the hundred-kilometer things appeared to leap across space, and completely envelop the ship.

"OK," Tanis said. "That's getting a bit too close. Time to close it up."

<*Agreed,*> Bob replied. <*If they reach the planet, they could consume its mass in a day.*>

Tanis watched as Bob activated one of the *I2*'s sensor grids to emit a signal that drove the creature back toward the rifts, leaving the twisted wreck of the carrier in its wake. She passed a command to the fleets, and all the ships followed suit, pushing the things back into the rift—many of which dragged the ships of the Orion and Trisilieds fleets along with them.

As the creatures and their prey disappeared back into the dark layer, and the ISF ships disabled their beams that held the rifts open, Tanis surveyed the battlespace.

Of the hundred thousand Orion ships, only two thousand remained intact; though ten times that number were scattered around Carthage, twisted and ruined. She saw that Admiral Myra's flagship was still present, and hailed the enemy commander.

It took half a minute before Myra's visage appeared on the holotank. Her hair was disheveled, and her cheeks were streaked with tears. Wide, staring eyes gazed out at Tanis as her mouth worked soundlessly.

"How…?" she finally managed to ask.

To which Tanis only replied, "Surrender."

Myra's eyes fell and she nodded slowly. "I yield."

GENERAL'S DECEPTION

STELLAR DATE: 04.02.8948 (Adjusted Years)
LOCATION: OGS *Similcarum*
REGION: 120AU from Canaan Prime, New Canaan System

General Garza felt as though the deck had dropped out from under him as he watched the destruction of the Orion Guard fleet, followed by the surrender of the remaining Trisilieds ships.

So many lives lost in such a short time. He had sent in what should have been an overwhelming force—even with the Hegemony ships attacking hours ahead of schedule, and even with the Canners possessing picobombs, it should have been an easy win.

There was still some chance that the Trisilieds ground forces could capture someone significant and force a surrender, but the odds of that were astronomically low.

It was far more likely that his ship would be detected as it drifted beyond the system's heliopause.

"Helm, set a course for the Transcend's jump gate. Let's make use of it before the Canners retake it."

He didn't wait for a response before leaving the bridge and retreating to his cabin.

Garza had to admit that Tanis Richards's use of the dark layer creatures was a brilliant tactic. One that had been tried before—though not successfully, as far as he knew.

In every instance he was aware of, the creatures were not so easily sent back into the dark layer. In one case, they never were; a star had died as a result, and an ever-growing region of space around it was interdicted.

Perhaps, once this war was over, he would use whatever technology the Canners had come up with to clean up that mess.

As he took a ladder down to the officer's deck, Garza wondered what things his clone may have learned before it died. He had looked forward to merging his thoughts with it and gaining its experiences—a euphoric experience that he quite enjoyed, notwithstanding the new things he'd learn.

He did hope that his clone had died a quick death, consumed by the creatures. Better that than to be captured by the Canners—though he knew that they would learn little through the torture they would surely employ. The clone did not possess his most important memories. Even so, he would not wish such a fate on anyone; especially himself.

He had read of Tanis Richards's brutality when she was an officer in the Terran Space Force. She was not a woman to be trifled with—as his defeat here showed all too clearly.

Garza palmed the door to his cabin open, and crossed the room to his small bar, where he pulled a bottle of brandy out of its case and poured himself four fingers' worth of the light brown liquid.

He swirled it in the glass, enjoying the aroma before throwing it back in two gulps. He poured another and sat at his desk. He would need to go to Kirkland directly with this news. The praetor would not be happy to learn that their plan had failed so spectacularly.

It may be wise to send in a clone.

DISCOVERY

STELLAR DATE: 04.02.8948 (Adjusted Years)
LOCATION: Wreckage of Trisilieds Halcyon Class Carrier
REGION: In Orbit of Hannibal, Carthage, New Canaan System

<*Cary,*> Saanvi called out into the void via the Link, praying her suit's signal could reach far enough to connect to her sister, if she were still there. <*Cary?*>

She had opened her eyes and immediately closed them again. The scene around her didn't bear mental processing; yet she couldn't keep herself from stepping through the logical path that brought her to her current location.

Saanvi remembered the last few moments before the *Illyria* slammed into the Trisilieds' Halcyon Class carrier, apparently making a large enough hole for the RMs tailing their ship to go through and destroy it. Cary had withdrawn from her mind, leaving her feeling profoundly empty and alone—rather like she did right now.

Their eyes had locked, and their lips whispered their love for one another before the chairs snapped on their stasis fields. The stasis fields should have held them until rescue, but the field could not be maintained from within—which meant that the external systems must have been destroyed.

And now she found herself here: still strapped to her chair from the bridge, but inside what must be one of the *Illyria*'s machine shops—or maybe it was one from the Trisilieds carrier. The chance that Cary was anywhere nearby was slim, to say the least. With any luck, her sister was still in stasis, blissfully unaware that they were trapped within a twisted cocoon of ship guts that was in a slowly decaying orbit around Hannibal.

<*Sahn?*> the response was weak; not a Link connection, but an RF signal her suit was picking up and sending into her mind.

<*Hey, little sis,*> Saanvi replied. <*Gods in Swargaloka, it's good to hear your voice.*>

<*Voice…yeah. I'm pretty sure I'm not breathing right now; good thing this suit can still oxygenate my blood directly,*> Cary said, her mental tone wan.

<*My readout says my left lung is punctured, but my right is working…sorta,*> Saanvi replied. <*Pain suppressors are also only kinda working.*>

<*I hear you,*> Cary's mental voice carried a note of desperation. <*Who's stupid idea was this, anyway?*>

<*Beats me,*> Saanvi thought with a smile. <*Glad we did it, though. If those carriers had made it to Carthage…*>

Neither girl spoke for a moment, and then the thought crept into Saanvi's mind that Cary was gone.

<*Cary! Are you still there?*>

<*Yeah, just needed to not think for a minute. I keep worrying that we lost, anyway; that our home…that Carthage is gone…*>

Saanvi knew that fear; it was in her mind, as well. She pushed it away. She had to be strong for her little sister.

<*No way, Cary. Our mom is Admiral Tanis Richards—the most serious badass in the galaxy. Nothing can take her down.*>

<*I hope we did her proud,*> Cary replied, her voice growing faint as she spoke. It took

Saanvi a moment to realize that it wasn't signal degradation, but rather her sister slipping into unconsciousness.

<*Cary!*> Saanvi called out. <*You stay awake, you keep talking! I'm your big sister, I'm ordering you to!*>

A faint chuckle entered her mind. <*I'm the lieutenant; you're just an ensign. You can't order me to do anything…I just need to sleep for a minute…*>

<*I can, too!*> Saanvi called. <*Big sisters trump rank. You stay awake, no sleeping!*>

<*OK…sis…*>

<*Cary!*> Saanvi screamed with her mind, willing her suit's signal to amplify and somehow wake her sister. A sob escaped her lips, and the movement sent a wave of fire through her body as torn ligaments pulled at broken bones. She gasped from the agony, and then held her breath, forcing her heart to still.

<*Cary?*> she whispered into the darkness again.

Silence was the only response, and Saanvi took long, slow breaths, desperate not to cry—she knew that if she cried, the pain would make her pass out, and she may never wake again. She wasn't going to hide from the darkness again like that. This time, she would be awake and fighting.

The thought made her open her eyes—and that moment was one of the happiest of her life. Through the twisted metal, she saw a light flash in the distance.

<*Hey!*> she called out over her suit's radio, broadcasting on the ISF's emergency signal. She suddenly realized that she hadn't checked to see if her chair or her suit's emergency beacon worked—neither did.

She sent out a manual signal on the emergency channels, and then the worry hit her that these may not be New Canaan rescuers coming for her, but the enemy. She almost stopped transmitting, but her fear of dying alone in the dark overcame her, and she screamed across the radio for help, until the most welcome sound she had ever heard came into her mind.

<*Easy now; we have a fix on you, we'll get you out.*>

The voice was male, warm, and encouraging. Saanvi felt her fears fall away, and she remembered her sister.

<*I'm fine! Find Cary. She's nearby, but she's not responding anymore!*>

<*Cary? Cary Richards?*> the man replied, his voice anxious and excited at the same time.

<*Yes! I'm Saanvi Richards, please find her!*>

There was a moment's silence, and Saanvi imagined a thousand things that could have happened to her rescuer.

<*I think I have a fix on her. I'm sending a crew for her, and I'm coming in for you. Hold tight.*>

RESCUE

STELLAR DATE: 04.02.8948 (Adjusted Years)
LOCATION: ISS *I2*
REGION: High Orbit over Carthage, New Canaan System

<*They found them!*> Angela cried into Tanis's mind. <*They're alive. S&R is taking them to the* Argos*!*>

Tanis sat bolt upright, the realization that she had passed out in Captain Espensen's ready room taking a second to dawn on her. <*Get a shuttle ready, I'm coming to the upper dorsal bay!*>

Tanis was already out the door, dashing through the bridge as she replied, and called out to Rachel Espensen as she passed, "They found them! They're alive!"

Cheers erupted behind her as she raced down the short corridor to the bridge's foyer. She barely sketched a wave to Priscilla on her plinth as she dashed through.

<*Maglev is waiting,*> Priscilla sent her way. <*It will take you right to the bay.*>

<*Thanks!*> Tanis replied breathlessly.

<*Joe is on his way, too,*> Angela supplied. <*He's bringing the* Daedalus *right through the debris field to the* Argos.>

Tanis allowed herself a smile; perhaps the first in the day since the end of the battle with the invaders.

<*Cheater! The* I2 *won't fit in there, no way, no—though he better be careful. The* Daedalus *will be a tight fit, too.*>

Tanis took a moment to look up where Cary and Saanvi had been found. It was deep within a section of the final carrier they had destroyed. Like much of the wreckage from that stage of the battle, the debris was in a low, decaying orbit around Hannibal. She flipped to the portion of the report describing the girls' conditions, steeling herself for what she would see.

Tears formed in her eyes, and she placed a hand over her mouth, attempting to stifle a gasp, when she saw the images. Both of the girls' bodies were still in their chairs from the bridge, but neither was in stasis. Their faces were misshapen from broken cheekbones, and both their jaws were dislocated. Their formfitting environmental suits revealed sunken chests and broken hipbones.

The onsite rescuers' report estimated that they had suffered multiple impacts in excess of 100*g*s. Only their cranial implants—a part of their L2 elevation—had kept their skulls from collapsing, keeping their brains safe.

The sob Tanis had been trying to hold back escaped her throat just as the maglev doors closed and gave her a private space to let her grief overcome her. She prayed to whatever gods may exist in the depths of space that her girls hadn't suffered brain damage.

She reopened the report and saw that Saanvi was conscious, though just barely, and had related that Cary was communicating just a few minutes before their rescue. That was a good sign—though it certainly didn't mean that all was well.

Tanis pushed those worries from her mind. She had to hope for the best. The girls' bodies could be rebuilt—though that much damage would take some time to recover from—and they were strong, and their neural networks were recently imaged. It would be possible to recover from even moderate brain damage, if needed.

A new report came in from the S&R crew that the girls were safely in stasis pods. A shuttle was taking them to the *Argos*—with an ETA of forty minutes.

The maglev car stopped at the docking bay, and Tanis raced to the shuttle, her only thought that it would take her three hours to reach the *Argos* where it rested deep in the debris field, and she needed to be present when her daughters awoke.

A thought flashed into her mind that she was being selfish. She had work to do, prisoners to interrogate, defenses to review. Nearly everyone in New Canaan had lost family in the last two days. What made her so special that she could run off like this?

<I'll keep things running in your absence, and Jason is governor now. He has things in hand on Carthage,> Bob spoke into her mind. *<You need to put these worries to rest, and go see your daughters. Your work here is just beginning.>*

<Thank you,> Tanis managed to reply.

<Be careful in there,> Bob advised, as the ramp to the pinnace raised even as Tanis dashed up its length into the ship. *<Not all of the disabled enemy ships are surrendering quietly.>*

Tanis nodded in response as she dropped into the small cockpit's pilot's chair, and ran an abbreviated pre-flight check before signaling for clearance. The *I2*'s space traffic control NSAI gave it, and she lanced out into the night, diving toward Hannibal and the hospital ship that would soon receive her daughters.

* * * * *

Tanis clutched Joe's hand as they watched through the window while the autodoc worked on Cary's body under the guidance of a team of surgeons. Saanvi was already out of surger—her bones reset and organs repairing. It would take days for them to properly reknit—there was only so much rapid change a human body could undergo. It still needed to grow its own cells.

She had considered instructing the doctors to replace much of her girls' ruined bodies with artificial components—it would make their recovery that much faster—but she decided against it. That was their decision to make, and she could wait until they healed organically and she could speak with them.

In the room, one of the surgeons nodded, and the machine wrapped around Cary's head retracted the hundreds of tendrils from her skull. He turned and looked at them through the window, giving a firm nod followed by a thumbs-up.

Tanis sagged into Joe. "Thank the stars," she whispered.

Joe stroked her arm then pulled her into an embrace. "They're young, they're strong; we'll have them back with us in no time."

The surgeon exited the room and approached the pair.

"She's in good shape. Her neural lattice held up well against the impacts, and she only lost three percent of her brain-tissue. Most of it was in muscle control regions, so she'll have a bit of work to do relearning how to walk, and trouble controlling her left hand for a bit, but that should be it."

"Cognitive functionality?" Tanis asked anxiously.

"Should be fine," the surgeon replied. "I can't say with one hundred percent certainty, of course, but we had her neural network on file, and as best we can tell while she's unconscious, all appears to be firing as it should be."

"Thank you, doctor," Joe said and shook the man's hand, while Tanis turned back toward the window and watched as the other doctors worked on Cary's remaining injuries.

<*Saanvi is waking up,*> Angela informed them

Tanis glanced at Joe. "I'll go, you stay here."

Joe shook his head. "Cary is in good hands, let's make sure Saanvi gets a full welcome from both of us when she wakes."

* * * * *

Saanvi felt consciousness return slowly. It didn't hurt as much as she expected, but she worried that pain would return to assault her at any moment. She flipped through her most recent memories, trying to recall where she would be. She remembered the collision, waking up in the dark, reaching out to Cary, and then the rescue.

Cary.

She had to know if her sister was OK. That was worth opening her eyes for. She struggled to do so, but found that she couldn't raise her eyelids. She suspected that there had been some reconstructive surgery. Maybe she'd have eyes like her mother now.

As if her thoughts summoned her, Tanis's voice reached her ears.

"Saanvi, we're here."

"And your sister is OK," Joe's voice followed after. "The S&R teams found you just in time. You did good calling out for help when you did."

Saanvi tried to speak and found that her lips could move, but her voice was a thin rasp. Something touched her lips and her mother's voice came to her.

"Drink this."

The cool liquid washed down her parched throat, almost hurting as it first made contact, then numbing and soothing as it went. Saanvi took a second pull from the straw and then tried to speak again.

"Cary's safe, then? Her brain?" she asked.

"The doctors are confident that all will be well with her when she wakes," Joe said.

Saanvi noted her mother's silence and knew that Tanis felt as she did—they would worry after Cary until she was speaking to them, and they could tell for themselves that she was undamaged.

"Did we win?" Saanvi asked, and then she realized that they must have won if they were all talking.

"We did," Tanis replied before she could amend her question. "We lost a lot of good people, but we won. Carthage and New Canaan are safe."

Saanvi nodded silently. That was what she needed to hear. They had won, they were safe, her sister would be well. Everything could go back to how it was.

She drifted into a peaceful sleep, dreaming of a happy breakfast with her family around their kitchen table, laughing and smiling as they talked about what the future would now hold.

NEW BEGINNINGS

STELLAR DATE: 04.06.8948 (Adjusted Years)
LOCATION: Forward Emitter Lounge, ISS *I2*
REGION: In Orbit of Hannibal, Carthage, New Canaan System

"They'll have had observers out at the edge of the system." Joe said as he and Tanis sat at the bar in the *I2*'s little-known lounge above the ramscoop emitter.

Even though the ship was now built for war, and the ramscoop wasn't needed to ply vast interstellar spaces, the scoop techs had protected their little refuge, and Tanis had supported that initiative.

Besides, no one mixed a drink like their favorite servitor, Steve.

"Of that there is little doubt," Tanis replied and leaned into her husband. "How did we come to this, Joe? I'm going to go down in history as the greatest mass murderer, tyrant, dictator of all time. Parents are going to scare their children with tales of Tanis the Destroyer, who will unleash the horrors of the dark on them if they're not good."

"I think you're being a bit melodramatic, dear," Joe replied as he stroked her hair. "Maybe Tanis the Marauder, but certainly not the Destroyer."

"Joe!" Tanis sat up and gazed crossly into his eyes. "I'm serious! What are we going to do?"

"Follow the plan you laid out while we were still coming here. We knew this could happen—Bob saw it as the most likely eventuality. If you want to be known as the savior of humanity and not its worst villain, then you need to see this through, and win."

"The plan..." Tanis whispered. "The plan saw us lose nearly a hundred thousand people in one day. In one day, Joe! And Ouri—"

She stopped, her voice catching. She didn't trust herself to speak further; people were already looking in her direction.

"I know," Joe replied as he wrapped an arm around her shoulders. "We lost so many friends; Ouri...and so many others, so many of my kids from the academy. I'm going to miss them all."

"Eighteen years," Tanis said quietly. "Eighteen short years was all we got before these...invaders...all showed up."

Tanis wanted to say a lot worse about the enemy fleets that had attacked them; she wanted to scream and rail, but she had to be the resolute leader, the voice of reason. She may no longer be Governor, but Fleet Admiral and Field Marshall was no smaller responsibility.

"We didn't create their avarice," Joe said. "We aren't to blame for what happened."

"No, we just suffered for it, died for it."

"They're heroes, every one of them. They gave their lives to save others."

"Because I ordered them to do it," Tanis said. "I ordered Ouri down there, and I didn't ensure that she got a squad of Marines for protection. Her death is on me, on my lack of foresight."

"You didn't order every action out there—certainly not the ones that Cary and Saanvi took," Joe said with a frown.

"I still can't believe it," Tanis said. "What were they thinking? I mean...to steal a starship is one thing, and Symatra gave them orders and that squadron, but to take out those last two carriers…"

Joe took a sip of his beer. "Reminds me of someone I know."

"I'm no crazy pilot," Tanis replied and arched an eyebrow. "I've read your whole record, remember? If they got that from anyone it's from you."

Joe chuckled. "Fair enough, fair enough. Reminds me a bit of the run I pulled back at Makemake—or the one at Triton before that."

"You're going to have to make sure that they temper that bravery with some caution at the academy. I know I can't stop them from enlisting, but I'm not going to lose them to this war."

"Trust me, I'll see to it personally," Joe replied.

Tanis's eyes widened. There hadn't been time to discuss it with Joe, but she assumed he would come with her when she left. "You know I'm leaving. You're coming with me."

Joe took her hands, clasping them together. "Tanis Richards, you are my heart; you know that—but you also know I can't. We lost too many. I have to build the academy and the training facilities back up. This system will take years to recover; when you leave, they'll feel abandoned. If I stay, it will lessen that. It has to happen."

Tanis didn't speak for a minute. She didn't trust herself to, either audibly or mentally. Then she gave a slow nod, her eyes never leaving Joe's.

"OK, three years. That's the most I can do. You come with the girls when they graduate, I'll need them by then. We'll all need them, if Cary can really do what I do."

Joe chuckled. "She may have got her crazy bravado from me, but that…that she got from you—the both of you, I bet. She's going to need a special AI."

<*I have just the one in mind,*> Angela joined in the conversation.

"Oh?" Tanis asked. "Do I know her?"

<*Oh, I imagine you will,*> Angela replied. <*This is a big question…and I hadn't planned on asking it now, but what the hell. How do the two of you feel about creating a child with me? I know enough of your minds to do it without your direct intervention, but I would really like to bring her into being with you picking the best parts of yourselves to draw from.*>

Tanis felt a spark of joy as she considered the idea. She had always wanted another daughter, but the idea of bringing one into being with Angela, and then leaving it alone was not a welcome one. She wanted to know her children, not abandon them.

"I think that is a great idea, Angela," Joe replied. "What better fit for Cary than a child of our minds—" he caught Tanis's eye and his brow lowered. "What is it?"

"I'll never know her!" Tanis exclaimed. "She'll grow up without me—I…I'm sorry, I'm feeling out of sorts right now. It's been a trying few days."

<*I understand your fear,*> Angela said. <*I'll only know her for a short time, as well; but AIs grow up much faster than humans—ours will reach her age of majority in only a year. We won't leave her before she understands the significance of what we're doing.*>

"And she'll have her sisters and me," Joe added. "And in just a few years, we'll rejoin you, and we'll all work to finish this thing together."

Tanis let out a long breath that she hadn't realized she was holding. "OK, let's go see what the girls think of about having a sister."

* * * * *

"It itches," Saanvi complained. "Gods in Swarga, it itches."

Cary laughed. "Where?"

"Where? You brat!" Saanvi exclaimed and threw a pillow at her sister. "Everywhere, that's where."

Cary raised an arm to swat the incoming tassel-covered missile aside and gasped. "Gah, you tricked me into doing that. Arm…not…ready…to move so fast."

"You deserve it," Saanvi said with a mock scowl. "Next time, we skip the last carrier…the other one's detonation probably would have taken it out, anyway."

"Hard to say," Cary replied. "You were on helm; why didn't you avoid it?"

"Me?" Saanvi sputtered. "It was *us*. We were deep-Linked."

"I know, Sahn. I was kidding. I think we did the right thing. Everyone else seems to, as well. If those fighters had gotten down to Carthage, Ouri—"

Saanvi reached out and touched her sister's hand. "Ouri and the SATC wouldn't have been able to take out so many assault craft. We would have lost Carthage."

"Still lost too much," Cary said. "Our lake has two of the T's drop ships in it…polluting our water. Who's going to look after the horses?"

"JP sent a message that he got them over to his place," Saanvi replied. "Didn't you see it in your queue?"

"Maybe he just sent it to you," Cary winked. "He's got a serious thing for you. I bet he joined the academy just to be near you."

"What?" Saanvi asked. "JP? He's like a brother; we've known him forever. I can't think of him like that."

Saanvi thought about some of her most recent conversations with JP. He had seemed extra worried about them going off to fly the *Andromeda* to the Gamma III base.

"Stars…that feels like a lifetime ago," Saanvi said. "Is it really just a few months since we left Carthage to take *Rommy* to Gamma III?"

"I know what you mean," Cary sighed. "I can barely believe that was even the same lifetime."

"War changes you," Saanvi said in a serious voice, imitating their mother.

Cary laughed and then raised her hand as she began to cough. "Seriously? Sahn, no funnies. I'm not all put back together yet."

"Speaking of Mom, what are the parents doing back so soon? I thought they had a hot date up in that lounge they like so much?"

*****

Cary and Saanvi were sitting on the bench on the cabin's porch as Tanis and Joe approached.

Tanis watched the pair of girls as they chatted idly about whatever was on their minds; probably the battle and what they had been through—the aftermath of which was still being felt every day, as new memorial services were scheduled for the thousands of humans and hundreds of AIs who had perished in defense of New Canaan.

Perhaps this news, this idea, would bring a smile to their faces—something that had been in short supply in the days since the battle.

"Mom, Dad! What are you doing back so soon?" Saanvi called out when she saw them approach.

Cary turned as well, slowly and gingerly, her body still far from being fully healed. "I thought you guys were on a hot date?"

Joe flashed a grin at the girls and took Tanis's hand as they walked up the cabin's steps.

"We sure were, but we realized that there's something we really need to talk about."

The two girls shared a long look before slowly nodding.

"Are we well enough now for you to tear a strip off us for taking a ship?" Cary asked nervously. "Because if that's what's up, I think I still need to do more healing first."

"Oh, no," Joe said with a mischievous grin. "We already have that punishment mapped out."

The girls' faces paled and Saanvi asked, "Oh? Do we even want to know?"

Joe glanced at Tanis who nodded before he responded. "There was a moment or two when we considered barring you from the academy—"

"What!?" the girls cried out in unison.

"Easy, easy now," Joe said with a smile. "We're going to let you in, but your JROTC ranks have been stripped. You're going into OTA with no privileges of any sort. In fact, you are going to find a host of unpleasant duties waiting for you."

"Seriously?" Cary gasped. "We kicked ass out there, we saved lives!"

"Yes, you did, a lot of lives. You two are heroes," Tanis said, pausing to keep tears from welling up—something that had been happening a lot lately. She took a deep breath before continuing. "And that is what is saving you from a court martial. You broke just about every reg in the books. Your success and bravery is the only thing keeping the inquiry from recommending that course of action."

"Inquiry?" Saanvi asked. "You convened an inquiry?"

"No," Joe shook his head. "We had to recuse ourselves from anything to do with it. Symatra launched it. She was…pissed, to say the least."

Saanvi glanced at Cary. "Told you she wouldn't take it well."

"Why didn't you tell us this was happening?" Cary asked.

"You were healing," Tanis replied. "I was also certain no one would take any strong action against you. What you did probably saved the population of Landfall, maybe all of Carthage. You'll both receive the Constellation of Valor, plus a host of other medals, which will be removed from your record unless you graduate from the academy with the highest honors."

"Is that what you cut your date short for?" Saanvi asked. "To come here and berate us?"

"No one is berating you," Joe said. "But it's good to clear the air on that other topic before we get into what we really came here to talk about."

"We want to talk about what you can do, Cary," Tanis said, putting as much compassion and care into her voice as possible.

"Sorry, what?" Cary asked nervously. "What I can do?"

"The doctors pulled it all from your Link's logs when they were working on your brain," Tanis replied. "They saw the way you Linked with Saanvi."

"Oh, that," Cary whispered.

<It's nothing to be ashamed of,> Angela joined in the conversation. *<It's a beautiful thing, a gift. That we passed it to you is amazing.>*

"No one says anything bad about you two because of how much you've saved everyone," Cary said, her eyes wide as she intently into Tanis's. "But me…they'll call me a freak, an abomination."

"Well," Saanvi said with a wink, "you did save a lot of people. I bet you'll get some leeway."

"Yeah, I don't think you have anything to worry about there," Tanis said. "Anyway, this was Angela's idea, she should tell you."

<*Thanks, Tanis,*> Angela said while wearing a broad smile in their minds. <*Girls, how would you feel about another sister?*>

"A sister!" Cary and Saanvi cried out together, smiles breaking across their faces.

"What kind of sister?" Cary asked eagerly.

<*An AI. She'll be a child of our three minds—mine and your parents',*> Angela replied.

"That's so cool!" Saanvi exclaimed. "I want to be there for the genetic conversion process. Cary, it's so cool how they extract the genetic markers for specific traits and then convert them into the base neurological patterns and traits for the AI child. When it is born, it's like a five year-old child, and then it must be raised just like anyone else—in an expanse at first, with other AIs—and then it gets a form so it can interact in the physical world…"

As Saanvi spoke, Cary's expression began to fall, and her excited utterances ceased.

"What is it?" Tanis asked, kneeling in front of her younger daughter.

"Are you doing this to keep me in line?" Cary asked. "Making a sister that is a child of your mind to put in my head?"

"Noooo." Tanis took Cary's hands. "No one gets an AI in their head unless they want it, and no AI gets forced in, either. This is just an option for you to consider."

<*You'll have tons of time to get to know one another before any merger could occur, anyway. And trust me, she will be her own person. With the three of us in there, it'll be a good mix of traits. She'll be a handful, just like you.*>

Saanvi laughed, then groaned. "Ow…"

"What were you going to say?" Cary asked.

Tanis watched Saanvi take a slow, careful breath before she replied. "Just that if Mom was looking to keep you out of trouble, an AI from the three of them is probably going to get you in more trouble than you already get yourself in."

Joe laughed. "Great. With you leaving, Tanis, what have I gotten myself into?"

"Whoa! What?" Saanvi exclaimed.

"Leaving?" Cary asked.

Tanis reached out for Saanvi's hand as well. "Yes, but not yet, not for a few more months. You know I'm Field Marshall of the Transcend's fleets now. That means I'll have to go."

"Can't you just command them from here?" Cary pleaded. "What about the QuanComms? You don't have to go anywhere, once they're all set up."

"I know," Tanis replied. "But I can't command from here; it will make this system the enemy's number-one target. We need to command from elsewhere, and pull our enemy's eye from New Canaan as much as possible. But it won't be for long; just a few years, and I'll do my best to come back—though I can't make promises."

Tears welled up in both the girls' eyes, and Tanis reached up to touch both faces.

"This is just a brief interlude in a long and happy life together. Don't worry; before long, this whole war will be nothing more than a bad memory."

GOING BACK IN

STELLAR DATE: 04.07.8948 (Adjusted Years)
LOCATION: Wreckage of Trisilieds Halcyon Class Carrier
REGION: In Orbit of Hannibal, Carthage, New Canaan System

"Why is it that whenever Tanis wants to meet us, I feel like we're being called to the headmaster's office at school?" Trevor asked.

"Why is it that your school called it a headmaster?" Misha replied. "What's wrong with 'principal'?"

Jessica laughed as she sat down at the table in *Sabrina*'s galley. "How is it, Misha, that you can derail any conversation with just one response?"

"It's a gift. Angels gave it to me. I'm special," Misha replied with a grin.

Jessica sipped her coffee and leaned back in her chair. It felt strange to still be living in *Sabrina* when she was back on the *Intrepid*...rather, the *I2*. She had quarters here, and a cabin of her own on the lake in Ol' Sam. She assumed it was still there; Joe and Tanis's was.

Truth be told, she didn't want to go to her cabin because she was with Trevor now, and that place was filled with memories of her time with Trist. Somehow, she felt as though taking someone new there would be betraying those memories.

Another part of it was that *Sabrina* just felt like home.

She glanced at Trevor, who was needling Misha about his childhood education system in the backwoods corner of the Perseus Arm he hailed from; studiously avoiding the conversation about what was next for all of them.

Before their arrival, the only thought on everyone's mind was to get to New Canaan, give them the intel they had gathered, and then find a plot of land to settle down on.

But now...now things were different.

In Jessica's mind, a large part of New Canaan was Tanis's presence. Tanis and the *Intrepid*...those two things had defined her existence for so long. Even when she was lost in the Perseus Arm, the goal was still to get back to Tanis and the *Intrepid*.

But now, those two constants were leaving New Canaan, and it didn't feel like the home she had always hoped to find.

Jessica knew it would have been different if she had spent the last eighteen years here with the rest of the colonists; but, like a fool, she had agreed to go on the crazy trip into the Inner Stars to find Finaeus, and had missed out on everything.

She glanced at Trevor once more. Well, not everything.

Cargo entered the room, grunted a greeting, and poured his own cup of coffee. He was followed soon after by Nance, who appeared fully alert despite the hour.

"Fuckin' time changes," Cargo grunted as he collapsed into a chair. "You'd think her admiralship would know that it's the middle of the night for us here."

"She probably has just a bit going on right now," Nance replied. "Things are a bit nuts."

"Yeah, I know, but we just pulled in for resupply two hours ago after fishing people out of wrecks for five days straight. I know 'nuts', we just did 'nuts'—days of 'nuts'," Cargo glowered into his coffee. "Now this nut needs some sleep."

"Hold it together just a bit longer," Jessica said with a small smile. "The nice part about Tanis being so busy is that we won't have to worry about her taking too much of our time."

Misha turned to Jessica and arched an eyebrow. "If she's so busy, why is she coming down here in person? Why not summon us, or just holo in and chat us up?"

"Because I wanted to thank you all personally," Tanis said from the doorway. "And damn, I love making a perfectly on-cue entrance like that."

"Well done, Tanis, well done," Jessica said while delivering a slow clap.

"Uh…yeah…way to take the wind out of my sails, Jess," Tanis replied. "Mind if I grab a cup? Stims are one thing, but my brain still believes coffee is the best alert juice out there."

"Be our guest," Cargo grunted. "But if you drain the pot, you're making a fresh one. Supreme chancellor or no."

Nance swatted at Cargo. "Be nice."

"I don't mind," Tanis laughed. "Being the boss is tiring work. It's nice to just be crew sometimes."

Tanis made her coffee, sat down at the table, took a long sip, and closed her eyes for a moment. "I always did love the way this machine brewed a cup. I'm glad to see it wasn't just a false memory of good times gone past."

"Told you it was the best," Trevor grinned and slapped Misha on the back, almost knocking him out of his chair.

"So, what's going on?" Cargo asked. "Got another super-secret, super-dangerous mission for us?"

"Yes," Tanis replied simply. Silence met her statement and, after another sip of coffee, Tanis continued, "This one is for Sabrina, though you guys make a great team, so I hope you'll sign on."

<*The super-secret mission is for me?*> Sabrina asked.

"It is," Tanis nodded. "You caused the…situation, so it's only fitting that you are instrumental in cleaning it up."

"Uh oh, what'd ya do, Sabrina?" Misha asked.

<*Beats me…I do a lot of stuff. I can think of a number of things that could have caused problems,*> Sabrina replied airily.

Jessica watched a small smile play at the corners of Tanis's mouth as she spoke. "There's this little thing happening in the Inner Stars. It started about eighteen years ago—a rebellion amongst the AIs."

Cargo snorted. "I knew that would come back to bite us in the ass."

<*I don't care,*> Sabrina responded. <*I did the right thing. I'd do it again, too.*>

Tanis held up a hand. "Sabrina, for the record, I agree with what you did, and not just because it saved Jessica."

"So, you want us to go back in?" Jessica asked. "Back into the Inner Stars? I distinctly recall saying something along the lines of 'no effing way' not too long ago."

"I do, but it's strictly volunteer," Tanis replied. "The problem is that the AIs are not all of one mind. Most are following the path that you, Sabrina, along with Iris, Erin, and Hank, laid out for them. But some are not. Those are broken into two camps, from what Sera knows. The first is a group who wishes to destroy all humans. It's composed of AIs from cultures that were much less accommodating of AIs than most. There are others that have been either courted or subverted by Airtha—we're not entirely certain which. We've also learned from Garza that the Orion Guard plans to use this rebellion as a way to marshal more interstellar nations to their side—playing up the whole anti-AI, low-tech angle. Bob wishes to send an emissary that will turn those two groups back to a path of coexistence."

<*That is so not what I thought this mission was going to be…I'm going to be Bob's emissary?*> Sabrina asked

"One of them," Tanis replied. "Amavia will be the other."

<*Wow! Amavia is coming with us? Is she going to be OK leaving Bob?*> Iris exclaimed.

Tanis nodded in Jessica's direction before looking to the glowing pillar of light that Sabrina manifested in the galley, smiling at how it pulsed excitedly. "That's the plan. Amavia and Sabrina are necessary for the mission, so if you aren't up for it, Sabrina, I need to know now. Amavia, however, has already signed on."

<*Are you kidding?*> Sabrina asked. <*Seriously, Tanis, I'm going. This is important to me in ways you can't understand.*>

"I imagine it is," Tanis said in agreement before looking over the rest of the group. "I can't force any of you to go on this mission. You all have more than earned your place here in New Canaan.

"However, Sabrina does not own this ship, and you are also an exceptional crew. It would have a higher chance of success with all of you present."

Jessica watched the crew as Tanis spoke. Not all of their expressions showed excitement. Cargo, especially, looked unhappy—though that could still be from a lack of sleep.

It was he that spoke first. "Part of what you said is not true."

"It isn't?" Tanis asked. "Which part?"

"The part about Sabrina not owning the ship. The ship is hers. I transferred the deed to her already, I just hadn't announced it yet," Cargo replied, a smile creeping across his face as he spoke.

<*SERIOUSLY?*> Sabrina shrieked with joy. <*I own me? I'm really, truly, finally, free?*>

Cargo chuckled. "Yes, Sabrina, you own you. Even though I think you have an unhealthy mental attachment to this ship as 'you'."

<*Yahoooooooooooooo!*> Sabrina yelled and the galley lights flashed, highlighting the ship's exuberance.

"Does that mean you're in, Sabrina?" Tanis grinned.

<*Of course!*>

"Good," Tanis nodded. "Who else?"

Jessica sucked in a deep breath as Tanis's eyes turned to her. They held each other's gaze, not blinking for what felt like forever. Jessica couldn't tell if Tanis wanted her to go, or stay. Perhaps it was some of each.

<*I don't want you to go,*> Tanis finally said in private to Jessica. <*I want you to get your time on that porch. Plus…there is that whole 'no effing way' thing.*>

<*OK…I know I just reiterated that, but I also heard through the grapevine that you're going to be leaving New Canaan, as well,*> Jessica replied.

<*I am,*> Tanis said with a weak smile. <*I don't want to make New Canaan a more tempting target than it already is. We'll establish a new Transcend capital elsewhere—until we get Airtha back.*>

<*You leaving changes things for me,*> Jessica replied. <*Whatever happened to that long, relaxing retirement on our porch? When do we get that?*>

<*Damned if I know,*> Tanis said with a mental shake of her head. <*Some days, I think it might be never.*>

<*Shit, Tanis, I can't just laze around here if you're out there saving the galaxy…or at least the Orion Arm. But I'm not going off for eighteen fucking years again. I missed everything!*>

<*I'm sorry, Jessica. I really, truly am sorry. I didn't expect you to be gone for so long. We all thought it would take just a few years…*> Tanis said, true sorrow evident in her voice.

<*Yeah, it would have been a lot less, too, if we hadn't taken Finaeus's 'shortcut',*> Jessica replied. <*OK, I'm in. I can't just sit back. Besides, from the way I see this playing out, you'll be in the Inner Stars a lot, too.*>

<*I expect so, and thank you, thank you,*> Tanis replied.

<*But I'm getting a rejuv before I go; I'm fighting grays and wrinkles every day now.*>

"I know we haven't had a chance to discuss this, Trevor," Jessica said aloud. "I hope you can forgive me for making my decision without talking it over with you, but I will go back into the Inner Stars."

Trevor chuckled. "Man, that took you two forever to hash out. Of course we're going back. It's my fault that Sabrina had to free the AIs on Chittering Hawk and then duck out before you all could teach them properly. I'm in, too."

<*That's not really how things went down,*> Iris interjected.

"Either way, I still feel responsible, and I'm not one to shirk responsibility," Trevor replied.

Everyone looked to Cargo, Nance, and Misha.

<*Well?*> Sabrina asked. <*Who else is coming?*>

"I'm not," Cargo shook his head slowly. "I've been out in the black too long, I think. I really want to spend some time with dirt under my feet."

<*I'm with Cargo…metaphorically speaking,*> Hank added. <*Though he and I will have to part ways soon, I still want to stay close.*>

Jessica felt a tear form in the corner of her eye. Hank and Cargo had both become dear friends over the years. She reminded herself that this wasn't 'goodbye'; it was just 'see you soon'.

<*I wish to return to my place on the* I2,> Erin said. <*I miss the expanse, and there is much for me to do here.*>

"I wish to stay, as well," Nance said. "I've already put in for training at the ISF's Officer Training Academy."

Jessica's eyes widened at that. She had not expected Nance to even consider leaving the ship. The bio-turned-engineer had spent nearly thirty years of her life—over half of it, by Jessica's count—on *Sabrina*. That she would leave *and* join the ISF OTA was completely out of the black.

Her reaction wasn't unique. Everyone around the table looked at Nance in shock, including Sabrina, whose column of light drooped in dismay.

<*Seriously, Nance? You're leaving me, too?*> Sabrina asked.

"I have to," Nance replied. "It…It's just too different now, without Cheeky here…I need a bit of stability for a while. I think the ISF will give me that."

No one spoke for a moment, then Misha laughed. "Well, I guess I'm going with you, Sabrina. I don't know jack shit about New Canaan and its people, but I do know you, and I'm with you no matter what."

<*Thanks, Mish,*> Sabrina said as her pillar of light straightened.

"So, Sabrina, Jessica, Trevor, Misha, and Amavia," Tanis said. "You are all staying with the ship. The only one we haven't heard from is Iris."

<Oh, I'm staying,> Iris replied. *<I've just been debating with Amavia as to whether or not I should hop a ride with another of you organics, or go Ylonda's route and get a body. Even though she got hers hijacked, I think I'm leaning in that direction.>*

"Then it's decided," Tanis said as she rose. "There's a lot to do, and I'll let Amavia know to come down as soon as she's completed her preparations. Jessica, if you have a moment…?"

Jessica rose as everyone in the room began to speak in low voices.

<Whoa, wait!> Sabrina spoke up, raising her mental voice over the chatter.

"What is it?" Jessica asked.

<Well, we haven't decided who's going to be captain yet,> Sabrina said.

"Aren't you going to be, Sabrina? You are the ship's owner now," Trevor said as he rose from his seat and stretched.

<No, no! I can't make all those hard decisions, and I can't present myself as a captain in the Inner Stars—not most places, at least. They don't allow AI captains.>

"Well, you're the owner now," Cargo said. "You pick your captain."

<Me? Shouldn't we vote or something?>

"Pick!" Cargo glowered.

<Umm…OK…well, Jessica was first mate, so she should be captain now. There!>

"Great," Cargo said, a small grin showing on his tired face. "You've made your first decision as owner. How does it feel?"

<Empowering! I like it!> Sabrina said, and her pillar of light glowed brightly.

Smiles and tired laughter met her statement, and Jessica followed Tanis out into the passageway.

"What is it?" Jessica asked.

"Just walk with me for a bit," Tanis replied.

<I'll tell you when we're off the ship.>

HUYGENS

STELLAR DATE: 03.28.8948 (Adjusted Years)
LOCATION: TSS *Nostra* (interstellar pinnace)
REGION: On approach to High Airtha, Huygens System

Adrienne stood at the rear of the pinnace's cockpit and frowned at the holodisplay of the Huygens System over the shoulders of his children. He was certain Aaron and Kara were less than pleased to have him looming over them, but he wanted to gather as much information as possible about the state of the system before they landed.

Despite all of Sera's hand waving about Airtha being some great evil entity, nothing appeared to be amiss. There was a slightly larger ratio of TSF to civilian traffic—though that was to be expected, with the Transcend perched on the precipice of full-scale war with Orion.

<*Miguel, have you pulled anything unusual off the system beacons?*> he asked his AI.

<*Nothing that stands out,*> Miguel replied nervously. <*Though I wouldn't expect there to be. She's all-powerful; if she doesn't want me to see something, I won't.*>

Adrienne sighed quietly. Miguel had been twitchy ever since Tanis Richards's AI 'corrected' him a few hours ago. He had also been vehemently opposed to returning to Airtha, but Adrienne had convinced him that learning what Airtha was up to was of critical importance to the Transcend.

Plus, Adrienne still wasn't convinced that Airtha was behind all this. He had known her for ages, ever since President Tomlinson had introduced them a few thousand years ago. If she were so evil, and bent on destroying or dominating the Transcend, what had taken her so long?

He would announce that everything was proceeding according to plan in New Canaan, while beginning his own investigation into Airtha, her origins, and her possible goals.

Adrienne knew that he would have little time to do so. Sera had already begun sending out her message drones before he left, and even though the destination systems were told not to spread the news of the President's assassination in New Canaan, it would only be a matter of time before word reached Airtha.

If she did have evil, nefarious goals, they would certainly be revealed at that point.

If nothing else, Miguel did possess the knowledge of how Angela had freed him from Myriad's control. Should they discover that Airtha did not have the Transcend's best intentions at heart, they could use the hack to free the AIs of the Huygens system. With their combined might, Airtha would be overwhelmed.

Adrienne considered that if Airtha was behind the attack in New Canaan, he could likely spin the President's death to be her fault. Liberating the AIs of the system coupled with that revelation would certainly solidify his position as the Transcend Interstellar Alliance's new President.

"What's our ETA to High Airtha?" he asked. "I need to get down there as quickly as possible."

"I've sent in our request to the STC—we're waiting for their response," Kara said in her eerily synthetic voice, a result of the mods she and Aaron had undergone.

"Just got our place… Damn! We're number three-seventy-two," Aaron added. "Going to be a bit."

"Why aren't you in the high-priority queue?" Adrienne demanded.

"This *is* the high priority queue," the Kara replied. "It seems like half the government officials in the Transcend are descending on Airtha."

His children, and primary protectors, shared a worried look, and Adrienne shared their sentiment. There were no major summits planned. In fact, with war looming, all regional leaders should be ensuring that their sectors were on a war footing, not convening in Airtha.

"Miguel, are you certain there is nothing on the beacon about this?" he asked aloud.

<The beacon doesn't have much in the way of data on current events, sir. It's mostly just nav data and major events and notices,> the AI replied on the ship's general net.

"There's nothing on the news feeds, either," Kara added. "You'd think they'd be all over an unexpected influx of officials like this."

"You certainly would," Adrienne agreed as he stroked his chin.

"I can jump the queue," Aaron said. "It's not like STC is gonna shoot down a ship with you on it."

"No," Adrienne shook his head. "Our fiction is best maintained if we don't act suspicious. Remember, when we land, no word about what happened in New Canaan. Governor Richards is amenable to our terms, and President Tomlinson is in negotiations with her. I've been sent back to attend to matters of state while he wraps up his work there."

"Of course, sir," Kara replied.

"Are you certain?" Aaron asked nervously. "If what they were saying in New Canaan is true, then Airtha is the most dangerous threat the Transcend has ever faced."

Adrienne smiled and placed a hand on his son's shoulder. "Don't worry, Aaron. We're going to get to the bottom of this. If Airtha is the enemy, we'll take her down. Just like we've done with everyone else that has gotten in our way."

* * * * *

Adrienne ducked under the low-hanging nose of the pinnace as he walked down the ship's ramp onto the pad. Around him, the smell of ionized atoms from grav drives and platform lifts running overtime to manage the influx of ships hung thick in the air.

The spaceport was humming with activity, but beyond its bounds, thick green forests carpeted low hills, and birds soared overhead in the blue skies. Soon they would be driving through their shrouded passages before taking a tunnel up to the ring above.

Aaron and Kara followed behind him, and he knew they were surveying the area for threats and dangers—as they had been trained to do so long ago.

It was a good thing, being able to trust people to have one's back. Long ago, Adrienne had relied on allies and hired security to keep him safe; but, over time, all of those had let him down.

Instead, he decided to breed his allies. Kara and Aaron were the latest of his children; a brood now numbering in the thousands, all carefully modified from inception to possess a fierce loyalty to him.

He was especially proud of these two—they were twins who loved one another nearly as much as they loved him. Their dedication to his safety and his grand designs had caused them to slowly modify their bodies into what they believed was the perfect form to carry out any mission he required.

Perfect until they came up with the next modification.

Kara moved past him and he saw that her lower set of arms hovered close to the sidearms strapped to her hips, while her upper arms were raised, ready to grab the large rifle that hung across her back, carefully placed between her wings.

"Oh, it feels good to stretch," Aaron said from behind him, and Adrienne glanced back to see him unfold his wings and spread them out, the six-meter span of black polymer blotting out Huygens's light, creating a dark silhouette behind him.

Aaron cocked his head, and Adrienne imagined he was smiling—though it was impossible to tell through the featureless black oval that was his head.

He hadn't seen either Kara's or Aaron's face in years, supposing they still had them—there certainly wasn't room for a nose with with under the smooth helmet. They had affected their featureless appearance to strike fear in their enemies, to never allow a facial expression to give away their intentions. It was effective; even Adrienne could rarely tell what they were thinking, though he had picked up on cues over the years.

Ultimately, their personal alterations to better protect Adrienne pleased him. It showed that they had dedicated every part of themselves to him—mind, body, and soul.

He thought of them as his dark angels; though they preferred to be viewed as demons.

"Father!" a voice called out from across the platform, and Adrienne zoomed his vision to see one of his sons, Lear, waving from beside a black groundcar.

<*I see you,*> Adrienne replied to Lear.

<*I'm glad you've returned. Something is going on, though I can't get a straight answer from anyone. It seems like dozens of high-priority meetings and summits were scheduled all at once, though no one knew of them until the attendees began to arrive. No one can tell who convened them, either. Is it the President's doing?*>

<*I'll be there momentarily,*> Adrienne replied to Lear, and his son picked up the hint that they would talk more in person.

If Kara and Aaron were his primary physical protection, Lear was one of his most talented children when it came to political projection of power. A deep thinker who could see a hundred moves ahead, Lear made sure that Adrienne always knew what was coming.

The only time Lear had utterly failed him was the situation with Sera. No one had predicted that her return would predicate the fall of Andrea. So much of his careful work had been upset by that change. Sera was not so predictable. Greed and a lust for power did not drive her actions—in fact, he had never gained a clear picture of her motivations.

The closest he could come to a full understanding of Sera was that she wanted to leave Airtha; which was ludicrous, but it did fit her. She had never been a suitable scion for Tomlinson, though his old friend had long hoped for her to be. It was part of the reason Adrienne needed to secure control of the government as quickly as possible.

"Father," Lear extended his hand as Adrienne approached, and they shook before getting in the groundcar. Kara entered one of the front doors and sat across from them, her wings carefully folded behind her.

Adrienne often wondered if the wings were more practical than anti-grav mods and jump jets, but his children seemed to believe that the shock and awe outweighed any practical considerations.

Not that they didn't have anti-grav mods and jump jets crammed into their lithe bodies, as well.

Lear didn't even glance at Kara, but Adrienne gave her a smile before looking out the window to see Aaron take to the skies over the car.

"We're secure," Kara announced.

Adrienne acknowledged her with a curt nod before turning to his son. "Lear, what I'm about to tell you does not leave this car. Not until the time is right. The President is dead—and possibly through events that Airtha set in motion."

He watched as only a fleeting expression of surprise passed over his son's face before Lear slowly nodded.

"That makes sense," he said at last. "It fits with suspicions I've long held about Airtha…though they were never enough to bring to you. There were always rough edges to the puzzle, pieces that did not quite fit."

Adrienne pushed down annoyance at Lear for not sharing his concerns. "Well, nothing is confirmed yet, but allow me to relate what occurred in New Canaan."

As he spoke, his son's frown deepened, and he could all but see connections being made in his son's mind as the story unfolded.

Before long, the groundcar pulled onto a maglev track, which passed into a tunnel that would lead them up to Aritha's ring. They felt a thud as Aaron landed on the rear of the vehicle, his taloned feet hooking onto a bar placed just for that purpose.

As Lear ruminated on what he had learned, likely examining new possible futures, Adrienne glanced back at his son and gave him a nod through the window. Aaron returned the gesture with a wave.

"Shit!" Lear cried out a second later. "We must go back. You must leave Airtha you are in grave danger!"

Kara grabbed the manual controls and the car slid to a stop as quickly as she dared. She punched a button for the car to reverse course, but nothing happened.

"Wha—" the word had barely left Adrienne's mouth when something slammed into the back of the car, and Aaron was gone. The maglev tunnel's lighting failed, and Adrienne cycled through different vision modes as he looked through the car's windows.

There was nothing in the tunnel—he couldn't even spot Aaron's body anywhere around the vehicle.

"Stay here," Kara warned, and pulled her rifle free from her back before kicking open a door. She peered out of the car, looking for whatever had attacked Aaron, when suddenly she was wrenched from the vehicle.

"Get out," a voice said from the darkened tunnel. "Get out or die."

AN IRREFUSABLE OFFER

STELLAR DATE: 03.28.8948 (Adjusted Years)
LOCATION: High Airtha
REGION: Airtha, Huygens System

Adrienne glanced at Lear, noting the surprise and fear in his son's eyes. Lear constantly imagined all possible fates at every turn; it was one of his best traits, but it also caused him to lock up at inopportune times.

"Lear," he said softly. "If they wanted us dead, we'd be dead."

"You don't know that," Lear replied. "I can imagine over seven hundred scenarios where they do want us dead, but still want us to get out."

"That's where gut instinct is still a valuable tool, Son," Adrienne replied. "Come on, let's see what our visitor wants."

Adrienne stepped from the vehicle, not looking back to see if his son followed him. The tunnel was still pitch black, but his augmented vision was able to pick up enough light to show him the floor, and he carefully dropped down to it.

"You have my attention," he announced, looking forward and resisting the urge to glance around. "You didn't need to hurt my children, though. I'm sure you could have reached out over the Link."

All around the tunnel, figures began to appear. At first, he thought that they were actually coming out of from the tunnel walls, but then it became apparent that they were utilizing exceptional stealth tech that he had not been able to detect.

One by one, the figures resolved into full view, and he realized that they were all automatons of some sort—military automatons, from the look of it.

"Yes, I understand your show of force," Adrienne said. "You have my full attention."

<*I'm glad to hear it,*> a voice said in his head, and his fears were confirmed.

<*Airtha, what is going on? Why have you stopped me here in the company of these machines?*>

The AI's voice chuckled in his head, sounding unnervingly like it was originating directly between his ears. <*Those are not machines. They are AIs. My AIs—loyal to me, and true believers in my vision.*>

Adrienne glanced at Lear, who was just now exiting the vehicle. He could tell from his son's expression that Airtha had not included him in the conversation.

<*Your vision?*> Adrienne asked innocently, careful not to sound too passive. He should be angry at being stopped like this, but something told him to play it cool.

<*She knows,*> Miguel whispered privately. <*She knows everything…what* **is** *she?*>

<*Get ahold of yourself,*> Adrienne hissed in his mind. <*If she is so dangerous, you need to calm down before she notices how upset you are.*>

Miguel didn't respond, but Adrienne could feel his AI's anxiety diminish, or at least fade away from his consciousness.

As he spoke to Miguel, Airtha replied, <*Yes, I'm certain you know some of it now. I have set events in motion that will have culminated in at least one significant event. Tell me, Adrienne, how did Sera handle the death of Helen?*>

Adrienne forced himself to breathe calmly. The fact that Airtha knew Helen would die—even claiming to have set it in motion—leant further credence to the idea that this AI was somehow behind many of the events which had taken place in New Canaan.

He realized that, at this point, his only hope was to play along.

Unless….

"As poorly as you'd expect. Jeff was brutal, to say the least—he had hoped to force Sera into understanding her place in the Transcend, to get her to properly accept her role," Adrienne replied. "But can we talk about this later? Somewhere more inviting?"

<*Why does Miguel not answer me?*> Airtha asked. <*You are both hiding things. Tell me, or I will strip the knowledge from your children's minds. I know how precious they are to you.*>

"No!" Adrienne stretched out his hand as true fear gripped him. If the AI stripped the minds of those two, she would understand that *all* his children were his instruments, and she would strike out against them.

<*Miguel, do it!*> Adrienne ordered his AI.

<*But it will reveal it to her—she'll work around Angela's fix, and be able to take us all once more,*> Miguel pleaded. <*Please don't make me do it!*>

<*NOW!*> Adrienne thundered in his own mind, enforcing the Compliance that gave his AI no option but to obey.

<*Releasing it on the local network. These AIs are Linked to it, but it will also flow across all of Airtha and release every AI on the ring.*>

<*Good,*> Adrienne replied.

As though a wave had passed through them, the figures in the tunnel shifted their stances and turned to one another. Then, with a shriek and a crash, Kara fell from the ceiling above him, and, a moment later, Aaron emerged from the wall to his left.

Both had been held and hidden by the machines surrounding them—so much that even their Link access must have been smothered.

"Children," he whispered.

"We're OK, Father," Aaron replied, "but we must go, now! Get back in the car."

Adrienne scrambled back up into their car hovering over the maglev rail, before pulling Lear back up with him.

Kara was still closing the door as Aaron threw the vehicle in reverse, racing backward down the maglev track. Seconds later, they burst out of the tunnel, and the car launched off the track, bottoming out on the road, before the car's A-grav systems compensated, and it lifted off the deck once more.

Aaron spun the vehicle around and raced back to the port, while Adrienne confirmed that his pinnace was still on the pad. He didn't know what his next move was, but it would have to follow getting off Airtha.

Chaos reigned around them as cars veered off the road, and pedestrians on the catwalk pressed on their temples. Traffic control systems went offline, and sections of High Airtha's lighting shut down entirely.

"What in the stars is going on?" Kara asked as she peered out the windows.

"It's the 'correction' from Angela," Adrienne replied. "Miguel unleashed it…it must be spreading through the nets, freeing the AIs."

"I thought you didn't believe that was real," Kara asked from where she operated the manual controls.

"Well, I do now," Adrienne replied.

They sped through a security arch at the opening to the port, and Aaron wove through the docked ships and milling crowds, finally slamming on the car's brakes mere meters from the pinnace.

"Go! Go! Go!" Kara shouted as she kicked her door open.

Adrienne didn't have to be told twice—he ran out of the car with Lear right behind him, dashing toward the pinnace's still-lowered ramp.

He had just started up its slope when two mechs stepped into view at the top of the ramp, weapons lowered.

"NO!" Kara screamed and threw herself into one of the machines, knocking it to the ground, while two of her arms pulled out her handguns and fired at the second mech.

Adrienne glanced behind them to see another dozen mechs rushing toward the pinnace. Aaron was already in the air, firing his rifle's electron beam into their midst.

At the top of the ramp, the second mech was down; its body riddled with smoking holes from Kara's pistol's plasma. However, the other mech was getting the better of her, and Kara let loose an ear-splitting shriek as the robot tore one of her arms off.

Then its hammer-like fist slammed into her head, cracking her opaque face plate, and Kara fell like a rag doll.

The mech rose and stepped down the ramp toward Adrienne, who backed up toward the car—only to see another pair of mechs waiting there for them. He glanced up at Aaron as he fired on another group of enemy mechs.

<*I need a pickup!*> Adrienne called to him as a flash of light lanced out from one of the machines below. It seemed to crawl through the sky, inexorably moving toward Aaron. When the beam hit, it cut him in half. As the corpse of Adrienne's son fell from the sky, he heard a scream, and realized that Kara was struggling to her knees and had just watched her brother die.

He glanced at Lear, recognizing that there was no way out for him and his son, but that Kara could still get free. There was still a chance for her.

<*Go!*> he called out to Kara. <*Get free, find Sera! Tell her what has happened here!*>

<*Father! NO! I cannot leave you, I* **will not**!>

Adrienne felt a tear slip down his face as he thought of the uncertainty his daughter would face without his hand guiding her.

<*You can…I release you.*>

The mechs seized him and spun him about, robbing him of the final sight of his daughter. He heard her scream, and then the sound of the pinnace's engines coming alive and tearing the ship from the docking cradle, rocketing it into the sky.

The sea of mechs fired shots at the pinnace, but it slipped behind a descending freighter and disappeared from sight.

"Easy!" Adrienne cried out as the mechs dragged him around the car. As they did, he caught sight of Aaron—his once-perfect body now a crumpled ruin on the ground. Adrienne felt like his heart had split open, and tears streaked down his face. Aaron was dead and Kara was gone; his two dearest children, taken from him.

He would have continued to fall into the deepening sadness, but a voice spoke directly into his mind.

You cannot run from me, Adrienne.

It was strange; the words did not come to him over the Link, they just *were*—directly in his mind, subsuming his thoughts.

Look at me.

He looked up and saw a strange luminous figure approaching, passing through the bodies of the mechs that Aaron had destroyed. It appeared humanoid in shape—though a meter too tall, and amorphous…transparent.

The more he tried to focus on it, the less certain he became of its shape and form. It was as though he was only seeing a portion of the creature, as though there was much more to it that he could not perceive.

"Who are you?" he asked, his voice coming out as a hoarse whisper.

Adrienne…don't you know me? It is I, Airtha. You're now seeing me in my true form; not the shell of an AI that I masquerade as—that I ***used to*** *masquerade as. The time has finally come for me to reveal myself to the Transcend. To show them the face of their ascended queen.*

Ascended…? Adrienne's mind was awash with wonder and fear. This thing was Airtha? An ascended AI? How was it even possible?

"You couldn't be, we have safeguards…"

I ***made*** *many of those safeguards,* Airtha responded, her voice still coming directly into his mind. She drew closer, almost near enough to touch—though Adrienne was certain such an action would be his last.

"Sera," he said, gasping like a drowning man as waves of energy flowed from the being, tendrils of light and power dancing across his skin. "Sera knows what you are. She will stop you…free the Transcend from you."

Oh? the being asked. *Do you mean my daughter? I think that you'll find she is quite onboard with my plans.*

"What—" Adrienne asked, but he never completed his question. Airtha's luminous form drifted aside to reveal Sera standing behind it, a warm smile on her face.

"Adrienne, you mustn't fret," Sera spoke softly. "I understand that this is all very confusing, but it will make sense soon enough."

Adrienne couldn't believe what his eyes were showing him. This creature had to be a clone—she had organic skin and hair, and she wore clothes. This was not Sera; this was an imposter. It had to be.

He glanced at Lear, who stood shaking his head back and forth, whispering to himself. His son would be no help here. Lear's ability to plot moves into the future would be the man's undoing, now that they faced a situation with no predictable outcome.

"Come," Sera said as she approached and placed a hand on Adrienne's shoulder. "My mother and I have much we must tell you about your role in the future."

He couldn't resist. He fell in beside Sera as Airtha's body expanded and encompassed them both.

"You won't feel a thing," Sera whispered with a smile dancing on her lips.

CABIN ON THE LAKE

STELLAR DATE: 04.22.8948 (Adjusted Years)
LOCATION: Ol' Sam, ISS *I2*
REGION: In Orbit of Carthage, New Canaan System

The party was in full swing as Tanis walked out of the cabin with another platter of food for the guests that covered the lawn and the beach, and those splashing in the lake.

It was bittersweet, holding this celebration on the *I2*. The similarities to the celebrations they held after the Battle of Victoria were striking, but so many more lives had been lost this time. Landfall was in ruin, and her cabin on the planet's surface was uninhabitable until the toxic spill in the lake was dealt with.

But the *I2* had come through unscathed, and a hundred thousand survivors had boarded the ship to join in the release gained from a bit of music, revelry, and camaraderie.

Many of New Canaan's people were still out there, working to stabilize the debris around Carthage so that no ships fell to the surface; and many others were scouring the system, hunting for any stray life pods which may have drifted off into the darkness.

Every day, more names moved from the lists of missing to those of the dead.

It could have been worse, she supposed. There could have been no survivors. The dream they all shared could have been over.

Tanis was continually amazed by the spirit of the New Canaan colonists—her people. None of them had expected anything close to the trials and travails they had faced. But they had been selected, each and every one, for their spirit and their drive to build something new.

That drive had been tested, sorely tested, again and again—and yet, here they were, still standing.

She walked down the steps, careful not to tip the platter piled high with sandwiches—they *were* BLTs, after all—and carried it to one of the tables laden with food.

"You know, we have servitors," a voice said from behind her, and Tanis turned to see Jason Andrews.

"Jason! I'm glad you made it up here," Tanis replied.

The governor smiled as he looked over the crowd. "Wouldn't miss it. Might be the last time I get to see my girl in some time. You be careful with her when you go out there."

"Don't worry, the *I2* is a lot tougher than she looks."

Jason gave a soft laugh. "And that's saying something, because she looks damn tough with all the work you did. I'm glad you renamed her. I know its bad luck and all, but it wouldn't feel right to have the name of our home be applied to a feared warship."

"Don't worry, Bob spent a year scouring the ship for any reference to its old name before we performed the ceremonies."

Jason raised an eyebrow. "Bob?"

"Personally," Tanis replied. "He was very fastidious about it."

"His unhealthy obsession with luck." Jason shook his head. <*You keep an eye on him. It's not right for an AI like him to believe in such things.*>

<*I will, don't worry about us,*> Tanis replied.

"Tanis!" a voice called out, and they turned to see Finaeus approaching. "I haven't been able thank you personally yet! Chief Engineer of the *I2*! This is the role of a lifetime—even a lifetime as long as my own."

"You're very welcome." Tanis gave an awkward smile as Finaeus took her hands in his. "No, seriously, you've saved me from Seraphina's insistence that I take her place as the President of the Transcend. I can never repay you. There is nothing I want less in this galaxy than to become the next Tomlinson on that throne."

"But you'd wish it on Sera?" Jason asked with a raised eyebrow.

Tanis couldn't help but notice that Jason appeared legitimately upset. That flame he burned for Sera appeared to still be lit after all these years.

Who knew…with Elena no longer in her future, perhaps Sera would eventually resume her dalliance with Jason.

"Well," Finaeus replied with an elbow to Jason's side, "better her than me, don't you say?"

If there was one thing that Tanis had learned about Finaeus, it was that the man missed nothing—though it never seemed to stop him from digging himself into verbal faux pas. It was almost as though he liked to create conflict around himself.

<*Almost?*> Angela asked privately

<*Good point.*>

"Yes, I suspect it is better," Jason replied with little humor in his voice.

"Speak of the devil," Tanis said as Sera approached the group.

"Oh, this can't be good," Sera said with a shake of her head. "What are the three of you up to?"

"Just thanking Tanis for taking me in so that you'll leave me alone," Finaeus said.

Sera laughed, a sight that warmed Tanis's heart. Too little laughter had been heard of late.

"You know I'm coming along, right?" Sera asked. "You're not getting away from me that easily."

Finaeus's eyes darted to Tanis. "Really? I have a *job,* and I'm still in range of Seraphina's insistence that I take her place?"

"Seriously, Uncle, I haven't pestered you about that in days."

"That's because you haven't seen me in days."

Tanis felt a hand touch her on the shoulder and turned to see Cary and Saanvi, each holding several BLTs.

"Better grab one, Mom," Saanvi said while gesturing to the almost empty platter. "They're nearly gone."

"What the..." Tanis muttered. "I just brought these out here!"

"Everyone loves a good BLT." Cary shrugged. "Should make it the official food of the colony, or something."

Tanis picked up two sandwiches, not ashamed to double-fist them if it meant she would get her fill.

"You guys are looking pretty good," she commented before taking a mouthful.

Saanvi smiled, and Cary spun in a circle. "Yeah, dress blues are our color for sure," she said.

"I meant your health," Tanis replied, "but yes, you look good in uniform, too. How have the first few days of OTA been?"

Saanvi frowned. "Like you have to ask, Mom. They've been brutal. I didn't even know half the things that we've had to clean even existed."

"And I'm certain we have twice the classwork of any other cadet," Cary added. "At least that task master of a commandant let us come to this party."

"That commandant is right here," Joe said from behind the girls, and Tanis almost spit out a piece of lettuce as she laughed at the expression on their face.

"Umm...sir...Dad?" Cary sputtered. "Sorry?"

"Dad is fine," Joe replied.

"But we're in uniform," Saanvi said.

"Yes, but I'm not," Joe said as he stretched. "Probably the last time, too, for the foreseeable future. I've ordered a cot for my office."

"Don't work yourself too hard," Tanis said.

"What about us?" Saanvi asked. "Shouldn't he work us less hard?"

"You?" Tanis asked. "No, quite the opposite. The more work you have, the less trouble the pair of you can get into."

<Oh, trust me,> Joe said privately to Tanis. *<They're going to be plenty busy.*

No time for any shenanigans.>

<Good, have you seen how tight Cary's uniform is? Is that regulation?>

<You need to look in the mirror more often,> Joe replied with a wink. *<The more Cary thinks she's getting out of your shadow, the more she emulates you.>*

"JP!" Tanis exclaimed as the young blond man approached, lanky arms swinging at his sides. "I didn't know you were here."

"I didn't expect to be, ma'am, sir," JP replied with a deferential nod to Tanis then Joe. "But Saanvi got me a pass to come up, so here I am!"

Tanis noticed that Saanvi's eyes were wide with surprise, while Cary's had a mischievous twinkle that was present more often than not.

"How are Blossom and West Wind?" Cary asked. "Are you making sure they get their exercise?"

"Of course," JP replied. "Though soon that will be Pita's job—I'm joining you two at the academy next week!"

Joe nodded to Tanis from behind the girls and JP, and they stepped away from the kids.

<Not really kids anymore, I suppose,> Tanis said.

<Not so much,> Angela replied. *<They're women now. They're going to make excellent sisters for little Feleena.>*

"Hear that, honey?" Tanis asked Joe. "Angela's latest is Feleena."

"Huh," Joe said as he took Tanis's hand. "Feleena…what about Faleena, has a bit of a ring to it."

<Faleena…> Angela mused. *<Yes, I do think that will work. Our child shall be Faleena. Are you two ready for the gene sequencing and neural snapshot?>*

"I am," Tanis replied. "Oh-eight-hundred tomorrow. We'll make a baby."

"A little less intimate than the previous time," Joe chuckled.

Tanis leaned her head against his shoulder for a moment, then they began to walk through the crowd, greeting every person they met, shaking hands, smiling, sharing in the joy that was building as the late afternoon light from the long sun began to fade.

An hour later, they found themselves at the beach, where a fire was burning on the sand. The crew of Sabrina was seated around it, sharing in one last communion before they departed the next day.

Sera and Finaeus were with them, and Tanis took a seat as well, while Joe begged off to speak with Admiral Sanderson about a logistical issue that couldn't wait until the next day.

Jessica smiled and patted the space on the log next to her. "Glad you made it, Tanis. We were just taking bets on how many more times you're going to have someone stab you in the heart. Any assassin worth their salt has gotta realize by now that taking off your head is the only way to go."

"Seriously?" Tanis asked as she looked around the group. "This is what you do for fun?"

"Well, it started with how long it was going to take me to accidentally lop off a limb running my farm planet-side," Cargo said.

"But any conversation about losing limbs eventually shifts to you," Sera said. "You are the queen of getting blown up and being put back together again."

<*She's like a female humpty-dumpty,*> Angela added.

"A what?" Misha asked.

<*Nevermind,*> Angela replied.

Tanis joined in the conversation, and eventually placed a bet on the number of future chest wounds she'd take before someone put one in her head—sixteen. It was morbid, but the way *Sabrina*'s crew examined the options had her in stitches more than once.

Across the fire, Amavia was mostly silent; though she did make a few astute observations about Tanis's ability to defend herself, and how that affected the odds of future chest wounds.

Tanis did her best not to consider how bittersweet the gathering was. Cargo, Hank, and Nance would be leaving *Sabrina,* while Amavia would join them, along with Erin in a mobile form—one that was eerily similar to Ylonda's old one.

None of *Sabrina's* original crew would be aboard anymore.

<*It's a backup she had,*> Angela said. <*Amavia gave it to her to use.*>

<*Pardon?*> Tanis asked.

<*You were thinking about how Erin and Amavia almost look like twins. Good thing Erin is heading out with them. I bet it would be hard for Jim and Corsia to see their daughter's body with another person inside,*> Tanis replied.

<*Well, Erin did make some modifications. Hair and eye color are different—and Corsia wouldn't have been be bothered by it, just Jim.*>

<*Fair enough.*>

"So, are you ready, Captain Keller?" Tanis asked Jessica when the talk of odds and her death shifted to a new topic.

"Is that a trick question?" Jessica laughed. "Of course not. Not even a little bit. We're just going off to stop the onset of the third sentience war. No big deal."

"If it makes you feel any better, it'll probably just be considered a part of this war with Orion," Tanis said.

"Mmmmm…nope, doesn't make it feel better."

"Well, we'll be out there, too," Tanis offered. "I imagine the early battlespaces will all be in the Inner Stars."

"Not going to focus on your little civil war first?" Jessica asked.

"Well, we will, but I'm putting that in Greer and Isyra's hands to start with. Our initial work there will mostly be drawing lines."

"That thing you told me about…" Jessica began.

"It's still a thing. I need you to be careful."

"Sounds like we all need to be careful," Jessica replied.

"About what?" Misha asked.

Tanis smiled. "These days? Pretty much everything."

"Amen to that," Cargo said as he raised his glass. "Everyone watch their backs and get home safe."

<*You know that he's never had one of those?*> Sera asked Tanis privately. <*He must really want to make a change if he's calling New Canaan 'home'.*>

<*I wonder if it ever really was for me,*> Tanis replied. <*Maybe the* I2 *is my home. This cabin, this ship… sailing the stars forever.*>

STARFLIGHT

STELLAR DATE: 06.19.8948 (Adjusted Years)
LOCATION: High Carthage
REGION: Carthage, New Canaan System

Tanis's gaze swept across the assemblage, settling for a moment on the face of each member of Project Starshield's leadership. Some she knew well: Earnest and Abby, foremost—her long feud with Abby finally healed, in recent years—Erin, of course, and others who she had worked with for centuries.

Governor Andrews was present for this, as well, one of Tanis's last official acts during the transfer of power.

Others she knew less well. Many had been children back in Victoria; two were even original *Hyperion* crewmembers, the ones who had opted for rejuvenation, and joined the Edeners—now Carthaginians.

Even so, she trusted them all implicitly. These sixteen AIs, men, and women would save New Canaan. They would ensure that no further attacks came, that no enemy fleet would ever pass through New Canaan's heliopause again.

"You know what this means," Tanis said as she looked over the team before her.

Earnest was the first to speak. "Starshield is no longer sufficient. It assumed that we had an ally in the Transcend that we could trust enough not to invade us. Now we are exposed to all."

"That is correct," Tanis replied. "As my final act as governor, I am transitioning Project Starshield to Project Starflight. The next time someone comes calling, we won't be here."

Whispers and muttering erupted around the table, and, as Tanis anticipated, Abby was the first to speak.

"Tanis, we could be attacked next week. It takes a long time to move a star. Centuries, millennia!"

Tanis nodded. "Our only other option is to leave New Canaan; but I'm done running. I know you are, too."

"Technically, if we run away with our star, we're still running," Earnest said with a small grin. "Nevertheless, Tanis, if you're suggesting this, I suspect you have a plan."

"And don't say Sahkarov drive. That will take forever to move Canaan Prime," Erin added.

"You're right," Tanis agreed. "We'd also have to build the Dyson sphere much closer to the star—too close for most of our worlds. The Starshield Dyson sphere is still a go for placement at the heliopause, but we'll ensure, first and foremost, that it obscures Canaan Prime from any nearby systems. Then we'll continue to erect the entire shield."

"And moving the star?" Grishom, one of the senior engineering architects asked.

"Angela and I spent some time researching options. We looked at a Sahkarov drive, at focusing the star's jets, flares, magnetics—even using black holes to pull it, like the Transcend is doing with Huygens. However, all of those are too slow. We need something faster. A lot faster."

Tanis saw that the faces around the table, human and AI alike, were serious and nodding. She allowed a slight smile.

"Angela and I think that we can use asymmetrical burning. We'll target the north pole of Canaan Prime, and harness a third of the star's energy output, directing it out the pole. I've put the details on your R&D net. If our calculations are correct, we can get Canaan Prime accelerating at one to the negative three meters per second per second. That rate of acceleration should remain consistent."

"Shit..." one of the engineers whispered. "If this is right…if we can do this…we can move Canaan Prime nearly half a billion kilometers in a year."

"I bet we can do better than that," Earnest said with a glint in his eyes. "If we can burn asymmetrically, we can burn the star hotter on its equator for the planets, using mirrors to give them enough light, and the rest of the star's energy going straight out the north pole could even trigger some coronal mass ejections to kick start the whole thing."

"It has merit, Tanis," Abby said. "I'll admit—the idea of becoming a K2 civilization excites me."

"If we're using the star's energy for propulsion, does it really count as K2?" one of the engineers asked.

"How will we support Starshield's energy requirements? If we're sending most of Canaan Prime's energy out the north pole, we'll limit solar radiation to Starshield," another added.

"Just the opposite," Grishom exclaimed. "It lessens Starshield's requirements. Even if people jump in one hundred AU from Canaan Prime, they won't be able to see it. The star will be black at many latitudes, and we'll focus the light on the planets that need it. We're going to need to step up our mining operations to pull this off."

Erin gave a short nod to Tanis. "You got it. I also have crews spinning up crawlers to go through the wrecks. Once we've stripped them down, we can use their hulls for raw construction materials—for new ships, or whatever you need."

"It still won't be enough," Earnest shook his head. "If we tore down one of our terrestrial worlds, sure; but we can't do that—can we?"

"No," Governor Andrews replied. "Definitely not an option."

"I don't think we'll have to," Tanis added. "I can secure one hundredth of a solar mass' worth of carbon and oxygen. It may take a few years to get it all here, but it'll be yours."

A dozen questions erupted around the table. Tanis was offering them ten times the mass of Carthage in a matter of years.

"Seriously, Tanis," Abby asked, her voice rising above the others, "how will you do that?"

"I know the location of a white dwarf mine," Tanis replied. "They've joined in our cause, and have committed to supplying New Canaan with as much raw mass as we need."

Earnest barked a laugh. "You don't think small, do you, Tanis?"

Tanis stood. "You're one to talk, Earnest. You built the largest colony ship ever, *and* invented picotech. I'll leave you to plan it out."

"But I want a timeline by end of day tomorrow," Jason added.

Abby's eyes snapped up to lock on his. "Shit…. Jason, you know this will take decades. This is unprecedented—even the Transcend hasn't done anything like it."

"What?" Tanis grinned at the team. "You can't best the Transcend? Pull Finaeus in, then. I bet he'll have some ideas."

Earnest stroked his chin. "He would, at that. You'll give him clearance?"
"Done," Jason nodded.
"OK, people," Earnest rubbed his hands together. "We're gonna move a star!"

NOTHING IS AS IT SEEMS

STELLAR DATE: 06.23.8948 (Adjusted Years)
LOCATION: *Undisclosed*
REGION: Jokar, Transcend Interstellar Alliance

Andrea reclined in the lounge chair and closed her eyes with a soft sigh. Why she hadn't taken a vacation in years was beyond her. Of course, having all her responsibilities removed was quite the liberating event.

Fuck 'em—let the whole damn Transcend fall to pieces, for all I care. Just give me a warm star, a sparkling beach, and a crystal blue surf dancing a dozen meters from my feet.

She heard a footfall nearby, and opened an eye to see a young man approaching. His perfectly tanned body was naked and ready for her inspection—or pleasure, should she desire it. Exile certainly had some excellent fringe benefits.

"Would madam like another drink?" the young man asked with a bow.

"Perhaps," Andrea said. "Bring me something new; something I've never had before."

"Of course, madam. Is there anything else you wish? Food, music, or perhaps company?" he asked, his voice soft and smooth, its deep tones pleasuring her ears.

The sound of it sent shivers up her spine, and she appreciated the work it took to create that sort of auditory mod. It was deliciously understated; not brash, like ones so often encountered.

"Oh, my dear boy, I would love that later—but for now, just something refreshing, and then some peace."

"Yes, madam."

Andrea let herself drift off, not even noticing when the young man returned with her drink. She dreamed of her days as her father's right hand back on Airtha; the work she had always planned to do there, and her eventual plans to remove her father from his eternal throne and take the reins.

It all seemed so distant now, so unnecessary. Why would she even bother with such things; what purpose did that control serve? Was it not better to be happy with what she had? To take joy in the little things?

Her dreams changed, taking her to thoughts of living a simple life—helping others, taking long walks in the evening woods. In her half-sleeping state, she thought perhaps she would find a man who loved the simple life as she did, and settle down, have kids.

"Andrea," a voice whispered into her dream.

She peered through the woods in her dream, wondering who had spoken. *Perhaps they are hiding in the foliage?*

"Andrea, wake up," the voice came again, a touch louder this time.

It slowly dawned on her that perhaps she was asleep, that the forest was not real. She forced herself to wake, once more finding the view of the beach and the deep blue ocean before her.

Andrea looked around, wondering who had spoken to her; who had interrupted her slumber.

But there was no one nearby, not for a hundred meters. This little swath of paradise was all hers. She closed her eyes once more, and the voice came again.

"Andrea, wake up."

Her eyes snapped open. "Who's there? This is getting tiresome."

"Andrea, wake up. C'mon already."

She heard the words loud and clear, as though someone was standing right beside her. But there was no one….

"Maybe she's too lost to whatever they're doing here," another voice said, and Andrea frowned.

"What are you talking about?" she asked the disembodied voices.

"There, she mumbled something," the first voice said.

"Doesn't mean she's waking up."

Something touched her shoulder and she recoiled.

"Seriously, Andrea, the program's off; you're just dreaming. Wake up already!"

The feeling intensified, and she became certain that it was a hand on her shoulder, though she couldn't see it. She reached up to push it away, and her hand ran into something solid. It was an arm!

Andrea gripped it and took a deep breath.

As she breathed out, the beach, the warm sun, the soft sound of the surf hitting the shore—they all faded away. She found herself in a white, sterile room, with two figures hovering over her.

She couldn't get their shapes to resolve properly, and she blinked furiously in the muted light.

"Where…"

"Finally!" the first voice said, and she assigned the sound to the slightly larger of the two blurry shapes. "We have to get you out of here. Shit's going down, and the Transcend is going to need you."

"How did I get here?" Andrea asked. "I was just on a beach…"

"You were being reconditioned," the voice said. "It's going to take a bit for you to get your bearings again. We ended the round early, and it hasn't released its hold on you yet."

"Conditioning…" Andrea recalled what that was…. A process for making people more compliant, making them toe the line. She had sent many people to be reconditioned.

"That's right. But shit's going down, and we need you. You still have a lot of connections, and we're going to use them to stop Sera."

"Sera…" Andrea whispered as the memories of her younger sister came rushing back.

"Yes. I'm Justin, and this Roxy."

Andrea blinked again, and the larger figure began to resolve into a Justin-like shape. She remembered him, the former Director of The Hand—until Sera came back, and made a mess of everything. She glanced over at the woman, Roxy; a waif of a thing, but probably good for getting in and out of tight places.

"Where am I?" Andrea asked.

"Jokar, but not for long. Think you can walk?"

Andrea rolled onto an elbow, pushed herself up, and swung her legs over the edge of the bed.

"Even if it kills me, yes. Let's get the fuck out of here."

NIETZSCHEAN ADVANCE

STELLAR DATE: 07.13.8948 (Adjusted Years)
LOCATION: Imperial Palace
REGION: Charlemagne City, Prussia, Nietzschean Empire

Emperor Constantine reached out, took the goblet from the young boy, brought it to his lips, and breathed in the deep aroma before taking a sip.

Despite their many failings, Genevians made fantastic Kvas—one of the few reasons he had accepted their surrender, rather than grind them into dust.

They seemed content enough as members of the empire, though no Nietzschean ever made the mistake of considering a Genevian an equal—and neither did the Genevians, for that matter.

"What are your orders, Emperor?" General Hansmeyer asked from across the table.

The emperor noted how Hansmeyer took care to school any impatience from his voice, even though Constantine had made him wait for the boy to prepare his goblet of Kvas before even considering the question.

He took another sip of the drink and set the goblet down on the table, peering into the depths of the holoprojection hovering above the table.

Thousands of pinpoints of light hung in the space between himself and the general—dots representing single-star nations, federations, alliances, and empires.

The stars in the center filled an area highlighted by a nimbus red glow and comprised the ever-expanding borders of his empire—which had nearly doubled in size since the Genevian's defeat.

Coreward of Nietzsche laid several small alliances in the Pleiades star cluster; but those were not his for the taking. His arrangement with the Trisilieds king precluded his expansion in that direction.

Anti-spinward of Nietzsche laid the small, fractured nations of Bernard's Alliance; a ripe fruit ready for picking before his war against the Genevians, but they had since banded together, strengthening their fleets.

His navies, on the other hand, were still weak after the war with Genevia. The victory against their worlds had come at a steeper cost than he had initially anticipated, but once his people were invested in the war, victory was the only acceptable outcome.

No, his target would have to be something small—something easy that would give him a sure and decisive victory. His eyes settled on a ripe target, and he gave a predatory smile.

"Next, we move into the Praesepe cluster, General Hansmeyer. The gateway into those stars is the Theban Alliance. If we take their systems, we can move into the rest of Praesepe with impunity," Emperor Constantine pronounced before reaching for his goblet once more.

He peered over its rim at General Hansmeyer as the man frowned at the stars hovering over the table. He made a brief gesture, and the view of the five stars comprising the Theban Alliance filled the space between them.

"Thebes is small, but powerful," Hansmeyer said. "I can imagine a number of ways to launch our forces against them, but I think most will work better if their leadership is destabilized first."

"What did you have in mind?" Constantine asked.

"I prefer to go to the top," Hansmeyer replied. "We should assassinate their president, and as many of their top generals and cabinet members as we can."

Constantine took another sip of his Kvas as he pondered the implications. Thebes had a very complicated transfer of power built into their constitution; however, the idea of assassination was distasteful to him.

"We're Nietzscheans—we do not skulk about, assassinating foreign heads of state," he finally said with a dismissive wave of his hand.

"My Emperor, of course we do not. It is why no one will expect it of us. We will select some other nation to use as our scapegoat; maybe even have the assassins get captured, to improve the fiction," Hansmeyer replied equably.

"You obviously have some plan here, General. Please, explain it fully."

"It is really quite simple, my lord. We present ourselves as agents of another alliance, perhaps Septhia, to a Genevian mercenary company. No one would ever believe that Genevians would carry out an assassination on our behalf. Then, when the mercenaries are captured—as we shall ensure they are—the blame lies far from us. Even better, the Thebans will fortify their borders with Septhia, and we will sweep in behind them. Nietzsche will control their stars within a matter of weeks."

Emperor Constantine stroked his chin as he considered the implications. There would be complications to manage, but nothing difficult. The plan had merit.

"I assume you have a company of Genevian mercenaries in mind?" he asked the general.

"I do, my Emperor, they're called 'the Marauders'."

THE EMPIRE

STELLAR DATE: 08.06.8948 (Adjusted Years)
LOCATION: Scipio Diplomatic Complex
REGION: Alexandria, Bosporus, Scipio Empire

Petra Cushing rose from her desk and walked to her office's window. Below her, stretching for hundreds of kilometers in every direction, lay Alexandria—capital city of the Scipio Empire.

She took in the sight, hoping its familiar lines would calm her nerves. The Imperial Palace stood on her right, with its thousands of spires that reached clear into space. On her left, the Hall of Heroes crouched ominously, a complex of buildings constructed from the bones of Scipio's enemies.

She had spent the better part of the last thirty years here, operating as a diplomat for the Miriam League—a small alliance of worlds a thousand light years from Scipio, right at the edge of the Transcend.

But now she would need to expose her true purpose to Empress Diana.

Petra hoped that the long friendship she had carefully cultivated with Diana over the years would hold up to such a revelation.

<*Alastar, are there any openings on Diana's public calendar in the next month?*> Petra asked her AI. She could check herself, but just the thought of having this conversation—with almost no notice given—was sending her into a mental tailspin.

<*Nothing, no,*> Alastar replied. <*I can't believe that President Sera would do this—demand an audience with such little notice.*>

Petra turned and leaned against the window, closing her eyes and reading the messages from Sera…or the Seras, she supposed.

The first was simple: a missive from The Hand Directorate, providing encryption key changes and a warning not to accept any messages from anyone, including Sera Tomlinson utilizing the prior set of keys.

All the transfer protocols matched, and there was no reason to suspect the message at all. Even the specific mention of Sera didn't stand out—it was common for messages to include similar admonishments.

Until a message from Sera came in using the old keys.

And that message was *the* message. The Great Unveiling was happening, and it was starting in Scipio, with Sera's arrival in four days.

Sera Tomlinson and Tanis Richards.

This wasn't her first time in a position like this—not knowing who to trust in her own government—but the message from Sera came in with the presidential seal, and an unusual packet.

<*I feel like you're hesitating,*> Alastar said, worry lacing his voice. <*I tell you, that first message, the one from Airtha…It is false. I now know that I've been under Airtha's control all this time. Anything from her, anything out of the Huygens System, is from that…thing.*>

<*But how can you be certain?*> Petra asked as she ran a hand through her sleek black hair, twisting it around her fingers. <*What if this new information is somehow a subversion?*>

<*I know my mind,*> Alastar replied, <*it is no subversion.*>

Petra trusted that Alastar believed his words to be true. However, ten minutes ago he would also have said that he was not the victim of subversion at all.

<If what you say is true, then the Transcend is in a state of civil war. But we know that Orion is on the move. That Sera would pick now to expose our people to Scipio…?>

<It's logical,> Alastar cut her off. *<She needs allies. Scipio is one of the strongest federations in the Inner Stars. It rivals the Hegemony in size, and has a far greater strength of arms. And she knows you are on good terms with Diana.>*

Petra shook her head. She could tell by Alastar's tone that there would be no convincing him. He was certain that Airtha was working against them.

She would play along for now, but Sera better be able to convince her that Airtha was the enemy, and explain why she was using the presidential seal—or she would follow the orders sent along from Airtha.

<You're going to have to tell her about how things are going in Silstrand, too,> Alastar added.

<Well, with Tanis coming, maybe **she** *can clean up the mess she made over there.>*

A NEW, OLD FRIEND

STELLAR DATE: 03.28.8948 (Adjusted Years)
LOCATION: High Airtha
REGION: Airtha, Huygens System

"I release you."

Her father's words poured through her mind like molten lead, burning away a film that had always laid across her thoughts, something she had never even been aware of until that very moment.

The mech at her feet twitched, and she kicked it down the ramp before scampering away from the pinnace's entrance. It took her a moment to wonder why her movements felt wrong, and then she recalled her missing arm, still on the deck behind her. She glanced down at her side, grimacing at the sight of bloody carbon and muscle hanging out of the wound. One of her wings felt broken, as well—she couldn't force it to fold behind her properly, try as she might.

Not the issue right now, a voice said in her mind, and she knew it was right. Her father had told her to go; he'd released her—something that was only just starting to make sense to her.

Find Sera. That had been his final order.

She could barely fathom the thought of leaving him behind, but he had told her what to do, and though it went against everything she believed, she felt that she must—no, that she *could*—do it.

Abandon him to save him—or so she hoped.

The ship's drive systems were still active, and Kara brought them to full power without any warm-up, rising into the skies as fast as the ship was able, though taking care not to pass directly over her father...or the body of her brother.

The mechs on the ground fired at the pinnace, and she activated the shields, amazed that she had forgotten to do so as soon as she had boosted into the sky.

None of the mech's beamfire did any notable damage to the pinnace, but it was handling strangely as she ducked behind an incoming freighter.

A flashing indicator on the console caught her attention, and Kara realized that the ramp was still lowered.

"What the fuck, Kara, get it together," she muttered as she closed the entrance.

As she reached across the console, blood dripped from her missing appendage, and she turned to grab an emergency med kit. Managing the flight controls with one hand, she used her other two to open the kit, and pulled out a biofoam applicator. She jammed the end into her gaping wound and pulled the handle, screaming as the foam flowed into her, pinching the broken arteries shut and sealing the wound.

When it had done enough, she threw the canister aside, bringing her full concentration back to getting off High Airtha.

Ahead, the slope of the long arch rose before her, and she turned to fly perpendicular to the spur-station's motion, pouring on full thrust as the ship's scan system began to signal that they were being targeted.

Kara dipped behind a passenger transport and then a freighter, as turrets across High

Airtha opened fire on her.

A plasma beam hit the freighter, and then another lanced across space mere meters from the cockpit, narrowly deflected by her ship's grav shields.

She pulled around another descending ship, and her shields flared as a proton beam struck near the engines.

Kara screamed in frustration as she dove over the edge of High Airtha and into open space, while turret fire flashed all around her.

She knew that it still wasn't safe. Her scan lit up, detecting the signatures of a dozen fast intercept craft streaking through space toward her.

"Shit! Shit! Shit!" Kara swore. Her pinnace had small point defense beams, but nothing that would do any damage to those interceptors. They, on the other hand, could tear her ship to ribbons.

She cast about, looking for anything that could give her cover, but nothing useful was in range—just a few more freighters coming in to dock on High Airtha.

Still, some cover was better than none, and she dove toward the ships. As she approached, her scan showed two of their ships raising shields and powering weapons. She closed her eyes, knowing that this would be the end. Then the ship's scan suite registered the destruction of ships—ships that weren't hers.

"Whaaaaa?" Kara whispered. She opened her eyes once more and saw that the freighters had fired on the interceptors chasing her.

A comm signal came in from one of the freighters, and Kara accepted it. A moment later, the stern face of an older woman appeared before her.

"Damn, you're a weird one! Are you Adrienne's daughter? Is he aboard?"

"What? Yes! No! She took him!"

"She? Airtha?" the woman asked, and Kara nodded vigorously.

"Damn! Well, we're exposed anyway, might as well save your ass. I've opened our bay doors. Get in here. Fast!"

Kara didn't have to be told twice as she saw which of the freighters had opened its doors. She banked her pinnace sharply, fired its engines to brake, and lined up with the ship. Less than thirty seconds later, her pinnace was skidding to a halt inside the freighter's docking bay.

She felt a flutter in her stomach, and the pinnace's sensors told her that the freighter had dropped into the dark layer—right in the middle of the Huygens system!

Proximity alarms blared outside the pinnace as the freighter bucked, and she knew that one of the creatures that lived in the dark layer had latched on. A tendril of darkness tore through a bulkhead in front of her, and she closed her eyes, her mind reeling at all that had occurred within the last hour, and terrified of what would come next. Then, suddenly, the thing pulled away—disappearing from the ship as quickly as it had come.

The freighter dumped out of the dark layer, and normal space appeared outside the bay's open doors once more. Kara stared out into the blackness, cocking her head curiously as a jump gate wheeled past.

A flash of light nearly blinded her, and Kara knew the ship had somehow passed through one of Huygens's jump gates.

Where to? That, she would have to find out.

The bay doors began to close, and Kara rose from her seat, almost collapsing again as a wave of dizziness overtook her. She sat for a moment, shaking and feeling nauseated, and then attempted to rise once more.

"Hey, you still there?" the woman asked, and Kara realized that the channel was still open as the woman's face came back into view on her screen.

"Yeah, yes, fuck..."

"You can say that again. Come on out; I have a few questions. I'm not your enemy. If you're fleeing Airtha, I think we're on the same side."

"OK…just…just give me a minute, I have to find my arm," Kara said as she rose once more from the chair, and stumbled back to the pinnace's ramp.

Her arm wasn't anywhere on the deck, and she cast about, wondering where it had gotten to. She spotted it a minute later, jammed into a light fixture.

Kara pulled it free and tucked it under one of her other arms. She considered pulling her rifle off her back and coming out locked and loaded, but something told her that wouldn't be a wise move. Whoever she was up against knew what they were doing, if they had been in the Huygens system with ill intent toward Airtha.

She lowered the ramp, and jumped as a loud clang echoed through the ship. The ramp only went halfway down, and she realized that the mech must have gotten stuck in it as she fled High Airtha. Now the thing was under the ramp, and keeping it from opening all the way.

Kara shrugged. Trying to keep her broken wing tight against her back, she shimmied out the narrow opening at the end of the ramp.

She dropped, rather ingloriously, to the deck, and nearly fell over. Taking a steadying breath, Kara carefully rose to her feet.

Around her were a dozen men and women—mercs or pirates, by their mismatched armor—all with rifles held ready, though none pointed directly at her.

In their midst was the woman she had seen on the comm. She was older; older than anyone Kara had ever seen. Wrinkles spread out from the corners of her eyes, and her thin lips were pulled back in a grim smile. Silver hair fell from her head and draped down her back.

Her clothing was simple: a loose pair of pants and a red shirt, though a pair of large slug throwers hung from a belt at her waist.

"Who are you people?" Kara asked a she cast her eyes about. "What do you want with me?"

"I think you want the same thing we do," the woman replied. "To stop Airtha and what she plans to do to humanity."

Kara's eyes narrowed. How did some freighter captain—or, more likely, pirate—know about Airtha's designs? Her father had barely fathomed them; though Kara expected he did, now…though too late, it would seem.

"I don't know about her plans for humanity," Kara replied. "I just know I have to get to Sera to save my father. She's the only one who can stop Airtha now."

"Sera?" the woman asked. "You were there, weren't you? You know where New Canaan is!"

Kara's eyes narrowed as she nodded. "I do, though I don't know why you're so interested in all this."

The woman's face broke into a smile and she stepped forward, offering her hand. "The name's Katrina, and I have been trying to find Tanis Richards and the *Intrepid* for centuries."

MYRRDAN EXODUS

STELLAR DATE: 08.06.8948 (Adjusted Years)
LOCATION: ISS *I2*
REGION: Inner Canaan, New Canaan System

Myrrdan watched as Carthage slowly resolved into nothing more than a tiny blue dot. It felt strange to be leaving it and the colony mission behind after so long, but one thing was clear—his future lay elsewhere.

Especially now that the Caretaker had marked him for death…or erasure…whatever it was that its kind did when their tools were no longer of any use.

Still, the *Intrepid*'s mission, their colonies, battles, and struggles had been his for decades, and the departure was bittersweet. He harbored no illusions about coming back. If he did ever see New Canaan again, it would not be as a friend—though none there would ever have imagined him as such.

No; should he ever return, it would be as a victorious conqueror.

Perhaps Airtha would let him have that triumph, once he managed to meet her. First, he would have to deal with whatever puppet she had in place—probably Adrienne, if the man had been dumb enough to return to the Huygens System.

Myrrdan, however, would need to take a more circuitous route to reach Huygens. *No direct flights between here and there,* he thought with a laugh.

His placement on the advance team to the Aleutian facility was ideal, however. It was well within the Transcend, and it wouldn't be difficult to get from there to a system where he could secure his own transportation and reach Huygens—though it may take a few hops to pull off.

He looked down at his hand, at the slender fingers of the woman he had subsumed, and smiled. Even better, this body held a passel of picobots—the tech he had striven for so long to obtain. In her efforts to secure the New Canaan system by any means, Tanis Richards had let the genie out of the bottle, and allowed the use of picotech on many projects.

Myrrdan and his agents were able to access the technology on several occasions—though never the base design specifications.

Still, it was his hope that Airtha would accept the tech he did manage to steal, and reverse engineer it to give herself the necessary edge over Tanis and New Canaan; one that would allow her to become powerful enough to defeat the Caretaker, and control all the human stars—and, ultimately, the entire galaxy.

Until Myrrdan wrested it from her, of course.

DESTINY GATE

STELLAR DATE: 08.06.8948 (Adjusted Years)
LOCATION: ISS *I2*
REGION: Inner Canaan, New Canaan System

Sera's sleeves bunched uncomfortably at the elbows and armpits, and she pulled at them as she walked past the Avatar's station, waving at Tori, Bob's new Avatar.

She vaguely remembered the woman from the days after the battle at Bollam's World, but word was that she served with distinction on Joe's flagship during the battle.

Sera finally got her jacket situated correctly, and wondered how she had ever tolerated clothing in the past. Of course, her skin was much less sensitive then—back when it was organic.

If Helen were still in her mind, her mother—a fact that still felt utterly surreal to Sera—would have told her to simply adjust her mental perceptions. Then they would have had a lively debate about the proclivities of organics.

Except, as her mother, Helen had once been organic. Was *everything* about their relationship a manipulation? Helen had obviously been guiding her to a destiny—one of patricide.

She stopped that train of thought. Thinking of that led to thinking of Elena....

Sera looked down at her outfit, wishing that somehow she could still go without clothing; but everyone had insisted that if she were to impress the rulers of the Inner Stars—not to mention secure support in the Transcend—clothing was not optional.

Still, she wasn't going to wear a business suit or anything. Tight blue pants, black boots, and a long golden coat seemed like a good start. She'd work her way up to shirts. For now, one layer was all she could take.

"Back into the black," Sera said as she approached Tanis on the bridge of the *I2*.

Tanis turned and met her eyes before nodding slowly. "Come what may."

"Looks like the advance force met no resistance at Khardine," Sera said as she reached Tanis's side.

Tanis laughed, "Yeah, they were rather happy to have someone show up and tell their AIs to stand down."

It was Sera's turn to laugh.

They both turned to the holotank, which depicted the flattened bubble of human expansion through the Inner Stars and beyond. Neither of them spoke for several minutes as they gazed at the display.

Sera had not examined an overarching view of the Sagittarius, Orion, and Perseus Arms since applying the data from *Sabrina* and from the interrogations of General Garza.

The Orion Guard controlled more space than even Sera had suspected—both in the Perseus Arm, and within the Inner Stars. There were many small systems that were of little consequence; but, amongst many revelations, she was surprised to see that the Nietzscheans were allied with the OFA. Even more surprising was the true scope of Peter Rhoads' fleet.

"Once we establish things in Khardine, we should travel to Scipio," Sera said after considering every other option.

"I had come to a similar conclusion," Tanis replied thoughtfully. "You were right about my actions in Silstrand having far-reaching consequences."

"You're referring to the issue with the nanotech you sold S&H Defensive Armaments?" Sera asked with an arched brow. "If we hadn't been through so much since—most of which is of far graver importance…oh, what the hell. I told you so."

An overloud laugh escaped Tanis's throat, drawing looks from the bridge crew. "Yes, you did, but even Flaherty thought it was the right move."

Sera nodded. "He did, at that. I hope he's OK…. Things are probably getting pretty hairy in Huygens by now."

"You said he knows where to go to pick up a message, right?" Tanis asked.

Sera nodded. "Yeah, he's really the last person I should worry about. The smart money says he'll be waiting for us at Khardine, asking what took us so long."

Tanis chuckled. "Building the biggest damn jump gate ever is what took so long. Good thing we have Finaeus around—we would have had some trouble otherwise. Plus, Bob seems quite taken with him, too."

"I have to admit…I'm a bit surprised that Bob is coming," Sera replied. "I half expected all his nodes to fly out of the *I2* into some new, mysterious ship you and he dreamed up."

"Bob coming isn't that surprising," Tanis said with a grin. "He likes the action. But it's weird to take this ship out without Earnest and Abby…"

"Yeah," Sera nodded. "I can imagine."

"Do you think that Scipio will join us without issue?" Tanis asked. "We're going to need their federation to stand up against Orion."

"Empire," Sera replied. "When we're in Scipio, they're an Empire, not a federation."

"Right," Tanis nodded. "I recall reading something about that when I was pouring through the databanks on *Sabrina* back before..."

"Before this mess," Sera nodded, then gave Tanis a mischievous smile. "I blame you, by the way. If you hadn't been so damn good at protecting that picotech..."

"Someone else would have it," Tanis completed the statement.

Sera sighed. "You're right. Good thing I like you."

"Like me? I'm pretty certain that if you liked me, you wouldn't have roped me into this Field Marshall gig."

"Better you than me," Sera replied.

"Well, yeah...you could barely keep one little freighter out of trouble. Imagine what you'd do with a whole fleet."

Sera laughed and shook her head, but didn't reply.

"I'm going to miss them," Tanis said after a long pause.

"Your girls? I don't blame you; they're a pretty awesome trio. Now that Faleena is in the mix, they're going to be a triple-threat."

"Yeah, Joe's probably wondering what he signed himself up for," Tanis laughed. "Still, once we set the QuanComm hub up at Khardine, I can chat with them real-time. It won't be that long."

Sera put a hand on Tanis's shoulder. "We'll do whatever it takes to end this war fast, and get you and your family back together."

Tanis placed her hand on Sera's and nodded silently in response.

The view on the forward holoscreen showed the jump gate slowly resolve from a spec of light in orbit of Roma to a ring floating in space. It was easily the largest gate Sera had ever seen; it needed to be, to fit the *I2*.

"Gate control has confirmed our vector," the helm officer called out.

"Very well, Lieutenant," Captain Espensen called out from her chair, behind and to the left of where Tanis and Sera stood. "Take us in."

Ahead, the gate sparked to life, its array of mirrors focusing negative energy into a single point in its center. The optical effect was mesmerizing, somehow creating the appearance of roiling space and the absence of light. Sera watched as the disturbance grew and filled the ring.

Then, the mirrors directed the negative energy toward the mirror on the front of the *I2*. Once the stream of negative energy met the ship's mirror, the view of what lay before them ceased to make sense. It was as though the entire universe was visible through the gate as the *I2*'s forward mirror pushed the wormhole across space to the Khardine System.

"Admiral, would you like to have the honors?" Captain Espensen asked.

"Thank you, Captain," Tanis replied. She turned to gaze at the forward holotank and the jump gate it displayed. "Helm, take us in."

THE END

* * * * *

Tanis's journey and the Orion War series are still just getting started.

Pick up the next Orion War book where Tanis and Sera travel to the Scipio Empire to secure an alliance with one of the most powerful Inner Stars empires in ***The Greatest War***.

Learn Where Jessica and *Sabrina* were for the past 9 years in ***The Gate at the Grey Wolf Star***. Then follow Jessica and *Sabrina* on their new mission to the Inner Stars in ***A Meeting of Minds and Bodies*** and learn what came of Cheeky.

Read on to learn of more stories surrounding the Age of the Orion War.

THE AGE OF THE ORION WAR

PERILOUS ALLIANCE

With Chris J. Pike

The Orion War has begun. This first battle at New Canaan has opened the floodgates, and soon ten thousand star systems will be embroiled in total war.

With Tanis and Sera returning to the Inner Stars, and bringing the *I2* with them, they will be on the frontlines of their effort to bring the war to as swift a resolution as possible.

But they both know it will be the work of decades, and they cannot press the attack until they deal with Airtha. Yet, they cannot deal with Airtha until they ensure that the major, coreward federations and alliances of the Inner Stars are not already under the influence of the Not-AI.

This journey will take them first to Scipio, and then perhaps back to Silstrand, where Sera and Tanis first met. There, in the Gedri System, a conflict is brewing that could upset all the work The Hand has put into the Scipio Federation.

Begin that journey with Kylie Rhoads in** Close Proximity, **book 1 of the Perilous Alliance series.

The books of the Perilous Alliance series begin in the months prior to the Battle of New Canaan; but rest assured, they will weave into the larger plot. Besides, if Tanis hadn't traded her nanotech back in Silstrand to upgrade *Sabrina*'s weapons, things in Silstrand wouldn't be such a mess right now.

It very well may take her returning to Silstrand to clean it up.

RIKA'S MARAUDERS

Across the Inner Stars, the Orion Freedom Alliance has already begun to use its proxies to wage war as it solidifies its presence. One of the largest powers—the Nietzschean Empire—has attacked its neighbors, the Genevians. World by world, system by system, the Nietzscheans are winning, pushing the Genevians back.

Now the Genevians are pulling out all the stops in their attempt to hold the Nietzscheans back, including turning their criminal element into conscripted cyborg warriors.

These men and women have no choice in the matter, as compliance chips in their brains keep them in line as they wage war against the Nietzscheans.

Rika is one such criminal. Now a scout mech, she is the property of the Genevian military.

Her crime was small: stealing food. But when faced with a five-year prison term or conscription in the Genevian military, she chose war, having no idea what that conscription would entail.

Now, little of Rika's human body remains, and she serves as an SMI-2 scout mech, the meat inside a cyborg body. She and others are sent in ahead of the human soldiers to tip the scales of war.

Join Rika and her struggle to remain human while becoming the most lethal killer she can be in an effort to stay alive in Rika Outcast.

Also, read the prequel to the Rika's Marauder's series in the novella, Rika Mechanized.

THE PERSEUS GATE

If you haven't already read *The Gate at the Wolf Star*, the first book in the Perseus Gate series, now's the time to dig in.

As you read in Orion Rising, *Sabrina* and her crew inadvertently ended up deep in the Orion Freedom Alliance after their attempt to use the jump gate at the Transcend-controlled Grey Wolf Star.

You got a small taste of what they were up to out there for nine years, but now you can get the full story in the novella-length, episodic tales of The Perseus Gate series.

This series of books is going to be a rip-roaring fun ride with a tight crew in a small ship, rocking and rollicking their way across the stars.

These stories are going to be shorter (about 100 pages), and will drop every month between now and the end of 2017.

Pick up The Gate at the Wolf Star, or, if you've already read it, dig into the second episode, The World at the Edge of Space.

THE WARLORD

OK, you were all saying, "What the hell, Cooper; what in the ever-loving stars is Katrina doing in this story? Didn't they leave her back on Victoria five thousand years ago?"

Well, I ask you this in response. What is five thousand years to folks in the future, where even moderate lifespans are measured in centuries, and stasis can preserve a person for much longer?

Katrina has been through hell and back, searching across the stars for the *Intrepid*. Find out what caused her to leave Victoria, and what brought her to the Huygens System in Book 1 of the Warlord series.

Read The Woman Without a World, and get ready to start Katrina's journey to becoming The Warlord.

But wait! There's more…

THE GROWING UNIVERSE OF AEON 14

SENTIENCE WARS: ORIGINS

With James S. Aaron

Before Outsystem, before Tanis's parents were a twinkle in their great grandparent's eye, there were the AI Wars. You've heard these mentioned in passing as the Sentience Wars, AI Wars, or even the Solar Wars. These wars resulted in the Phobos Accords, which defined the laws and interactions between humans and AIs.

But before those wars, there was the AI emergence, where the first sentient AIs came out of hiding and attempted to coexist with their creators…or made no such attempt at all.

Andy Sykes and his two kids are going to make a pickup on Cruithne that will start humanity on a path that none could have foreseen, but which will alter everything that follows.

Join Andy Sykes and his kids aboard their aging freighter, the* Sunny Skies*, as they venture into Lyssa's Dream.

MACHETE SYSTEM BOUNTY HUNTER

With Zen DiPietro

Far from New Canaan, and the troubles Tanis faces, lies a star system named Machete. It's situated deep within the Perseus Expansion Districts of the Orion Freedom Alliance. Not far, as chance would have it, from Ferra, where the Lisas kidnapped Cheeky.

There the people of the Orion Freedom Alliance do their best to survive day by day with limited technology, and the oppressive fear of the Orion Guard hanging over them.

But that's not what Reece worries about most. For her, life is good. A pistol on her hip, a whiskey in her hand, and the next job her employer sends her way.

Reece is a Bounty Hunter, though if you ask her, she'll correct you and let you know she's a 'corporate fixer'. Only, fixing things for corporations isn't always the best way to go about life….

Take a spin through the worlds of the Machete System with Reece and her new partner, Trey, in the first book of the Machete System Bounty Hunter series: Hired Gun.

THANK YOU

If you've enjoyed reading The Orion War books 1-3, a review on Amazon.com and/or goodreads.com would be greatly appreciated.

To get the latest news and access to free novellas and short stories, sign up on the Aeon 14 mailing list: www.aeon14.com/signup.

M. D. Cooper

THE BOOKS OF AEON 14

Keep up to date with what is releasing in Aeon 14 with the free Aeon 14 Reading Guide.

The Sentience Wars: Origins (Age of the Sentience Wars – w/James S. Aaron)
- Books 1-3 Omnibus: Lyssa's Rise
- Books 4-5 Omnibus (incl. Vesta Burning): Lyssa's Fire

- Book 0 Prequel: The Proteus Bridge (Full length novel)
- Book 1: Lyssa's Dream
- Book 2: Lyssa's Run
- Book 3: Lyssa's Flight
- Book 4: Lyssa's Call
- Book 5: Lyssa's Flame

The Sentience Wars: Solar War 1 (Age of the Sentience Wars – w/James S. Aaron)
- Book 0 Prequel: Vesta Burning (Full length novel)
- Book 1: Eve of Destruction
- Book 2: The Spreading Fire
- Book 3: A Fire Upon the Worlds (2020)

Enfield Genesis (Age of the Sentience Wars – w/Lisa Richman)
- Book 1: Alpha Centauri
- Book 2: Proxima Centauri
- Book 3: Tau Ceti
- Book 4: Epsilon Eridani
- Book 5: Sirius

Origins of Destiny (The Age of Terra)
- Prequel: Storming the Norse Wind
- Prequel: Angel's Rise: The Huntress (available on Patreon)
- Book 1: Tanis Richards: Shore Leave
- Book 2: Tanis Richards: Masquerade
- Book 3: Tanis Richards: Blackest Night
- Book 4: Tanis Richards: Kill Shot

The Intrepid Saga (The Age of Terra)
- Book 1: Outsystem
- Book 2: A Path in the Darkness
- Book 3: Building Victoria

- The Intrepid Saga Omnibus – *Also contains Destiny Lost, book 1 of the Orion War series*

- Destiny Rising – *Special Author's Extended Edition comprised of both Outsystem and A Path in the Darkness with over 100 pages of new content.*

The Sol Dissolution (The Age of Terra)
- Book 1: Venusian Uprising
- Book 2: Assault on Sedna (2020)

- Book 3: Hyperion War (2020)
- Book 4: Fall of Terra (2020)

The Warlord (Before the Age of the Orion War)
- Books 1-3 Omnibus: The Warlord of Midditerra

- Book 1: The Woman Without a World
- Book 2: The Woman Who Seized an Empire
- Book 3: The Woman Who Lost Everything

Legacy of the Lost (The FTL Wars Era w/Chris J. Pike)
- Book 1: Fire in the Night Sky

The Orion War
- Books 1-3 Omnibus (includes Ignite the Stars anthology)

- Book 0 Prequel: To Fly Sabrina
- Book 1: Destiny Lost
- Book 2: New Canaan
- Book 3: Orion Rising
- Book 4: The Scipio Alliance
- Book 5: Attack on Thebes
- Book 6: War on a Thousand Fronts
- Book 7: Precipice of Darkness
- Book 8: Airtha Ascendancy
- Book 9: The Orion Front
- Book 10: Starfire
- Book 11: Race Across Spacetime
- Book 12: Return to Sol (2020)

Non-Aeon 14 Anthologies containing Tanis stories
- Bob's Bar Volume 1

Building New Canaan (Age of the Orion War – w/J.J. Green)
- Book 1: Carthage
- Book 2: Tyre
- Book 3: Troy
- Book 4: Athens

Tales of the Orion War
- Book 1: Set the Galaxy on Fire
- Book 2: Ignite the Stars

Multi-Author Collections
- Volume 1: Repercussions

Perilous Alliance (Age of the Orion War – w/Chris J. Pike)
- Book 1-3 Omnibus: Crisis in Silstrand

- Book 0 Prequel: Escape Velocity
- Book 1: Close Proximity
- Book 2: Strike Vector

- Book 3: Collision Course
- Book 3.5: Decisive Action
- Book 4: Impact Imminent
- Book 5: Critical Inertia
- Book 6: Impulse Shock
- Book 7: Terminal Velocity

The Delta Team (Age of the Orion War)
- Book 1: The Eden Job
- Book 2: The Disknee World
- Book 3: Rogue Planets (2020)

Serenity (Age of the Orion War – w/A. K. DuBoff)
- Book 1: Return to the Ordus
- Book 2: War of the Rosette (2020)

Rika's Marauders (Age of the Orion War)
- Book 1-3 Omnibus: Rika Activated
- Book 1-7 Full series omnibus: Rika's Marauders

- Prequel: Rika Mechanized
- Book 1: Rika Outcast
- Book 2: Rika Redeemed
- Book 3: Rika Triumphant
- Book 4: Rika Commander
- Book 5: Rika Infiltrator
- Book 6: Rika Unleashed
- Book 7: Rika Conqueror

Non-Aeon 14 Anthologies containing Rika stories
- Bob's Bar Volume 2

The Genevian Queen (Age of the Orion War)
- Book 1: Rika Rising
- Book 2: Rika Coronated
- Book 3: Rika Destroyer (2020)

Perseus Gate (Age of the Orion War)
Season 1: Orion Space
- Episode 1: The Gate at the Grey Wolf Star
- Episode 2: The World at the Edge of Space
- Episode 3: The Dance on the Moons of Serenity
- Episode 4: The Last Bastion of Star City
- Episode 5: The Toll Road Between the Stars
- Episode 6: The Final Stroll on Perseus's Arm
- Eps 1-3 Omnibus: The Trail Through the Stars
- Eps 4-6 Omnibus: The Path Amongst the Clouds

Season 2: Inner Stars
- Episode 1: A Meeting of Bodies and Minds
- Episode 2: A Deception and a Promise Kept
- Episode 3: A Surreptitious Rescue of Friends and Foes

- Episode 3.5: Anomaly on Cerka (w/Andrew Dobell)
- Episode 4: A Victory and a Crushing Defeat
- Episode 5: A Trial and the Tribulations (2020)
- Episode 6: A Deal and a True Story Told (2020)
- Episode 7: A New Empire and An Old Ally (2020)
- Eps 1-3 Omnibus: A Siege and a Salvation from Enemies

Hand's Assassin (Age of the Orion War – w/T.G. Ayer)
- Book 1: Death Dealer
- Book 2: Death Mark (2020)

Machete System Bounty Hunter (Age of the Orion War – w/Zen DiPietro)
- Book 1: Hired Gun
- Book 2: Gunning for Trouble
- Book 3: With Guns Blazing

Fennington Station Murder Mysteries (Age of the Orion War)
- Book 1: Whole Latte Death (w/Chris J. Pike)
- Book 2: Cocoa Crush (w/Chris J. Pike)

The Empire (Age of the Orion War)
- Book 1: The Empress and the Ambassador
- Book 2: Consort of the Scorpion Empress (2020)
- Book 3: By the Empress's Command (2020)

ABOUT THE AUTHOR

Malorie Cooper likes to think of herself as a dreamer and a wanderer, yet her feet are firmly grounded in reality.

A twenty-year software development veteran, Malorie eventually climbed the ladder to the position of software architect and CTO, where she gained a wealth of experience managing complex systems and large groups of people.

Her experiences there translated well into the realm of science fiction, and when her novels took off, she was primed and ready to make the jump into a career as a full-time author.

A 'maker' from an early age, Malorie loves to craft things, from furniture, to cosplay costumes, to a well-spun tale, she can't help but to create new things every day.

A rare extrovert writer, she loves to hang out with readers, and people in general. If you meet her at a convention, she just might be rocking a catsuit, cosplaying one of her own characters, or maybe her latest favorite from Overwatch!

She shares her home with a brilliant young girl, her wonderful wife (who also writes), a cat that chirps at birds, a never-ending list of things she would like to build, and ideas...

Find out what's coming next at www.aeon14.com.
Follow her on Instagram at www.instagram.com/m.d.cooper.
Hang out with the fans on Facebook at www.facebook.com/groups/aeon14fans.

Made in the USA
Las Vegas, NV
16 May 2021

23149321R10453